I0788546

THE WOLVES OF FOREST GROVE

ELENA LAWSON

AUTHOR NOTE

This series takes place over a span of several years, beginning when the FMC is younger, and ending when she is in her twenties. So expect a slow burn with a *ton* of angst and build-up, but don't expect there to be open door scenes until nearing book four <3

SHIFTED FATE

BOOK ONE

I followed the white wolf into the woods. I went into his cabin. And there's no going back.

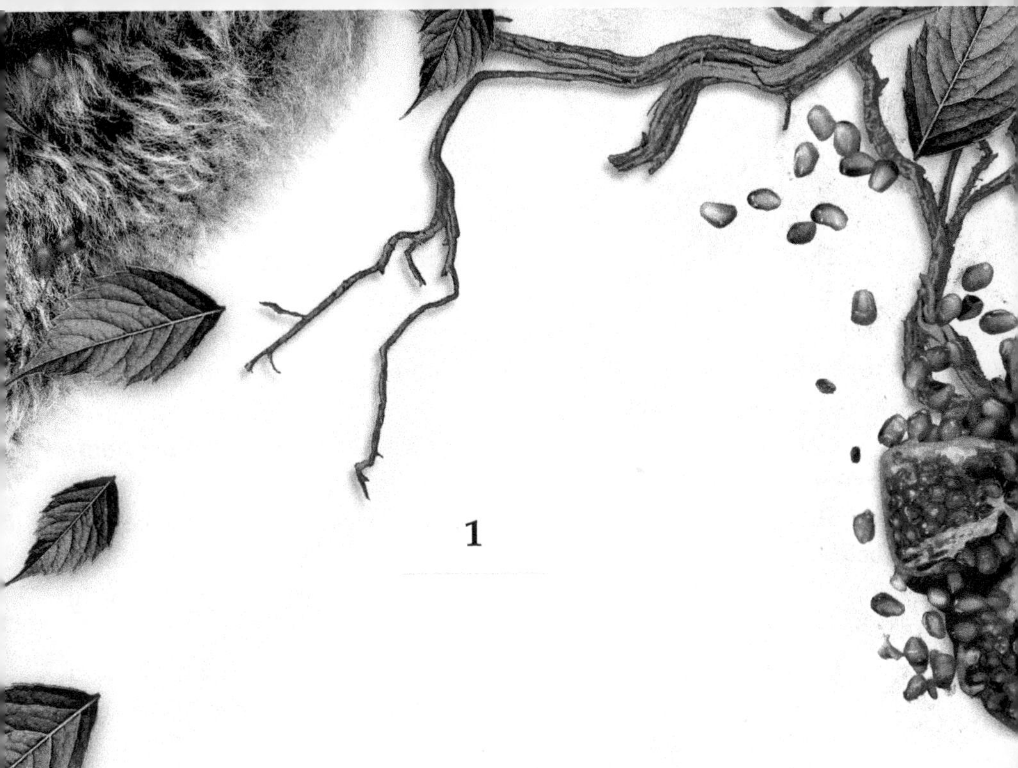

1

The bus only goes to the edge of town. Then it's another twenty-five-minute hike on rough terrain to get to Dad's old hunting blind in the woods overlooking Forest Grove. When he died last year, the small camouflaged tent became the last place that felt like home.

"Take this, sweetie," Maggie, the elderly driver called before I could step off the bus at my usual stop; the end of the line. "There's a storm comin'."

She looked ominously into the gray sky and clucked her tongue.

"It isn't supposed to rain," I told her, readjusting the strap of my pack so it wouldn't dig into my shoulder so much. Weighed down with my schoolbooks and two new ones from Jacqueline's shop, it felt heavier than usual.

Maggie shook the nondescript black umbrella at me and narrowed her warm brown eyes. "These old bones don't lie."

I shook my head but reached out and took it. "Thanks, Mags. I'll get it back to you tomorrow."

She nodded tightly before turning back to the road. "Be careful out there, Miss Allie."

My lips pursed and I turned away quickly so she wouldn't see how her words struck me. I pressed my lips into a tight line; Maggie didn't know I lived alone in the woods.

No one did.

The folding doors closed, and I watched the tail lights of the old city bus jar as it went over the bumpy, pockmarked road. I barely got fifty feet onto the slender trail before the first droplets of rain hit the top of my head. I snorted as I opened the umbrella. I'd have to remember to thank Mags tomorrow.

It wouldn't be the first time I'd arrived at my makeshift home soaked to the bone, but I couldn't afford to get sick like last time. It would be winter soon. I figured I had about two months, maybe less, before the cold got so bad I wouldn't be able to stay in the blind anymore. That meant I needed every shift I could get at the book shop in town.

I'd been looking for a second job for ages. One where I could earn tips. But seventeen-year-olds can't serve liquor, so I'm not exactly a prime candidate for that sort of job.

I sighed as my calves burned, the muddy terrain making the climb into the trees more arduous than it had been yesterday. At least the exertion was keeping me warm. It seemed a lot colder than it should've been for mid-September and my hard breaths clouded the air around my face with each step.

The weekend couldn't come soon enough. I had Sundays off work and school and couldn't wait to cuddle up and read for the entire day.

No six am wake up to get to Forest Grove High in time to shower before first period.

No running to the bus stop to make it to the book shop for my 3:30pm shift.

No long, bumpy bus ride.

No twenty-minute hike into the trees at dusk. I *loved* Sundays.

A creak in the trees to my right had me spinning and squinting into the growing dark. I had the bear mace out and the safety clip removed in less than a second. My skin bristled. But a long neck and black eyes lifted from the brush instead. Only a deer. I smiled at the creature as its jaw worked to chew what remained of its dinner.

"Better get home," I told it, and its ears pricked, noticing me. "Storm's coming."

I could feel it in the atmosphere now. Mags was definitely right. The rain was coming harder, and the wind whistling through the old pines on the mountainside was growing louder. "Go on," I said a bit louder and it took off in the opposite direction, its white tail bobbing as it vanished into the greenery.

Shoving the mace back into the side pocket of my pack, I picked up the pace, eager to get home before night fell in earnest and the storm truly started.

I closed the umbrella as the blind came into view. A camo shelter no bigger than your average closet, set fifteen feet from the ground, nestled between two trees. Hurriedly, I climbed to the hatch set into the floor and closed it firmly behind me. Where the walls and roof were made of good quality waterproof canvas, the floor was a solid wooden platform, bolted securely into both trees.

My sodden bag dropped to the floor and I rushed to remove the books from it, not wanting them to be ruined from the damp. I set them into the small nook in the corner and set to removing my damp sweater and muddy boots.

The wind howled outside, making the thick canvas walls snap and ripple. I gritted my teeth as I tugged on a dry sweater and pulled the sleeping bag from the floor to wrap around my shivering shoulders. The scents of cold pine and musty earth enveloped me. I considered lighting the camp stove for a bit to get some warmth into the tent but thought better of it.

I didn't have very much propane left and if I wanted a warm breakfast in the morning, I'd better save it.

The buzzing of my cell broke through my daydreams of warm oatmeal with huckleberries. I clicked to my messages and ignored the fifty-three unopened texts from Devin, my stomach souring at the mere sight of his name. My fingers absently went to the still tender skin along my neckline.

Swallowing past the lump in my throat, I opened the new message from Vivian at the top.

Vivian: You get into the city ok? Looks ugly as fuck out there.

Allie: Yep. Home safe and sound.

Vivian: You going to Thompson's party this Saturday?

Allie: I'm not sure yet.

Vivian: Yes you are.

I rolled my eyes, thinking about it. Devin and Thompson didn't really hang out. What were the chances he would even be there? *Slim*, I thought, biting my lower lip.

Allie: Only if I can crash at your place?

Vivian: Deal.

Allie: Night Viv.

Vivian: xo

I clutched the phone tightly in my palm. The guilt of keeping up all the lies made my stomach churn. Vivian was one of my best friends. Along with Layla. If I thought I'd have been able to stay with either of them when my aunt and uncle decided to up and move to Florida until spring, I'd have asked. But I knew it wasn't a possibility.

Layla had seven brothers and sisters and they were already three to a room.

Viv's parents fought like hyenas, and her dad was a loud, and sometimes mean, recovering alcoholic. They wouldn't want me around that. It would make them uncomfortable.

The solution seemed simple enough at the time. My aunt and uncle made it clear they wanted to go. My uncle thought it would save their marriage. My aunt wanted to drown her sorrows in cheap strawberry wine by the pool. Who was I to stop them?

So, when they said they wanted to Airbnb their pristine digs in the city to fund their trip and asked if I could stay with a friend until spring, I didn't hesitate. I was already enough of a burden to them since Dad passed; I could give them this one request.

Now they think I'm staying with Viv. And Viv and Layla, and just about everyone else, thinks I take the bus back into Portland every night after work.

No one needs to know the truth. Besides, by the time they got back, I'd be eighteen. Hopefully have my own place. Maybe, just maybe, I wouldn't have to move back into their fancy condo in Portland at all.

I grimaced when I noticed my battery only had a ten percent charge left and switched to battery saving mode. I'd forgotten to charge it in History this afternoon like I usually did.

Damn. I just had to hope it would last until morning. Without my alarm, I wouldn't wake up at the ass crack of dawn to make the bus into town.

A violent gust of wind rushed over the tent and the window flap came loose, lifting to let in a hard gush of cold wind. I rose to secure it back into place, the boards beneath my feet creaking under my weight. I glanced out into the night and my lips parted in a silent gasp.

Over the boisterous sounds of the howling wind and rustle of leaves and needles, was the unmistakable rumble of thunder. The rain was sheeting in sideways, misting my face with its chill through the mesh window lining.

In the distance, between the branches, the storm approached rapidly from the north. Racing over the sky like a band of wild horses, each of their hoof falls striking the clouds like a blacksmith's hammer against hot metal, shooting sparks into the night.

Lightning snaked through the clouds like veins beneath pale skin. The groan of a tree falling somewhere far in the distance ended with an earsplitting crash.

Hurriedly, I fixed the flap back into place, knotting the string twice to make sure it stayed put. My heart in my throat, I dug through the rumpled heap of my sleeping bag until I found my phone. I winced when I saw the battery had already gone down to eight percent.

Shit.

I flicked over to the weather app on my phone. It took a second for the app to update, and I had to hold my phone high to get the second bar of service I needed.

High wind alert. Heavy rain. Flood watch.

I shut off the phone, needing to conserve the battery in case—

No. I'd been through worse out here.

"It's going to be fine," I told myself aloud, my voice sounding muted in the deafening roar of the wind. The grumble of the sky above grew louder as though it were trying to disagree. I flipped it the bird and patted the photo of Dad I kept pinned to the canvas wall. It batted against my fingers, but I found the strength I needed in his watchful stare and set my jaw. "We got this."

We don't got this.

Water poured into the hunting blind from the tear in the roof. I rushed to move everything out of the way so I could patch it up, my fingers growing numb and stiff from the wet cold.

The lightning turned from a low rumble far away to sharp loud *cracks* that illuminated the tent in startling blue hued clarity. I flinched as each one struck earth, the creaky boards under my feet trembling with the force of their impact and the near constant vibration of resonant thunder.

I tore a strip of duct tape from the roll with my teeth and struggled to get it into place to stop the deluge of water. Already, my sweater and jeans and most of the floor were soaked. If I didn't get it patched up fast, I wouldn't have a single dry thing left to wear when the storm passed. The idea of having to curl up wet and cold had me pushing myself. Working harder. Faster. I forced my clumsy fingers into obedience.

Finally, after three more strips, I got the tear patched. I wasn't sure how long it would hold with it still raining so hard, but I *prayed* it would last through the rest of the storm. It had to be over soon, right? How much longer could it possibly go on?

My trademark ponytail had come undone and I had to move my long dripping hair from my face, bending to catch my breath as I felt around in the dark for the fallen hair elastic.

Until the unmistakable sound of canvas tearing made ice water flood back into my veins—and into the tent. A branch had pierced the roof on the opposite side and was hanging over the nook where I kept all my schoolbooks and the ones from the shop.

Water and dead leaves rushed in, covering them.

Not my books!

I lunged to stop the slaughter, but as I reached them an even louder *crack* stole my breath. The light from the lightning strike was vibrant neon right above the tent. It blinded me. Sparks flashed like fireworks into the inky dark.

The only warning I had was an ominous groan before the sharp sound of splitting wood broke the spell that had me frozen in place. It was like an ax coming down on a block. And it could only mean one thing.

I dove out of the way just as a large section of the great tree holding the hunting blind in place broke off from the whole and came smashing down, taking me and the tent with it on its descent to the ground.

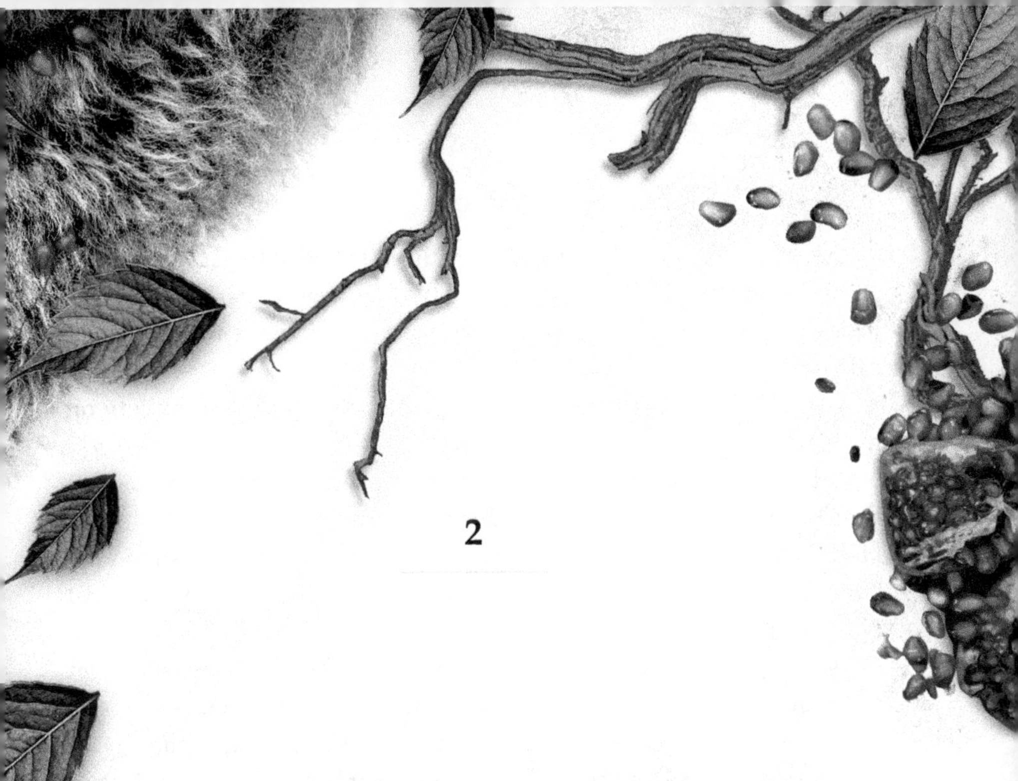

2

S omething heavy pinned my leg to the muddy earth. It took a full minute for me to come back to myself. My vision was blurred, and my head spun. I coughed, tasting the foul metallic tang of blood on my tongue. I must've bitten it in the fall.

Trying to get my bearings, I took stock of what'd happened. Between the cloud cover and the rain there was almost no light. I had to rely on the flashes of lightning to see by, and they seemed to be growing sparser. The bolts hitting further away. That was a good thing, at least.

Ok, this isn't so bad, I told myself, shivering as rivulets of rainwater cascaded down my face and the icy wind whipped sharp leaves and debris at my head.

Shielding myself from the brunt of it, I saw that the hunting blind had fallen, the metal bolts that were holding it in place had been gouged out of the tree. My leg—or more accurately, my ankle was stuck beneath the wooden platform that made the floor.

But the blind was still more or less in one piece. When the lightning flashed again, I could see that the roof was torn and flapping. But it could be repaired.

I'd never get the damned thing back up into the trees, but shelter was shelter. I'd just have to be extra careful with open food if I had to be earthbound.

This is ok. I'm ok.

My teeth began chattering and I realized I needed to get free if I was going to be able to do anything. Surely there was something still dry inside the tent? Maybe I should try to make it back to the main road. Or call—*no,* I couldn't call anyone.

I grit my teeth together to stop the chattering and tried pulling on my leg.

I bit back a scream, only able to rein in the worst of the pained keening sound. I moved it again, this time remaining conscious of what I felt, like Dad taught me. There was no grinding. The pain wasn't in the bone itself, or at least, I didn't think so. A sprain then. A bad one, but I didn't think the bone was broken.

Moving myself in closer to the corner of the blind, I managed to get my fingers beneath the base, earning myself a nasty splinter.

I heaved the wooden platform with everything I had, grunting as my shoulders felt like they were going to tear. I couldn't move it. Not enough to get free. I hastily wiped the water from my eyes, but only managed to add mud to the mix.

Groaning in frustration, I clenched my fists and closed my eyes, listening to the sound of my own heartbeat and the blood rushing in my ears. I was reminded of a time when me and Dad were out here in a storm. It hadn't been as bad as this one.

I'd been so frightened. My little seven-year-old mind had conjured all sorts of terrifying images. Of tornadoes. Of monsters in the dark. Of dying, or worse; losing the only family I had left. But as he lit the small lamp in the blind, casting his long shadow over the wall as it rippled in the wind, I remembered what he told me.

It's only a storm, Allie Grace, he said in that soothing deep timbre he had. *Just close your eyes. It'll be over soon, and then the sun will come out just like it did yesterday.*

Promise? Promise, kiddo.

I took a deep, stabilizing breath and pushed it out, determination setting my jaw. I felt around in the grass, finding as the lightning struck again that there was a thick branch a few feet away.

Sliding in the mud and molting leaves, I reached for it with trembling fingers, stretching my arm as far as it would go. My fingers closed around the tip and I pulled, dragging it over to me. I felt the solidness of the branch in my hands. It was heavy. At least four inches thick.

It would work.

I jammed the end of it under the base of the blind and used all my body weight to pull it down, lifting the platform the few inches I needed to wriggle my ankle free.

As soon as it was out, I let go of the branch and collapsed against the ground, grinning like a fool. "*Fuck you,*" I called into the howling wind and whipping rain.

I laughed.

"*That all you got?*" I shouted into the trees, up at the sky.

When my breaths steadied, I hobbled to my feet and went to see what I could do to salvage my makeshift home and its contents. Though the rain still poured down in a fury, it seemed the worst of the storm was passing. The sun *would* come out tomorrow, and I *would* get through this.

It was just a hiccup.

The annoying kind that stuck around for a while, but still only a hiccup.

Peering into a slit in the heavy canvas fabric, I saw that all my clothing, bedding, and books were completely soaked. *Fuck my life.*

A glimmer of silver caught my eye and I snaked my hand in to retrieve my cell phone. It was beyond dead. Or worse, maybe it was water damaged. I couldn't afford another one. It would take all the savings I had left.

I jammed it deep into my front pocket, hopeful that I could find a way to fix it.

That's when I heard it. Higher up the mountainside.

A sort of rumbling, rushing noise. Growing louder by the second. It wasn't thunder. I could still hear the deep growl of the clouds as they moved further south. This was something else.

I limped to the edge of the tent and tried to see past it into the forest.

Were the trees further up *moving?* I shook my head, wondering if I'd hit it too hard in the fall. I blinked rapidly to clear my eyes of rainwater and tried to make sense of it. The trees *were* moving.

I gasped.

It's a mudslide...

My heart leaped into my throat and I took off into the trees. It was coming down the slope of the mountain fast. But if I could just get to the outside edge of it before it hit, I could...

Dad.

I stopped, my hard breaths clouding in the night as I stared sadly back at the battered tent laying in the brush. I clamped my mouth shut with an audible click. Cursing myself, I ran back, my ankle protesting each step. It took me a second to get the photo unpinned from the tent, and by the time I did, the mudslide was nearly upon me.

Stupid. So fucking stupid.

The ground under my feet shifted as I ran, trying to make me lose my footing. Trying to suck me down. I just had to get to the edge of it. I'd been caught in one of these before, but I'd been on my old Yamaha 250.

Go diagonal, I remembered that much. *Run down and away. Don't stop until it's far behind you.*

Except my ankle was about to give out, and any second now a heaving tree root was going to send me sprawling. I couldn't move fast enough.

A streak of white to my left caught my eye and I saw an animal running in the same direction and pattern I was. As it neared, its front paws tearing up loose dirt, its snout twisted in an angry snarl, I saw what it was.

A wolf. *Huge* and powerful with muscles rippling beneath its fur. Its eyes seemed to glow in the dark. One of them somewhere between copper and gold. And the other the same but with a bright fleck of green. It was the most beautiful thing I'd ever seen.

Pity then, that the beast would probably eat me if we both made it out of the landslide in one piece.

I tried to put distance between me and the wolf, but as I side stepped to the right, my foot caught on something sharp in the dirt and I went down hard, losing my breath.

The wolf charged the last few feet to me, its glowing gold and green eyes fixed to mine. I couldn't breathe. The mudslide was sucking me down, pulling me away. And every time I tried to yank my legs free to stand up, they got sucked back down again.

I realized too late that the photo was no longer in my hand and scanned the shifting dirt for it. But the last picture I had of him was already being sucked down into the mud more than six feet away. His grinning face vanished beneath the cold earth.

A vice gripped my heart and hot tears carved twin trails down my cheeks.

My entire body was covered in cold grime and I coughed as some made its way into my mouth. When I looked up again, the wolf was there. Close enough that I could smell its loamy breath and feel its warmth. The thing was larger this close up. Double the size of a normal wolf. The fucker must have been on goddamned steroids.

Make it quick, I thought, my throat going dry as I closed my eyes.

A cold nose pressed insistently against my temple and I jerked back, my eyes snapping back open. The wolf made a pained sound in its throat and something in its eyes struck me.

A kindness.

Was it...was it trying to *help* me?

The ground beneath us shifted again, heaving up from beneath. It was enough to jostle my legs free as we continued to slide down the side of the mountain. The ground shook as a tree fell five feet to my left.

I had to move. I couldn't stay here, or I'd be killed.

Tentatively, I reached out a hand, pushing it into the wolf's thick fur. It lowered its head, still making small sounds in its throat and shuffling its feet to keep them atop the moving dirt.

When it made no move to attack me, I fisted my hand into its fur. Then reached my other hand up and did the same. As soon as my hand was secured, the wolf began to pull. It dragged me over the dirt, between moving trees. I resisted the urge to scream as all manor of rocks and dirt and sharp debris scraped my side. It stopped suddenly and put its body lower for me to readjust my position.

I moved one hand so I could grip its opposite side, and when the wolf lifted its body the second time, I was laying over its back. Its knobby spine jabbed into my breastbone, but it was a hell of a lot better than being drug over the forest floor.

The wolf had us out of the brunt of it faster than I could have dreamed, its sides heaving with the additional effort of hauling a second body. When the groaning sound of moving earth stopped and I thought it was clear, I let go and slid from the wolf's back, feeling like the whole world was spinning. My shoulders and biceps ached from clinging to the animal that'd saved my life. I rolled over and retched into the bushes.

Please don't eat me. Please don't eat me. Please don't eat me.

The words were like a mantra in my head, but when the spinning finally subsided and I chanced a glance at the enormous wolf, I found it watching me.

And not in an *I'm going to eat you* way. In a curious way, with its head tilted to one side. There was something unnerving in its stare, though. Something intelligent that made my skin crawl. Wolves were smart. Most animals were. But this was more than that.

I spat bile into the mud and wiped the corner of my mouth. "*Um...*" I started, afraid if I spoke too loudly it would break the spell and jerk the string that would ring the proverbial dinner bell. "Thank you."

It continued to stare. "You...you can go now." It didn't budge.

Okay then.

I used a nearby tree to help me stand, gripping the rough bark hard enough to aggravate several cuts I didn't know I had on my hands. I winced, hopping on one foot. It felt like my ankle had swelled to double its size.

When I finally dared to take my eyes off the wolf still watching me intently, I noticed three things.

1. I couldn't feel my toes or my fingertips.
2. I had *no fucking idea* where I was.
3. The storm had finally ended.

Great.

The wolf turned and lumbered into the trees. I watched it go and something tugged at my chest. Without that wolf, I'd probably be dead right now. Buried beneath a good six feet of earth. No one would've ever found me.

My eyes burned, and I wasn't sure if it was more from the dirt still inside them or the threat of tears. "*Bye,*" I whispered as it vanished into the dark, and scanned the trees around me to try to figure out where I was.

If I just kept moving down, I would make it to the main road. The mudslide had probably taken me most of the way already. It shouldn't be far.

I started to move and cried out at the pain in my ankle. Pins and needles from the numbness radiated up my calves like little daggers.

The sound of the wolf's panting alerted me that it'd returned and the hairs on my neck rose as I spun. It was holding a long stick in its jaws. Long fangs stark white against the damp wood. It dropped the stick at my feet, and I reached down for it, careful to keep my movements slow.

It was long and sturdy. Mostly straight except for a crook near the top. The perfect walking stick.

"Smart pooch," I muttered under my breath, side eyeing the huge wolf.

It moved several steps to the east and then waited. I narrowed my gaze. When I tried to move a couple steps south, the wolf let loose a low growl. I stopped. It moved another two steps to the east and then paused, waiting with its head tilted back to watch me.

"You want me to follow you?" I spoke through chattering teeth, my voice hoarse.

With ears pricked to listen for my advance, it began to move further into the woods with slow steps.

"Uh...I need to get to town..." I told it, not really knowing why the hell I was arguing with a wild animal. Truth be told, I wasn't really sure what I was going to do when I got to town, but at least there would be shelter in case the storm came back. Judging by the sky, it was only a couple more hours until sunrise. I could wait outside the school until the janitors went through.

Then what? The other part of my brain rationalized. You have no clothes. No money for food. Your schoolbooks, boots, and wallet are all back in the blind, probably buried somewhere in the mountainside.

And if someone sees you covered in mud and leaves from head to toe, they're going to think they've just sighted bigfoot.

The seriousness of what happened finally hit me like a punch to the gut. A weight on my chest made it hard to breathe. What was I going to do?

The wolf barked, still waiting for me to follow it.

I pursed my lips, looking to the direction I *thought* was south, and back to the wolf.

*What the hell...*I thought. I didn't know where the fuck I was anyway, and the wolf hadn't eaten me yet. I had to hope it was leading me to shelter and not to a pack of other wolves it wanted to share its dinner with.

It barked again.

I used the walking stick to help me along, limping to follow the oversized fleabag with all the strength I had left. "*Yeah, yeah,*" I muttered. "I'm coming. But if you eat me, I'm going to make sure the devil saves a special place for you in hell."

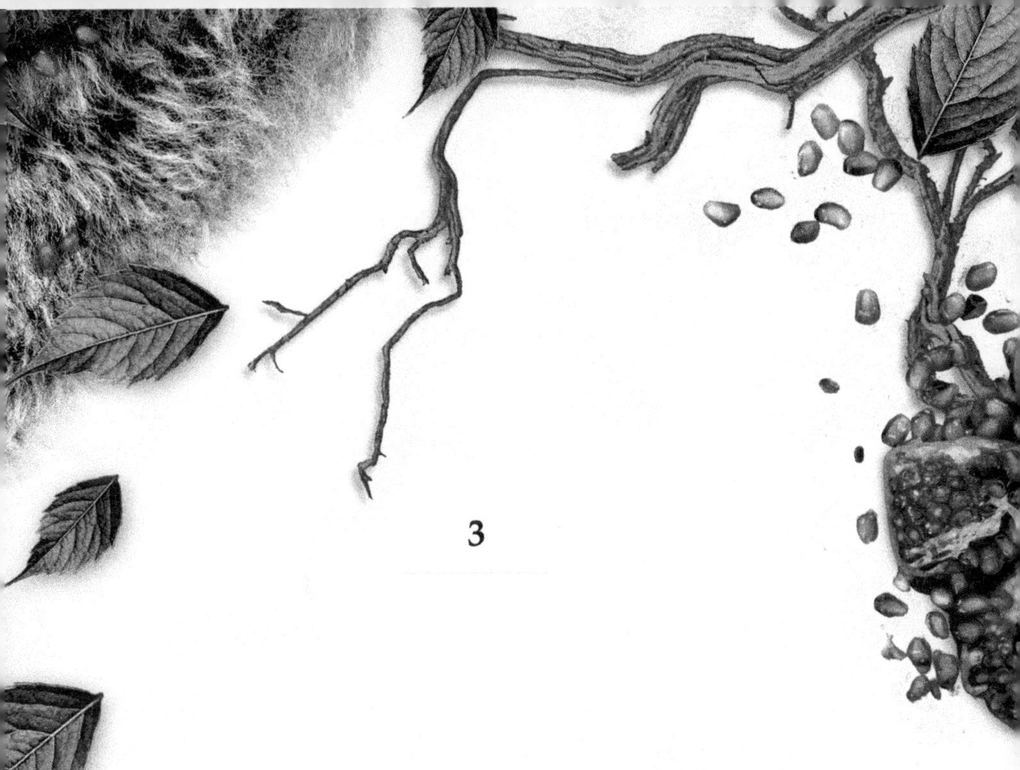

3

W e walked for what felt like at least an hour but was probably
less. By the time I saw the mellow orange glow of artificial light
through the trees and caught the scent of burning firewood on the
breeze, I was half unconscious.

Between the cold, the adrenaline crash, and all the exertion, I was
past the point of no return. I had just enough presence of mind to recognize shelter and sigh in relief before my body gave out under its own
weight and the darkness at the edges of my vision started to spread.
Come on, I shouted in my mind. *You're almost there.*

Call out for help or something.

I parted my lips to call out, but my voice rasped out barely above a
whisper. I tried to push my body up, but the numbness had spread to
cover most of my hands and forearms. They were practically useless at
this point.

Army crawl it is...

I pulled myself forward on my forearms, using all my shoulder
strength to move the rest of my aching body. As I nudged a particularly
spikey shrub from my path, I saw it.

Nestled in a grove in the trees, down a gently sloping hill. A wooden
structure, like a modern hunting cabin, or maybe a private chalet,
crouched among the foliage. It had two levels, each with their own

wraparound deck. A big peaked roof with a chimney puffing out coils of dark smoke made me shiver, anticipating the warmth it would provide.

If only I could make it there...

I glanced around for the wolf, hoping it could help me get the rest of the way. Pull me like it had when I was stuck in the mudslide. But it was gone.

I sent a silent thank you to the white beast, bowing my head for a moment of rest. It had gotten me this far. I could make it the rest of the way. I just had to try to stand back up. I'd never get there dragging myself across the mud.

"I've got you," the rich male voice made me gasp and recoil as a strong, warm hand curled under my left arm to help me up. "It's okay, Allie. It's me. It's Jared."

I all but squealed, wanting to wrench my arm away, but he was holding me tightly as he braced my body with his other hand around my middle and lifted me to standing. He pulled my left arm around his neck and then held my hand there to keep me in place, securely against his toned torso.

His *naked* torso.

A pair of beige khaki shorts hung low on his tan hips. He was barefoot and when I turned in horror to meet his gaze, I saw that his eyes, a beautiful caramel color with a bright fleck of green in the left one, seemed to be lit from within. Glowing.

He smelled of cedar and birch with an undercurrent of something not entirely unpleasant, but *unusual.* Something musky and animal that I couldn't place. "Jared?" I croaked, blinking away the black spots from my eyes and craning my neck to see him better. Had I passed out? Was this a vivid dream?

"Come on, we need to get you inside before you get hypothermia," Jared said, helping me to move slowly down the slope to the cabin.

Hypothermia? Hypothermia caused confusion. Could it cause hallucinations? I couldn't remember. But maybe that's why his eyes seemed to be glowing? Maybe that was why I was seeing him here in the first place. Maybe he wasn't really here at all.

What the hell would Jared *freaking* Stone be doing out here in the woods half naked and alone in the hours before dawn? He was in his senior year at Forest Grove High. Everyone knew him. And it wasn't hard to see why. You couldn't exactly miss the guy. With those striking eyes and high cheekbones framing an unnaturally symmetrical face with a dimpled chin. The perfectly tousled dirty blonde hair. Jared Stone could have any girl at Forest Grove he wanted, but he'd never dated any of them.

He'd never even *spoken* to me before I didn't think. Not that I cared. I'd only dated one guy in my high school career and that turned out to be a big fucking mistake. Maybe Jared was on to something by taking himself irrevocably off the market.

"*What,*" I started, swallowing to ease the scratchy feeling in my throat. This was suddenly *mortifying.* I was covered in mud and leaves and god knew what else. I probably smelled like a sewer.

Fuck. My. Life.

"What are you *doing* out here?"

He paused and cocked his head at me, his brows drawing together in confusion.

A feral growl had me turning back to the cabin ahead, clinging to Jared as a wolf approached. Not my white wolf. Not my savior.

This was another beast. Bigger. I almost thought it was a bear, but it wasn't. Its face twisted in a feral snarl.

The dark gray wolf skidded to a stop a few feet away and I let out a small sound of fear. Its hackles raised and it snapped in my direction, its piercing blue eyes locked on me as though it wanted to tear my throat out.

Jared squeezed my hand, stopping me from screaming and drawing my attention back to him. My heart was thudding so loudly I'd have been surprised if he couldn't hear it. The black spots were coming back, now. The adrenaline too much for my body to take. But Jared stood calmly at my side.

In fact, he was staring daggers at the wolf.

Completely unperturbed.

"Fuck off, Clay. She needs help."

The wolf snapped at Jared and I yelped.

His hand around my waist held me closer, as though trying to reassure me.

My mind raced to make sense of what was going on. Was this...was this Jared's *pet* or something? Some rare breed of domesticated giant wolf I'd never heard of?

But that still didn't explain what the *hell* he was doing out here. Did he...*did he live out here?* That couldn't be right.

"I'm bringing her inside. *Move.*"

The wolf snarled at Jared.

Sweat broke out over my brow, moving lower to coat my chest in a slick layer of ice.

The intense stare down lasted several more heartbeats before the wolf snapped its gaze away from Jared and tore off into the trees.

Relief flooded my body like a sedative injected into my veins. And once I couldn't hear the wolf's footfalls any longer, I slumped against Jared and gave in to the dark. The haunting sound of a lone wolf's howl carried me into oblivion.

I AWOKE TO THE CRACKLE AND HISS OF FIRE AND THE LOW HUM OF DISTANT raised voices. It was bright and I was warm beneath a heavy quilt atop a bed I didn't recognize. In a *room* I didn't recognize, I realized as my eyes adjusted to the sunlight streaming in from the large rectangular window several feet from the bed.

Panic lodged in my throat, and I shoved the quilt off and swung my legs over the edge of the bed to rise, wincing as I set my feet down on warm wood. I swallowed hard and breathed through the anxiety rushing to my head like a loud swarm of bees.

My clothing was stiff with caked mud and grime. There were scrapes up my arms and over my hands. When I reached a hand up, I found my long hair to be crunchy with bits of leaves in it.

Shifting, I found my left pant leg was torn to the knee. A tensor bandage wrapped around the swollen joint of my ankle.

The storm.

Dad's blind had been destroyed. And I...I'd followed a wolf here.

And then Jared...

I inhaled deeply through my nose and tried to calm down and remember how I got here.

I was in a cabin in the woods. A cabin that must belong to Jared. He had to have carried me up here when I passed out. Judging by what I could see outside, I was on the second floor. And this must be a guest room, because there was nothing identifying it as belonging to anyone.

No photos.

No band posters, or school binders or textbooks.

It had the plain wooden double bed I was sitting on. The quilt looked to be hand-stitched. I immediately prayed the smears of mud and specks of blood from my scrapes would come off. I didn't want Jared's parents to give him hell because I'd ruined it.

There was a low nightstand beside the low bed, and a fireplace across the room—a low burning fire, mostly embers now, in its hearth. A metal grate was set around it, and a threadbare rug adorned the floor in front of that.

There wasn't anything else.

Except...was that?

My phone! It was cleaned off and plugged in beside the bed. It had been tucked away on the wide ledge of the wooden bedframe. I snatched it up and sent a silent plea to whatever gods would hear me that it would still work.

I held my breath as I pushed the side button and tipped my head back in a sigh of relief when it powered on.

My relief was short-lived, though. It was one in the afternoon. And I had thirty-three text messages and three missed calls. *Damn.*

I fired off two quick texts. One to Layla, and one to Viv. I ignored the new one from Devin and didn't bother to read the million messages from my two friends. I just told them that my phone needed to charge, and I was fine. The battery died and I'd just slept in. That's all.

I could find a way to explain away how I sprained my ankle later.

The raised voices grew louder, and I strained my ears to hear what they were saying. I set my phone down, ignoring the double vibration that told me I'd just gotten another message. Limping, I made my way over to the window and peeked outside, my breaths clouding the windowpane.

Jared was out there talking animatedly with another guy that sparked something in my memory, but from this far away, I couldn't place his face. Maybe he went to Forest Grove, too? No, that couldn't be right. He looked too old to be a student. A family member of Jared's, maybe? A cousin.

Oh shit. Maybe this is that guy's house and you just rubbed a bucket of mud into his clean sheets.

I reached for the knob at the base of the window and turned the crank slowly and as quietly as I could until the window cracked open.

"...can't stay here." A deep gravelly voice growled at Jared.

With bated breath, I gripped the sill with both hands and squinted down at the front of the house where they were arguing. Jared had a shirt on this time, but the other guy...he sure as hell didn't.

He was hulking in size, tan, and with short cropped dark hair. From this angle, I couldn't see his face, but from the sound of his voice, I had to imagine it would be just as scary and intimidating as his growl.

"She's been living in that fucking hunting blind in the woods for months, Clay. It's destroyed. I went and checked for myself. That bag is everything that she has now."

I saw where he gestured to a muddied brown sack on the edge of the front deck. My heart pounded hard against my ribcage, and hot tears stung my eyes. The picture of dad. I'd dropped it during the mudslide. I wanted to hope it was in there, but I knew it wouldn't be.

"We aren't a *goddamned shelter,*" the other guy seethed, rubbing a wide hand over the back of his thick neck. My toes curled and a hot flush stained my cheeks. *What an asshole...*

He was right, though. I wouldn't be anyone else's burden. It was why I'd moved out into the blind to begin with.

Jared stepped in closer to the other guy, his shoulders squared. The guy called Clay took two steps back and rolled his shoulders, limbering up as though for a fight.

Oh no. Hell, no.

I hobbled to the door, using the wall for support. Outside was a wide hallway with an open balcony at the end that allowed someone upstairs to see the living area downstairs from above. I didn't bother to look around, rushing to get downstairs.

The stairs were hard to navigate, but I managed.

Once I got to the ground floor, I found the front door next to a kitchen I couldn't see from up top and wrenched it open, stepping outside to a snap of cool air and the brush of a warm afternoon sun on my cheeks.

Their conversation stopped immediately as I made my way across the deck, shielding my eyes from the worst of the sun's rays.

I snatched up my bag from the edge of the deck and tried to figure out what to say as my eyes adjusted. Jared was staring at me with a pained expression, his beautiful amber eyes going first to my hair, and then to the tear in my shirt that exposed most of my midriff.

The other guy stared, too, but not with anything that looked like pity.

Good, because I didn't want any.

The guy's fists were white-knuckle sandwiches as his sides, and he looked about ready to blow a gasket with the vein in his neck sticking out so much. I was wrong about his face, though. His apprehensive stare was chilling, but he didn't look like the monster I thought he would from that gravelly voice. Scary, yes, but with incredible blue eyes like a frozen lake under bright sunlight.

They looked...familiar. In fact, *he* looked familiar.

"I—I heard you arguing and..." I stuttered. "You don't have to fight. I'm going." I turned to Jared, averting my stare, completely unable to meet his gaze. A hot blush rose to heat my face. "Thank you," I said earnestly to him. "For what you did. I think that wolf would've eaten me if you hadn't been there."

I began to walk away, limping heavily. But as my feet connected with still-damp earth, I realized I was missing something, or a few something's.

My boots for one.

And I'd left my damned cellphone upstairs in my rush to get outside and stop them fighting.

Jared moved to stand in front of me, unapologetically blocking my path as he shoved his hands deep into his pockets. "You aren't going anywhere, Allie. Don't worry about Clay," he said, his amber eyes flicking to his friend. "He's an ass in general. It isn't you."

Clay scoffed, but I didn't dare turn around to see the look on his face.

Wait...*Clay?*

Isn't that what Jared had called the wolf from last night? I glanced up into Jared's eyes again, seeing the small fleck of green in the left one. Gulped.

Slowly, with my heart hammering in my chest, I turned back to Clay, flicking my gaze up only long enough to catch the unmistakable color of his eyes.

No. I almost laughed, giving my head a shake. *That's crazy, Allie.*

"I—I left my phone upstairs. If you just let me run back inside and get it, I'll be out of your way."

"Allie," Jared said, his tone hard with a warning. I chanced another glance up to see his jaw was set. "You're covered in mud from head to toe, you have a sprained ankle, and...I don't think you have anywhere to go."

The truth of what he said hit me like a blow to the chest. I rocked back on my heels from the force of the impact. "You can stay here for now. We don't use the guest room you were sleeping in. The only thing we ask is that you don't tell anyone."

My brows furrowed. *Don't tell anyone...what?* I wanted to ask, but Clay growled behind me and I turned in time to see his icy blue eyes light from within. My breathing hitched.

What the hell *is going on here?* Panic made my fingers clasp tighter to my backpack as I backed away from Clay, closer to Jared.

"*Clayton,*" Jared hissed. "Control yourself."

It clicked in my mind who he was. Clayton Armstrong. Bad boy extraordinaire. He was a senior when I was just a junior at Forest Grove High, but that face and hulking form was hard to forget, even if he did skip more classes than he attended. The juniors still whispered about him in the halls.

"You're a fucking idiot," Clay spat. "If Ryland finds out—"

"He *won't.*"

Clay looked like he was using every last ounce of his will to keep from losing it, and I found myself still backing away, trying to get out of the line of fire before he exploded. Until Jared circled my wrist with his warm hand, stopping me.

"*R-Really,*" I stammered. "This isn't necessary." I swallowed past the ever-growing lump in my throat, trying unsuccessfully to tug my wrist away from Jared. "I'll just go. Town can't be far. I can crash at Viv's place. I—I'm sorry, I didn't mean to cause so much—"

"Stay," Jared commanded, never breaking eye contact with Clay. When I chanced a look at his face, I saw that his eyes seemed to be glowing, too. The amber lit with a golden hue, only broken by the fleck of glowing green.

I rubbed my own eyes, taking another look before I decided I *wasn't* imagining it.

"What are you?" I breathed and Jared broke his stare with Clay to look at me with furrowed brows. With his eyes on me, there was no doubting their other-worldly glow.

"You don't remember?"

I tugged my wrist away and bolted, forgetting that my ankle was completely fucked. I got maybe twenty yards before I fell on my face and the contents of the pack spilled all over the dirt drive. I coughed and inhaled dirt, coughing some more. A bloodcurdling animal snarl had me scrambling away on all fours as an enormous black wolf skated to a massive black wolf have Clay's piercing eyes? Why did the white one have Jared's?

I struggled for breath as they continued their animal conversation. My head began to spin again. My breaths came slower...*and slower* until I was sure I was on the cusp of passing out, but I fought against the pull of the dark. This was *not* the time to be unconscious. I wasn't raised to be a sissy. I could change a transmission in a single afternoon. I could shoot a bow into a target at two-hundred yards and hit it dead center.

I could deal with a couple overgrown wolves.

Couldn't I?

Even if they were...*what the hell were they?*

Werewolves?

I tried not to laugh, but the sound started to burble up of its own accord. I pressed my lips tightly together to stop the sound from escaping, but my shaking shoulders and small noises gave me away.

The black wolf snapped at me one last time before it tossed a disgusted stare to Jared and stalked off into the trees.

I let the laughter out as soon as Clay was out of sight, tears springing to my eyes from the force of it. It was making my sides hurt. My abs were getting a work out. I snorted and wiped at the tears.

Was this what it felt like to go insane?

The wolf, *Jared,* sat gracefully with his paws at his front and cocked his big white head at me. It only made me laugh more.

"Allie?"

In the span of a single blink the wolf was gone and sitting buck ass naked in front of me was Jared. With one hand covering his junk and the other reaching toward me.

I shied away from his touch, the laughter dying on my lips as I took him in. As my mind tried to rectify what it was seeing from what it knew to be possible and *im*possible.

"Are you..." he trailed off, drawing his hand back with an apology in his still-glowing eyes. "Are you alright?"

"You were a wolf," I blurted. "Like a second ago. I saw you. And now you're..."

"It's a lot to take in. I know. But I thought you saw me shift last night, and if you're going to stay here—"

"I need a minute," I interrupted by putting a hand up to stop him, feeling faint again. "And...a shower. Do you have coffee?"

"Don't you want to talk about this?" Jared trailed off. The surprise unmistakable in his expression.

I eyed him. It was nearly impossible to stop my gaze from wandering low into his lap, where his torso tapered into an eight-pack and a sharp Adonis belt, and lower to...

"You need to put some clothes on," I said plainly, not allowing my mind to wander back to the land of fairy tales made real. I would think about it, just...later. Not right now.

I needed that damn minute of peace to process before I lost my fucking mind.

I needed him to stop looking at me like *I* was the one who was crazy when he'd been a wolf five seconds ago.

Jared's brows raised and he looked away, but not before I caught the start of a red flush in his cheeks. "Yeah. Right. Go take a shower. It's the door next to the room you slept in. I'll make some coffee." He cleared his throat. "And uh..."

I stood and waited, unable to take my eyes off him now, wondering if at any second I would blink, and he'd be canine again.

This was madness.

"Then we'll talk?" he asked, peering up at me beneath a set of thick caramel lashes.

I pursed my lips. "Yeah. You can start with telling me how long you've been watching me."

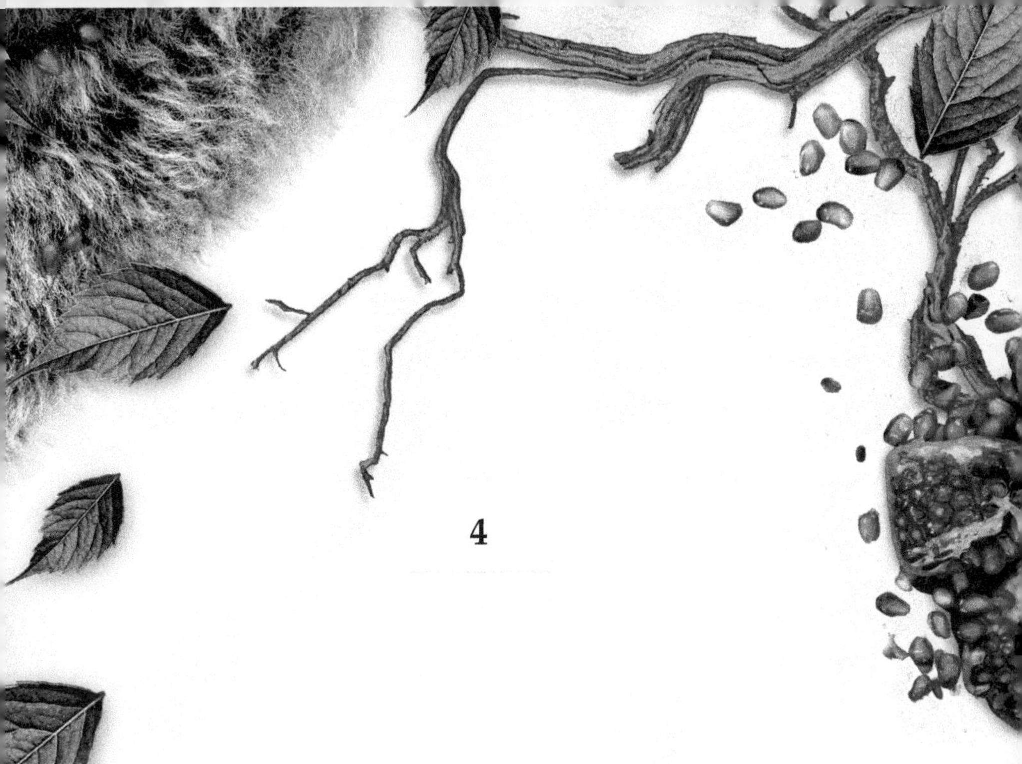

4

I took my time in the shower. There really wasn't any point in trying to make it to school for the end of the day. I was hopeful that I'd still be able to make my shift at the bookstore later in the afternoon, but I knew it was doubtful. I already gave Jacqueline a heads up that I might be late. I couldn't afford to miss the shift entirely. Especially not now.

"Perfect timing," Jared said as I hit the bottom step. I bit back a snide comment and followed the sound of his voice to the kitchen. "The coffee's just finished."

I pressed my lips together in discomfort. This was *weird*. Why was he acting like everything was alright? Like I didn't just find out that he and his buddy could turn into wolves?

He pulled out a chair for me at a small breakfast nook near a tall, wide window at the far end of the kitchen. His stupidly perfect smile made my jaw clench.

Hey Allie. Come sit and have some coffee. We should catch up, Allie. Everything is alright, Allie.

Except I didn't know him any more than he knew me. We weren't friends.

"Thanks," I said, unable to keep the lilt of apprehension from tainting my voice as I sat down.

"Glad they fit alright," Jared said, stuffing his hands deep into his pockets again.

I looked down at the outfit I'd found in the spare bedroom when I'd come out. My muddy clothes had vanished and in their place were a pair of sweats with an elastic waistband that I would've been drowning in if it weren't for the fact that I'd rolled them up several times at the hem and the waist. That along with a pair of red plaid slippers and a nondescript gray t-shirt was all I had on.

I kept my arms crossed over my chest, trying to hide the fact that I wasn't wearing a bra, though I supposed since he took my sodden one while I was in the shower, he already knew.

He didn't need proof, though.

When I didn't respond, mostly because I was uncomfortable *as hell* wearing *his* clothes in *his* house, his eyes flitted to the oak countertop in the kitchen where a coffee machine looked to have just finished brewing a full pot of glorious java.

My stomach rumbled.

"Are you hungry, too?" he asked. "I can make—"

"No," I interrupted. "Just coffee for now. I'm not feeling so hot."

It was the truth. At first, I thought I was getting sick from being out in the cold, but I knew the feeling well enough to recognize what it was. Anxiety. I'd suffered from it as a young child. And when Dad died last year, it'd come back. The hazy thoughts. The shaking fingers. The hollow pit in the bottom of my stomach that made me feel like I would throw up if I even *tried* to eat. The tense shoulders that I couldn't relax no matter how hard I tried.

I hadn't had a panic attack in six months, though, and considering what I'd just gone through and seen... well, let's just say I was shocked it hadn't happened already.

The power breathing in the shower had helped some.

"What do you take in your coffee?"

"Nothing," I answered him. "Just black is good." His brow furrowed. "Ok."

He poured me a coffee and one for himself, adding half a sugar and a splash of cream to his mug before he sat down across from me.

My hands clasped tightly together in my lap. "You're not going to turn into a wolf again, are you?"

Jared's lips tugged up into an understanding smirk. "No—no we try not to shift in the house. Too many things end up getting broken."

Good to know...

Note to self: stay *far* away from shifting wolves. "This is fucked," I muttered as I sipped the piping hot coffee, wincing as it seared a path down my throat. I wrapped my other hand around the tall mug and let the warmth of the heated porcelain seep into me, shivering.

"It's a lot to take in, I know."

"How long? I mean, how long have you..."

"Been a wolf?"

I clicked my jaw shut, unable to meet his stare. I nodded.

"Forever. I was a born wolf."

"A what?"

Jared took a drink of his own coffee and leaned against the table between us. I moved to lean back against my own chair in response. He didn't miss my aversion, pursing his full lips. "A born wolf," he repeated. "A shifter is made one of two ways. They are either born, or they are made."

I raised my brows, waiting for him to elaborate.

"A bite," he told me. "A bite from a shifter can trigger the change."

"Can?"

"It doesn't always."

"So, if Clay had bitten—"

"He wouldn't."

I found that doubtful. He looked pretty damned close to doing just that last night, and again this morning.

I snorted, setting my coffee down, my mind racing. I had about a million questions, but I wasn't sure I could handle all the answers right now. Already, my insides felt like they were ready to turn themselves inside out. I needed to take this slow or Jared would either be holding my hair over the toilet or helping me to breathe into a paper bag. I didn't relish the idea of either of those.

"Can I ask you something?"

I glanced up from the table. "Hmmm? Oh. I guess so."

"Why green?"

The question took me by surprise. "What?"

"Your hair. Why green?"

My hand unconsciously went up to finger a still- damp lock of it. "It's not green," I told him. "It's turquoise. But I guess it's a little faded."

"Your hair was blonde before, right? Almost white if I remember right."

I nodded.

"You've had it at least four colors since junior year.

Why dye it at all? It was beautiful."

I looked away, trying to hide a blush.

"I mean, it's beautiful now, too. It's beautiful no matter what you do with it," he rushed to cover his mistake.

I smirked, realizing what he was doing. I was visibly freaking out, and he was trying to calm me down by distracting me. Dad used to do that, too. Ask me a bunch of random, meaningless questions when I started to freak out. My heart gave a sorrowful squeeze.

"My mom had light blond hair, too," I blurted before I could stop myself. "My dad said that I looked like her and I..."

"Didn't want to look like her?" He offered, the crease back between his brows.

I drew in a long breath. "I didn't think he could stand it," I whispered, my throat growing tight. Why did I just tell him that? I snapped my mouth shut and licked my dry lips, suddenly eager to change the subject back to more comfortable territory.

"So, it's my turn," I said before he could comment on what I told him about my mother. "How long were you watching me?"

This time, I didn't avert my gaze. I didn't want to give him the opportunity to lie to me. There was no way he could have known that I'd been out there for months unless he'd been keeping an eye on me. My skin bristled again at the thought that I was being watched.

Jared began picking at a chip in the top of his mug. "A while."

"A while?" I prodded, unable to keep the ire from my voice. My blood was beginning to heat, chasing what remained of the anxiety from my veins. "How long is a while?"

The door crashed open at the other end of the kitchen. I whirled in my seat, gasping as I sloshed coffee all over the table.

Clay stormed into the cabin. His bulky arms were wrapped in thick corded veins. The tendons in his hands stood taut beneath the skin as he tightened his fists.

"Can I talk to you for a minute," he growled at Jared, cutting me a scathing look, his face pinched as though he was holding back. "*Alone?*"

"Dude, come on—"

"*Now.*"

My heart was hammering beneath my breastbone again, and I reached for the napkin holder on the table and quickly began to wipe up the mess of coffee. I swallowed, wincing from the pain in my ankle as I stood to toss the sodden tissues into the trash. "I have to get to work," I said absently, trying to settle my frayed nerves.

The guy made my body rigid with unease. He had this disquieting air about him, and when he entered a room, the atmosphere changed. Like he was a storm cloud threatening rain. Or the swell of the ocean when the winds change.

"Maybe you should take the night off ?" Jared said, rising from the table.

I shook my head. Nope. Not a freaking chance I was staying there with Clay. He looked like he wanted to take a bite out of me, literally. And as beautiful as I'd always thought wolves were, I definitely didn't relish the thought of becoming one. The thought brought with it about a million questions, and I wondered if I'd ever get the answers.

Did they have to shift during a full moon? Did it hurt?

Could they control themselves?

Oh my god...

Are there *other* things in this world that I don't know about?

My stomach roiled. "Uh...Jared, do you think my clothes are dry yet?"

I really needed to get out of here. I wanted the peace and solitude I could only find surrounded by shelves of books. Surrounded by thousands of stories with happily ever afters. With words that could whisk you away to another world, to make the one you're living in bearable.

"Are those my sweats?"

My blood froze to ice in my veins. I glanced down at the sweats I had rolled at both ends hanging low on my hips. And then I glanced up into the murderous stare of Clayton Armstrong.

I shot a look at Jared that I hoped conveyed the depth of my furious accusation.

Jared shrugged. "All my sweats were dirty," he said as though it were the simplest thing in the world. "I'll go get your clothes, Allie."

A tiny sound of protest rose up my throat as he left the room. As he left me *alone* with Clay.

The bastard.

"I—I'm sorry, I didn't know they were y—"

"Save it," he barked, pinching the bridge of his nose.

Much as I tried not to look, I couldn't help but notice that he was still barely dressed. In low-hanging shorts and bare feet. His torso was *huge,* the muscle more defined than an airbrushed actor in a gladiator movie.

Intimidating as hell.

"I'm not staying," I added when he continued to stand there stoic, purposefully not looking at me, but staring at a spot on the wall in the living area as though it were the most interesting spot in all the world. "You don't have to fight with Jared. I—I won't be anyone's burden."

His gaze dropped and some of the fury dimmed in his eyes. His jaw twitched as he ground his teeth together before he responded. "Do you have somewhere else to go?"

The question caught me by surprise and what he said earlier replayed in my head, making my own hands curl into fists.

"That's not your problem," I said, astonished at how level my voice came out. "This isn't a shelter, after all..."

His head snapped up and I saw a flash of something beneath his haughty stare.

"Here it is," Jared said, coming around the corner with an armful of clothing fresh from the dryer. He looked between Clay and I, pausing with a quirked brow. "What'd I miss?"

Clay's upper lip curled back in disgust before he stalked up the stairs, each of his heavy footfalls reverberating in my chest.

Jared passed me the bundle of still-warm clothes and gestured to the foot of the stairs. "They should be your size, but if they don't fit, I can get another pair."

A pair of simple black converse sneakers rested on the bottom stair. They looked like they were brand new. "I found one of your boots in the wreckage," he continued. "But I couldn't find the other one, so..."

"Did you buy those?"

Could he have left this morning while I was asleep to buy me shoes?

My shoulders tensed. That was...*weird*. Why would he do that? *He doesn't owe me anything.*

We aren't even friends.

"You can't go anywhere without shoes," he said with an awkward laugh, rubbing the back of his neck.

He was right. I'd been so pre-occupied with needing to change out of *Clay's* sweats and get to work that I'd forgotten I didn't have any shoes. How was I supposed to get to work? Walk through who knows how many miles of forest barefoot?

I swept the hair from my face and tucked it behind my ear, praying there was at least one hair elastic in my bag by the front door. "Um... *thanks.* I'll pay you back for them."

"You don't—"

"I do. I'll take some money out after work and bring it to school for you tomorrow."

His brows lowered. "Tomorrow?"

My gaze unconsciously flicked to the stairs, where Clay had disappeared down the corridor, my throat going dry.

"He'll come around, Allie," Jared said in a silky soft voice that almost made me forget he was half beast. I shoved the image away, my mind still trying to rebel against it even though I'd seen with my own eyes. Dad always told me that if the truth was looking me dead in the eye that I should believe it. But he was talking about people and their true colors...not men who could transform into wolves.

"Please tell me you'll come back after your shift?"

I dropped my stare, digging my fingers into the denim of my torn jeans. "I have to go," was my response before I brushed past Jared and up the stairs against my better judgment. I didn't want to go anywhere near Clay, but the bathroom next to the room I slept in was the only safe place to change. The bedroom didn't even have a lock on the door.

"Wait—" Jared said, stopping me with a hand on my arm. I shivered at the contact. The warmth of his skin and his hard calluses reminding me of wolfish paws.

He let go of me as though burned on contact. "At least let me drive you to work."

I tightened my jaw but nodded. It would be hell walking on this ankle if I didn't accept his offer, and I had no idea how far town was.

"And Allie," he added when I took another step up the stairs.

I turned, finding him watching me closely with those amber eyes, his face slightly pale. "I need your word." His adams apple bobbed in his throat. "I need your word that you won't tell a soul what you saw."

It was suddenly hard to breathe. Jared had phrased the words as a request, but by the loss of color in his face, and the hardness in his eyes, I knew it wasn't a request at all. It was a demand. I shuddered to think what would happen to me if I didn't meet it.

There was a reason I didn't know these sort of things existed—that *no one* knew. Maybe they didn't leave people like me alive to go blabbing? What was it Clay said? About someone named Ryland finding out...

Was he a wolf too?

I shook my head and held my breath, trying to stave off the rise of anxious thoughts.

"If you keep my secret, I'll keep yours," he added when I didn't respond right away.

I tilted my head at him, unsure what he meant.

"I don't think anyone else knows you live out in the woods...do they?"

Was that a threat?

I straightened my spine and lifted my chin. "I won't tell."

I turned on my heel and used the banister to help me limp the rest of the way to the top of my stairs, my blood chilling. As if I would tell anyone, anyway.

Who the hell would believe me?

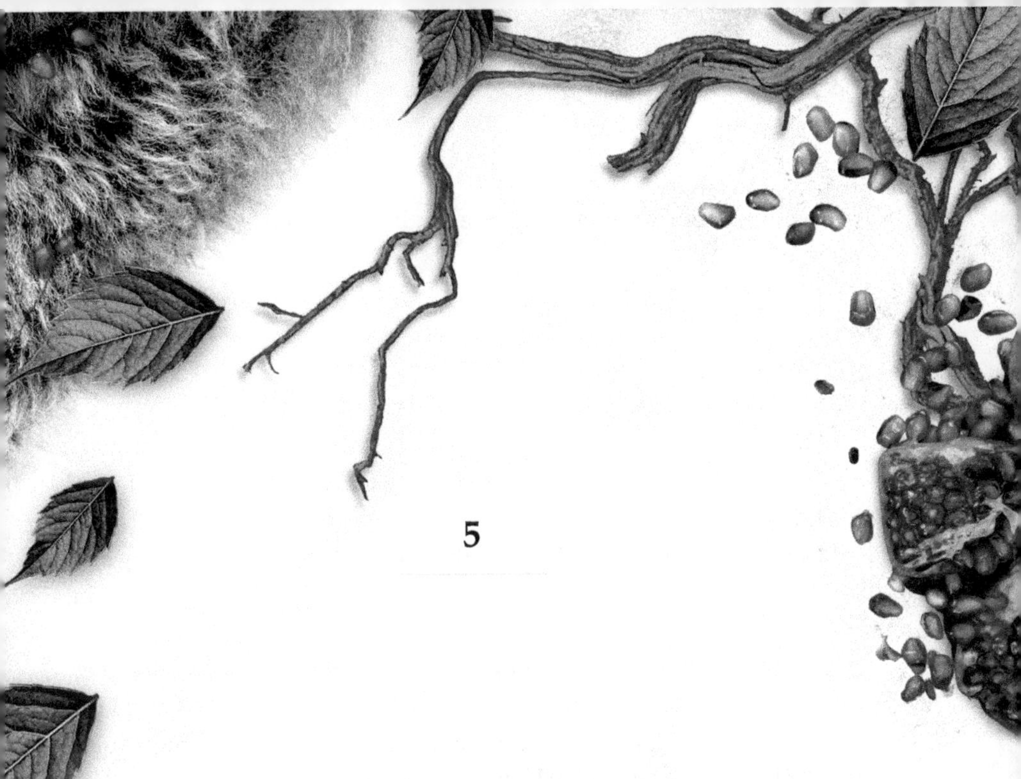

5

Jared and I didn't speak for most of the drive. He'd made a lame attempt at conversation during the long walk through the woods to where he parked his jeep in a small lot at the edge of a hiking trail, but my mind was elsewhere. And I needed to focus to keep my eyes from tearing at the pain in my sprained ankle. I had the walking stick from the night before, and luckily the shoes fit, but it still hurt to put weight on it.

I wanted to ask Jared why he didn't have a proper driveway leading up to the cabin, but I could guess the reason. Couldn't have visitors showing up when you could be caught morphing into a fucking over-sized dog. Jared pulled his Wrangler up to the front of the shop, putting it into park in one of the many empty spaces along the street. "Where will you go?" He asked, his hands gripping hard on the steering wheel.

I opened my mouth to say something but ended up closing it again. The truth was that I had no freaking idea where I was going to go, and I was a shit liar. I licked my dry lips and pulled the backpack from the back seat, slinging it over my shoulder as I stepped outside. "Thank you," I told him, meaning it. I'd had the time to think on the drive into town and I realized that even though the hours since I awoke this afternoon had been some of the most fucked up I'd ever experienced, he'd still saved me.

Even if he *had* been watching me out in the woods. Even if he was a wolf in human skin.

Without his help, I might be dead. "Thank you for saving my life," I said earnestly.

His jaw tightened.

"Your secret is safe with me. I won't ever tell."

"Allie, I don't—"

"*Please,*" I interrupted him, that panicky feeling rising again. "I need you to go now."

Before he could answer, I closed the door to his Jeep and did my best to hurry into the shop, but I barely managed a waddle, cursing the entire way as my ankle protested.

The bells inside the door jingled as I entered, the familiar sweet, musky scent of paper and ink greeted me like a warm embrace, and I felt my nerves calm. I didn't turn around as I heard the Jeep's engine purr back to life as Jared pulled back out onto the road.

Jacqueline squinted up from the front counter, her small glasses perched low on the tip of her nose. "Oh, Allie. You made it. I wasn't sure if…" she trailed off, and something registered in her eyes. "Is everything alright?"

She eyes me from bottom to top, taking in the torn jeans and the limp. Jared managed to rescue several clothing articles from Dad's hunting blind, so I at least had a clean sweater over my tattered tank top. But I knew I looked half dead. Much as I tried to avoid it, I'd seen my reflection in the mirror at Jared's cabin.

"Sprained my ankle," I said with an impish grin. "Hurts like hell, but I'm fine."

"Oh," she said, pushing back her graying dark auburn hair from her face as she came around the counter. "What happened? If you would prefer to take the night off and keep it elevat—"

"No," I blurted, reeling myself back in. "No, I—I want to work. It's not even that bad."

She seemed to consider and then nodded. "Alright. Just don't overdo it. I haven't gotten around to scanning in today's deliveries, if you want to do that, I'll get them on the shelves in the morning."

"Okay," I replied, knowing full well that I would get all the deliveries scanned in *and* shelved before I left tonight. I needed this job, and I wasn't about to shirk any of my duties, sprained ankle or not. The book shop wasn't just my only source of income. There was an apartment above it. Occupied, but only until December. Then, when the guy moved out, I was hoping Jacqueline would let me rent it. It was what I'd been saving for. I'd have first month's rent and a deposit ready to go. Who better to rent the space than your only employee, right? I hadn't asked her yet, but only because I wanted to have the deposit ready to give her when I did.

And now, after losing almost everything last night, that might take longer than I had planned. I sighed.

"Is everything alright?" she asked, leaning over the counter to pull her purse and jacket from the coat rack.

"Huh?" I blinked. "Oh. Yeah. Just a little tired."

"The coffee in the back room is still pretty fresh."

"Thanks, Jacqueline."

"Oh!" Jacqueline exclaimed, pulling a folded slip of paper from her purse. "I almost forgot. Devin was here earlier. Around the time your shift normally starts. I told him you were going to be a bit late and he said he couldn't wait."

She held the note out to me.

"He left this for you. Said he was worried your phone wasn't working."

She lifted a brow when I didn't immediately move to take it but made no further comment. Jacqueline knew my phone was working just fine. I'd sent her a message that I'd be a bit late today just a few hours ago.

I gritted my teeth as I limped the three steps between us and gingerly took the paper from her slender fingers with a tight smile. "Thanks."

"Right," she said, snapping back into motion. She tugged on her coat and belted it in the front. "Well, I've got about a million errands to run. Take it easy on that ankle, hey?"

"I will."

"Good."

I crumpled the note in my fist as the door shut behind her, the sound of the bells loud in the quiet shop. I chucked the balled-up note onto the desk and slumped into the tall stool behind the counter as the bells jingled again, signaling the entry of the first customers of the evening.

I pressed my palms into my eyes and yawned. It was going to be a *very* long night.

I finished scanning the new stock into the system and had it all shelved and the entire store dusted and swept before seven, as usual. It was simple work, and even with a bum ankle, it wasn't so hard.

But I'd almost hoped the work would take me longer tonight, now I had two hours to sit here and contemplate my bleak existence. I should've been using the time to think about where the hell I was going to stay tonight. Or, you know, until December when the guy upstairs *hopefully* moved out.

Sighing heavily, I continued going through the fall catalog from Random House. It was my job to keep the young adult section up to date on all the newest releases, and I took that responsibility *very* seriously. It showed in the surgency of teen clientele the store had gained since I started here last year.

Unconsciously, my gaze slipped to the crumpled note atop Jacqueline's desk behind the main counter. I clenched my jaw, trying to distract myself with options for places to stay.

I could go back to the blind in the woods. Jared said it was destroyed, but how destroyed was destroyed? Was it salvageable? If I brought a tarp and some duct tape, could I make it work?

My heart ached for the last place I had that reminded me of him. After the house sold and my aunt and uncle boxed up all his things, all I had left was that one photo and the old blind. Now I had neither.

My chest ached.

What else? I asked myself, trying to distract from the pain. *Where else could you go?*

Not Viv's or Layla's. *Then you'd have to explain that you've been lying to them for months.* I was just glad that Layla had to watch her younger brothers and sisters on Thursdays, and Viv always went to visit her Nona at the senior's home. Otherwise, they'd both be here demanding answers I didn't know how to give. I groaned, dropping my head into my hands.

This was all getting so out of hand.

My gaze flitted back to the paper on the desk and before I could change my mind, I leaned over and snatched it up, huffing before I uncrumpled the page and flattened it against the counter with my palm.

Allie, I'm sorry for what happened. Please stop ignoring me. You know it wasn't really me. I wasn't myself. You know me. You know I'd never hurt you. I love you. -Devin.

My hands began to shake as I read the words over again. My fingers curled in, my stubby nails like talons as I tore the note to shreds, letting the anger chase away all the other ugly thoughts.

You know I'd never hurt you... What a joke.

My fingers absently went up to trace the line of tender flesh along my collar. It was almost healed. It barely hurt to touch now, but that didn't erase the memory of how I'd gotten it. What he did.

Little tremors raced up my spine and I took another sip of warm coffee to subdue the rise of anxious energy. The first flash came, and I winced.

An image of Devin in the dark of the basement at his Dad's house. In the middle of the night.

I'd been asleep. Peacefully dreaming while he was going through my phone.

I had no idea what awaited me when I awoke to the sound of his heavy breathing. Barely able to see save for the strange greenish glow of my cell phone like a halo framing his head.

"Devin, what are you doing? Come back to sleep," I'd murmured, my voice breathy with a yawn.

I pulled myself out of the flashback, and a small whimper made my bottom lip quiver. I wiped the note confetti from the desk into the recycling bin, some of the pieces scattering to the floor in my haste.

We only dated for three months, but I thought I'd loved him. He was handsome, in a devil may care sort of way. With a shock of dark hair and arresting green eyes. He was tall and lean. He thought my love for books and anime was silly and childish, but we both loved hockey and shared the same taste in music.

I couldn't even listen to those songs anymore. Preferring deafening silence to a single note of any song we once sang together.

It was only three months. So then why did this hurt so much?

I could still picture him. The new boy at Forest Grove high last year.

He was all anyone could talk about for a while. In a town as small as ours, any newcomers were regarded with a sort of scrutinizing awe. How did they come to live in a place like this? What brought them here? Where were they from? The rumor mill churned out its own theories, but I knew somehow that none of them were correct.

When I began to notice him watching me as I curiously watched him, I couldn't believe that someone like me had caught his eye. Outgoing and handsome as he was, what could he possible want with a quiet girl like me?

He was a mystery I wanted to unravel.

Why couldn't I have seen the that way lay beneath the surface wasn't the treasure I'd been seeking, but a broken soul that relished inflicting pain on others?

As I bowed my head, another flash came, and I gripped the edge of the counter to steady myself—to try to chase away the bad memories. But in the last week since it'd happened, I couldn't seem to stop reliving it.

"Why are you texting with Quinn? Is something going on between you two?" he'd asked, the question rousing me from sleep only enough to give him a playful shove and murmur for him to stop being ridiculous.

Quinn was in my elective culinary class. We had been assigned to do a project together on Moroccan cuisine. We were texting about that. And I didn't think it would be too hard to see that if Devin was *actually* reading the messages.

"Go back to sleep," I'd urged, completely unprepared for what would happen next.

Devin grabbed my wrist painfully hard and yanked me to sitting, making my head spin as my eyes tried to open and adjust to the lack of light. Heart pounding and blood suddenly pumping.

"What are you—"

"*Tell me,*" Devin had hissed, his face illuminated in the cell phone light. My eyes strained from the green- tinted brightness. "Tell me the truth."

I yanked my arm free of his grasp, rubbing out the ache in my joint. "What the hell, Dev?" I'd snapped. "That hurt."

I was still trying to figure out what was happening, my sleep addled brain needing a minute to catch up, when the first blow knocked any sense from my mind, making the rational part of me retreat somewhere deep within. Huddled with her knees to her chest, trying and failing to understand what she'd done wrong. Why she hadn't seen this coming?

Who this man was. Because it wasn't her Devin. It couldn't be.

I came out of the memory and ran for the front of the shop, flinging the door open to the stairway that led down into the storage area. The jingle of bells alerted me there was a customer entering the shop, but I didn't stop. I stumbled down the last three steps and barely made it, limping, into the bathroom before my stomach heaved and its meager contents were swallowed up by the toilet.

I dry heaved until there was absolutely nothing left.

Until my sides were splitting and my head pounding.

"Hello?" A voice echoed from upstairs.

Shit. I needed to get myself together. I couldn't puke every time I thought about what happened. I'd already lost almost ten pounds since last week. I couldn't afford to start losing muscle, too.

I needed to get over it. Rising, I rinsed out my mouth in the sink and lifted my chin. Set my jaw. It wasn't that he hurt me. I could handle the pain. A good body check on the ice did more damage than what he did to me. It was the fact that I *trusted* him. That I *loved* him.

...that I thought he loved me back... That was what made me sick.

The memory of gentle caresses and warm embraces, of tender kisses stolen beneath the bleachers was at war with the new violent imagery that had taken up my brain space where the softer things used to be. I couldn't reconcile one with the other. It was impossible. It was like Devin Wright was two completely different people. The mischievous, but *kind* guy I'd fallen for...and the animal who ripped my heart out.

I hauled ass up the stairs and pasted on a more pleasant expression than the one I was wearing. "Sorry about that," I said, rounding the corner without a trace of the weaker girl I'd left to desiccate at the bottom of the stairs.

I went to the counter and began ringing in the man who was trying to hide the fact that he was purchasing an erotic novel by buying the newest John Grisham. I didn't comment on his tastes. I never did. He would only say it was for his wife even though he wasn't wearing a ring and then he wouldn't come back in. I knew his type.

Instead, I told him to have a nice day and enjoy his books. To come back again soon.

I'd gotten through the bulk of the thick fall catalog for Simon and Schuster by the time the next customer came into the shop. I glanced up with a ready smile and a greeting on my tongue, but the words dissolved before I could speak them, and I was left with a sour taste coating my mouth.

Devin sauntered into the shop, dipping his head low so he didn't hit the bells atop the doorframe. When his eyes met mine, something in my body died and came alive all at once. I wanted to run.

But I couldn't move.

I wanted to punch the stupid demure smirk from his lips.

But then I wouldn't be any better than he was.

I swallowed hard and flipped the catalog closed with a thud.

"Allie, just let me talk." Devin stepped further into the store, approaching the counter with slow, measured steps as though I were the dangerous one. As if *he* was the one afraid.

How fucking ludicrous. "No."

"Allie," his eyes darkened, and there was a note of warning in his voice.

Hastily I looked around, but as was usual for a weekday evening, there wasn't anyone in the shop. And no one on the street outside, either.

I rose from the stool and grimaced from the pain in my ankle, pulse quickening. "I think you should leave. I have nothing to say to you. And I don't want to hear any—"

"What happened?" Devin growled as he came around the counter to inspect my ankle. His green eyes suddenly bright and cutting. "What did you do?" He kneeled to inspect the bandages, reaching out to take hold of my calf.

I shrank back, backing into Jacqueline's desk. A metal stapler fell from the ledge and clattered to the hardwood, the loud noise sending a tremor racing up my back. "Y-you aren't allowed back here, Dev. I could get fired."

He backed up a step and looked down at me with a tilt to his head. Looking at his thick brows and shadowed eyes, that wide chin, and sharp nose, I wondered how I ever found his severe features to be anything less than menacing.

Devin Wright was handsome, yes. But it was there in his eyes, had been there all along and I just hadn't seen it. He'd kept the ugly bits of himself concealed from me. From everyone.

Now that I'd seen it, I couldn't unsee it.

Devin turned on me with an accusatory stare. "What's going on with you, Allie?"

What's going on with me?

He was the one who turned into a fucking monster. "Nothing," I said, keeping the spite from my voice. When I'd tried to fight back last week, it'd only made it worse. When I told him to go to hell, he'd only hurt me more. This time I wasn't going to give him any ammunition. "Nothing is wrong. I just hurt my ankle walking home from the bus."

His jaw twitched and something hot and angry flashed behind his eyes. My hand went to my stomach, feeling the threat of vomiting all over again coming back.

"I really need to get back to work, Devin."

"Work? Is your work more important than *us*? *Christ, Allie!*" His face soured and I felt around on the desk behind my back until my fingers wrapped tightly around a pen. "I just came here to talk to you and you're acting like...like you don't even *care*."

He closed the last few steps between us and I flinched when he raised his hand.

Devin didn't like that.

He glared down at me, gently brushing several strands of faded turquoise out of my face. My heart skipped a beat and I struggled to keep down the bile rising in the back of my throat. "I'm not going to hurt you," Devin said with a scowl twisting his features. "How could you think I would hurt you?"

My mind raced. I couldn't help the furrow from forming in my brow. *But you already did hurt me...*

What the fuck was he playing at? "But you di—"

"That wasn't me," he interrupted, his eyes drawing down at the corners, some of the lines in his forehead smoothed. "You know it wasn't."

Wasn't it?

I managed to squirm out of his grasp before he could lean his forehead against mine. I put two feet of space between us, my chest rising and falling faster than it had been a moment before.

He needed to leave.

I couldn't deal with this right now. Not on top of everything else.

Devin had shown me his true colors. The truth of him, of who he was deep down inside, had looked me dead in the eye that night, and I believed what I saw.

He couldn't take it back.

"Get out," I said, ready to try to hurt him if that's what it came to. Just because I was taught not to use violence as an answer, didn't mean I wouldn't protect myself. I was surprised last time. I shut down. I didn't know what to do. I was in shock.

Not this time.

"If you don't leave, I *will* call the police and I *will* tell them what you did to me." My voice didn't waver even once and I gave myself a mental pat on the back, squeezing the pen behind my back until I thought I might snap the damned thing right in half before I even had a chance to use it.

Devin's eyes widened in fury, and under the fluorescent light above the counter, they almost seemed to glow. I shook my head and the illusion vanished. The bells on top of the door sounded just as Devin took a step toward me and my body tensed to strike him.

"*Wright*," a familiar voice cautioned from just inside the doorway. "I believe you were asked to leave."

Jared was wearing the same clothes he had been earlier, but he looked different. Angry. Even with Clay barking at him earlier he hadn't seemed angry. His hands weren't balled into fists like they were now. His nostrils weren't flaring. There wasn't a fire burning beneath his stare.

Devin never took his eyes off me. "*Mind your fucking business, Stone*," he hissed at Jared. "This is between me and Allie."

I tried to move a little further laway, to get out from behind the counter and closer to Jared because somehow in that moment I was less afraid of a wolf- man than I was my eighteen-year-old ex-boyfriend.

How fucked is that?

Devin stopped me with a hand wrapped roughly around my upper arm. "Where do you think you're going? I wasn't done talk—"

Reflexively, I stabbed the pointy end of the pen into the flesh of his hand. Not enough to do much more than draw tiny droplet of blood, but enough to make him loosen his hold, and for me to scramble out of his grasp and fall to the floor.

Jared was there faster than humanly possible, and I had to remind myself that it was because he legit *was not human*. He was helping me to stand when Devin growled at both of us, stomping out from behind the counter. "She's *mine*," he roared at Jared, his voice taking on a tone that made my stomach drop to my toes.

His? Was he fucking kidding me?

I didn't know if it was because I had Jared at my back, or if the words themselves had just gotten me that enraged, but I *snapped*. I pulled away from Jared only enough to get in Devin's face. "*I am not yours! I belong to no one.*"

Devin stumbled back a step, his lips parting in wordless protest as he took me in like he was just seeing me for the first time. "Allie..."

"Get the fuck out of here. Don't come back," Jared added, moving to stand next to me.

Devin looked between Jared and I, a wrinkle in his brow. He looked like he might hit one of us. I could practically feel the fury rippling off of him in waves of heat, but he just made an angered sound in the back of his throat and turned his back to us.

He slammed the door to the shop behind him, making the glass pane in the door shake.

I slumped, suddenly unable to get my breath, and leaned heavily on the edge of the front counter. I breathed in deeply through my nose and pushed the air out through my mouth. My hands were shaking, and I desperately wanted them to stop. I wanted to shuck off this weaker Allie like a dead skin and be the stronger one I knew was there somewhere. But she'd been hiding for a long time, and I didn't know how to get her back.

"Hey," Jared said, brushing a hand over my back. I recoiled from his touch at first, but then settled, letting his stillness help to soothe my nerves. "Can I..." he trailed off awkwardly. "Can I get you some water or something?"

My throat was dry as a bone from breathing so hard, but I didn't say that. I didn't answer him at all. His touch was helping, and the truth was, I didn't want him to move.

After I got my breath back and my stomach stopped trying to propel itself up my throat, I felt my muscles go, and my body sagged in relief. "No. I'm fine. I mean, I'll get it myself."

"It's water, Allie. I know you can get it yourself, but it's okay to need help sometimes."

I pressed my lips together.

"Alright," Jared breathed, removing his hand. "No water, then. When is your shift over?"

Spinning, I cocked my head at him.

Jared shoved his hands in the pockets of his jeans and lifted his shoulders. "If it's alright with you, I'd like to stay."

What?

"Did you find a place to stay tonight?"

I gulped, looking away. I'd actually been thinking I would stay here. There was a couch in the back of the shop. And if I left before dawn, there was a good chance no one would see me. But even I knew that was a bad idea.

If someone *did* see me, it would be hard to make up an excuse to why I was leaving the bookshop at five AM when my shift didn't start until 3:30 in the afternoon. I couldn't afford to lose this job.

I shook my head.

Jared nodded. "Alright."

"Alright?"

"Then you'll come home with me." I opened my mouth to protest.

"Please," he said, an earnestness gleaming in his amber eyes when he lifted them to mine. My chest tightened. "I know you have more questions. I'll answer them all, if you want." He kicked at a spot on the floor and I noticed he was watching the front window with a keen eye, making sure Devin wasn't waiting outside. "And maybe you could answer a few more of mine?"

I bit my lower lip, feeling awkward and hating it. My face hot and fingers numb from knotting them together. I didn't know what to say.

"Just...let me help you. Please."

"Why?" I asked, voicing the question I'd been afraid to ask before. "Why do you want to help me? You don't even know me."

The hint of a smile pulled up the corner of Jared's stupidly perfect mouth, showing off a slight dimple on his left cheek. *Damn.*

"Because you're a good person who doesn't deserve all of the bad things that've happened to her," he said, the tips of his ears staining pink.

My breath caught and I couldn't look at him anymore. Could hardly breathe.

Because Jared was wrong. I deserved it all.

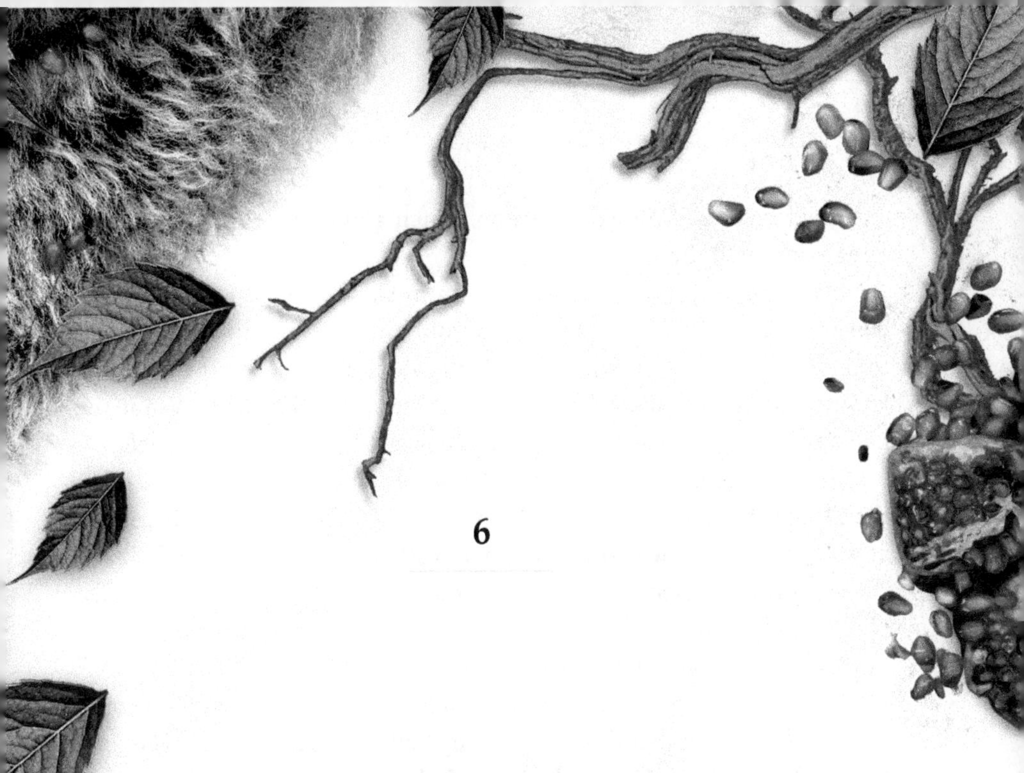

6

"Don't take that road," I all but shouted as Jared made to round the bend onto Lofty Pines Drive.

The tires of his Jeep screeched as he righted the vehicle and continued straight. "Something against short cuts?" he asked, his voice pitched high from surprise.

I shook my head. "No. I just—I don't go that way."

Understanding settled in his eyes and I hated the pity I found in his stare. "Don't look at me like that," I told him.

"Sorry, I forgot the graveyard was dow—"

"It's fine. Just drive, okay?"

If you looked hard enough into the trees out the passenger side window, you could see it; the graveyard where my mother and father were buried. I didn't look, of course, I never did. I kept my eyes straight ahead as we passed, wringing my fingers in my lap.

I killed them.

Both of them.

But they weren't the first lives I took. No. I took my first before I was even born.

"You okay with pizza for dinner?" Jared asked, changing the subject.

"There were a few packets of ramen in my bag. I can just have that and some berries from the mountain."

53

Jared snorted. "You can't live on ramen and berries, Allie. Besides, I already ordered three large pizzas."

My eyes widened as I watched him in the darkened vehicle. In the close quarters I could smell his cedar and birch scent—and that undertone of something else, the thing I couldn't place before, but that now I knew was an animal smell. Like fresh air and loamy earth. "What the hell are you going to do with three large pizzas?" I asked in disbelief.

He shrugged. "I can eat one by myself usually. Clay can eat more than that. I figured you'd at least have a couple slices, so I got three. You aren't going to let the extra slices go to waste, are you? I hate cold pizza."

My brows raised. "Who hates cold pizza?" I asked suspiciously. "Cold pizza is the best."

"Nah," Jared said with the ghost of a smirk on his lips. "Shit's nasty."

"Well, I won't let it be wasted," I said, rising to his bait and knowing it. I couldn't remember the last time my belly felt full. Probably the time I spent the night at Viv's, when her dad was out of town visiting her uncle. We'd had lasagna, and I think I ate more than Viv and her mom, combined. The idea of having not *one* slice of pizza, but *several* made my mouth water and my stomach growl audibly in the cab.

Jared stifled a laugh and I chortled, pressing a hand to my abdomen to try to quell the loud noises, but that only made them louder.

By the time my stomach stopped yelling at me, we were parked at the end of the bumpy dirt road in the small lot at the foot of a hiking trail not often used. In fact, I didn't even think it was on a map.

I gasped as I turned to get out of the Jeep, finding Jared there opening my door, his tan face popping up in the window shocked a short squeal from my lips. "Sorry," he said, holding the door open and a hand out to help me step down from the jacked-up height. I took his hand, if only because I was afraid to twist my ankle more if I jumped to the ground without something to stabilize me. "Didn't mean to scare you."

I reached back inside to grab my bag once my feet were on solid ground and turned to close the door, finding Jared watching me curiously.

"What?" I asked, squinting up at him in the growing dark, shivering against the autumn chill.

He shook his head. "It's nothing. Here," he said, holding out a hand for my bag. "Let me carry that. We should get moving before you freeze. I think your walking stick is still over by the trail."

He was right, and after I grudgingly handed over my bag, I hopped over to the wide pine and snatched the walking stick he'd fetched for me when he'd been a beast on all fours. I squinted down at the length of wood, pursing my lips. Was that really just last night?

It felt like it'd been days since the mudslide, already.

My breath clouded around my face when I huffed, and I made a mental note to go to the storage unit my aunt and uncle had rented and grab my jacket and a couple sweaters. I didn't have much in there, and the bus ride and hike to get to the unit was grueling, but it was better than having to buy new stuff—even if it was from the thrift shop. I'd left a bunch of stuff in there when I'd decided to move to the hunting blind in the woods. Not only did I not have the space for anything extra, but anyone who stumbled upon the tent in the woods would be able to steal from it what they wanted. Not worth the risk.

We went in the opposite direction of the trail, deeper into the wood to the east instead of the northwest, where my blind used to be. Once my ankle was healed, I planned to go and find it. Make sure there wasn't anything else I could salvage. Make sure it really was beyond repair before I floundered to try to find some place else to stay.

"I'll get you some ice for that when we get back," Jared said, eyeing my swollen ankle. "It looks worse than it was this morning."

I didn't reply, my mind elsewhere. I couldn't believe I'd agreed to come back here with him. Every step I took towards the hidden cabin in the woods felt like another nail being hammered into a coffin of my own making. What was I doing?

Jared was hot as hell. The most sought-after piece of man flesh at Forest Grove High School.

But he was also a goddamned *wolf*. And his friend, Clay was an *even bigger* wolf who wanted to eat me.

I'd have been better off crashing in an alleyway. "What's wrong?" Jared asked, and I found myself wishing he was less intuitive. Wishing he would stop looking at me as though I was this foreign creature he wanted to study under the lens of a microscope. To pull me apart and find out what makes me tick.

There were things I didn't want him to know.

I bowed my head. And some things no one knew... I wanted to keep it that way.

"Do you think Clay is going to eat me?"

Jared laughed, and the sound lightened a weight that'd been pressing on my chest. "No," he said between fits of laughter. "No, he's all bark. No bite. Trust me."

Trust him?

Could I?

I watched him under the cover of the darkening sky from beneath my lashes. He was smiling to himself as he walked.

"Jared?" I tried again, forcing myself to ask him the question I was afraid to find the answer to. Because I found myself wanting to trust Jared Stone, but depending on his answer to this one question, I wasn't sure if I could.

"Hmm?"

"You never answered me before," I whispered, grunting as the terrain began to slope upwards and it became more difficult to navigate with the walking stick. "About how long you've been watching me..." I swallowed, my hand tightening on the smooth wood in my hand. "... and *why* you were watching me."

Jared's posture changed, his spine growing rigid beneath his thin sweater. "I wasn't *watching* you," he began, his tone uncertain. "Well, I guess I was. Sort of." He ran a hand over his tousled dirt blond hair and sighed. "I picked up your scent in the woods about two months ago, maybe a little more than that.

I followed it and found you walking alone with a backpack and bear mace clutched in your hand. I was curious, so I followed you. I thought you might be lost. Or, I don't know, maybe you were running away from something— or *someone*," he said pointedly, and my chest squeezed at the mental image of Devin.

"So, what? You were just making sure I was alright?"

For some reason, I seriously doubted that. His adams apple bobbed. "At first, yes."

"And then after?"

He looked uncomfortable as he shrugged. "I don't want you to get the wrong idea, Allie. I'm not a creep. I wasn't stalking you."

Kind of sounds like it...

"But you were watching me?"

"Sometimes," he admitted after a beat of silence. "Not watching, really. Just checking. It started to become habit when you kept coming back every day. I usually go for a run in the evening before bed. So, I started running near where that hunting blind was. I checked to make sure you were inside, that the hatch was closed. Sometimes, I followed you when you walked from the bus stop."

I shuddered. The idea that someone had been following me made my skin crawl. I didn't like this. Not one bit.

"But I only did it to make sure you got there safely.

That's all. Then I would leave. *I swear.*"

Jaw clenched tight, I nodded, wanting to believe him even though everything I'd known in this cruel world had trained me to always think the worst.

"And then when you came to school with the bruises on your neck —" he cut himself off, fuming. "I *knew* it had to be him that did it. I followed you to make sure he *didn't* follow you, and to scare him off if he tried."

My mouth went dry. What would he think if he'd seen the other bruises? The ones that were hidden beneath my clothes... those ones were worse.

"Why didn't you go to the police, Allie?"

I flinched. "He was drunk. I don't think he—"

"Don't do that," Jared all but snapped, turning on me with passionate fury in his eyes. They'd begun to glow around the edges, and I stumbled backward, almost falling. My reminder to myself from earlier played back in my mind. *Stay back when they shift.* "Don't make excuses for him. There's no excuse for that. *Ever.*"

I bit down, clenching my teeth to try to quell the urge to justify what I did, and the embarrassment because deep down, I know I should've told someone. If not the police, then Viv or Layla. Someone who could've helped me. Convinced me to do the right thing.

But I didn't want to be convinced. I didn't want to believe what happened was real. I just wanted Devin to leave me alone and to move on. Say fuck dating and resign myself to being single forever.

"Look, I'm grateful for your help. Really, I am. But can we not do this?"

The fire in Jared's eyes went out and he backed away a step, conscious that he'd frightened me. "I'm sorry. Sometimes when I'm angry—"

"Yeah, I figured that out already," I said with a sad smile. "When you're angry your eyes glow. And when your eyes glow it means your uh...*wolf side?* wants out. Is that right?"

I started walking again and Jared followed. "Pretty much, yeah. You catch on quick." I wished I didn't...

The orange glow of firelit windows could be seen through the trees now, and I sighed heavily as we stepped out of the tree line and onto the hard-packed dirt of the yard. The lights were on, which meant that Clay must be inside.

I paused before going up the steps and onto the deck, gathering some courage. A warm bed and a full belly were worth it, right? I could endure some glares and snide comments as long as Jared kept Clay's wolf at bay, couldn't I?

"It's going to be fine," Jared said, reaching out a hand for me as I rested the walking stick against the rail. I took his warm hand and hopped up the steps. "I talked to him earlier."

But he hadn't known I would be staying here earlier...

Or had cornering me at the shop and prodding me into his Jeep been the plan all along?

Bugger.

"He's not happy, but he's never happy, so don't take it personally."

Jared winked at me and opened the door.

"Honey, we're home!" He called into the warm cabin, making me want to swat him.

"The fuck took so long?" Clay called from above and I craned my neck to see him at the top of the stairs, looking a tad less angry than the last time I'd seen him, but still menacing as fuck.

Jared set my bag down by the front door and turned to his friend. "Ran into a small...*problem,*" Jared said, his gaze flicking up to meet Clay's as though telling him something he couldn't say aloud. "So, I stayed at the shop until she finished her shift."

Clay glared at Jared, his icy blue eyes flitting to me for the briefest second. "You deal with that *problem?*"

"For now."

Clay rolled his shoulders back. "You let me know if anything else happens."

Were they talking about Devin? What the hell were they going to do about it? And what did *Clayton Armstrong* care if some douchebag guy was bothering me? He'd made it *very* clear he didn't want me here.

"You hungry?" Jared asked Clay, pulling off his boots. I noticed how they were completely undone. The laces loose and tongue flapping down. I cocked my head, remembering the tattered clothes on the lawn this morning. Did he wear them that way so he didn't ruin them if he shifted? I bet it would hurt to get wolf-sized feet jammed up in size twelve shoes.

Clay rubbed the back of his neck, and I noticed he was pointedly not looking at me. In fact, he was kind of ignoring that I was here at all. It was...weird. Did he need to smell the back of my hand first to make himself more comfortable? I stifled a snort at the thought.

"Starving," Clay said.

"Good," Jared said with a devious grin. "Because it's your turn to go pick up the pizza."

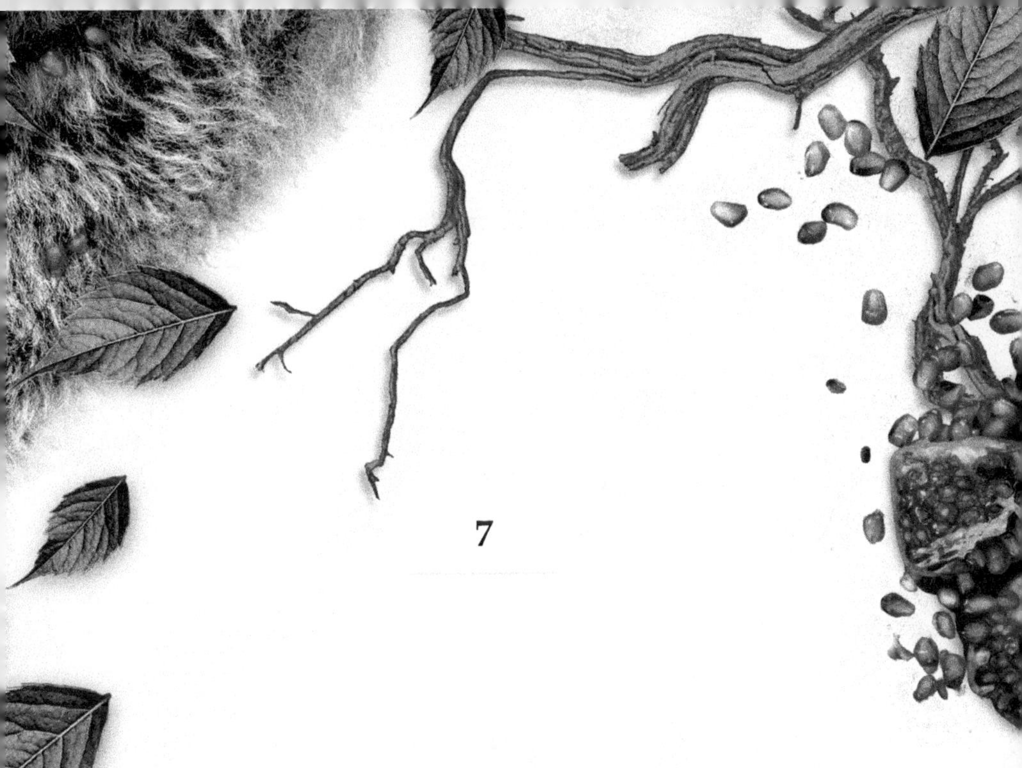

7

We didn't talk much last night. I'd wanted to. Watching Clay and Jared inhale entire large pizzas by themselves in the span of ten minutes only made my mind swirl with *even more* questions. But with a full belly and the promise of a clean bed, Jared had washed all the sheets and blankets, because *of course* he had. I was starting to think the guy had no flaws, I wandered upstairs and passed out fully clothed.

I bounded down the stairs, wearing yesterday's jeans and a clean shirt and sweater from my pack. I'd need to go to the storage unit *today* if I was going to avoid wearing the same outfit to school two days in a row. I couldn't remember the last time I'd felt so rested, even though my dreams weren't exactly filled with gumdrops and unicorns.

While we ate, the prospect of sleeping in a house with two *literal* wolves had made me think I may not sleep at all, and agreeing to come back with Jared at all was a very *very* bad idea. But I'd been wrong.

Other than Clay shooting me daggers while he ate, it wasn't all that bad. And by the time I crawled into bed, I was too tired to care about much of anything. I whispered to myself that they were just overgrown dogs. Puppies. Yeah. They were massive puppies in super-hot human skin sacks. That's not so scary, is it?

Lying to myself only helped so much, though. I dreamed of wolves. And not the kind that came to the rescue of homeless girls in the forest.

No, I dreamed of wolves skinned and left for dead against the warm earth, like the ones Dad and I found deep in the mountain when I was only eight. Their massive carcasses left behind by the hunters who stole their furs.

I dreamed that the rest of that pack found us. My dad and I standing over the carcasses. The gun slung over my Dad's shoulder, the one he only used for partridge and wild turkey because I cried if he killed anything else—making him look mighty guilty. The wolves circling. Snarling. Snapping their great teeth.

I woke up just as the pack alpha lunged for Dad's throat.

Despite the bad dream, I couldn't remember the last time I'd slept through the night without waking and that was a damn good night in my books.

I wandered into the living room, admiring the massive stone hearth that reached floor to second story ceiling in front of the long brown leather sofa, matching armchairs, and low coffee table where we all ate last night.

"Jared," Clay called, coming around the corner from the kitchen with a steaming coffee mug in his hand. He paused when he saw me. "Oh," he grumbled, his face darkening. "Thought you were Jared."

"I think he's still in the shower," I said, the hairs on the back of my neck standing on end as I bent to retrieve my cell phone from the coffee table. I'd forgotten it downstairs when I did my zombie-walk up to the guest room after gorging on half a large pizza.

Clay sipped his coffee. "That thing went off about a million times last night," he said accusingly, glaring at my cell phone.

My face heated. "Shit. I'm sorry if it woke you—"

"Maybe just remember to shut the ringer off if you're going to stay here," he said, glaring down the bridge of his nose at me as though I were two inches tall. "I'm a light sleeper."

Noted. "Yeah. I mean, I will. Sorry."

He rolled his eyes and turned back into the kitchen. "Hey," I called to stop him, going out on a limb. "Is there any more of that coffee?"

He eyed me, his lips pressing firmly together. I held my breath.

"Yeah," he said finally. "But you can get it yourself." I didn't tell him I wasn't going to ask, that I wasn't the sort of girl who needed to be fucking waited on hand and foot. He could just figure that out on his own. Steeling myself, I pressed forward, following him into the kitchen to grab a mug from the cupboard where I saw Jared grab a couple yesterday morning.

Clay went over to the table and grabbed a carbon vented front disk protector off the surface. For the first time, I noticed how his hands were dark with the stain of engine grease. How the stains collected around his calloused fingers and in the cracks of his chapped skin.

"What are you working on?" I attempted conversation, pouring myself a cup of coffee and taking a sip. The question was more to start a conversation than anything. I already knew what the part was and what it was for. Though, he didn't have the bike specific mount kit with it, so I didn't know what kind of dirt bike he planned to put it on. He looked like a Honda guy to me, though.

I'd installed a similar part on my Yamaha a couple years back. But I stopped riding after Dad died. And my aunt and uncle didn't think dirt biking was a *normal* activity for a then sixteen-year-old girl, so they sold it, along with all Dad's shop tools. I didn't let them sell his bike, though. It was in the storage unit along with all the rest of my things and their furniture.

It was a Maico 620 and I intended to ride it someday. Whenever I could stomach the idea of riding without Dad.

Clay eyed me up and down as though measuring my hand and foot. He could just figure that out on his own. Steeling myself, I pressed forward, following him into the kitchen to grab a mug from the cupboard where I saw Jared grab a couple yesterday morning.

Clay went over to the table and grabbed a carbon vented front disk protector off the surface. For the first time, I noticed how his hands were dark with the stain of engine grease. How the stains collected around his calloused fingers and in the cracks of his chapped skin.

"What are you working on?" I attempted conversation, pouring myself a cup of coffee and taking a sip. The question was more to start a conversation than anything. I already knew what the part was and what it was for. Though, he didn't have the bike specific mount kit with it, so I didn't know what kind of dirt bike he planned to put it on. He looked like a Honda guy to me, though.

I'd installed a similar part on my Yamaha a couple years back. But I stopped riding after Dad died. And my aunt and uncle didn't think dirt biking was a *normal* activity for a then sixteen-year-old girl, so they sold it, along with all Dad's shop tools. I didn't let them sell his bike, though. It was in the storage unit along with all the rest of my things and their furniture.

It was a Maico 620 and I intended to ride it someday. Whenever I could stomach the idea of riding without Dad.

Clay eyed me up and down as though measuring my worth. I refrained from balking at his stare. "It's for a Honda CRF 450 R."

Big fucking bike. But then, I supposed with his size, he'd need something that big. "Nice. Looks like you're missing the mount kit, though."

His gaze only narrowed further.

"Hey," Jared said, entering the kitchen with his hair still damp from the shower. He glanced between Clay and I, his brow raising.

Clay shot me one last curious glare before he shouldered past Jared and out into the yard. I saw him pass by a window across the cabin in the living room as he went around to the back of the cabin. I wondered if he had a shop somewhere back there. I'd only ever seen the front of the cabin. There hadn't really been time to explore.

Jared poured himself a coffee and filled the toaster on the counter with four slices of whole wheat. "Hope he wasn't being too much of a dick," he said, the words more a statement than a question.

I shrugged. "I wouldn't want some homeless person living in my house, either. I get it."

Jared's brows lowered. "You aren't homeless, Allie.

You *chose* to live in that blind."

"How would you know?"

"It was a guess. You just confirmed it." I rolled my eyes at him.

Jared tossed two pieces of toast on one plate, and the other two on another and passed me one. "Eat fast or we'll be late."

Right. I still had to go to school. Though, on the bright side, at least I had a ride.

My blood chilled as I took the proffered plate from Jared. I couldn't show up to school in Jared *freaking* Stone's Jeep. I'd never hear the end of it from Viv and Layla. I'd be the target of every glare, the butt of every joke.

I could already hear the senior's snide remarks in my head. Their disbelieving expressions as they rationalized to themselves why someone like me would be with someone like Jared. And Devin. Fuck...if Devin saw me with Jared *again*...I shuddered to think what he might do.

Seemingly unperturbed, Jared took a seat at the table and opened up a jar of raspberry jam. He cocked his head at me when I didn't move to sit down. "What? You don't like jam? There's peanut butter too if you want."

Unbelievable.

Thank god by the time we pulled up to Forest Grove, the parking lot was all but empty, everyone rushing to make it inside for the bell that would ring in two minutes. I managed to put distance between Jared and I and make it into first period class before I would be marked late.

The teacher for Forest Grove's culinary arts class was super laid back, though. I doubted he would have marked me late, especially given I'd had to limp into the classroom. My ankle felt about a million times better, but the hike from the cabin to the lot where Jared's Jeep was parked had made it start to ache again. I'd need to ice it really good tonight if I planned to be walking that distance daily to get into town.

My skin bristled. Would I really stay with Jared and Clay that long? Jared was insistent that I didn't need to go anywhere. That I could stay as long as I needed until I was able to find a place of my own. But, how long would that take? And what happened if one of them lost control around me? What if I went insane from all the questions wreaking havoc in my head?

I watched the teacher pace in front of the chalkboard but didn't hear him. I always hated this part of the day's lesson. We always spent the first twenty minutes of class learning theory before he allowed us into the adjoining kitchen to start cooking.

Quinn slid into the seat next to me quietly, not saying a word. I blinked, pulling my head out of the storm clouds and back down to earth.

"Hey, Quinn," I said, turning in my seat to face him as I resumed taking down notes about proper cooling methods. But my hand froze before I could write a single word.

Even though he had his head bent, and the dark flop of brown hair covered most of his face, I could see the purplish-blue hue of an angry bruise on his jawline, and what looked to be a swollen eye.

"Shit Quinn," I whispered, careful to keep my voice low. I didn't want to draw attention I could tell Quinn *clearly* didn't want. "What the hell happened?"

His jaw twitched. "Quinn?"

My heart started to pound. A clammy sweat coated my palms.

He wouldn't have...

"Why don't you ask your boyfriend," he said, finally turning to me. My stomach heaved as I took in his pummeled face. I didn't miss how his eyebrow ring was missing, the line of dried blood telling me how Devin had ripped it from his head without Quinn needing to say anything.

What. The. Fuck.

I didn't want to believe it.

My mind rebelled. Hands clenching into fists in my lap.

I thought I knew him. I thought he was *good*.

How could I have been so wrong? "I—I'm so sorry, I didn't know that—"

"Save it, Allie."

Tears pricked in my eyes and I spent the rest of class going over what I would say to Devin in my head when I saw him in the hall today. Messing with me was one thing, but this was Quinn. Fun-loving, not-a-care-in-the-world Quinn. My cooking partner for this class who now couldn't even look at me, let alone smile or crack jokes like he usually did.

I was still fantasizing about hunting him down with my damned bow and putting a couple arrows in places that would hurt, but wouldn't kill him, when I ran into Viv in the hallway.

"There you are," she said accusingly, pulling me out of the surge of students and into an alcove between lockers. Her short honey blonde hair made her look more severe than her slight features would otherwise allow. Her brown eyes took me in appraisingly. "I texted you last night, did you get it?"

"I fell asleep super early," I told her. "I was exhausted. Sorry, Viv."

She squinted at me. "Oh yeah?" she asked. "And I suppose you have an equally lame excuse for why you're limping?"

I shrugged. "Missed the last step on the bus and fell on my face," I lied, rolling up my sleeves to show her all the scrapes there as further evidence.

Viv tapped her finger to her chin. "You're lying." Why did she always have to know when I was lying?

Was it that easy to tell? "I'm not," I insisted, my spine straightening as the throng of students in the hallway began to thin out. If we didn't hurry, we weren't going to make it to the next class on time.

Viv didn't budge.

On first meeting her, you'd think Viv was overbearing, and that's because she was. You might also think she was kind of a bitch, which she also was. And I suspected those two things were the main reasons why she didn't have many friends. But once you got over her filterless ranting, her overbearing nature, the third- degree questions and need to know *everything* that's going on, she was the nicest, most loyal friend I thought I would ever have.

"I'll explain later?" I offered, not really intending to explain anything at all, just hoping to put her off the scent for a while until I could figure out *how* exactly to explain.

I side-stepped her and rushed in the opposite direction.

"Hey!" she called after me. "See you for lunch?"

"You know it!" I called back, rushing around the corner to my locker before the second bell rang and I was late for AP History. Mr. Brown didn't just mark you late for that class—he made you stay behind a minute for every minute you were late, effectively making you late for your next class, too.

I already had a voicemail from Uncle Tim I was dutifully ignoring for now. The school still called them when I missed classes and he was probably wondering why I didn't go yesterday. I didn't want them getting another call today saying I was late. I didn't want to give them any reason to suspect anything at all.

They hadn't bothered to contact Viv or her parents at all so far to make sure I was actually staying there, and I didn't think they ever would so long as I stayed in line and didn't cause them any hassle.

I just had to last until the guy above the bookshop moved out and then I was home free. Even if they found out about the lie anytime after I turned eighteen, it wouldn't matter. There wouldn't be anything they could do about it then.

I managed to make it to lunch without much incident. I crossed paths with Jared in the hallway once and kept my head down. I kept expecting to run into Devin, but I never did, not even between third period and lunch, when I always saw him at his locker. He must not have come today.

On my way to lunch, I took out my cell phone and jammed the screen until I had his text conversation pulled up. Ignoring the zillion messages from him, I typed out one of my own.

Allie: What the fuck is wrong with you? Quinn didn't do anything to deserve that.

My cell phone buzzed with his reply almost immediately and I pulled it angrily back out of my pocket. It slipped from my trembling fingers and skidded onto the floor between the lines of moving bodies on their way to lunch. I sucked in a breath and darted between people to grab it, but someone else was faster.

A tan hand closed around the cell and I looked up to find Jared watching me with a worried furrow in his brow. I snatched the phone from him, my gaze shifting to make sure no one was watching us.

"Thanks," I chirped, trying to shoulder past him.

He stopped me with a hand lightly on my shoulder and whispered my name. I shivered. "Are you avoiding me on purpose?" He asked the question so quietly; I was hopeful that no one heard. But if I didn't keep moving someone would notice us talking and I didn't want the drama that would surely come with being publicly involved with Jared Stone. Already, I heard Amanda Schmidt whisper under her breath to Stella Baker, her eyes sliding over me with a question in them.

"I need to go meet my friends," I rushed to say, unable to look him in the eye.

"I was hoping you'd have lunch with me."

My eyes widened and I snapped my head up to see that he looked *dead* serious.

"What?"

He cocked his head. "I said I was hoping you'd have lu—"

"No, I heard you," I whispered, tucking my phone away. "But I told Viv and Layla I'd eat with them. See you later, kay?"

I rushed off before he could reply, weaving through the front atrium and up the stairs into the cafeteria. I sighed as I entered, finding Viv and Layla at our usual spot in the far-left corner, just next to the small raised stage that didn't make any sense to have in a cafeteria. It was literally *never* used, but it made our spot a little more private than the rest of the wide-open space.

"Did you really come to school this morning with *Jared?*" Layla asked the second I sat down.

Couldn't anyone keep shit to themselves in this fucking town? I groaned and let my head fall to smack against the table.

"Guess that means it's true," Viv teased, knocking her shoulder into mine. "Spill. Now."

"It's nothing alright," I muttered without lifting my head. "I missed the bus connection and he saw me walking."

"And he offered you a ride?" Layla asked, her voice giving away her shock.

I lifted my head, trying my best to keep my expression neutral. "I was as shocked as you are. But I would've been late if I hadn't accepted the ride."

It sucked having to lie to them. Each time I did, I felt the hollow pit in the bottom of my stomach yawn open a little more. Sucking a little bit more of my soul down into the dark. *Soon, I wouldn't have to lie* I told myself.

Soon.

Viv studied me and I hoped to hell I was passing whatever weird lie-detector thing she had going on. After a minute, she gave a one-shoulder shrug and went back to her mac 'n cheese. Layla, however, spun in her chair and watched as Jared walked into the cafeteria. I watched him, too, unable to help myself.

When our eyes met, I hurriedly turned back to the table and stole the clementine off Viv's tray and began peeling it.

"There's something off about him," Layla mused as she brushed her long jet-black hair from her face and spun around. "I don't know what it is. But I get a weird vibe from that guy. Like he's radioactive or something."

I barely managed to keep my composure at her comment. She had *no* idea.

"So, about Thompson's party..." Vivian said, speaking around half a mouthful of cheesy noodles.

And just like that, I got away with another lie.

Walking to the bus stop after I locked up the shop for the night felt familiar, and if it wasn't for the feeling of unease skating over the back of my neck like a warmth breath, I would have been skipping.

I couldn't help but keep glancing over my shoulder, afraid to find a wolf's glowing eyes or Devin following me.

I'd hauled ass to the bookshop after the final bell. Declining the ride offer from Jared. I told him I'd meet him where he usually parked his Jeep. There was a bus stop near there and I needed to replace Maggie's umbrella, anyway.

After a quick stop at the ATM to get Jared some cash for my new kicks, and another stop at the pharmacy to pick up a plain black umbrella, I had to sprint to the bus stop—which proved to be harder than anticipated with my ankle still causing me a stupid amount of grief.

I pounded on the glass of the door a split second after Maggie closed it.

"Miss Allie, you done gave me a heart attack," she exclaimed, her warm brown eyes widening at the sight of me as she opened the door again. "Where've you been, child?"

Out of breath from the run and weighted down with the tattered old textbooks I'd been given to *temporarily replace the ones I irresponsibly misplaced*, I stepped up the two steps and onto the bus. "Hey, Mags."

She eyed the umbrella in my hand, her gaze zeroing in on the price tag. Then her eyes trailed to my scraped- up hands, and down to my foot. "You got caught in that storm, didn't you?"

I handed her the umbrella and swiped my bus pass in the reader.

There wasn't really any point in lying to Mags at this point. She may not have known that I lived alone in the woods, but she knew I walked into them every evening when she dropped me off.

"Yeah. Slipped in the mud and twisted my ankle really bad." It was only a half lie.

She pursed her lips, taking the proffered umbrella. "And just what happened to my umbrella?"

"It—uh...it broke."

"*Mmmmmmmhmm*" said Mags, releasing the airbrake as she pulled away from the stop and onto main street. "Sit down, Miss Allie. I got a route to get to."

I did as she said, sitting where I usually did just behind where the blue seats reserved for commuters traveling with children or seniors. Neither rode the bus at this hour, in fact, I usually rode entirely alone—but I felt strange taking up one of those seats anyway. "You didn't have to go and buy a new one, you know," Mags said after a few more minutes.

I saw her watching me from the rearview. "It was yours. Of course, I did."

Mags kept glancing up at me in the mirror for the rest of the ride, as though trying to figure out if she should say something. I beat her to it. "I'm getting off at Carpenter Creek today instead of my usual."

"Alright," she said after a pause, and I could tell she was wondering why and knowing it wasn't her place to ask.

Maggie made the stop and opened the door, I paused as I walked by her. "I don't know if I'll be on the bus much anymore for a while," I told her, watching her graying brows furrow. "I found a better place to stay."

Her shouldered visibly sagged. "Thank the lord for that," she said with a laugh. "Child, I was about this close to taking you home with me." She pinched her fingers together with about an inch of space between them to illustrate her point.

I cocked my head at her, a chill gripping my chest. "A girl your age shouldn't be out there in those woods all alone. I know it's none of my business, but it ain't right."

I snorted. I should've figured she would know. There wasn't anything around my usual stop for miles except for a car-pool lot and she knew damn well I didn't drive. "Thank you," I told her earnestly. "For not telling anyone...and well...for everything else."

"You're welcome. Take care now, hear?" I nodded. "I will."

It didn't take long for me to find Jared leaning against his Jeep in the space he usually parked in at the mouth of the hiking trail. "There you are," he said as I approached. "I was just about to go look for you."

My ankle had started to hurt again from the walk, and I winced as I made my way over to Jared. I was still feeling a little awkward after turning down his offer to have lunch today and could barely look at him. Which made what I was about to suggest a lot harder. "I guess we should exchange numbers," I said sheepishly. "I mean, if I'm going to be staying with you for a little while, anyway."

I didn't miss his slight grin. "Yeah," he said, tugging a slim black phone from his back pocket. "Good idea. What's yours?"

I told him my number, my gaze flitting toward his face as it was bent over the glowing light of the cell, punching in the numbers as I said them. "There," he said after he was finished, raising his head with a smile. "I just texted you."

I felt my bag vibrate. "Great," I said, adjusting my pack. There was one more thing I needed to ask him, and the chill of the evening gave me the courage to do it. "Do you think you could give me a ride to the edge of town?"

His brows furrowed.

"To my aunt and uncle's storage unit. I—I need to grab my jacket and winter stuff...and whatever is left of my clothes."

"Oh. Yeah. Of course. Do you want to go right now?"

"If that's okay?"

Jared nodded and nudged his head toward the Jeep. "Hop in."

On the way to the unit, I returned my uncle's phone call. It was awkward as fuck with Jared in the car, but I didn't foresee another time to call, and if I didn't return his call soon, he might try to call Viv or her mom. I couldn't have that.

Jared shifted in his seat as I lied to my uncle, telling him that I wasn't at school the day before because I came down with a bad cold and that I was completely fine now and not to worry about it. Placated, Uncle Tim told me they were going to try to come home for Christmas in two months, but that the plan wasn't concrete yet. I gulped. I didn't really care to see them for Christmas, or anytime really.

I didn't even feel like I *wanted* to celebrate Christmas this year. Besides, I knew Uncle Tim was just saying that to give me false hope. If my aunt wanted to stay in Florida, which I knew she did, he would stay too.

"Is this it?" Jared asked about an hour later, after I'd finished gathering up the last vestiges of my belongings from the packed storage unit. His eyebrow was raised as he glanced down at the small box in his arms. He was kind enough to offer to carry it back to the Jeep for me after I nearly dropped it with all my limping.

I dropped my gaze and brushed my hair from my face. "Yeah," I told him, looking around at the vacuum- sealed Hermes pillows, and the

Tiffany lamps. The dusted jade Ethan Allen sofa set, and glittering gold coffee and end table set. Not to mention the bagged-up winter parkas and boots that were worth more than everything I owned in all the world. I mean, who the fuck needed a nine-hundred-dollar jacket, anyway?

Jared seemed to be doing the same thing I was, looking around all the fine things gathering a fine layer of dust in storage. Meanwhile, everything I owned in here could fit in the little box in his arms. "Is any of this stuff your dad's?" Jared asked in a breath, his voice neutral even though the distaste was clear in his expression.

I gestured to the massive Maico bike covered in a taupe sheet back behind a fancy ottoman and mahogany headboard. "That's Dad's," I told him. "But my aunt and uncle don't want me riding it, at least until I'm eighteen."

"That's it?"

I pursed my lips. "Yeah. That's it."

They'd gotten rid of everything else when he'd passed. Saying there wasn't space in storage, and they didn't want to pay for another unit. My father hadn't been able to leave me much, either. Ours being a single income household my entire life, his medical bills took every last cent before his illness finally took him. Leaving me with almost nothing.

I'd wanted to look for a new picture of my dad to take with me, but with stacks of boxes piled ceiling high, I knew it would take too long. Besides, I couldn't even be sure my aunt and uncle kept any...

I hoped they had, though.

The only photos I had of his now were the ones on my phone, and they were taken just before his passing. I didn't want to remember him like that. I wanted to remember him healthy and happy and full of life.

"You ready?" Jared asked gently, pulling me out of my head.

"Hmm?" I murmured, swallowing hard and spinning on the spot, not realizing my eyes were damp with tears until Jared had already seen them. His jaw clenched. I sucked in a breath, easing the ache in my chest. "Yeah. Yeah, I'm ready. Let's go."

Jared set down the box atop a gilded table and closed the small gap between us. I looked up at him, my heart suddenly aching for an entirely different reason. He wasn't looking at me with pity like he did before. This time the emotion buried deep in his amber eyes was something more like understanding. Like...like he was sharing my grief.

I parted my lips to say something, but his arms came around me. I stiffened at first, but then his cedar and birch scent filled my lungs and I sagged into his embrace, pressing my cheek against his warm chest. My chin quivered as I tried to erect a dam to stop the swell of emotion rising within.

He rubbed wide circles into my back.

I fisted my hands in the material of his soft t-shirt.

The dam broke, and I let go, shaking as the first of the tears came.

It was like he'd given me permission to feel the pain, and I hadn't had that in a long time. Not ever, really.

I couldn't cry like this in front of my aunt and uncle. And I didn't want Viv and Layla to worry about me, so I kept the pain at bay.

They'd seen me cry once and only once—at his funeral. Then I had to be strong. I had to hold back my pain so I could get through going to school and to work. So I could get to my refuge in the woods each night without collapsing.

I had to be strong. I didn't have a choice.

But for the first time, with a perfect stranger holding me, giving me permission to feel my pain, I let it out. It was like letting something go, a weight that I'd been carrying but unable to put down even for a second, finally hit the ground and I felt heavier and lighter all at the same time.

I cried for what felt like only a few minutes, but when the tears finally dried and I began to pull away, I knew it'd been a lot longer. My shoulders were stiff and the wide circle of damp on Jared's t-shirt spoke of more tears than I cared to admit. I sniffled, completely unable to look at him as I withdrew my arms, using my sleeves to get the worst of the wetness and snot from my face.

A warm touch beneath my chin made me tilt my head up. I met Jared's amber eyes with an angry red blush clawing up my neck. I was surprised to find that his own eyes were damp—my own chaotic emotion had drawn some of his own pain to surface. For the first time I wondered about Jared's parents.

He lived in that cabin with Clay. Neither ever mentioned their families. I'd never even seen Jared with his mom and dad. His uncle came to pick him up from school once, though. I only knew that because I was in the office when he came to call him out from class.

What had happened to him? To his parents?

"You don't need to hide your pain from me, Allie. We all carry scars. Some people wear theirs like armor. Some hide beneath them. Neither works. You have to *own* your pain. Accept it. And maybe find someone who understands it to share it with, so the burden isn't so heavy to bear."

My heart swelled in my chest and I had to blink away the new tears trying to form. "Thank you," I whispered, truly meaning it.

Jared brushed the hair away from my face, tucking it gently behind my ear before he stepped back and lifted the box from the table. He winked, trying and succeeding to lighten the mood. "Anytime Allie. Now come on. I don't know about you but I'm starving."

"You're always starving," I muttered under my breath as I drew down the metal door and latched the lock.

"I heard that."

I chuckled, stepping up into the warm Jeep and shutting the door behind me. Excited to get back to the cabin. The fear I'd felt the day before at the prospect of sleeping in a house full of wolves all but vanished. They may have beasts inside them, but that didn't have to mean they were monsters...and I was starting to see that.

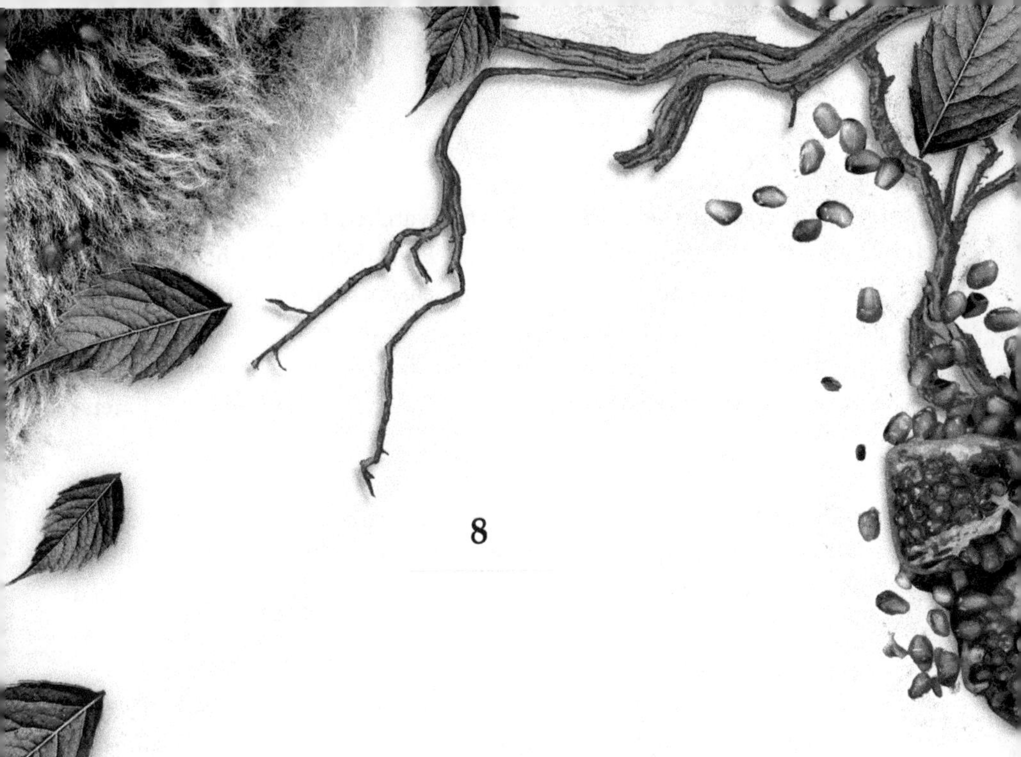

8

The rest of Thursday and Friday came and went without incident. Jared and I shared a late-night dinner of spaghetti with meat sauce that I'd offered to cook. We set a plate aside for Clay who was presumably still in the shop out back working on something.

Friday felt almost...normal.

I gossiped with Layla and Viv at lunch. Almost got trampled in the hallway. Quinn actually helped with the day's task in culinary class, though he still wasn't overly chatty—and I didn't blame him. And lucky for me Devin didn't seem to be at school again, which meant I didn't have to deal with seeing his unsettling face in the crush of students between classes. A part of me wondered where he was, but the other part—the angry *rational* part told me it didn't matter where the hell he was, just that he wasn't at school.

After his reply message yesterday, I didn't know what to think. I'm not sure what I expected, but an *apology* was not it. After I'd asked him what the fuck was wrong with him and told him Quinn didn't deserve to be treated like that his response was all of two lines.

I don't know. I'm sorry.

What. The. fuck.

But no new messages came in. Not that day at school, or during my shift at the bookshop. Not at all that evening while Jared and I sat on

77

opposite ends of the living room and watched the new Star Wars TV series. I didn't peg him for a sci-fi guy. But I didn't think he pegged me for a sci-fi lover, either. We were both pleasantly surprised to find such a mundane commonality after all the chaos of the week.

The fact that he also liked to mix Milk Duds into his popcorn only made him seem even more human. My dad taught me to do that when I was barely four years old. It was the best.

We hadn't talked much about the heavier stuff since Thursday. He hadn't asked me about my breakdown at the storage unit, and I didn't ask him any more questions about being a wolf. It wasn't that I didn't have the questions, it was just that it was kind of hard to work into a conversation.

Hey Allie, want some more coffee?

Yeah, Jared, another coffee would be great...oh and by the way, were you a wolf or a human first? Who else knows? Who's Ryland and why would he be angry if he knew you had me here? How many of you are there? Are there other things I don't know about?

I shivered in the early morning chill as I stood outside on the front deck with my hands wrapped around my coffee mug, leeching the warmth from the porcelain. I wanted to know the answers to all those questions and about a million more, but I was afraid to ask.

My perception of this world had already been shattered once this week and I'd survived it. I didn't want to tempt fate by shattering it again. The pieces of me might not come back together properly if I pushed it too far too fast.

I inhaled a deep breath of molting leaves and cold pine. The air was so clean at the cabin, like it had been at the blind when I left the window flaps open. If I closed my eyes I could almost pretend that I was still there, up on that platform between the trees, nothing but a canvas wall separating me from the surrounding universe.

"Hey," the brusque voice caught me by surprise, and I reeled back, sloshing my coffee over my arm, hot trails of it ran down my sleeve to my forearm.

"God damn motherfucking shit balls," I cursed, trying to flick off the scalding liquid as I breathed in hard through clenched teeth and did my best not to spill any more of it. I didn't have time to make another pot before I had to leave for my early afternoon shift at the shop.

When I finally looked up, blushing, it was into the stunned icy blue eyes of Clay as he came around the cabin and up onto the deck. "Didn't mean to scare you," he said, not seeming to care at all that I'd just spilled boiling coffee all over myself and effectively ruined my light gray sweater—probably the nicest article of clothing I owned.

"Yeah. Sure."

He narrowed his eyes at me. "I don't think I've ever heard a girl curse like that."

I tried to reign in my temper. It got easier as the burning sensation dissipated.

"Well I'm *not* most girls. And most *humans* make noise when they walk. They don't just fucking *appear.*"

It was the truth. I should have heard him coming if he'd walked from the shop around back over the dirt and gravel drive, but I hadn't heard a sound. "Well I'm not human," he said in rebuttal, lifting a brow. "But you already knew that."

His blue eyes pulsed with an otherworldly glow, a warning. I stood my ground and didn't flinch away from his hard stare. Jared's words replayed in my mind. *He's all bark and no bite.*

Clay backed down after a moment, some of the ire in his expression melding into something more like indifference, but with a hint of something else. Respect.

He'd challenged me. Tried to scare me with his stupid unfair wolfishness, and I hadn't backed down. He cocked his head at me. "You aren't what I thought you were."

I snorted, but didn't answer, raising the mug to my lips for a sip as I looked away from him and out into the misty trees. My spine tingled as I felt his gaze sweep over me one last time before he vanished into the cabin without another word and I let loose a breath, unfurling my tense muscles.

I zipped my sweater the rest of the way and I sat down on the top step of the porch, draining what was left of my coffee and then set the mug down and curled my arms into my chest, taking in the silence, or rather the peaceful sounds of the forest that passed as silence in an otherwise boisterously loud world.

The gentle rustle of dry leaves. The whistling of wind through branches. The calls of songbirds in the gray light of early morning. It was my favorite part about being out here. The sound of nature's silence.

Clay ruined it the moment he stepped back outside, the screen door banging loudly closed behind him. I scooched to one side of the stairs so he could pass, trying not to flinch at his stomping approach. If he was any louder, he'd wake up Jared. And I had been trying really hard to be quiet this morning as I showered and made coffee to let him sleep in. Just because I couldn't sleep last night and had to work today didn't mean the whole house had to wake up with me.

"So," Clay said, and I craned my neck to see his jaw twitch as he spoke. "You know bikes?"

"Most."

"Cars?"

"The older models. I don't touch any of that new computerized bullshit."

His lips twitched. *Was that...*

Was that a smile?

He nodded, but the motion seemed to be more for himself, as though he was agreeing with a thought thunk within the confines of his own mind. "Okay."

I squinted up at him. "Okay?"

He nodded again. "Okay," he repeated without elaborating and jumped down the four steps to the ground and began to walk off towards the back of the cabin. That was...weird.

He's so...I couldn't think of the word just yet, but it was there on the tip of my tongue. Closed-off? No, that wasn't it. Hostile? Yes, but that wasn't it either.

I didn't really know *what the hell* Clayton Armstrong was, but he was really *something.* Not just the bad boy who graduated a few years back that *supposedly* took on an entire football team once in a straight-up brawl on the field. Not just the guy who broke the hearts of at least five girls during his high-school career. Or the guy who allegedly black-mailed a teacher and told off Principal Dane to his face on his last day of school. There was more to him. And I didn't think it was all bad.

No one was all bad.

Not even me.

No matter what my mind tried to tell me when I fell asleep at night.

I didn't *only* cause pain and devastation everywhere I went. Not always. If I could make a guy like Clay smile even for an instant, I couldn't be completely *bad*. I wasn't rotted inside like the version of myself I saw in my nightmares. Those were silly manifestations of my own thoughts.

At least, that's what the therapist my dad had me see for two months before he passed told me. He'd paid her a pretty penny to see me every Wednesday evening after school during those months. He wanted me to be *properly prepared* he said. To be able to handle his death.

Handle it, like grieving his loss was the same as cleaning spilled milk or acing an exam. Like getting stitches to close a deep cut. It was when he suggested the therapist that I knew he wouldn't survive. And not because he didn't have a good chance of it. *No.* Because he didn't want to.

Because he was tired of fighting.

I guess everyone gets tired sometimes. "And just who might you be?"

If I had had any more coffee to spill, I would've as I jolted at the sudden appearance of an older woman at the edge of the trees and knocked over the empty mug. "*Uh...*"

I struggled to find the words for an excuse. But found nothing.

The woman at the edge of the woods looked so out of place among the dark wood and gray mist. She had long brown hair that was mostly gray now, swept to the side in a loose braid down her front. She wore a simple thin white dress that almost looked like a nightgown with a deep jade green shawl over top of it. She was carrying a wicker basket covered in a red cloth.

I noticed as she drew near that she was sort of hobbling, and her feet were bare. The age spots around her dull blue eyes spoke of an age far beyond what I'd initially thought.

"Grams?" Clay said as he came crashing back around the cabin. He looked between me and the older woman. He gestured roughly for me to go inside and I rose as quietly as I could to excuse myself. "Grams what are you—"

"I was just about to introduce myself to your friend," the older woman said as she reached the bottom step of the porch.

She's blind, I thought to myself as I watched her speak to Clay—

looking in his general direction, but not directly at him. Not meeting his gaze. The dullness in the blue of her eyes wasn't from age at all. What the hell was a blind old lady doing walking around with a freaking basket in the forest? She could be mauled by a bear, or trip and break her hip.

I'd been about to turn back to the cabin when Clay's jaw clenched and he stopped me with a look, jabbing his head in the direction of the woman he calls *Grams*. I wondered if she was his actual grandmother and where the hell she came from. Clay seemed exasperated, rubbing a wide hand over the scruff on his face.

"Grams, this is Allie."

Clay's gaze prodded me forward to meet the woman and not knowing what to do, I gulped and stepped down onto the dirt lawn, reaching out my hand to her. I quickly dropped my hand an instant later, feeling like an idiot for offering a handshake to a blind woman. God, I could be so dense sometimes. "Um. Hi. I'm Allie. Allie Grace."

The woman bent to set down her basket on the bottom stair of the porch and stepped forward, reaching her slight wrinkled hands forward. I nervously eyed Clay, unsure what to make of the woman who came from the trees. He looked thoroughly amused at my discomfort.

I glared at him and turned back just as the woman set her cool hands on my arms just near the elbows. I did my best not to flinch away as she drew my hands forward to hold in hers. Her milky gaze found mine, and for a heartbeat it was like she could see me after all. Her stare was piercing. "So much pain," she said so quietly I almost didn't hear her. Wasn't really sure if I had.

"Pardon?"

She frowned and bowed her head, examining my palm. "Strange."

"What is it Grams?" Clay asked, looking at me with an accusatory stare.

The woman ran her index finger along a line on my palm, making me begin to doubt whether she was actually blind at all. "You were two once."

"What?" Clay cocked his head, confused.

But I wasn't. I didn't know how she knew, but I understood her perfectly. I knew exactly what she meant. A shiver ran up my spine and my lungs squeezed painfully. I ripped my hands away from her and bent to retrieve my mug. "It was nice to meet you," I said, maybe a little too hastily and made to run inside and grab my bag, not wanting to stay here another minute longer than I had to.

I was going to be late for work. I needed to go.

"Here," the woman said, stopping me. I clenched my fists. She bent to retrieve the basket and stuck her hand beneath the red fabric to retrieve two cookies. They smelled of oranges and cranberries. My mouth watered. "Take some cookies." Her smile was bright and made it impossible to be upset with her. Her gaze was blank again and her eyes stared at a spot just over my right shoulder. "I didn't mean to overstep. Please. Have some."

I took the proffered cookies, careful not to touch her this time and muttered a hasty thank you before I retreated inside, falling against the door to catch my breath the moment it closed.

"Allie?" Jared said from the bottom of the stairs. His dirty blond hair was sleep tousled and his eyes were droopy at the corners. His shirtless torso stole my breath and his baggy plaid pajama pants hung on his hips showed off the dips of the deep 'v' shape that disappeared beneath his waistline.

I choked on my response, wanting to avert my eyes, but knowing that would only make it more awkward.

"You alright?"

I rushed to conceal me expression, pushing off from the door to grab my bag. "Yeah. I'm fine. There's a...an old lady outside with a basket of cookies."

His gaze snapped to the window next to the door. "Hazel?"

"Is that her name? I—I didn't catch it."

I tucked the cookies into my pack with shaking fingers. "I have to get to work. I'm going to miss the bus."

"The bus?" Jared squinted at me, perplexed. "Don't rush. I'll drive you."

I shook my head. "No!" I said hastily and then rushed to correct the tone of my voice. "I mean, *no*, that's alright. You can't be driving me everywhere."

I slung the pack over my shoulder and turned back to the door.

"Allie, I have to go to town, anyway. It's no big deal, if you just give me five—"

"You don't need—"

"I *want* to," he interrupted, his voice harder than it had been a moment before. Hard enough to make me pause and turn to see him shaking his head at me. "You are so frustrating," he said smirking.

I crinkled my brow at him.

"Would you just give me five minutes?"

I licked my lips and loosened the grip on my pack, setting my jaw. "Fine." I ground out. "I guess if you have to go to town anyway—"

"Good." He nodded and turned to bound back up the stairs.

"Thank you," I hollered up to him as an afterthought. I mean, I hadn't asked for the ride. Hadn't really even wanted it, but with my ankle still a bit tender and only fifteen minutes standing between me and the bus stop, I was already liable to miss it.

Just then Clay pushed through the door and it bumped into me from behind, hitting me hard on the shoulder. "Fuck!"

Clay glared at me as he entered, and I shuffled out of his way as the giant brute filled the entryway. The basket was clenched in his hand. Where it looked large and heavy in the arms of the woman named Hazel, it looked like a toy in Clay's. Like a giant with a toddler's toy between his two fingers.

I bit back a laugh at the esthetic.

Clay shouldered past me and into the kitchen, discarding the basket atop the table before he set to making more coffee, getting the engine grease still coating his fingers all over the silver knob of the cupboard.

"Is she not staying?" I asked, pushing back the sheer curtain of the window beside the door to peer outside. I didn't see the old woman anywhere. Had she already left?

Had she really only come to bring some baked goods?

How strange.

Clay never answered me, his brows were pinched as he viciously scooped massive mountainous spoonsful of coffee into an askew coffee filter.

"If you don't fix that filter, you'll have grounds in your coffee."

He turned on me with a snarl, his blue eyes aglow. This time, despite myself, I *did* flinch.

"Did I ask for your opinion?" He snapped.

"Wow dude," Jared said, coming back downstairs. The sight of him and his calm demeanor soothed the suddenly erratic beating of my heart in my chest. "Who shat in your corn flakes this morning? Chill." He turned to me. "Sorry, Allie."

Clay muttered something but I didn't catch it. "What did you just say?" Jared snapped at Clay and I thought I saw his face pale.

Clay didn't answer him, and I was about done with this whole conversation. "Um, if you're ready, I have to get to work..." I trailed off, eager to leave the aura of rage in the room.

Jared snapped out of whatever had shaken him and moved with me to the door. "Oh," I said as I pulled on my new shoes, figuring I might as well tell Jared in front of Clay so he would know, too. It might make him less agitated to know I wasn't coming home tonight. "I almost forgot to tell you; I'm going to a party tonight with Viv so I'm going to stay at her house."

From the corner of my eye, I saw Clay pause for an instant before jabbing the button to brew.

Good, he'd heard me.

"Oh," Jared said, and I could tell he was trying to sound indifferent.

"Which party?" Clay asked, and Jared and I were both taken aback by the question.

I shared a look with him, hesitating before I answered Clay. I cleared my throat. "Um...it's Thompson's."

Clay nodded, but his lips were pursed in distaste. I knew that he knew Thompson's older brother who'd moved away for college, but they weren't friends. Or at least, I didn't think they were.

"Sounds fun," Jared said offhandedly, stuffing his hands into the pockets of the jean jacket he'd just finished pulling on. "Think I could tag along?"

My lips parted, but no sound came out. "Um..."

I couldn't show up to a party with Jared Stone. No freaking way. But looking into his soft amber eyes, something in my chest pulled and my traitorous lips were already forming the words... "Sure." And then more strangled, "Sounds good."

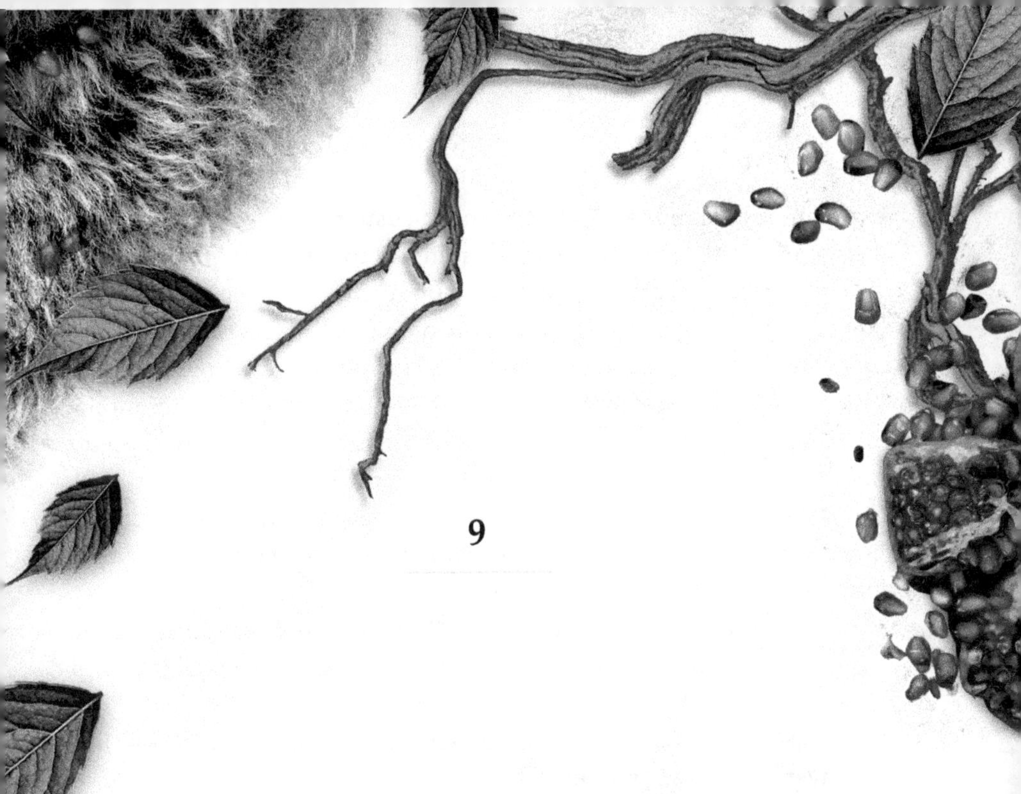

9

I was bouncing in anticipation my entire shift.

It's not a date, I told myself for the fourteenth time since Jared dropped me off.

He just wanted to come to the party. He went to parties sometimes.

Not often, but sometimes. He would probably meet his friends there. He wouldn't even really be hanging out with me. We would just be at the same party. No biggie.

So then why couldn't I relax? Why did what other people thought if they saw us together bother me so much? Was it just because I was so bent on flying under the radar and coasting to graduation without any more incidents? Or was there something else to it?

I finished sweeping and set the broom and dustpan in the nook behind the door leading down to the basement. All the lights down there were already off. There wasn't anything left to do, so I grabbed my jacket and bag and waited out the last five minutes before the official closing time. I'd already locked away the cash box in the safe downstairs fifteen minutes ago. Hardly anyone ever came in this late and if they did, they usually paid with debit.

Not many cash sales nowadays. Which was good because if there was one thing I sucked royally at; it was math. If I didn't punch in the exact amount of money, I'd taken from a customer to get the calculated change, I'd be standing there for five minutes counting out pennies.

The instant the clock struck 6:00pm, my phone pinged, and I stepped outside and locked the door behind me. Headlights wiped their off-white light across the windows, and I turned to see Viv pulling up in her moms Volkswagen beetle. The thing was more hers than her mother's these days. With her working from her home now, Viv was pretty much the only one who put miles on that thing.

She rolled down the window as I approached. "How much for an hour?" she said and waggled her eyebrows, skimming my frumpy attire with a predatory gaze.

I opened the door and hopped in. "I'm way out of your price range buddy," I joked back. "But I'll let you take me home, anyway." I winked at her.

"Missed you, bitch," Viv said and put the beetle into drive. "I feel like we haven't done this in weeks."

I snorted.

I didn't say so, but she felt that way because it *had* been weeks. Over a month, actually. We used to hang out every weekend, but now with my supposed move into my aunt and uncle's condo in the city, we hung out outside of school less and less. If Viv or Layla asked to come over, I'd make up an excuse. My aunt and uncle have company, or they're remodeling the bathroom. Eventually, she stopped asking.

And Viv only invited me over when her dad was out of town, which wasn't nearly often enough.

"It's been a while," I agreed.

Viv scanned my attire as we pulled onto a side street toward the south end of town where Layla lived. I figured we were going to pick her up on the way to Viv's so we could all get ready together like we used to. A weight settled on top of my chest as though a fat elephant had taken a seat there once I remembered *why* we didn't do this so often anymore.

It was because I was lying to them.

"Please tell me you have something else to wear in that bag. Is that coffee on your sleeve?"

"No," I'd left my other clothes in the dryer at Jared's cabin. I had to wash them every few days if I wanted to wear clean clothes every day. "Why?"

"We really need to update your wardrobe. I feel like you have the same three outfits you wear, like, every day. Did you grow or something?"

I shrugged. "Yeah, I guess. Lots of stuff doesn't fit anymore."

"Then maybe you'll fit into some of my stuff," she said. "I have a box of shit that I grew out of last year. You can have it if you want."

My eyes lit at the idea of an entire box of clothes all to myself.

Viv bumped my shoulder. "Jeeze Allie Cat, they're just clothes. You didn't win the lottery or anything."

"Right," I said lamely. "You just know how much I hate shopping. You'd really be saving me."

It was easier to lie when I mixed in some truth. I really did hate to shop, and she really was saving me. She just didn't know the extent of it.

Even if her clothes were a bit too big because she was a freaking giant, or if I thought the way she dressed sometimes was a little too revealing for my taste...an entire box of clothes would mean more money I could save to get the little apartment above the bookshop and that was a *massive* win in my books.

"It's yours. We can go through it when we get to my place," she said, waving off my thanks as we pulled into Layla's driveway and she laid on the horn.

Layla came out a few seconds later as though she'd already been waiting by the door and knowing her it was possible she had. Any excuse to get out of her chaotic single-story house and she was running out the door. With seven brothers and sisters, all of them save for one younger than her, it was hard to find a single private minute any time she was home.

At least she didn't have to babysit for her parents tonight. I couldn't even count how many times she had to cancel plans or swindled us into helping her with her siblings on the weekends last year.

Both her parents worked two jobs apiece to support their massive family. I don't know how they did it, but they did, and with smiles on their faces, too. They loved their kids more than life itself, evidenced by the fact that neither actually lived any semblance of a life outside of their children and work.

"Hey," Layla said, jumping into the backseat. "Drive before my mom changes her mind and decides to take the shift her boss just offered her."

As we pulled out, sure enough, I watched the door crack open and Mrs. Esposito poke her head out. I quickly averted my gaze before our eyes could meet and Viv turned up the music as she swiveled the beetle out onto the road and pulled away.

"Is she going to make you go back?" I turned to ask Layla, wondering if trying to escape was even worth it.

Layla grinned at me mischievously and flounced her dark hair back over her shoulder. "Can't," she said with a little shrug. "I accidentally left my phone at home."

Viv snorted, pounding her palm against the steering wheel as she whooped loudly and wiggled to the beat of the pop song blaring out of the speakers.

"Oops," Layla said innocently, and I rolled my eyes at her.

I could only imagine the earful Layla would get from her mom tomorrow, but at least she had tonight.

At least she had a mom to begin with.

No one was there to worry for me. To make sure I got home safely. Not anymore.

"Loosen up, would you?" Layla said between belting lines of the repetitive chorus, swatting me on the arm. "You act like you've never lied to get out of the house on a Saturday night."

I laughed, trying to loosen up. I didn't think I had ever had to lie to get out of the house, actually. Dad was easy going when he was around, and my aunt and uncle didn't care when I came home as long as I wasn't loud when I came in and woke them up. But Viv was right... and I knew she was only trying to cheer me up.

And honestly? It was working.

I had an actual roof over my head. Access to fresh running water. The ability to sleep past the six am bus because I didn't have to rush to shower at school before the other students started arriving. I hadn't had to eat ramen in days. I had a ride pretty much everywhere.

The situation wasn't ideal, but even I had to admit, it was far better than what I had, even if I had to share it with two wolves. One who seemed bent on helping me whether I liked it or not, and one who still looked like he wanted to eat me for lunch. But hey, beggars can't be choosers, right?

I turned up the music as an Imagine Dragons song came on, determined to have a good time with my best friends tonight. I hollered over the music. "So, what are we drinking tonight?"

Layla and Viv answered at the same time, shouting over the music to be heard, "Tequila!"

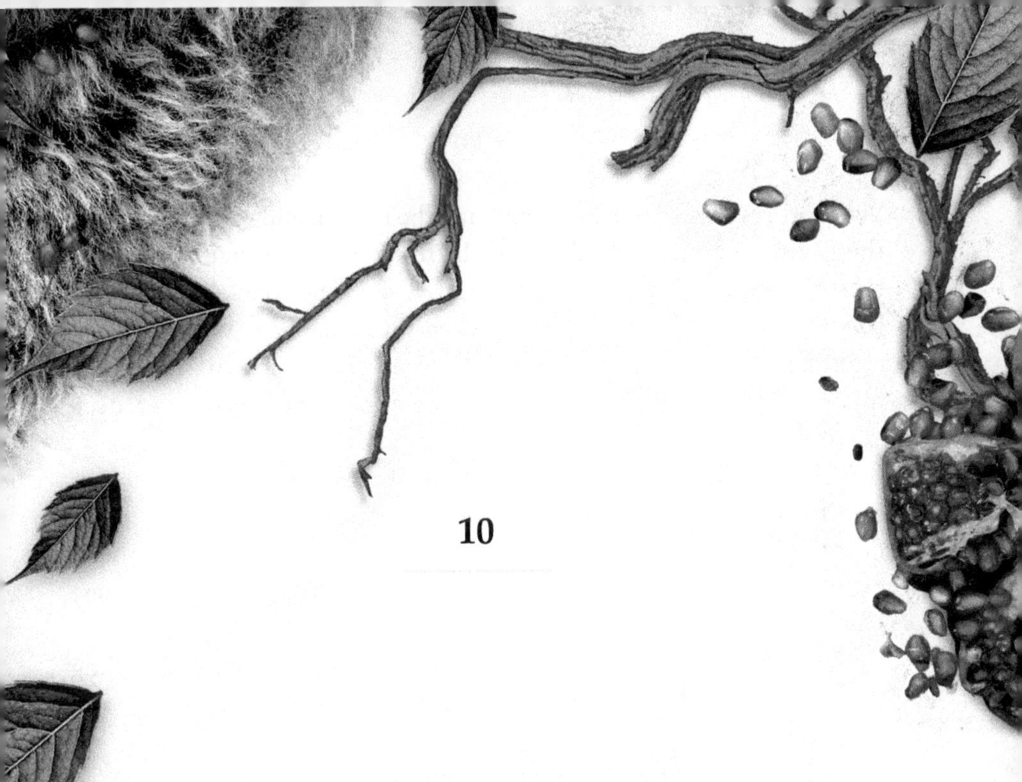

10

To be clear, I hated tequila.

It tasted bad no matter how much salt and lime you ingested with it. It left a horrid taste on your tongue and felt like it was burning your insides when you swallowed it. But Layla's parents kept a massive store of the stuff in the basement under lock and key. And Layla, being the sneaky ninja she's always been, knew *exactly* where that key was kept, and *exactly* which bottles to take that wouldn't ever be noticed.

So, tequila it is.

I grimaced as I downed my second shot, shaking as I made a face. "Ugh."

"You aren't allowed to drink tequila in front of anyone but us," Layla said, watching me with apprehensive wide doe eyes. "I've never seen anyone make a scarier face than the one you just made."

"Layla!" I said, chucking a t-shirt at her from the box of clothes Viv had plopped in front of me two hours before. I was now dressed in jeans that fit snuggly around the waist, but that were just an inch or two too long. They were brand name and nicer than anything I owned even though they had a tiny oil stain on the butt that Viv couldn't get passed, but that I hardly noticed. With it, I was wearing a shirt from the box that Layla insisted I *had* to wear.

It wasn't really my style, but even I had to admit that it looked good.

Viv hadn't even ever worn it, it still had the tags on and wasn't really her thing, either. It was low-ish cut in the front and accentuated my small breast. It was a deep navy fabric printed with the constellations on it that looked killer with my freshly dyed turquoise hair. With the deep coal I let Layla put on my eyes and the deep plum color Viv lent me for my lips. I looked like the night. Like the aurora borealis or deep deep space.

I always ended up overdoing it when I was out with them. It was nice to be girly sometimes even though I felt more myself in looser fitting jeans, simple t-shirts, and hoodies. Sometimes I forgot that I could be the pretty Allie and it was nice to see that she was still there after all the ugly I'd gone through.

"We should probably go outside soon," Viv said, finishing styling her short blond hair with the little jar of wax on her desk. "The uber will be here soon."

"Allie, I'm going to shove this in your bag," Layla said as she opened the top of my pack to slide the bottle of tequila inside.

"Lay—"

Layla silenced me with a raised hand, and I froze, afraid she'd found something incriminating in my bag that I didn't remember putting there. Except, she wouldn't be able to tell I'd been lying to them and living out in the woods just because I had some extra clothes and a bar of soap in there. I was being paranoid, and I knew it, but when she drew out my cell phone with wide eyes, I worried for an entirely different reason.

Where I lived wasn't the only thing I'd been lying to them about.

Shit.

Was it Devin?

Or...*shit...*

"Allie..." Layla breathed, pausing for dramatic effect to get the attention of Viv, too.

I shrank into myself.

"Why is *Jared Stone* wondering when you're heading to Thompson's?"

Viv dropped the jar of wax back onto the desk and whirled with an overly dramatic intake of breath. "I *knew* it," she said in an accusing tone.

I tried an innocent smile, but I was sure it looked more like I was constipated or baring my teeth. "I—"

"Spill. Now."

I was careful to dance around the truth. He just offered me a ride, I told them. And we got to talking a bit. He stopped by the shop the other day too and told Devin off for me. I told them he wasn't what I thought he was. Not the standoffish super-hot guy who acts like he doesn't have time for anyone but himself and his closest friends.

"He's actually...really nice. Maybe too nice," I told them, wishing I could hide my expression that I knew would be telling them all the things my voice did not.

I liked him.

I liked Jared Stone.

Not in the way they were thinking, or at least I didn't think so, but I did like him. In fact, after bingeing the new Star Wars TV show with him the other night in companionable silence, I thought maybe we could actually be friends.

It would be annoying at first, with the all-girl Jared fan- club patrolling the halls, ready to lap up even the tiniest morsel of gossip related to him at any given moment. I would be the butt of many a joke and scrutinized for being the only girl he cared to spend any time with, but I was starting to think maybe I could deal with that.

It wouldn't last forever. Eventually they would see that Jared wasn't into me that way and I would go back to being the invisible girl I wanted to be...just one friend richer.

"Nice?" Layla accused. "He's *nice*? The guy is a total recluse. I think he's hiding something. He's too pretty... like—oh! Like those serial killers you see in old newspapers, the ones where people are so shocked that someone who seemed so *nice* and so well put together could do something so awful. Like that."

I rolled my eyes to the ceiling. "Layla, I really don't think he's a serial killer."

He's part giant wolf, but I stopped seeing him as being dangerous over the past few days. I was starting to forget how terrifying his wolf form really was. In my memory, the vision of him had morphed from huge dog that could eat me in a few bites to something far less threatening.

"Well, either way, I don't trust him." I pursed my lips and nodded.

"You're not into him, are you?" Viv asked, her face puckered.

I shook my head. "No. I mean he's really good looking—anyone can see that, but I'm not attracted to him like that."

Not even I fully believed that lie..

I cleared my throat. "He's just a nice guy who I have some things in common with and who offered me a ride, that's it. Besides, I'm still working through shit with Devin."

I could barely rein in the disgust from coloring my tone.

Viv began to pull on some socks and tapped her phone to check and see where the Uber was. "You think you'll work it out with him?"

"No," I said, maybe too quickly. "No, I'm done with him. He turned out to be a royal dickhead."

Viv's thick blonde brows drew together and down, there was worry in her gaze. "What do you mean? I know he accused you of cheating, which is super fucking stupid and a total dick move, but that's all that happened, right?"

I didn't answer right away, and Viv didn't budge, her gaze cold and calculating, daring me to lie to her.

My throat felt tight and my lips parted to tell her the truth. To tell her what Devin did to me and how I didn't want them to worry. How I didn't want to make a huge deal out of it. Devin's father was a judge. I knew if they forced me to go to the police, he would never be charged. His father wouldn't ever allow his precious boy to be slandered in that way.

"I—" I started, but was saved by the dinging of Viv's phone as it notified her the uber had arrived and was parked outside.

Viv still didn't move, her eyes searching mine for an answer I wasn't yet ready to share. I dropped my head. "Yeah. That's all that happened."

"Come on," Layla said, her voice a little more tense than it had been a moment before. "We should go before the uber takes off and we have to wait an hour for the next one."

Viv watched me quietly as we all rushed to put on our boots and jackets and scarfs and run out the door. After we called a goodbye to her mom who lifted her hand in a lazy Xanax wave in reply and shut the front door behind us, Layla ran to stop the uber from driving away and

Viv turned to me. I could tell she was reading the truth in my heavy stare.

Her face pinched.

"If that bastard comes near you again, you call me," she said. "I'll teach him to mess with my best friend."

I reached down and squeezed her fingers in my hand. "Thanks, Viv."

"Of course, Allie Cat," Viv said with a warm smile and wink. "We're family."

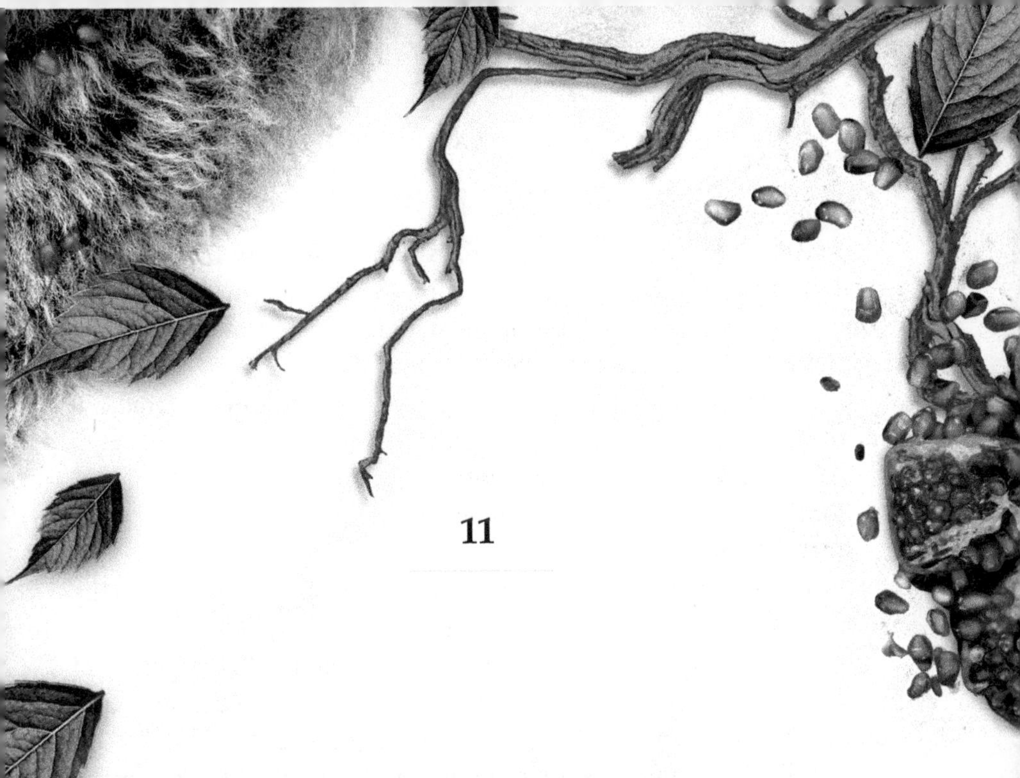

11

Thompson's place was just at the edge of town. His house backed onto a quiet wood which made it the perfect place for house parties. The nearest neighbor was three blocks away and was a partially deaf older man who went to bed at eight. No one to call the cops. And the cops had little reason to drive down a dead-end road without a call.

The uber let us off near the old man's house a few blocks away. It was Thompson's only rule when he had a party. If you're getting a ride, you don't get it right to the house. People in the small town of Forest Grove could be nosey.

The uber who drove us was a girl named Jess' uncle's best friend, Jack. Even though it was unlikely he would rat us out, especially since I saw the creep checking out my minimal cleavage in the rearview, it was possible he could tell someone about the party who would.

We hopped out and took a breath of the crisp air after being stuffed in the cab for too long with the stale smell of tequila on our breaths and the faint odor of cigarettes clinging to the fabric seats.

The last time Layla, Viv, and I had been to a party together it was the height of summer and people were shooting water guns full of raspberry vodka into other people's mouths. The pool in Thompson's backyard was warm and filled with half-naked bodies. That wasn't the reason we came tonight.

It was cold as fuck.

And as we hustled down the road under the glow of the uber's retreating headlights, I could see my breath clouding in the air. The thrumming bass drew us nearer like a moth to a flame. The prospect of a warm house full of bodies spurring us faster.

I tugged out my phone and thumbed a quick reply to Jared. I'd meant to do it in the cab, but I'd forgotten.

Allie: We just got to Thompsons

Jared's reply came in almost immediately.

Jared: Almost there

I peered down the street for the headlights of his Jeep coming up the road but didn't see any car approaching.

The music grew louder, accompanied by the indignant whine of someone who probably just had beer spilled on them. I felt for them. No one liked to wake up the next morning smelling of stale beer. *Barf.*

"Looks like the party started without us," Viv called back over the music as we picked across a once pristine lawn now littered with cigarette butts, empty beer cans, and what looked like the remnants of a stuffed unicorn...I raised my brow at that one.

My new converse shoes stuck to something sticky on the wooden steps leading up to the open door and the crush of bodies milling around inside the large house.

Viv's height and broad shoulders came in handy in a crowd. She always went first to clear a path for Layla and I to trail behind in her wake. Her size coupled with her very *loud* attitude usually did the trick. If you didn't see her and move, she would bark at you to get the fuck out of the way without batting an eye.

I loved her for it.

I shivered as my body adjusted to the temperature difference, my cheeks flushing as I tore off my jacket, almost tripping over someone's discarded boot on the hardwood in the hall.

It seemed like the entire eleventh and twelfth grade classes were here. I coughed as we walked through a haze of pot smoke near the back of the house. It wasn't much worse than the general cloying reek of hair product and dollar-store aftershave. Viv saw someone from her lacrosse team and vanished into the kitchen, rushing to whisper a hasty *be right back* before she vanished.

I turned to Layla and gestured to the only empty nook I could see in the house. A wide window ledge looking out into the back yard that stood directly across from the wide, dim stairwell leading down to the basement. The clinking of pool balls and the sound of a TV blaring could be heard below. "Drink?"

"*Please,*" she said, her body tensing as she craned her neck to get a look around the corner of the wall and up the stairs that were positioned directly above the ones leading down. "Pour me one?" she asked, raising her voice above the thumping music. "I'm just going to run to the washroom. Be right back."

I nodded, tugging off my pack to set it down on the window's ledge. I dug around for the bottle of tequila, wondering if it would be safe to leave the bag for a second while I dipped into the kitchen for a couple of plastic cups to pour the tequila in.

"Viv," I hollered into the kitchen, stepping back from the bag to get a look inside. I was about to shout again when a loud curse behind me made me whirl around in time to see a fist connect with a face and for a guy I didn't know to stumble backwards, knocking me hard in the middle of my chest. I fell back, my feet leaving the floor as I lost my balance. Gasping, my eyes widened as I plummeted backwards down the stairs.

Except, I didn't hit the hard edges of stairs. Didn't break my neck as I tumbled backward into the basement. The breath was knocked from my lungs as I connected with warm, hard flesh instead. His arms caught me, righting me back on shaking feet. My knees quaked.

Engine grease and spice filled my nose.

"*Break it up,*" Clay growled, pulling the one guy off the other as though they were half as big as they were. As the guy who had clearly been the instigator leveled his glassy stare at Clay, his eyes widened.

"Clayton?"

Clay jabbed two fingers hard into the guy's chest as I bent with shaky fingers to help the other smaller guy stand up, his eye already swelling shut. "You could've fucking *killed* her," he was practically frothing at the mouth. "If I hadn't been watching, she could have a broken neck!"

I opened my mouth to say something. To stop him.

But I was still in shock. What was Clay doing here? He never went to these kinds of things anymore. Had he just...

Had he just *caught* me?

"Fuck off, man" the guy I recognized to be a senior named Jason spat back at Clay.

Clay rolled his shoulders back and I saw a flicker of something cross his face. His fists clenched at his side, the big knuckles stark white against the olive tone of his hands. *Shit.* A spark of blue glow was beginning to ring his iris'.

In a knee-jerk reaction, I stepped between Clay and Jason, placing my hands firmly on Clay's chest even though Jason was the one who was swinging only a moment before. I knew who the real threat here was. If Clay lost control, Jason would have more than a black eye.

"Calm down," I whispered to Clay, breathless and with my heart thrumming wildly in my ears. "I'm fine."

Clay glared down at me with a set jaw, the slightest glow that'd been starting in his eyes was already fading, and I doubted anyone noticed it. Just a trick of the light, they would think. Clay jabbed a finger over his shoulder at Jason one more time, turning his haughty stare back at the drunken idiot who's desire to pick a fight almost had some serious collateral damage. "*Leave*," he all but roared.

Jason's expression hardened.

"Let's go man," one of his buddies said, grabbing Jason by the shoulder. "This party fucking blows anyway."

When Jason didn't move to depart with his friend right away, Clay gripped me by the shoulder and gently, but forcefully, shoved me from his path, his big barrel chest rising as he stared with murderous intent down at Jason. "Get the fuck out. *Now.*"

Something within Jason seemed to recognize the predator standing before him. Seemed to recognize that he was the prey. His lips parted and he fell back a step as though seeing Clay for the first time. Then he shook it off. "Yeah, whatever man. This shit's lame, anyway."

Jason turned and fled with his friend and I sagged against the windowsill where the other guy with the black eye was wincing at the ice-filled rag a girl was pressing to his eye. The girl kneeling in front of him holding it to his face was grimacing as she looked at the garish swelling and small cuts around his eyebrow.

"What's your name?" he asked her. "Myra," she said with a pained smile.

"Want to go upstairs?" He blushed. "It's quieter there and we can rinse off the blood in the bathroom."

She smirked and nodded, rising with a little difficulty from the ledge. The guy thanked Clay quietly as he passed. "Don't know what that guy's problem was."

Clay grunted as a response and then turned back to me, his shoulders still tense and raised. His body still tightly coiled and ready for a fight. "You alright?"

His icy blue eyes had softened, and he was staring at me intently, waiting for my response. He was so unlike Jared. Where Jared seemed unsure and was always gentle, thoughtful—Clay was all hard edges. A straight shooter if I ever saw one. He held my gaze with a fire in his eyes as though if I told him I wasn't alright he would go hunt down the guy that almost knocked me down the stairs and throw *him* down them instead.

"I'm good," I said and he visibly relaxed, nodding.

I barely heard his response as the song switched to one that seemed even louder, as if that were even possible. "Good."

"What are you doing here?" I asked him after a beat of silence between us, and when he showed no signs of leaving.

Clay paused and I saw his gaze fix on something behind me out the window. "Could you just...find someplace else to sit?" he said, though his tone told me it wasn't a question. He was telling me I needed to move. That sitting across from a stairwell in a house full of drunk teenagers wasn't safe.

But that also meant that Clay—the guy who almost chewed my head off a few nights ago, the one who told me the cabin wasn't a shelter for the homeless and that he didn't want me there—*cared* about me enough to not want me to fall and hurt myself.

That was progress.

I couldn't help the small smile that climbed onto my lips.

"Don't look so smug," Clay said, the ire I'd grown used to back in his stare. "You could have been seriously hurt."

"But I wasn't," I said.

He rolled his eyes at me. Just then Viv appeared in the doorway to the kitchen, "What happened?" she demanded. "Someone just told me you got shoved down the stairs."

She searched me for injury, and I shook my head. "Nearly, but Clay—"

I turned to gesture to him; to give him the credit for saving me, but he wasn't there. I stood on tiptoe to see over the crowd, but he was gone. That was when I noticed the sliding door several paces down the wall was slightly ajar, letting the cool air of the night into the house. I turned to the window just in time to see him vanish into the tree line.

"*What?*" Viv asked, her brows lowering. Her eyes were unfocused, and I knew she'd likely had a few shots with her lacrosse buddies in the kitchen while the whole ordeal played out.

"Never mind," I said instead of explaining. "I'm good."

She squeezed my shoulder, letting loose a very exaggerated sigh. "Good, because I just saw Devin come inside."

I stiffened. He wasn't supposed to be here. Why was he here? Could she have mistaken someone else for him?

"He looked pissed. He was asking Thompson if he'd seen you."
Shit.

"Thanks, Viv," I said, rushing to sling my pack over my shoulder again, but leaving the tequila behind on the sill. "Layla just went to the bathroom. Said she'd be right back. If you see him, can you tell him I left. I don't want to deal with that tonight."

A little whining voice in my mind bleated *this was supposed to be fun.*
This was supposed to be like old times.

Viv just nodded. "Okay, where are you going?"

"Just out back," I told her, squinting out the window into the trees to see if Clay was still there. Hopefully Devin wouldn't think to look outside for me. And hopefully if he did, Clay was still around.

I couldn't fathom why, but I felt like if I was in trouble and Clay was there, regardless of what he thought about me, he wouldn't let Devin hurt me.

He may be a brute and total ass. But the reason he'd fought an entire football team that summer a few years back was because one of the guys thought it would be funny to get a girl named Stacy drunk and fool around with her. Except from what I heard, it wasn't only the one guy, but the whole football team who'd planned to have their way with a drunken female student a couple years younger than most of the players.

I didn't know if that was true, and I doubted Clay did either, but that didn't stop him from knocking out three guys and sending two more to get stitches. He was suspended for two weeks and nearly flunked that year because of it.

I slipped out the sliding door without saying goodbye to Viv just as I spotted Devin coming through the doorway to the kitchen. I jumped back from the door before he could see me and took off at a sprint into the shadows of the trees.

"Clay," I whispered harshly into the woods.

There came no response and I listened for the sound of his footfalls, or his wolf's hot, heavy breaths from the brush, but there was nothing. He was already gone.

I shivered.

Once I was fully under the tree's canopy and the dappled moonlight was blocked enough to conceal me in the embrace of prickling pines and withering elms, I took a steadying breath.

I could hardly see a thing through the window, but I tried to make out the shapes of Viv and Devin standing together as he questioned her. If it was Layla he was grilling I'd have been a bit more worried, but Viv could take care of herself. I had no doubt that if Devin even made a move to hurt her, she'd have him on the ground faster than he could blink.

She wasn't held back by the same constraints I was. She wouldn't be thrown into a state of hurt and shock if he raised a hand to her. She wouldn't vanish into herself, diminishing into a back corner of her mind while her body quaked like an empty husk in a strong wind.

"Allie?"

I screamed, whirling around at the sudden sound.

His hand came over my mouth, muffling the last of the scream. His lightly calloused hand was warm against my mouth and my eyes took in his glowing amber ones in the dark. He was shirtless but had a pair of jeans riding low on his hips. A belt, a pair of flat converse shoes almost identical to mine, and wrinkled t- shirt lay against the cold earth by his feet.

He seemed to be studying me almost as intently as I studied him.

Taking in the low cut of my navy top beneath the unzipped jacket and the tight-fitting jeans with hunger in his stare.

The *bang* of a door flying open back at the house made me jump and Jared's hand was jostled away from my face. I looked between him and the house where Devin was frantically scanning the forest, his eyes bright and shifting.

It took me all of a heartbeat to realize how this looked.

I knew Jared had run here in wolf form. That was why he was carrying clothes with him. That was why his jeans were barely on and his warm, solid chest was bare.

But that wasn't what others would see...

Jared glared at the place where Devin stood in the doorway, his upper lip curling back into a snarl. "What did he do to you?" Jared hissed.

I shoved his chest back and he barely moved, but his glare broke and he focused his gaze on me, confused. "*Go,*" I urged him, breathless as I heard Devin's descent down the steps and onto the lawn. "Go!" I whisper shouted a little louder, trying to get through to him.

Jared was barefoot, with his jean all but falling from his hips. He was shirtless and his clothes were in a pile on the ground. He was with a girl in the woods, and the girl had screamed.

It didn't matter what I said now to defend him. I knew what it looked like and Jared's eyes widened as he finally figured out why I was urging him to *fucking move.*

"I won't leave you with him, it isn't safe."

"No fucking shit," I managed, still shoving his stupid hard chest without being able to move him more than an inch at a goddamned time. *Damn,* it was like trying to shove a man-sized block of cement. "Get the fuck out of here, Jared."

"No."

"I'll get inside. I won't stay out here alone with him, now go," I urged him as I saw Devin stalking toward the trees, his head lifting as though he caught the scent of me on the air. A group of a few people followed behind him, wondering what all the fuss was about. "Look, he isn't alone. Go around to the front and meet me inside," I added, thinking maybe the suggestion might make him move if nothing else did.

Jared tore his gaze away from Devin and his jaw flared as he clenched his teeth. "If he hurts you, I'll kill him."

Jared backed away and shifted in the blink of an eye. One second he was man, the next he was wolf. Somewhere in there he'd managed to pull down his pants and avoid shredding them to denim ribbons and I somehow managed to be both relieved and a little disappointed I hadn't caught it. The enormous white wolf flashed its amber eyes at me before it lifted the pile of clothing into its mouth and sprinted away into the dark, like a white streak of lightning through an inky sky.

But I was still reeling from what he'd said to wrap my mind around the fact that this time I'd actually watched as a man became a wolf. In the same breath. In the same heartbeat. *If he hurts you, I'll kill him.*

It was what my father had said to me when I had my first date. Bobby and I were only fifteen. He was taking me to see a movie at the park.

My eyes stung at the memory.

It seemed so unlike Jared to say something so insidious. It was something I would expect to come from the foul mouth of Clay, not the sweet, sensitive Jared. But when he'd said those words, there had been no trace of doubt in his gaze. He'd meant it. And I believed him.

My pulse was still pounding when Devin found me standing there dumbstruck with my breath clouding the air in front of my face.

"Allie."

I flinched away from his touch and stumbled back, shaking off the gloss of incredulity and almost falling in my haste to get away from him. "Don't touch me," I managed before I bumped into someone else.

Her name was Mandy—she was super drunk, but I knew her, she was in my Philosophy class. "Are you, like, okay?" she trilled in her high-pitched nasally voice. "Devin said he heard you screaming."

I didn't know how the hell he could have heard me. I distinctly remembered closing the door behind me and the music in there was too loud to hear the person next to you, never mind what was going on fifty feet away *outside*.

Someone must have opened the damned window.

Fuck, Allie, why did you have to scream?

"Babe, look at me," Devin said, reaching for me again with a crease between his brows and a worried depth in his gaze. Fake. All of it was fake. He didn't fucking care about what happened to me. He couldn't. Not after what he did to me, himself. "Did someone hurt you?"

Did someone hurt me?

He had to be fucking with me.

Maybe it was the tequila still lingering in my bloodstream, or maybe it was the fact that I wasn't alone out here with him, already a group was forming near the back door of the house and I could see Layla and Viv hustling out onto the back lawn.

But no matter what sparked it, what I was feeling was pure rage and I couldn't contain it any longer. The fucking audacity.

"*Did someone hurt me?*" I repeated the question back to him, urging him to see his colossal mistake in asking me such a rhetorical question.

Devin's eyes flashed at me in warning, his gaze darkened.

I didn't care.

"Yeah," I spat, twisting out of Mandy's clammy grasp. "*You did,* asshole."

My chest ached at the admission and something in my heart snapped. "You did," I whispered again, and my voice broke.

The warning in Devin's eyes vanished and his face fell. The devilish Devin I'd seen him a moment before gone and replaced by the one I knew. "I..."

"Save it."

He stepped forward. "I'm so sorry, Allie, I—"

"Just leave me alone," I managed through the bleary haze of tears coating my eyes, rushing to meet Viv and Layla halfway across the lawn.

Viv folded me under her wing and Layla wrapped an arm around my other side, the pair of them effectively shielding me from the prying eyes of the drunken students watching from all sides.

"Fucking prick!" Viv snarled back at Devin over her shoulder and I flinched, imagining how many eyes would be turning on him with accusing stares.

I couldn't help myself, just before we reached the door, I turned, catching a glimpse of Devin standing with his face pinched and hands like talons at his sides.

He wasn't looking at me, though, he was looking back into the trees, to where I could just make out the gleaming white of Jared's converse sneakers discarded against the brackish leaves on the ground.

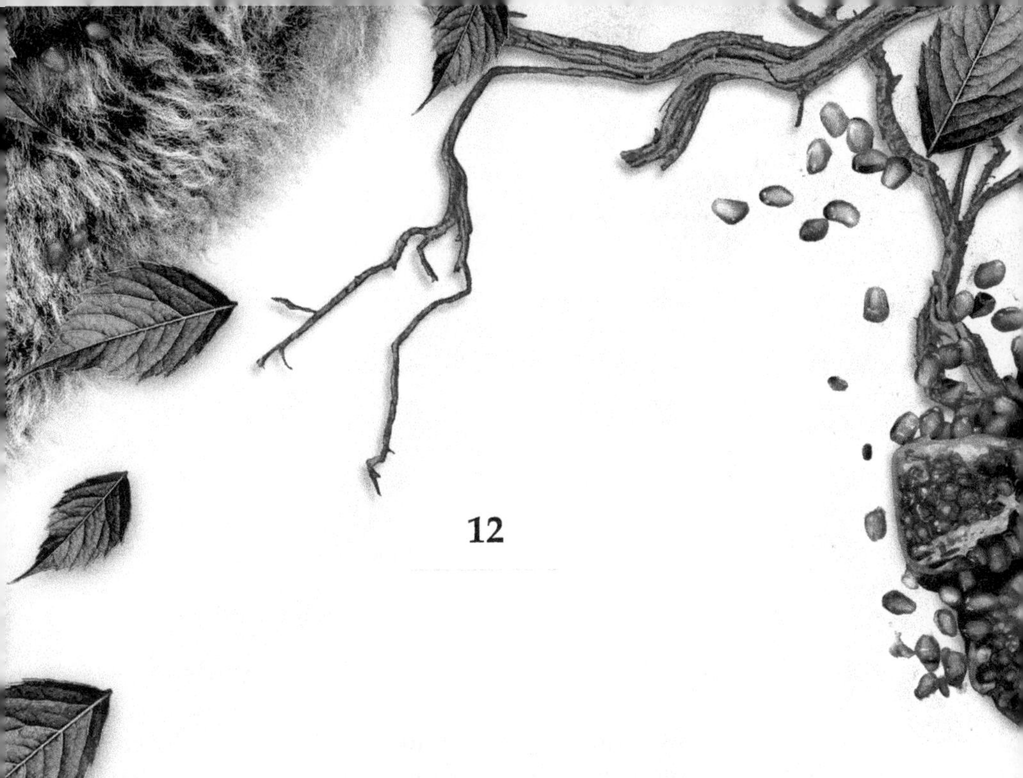

12

I told Thompson I was sorry for making a scene on our way out the door. I also told him that if he saw Jared to tell him I was leaving with Viv and Layla. I was about done with the stupid party. I could explain to Jared later.

I hadn't even had a single drink and yet somehow, I still managed to ruin the whole night.

It was law in my life; that every good thing had to be paid for by at least one bad thing. It was like I wasn't allowed to be *too* happy. Not able to be relieved for any length of time. The beef karma had with me would be everlasting. To be paid in installments over the course of my existence.

It was only fair, since I'd taken life, I had to pay for it with great big awful chunks of my own. I'd accepted this a long time ago.

"You're sure nothing happened?" Layla asked for the second time as she rubbed warmth into my arms in the backseat of the uber. "Someone said Devin heard you screaming."

I shook my head. "I just freaked myself out," I lied. "I thought I saw something in the woods."

"It's wolves," the driver chimed in. It wasn't the same one as earlier. This one I didn't know. His eyes flitted to meet mine in the rearview. He was old with silver eyebrows and crinkled brown eyes.

109

"Wolves?" Viv asked with a raised brow from the front seat, her tone doubtful.

"I saw one out there last summer. Giant sucker," the driver said, his tone now defensive, knowing he was being mocked. "I saw it. I know what I saw. Best you young girls stick indoors."

"*Right*," Viv replied to him, drawing out the word. "We'll definitely watch out for those giant *wolves*."

She twirled her finger against her temple when he wasn't looking, and Layla stifled a giggle. I, however, was paying attention. I was about to ask the guy where he's seen the wolf, what color it was, when Viv's hand snaked into the backseat and patted my lap. "You sure that's all it was?"

I nodded, unable to utter another lie tonight. I just wanted to go to sleep.

The driver pulled up in front of Viv's house and I heard a loud groan that made me squint out the window to see what she was so upset by.

Her dad's truck was there. And by the look of the smashed rear left taillight, he'd driven it home drunk.

"You can sleep on my couch?" Layla offered with a shrug. None of us ever talked about Viv's asshat of a sperm-donor, we didn't have to. It was universally acknowledged that he was a dick no one wanted to be around if they didn't have to. We didn't need to hash out the details.

"Can I come too?" Viv whined as the front door creaked open and her father staggered out onto the front step.

"Hey, get out of my driveway," Mr. Cole yelled, shaking a fist at our uber.

"It's me, dad!" Viv called. "Vivian?"

A pause.

"The hell you been? Get in before I let all the hot air out," he hollered, taking another swig of his beer as he swayed back into the house.

Viv bowed her head. "I better go before he gets pissy. There's no stopping him once he starts ranting. You going to be okay at Layla's?" she asked me, the spark in her eyes suddenly diminished.

"Yeah. Of course."

"That may not be necessary..." Layla trailed off as her and I stepped out of the uber and the driver sped away from the house with the crazy drunk guy. I followed Layla's gaze and found a white Jeep was pulling to a stop on the opposite side of the street. The window rolled down and Jared's face appeared as he leaned over toward the window.

"Want a ride home?" He called, and my heart lifted at the sight of him, and at the prospect of not having to wake up with Layla's seven younger brothers and sisters crawling all over me on my Sunday morning off work.

"Did he follow us here?" Layla whispered harshly. She squeezed my hand, holding me back where he couldn't see. "And is he actually going to give you a ride all the way back to the city right now? It's after midnight."

I batted her hand away playfully. "I *told* Thompson to tell him I was spending the night at Viv's, remember?" I purposefully ignored the second part of her question.

But even the first part wasn't entirely true. I had only said I was spending the night with Layla and Viv. I hadn't told him which house we would be sleeping at. And I definitely didn't tell him where Viv lived. But it was a small town and wouldn't be so difficult to figure out. Viv and her family had always lived in the small bungalow on Glenwood Drive.

"Just a sec!" I called to Jared, who nodded before turning back to the front and rolling up the window.

"You really don't like him, do you?" I asked Layla, tilting my head to better see her expression under the single street lamp set ten yards away on Viv's street.

"Do you?" she asked me.

I fumbled for a response, glancing back at the idling Jeep.

"Oh my god, *you do!*"

"I—"

"I say go for it," Viv chimed in, already making her way to the ajar front door of her house so her dad didn't have a reason to come back out and embarrass her even more in front of her friends. "He's *hot.*"

"Vivian!"

She turned and ran up the last two steps, hollering back, "Later bitches," before she vanished inside.

"Come on," I told Layla, jerking my head toward the Jeep. "I'll ask him to give you a ride home, too."

Layla didn't live far from Viv, but I didn't want her walking alone, not tonight.

I could already tell she was about to refuse, so I rushed to add. "It's freezing out here and I'm not going to let you walk." I took her hand and dragged her over to the Jeep and opened the door to the backseat.

She was positively rigid, but when I told Jared he needed to give her a ride home too and he didn't bat an eye, she reluctantly hopped into the cab.

I jumped in the front seat and rubbed my hands together, trying to get some warmth back into my prickling fingertips.

Jared cranked the heat and positioned the heaters to point at me. I shivered as hot air rushed over my icy hands and began to thaw my bones.

"Thanks," I muttered as he pulled away from the side of the road.

He didn't respond, instead tilting his head back to Layla. "You still live on Brown?"

Layla cleared her throat. "Um...yeah. 34 Brown near the corner of Stanley."

She didn't seem to be surprised that he knew where she lived, and I wondered why. I looked between her and Jared, thinking I could sense something off between them, but not sure exactly what it was I was sensing.

Jared took Stanley down to Brown and turned left onto her street. The air in the Jeep was stale and quiet as we drove. In an attempt to make conversation, I swallowed past the hard lump in my throat and lamely said, "Well that was an interesting night."

"Yeah," Jared replied.

"Mhmm," Layla murmured, then she inhaled sharply, and I saw her shift in my peripherals. "So," she began, drawing out the word and I thought I knew what she was going to say, but I wasn't fast enough to stop her. "What exactly are your intentions with my friend?"

"Lala!" I barked, whirling to give her a pointed glare. Her old nickname had just slipped out of habit.

Jared's hands tightened on the wheel. I was too worried to look at the expression on his face. "Uh..." he said. "Well I—"

"Oh, look, we're here," I said interrupting him as we pulled up to Layla's house. The moment the Jeep stopped, I unfastened my seatbelt and climbed out, ripping Layla's door open, ready to drag her from the vehicle if I had to. "Time for you to go home, *mom*."

Layla got out without a fuss, but not before she turned back to Jared and said ominously, "I'll be watching you."

I made a strangled sound in the back of my throat and dragged her the rest of the way out of the Jeep and slammed the door. "Can you *be* any more embarrassing?" I said in a high-pitched tone as I walked her up to her door.

"It's not too late you know. My couch is just inside.

You can stay—"

I groaned. I'd almost rather stay here now if only to avoid the awkward ride back to the cabin. But... "No. I should go home. The buses don't run tomorrow. But thanks for making sure I have a super awkward ride."

She shrugged innocently, brushing her long dark hair back from her doe eyes. "Your welcome."

I tipped my head back in frustration, but when she came in for a hug, I hugged her back. I wanted to tell her that Jared wasn't the enemy, that if she got a bad feeling about someone, it should've been Devin. But I couldn't tell her that. She would blame herself for not paying closer attention. Her and Viv both would.

"Night," she said just as a light turned on inside the dark house. I really hoped it wasn't our fault that one of her siblings had woken up.

Layla sighed. "I should get in and get whoever that is back to bed before they wake up mom and dad."

I nodded. "See you Monday."

She eyed the Jeep one last time before she stepped inside. "Text me when you get home?"

I shook my head at her but nodded. "I will."

Like a total creep, she put two fingers up to her eyes and then pointed them at Jared in a silent reminder that she would be watching. I shoved her hand down and pushed her inside, hoping Jared hadn't been looking.

She giggled as I pulled the door closed and I blushed like a maniac on my way back to the Jeep.

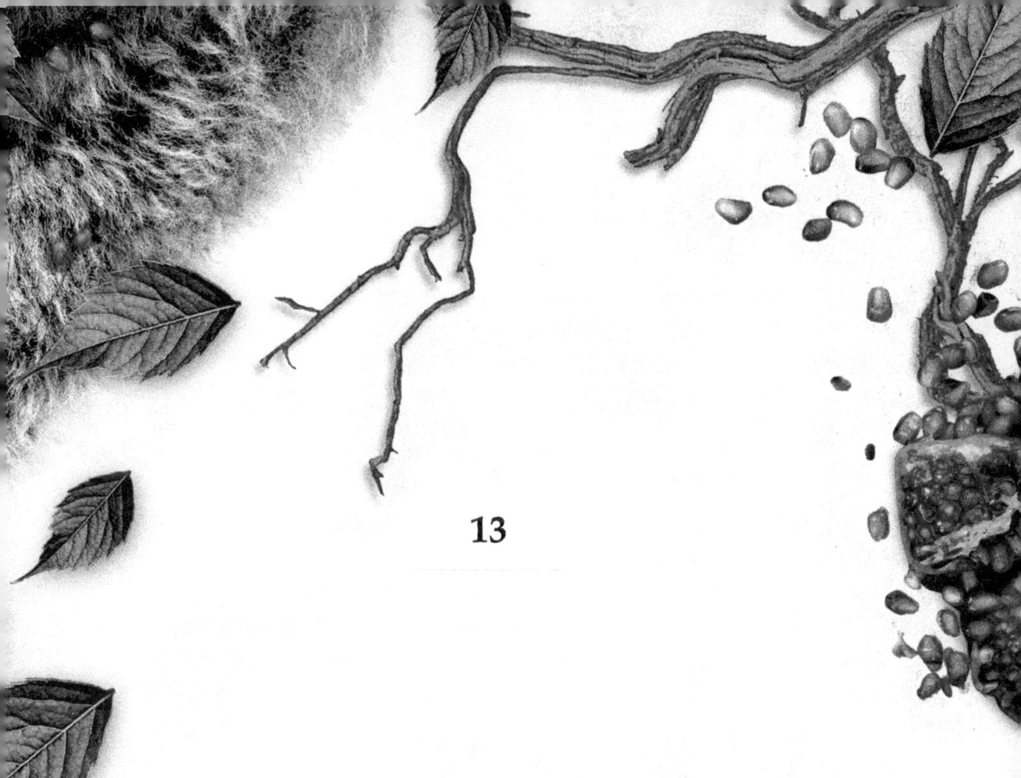

13

Jared was smirking when I tucked myself back into his Jeep.

He kept glancing at me as we started the drive to the edge of town and the invisible trail he seemed to have memorized that lead to the cabin in the woods.

"So," he began, and I knew where he was going, what he would ask.

Suddenly, the idea of asking him the questions that'd been burning in my mind for the past few days didn't seem so daunting. Having *that* conversation was a hell of a lot better than having the one he was about to try to have.

I didn't need him asking me *why* Layla would ask him what his intentions were. Or why Viv told me to *go for it*. Even though the window was rolled up at that point, I had no doubt that his canine ears had heard her.

"So, I've been thinking about it," I eeked out in a pitchy voice, cutting him off before he could continue with no remorse. "And I *do* have some questions for you." I reached for the half-empty bottle of water in the cup holder between us. "Do you mind?" I asked him.

He pouted his bottom lip and shrugged. "No. Go ahead."

I took a swig of his water to clear my throat.

"So, shoot," he said after a moment. "What is it you want to know."

Thankful that he'd dropped the former topic, I racked my brain for

115

all the questions I'd been gathering there since I'd first realized he was a wolf. I came up empty handed.

"*Uh...*"

I watched Jared's brow raise from my periphery and scrambled for something. Anything. The moon outside caught my gaze. It was big and round in the sky, lighting the way along the back-country road we were driving. It had to be almost full. Maybe only days away.

I gulped. "Do you have to turn during a full moon?"

Jared shifted in his seat and I watched his jaw clench. *Shit.* Was that the wrong thing to ask?

"Y—you don't have to answer—"

He shook his head almost imperceptibly, never taking his eyes from the road. "No, it's alright. The simple answer to that is *yes*."

"And the complicated answer?"

He seemed to consider something before responding, deciding how to best explain something. I waited with my fingers clasped tightly in my lap, chewing my bottom lip. "Your myths and legends and fairytales. They are all steeped in truths. But it's like...*it's been diluted*. The bag has been used too many times. And then people add their own flavor to it. Cream and sugar. Vanilla syrup..."

"You're losing me," I said. It wasn't that I didn't understand the analogy. I did, but I wished he would just tell me without beating around the bush.

He ran a hand over his tousled hair. "We aren't *werewolves* like the ones you see on TV. Silver does jack shit to us. We aren't mindless beasts. We weren't even always shapeshifters."

My curious self, the one who loved a good story and spent the bulk of her days reading at work and in the hours after dusk came out of her hidey hole. I was sitting up straighter, my mind sharper, readying itself to take in what Jared would tell me without anxiety. If I thought of it like a story, like fiction, maybe I could understand it better. Accept it.

"Go on," I urged him, worrying a frayed string at the edge of my hand-me-down top.

Jared sighed. "We were once known as Endurans. We were our own race before our people were cursed, and before our homeland was destroyed."

"Your homeland?"

"Emeris," he said. "The immortal lands."

Okay...

"And where is that?"

I may have nearly flunked geography, but I knew *Emeris* wasn't on any map I'd ever seen.

He licked his lips. "No one really knows anymore except for the elders. We've been here over a thousand years. All I know is that the Immortal lands are and always have been concealed from mortals. They wouldn't be on any map or known to any human."

My mouth was dry again and I guzzled the rest of Jared's water, positioning myself in my seat so I could see him better. "So, you're telling me that there is a whole other continent out there somewhere? One that people, normal people like me, can't see?"

I saw him flinch a little and I realized my mistake. "I didn't mean—"

"No, that's okay. I'm not normal. It shouldn't bother me for it to be pointed out."

Except clearly it did.

"But yes," he continued. "There are two actually.

Emeris and Fae lands of Meloran." I gaped at him.

"F-Faeries?" I managed after a heartbeat. "Fucking faeries?"

He snorted. "Yeah. They just call themselves *Fae* mostly."

I was still gaping. I didn't think I would ever be able to pick my jaw up from my lap again. I fucking *loved* faeries! I mean...the myths about them. Stories about them. The legends and all that. Somewhere deep down inside myself, I'd always thought those kinds of things were real, I realized.

I mean, how could there be so many stories from all sorts of different places all about the same thing if there wasn't at least *some* truth to the myths? But I didn't expect to ever be proven right. It was fantasy. A fairy- tale...no pun intended. It wasn't supposed to be real.

"You okay?"

I nodded rapidly, making a strangled, "mhmmm" noise that ended up sounding like I was in pain. With my brain on fire, I managed to remember another of the questions I'd wanted an answer to. He'd just answered it in part, but...

"Are there...other things?" He paused.

"Jared?"

He turned his gaze to me as he pulled the Jeep off the main road and onto the bumpy drive that led to the parking lot where he would leave his Jeep and we would continue on foot to the cabin.

"Jared!" I was dying to know now. Why wasn't he answering me?

His adams apple bobbed. "I could get in a shit ton of trouble telling you this, Allie, but yes, there are other things."

"Like?"

He put the Jeep in park and shut it off. He stepped outside and I rushed to unlatch my seatbelt, fumbling in my rush to get out of the car. "Isn't that enough for one night?" he asked, his expression pained as he hopped out and shut the door.

Oh hell no.

"Hey!" I all but shouted, finally getting myself untangled from the seatbelt and out of the cab. I stomped around the vehicle and grabbed him by the shirt. "You don't get off that easy. You just told me other *beings* exist. I can't just let that shit go, Jared."

Every book about every being I'd ever read about flashed behind my eyes. Oh my god, angels? Were angels real? What about demons?

I shuddered.

"Okay, okay," Jared said, prying my hand from his shirt, except once he had my claws retracted, he didn't let go right away, and I shuddered for a completely different reason as he brushed his thumb over my knuckles. "There are also Vocari—what human know as Vampires."

Shit. I held onto his hand and he brought his other hand up to cup on the other side of mine, leaning down to breathe warm air into my palm to thaw my icy fingers. "Okay. Vampires. Cool."

He tilted his head. "Not really."

"Okay. Not cool. Noted."

"And there are witches."

My eyes lit up. "Also, not very cool."

I extinguished the excitement from my expression. "Oh?"

"They're the ones who did this to us. To the Enduran people and the Vocari a thousand years ago."

Jared drew my other hand up to join the one he still held and rubbed warmth back into that one, too. Cautiously, I studied his silhouette in the shadows of the night. His warm amber eyes set into that unnaturally symmetrical face. The high cheekbones and pouty lips. The line of his jaw and the subtle bits of gold in his hair. He didn't even look human, not when you looked this closely.

He seemed almost...ethereal. Too good looking to really fit in with us mere mortals.

And he was holding *my* hands. Looking into my eyes with a quizzical interest, as though trying to read how I was handling all of what he'd told me. As though *I* was as equally enthralling to him as he was to me.

"We should get going before you freeze. It's really cold tonight."

I nodded, unable to tear my gaze away from him. "Jared," I stopped him as he lowered my hands.

His eyes searched mine. "Yeah, Allie?" He stepped back in closer and I tipped my head up to see his expression. Something flipped low and hard in my belly. He was looking at me like he had in the woods outside of Thompson's party. Hungrily. Like a wolf.

Except, it didn't scare me. Not anymore.

I blinked and a weight pressed into my chest, bringing me back to earth. I stepped back and gave a half-hearted chuckle. Fuck...what had I even been about to say?

"Never mind," I said with a forced smile. "You're right. It's freezing out here. We should go."

He held out his elbow to me and I looped my arm through his. Even with the moon, it was hard to see under the canopy of the forest in the dark. I usually ended up tripping at least a dozen times before we made it to the cabin.

"Thanks," I muttered, matching his pace as we walked arm in arm into the trees. The ominous hooting of an owl in the distance made a shiver run down my spine. A twig snapping several yards away had my mind shooting to images of Dracula and the Wicked Witch of the West. I imagined fanged faces emerging from the dark.

Aw fuck...I just had *to know. Now I couldn't exactly* unknow...

Good going, Allie.

Jared patted my arm, pulling me closer to him. "Don't worry," he said with a devilish grin as he dipped his head low to whisper in my ear, his breath caressing my cheek. "You're safe with me."

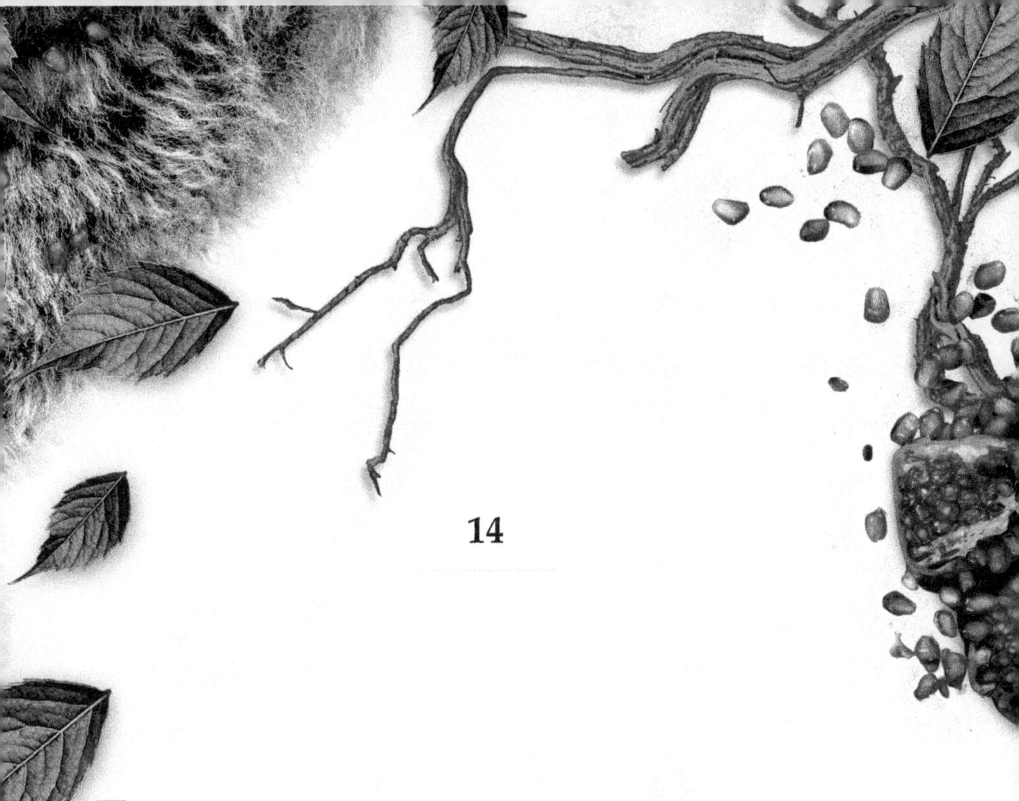

14

Jared cursed.

I almost gave myself whiplash snapping my head around to see why he'd suddenly stopped only fifty feet away from the cabin.

I could just see it through the tall pines as close together as the teeth in a comb. The orange glow of light and warmth had me practically aching to get inside after the long walk from the Jeep.

"What?"

He hushed me sharply.

My heart started hammering and all the thoughts of monsters in the night I'd been working so hard to suppress came rushing back. What was it? Why did he look so distressed?

He was positively rigid. His irises had flooded with a fiery amber glow and his nostrils were flaring.

"Jared?" I croaked, hoping he was messing with me. "If you're messing with me, I swear—"

"I'm not."

My throat closed.

I scanned the darkened woods.

"It's Ryland," he said after giving the air a good long sniff. "But why is he here?"

"W-Who's Ryland?"

It was another of the questions I'd neglected to get an answer for, but I still remembered what Clay had said that first morning. *If Ryland finds out...*

He won't, Jared had replied.

Why did I get the feeling that this Ryland person being here was a very *very* bad thing?

His eyes hardened and his lips pressed into a firm line. "He's pack alpha."

He's *what?*

Jared tugged me away to the east, so we were skirting around to the back of the cabin. I tripped in my haste to keep up with his long strides. "Where are you taking me?"

"To the shop. I can hide you in there."

Hide me?

"Jared," I pulled back on his hold around my wrist. "Jared, stop," I hissed when he didn't let go.

He turned on me with his teeth bared, and I didn't miss how his canines seemed to have grown longer and larger in the last two seconds. Or how his pupils had dilated.

I couldn't help the talon of fear tearing through my chest. I managed to break free of his hold and fell back a step, trying to keep my breaths under control.

"Allie, I'm sorry, I didn't mean—"

"You can't hide me," I told him, glossing over the fact that the sight of him partially wolfy had just freaked the shit out of me. I didn't want him to think I was afraid of him, even though a very small part of me was still more than a bit apprehensive about spending the bulk of my time among wolves. "If you could smell Ryland from fifty feet away, don't you think he's going to be able to smell me if I'm just around back?"

He blinked, taken aback. "You're right," he said, exhaling loudly in frustration. "Fuck. You're right. What was I thinking?"

Giving myself a little mental pat on the back, I stood up a little taller. "Look, he can't know that I know about you, right?" I asked, taking a stab in the dark, trying to keep my voice very *very* low.

Jared nodded.

"Okay, then I don't know," I said, shrugging. "I'm just…a friend. A friend who had a rough night at a party who needed a place to go."

He didn't answer right away, staring at me with mild shock.

"Will that work?"

Jared opened his mouth, then closed it, and eventually opened it again as he scratched at a spot at the base of his neck and his brows drew together. "Yeah, actually.

It might. But the whole cabin already has your scent. We'll have to say you've been staying a while. You'll just have to play dumb about any of the…*things* you shouldn't know. I'll deal with Ryland."

I smiled.

Jared smiled back and reached out his hand to me, sighing as the last bit of glow in his eyes was snuffed out and his body had stopped trembling with what I assumed was his urge to shift. "Come on," he said as I slid my hand into his. "It's time for you to meet my uncle."

The door banging open as we entered shattered any bit of confidence I'd managed to construct on the slow walk up onto the porch and into the cabin. I flinched and immediately regretted my choice, wanting to tuck tail and run back outside.

The feeling was even more intense as two sets of eyes zeroed in on me from the living room.

Holy. Fucking. Shit.

If I thought Clay was big, he had nothing on Ryland.

The man sitting opposite Clay in the living room cocked his head at me and I didn't miss how his jaw ground together and his deep brown eyes flashed with a dangerous glint in the light of the fire crackling in the stone hearth to his left.

He was massive. His shoulder span was nearly as wide as the enormous leather recliner he was sitting in. His posture was rigid as he leaned forward with his elbows resting on his thick knees. Ryland's face could've been called handsome, if it weren't for the jagged scar running down one side of his face. It split his thick chestnut brow in two and puckered the flesh on his cheek. He had thin lips and a strong chin, made to look wider and rougher by the week-old scruff coating in varying shades of browns and golds.

"Uncle Ryland," Jared said by way of greeting, not so much as though he was surprised to see him but edged in a question as though to ask why he was there.

"Jared," Ryland replied in an equally questioning tone, his voice seemed to carry its own form of breathy echo and I could feel it deep in my chest.

Immediately, I decided I didn't like him.

I didn't know why. It wasn't that he just looked big and scary. There was something else about him that just felt wrong even though I couldn't place it.

Funny enough, it was the same feeling I got around Devin all those months ago, before he charmed me into dating him and that feeling eventually dulled.

It clicked in mind that it was the feeling of recognizing someone further up the food chain than yourself. Like looking into the eyes of a lion while knowing you're nothing more than a field mouse.

"And who's your friend?"

I licked my lips, trying to find my voice and my spine. "I'm Allie," I said before Jared could speak for me. Gulping down a breath, I moved from Jared's side into the living room. Clay's jaw twitched as I passed, but he managed to refrain from looking at me as I planted myself in front of Ryland. I stuck out my hand. "Nice to meet you."

Ryland glanced at Jared and then back at me before he folded my hand between the two of his. They were large and warm and calloused and swallowed mine up easily. I suppressed a shudder when he smiled up at me. It wasn't a kind smile.

Nor was it welcoming. More of a grimace.

I tugged my hand out from his and turned.

Clay rose from his seat and I held my breath. I wondered what Clay had already said to Ryland about me. Surely, he wouldn't have told him everything?

"I was just telling Ryland that you've been staying with us for a couple days," he said gruffly, his eyes flashing in warning.

It was like there was a block in my throat. I couldn't swallow. I coughed instead.

"Right. Yeah. Your, um, nephew said I could crash here until...well, until I move into my new place above where I work."

My stomach roiled as I realized I didn't know what Clay had told him. I prayed he hadn't said anything about why I was there, or at the very least that our stories didn't conflict. I might have just ruined everything with my big mouth.

The thought of being kicked out of the cabin out into the cold set my teeth on edge and made my chest ache. I didn't realize how comfortable I'd gotten here. So comfortable, apparently, that the thought of leaving made me physically ache. I realized, even though being here was insane, I didn't want to leave.

Even if I did, where the hell would I go?

Ryland's gaze never wavered as he watched me. "Is that so?" he asked with a saccharine sweetness.

Jared had joined us in the living room now and was nonchalantly putting himself between his uncle and me. I didn't know if I should be worried or not, but I didn't like the tight set of his jaw, or the way his hands were splayed at his sides as though anticipating an attack.

"Why don't you go take a shower and get to bed," Jared said in a monotone voice. "It's late. I bet you're tired."

Even though he was staring at his uncle, I knew the words were meant for me.

I cleared my throat and nodded, doing my best to procure one last innocent smile for Jared's uncle. "Okay," I muttered and then added, "I-It was nice to meet you in person, sir. Goodnight," before I rushed around the furniture and past a silently brooding Clay, up the stairs and down the hall. I paused just shy of going into the bathroom. I opened the door and then closed it again, but didn't go in, silently settling myself against the wall, straining to hear.

The moment the door closed, their conversation began again, but now it was in hushed tones and dangerous whispers. I couldn't quite hear what they were saying, and I stooped low into a crouch and skirted along the edge of the wall a bit closer to the top of the stairs. I listened with bated breath, not wanting Jared and Clay to get into trouble for helping me.

And he wasn't just their uncle. Jared had said he was their *pack alpha*. I would be the first to admit how little I knew about their kind, the Enduran race. But if they were anything like regular wolves, then the pack alpha was sort of like the boss, right?

They had to listen to him. Do what he said, or else...

Or else, what? I wasn't sure what sort of punishment could be in store for them if he told them I needed to leave, and they didn't abide by his orders. Which was why I was listening.

If Ryland told them I couldn't stay, they no matter how much Jared insisted, I would leave. I wouldn't have them getting into a literal dog fight over me.

Ryland's voice rose above a whisper, his tone calmly authoritative. "What were you thinking bringing her here?"

I tensed.

"She had no place else to go," Jared replied.

"That's not your problem," Ryland snapped back, his voice raising into a scathing hiss. "You know the rules. *No one* was to know of this place. This is *our* place. And now you've tainted it with mortal presence."

There was no response from Clay or Jared for a minute, then a groan as someone sat back down. "She won't be here forever." Clay said, surprising me. He wasn't exactly defending me, but the fact that he spoke up at all was reassuring.

"Has anyone else been here?" Ryland asked. "No," Jared replied.

"Good."

"What are you going to do?"

There came no immediate reply and the floorboard beneath my knee creaked. I held my breath, screaming inside.

Shit. Shit. Shit.

"I'm going to fix your mistake," Ryland said, and I allowed myself to breathe. They hadn't heard. And if they had, they attributed it to fluxing wood in the cold.

There was a strange scuffling sound and a grunt. My heart stopped. "Make sure she's here at mid-day tomorrow. I'll call in the favor."

With his voice strained as though there was a boot on his throat, Jared replied in a hiss, "You don't need to—"

"*That's an order,*" his uncle all but shouted, and the sound of his echoing voice burrowed itself into the marrow of my bones. A cool sweat broke out along the back of my neck, raising the small hairs there and setting every inch of me on high alert.

Why did he want me to be here at high noon? What was he going to do to me?

Oh my god.

Oh my god.

I retreated on my hands and knees, trying to quiet my breaths as I silently turned the doorknob tucked myself into the bathroom, careful not to make a sound as I closed the door behind me.

Downstairs, I heard the front door slam and I scrambled to my feet to look out the bathroom window, watching as Ryland stalked out onto the dirt lawn. My breath clouded the glass and my fingers shook as I clutched the sill to steady myself.

He turned back, his head snapping up as though he already knew exactly where I was, that I would be watching. His glowing orange eyes met mine and I gasped, throwing myself away from the window. My foot caught on the bathmat and I tripped backwards, falling *hard* into the edge of the tub with an *oomf*, the breath violently expelled from my lungs.

A loud knocking came at the door and I scrambled back, thoroughly shaken.

"Allie?" Jared's voice came through the thin wooden door. "Allie, are you okay?"

It took me a second to get my breath back, my chest tight and burning from the lack of air. "Yeah," I said. "Just tripped. I'm fine."

"Are you hurt?"

"No," I rushed to say, my mind still whirring. "I'm good."

I looked at the door as though I could see Jared through the wood panel. I could imagine him standing there on the other side, at war with himself. Needing to follow the order of his uncle, but also wanting to save me from whatever fate the man had devised. With bated breath I waited for him to make up his mind, my heart in my throat.

"When you're finished," he said finally. "I need to talk to you."

I bowed my head. "I'm really tired," I lied. "Can we talk in the morning?"

A pause.

"Yeah, Allie. Of course."

"'Night, Jared."

"Goodnight. See you in the morning."

My eyes stung and it felt like someone had shoved a bucket of razor blades down my throat. I held back until I heard his footsteps move away from the door to allow the first of the tears to fall. Jared wouldn't be seeing me in the morning.

I'd already be gone.

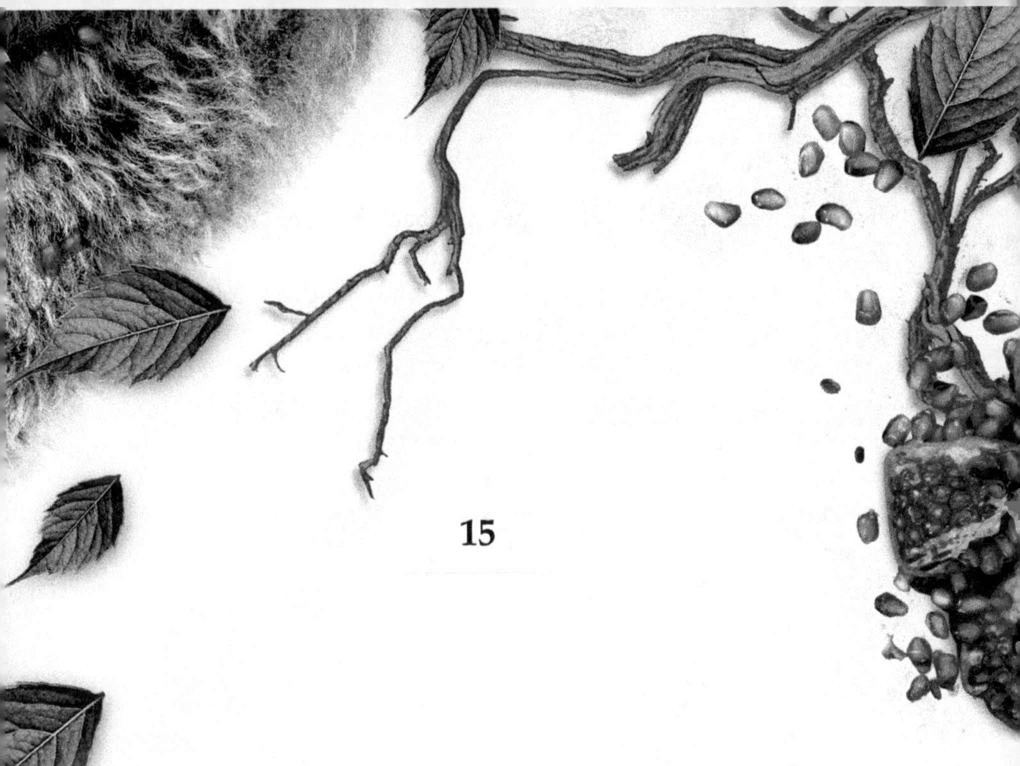

15

I waited until I was certain they were both asleep. It took a lot longer than I thought it would. They stayed up conversing in rough whispers for hours before I heard their heavy footsteps ascend the stairs and enter their bedrooms.

Funny, I'd been here for days now and I still had yet to see much of the house. I hadn't seen the inside of either of their rooms. And other than the laundry area, I hadn't explored much downstairs, even though there were several other doors leading to god knew where.

And I hadn't seen Clay's shop, either.

I debated going to have a peek inside before I left but thought better of it. I needed to get away as quickly and quietly as I could. Knowing my luck, if I tried to go into his shop, I'd end up knocking over a bin full of ratchets or falling into a bike he'd just finished decaling.

No. It wasn't worth the risk.

I finished shoving the last of my things from the bathroom into my bag and moved into the spare room I'd been using as a bedroom since I arrived.

Could that really only have been *days* before? It seemed like so much had happened in such a short time. It could have been weeks instead, even a month.

I steeled myself as I shoved the phone charger Jared had loaned me into the pack. I'd find a way to pay him back for it, or I'd buy a new one and give this one back when I saw him at school.

I gritted my teeth together. I'd hardly thought this through.

Of course, I'd still have to see Jared at school. He could still try to convince me to come back. And then there was the chance that whatever Ryland had planned for me wouldn't be stopped or even staved off just because I'd decided to leave of my own volition.

But it was worth a shot, wasn't it? Maybe once I'd gone, once I'd been removed from the equation Jared and Clay would be off the hook. Ryland would change his mind about whatever he had planned, and we could all just go back to our lives.

Maybe.

It was better than doing nothing.

Ever since I heard what Ryland said down in the living room when he thought I wasn't listening, I'd been eager to get the fuck out of dodge. My first instinct was to run. Which was strange for me.

I was a fighter. I'd wanted to run when dad was sick, but I hadn't. I'd wanted to give in and go crawling back to my aunt uncle, or to tell Viv and Layla the truth and beg them to take me in after my first few weeks in the blind out in the woods. But I didn't.

I fought.

I kept fighting. I didn't give up. But this...

This was different. I didn't know what would happen to Jared and Clay if they decided not to allow Ryland to do whatever it was he had planned for me, and I had this sneaking feeling that they wouldn't. That Jared at least wouldn't stand by while Ryland...

While Ryland what...? Bit me?

Would he really do that? Surely, he wouldn't kill me. Then what?

I remembered Jared telling me about witches and vampires and fae and wondered what sort of powers they had, or if they had any powers at all. If there were witches, then I had to assume there were spells.

Was that it then? Did he plan to *call in a favor* with a witch? To put a spell on me?

My stomach flipped and I shouldered my heavy pack and crept from the room, creeping on my sock feet past Jared's room first, and then Clay's, where I could hear him snoring softly through the door. His door was open just a crack and unable to help myself, I paused, squinting through the slice of open air between the two chunks of wood.

The angle was just right for me to see him atop a double bed, laying on his back with his mouth slightly ajar—in nothing but a pair of loose boxers. The moonlight streaming in from the window to his right painted his strong features in shades of brilliant white and darkest gray. Making him look as though he could be hewn from stone.

He didn't look peaceful, not even in sleep. There was a crease in his brow and where his arm rested atop his stomach, I could see that his hand was slightly fisted, as though he anticipated an attack.

I wondered what he could be dreaming about.

Before I could wonder any more, a creak from behind me stole my attention and a sharp gasp escaped my lips. I whirled around, but there wasn't anyone there. It was enough to make me get moving, though, rushing now to put distance between myself and the wolves who'd taken me in.

I allowed myself a momentary pause when I finally made it outside and down the porch steps, onto the dirt yard. I turned to look back at the slumbering cabin crouching against the tall pines rising to brush the navy sky. The night was still, and the only sounds were the long chirps of crickets in the grass and the ominous rustle of leaves.

Closing my eyes, I tore myself away and set off. I didn't look back again. I couldn't—afraid that if I did, I would lose my nerve entirely and end up going back inside.

I walked numbly over the dead leaves and bed of pine needles; head bent as I ran through my limited options for places to go. The moon-dappled canopy above created flickering shadows on the ground, keeping me on edge. At least the big, round moon made it easier to see. Gratefully, I didn't need to use my phone torch to be able to avoid the rounded tree roots curling up from underground, or the pinecones and branches scattered like discarded toys over the rough earth.

The fresh dewy smell of the forest in the hours before dawn kept my head clear as I walked, still unsure of my direction. I was used to the sounds of the forest at night, but now they carried with them an edge they hadn't before.

Was the scrabble of animal claws on frayed tree bark actually a beast lingering in the shadows? Was the hum of insects actually the buzzing of magic from a witch's spell? I shivered and it wasn't because of the cold.

I'd been right. Now that I knew, I couldn't *unknow*. And fuck if I wished I could. Digging in my pack, I procured the sole bottle of water I'd brought with me and took a small sip, not wanting to guzzle it all and leave myself without any to drink in case I wound up staying in the woods tonight.

I realized the direction I was going when the landscape began to change. Trees leaned drunkenly against one another, and others lay fallen against the earth. Uprooted tree bases showed their unmentionables above ground. And the ground itself was not the carpet of nettles and moss and leaves it was ten feet before. It was dirt, loose, and squishy underfoot.

This was the edge of the mudslide. Which meant that dad's blind, or where it once sat was just up ahead. Except I knew it wouldn't be there, instead of moving northwest to where it should be, I moved south, following the flow of churned earth down the mountain to where it would have been carried.

I'd been wanting to go back, to see that there was truly nothing else to be salvaged. I wanted to see the state of the blind myself. Jared had said it was completely destroyed. But was it still salvageable? If it was, it would save me the massive headache of figuring out where to go. The sickly stink of rotting wood in a nearby marshy patch made my nose wrinkle as I stepped around it and peered through two steepled trees ahead. The unmistakable *snap* of fabric in the cool autumn breeze drew menearer.

As I passed through the natural arch, I saw it, instantly deflating.

Jared had been right.

The old hunting blind was vertical, sticking up like a sore thumb from the earth where half of it was entirely buried. It leaned against a wide birch tree, coils of white bark fraying this way and that.

The canvas wasn't just torn now, either, it was in tatters like frayed ribbons flapping in the wind.

Well fuck.

Readjusting my pack, I sighed, going to have a quick look to make sure nothing else could be salvaged. The contents of the blind were entirely missing when I kneeled against the damp ground to peer beneath the flaps. I thought I could see the edge of one my old textbooks sticking up from the ground, but it wouldn't be worth the trouble of digging up. It would be too damaged to use now.

I'd been hoping at least my camp stove had survived. I could get another one relatively cheap, but a breakfast of warm oatmeal would have been nicer than the single banana and half a loaf of bread I'd pilfered from Jared's place.

The snap of a branch behind me made me whirl around, my heart jumping into my throat. I scanned the area but found nothing. I looked over the ground but saw only the unmistakable press of enormous paw prints in the upturned dirt.

They had to be Jared's from when he'd come back to get my things. But as I leaned in closer to inspect the nearest one, tracing the edge with my finger, I realized they looked *much* fresher than a few days old.

Had he come back here again?

My lungs seized. Or were they another wolf's?

Rylands?

I jolted back to my feet and swallowed, glancing around frantically now.

I couldn't stay in the woods tonight. What was I thinking?

With a shake of my head, I turned south, intending to go straight to the main road and make my way into town. I'd go to the bookshop. I could sleep for a couple hours and then leave before daybreak.

"I knew you'd come back here."

My body went rigid. A cold feeling of dread slithered up my spine, forcing the hairs on the back of neck to standing. My lips parted in a silent gasp.

It couldn't be.

Unable to conceal the tremor in my fingertips, I shoved my hand deep into my pocket and kept the other one tightly clasped around the strap of my pack as I turned. "Devin?" I asked incredulously, *praying* I was dreaming, or hallucinating, or anything other than the truth. "What are you doing out here?"

The other question I didn't ask was whispered in the back of my mind. *And how did you know I'd been here?*

I'd never told him about the hunting blind in the woods. He thought

I went back to Portland every night after work just like everyone else, hadn't he?

His green eyes were shadowed in the dark, and beneath the heavy leather coat he wore, I could see that he was shirtless. I backed up a step, noticing too how he was barefoot.

There was a connection forming at the edges of my mind, but it wasn't fully formed yet. I couldn't quite piece it together, but I could feel it in my bones.

There was something very wrong here. "Did you really think I didn't know?"

My breaths were coming faster now. I wished he would step into the light so I could see him, his expression. As he was now, cloaked in shadow, he seemed even more menacing than that night weeks before.

"Know what?" I asked foolishly, knowing exactly what he was getting at, but not wanting to admit to the lie. He didn't like it when I lied to him, or more accurately, when he *thought* I was lying to him.

With inhuman speed, Devin cleared the space between us in the span of a single breath. My jacket was fisted in his hand, pulling me to him, forcing my head up to look into his furious gaze. "Don't lie to me," he growled.

"Devin, stop," I managed. "Y-You're hurting me."

His knuckles were digging into my chest and it was beginning to be difficult to breathe. I fisted my own hand, ready to swing. "Please, let go."

He did, and I unclenched my fist, my broken breaths sawing in and out through chattering teeth.

He straightened his jacket and pushed back his dark hair. "I didn't mean—" he started but stopped himself. "You just...*you just make me so angry* sometimes."

Yeah, I fucking noticed, I wanted to say. *I have the bruises to prove it.*

I could feel the beginning of that fluttering sensation in my chest. The cold lick of anxiety like an ice cube down my neck. I grit my teeth and forced lungs full of air into my chest to quell the feeling. If I started hyperventilating right now, it would only make matters worse. I was alone in the woods with Devin Wright. My ex.

The guy who only weeks ago had wrapped his hands around my

neck and squeezed, the one who's knuckles rapped against my chest, leaving stippled purple bruises in their wake.

"But that's okay," he went on, his eyes unfocused as he spoke, gesturing wildly with his hands in a way that made me flinch back every time he raised them. "It's okay because you're my mate. Once the bond is made, you'll belong to me forever."

I shrank back, my eyes widening. "What are you talking about?"

Devin stepped in again and I readied myself to swing and run. If I thought angry Devin was scary, crazy-talking Devin was even more terrifying. "You aren't making any sense."

Devin snarled. "*You smell like* him," he barked. "When you're mine, you'll only bare *my* scent. You won't even look at another—"

I swung, decking him hard in the nose. He stumbled back and I saw the arc of red spray as blood poured from his face. My daddy taught me how to punch, but he forgot to mention how much it fucking *hurt*.

With my fist smarting, I tore off into the trees, discarding my pack without a second thought to gain the speed I would need to outrun a six-foot-four Devin.

Fuck. Fuck. Fuck.

I ducked under a low-hanging branch, moving through a spider's web and grimacing as I slid in the mud. I almost fell but caught myself at the last second.

A bellowing roar behind me made my entire body scream, the burst of adrenaline setting fire to my nerve endings as my legs pumped harder, *faster*, zigzagging downhill.

My hair whipped around my face, blinding me as I craned my neck to look back. He wasn't there.

No. no. NO.

I took a giant lungful of air, readying myself to scream as loud and as long as I could. But the tears stinging at the corners of my eyes were there because I knew no matter how loud I screamed, this far out of town—this far up the mountain, no one would be able to hear me.

Loud snorting breaths from behind and the unmistakable sound of thumping footfalls were the last things I heard before a hard object bashed into the back of my skull and the lights in my world went out.

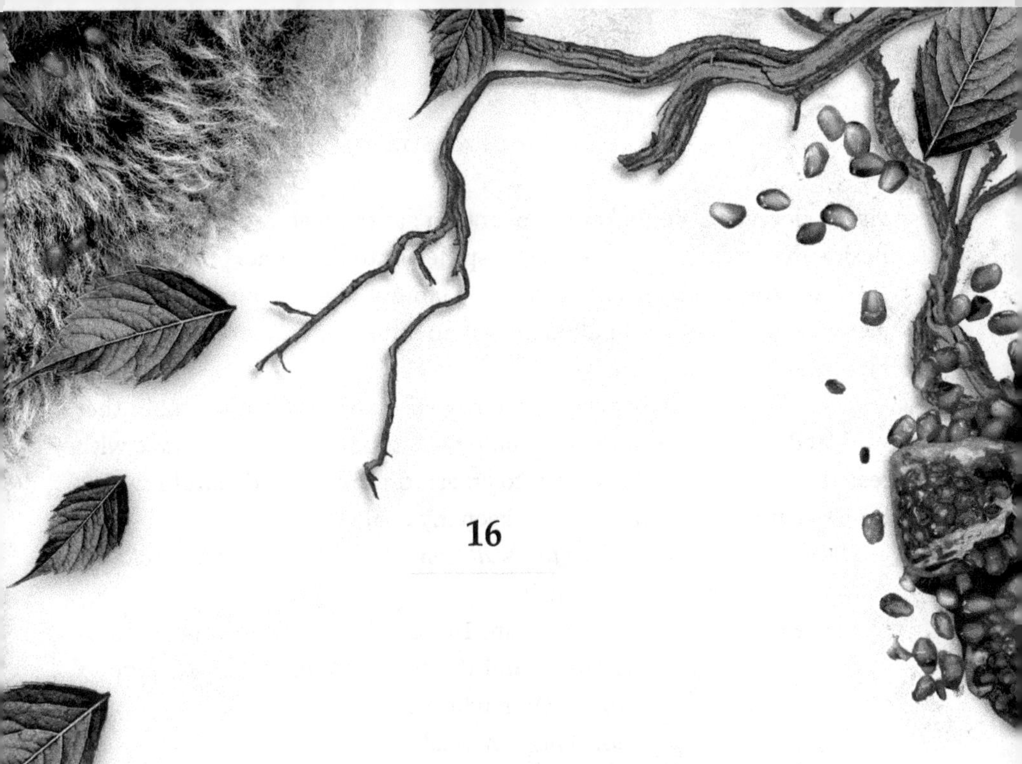

16

My hand slid over damp, bumpy stone. The jangle of metal was loud in my ears as I moved. I winced as I attempted to lift my head from the hard, cold surface beneath it. The ache in the back of my skull radiating out over the entire surface of my scalp in a thudding, stabbing migraine.

The scents of stagnant air and musky animal fur clogged my nostrils, mixed with the unmistakable tang of body odor that I was afraid was my own. A moan eeked out of my mouth before I could contain it and I reached a hand up to clutch the front of my skull in an attempt to stop the pounding pain. But my hand came up short, jerked to a stop only a few inches from my forehead. The bite of unyielding metal against my wrist made me snap into wakefulness.

I scrambled to sit up, disoriented with enormous black blobs crowding in at the edges of my vision. The world tipped up and the floor fell away as a wave of vertigo claimed me, forcing me to fall back onto the cold stone, gagging as a wave of nausea twisted my stomach. My stomach heaved, but it had nothing to expel. My sides ached at the pressure until it was finally lifted and the dry heaving stopped, leaving me to shake uncontrollably against the stone.

There was little light in the space, but it was enough to see by as my vision cleared. A single kerosene lantern sat ten feet away atop a crate. Beside that was my pack, open and spilled onto the stone.

A slim black device laid next to the lantern and my spirits soared as I recognized my phone. I pulled myself up but stopped short as the metal bit into my wrist once more.

I lifted my arm, inspecting the rusted manacle, and the chain that vanished behind me into the shadows. I tugged it but was met with resistance. My pulse skittered into an erratic pattern and I shut my eyes for a second, gulping down air to keep my cool.

Okay, Allie. You're chained to a wall. Don't freak out. Do not freak out.

Except I was already losing it.

When I opened my eyes again, I noticed there were mouse droppings scattered over the stone, and the flickering light threw shadows over the space. It was a room. Or maybe a cave?

Focus. You need to focus. Where are you?

It was like it was carved out of the rock on purpose, the corners too precise, the floor too smooth. A man-made cave, then?

Water dripped from some unseen crack in the ceiling and suddenly I was dying of thirst.

How long had I been in here? What happ—

It came back in a burst of clarity. The woods. Devin.

He...he'd knocked me out.

He must have taken me here. Chained me up.

I tugged harder on the chain, rising slowly to stave off the dizziness as I pulled myself along the chain to the wall. It was made of stone, too, lending credit to my theory that this was some sort of cave. I found where the thick chain was fixed to the wall at around chest level with a strong metal loop that was drilled deep into the stone. Using both hands, I pulled on it, but wasn't able to make it so much as budge.

I felt around the wall as my eyes adjusted to the dim, finding one, two, *three* other chains discarded near the base of the stone wall. Another at the same level as the one around my wrist. And two more nearer to the floor.

What the hell is this place?

A shrill ringing made me yelp and I spun to find my cell phone illuminated where it sat on the crate. It buzzed over the surface, moving slightly as the call came in.

Oh my god.

Wherever I was, there was cell service. I rushed to answer the call but tripped against the stone when my wrist was snapped back, the air knocked from my lungs as I hit the ground.

The crate was too far away. I reached with everything I had, gasping for unrestricted breath, but it was still several feet from my fingertips.

My phone buzzed insistently, the loud ringing echoing back to me from the stone walls. A lick of fury chased the anxiety from my veins, and I spun, positioning myself with my wrist pulled against the chain as far as it would go, and my legs inched toward the crate. I stuck out my right leg and the toe of my shoe just scraped along the edge of the crate. I pulled harder on the chain and lifted my body, giving it the last few inches of length I needed to nudge the phone. Grunting, I managed to shove it inch by inch to the edge of the crate, and then to the floor.

I grinned, pressing on it with the sole of my show and scraping it over the stones as I pulled it to where I could reach with my free hand. With clumsy fingers, I flipped it over and saw the caller ID flashing with a name.

Jared.

I could have kissed the screen, tears bloomed in my eyes as I answered the call.

His voice came through distorted, and I saw that I only had one bar, and even that was wavering. "Allie?"

"J-Jared," I cried, "I need—"

A door that'd been concealed in shadow across the room banged open and I screamed as the shape of a man swept into the cell and the phone was torn from my grasp, a sharp explosion of pain and mottled stars in my vision alerted me to the fact that I'd been struck.

"Stupid bitch!"

The voice belonged to Devin, that much was certain, but it was laced with an animal growl that twisted the words until they sounded less than human.

I tasted blood on my tongue and spat onto the rock, holding myself up with weak arms.

I shed a tear for the lost opportunity. If I'd just spoken faster, I could have told him I was in a cave somewhere. He might've been able to find me. He'd at least have known I was in danger. He could've alerted the police.

Idiot.

"Where am I?"

"What have you done?" he bellowed.

I craned my neck to look at him, shrinking back from his tone and utterly unprepared for what I saw.

Green glowing orbs watched me with crazed fury. His face was half set in shadow and half alight with the orange glow of flame. His hands were talons at his sides and his body heaved with each hard breath he took, nostrils flaring.

A glimmer of white betrayed his elongating canines. Breathlessly, I searched for the other signs with a hard ball in my throat. The thickening of the hair on his hands, the lengthening of his fingernails.

He couldn't be. No.

Jared would've told me. Surely he'd have known.

"You could have ruined everything!" he shouted, making to strike me again, but I lifted my arms to block the blow and he stopped himself, seeming to hold his breath. "Why Allie..." he trailed off, his voice breathy now. Subdued.

"Why did you have to make this so difficult for us?"

He fell back to sit on the edge of the crate and buried his face in his hands, when he looked up at me again the glow was gone from his eyes, and his canines were back to a regular *human* length.

Once he had himself under control, he let down his hands and pulled my phone from the floor, illuminating the screen as he tapped it and began to type out a message.

"What are you doing?" I blurted before I could stop myself.

His head snapped up and glared at me. I pushed myself back over the damp stone, my hands moving over loose bits of rock and mouse droppings until I had my back pressed firmly against the wall furthest from him.

"I'm fixing your *mistake*," he replied tersely, jabbing his thumbs into my phone screen. One last hard tap and he hit the side button to turn it back off. "There."

I didn't have to ask him to know what he'd done, what he likely had been doing since he first brought me here however long ago. He was keeping up appearances. Replying to the texts I'd probably gotten from Viv and Layla by now. We always chatted via text on Sunday and they would want to know how my night turned out with Jared.

Would they know it wasn't me who was answering them?

Devin chuckled darkly. "Jared's going to get the fourth-degree tomorrow. Fucker deserves far worse for trying to steal what's *mine.*"

"What did you do?" I breathed.

He leaned in and tilted his head so I had a fully unobstructed view of his face in the lamplight. I pressed myself into the wall.

I'd broken his nose, hadn't I?

I'd seen it split. Seen the blood spray from his nostrils.

But as I watched him carefully from my place against the wall, I noted there wasn't even a scratch on him. Not even a drop of dried blood.

Apparently, they healed *very* fast. *Noted.*

"I can't believe you were staying with *him,*" Devin snarled in disdain. "Of all people, Allie. Why him?"

I was afraid to answer. I didn't want to provoke his wrath. I decided to lie, instead. "H-He offered, that's all. I didn't have any place else to go."

Seemingly placated by my response, he pursed his lips and tilted his head, sighing. "It doesn't matter now, anyway..."

My heart was battering at my ribcage. I thought for certain he would be able to hear it in the echoing space. It was all I could hear in the intermittent silence.

The drip of water from some unseen source above and the constant, hurried thudding of my pulse shoving blood through my veins seemed loud in my own head.

"Devin," I pressed, trying to maintain a façade of calm even though a million other emotions were clawing for their chance to be heard. Pain. Anger. Fear. Hurt. The list was endless.

I could show none of them. I could show nothing that would provoke the demon slumbering beneath the surface of Devin's flesh. If he lost it in here, I'd never make it out.

"Hmm?" he replied absently, pressing his thumb and index finger into his eye sockets.

I swallowed hard and dug my fingernails into the stone to steady myself. "What am I doing here?"

He didn't answer, only released his hand and gazed up at me from his perch between his knees curiously.

"What are you going to do to me?"

Devin clucked his tongue and sat up straighter. "He really didn't tell you about me, did he?"

A lance of hurt made my shoulders curl inward. "No," I replied. Jared hadn't told me about Devin, and now I knew that he *did* know. Why didn't he tell me? Did I not have a right to know he was a wolf inside, too? It was easy to see it now, and I wasn't sure how I hadn't before.

There were so many times. *So many times* where I'd felt as though I was being watched and I'd shucked off the feeling. Now I knew it wasn't paranoia. Devin had known I was living out in the blind in the woods. He followed me there.

Like Jared had.

Except, unlike Jared, Devin had dangerous intentions...and Jared only watched me to stop Devin from seeing those intentions through.

Why didn't you tell me, Jared?

"Too bad..." Devin trailed off, flicking something from his fingers onto the stone floor. "I would've loved to have him hung for that."

I narrowed my eyes at him. *Have him hung?* Was he saying that if Jared had told me about Devin, he'd have been...what? Killed?

What the fuck was this world we were living in?

It wasn't what I thought it was... "Guess I'll just have to do it myself."

I sprang forward in a knee-jerk reaction. "You won't touch him!"

Hard breaths were escaping from between my clenched and bared teeth as I pulled on the metal binds, surprising myself with my reaction.

Devin's expression soured. In a flash, he was on his feet, his face a breath from my own, but I didn't flinch this time. I stared right back into his glowing green eyes with a defiance I didn't know I possessed.

"You. Are. *Mine.*"

I spat in his face, realizing a millisecond too late that it was a colossal mistake. A flurry of movement from the corner of my eye was the only warning before the back of his hand connected with my cheek, sending my head jerking to the left. An explosion of stars burst in my eyes and the metallic tang of blood on my tongue made me want to gag.

"Fuck you!" I shouted, but the words came out discordant and broken. "I will *never* belong to you."

Strong hands came around my shoulders with a bruising grip and shoved me back until my spine connected with the stone wall. I exhaled sharply and slumped to the floor when he released me, blinking rapidly to clear the wave of dizziness.

Devin was heaving with the effort of keeping himself contained. It reminded me of that night. How he'd kept clenching and unclenching his fists, breathing heavily as he shook his head over and over.

Like he couldn't make up his mind whether he wanted to kiss me or kill me.

It was the uncertainty that made it the most terrifying. In one moment, I felt like it was over, that I could trust that he wouldn't hurt me again, and then in the next second, the beast could return, and he would descend upon me with a renewed fury.

Had his eyes been glowing that night and I just didn't notice?

Because they were glowing now.

Bright and vibrant in the dim. The clearest shade of green I'd ever seen.

"You *are* mine, Allie. I've known it from the first time I saw you. Right after your father died. He was weak, you know. So weak it was pathetic."

I struggled to rise, lashing out with my legs to try to kick him. How dare he! I muttered a string of curses under my breath, whimpering against the stone.

"But you…"

He licked his lips, and suddenly his eyes were alight. "You were so strong, Allie. You took his death in stride. You never let anyone see your pain, but I saw it. I saw *you*. The *real* you. I saw you working every day to make your own way. I saw you when you lied to your selfish aunt and uncle so they wouldn't have to feel guilty for leaving you. I followed you when you moved out into your father's old blind in the woods. And bit my tongue when you lied to everyone you knew about it…even me." He was shaking his head now, his hand coming up to rub his chin as he inhaled deep, expanding his chest. His eyes gleamed.

"Can't you feel it?" he asked me after a momentary lull, kneeling several feet away so he was at eye-level with me. "We're fated mates, Allie. And once you've completed your first shift, we'll be together. Forever."

I clutched my stomach, afraid I might hurl. "I-I don't understand..."

Devin reached out to me and with no place left to move away, I turned my face into the stone. His fingers gently stroked the side of my face unmarred by his knuckles. I shuddered and my stomach heaved at the contact. "You will," he said softly and then his fingers vanished, and I sensed him moving away. I opened my eyes again cautiously, wishing more than anything else that he would leave. Just leave me in the dark and cold alone to rot away.

I'd prefer that than to live a life of servitude as his... as his what? His *mate*?

I didn't know what the fuck that meant, but I didn't think I wanted to.

He pointed up toward the ceiling. "This is a moon room," he said, and his expression was placid, almost kind. It was scarier than when he looked angry.

"You see...when a *changed* wolf first shifts, their animal urges can be...*uncontrollable*. People can get hurt. Or worse, *they* could capture us on video. The witches don't like that. It creates a big mess for them to clean up."

With no other option, I shifted to lay my aching head back against the wall and wrapped my arms around myself, suddenly colder than I think I'd ever been in my entire life. I listened even though I wished I could stuff my ears full of cotton and not hear any of it. "So, my people —*our* people—created these. For the first year or so of moon-triggered shifts, we'll keep you in here. Until you can control yourself. That circle up there," he said, eyes peering above where he stood. I craned my neck to follow his gaze and found I could just make out the smallest crevice in the rock, forming a near perfect circle. It was damp and therefor darker than the rest of the stone ceiling. Water dropped from one side to splash against Devin's face. He wiped away the moisture, unperturbed. "It opens to allow the moonlight inside. You'll shift with or without it touching you, but it's faster this way."

Devin pocketed my cell phone and I stifled a whimper. He went to the hidden doorway across the room and procured a plastic bag, moving in close to set it down next to me.

"And then we'll start our own pack. Ryland thought he could kick me out without retribution...he was *wrong*. We'll build our own force." Devin shook as he began to pace, and I watched his fists curl until the knuckles turned white. "A force bigger and *stronger* than his. He'll see his mistake in forsaking me." His leg reared back, and he kicked the crate hard, sending it sailing into the wall. The kerosene lantern careened into the air, but as the wooden box blew apart into small wood fragments, some of them hitting me in the shins and forearms, the lantern didn't break.

Devin caught it before it could. He set it down with shaking fingers.

His outburst could've just cost us both our lives. If the kerosene had spilled and the flame had been exposed, we'd be burning right now. As it was, I only had a few more scrapes and cuts to add to my growing collection.

He turned numbly to the door, scooping up my pack and its spilled contents and shouldering it. "I'll be back," he said in a monotone voice. "Eat. Drink."

I eyed the plastic bag, realizing it had the mark of a grocery store on it, but it wasn't one I knew. It wasn't a store in Forest Grove. My heart sank. Where the hell had he taken me?

"The full moon is in two days," he said, vanishing into the shadows on the other end of the space. "That is when I'll awaken your wolf."

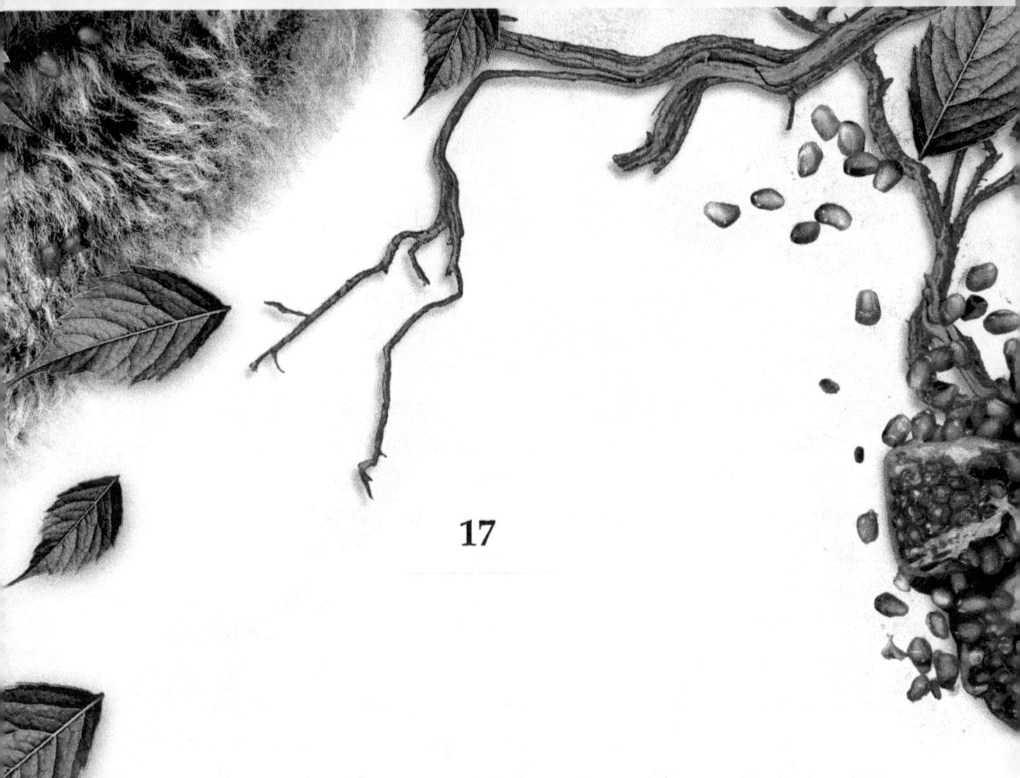

17

I awoke with a sting in my cheek and aching bones, but the migraine I'd had prior to falling asleep had gone.

It was a small mercy, but one I couldn't be grateful for since when my eyes adjusted, I found myself still inside the cave-like space. Without the presence of light, it was impossible to tell what time of day or night it was, let alone if I should be awake or sleeping.

The meager meal of sliced fruit in a plastic cup and a box of crackers Devin had left for me lay open a foot away where a mouse feasted on the corner of a discarded bit of cracker, its beady eyes watching me as its body shook.

My first instinct was to shoo it away, but who was I kidding? It wasn't like I could stomach any more than a few tiny morsels I'd already managed to get down *and keep down* before I eventually passed out. "Someone might as well eat it," I whispered to the tiny rodent instead. I reached over and grabbed another few crackers from the open bag.

The mouse began to scurry away but paused before it vanished from view. I held out the crackers to it. "Here," I told it. "Don't be afraid. I won't hurt you."

The little critter hesitated, running this way and that on a zigzagging path that eventually led it back to the discarded cracker. It resumed eating the small piece that was left and then came for more, inching slowly closer.

"Go on," I told it, a small smile tugging at my lips made the bruises on my cheek sting. The little mouse drew forward and took the proffered crackers. It stared at me as still as the bits of wood and stone around it, and then it skittered away with its bounty.

I stared at the spot it'd vacated, the smile slipping from my lips in favor of a frown. I didn't know how long I'd been asleep, but it wasn't the first time I'd passed out since Devin left, which made me wonder if it'd somehow already been two days.

My stomach growled and ached painfully, and my bladder felt about ready to burst. I'd had to relieve myself twice already, afraid I'd burst if I hadn't. But the acrid stench of my urine was gone, which meant Devin must've come in at some point to clean it away while I slept.

I eyed the crackers and fruit suspiciously and then saw another mouse, different from the one who I'd just shared my meal with. It was smaller, it's color a darker gray. And it was dead.

Laying only a handful of feet away from the bounty of food it'd clearly been feasting on.

"*Shit,*" I cursed, wanting to cry and barf and scream all at the same time.

I felt around my clothes. Beneath my dirty and torn jacket, I was still wearing the jeans and long sleeve shirt I'd had on when I left Jared's cabin. My bra was still in place beneath my shirt. My zipper was done up, the button buttoned.

He'd drugged me, that was why I kept passing out. There was something in the food. Had he injected the fruit? Sprinkled sleeping pill dust over the crackers? There'd been a funny taste in my mouth after I'd eaten, I remembered that, but I'd attributed it to the blood still in my mouth and not having brushed my teeth in a couple days.

I'd been wrong. Whatever the drug was, it'd killed that mouse...and it would kill the other one I'd just fed. My chest burned.

Sorry little guy...

I groaned in fury, kicking at the wall. I could feel it now, the grogginess. My body felt heavy and sagging. My mind foggy and swaying.

I held my head between my hands and tried to clear it, taking in deep breaths.

At least he hadn't touched me.

He hadn't, right?

My body didn't *feel* violated. My clothes were still in place and there was no pain *down there*.

I needed to get my wits back before I passed out again. Shoving my fingers deep down my throat, I upturned what little sustenance I had left in my body. I reached for the last dregs of water left in the large one-liter bottle that'd been in the bag to wash out my mouth, but paused. Noticing for the first time a strange shimmer in the water.

I chucked the bottle across the room and it hit the opposite wall with a noisy plastic crunch before rolling to the floor and spilling what was left its contents over the stone. He'd drugged *everything*.

The fucking bastard.

In my rage, my vision wavered between blurred and crystalline sharpness as I seethed alone in the dark. Something small, slim, and metal caught my eye next to where the dead mouse was laying motionless amid the debris from the wooden crate Devin had shattered against the wall in his rage.

It was a nail. A slightly bent, slightly rusted nail, but the sharp tip of it sparked an idea. I lifted the manacle on my wrist and inspected the keyhole with shaking fingers. I'd never picked a lock before, but this one was old and wide. Surely it wouldn't be so difficult. With a renewed fervor, I clambered over to the nail and snatched it up, dropping it twice before I was able to settle my nerve-racked body enough to hold it steady.

Fuck. I needed to get control of myself. The dull knife of anxiety was creeping over me, made stronger by the fact that my body was weak. It was always worse when I hadn't eaten right. Wasn't hydrated.

Forcing myself to vomit up what little I had eaten probably only made it worse, but I prayed it had the effect of turning up any leftover drugs that hadn't already been absorbed into my bloodstream.

I just needed to focus. To get out. Then I could stuff my face with all the huckleberries I wanted—*after* I was done running the fuck away from here. Wherever *here* was.

I couldn't think about that now. I couldn't focus on what I would do once I was free or what other trial might face me once I got through that door. I needed to take the first step. *Exit.*

Then figure out the rest.

Fitting the end of the nail into the rusted opening was like trying to thread a needle with my vision swimming so badly. But eventually, I got it in. I wet my mouth, shirked off my jacket, pressing my back against the cold stone. The chill seeped into my skin and had the desired effect, lending me the momentary alertness I needed to do this.

From what I knew of locks, very little I had to admit, there was a tumbler thing inside that needed to be pushed up and rotated out of the way for the lock to come undone. I didn't even know if this was true for all locks, or if, like the movies, you needed two slim pieces of metal to pick a lock properly.

Grunting as I pressed upward into the narrow channel of the lock, I heard a little click and nearly cried with relief, dropping the nail.

Except when I pulled on the manacle, it didn't come free. Instead a small bit of something fell from the keyhole.

My fingers were trembling too badly for me to be able to pick it up, but on closer inspection, I saw that it was a small bit of metal.

Please don't tell me I just broke the damned lock...

I threw my head back and let the hopeless moan I'd been trying to hold back escape. It rose in tempo and volume all on its own, the fury chasing out the weakness.

Fuck him, I thought to myself. *Fuck him!*

That fucking bastard wanted me to sit here, loopy and out of it on drugs until he came for me. Was I really going to give him what he wanted? Was I really going to make it this fucking easy?

My father's voice answered the question for me in my mind, as though he was sitting in the makeshift jail cell with me.

Hell, no.

You pick your ass up, Allie Grace, and you keep going.

I nodded to myself, wondering offhandedly if this was the onset of hysteria.

I didn't bother with the nail this time. I didn't know how to pick a lock. It was a stupid idea. But there was something else I could do.

I cursed myself for not having thought of it sooner. There were a couple centimeters of space between my wrist and the manacle. If I pulled as hard as I could on my arm and tried to slip my hand through the circlet of metal, it was close—the bind was clearly made for a larger wrist. But no matter how hard I pulled, I couldn't quite get it off, not even when I greased the thing with water, and later, when I'd tried saliva instead.

I tenderly pushed against the spot where my thumb connected to the base of my hand, wincing at the tender flesh just below, where the manacle had been rubbing in my sleep. If it didn't have the bump of my thumb joint to go over...

My stomach roiled.

Was I really going to do this?

This time it was Viv in my mind. *Fuck yes, you're going to do this*, she hissed in that lovingly neurotic way only she had.

Viv would do it. Hell, she would have already thought of it and done it and escaped.

So, then why was I hesitating?

Goddamnit.

Before I could change my mind or really think it through, I snatched up an errant piece of broken crate and slid it between my teeth. Then pushed the manacle as far down my forearm as I could and bent my thumb inward, pressing the palm of my opposite hand flat against it to hold it in place.

I could feel the joint straining already. All it would take is one good thrust with all my body weight and it'd be done.

I closed my eyes and bit down.

...and did what had to be done.

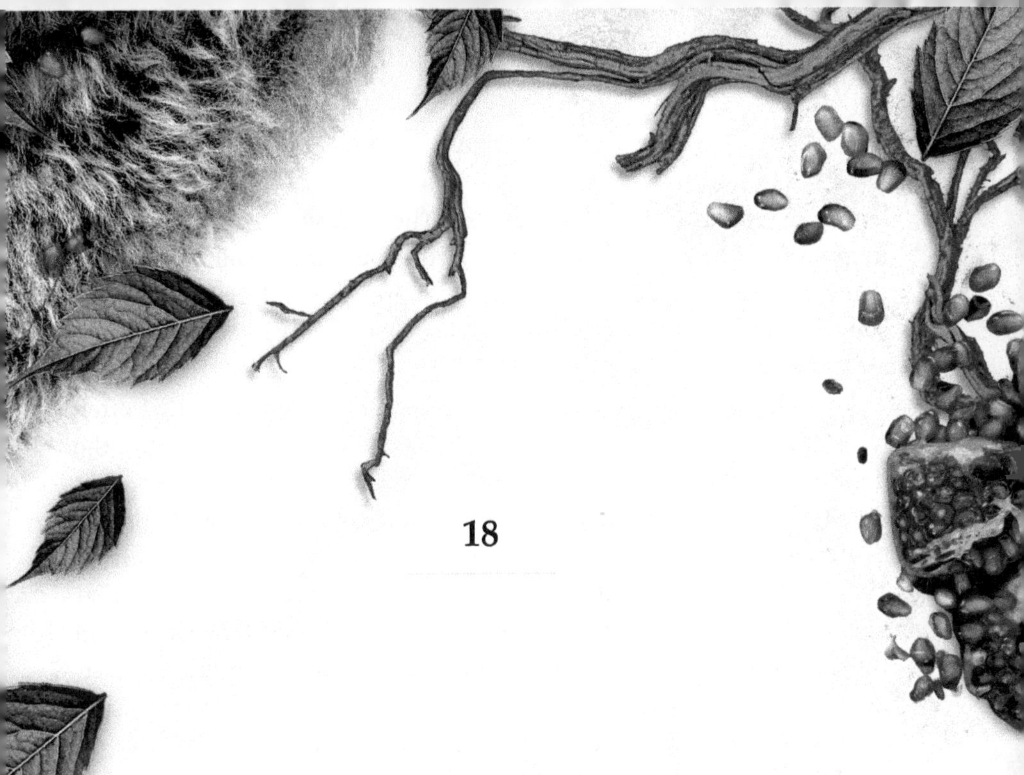

18

My hand slipped free of the manacle with only a slight tug, but the pressure of the metal against my newly broken digit almost made me scream. I clutched my hand to my chest for a moment to catch my breath and spat out the bit of wood, letting it clatter to the floor.

Time to move.

Taking in a lung full of air through my nostrils, I rose from the floor and took two steps, nearly falling over as another wave of vertigo swept over me. I caught myself before I could fall and shook my head sharply, turning back to scoop up my jacket and put it on. It took longer than I would've liked to get my injured hand down into the sleeve.

Okay, I reassured myself. *You did the hard part, Allie. It's done. Now you need to get out. Then...you need to run.*

I didn't quite know how in the hell I was going to do that. I was weak and tired and aching all over. Dehydrated and twitching with anxiety.

But you can *do this, Allie Grace,* my father reminded me like he had so many times before when I'd wanted to give up. He was the one who molded me into the fighter I am today. And I would make him proud.

It took a moment to steady myself, to gain my footing and my head, then I was moving. I crossed the cell on clumsy feet and drew the

153

lantern nearer so I could see the door. The wick was nearly all burned up now—only a small tail remained jutting out into the oil beneath the flame. We used to have one of these lamps, me and dad—when we stayed in the blind. I knew from then that the wicks generally lasted about eight or so hours.

Which had to mean that Devin had been coming at least that often to replace the wick because to my knowledge I hadn't been left in the dark. Each time I awoke, the lamp had been lit. Judging by what remained of the wick, there was an hour left of burn time, and I prayed that meant I had at least an hour to escape before Devin would return.

The door wasn't really a door at all, I found, just an archway that had the illusion of looking as though it were sealed off. The air beyond was just as dark as it had been inside, there was no discernible breeze. But as I drew in great gulps of air in my panic, I realized it was fresher than it was deeper into the cell where I was being kept.

There had to be a way out through here.

I used the wall to help steady myself, regretting leaving the lamp behind in the cell when the inky dark grew so thick, I couldn't even see my cold breaths in the air anymore.

But after several more paces and following the wall around a bend and up three jagged steps, the stone corridor plateaued, and light could be seen at the end of a long upward sloping tunnel.

Tears pricked at my eyes as I hurried faster upwards, almost to a jog now. The light was coming from a slit in the stone, and when I was close enough, I saw that it was definitely an opening. I pressed against the wall with my shoulder, but the heavy door barely budged.

I felt around it with my hands. It was...stone. The opening had been mostly covered over by a stone door. I felt the edges, top and bottom. It had been rolled into place concealing the opening of the cavern.

Fuck.

I knew I couldn't move it alone. Even though it only came to my chest in height and didn't seem to be particularly thick, it was still solid rock and probably weighed at least two-hundred pounds, if not more.

But...maybe I could roll it. The gap in the stone was just big enough for me to slip my fingers in and get a good grip, but with only one hand I could use to do the job, it wouldn't work. And after several pulls with everything I had in me, gritting my teeth and growling at the exertion, I knew it was no use.

When you couldn't lift the hunting blind off your ankle, you found a way. You can find a way to do this, too, I told myself. The false sense of security I kept trying to give myself was starting to disintegrate. If I couldn't open this and Devin found me freed from his chains, what would he do to me?

I had a flicker of an idea, maybe I could go back, pretend I was still chained up and then when he came for me...

When he came for me...what?

I couldn't take him down. I knew that now. He was half wolf. Stronger than I could ever hope to be. But with the element of surprise, maybe I could incapacitate him. Maybe I could kill—

I stopped the thought before it could take hold.

No. I couldn't do that. Not even after what he did to me. I couldn't end someone else's life. *Fuck!*

Gritting my teeth, with my hand throbbing as I moved, I settled myself down on the floor, pressing my back flat against the wall to the left of the door. Rough stone jabbed into my back, but I paid it no mind. It was the least of my worries. I could deal with a few more bruises if I could just get out.

Pressing both my feet against the tiny lip of the door, I used the wall to help push my legs, straining muscle and sinew and tendon as I bared my teeth and pushed with everything I had.

The door rolled an inch. I took a breath and pushed again, stifling my urge to cry out from the strain. It rolled again, another two inches. I kept pushing, and soon, its own momentum propelled it until it connected with some other stone outside, the loud *crack* deafening in the silence of the night, reverberating through the deep navy of early night and the forest below the ledge I was peering over.

It was a mountain. Not a large one, the downward inclination wasn't incredibly steep, and only about ten feet away, small trees grew out from the dirt covered stone sloping all the way down to the forest floor about forty feet below.

I didn't recognize it, I realized, but I was high up and had never seen *my* forest from this angle. I squinted into the horizon above the trees, still trying to catch my breath, and saw the glow of a city's lights in the distance. I was so turned around I had no idea which way was north, but if those lights were Forest Grove, and I prayed they were, then that was the way I was headed.

As I scrambled out of the mouth of the cave and onto the ledge, the crunch of plastic made me squeal and I nearly fell off in my haste to back away. It was a plastic water bottle, much like the one Devin had left for me except as I twisted the cap, I realized the seal was still intact. With stiff fingers, and using my underarm to hold the bottle steady, I untwisted the cap and spilled almost half the water over the rock at my feet in my haste.

Cursing, I righted the bottle and gulped it down greedily, finishing its entire contents in three long swallows. It was icy cold and hurt my teeth, but I didn't care. I could feel it carving a cool path down my esophagus and through my belly. It was fucking glorious.

In hindsight, I should have conserved it, but as I tossed the bottle back to where I'd found it against the exterior of rock, I found I couldn't bring myself to give a shit.

The sting of crisp autumn air on my cheeks and the feel of the moonlight against my closed eyelids was absolute bliss. *I did it.*

And mercifully, it seemed, Devin had yet to return. I half expected him to jump at me from the shadows, or for him to have been sitting out here smugly waiting as I struggled to roll away the stone door. But he wasn't. And I was free.

I managed to maneuver myself from the ledge and down onto uneven rock, glancing back at the black hole I'd just emerged from with a gulp. *No time to waste.* I hurried as quickly and quietly as I could down the slope, only slowing once I had the cover of trees.

My vision blurred and fell against the rough bark of a tree, scraping my palm. I bowed my head for a breath and stumbled to the next tree, falling against it harder than I had the last one. It was like gravity was stronger here. My weight twice as heavy as it was normally. The magnetic pull of the earth trying to drag me down was a physical force and I had to grit my teeth to press on. I had to get *far* away if I was going to truly escape.

Jared scented Ryland outside his cabin from fifty feet away. If he'd been trying, I was willing to bet he'd have scented him sooner, and that was in his *human* form. It would be easier as a wolf, wouldn't it?

There was no time for a break. I couldn't afford the luxury of pause.

Devin would be on his way back to the *moon room* to turn me any time now. My head whipped up to the sky. I'd slept twice. The moon was fat and round in the caress of wispy gray clouds in the sky. It seemed bigger than usual. The stars around it brighter.

It was full. There was no doubting it.

If Devin found me, he was going to *turn* me.

*Or try to...*my mind corrected. Jared said that not everyone completed the change. There was a chance that it wouldn't work even if Devin *did* find me and... what? Bite me? Was it that simple?

And if you don't change?

Then what do you think he'll do to you? If he can't have you how will he react?

I cursed in a whispered string of profanity as I pressed on, seething with rage, and shaking from cold and fear.

I just needed to get to town. *Just get to town and then you'll be safe.* You can call the police. You can find Jared and tell him what happened. Surely if the police couldn't apprehend him, a pack of other wolves would be able to hunt him down? There had to be rules against this sort of thing, right?

Even in fucked up paranormal land?

The sound of trickling water caught my attention and I followed it to a small creek hemmed in by low hanging brush and stumpy trees. I sagged to my knees in the dirt and lifted a handful of icy water to my lips, taking a drink before wiping the rest of it over my sweat-beaded brow. I repeated the motion three more times before I felt the sharp edge of alertness return enough to rise once more.

But before I could, I dipped my hand deeper into the water, reaching all the way down to the muddy creek bed. I dug my fingernails into the cold, wet earth and drew out a handful of algae filled mud. I ran my hand over my forehead first, shivering as the mud slid over my skin as though it were a grainy ice cube. I did my cheeks next, then my neck, regretting that choice as small drips of mud found their way between my breasts. I scooped up more and coated the outside of my jacket in streaks of reddish brown. Then the front of my jeans and with a mournful pout, my new converse sneakers.

The mud should help to conceal my scent, I rationalized to myself, regretting my decision as a biting breeze passed over me, clinging to the wet mud and shooting pins and needles into my skin.

"This better fucking work," I muttered to myself, setting off in the direction of the city lights with a set jaw and renewed determination.

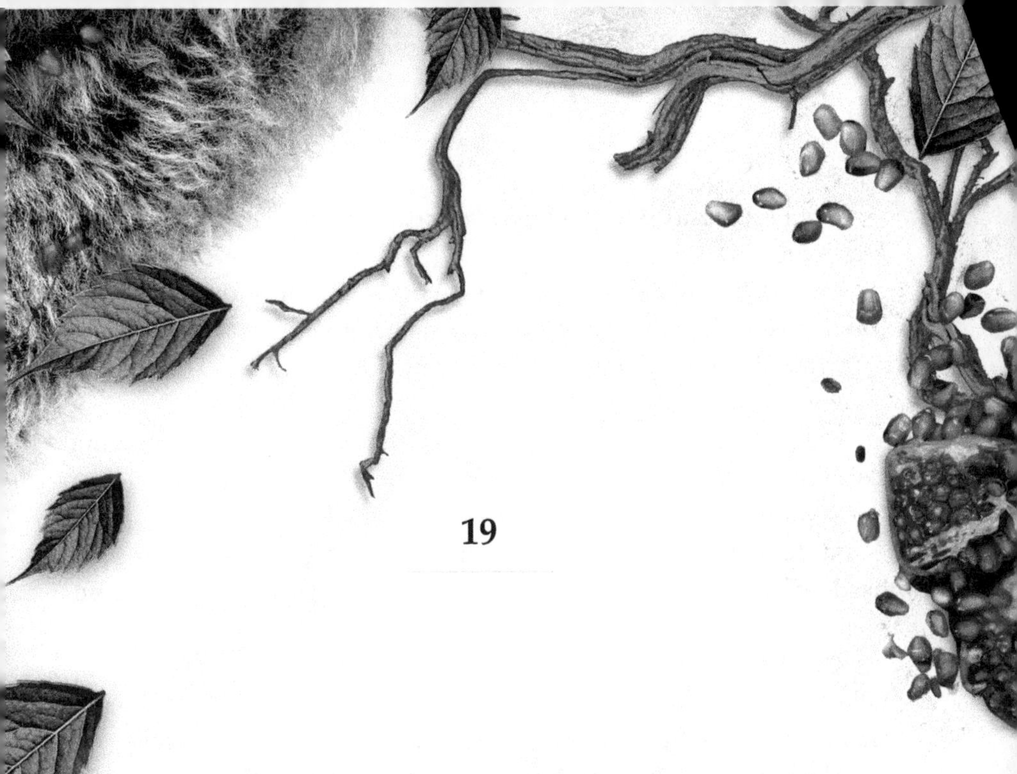

19

About thirty minutes later, I was drifting in and out. I kept blinking hard as I tried to keep up a brisk pace, but barely managed a slogging one, and each time I blinked, I had this strange feeling as though more time had passed than I realized.

Surveying my surroundings every so often only made me feel more disoriented. I couldn't even be certain I was going in the right direction anymore. My throat was raw and sore from the cold. My feet were aching, the pain in my heels starting to overtake even the throbbing ache in my hand that I kept clutched to my chest, elevated to stave off the worst of the pain.

I had to be getting close by now.

Just a little further, I urged myself, imagining the warm hearth in Clay and Jared's living room. My cozy bed. Viv and Layla pulling me into a warm hug, so glad to find that I'm alright.

Except...they didn't even know I was missing.

If Devin had succeeded in keeping up appearances, no one did.

My face pinched as my chest tightened and I rested for a moment against the peeling bark of a thin birch tree, finding the soft texture and scent so incredibly soothing that I found myself wanting to curl up at its base and sleep. I was so *so* tired.

Just a little break. Five minutes. I just needed five minutes and then I can keep going.

It was a lie. I knew even as I pressed my back against the base of the tree and settled my bottom against the damp ground that I wouldn't be getting back up. At least, not much more than five minutes.

But you have to...

I tipped my head back to rest against the tree and looked up at the sky between the branches of the forest's canopy. It was so beautiful. The forest was so peaceful. If I closed my eyes, I could just drift—

An eerie tremble rolled up my spine and I straightened, bringing my head off the bark with slow, measured movements. I wasn't even breathing.

The forest had been peaceful. Filled with sounds I'd grown used to falling asleep to over the past months. The rustle of leaves. The skitter of small animals in the underbrush. The crickets and other insects.

There was none of that. It was spine-tinglingly silent. Not even the wind dared interrupt the miasmal sense of foreboding that slithered over my mud caked body like a serpent scenting its prey with its forked tongue flicking before scaled lips and shining black eyes.

But the eyes I saw in the wood were not beady. And they were not black.

They were brightest emerald. And they were trained on me with an unwavering focus.

The wolf strode from the shadows with a hunter's grace, its massive paws silent against the mossy carpet of the forest. Its canine lips were curled back over shining white teeth. Its hot tongue snaked out from its jaws as it neared, a low growl reverberating out from its muscled chest.

This wolf was not Jared. And it was not Clay.

I whimpered, pressing my back into the tree. My hands clenched fistfuls of crackling brown leaves as I braced for an attack.

I had the presence of mind to *want* to feel around for a weapon on the ground, but I couldn't peel my gaze from the beast stalking ever closer. I was afraid that if I did, he would lunge.

"P-Please," I croaked. "Don't."

He was only a few feet away now, his deep gray and brown fur rippling as he blew steam from his nostrils and planted his front paws firmly against the earth.

The wolf that was Devin lifted its head to the sky, its wide green eyes reflecting the full moon against their glassy surface. When those green eyes fixed themselves back on me, it was with an apology and I knew what he was trying to say without the need for a human voice box.

It's time.

I screamed.

I screamed loud and hard, shocking myself with the volume I was able to manage even though the sound was raw, and scratching and my chest twinged from the pressure.

The scream was cut off midway when Devin lunged. His eyes were sharp and wild. His jaw agape. I threw my body to the side and rolled. A wolfish yelp told me he'd hit the tree and I was up and running, fueled by pure unfiltered adrenaline.

My vision was no longer dull. My body no longer ached. I felt nothing except for the wind in my hair and the passage of my feet over earth, my heart bleating out a thudding rhythm in my ears. For three blissful seconds, it was like I was flying, until I wasn't.

I was pushed forward and sailed five feet before I landed on my chest, splayed like a goddamned starfish in the dirt. Devin was on me before I could blink, and pain exploded through my shoulder. His jaws clamped down and warm liquid ran over my skin as I cried out, trying unsuccessfully to buck him off me.

All the while inside I was screaming.

No. No. No. Please god no.

My eyes stung with the welling of hot fat tears as I silently pleaded, not for the pain to stop, but for whatever was in his stupid magical wolf saliva to *not* work.

There came a savage snarl to my right a split second before Devin's weight was shifted off of me. Without the pressure of him on me, my lungs rushed to fill with air, inhaling a mouthful of dirt and debris. I coughed, scrambling to get myself on my feet. My hand went up to staunch the blood flow from my shoulder.

The jacket was slick with blood and I pulled my injured hand threw the sleeve so I could remove it from that arm and get a better look. My shirt was torn and wet and I ripped it more, needing to see the damage, as though if I were able to see the bite mark itself, I would somehow know if I was going to shift.

My tiny, gasping breaths halted as I assessed the wound. It was so gross I had to stifle the urge to be ill. But the torn and puckered skin, the welling of blood, and smattering of dirt made it look mundane. It could have been a dog bite. It was nothing. It would heal.

I was going to be alright—

The strangled keening of an animal had me coming back to myself, finding the source of the cries just as a howl shattered the air somewhere behind me. I pressed myself against a tree, breathing heavily.

A wolf—*a shifter*—had his jaws around Devin's throat, squeezing as it held him down with a strong paw. It was bigger than Devin. Bigger even than Clay's black wolf. This one was matte gray with black markings around its hate-filled orange eyes. I knew without seeing his human form, it was Ryland. Jared and Clay's pack alpha.

I whirled, emitting a startled chirp as a blur of black barreled into the small clearing, growling at Devin's wolf and then at Ryland, restless as it drug its claws over the ground, turning up dirt. At first, I thought the wolf was wanting to protect Devin, but when it lunged to take a bite out of him itself, I realized it just wanted the chance to tear Devin apart.

Its great black head caught the moonlight and I saw its icy blue eyes. *Clay*—my heart gave a little start.

A white wolf sped into the clearing as though a bow loosed from an arrow, surveying Ryland as he pushed Devin's canine head into the earth and bit down harder on the scruff of his neck with unrelenting jaws. Then taking in Clay with a low whine. And then...its amber eyes. One shining with the glow of a sunset, and the other with a fleck of green in the lower left corner.

"Jared?" I choked and the wolf sped to me, skidding in the dirt as it stopped, whining high in its throat as it pressed its big furry head into my belly, almost knocking me over. I buried my bloodstained hand into his fur, dropping to my knees to pull his head further into my chest. I tried to loosen my fist in his fur, but couldn't, and he didn't seem to mind. His cold nose nudged a spot under my neck, as though trying to lift my head.

I lifted it to look into pain-filled eyes, wide and searching.

"I-I'm alright," I told him. It wasn't exactly the truth. But I was alive, and that was a win in my books.

Jared sniffed my throat and I felt his canine body go rigid beneath my fingers. Reflexively, my hand fell away and he broke free of my embrace, sniffing a trail along my breastbone and up to my collarbone, and eventually, to the wound in my shoulder.

He barked, his hackles rising as he jumped a foot backwards, his amber gaze sweeping over me in horror.

My jaw tightened. I was about to reassure him that the bite didn't have any effect when three other wolves flew past us from behind, moving to inspect the scene. My pulse pounded in my ears. They were all shifters. They had to be. They were too big to be normal wolves. Two of them watched me curiously, making low noises in their throats, while the other took over for Ryland, wrapping his jaw around Devin's throat so Ryland could retract his.

Devin yipped and then went still under the pressure of the larger wolf atop him, giving in to the dominance of the other wolf. For a fleeting second, I wished the wolf atop him would just tighten its jaws a little more.

No, not just tighten his jaw…I wished he would tear the fucker's throat out and leave him to bleed out over the drying moss.

I gasped a little at the malice of the thought and tried to shake off the feeling, finding my vision had begun to blur again.

Ryland stalked over to where Jared still stood rigidly in front of me. Clay was still snarling and looking back at Devin every few seconds, but he followed Ryland until the three wolves had formed a line in front of me.

"Th-Thanks," I murmured, not knowing if they were able to understand me in this form. I thought they could, though. "I need—"

I curled over, clutching my stomach as a stabbing sensation stole my breath away. I moaned, curling my fingernails into the earth as the aching spread. Colorful spots dotted my vision and I heard Jared whine.

Squinting, I looked up at him. He was trying to come closer, to help me, or maybe to comfort me, but Ryland stopped him with an outstretched paw and a short growl.

Clay's wolf watched me with a stony expression, as though he was watching something he'd rather not see, but that he had no power to stop.

I looked past them to the other three wolves. All were watching me. I cried out as another wave of pain like a thousand knives tearing me apart from the inside out washed over me. My eyes blurred with tears, and my body heaved with a great tremor and a sudden wash of intense nausea and burning heat.

My chest felt like it was on fire. The back of my neck burned. The heat raced through me like my veins were filled with gasoline instead of blood and I shuddered, falling to the ground to curl up into a ball.

"P-Please," I begged through the searing agony, not even sure what I was asking for. My head was spinning, or maybe it was the earth that was spinning. Whatever the fuck it was, I needed it to stop. I couldn't take it.

The pain stopped for one blissful second and I slitted my eyes open to see the wound on my shoulder had healed. Not fully, but the bleeding had stopped, the tears in my flesh had closed. All that remained was the puckered ridges of four large holes and two smaller ones. As if the bite had happened months ago, instead of minutes.

A *slap* of pressure and sizzling pain like a punch to my chest made me flip onto my back. The moon stared down at me from her perch in the black sky and my eyes widened as though I was seeing her for the first time.

The air had a sudden crystalline quality. I could see every speck of dust like tiny shining specs of gold and silver in the moonlight. I could hear the scurrying of a critter that had to be half a mile away. The trees groaning in the bend of the wind felt louder than it ever had before.

My heart in my chest felt larger, it's beating harder, louder, and *faster* than was humanly possible.

A scream tore from my throat as the first bone snapped. The rest followed in a symphony of torment. My screams warped. Changed. And before I had time to consider the inhuman quality of my own voice, the pain stopped in a blinding flash of pure white over my eyes and I scrabbled to my feet, a soft whining sound coming from some-where close by.

I spun, searching for the sound, but it wasn't anyone else. The sound had come from me. My great sides heaved to draw in a breath. Breath that clouded in front of my jet-black snout. My heart was still thudding like the beating of war drums in the deep. But now it beat within the chest of an animal.

I bowed my head, moving back as I whined, until I backed into a tree and yelped, scampering away as though scorched by its cool bark on my flank. *It happened.*

Holy fucking shit. Oh god.

Oh no.

How do I turn back?

Disjointedly, I realized I could still have rational thought. I was still here, I just had very little control over my animal urges. The whining sound was still pressing out through my jaws, but I wasn't aware that I was doing it, and I was powerless to stop it.

I saw my clothes laid in tattered ribbons over the dried leaves and had the gripping sense of being naked. I flinched back, realizing how ridiculous the feeling was since I was covered in a coat of thick fur.

With my sharper canine eyes, I took in my surroundings. When my jerking gaze fell on Devin, still pressed hard into the ground, my wolf lunged. A terrifying growl thundered out of my chest, viciously savage even to my own ears.

One of the other wolves blocked me, knocking me back to land hard on my side until I managed to get my footing back under me. I growled at him.

Devin whined, and I looked at him again, this time seeing just how pathetic he looked subdued by the other wolf. His green eyes met mine and I felt nothing but an overwhelming fury that my wolf had to work to contain with nasally snarls and chuffs, knowing I would only be rebuffed if I tried to attack again.

But my wolf was difficult to contain. As though she was a completely separate entity, she prowled and pacing, eager for the taste of his blood on her tongue.

The creak and snap of a twig behind me drew my attention away from Devin and my wolf reared back in anticipation of an attack.

Two wolves, one white and one black drew forward while the other larger gray wolf remained sitting sentinel behind. I knew they were Jared and Clay, but they were something else, too.

A roaring voice not unlike my own echoed in my skull. *Mine,* she said as she watched them approach somberly, with measured steps as though approaching a beast much larger than I was.

I met Jared's amber eyes and the breath *whooshed* from my lungs as though sucked out by a cosmic vacuum, and I tipped my head back and howled long and loud into the night as my heart expanded in my chest until I thought it would burst from the pressure.

Jared's howl rose to meet mine, the duet creating a haunting harmony of sound that filtered down deep into my ear canals and reverberated through every nerve ending in my body.

When I lowered my head, my skin bristled, sending my fur rippling over my body as something I could not name settled into the marrow of my bones.

Jared moved in closer, and though I wanted to retreat, I found I couldn't. My wolf wouldn't budge. And when Jared pressed his head against mine, rubbing it as though in an animal embrace, my wolf shivered at the sensation and something warm spread through her belly. *Mine,* she growled again.

Mate. Jared's unmistakable voice flooded my thoughts and I perked up, searching his eyes. *Mate,* he spoke again in my head.

Mate, my wolf responded, as though agreeing.

Movement from the edge of my periphery sent a chill skating down my spine.

Mate, a separate voice entered my thoughts. This one gruff and deep with a reverberating timbre that pressed down on me like a physical weight. When I lifted my gaze to Clay and our eyes locked, I whimpered, feeling the same breathlessness as my body awakened to him.

Unable to help myself, no matter how hard I tried to fight it, head bowed, and teeth bared, the howl tore out of me. It ripped from my chest, even louder than before, twisted with the anguished sounds of my resistance.

But as Clay's howl diminished with mine, there was no doubting the settling of something else in my bones.

Jared bent his head and upper torso low, growling furiously at Clay. Clay only watched him with a steely indifference and made no move to return Jared's challenge.

Ryland and the other wolves were watching from the shadows, and it was like I could hear their thoughts.

Impossible. Not right. Two tails?

But when Clay, ignoring Jared's snarling from only a few feet away, moved in, I buckled under his stare. His bright blue eyes glittered dangerously, and he bent his head to me, as though unwillingly bowing to a queen.

No. I don't want this.

I don't want any *of this.*

I managed to get a modicum of control back and though my inner wolf was chanting *Mate! Mate! Mate!* The part of me that was irrevocably still Allie took hold of the reins.

My strong hind legs launched me over Clay's bowing form. Past Jared's coiled beast. And away into the night.

No one followed, and I let the gravity of what'd happened finally sink in. I cried out inside and my wolf let out inhuman sounds that matched what I felt within...until I pushed it all away, unable to think about it anymore. Not yet. Not right now. I didn't want to ever think about it. Didn't want it to be real.

I focused instead on my light footfalls. The cold air in my lungs. The burn of my pumping muscle.

The wind whipped past my lithe body as I raced over the earth. It filled my ears and funneled through channels of my fur.

If I told myself all of it was a dream. That I was still Allie and still my own, I could almost pretend I was flying. It was the tiniest thread of bliss in a tapestry woven of dread.

It was enough...for now. To keep going until I figured out how to live as something less than human.

BONUS SCENES

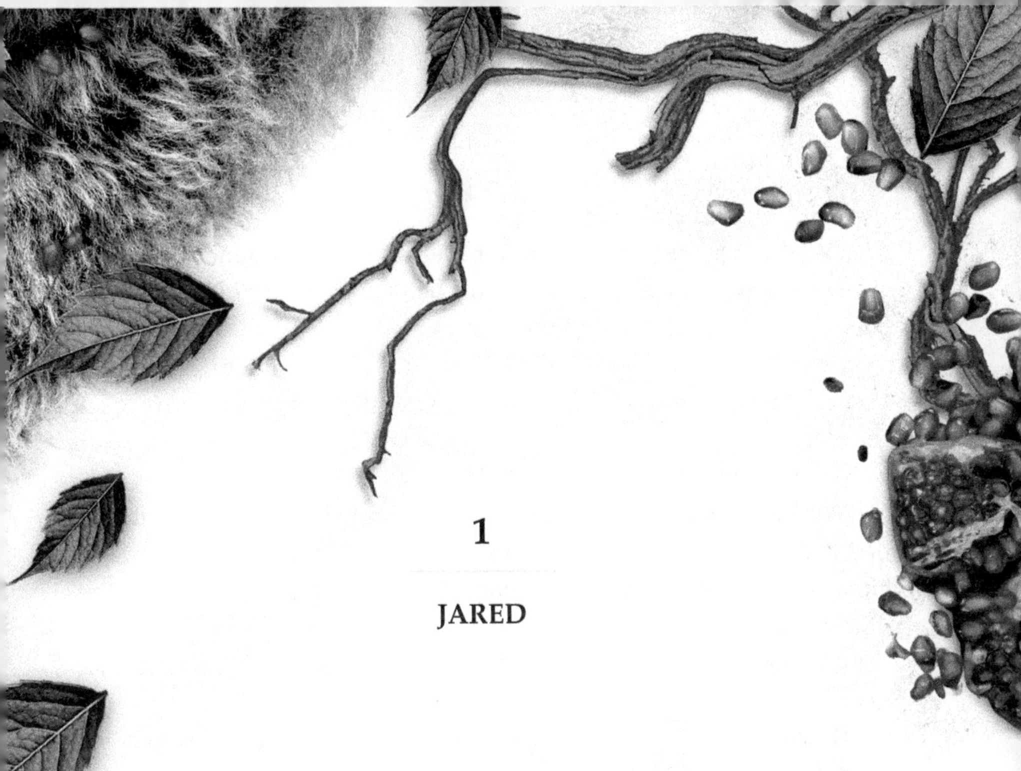

1

JARED

Her door loomed near the end of the hall, sealed shut, but not locked.

Allie hadn't come out for anything more than using the restroom in days. And I hadn't tried to enter, doing my best to give her the space she obviously needed.

But I couldn't wait anymore.

Every tray I brought up for her, weighed down with a meal fit to satisfy her new more ravenous appetite had been left untouched outside her door. I wouldn't let her starve herself.

"Hey," Clay called as I mounted the top step. He surprised me and my jump almost spilled the full glass of orange juice onto the mountain of macaroni and cheese with bacon I made for her.

"*Shit*, Clay," I hissed, shoulders tensing.

Clay's face hardened and his stark blue eyes bored a hole in the floor. He'd barely been able to look at me since the other night in the woods. We'd hardly spoken, either. This was new territory for us. Things like what happened with Allie weren't supposed to be possible. In the history of the Enduran race, as far as we knew anyway, there wasn't a single other case of two wolves bonding to the same mate.

It just wasn't a thing that happened.

It was...*unnatural.*

A ball formed in my throat.

"What?" I bit out when he didn't speak, speaking around the lump.

He reached back to palm the short hairs on the back of his neck. "Is she...I mean," he corrected. "Has she eaten anything yet?"

I clenched my jaw and a fire licked up my spine, igniting the spark that began the process of bringing my wolf to the surface. I squelched the primal urge to stake a claim on what was mine. How could I when what was mine was also *his?*

With a longing glance down the hall to where Allie lay huddled in bed, I deflated, a short growl coming out with my exhale. Allie wasn't either of ours. The magic of the curse had bound us together, but that didn't make her anyone's property.

"No," I said without emotion. "But I'm going to see if I can convince her to."

He nodded mutely as though agreeing with a thought in his own head. "Good," he said. "That's good."

Clay's fists curled and he gave me one last sharp nod to acknowledge the end of the conversation before he stormed off and I heard the screen door bang closed behind him.

He hadn't been around much since it happened, preferring to spend his days in the shop pummeling his heavy bag and tinkering with his motorcycle. And his nights out in the woods, sleeping in his wolf form.

The only real thing he'd said to me since it all happened—and the only reason my wolf wasn't going for his throat—was that he would step back. Clay wasn't going to lay claim to Allie. He promised to keep his distance as much as possible. It was more than I expected.

The floor beneath my feet trembled slightly as I hesitantly stalked to Allie's door. Clay was going extra hard on that heavy bag today. If he wasn't careful, he was going to have to replace it...*again.*

I coughed a little to clear my throat and tapped on her door with my knuckle. "Allie," I said gently, but loud enough that I knew she would hear me. I doubted she was asleep since it was just past dinner time, but for all I knew she could be.

No answer came.

This is what I was afraid of. I didn't want to encroach on her territory. I didn't want to force her to face me.

But...I wouldn't let her keep doing this to herself, either.

Grimacing, I balanced the tray on my wrist and turned the handle, stepping inside cautiously. She had all the lights out and her hearth was cold even though I'd stacked enough wood next to it to keep her warm for weeks.

Allie was sitting atop her bed, as disheveled as the crumpled sheets and blankets beneath her. Her turquoise hair was matted in the back and curled up in a cowlick on one side. Her cheeks looked sallow and her eyes dark. She stared unseeing out the window at the thick cluster of trees lining the property.

My chest ached and the pull of the bond coiled in my chest like a fist curling around my heart, forcing me to feel her anguish whether I wanted to or not. Which meant that she could also feel *my* emotions. I dampened them down, dulling my worry and pain so she wouldn't be saddled with the extra emotional baggage. She had enough on her plate as it was.

"What do you want, Jared?" she asked me in a hushed tone, her voice a little hoarse. She didn't bother turning from the window, just watched with glazed eyes as the sun began to slump low and hang heavy and bright orange in the sky.

The light made her gray eyes gleam with flecks of amber as I drew near enough to see them.

I set the tray down on her bedside table, nudging her cellphone out of the way to get the tray down in a position where it wouldn't fall. "Allie," I whispered, both hoping she would look at me and dreading it at the same time.

So, I didn't know whether to be disappointed or relieved when her gaze never faltered from watching the sun fall down to the horizon.

I stuffed my hands deep into my pockets, fisting them. "You—" I began, but was cut off by the violent buzzing of her cellphone atop the table. It rattled against the metal tray loudly and, in a trancelike state, Allie dropped her gaze from the window and reached out with a shaking hand. She pressed the side button to silence the call and pulled her arm back to rest in her lap.

Her vision grazed the tray of food and her stomach rumbled loudly, but her top lip curled back in disgust and she pressed her palm flat against her thin stomach.

The screen flashed with her notifications a second later. I didn't want to pry, but I couldn't stop myself from looking.

New Voicemail

Sent from Vivian Cole

And below that were a slew of others.

Text Message

Vivian

Are you sure I can't bring you anything? My mom made so...

Text Message

Layla

I tried calling you at the house, but the line has been disconnected. Where are...

New Voicemail

Sent from Layla Esposito

Messenger

Seth Green: Haven't seen you in class, everything okay?

If Allie didn't start responding to her friends, someone was bound to try to get ahold of her aunt and uncle. Then the secret she'd worked so hard to keep would be exposed. She'd be forced to move back with them until she turned eighteen.

It was like someone had doused me in ice-water.

"What have you—"

"They think I'm sick." Her voice was deadpan, and finally, she looked at me. In her eyes I saw all the hurt she was trying to numb—trying so desperately not to feel—and it was like someone was pressing down on my windpipe.

This was all my fault...

If I'd just left her alone in the woods...

Or hadn't convinced her to stay here...

If I'd just fucking *told* her about Devin when I had the chance and damned the consequences...

This could have been avoided.

"I told them I have a nasty flu and that I don't know when I'll be back at school. I told my aunt and uncle the same."

Still tense, I managed a nod. "That's good."

"Is it?" she snapped, her damp eyes narrowing on me. "How the hell is any of this *good*, Jared?"

Her eyes welled and she looked away just before a hot tear could fall on her cheek. "How am I supposed to live like this?" She'd said it so quietly that if I wasn't part wolf, I wouldn't have heard her.

I couldn't relate, not how I wished I could. I was a born wolf. So was Clay. There were a few changed wolves in our pack, but they were more rare. I would never know what it was like to lead a normal life before having it torn out from under me because I'd never had a normal life.

Damn, I hated it when she cried. My fingers itched to wipe away her tears, the mate bond calling for me making it even more difficult than it had been before.

"It's not," I finally replied, even though her question was clearly rhetorical.

I just stood there stupidly while she cried quietly for a minute, unsure what to do. I couldn't leave her like this. And I couldn't comfort her. She'd made it pretty damned clear when I coaxed her into coming back to the cabin with me that night. Every time I got anywhere near her, she'd growled at me. Her mouth frothing and teeth snapping in warning.

I'd never seen a wolf as beautiful as she was—though I'd have expected no less. Looking at her now, even gaunt and matted with her eyes red-rimmed from crying, she was still the most beautiful girl I'd ever seen.

I'd wanted her for as long as I could remember, but would never allow myself to get close to her for fear of this very thing happening.

She tilted her head and I was struck with a memory of her. Her little gray eyes looked as they did now, both sad and horrified. She couldn't have been more than seven or eight. I wondered if she remembered me.

I shuddered as the memory of my parents' blood, cold and sticky and starting to dry into my fur bombarded me. I sealed my eyes against the memory and clenched my teeth together. If it weren't for Allie I don't think I would have survived.

Her father hadn't wanted her to help me. I remembered him, big and burly with a thick beard and a kind but hard gaze. I'd growled at him when I saw the shotgun slung over his shoulder, but he wasn't the one who killed them and taken their furs to be hung like a morbid deco-ration on a wall, or to be forever walked on as a rug by someone's fireplace. Or worse—*worn* as though a jacket on the back of some rich gold-miner's daughter.

She helped me despite his warnings and had cried when he tried to pull her away. She was strong even then. And stubborn as hell.

The bright thread of hope in the dark memory lessened the gripping pain of it and my shoulders sagged. It was my turn now. I needed to help *her* this time. No matter what it took.

Bond or no bond.

I owed her and she didn't even know it. Couldn't remember. Or maybe, just preferred not to.

I knelt next to the bed but didn't dare touch her. "Allie, I'm *so* sorry."

She sniffed and wiped at her nose with the sleeve of her sleep-rumpled plaid shirt. "It wasn't your fault," she said, but from her tone I knew that she didn't mean that. She was saying it to placate me. Even now, in the amount of pain she was in, she still had it in her heart to not want *me* to feel guilt.

How was I ever going to deserve her?

"It is," I rebutted. "And you know it is."

She looked at me then, curiously, but with her jaw locked, the spark of her wolf faintly coming into her eyes.

"And I'll never forgive myself for allowing this to happen to you. But it *has* happened, and there's no going back."

She whimpered and it was like a punch to my gut.

"I'm doing to everything I can to help you. I promise. But you need to eat, and you need to—"

"Where's Devin?" she asked, her voice breaking on his name. A muscle just beneath her left eye twitched and the glow around her iris' brightened.

I held her gaze as best I could as I answered. "His punishment hasn't been decided yet." Much as I tried, I couldn't keep my own wrath from tainting my words. I'd have torn his head off by now if my uncle Ryland had allowed it.

And I knew Clay was plotting something to do just that. Normally, I would try to stop him, but not this time. If Ryland wanted to punish Clay for doling out the sentence that fucking bastard deserved then he'd have to punish me, too, because as soon as I was able to look my best friend in the eye again, I vowed to help him in whatever way he needed to see justice served.

Devin couldn't be allowed to walk free. He would do it again. And if it wasn't Allie, it would be some other girl.

Her nostrils flared and she glared at me. "Why not?"

"It takes time," I attempted to explain. "Ryland doesn't deal out death unless it's warranted. He—"

"So, he's going to kill him?"

I couldn't tell if she was relieved or paralyzed with fear. It really could have been either. "Maybe," I said carefully. "It's either that or he'll be forced to leave Forest Grove with a warning that if he steps back onto the lands our pack controls—he'll be dealt with on sight."

"*Your* pack," she corrected, seeming to miss what I was saying entirely. "*Yours*," she repeated. "Not mine."

I reached out unconsciously and placed a hand on her knee. She flinched a bit, but softened after a minute and I sighed, not pulling away. "It could be yours, too. We're the only pack in the area. And the only other lone wolf in these parts that Ryland allows to live not under pack law is Grams."

Her brow furrowed. "So, what you're saying is that if I don't join your pack...what?" Allie snorted in a dark laugh. "Ryland will kill me?"

My eyes widened. "No," I said, more fiercely than intended.

She batted my hand from her knee, recoiling at the harshness of my tone.

I soothed the pounding in my chest with a measured breath, excavating the nerves from my flesh. "No, he wouldn't do that. We wouldn't let him. But he could try to make you leave."

"*Gladly*," she said, crossing her arms.

Her rejection stung. "It isn't safe out there as a lone wolf."

"I'm *not* a wolf," she replied, but her voice was already wavering again, and her eyes began to glow more brightly in direct contradiction to her words.

"You are," I told her. "And the more you hold back from shifting, the harder it will be for you. In the beginning it's important to shift as much as you can by will so that you can learn how to control it."

She didn't respond for a while, but then she choked out, "*I can't.*"

We both knew it was more a matter of *won't* than *can't*, but I didn't correct her.

The silence hung between us for long enough that I started to feel the bristle of awkward tension on the back of my neck. "I don't want to keep upsetting you," I told her, taking in a lungful of air. "I'll go, but can you please," I started, gesturing at the tray of now cooling and slightly congealed macaroni and cheese. "Can you *please* eat something?"

Her nose wrinkled.

"I can make you something else," I tried. "Anything you want."

She gulped and with her eyes downcast, thick lashes brushing her cheeks, she said in a small voice. "A steak?"

My brows rose.

"Never mind," she rushed to say, turning her body away from me.

I snapped myself out of it and reached my hand out again, more tentatively this time. I brushed the curve of her arm to get her attention and she turned back to me; her cheeks flushed. "It's what *it* wants," she said helplessly.

"I have two steaks in the fridge," I said encouragingly. "Why don't you come down with me and get a drink while I grill them?"

She frowned.

"Just the two of us. And you can come back upstairs whenever you want."

Her resolve was wavering, and I held my breath for her answer, whispering a mantra of pleases and promises if she would just say yes.

"Okay," she said finally and moved to get up on shaking limbs. She almost stumbled, but I caught her before she could fall. The press of her body against mine made my blood race through my veins and my breath come heavier in an instant.

Allie couldn't get herself disentangled from my arms fast enough. She stepped back, shivering.

"*God,*" she shouted accusingly. "*What* is *that?*"

I took a step back from her and pushed my hands back into my pockets, not trusting them to behave themselves. "It's the mate bond," I offered with an impish smile. "Don't worry, you'll get used to it."

She looked like she wanted to do anything but get used to it, but I reassured myself that all she needed was more time and everything would be alright. It had to be. I was only going to mate once in my life, and I'd wanted it to be her since she set the food and water from her little camo backpack around where I laid curled into the corpses of my parents.

I knew she was goodness incarnate from that moment and had watched her from a safe distance ever since.

A lot of good that did me.

"Shall we?" I pressed, holding out my hand to her, my throat suddenly parched.

Allie studied my hand in the orange glow of the sunset and her lips parted as though she was going to say something, but then she closed them again, maybe thinking better of it.

Instead of taking it, she grimaced and walked past, wandering down the hall on wooden legs as though no more than a phantom of the girl I fell in love with a long time ago.

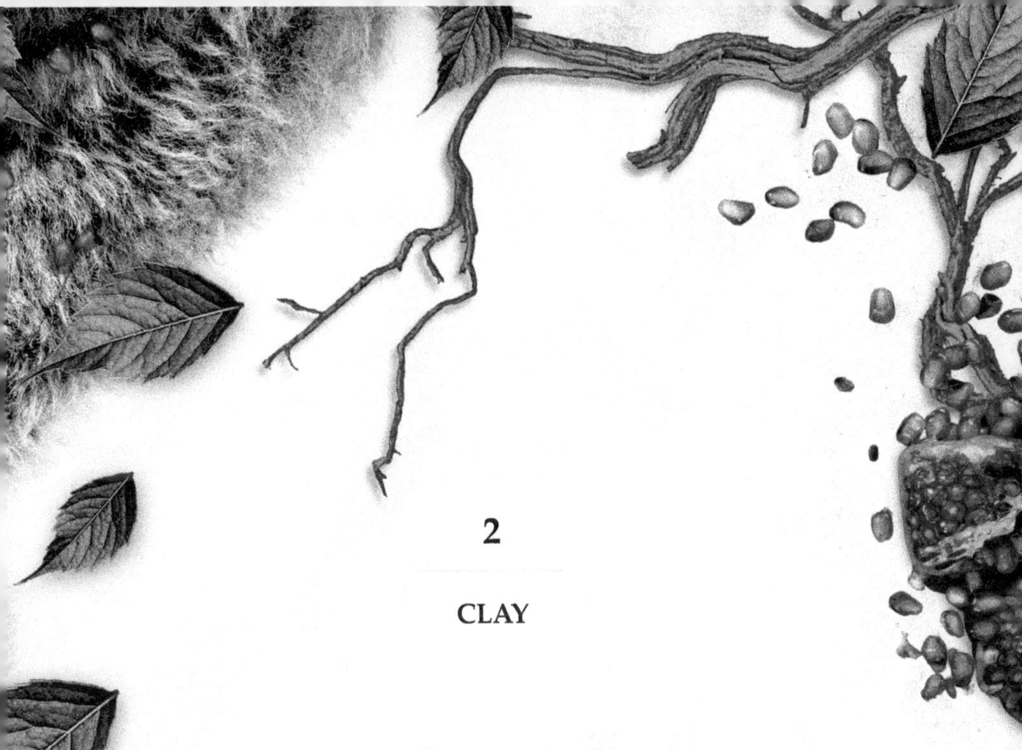

2

CLAY

The uneven terrain of the forest passed beneath me in a blur of greens and browns. I'd never run so fast in my life. I was a good half a mile ahead of Jared now, and only a few hundred meters behind Ryland.

We were close.

We'd been searching for her for hours, following her scent over land, through jagged creeks, and up steep rock. Jared had been right. There was something wrong. And I was willing to bet that asshole ex-boyfriend of hers was the one responsible for it.

After Ryland forcefully removed him from the pack, he changed. He was already a total scumbag—but once he didn't have an alpha, no one left to answer to, he became dangerous. If what Jared said was true, and he'd *hurt* Allie before, I could only imagine what insidious plans he had for her now.

If I'd known before...

If Jared, or Allie herself had told me, I'd have dealt with him before this happened.

It was probably *why* neither of them told me. They knew I'd tear him to shreds. After what happened to Sam—

I cut the thought short. I needed to keep my head. Once the red tinge of my anger began to crowd my vision, painting everything in shades of fury and unbridled *hate*, there was no coming back from it. I already had enough blood on my hands and fuck if it didn't keep me up some nights...

But I couldn't bring myself to ever fully regret the actions I took to avenge my sister. The bastard deserved what he got. If I had to, I'd do it again. Without blinking.

Allie's screams rose from the earth like a bolt of hot lightning, punching a ragged hole in the atmosphere. It was her. I could feel it in the marrow of my bones.

A howl tore from my chest and I changed direction, chewing earth beneath my claws as I worked my muscles to their breaking point. Following the pained sounds of the girl I had all wrong.

I didn't want her in my house at the start. I didn't care to know her. Didn't *want* to.

But she wasn't what I thought she was. It took mere *days* for Allie to burrow into me. And my wolf, despite my protests, made the decision for me when Jared requested the help of the pack to find her.

I couldn't say no.

Another scream, louder this time, had me adjusting course again. My blood hummed in my veins. A low sound vibrated in my chest. It fucking *hurt*.

I ran harder, my sides heaving with the effort. I couldn't stand the sound of her cries. Each one was a knife in my chest, twisting and grinding. Piercing.

And all the while, I couldn't help thinking; what if Grams was right?

"Careful with that one," Grams told me in that ominous way she had after Allie went back inside that day. She was always speaking in riddles and not making any sense. It was part of the reason Ryland allowed her to leave the pack.

He couldn't stand her ramblings. He couldn't stand them even more when they started to paint him in a less than *clean* light...but I had my own suspicions about that.

Regardless of her ravings, though, the woman was sweeter than molasses. She brought fresh baked cookies once in a while and usually stayed to give us heck about something or other. The loaded chocolate chip cookies and sugary sweet fudge squares helped cut the bitterness of her nagging. Or at least, made it easier to ignore.

Grams was one of the few people in this world I could stand to be around for more than ten minutes without wanting to have a go at my heavy bag.

I'd raised my brow at her, amused at her comment about Allie.

"What? She a serial killer, Grams?"

I bit back a laugh. Allie was about as dangerous as a field mouse.

Grams frowned. "No," she told me plainly and placed a weathered hand on the center of my chest. I flinched at the contact, my jaw tightening.

I don't like to be touched.

Her unseeing eyes watched me as though they could peer into my soul.

She tipped her head as though following an invisible trail between where I stood, and where Allie just vanished inside the cabin. I thought she was back to her usual cryptic self, but then she spoke, and there was no mystical tone to her words, no riddle. Her words were blunt. "She's your mate."

I stepped back as though struck, a growl clawing up my throat. "She isn't a shifter," I snarled at Grams, immediately going on the defensive.

A million splintered thoughts raced to discredit her words. *She isn't right in the head. She doesn't know what she's talking about. It isn't true.*

Did I even hear that right?

Grams only shrugged. "Not yet," she said. "But fate always finds a way, my boy. You'll see."

I could feel the beginning of my wolf surfacing, responding to my quickened pulse and the fury coiling up through my core like the hot lick of flame. My face heated. I quashed the urge to shift, needing Grams to explain herself, but unable to find the words.

"You're wrong."

"Fate has already brought her to you."

The truth in those words dropped like an anvil in my gut and I straightened my spine against the force. *No. She's wrong.* I didn't have to listen to this shit. "You need to leave, Grams. I'll tell Jared you stopped by."

Grams smirked, her wrinkled skin pulling into rivulets on her cheek. "Still as stubborn as ever, I see."

I ground my teeth.

"Forget I said anything," she said, and the hint of condescension in her tone was almost enough to send me over the edge. Grams patted my arm in a comforting gesture that only served to stoke the flames. "I'm not *always* right, you know."

I didn't stick around to watch her vanish back the way she'd come. I was around the cabin, the door to the shop banging loudly as I entered, fisting my hands as I stormed to the back corner, where the heavy bag hung, beckoning me to give it a good and thorough pounding.

But she isn't *always right,* I told myself as Allie's scent filled my nose, pulling me back to the present. The smooth smell of lily of the valley in spring and fresh green moss...along with the coppery tang of her blood and the cloying odor of cold sweat.

And...*Devin.*

The reek of his wolf mingled with the smell of her in a way that made my flesh crawl beneath the heavy coat of my black fur.

My wolf itched to stop and investigate the smell, to make sure there really was blood amid all the other things I was scenting. But something in my body told me there wasn't time. I needed to hurry.

Kill, my wolf hissed, and I tried to maintain control with detailed images of all the ways I'd make him suffer once I found him. Yes, that was calming.

I scented Ryland an instant before I saw him, a blur of deep gray wavering across a backdrop of trees. A savage snarl rang in my ears, followed by a strangled keening and my wolf reared back his head and howled, thirsty for blood. All traces of my soothing torture plans slipped through my fingers.

The trees cleared in an instant and I burst through into a small clearing, shredding the ground with sharp claws as I skidded to a halt. It took me less than a second to assess the scene. There was Allie. Bleeding, reeking of fear, injured on a deeper level than what I could see of the wound gushing blood so dark red it seemed purple from her shoulder—but she was *alive.* And there was Ryland, his jaw clamped around Devin's throat, growling in warning as he held Devin down.

The pathetic swine whimpered pitifully beneath the strength of my alpha. He smelled of piss and rapidly receding adrenaline. I dragged my claws over the ground, growling low at Ryland.

Let him go, I spoke through the pack bond in a hiss. *Come on, Ry, I'll even give him a head start! Let me tear him—*

Clay, my name was a command and I strained against the force of my alpha's will, snarling as I attempted to shake it off.

If things had been different, *I* would be *his* alpha. I should have been. It was my birthright. And if I was then it would be *my* call what was done with Devin. But shit hasn't been panning out in my favor for a long time. Karma obviously isn't finished kicking my ass yet.

My gaze fell on Allie as I bowed my head to the alpha and the raw fear I saw there sobered me. Made Ryland's irrefutable command easier to swallow.

I'll rip him apart, I pledged, steeling myself. Every muscle was engaged and coiled as I worked to rid myself of the rising fury that would be my undoing if I allowed it to consume me. I *would* make Devin pay for whatever he did to her. But I wouldn't make her watch the carnage. She'd clearly been through enough already.

I shuddered at the images my mind conjured. Of all the things he could have done to her in the three days she'd been missing.

With one last snap in the direction of Devin, making him whimper even louder, I turned, ready to go to Allie. Something loosened in my chest and I was calmer now that I'd made my decision. Devin didn't have to pay for his sins just yet, and maybe the fear of knowing what was coming to him would make it even sweeter when I doled out vengeance.

Before I could take more than a step in Allie's direction, Jared shot into the clearing, his amber eyes wide and searching. Landing first on Ryland and Devin, then on me with a low whine as his thoughts permeated my mind.

Allie, he cried. *Where's Allie?*

I allowed my eyes to rest on her by the tall tree just behind him and he whirled, clearing the space between them in three quick strides.

I watched with a weight on my chest as her bright gray eyes took him in, recognizing him in his wolf form only an instant before he burrowed his head into her tiny chest and her blood-coated hands delved into his thick white fur, gripping tightly as a sob swelled in her chest.

My own chest tightened in response and I locked my jaw.

She didn't need me right now. She needed *him.*

"I'm alright," I heard her whisper to him, but a strange scent on the breeze flared my nostrils and my body went rigid. I knew that scent.

It could only mean one thing.

Jared barked and I lifted my snout, narrowing my canine eyes on the exposed wound in Allie's shoulder. The unmistakable mark of a wolf's bite punctured her flesh there.

The enormity of what it meant settled in my veins like lead.

She's your mate...

Grams' words echoed in my skull.

No.

No.

But as much as I ached to get the fuck out of there, I couldn't seem to take my eyes off her. My gaze remained fixed as though I was watching a train wreck about to happen with no possible way of stopping it. The tires screeching, the horn blaring. Barreling down the tracks to a break in the rails.

I was transfixed.

It was going to happen. Any second now. And she had no idea.

Being a born wolf, I couldn't even remember my first shift. I wasn't plagued with the memory of the most horrifying—most *painful*—thing I'd ever had to endure. But I'd seen the agony of the first shift once before, and it wasn't something I would wish on any living being.

Charity, Harrison, and Forrest entered the clearing then, breathless, with their hair matted down in sweat.

Charity and Forrest surveyed the scene, their glowing eyes finally taking a rest on a shocked Allie while Harrison moved to take over for Ryland, their hushed internal conversation prickling at the back of my mind. But I wasn't paying any attention to them.

Ryland stepped up beside me and as Devin yipped under the pressure of Harrison's jaws, I turned just long enough to loose a warning growl from my throat.

He's mine, I spoke into Harrison's mind before moving to follow Ryland's slow steps closer to Allie with stiff legs and icy dread pouring down the back of my neck. We moved into a line next to Jared, only a few steps separating us from Allie now.

The smell of her stale fear was so pungent I almost choked on it.

I ignored the urge to go to her. She didn't want me right now. Judging by the look in her watery eyes, I didn't think she even wanted Jared anymore. She wanted to get out of here. Away from us.

The realization only made it even more difficult to watch.

Jared whined low in his throat and Allie came back to herself, chest rising and falling heavily as she took the three of us in. "Th-Thanks," she stammered, eyes flitting to Devin with a flash of something I couldn't name. An emotion someplace halfway between fear and malice. "I need—" she sputtered, and I willed my expression to remain placid, taming my inner wolf into rigid obedience.

She was afraid enough. She didn't need to witness my fear, too. It would only make it worse.

The contagion took Allie swiftly. She curled in on herself, folding as though made of paper. A strangled cry slipped past her lips as her fingernails desperately clutched her stomach.

Jared whined again and I saw him attempt to move forward, but he was stopped by Ryland's short growl and left whimpering quietly to himself.

I shut out his thoughts. Not wanting his panic to take hold within me.

This is our fault.

I shouldn't have allowed her to stay. If I'd forced her out, this wouldn't be happening. It was my punishment now to watch her body writhe against the cold earth. To listen to her screams of torment. Just as it was Jared's.

Her tiny body heaved and shuddered. "P-Please," she begged in a broken voice that threatened to shatter what little resolve I still possessed.

Knowing Devin was only yards behind us, *still breathing,* wasn't helping.

A second later, she gasped and her back arched high and fast—flipping her over body onto. The convulsion was so strong her face crumpled and her hands contorted.

The snapping of the first bone harrowed the beginning of her shift and dragged a long and blood-curdling scream from her lungs. She shook as the rest of her bones broke and reformed. The cacophony of snapping and popping sounds would have both Jared and Ry closing their eyes. But I wouldn't shut mine. No matter how terrible the scene before me.

Her screams changed as the shift claimed her voice box and shortly after, her mouth.

The shift was over in a matter of seconds but might as well have been hours of torture for the black, throbbing ache in my chest where my heart used to be.

Allie was up and on all fours, whimpering and mewling. She looked down at herself—at her new form—and began to back away, not only from us, but as though she could back away from herself.

Her backside bumped against a tree behind her and she yipped, tripping over her own paws as she prattled away. Her tails whipped back and forth behind her and I blinked hard, taking a tentative step forward. But I wasn't imagining it. She had two. They were tipped in white as though dipped in bleach. The rest of her was midnight black save for white socks to match her white-tipped tails, and a band of silver like a crescent moon over the back of her shoulders.

She was magnificent.

But...

Two tails?

Disjointedly, I could hear the murmur of her thoughts. They were unclear, as though spoken through a mouthful of cotton. They would only become clear once she was pack—*if* she became pack, I corrected myself.

But even as muffled as the words were, I could make out the string of profanities marching through her thoughts and something at the center of my being tugged.

Fuck.

When her fleeting gaze finally found Devin, I watched her glowing silver eyes narrow and her wolf snarled viscously, lunging for his throat with a strong thrust of lean hind legs. I lunged to protect her flank, but Charity was faster, checking Allie's body out of midair to send her sprawling to ground in a heap of long limbs. I snarled at Charity, but she only barked at me, a warning to get ahold of myself.

I snorted and stomped in her direction, warning her right back.

Don't touch her.

Allie didn't look like she was finished, and if it were up to me, I'd have let her have the kill. But Ryland wouldn't allow it.

Jared, ears low and tail stiff, moved to follow me, and together we approached Allie. That tugging sensation in my chest was growing stronger, infuriatingly difficult to suppress. It pulled me to her against my will, and small sounds of straining effort chuffed out past my jaws.

She spun at our advance, quick breaths clouding in front of her snout. Her eyes fell on Jared and the static in the atmosphere was enough to make each and every one of my hairs stand on end. My spine tingled as my hackles went off like falling dominoes down every vertebra. My ears pressed flat against my skull.

This isn't right.

Allie stilled and her lithe body tightened as the roar of the mate bond fused to her soul. She tipped her head back and a long, haunting howl ripped out of her core. Jared's answering howl coalesced with hers, creating a harmony that made the very air tremble.

The bond took hold, and their twin howls dimmed until the absence of sound became almost unbearable. Jared pushed his head against hers, claiming his mate. My gut twisted.

The strength of the conviction in his voice as it echoed through my mind made my stomach turn. *Mate,* he spoke to us all. Rejoicing in the newly formed bond.

This was a good thing. I didn't want a mate, I told myself. Never had. Never would.

But the tugging at my center wouldn't fucking quit. If anything, it was getting *stronger*.

Regardless of what I did or didn't want—or of what I'd just witnessed with my own eyes, I knew it deep in the abyss of my soul; Allie couldn't be his.

I could feel it as surely as I could feel my own goddamned heartbeat.

Allie was *mine*.

Mate, my wolf bellowed, and Jared broke contact with Allie. Her head lifted and finally, her eyes met mine.

Jared, confused, backed away as I approached. And Allie, *poor* Allie, fought with everything she had to stop the fusing of the bond. But I wasn't fighting it anymore. It wasn't something you *could* fight. It was useless to try.

She bared her teeth with the effort, but I could hear her inner wolf responding to my call, untethered by Allie's own wishes. *Mate,* her wolf replied before a heaviness crushed my chest, forcing out my howl to meet hers. Louder and stronger than anything I'd ever heard.

A primal calling that neither of us may ever be strong enough to resist.

But I'd be damned if I wasn't going to give it my best try.

SHIFTED SOUL

BOOK TWO

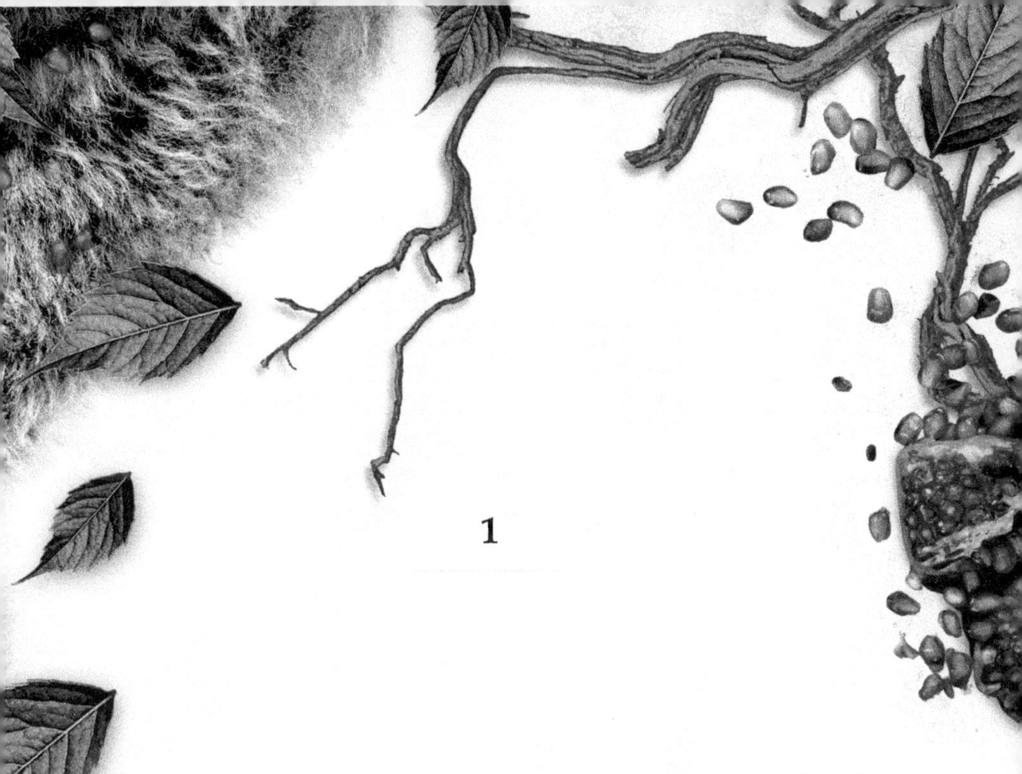

1

The scent of fresh red meat searing in a pan downstairs roused me from a troubled sleep.

I awoke salivating. My eyes burned in protest at being forced open, and my body ached with stiffness from having fallen asleep curled in front of the hearth in the cabin's guestroom.

I palmed the damp spot at the corner of my mouth and shook my head, trying to haul my thoughts out from the haze of sleep and into reality. Like every morning, it took a few seconds before the grip of anxiety latched back on. A dark cloud of thoughts stampeding down into the forefront of my mind.

My jaw clenched as I limbered my legs with a stretch to rid them of their numbness, snatching my phone from the nightstand.

Monday.

I'd been dreading this day all weekend. It became clear on Friday after I received not one, but *two* calls from Uncle Tim about missing school I had to return to my life, ready or not.

I couldn't be 'sick' forever.

Layla and Viv threatened to come into the city to see me this weekend where they *thought* I lived with my aunt and uncle. It took several phone calls and an entire afternoon of texting to convince them not to. That would have been a whole other headache I wasn't ready to deal with yet. I couldn't lose them, too. They were all I had left.

The thought reminded me I may not have a choice what I kept or lost anymore.

A sharp jab behind my ribcage made me double over and I bit back the burning in my throat, refusing to allow a single tear to fall.

I'd done enough fucking crying since Jared and Clay herded me back to their cabin last Tuesday night. It was practically all I did now, other than eat my own body weight in red meat. That was the only thing that seemed to keep the trespassing entity now residing within me at bay.

I checked my phone again, already having forgotten the time I'd just checked two seconds before.

An hour. I had an hour before Jared and I would have to leave for school. And if I survived the day there, I'd have exactly thirty minutes to collect myself before I needed to show up at the book shop for my afternoon shift. Missing an entire week of work was going to make saving up enough for first and last month's rent by December a *lot* harder. I couldn't miss another shift. Not if I wanted to be first in line for the apartment above the shop when the guy who lived up there now moved out as planned in December.

I only had to stay with Clay and Jared for another two months. I could do that, right?

I chuffed out a dark laugh. It wasn't as if I had a damned choice. They were the only people—*er, shifter*—I knew that could help me get control of the beast now slumbering beneath the surface of my skin. Which I was now determined to do. It was the only way I'd be able to go back to my life. Or at least something close to it.

Jared promised me in time, and with a *lot* of practice, I'd live a mostly normal life. Eventually, I wouldn't be a danger to my friends. I would have full control over my new urges and impulses. It was going to take time. And like it or not, Jared would be stuck to me as irrevocably as my own shadow until I figured it all out. Couldn't have me shifting into a beast in the hallways or growling at people when they pissed me off.

Grabbing an armful of clean clothes from the basket Jared brought up, I spied the arm of the denim jacket I was wearing that night in the woods. There was a tear in the shoulder, gaping and fringed in blue and white threads. Faded red stains ringed the mangled hole.

A cold fear gripped me at the memory of slick stone and the smell of stale urine; of the sting of frigid mud on my skin to mask my scent, and the delirious trek through a blur of greens and mottle browns that was all for nothing.

He'd found me anyway. Devin had followed through on his promise. Except he was *wrong*. We weren't meant to be together. I wasn't his mate.

I was Jared's. And Clay's.

My chest vibrated with a growl and I shrank back as my wolf tried to claw to the surface. I held my breath and pushed her back down with deep breathing and a cleared mind. A lick of heat lapped up my spine, making my hands tremble and the tiny hairs on my arms and back stand on end. For a second, it almost looked like my nails were growing.

In a knee jerk reaction, I dropped the clothes I was holding and ripped the jacket from the basket, stomping over to the hearth to toss it onto the still red embers in its maw.

Hard breaths sawed out through my clenched teeth and my vision came in flashes of red. Then, as the embers sparked the denim to flame, my body relaxed, clenched fists unfurling. My inner wolf receding.

My rage simmered back down to a manageable warmth in my belly and I sighed, the weak sound coming out brittle and uneven.

I turned, gaping as an identical Allie appeared across the room. This one frazzled, with crazy sleep-mussed turquoise hair and brightly *glowing* gray eyes. I stared unblinking, willing the reflection in the mirror to change. With each long breath, the glow dimmed until my eyes were back to their normal dull shade.

My shoulders sagged in relief.

How the *hell* was I going to get through today?

Checking one more time to make sure the jacket was good and thoroughly burned, I lifted the discarded outfit from the floor and stepped out into the hall. Pulling the door closed behind me, I turned the knob silently, not wanting to draw attention upstairs.

The catch clicked into place and I spun to pad to the bathroom, coming face to face with Clay as he crested the top of the stairs. A red-hot blush flared in my cheeks as our eyes locked for the briefest instant. Why did he never make any sound when he walked? For a guy as large as Clay was, you should've been able to hear his approach from a mile away.

He was clearly just as surprised to see me as I was to see him. Except where I thought I probably looked like a deer in the headlights, he looked downright furious. But that was common for Clay. I'd only seen him smile once in all the time I'd been staying with them in the cabin, and it was more a smirk than anything.

And that was *before...*

Now, he couldn't even look at me. Wanted nothing to do with me, either. Or at least, that's what I assumed since he now spent 99% of his time *not* here. Preferring to sleep in his wolf form out in the woods, eat around back in his shop, and bathe in the stream several miles away instead of using the perfectly good shower in the cabin.

His shirtless body almost seemed to steam in the tight hall.

The wide expanse of his shoulders was tense, and the muscle there and in his ripped stomach flexed and shimmered beneath a fine sheen of sweat. I tried to avert my stare, the hot flush in my cheeks turning a shade of scarlet but found it impossible to look away.

I hadn't seen him since Tuesday night, and it was like I was seeing him for the first time all over again. He was at once a stranger and so familiar it sparked something deep in my core.

A muscle in Clay's jaw twitched and something inside me tugged at the sight of his discomfort. *No*, not the sight of it. The *feel* of it.

I felt the same thing with Jared. But I'd half hoped the mate bond *thing* that'd happened in the woods would have faded between us. Or maybe that it wasn't real at all. But as Clay approached, his gaze locked not on me, but on his bedroom door a few paces away, I knew it was foolish to hope.

With each step, that stubborn pull in my chest grew. With each step, my skin came alive with electricity, bristling and shivering no matter how hard I tried to make it stop. I'd been about to dash into the bathroom, praying that a closed door would help block whatever the sensation was, when Clay froze in the hall.

His head snapped up, cutting blue eyes searching as he drew in a hard breath through his nostrils, sniffing something on the air.

He cursed and changed course, rushing past me to barge into my room.

"It's just," I tried to explain, realizing belatedly that I'd just been burning denim. Probably *not* a scent he was used to catching in his house. "My jacket," I finished, but he was already inside.

I peered around the door frame; my lower lip caught between my teeth. "I'm sorry, I just—"

Clay's expression as he took in the mostly charred jacket in the hearth was hard and cold, shocking me back into silence. His stony gaze registered recognition. A vein in his neck stood out against his tan flesh, thick and pulsing.

He whirled to face me, and I saw something like guilt cross his expression before it was gone, replaced with his usual tepid fury. "I didn't mean to..." he grunted, trailing off as discomfort twisted his face.

The glow in his eyes died before it could truly be born. But the momentary presence of it was enough.

At the rise of his wolf, my own wolf jumped to the surface, shocking a startled whimper from my lips that I fought to conceal. My fingernails dug into the wood of the door frame, steadying the erratic beating of my heart.

Mate, the word reverberated through my skull, dragging a shudder from my bones. The voice was my own, but also...*not.* I didn't think I would ever get used to it.

"Thought something was burning," Clay finished, seemingly oblivious to the havoc he was wreaking on my body and mind as he shouldered past me into the hall.

The brush of his skin against mine was no more than a whisper, but the contact made my insides squeeze and flip, drawing yet another strangled sound from my throat.

I stayed there, unmoving and squeezing my eyes shut until I heard the click of his door closing behind me. Only then did I straighten, tugging my fingers out of the wall.

Oh god.

Where my hand had been on the door frame, there were *finger holes.* The wood dented a good half an inch where they'd burrowed into the treated grain.

My mouth fell open and I stared incredulously from my slender fingers, unmarred, back to the wood. Snapping my lips shut, I blinked, reaching back up with unsteady fingers to place them back into the small hollows I'd created. How had I done that?

I withdrew as though burned and all but ran into the bathroom, sequestering myself inside. I leaned against the sink for support, being mindful of where my fingers gripped the porcelain, afraid that I might shatter it if I wasn't careful.

"Allie?" Jared's voice floated up the stairs from the kitchen below. "You up? Breakfast is ready."

As though on cue, my stomach burbled loudly, and I put a hand to it in an attempt to suffocate the animal sound. "Yeah," I called back; my voice weaker than I'd have liked.

I cleared my throat and straightened, relaxing the contorted expression straining my face in my reflection in the mirror above the sink.

It took a minute, but...*there*.

There was the Allie from a week before any of this happened. Battle hardened and with more pain in her eyes than there had been before, but there she was.

She was still there. She could do this. "I'll be right down."

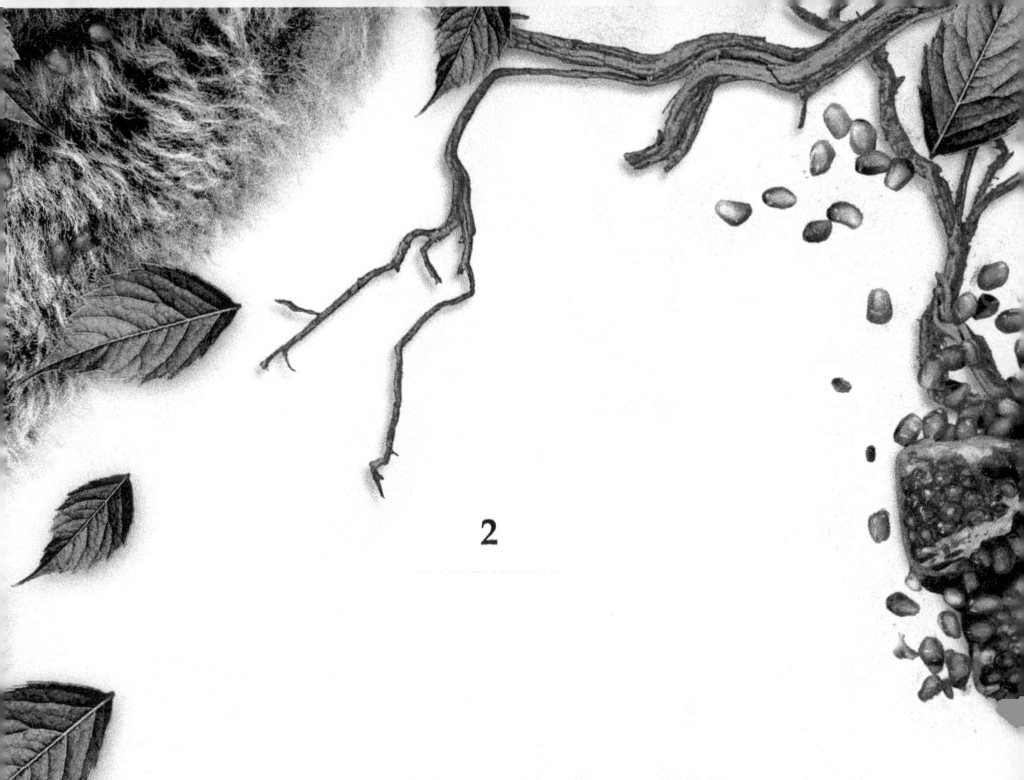

2

Jared cooked a breakfast of steak and scrambled eggs. As much as I wished I'd be just as content with my usual huckleberry oatmeal or a slice of toast, that just wasn't the case anymore.

Only red meat truly sated me. If I had oatmeal, I'd be hungry again in five minutes and my inner wolf would be testy and impatient. Since I was finally going back to school today, I had to take every precaution.

Jared slid a plate to me as I folded myself into the seat opposite him at the table. I didn't miss how he gave me the larger of the two steaks. When the scent of the meat coiled up into my nostrils, it was almost impossible not to dig in with my bare hands. I could feel the phantom press of sharp canines trying to dislodge themselves from my gums. I shook my head, swallowing back the urge to tear into the meal like a beast.

My skin bristled at Jared's nearness. Every time he looked at me, white hot currents ran through my veins. Sizzling. The brush of his eyes tantalizing, like the ghost of fingers playing on soft skin.

I hated it.

Or...more accurately; I hated that I couldn't control it. That I had no say in what my body felt around him. But I think he knew that. It was why he mostly kept his distance. He'd only touched me once since they brought me back here and I hadn't reacted well. Now he kept a consistent minimum amount of space between us, never getting within less than a foot away from me.

He had no idea how much I appreciated that. Or how much my inner wolf *loathed* it.

"Thank you," I said and lifted my knife and fork with shaking fingers. Fingers that wanted to tear into the meal like a starved dog. Tail wagging. Ears pressed flat. Growling when any other dogs came near.

I stabbed the meat with my fork and poised the knife to cut, swallowing hard.

A clatter on the other side of the table made me glance up to find Jared had set his own cutlery back down against the oak table in favor of using his hands.

His amber eyes flicked to me and back to the steak now gripped between the thumb and forefinger of each of his hands. The green fleck in his left eye glinted in the light of the morning as it turned from the pale hue of dawn to the shining orange glow of a new day poking through the trees.

Brownish red juices dripped loudly back onto his plate as he tore a bite from one edge, seemingly as though it were the most natural thing in the world.

Before I fully realized what I was doing, I found I'd discarded my cutlery too. A bolt of icy shame lifted the hairs on the back of my neck as I ripped off my first bite. But the shame melted away as that first bite found its way down my throat, sitting heavy in my stomach. Soothing the wolf within. I sighed audibly, completely unable to help it.

"So," Jared said between bites. "Are you excited to see your friends?"

I almost choked. Finishing off the last bite of my steak, I took the paper towel Jared offered and cleaned off, ready to switch to my fork to eat the eggs like a normal human being. "More like terrified," I blurted.

He cocked his head at me, sunlight staining his dirty blonde hair with threads of copper and gold. "If you aren't ready—"

"No," I interrupted, pushing the eggs around on my plate. "I mean, *yes*, I am ready. I have to be."

I didn't have to explain in any more depth than that. He knew just as well as I did that if I stayed MIA much longer, it was only a matter of time before someone found out I was living here.

And before they found out I wasn't even *me* anymore.

"I'll be right there the whole time," Jared said after a second, his tone soft and encouraging.

I winced. "Did Layla and Viv say anything to you last week?"

Jared's lips tightened, pressing into a thin line that told me everything I needed to know.

Still cringing, I asked, "What did they say?"

I'd done my best to erase the damage Devin had done while he had me captive in that cave out in the mountains to the north. He'd been keeping up appearances while I was chained up. And part of that was texting Viv and Layla to tell them I was ill...and *also* that Jared was a total asshole.

Devin texted them from my phone. Told them that when Jared had *'driven me home'* after Thompson's party that he'd been rude and tried to make a move on me. And that when I told him *no*, he'd turned into a total dickwad.

I'd done all the damage control I could via texts and calls from my room upstairs. But Jared had had to deal with them face to face at school last week. We couldn't *both* be missing from classes for days on end at the same time. That would be *way* too suspicious.

"Jared?" I prodded when he still wasn't answering.

He huffed, pushing the last of his scrambled eggs away as he leaned back into his chair. "They didn't say much. Don't worry about it."

I really hoped he was telling the truth, but I got the feeling he wasn't. I'd done my best to fix it by telling them that I was overreacting. That Jared hadn't even made a move on me. I was just on edge because of running into Devin at Thompson's party and had taken it out on him. I told them *I* was the one who should be sorry. Not Jared.

But I doubted they believed me. Which was why it was going to be... *difficult*...today when Jared was stuck to me like glue between classes and at lunch hour.

I could already see their disapproving faces. And I could already hear the curious whispers I knew would follow Jared and I wherever we went.

Jared rose from his seat and collected my plate with his, scraping both of our uneaten eggs into the compost bin. He cleared his throat before speaking again. "You sure you don't want to try shifting first? We could go in after lunch. It might help."

My shoulders pulled inward at the suggestion, my chest suddenly tight and throat parched. "No," I said weakly, shivering at the memory of the first and only time I'd shifted since Devin bit me.

I remembered the agony of every bone in my body fracturing and breaking. The dizzying displaced feeling of everything inside me being disjointed and rearranged. The *burning* in my blood. The aching.

My lips parted in a little gasp at how vivid the memory still was inside of my head and I pressed my hand back to my stomach, quelling the urge to vomit.

Jared crouched down beside me in the chair, keeping the foot of distance between us, but putting our eyes level. "It's not like that when you shift on your own. The moon *forces* a shift and it sucks. It's always the worst the first time. But *choosing* to shift," he said, his eyes pleading with me to understand. "It's different. It's accepting your wolf and letting it out of your own volition. It hurts a little until you get used to it, but it's *nothing* like the first forced shift."

He must have seen how my jaw was tightening. Maybe even felt my unspoken denial of his offer because he added. "But if you don't shift on your own, it *will* be just as bad as the first time. If you wait until your wolf is so suppressed that it explodes out of you, it'll never get easier."

Hot tears dampened my eyes, stinging at the edges. "Not yet, okay?" I managed, wanting to cry and scream and growl all at the same time. I wanted to tell him that I didn't *ever* want to shift again. Despite the brief moment of feeling like I was a spirit flying over earth, it had been utterly terrifying. Not having full control over my own body was one of the worst things I'd ever felt.

Jared's hand lifted from his knee and I thought for a second he was going to reach out and touch me. I ached to feel him. Whatever piece of my soul now residing within him called out to its counterparts within me. My heart twisted painfully in my chest as he pulled away, remembering to keep his distance with a sudden hard blink of his eyes.

He stood again and shoved his hands deep into his pockets. "Okay," he said. "When you're ready."

Jared turned to glance at the clock on the stove and hauled in a shaky breath, his muscled chest expanding beneath his shirt until I could see the outline of his pecs and sharp collarbone beneath. "We should get going or we'll be late."

WE PULLED UP TO THE SCHOOL WITH ALMOST TEN MINUTES STILL TO SPARE. Jared told me that running—even in my human form— would also help to expend some of my wolf's energy, therefore making it more docile. So, we'd run to where he kept his lifted white jeep parked at the end of an unmarked trail through several miles of trees.

A walk that usually took me and Jared twenty minutes had barely taken us more than two this morning. The trees whizzed past in a blur of green needles and leaves in varying shades of greens and golds. Autumn had swept over the mountain in earnest while I'd been hiding out in the cabin, it seemed.

There was more color than I remembered. And the air was thick with the distinct aroma of fall. The scent so much stronger than it'd been before. But everything was now. Sounds were louder. Certain smells were almost unbearable in their intensity. My vision was sharper, too. Even running at a speed I had to guess was something north of thirty-five miles per hour, I could see everything around me with a crystalline sharpness.

It helped that since shifting into my wolf and back, my ankle had been completely healed. The sprain I'd gotten in the storm a couple weeks ago was entirely healed. So were all the cuts and scrapes. Even the thumb I'd forcefully broken to get out of the manacle in the cave was good as new when I'd reverted back to my human form.

If it wasn't for the silky pinkish-white skin of the puncture wound scars on my shoulder, I could almost pretend none of it ever happened. *Almost.*

Jared shut off the ignition and peered over at me in the passenger seat. "You did good on the run," he said, his eyes shifty and back stiff. "If you want, we can go for another after school? Maybe a bit longer?"

I nodded, offering up a small smile. "Yeah," I breathed. "Sounds good."

It *had* helped. Some of the anxiety trying to rise in my blood, making my breaths come out stippled and shaking, had subsided after we'd come to a screeching stand still next to Jared's jeep. I'd probed around inside of myself, searching for that *other* entity that had been a constant since last week in the woods and found almost nothing.

There only remained a whisper of the wolf within. As though the thing was taking a nap, giving me full control of the reins for a while. I just hoped it would last for an entire school day, and hopefully, for my shift at the shop later this afternoon, too.

"Maybe I'll even let you drive the Jeep back to the trailhead if you want," he added in a teasing tone, opening his door to step out. I knew he was trying to lighten the mood, but his offer only made me shrink more into myself.

I stepped out of the Jeep and pushed the door closed behind me as Jared came around to my side. When he caught my expression, his brow wrinkled, "Did I say something wrong?"

"No," I assured him, slinging my backpack over my shoulder and wondering in the back of my mind how I ever found it to be heavy. It felt like carrying a bag of air now. "It's just..." I trailed off, trying to fight a blush. "I don't know how to drive."

Dad got sick a couple of years back and he'd died just last year, leaving me all alone with my aunt and uncle who couldn't be bothered to teach me. Most high school seniors I knew either had their full license or were at least on their way to getting it.

I didn't even have my learners permit.

What was the point? I couldn't afford a car and Forest Grove had decent public transit. Besides, both Layla and Viv could drive. I didn't need to.

Jared looked at me like I'd grown a second head. I thought about offering some sort of excuse but thought better of it. I didn't owe him an explanation.

Once Jared was rid of his initial surprise, he shrugged. "Then you'll just have to learn," he said simply.

I opened my mouth again to protest, not wanting to take up any more of his free time than I already was these days, but he continued on talking as though I wasn't about to say no. "Clay's a good teacher," he mused, and a fraction of a second after he said it, I saw something in his eyes darken. The twitch of a frown turned down the corners of his mouth.

Jared coughed. "I mean, he's the one who taught me. But I think I could be a good teacher, too. If you'll let me?"

I didn't miss the change of tone when he mentioned Clay. I wanted to ask him what Clay's problem was. Why he wasn't talking to either of us. Why he was never home anymore. But I was afraid I already knew the answer.

It was because of me.

Because he couldn't stand the thought of being mated to me.

Even though I never asked for it—didn't *want* it either, the rejection stung.

Rushing to match Jared's strides as we crossed the lot, I stuttered my response. "You don't have to," I told him. "Actually, I'm perfectly fine not driving. It sort of freaks me out. Besides, I can't afford a car anyway and—"

"Allie," Jared interrupted again, slowing to look down at me. The sound of my name from his lips rendered me momentarily mute, a warmth blossoming in my belly. *Fuck.*

Why did being around him have to feel so fucking *good?*

I grit my teeth, waiting for him to finish while I collected myself.

"It's no big deal. So, don't make it one, 'kay? I don't mind."

I nodded numbly, pressing my lips together. "Alright. Thanks."

"You're welcome." Jared grinned down at me. "See?

Was that so hard?"

I snickered at him. *Let me help you,* he'd said to me once. He'd also called me stubborn and he was right. I didn't know how to accept help when it was offered to me. I'd felt like I was a burden since the time I was old enough to understand the meaning of that word. And it wasn't because Dad made me feel that way. I just knew I didn't *want* to be a burden to him or to anyone else.

Not after what happened.

I didn't want to be a burden to Layla and Viv. Or my aunt and uncle. All this *help* Jared was giving me since he rescued me in the woods a couple weeks ago made me hideously uncomfortable.

But also sort of *warm.* Buried beneath multiple layers of discomfort there was something there I hadn't felt since before Dad got sick; a sense of belonging.

Like, because it was *Jared* who was helping, it was okay. Or at least, more okay than if it were someone else.

"Hey," Jared said, turning and coming to a stop only a stone's throw from the side entrance to Forest Grove high. He adjusted the strap of his pack and searched my eyes. "You okay? You went somewhere dark there for a second."

"Hmmm?" I murmured, suddenly acutely aware of all the people staring at us as they rushed into the school at the sound of the bell's ringing. My neck was on fire as stare after stare penetrated my personal space. This was going to be a long ass day.

"Yeah," I told him, a long sigh coming out with the word. I'd have to get used to him being able to pick up on my emotions now. "I'm good."

"It isn't Devin, is it? You don't have to worry about seeing him here."

I shuddered. For once, my abusive ex-boyfriend who turned out to be a clinically insane wolf shifter was *not* what I'd been thinking about. But I sure was now. *Thanks, Jared.* "Did Ryland decide yet?" I asked, unable to help myself now that he'd brought it up. I'd been afraid to ask, but maybe knowing one way or the other would help me get through today.

The memories came back in a flood of dread and my panic rose.

I still didn't know...

I still wasn't certain if he'd touched me while I was unconscious in that cave. The warring emotions of anger, disgust, and fear swirled in my belly. A tremor racked my spine and I had to shove down my wolf's urge to jump to the surface, trying to defend itself from an invisible assailant.

"Did he decide what to do with him?"

Jared frowned, "No. But it's looking like Ry's going to banish him like we thought. He won't be allowed anywhere near Forest Grove ever again. And if he *does* come back, any one of our pack has the authority to deal with him on sight."

I knew what he meant by *deal* with him and I couldn't deny that was exactly what my wolf—and to some extent, *I*—wanted. I had this horrible feeling that he wouldn't leave so easily. Maybe for now he would, but one day, when he was stronger and maybe had a pack of his own, he would be back. People like him didn't quit until they had what they wanted.

What they thought *belonged* to them.

My knees quaked and a flashback of the dank, cold cave flashed vividly against my eyes.

"Right," I said, unsure what else to say. There was nothing I could do about it and I couldn't think about it anymore or else I wouldn't be able to keep myself in control.

You're safe, I told myself, trying to ease the tightness in my chest. *He's not here. Focus on the things you can control.*

It was what the therapist dad hired to see me every Wednesday last year had taught me as a way to cope.

Don't worry about things you can't do anything to change, she would say as she talked me down from a panic attack over the phone. *Instead, think of everything you* can *control. What can you control, Allie? List the things within your control.*

I swallowed hard and pulled the heavy metal door open, but I tugged it with too much force, and it banged loudly against the brick exterior of the building, sending a sprinkle of brick dust to scatter over the blacktop. I grimaced. Jared did too.

"Let's just get to class before I change my mind."

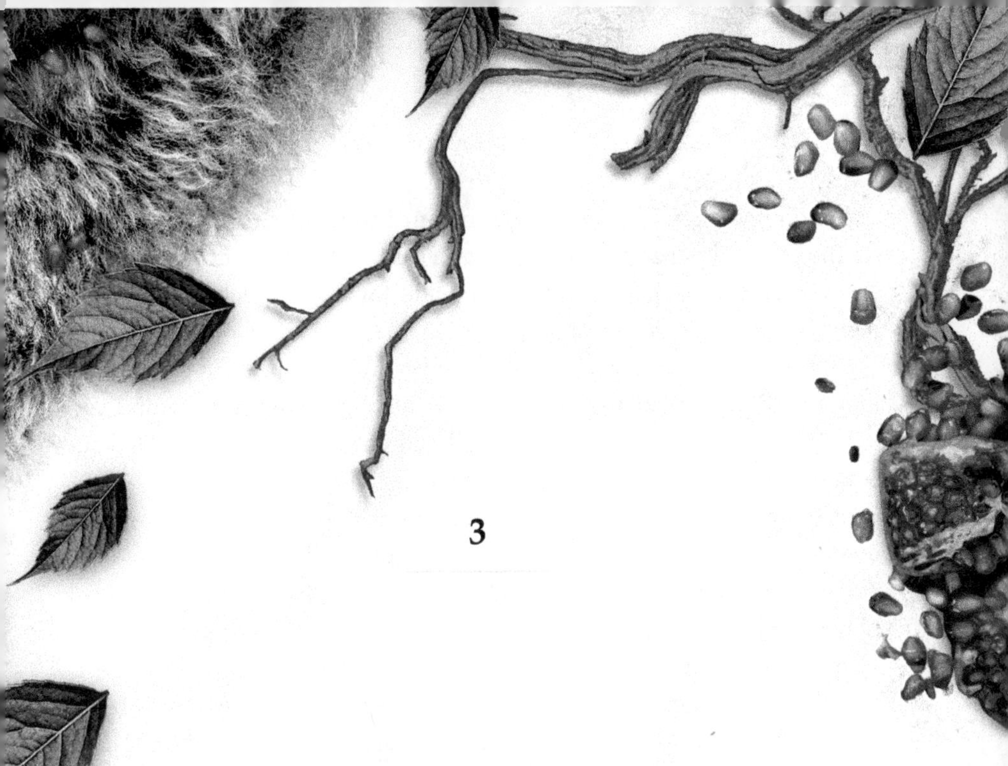

3

"Allie Cat!" Viv's shout from down the hall between first and second period almost gave me a freaking heart attack. I whirled around and slammed my locker closed just in time for her to crush me against her in a tight hug. Her scent, a combination of the strange smelling shampoo she liked to use, and powder scented deodorant enveloped me and I was able to take a full breath. A first since I woke up this morning.

"Hey Viv," I said as she pulled away, holding me at arm's length to inspect me with a critical eye.

"You're not still contagious, are you?" she asked with a lifted blonde brow. Her hair was shorter than it had been the last time I'd seen her. No longer a bob, but more of a messy pixie cut. It suited her.

"No," I replied with a forced laugh and tugged at one of her blonde strands. "Hair cut?"

"You like?"

"Suits you."

"Thanks," she said and did a little gangsta pose in the hall, drawing several side-eyed glances from the students milling about. "You look different, too," she added after a second, nudging me to walk next to her on the way to class. "Did you do something different?"

"Nope," I rushed to say. "But I must've lost at least five pounds from the flu."

Viv pursed her lips, and for an instant I thought she would call me on the lie, but instead she shrugged and said, "Yeah, that must be it. But you've been looking on the scrawny side for a few weeks now. They feeding you properly over there?"

By *they* she meant my aunt and uncle, and I suppressed a flinch at the reminder of all the lies now building into a wall between me and my best friends. After last week, that wall had gotten even higher. Thicker. Soon, I wouldn't be able to tear it down even if I tried.

I made a sound in my throat that was neither an agreement nor a denial, just a short awkward laugh. The truth was I'd been eating less and barely able to keep my meals down since that night at Devin's house all those weeks ago. When he'd accused me of there being something going on between me and a fellow classmate.

When he'd shown me the truth of who he was deep down inside.

I should have reported him after he hurt me that first time. Then maybe none of this ever would have happened.

"Want to come over tonight?" Viv asked suddenly. "Dad's out of town for a few days. I can get you caught up on Geo?"

Geography was one of the few classes Viv and I shared. She was in all the *advanced* level classes save for that one. I barely passed the regular level in several subjects.

Think of an excuse, Allie. You can't be there alone with her.

"Um," I started, floundering for some kind of reason why I couldn't go over and coming up empty handed. "I..."

I was saved when Jared found us in the hall and sidled up next to me, falling into step at my shoulder.

"Hey Allie," he said. "Feeling okay?"

I nodded, though I was sure the panic was clear on my face.

"Stone," Viv said by way of greeting, clearly unimpressed he'd found us.

"Vivian," Jared replied.

Jared was still waiting for a response and I didn't really know what to say. He wasn't asking me because I was getting over the flu. He was making sure I was keeping myself *contained.* I'd been doing pretty good so far. Quinn wasn't in our shared culinary class this morning, so I'd been able to focus on doing all the work alone, without any distractions. I didn't think I'd be as lucky for the rest of the day, but so far, so good.

"So far, so good," I told him, hastily adding, "Thanks for asking," as a blush worked its way into my cheeks.

Stella Baker openly gaped at us walking side by side from her locker as we passed and my skin bristled.

The second bell sounded, and I used it as an excuse to rush away. "See you at lunch Viv?" I asked, moving to go down the corridor to the left towards Mr. Brown's history class.

"Yeah!" she called back, going the opposite way. "Jared?" I added, knowing he was coming to sit with us at lunch today whether I liked it or not. Better Viv think it was my idea. "Want to have lunch with us?"

He smiled. "Sure thing, Allie."

Viv's eyes widened as she looked between Jared and me. She was looking at me like I was insane, and a little like she was pissed.

Viv was not someone you wanted to piss off. But since I was one of her best friends, I got Vivian rage immunity. I shrugged innocently at her and mouthed *sorry* before turning to rush into class.

I HAD TO STAY EXACTLY TWO AND A HALF MINUTES AFTER CLASS TO MAKE UP FOR the two and a half minutes I was late. It was a rule of Mr. Brown's, and made me miss catching up with Viv and Layla on their way to lunch. When I exited the classroom, though, with a sour attitude and way more irritation than I should have been feeling, Jared was there.

"Figured Brown would make you stay late," he said as the door shut behind me. "I had him last year and spent half my lunch period in there some days."

"You didn't have to wait for me," I told him. Well, more like snapped at him. The irritation at being made to stay behind and listen to Mr. Brown's nasally voice tell me that I *owed* him 'two-point-five minutes for tardiness,' still hadn't gone.

Jared made me pause with a hand on my wrist. The contact made me immediately reef my arm away, gasping as a sizzling bolt of electricity struck something deep in my belly. "Don't," I shouted, too loudly.

It took me a second to get control back before I could finish, nostrils flaring. "Don't touch me."

He held his hands up in a placating gesture. "I-I'm sorry," he said, amber eyes downcast.

I swallowed, calming my breathing. "Are my eyes okay?" I asked, suddenly afraid to look up. There were still a few students down at the other end of the hall putting their things away before lunch. I couldn't have glowing eyes at school. I flitted my gaze up to Jared for a second so he could get a good look.

"Yeah. You're good."

I relaxed a little, the irritation leeching away.

"I'm sorry I snapped at you, I was just..." I struggled to find the word.

"Frustrated?" he offered.

"Yeah," I admitted.

Jared's lips twitched into a sad smirk. "I know you don't want to hear it, but that's normal. Heightened emotional responses are common, especially in the begin—"

"Jared!" a girl's melodic voice called from behind me. Amanda Schmidt walked up to us, all hips and grace in her two-inch black heels.

Jared's face turned stony in the span of a heartbeat, and I realized it was a face he put on for everyone else. In a beat he went from the Jared I'd come to know over the past couple of weeks, back to the closed off Jared I recognized from the last few years of school.

"Hey," Jared said, rubbing at a spot at the back of his head.

Amanda Smidt looked me up and down, making no secret of her disbelief. Her low-cut top accentuated perky B's and it was a wonder you couldn't see the top of her underwear for how low the waistband of her jeans rode on her bony hips. "Oh, hey Allie," she said, overly chipper before turning her attention back to Jared.

"Did you need something?" Jared asked her, and even though his tone wasn't unpleasant, I could tell he wanted her to leave. I could feel the discomfort drifting off of him in waves, eliciting the same response in me.

"I was just thinking," Amanda said, leaning into Jared's side. "Since you missed a couple days of Philosophy that I could help fill you in before the test on Friday."

Before Jared could work up a response, she went on. "I'm free

Wednesday," she told him, pulling her bottom lip in between her teeth as she pressed her chest into his side and put her lips to his ear.

If it weren't for my new canine hearing, I may not have heard her. I wished I hadn't.

Amanda whispered, her voice husky in Jared's ear. "My parents will be out," she said. "All. Night."

A sharp growl ripped from my chest and I felt the swell of something *other* behind my breastbone, expanding my lungs to the point I thought they would start cracking ribs.

Mine, that foreign voice hissed in my mind. My hands tightened into claws at my sides.

What the hell was she playing at? I was standing right here, and she was acting like they were completely alone. Her fingers drew lazy circles on the soft skin of Jared's forearm as she continued to lean into him.

Her cloying perfume clogged my nostrils. An assault of sugar sweet cotton candy and choking florals.

It was clear Jared wasn't interested. Couldn't she see that?

Couldn't she take a fucking hint?

Jared's gaze snapped up to meet mine and he flew into action, shoving Amanda away with a hastily called, "Some other time," as he nudged me to turn away from her and herded me down the hall at a brisk pace.

"Call me!" Amanda called after us as we rounded a corner, and it took everything I had in me not to turn around and rip her fucking throat out. Small growling sounds vibrated in my throat and chest and I had to work to keep my lips tightly closed to trap the sounds inside until Jared kicked open the door we'd come in this morning and tugged me outside, letting go as soon as it closed behind me.

Distantly, I was aware that my cell phone was vibrating in my pocket and that Viv and Layla were probably wondering where I was. Why I wasn't meeting them at our usual spot in the corner of the cafeteria. The fact that Jared was *also* not at lunch right now would only raise even more suspicion.

But I couldn't care about that. I needed to breathe.

Jared was saying something, but I was beyond hearing him. My mind kept going back to the thought I'd had only a minute before. I'd wanted to rip her throat out.

Not figuratively.

Literally.

My stomach turned and a sour taste coated my tongue.

"Allie?" Jared said, his voice louder now. I didn't think it was the first time he'd said my name.

I looked up, my shoulders and chest still heaving slightly. The sky threatened rain. Big ominous clouds blotted out the afternoon sun and painted everything in shades of muted gray. But still Jared looked like the sun.

Even surrounded by a world bleached of color, he was vibrant with life. Burning bright.

I found myself drawn inextricably to his warmth. It wasn't quite a tether drawing us together so much as it was something more like gravity. Like I wasn't tethered to the earth anymore, but to *him*.

"Jared," I choked, disgusted at the thoughts in my head that were mine and not mine at the same time. There was still a small part of me, the animal part, that wanted so badly to go back inside and chew Amanda's head off. "I can't do this."

"I'm sorry, Allie," he whispered, as though it was his fault a pretty senior wanted to fuck him. As if he'd asked for it. As if my reaction was his fault too.

I shook my head. "Stop it," I muttered. "Just stop being so fucking perfect all the time."

"Perfect? Allie, what are you talking about?" he asked with a dark laugh. "I'm far from perfect, and once you get to know me a little better, you'll figure that out."

I seriously fucking doubted that. My chest burned with the urge to cry a thousand frustrated tears, but I fought it. "I think I need to go," I told him after a minute. "I wasn't ready to come today."

Part of me didn't want to give up. I couldn't just run away every time this got hard. I'd never run away before. I always faced my shit. But this was different, wasn't it? What if I'd actually acted on my wolf's instinct to attack Amanda?

Like...*fuck*.

"You can do this," Jared held out his hand to me as the first droplet of rain landed with a cold bite to my forehead. His jaw was taut and shoulders rigid.

I looked down at his open palm, studying the lines and the small ridge of calluses below where his long fingers connected. "Let me help you," he said. "No strings attached."

Hesitating, I bit the inside of my cheek.

"We're stronger as one," he said. "Do you trust me?"

My heart in my throat, I bobbed my head. I did trust Jared Stone. As much as you could trust someone you'd only properly met two weeks before. I held my breath, lifting my trembling hand to place in his large, warm one.

The initial contact sent sparks shooting through my nerve endings and I clamped my jaw down tight against the sensation. Jared ran his thumb over the back of my knuckles, and it was like someone injected my legs with a sedative. My knees didn't want to work anymore. I wobbled and Jared caught me with his other hand, clasping firmly to keep me upright.

His eyelids grew heavy and he blinked slow as he watched me through the haze of whatever strange magic drew us together.

"Jared," I whispered, about to ask him to let me go when the sensations wreaking havoc on my body began to level out. The lustful haze that had been making my breaths come shallow and my mind wander to his lips was lifting. In its place, a steady sort of structure formed. Like a bridge between body and mind.

That piece of myself that was missing was returned, or at least borrowed back, lending me a rush of strength and clarity.

"As long as *I'm* calm," he told me, his voice a low timber that I could feel in my bones. "It'll be easier for you to be calm, too."

I looked at our linked hands and back to him, still trying to make sense of all the new riotous emotions vying for dominion over me. "Like this?" I asked him. "I mean, we have to be touching?"

Jared licked his lips, considering. "No, I don't think so, but it doesn't hurt."

We stayed like that for another few seconds before Jared spoke again. "Do you still want to leave? If you do, I can cover for you."

I huffed a sigh and released one of his hands, keeping the other in mine, afraid if I let go that the rage and anxiety would rear back up again. He brushed his thumb over the back of my hand again and I sighed. "No, I should stay."

How else was I ever going to get my life back? "There she is," Jared said with a coy smirk, tipping my chin up to search my gaze. "I was starting to think I lost you there for a second."

Despite myself, I grinned back at him. "Come on," I said, tugging him back to the door. "If we don't show ourselves soon, Viv is going to send a search party."

"They really don't like me, do they?" I shrugged. "You'll grow on them."

I pulled the door open and stepped back into the empty hall, towing Jared inside with me. "Like I grew on you?" he asked with a lifted brow.

Rolling my eyes, I finally let go of his hand, not ready to deal with the implications if someone saw us like that. I glanced around to make sure no one had seen and exhaled when the coast was clear. "Yeah. Like that."

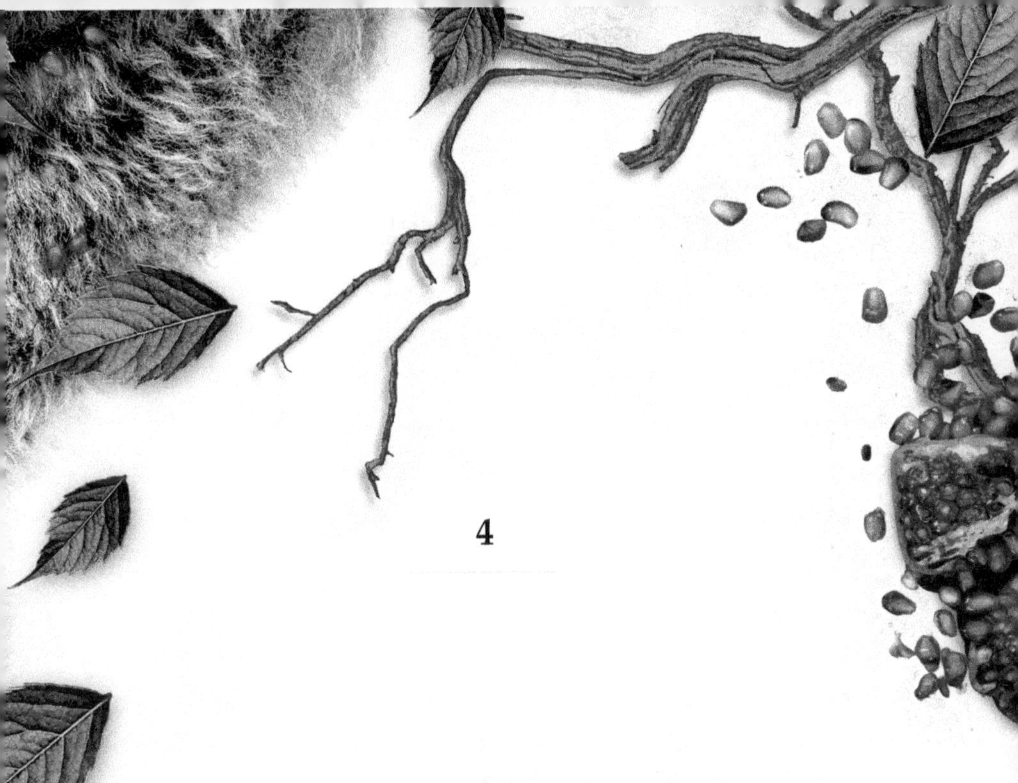

4

ayla noticed something was off with me, too.

She'd eyed me with poorly veiled suspicion at lunch and the moment Jared walked away from the table to grab a third plate from the cafeteria, she voiced her concern.

I spent most of my shift at the bookshop texting back and forth with both of my best friends. They wanted to know what was going on between Jared and me.

I didn't know what to tell them.

Even just imagining the exchange was a total joke.

Are you guys dating? Viv would ask, disapproval coloring her tone.

I don't like the vibe I get from him, Layla would add, crossing her slender olive toned arms over her chest.

I'm not dating him, I would say. *I'm just mated to him. You know, because I'm a freaking* werewolf *now and that's a thing that happens... apparently. I have no choice in the matter. We're just destined to be together. Like it or not.*

Except...I wasn't really sure if I *dis*liked it.

And I couldn't tell if that was because I actually did like Jared Stone or because of my wolf's desire for him messing with my head. I'd liked him before I'd been bitten, hadn't I? As a friend, definitely. After everything Jared did for me, I owed him at least that. But there was something else between us even then, wasn't there?

I hefted the last stack of new orders onto the shelf and sighed. I didn't know what was real and what was a byproduct of being part wolf anymore.

Another text buzzed in my pocket and I drew it out, groaning in anticipation of yet another unimpressed text from Viv or Layla. But it was Jared's name that flashed on the screen.

Jared: Thought we'd run home if you don't mind getting a little wet. Be there to pick you up in an hour?

My fingers hovered over the keypad. I could just take the bus to the unmarked trail and walk myself back to the cabin. I didn't really need him to come and get me.

But the idea of being alone in the dark—*in the woods*—didn't sit well with me anymore. Alarm bells went off in my mind, sending my pulse skittering into a quicker rhythm. What if Ryland let Devin go?

If he banished Devin, would he give my ex time to collect his things? Would Ryland send an escort with him to make sure that was *all* he did?

My throat tightened and I hated myself for being such a coward, but I thumbed out the reply anyway.

Allie: Okay. Thanks.

Then I clutched the phone to my chest and closed my eyes, taking a soothing breath. My inner wolf, which had awoken to the surge of fear pumping through my veins, settled back down.

I was starting to think there was no way around it. Jared was right. I needed to shift again. If I didn't, I knew my wolf would make that call for me.

The risk of that happening in front of someone normal wasn't one I was willing to take. And not because I'd be in some sort of trouble, but because I couldn't stand it if it happened in front of someone like my boss.

Jacqueline would probably have a goddamned heart attack. It would be even worse if it were Layla and Viv. I could picture their horror-stricken faces so vividly it made my stomach turn.

And someone seeing me wasn't even the worst part. No, the worst part was imagining what would be done to them if they saw. There was a reason normal people didn't know about this stuff.

With only one person browsing the shelves of the small used book section near the back, I stepped outside for a second, wanting a breath of fresh air. The cold breeze helped snap me out of it and I inhaled a lungful, chafing my arms for warmth.

The Monday evening was quiet, like they always were in Forest Grove. At almost seven o'clock most of the shops had already closed and there were only a few stragglers left on the streets. Most hurrying home, not stopping to shop. Sometimes I wondered why Jacqueline bothered staying open past five, but I'd never ask her.

If she decided to take my advice and close earlier, I'd be out of a job. And those were hard to come by in as small a place as this town. My breath clouded in front of my mouth and I peered back over my shoulder to check that the customer was still browsing and not waiting for me by the counter.

As I tilted my head, I caught a scent on the wisp of autumn wind dragging its long fingers through my hair. I knew that scent. What was it?

I sniffed the air in that direction, moving away from the shop to follow its trail. It was a musky smell. Like engine grease with an undercurrent of spice. I didn't realize I'd moved nearly half a block down the street until the scent began to fade and I came back to myself with a start.

Shit.

I blinked rapidly, wrinkling my nose as I bolted back to the shop and flew through the door. The customer who'd been browsing the stacks at the back was tapping his foot at the front counter.

Double shit.

"Sorry," I called sheepishly, rushing to get behind the register. "Thought I saw a stray outside."

I wasn't nearly as out of breath as I should have been from running almost twenty miles. When Jared and I broke through the last copse of trees before the cabin came into view, I was only just beginning to get winded.

"You're fast," Jared mused as we slowed to a walk and started down the gentle slope that led to the cabin's dirt lawn.

I didn't really know what to compare it to, so I took the compliment with a nod.

"Feel better?" he asked.

I thought about it, feeling around for the wolf within, and decided I *did* feel more myself than I had before we'd left the shop together. "Yeah, actually. I feel more myself than I have since last week."

"Good," he said with a smile that glinted in the exterior light as we stepped up onto the deck.

That smile...

The screen door banged open ahead of us, slamming against the outside wall of the cabin. I reared back instinctually, my hackles raising.

Clay stood in the doorway, hulking and just as angry looking as ever. The light behind him threw his face into shadow, so I could only make out the shape of him in the dim.

"Clay?" Jared said, surprised.

"I thought you were staying out in the woods tonight?" he added when Clay didn't respond right away, this time his tone was different, and I sensed something charged in the air between them. My wolf didn't like it. I backed away a step, trying to put distance between myself and the guys that made my nerve endings go haywire.

"I need to talk to you," Clay growled at Jared. "Alone."

Jared's shoulders tensed and I got the feeling they were doing that thing again—the thing where they were having a silent conversation I couldn't understand.

"Does it have anything to do with me?" I asked before I could stop myself.

Neither answered me, and their lack of response was enough to tell me what I wanted to know.

A low growl shook behind my ribcage. "Because if it is then I have a right to hear it," I snapped at them both, my fists curling.

It was about Devin, wasn't it? Ryland had finally let him go.

That must be it.

My breaths came harder and my nostrils flared, taking in the scent of stale sweat and something else... engine grease.

And spice.

"You were at the shop earlier," I said, the accusation in my tone clear.

Jared snapped his gaze to me and back to Clay, his jaw tightening.

Clay didn't deny it, but he didn't admit it either. "We need to talk," he repeated, more slowly this time.

"Spit it out," I all but shouted, fuming now and completely unable to help it. "It's Devin isn't it?" I asked, storing the fact that Clay was keeping an eye on me while I worked in the back of my mind for future contemplation. Right now, knowing what the fuck was going to happen with Devin was my priority.

Jared's spine stiffened. "Ryland was here," he said, more a statement than a question. I wondered if he'd scented his pack alpha and I sniffed the air to see if I could discern the unique smell like I had with Clay's back at the book shop.

There was a faint peppery odor with an undercurrent of something smoky that was different from the smell of the fire burning in Clay and Jared's hearth in the living room. This was more like an outdoor fire scent. Like the fires Dad and I used to burn at camp when the wood was a bit damp and there were too many leaves in the pit.

It left a bad taste in my mouth.

Clay turned and stormed back inside, leaving Jared and I to follow. I let Jared go inside first, following in his shadow and pulling the screen door closed behind me.

Clay went to stand in the dim living room, snatching a short glass from the fireplace mantle to swirl the amber liquid within. He knocked back the drink in one long swallow and set the glass back down with a hard knock against the wood. He huffed out a breath and moved to stand behind the large armchair where Ryland had sat the last time I'd seen him here.

Instead of sitting in the chair, Clay splayed his fingers over the ridge of its leather back and breathed deeply.

Keeping my distance, I stood by the couch only a few feet away from Jared. I didn't think I could sit yet, either.

"What did he say?" Jared asked, his voice deeper than I was used to.

Clay looked up at Jared and I, his startling blue eyes flickering with the reflection of the tall flames to his right. "A lot," he replied. "But I guess it was nothing we shouldn't have already expected."

His mammoth hands tightened on the armchair, straining the worn leather.

"He's letting Devin go," I breathed. "Isn't he?"

My heart leaped into my throat and the swell of panic behind my breast made it hard to swallow; difficult to breathe. I needed to move.

Staying still always made it worse. I walked a few steps toward the kitchen and then turned back, my breaths coming faster. I turned and paced the length of empty floor again. "Clay!" I shouted, stopping for just a second so I could glare at him. "Is he letting him go?" My voice broke on the last word and I hated it.

My wolf roiled and snapped within. She was growing, starting to press against the limits of my human flesh. I knew if I looked in the mirror right then my eyes would be glowing bright and angry.

"He is," Clay said finally, and it was like something inside of me snapped. My blood went cold.

Ice cold.

Sweat broke out over my chest and darkness swept in at the edges of my vision.

Think about the positives. Focus on the things in your control. List them.

My breathing spiked and I fought for control. I couldn't think of a single thing. All of my thoughts were scrambled and incoherent, fraying at the edges.

"Allie?" I distantly heard Jared call out to me as though we were all underwater.

"Hey," he said, and his face appeared before my eyes. His hands curled around my arms and for once I didn't feel anything. I was numb on the outside and brimming with too many feelings on the inside.

"Breathe," Jared ordered. "Everything is okay. You just have to breathe."

But I couldn't. It was a fight for every breath. Ryland *let him go...*

But what had been the alternative? Kill him?

Did I really want that?

Yes, an animal voice hissed in my ears, making me shiver.

"Ryland banished him like we thought he would," Clay continued. "He's been given twenty-four hours to collect his things and leave town...then he's fair game."

I craned my neck to look up at him as Jared guided me to sit on the sofa opposite Clay. "What?"

Clay's face reddened. "He can't be allowed to live," he said simply. "Scum like him shouldn't be *free*."

I understood what Clay meant. The implication he didn't want to say aloud. Just because Devin wasn't *here* in Forest Grove, didn't mean he wouldn't do the same thing he did to me, to someone else, some place else.

Take a liking to a girl. Stalk her. Accuse her of cheating and hurt her. Take her captive and...

I almost threw up but stopped the train of thought before I started gagging.

"There will be consequences," Jared muttered, his gaze searching the pattern of the rattan carpet beneath him as though it held the answer to an unasked question.

"So be it," Clay's voice was a monotone rumble in the cabin.

My pulse slowed and bit by bit, the darkness at the edges of my eyes cleared. The hollow pit in my stomach filled. The swell of anxiety that almost had me passed out against the sofa cushions was abating. "You can't," I whispered.

"Can't what?" Clay barked.

"You can't kill him," I told him, meeting his piercing stare with a hard one of my own, shifting that stare to Jared once I was done with Clay.

"Allie, I think Clay is right, we should—"

"No," I said with more force than I thought I could muster. "It's murder. You wouldn't be any better than he is."

Clay recoiled, his fingers coming free of the armchair as though I'd struck him. "And letting him live is better?" he demanded. His eyes blazed with the glow of his wolf as he stepped back again, away from Jared and me.

I shook my head, unable to look at him anymore. My canines were pressing painfully against my gums. My wolf wanting to join his. "It's not just that," I croaked, "It's like Jared said, you'll both be punished if you go against Ryland's orders."

I gulped. "I'm not going to pretend I know anything about how any of this works, because I fucking don't. But I do know that if you guys get banished, then I—"

I couldn't say it. Didn't want to admit how terrified I was of all of it. Of myself.

Then I'll be all alone... because after everything I'd done, everything I'd sacrificed to stay in Forest Grove, I couldn't leave.

Clay snorted, making me peek up to see his dark expression. The glow in his eyes dimmed. I thought he was mocking me. Poking fun at my weakness. And my wolf snarled, coming alive in a lick of heat up my spine. "It might not matter," Clay said, throwing a fist over his skull, through the short dark hair there. "Ry also gave me a message to pass on to you."

From the corner of my eye, I saw Jared's hand curl into a fist. "It's too soon," he almost shouted. "She isn't ready."

Clay sneered at his friend, though I could tell the anger wasn't wholly directed at Jared. He was furious, but that fury was directed at something, *or someone* else. And I bet I could guess who.

"This is *his* territory," Clay reminded Jared and I got a feeling I knew where this was headed. I didn't fucking like it. Not one bit.

"Either she submits," Clay trailed off, and I found his gaze again, this time a real chill creeping over me at his stare. "Or she'll be forced to leave."

"Bastard," Jared breathed, his hands moving up to clasp his head between them as he slumped into the armchair across from me.

What the hell did that mean?

Clay reached for the bottle of amber liquid on the side table, snatching it up on his way out of the cabin. No longer looking at either of us.

"She has until the next moon to decide."

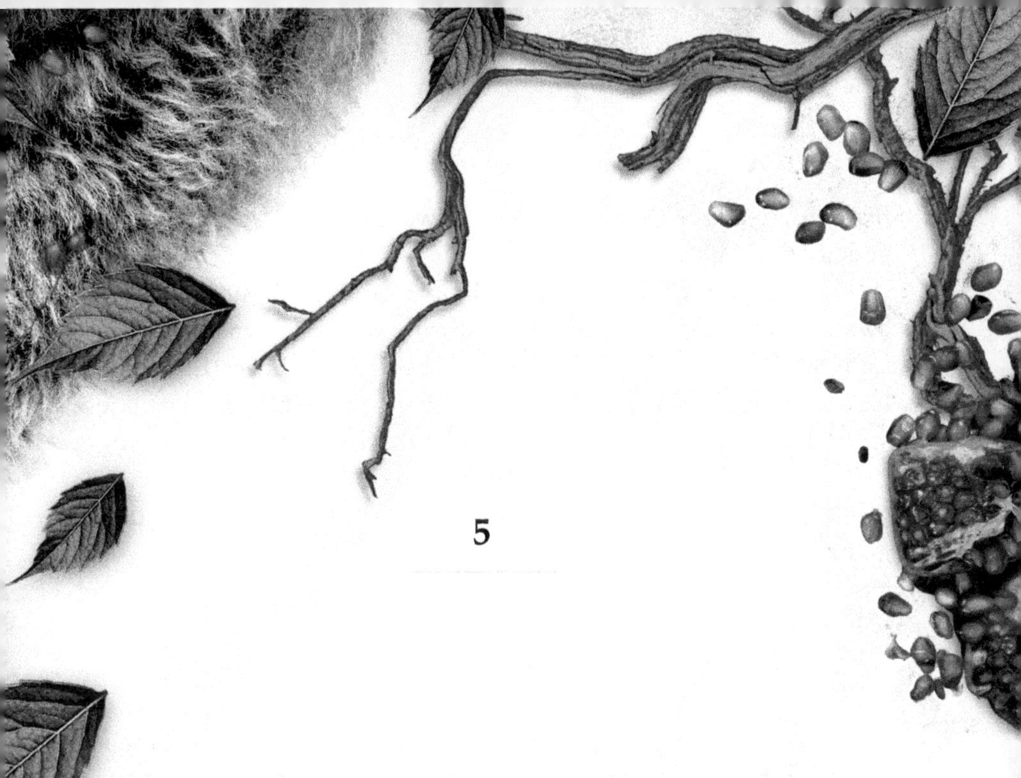

5

"A llie," A soft voice crooned in my ear.

My eyes flew open and the swell of panic lodged in my throat, blocking off a scream. A large hand covered my mouth before I could draw enough breath to project a shout for help. I twisted in bed, the covers tangling between my legs as I tried to lash out; to defend myself.

My wolf sparked into a hot flame and I thought for a terrifying second that I would shift right there in my bed. Tear my clothes and Jared's covers and mattress to ribbons...

"Allie," the voice urged again, and the sharp edge of panic abated as I realized who it was.

"Jared?" I breathed as he pulled his hand away from my mouth. "What the hell are you doing?" My hand pressed into my chest, feeling the quick thumping behind my ribcage. "You scared the fucking shit out of me."

Now that the fear ebbed away, the sense of his nearness fell over me like a warm shroud.

"I'm sorry," he rushed to say. "I didn't think—" he cut himself off. "I was just..."

"Just *what*?"

"I got something for you," he said, tugging his lower lip in between

225

his teeth, clearly re-thinking the idea to wake me up in the middle of the goddamned night.

I cocked my head at him, pushing myself up to sitting. Acutely aware that the thin tank top I was wearing with *no bra* made it impossible to miss the hardened pebbles of my nipples beneath the sheer fabric. I kept the blanket raised to cover myself, wishing he would just spit it out so he could leave, and I could go back to sleep.

If he could see me as well as I could see him in the dark, then it wouldn't matter, though. There was only a sliver of moonlight illuminating my room through the window, but still I could make out every rise and hollow of his face. The delicate curl of his tousled dirty blond hair. And even the bobbing of his throat.

"Will you come with me? It'll be dawn soon and we can—"

"Wait," I said. "Go with you *where?*"

Jared lifted something from the floor by his feet and placed it in my lap. It was heavy, and I knew exactly what it was at first glance. A bow.

"How did you—"

"I got it last week," he said with a little smirk. "I remember you used to use one. When you were younger," he gulped. "With your dad."

My heart gave a throb of hurt and I moved my hands over the bow, feeling the solid strength of it beneath my fingers. It was big. Bigger than the one I'd had before my aunt and uncle sold it. Apparently teenage girls *shouldn't have weapons.*

"I told the guy at the store how tall you were, and he said this should be good for you. He looked at me like I was crazy when I told him you could handle an eighty- pound-draw but..." Jared shrugged.

My brows furrowed. "I *can't* handle an eighty- pound-draw," I told him, a swift disappointment settling into my bones when I realized I couldn't use it. At most I could *maybe* pull a fifty. Definitely not eighty.

"You can," Jared said with a wicked smirk and his left brow raised. A glimmer in his amber eyes.

A slow smile spread over my lips. He was right. I remembered how I'd notched the wooden door frame with my bare fingers—without even *meaning* to.

I'm stronger now.

And I have better senses.

"This," Jared said, brushing my messy hair away from my face, leaving a trail of embers against my cheek where his fingers brushed just above the cheekbone. "What happened to you—becoming a shifter—it isn't *all* bad. Let me show you?"

FIFTEEN MINUTES LATER WE WERE OUTSIDE IN THE GROWING LIGHT OF EARLY dawn. The sun hadn't risen yet, but the evidence of its approach stained the sky in shades of deep purple and streaks of pink-bellied cloud.

I had the bow Jared gifted to me slung over my right shoulder. He carried with him a small quiver. The ten arrows inside rattled as we walked. I had no illusions about how much it must've cost him. A bow of this quality would've had to be purchased in the city. It must have been at least several hundred dollars.

At least the bow had been freshly strung, and the string waxed. I doubted Jared would have known that he needed to purchase a bow stringer and a good quality bow wax to take proper care of it. I usually used gloves and an arm guard, too. They helped keep my fingertips from blistering and my wrists from being turned to mince meat from the snap back of the string.

I wouldn't mention any of that though. I'd quietly go and purchase the things he didn't know better to get later...unless I could convince him to return it after I got a few good shots in. The desire to see how my new canine senses would affect my ability to shoot was too great to pass up.

"Do you work?" I asked Jared once we were in the thick of the trees, heading north into denser forest, skirting the slope of the mountain. I was curious to know how it was that he could just afford to go and get a brand-new bow when he liked. Or a brand-new pair of converse sneakers. Or afford to buy rib eye steaks on a daily basis.

I'd offered to buy our steaks over the weekend and balked when he said they cost him about thirty dollars—for only *two*. And he usually bought three even though the one intended for Clay usually went uneaten and ended up split between us for the following breakfast.

Jared shook his head. "No," he said, though he didn't seem sure. "I mean, I guess technically yes, but not really."

A short laugh broke the silence between us. What did that even mean? "Care to elaborate?"

A twig snap in the distance made my spine stiffen and I tried to nonchalantly move a few inches closer to Jared beneath the shadowed canopy. Jared assured me that even though Devin had been released to gather his things, Ryland would have at least two pack members with him at all times until he was out of town. Even when he went to the bathroom—I asked to be sure. But I still couldn't help the foreboding feeling the forest at nighttime drew out of me.

It was always *my* place. The forest was where I found peace. Comfort. It was where I felt at home. Now, even that, it seemed, had been taken from me.

"I help my uncle Ryland sometimes when he needs it. My family owns a quarry. If he needs to go out of town or anything like that, then he'll sometimes ask me to check up on things there. That sort of thing. I'm the only one who knows how to run the place. And the only one he trusts to handle the payments when he isn't around to do it himself."

"So..." I trailed off, unsure how to ask without sounding like I was prying or judgmental. In the end I figured it was better to just come out with it. "Are you rich then?"

He laughed. "My family is, I guess," he admitted. "I was left with a small inheritance when my parents died." Jared shoved his free hand into his pocket and looked on. I sensed he was remembering something. Maybe something he didn't want to remember. "And the quarry. But I was just a kid, so my uncle took over all of that for me."

"But you're eighteen now," I reminded him. "Shouldn't it be yours?"

Jared shook his head. "I've never had an interest in it. I mean it's mine now if I ever wanted it, but—"

"You don't want it?" I ventured a guess.

"No. I don't think so. Uncle Ry uses the money for the pack, and I think that's how mom and dad would've wanted it, anyway."

"What happened to them? Your mom and dad?" I asked before I could stop myself. I'd never known Jared's parents. I'd only seen his uncle once besides that night in the cabin and in his wolf form in the woods last week, and I hadn't really ever wondered why his uncle had come to collect him at school that day instead of his parents.

Jared visibly paled and I worried I'd overstepped. "You don't have to tell me," I assured him. "I just...wondered."

Jared paused and turned to face me, his eyes looking everywhere but into mine. He swallowed. "I do want to tell you," he said, his voice a low whisper. He sighed. "It's just—"

"Hard to talk about?" He smirked. "Yeah."

"I get that."

"Tell me when you're ready, then."

"I will," he said and then reached out his hand to me. "Come on, it's just a little farther."

I took his hand with a little shiver as that *zap* of energy fizzled between us and then followed him further into the brush.

The dense trees grew sparser as we walked, and the dawn came swiftly in shades of orange and blush pink. It was only another couple of minutes before we came into a clearing. I grinned as broadly as Jared when I saw the two targets set up at the other end.

I'd been a little afraid he expected me to shoot something with a heartbeat and I'd have to refuse, even though he'd gone to the trouble of getting me the bow.

My smile dimmed when I realized the targets were brand name. The really good ones dad could never afford to get me. I practiced on hay bales and trees on our property when I'd been really into my bow. I'd *begged* him to buy me one of those targets.

Now Jared had bought me two.

The bow was enough already. This was too much.

"I can't fire on those," I said, my voice betraying how upset I was that I wouldn't get to use them. "You have to return them, Jared."

His face screwed up into a confused pucker. "I thought you'd be happy."

I opened my mouth. Closed it. "It's not that. I just—I can't accept all this. I don't have the money to pay you back right now."

Probably wouldn't ever.

"You don't have to pay me back."

I took the bow from my shoulder and pressed it into his hand. "I don't need you to take care of me, okay?"

Jared reeled back as though my words had been a physical blow. "Allie, I'm not trying to—"

"Just stop, okay? Stop trying to make everything better. Stop being so...so..."

I couldn't find the word, but my frustration was mounting and the itch to shout was starting to be too much to ignore.

What was he doing anyway? Trying to *buy* my affection since the stupid mate bond bullshit didn't have the desired effect? What did he want from me?

"Listen," Jared said, setting the bow down slowly on the ground as though he feared a sudden movement might spook me. He may not have been wrong. "I *know* you don't need me to take care of you. I know that. But sometimes—"

"But what?" I demanded, my breaths sawing in and out through clenched teeth now. A heat was rising within me and it was out of my control. I didn't want to be angry. Knew somewhere inside that I shouldn't be, but I couldn't stop it.

"Christ, Allie," Jared said, his temper rising to meet mine. "Why can't you ever just let someone in? Why don't you let *anyone* help you?"

"Because I don't deserve it!" I shouted, the words almost a growl. Once they were spoken, I couldn't take them back, and the weight of them pressed heavily on my shoulders. It extinguished the fire in my blood, and I sagged, feeling numbness where there was pain only a second before.

I remembered what Jared told me, about how my emotions were going to be out of whack for a while. If it was like this every day, things were going to get *very* interesting. A broken laugh came out before I could stop it.

Once I had my breath back and I was sure all the rage had escaped, I peered up at Jared, dashing away a tear before it could run down my cheek and he saw it. "I'm sorry. I didn't mean to yell at you."

"I know, it's your wolf. It's a completely normal reaction."

I laughed again, sure now that I was going insane. "How about this," Jared said, picking the bow back up from the ground to hand to me. I took it reluctantly and glared at him—though this time there was no true anger behind it.

"I'm going to let you borrow *my* bow and all this... stuff," he said, pointing to the arrows and the targets set at fifty and about eighty paces away. I rolled my eyes.

"And in exchange, you can teach me how to use it."

I thought about it and even though I knew what he was doing, it *did* make me feel better. If only a little bit.

"Do we have a deal?"

"Okay," I told him, a trace of mischief seeping into my tone. "Deal. But you're going to need a wrist guard and some gloves."

"A what?"

I rolled my eyes again. "To keep the bowstring from—"

"You're forgetting," he said, the same glint of mischief now shining in his eyes. He jabbed a finger toward himself and then at me. "We're not human," he said with a coy smile. "The sales guy tried to upsell me on all that stuff, too. Didn't think we'd need it."

I looked down at my hands. My wrists. Considered their strength. They looked the same as they always had, but Jared was right. I didn't need precautions like that anymore. Yet another thing to add to the slowly growing list of positives. "No," I said, tugging a bow from the quiver in Jared's hand to notch it for a shot at the first target. "I don't suppose we do."

Jared was hopeless.

No matter how many times I demonstrated the proper stance and how to hold the bow and how to look down the length of the arrow to make aim, he just couldn't do it.

"It's no use, I'm hopeless," he said after the sun had risen in earnest, flopping onto his back on the dew- coated dead leaves and grass. "How do you make it look so easy?"

I'd actually sucked, at least for the first ten shots. It took me a minute to get used to the bow—but more than that—used to my own strength. I also broke the string twice before I found the proper amount of effort needed to pull back the eighty-pound-draw. It was *much* less than I thought I would need. Almost too easy.

In fact, I might need a heavier draw.

But after I sorted all that out, it had been a relative breeze. Like muscle memory snapping back into place, even after over a year of not using those muscles. It would take time before I was bullseye-good again, but I was hitting the fifth and sixth rings, so I knew I'd get there with a bit more practice.

"*Ha ha,*" I teased. "I'm super rusty and we both know it, but you are right about one thing."

Jared looked at me questioningly. "You are hopeless."

His mouth fell open in mock dismay and before I could see what he was doing, he'd curled a hand around my ankle and pulled my legs out from under me. I caught myself on my palms. They pressed into the wet, mucky earth next to Jared and I gasped at how cold the wetness was seeping into my jeans at the knees. I pushed him roughly in the arm.

"Jared," I cried indignantly, flipping over onto my ass to inspect the new dirt and grass stains on my knees. *Bastard.* "You're going to pay for that," I warned, ready to grab myself a good handful of mud and grass to rub into his crisp light gray long sleeve.

But I paused. Jared lay still in the grass and something pricked at the edges of my hearing in the distance. A scent not common to find in the woods tickled my nostrils. I knew that smell.

"Is that...chocolate chip cookies?"

"And oatmeal raisin," called a willowy voice, like a phantom song carried on the wind. I whirled around but couldn't find the source. "But I suppose the chocolate chip ones do smell better."

Then she was there, emerging from the brush not more than ten feet away. She looked almost identical to the last time I'd seen her. In a dress that looked more like a nightgown, though the material looked thicker. Warmer. With a deep purple shawl this time instead of jade green. It made the silver strands in her long brown braid stand out even more than they already did.

"Hazel," Jared said, her name sounding almost like a question. He rushed to get off his back and onto his feet, brushing the decay of the forest from his back and sides as though the blind woman could see him.

"And where is my grandson?"

"Uh," Jared said, clearing his throat. "I'm—uh...not sure. Maybe back at the cabin."

The old woman *tsked* Jared, but made no comment, moving out from the brush cover and into the clearing. A branch tugged at her arm, drawing a small drop of blood from the papery skin just above her wrist. The cut wasn't deep, but it was long.

"You cut—" I started, but before I could finish the sentence her small wound healed, and she brushed the droplet away, smearing red over her faded tan skin.

"What's that dear?" she asked, walking with a little limp until she was right in front of Jared and me.

I rushed to move the bow out of her way and stood awkwardly next to Jared. It was hard to imagine that somewhere lurking beneath the flesh of this old, frail woman, there was a wolf slumbering. Just like mine.

Was she blind in wolf form, too, I wondered?

Why hadn't the transformation healed her blindness how it'd healed my ankle and broken thumb?

"Never mind," I muttered.

The woman called Hazel set the basket down on the ground and opened her arms. Jared coughed and then embraced the woman. "It's getting cold, Hazel," he said against her shoulder. He looked like a giant with her withered arms around his middle. "You don't need to be bringing us things."

She tutted again and pulled back from him. "Nonsense," she said with a sour pout. "You're as much my grandson as Clayton is, you know, and I'll bring my family cookies when I damn well feel like it."

Jared laughed, some of the tension leaving his posture. Hazel took his hands when he pulled back and I saw something in his jaw twitch, but he didn't pull away.

She flipped his hands palm up and the strange faraway look in her eyes sharpened and for a second her pupils constricted, staring not just straight *at* Jared, but into him.

It unnerved the shit out of me.

"Ah," she said, dropping his hands after a second, her milky gaze going back to looking somewhere over his shoulder. "So, it's true then."

"What is?" Jared asked, though I think both of us know.

"Your friend has completed the transformation."

Jared glanced at me with an apology in his eyes and a tiny shrug as though to say *she's just a crazy old lady, don't take it personally.*

"And she has bonded to *two* mates," Hazed added with a thin brow arching over her right eye. "Can't say I'm surprised."

Jared's mouth pressed into a firm line at that. "What do you mean?"

I remembered what she said the first time I'd met her. *You were two once.*

I don't know how she could've possibly known, but there it was. One of the things I worked so hard to forget about. One of the deaths I'd caused before I'd even drawn my first breath.

"How did you know?" I asked Hazel, my hands worrying the hem of my shirt, unable to look her or Jared in the eye.

Hazel smiled, showing off two rows of age- yellowed teeth. One missing in the upper right side. "It's my blessing," she told me. "And my curse. To see the inner workings of people. Their gears and cogs. The way they tick."

"By touching them?"

Hazel tipped her head this way and that. Her silver- threaded hair gleaming in the light of the rising sun. "Such a curious one, you are," she said. "That will be your downfall, I fear."

"Hazel," Jared said, clearly trying to end this conversation, but Hazel ambled forward, reaching out her hands in my general direction. I looked between her and Jared.

"It's easier that way, but not necessary," Hazel said in a gravelly voice, answering my previous question. "I was born blind, you see," she told me, still holding her wrinkled hands outward. "And when the transformation claimed me, *this*," she said, shaking her hands for emphasis. "Was how it compensated for that. By giving me a *different* sense."

Jared looked up at the sky and cleared his throat again. "We've got to get going, Hazel. School."

Hazel kept her hands outstretched for another second before letting them fall.

"Take the basket," she ordered Jared. "I'll come and retrieve it later. I haven't had Clayton's lasagna in a while. Tell him I'll be by for dinner soon. It's been too long since we all shared a meal, wouldn't you say?"

Jared lifted the basket and leaned in to give Hazel another small squeeze and little peck near her temple. "I'll tell him."

"Thanks for the cookies," I managed, already backing away.

"Be sure and eat some, will you," she replied. "Can't have you wasting away from stress. My Clayton will need a strong mate. As will Jared in the times to come."

My spine went rigid at the suggestion and I struggled not to spout back at her with a scathing retort. *This is just how it is for them,* I told myself. *She didn't mean anything by it.* I collected the rest of the arrows as Hazel retreated back into the woods.

"She means well," Jared said as he caught up with me, the basket clutched in his hands.

I gave him a tight-lipped smile.

"Plus," he huffed, turning on me with a wide grin. The light of the now risen sun caught those gold and copper strands in his hair, making it look like he had a halo atop his head. "The woman makes a mean chocolate chip cookie."

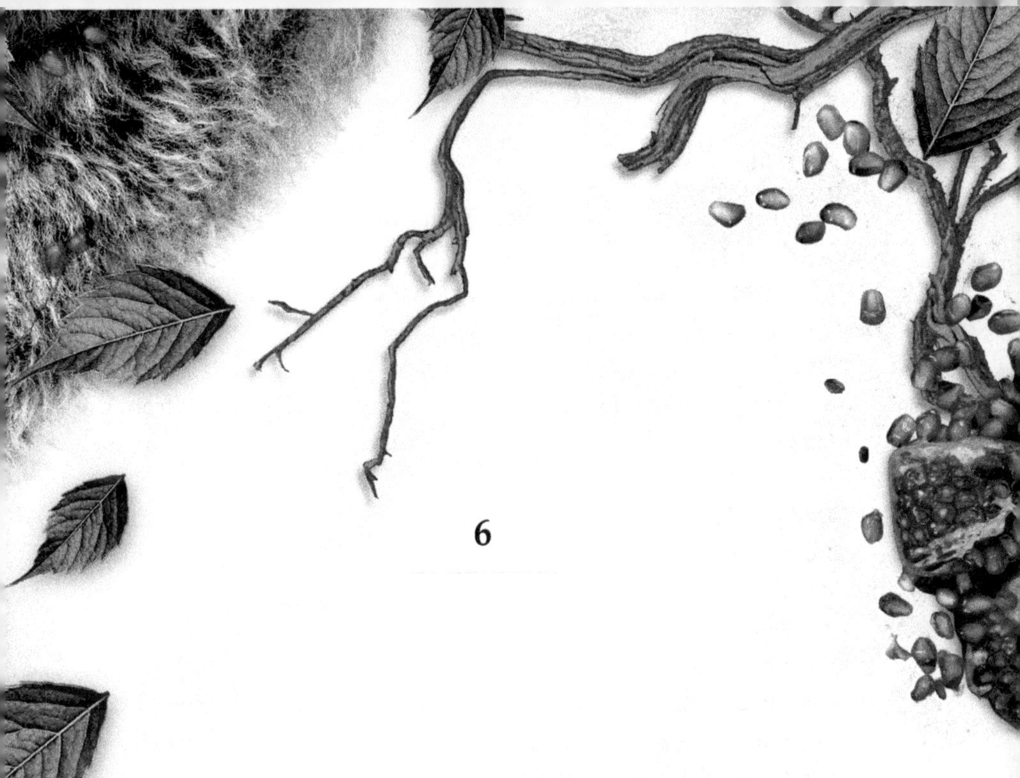

6

There was a strange scent on the breeze as we neared the cabin.

The temperature had risen with the sun, but the air was still cool and scented with pine and molting leaves...and that shampoo my aunt used that I always thought smelled terrible. Like burned hair and chemicals. For a single heart-stopping second, I thought they were back. That they'd found me.

But then my nose picked up the scent of Axe body spray and just a hint of lavender. My aunt *hated* the smell of lavender. She wouldn't be caught dead using that to perfume herself.

"Is someone at the cabin?" I whispered to Jared, trying to peer through the gaps in the trees for a better look. We were still at least fifty yards away though and because of how the forest floor sloped into the tiny valley where the cabin squatted on a patch of dirt, I could only just make out part of the roof and upper balcony.

Jared lifted his head and blinked. "What?"

I didn't really know how else to say it, so I just spat it out. "I...smell people. Like, *other* people. Not Clay."

Jared's eyes narrowed on the trail ahead and he breathed deep in through his nose, halting mid breath. "It's Forrest and Charity," he said. "And Seth too, I think."

I regarded him with lifted brows, urging him to tell me who they were.

"Oh, right," he said. "Sorry. They're pack. Charity and Forrest were there when you…"

"Oh," I breathed. "What are they doing—"

"She has until the next moon," Clay's distinct voice roared from the cabin, sending birds tripping from branches to take to the sky. "So fuck off."

Jared and I shared a look.

There was an apology in his stare, his face pinched around the nose and mouth.

Guess now we knew why they were here.

"You can go around if you want," he tried. "I'll grab your backpack and meet you at the Jeep after I deal with them. We can grab breakfast and coffee on the way to school."

It was tempting. Like, *really* tempting.

But from how the area where the cabin was had grown silent, I thought it might be too late for that. "If we can smell them, then I think they can probably smell us."

They would likely already know I was here, and if I avoided them— went around the cabin in the woods to go and hide by the Jeep and wait for Jared, then I was a coward.

And if there was one thing on this earth I never wanted to be—it was that. Dad taught me better.

Face your fears, Allie Grace, he used to say. *Or they'll gobble you up and spit out your bones.*

"No. I'll go with you."

I started walking again before Jared did and he rushed to catch up with me, making no comment. Though from the corner of my eye I saw his jaw twitch with strain and his eyes begin to glow a ruddy orange at the edge of his irises.

That fluttery feeling began in my chest again and it was hard to catch my breath. I forced my shoulders to relax and inhaled deeply through my nose, quelling my wolf and the rise of panic like a cork in my throat.

"You're freaking me out," I hissed quietly to Jared as we ambled through the trees. "Calm down."

For a second when I looked at him it was like I could see the wolf inside. Snarling. Hackles raised. Tail erect and ears flat against his skull. My own wolf was prowling now, too. Shocked awake by the scent of new beasts in her territory.

Jared nodded once to indicate that he'd heard and the glow in his eyes dimmed. He unclenched his fists.

"Word has spread," I heard a voice say as the trees thinned and the cabin and yard came into full view. "Other packs know about her now."

The girl who was speaking stood between two males. She was of average height, with a thick, muscled frame and long blond-tipped, brown dreads that hung to her mid back, pulled back with a leather tie. She and the others turned as we approached. Her face was heart shaped and almost painfully pretty—not at all what I would've imagined from seeing her back profile.

Her eyes were a shade of green that bordered on turquoise and she watched me with a fixed stare. Her emotions unreadable.

The other two males with her watched our approach with differing expressions. The one on the right with a stoic expression and rigid stance. And the other with a wide smile and bright hazel eyes that brought out the olive tones in his skin and the shine in his jet-black mop of hair.

There was nothing false in his smile. It wasn't forced or pinched, but genuine. And he wasn't looking at me, he was looking at Jared.

"Jare," he said, rushing to greet Jared with a manly embrace.

"Seth," Jared said, returning the hug with a hard pat on Seth's back. "It's been a while."

Even though they were acting friendly, I could hear the tension in Jared's words, and when mine and Clay's eyes locked, a shiver ran down my spine. My massive mate was standing on the front porch just outside the door, his arms crossed, face reddened, and a thick vein jutting out of his neck.

I took two steps before I even realized what I'd done and stopped. My body had wanted to go to him.

When I peered up at him again, I found him looking away, his arms flexing at his sides.

"And this must be Allie," the one called Seth said as he made his way over to me, flipping his hair away from his brow.

He stuck his hand out, towering a full head over my height. Why were they all so freaking tall? "Seth."

I lengthened my spine and took his hand, shaking it like Dad taught me. With a firm grip and eye contact even though my first instinct was to look away. "Allie Grace," I said in reply, dropping his hand.

"Good handshake," Seth said with an impressed smirk, raising one brow at me as though trying to read what I was thinking. "Strong will, too, I think."

I cocked my head at him. A strong *will?* Kind of a weird comment, wasn't it?

"You've spoken your piece," Clay barked from the porch. "It's time for you to go."

The other male stood straighter, rolling his shoulders back like Clay did sometimes. I'd come to recognize the motion as a sort of defensive stance. Like the person doing it expected a fight. "Not so fast," he said.

"*Forrest,*" Clay warned.

"What's going on?" Jared asked, staring pointedly at the one called Forrest. He wasn't as tall as Seth, but he was stocky. Dad would have said he was built like a brick shit house. Whatever the fuck that meant. He even had the square jaw and boxy calves to go with the description.

"She's unclaimed," he said, turning slightly to face Jared while also being able to keep a wary eye on Clay. Probably a smart move.

"Un...*what?*" I asked, unable to help myself. I didn't like the sound of that word, or what I thought it implied. A hot swell of anger bubbled in my chest and up my throat, leaving an acrid taste on my tongue.

The girl, Charity, cast a long glance my way. "Unclaimed," she repeated with none of the ire Forrest had, but with patience instead. "You don't belong to a pack," she explained in a level voice. "You have no alpha. We call that being unclaimed."

"So? Ryland said I had time to decide, right?"

She nodded with a little sigh. "He did, but," she looked from Jared and back to me again. "That might change."

"What do you mean?" Jared demanded.

Clay groaned and threw a fist through his hair before turning and vanishing back into the cabin, letting the screen door bang loudly closed behind him, effectively telling us he was *done* with the conversation. But I doubted he would go far. In fact, I could see his shadow pacing the length of the cabin by the front window.

"Word is spreading about her," Forrest explained, his eyes sharp. "About the new wolf in Forest Grove who is unclaimed and who has *two* tails."

Jared stiffened.

"They're curious," Charity added hesitantly. "Ry's already had to chase a few off our lands who were trying to sneak a peek."

I didn't like the way Charity had said *curious*. Like it was a bad thing. Like the innocent word could be concealing something more sinister but she didn't want to come out and say it.

"She's *mated*," Jared growled, and my wolf shifted in response to his use of the word.

"Yeah," Seth said with a shrug. "They're curious about that too. But who isn't?"

My mouth went dry.

Jared brooded in silence. I could tell he was trying to find a solution right there on the spot but coming up blank.

"You're going to join anyway, right?" Charity asked, moving past Seth to come nearer.

I met her kind stare with defiance. "I don't know," I said between clenched teeth, trying hard to keep control even though it felt like I was being backed into a corner.

"But you want to stay here don't you? This is pack territory. *Ryland's* territory. And your mates are pack—"

"I said I don't know," I snapped.

"Okay," Charity said, backing away a step with her hands raised. "I just thought—"

"She needs more time," Jared growled, breaking free from his stillness to curl a hand around my arm and lead me toward the cabin. "You all need to leave."

"Awe man, come on," Seth whined halfheartedly with an overstated pout.

Forrest stepped up to stop Jared and I from passing. Jared's nostrils flared.

"That's not the only reason we came," Forrest almost shouted. I noticed the fine lines around his eyes and decided he must have been the oldest of them. Where the other two looked like they could be in their early twenties or even younger, Forrest seemed older. Maybe late twenties or early thirties.

My wolf wanted…I don't know what she wanted. But with him so close it was like she wanted to challenge him for dominance. An urge to see him beneath my paws against the dirt—to see him *submit* rushed over me. I wanted to show him who was stronger, and it seemed, my wolf thought that was *her*. Not him.

I let out a shaky breath and shrugged off Jared's hand to run up the steps onto the porch past Forrest, needing to put distance between us before my wolf jumped out of my throat and went for his.

The further away I got, the more the feeling subsided. It helped even more when I looked away.

"What then?" Jared sighed. "What do you want, Forrest?"

"Ry needs you."

"What for?"

"As long as your *mate* refuses to join the pack, we're all on damage control. Like Charity said, he's already had to chase two off our lands. More will come. Some might want to claim her."

Jared's eyes ignited in amber and jade light.

I had to look away again, my pulse thumping in my ears.

"Not a fucking chance," Jared hissed. "No shit," Seth said from behind him.

Charity stepped into place between and beside both Jared and Forrest, as though making herself a physical buffer between them. "He needs you at the quarry," she said, and I saw how even though she had a fighter's stance, her tone was cool, trying to keep the peace.

I liked her.

But I didn't like how Forrest was looking at Jared like he was a fucking snack. My wolf didn't like it, either.

"I-I need you to move away from Jared," I warned Forrest and he turned to glare at me. My voice came out pitifully unsteady, but I did need him to move away. I didn't want to shift right now.

I wasn't ready. Not yet.

I needed more time.

And if he didn't get the fuck away from Jared, then my wolf was going to make him.

Charity held her hand out. "Forrest isn't going to hurt Jared," she said soothingly. "It's okay. We're just talking, right boys?"

Forrest turned back to Jared. "Yeah," he spat. "Just talking."

"Isn't there someone else?" Jared asked, thought I could see the wind had left his lungs. He looked completely deflated, like he already knew the answer to his question.

"What do you think?"

"Fuck."

I didn't want Jared to go, but we'd just talked about this. He said his uncle needed him sometimes to help with his parents' business. I just didn't expect it to happen so soon.

"When?" Jared asked. "Tomorrow."

"Until?"

"As long as it takes," Forrest replied, cutting a sidelong glance toward me and then back to Jared, illustrating my role in exactly how long that was. I wanted to punch the smug look off his face.

I staggered forward, seeing red, and stopped only when a heavy hand clamped down on my shoulder, sending a bolt of heat and electricity rushing through my blood. I gasped and turned, finding Clay had come back outside.

"Easy tiger," he warned and then flicked his gaze back to the other pack members.

"It's time for you all to leave."

When no one moved, Clay rolled his shoulders back and glared at each one in turn, his sharp blue eyes rimmed in an otherworldly glow. "*Now.*"

Jared shouldered past Forrest to join Clay and I on the porch.

"What should I tell Ryland?" Forrest demanded. Jared paused and his eyes turned down at the edges.

He bowed his head. "Tell him I'll be there."

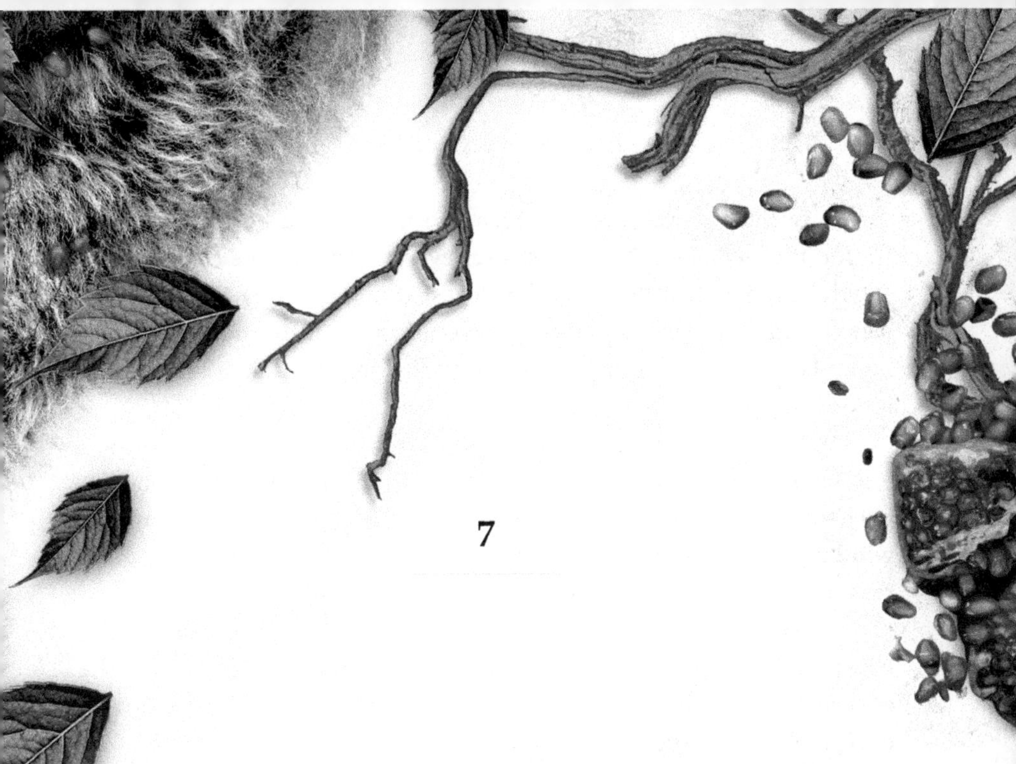

7

Maybe I should just join the stupid pack. Even though I *hated* the idea of it down to the marrow of my bones, it really would solve all the problems. Ryland would leave us alone. Other packs wouldn't be crossing the borders of his land. Jared wouldn't have to leave.

But...I wouldn't *belong* to myself anymore.

I would be bent to the will of another. I would have to do what Ryland commands. Jared hadn't sugar coated it for me. He told me on the way to school in the morning exactly what it would mean if I joined.

"Ryland is a decent alpha," he'd said.

"But I would have to do what he says," I'd pressed. "Even if I don't want to?"

Jared nodded solemnly.

"So, if he told me to kill someone, I'd have to do it?"

"He wouldn't—"

"But if he did?"

It was a shit example, but I wanted to know just how *much* control he would have. Was it really that bad?

Jared's eyes had darkened. "Yes. Technically. You could fight it, but it's almost impossible."

That made up my mind.

Or rather—it made up my mind to *not* make a hasty decision. I couldn't leave Forest Grove. Not after everything I'd done to be able to stay here. Layla and Viv were the closest thing to family I had left. If I was forced to leave, staying in that hunting blind for months, all the hours I'd put in at Jacqueline's shop, all the lies; it would all have been for nothing.

I would lose everything I worked so hard to keep.

But staying meant giving up a part of myself. A very important part; *my free will.* That wasn't something I was going to toss out the window so easily. Not without a lot of thought and a damn good reason.

A part of me held out hope that maybe, just maybe, I could live in Forest Grove like Hazel does, without a pack. A lone wolf. I knew the circumstances were much different, but if Ryland made an exception once, maybe he would do it again.

Maybe.

"Are you going to leave her the keys to your precious jeep?" Clay arched a brow at Jared as he shoved his running shoes into a messenger bag to join the clothes and bare necessities he'd packed after we returned from our run home together from the bookshop.

Other than the drive to school and a few exchanged words after work, before the run, we'd barely spoken. There hadn't been time. And it felt like it was all happening so fast.

Jared was leaving in less than twelve hours and he couldn't tell me when he was going to be able to come back. He told me he was going to check in at night when the quarry quieted down, if he could get away, but he couldn't make any promises.

Jared was leaving me alone.

With Clay.

There was no other option. I had no other place to go.

And Ryland had given a command—albeit a second-hand one—but it was still a command. Jared needed to go. I needed to stay.

Jared looked at the keys hung on the hook by the door and to me. "Shit. I forgot," he said, grinding his teeth. "Will you be okay to run?"

"Are you really not going to let her drive your jeep?" Clay growled at him.

Jared opened his mouth to speak but fumbled for the words.

"I can't drive," I said for him. "It's okay. I'll run. I need the exercise anyway."

Or, more accurately, my wolf does.

Clay narrowed his eyes at me but said nothing.

"When are you leaving?"

"Before first light," he replied, casting furtive glances at Clay. "Ryland will want me there by daybreak."

I nodded my understanding.

"Allie," Jared said after placing the packed bag by the front door. His jaw was taut and something in his expression set my nerves on edge. "Can I have a minute with Clay?"

"Oh. Uh—yeah. Sure. I'll just go outside."

"Stay in the yard," Clay growled at my back as I left the cabin. I refrained from shouting something back at him. I didn't want Jared to worry about us getting along while he was away. I was already worried enough for the both of us.

I padded down onto the dirt lawn and shivered as the cold dirt brushed against the pads of my bare feet. Unable to help myself, I peered back toward the cabin, trying to see them through the crack in the blinds where one of the slats was missing.

A pair of bright blue eyes locked onto mine and I started, tearing my gaze away and rushing further from the house. I rounded the east side and attempted to quiet my mind, hoping Clay wasn't about to rip Jared's head off.

There was a reason Clay didn't want anything to do with me; a reason why he was keeping distance between us.

He'd made it clear as crystal that he wasn't at all fucking impressed that he was going to have to *babysit* me. That would mean he would actually have to be near me. Maybe even talk to me. Hell, he might even have to sleep in his own bed down the hall from me at night instead of as a wolf in the woods.

Fuck.

I wasn't exactly thrilled about it either, but that was for an entirely different reason. As I rounded the back of the house, I saw that both Clay and Jared's rooms shared the large second-floor balcony that wrapped around the western exterior. My room didn't have access to it, but it seemed mine was the only room that didn't.

Though, I thought if I crawled out my window, I could probably get to it.

Surveying the back of the cabin, I saw where a different structure, one comprised of a different sort of wood and a tin roof jutting out from the rear. It was a good size. Maybe fifteen by twenty feet with a large garage door and no windows. From the smell of engine grease and carburetor wafting out from it, I had to guess it was Clay's shop.

Glancing behind me, I listened for approach and found no sounds save for the chirping of crickets and the rustle of dried leaves still clinging to their branches.

Just a peek, I told myself, and crept to the door. It was open. Clay must've been working in there before he heard us get back.

There was a lantern hanging crookedly in the back corner of the space, casting light and shadow over the shapes in the shop. The silhouettes of two bikes were visible near the back, covered by rough canvas sheets.

Ahead of those, perched proudly among the meticulously arranged tools and parts hanging on the walls and arranged in straight lines on the rough wooden counter's edge, was a Sportster forty-eight. A beast on wheels.

The Harley was done up in chrome and midnight black with shocks of shimmering blue.

She'd been polished to within an inch of her life. There was no doubt in my mind who it belonged to. "Get a good look?"

I yelped, spinning around to find myself face to face with Clay.

"Fuck!" I shouted, springing back from him until my back was pressed against the wooden exterior of his shop.

Once I caught my breath, a rush of heat flooded my cheeks. "I was just..." I started, but the words eluded me. What *was* I doing?

"Snooping?" Clay offered with a snide look.

The blush was gone in an instant, replaced with a different sort of hot flash. "Sorry," I grunted, pushing off from the wall to leave. "Won't happen again."

"You said you ride, right?" He said, making me pause mid step.

My jaw clenched and I closed my eyes. Vivid images of my Dad and I tearing up the dirt together flashed like projected images against the backs of my eyelids. My stomach rolled.

I got the sense he was trying to offer the proverbial olive branch. To find something in common between us. This was his apology for snapping at me. But I couldn't take it.

"I used to," I corrected him. "I don't anymore."

"Pity," he said.

"Why did you—" I started, but by the time I turned around to face him again, wondering why he'd asked, Clay was gone and the absence of him was a cold sting in the air.

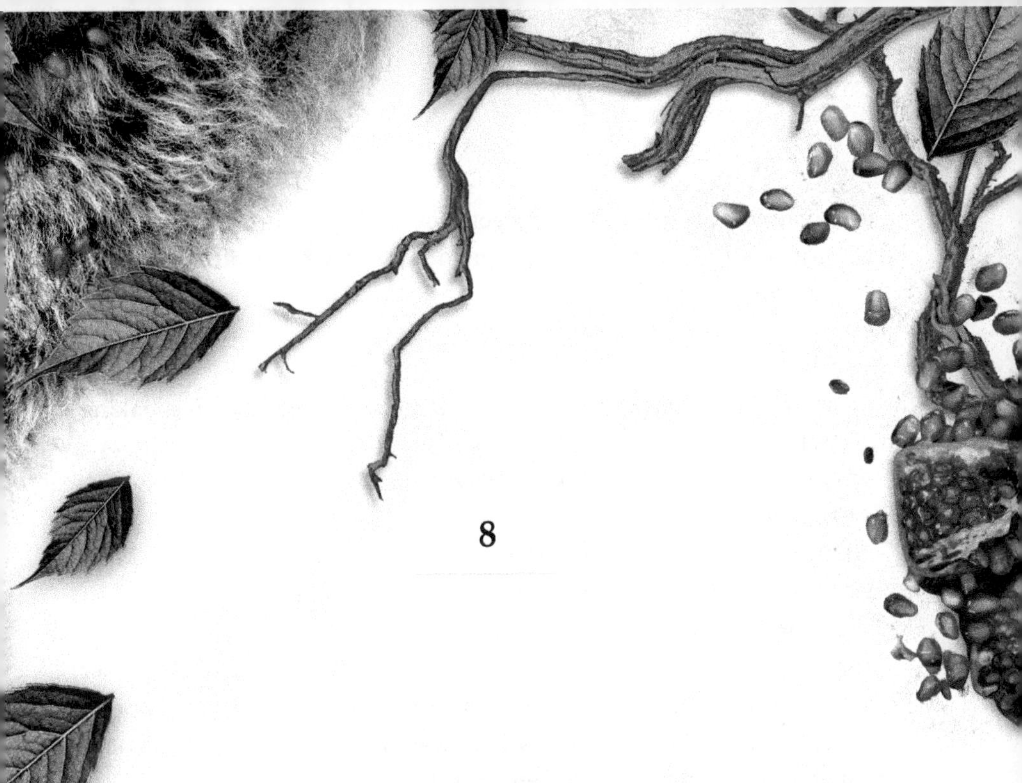

8

E ven though I'd fought him on it, Jared left a hefty stack of twenties in the drawer in the kitchen. *For necessities*, he'd said.

I wouldn't be touching a cent of it.

After work I planned to hit up the small grocery at the edge of town and get my old staples. Apples. Oats. Ramen. You'd be surprised just how long a person can live on those three things.

There was enough left in the fridge and cupboards still that Clay would be alright for at least a few days. But we really had no idea how long Jared would be gone for. A few days for sure, though he'd warned this morning before he left that it could be closer to a week. Even more if his uncle didn't get the message out that the Forest Grove pack wouldn't tolerate rogue wolves on their lands.

It all seemed a little silly to me, but then, I wasn't born into this life like Jared was. I was snatched away from my mortality—my normalcy—and *thrown* into it.

"Hey," Layla snapped in front of my eyes. "Where's your man friend today? You guys have been joined at the hip since you came back to school, I thought maybe..." Layla trailed off, brushing her long near-black hair away from her face to hang down her back.

"What?" I asked, trying to get back to the conversation at the lunch table and having a hard time focusing. Without Jared with me at school,

251

I was walking on eggshells. I'd been doing alright so far, but I had a feeling it was only because I'd run a good twenty miles after Jared left this morning.

I would run the same or more every day that he was gone to placate my wolf.

"*Jared*," Layla repeated, saying his name slowly as though speaking to a deaf person. "Where is he?"

"Oh, um...he's helping his uncle with something. He won't be back for a little while."

I bit my lower lip after I said it, hoping that was alright to say. I had no idea what was safe to say to people and what wasn't anymore.

"So, he's just going to miss school?"

Quinn saved me from having to come up with a reply when he set his lunch tray on our table, the plastic clattering against the chipped enamel. I winced. I didn't know which was worse between the cafeteria at lunch time or the halls between classes...

Both were on the verge of making my ears bleed, or at least, that's what it felt like.

Yet another thing to get used to.

Quinn slid into the seat next to Layla and bumped her shoulder. "Hey," he said, glancing around the table at Layla first, with a smile, and then Vivian, who stopped scrolling on her phone to raise a brow at him, and then to me.

"Um, what are you doing?" Viv asked, eyeing Quinn with unconcealed disdain.

Layla went scarlet.

I turned in my seat. Quinn was almost pressed against Layla they were sitting so close. His dark flop of hair looked like it had some gel in it. The bruising around his eyes and mouth from what Devin had done to him looked to have mostly faded. And though the cut in his eyebrow from where the asshole had ripped Quinn's eyebrow ring out was mostly healed, he wouldn't be able to put a new ring in there any time soon.

But he had a shiny new piercing. A simple silver lip ring on the left side of his mouth. It suited him.

"Hey Quinn," I said, trying to soften Vivian's blow. Quinn and I were back on relative speaking terms, though I didn't think we'd ever get back to our easy banter in culinary class ever again. Even if Devin was gone for good.

"Hey Allie."

"Did I stutter?" Vivan prodded, cocking her head at Quinn.

Layla rolled her eyes. "Oh, calm down, Vivian," she chastised. "I invited him."

Vivian's eyebrows shot to her hairline. She turned her light brown eyes to me, a question in them. She was wondering if I knew what the hell was going on. I shrugged.

It seemed a lot could happen in a week away from school.

"I can leave," Quinn offered with a one-shoulder shrug, trying for nonchalance even though it was clear Viv had made him uncomfortable. His throat bobbed with a deep swallow.

Layla placed a delicate hand on his arm to stop him, her painted black nails denting the fabric of Quinn's long sleeve band tee. "No," she said. "Stay."

Then she turned to Viv. "Allie broke the rules first," she added with a little smirk. "So, I figured the no-boys-at-the-lunch-table rule didn't apply anymore."

"You had a no-boys rule?" Quinn asked, clearly amused.

Layla swatted him. "We were thirteen when we made that rule," she pointed out.

Vivian sighed. "It's the beginning of the end," she said dramatically, crossing her arms over her chest and leaning back in her chair to push her tray away.

I reached over and stole her chocolate milk and the rest of her uneaten mac and cheese. She shook her head at me. "At least some things never change."

I DODGED ANOTHER OF VIVIAN'S ATTEMPTS TO GET US ALL TOGETHER THIS weekend, but only barely. I wasn't going to be able to keep turning her down or giving excuses for much longer without her thinking something was up.

But knowing what needed to be done and actually *doing* it were two completely different things. If I could just grow the kahunas to shift again, I could start to get control of myself. Or, I guess, to become one with my wolf, which should make her more malleable to my human will. Or...something like that.

With Jared gone though, well, I wasn't sure if I could do it alone. Asking Clay for help was definitely out of the question. He'd stayed out in his shop all night last night and only came inside after Jared left. "Want me to drive you to school?" he'd grunted as he poured himself a coffee.

I'd said no and he hadn't said another word. He didn't offer to run with me, even though running in the dark alone until sunrise had almost sent me spiraling into a panic attack at six am, but I'd caught his scent on the way back to the cabin. Somehow knowing he'd been following me made me feel both relieved and violated at the same time.

"Where are you going?" Viv asked as I peeled off from our group after lunch, heading in the direction of the main office.

I spun, walking backwards in the crush of students rushing to their lockers before class started again. "Dane wants to see me," I replied.

Viv stuck a finger in her mouth and pretended to gag, illustrating her sympathy. I didn't think *anyone* at Forest Grove actually *liked* Vice Principal Dane. Except maybe Stella Baker, but she was widely known as all the teachers' pet. There was even a rumor last year that she got with Mr. Cavelli—the math teacher. Apparently, there was no other possible way she could have gotten a ninety-seven percent in that class. The girl didn't even know her basic timetables.

But who knows, maybe her rich mom and pop had shelled out for a private tutor. You really never know what's going on in other people's lives. Which is why I *try* not to judge or listen to the churning small town gossip mill.

I shouldered the office door open and stepped inside.

"I need his *goddamned* transcript. *Christ*, I've been standing here for twenty minutes. I have court in less than an hour and need to let the movers into the house. I don't have time for this shit."

Mr. Wright was standing over Susan, the tiny office admin at the front counter, his wide fingers splayed over the glass top.

"I-It'll just be a moment, Mr. Wright," Susan stammered, backing away from the counter. "I'm sorry to keep you waiting."

I craned my neck to look around, my heart in my throat.

There was no shock of dark hair. No steely green eyes watching me. Devin wasn't there.

"If you'd like to have a seat," Susan gestured to the short row of plastic bucket seats along the wall next to where I was standing.

Mr. Wright loosed an exasperated sigh and turned. I backed toward the door to leave but wasn't fast enough.

His speckled green eyes found mine and he straightened to his full height. A few inches taller than his son, Mr. Wright was a goddamned giant. With wide shoulders and a lanky frame.

Dark pepper hair salted with strands of silver and cropped short framed his square face.

The lines around his bloodshot green eyes deepened. His upper lip curled up at the sight of me and I didn't have to guess to know that Devin had blamed me for whatever story he must've told his father about why he needed to leave town.

I could tell straight away Mr. Wright was human. I didn't know whether or not he knew what his son was, but regardless, it was clear who he blamed.

I didn't have to wonder anymore why Devin went to seven different schools growing up. When he told me, I assumed it was his father moving them around for work or something like that. I'd felt *sorry* for him. That he wasn't able to grow up in one place, make lasting friendships.

But now I knew the truth. It wasn't his father. It was Devin running from his mistakes and dragging his father into his messes with him. Though Mr. Wright was definitely guilty of feeding into it. Being a judge, he probably got his son out of trouble more often than trouble caught up with them. The perks of being son to a powerful and complaisant father.

I pitied the man.

My mouth opened as if to speak, but I really didn't know what to say. My wolf was snarling inside, and I averted my stare in case my eyes betrayed the truth of what lay within.

"I hope you're happy," Mr. Wright growled and when I chanced a glance at him, my heart stopped. With the light directly over his head, casting his face in shadow, I didn't see him.

I saw Devin.

A sound something like a whimper clawed up my throat and my wolf launched to the surface. A bone in my hand popped and I cried out.

"Dear?" Susan called from behind her computer screen. "Are you alright?"

"You little bitch," Mr. Wright whispered low enough that no one else would hear.

Another bone snapped audibly, and my knees weakened.

He sounded so much like his son when he whispered like that.

A shiver raced up my spine and a forceful swelling in my chest rocked me back like a punch. "I-I'm not feeling well," I eeked out, turning away toward the door. There was a garbled quality to my voice and pain burned through my jaw as my teeth slid low, cutting into my lower lip. "I have to go."

"Wait! You need permiss—" Susan called after me, but the door shutting on my heels cut off her voice and I sprinted to the front exit, tripping as I went through the door when my ankle snapped.

I screamed, earning myself a horror-stricken stare from two students rushing inside late from lunch. With tears in my eyes, I hobbled around the building, crashing onto my knees when my other ankle gave out. My spine stretched and flexed. I prayed my thick sweater and baggy jeans were enough to cover what was happening beneath them in case anyone could see me from the windows.

"Fuck," I ground out, trying to stop the shift from claiming me. But my wolf was tired of playing nice. With images of Devin in her mind and the whisper of his voice trapped in her ears, she would not be controlled.

"*Allie*," the growl was so close, I flipped back and landed hard on my tailbone, staring up into the stunned ice-blue eyes of Clay. He was shirtless and his body steamed in the chilly fall air.

"Fucking hell," he cursed, scanning the area before he reached down and grabbed me around the arms.

A sizzle of warmth exploded through my belly at his touch and I whimpered.

"We need to go," he hissed in my ear as he wrapped his wide arm around my waist and hefted me into his arms as if I was a babe.

I wanted to protest. To kick and scream and *demand* he put me the fuck down. But it was all happening so fast. I was being washed out with the tide, tumbling and spinning. My head throbbed as I tried and *failed* to breathe.

Clay ran.

I didn't know where he was taking me, but after three more bones snapped, we were in a shaded place and when I opened my eyes, I saw dark green pine and withering autumn leaves.

"Is...safe?" I managed; my voice unrecognizable.

He kneeled and set me down on the carpet of the forest. The cold damp soaked through my jeans, shocking me back from the edge. The clarity brought with it the crushing realization of what was happening. I was shifting.

I didn't want to shift.

I pushed back against the wolf, a sound like a groan pressing out through my lips as I fought it.

No.

No, no, no.

Please, I begged. *I can't...*

Think about the things you can control, Allie. Think about the positives. Breathe.

I'm safe. Devin is gone. He can't get me. Everything is okay. I am in control.

I am in control.

Another pop of bone somewhere in my leg and my lungs were on the verge of giving out.

"You need to shift," Clay barked. "Stop fighting it."

"Fuck. *You.*"

"You're only going to make it worse."

I roared, rearing up onto all fours and then onto my aching feet. My ankles protested, but I forced them to hold my weight. "*No.*"

Clay shook his big head at me, and I saw how his eyes were shining with his own wolf's urge to shift. It made something inside of me quake.

"I have to go back," I said, my voice sounding like something spoken through a garbled radio. I needed to get to class. If the school called my aunt and uncle again, I would be in deep shit. I couldn't keep lying to them. They were going to figure it out. They would catch me. Then what?

I blinked and shook my head. I couldn't let that happen.

Clay moved to block the way, stopping me. "Don't be an idiot."

Inside, I was screaming, but on the outside, all I could do was keep breathing as the anger filled me. As the unfairness of what was happening to me—the helplessness sunk in.

Three weak steps and I was shoving him. Hands screaming from the broken bones beneath my skin.

I shoved him again, becoming numb to the pain.

He let me shove him a third time before he caught my hands and held them tightly between his, stopping me. "It isn't fair," he said in a low voice, without the anger that usually tainted his tone. "*I know.*"

How could he?

"But this is your life now. Like it or not."

His hard gaze found mine and he held me there, captive in the fathomless depths of his eyes. "Don't fight it, Allie. Just...fucking *let go.*"

The soft command was like a rip cord, sending me falling headfirst into the dark. The instant I gave in and stopped fighting, too weak to keep pushing and *pushing* against the growing being within me, she leaped out. It could have taken a second, or a minute, I wasn't sure.

But it was *fast.*

When I opened my eyes again, my lithe body rippled. Hot air clouded out from an elongated snout. My canine legs twitched with the urge to run. A muted whine strangled my lungs. I turned at a sound behind me and scrambled back on all fours.

My clothes lay in tatters against the ground and standing amid them was a large wolf. Deepest gray with eyes like backlit sapphires. My twin tails whipped around, catching my flank and startling me.

It was done then.

It hadn't been even half as bad as the first time, but...I could already feel my wolf getting restless. She wanted to run. She wanted to *chase.* She wanted...

Mate, the word echoed in my skull and the whining stopped.

The dark wolf bowed his head.

Come, his voice spoke in my mind and I startled, my ears pricking at the intrusion.

Clay, I tried, speaking his name in my head as though trying to speak to him without the ability to form words.

He nodded.

I reeled back, my claws dragging over leaves and dirt.

Oh god...

Could he *hear* my thoughts?

Oh god, could he hear *all* of my thoughts?

Clay stepped forward and snapped in my general direction, getting the attention of my wolf. Her body going rigid. Then he turned tail and pressed off with his strong back legs, launching himself into a run through the trees.

My body quivered in anticipation and my wolf let out a loud yip before she tore off after him. The primal instinct to *chase* was too strong to deny.

The exertion pumped my muscles and sang in my blood. The cool wind whistled through my fur and reminded me distantly of being a little girl again.

Sticking my arm out the window of Dad's truck, feeling the press of air as it rushed over my skin. Belting *Don't Stop Believing* along with the radio as I pretended to fly.

Unable to stop it, a howl pushed out from my center, loud and haunting as it echoed all around me.

Clay's howl rose to meet mine, melding with it until the harmony of our matched voices converged in my ears, sounding like one instead of two.

It didn't take me long to catch up to Clay. I didn't think I cared one way or the other whether I could beat him, but the same couldn't be said for my wolf. She wanted to best him. She pushed herself until our lungs burned and our legs began to ache.

And when Clay saw us coming up alongside him, the startled look in his wolf's eyes and the short sound of indignance chuffing out through his lips was worth it. My wolf's pride and glee at her accomplishment made me smile inside. For a fleeting second, her happiness became my own.

Clay changed paths and I recognized the change in scent before I visually realized where we were headed. We were almost back to the cabin now. I could already see the break in the trees.

But another scent stopped me dead in my tracks. My wolf skidded over the molting leaves, almost tripping in her haste to stop. She lifted

her head, sniffing the air, and then the forest floor, finding traces of...
something.

What *was* that?

Crunching in the distance and my ears pricked. I stilled.

There it was again.

Movement to my left. So far, I couldn't truly make out what it was,
but my wolf seemed to know.

She launched herself into the brush, taking off at a break-neck
sprint past the trees. Soaring over fallen logs as though she had
wings.

Black eyes lifted from the ground. Black-tipped ears pricked up to
listen.

I could see the deer's spotted brown coat now. I could also see the
dawning realization as it came into the deer's eyes when it saw me.

No.

It bolted.

But that only made my wolf hurry harder. Faster. My mouth
watered at the feast, bouncing through the underbrush with a white
bobbing tail. Like a little beacon popping up and down screaming *here I
am, here I am, here I am...*

No!

My wolf slowed for an instant at my command but sped back up
again a second later.

Allie, I heard Clay's bellow in my mind.

How do I make it stop? I shouted back, frantic. Silence was my answer
—I knew what that meant. I couldn't.

We were gaining on it. Another fifteen yards and my jaws would be
around its neck.

Fucking run, you stupid dear!

I imagined it: watching helplessly as my wolf—*as I*—consumed an
innocent creature. Hot blood and meat in my mouth. I gagged.

A black blur passed me, thudding over the earth.

My wolf snapped at Clay, but he didn't stop.

He attacked the deer, pressing down hard on its back as his jaw
clamped around its neck, biting down and twisting until the wrenching
sound of snapping bone silenced the sharp grunting sound coming from
the deer's tiny mouth.

My wolf growled and snarled. Distantly, I could feel hot saliva dripping from my jowls.

I felt my wolf's anger at her mate.

She'd wanted that kill and he'd stolen it from her.

Clay growled back, removing his teeth from the deer. His fur was matted with blood around his snout. It dripped onto the deer, leaving ruby red spots between the white ones on its back and side.

Go home, Clay spoke in my mind. *I'll meet you there.*

My wolf was still snarling, but I got the feeling she wouldn't challenge Clay for the meal at his feet. He'd made the kill. It was his feast, not hers. And he clearly didn't want to share.

Aghast at my warring thoughts, I managed to prod my wolf into leaving.

My thoughts clashed and spun out of control. How could I want to eat it and want to barf at the thought of eating it at the same time? How could I feel both sad the deer had died and angry that Clay had been the one to kill it first?

At her loss to Clay, my wolf began to recede. She was tired, I realized.

I wondered if it was just as hard for her to fight me as it was for me to fight her when I was in my human form.

It was easy for me to point her toward the cabin now. She bounded along without protest. It was *almost* as if *I* was in complete control. *Almost,* but not quite. When my paws went from sticks and leaves to hard packed dirt and the cabin loomed in front of me, my wolf was ready to give in to my demands to shift back.

She laid with her belly against the dirt and set her chin down against her paws.

A flash of my last shift bombarded me. It had been gruesome.

I gritted my teeth, ready for all my bones to snap back into their rightful place. Ready to throw up until there was absolutely nothing left in my body to expel and then to pass out from the pain and the emptiness.

Jared had wrapped me in a blanket and put me in bed. Or, at least I assumed that's what he did, because that's how I awoke the next morning. Naked with traces of leftover vomit in my hair—even though it was clear someone had tried to wash it out—with a blanket tucked around my nude body.

I never asked him about it because I was too embarrassed. But I was starting to get the feeling that being part wolf meant getting used to being naked at inopportune moments.

I held my breath and did what came naturally, pressing myself against the boundaries of my wolf just as she did when she was trapped within me. I imagined myself expanding out from where I felt like a prisoner in my mind, my consciousness expanding until I was whole again. Human again.

Me again.

There was a loud popping sound and a blazing heat ripped down my back, arching it sharply.

Then my fingers were brushing against dry dirt. Hair tickled my shoulders and chest where it fell, brushing against naked skin. Squinting my eyes open, I sighed, tears welling when I recognized my arms, my wrists, my hands.

My *human* hands.

There was no pain, but my stomach was uneasy, and my vision swam at the edges.

I swallowed back bile, trying to maintain control, and flexed my fingers in the dirt to ground myself until I felt ready to stand. Breathing heavily, I got to my feet and stumbled before gaining stability. There were streaks of dirt over my abdomen and chest. Muck crusted the inside of my fingernails.

I turned, as though I would be able to see the wolf version of myself, I'd left behind, still not fully believing her and I were one and the same. She was going to *kill* that deer. *Eat* it.

My skin bristled and the bile came back, threatening to expel itself from my lips.

I would never kill an animal.

Dad took me hunting when I was younger, but even then, when I was there, I only allowed him to shoot partridge and wild turkey. And I only *ever* shot my arrow if the animal hadn't been killed by Dad's shotgun and was lingering in pain. Only then did I deliver the killing strike. Because that way I could at least pretend I was merciful instead of murderous.

My gaze rested on a shape in the trees. A dark wolf watching from a distance, his paw frozen six inches from the ground. As though the sight of me had turned him to stone mid step.

Shit.

"*Clay,*" I snapped at the massive beast. "Jesus Christ, turn the fuck around or something."

His eyes widened and he spun, falling onto his side in his rush to look away. He scrambled up and sat with his back straight and ears sticking straight up, staring straight ahead, away into the trees. His near-black tail thumped twice before he schooled that into stillness too.

I rushed to cover myself as best as I could and bounded up the porch steps and into the cabin on wobbly legs, cursing under my breath the whole way to the shower.

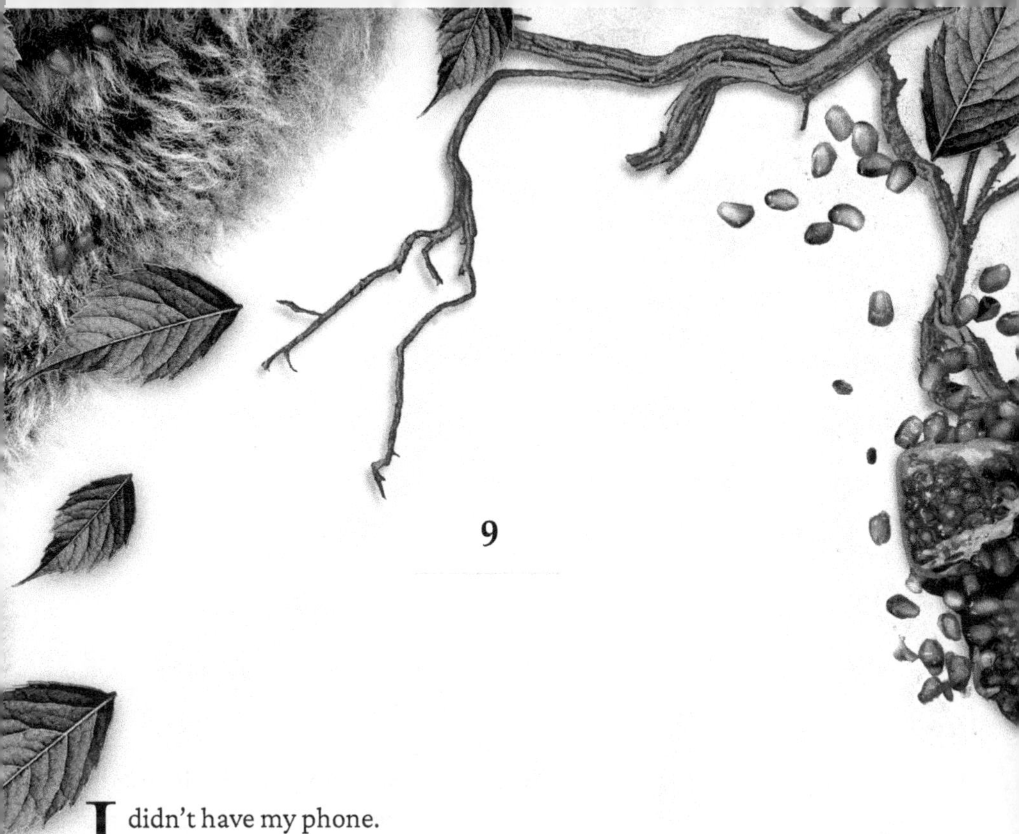

9

I didn't have my phone.

Fuck.

Layla and Viv weren't in any of my classes for the rest of the day, but I was sure Viv would have texted me to ask what happened with Principal Dane. She would wonder why I wasn't answering.

Had I had it with me when I ran out of the school? It had to have been in my pocket when I shifted. But I distinctly remember seeing all my clothes on the ground, shredded beyond recognition. I wasn't sure if I'd seen it there.

I toweled off with shaking fingers and rushed to get dressed and pull a brush through my hair. Would the school have phoned Uncle Tim yet?

Was he trying to call me right now, too?

Was he calling Vivian's house looking for me?

My heart thumped wildly against my ribcage, beating out a discordant rhythm that made my breaths come shallow and quick. The swell of panic was making it hard to think straight.

I stopped and set the brush down, inhaling deeply through my nose. *Okay, Allie,* I told myself. *Go find your phone. Just do that first and then work on the next thing.*

I nodded sharply to my reflection and left the room. "Hey," Clay said

265

as I ran down the stairs. Out of the corner of my eye, I saw his face was red, and he was avoiding looking at me.

The look in his wolf's eyes when he saw me in the yard buck naked flashed in my mind and I grimaced. "Not now, Clay," I bit out. "I need to go find my phone."

I looked around the front door and groaned. "And my goddamned *shoes.*"

They'd better not be torn apart.

My breaths quickened and I dropped the sweater I lifted from the hook by the front door twice before I was able to get my arm in the sleeve.

"Allie."

I got my arm through and held it with my numb fingers as I elbowed my arm into the other sleeve and reached for the door.

"Allie," he repeated, firmer this time.

"What?" I whirled on him, teeth clenched and head beginning to spin from the lack of air. This was the scariest part of having a panic attack. That no matter how much I seemed to be breathing, it was like my body didn't compute the O2. Like it was rejecting the air it needed to sustain itself.

I had to move. To walk. I needed fresh air against my cheeks. Then maybe my heart would stop beating like it might jump right out of my chest or stop completely any second.

Clay held up something slim and black in his right hand. "I have your phone," he said. "The screen's cracked a little, but it still turns on."

I hiccupped at the sight of it. My eyes burned.

"And your shoes are in my shop. The sole came loose on the right one and I had to glue it back on. It's in the vise until it dries."

My lips pursed to keep the tears at bay. I would *not* cry in front of Clay.

Acutely aware that my breathing had begun to level out and the shaking in my fingers had lessened to a slight tremble, I swallowed. Tried to force the tension in my shoulders and spine to ease.

"Th-thank you," I whispered, closing the gap between us to reach out for my phone.

He didn't give it over right away, still holding it up just out of reach as he searched my face. "You did good," he said.

I cocked my head at him, lips parting in surprise. "What?"

He jerked his head toward the window. "Out there. You did good. The shift was relatively clean, and you were able to hold off for a long time to keep from shifting in front of people. That's good."

I snapped my mouth shut, resisting the urge to tell him I didn't give a *fuck* if I was *good* at it. Partially because I was still angry at the world literally tossing me to the wolves, and partially because I knew I *needed* to be good at it if I ever wanted my fucking life back.

"You shifted back pretty easily, too. Usually the first voluntary shift lasts a lot longer. A full day at least. That was barely an hour."

"Should I be grateful?" I seethed, happy to replace some of the panic in my blood with the burn of anger. My wolf, who'd been all but gone since I shifted back, stirred in my belly.

Clay smirked but said nothing. He dropped the phone in my hand. "I called the school for you," he added as he walked toward the kitchen. "You don't have to go back today."

I looked at my phone and then back at him. I illuminated the screen, wincing when I saw the spiderweb crack in the upper corner. But it did still seem to work fine. There was only one text from Viv, sent thirty minutes ago.

Vivian: How'd it go?

No texts from Uncle Tim. No phone calls from the school. Nothing.

The last of the panic ebbed away.

When I glanced back up, I found Clay carrying a plate of raw chicken and a pair of tongs toward the door.

"What do you mean you called the school?"

He paused, and something in his jaw twitched. "I told them you weren't feeling well. That I came to pick you up."

"You *what?*"

"Your Uncle," he said, raising a brow. "Tim Adams, right?"

My mouth fell open.

"Don't know about you but a good shift always makes me hungry." He lifted the plate toward me—an offering. My stomach growled. "I'll save you one."

Then he vanished outside, and I felt the vibrations of his footfalls on the deck as he made his way to the barbeque with his massive plate of meat.

I gripped my phone, feeling the tiny shards in the top corner dig into the crease in my index finger. Had he *actually* called the school pretending to be my uncle to get me off the hook?

What the hell?

Why would he do that for me?

The whoosh of the barbeque being lit outside snapped me out of the confused daze. I texted Viv back.

"By the way," Clay called from outside, his deep, gravelly voice carrying on the air. My fingers paused over the keypad. "You're failing Math."

I groaned.

"And geography." Fuck. My. Life.

I WAS GLAD CLAY DIDN'T ASK WHAT SET ME OFF AT THE SCHOOL. WE TIP TOED around the whole subject as we ate at opposite ends of the deck off of paper plates. Not speaking. When we were finished, Clay went around back to retrieve my shoes and lifted Jared's keys off the peg inside the door with his pinkie finger.

"Come on," he said. "I'll drive you to work."

"You don't—"

"I do," he interrupted, twirling the keys around his finger. "Jared's orders."

I quirked a brow at the giant. "You don't seem like the type to take orders," I grumbled, crossing my arms when he took the soiled plate from my hands to dump it into the trash bin inside.

A throaty grunt was his only reply to that.

I was starting to like Clay. Or at least, starting to think I could tolerate him. That was until the first slew of texts came in from Jared while I was at work.

I'd asked—no—*begged* Clay not to tell him what happened today, and the bastard had done it anyway.

I didn't know how Clay got my number or how his number got saved into my phone, but amongst all the worried, sporadic texts from Jared was a single one from Clay. One Word.

Clay: Sorry.

I rolled my eyes at the screen, punching out a reply to Jared's texts.

Allie: I'm FINE. Clay is being dramatic about it. I shifted. It sucked, but it wasn't as bad as I thought it would be. Everything is good. You don't have to come back.

Jared: Are you sure?

I hesitated. Truth be told, the first thought that crossed my mind when I started to shift yesterday after realizing I wouldn't be able to stop it was that I wished Jared was there. He would have gotten me through it. Eased me into it.

But...it might have been worse that way. Clay's emotionless demeanor and command to shift was what had finally spurred me into letting go. If Jared had been there—gentle, patient Jared—would I have fought it longer? Would it have hurt *more*?

Maybe it was for the best that he wasn't there after all.

Allie: I'm sure. How are things at the quarry?

There was a long pause before he replied. I was able to help a customer and face up two whole stacks of books before his reply buzzed in my pocket.

Jared: As good as they can be. Everyone's on edge right now with Ryland away dealing with the trespassing wolves.

A cold fist of guilt twisted in my gut.

I hoped he wasn't fishing for me to give him any reassurances that I would give away my free will to his uncle. I hadn't thought about it much yet and honestly, I didn't want to. There had to be some other way.

Grimacing, I thumbed a reply.

Allie: I'm sorry for causing trouble. Jared: Not your fault.

Sure as hell felt like it was.

Jared: Don't rush the decision. It can't be undone.

I put my phone away and began to start the closing routine. Sweeping and vacuuming the front mat.

My pocket buzzed again.

Jared: What triggered the shift, anyway? Everything okay at school today?

I started typing out a reply but wound up erasing it.

I didn't want to tell Jared what Mr. Wright said to me. It would only make him angry he wasn't there. He would probably blame himself for the whole thing. I went with vagueness instead.

Allie: Mr. Wright was in the office today getting Devin's things. I ran into him and panicked. That's all.

Jared: Devin is gone. As far as we know he's already two states over. If he's smart, he won't come back.

Was he smart? I swallowed hard. At least with Jared preoccupied at the quarry and Clay relegated to babysitting duty, they weren't trying to come up with a suicide mission to go after my ex anymore.

Jared: How are things with Clay? I hope he's not being a dick.

Well if that wasn't a loaded question, I wasn't sure what was. I bit my lower lip, doing my best to find a good response. I knew he and Clay were going through their own problems since I was turned.

They'd both mated to me, and from what I gathered, it was kind of a big deal.

I mean, I knew it was too on some level. What I felt any time I got near them or touched them was no joke. But surely that would fade, right? Or I'd get used to it.

We'd be able to go on as if it never happened, wouldn't we?

They'd get over whatever rift that'd formed between them, right? They were best friends after all.

I shivered at the memory of Jared's hand in mine and the warring feelings of relief and anticipation that it'd brought. And Clay—when he brushed past me in the hall at the cabin the other day. And when he'd carried me into the trees just this afternoon as the urge to shift shook me.

Even through the haze of pain and panic, I'd felt him. Like an anchor keeping me steady enough to get through the shift.

Jared: Allie?

I cleared my throat and set the broom into its nook behind the door.

Allie: Everything's good. Don't worry. I can handle him.

Before I could tuck the phone back into my pocket, it buzzed again, and Clay's name flashed beneath the fractured glass, surprising me.

Clay: I'm outside.

Sure enough, when I glanced up and peered out the window, I saw Jared's white jeep idling across the street. The bulky shadow of Clay in the driver's seat— his cell phone illuminating the silhouette of his face in the dark. The sharp angle of his thick jaw. The line of his cheekbone. The soft curve of his full lips. His dark lashes and thick eyebrows against tan skin.

He turned, blue eyes meeting mine through the glass.

I stilled, a furious blush coiling up my neck and into my cheeks. I gave a little wave that Clay didn't return and quickly turned away, cursing myself under my breath as I finished locking the till into the safe and began shutting off all the lights.

Get your shit together, Allie Grace.

I SLID INTO THE PASSENGER SIDE AFTER DOUBLE CHECKING EVERYTHING WAS finished and splashing some icy water over my flushed face. The inside was warm and after the cold slap of walking from the shop to the Jeep, I shuddered.

It was getting *really* cold out there. I'd need to wear two sweaters or get a warmer jacket soon. "You can turn up the heat if you want," Clay grunted as he pulled away from the curb and into the mostly empty street.

"No," I rushed to say, clicking my seatbelt into place. "It's perfect."

Clay filled up the driver's seat and then some with his tall, wide frame. He rested his forearm on the center console to give himself a wider berth and when I bent over to find the buckle, my hair brushed his arm. He jerked it away as though the harmless hairs were something far more sinister.

He put his arm back when I moved away, but the damage was done. My inner wolf was sitting up now, paying attention. The cab was filled with the scents of engine grease and spice. Packed with the weight of his presence.

Leaning casually against the window, *away* from him, I cleared my throat. "You didn't have to come and get me, you know. I could've walked."

We passed the small grocery store on the main drag and turned off onto the side road that would lead us to the edge of town. So much for grocery shopping.

I'd have to find the time to go tomorrow. Jacqueline didn't need me at the shop—which was odd for a Wednesday—but at least it would give me a chance to catch up on some homework that was piling up and to stock up on some essentials. If I got my period right now, I was *fucked*. Good thing it wasn't due for another few days.

Clay snorted. "Yes. I did. I already told you—"

"Yeah, yeah," I said, remembering with a sigh.

"Jared's orders."

"Not just that."

I rested my chin against my closed fist and tilted my head to watch him as he drove. My lips parted to ask him what he meant, but then I closed them again, afraid I didn't want to know. He was probably referring to my little panic attack earlier. Or the fact that I nearly had a panic attack when I went for a run this morning before school. He was following me. He would have seen.

The drive seemed almost painfully slow. When we finally turned the last bend and I could see the narrow entrance to the unmarked trailhead where Jared usually parked, I sagged with relief. Clay's nearness was wreaking havoc on my nerves, and it took everything I had not to jump out of the Jeep before he even put it in park.

I slammed the door behind me, not realizing my own strength. The loud bang made me wince and the Jeep shudder.

"The fuck," I heard Clay whisper from the other side.

"Shit. Sorry, I didn't mean to slam it so hard."

Clay appeared around the back, the still glowing tail lights casting their red light over his face. His nostrils flared for a second then he shrugged. "Not my Jeep," he said with a one shoulder shrug. "But I *will* be the one fixing it if you break it."

I shrank back as he stepped forward toward the trail.

Clay bristled. "Why do you do that?"

"Do what?"

"Back away from me like you think I'm going to—"

He cut himself off and it took me a second to put together what he was stopping himself from saying. His cold blue eyes watched me, only the moonlight illuminating him now, but I could see better than I ever had been able to in the dark before. I could see the strain at the edges of his eyes and the tightness in his jaw.

I could see the web of veins in each of his forearms as he flexed them beneath the rolled sleeves of his black long sleeve t-shirt.

"Oh. No," I shook my head. "It's not that. I mean, you're scary, don't get me wrong. You got this whole *I could eat you in one bite* thing going on, but I don't think you would...um..."

"Then what?" he demanded, clenching and unclenching his fists. His gaze unwavering. "Do I fucking smell?"

I readjusted my backpack and took a breath. "No. It's the um—the mate bond thing."

His jaw went slack, and he stepped backward. Clay narrowed his eyes at me, and I could have been wrong, but I thought I saw something like hurt flicker there before it was gone, leaving me to wonder if I'd seen it there at all.

"It's just that when you get close to me," I trailed off, unsure exactly how to describe it. Surely, he could feel it too. From what I understood, a mate bond wasn't a one-way street.

"Got it," he grunted, his mouth twisting as he moved in a wider arc around me and into the trail. "I'll keep my distance."

"I just meant—"

"It's fine," he snapped and then stopped, but didn't turn. His back lifted with a deep breath and he turned his head so I could see the profile of his face in the dark, backlit in shades of silver from the moon. "I didn't ask for this, you know." He growled; eyes blank as he stared at the ground. "I didn't want it."

"I know."

He nodded once and then continued into the trees. "Come on. It's late."

I hurried to catch up, keeping about six feet of space between us. My hair fell into my face and I flipped it out of the way, my foot catching on something. The toe of my newly glued back together shoe jammed into the hollow beneath a tree root and I went sprawling face first toward the ground.

My backpack thudded to the dirt and I put my hands out to catch myself, but Clay was faster. He caught me by the wrists and steadied me, his burly chest inches from my face. My body screamed at the warmth emanating from him. Where his hand circled my wrists, they tingled.

He let go of me and knelt, reaching down to snap the curved tree root from the earth, freeing my foot. "Can you *please* watch where you're going."

I was still trying to school my face out of its *I'm about to scream* position when he rolled his eyes and stepped away. He gestured an arm forward and waited off to the side of the trail. "After you," he said with an unnecessary flourish. I stepped past him, realizing the frustration I felt as I did wasn't my own, but *his*. My eye was twitching because *he* was frustrated. I hoped he felt the hollow pit of my embarrassment in retaliation.

Clay fell into step behind me, keeping a safe enough distance away that the twitching stopped.

This emotion sharing thing was getting to be a bit crazy.

If I hung around Clay for too long, would I become a sour-faced grump, too?

Clay clucked his tongue and a prickle of unease made the hairs on the back of my neck rise.

"You can't read my mind when we're human, right?" He let the question linger in the air long enough to make my stomach knot and my chest freeze over in a layer of cold sweat. "No."

"And can you hear *all* my thoughts when we're wolves?"

"No."

"Well aren't you a wealth of information."

He sighed. "I can only hear what you project, but sometimes things slide through accidentally. Usually if you're thinking something really strongly, or if you're afraid."

We fell silent for a while and I thought Clay was done talking to me for the night, but he spoke again when we were only a few minutes away from the cabin. "I was thinking," he said, and the note of trepidation in his voice made me nervous. My steps faltered before I resumed the same speed again.

"You were?" I prodded, letting sarcasm drip into my tone.

"Ha. Ha."

"What?"

"Would you want to meet the pack?"

I remembered the pack members who'd come to try to pressure me into a decision. The same ones who took Jared away on Ryland's orders.

I wasn't sure I wanted to see them again—never mind meet *more* shifters like them.

Sensing my hesitation, Clay added, "You don't have to, but they'll just keep coming. Some of them are just curious. And some are stubborn pricks. I already chased off Harrison yesterday afternoon when I found him sniffing around."

I had no idea who the hell Harrison was, but I nodded, my mouth going dry.

"If you go to them. Meet them and tell them you intend to make your decision soon, then there's a better chance they'll leave us alone."

Couldn't they just mind their fucking business?

I gulped.

"You don't have to decide now," he continued as the cabin came into view. "Just think on it."

"Okay," I said as I moved toward the porch. Clay didn't follow. "Are you not coming inside?"

He shook his head. "Nah. Going to crash in the shop tonight. I have work to do."

I bit the inside of my cheek. My body ached for my bed, but the thought of sleeping in the cabin alone frayed my nerves. "Is it okay if I lock the door?"

Clay raised one brow at me, and I instantly felt stupid for even asking. If anyone wanted to get to me, they could just bust through a window or probably kick the door right off the hinges. Locking the door wouldn't help, but it would give the measure of control I needed to be able to close my eyes.

"Sure. I've got a key if I need to come in."

I nodded and wrapped my arms around myself, a sudden chill on the breeze digging into my bones.

"Allie," Clay called.

I looked up at him from beneath the cover of my lashes.

"You're safe here," he said. "I'm not going to let anything happen to you."

When I didn't answer, unsure what to say to that, Clay nodded tersely and vanished from view. I heard the garage door to the shop roll open, and I didn't hear it close again.

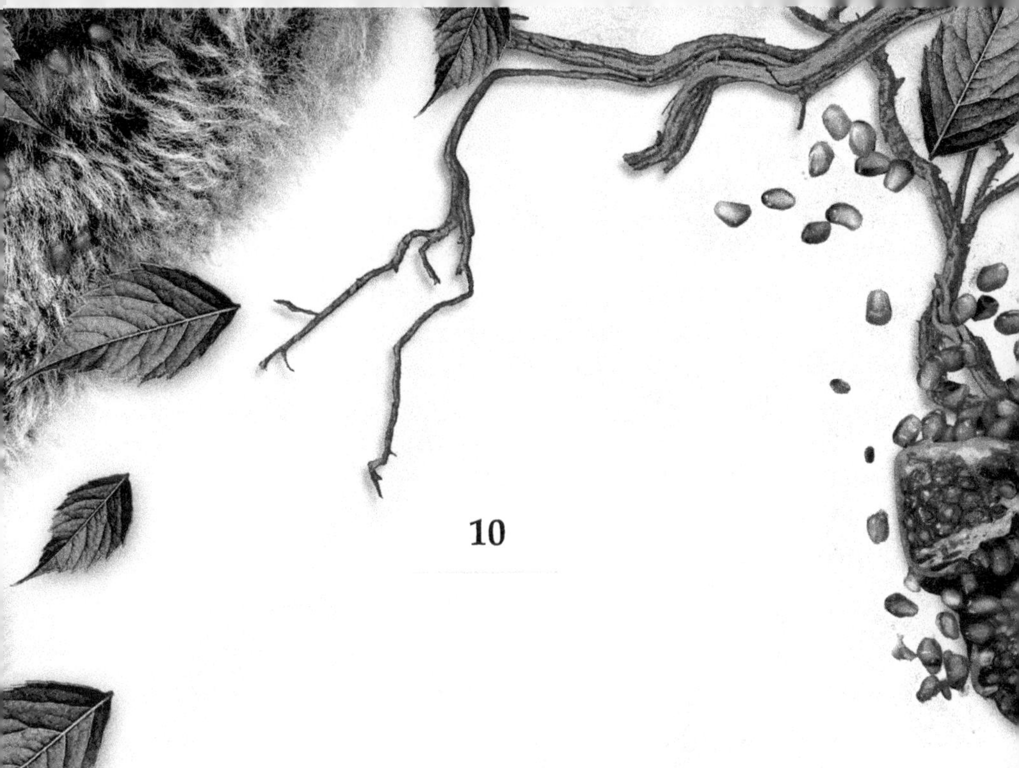

10

The bite of cold metal around my wrist awoke me. It stung—the tender skin beneath the manacle red and raw. The clanking of a metal chain over stone as I tugged at it rang like warning bells in my ears.

I tried to open my eyes, but my vision was out of focus and wavering in and out. A pale cheek and shock of black hair came into focus before it was gone again.

I tried to pull at the bind again, but my mind and body were groggy and heavy. It felt like someone had pumped my body full of heavy iron —the weight of it on my chest was crushing. My breaths whispered in and out through limp lips.

Where am I?

A familiar scent permeated the air. A musky vanilla. I knew that smell. I sighed in relief, searching for its source. I tried to speak, to call out to him, but the words came out disconnected and too soft for even my own ears to capture.

"I'm here, baby," he said, his voice husky and deep.

I rolled my head around and blinked past the substance in my eyes, trying to find him in the flickering light. It was so *cold*.

"You're shivering," he said, and I felt the distant pressure of a body pressing into mine. I felt the tingle of warmth where a hand rested on my waist beneath my shirt. I shuddered again.

I found him in the haze a second later. His sharp angular features watching me with heavily lidded eyes and full parted lips. His hand moved up my waist, following the contour of my body until his fingertips pushed beneath the underwire of my bra and found my breast.

The ring of metal as I twitched under his touch brought me a moment of clarity. I knew where I was.

I was in...*in a cave*.

Devin had carried me here, hadn't he?

"That's it, Allie," he whispered, and I felt his hot breath against the base of my ear. "Move for me baby."

There was a tug at my waist and the top button of my jeans came free.

This wasn't right.

Devin squeezed my breast hard, bringing a soft cry from my lips.

Why couldn't I move?

Why couldn't I tell him to stop?

His fingers grazed the top of my panties, pushing lower beneath the lip of my jeans. I tried to squeeze my legs together, to say *no*, but I couldn't.

His mouth pressed against mine and I gagged. When he pulled back, I saw his eyes were ringed in halos of glowing green.

I remembered.

A broken cry echoed back to me from the stone.

No.

My heartbeat was a thunderous roar in my ears, blocking out Devin's next words as he struggled with removing my jeans. My limp body not cooperating.

The water bottle I'd been drinking from earlier was laying against the stone ground, and I saw something inside of it shimmer in the light. A trace of some other substance lacing the contents of the bottle.

My jeans came off and my feet slapped back down against the rock.

Devin's calloused hands wrapped around my knees, nudging them apart.

I screamed, but the sound that came out was a forced expulsion of air with no sound. My lungs didn't have the strength to produce sound.

I screamed again and again.

I kept screaming silently until my body began to wake from its drug addled slumber. Hard hands gripped my shoulders, shaking me.

A loud voice bellowed angry words in my ears. Shouted my name.

I inhaled sharply and the scent of birch and fire assaulted my senses. My body moved, jerking upright until my head connected with something hard and unyielding. I flopped back down, dazed for a second, but elated to find my wrist was free.

Kicking out, I scrambled to the right, and fell, landing in a heap against...against *wood*.

My fingers stroked the floor, and my hard breaths began to slow. Ahead of me there was a hearth. The fire I'd lit in it before bed was nothing but a pile of ash and near-dead ember now. I wasn't in the cave.

I wasn't with *him*.

Someone groaned behind me and I flipped onto my side, my fists clenching.

His hunched shape loomed over me like a shadow and a new scream lodged in my throat, but his dirty blond hair caught the moonlight streaming in through the window and I sagged.

"Jared?"

A loud *crack* and banging downstairs made me jump, my heart in my throat. Jared froze, glancing between me and my open bedroom door.

Running steps tore through the house and up the stairs.

Jared removed his hand from his face and straightened revealing a smear of blood over his lips and a painful looking crook in his nose. He moved in front of me just as the intruder appeared in the doorway.

Clay's massive body was heaving with animal breaths. His blue eyes were so bright they made the rest of his face indiscernible, casting it in shadow. When his eyes found me on the floor, he growled.

"What the fuck happened?" he demanded, gripping either side of the doorframe as if to keep himself from losing his shit. His fingers burrowed into the wood, adding more dents to the frame to join the ones I'd put there.

"Bad dream," Jared said, deflating when he recognized his friend in the hall. "Just a bad dream. I was trying to wake her up."

Clay was still trying to get control of himself. His mostly naked body rippled with flexed muscle. But his shoulders were slowly lowering. His breaths were evening out.

"You good?" he asked, this time directing the question to me.

I swallowed, nodding. "Yeah. Yeah, I'm good. I-I'm sorry, I didn't mean to wake you—"

"We're good here, man," Jared interrupted, bending to offer me his hand.

I took it and he helped me up. I went for the blanket on the bed and covered myself, wrapping it around my shoulders for warmth and to conceal my Naruto panties from their view.

Clay ripped his fingers away from the doorframe and walked away. A door down the hall opened and shut so hard I could feel the rattle beneath my toes in the floor.

Jared turned to the mirror in the corner of the room and bent to see into it. With a gag-worthy *snap* and a wince, he had his nose straightened, but as he turned, I saw a new drop of blood snaking a path down his chin.

"I'm *so* sorry," I said, still shivering from the cold and the nightmare Jared woke me from.

He was saying something—something about how it happened all the time and that he'd lost count how many times he'd broken his nose, but I wasn't hearing him. Not really.

I could still feel the press of Devin's fingers on my skin. I could still *smell* him.

It was just a dream. Just a dream.

But then why did it feel so *real?* Devin had drugged me. Who was to say he hadn't touched me?

Just because I didn't *feel* any different or...or... Oh god.

I ran for the bathroom, sliding onto my knees against the tile in front of the toilet to wretch bile into the porcelain bowl. I jerked at Jared's touch, but was grateful when the hair vanished from my face and he held it in a knot against my neck.

He said nothing as I brought up every last ounce of liquid in my stomach. It wasn't until I finally sat back against the wall that he released my hair and handed me a wet cloth, leaving only to return with a cup of cool water that he pressed into my other hand.

I cleaned out my mouth, so spent from all the vomiting that I didn't have the energy to feel embarrassed. "I'm sorry you had to see that."

He shook his head. "Don't be."

He took the cup from me after I drained it and refilled it in the bathroom sink before placing it on the floor next to me. I pressed the cloth to the back of my neck and sighed as my pulse began to slow.

"Do you want to talk about it?"

His amber eyes watched me patiently from where he crouched next to the tub. I handed him the cloth and looked away. "You should get that blood off before it starts to crust."

He took the cloth and cleaned himself off, leaning to rest his back against the vanity. "It was him, wasn't it?"

My teeth clenched.

My non-denial was all the answer he needed.

"He's gone, Allie," Jared reminded me, brushing his hair away from his forehead. "He can't hurt you anymore."

"It's not that," I managed after a second. "It's...he drugged me, Jared. What if he—"

I cut myself off, not wanting to say it aloud. I didn't want to give any more credence to the thought. It was bad enough that he'd kidnapped me and chained me up. That he turned me into a beast and was going to try to force me to be his *mate*. I couldn't handle it if he also...

Jared's eyes widened and he was suddenly there, angry and pained. His eyes searching mine. When I met his gaze, he shook his head.

He pulled my hands into his and I shivered at the contact, wanting to pull away and melt into him all at the same time. "Hey," Jared said when I tried to look away, too sickened and ashamed to meet his stare. "That didn't happen."

"How do you know?" I whispered, angry tears burning at the corners of my eyes.

He gripped my hands, rubbing a thumb over the back of my right hand. "If you really need to know," Jared paused, gulping. "I would have scented him on you. His..."

I looked up, confused.

Jared's face twisted as he continued. "I would have scented his *seed* if he had..."

"Are you sure?"

I couldn't seem to get enough air into my lungs. My breaths were cut-off and my body still trembled.

"I'm sure. I'm *one hundred percent* sure."

A tear fell and then another. I squeezed Jared's hands back.

I didn't realize how badly I'd been worried that Devin violated me until now. Until Jared could tell me with certainty that he didn't. It didn't ease the disgust that he might have touched me. And if the dream was any proof, then I didn't doubt he had.

But he didn't do *that*.

And that was a small comfort.

Jared released me and turned on his knees to the tub. He twisted the knobs and water gushed into the drain. Once he had the shower started, he stood and held out both hands to me.

I stood, aware that when I'd rushed to the bathroom, the blanket had been discarded somewhere in the hallway and my Naruto panties were *clearly* visible. But he wasn't looking there. His eyes remained fixed on mine as he jerked his chin in the direction of the shower.

Steam rose from the slim gap in the curtain and suddenly I *longed* to scrub my body until at least five layers of skin came off. How did he always know exactly what I needed?

"I have to go soon," he said.

"Stay until I get out?" I blurted, surprising myself. I opened my mouth to correct myself. To tell him never mind, that he didn't have to stay. I'd be okay.

But Jared smiled and something in my belly flipped low and hard, spreading warmth all the way down to my toes at how his eyes lit from within.

"Okay," he said and turned away from me, trying to hide his grin. "But I have to leave by sunrise or my uncle will have my head."

He closed the door behind him, and I stepped into the shower, clothes and all, letting the hot water wash away the memory of the monster who tried to claim me.

JARED WAS SIPPING COFFEE BY THE WINDOW IN THE KITCHEN WHEN I went downstairs. I could smell the nutty aroma of it over the smell of their Irish Spring soap in the shower.

A gush of cool wind funneled into the cabin and I wrapped my arms around myself, finding the front door hanging precariously by its top hinge, leaning against the kitchen cupboard for support.

Only the screen door remained intact and I felt a bolt of dread in knowing that the damage was my fault. Clay must have assumed the door would be locked like I told him and didn't want to waste time fumbling with a key. I'd been screaming bloody murder upstairs. If the tables were reversed, I'd have broken it down, too.

"Hey," I said, grabbing myself a mug only to notice there was already one next to the coffee machine. Black—the way I liked it. "Is this for me?" I asked, even though it was pretty obvious.

Jared turned, leaning against the glass to watch me with a smirk playing at the corner of his mouth. His eyes traveled the length of me from toes to tip before he spoke. "No, it's for the other girl living upstairs."

"Very funny," I said as I scooped up the mug and joined him by the window, blowing over the surface of the coffee to make tiny black tidal waves before I took a sip.

"Why does it always taste better when you make it?" I whined, drinking down a larger gulp.

Jared just shook his head. "Are you feeling better?"

I nodded. "Yeah. Thank you. You really didn't have to stay, I was just..."

I was just *what*?

I really wasn't sure.

In that moment, I just knew I didn't want to be alone. And after Clay slammed his bedroom door behind him, not a peep had come out of his room. I doubted I would see him again until morning, or maybe not even until later today since I'd ruined his sleep. I certainly wasn't about to go knocking on his door for comfort.

"It's no problem. I didn't want to leave yet, anyway and the quarry stays pretty quiet at night. No one will even be there for a couple more hours."

He sipped his coffee and grimaced. "I think the cream's bad."

"Will you be coming back soon?" I hedged. "I can go pick up some fresh cream after school if you want."

The note of hopefulness in my voice was apparent even to my own ears, but Jared's frown dashed it away. "I don't know when I'll be back," he muttered, swirling his coffee. I could see little cream colored floaters in the brownish liquid. Ugh. "Hopefully soon."

There were dark circles under his eyes, I noticed. And as he tilted his face back into the wan light of pre- dawn, I could see just how tired he was. How stressed.

There were lines around his eyes and in between his brows that I didn't think I'd ever seen on him before.

"Come here," he said after a second, eyes fixing on something above the trees.

I set my coffee down on the little half-circle table and stood next to him. "Do you see that?" he asked, pointing upward, but I couldn't tell what he was showing me.

I shook my head.

Jared set down his mug next to mine and moved behind me, making my skin bristle as he moved in close, leaning down to my eye-level. Reaching around, he tilted my chin up and pointed again. This time, I was able to look down the clean line of his extended arm as though it was an arrow. And there, above the trees, cradled in the sky, was a little cluster of stars.

They were dim as the night began to turn to day, but with my new canine eyes, I could see them clearly. More clearly than I thought I ever could've even on the darkest of nights.

Jared flicked off the oven-light behind him, plunging us into dark-ness, making the small constellation even brighter.

"It's called Aurus," he said.

I tilted my head to see it better, brushing against his cheek. I knew some constellations, but I didn't think I'd ever heard of that one. "I've never heard of it."

I felt more than saw him smile. "You wouldn't have.

It's not one of yours."

One of mine?

"What do you mean?"

"My people—*our people*—have been around a lot longer than the human race," he whispered against my ear. "My ancestors named the stars long before yours did."

"Do they have stories, too?"

"Lots. But most are a bit grim."

"Will you tell me about them sometime?"

I settled against Jared's chest, almost like my body had been slowly gravitating toward him this entire time. He stilled under my touch, but then tucked his chin against my shoulder and dropped his arm. "I'll tell you everything," he said in a low voice that made my toes curl. "Everything you want to know."

His heart beat steadily against my back and I allowed him to anchor me like he had at school that first day. His smooth birch and cedar scent filled my lungs and I let his strength wash over me, chasing away what remained of the shadows. His wolf snapped at the heels of my anxiety until it was only a distant whisper at the edge of my mind. My coiled muscles unspooled and I sighed.

"Do you want to go back to sleep?" he whispered. "No," I replied, my blood buzzing audibly in my ears. The low, rushing hum of it a sort of primal music. The truth was, I wanted to stay right there in his arms. I wanted to borrow his strength and relax in the security of his embrace. Whether it was just what my inner wolf wanted or some byproduct of the mating bond I never asked for, it felt *good*. And I could use some of that right now.

The first rays of sunlight poked up through the tops of the trees, like ribbons of rippling gold cast over dark waters.

Jared sighed. "I have to go."

He released me and I spun, my lips parting in silent protest.

"I'll come back to check on you," he offered. "As soon as I can."

"This weekend?" I asked, remembering my conversation with Clay before we each went our separate ways last night.

He cocked his head at me. "Why?"

"Clay," I said, watching Jared's jaw twitch at the name. "He suggested I should meet the pack. He wants to take me to them."

Jared's eyes darkened.

"I haven't decided yet. Do you think it's a good idea?

If I go, will you come too?"

He thought about it for a minute and then nodded. "It's not a half bad idea, actually."

I couldn't be sure, but I thought he was cursing himself for not having been the one to come up with the idea. He nodded to himself. "I'll go with you if you decide to go."

"Then I'll go," I said before I could change my mind.

I needed to see what I was getting myself into if I was ever going to be able to make a choice like the one I was being forced to make.

Jared smiled, something like pride in his gaze as he looked at me. "Okay. I'll arrange it."

"Okay."

There was a charge in the air as Jared looked between the door and back to me again. He stuffed his hands deep into his pockets and then took them out again, balling them to fists.

Just say goodbye, Allie.

"Bye Jar—"

He closed the short gap between us and cupped the back of my head, pressing his lips to the top of my forehead. A small sound hitched in my throat at the surprise and a warm tingle raced across the back of my neck where his fingers pressed against the sensitive skin there.

"Be safe."

His words rested in my ears and when I blinked, Jared was gone.

Movement caught my eye out the window, and I turned just in time to see him fade into the forest at the edge of the yard.

I lifted my hand to brush the spot where he'd kissed me, finding the ghost of his lips was still there.

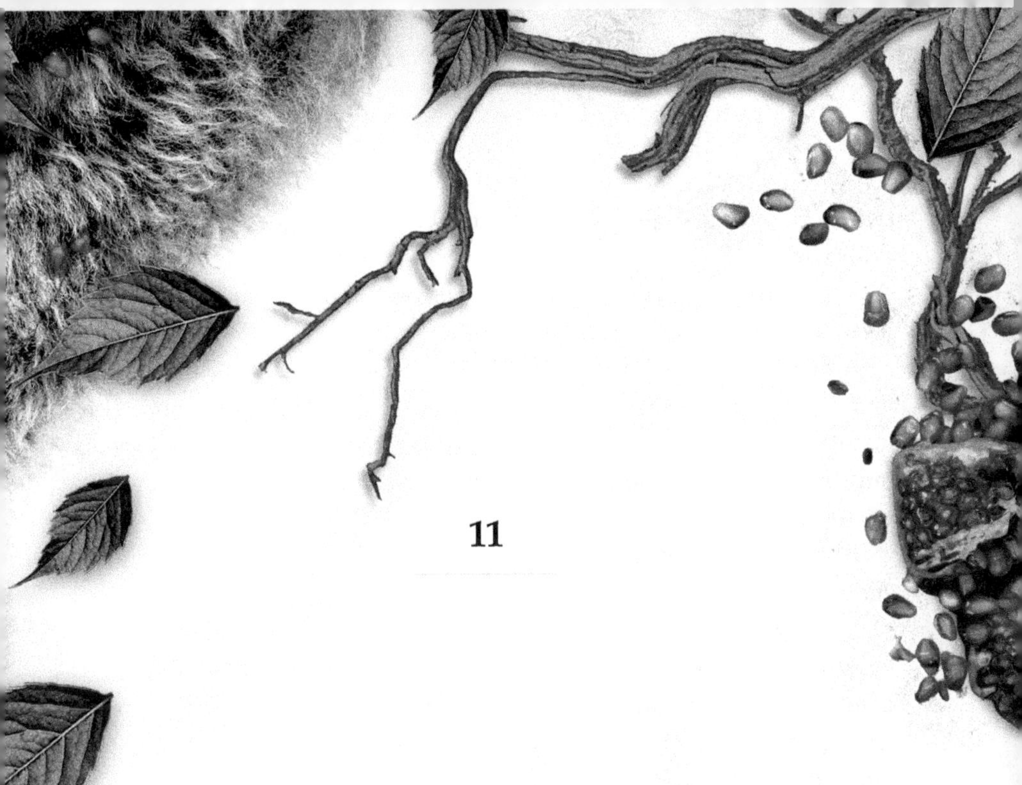

11

I wouldn't have time for a run anymore, but as I leaned back to look at my handiwork, I smiled. Having limited friends growing up and being an only child, I followed my Dad around like a barnacle on his haul.

Bike needed a tune up? I was there, passing him the ratchet.

Dinner caught fire on the stove? I was there, pulling the pin out of the fire extinguisher.

Busted door? I was there, holding it steady while he screwed in the new hinge-plate.

Jared and Clay's door wouldn't lock anymore. Not since the hard bar of metal broke through the wall and the door frame when Clay kicked it in. I couldn't even reuse the locking mechanism and bore out a new hole because he'd bent it beyond recognition. But with some stolen tools from his shop around back, I was able to make it at least close for now.

I'd stop by the hardware store and get a new lock later today. I'd install it before bed.

Placing the tools and extra screws back into the box at my feet, I rose and went to the sink to wash up.

A stair creaked behind me. I didn't turn. I knew it was Clay. How the hell he'd made it out of his room and down the hall without my hearing was a mystery. I swore he must be hollow inside. There was no way a two-hundred-plus pound giant could be so goddamned quiet otherwise.

One of these days he'd be the reason I dropped dead from a heart attack.

I finished getting the rest of the grit from beneath my fingernails and turned off the water, turning to lean against the countertop with unease rumbling in my belly. I hadn't exactly *asked* to borrow his tools, but I was hoping he would be happy to have one less thing to do today when he saw the fixed door.

When I gathered the courage to look him in the eye, my lips tightened into a frown. Maybe I'd been wrong.

Clay stood, with a shirt on for once, at the bottom of the stairs. The light blue color of the tee was so different from his usual all black and denim look that it caught me off guard. It made his eyes seem impossibly blue and his hair even richer in color. The way it offset his tan didn't hurt either.

But as ridiculously good looking as Clay Armstrong was, right now he looked like he was priming to kick the door down all over again. His fists were white knuckles at his sides. Veins coiled up to the creases in his elbows. His wide jaw was set, and his lips pressed into a firm line.

"Did you do this?"

His icy stare flicked to the toolbox and up to meet my stare before flitting away, his face reddening.

"I-I'm sorry for touching your tools, I just couldn't go back to sleep, and it was something to do—"

"You didn't have to—"

"I did."

Clay clamped his mouth shut and some of the tension in his expression eased. The redness in his cheeks faded.

"I'll grab a new lock from the hardware store later. Do you have a spade bit to drill out a new hole for the latch? Or do you just want to get a whole new—"

"You've done enough," Clay snapped and then unclenched his fists, wiping a hand over the stubble on his chin. "Let me worry about it."

"But—"

He gave me a hard look and I knew it was time to shut up and stop arguing. I nodded once to tell him I understood and dried my hands on the dish towel next to the sink. My hair was still a ratty mess from not brushing it after last night and I thought I should probably put some concealer under my eyes today if I looked as exhausted as I felt.

Clay went over to inspect the door and grunted his approval as he ran a finger over the hinges, including the new one I'd installed in the middle to give it a little more support. I'd also found some leftover weatherstripping and used it to repair the piece that'd come loose at the bottom of the door.

He lifted Jared's keys from their hook by the door and tossed them to me. I almost dropped them but managed to catch the ring on my pinkie finger.

I cocked my head at him.

"You can drive, today," he said without looking at me.

"But I don't have my license."

The fact that I also *couldn't drive* was implied.

He shrugged. "Drive us to the edge of town. I'll take it from there. How are you going to learn if you don't practice?"

I chewed my lower lip, picturing all the different ways I could damage Jared's Jeep from here to the edge of town.

"You working today?" he asked. "No. Not until tomorrow."

He grunted. "Good. Then we'll go get your learner's permit after school."

Confused, all I could do was stand there with my mouth slightly ajar and my eyes wide as I stared at him.

Clay craned his neck to one side to raise a brow at me. "Is there something on my face?" he asked gruffly, but I could see the hint of a self-assured smirk on the corner of his mouth.

Prick.

"Fine," I said finally, heading for the stairs. He wanted to put me behind the wheel of a car as jacked up and muscled as Jared's Jeep, then fine. It was his funeral.

I hid my smile as I bounded up the steps and called back, "But I hope you're as durable as you look."

After a quick crash course on which pedal did what and how to properly ease up on the clutch while alternately pressing on the gas, we were off.

I stalled it four times trying to reverse before Clay offered to back us out of the parking area and point us forward onto the road. Strangely, he didn't seem at all flustered or annoyed that I couldn't seem to get it like I thought he would be.

He gave me clear instructions and repeated himself each time I failed.

The only reason he took over for a second was because if he didn't, I was going to be late for my first class.

But how well he was handling my complete inability to figure it out was at completely odds with how *I* was handling it.

My teeth ground together as I rolled to a stop at the entrance to the trail, flicking the blinker to go right, toward town. I cursed when the Jeep stalled *again,* shaking as it rumbled to a sputtering stop. The fact that Clay was squished into the cab beside me, sending warning bells blaring and little fluttery sensations skittering beneath my skin wasn't fucking helping.

How the *hell* was I supposed to focus?

A lick of heat snaked up my neck, warming my cheeks.

"You *did* use to ride bikes, right? That wasn't bullshit?"

I glared at Clay.

"It's not the same," I bit out.

He put his hands up in mock surrender.

"Besides," I added, trying to get control of my anger. My wolf was starting to get edgy from my frustration and I doubted Jared's Jeep would survive me shifting while buckled into his drivers' seat. "It's been a while."

I started the Jeep for what felt like the millionth time, trying hard to focus on putting *just* the right amount of pressure on the pedals as I looked both ways and made the sharp turn onto the road.

I smoothly shifted from first to second and then from second to third, sighing as the Jeep cruised down the long and straight back road leading toward town. Now it was just a matter of staying inside the lines. I wouldn't worry about downshifting for another few miles until we were closer to the last turn before the tree-covered Forest Grove population sign came into view on the shoulder.

"I have an older bike," Clay said, his eyes fixed on the road. "It's about your size."

My heart gave a little pang and the Jeep slowed before I realized I'd eased up on the pedal and gave it a more insistent push.

"You could use it," he said. "If you wanted." My throat went dry. I wanted to.

I *really* wanted to.

I missed riding more than I could say, but... "I only ever rode with my Dad," I found myself saying, the words trailing off, leaving Clay to take from them what he would.

I glanced at him from the corner of my eye and saw his head bow. "Well, when you're ready then. I'll hold on to the bike in case you change your mind."

My brain cramped trying to make sense of Clayton Armstrong. How could he be such an asshole and so...*kind* at the same time? How could he be so intimidating but also so...*not.*

How is it that I can want to punch him while also wondering what his stubble would feel like beneath my fingers?

"Allie," Clay's shout brought me back to the present and I swerved back between the lines, pulling the tires away from the crunch of gravel that almost led us into the ditch.

"Shit," I cursed, hands tightening on the wheel. "Sorry."

"Allie, speed up."

"What?"

I was still on edge from almost putting us in the ditch, but something in Clay's tone made my wolf stir and a stone drop in my belly.

His eyes were glowing like blue flame, fixed on something out the window. A blur of light gray blinked in and out between the trees at the side of the road. An animal.

A wolf.

"Clay," I croaked nervously. "Who is that?"

I struggled to keep my eyes on the road, watching for the wolf blur into and out of focus and worried Clay might burst out of his skin at any second.

"Clay!"

"I don't know. *Drive faster.*"

I did as he said, panic lodging like a cork in my throat as I pushed the Jeep from thirty to sixty.

"Don't move your foot off the gas," Clay barked and before I realized what he was doing, he had the center console pushed up and out of the way and was sliding toward me.

My seat belt came undone and his hands lifted me at the waist. I yelped, accidently letting off the gas.

"Don't stop."

The seat fell back as he adjusted its position for him to fit. If he wasn't holding me up, my foot would've completely come off the pedal.

Spice and engine grease filled my senses as Clay positioned himself under me in the driver's seat and reached for the wheel with his left hand.

I felt his foot nudge mine on the gas pedal. "Move over," he ordered.

Using the dash to stabilize myself, I shifted from his lap and into the passenger seat and Clay punched the gas, shooting us down the road at a speed that had my stomach pressing flat against my spine as I fumbled to buckle myself back in.

"What's going on?" I demanded, peering outside to try to find the gray shape in the trees again. I couldn't see it, but that didn't mean it wasn't there.

When Clay didn't answer, I shoved his arm, trying to get his attention. "What do they want?"

"They aren't pack," he hissed. "They're trespassing."

And they were following us.

Following *me.*

My wolf ached to chase. To bite. To *maim.*

I bent and put my head between my knees, getting control of my breaths and fisting the hair at my scalp so I had something to focus on other than the urge to shift. "It's okay, Allie," Clay said, surprising me with the tenderness of his tone. "We're almost there."

The Jeep jerked to one side and I sat up, thinking something had hit us, but Clay had just taken the corner too sharply and the tires bumped to get a grip on the blacktop.

He visibly relaxed once we were off the mostly barren back road and onto the main roads of town. There were people here. Kids walking to school. Their parents rushing to work. A post woman stuffing a mailbox with junk fliers and bills.

"Sorry," Clay said. "Didn't mean to freak you out." My heart was still hammering behind my ribcage,

but watching the normal people go about their normal morning routines outside the windows, like an animal looking through plate glass, brought me a measure of calm.

I wanted to laugh.

Him freak me out. No, it was the goddamned bear- sized wolf chasing us down the road that freaked me out.

A short bubble of laughter escaped my mouth, and another followed it.

"Allie, are you okay?"

"I don't know, am I?" I managed between fits of laughter that were starting to turn into something dangerously close to tears.

I'm going insane.

And the look on Clay's face told me he thought so, too.

By the time we pulled into the school lot, I had control of myself— for the most part, anyway. The adrenaline had dissipated, leaving me bone-weary and a little shaky. I wondered if I could get away with napping in class if I set my textbook at just the right angle.

When I jumped out of the Jeep, Clay was already there, waiting outside the door for me.

I surveyed the lot, finding more than one set of eyes peering curiously at the massive former student. Thankfully, their curious looks hadn't extended to me yet. "Clay," I warned between clenched teeth, trying to keep my voice low. "Get back in the Jeep."

I shouldered my pack and headed for the door. Clay followed on my heels.

I spun. "What are you doing?"

A muscle in his jaw twitched. "I'm walking you inside."

"No, you're not."

He tilted his head, a challenge in his gaze.

I stared right back. The whispers about me and Jared Stone were enough to deal with. I didn't need people asking questions or making up gossipy stories about why Clayton fucking Armstrong was *walking me to class.*

"Not a fucking chance," I hissed.

Clay scowled, but when I took a backward step, he didn't immediately follow. "Fine," he said. "Go straight inside and stay there until I pick you up. I'll find out who that was... *Got it?*"

An inner light flared beneath his irises for an instant before it faded.

Both me and my inner wolf agreed that we didn't like him trying to tell us what to do. Both of us had our lips curled back, a rumble vibrating behind our breastbone.

"Got it," I begrudgingly replied, eager to end the conversation so I could escape before the lot filled with even more students rushing to make the first bell.

When I looked back over my shoulder as the heavy steel door shut on my heels, I found the Jeep still parked in the same space and the parking lot. Short one tall, broad shouldered guy.

Where the fuck did he go?

Something blue caught the wind at the edge of the lot that backed onto the cross-country running trail. Clay's t-shirt caught in a low branch, flapping like a flag in the chilly autumn breeze.

My breath caught as I remembered the lithe animal matching our pace through the trees at the side of the road. There had only been one, right?

But it was a *big* fucker.

And if it wasn't part of the Forest Grove pack. "*Idiot,*" I hissed.

Why would he go out there after it alone?

My wolf itched to follow. The flapping blue swath of fabric like a matador's red cape, drawing her to charge.

I tore my eyes away and dug out my phone, sloppily thumbing through contacts until I found Jared's name. I punched it and brought the phone to my ear, wordlessly grumbling to myself as I cursed Clay for making me be the one to rat him out. It was either this or go after him myself and I doubted I'd survive the latter.

If the wolf chasing us didn't kill me, I was sure Clay would.

Jared answered on the third ring. "Allie? Is everything okay?"

"Define *okay.*"

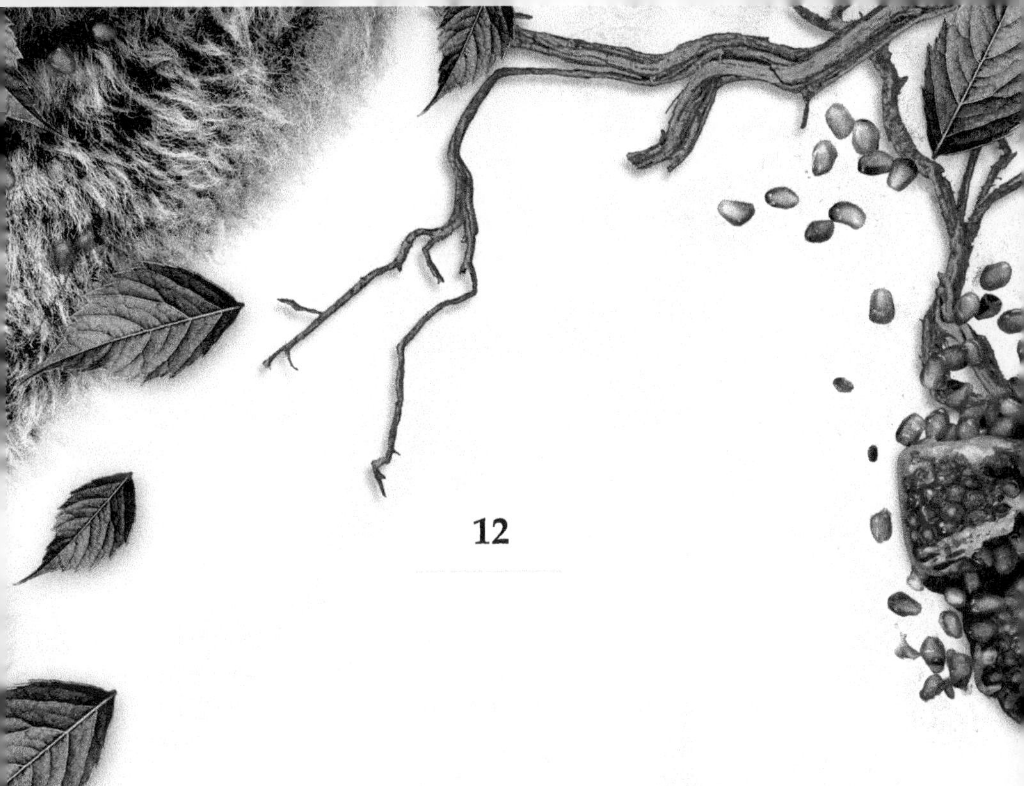

12

They weren't answering.

I'd texted Clay right after I got off the phone with Jared. And I'd texted Jared after an hour of not hearing back from Clay or getting the callback Jared promised.

When I called them both between classes both of their phones went to voicemail. I was giving them until lunch to get back to me before I would allow myself to freak out.

They can't very well answer their phones in their wolf forms, I rationed. And in Clay's case, I had to assume that was why he wasn't answering. His discarded shirt was proof of his intent to shift.

And Jared...well, he was working at the quarry.

Overseeing deliveries and whatever the hell else he was supposed to be doing there to help his uncle run the place.

He was busy. I couldn't expect him to be available every second.

I just needed to breathe. That's all. Just chill the fuck out.

They're fine. It's all fine. *Fine.*

But the minutes were ticking away towards lunchtime and with each slice of time cut away, another crack formed in my resolve. At this rate, my wolf would stop cooperating before the end of the day *for sure.*

Strangely, though, I found reassurances helped. Instead of fighting

295

against her and trying to force her into obedience, my own internal monolog of reassurances seemed to calm her, too.

I spoke to her as though she could hear me. Telling her—and in a way, *myself,* at the same time—that everything was alright, and I was just being overly paranoid.

It felt like it was working, so I kept it up all through first and second period. I focused on the driver's handbook I had concealed behind my textbook, inhaling page after page of information in between self-reas-surances.

I doubted Clay still wanted to take me to get my learner's permit after what happened this morning. And after I'd snapped at him. But if he did, then I wasn't about to waste his time by failing the test.

By the time the lunch bell rang, and I still hadn't heard from either Jared nor Clay, I was able to handle it without totally freaking. I dumped my books in my locker and checked my phone again, grimacing when it flashed with my lock screen picture—a photo of Layla and Viv and me two years ago, before everything fell apart—not a single notification superimposed over the image.

Unruffled, I tucked it back into my pocket and scanned the crowd of students for Viv's tall blond head above the others. I couldn't see her yet and wondered if they were already in the cafeteria.

A pair of light gray eyes met mine from down the hall. They belonged to a girl with a mess of dark purple hair piled in a knot at the top of her head. She held her arms folded over her chest and her expres-sion was one of open disdain.

I knew right away she wasn't human.

I didn't understand why, but there was this *otherness* around her like an aura. Invisible to the eye but I could feel it. Sense it.

Or maybe it was my wolf that could sense it.

A circle hoop of silver in her nose twitched as she smirked, turning away to leave the corridor and head into the main atrium.

She didn't go to school here; I knew that much. I'd never seen her before. That hair would be hard to miss.

"Sorry," I muttered as I shouldered past a gaggle of girls blocking the way and almost tripped over Trip Thompson's gym bag.

He called something after me, but I didn't hear him, I was already in the atrium, whirling as I scanned the area.

She was by the doors, waiting.

When our eyes locked, she pushed open the door and stepped out.

Clay's warning made me pause, but if they were getting ballsy enough to come and approach me at school then I had to do something about it, right?

Jared isn't here to stand up for you, Allie. Clay's already busy with another one.

I'd have to handle this one myself. I shoved the door open and cool air stung my hot cheeks.

"Allie, right?" The girl asked, and I found her just outside, several feet away from the doorway, but still in plain view of the front parking lot where there were other people and teachers getting things from their cars and driving past for their afternoon Starbucks run.

At least we weren't alone.

Easy, girl, I whispered to my wolf as she readied to force her way out if necessary. *We're safe.*

"And you are?"

She smiled. It wasn't a kind smile. "Call me a concerned pack member."

"Okay *concerned pack member*," I said, spitting her words back at her, struggling to smother my rising temper. "Why are you here?"

She narrowed her gray eyes at me as though she could see inside my soul and read what was written there. It unnerved me enough that I took a step back.

She laughed. "A bit skittish, aren't you? I don't know why Ryland doesn't just make you leave. Save us all the trouble. Samson's pack can have you as far as I'm concerned."

Samson?

"Wait," I said, reminded of the other wolf from this morning. The gray wolf in the woods. "Did you follow us this morning?"

She tilted her head to one side and gave a little forced laugh. "Follow you? Why would I follow you?"

No, it couldn't have been her. She said she was a concerned pack member. She was part of the Forest Grove pack. Ryland's pack. And Clay had said that the wolf in the woods was *not* pack.

The girl narrowed her gaze at me again, stepping in close so I met her steely gaze.

Before Layla and I became good friends, she always said my grayish colored eyes were unnerving. Now, looking into the heated gray eyes of this perfect stranger, I thought I might know what she meant.

When they caught the light, they almost looked see- through.

This time, I didn't balk at her approach. She called me a coward once, I wouldn't give her a reason to do it again. I was *not* a coward.

"The one who was following you," she hissed, her gaze shifting between my eyes. "Wolf or human?"

"Wolf."

"Not pack?"

"Not your pack."

She cursed. "I have to tell Ryland," she started, pulling out her phone. "When was this? What did they look like? Where—"

"Clay went after it," I told her, suddenly exhausted with this conversation. "And I already called Jared, so Ryland probably knows by now."

She squinted at me. "Not as stupid as you look then," she amended, staggering back a step, but keeping her cell phone in her hand.

"If you're done now," I began, turning away from her. "I think I'll go eat my lunch."

"Just choose," the purple-haired girl said, her expression fierce. "I don't know why they're all so interested in you—so you have two tails, *whoop-dee-do*—but they *are*. And now everyone seems to think your will is crazy strong, too, which, honestly? By the look of you, I seriously doubt that."

She was rambling and I had trouble keeping up. I was about to ask her what the hell this *will* business was everyone seemed to be talking about, but the door banged open and Vivian appeared outside.

She found me and glanced between the girl who was only a few inches away from my face and back to me.

Vivian put her lacrosse face on. The one that made the girls on opposing teams get the fuck out of the way when she made a run. I was tempted to put myself between the stranger and my friend, knowing Vivian was really no match for the other girl, even if she was half a head shorter and leaner than my best friend.

"You don't go here," Vivian said, eyeing the girl. The girl eyed Viv right back.

"Allie, do you know her?" I shook my head. "Nope."

Grabbing Viv in the crook of her elbow, I tugged her in the opposite direction, back toward the door. "Come on, Viv, I'm starving."

But Viv was still staring curiously at the girl.

I wondered if *Viv* recognized her for a second, but then the girl dragged her unnerving eyes over my friend again, this time, lingering over her with her bottom lip caught between her teeth.

Viv stiffened as though she was just jabbed with a hot poker.

"See you around," the girl called back to us as she walked away.

"Viv, come on," I urged, trying to jar her out of whatever was holding her in place.

"You sure you didn't know her?"

"Positive."

Something in Vivian's face hardened and I punched her shoulder just as Stella Baker pulled into the lot in her shiny red Volkswagen beetle, trying to bring her back to the present. "Punch buggy no punch backs!" I squealed, bounding away from her and into the school as she glared at me.

"What are you, twelve?" she groaned, but as she followed me inside, Vivian peered back over her shoulder one last time, her face flushing with something I couldn't name as she searched for the girl.

"So, are you guys, like, an item now?" Viv drawled at the lunch table, her unimpressed stare taking in Layla and Quinn practically on top of one another on the other side of the table.

Beneath the table, I had my phone out, texting Jared *again*.

Allie: Is everything alright? I haven't heard back from you since this morning and I'm starting to panic. Can you just answer this as soon as you get it? Please.

Right after I hit send, I realized I should probably mention something about the girl who came to ambush me at school, but I didn't want to worry him. Instead, I flicked over to Clay in my contacts and typed out another message.

Allie: Are you okay?

I deleted the message before sending it. I didn't want to sound, how did that girl put it? *Skittish.*

Allie: Text me back when you get this.

There. Now when he texted me, I would know he was okay and I could just say...well, I would figure that out later.

"You in, Allie?" Viv asked, staring daggers at me.

I set my phone face down on the table and winced. "Sorry, what are we talking about?"

"My birthday," Layla chimed in. "Viv wants to have a girl's night."

"But your birthday isn't until next week."

Layla adjusted herself on the bench and as she did, I noticed Quinn's hand wrapped around hers beneath the table. She flushed when she saw me looking and let go.

Layla pushed her hair back from her face, brushing it behind her ear. "Yeah, but you know how my parents are. They want to do the big family thing."

Viv locked her arms over her chest and leaned back in her chair. "So we're going to celebrate *this* weekend. Besides, her birthday is on Tuesday so it's closer to this weekend than it is to *next* weekend," she said pointedly. I bristled but managed to calm myself with my hands wrapped around the base of the bench seat, pressing my fingers into the hard, cold metal. The truth was, I'd forgotten all about Layla's birthday.

We mentioned doing something together a few times last month, but we hadn't really talked about it since.

"Don't you want to go into the city or something?" I asked. "We could plan something for later in the month. Maybe hit up that new arcade that has the laser tag and go karts that you were talking about."

"Actually," Quinn butted in. "I already took her to that. Last weekend."

Layla blushed.

I had just been trying to put it off a bit longer. My wolf had tamed some since I let her out, but the pressure of her would build again. I could already feel her growing restless by the hour. I needed more time.

"Of course, you did," Viv rolled her eyes at Quinn. "Well, Al? You in? Or do you already have plans?"

I told Jared I'd go meet the pack, but...this was more important.

This was Layla. And Viv.

The two reasons I wouldn't be easily forced out of my hometown. My family.

I could shift again before the weekend. For them. I gulped. "Of course, I'm in."

Viv grinned and I saw some of the tension leave her shoulders. "Good," she said. "We're watching that movie La La loves that always makes her cry. That Fault Line Stars one or whatever it's called."

I suppressed a laugh. "Oh, you cried too. Admit it." She looked away, brows drawing together. "*Never*."

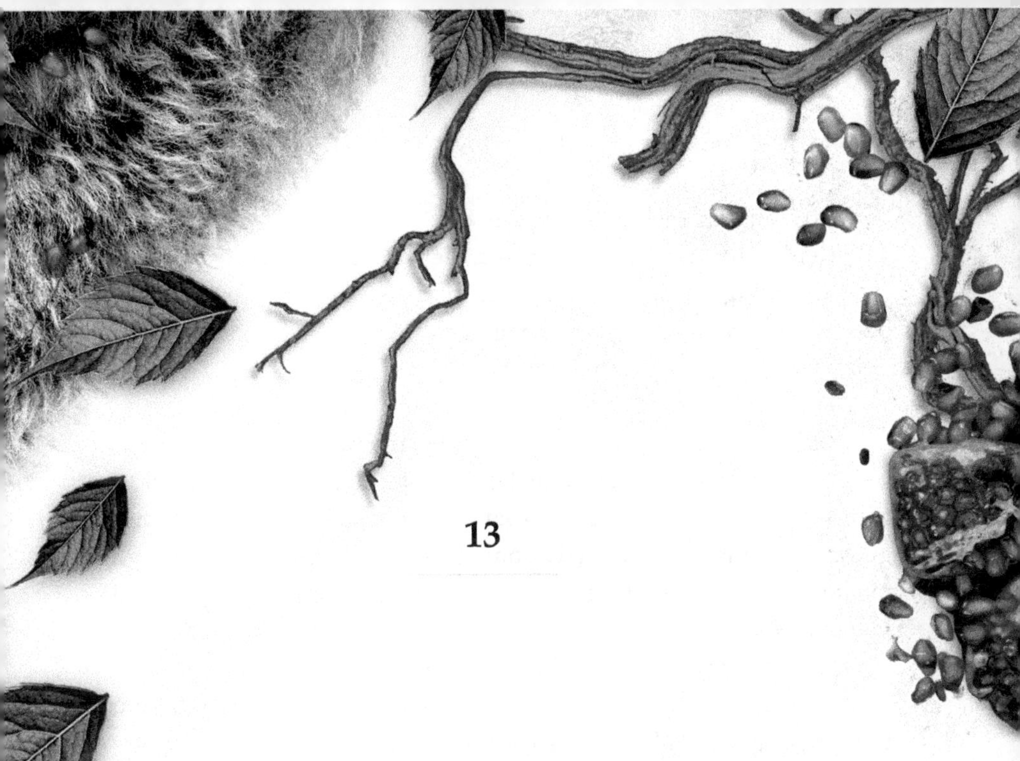

13

Clay stood outside the Jeep, leaning against the driver's side door in a pair of aviator shades like he didn't have a care in the world. He flicked a bit of dirt from beneath his fingernail and looked up, finding me rushing out with the rest of the students after last bell.

The first thing that hit me was a wave of spine- tingling relief, the second was fury.

"What the *hell* Clay?" I demanded in a harsh whisper when I was close enough that no one else would hear. "Where did you go?"

The mirrored lenses shielded his eyes so I couldn't tell if his lips were parting in surprise or disdain.

"I've texted you like five times."

"I don't have my phone."

"What happened?"

He jerked his head toward the Jeep and opened the driver's side door, lifting himself into the seat with a hand curled around the roof. He'd changed. That, I noticed.

He wasn't wearing the same jeans and t-shirt he had been earlier. Now he was in a black muscle shirt that made me want to avert my eyes and drool at the same time. Why did he have to flex his arms like that? Wasn't he cold?

Could he wear a fucking jacket like the rest of the world did in fall?

303

Between him and Jared, I was *fucked.*

"Get in," he said. "We can talk on the way to the DMV."

Grumbling, I made my way over to the passenger side, scooting the door closed and ducking low when I saw Viv and Layla exiting the main doors with Quinn in tow behind them.

"Fuck," I cursed. "Can you hurry please?"

I did *not* need to have to explain this to them, too.

Clay smirked as he drove us from the lot. I didn't sit up until I was sure we were far enough away that no one would see me. But I had to guess the damage was already done. Someone would have seen. Which meant that Viv would find out one way or another and there would be hell to pay.

I groaned, pressing my palms into my eyes.

"Does it get any easier?" I asked, more for myself than because I thought Clay would have the answers.

"Lying to your friends?"

I moved my palms to look at him from the corner of my eye, studying his stoic profile. "No," he said. "It doesn't. Which is why I stuck with Jared after I left school. Relationships with humans are—" he seemed to be searching for the right word. I didn't think I wanted to hear it. "*Difficult,*" he decided, finally, giving me a tight-lipped frown.

My stomach turned and I wanted to lash out at him for dashing what little hope I had. But what did he know? He was bitter and...and... *mean.* Maybe it would be difficult, but you didn't turn your back on family just because it was *difficult.*

"So," I said after a few miles of silence stretched between us with me scanning the trees for the wolf that had been chasing us this morning. There was no sign of anything out there at all. The only movement the occasional leaf falling to desiccate with its relatives on the forest floor. "Are you going to tell me what happened this morning?"

Clay snorted. "Haven't you spoken to Jared?"

I pursed my lips. "No. He isn't answering my calls, either."

Clay shrugged. "I wasn't able to catch him. He was definitely from another pack, though. Not an alpha. A scout."

"A scout?"

"Probably sent here to see if the rumors were true about you."

"Why?"

Clay's grip tightened on the wheel. "Don't worry about it. It's being handled."

"Clay," his name came out through clenched teeth, my anger rising again.

Clay reached for the radio and flicked it on, turning up the volume. A song I knew only because Devin used to like it blared to life through the speakers. I punched the power button.

I glared at Clay.

He sighed. "The only reason an alpha would send a scout would be to see if it was worth it for them to breach our territory. A scout or a low in rank pack member on our lands is a nuisance. We kick them out, give them a warning not to come back, and it's done," he paused. "But an alpha on our lands is different. If an alpha from another pack steps foot in or around Forest Grove without permission, it's not just a nuisance—it's a direct challenge."

I wanted him to explain more, but Clay put the Jeep in park in front of the DMV and nodded to the building in front of us. "DMV's closing soon," he said, reaching over me to push open my door. He was kicking me out. "Better hurry."

My phone buzzed as I entered, but I didn't bother checking it. Clay was right. If I was even going to finish the damned test before they closed, I needed to get signed in. And I didn't spend all afternoon studying for nothing.

I walked up to the counter and told the lady what I was there for, providing a form from school that had my *incorrect* address on it and a photocopy of my birth certificate I'd printed from my documents folder in the computer lab during Geography class.

"Allie?" The woman behind the counter asked.

I nodded, pulling out my debit card to pay the testing fee with a wince when I saw the amount on the screen.

"No need for that," the woman said, holding up a hand at my raised debit card. "It's already been taken care of for you."

My stomach dropped.

I stuffed the card back into the zippered pocket of my bag and pasted on a smile for the woman as she entered the information from my documents on the computer. "I'm sorry," I said, clearing my throat. "But who paid for this?"

The woman looked at me curiously, but grinned. She pointed past me out the window at the white Jeep parked in the lot right out front. "That young man came in about an hour ago to pay in advance for your test."

When I didn't answer, too stunned to form words, the woman gave a little laugh and waved me toward a cordoned off testing area. "Good luck," she called as another woman herded me to a desk and set a slim stack of paper in front of me and handed me a pencil. She was saying something, but I wasn't hearing her, all I kept thinking was *that mother fucker...*

THE SLIP OF PAPER CLUTCHED BETWEEN MY FINGERS WHEN I EXITED THE building was almost enough to make me forget I was pissed at Clay. He was waiting outside of the Jeep with a smug look on his face, the keys dangling from his index finger. "On the first try?" he asked. "I'm impressed."

I swiped the keys from him and resisted the urge to shove him out of the way. "I'm paying you back for that I hope you know," I said instead as he sidled to the other side of the Jeep, rocking the whole vehicle with his weight as he got in.

Clay just grunted and buckled his seatbelt, curling his other hand around the holy shit handle above the window.

"I'm not a charity case," I added as I started the Jeep, feeling like the message hadn't fully sunken in.

"I mean it," I said, pausing with my hand on the gearshift to stare at him.

Clay finally rolled his head to look at me. "I *know* you're not a charity case," he said. "It was my way of saying thank you—for fixing the door. That's all."

My lips pursed, but I nodded.

"Thank you," I ground out, realizing a little belatedly that it was rude not to thank him regardless of how his misplaced charity made me feel. The truth was, I couldn't really afford it. The fee would have set me back at least a week of saving towards my goal of getting the apartment above the bookshop. "If you're sure, then—"

"Positive," he replied instantly, shuffling in his seat. "Now can we go?"

THE TWO OF US DIDN'T SPEAK MUCH ON THE WAY BACK TO THE CABIN OTHER than for me to ask if he'd heard from Jared. I was trying to figure out how to make a proper meal out of what we had left in the fridge at the house, since I'd forgotten to stop at the grocery store *again*.

I blamed Clay for that. He was distracting as hell.

And besides, I didn't want to drag him with me.

After I parked the Jeep, only having stalled it *once* on the way back to the trailhead, we set off for the walk through the trees. Somehow, I needed to ask Clay if he would help me out with another shift before the weekend. That meant I'd either have to do it tomorrow, or early Friday if I was going to feel confident enough to spend an entire evening among my mortal friends.

I also needed to tell him that I wouldn't be free to go to meet the pack until later in the day on Saturday. Viv always cooked a big breakfast spread when we did girls night and none of us usually left until well after lunch time.

"Clay," I began, ready to have the conversation now and get it out of the way so we could get back to our respective corners of the house and back to ignoring one another.

"Hmm?"

"I was wondering—"

We weren't even all the way back to the cabin when I caught a peculiar scent on the wind. I stilled, lifting my head to inhale it more deeply. The peppery aroma was distinct. I'd smelled it before. "Wait," I said, holding a hand out to Clay to stop him, too. "Do you smell that?"

Clay was immediately on the defensive, his thick muscle flexing as he too lifted his head and sniffed the southbound breeze. He relaxed a little after a second, but the tension around his eyes never eased. "It's Ryland," he said. "And Forrest."

My jaw tightened.

"It's okay," he said. "Just go inside when we get there. I'll deal with it."

I wanted to disagree, but I was still so out of my element with all of this. I didn't even know where to begin. And if Ryland still set me as much on edge as he did when I was still human, I wouldn't be able to keep my wolf from barging through.

"Okay," I said, swallowing to wet my throat as we pressed on. My phone buzzed in my pocket and I drew it out just as the cabin began to come into view. The cracked screen flashed to live with two missed calls and three text messages from Jared.

I thumbed through the texts, a stone dropping in my gut.

The first was a reassurance that he was fine and an apology for worrying me.

The second told me that there'd been a complication and he needed to talk to me right away. He asked me to call him back.

The third told me not to go home.

Shit. Why hadn't I checked my phone earlier when I felt it go off?

Reading the messages had made me lag behind Clay's long strides. I rushed to catch up, curling my hand around his forearm. He jerked as though I'd shocked him and stared down at me, reading my face. "What is it?"

"It's Jared," I said, holding the phone out for him to see, my heart hammering heavily in my chest. "He said not to—"

"Welcome home," the gruff voice interrupted and as one Clay and I glanced toward the cabin to find Ryland sitting on the top step of the porch. Forrest leaning against the post below. Ryland stood as he spoke. "We were just thinking about coming back another time. Glad we waited."

My fingers curled tightly around my phone and I lowered it from Clay's line of sight. I didn't realize my fingertips were also digging into the flexed muscles of Clay's arm until he removed my hand with his, giving it a tiny squeeze before dropping it. "Just go inside," he said in a low voice.

"No need for any of that," Ryland said, waving his hand as though to swat away a fly. He'd clearly heard Clay. "I'm just here to have a little chat. No reason to get all defensive."

Ryland stepped down onto the dirt lawn, making the steps creak and groan under his weight. I'd forgotten how big he was. Broader through the shoulders than even Clay. Taller, too. With shifty brown eyes and that scar running down through his left brow, puckering the skin on his stubbled cheek.

Clay was positively rigid, and his energy was contagious, setting me on edge. This was Clay's alpha. Jared's alpha.

So then why did I get the feeling that Clay didn't trust him. How could he have given his allegiance to a man—a beast—he didn't trust? How could either of them expect me to?

I rationalized that Ryland was sort of like a boss. He had to keep a large group of people that turned into wolves in line. I imagined that was a difficult job and would require a heavy hand at times. Ryland was just the shifter equivalent of a stern CEO.

Lots of employees feared their superiors. Nothing to get your panties in a knot for, Allie.

"Why are you here?" Clay asked up front, stopping several feet away from his alpha. I didn't miss the space he kept between them. I stayed with Clay, catching Forrest watching me from where he was still leaning against the post.

His square jaw twitched as he pushed off from the railing to stand with his beefy arms crossed over his chest.

Ryland met Clay's stare. "I've no doubt you've heard about the *problems* your mate's indecision have caused our pack."

Clay paled.

Ryland cut his gaze to me and I balked, unable to meet his deep brown eyes. My wolf's hackles raised. As I suspected, she was immediately on the defensive, making anger rise like steam in my core. I balled my hands into fists, digging my fingernails into my palms to keep myself steady.

I got the feeling shifting into a wolf right now would be a bad idea. Ryland was an alpha. From what I understood, you *did not* challenge an alpha. Not unless you wanted to die.

"There's still almost two weeks until the next moon," Clay growled.

Ryland never took his eyes off me. I didn't have to lift my head to see him staring, I could feel it. "And that's the problem."

"Ry," Clay began, his tone changing to one I didn't recognize. His alpha's name almost a plea.

I glanced up at Clay, surprised to find his expression pained. Tense.

I didn't like it. Not one fucking bit. My wolf didn't like it, either.

Ryland held up a hand to silence Clay. "I'm afraid we can't wait any longer. One of the pack was injured this morning trying to chase off one of Samson's pack from our lands. If Charity had been more gravely injured, I would've had no choice but to retaliate."

Ryland's gaze was back on me now, making my skin itch. "I know you don't understand the implications of your indecision," he said, and I gulped, finally gathering the courage to look him in the eyes.

When our gazes met, Ryland's brows lowered and his eyes narrowed, as though he recognized something in the gray hue of my stare. Something he didn't much like.

"Our race is a dying one," he explained. "The number of born wolves declines every year and it is forbidden to turn a human. The witch's council looks the other way for the most part, but if they are feeling particularly nosey, the offense is punishable by death. Effectively, if an Enduran bites and changes a human and it can be proven that it was *not* an accident, then that shifter will pay with their life. So, you see why a shifter who has not claimed her pack would be something of a commodity."

"Packs made up of mostly born wolves are *families*. Brothers. Sisters. Cousins and the like. You can understand how important it is to inject new bloodlines into packs to prevent..." he trailed off, thinking of the right word. "Inbreeding."

Ugh.

A low growl emanated from Clay's chest and I saw his eyes spark to light.

"She's *mated*," he hissed at Ryland.

"Which is why I don't understand why she hasn't simply agreed to submit herself to my rule and become *pack*," Ryland spat, getting impatient.

My wolf battered against my resolve. She wanted to show him who should be the one submitting.

"She needs more time," Clay demanded.

"She needs to speak for herself," Ryland seethed at Clay before turning his hard stare back at me. I had to physically resist the animal urge to growl at him. My upper lip twitched, wanting to curl back over my human teeth. My nostrils flared as I inhaled deeply.

"I don't want to leave Forest Grove," I managed, giving myself a mental pat on the back for not sounding as angry or as afraid as I did inside.

Ryland stepped in closer to me and Clay, stopping only when he was so close I had to lift my face to meet his stare as he curled his massive body over me. "Is that your answer then?"

My mind raced. I wasn't ready to do this. Looking into Ryland's eyes, I knew I didn't *want* him to have that sort of power over me. I didn't want *anyone* to have that sort of power over me. And it seemed my wolf heartily agreed.

"No," I replied, my voice strangely steady. The tone thick with the animal quality of my wolf trying to get free.

Ryland's expression shifted. His dark brown eyes flickered with rage. "You can't have it both ways."

"I'm taking her to meet the pack," Clay said, shifting his stance so he was nearer to me, in reaching distance of Ryland. Forrest, who'd been still and silent until just now, moved in closer, putting himself on Ryland's right flank.

When Ryland didn't budge, refusing to back up off me, something in Clay's expression snapped. He clapped a hand hard onto Ryland's shoulder. "She isn't going to make a decision right—"

Ryland turned on Clay, knocking his hand away. His eyes glared vibrant orange and his jaw unhinged in a halfway shift. "Back," he growled at Clay and my mate bared his own teeth. And even though I could see how hard he struggled. Even though I could see the strain in his muscle as he fought against the command from his alpha, Clay fell back a step as though he'd been shoved by a physical force, bowing his head with a dark grimace.

My wolf roared.

Before I could stop it, my body splintered into a thousand pieces.

It fractured and bent and broke. But this time I didn't feel the pain. I hardly noticed it. The fury was white hot, and my wolf was stronger than I'd ever felt her. She forced herself to the surface in one great push and when she made the decision to take the reins, I didn't stop her. I didn't think I could've even if I'd tried.

No one would make Clay bow to them. Not in front of me.

Not while I could do something about it.

The other three humans in the yard shifted quickly. Their bodies exploding into their larger wolf counterparts. Clothes flew in the breeze and settled over the dirt like tattered flags.

I heard Clay's voice in my mind, but it was distant, my wolf wasn't listening. She was beyond hearing reason. She was fucking *pissed*.

Allie, Clay urged. *I can't help you. Back down. Back down!*

His growl made my wolf turn to him and snap at his ankle, surprising him enough that he backed up a step. The sounds coming out of my mouth were viscous. They scared even me.

Clay tried to put himself between Ryland and I, but Ryland gave him one look and pulled his canine lips back over his teeth, growling as drips of hot saliva fell from his exposed tongue. Clay's upper body bent under the pressure of his alpha's stare and he made a pained keening sound that made my wolf lose her fucking mind.

As though anticipating that I was about to attempt to rip Ryland's head off while he was busy with Clay, Forrest sped forward. He was a blur of dark fur and small glowing yellow eyes. He lunged for me, but I was faster, parrying to one side a fraction of a second before he'd have had me. My jaws found a hold on the back of his neck and I tossed him like a rag doll several feet away.

He scrambled to his feet and came for me again, this time taking up a warning stance, his eyes meeting mine in challenge. His growl was loud, but mine was louder, echoing in my ears.

My wolf raised her head, looking down at Forrest. She held his furious stare, digging her claws into the dirt, stamping them to assert her place. Forrest skidded back a step, his head bending lower until we were over him, *daring* him to touch us again.

He lay with his chest against the earth, still growling softly, but no longer a threat.

Allie, Clay's voice in my mind was different. Breathless. It was enough to break me out of the strange trance-like state that'd taken over. I backed away from Forrest, but he stayed down, his teeth still bared as he growled softly to himself.

When I turned, I found Clay in a similar position to Forrest...and Ryland, staring at me like he was only just seeing me for the first time.

My heart launched itself up my throat when my eyes locked with Ryland's. His hackles shot up in a ridge of black fur rippling down his spine. I was sure I looked the same. I could feel my skin shifting beneath my fur. Fluttering with anticipation. I shook as I approached him.

Somewhere, deep in the back of my mind, I was screaming for my wolf to back down now, too. Something told me she would not survive this. That if she openly challenged the alpha, she would lose.

We would die.

She wasn't listening though. She watched Ryland with a singular focus. Our body breathed tightly, conserving energy, restricting my urge to panic.

Trust me, she seemed to be saying. *Trust that we are stronger.*

But I'd never been strong. Not like this.

I could live in a hunting blind in the woods and withstand the cold. The elements. I could withstand the loneliness of my existence. The death of my parents. The abandonment of my guardians. But this was something else.

This would require a physical strength I didn't think I possessed in either of my forms.

Clay was still whispering pleas in my mind, but we blocked them out. We needed to focus.

We needed to show Ryland that he didn't own us.

He doesn't own me.

An image of Devin flashed before my eyes. His words came back, strengthening us instead of weakening us. *You are mine.*

It wasn't true then. It won't be true now.

We belong to no one.

Ryland snarled at me and a pressure formed in my chest. My head wanted to bend to the force of his will, and it took everything inside of me to fight the urge to lay flat against the earth and quiver in his shadow.

But we were done living in the shadows. We didn't want to bow.

And in a burst of clarity it was like me and my wolf were one. Just for a second. Just long enough for us to combine our strength and raise our weary head. A vibrating growl reverberated through our rib cage and we snapped back at Ryland when he snapped at us.

His voice *boomed* in our skull. *Concede!*

But we were gaining strength. Our muscles burned from fighting his command, but he was *not* our alpha. Not yet.

Ryland's ears lowered and his growls became lower. His glowing orange eyes were crazed with shock and fury. Any second now, he would attack. I could feel the threat of it like a pressure in the air. I could see how his body was coiling for the strike.

We were ready.

As we lifted our head to stare down at him, his body pressing slowly down toward the dirt, we had a fleeting moment of satisfaction. He'd bent to *our* will.

Ryland lunged before he fully submitted. His muscled form leaped from the earth only to be tackled by another body. A white streak against the bleak dusk. Jared sent Ryland sprawling onto the dirt. Their bodies skidded over loose gravel and debris, black and white bodies coming up smeared with swaths of earthy brown. Ryland snapped at Jared, missing his throat by barely a hair.

Jared was up in an instant, standing with his shoulders lowered and a fierce growl echoing all around us. He had positioned himself between Ryland and I, but I knew that with one word from Ryland, Jared would be rendered just as immobile as Clay was.

The dark gray wolf was panting with the effort of crawling his way over to me, attempting to break his alphas command to back down.

Forrest moved as though to sneak up on Jared from behind, but with a look from my wolf, he stopped, dropping his big head back to the dirt with an indignant snarl.

I couldn't hear them, but somehow my wolf knew Ryland and his nephew were having a conversation. It was agonizingly slow, but after a minute, I noticed some of the heat leave Ryland's eyes. And I noticed how Jared's body loosened, reverting back to the soft, gentle wolf that'd saved my life all those nights ago.

Ryland moved past Jared a moment later, ignoring me as though I wasn't even there. My wolf shivered with something like ecstasy. We knew why he wasn't looking at us. He was afraid.

And maybe he should be.

I was surprised at the malice seeping into my thoughts, poisoning my mind. As Ryland growled at Forrest to get him moving, I walked to where Jared was now standing next to Clay as his friend was finally able to pick himself up from the ground.

When Ryland was gone from view, I sighed inwardly, my sides heaving as my wolf let go. She was beyond exhausted and ready to hand back the reins. I slumped against Jared, and Clay, still panting, slumped against my other flank, resting his head on my back to stare at Jared.

As one, they both turned their attention to me, looking at me as though only just seeing me for the first time. Their emotions raged within them, spilling over until I could feel them pushing at my barriers.

Surprise. Pride.

Fear.

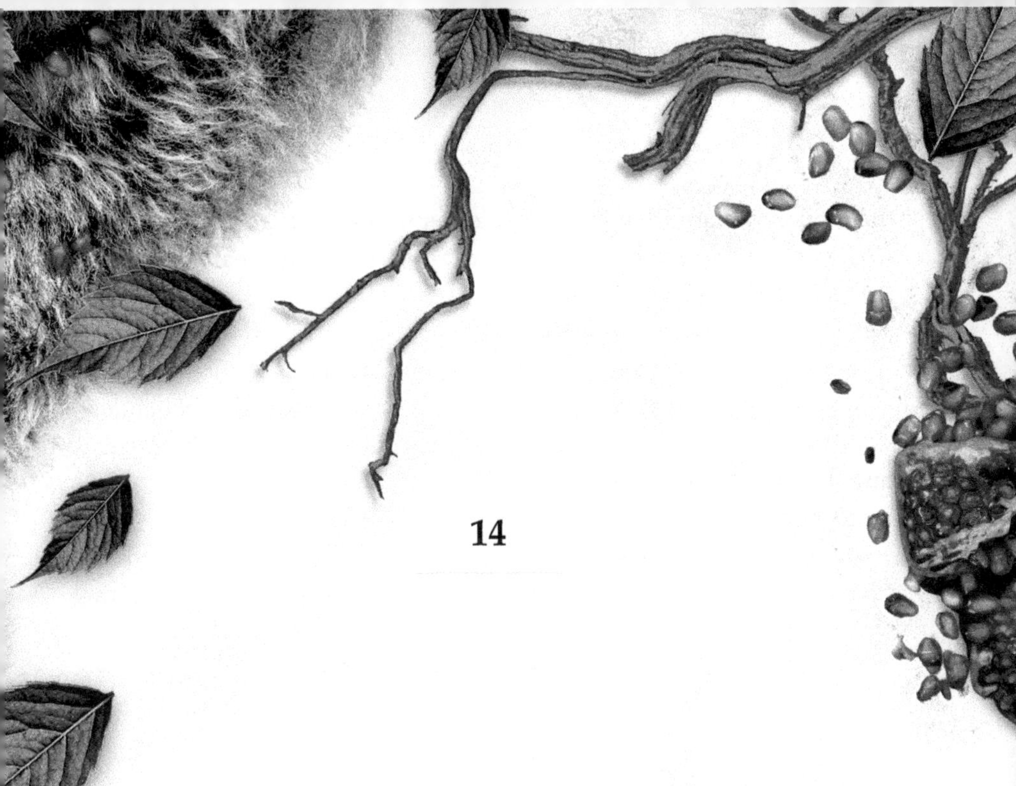

14

"Pretend it never happened."

That's what Jared told me after we'd all shifted back the other day. "Ryland definitely will, and if you don't—"

"Ryland will accept your challenge," Clay had finished for him. "A fight to the death. Winner takes the place of alpha."

Jared and Clay had been reeling and barely able to utter more than a few words to me for hours after we shifted back. Both of them had worn pinched faces as we sat together in the kitchen. Them in those infuriatingly low-hanging shorts they liked to throw on after a shift and me wrapped in a towel because all of my clothes were in the laundry.

They said it was impossible.

Muttered how there had *never* been a female alpha before. Not since before their people left the immortal land of Emeris and came to the mortal lands. And even then, there was only one known female alpha in the history of their race.

It just didn't happen.

Apparently, gender equality wasn't exactly a *thing* for immortals— aside from the Fae race who were apparently ruled by queens instead of kings.

Females were rare in the vampire race and they didn't generally have the power to compel, which from what I understood meant that

317

they could implant thoughts into another mind. Make you think and do whatever they wanted you to. So, basically, they were weaker than the males as a rule of their genetic makeup.

Witches were ruled by a hierarchy of male leaders and councilmen.

And shifters—apparently—only had *male* alphas.

I was happy to break the mold on that one, but the idea of actually *killing* someone—*Jared's uncle*—to do that, made me abort the premature thought without hesitation.

I was not a murderer.

"If you agree to accept Ryland as your alpha, he'll still accept you as pack," Clay had said, but I could see that it pained him to speak the words.

"You might even get a prime position," Jared added, trying to make light of it. "With your strength, you'd be an invaluable addition to any pack."

A prize to be won.

A tool to be used.

Ryland had given me until Monday night to decide. So, I had the weekend. This last weekend as a free wolf before I either chose to submit or chose to leave. I wouldn't leave, which left one option. I just prayed my wolf would allow me to do it. If she had her way, she'd tear Ryland's throat out without hesitation and take the position of alpha. I couldn't let her. Not only might I *die,* but I had no right to, and no *idea* how to run a pack as an alpha.

Besides, as I'd already established; I was not a murderer. I couldn't kill a goddamned mouse, let alone a human wolf man person that was related to someone I cared about.

At least it was a long weekend, I reassured myself. With school closed on Monday for a PA day I would have that whole day to prepare myself before meeting with Ryland and bending the knee under the light of the moon.

Pretending it never happened meant going about life as usual, even though everything felt more than a little *unusual* now. My wolf was mostly behaving, which was...*odd.* And no one else came to harass me at the cabin or at the school about joining the pack. No one chased me and Clay in the Jeep on the way to school on the day we drove, or on foot on the day we ran together.

Jared had needed to go back to watching the quarry for his uncle while Ryland was still busy expunging the other wolves off their lands.

And with me busy between school during the day and work in the evenings, it wasn't until Friday just before I was getting ready to leave to meet Layla and Viv at her house when Clay came to talk to me. "You sure you should be going?" he asked, fists curled at his sides and stained in the creases with black grease. He'd been in the shop a lot over the past two days. Only coming out to sleep inside at night and to share mostly silent meals with me in the living room before I went to bed.

We chatted, but not about anything important. Not about what I wanted to talk about, nor, I didn't think, what *he* wanted to talk about, either.

They weren't asking me to choose anymore. Jared and Clay didn't even mention it. But since the incident with Ryland, they were both on high alert. Like they were expecting something bad to happen at any second. It was driving me up the goddamned wall.

I wished they would just *tell* me what they were so worried about. But, being the coward I was when I wasn't propped up by the strength of my wolf, I was afraid to ask. Partially because I thought I may already know.

They weren't pushing me to choose anymore because they just *expected* me to submit to Ryland. As if there wasn't any other choice.

And they were acting like there wasn't any other choice because there probably wasn't anymore. I may be immortal bullshit illiterate, but even I could piece together that if I didn't submit to Ryland, give him permission to control me, then I would be a potential threat.

An alpha on his lands.

And what had Clay said about alphas crossing pack territory?

Oh, right. "It's not just a nuisance—it's a direct challenge."

Which meant a fight to the death.

All hope of Ryland allowing me to remain in Forest Grove *without* agreeing to be part of his pack had vanished. It was join or leave. And I wasn't even sure if leaving was an option anymore, either.

I'd been sick with anxiety and barely sleeping for days.

"Allie?" Clay prodded, getting my attention again as he walked closer to where I was at the bottom step of the porch.

I shook my head, clearing it so I could think. "I have to," I told him. "It's Layla's birthday. I promised I'd be there."

He blew out a breath that clouded in the chilly air around his face and passed me on the steps, sending a jolt over my skin as his wide frame brushed against my arm. "Give me a couple minutes to wash up. I'll take you."

"I was going to run."

He looked out over the yard and into the trees as though he could see around for miles. Frowned. "No. It isn't safe right now. We'll drive."

I didn't like the expression on his face. Like he was deflated. The anger was still there, evident in the crease between his brows and the stiffness in his neck, where a thick vein had been present against his tan skin for days.

"Hey, Clay?" I ventured, my throat drying. "Are you okay?"

He didn't turn, but his back stiffened at the question. "Fine," he grunted and then swung open the newly repaired door. "Don't move. I'll be out in two minutes."

With nothing else to do and absolutely no energy to argue, I slumped down to sit on the bottom step of the porch, setting my bag beside me to wait. Clay was right, of course. After what happened, it was only logical that the outside packs interested in me would be ten times more curious if they found out about my apparent *strength of will*, as Jared put it.

And also, Forrest is something of a loudmouth, or so Clay said. Unless Ryland thought to give him a direct order to keep his mouth shut, everyone would know about what happened in a matter of days.

The forest wasn't my safe haven anymore.

I longed for the ease of walking across sodden earth, waving to the deer and hares picking through the brush, toward my little canvas dwelling in the trees.

I'd never take the simple things for granted again, I decided.

I'd give almost anything to go back to that hunting blind, remain oblivious to the world of immortal beasts hiding right beneath my nose.

But, and this was a major *but*; then I wouldn't know Jared. He would still be the handsome loner that everyone wanted, and no one could have. I'd only know him from a distance. And Clay. I wouldn't even *know*

Clayton Armstrong at all. And the idea of forgetting either of them left a sour taste in my mouth and a hollow pit in my gut.

"Ready?" Clay barked, standing directly behind me on the stairs.

I yelped and jumped to my feet, knocking my pack onto the dirt. "Fuck, Clay!"

He laughed.

Like a *real* laugh. The kind that have deep roots, drawing sound up all the way from your belly. It was cut short, but for one blissful second, I smiled, because I had made *Clay* laugh. And it was probably the best sound I'd heard in days.

"Come on," he said, getting control of himself while sliding back on his mask. "Let's get going before I change my mind and leave you hog-tied in your room." A little *zip* of surprise unwound down my back and I stared at him in morbid shock, my cheeks heating. "I *can* joke, you know," he said with a wink.

A wink!

"I know," I rushed to say, but honestly, I thought it was the first time he'd *ever* joked with *me*.

"*Allie*," Clay urged, almost to the trees now.

"Coming!" I called, following him as he grumbled something unintelligible under his breath.

"Look what the Alley Cat dragged in. Was starting to think you abandoned me to the pits of despair with this one," Viv jabbed a thumb behind her.

"I heard that!" Layla called back from somewhere deeper in the house. "And it's a *good* movie, that's why it makes you cry!"

Viv rolled her eyes exaggeratedly and shut the door behind me as I stepped inside.

I slid off my shoes and waved to Mrs. Cole on the sofa in the small living room. "Hi, Mrs. Cole. Thanks for having us."

Mrs. Cole waved a lazy hand through the air and then lifted her remote to the television, turning up the volume on a Dr. Phil rerun. "You're always welcome, Allie Grace. You know that, hon." Her words were disjointed and oddly soft and I knew without looking at her that she was mixing the wine in her *large* glass beside the sofa with the pills inside the prescription bottle next to it.

Some things really never change.

Viv blushed, but led me past her mom and down into the hallway, tugging my arm into her bedroom.

Layla was laid out on the bed, surrounded in bowls of barbecue chips, Swedish Berries, and m&m's. Viv's, mine, and Layla's favorites, respectively. She was fiddling with the DVD case, leaning over to get the movie queued up on the box TV atop Viv's dresser, a handful of m&m's already stuffed into her mouth.

The whole scene brought with it the sort of nostalgia that made me want to cry after the last couple weeks I had. When was the last time we'd done this? It had to have been months. Maybe half a year or more.

Suddenly, I realized why *this* was what Layla wanted to do for her eighteenth birthday with her best friends. I couldn't think of a better way to spend mine, either.

And I was next in line for the big one-eight. Just another month to go and I'd be free. *Really* free.

Viv nudged me, bringing me back to earth.

You okay? She mouthed, eyes dodging between Layla and me like she wanted to make sure, but also didn't want anything to ruin Layla's night.

I nodded. "Completely," I told her and tossed my bag onto the bed, rushing to tackle Layla from the side in a bear hug. She squealed and fell to the carpet, trying to kick me off her. But I just hugged her tighter. "Happy birthday, bitch."

She stopped struggling and hugged me back. "Yeah, yeah," she said. "Thank you, now get off of me before I go nuclear on your ass."

I snorted. Layla's idea of *going nuclear* was using her black painted cat claws against me. Once, I might have been *very* afraid. Now, I doubted I'd even feel them.

"I got you a present," I told her, letting her shove me away and push the curtain of dark hair away from her face. She spat a few strands from her mouth and stood, glaring down at me.

"I told you not to get me anything," she protested, putting her hands on her hips.

I shrugged. How could I take her seriously when she was wearing a black sheep onesie with golden horns on the hood? *"Please,"* I said, tossing my backpack at her. "Are you really telling me you didn't *already* get me something even though my birthday isn't for another month?"

She narrowed her eyes at me. Layla was the sort of person to start buying Christmas presents in July, the practice completely at odds with her outwardly projected persona of doom and gloom.

"Thought so," I said with a grin. "Now open it."

"Might as well open mine, too," Viv said, flicking a small box onto the bed to join my bag and Layla where she sat cross-legged in one corner.

She cut Viv a glare, but said nothing, pulling the hastily wrapped gift from my bag to set next to her other gift. "Fine," she said and lifted Viv's gift, searching for a loose corner to pull the wrapping off without damaging it. "But *then* we start the movie. You can't put it off all night."

Viv and I groaned in unison. Truth be told, I didn't mind the movie. I actually thought it was pretty good. But I'd already cried a river of tears in the last few weeks. I had no interest in watching something that was going to make me cry even *more*. But for Layla...

Layla slid her finger beneath the paper, struggling to contain her excitement, when the landline let out a shrill ring from the living room. Layla halted and looked with a wince toward Viv.

The phone rang again, and Vivian groaned, shoving off from the bed. "Hold that thought," she said with a sigh. "I'll be right back."

We all knew Mrs. Cole was in no condition to get the phone and if it was Viv's dad, they'd never hear the end of it if one of them didn't answer before the answering machine picked up.

Layla shook the small box from Viv, bringing it up to her ear to listen to the tinny jangle of something metal inside. She pursed her lips, leaning in to whisper. "You don't think she got me jewelry, did you?"

I shrugged. "Doubt it," I whispered back as she traded the small box for my larger one and shook that, too. I'd just picked up the gift yesterday, forcing Clay to wait outside the small independent antique shop down the strip from the bookshop while I browsed for the perfect item. Something that she would love, that wouldn't put me more than an *additional* week behind my saving's schedule than I already was.

"Mr. Adams?"

Those words from Viv's mouth as she answered the call carried down the hallway and filtered into my ears like acid. My stomach turned and I couldn't jump from the bed fast enough, leaving a confused Layla to follow concernedly in my wake as I tripped into the hall, banging hard against the opposite wall before getting my footing back under me.

No.

It was a mistake. Why would he call?

I gave him *the wrong number* for Viv's parent's place. He wasn't supposed to ever call it. He wouldn't. Clay covered for me the other day. There was no reason to—

"Uh," I heard Viv say, her tone changing from surprise to the one I knew her best for—defensive. "What do you mean?"

Oh fuck. Fuck!

"Well, I—" she started, but my uncle must have cut her off.

Please. Please. Please.

I cleared the end of the hall and stood, chest heaving in the light of the kitchen where Viv stood, her face flushed with the receiver against her ear.

I held my hands up against the physical blow of her glare, trying to convey a million apologies with a single look. "Please," I whispered just as Layla rushed by me into the kitchen, staring between me and Viv and the phone in Viv's hand.

"What's going on?"

"*Please*," I urged Viv and she shut her mouth, her expression and body hardening until she could have been carved from stone. But that wasn't the worst part. The worst part was the way she was looking at me.

Like she didn't recognize me.

"Yeah," she finally snapped down the receiver. "Of course, she's here. She *lives* here after all."

Layla's face screwed up in a confused pucker. "What?"

"Here Allie," Viv said, tearing the phone from her face to me. "Your uncle wants to know why you're failing Math and Geo."

My blood ran cold. That day in the office.

When Devin's father cornered me and I ran away, unable to contain my wolf. Principal Dane had wanted to speak to me. I'd never gone back in to talk to him like he asked. *Shit.*

And then the assistant told Clay when he called in pretending to be my uncle that I was failing. That's what the principal wanted to talk to me about.

That's what he obviously took it upon himself to chat with my uncle *directly* about.

Why hadn't he called *me*?

Why did he phone Viv's house?

Why? Why? Why?

It didn't matter now. The damage was done.

As I reached out for the phone, Viv dropped it into my waiting hand disgustedly and shoved past, dragging Layla with her.

They left me alone with only my own voice to echo back to me as I lied to my uncle. Each word was another nail in the coffin I'd built for myself.

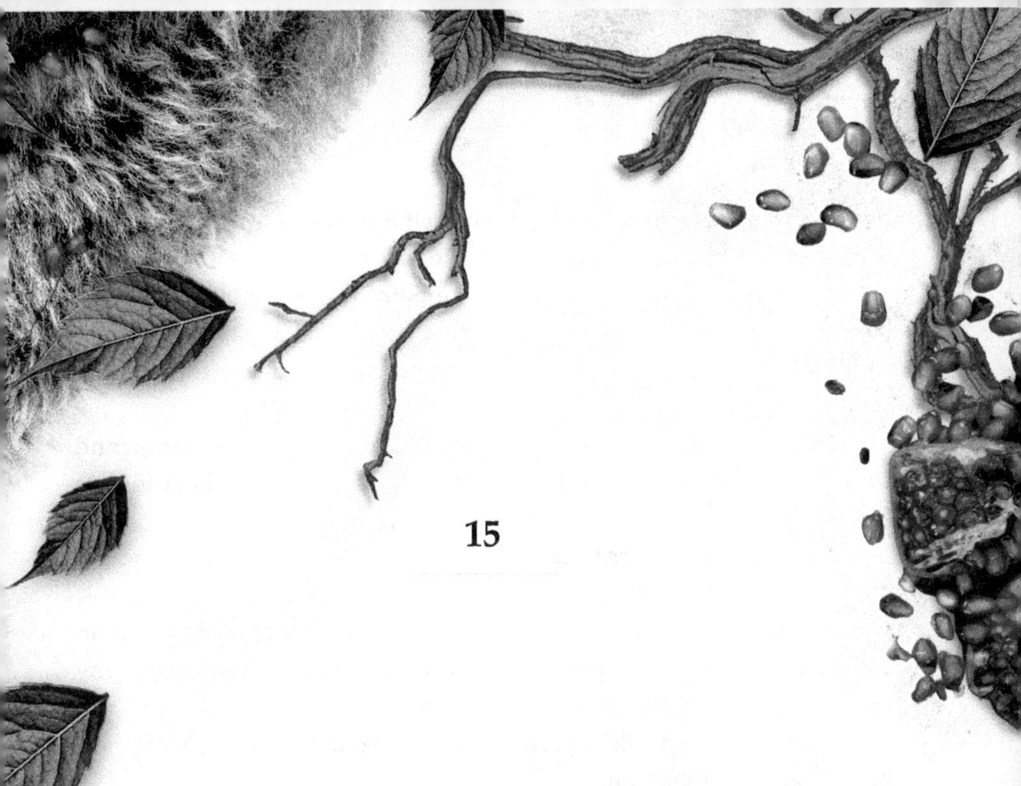

15

I'd been both right and a little off base about why Uncle Tim had reached out to Vivian.

He *had* been notified about my failing grades. That was why he'd phoned the principal himself to speak about what could be done for reparations. At the onset of that call, Susan, the receptionist, had mentioned that she hoped I was feeling better after leaving suddenly from the office on Tuesday.

Susan had reminded Uncle Tim that he'd called to vouch for my absence.

What a shitty fucking time for him to suddenly decide to be *involved*. When Uncle Tim demanded to know if it was Devin who'd called pretending to be him, I was all too happy to point the finger at my ex. And then to explain that we'd since broken up and he'd moved away. That set Uncle Tim's mind at ease.

You're a good kid, Al, he'd said. *I'd hate for someone else's bad influence to get you into any sort of trouble.*

Little did he know I'd gotten *myself* in all the trouble I'd been in. It was *my* actions that put me here, caught in a tangled web, trying to claw my way out of the lies I'd been spinning for months.

The receiver fit into the cradle with a dull click as I hung up. With a

327

promise to behave myself and *apply* myself more in class, Uncle Tim had let me go. My friends wouldn't forgive so easily.

All the turmoil had upset me to the point that my wolf was pacing steadily in my belly. I hushed her as best I could, taking a spare minute to fill a glass of icy water from the tap and gulp it down slowly before leaving the kitchen.

I needed to do this now. Layla and Viv deserved an explanation and they wouldn't be convinced to wait. If I left now, they wouldn't forgive me. And I *needed* them to forgive me.

Rolling my shoulders back, I walked back down the hall, toward the glow cast against the worn hardwood from Viv's open bedroom door. It was like a game of the floor is lava, but there was nothing to jump on and save myself. Each step was painful and deliberate. I had to force my feet forward, dragging my heavy form with me.

Stay calm, Allie, I told myself, pausing for one last steadying breath before I entered the room.

"I just don't understand what could—" Layla had been whispering harshly to Vivian atop the bed but halted when she spotted me in the doorway.

Viv whirled on me, her jaw set. "Go ahead," she snapped. "Tell her."

I should have known she wouldn't explain what was going on to Layla. She would want me to do it myself. To admit what I'd done in betraying them both.

"I lied to you," I began, a ball forming in my throat, unsure of what to do with my hands. "I've *been* lying to you both for months."

Layla frowned, a crease deepening in her forehead. Sighing, I lowered myself into Vivian's chair by her desk and toed the bedroom door closed. Viv's mom was out of it still in the living room, but I couldn't risk her overhearing this conversation.

I leaned forward over my knees, breathing raggedly as I settled my head into my hands. "Just...don't hate me, okay."

Neither said a word. So, I began.

I told them about my aunt and uncle moving away to Florida *temporarily* to try to save their marriage. I told them how my guardians asked me if I could stay with a friend for a while and how I knew Layla's house was full as it was and that Viv...well, she wouldn't want me around because of...I didn't go into detail there, she got the gist. I couldn't live here for the same reason Viv only invited us over when her dad was out of town.

I explained where I *had* been. In my dad's old hunting blind in the woods. How I'd been going into town at the crack of dawn to use the school showers after the janitors went through. I made it sound much more *comfortable* than it actually was. They didn't need to know the bleak truth of how I'd felt near to freezing to death several nights.

I told them everything I possibly could. Everything I was *allowed* to tell them.

When I was finished, Viv looked like she was ready to kill someone.

Layla looked like she was going to cry.

Viv ran a hand through her newly cropped pixie cut and inhaled deeply through her nose. "So, you've been secretly living in your dad's old hunting blind because you didn't want to put *us* out."

I nodded.

"And then when the hunting blind was destroyed in that storm, Jared took you in and you've been staying with him since."

I nodded again.

"Well that explains *that* mystery, at least."

I couldn't tell them about Devin. Or about *why* I continued to stay with Jared and Clay. They would have to draw their own conclusions. There were some truths that were not mine to tell. And if telling them would put them in any sort of danger, then those were lies I'd have to uphold, no matter what it cost.

"Fuck, Allie," Vivian said, dropping her head to pinch the bridge of her nose.

Layla rose from the bed stiffly and came to pull me into a hug. Her light jasmine scent comforted me, and I felt tears stinging at the corners of my eyes. "Those bastards," she choked against my shoulder and then pulled away. "I can't believe they just *left* you."

My mouth fell open at her words. *This* was what she was most upset about? Not the fact that I'd been lying to them for months?

"I ought to fucking call child services on those motherfuckers," Vivian grumbled.

"But...I *lied* to you guys."

"Yeah and you're a goddamned idiot for not just telling us the truth," Vivian said through clenched teeth.

"Are you sure there isn't anything else?" Vivian added, leveling a hard stare at me.

My chest tightened. It took me a second longer than it should've to answer her. She noticed, too. "Yeah. That's it."

Vivian shook her head. "Seriously, if there's something else, if you're in some sort of trouble, you have to tell us."

My brows furrowed. Some sort of trouble? "What sort of trouble do you think I'm in?" I scoffed, confused.

"The kind that makes you miss school for a whole week and vanish from class halfway through the day."

I buckled under her stare.

"The kind of trouble that makes Devin Wright up and vanish from Forest Grove. Or the kind that makes weird gang-looking chicks come and confront you at school? Oh! Or makes people like Clayton *fucking* Armstrong give you a lift home from school?"

Layla looked between Viv and I, clearly not following.

Leave it to Vivian to connect all the dots I didn't want her connecting. Fuck my life.

"I was *sick*," I insisted. "And I told you, I didn't know that girl. And Clay *lives* with Jared, that's why he was there picking me up."

Layla gasped. "Wait, so you're living with Jared Stone *and* Clayton Armstrong?"

I grimaced.

"How the *hell* did you manage not to spill the beans on that?? She was watching me incredulously.

I didn't have an answer for her. I'd wanted to tell them so many times.

Vivian was still watching me like she wasn't quite sure she recognized me. Like she still didn't fully believe me. I hardly blamed her.

"I'm sorry," I told them, feeling an ache behind my breastbone. "I'm *so* freaking sorry. No more secrets, okay?"

...except the ones I had no choice but to keep.

Layla cast her eyes to the floor and Viv's face pinched.

There was a pause where I held my breath, praying to whoever would listen in the back of my head that I would do anything if it meant keeping my best friends.

Please.

Please.

Layla moved away and sank onto the edge of Vivian's bed. "If we're being honest, then I have something to tell you both. I—I haven't exactly been honest, either."

Viv's spine went ramrod straight and her eyes bored into the back of Layla's head and then glanced questioningly at me as though I should know what she was talking about. I shrugged to show I didn't.

"What?" Viv pressed.

Layla winced and I saw a slight tremor roll over her shoulders. It made my insides twist. This wasn't some small lie. I braced myself for it, somehow ending up kneeling next to her on the floor, putting my hand on her lap. "What is it, La La?"

She smiled sadly at me. "I'm sick," she said. It was like a physical slap.

Vivian turned white as a sheet.

I could hear my pulse in my ears.

"Huntington's?" I asked in a breath when she didn't elaborate.

Her mouth pressed into a firm line.

"But you said the test came back negative."

When she looked up again her eyes were red rimmed and brimming with tears. "I'm sorry," she blurted. "I didn't want you to know. I didn't want anyone to know. They said I might not even show symptoms at all for another twenty years, maybe even thirty. I could be fifty before it starts."

She was rambling now, but the important part she left out was that it *would* start. Her grandmother had Huntington's Disease. It was genetic. And there was absolutely no escaping it. Eventually, someday, Layla would begin to deteriorate. She would lose her fine motor skills. Then her ability to walk. Her speech would become garbled and disconnected until she may not be able to speak at all. Then the dementia would set in. And eventually, Layla would succumb to it.

"My parents and I decided before the results came back not to tell my brothers and sisters. It would be too hard for them. And then when the test was positive, I just couldn't bring myself to say anything to either of you right away. I told myself I would tell you later, when it wasn't so fresh and raw. But...then it was a month later. And then six months later. It was never the right time. And, I mean, it's not like it matters anyway, right? I might be *totally* fine until I'm, like, super old anyway."

Viv tugged Layla back into a hug and I crawled up onto the bed to join the group hug. Layla shook between us as we all cried. "We'll take care of you if it comes to that," Vivian said against Layla's hair, meeting my eyes over her head. I nodded my agreement.

"Yeah," I added. "We'll all buy a big house together and get jobs working from home. It'll be perfect."

The beginning of an idea was forming in my mind and I held tightly to it, daring to hope.

If shifters and vampires and witches were real, then magic was real. And if magic is real then maybe, *just maybe* there was a way to fix this before Layla would ever have to feel the effects of the disease she'd inherited from her grandmother.

I can fix this.

We pulled away after a while, all of us wiping our eyes. Viv trying to hide the fact that she'd been crying at all.

"So," Layla said awkwardly, pushing out a breathy laugh. "Are we going to watch this movie, or what?"

I shifted, going to get up and start it for her, but Vivian stopped me, curling her fingers around my wrist.

Her pallor was almost green when she spoke. "One more thing," she said, gulping hard, her eyes shifting, not resting on either of us for more than a second.

"If you say you're sick, I swear to god—"

"No," she hurried to say, shaking her head. "It's not that. But we did say no secrets and I guess I haven't been honest, either. Not even with myself for a long time."

Layla and I waited while Viv struggled for the words. She worried the edge of her Paramore t-shirt until it started to come apart at the seam. "I'm gay," she said in a gush of air, snapping her mouth shut as soon as the two words flew out. Like they were a caged bird she hadn't meant to free.

Me and Layla shared a look.

She smiled first. My smile followed.

Vivian, finally looking at us now, was beat red and clearly confused as to why we were grinning like idiots. "We know," Layla and I said at practically the same time.

I gripped Viv's shoulder, giving her a little squeeze. "But we're glad you figured it out."

She choked on a laugh and laid her hand overtop of mine, squeezing it back while she fought not to start crying again. "Okay," she croaked. "Put the stupid movie on. Might as well cry some more now since the floodgates are open."

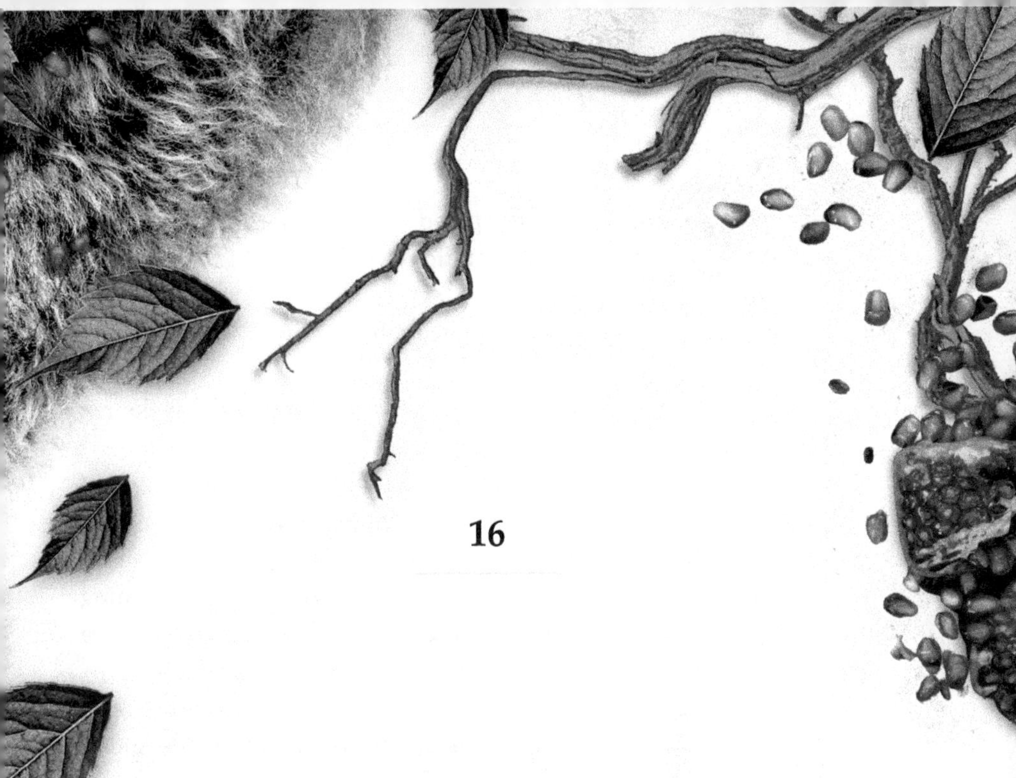

16

I shouldn't have been surprised to find Clay parked outside in the morning. I was the first one up, and when I left the room for water, I stopped in the living room to clear away Mrs. Cole's empty wine glass and the dish of candies she'd accidentally knocked to the floor in her sleep. She was splayed in a pink bathrobe with purplish stains dotting the collar over the sofa where she'd been when I came in last night.

That was when I saw him. Or, rather, the jeep. Parked across the street a little way down behind a black SUV. I smirked, rushing to the kitchen to put away the dirty glass and swish some water around my dry mouth. I really hoped he hadn't been out there all night but judging by how he wouldn't even let me run to Viv's alone last night, I thought he probably had.

Jared's orders.

Guilt ate at me as I rushed into the bathroom to change and quietly put together my backpack in Vivian's room to the soft sounds of Layla's snores. Viv's eyes snapped open as I collected my brush from her nightstand.

"Morning sunshine," I whispered, shoving the brush deep into my pack.

She grimaced, twitching into a deep stretch and a yawn. "Leaving

335

without saying goodbye?" she whispered back, a little sleepy smirk on her face. "Were we just a one-night-stand to you?"

I snorted.

"My ride's here early," I told her with a little frown. "Raincheck on brunch?"

She sighed, rolling over. "Ugh. *Fine.* Go before you really wake me up. I'm not done sleeping yet."

I lifted Layla's gift from the nightstand and set it between her and Layla on the bed. "Tell her she can open it when she wakes up," I added before slipping from the room. After everything went down last night, the gifts had been brushed aside. Layla wasn't exactly in a gift-opening mood and we were all too happy to get lost in the tragic romance playing out on the screen instead of lingering on our own drama.

The morning was uncharacteristically warm for autumn and I inhaled the crisp scent of dry leaves as I stepped outside and bounded down onto the sidewalk. If Clay was really there all night, I didn't want him waiting there until the afternoon, too.

With the early morning sun on my face, I went straight to the driver's side of the Jeep, ready to give Clay hell for creeping in front of Viv's house. Did he *really* think the threat was so great that I wasn't safe inside of a house? With a family of mortals?

I reached up to tap on the window, but my hand stopped just shy of its mark.

It was Clay, alright. But he was asleep.

The driver's seat was laid against the back seats and he was passed out with his arms up behind his head. With his blue eyes shuttered and his muscles relaxed, he looked so different from the Clay I knew. But like I'd seen once before, Clay didn't look fully relaxed even when he slept. There was a crook in his brow and a tightness around his jaw that made him seem like he could have only been pretending to sleep.

Back in his signature black tee shirt, I stifled a laugh at the sheer amount of convenience store food wrappers splayed over his chest and across the passenger seat. Pepperoni and cheddar sticks, several bags of Doritos, and one of those god-awful gas station sandwiches were the staples amid the smaller chocolate and candy items he'd had for his evening feast.

Briefly, I thought about turning around and going back inside.

Maybe texting him first? That way he could wake up on his own instead of me startling him.

I bit my lower lip, about to back away when he stirred. His left eye slitted open and then widened when he saw me. He stilled and then jolted bolt upright, smashing his head against the roof in his haste to sit up. Bits of plastic and paper scattered from his chest onto the floor of the jeep and he cursed loudly under his breath.

My face pinched when he turned his furious gaze on me. "Sorry," I offered, backing away from the Jeep as he shoved the door open and stepped out, still rubbing the top of his head.

"Hey," he said awkwardly, a blush staining his cheeks red. "I—uh—was just—"

"Spying on me?" His eyes widened.

"No," He bit out, straightening and removing the hand from his head to ball it at his side. "I just didn't think I should leave you alone."

"I wasn't alone."

"You know what I mean."

"Were you *worried* about me?" I teased him, but that only made his blush deepen and his knuckles turn white against the tan skin of his massive hands.

He muttered something about never doing something nice for someone without something and I laughed. "God, Clay, I was *joking*."

"Just get in the damned Jeep," he growled, getting back in himself and shutting the door with a loud resounding *bang* that echoed in the empty streets of early morning. Probably waking several of the neighbors. He was still muttering to himself when I slid into the seat next to him and he started the engine.

As we walked up to the cabin about a half hour later, Clay groaned to himself and tipped his head back as though suddenly exasperated.

"What?" I asked, confused as I rushed to match his pace through the sun-warmed brush.

"It's Grams," he moaned, and I twirled in a quick circle, wondering how I'd missed her. But I didn't see her anywhere at all.

I raised a brow at him, and he pinched the bridge of his nose. "She stopped by yesterday while you were at work. I completely forgot she was coming today."

"She is?"

Vaguely, I remembered the older woman mentioning something about coming over to get some of Clay's lasagna, but she hadn't come, and it'd been a week. I thought maybe she'd forgotten. I know I had.

"Oh, right," I said, cutting him off before he could answer as the cabin came into focus in the distance. "She wants your lasagna. I totally forgot."

He screwed his face up at me and I mirrored the look, shrugging. "I figured she would have told you. Or that Jared would have. We ran into her last week when I was practicing with my new bow."

He only seemed more confused by that. "Your...*bow?*"

Not for the first time, my chest panged with guilt at the rift I'd inadvertently caused between Clay and Jared. Then and there, I resolved to do what I could to fix that rift, no matter what it took. I wouldn't be the reason their friendship was destroyed.

I thought they'd get over it. Take some time to stew and moan and then shake hands and make up. But they were still barely speaking. It was getting to be a bit ridiculous and I wondered if the rift would ever heal itself.

"I'll explain while we cook," I offered. "I hope you have everything to make one. The pantry was looking a little...bare."

Clay wrinkled his nose. "It's not anymore. Jared made me shop yesterday while you were out. Said you probably wouldn't touch the cash he left you and I'd have to do it."

Bastard.

"Have what you need then?"

He tipped his head this way and that, considering. "We can make it work."

My mouth pulled into a smile. "Does that mean you'll let me help?"

"I'd rather you didn't."

"Too bad. I've got nothing better to do."

"I can think of a few things. Like Math and Geography homework for one," he said with an infuriating smirk and the glimmer of mischief in his eyes.

I gasped, putting a hand to my chest in mock horror. "On a *Saturday?* Blasphemy."

AFTER EACH OF US TOOK A TURN IN THE SHOWER, CLAY TURNED ON THE RADIO IN the nook by the door in the kitchen and we began to cook. I'd had to switch the station three times in the last two hours since we started with the chopping of the veg and browning the meat.

Wincing when a Timberlake song came on, I went to the radio for the fourth time and hit the preset button for another station. A horrid country song filtered out through the speakers and Clay made an annoyed grunting sound behind me. Guess he wasn't a country fan. Which was fine. Neither was I.

I switched to another station and then another until there was a song playing that didn't make me cringe and images of Devin parade through my mind. I'd been doing so well today. I was...okay. Feeling lighter than I had in weeks.

I didn't want to ruin it.

"You're one of those girls who can't get through a full song without skipping to the next one, aren't you?" Clay asked with a slight eye roll as he layered the meat sauce atop a set of noodles in the massive glass Pyrex dish.

I'd been surprised while watching him cook. He didn't cook often and when he did, what he made was usually simple, or pre-cooked, but this was different.

His knife skills alone were enough to tip me off that he knew his way around a kitchen far better than I'd assumed. And the sauce was *incredible*. I'd suggested the addition of mushrooms, but the rest was all him. A recipe only he knew, tucked away in his mind.

I wondered where he learned it.

"It's not that," I said, trying to conceal a slight blush when I turned around. "There are just certain songs that I...just can't listen to anymore." I shrugged, going back to washing out the pot we'd cooked the sauce in while blowing a stray chunk of turquoise hair from my cheek.

Clay had gone silent behind me, and when I peered back at him, he was still. His brows drawn down as his hand hovered with a ladleful of sauce over the noodles, thinking something intently.

He put the ladle back into the bowl and rubbed his hands clean on the tomato stained dishtowel we'd been using. Then he left without a word and returned once I was finished with the pot, setting a small black box down on the countertop and switching off the radio.

He thumbed through something on his phone—the device looking miniscule in his grip—and then pressed a button. The little Bluetooth speaker came to life with a song I didn't recognize.

But a voice that I did, I realized after a second of listening.

"Is this Banners?" I asked, shaking the excess suds from my fingertips.

"Damn," he cursed, scrolling for something else. "I was banking on you not knowing most of these. How about—"

"No, wait," I stopped him, grinning as the song progressed. "I haven't heard this band in a long time."

I frowned, realizing more than a few things had changed in the course of a few months dating Devin. I'd stopped listening to all the indie bands I loved in favor of the Top 40 songs *he* liked. I gave away tickets to a Dan Mangan concert I'd been dying to go to because he turned his nose up at the artist's music, telling me we should splurge and see a Chris Brown concert instead.

I had nothing against those artists. I loved a lot of their songs, too. But I'd sacrificed a small part of myself when I gave those tickets to Vivian and went to the other concert instead. I'd had a great time. But it was bittersweet.

There was a divide between Devin and I and there always had been, I just didn't see it. We were two very different people. More so than I could've ever imagined, actually. Since one of us wasn't even human.

Devin had only wanted to *change* me to fit his mold and I'd let him. I'd offered up bits and pieces of myself to be twisted and warped until some nights when I looked into the tiny mirror in my hunting blind in the woods, I wasn't sure who the girl was looking back at me.

With a sudden burst of curiosity, I snagged the phone from Clay's fingers and looked at the playlist, hungrily taking in all the artist names I'd forgotten and some new ones I'd never even heard of.

I wanted to *cry* as I played one of my favorite Glorious Sons songs. The opening lyrics telling about summertime on a main street in a small town washed over me like a balm.

Clay stole back his phone and I blinked up at him in surprise. "Is this *your* playlist?"

He raised his brows at me, a hard edge to his stare. "Last I checked."

"Can you share it with me?" I asked, "Please?"

When his unhinged jaw came up off the floor, he nodded. "Sure."

Before long, I was singing along to another of my old favorites, cursing myself for forgetting how easily a good song could brighten a bad day.

Clay hummed along and sang a few lines really low when he thought I couldn't hear him. I was surprised to find that he could really work his voice. The usually deep, gravelly cadence sounded rich and throaty when he sang—it made me shiver.

I used to think of Clay as being all hard edges. But I was starting to see something more beneath all the layers he kept himself concealed with. The protective armor he wore around me—around everyone as far as I could tell—was peeling back a bit and I was curious what was beneath it all.

If it was more of what I saw in him today, right now, then I was in deep *deep* shit.

Clay finished covering the top of the lasagna with a layer of foil and stuck it in the oven, checking the time.

"Here," I said, reaching out for the ladle he was about to clear away. "I'll take that."

I misjudged his grip when I tried to grab it and my fingers slipped off the plastic handle, sending what remained of the cooled sauce flying in a sling-shot arc all over his chest, neck and bottom half of his face.

Ground beef dripped off his chin and the oily red stain of tomato sauce was already staining the skin beneath the stubble on his jaw.

His eyes sparked with blue flame.

I *burst* into laughter at his dumbstruck expression, doubling over when my ribs began to hurt. Tears stung at my eyes. He was *covered* in it. And that face.

Oh my god, that face. Like he'd been hit in the back of the head with a frying pan instead of spattered with sauce. His mouth was open in a slack 'o' shape, completely at odds with the frustrated, honestly slightly *constipated* look he had in his eyes.

My sides were splitting as I backed away, the look on his face turning less constipated and more angry by the second.

"You're going to pay for that," he growled, and I lunged away with him on my heels, a handful of sauce from the bowl still atop the stove in his hand.

I squealed, shouting *shit, shit, shit* as I careened past the sink and out into the living room, trying to find something to put between us. But I could barely see through the tears of my laughter and I tripped, landing face first onto the carpet just as Clay caught up with me, his sauce covered hand raised and ready to strike.

"Clay," the bark was loud and had both Clay and I spinning to the door, the laughter sharply cut off.

Jared stood in the entryway with Grams just behind him—a strange little smile on her thin lips.

"You best not be tormenting your mate," she chastised her grandson in a playfully stern tone.

Clay cleared his throat and backed down, lowering the dirty spatula. "Grams," he said, tossing the ladle back toward the kitchen. It landed in the sink without ceremony, splashing a little of what remained of the sauce over the wall behind the sink.

"Is that your lasagna, I smell? Wasn't sure if you'd indulge this old bird with her favorite."

She rubbed her hands together, brushing past Jared to find Clay and embrace him. He held the frail woman at a tentative distance in an awkward half hug, trying not to get the sauce from his neck and jaw on her.

Red cheeked, I finally got to my feet, finding Jared staring at me from the doorway. There was something about the look on his face that ate at me. He was...sad?

No. He was *hurt*.

But just as quickly, his adams apple bobbed and the illusion was gone. His easy smile was back in place. The perfect one I used to hate because it made my toes curl when he flashed it my way. Now, though, he wasn't looking at me. He was smiling at Grams as Clay released her and excused himself to go wash off the mess I'd made.

He cast me one last glare before vanishing upstairs. "Here, Hazel," he said, kicking off his boots to help guide her to the living room until she sat in the armchair closest to the fireplace. Jared then set to work building a fire in the stone hearth while Hazel stared unseeing in my general direction.

"I didn't know you were coming," I managed around the lump in my throat as Jared struck a long match and lit the paper and kindling.

"Disappointed?" he asked, and I hardly recognized his tone.

It was like a stab to the gut and my wolf woke at the attack.

As though she could sense the tension in the air, Grams scoffed, flipping her long braid away from her chest to lean back into the plush armchair. "Now, now," she said. "We'll have none of that this evening. It's been a good long while since I've had company for a meal."

Jared deflated. His crouched form in front of the slowly building fire lost most of its tension at Hazel's words—his shoulders sagged.

Jared stood when the first bit of the log caught and met my stare. There was still a sadness drawing down the corners of his eyes, but this time the smile he gave me was real, albeit much less bright than his usual. "Help me bring in the table?"

I nodded. "Sure. Of course."

"Glad to see you adjusting dear," Hazel called after me as I followed Jared from the living room and out the front door.

I wasn't sure exactly how well I was adjusting, but I suppose there had been *some* progress since she last saw me. It was something.

"Thanks," I muttered. "It's good to see you again, too."

But I'll be keeping my distance. A wide *distance.*

When we stepped out, Jared's back lifted with a long breath of the crisp near-evening air. He let it out slowly and then turned. "Sorry," he breathed. "I had no right to be—"

I hugged him.

A little *oomf* sound puffed from his lips at the force of it. I buried my face in the crook of his neck, inhaling the cedar and birch scent of him that I loved. My pulse picked up as the nearness of him washed over me, making my belly ache and my skin prickle. Then it slowed as I breathed him in and his hands held me close against my upper and lower back, pressing me into him.

"I'm so glad you're back," I said, my voice muffled against his collar.

I could sense more than see his grin, the compromising position he'd found me in with Clay when he first arrived was forgotten for the moment. "Me too."

"Do you have to go back?" I asked as I pulled away, peering up at him.

His amber eyes shone in what remained of the daylight, that little green fleck more pronounced now than ever. The orange glow of the sun on the planes of his face cast shadows beneath his cheekbones and lent alternatingly darker and lighter shades to his dirty blond hair.

Jared shook his head, still holding me loosely around the waist. "My uncle isn't exactly *thrilled* with me right now."

And then I remembered what happened in the yard.

Right.

"I'm sorry."

He looked at me incredulously. "It's not your fault."

"Am I still going to be able to meet the pack before tomorrow? Before I have to...choose?"

An ugly pit of foreboding darkness yawned open in my gut. I swallowed and stepped back to rub my arms, trying to bring warmth back into the icy limbs.

Jared nodded. "Yeah. They're doing a bonfire at camp tomorrow. It'll be a good way to meet everyone."

He must've sensed my unease because he tugged me back in for one more quick hug, pressing his chin on the top of my head. "It'll be okay, Allie. Clay and I will support whatever you decide. If you leave," he paused, swallowing hard as though to digest the possibility. "Then so will we. We can request to be released from the pa—"

"Whoa," I said, tugging myself away with my hands up. "You are *not* going to do that."

"But if you leave then—"

"Jared," I interrupted him. "After everything I did to stay here, do you really think I'm just going to *leave*."

"But if you stay, that means you'll have to become pack. Accept Ryland as your alpha."

My wolf whispered that there was another way. She wanted blood. Ryland's blood. She wanted to take his place. I shook off the rising feelings of malice and blinked back to the present. "I know," I whispered. "I just need a little more time and then…" I let the sentence trail off.

I didn't want to bow to Jared's uncle, but I really didn't think I had much fucking choice if I wanted to stay here. Not anymore.

The silence hung between us for a long moment before Jared spoke.

"Come on," Jared said, jerking his head toward the side of the house, changing the subject. "We keep the big table in the shed out back."

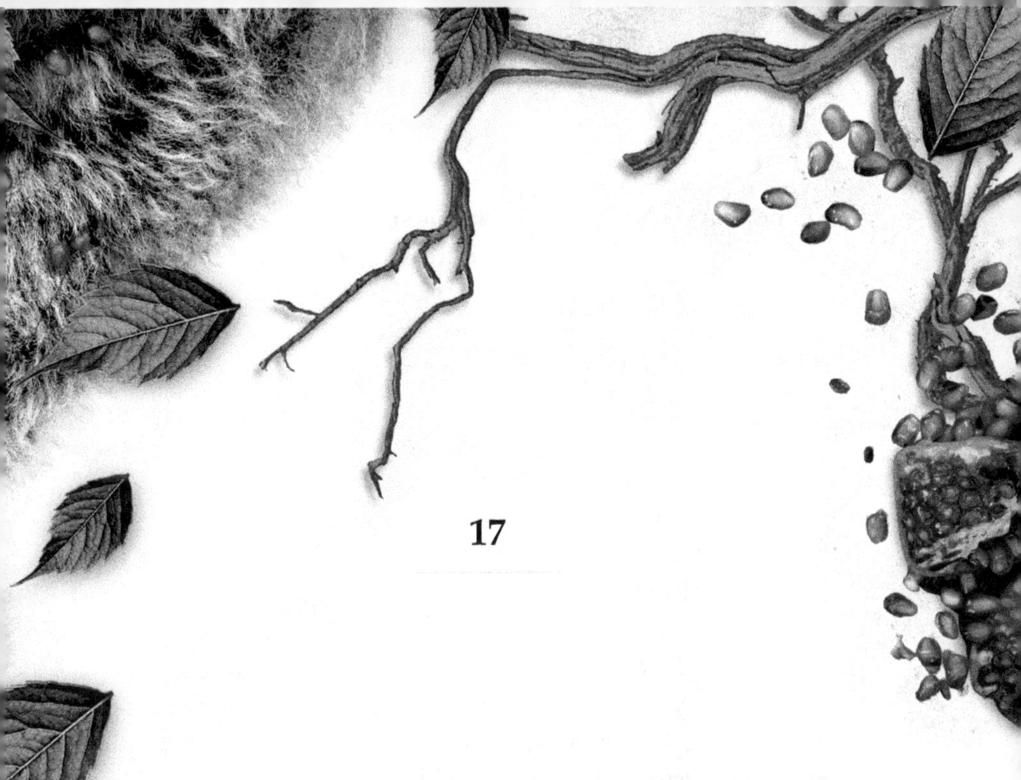

17

Jared and Clay sat at opposite ends of the rectangular table, with Hazel and I sitting opposite one another on the longer sides.

The meal was almost suffocating, with words left to stagnate on tongues instead of gracing the air. At least the lasagna was fucking *amazing*.

"It's really good," I told Clay, giving him a small smile as I shoveled in another bite.

A part of me acknowledged it was no fresh ribeye, which I'd become partial to since my transition, but still—*super* good. Easily the best lasagna I'd ever had.

Clay grunted his thanks and went back to chewing, eyeing Jared across the table every so often. It was setting my teeth on edge. The quiet was getting to me.

And it seemed, it was getting to Hazel, too. After another few minutes of quiet eating, she slammed her cutlery down and looked between Jared and Clay as though she could see them.

"Alright," she croaked, wiping the back of her hand over her mouth and then crossing her arms. "Out with it. Come on. Normally I can't shut the pair of you up when I come for dinner, now I might as well be eating in a godsforsaken mausoleum."

"*Grams,*" Clay groaned around a mouthful. Jared paled.

"Don't *Grams* me, young man." No one spoke.

You could cut the tension with a freaking knife. It was so thick. I itched to flee. Scarf down the rest of my plate and claim fatigue. Plead the fifth. Blow this popsicle stand as Dad would've said.

But I had a feeling I wouldn't escape so easily, because now Hazel was looking directly at *me*.

"Alright, fine," she said, the wrinkles around her milky eyes deepening. "If you won't tell me what the problem is then I'll tell *you*."

Clay rolled his eyes.

"You've both bonded to the same mate," she said. "It's not how that sort of magic usually works."

"Grams, could you not."

"*Hush*," she scolded, casting him a blind glare. He hushed.

"It's not Allie's fault," she continued, and I felt a prickle at her mention of me. I'd been hoping she would keep this conversation between her grandson and his friend and leave me the hell out of it.

"And it's neither of *yours*, either," she finished.

"We know, Hazel," Jared said tightly, moving what remained of his meal around on the plate in front of him.

"Do you now?"

Clay pushed away from the table to snatch the decanter from the fireplace mantle along with a glass. He poured himself a healthy half-glass and downed it in one gulp.

I drained the rest of the water from my cup and carefully skootched it his way.

His lips tightened, but he lifted the decanter to refill his glass and pour a measly ounce or so into mine. I swallowed it down, letting the burning warmth chase the anxiety from my veins.

He raised a brow at me. I mouthed *what?*

He shook his head.

Across the table Jared had his right hand fisted atop the polished wood. "He said he would back off." Jared's slightly glowing amber eyes flicked up to Clay for a second before falling back to the table.

Hazel cocked her head at Jared, then frowned. "And it was unfair of you to ask him to do so," she chastised. "You know as well as anyone how the mating bond works, Jared."

"I didn't ask," Jared spoke through gritted teeth.

I *really* didn't like to see him so angry. He was kind. Patient. Thoughtful. I wanted that Jared back.

"I offered," Clay injected. "He didn't ask me to."

"What did you mean?" I interrupted before Hazel could say whatever it was that had her scowling at her grandson. "About Jared knowing how the mating bond works…" I trailed off. "I mean, *how* exactly does it work? I thought it was just this—*uh*—*feeling*. Like the bond makes you feel something for another shifter even if you don't want to."

Hazel's mouth dropped open. She reached over and swatted her Grandson on the arm, missing on the first attempt, but finding flesh on the second.

I winced.

Oops. Had I said something wrong?

"Do you *really* mean to tell me that neither of you have told her *anything* useful?"

Clay rubbed the back of his head, subdued.

Jared sighed. "There hasn't exactly been time, Hazel."

And I hadn't even been ready to talk about any of it until very recently, and that was only because I was too busy being a coward. Too busy pretending nothing had ever happened. That I wasn't part wolf, when *clearly*, I was.

"Well, dear, allow me to enlighten you."

Jared grabbed his plate and rose from his seat, reaching out a hand for mine. I passed it to him with a hastily whispered *thanks* and watched his stiff back as he retreated to the kitchen, away from this conversation.

Clay sat still, sipping his whiskey, not looking at either his grandmother, nor me, but at a water spot in the tabletop.

"A wolf only mates once," she began. But that didn't make sense. "But—"

"You're an exception," she added. "And I think you know why."

My stomach turned.

"*Why* is that exactly?" Clay asked, his voice a dark whisper as he stared at me, imploring me to explain myself.

I opened my mouth, but no sound came out. It was like there was a cork there in my throat and the words couldn't get past.

Hazel waited; one brow slightly raised. She, too, was pushing me to tell them.

An ache formed in my chest and I pushed my cup back at Clay, who filled it again, this time with two ounces of whiskey. I sipped it and took a long breath.

The clatter of dishes in the kitchen had paused and I knew Jared was now listening too.

"You don't have to tell us," Jared called in a light tone.

But he was wrong. He deserved to know why this had happened. That it was my fault.

My fingers tightened around the glass in my hand atop the table until I was afraid it might break and released it, clutching my fingers together in fists instead. "I was two once," I said in barely a whisper, repeating the phrasing Hazel had used that first time we met. When she read something in my palm, or maybe in my *soul*.

"What does that mean?" Clay asked.

I gulped. "I was a twin," I explained, finding that now that the cork had been released, the words were there, ready to gush out. "My mom was pregnant with twins. Her and my Dad were so happy. They had names picked out almost as soon as they found out. One would be Allie, and the other..." My voice broke. I hadn't spoken her name out loud, not ever.

I took another pull of the whiskey to steady myself and then pushed the glass away. "April."

Clay didn't push me any further, but I had to tell them the rest. The rest was the reason this had happened to me—to *us*.

"It's called *vanishing twin syndrome*—when one twin *absorbs* the other." I told them; my voice oddly disconnected now. "April was never born."

"Because she became a part of *you*," Hazel said, and even though I knew her words were meant to be reassuring, uplifting, they only stung.

One crib had to be given away. One little wooden stool with the name *April* carved into the top was tucked away in the back of the closet, not to be found until I was eight years old. I found other things then too, in that same closet. A box of old ultrasound photos depicting *two* fetuses'. A photo album with a hand stitched cover that read in a delicate script *April and Allie*—devoid of any photos.

When my father went to the hospital that day with my mom, he already knew he would be leaving with one baby instead of the two they had originally thought they would have. A later ultrasound confirmed that I'd *absorbed* my sister.

But what he didn't know was that the daughter he would take home with him would be at fault for not one death—but *two*. Complications in the birth had taken my mother from him, too.

And so, a man raised a daughter without his wife.

And a daughter grew up without a mother or the sister she was promised.

I flicked away a hot tear from my eye before anyone could see it. There was a reason I didn't think about it. My mind fought against the swell of guilty thoughts and dark clouds. *It's your fault they're dead.*

"And this is why you've both mated to Allie," Hazel told the guys, her voice holding none of the acid it had before. Now she was speaking softly, *gently*. "The mating bond is fused to the immortal soul."

Jared fell back into his chair at the table. I could feel his eyes on me but didn't look up to meet his stare. "And Allie has two," Jared finished for Hazel, exhaling long and hard.

"Exactly," Hazel said. "And you both mated to her. Each of you holds a part of her soul and she a part of each of yours. It cannot be undone. It cannot be changed. Only death can sever it."

I peered up at Hazel, a weight on my chest. "You mean they'll never mate with anyone else? Like, *ever*?"

Hazel shook her head solemnly. "I'm afraid not, dear. Not as long as you're living." She crossed her arms over her chest and leaned back. "If my grandson *idiotically* tries to fight the bond and allows Jared to have you, then he will never mate to another. He will be *alone* for as long as you live."

Clay's expression darkened and he looked into the bottom of his glass like it might have an answer for him. A way out of this mess. I wished it was that simple.

Hazel tilted her head to the side, cracking her neck and sighing. "I suggest you lot get used to the idea of sharing."

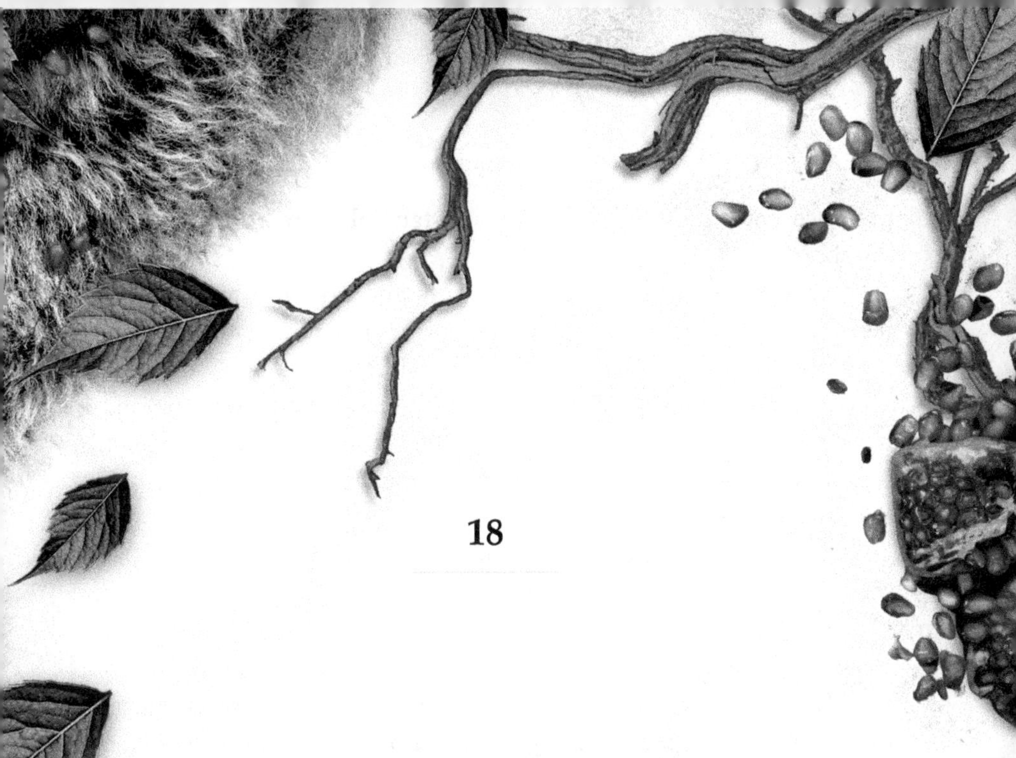

18

ey Allie?" Jared called through the door, knocking softly against the grain. After dinner I'd helped to clean up, mostly just so I had something to do to keep my mind off everything, and then Hazel had left. Clay offered to walk her home through the woods when she refused to stay the night.

She bristled at being babied, but eventually relented, saying she would be glad of the company. I'd retreated to my room shortly after they left, needing to fill my head with other things to stop it from straying back to the dark thoughts trying to creep back in after years of my keeping them away.

I set down the math text against the bed and called to Jared. "You can come in."

He pushed on the door and it stuck on the warped wood of the doorframe. He had to give it a good shove to get it all the way open, eyeing the grooves in the frame as he did. "I'll fix that for you," he said awkwardly as he entered, shoving his hands deep into the pockets of his jeans.

I let out a little laugh. "Some of those are from my fingers, too," I muttered. "I'll fix it."

He didn't argue with me, just moved into the room, filling it with his presence until the weight of *him* was a tangible aura brushing against my skin.

I peered up at Jared from the papers and texts on the bed. Geography and math, mostly. But also History. I may not have been failing Mr. Brown's class yet, but I was close to it after all those missed days.

Jared paused by the bed and I hastily brushed some papers and a binder away so he could sit down. The mattress creaked under his weight and I suppressed a sigh at the riotous feeling flitting around in my belly like a swarm of bees.

Jared lifted the text closest to him—math, and peered at the page, scanning its contents. "Homework?" he asked with a raised brow.

I pursed my lips. Nodded and then sighed heavily. "I'm failing two classes this semester," I admitted, wiping a hand over my tired eyes. They felt almost as if they were bleeding. Whether just from exhaustion, from staring at the small text on the pages of the textbooks, or from the half hour of silent crying I did when I first came up here, I wasn't sure.

Maybe it was because of all those things combined. "I can tutor you if you want," Jared offered, setting the textbook back down against the quilted blanket. I must have looked surprised because he added.

"Why does everyone always seem so shocked that I do well in school? Even my uncle thinks I cheat to get my grades."

He wasn't complaining, or even truly upset—Jared's tone was playful. Light.

"Because you're too pretty to be smart," I blurted before I could stop myself, my hand flying to cover my mouth as though it could stuff the words back in—but they'd already escaped.

He cocked his head at me, eyes narrowing curiously. A slight blush staining his cheeks.

"You think I'm...pretty?"

Now he was just being ridiculous. There was a reason Amanda, and every other girl at Forest Grove, wanted to get into his pants. I dropped my hand from my face to shove him. "That's not what I meant," I whined.

His gaze narrowed in silent challenge. "So, what you're saying is I can't be pretty *and* smart. That's just not allowed?"

"It shouldn't be," I grumbled to myself, folding my arms over my chest.

Jared laughed and the sound was like a balm to my nerves. Unlike Clay's coarse belly laugh, Jared's reminded me of someone else's laugh, but I couldn't place who it was. Regardless, I loved it and couldn't stop my face from breaking into a tentative smile, however strained that smile was.

That darkness in the back of my mind whispered that I shouldn't be allowed to smile. Not when there were three other people who wouldn't ever smile again—their blood on my hands and my hands alone.

A lump formed in my throat and I looked away from Jared, trying to get a hold on myself.

"Hey," Jared said, his laughter dying as he placed a hand on my knee. "I don't have to tutor you if you don't want me to. I just thought—"

I shook my head, stopping him from continuing. "It's not that," I told him. "I could really use a tutor."

He squeezed my knee until I glanced up at him again, my chest aching at the mirrored pain in his stare. I almost forgot that he could feel my emotions. The mating bond linking us together making him feel my unspoken pain.

"It's about what you told Hazel, isn't it?"

I bowed my head, not wanting to talk about it anymore, but not knowing how to tell him that.

It was about more than that, though. It was also about what Hazel told me about the mating bond. How Clay would *never* mate to another wolf for as long as I lived. I decided to pick at the lesser of the two wounds. "Why didn't you tell me how it all worked?" I asked Jared, not meaning to sound accusing, but finding the words came out that way regardless of my attempt to soften them.

Peering up at him, I watched his adam's apple bob before he replied. "I'm sorry. I should've explained it better. I just didn't know if you were ready to hear it."

I chewed my bottom lip. "Don't...don't hide things from me that are important. It doesn't matter if you think I can't handle it. Okay?"

Jared nodded. "Okay."

"So, it's true then, what Hazel said? If Clay refuses the mate bond between us, then...he'll never mate to anyone else?"

Jared's expression darkened and he removed his hand from my

knee, leaving me with a chill in the absence of his warmth. "I mean, you aren't supposed to be able to mate to two shifters, but you did. Maybe..." he trailed off and then blew out a gush of air.

We both knew he was grasping at straws.

The only reason I mated with both Clay and Jared was because I had a twin soul. I didn't want to think that meant what I thought it did. That my dead twin sister's soul *lived* within me. That *she* was the one who mated to either Jared or Clay. *Her* soul. Not mine.

And I'd never know which one of them was meant for me, and which one, meant for her. Because we were one now and there was no separating us.

"And the bond," I pushed on, needing to hear it from him. "It's *important*, isn't it?"

At first, I'd only thought it was a nuisance. That the bond tying me to Jared and Clay was just this annoying tether that I had to withstand. That I had to learn to live with.

But how they treated it—how the other shifters spoke about it—how *Hazel* spoke about it—I was starting to see it was something much bigger than I originally thought.

"It is," Jared admitted, flashing his amber eyes up to look into mine, setting my soul on fire.

A heavy breath pressed into my lungs and something flipped in my belly. I pressed my fingers together in my lap, trying to fight the sudden urge to kiss him. I didn't like the pain in his eyes.

I didn't like the tension in his shoulders or the way he nervously drummed his fingers against his thigh.

But I needed to know this. I needed to understand it if I was going to figure a way through this mess my life had become.

His adams apple bobbed again and he rubbed the back of his neck as though his head, or maybe the thoughts inside it, were suddenly too heavy to bear. "It doesn't always happen," he explained. "Some shifters go their entire lives searching for their mate and *never* find them. Some give up and form a bond to another shifter—their girlfriend or boyfriend or whatever—on their own. It isn't the same, but it *does* link the souls together. It's a sort of ceremony that some couples do later in life if they never find their mate or if they've fallen in love with someone they never mated to."

I tried to wrap my head around that.

"But this," Jared said, pulling my hands apart to hold one of them between his. I shivered at the radiating warmth as it ran through my veins like liquid fire, racing up my wrists and forearms from where our hands connected, all the way through my chest to that place deep within that I couldn't name. "*This* is rare. The mate bond connects souls who were made for each other—or at least that's how the legends go."

I swallowed hard, reveling in the feel of our connected souls now that I wasn't fighting it anymore. It was so much easier *not* to fight it.

"It's why we can make each other stronger. It's why I can hear your thoughts when we're in our wolf forms. Why you can hear Clay's, too."

"Is that why I can't hear anyone else?" I asked. "I thought I did before—when...when it first happened, but now I can't hear anyone except for you guys anymore."

"That was just the magic of the transformation taking hold, I bet. But Ryland isn't your pack," Jared explained, still running his fingers over the back of my hand, eliciting little shivers every time he did. "When you accept him as your alpha and become pack, you'll be able to share your thoughts and hear the thoughts of the entire pack."

Still so much to learn...

I thought I heard the door opening downstairs. It was long past dark, and I wondered if Clay would spend the night in his room, or because Jared was here, out in the shop.

"And Clay?" I asked, unable to look him in the eye anymore, keeping my voice low so hopefully Clay wouldn't hear me from downstairs. "*He's* pack too. If he refuses the mate bond, he'll be trapped here—with us."

I hoped he understood what I was implying. It was getting more and more difficult to deny the bond between Jared and me. I wanted him more every day. Every time I saw him. Touched him.

Eventually, I knew it would be impossible to stop the force drawing us together, even if it wasn't really *me* who wanted him. Even if it was just our wolves who'd mated, dragging us into the fray with them.

But Clay...

If he stepped back and allowed me and Jared to be together, then he would be relegating himself to the sidelines. Forever forced to watch his best friend and his mate together.

I couldn't imagine it. How *hard* that would be.

Even just keeping myself away from Clay day to day was a challenge. Sitting next to him in the Jeep was like trying to force two mega strong magnets apart. It was like ignoring an entire part of myself. Pretending it didn't exist.

I'd done it before. Hell, I'd done it for most of my life. But this was different. Because I wasn't just ignoring a part of myself, I was denying *him.*

"I don't think he would stay," Jared said, his voice so low and muted that I barely heard him, still lost in my own thoughts.

I recoiled from him, realizing a second later what he meant. "Are you saying he would *leave?*"

Jared nodded solemnly. "And Ryland would let him?"

"Probably. He's never really *liked* Clay. And Clay is only even part of this pack because he was grandfathered in."

"What does that mean?"

"Clay's dad was the pack alpha before Ryland. When Clay's dad died, technically, since he wasn't challenged and beaten by another alpha, the role of pack alpha went to the second in command. The wolf with the strongest will."

"Your uncle?"

"Yeah. My uncle. And this house is all Clay has left of his family, so he stayed with the caveat that he be allowed to live here, in their house, instead of on pack land with the others. So, Ryland declared the house to be pack property and allowed it."

"Wait," I said, backing away from Jared and removing my hand from his, staring around at the room with new eyes. "You're saying this is *Clay's* house?"

I'd thought it was Jared's. Maybe it belonged to *his* parents before they passed away. Or maybe it was his uncle's. Knowing it was Clay's house—that he grew up here as a boy made it seem somehow as if I was trespassing.

Jared smirked at me. "Yeah. Technically."

Well, fuck.

Once I was done digesting that, my mind circled back to the main problem that Jared was clearly now trying to avoid. "And you think he would leave, anyway? If I join the pack, do you really believe he would just abandon this? His home?"

Something panged in my chest. A dull aching throbbing with each beat of my heart.

I knew that when my father died, if there was any way I could've possibly kept the house, I would've. And I *never* would have left it. Not in a million years.

Jared's face pinched and his lips pressed into a firm line.

"He's your best friend," I breathed, not bothering to hide the accusation from my tone anymore.

Jared bristled. "I *know*," he said, his voice tainted with emotion. "You have no idea how impossible this is, Allie."

I had no idea? He had to be fucking kidding me.

"I see you together, Allie. You and Clay. I'm not blind. I know there's something there, too, whether I like it or not."

My stomach dropped.

"And Clay *deserves* to be happy too. Hell, he deserves it as much as I do or even more after everything he's been through."

As he spoke, Jared's hand curled into fists, tightening and tightening with each word.

His mixed emotions blasted over me like a hurricane. Guilt. Shame. Anger. And the kind of frustration that could blow you apart at the seams. I choked on it all, having to inch away little by little until my back was against the wall, unable to handle it all.

It was like trying to stand too close to the sun. If I didn't move away, I was going to get burned.

"And it's selfish of me and I know that."

He shook his head solemnly, eyes unfocused as he stared into his lap.

Jared snapped his head up, watching me with amber eyes aglow.

My wolf responded, trying to search for the source of his anguish and extinguish it.

"It's selfish, but I can't help it. I want you all to myself, Allie."

He reached out to me and it took *everything* in me not to take his outstretched hand. Not to fall into his arms and say he could have me. That he could have *all* of me. But I couldn't do that.

I managed to get up from the bed and get halfway across the room. "No," I breathed.

"No?"

"We can't, Jared."

He buckled as though my words had struck him like a physical blow.

"I won't make Clay leave his home. We can't do that to him."

I didn't speak the other thought aloud, but it was implied, the weight of it hanging in the air between us like a cloud of dread.

I would have neither of them. Not at the risk of the other's happiness.

Cooking with Clay today, listening to music together, I'd seen a side of him I didn't know existed. I'd seen him smile. Heard him sing and laugh. How could I want anything less for him?

Jared stood and in the low lamplight, I could see how his face paled. He looked like he'd aged ten years in this moment. "You're right," he breathed, as though he'd just come to some earth-shattering revelation. "You're right." He wiped his hand over his face.

"I'm sorry. I don't know what I was thinking, I just—"

He looked at me then and everything he couldn't say was written in his stare.

I understood.

In a knee-jerk response, I closed the gap between us and hugged him, pressing my face into his chest to inhale his woodsy scent. He wrapped his arms around me, gathering me to him like he wished he didn't ever have to let go.

"I'm so sorry for all of this," I choked, the words muffled.

"Don't be," he whispered against the top of my head. "It isn't your fault."

But it was.

It was always my goddamned fault.

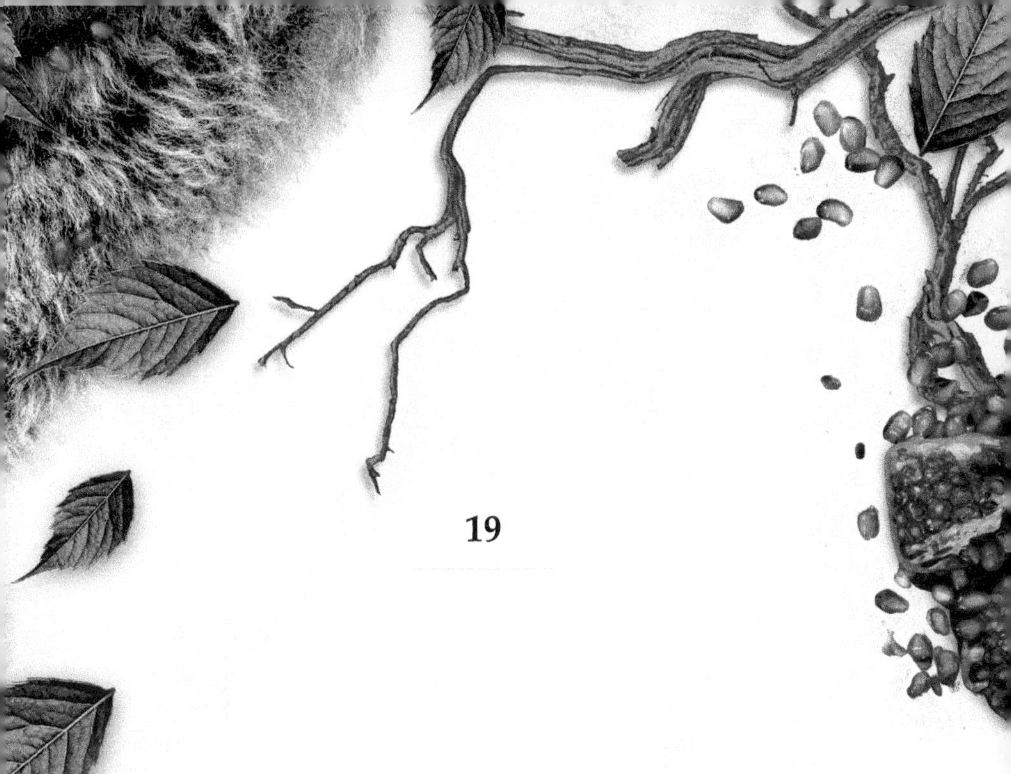

19

W here's Jared?" Clay asked brusquely as he came inside.

It was warm again today and like I assumed he would, Clay had been out back in his shop the entire day. But unlike what I assumed; Jared was *also* M.I.A. He'd been in his room since I woke up this morning and other than a creaking in the hallway upstairs that told me he was going to the bathroom, he hadn't left.

Not to eat. Not to go outside—even though it was *gorgeous* out. Not even for a glass of water as far as I knew. I'd spent the day between the living room and the front porch. I'd even dragged a chair from the kitchen table to sit just outside the door to soak up the last dregs of the sunlight before dusk fell.

It was near dark now and I couldn't believe the entire day had passed without me saying a word to either of them. I was left wishing I hadn't asked Jacqueline for Saturday off. Had I known we wouldn't have been going to meet the pack until after dark and that both Jared and Clay would be completely unapproachable for the whole day, I'd have gladly kept the shift.

As it was, the only people I spoke to were Layla and Viv, and only via text. They teased me about how my weekend was going in a house full of hotness and wondered when they were going to get their formal introductions to the infamous Clayton Armstrong.

361

My phone buzzed in my hand and I shrugged at Clay. "In his room, I think," I replied, leaning back against the sofa to open a new message from Vivian.

Vivian resent the last text I left without a reply an hour ago. I'd been hoping she would just drop it but staring at the duplicated message I almost laughed at myself. Why would I think she of all people would just let it go?

Vivian: I know there's something you're not telling us. You know you can talk to me, right?

Clay grumbled something unintelligible to himself and stomped into the kitchen to pour himself a tall glass of water. "We need to get going," Clay said as he set the glass into the sink and it tipped over, rattling loudly against the stainless steel.

My throat dried and I pushed myself up off the couch, wiping a sweaty palm against my thigh. "I'll tell him it's time to go," I offered.

Clay grunted to himself and then vanished back outside without another word.

My spine tingled with the whisper of some unnamed emotion coursing down it like an electrical current, heating and souring my belly. I paused to watch Clay go through the window in the living room as he made his way back around to his shop. His face was pinched. Eyes dark. Was it *his* emotion I was feeling, or my own?

It was hard to tell the difference these days.

My phone buzzed again, and I glanced at the new message.

Vivian: Is it drugs? Or did you borrow money from someone sketchy or something?

I rolled my eyes. Viv clearly watched way too many movies.

Allie: Jesus Viv. NO. I'm not on freaking drugs.

Vivian: I knew you were ignoring me on purpose.

I pocketed my phone with a groan and dragged my ass up the stairs, my pulse picking up as I approached Jared's bedroom door. I lifted my hand, but the fluttering sensation in my belly made me pause, trying to catch my breath.

That's when I noticed it was slightly ajar, and when I tilted my head, I could just see Jared on the far side of the room, sitting at a beat-up desk covered in a plethora of random stickers. Some peeling and others faded. He had his feet up on the edge and a book spread open between his hands.

No. not a book. The cover was on the wrong side.

Unable to help myself, I pushed the door open. "Is that Naruto?"

Jared fumbled and dropped the book into his lap, a little pain stricken gasp blowing out between his lips as it landed directly on his junk. He bent over, shoving the heavy manga from his manly bits, and his legs fell from the desk top, propelling him too far forward. He slipped from the chair and lay in a moaning heap on the floor.

"Oh fuck. Fuck!" I ran over to him and wrapped my hand around his arm. "I'm so sorry. I should have knocked. Jared?" I shook him. "Jared, are you okay?"

He groaned again, wincing as he tilted his head sideways to look up at me, his hand still clutching at the space between his legs. "Fine," he gasped. "I'm good."

Jared slowly moved to stand, righting the desk chair and pushing it back into the little nook beneath the desk.

"Is it time to go?" he asked, still wincing.

But something had caught my gaze and I found myself staring at a bookshelf beside his desk, tucked into the small span of wall between the desk and a tall armoire. A bookshelf filled with manga. Naruto and Fullmetal Alchemist. Black Butler and Bleach. And was that...Fruits Basket?

"Hmm?" I said, trying to claw my way back to the present.

For a halting second, I was back in Devin's basement, sitting next to him as he played a video game on the flatscreen. I'd been reading the newest Black Butler, so absorbed I hadn't heard his talking to me.

That was the day he'd asked me why I read *that stuff*. Why I watched stupid *childish* anime shows. He said he couldn't understand what I liked about it so much.

They're just glorified picture books and cartoons.

He was wrong, of course, but I'd been so eager to please him then. I'd returned the book to the library the next day at school without finishing it.

And there it was—right there on Jared's bookshelf. Something in my resolve cracked and I swallowed, turning quickly so he wouldn't see.

"I asked if it was time to go," Jared repeated, and I cleared my throat.

"Yeah," I said, more cheerfully than I felt. "Meet you downstairs, 'kay?"

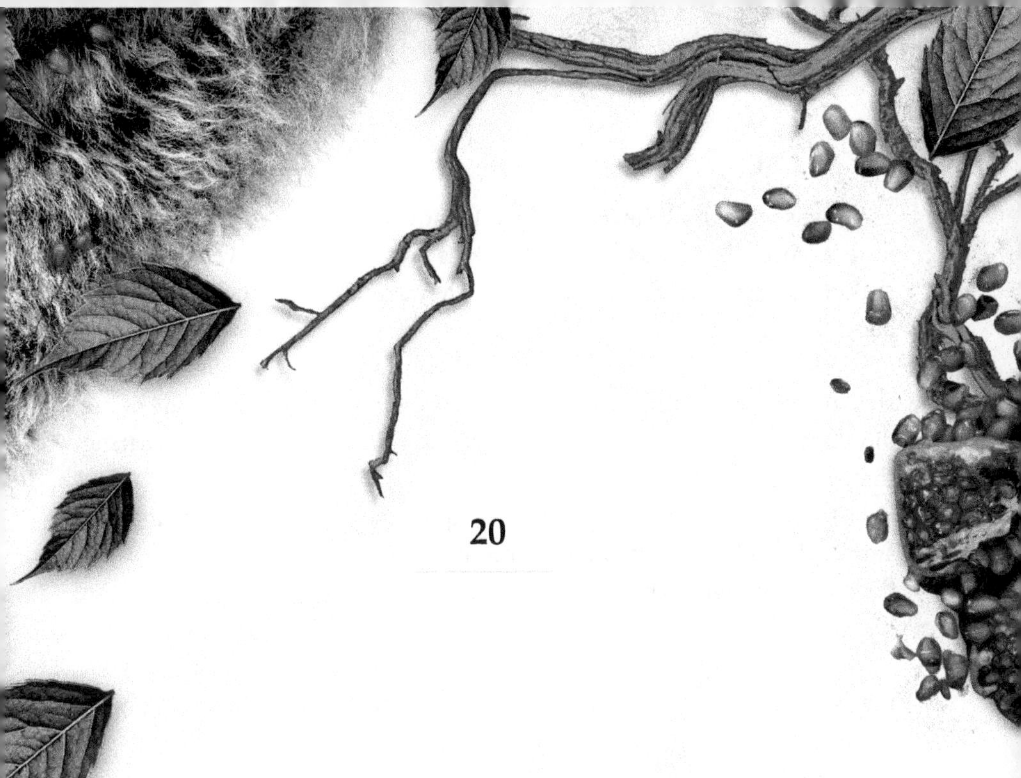

20

I hadn't wanted to shift and run, so we drove. Clay tried to insist that I drive for the practice, but it was dark, and I could tell Jared was eager to get behind the wheel of his Jeep again after a week away.

When we couldn't drive any further, we parked on the side of a bumpy back road and started on foot. I wasn't convinced we were even in Forest Grove any more with how far we'd walked through the trees.

I tried twice to start up conversations. Once with Jared and once with Clay. Neither took. There was this awkward tension between us all now and I *hated* it. When I was with just Jared, *before*, it was easy.

And Clay—we'd gotten somewhere hadn't we?

When I first came to stay at the cabin after the storm that destroyed my home, Clay hadn't wanted me to stay. He'd even gone so far to say that they weren't running a fucking shelter. He'd hated me without even properly knowing me. But just two days ago, he'd shown me another side of him, and it made me wonder whether he ever truly hated me at all or if it was just his way of defending himself from the world.

Make everyone think you hate them, that you don't *care*, and eventually they won't care, either. Not allowing anyone to get close meant not getting hurt.

I understood that more than most people.

365

It was why I had the two friends I made in elementary school and no others. After Dad passed, it was like I forgot how to even go about making a new friend. How could I? They would want to know things about me. And no one wanted to hear my sob story.

Noises pricked my ears in the dark forest and my spine went ramrod straight, pulse kicking into overdrive. Clay and Jared to either side of me didn't seem perturbed so I had to assume this was it. We were nearing the pack camp.

As if in answer to my unasked question, the smell of campfire smoke drifted to us on the cool night's breeze and I began to see the flicker of orange light tossing shadows over the thick pines in the distance.

"Don't worry," Jared whispered. "They're just curious about you, that's all. We'll just say our hellos, you can meet some of the pack, have a drink, and then we can head back."

I nodded.

Clay made a strange sound in his throat and added, "Stay close," in a low growl.

Jared rolled his eyes but didn't argue as we cleared the rest of the short distance between us and a massive break in the foliage. It came into view in snippets and pieces between thick, heavy branches. Lit with only the light of the fire and torches spaced every so often around the huge camp.

Directly in front of us was a small cabin. Nothing more than a squat square of wood and a shingled roof. Beside it was another and beside that, another. The cabins clung to the earth in varying sizes spaced fairly evenly all around as far as I could see. Small footpaths snaked between them, all leading toward a central area where the orange glow of fire and the bulk of the noise was coming from.

How could all this be out here? I wondered. Did they have power? Internet?

Or were they completely off grid?

Dad and I had been hunting out this way a few times when I was younger. How had we not stumbled on this place?

"Come on," Jared said, and I shut my gaping mouth, letting him tug me over the gravel covered footpaths toward the inner ring. We passed a few people on our way. Jared waved as we went, and Clay nodded toward them. I didn't miss how their gazes cut to me like missiles zeroing in on a target.

I tried not to look at them too closely, afraid my wolf would try to assert her dominance again.

"There you are," a feminine voice called out from the shadows, appearing like a ghost from their depths. I jumped and Charity laughed. Her blond-tipped brown dreads swung behind her back and her pretty heart- shaped face beamed with a wide grin. "Was starting to think maybe you'd chickened out."

My wolf calmed, seeing there was no immediate threat and I swallowed hard, remembering that of the three who came to see why I hadn't agreed to join the pack yet all those days ago, Charity was one of the nicer ones. So was the other younger guy. What was his name again?

Seth, I thought.

"Hi," I said sheepishly. "It's Charity, right?" She nodded. "That's me."

"Come meet everyone," she trilled, looping her arm through mine and dragging me out from between Clay and Jared. Out of my comfort zone.

"I—uh," I sputtered, unsure.

"She stays with us," Clay said, his tone laced with venom.

Charity just waved a hand at him as though swatting a fly. "Oh hush. She'll be fine. *Mates,*" she said with a slight eye roll. "Am I right?"

I let out a nervous chuckle and Jared and Clay followed behind Charity and me from a distance.

She led me through the winding pathways through the small houses and cabins until the center ring opened before us. A bonfire bigger than any I'd ever seen before stretched at least six feet in diameter in the very middle. The flames reached heights taller than my head.

Around the fire, bodies milled about, chatting and drinking. Red solo cups and beer bottles in hands. Picnic tables around the perimeter. And on the far side, another cabin, this one bigger than all the others. More like a bungalow style, with a long front porch and two levels. In my gut I knew that it was Ryland's cabin.

Music played from two speakers, one on either side of the space. A song my dad used to play in the truck drifted out over the crowd, shouting about being born to be wild.

Charity pulled me toward a smaller group further away from the fire and the larger group gathered on the other side. But they'd all sensed my presence now, and the song seemed louder in the lack of conversation as heads swiveled one by one to take me in. Measuring me head to foot.

Easy girl, I crooned to my wolf as Charity and I approached the smaller group and she released me to fill two cups from the keg set atop a makeshift table made from two tires and a flat piece of wood. She pushed one into my hand and winked at me. "Here, you look like you could use one," she said in a lower voice before turning to the others and adding. "Everyone, this is Allie. Allie—everyone."

I felt Jared and Clay behind me, near enough that some of the panic rising in my throat dissipated. "Um... hi," I said, dying inside at how awkward I sounded. "It's nice to meet you."

A face I recognized moved in front of the others. A mop of black hair was tossed from his bright hazel eyes and he gave me a warm smile. "Welcome to paradise," Seth said with a wide sweep of his arm and a dramatic half bow, "Grab a seat. Stay a while."

I laughed.

"Um, thank you...I think," I said, sipping my beer as the other shifters from the group greeted me with slightly less enthusiasm, but it was nothing compared to the vibes I got from the other *larger* group across the fire. Like Jared said, they were watching me curiously— everyone was—but the vibe from them was different. Closed off. The exact opposite of welcoming.

I suddenly hoped I didn't have to meet them at all. Charity and Seth helped introduce me to the others.

There were two other girls and besides Seth, three guys. "And that's Jenna, and those two are Trey and Todd,

they're mated. And that's Kyle."

I knew I'd never remember all their names, but I nodded and smiled, repeating variants of 'nice to meet you' for each of them.

As the group resumed their conversations, Charity turned her attention back to me. She must have noticed my puzzled look as something she'd just said sunk in. I glanced back at the two guys talking to each other and noticed how their fingers were interlaced. How the guy who I thought was called Trey brushed his thumb over the other's knuckles.

Had Charity said they were mated?

Charity leaned into my shoulder and I jerked as she whispered in my ear. "The mate bond is not hindered by gender."

I tried to wrap my brain around that. I'd assumed the mate bond was to do with...well, *mating.* As in, procreation and all that.

"Does that happen often?" I asked instead, my curiosity piqued.

Charity shrugged. "They're the only same sex mated pair we have, but some packs have a few. It was tough for them in the beginning, though," she breathed, still keeping her voice low even though it seemed like Trey and Todd were so engrossed in their own conversation that they wouldn't have noticed if the person next to them caught fire.

"Why?"

"Todd was so deeply closeted that he denied Trey for over a year. He said he wasn't gay. That the mate bond had chosen wrong."

"But now?"

"Well, look at them. You'll never meet a happier couple."

Clay cleared his throat from behind us and I whirled, having almost completely forgotten they were still standing there.

"Would you two quit hovering? Go water a tree or something," Charity said, making a disgusted sound in the back of her throat.

I'd drained my beer and Charity refilled it for me, letting the foam tumble over the side of the rim.

Jared glanced between Charity and me and finally said he'd be right back.

Clay stayed sentinel for another few minutes before jabbing his thumb toward the other side of the fire and the group gathered there. "I'll be right over there. Stay put."

"Okay," I said, feeling a new wave of nerves set in as they both moved away.

This is going to be your pack soon, Allie, I told myself. I'd have to get used to them—get to know them—if I was ever going to find my place here.

"So," Charity began as Seth turned away to talk to a girl close to my age whose name I'd already forgotten.

"Hmm?"

The mischievous glint in Charity's eyes vanished and she looked at me with a gentle sort of calm. "How are you? I mean, how are you handling things?"

I appreciated that she kept her voice low, but if all of their hearing was even half as good as mine was now, I knew they could probably hear us from across the fire if they tried hard enough.

I swallowed another gulp of beer, grimacing, and chewed the inside of my lip. "Okay, I guess."

She gave me an impish grin and shrugged. "It's hard in the beginning."

"Were you changed, then?"

"Yeah. A few years ago now, but I remember those first few months more vividly than I'd care to."

Feeling bold, I asked the question I'd been wanting to know the answer to since shortly after I'd transitioned. The question Jared and Clay couldn't answer for me because both of them had be *born* wolves. Not changed. "How did you, you know, get control of it? Your wolf, I mean? I'm pretty sure mine is insane."

Charity almost spit out her beer in a short laugh but choked it back and coughed before answering. "I thought the same thing," she told me. "But you're thinking about it the wrong way."

"What do you mean?"

She swiped the back of her hand over her glistening lips and seemed to be thinking about how best to explain. "Your wolf," she said, her eyes boring into mine. "It's not separate from you. I thought that too at the start, but it was that kind of thinking that made it take so long for me to be able to control that part of me."

She was losing me. My wolf was *definitely* a separate entity from myself.

"It's like this," she continued, setting her beer down atop the keg so she could use her hands to help illustrate her meaning. "You think there's you and there's your wolf. But that's wrong. There's the *you* that you've had—what, eighteen?—years to grow into, to learn to control. And there's this other part of you that's been newly born. It was always there; it was just never awakened. That part—the wolf part—is ruled by basic instinct. *Your* instincts. They just seem foreign because you know how to rationalize and separate feelings from actions. Your wolf *is* you. It's a manifestation of your most primal urges and animal desires. It just needs nurturing and guidance."

"I don't think—"

"Look," she said. "I know it doesn't seem like it right now, but the longer you fight against that part of yourself, the longer it will take to control those urges."

I bit my lip. She had to be wrong. "But there was this deer in the woods," I explained, grasping for something to use as an example. "I almost killed it. I wanted to *eat* it. I would never—"

"Your instinct was to chase it," she interrupted. "It ran away, right?"

I nodded.

"But you don't know whether you'd have killed it for certain."

"My wolf sure as hell wanted to."

"And you might have," she digressed. "When you're in your wolf form, especially at the start, those kinds of responses are natural. Deer equals prey. Prey equals food." She shrugged. "Simple."

She knocked back her beer and belched loudly. The other shifters in the group cheered, raising their cups to her.

It was so ridiculous and unexpected that I laughed. "You'll like it here," she said, changing tact, a fresh grin on her lips at my laughter. "The others seem scary," she said, nudging her head in the direction of the gathered crowd opposite us. I glanced over to see Clay chewing out two of them, his face reddened and a thick vein popping out of his neck. I winced, hoping that wasn't about me.

"But they just don't like outsiders. Especially outsiders on pack land. At pack *camp*. This sort of thing isn't usually done. You are only invited onto pack land *after* you've chosen your pack."

I could hear what she wasn't saying laced between her words. *The only reason you're allowed to be here is because Ryland expects you to bend the knee and join the pack. If he didn't, you'd never be allowed here.*

That heavy feeling of dread crept back in and I shivered, the warmth of the fire doing almost nothing to banish the chill creeping like frost up my arms. "I have to use the bathroom," I said, needing an escape—a minute to myself to gather my thoughts and calm my wolf's sudden urge to flee. We felt backed into a corner and we didn't like it.

Not one bit.

"Yeah. Use the one in the main house," Charity said. "Ry lets us use it when we have bonfire nights. Go inside, down the hall to your right and it's the door at the very end."

I opened my mouth to protest, but Charity gave me a sarcastic eye-roll and began pulling me in that direction. "I'll go with you."

I sighed, relieved that she wasn't going to try to make me go into Ryland's house alone. That would have been a hard *nope*. I'd have held it the whole night if I had to. But I felt I had to ask anyway because of how we'd left things that last time we saw each other— with me growling over his prone form in Clay and Jared's yard. He'd been forced to submit to me, and I seriously doubted he would soon forget that.

It was clear Charity didn't know about that and I hoped Forrest had kept his mouth shut and no one else did, either. I was willing to bet that would only cause more problems. Would they even want me in their pack at all if they thought I was any sort of threat to their beloved alpha?

I let Charity guide me up the three steps onto the porch and through the front door. She hadn't even bothered to knock. She pointed down the hallway toward a door I could see at the end. It was slightly ajar, and the light was on. "It's just down there."

She leaned against the wall in the entryway and shooed me down the hall. I left the entryway, noticing a small living area ahead and further back, a small kitchen. It didn't look like a place someone like Ryland would live. It was too...*homey.*

Sighing, I made my way toward the bathroom, the feelings of unease I'd had outside now dialed up to a hundred. Exactly the opposite effect I was going for when I said I needed to use the restroom. I hadn't even really needed to go, but as I drew nearer the bathroom, I found the beer *had* in fact worked its way down into my bladder already.

"...like an accident. Like you did before." Ryland's deep baritone echoed from within a closed door and I stopped dead in the hallway, stricken with panic. My chest fluttered with an erratic pulse. My wolf roared to the forefront of my mind and I was hit with an image of Ryland beneath our paws—his face pressed into the dirt.

I breathed through the urges, balling my hands to fists.

"I may not have to," another voice answered him, this one rich and smooth as velvet, the cadence breathy. A zip of some unknown sensation raced up my spine and my upper lip curled back of its own accord, as though anticipating an attack.

Recognizing an enemy.

"I did what you asked. The other packs already want her out of the picture. All we have to do it sit back and wa—"

"What's that?" Ryland barked and I held my breath. A pause.

"Someone's outside."

Oh my god. Oh my god. Oh my god.

I ran on tip toe toward the bathroom, a hot blush searing the back of my neck, slicking my chest with sweat.

"Allie," Ryland called, his voice a growl. I froze.

Fuck. My. Life.

Stiff as a corpse, I spun on my heel and faced him. "I—I was just going to use the bathroom," I stammered, gesturing to Charity where she was still leaning against the wall in the living area, her phone screen illuminating her pretty face. "Charity said I could use—"

"Did she now?"

Charity, finally noticing what was going on in the hall, lowered her phone and gave a little wave. "Oh, hey Ry," she said with a tight smile. "Sorry if we disturbed you."

Ry smiled back at her; the expression packed with a saccharine sweetness. "Not at all."

Another form moved from the room, a tall shadow filling the hall.

My hackles raised.

He slid past Ryland as though he were gliding on air. He looked between Ryland and I, and I could have imagined it, but I swear I saw Ryland give the guy a tiny nod. As if giving him permission for something. Maybe to introduce himself to me.

I backed away a step, not sure I wanted to meet the stranger that was making warning bells go off all over my body.

Ryland said something else to Charity, and she laughed as he left me and the creepy guy in the hall and went to talk to her. There was a buzzing in my ears, and it drowned out their voices.

"I should get back outside," I said to the stranger, not lifting my head to meet his gaze.

He was dressed in all black. A silver ring glimmered on his left index finger, laden with a bright blue stone.

"A pleasure to meet you," the man said, completely ignoring my plea to leave.

He held out his hand to me and I couldn't help noticing how *pale* he was.

Steeling myself, I lifted my chin and met his stare. Black orbs stared down into me from a blank face. High cheekbones and deep-set eyes made him seem even paler than he was—the shadows offsetting his pallor. Thick lips crooked into a sly grin, turning up at the right corner.

Inside, my mind was screaming that he wasn't human. But my wolf knew he wasn't wolf, either.

When his lips pulled back, I saw that a set of fangs were hidden behind them.

Before I could back away, the vampire grabbed hold of my hand and shook it, never breaking eye contact. "Grey," he said, and I struggled to understand what he meant, his cold grip throwing my thoughts out of sync.

His name. He was telling you his name.

"Allie," I replied, trying unsuccessfully to pull my hand back.

The vampire smiled and cocked his head, narrowing his gaze. "You didn't overhear anything just now," he said.

What? Vaguely, I remembered overhearing them talking, but I thought it best not to admit that. Besides, it wasn't like I heard anything private or whatever. "No," I replied, shaking my head slowly. "I didn't hear anything."

The vampire clapped his hand over mine from the other side and shook it again, just once, lifting his gaze from mine. "Good," he said. "Off you go now."

When he let go, I couldn't get away fast enough. I tore past him, away from the bathroom and toward where Ryland was chatting with Charity, saying something to make her blush.

"All done?" she asked me, pausing their conversation.

I gulped, still bristling from the whole ordeal in the hall. It left a sour taste in my mouth. "Yeah. Done. I'm going to head back out, okay?"

"I'm right behind you," she called after me, turning back to Ryland.

My hand closed over the knob, but it was pulled away when the door was reefed open from the other side and I was left staring at a heavily breathing Clay. He froze when he saw me and let out a little growl. "*Fuck, Allie,*" he said between gritted teeth. "I told you to stay put."

Before I could reply, Jared appeared beside Clay, equally breathless, but he wasn't looking at me. His eyes darted through the cabin until they found Ryland. Two other guys piled in behind Jared.

Clay bristled and barked, "Watch it!" as they shouldered past him.

"Territory breech," Jared all but shouted.

Ryland's face twisted into a sneer. "What?" he bellowed, and Charity removed herself from his side, tip-toeing closer to me and out of the range of his anger.

"Come on, we should go outside," Charity whispered.

"Two different packs," the one I recognized to be Forrest growled. "One to the north and one to the east. Dylan saw at least six of them to the north. We don't know how many are breeching to the east."

Ryland cursed, casting me a withering glare.

A hand wrapped around my arm and tugged me toward the door just as Ryland shouted "Out!"

Clay pulled me out of the fray and into a half embrace, shielding me as Ryland and others burst out of the cabin and someone cut the music.

"Breech," Ryland roared, and silence fell on the gathering, all attention turned to their alpha. The only sound was the ominous roar of flame. "Dylan," he called and a blonde guy in his early thirties, buck ass naked, stepped forward from the fire.

I blushed and averted my stare. "Gather a group and head east."

The shifter called Dylan turned and shifted in the blink of an eye, becoming a mottled light gray wolf. Four others burst from their human flesh, scattering clothes over the dirt, and followed him.

"Forrest," Ryland ordered, "Go find Harrison and Seth. You're with me. We go north."

Forrest glared at me before he ran at full speed from the porch and past the fire, down one of the footpaths.

Jared came to stand beside Clay and me, wrapping my shaking hand into his. *You okay,* he mouthed.

I nodded, not trusting myself to talk. "Party's over," Ryland bellowed. "Stay alert."

"Ry—" Jared started, and his uncle whirled on him, eyes aglow and shoulders rigid, his wide frame blocking out the light of the fire.

"Get her out of here," he hissed. "Tomorrow night we *end* this."

He turned his burning stare on me. "I hope you've made up your mind, girl," he snarled. "Or I'll have to make it *for* you."

The only thing keeping me in my human form and stopping my wolf from trying to rip his head off was Jared and Clay. My anchors. Lending me their strength. I didn't breathe until Ryland took off at a jog after Forrest, barking orders at the others still around the fire as he passed them.

"Well that escalated quickly," Charity said with a bit of a slur, stepping away from the cabin's door.

Jared shook his head. "Not funny, Char."

She shrugged. "It's not usually so exciting here," she assured me with a wink. "See you again soon I hope?"

How was she so freaking calm? I just gaped at her, open mouthed, trying to wrap my brain around how the night had gone from awkward drinks and conversation around a campfire to *this*.

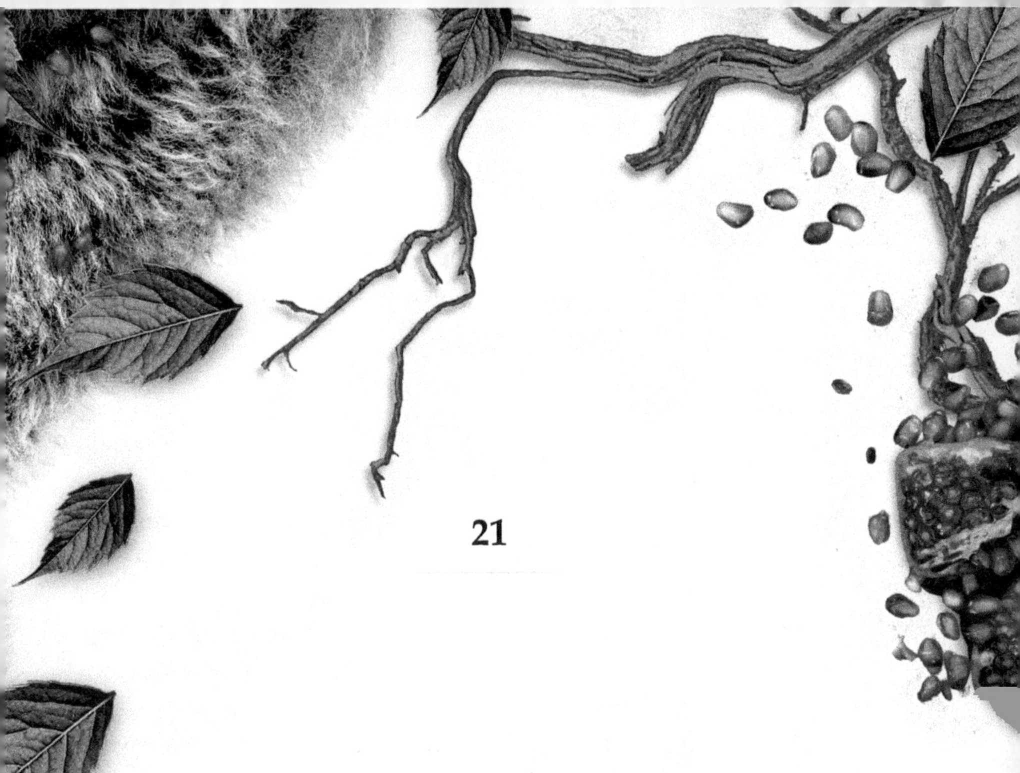

21

"Would you stop," I tugged my arm away from Clay as we finally neared the Jeep. He'd been hauling me at a breakneck speed through the trees after we left. If he'd gripped me any tighter, he'd have left bruises, and in my new, tougher skin, that was saying something.

Jared unlocked the Jeep and froze with his hand on the handle as a long howl rose up into the sky to the South.

"Seth," Jared choked, his eyes going wide and breaths coming harder than they had been a minute before.

Clay's gaze hardened on him and he held out a hand to Jared. "Go," he growled. "I'll get her home safe."

Jared considered the keys in his hand and then his friend in the moonlight. Then me.

"We'll be alright," I told him. "Go help them."

"*Fuck*," Jared cursed, his hands beginning to shake. "No. I need to stay with you. Get in the Jeep."

He pulled on the door and I cleared the four steps between us and slammed it back shut. "*Go*," I told him. "They need you."

I hoped my eyes conveyed what I couldn't bring myself to say. *Don't stay because of me. Don't let them get hurt because of* me.

Jared's face bleached of color and he tossed the keys to Clay and met my eyes. "I'll be there soon. Stay on the property—it's protected."

"What?"

"I'll explain," Clay told me and then stepped up into the driver's side, pushing the seat back to accommodate his size. "Get in."

"Be safe," Jared whispered to me and I hugged him, tightening my arms around his back.

"*You* be safe," I countered. "Okay?"

"I will."

Swiftly, Jared kissed the top of my head just as Clay started the Jeep and then he was off and running, removing his shirt as he went. His twin footfalls turned to the canter of an animal working into a full sprint within seconds.

"Come on," Clay barked out the window and I raced around the Jeep and hopped inside, shivering as a blast of warm air washed over me from the vents. I hadn't even realized I'd been cold.

Clay turned up the heat and peeled out of the little nook we'd parked in at the side of the dirt road. Bits of loose earth and gravel spat from the Jeep's tires as we barreled toward the main road. Of its own accord, my hand shot up and curled around the holy shit handle just as we went over a bump in the road that would've had my head bouncing high enough to hit the roof.

"Should I be worried?" I almost shouted over the roar of the engine and the sound of the tires munching gravel.

There was a pause, then, "No."

"You hesitated."

No reply.

Well, fuck.

The Jeep bumped onto the main road and the feel of smooth pavement beneath the tires made some of the tension flee from my muscles. My pulse slowed and the glow cast by my eyes over the dash was fading. The things were like goddamned flashlights in the dark.

"So, the cabin is protected?" I asked, still a little more breathless than I'd like, but slowly gaining back control.

Clay cut his blue eyes toward me for a second before training them back on the road, only looking away to scan the tree line on either side periodically. "Yeah," he said. "A friend of my parents did it a long time ago. She's a witch."

I realized now wasn't the time, but a little blossom of hope formed in my chest that he might actually *know* a witch. Witches could do magic, right? And magic might be able to heal something like Huntington's Disease.

Later, I told myself—when this is all over. *I'll ask him later.*

"It's a warding spell that's tied to the cabin itself, but it's only activated while we're inside. It draws its energy from us."

I squinted, trying to wrap my head around that. "So, the magic keeps people away by sucking energy out of the people who live in the cabin?"

I grimaced. I didn't like the sound of that. I'd been an unwitting participant in some spell I didn't even know existed.

Clay pursed his lips, considering how best to respond. "Basically, yeah. Only those who know where it is can find it. For everyone else, it's like it's not even there. It's invisible."

"But I've always been able to see It," I argued, thinking back to the very first time I'd laid eyes on it like a beacon of safety through the trees, dragging my battered body over muck and leaves.

Clay peered over at me curiously but said nothing.

Finally, he shrugged. "I'm no magic expert."

Ww made it back to the cabin without any problems and I didn't take a full breath until we were both on the dirt lawn. I sighed. "So...we should be safe now?"

He grunted.

But then something else prickled at the edges of my mind—something that didn't make sense. "Clay?"

"Yeah?"

"Why did you have to sleep inside when Jared was gone? I mean, if I was totally safe being in the house alone."

His body stilled and I could see his mind working in the way he shifted his eyes over the dirt at his feet. "Some enemies don't wear masks," he replied. "Some hide in plain sight, wearing the faces of people you trust."

He ran a hand over the back of his neck, and I could tell the question had made him uncomfortable. "Besides," he added after a beat of silence. "I thought it might make you feel safer. The one night I didn't sleep inside was the night you woke up from that nightmare and I..."

My brows furrowed. "...busted down the door," I finished for him.

He nodded.

I hadn't even realized it, but he was right. I only had the nightmares when he wasn't there. In the first week when he slept out in the woods, I'd woken shaking from nightmares almost every night. And then that night when I was alone in the cabin and he was out sleeping on the sofa in his shop—that'd been the worst nightmare of all.

I looked at Clay like I was seeing him for the first time. I smirked. "You aren't so bad, you know," I told him, trying to lighten the conversation. "You act like this big tough guy with your mean words and your angry face, but deep down, you're just a big softie, aren't you?"

His brows lifted for an instant before his face settled back to its usual hardness. "Nah. I really am just a giant asshole."

I laughed.

Clay nudged his head toward the dark cabin. "Think you can sleep?"

I thought about it. "No. Not until Jared comes back, anyway."

Clay didn't say anything right away, so I asked the question that'd been eating at me most of the drive and walk back home. "He'll be alright...right?"

Clay smirked. "He always is. We joke that the guy has horseshoes stuck up his ass. He's basically unkillable."

I cocked my head at him, laughing and wincing at the same time at the mental image that provoked. "What? Why?"

"He always finds some way to get himself out of trouble," Clay explained. "Add in the fact that he's cheated death a good half dozen times and..." Clay shrugged, trailing off.

Unkillable.

It was enough for me to shrug off the foreboding feeling weighing on my shoulders and my mind. I knew deep down that *no one* was truly unkillable, but Clay's confidence that Jared would be alright would have to do for now. Until I saw he was unharmed with my own eyes.

Clay nodded to himself, as though making a decision. "Come on, then," he said, lumbering off down the side of the cabin. "I could use an extra set of hands in the shop."

I grinned, biting the inside of my cheek as I followed after him.

We worked on a Honda CRF450R. It was one Clay was fixing for someone named Jack—who was apparently someone I'd briefly met around the campfire, but all the names blurred together, and I couldn't recall his face.

The bike was an older model. Maybe a 2015. Dad had one similar to it before he bought the Maico, and we'd worked on that one together lots of times before he got sick.

I was surprised to find, like archery, the muscle memory of working on bikes had never truly left, either. Clay and I settled into a rhythm as we changed the air filter which was just as much of a pain in the ass as I remembered. I went to wash up, letting Clay finish adjusting the intake valves since it was really a one-man job.

Dirt, grime, and engine grease stained the sides of my hands and the creases in my fingers. I rubbed the grit between my fingertips, a million memories of Dad surfacing in the back of my mind. But unlike most times, the memories didn't trigger the cloying darkness.

Instead, I smiled at my dirty hands. At the metallic shop smell and the tang of Fast Orange as I rubbed the abrasive soap into my palms and scrubbed the grease from beneath my nails.

I breathed deeply. I'd forgotten how much I *loved* that smell. I felt... strangely peaceful as I dried my hands on my jeans and lifted myself to sit atop the counter, waiting for Clay to finish.

Jared still wasn't back, and I began to bob my knee, hoping Clay had more work I could help with. It was doing wonders for keeping me distracted and I didn't want to be alone with my thoughts just yet.

There were too many places my mind wanted to wander.

To Jared and whether he was safe. To Layla and her illness.

To the inevitable choice I would have to make tomorrow.

And to the way the light and shadows played over Clay's face as he fit his big fingers into the cavity of the bike, adjusting its valves. His expression focused and without the pain it usually held.

This was his solace, too.

This and the mangled heavy bag hanging in the corner of the room. It was streaked with ribbons of shining silver duct tape, holding it together in the place where Clay had blown it apart. I'd felt the rattle of his fury in the floorboards on more than a few nights since I'd come to live here. It was a wonder the thing didn't need daily replacement.

There was a tarp behind it and to the right, hung using its silver eyelets to cover part of the wall above a sofa strewn with a ratty knit blanket and flat pillow. At the edge, a curling piece of paper jutted out, and when I squinted, I thought I could just make out a little slice of black string tied to a pin. The paper was bluish in hue with streaks of red and white. Tiny text dotting the surface. A map.

I glanced at Clay, who was still intently focused on the bike and back to the wall.

Jumping down from the counter, I strode over to it, my curiosity winning out. I kneeled on the sofa cushions, feeling the hard coil of metal springs beneath as they dug into my knees. I peeled back the tarp.

"Allie, what are you—"

Clay abruptly stopped speaking and I heard a tool drop from his hands to clatter against the ground.

It was a map alright. Of the continental US.

A silver pin was stuck in the spot that I knew to be Forest Grove near the west coast. Attached to it was a black string leading to another pin, this one in a neighboring state. From there was another string leading to another place, and another, where it finally stopped. The trail ending.

Above that series of strings and pins was a photo of Devin. His face shrouded in a hoodie—eyes hollow and shadowed with purplish half moons beneath. The picture was taken in secret. Devin didn't know he was being watched, his gaze was fixed on something in the distance and his cell phone was clenched tightly in his hand.

Bile rose in my throat and a little flutter of panic took wing in my chest.

Something red in the upper corner caught my eye and I peered up to the top left corner of the map, to where a red pin was stuck in a spot just below Fairbanks, Alaska.

I wondered what it was, but it was clear to me what Clay was doing. Why he had pins in a map on his wall and a picture of my ex taped above. "You're tracking him," I breathed, unsure how to feel.

Clay appeared as if from thin air, a dip in the cushion the only evidence that he was there at all until he cautiously took the tarp from my fingers and drew it back closed over the map.

Was this why he'd been so busy in the shop lately? Was it not because of me, but...because he needed the money to hire whoever took that photo?

I was afraid to ask.

My heartbeat thrummed in my ears and when I finally looked away from the covered map and shakily got back to my feet, I fumbled to figure out what to say.

Why are you tracking him? That would be a good place to start.

Are you still planning to kill *him? Tracking him so you can tear his throat out if he ever gets close enough again?* That would be another valid question.

Or are you making sure he's far *away from me? That he can't hurt me.*

Something in his hard, solemn gaze told me it was a combination of the two and my breathing hitched. Something that'd been tightly wound in my chest began to unravel.

"I may have told Jared I would step back," he said through tight lips, his left brow twitching as though he was working very hard to keep himself restrained. "And I have. But that doesn't mean I won't protect you. I'll *never* allow anyone to hurt you again. Never."

"Clay—" I breathed, my legs moving all on their own, hands outstretched to touch him. I felt an uncontrollable urge to comfort him. I wanted him to stop looking so hurt. This whole time I thought he hated me. Wanted me gone. I thought he was sickened by the bond tying us together. Disgusted.

I thought he didn't care. I was so, *so* wrong.

He took a sharp step back, putting himself out of my reach. "*Don't,*" he barked, nostrils flaring. "I can't," he said, but I could see his resolve weakening. His fists shaking. "You shouldn't—" he stammered, cutting himself off, shaking his head. "I'm not—I'm not *good* for you, Allie."

I could've laughed.

If anyone wasn't *good*, it wasn't Clay. Couldn't he see that? Death and destruction followed me wherever I went. I was a plague on the people I cared about. If anyone wasn't *good* for someone, it was me.

"No," I argued in a whisper. "You're wrong."

For a second, I stop denying the connection between us. I let myself feel it in full force and gasped as the sensation washed over me like the brush of fingers over my flesh.

He didn't step away when I closed the gap a second time and tentatively placed my palm against his cheek, coaxing him to look at me. His eyes, like a frozen lake under a winter sun, pierced me straight through. I saw in them something I hadn't ever before. For a fleeting second, he wasn't the *beast*, he was just a man. A man in pain. Tortured by the intensity of the emotions he tried to pretend he didn't possess.

He bristled under my touch and my lips parted as I tried to find the words to thank him. I realized there was *so much* I needed to thank him for.

The words had only just begun to form on my tongue when they were stolen along with all the breath in my body. Clay snatched me up with strong hands around my waist, fingers pressing into the exposed skin at my lower back. I fought for breath as he lifted me onto my toes and in one swift motion, pulled me against him, his lips finding mine.

An explosion of impossible sensations sent stars bursting behind my eyelids, and a surprised moan coiled up from within, trapped between our lips.

A long-suppressed desire flooded my veins and I found myself kissing him back, hands hungry and grasping. Hearts pounding and crashing.

He was breathing too fast.

I wasn't sure I was breathing at all.

My head spun with dizzying desire and my whole body *ached* and hummed. I felt...alive. There was so much energy—so much *life*—gushing through my veins, I thought I might burst at the seams from it.

I'd been terrified I might recoil the next time a man tried to kiss me. That maybe I'd be repulsed by his touch. I was thrilled to find I'd been wrong. I wasn't afraid. I didn't want him to stop.

Clay tipped my head back with fingers pressed on the base of my skull, his fingers wrapping around the back of my neck, holding me there against him. Fastening us together.

Time ground to a halt as he lifted me again, this time taking my feet from the ground. My back knocked hard into a solid surface behind me and the crinkle of the tarp shimmied in my ears. He had me pinned against the wall.

My composure and sanity were fighting each other to be heard, to be heeded, but one chased the other out the window until both were long gone and only *heat* remained.

Hot—where he touched me.

Hot—where he kissed me.

A blazing inferno that ran so deep it was a wonder I didn't catch fire, burn to ashes from the inside out.

His tongue slid between my lips and his thigh pressed between my legs, brushing against me in the most beautifully *agonizing* way. He filled all the gaps between our bodies just as he was filling some of the hollow places in my heart—vaporizing the darkness living there.

There was only Clay. There was only—

He broke the kiss, drawing back to look at me with heavily lidded eyes that glowed with blue flame and too many emotions to decipher even a single one.

A sliver of ice lodged itself in my chest as the stark reality of what I'd just allowed to happen slapped me. Clay released me, and I saw a similar shock mirrored in his gaze.

The hands that had been holding me tightly a second ago, were stiff now. The lips that'd kissed mine were a hard line.

"We shouldn't have—" I choked, sick with guilt. It didn't matter that nothing had happened between Jared and I—that we weren't *together* no matter how much this magical bond tried to argue that we were.

It didn't matter because I'd just finished telling Jared that I would have neither of them. And now...

And now...

Frustrated tears burned at the corners of my eyes, blurring the edges.

I shouldered past Clay, unable to speak, too afraid that if I opened my mouth all the confusion and frustration and *anger* would come out and I wasn't sure what I'd say. What I'd do.

Because I wanted Clay to kiss me five minutes ago.

And if I was being honest with myself, I wanted him to do it again.

To not ever stop.

I tripped in my haste to get out of the shop and inside the cabin. I didn't stop until I was up the stairs, down the hall, in my bedroom. The door slammed behind me and my boots came off, kicked into a corner as I numbly climbed onto my bed.

I drew the covers up to my chin, as if I could hide from the truth I'd been trying to fight since *before* I became a shifter. Since before *any* of this had happened.

Because even then, I had feelings for them both.

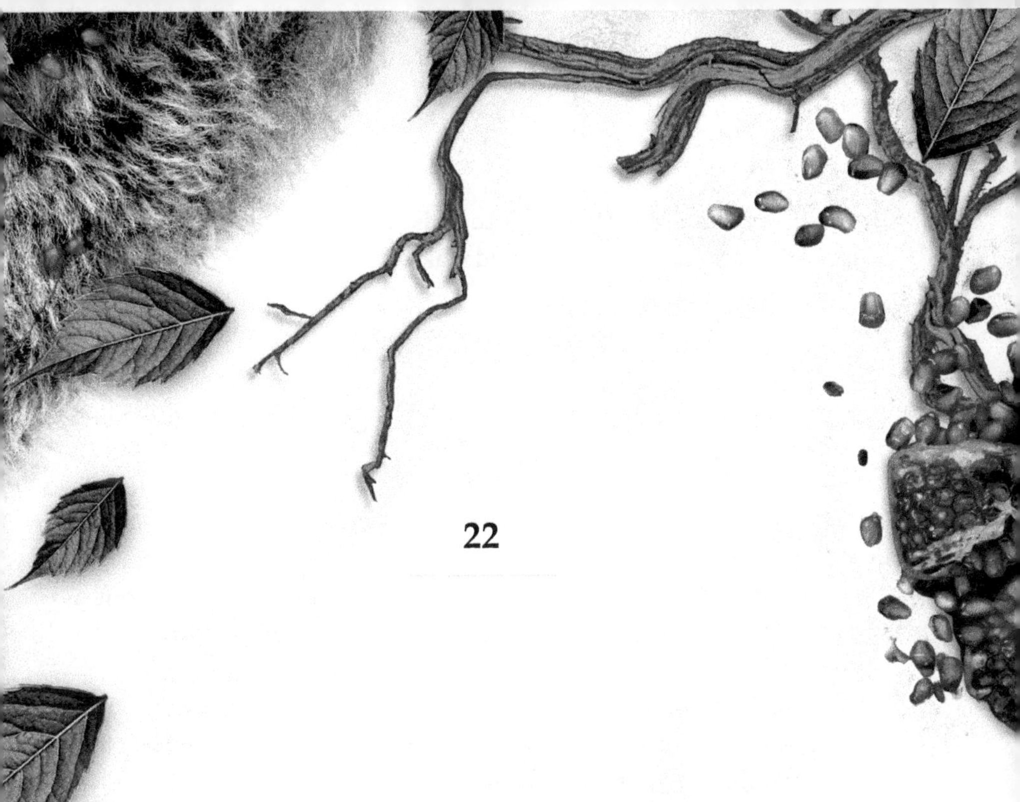

22

I didn't mean to fall asleep.

The minutes stretched into hours as I waited for Jared to return home last night. The last I could remember was the burning in my eyes and the heaviness of my eyelids before I must've passed out.

Something woke me, though. A shifting movement that wasn't my own. My eyes didn't want to open yet, and I had to force them, my pulse quickening as I startled into wakefulness to find the source of the movement.

I stilled, noticing the hand slung over the lower part of my leg. Propping myself up on my elbow, I gushed a sigh of relief when I found Jared there, sprawled at the end of the bed with one leg sticking off the side and one side of his face pressed into the covers.

He breathed deeply in his sleep. A streak of dirt ran up from his lip to curve over his cheek like war paint. His dirty blonde hair flopped over his forehead, shining in the dawn light filtering in through my window. Unconsciously, I reached over to brush it away from his eye, wincing when I saw a small trail of blood beneath.

He'd been hurt. But he'd healed—leaving only the blood behind as evidence he was injured at all.

Jared didn't stir. Not when I woke or when I brushed his hair away.

He was in such a deep sleep I had to resist the urge to double check his pulse and check to see that he would wake.

Let him sleep, I told myself.

"I have to tell you something," I whispered, my voice so quiet I wasn't sure he'd have properly heard even if he *were* awake.

I shivered as the memory of Clay's fingers on my body—of his lips on mine—raced across my thoughts. How was I going to tell him?

How could I tell him he was right?

That there *was* something between Clay and me. And that I couldn't deny it any more than I could deny what was between me and Jared.

I gulped, running my fingers through his smooth hair. He let out a small sound, something halfway between a sigh and a groan, and I pulled my hand away, not ready to wake him.

Not ready to face him.

Even though my body had begun to buzz with anticipation for what the day would bring, I found my eyes were still heavy. It couldn't have been very late yet. I yawned.

I could sleep just a little bit longer.

I adjusted the blanket to cover Jared, though it felt like a crime covering up his naked chest and abs. I had to look away before my gaze strayed too low. His khaki shorts were hanging so low on his hips I could tell with a single glance that he wasn't wearing *anything* under them.

Once he looked at least a bit more comfortable, I sunk back down into the mattress, pressing my legs against his body and allowing his exhaustion and sense of calm to drag me back under.

THE SECOND TIME I AWOKE, MY HEAD FELT HEAVY, AS THOUGH FILLED WITH lead. It always happened when I let myself go back to sleep after waking the first time. With a groan, I turned over, feeling around the bed with my legs for Jared. But when my toes poked through the edge of the blanket and found empty air, I forced myself up.

"Jared?" I whispered, wondering for a fleeting second if I imagined him there. But when I drew back the covers at the end of the bed, I found that little traces of dirt beneath and his scent still lingered in his absence.

I rubbed the backs of my hands over my eyes and noticed my phone next to my elbow in the bed, flashing with missed notifications.

Shit.

Had he needed to leave again?

With sleep-numbed fingers I lifted it, squinting at the screen's brightness before my eyes adjusted.

I had a missed call from Uncle Tim that I'd need to return later, and three texts. One from Layla and two from Vivian.

Nothing from Jared. I strained my ears to reach the lower level of the cabin, trying to hear for anything downstairs, but heard nothing.

Where the hell did he go?

The time glowed white in the upper corner of my phone, telling me it was almost one in the afternoon. I couldn't remember the last time I'd slept past nine in the morning, never mind all the way until the afternoon. No wonder I felt like shit warmed up.

I punched my pillows into a backrest and leaned against the creaky headboard to open the texts from my friends.

They were both asking me to go with them to the drive-in tonight. Layla texted to ask if I got Viv's message and if I could come, and Viv texted begging me to save her from being the third wheel because Layla was insisting on bringing Quinn.

I wondered if she was using the fancy new phone case I'd given her for her birthday. It was matte black with shining gold stars and some sort of runic design on the back. It had screamed *Layla* when I spied it in the shop and I was a little disappointed I hadn't been there when she opened it. But the gushing thank you text told me what I wasn't there to witness myself.

I smirked, but then paused before replying, remembering in a rush what was happening tonight as my mind caught up with my body and woke. *Fuck.* Grimacing, I thumbed a quick reply to Viv.

Allie: Sorry, can't. There's something I have to do.

See you guys tomorrow, k?

I left it at that, hoping the final tone of the message would let them know my mind couldn't be changed and save me from five more messages trying to convince me.

I'd put this off long enough.

I remembered the crimson smear on Jared's brow and shuddered. No one else was going to get hurt because of me. I'd already caused enough pain and suffering and *death* in my seventeen years. I could get over my issue with submitting to Ryland if it meant peace.

I could live with that choice. Right?

I rolled my head around to get the crick out of my neck as I hauled my heavy bones from bed and dug through the pile of too-clean-to-wash-but-too-dirty- to-put-away laundry on the wooden chair in the corner. I picked out a fresh(ish) pair of jeans and a t- shirt of Viv's that was a bit big on me, but comfy as hell and stumbled into the shower. Eager to get the campfire smell out of my hair.

The telltale bang of the screen door against the frame was what finally drew me out of the warm embrace of the water and out into the chill of the bathroom, feet protesting the icy tile.

"Jared?" I called as I wrapped a towel around myself and set to quickly brushing my hair.

When he called back, "Yeah, I'm down here," I didn't know whether to be relieved or start panicking. Relieved he was still home. Panicked because his tone was uncharacteristically drawn, and I had a pretty good idea why that might be.

Time to face the music, Allie.

"I'll be right down," I hollered back, rushing to make myself presentable. I pulled the brush through all the tangles in my hair, wondering if some of them were caused by Clay's fingers, feeling alternatingly guilty as hell and turned on at the thought.

It's not right.

Nothing about this is normal.

I shouldn't be falling for *two* guys.

I felt dirty and slimy and almost got back in the shower to try to rid myself of the feeling but didn't. It wasn't my fault, or at least that's what I tried to tell myself. It was my wolf. *She* bonded to them both. Not me. She wasn't giving me a choice and I was tired of fighting.

The excuses did little to assuage my thoughts, but I kept pumping them out anyway, hoping for one that could stick. One that I could make myself believe.

Quit stalling, I told myself, fingers curled around the porcelain sink. *Jared's waiting. Get your ass out that door.*

Walking down the stairs was like walking the fucking plank. Each step drawing me nearer to certain doom. When I found Jared sitting alone at the small table beside the window—the one we'd eaten at together that very first morning here, I was reminded of everything he'd done for me since I came here and that only made it ten times harder to slide myself into the seat opposite him and bring my chin up to meet his eyes.

"So," I said, hating the awkward tone of my voice. I wasn't any good at this kind of stuff. Never had to be before. "What happened last night? You were bleeding? Did—uh—did anyone get hurt?"

My hands clasped and unclasped in my lap beneath the table.

Jared shook his head. "Nothing bad. Just some scratches. Seth got bit pretty bad, but he's already mostly healed."

I would've asked what they wanted, but I had a feeling I already knew. "They were looking for me, weren't they?"

Jared didn't answer, his face turning to stone as he shifted his gaze out the window to the subdued light of a cloud-covered day.

"Don't worry about it," Jared said in a faraway voice. "We won't let anything happen to you."

My stomach soured. "Jared, I need to—"

"Clay already told me," he countered, eyes still trained on something outside.

That was what I was afraid of. I knew Clay wouldn't hide something like that from his best friend. *Of course,* he would tell him. But what exactly had he said? Did he apologize? Did he say he wouldn't ever do it again? Or...had he said what I'm about to say?

The words were caught in my throat, dancing on the tip of my tongue. He needed to know the truth. My truth. Regardless of what Clay said.

I bowed my head. "I'm sorry."

"Don't—"

"Wait," I interrupted, glancing up to find him watching me. It took all my will to keep from looking away from his pain-filled stare. "Let me get this out."

His adams apple bobbed and his brows lowered, but he waited.

Without knowing how to put it delicately, I just blurted the thoughts as they came, needing to break the dam and get it all out in the open. It was the only way we would ever be able to find our way through this mess. We had to be honest.

"You were right," I began. "There is something between Clay and me. I just didn't know exactly what it was until last night. Or, wait, that's not actually true. I did know before, I just didn't *want* it. I was trying to fight it. Just like I was trying to fight what was happening between me and you."

Jared paled and his knuckles whitened where they gripped the handle of the mug on the table.

"I can't choose," I told him, evicting the words quickly to get this over with. "It would be like..." I fought to find a way to explain. "Like cutting off a limb or something. And even if I wanted to, my wolf would never allow it."

"It's not your wolf," Jared said. "It's the mate bond."

He sighed. "I shouldn't have ever put you in this position. I shouldn't have been glad when Clay said he would back down. I shouldn't have let him do that. The bond is sacred. We're taught that from pups," he gave a tight, strained laugh, shaking his head.

"And I completely disrespected it. And him. And *you*."

This...was not what I was expecting. He was too good. Way *too good* of a person. I didn't deserve him. I didn't think I could *ever* deserve him.

"Don't be sorry," was all I could think to say. "It's a fucked-up situation."

He licked his lips. "Yeah. Super fucked up."

There was a long moment of silence between us and the tension started to make the hairs on the back of my neck raise. "So," I said tentatively. "Where does this leave us?"

We could just all be friends. Ignore the urges to be more.

Or...*and this one hurt*...I could leave. It was an option I'd been toying with for a couple days now. My leaving would save everyone a lot of grief.

It would stop virtually every problem with the pack. It would leave room for Jared and Clay's friendship to heal. They could find other girls to date. It wouldn't be the same, but at least those relationships would be easier.

They would be normal.

And I could still see Layla and Viv. They would come visit me. We could FaceTime. I'd be eighteen next month. I could leave and no one could stop me.

"I don't know," Jared said, taking a steadying breath. A breathy laugh came out with his long sigh. "Maybe Hazel was right."

I cocked my head at him, wondering about which part. "What do you—"

The door banged open and Clay appeared in the kitchen, rubbing the dirt from the bottom of his boots. His eyes flitted to mine for a fraction of an instant. There was a question in them—in the tight line of his mouth.

He seemed to be asking without the need for words,

we good?

The relief was like a baby grand piano had been lifted from my chest. When our eyes met again, I gave him a tiny nod, and his posture relaxed.

Then his brows drew together. "Hey," he said, peering over to look at something in the kitchen. The clock on the stove. "Don't you work today?"

I groaned, letting my head drop like a stone into my hands. "Fuck, I completely forgot."

I'd taken an earlier shift since it was a PA day to make up for missing Saturday. I was practically already late.

"What time are you working until?" Jared asked, and I didn't miss how he was carefully avoiding making eye contact with Clay.

"Eight. I have to do returns after hours tonight." Jared nodded. "Okay. I'll take you if you want."

Clay busied himself getting a glass of water and Jared got up to grab his keys from the hook. "And I'll pick you up after with Clay—we'll have to go straight to the four corners to meet with Ryland after. I told him I'd have you there by nine."

The what?

"*Uh,* okay, yeah. Sounds good," I said, even though warning bells were ringing, and my wolf was waking, and it definitely *definitely* did not sound good. "I'm going to run up and change really quick. Meet you outside?"

I left before either of them could see or feel the panic rising within me like an evening tide. By the time I came back downstairs, I'd be calm. Collected. They wouldn't know that I was on the verge of total meltdown.

I can do this.

I can do this.

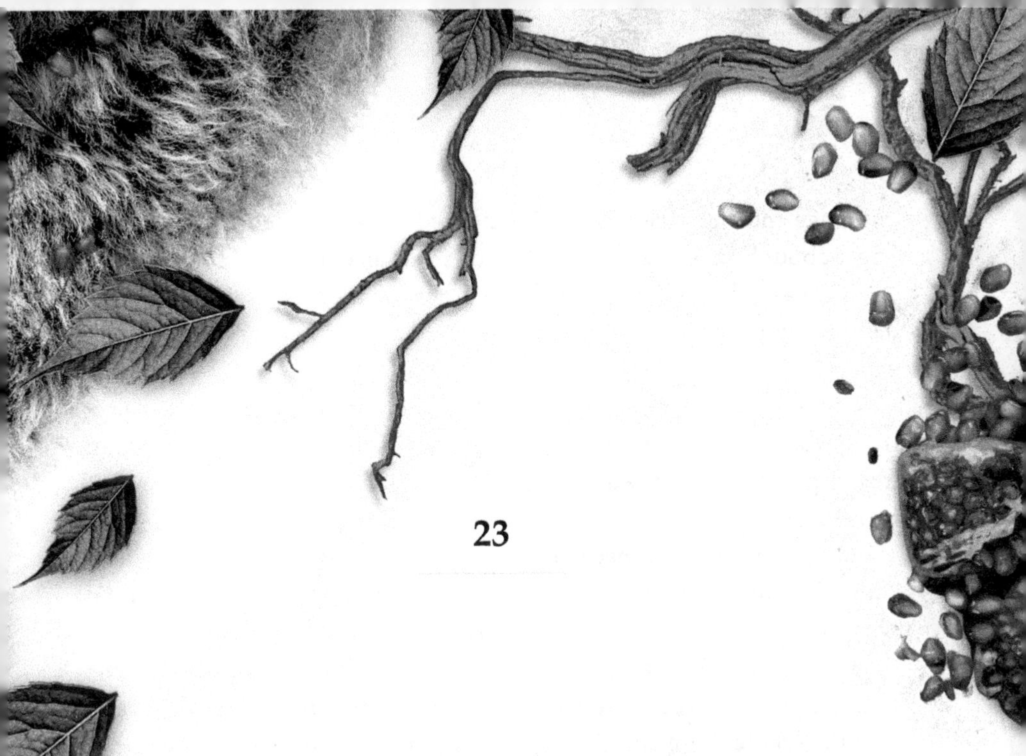

23

Much as I tried to draw it out, the shift at the shop went by so quickly I swear one minute it was three o'clock and I was fielding texts from Layla and Viv while dealing with an uncharacteristically busy shop, and the next I was packing away the last of the returns in a box behind the counter, glaring at the clock that told me I only have five more minutes before it was time to go.

Three minutes early, Jared's white jeep pulled up out front. Two shadows crowding the front seats.

It's going to be a cakewalk, I told myself as I shut off all the lights and triple checked that the safe was properly locked with the cashbox inside. *Just agree to submit, accept him as your alpha. Do the whole ceremony thing and be done with it.*

I made a mental note to ask what exactly the ancient ritual of being inducted into a pack entailed on the way so I would know what to expect. I assumed it would just be swearing an oath or something, like in ancient times when men swore fealty to their lords and kings. Or something equally symbolic and ridiculous. But who knew?

I'd also been wondering about the vampire guy I'd run into at Ry's cabin. No one else seemed even mildly curious as to why he was there. Jared and Clay didn't even mention him. I assumed that meant it wasn't a big deal. Maybe he was even a friend to the pack. But either way, the guy gave me the creeps and I wondered what Clay and Jared might know about him. I'd ask them when this was all over.

If I was going to be running into other paranormal creatures on the daily when I joined the pack then I wanted a bit of heads up on what to expect.

I locked the door behind me and took my time making sure everything was finished, checking off the mental list in my mind to keep from freaking out. I didn't want to get in that Jeep until I had control of myself.

My inner wolf had been prowling like a caged beast for the whole shift. She knew what was coming as well as I did, and even though I'd accepted my fate, she wasn't ready to bow so easily.

I remembered what Charity said about me and my wolf being one. That she wasn't truly a separate entity from me, but then why was I over the whole thing and she was still fighting it? It didn't make sense.

Once I had my breathing steady and the shaking in my hands down to a barely noticeable tremble, I shook the door handle one last time and then tore myself away from the shop and climbed into the back of the Jeep.

"Hey," I said, clearing my throat when my voice came out shaky and uneven.

"You ready?" Clay asked. "Ready as I'll ever be."

"It's going to be fine," Jared reassured me, but not even *he* sounded certain. "We'll be finished and back at the cabin before you know it."

Back at the cabin before you know it, I repeated to myself in my mind, the reassurance sinking in.

Piece of cake.

We drove in silence out from the main street and to the edge of town, me in the middle of the back seat, rigid with nerves. It didn't help that the car behind us seemed to have their high beams on, the light bouncing off the rearview straight into my damned retinas.

When it didn't seem like they were going to get off our tail any time soon, I unbuckled and moved to the seat behind Jared, I'd never fit in the narrow gap behind Clay's seat. He had to have it pushed the full way back just to fit his bulky frame in the vehicle.

I rubbed my eyes and sighed. "Are we almost there?" My stomach was sour with nerves—leaving a foul taste on my tongue. I needed to get this over with before I went into full blown panic attack mode. I couldn't exactly swear my allegiance if I was vomiting or couldn't fucking breathe.

Why was this so stressful? Why did it feel so *wrong*?

"We're here," Clay said a moment later and Jared pulled the Jeep over into a small dirt inlet at the side of the back road. The car that'd been behind us finally whizzed past, their blinding lights vanishing behind a bend in the road. It took forever for my eyes to adjust to the dark after they'd practically been seared the whole way here.

"We go on foot from here," Jared said as we picked our way to the front of the Jeep and onto a tiny footpath no wider than the width of my palm. "It isn't too far."

Jared led the way and Clay fell into step behind me, protecting my front and back, I realized as their chaotic energies soaked into me. They were on edge. As much as I was or even more so. I didn't have the gall to ask why.

Hating how quiet they both were being, I tried to come up with something to say as we walked in a straight line further and further into the cold and the dark. I brushed my hands over my arms—the sweater I'd worn not enough to keep out the chill. My breath clouded in front of my face in little wisps of steam. My teeth chattered. "So," I said. "Why is it called the four corners?"

"We shouldn't talk," Clay said, low and dangerous— his tone making me shiver even more.

I was going to ask why not, but that would require more talking, so I zipped my lips, grinding my teeth together to ward off the foreboding feeling trying to take hold in my bones.

I jumped as something heavy fell onto my shoulders and steadied when I found it was just Clay's sweater. The smell of engine grease and spice filled my nose, almost immediately putting me at ease. I pulled it closer around me and breathed deeply, turning to give him a tiny nod of thanks.

He nodded back, and I noticed how his eyes were white hot with the glow of his wolf. How the steam didn't only come from his mouth in the cold but rose from his shoulders as though he were on fire.

The illusion made him look like something you might find hiding in your closet or clawing its way out from beneath your bed. But a break in the trees revealed his face, the moon chasing away the shadows until I could see that it was just Clay.

Ahead of us, I could just make out a clearing. Much like the one Ryland's camp was built in. Except where his was man made, this one was a natural break in the trees. Packed dirt and brush gave way to tall grasses and ferns brushing against my knees. The grasses rippled in the light breeze, making the almost perfectly square-shaped meadow look like it was an ocean under moonlight. The grass moving in perfect sync to look like waves lapping towards a far-off shore.

If we were here for any other reason, I'd have been in awe of its beauty. As it was, the space was filled with an eerie tension. Like the air was charged with static electricity and any second lightning could strike even though the sky was so clear I could see every constellation for miles around.

My heart in my throat, I moved nearer to Jared, gripping his arm to keep myself steady. Needing his strength to hold me up. "Now what?" I whispered.

"We wait," Jared whispered back. "Ryland will be here any minute."

We waited.

I knew somewhere in the back of my mind that it was probably only a few minutes, but it felt more like closer to an hour or more. By the time I sensed Ryland's presence and caught a whiff of his peppery scent, Clay had positioned himself on my other side, his shoulder pressed against mine. Making all three of us connected. It was the only thing keeping me sane.

It wasn't lost on me that only weeks ago I could barely get near them without my nerve endings screaming, and now all I wanted was the solace and warmth they lent me.

Funny how things change.

Ryland came with a group of others. I recognized Charity to his right, and the purple-haired girl from school next to her. Beside them was Forrest and that guy I thought was called Harrison. The one Ryland had called Dylan was there, too, scanning the clearing for threats with backlit green eyes.

"Good," Ryland said cheerfully as they neared. "You're here."

Jared's hands clenched. "I said I'd bring her," he retorted, all traces of my gentle Jared gone. "I did what you asked, now let's get this over with."

Jared's hand found mine, and he squeezed it tightly, twining our fingers together.

"Come forward," Ryland said with a sweep of his arms and a smirk that had my wolf trembling for release.

Hush, I soothed her. *We have to do this.*

It was almost as though I could hear her whispering back to me. *No, we don't. We won't bow.*

But we had to.

Jared let go of my hand and I shrugged off Clay's sweater, handing it back to him as the fire of my wolf made it feel almost stifling beneath too many layers of clothing. Like Clay, I found that my arms almost seemed to steam as my wolf pressed against my bones, trying to force herself from my flesh.

I realized, a little belatedly, that I'd forgotten to ask how this would go and gulped, praying whatever the process was that it would be quick. I wouldn't be able to hold my wolf for much longer.

The purple-haired girl handed Ryland a flask and he took it, his long fingers curling around the brushed silver. He seemed to be almost moving in slow motion and I wondered why he was drawing this out. I wanted it to be over.

I shook with anticipation.

Just do it. Come on. Faster.

I groaned as my wolf twisted inside me. The pressure of her on my ribcage was going to crack bone. I hunched, pressing my hands into my gut to attempt to hold her inside.

"Thank you, Destiny," he said to the girl with the purple hair.

Charity stepped forward, her hand outstretched as if she intended to help me remain standing, but she was stopped with a glare from her alpha.

"Not yet," he barked at her and she backed away again, mouthing *sorry* to me followed by what I thought was *you got this.*

I shuddered and pushed myself back to my full height, keeping just one hand to my stomach, fisted into the fabric of my thin gray sweater.

I could feel Clay and Jared at my back, but they were too far for me to draw from their strength. I doubted they had much more to give in any case. I'd probably drained them dry.

"When Endurans are pups, they take the blood of the alpha to be taken into the arms of their pack. It is done as soon as they are able to speak the binding words."

Ryland tugged the v-cut neckline of his black long sleeve shirt, revealing a patchwork of scars. Tiny bite marks. The fangs of adolescent wolves forever scarred into his flesh.

If I had to shift right now to do this, one of us wouldn't be leaving this clearing.

I opened my mouth to tell him as much, but he held up his hand to stop me and I closed my mouth again, swallowing to wet my dry throat.

"The process is a bit different for changed wolves. Sometimes, adult wolves can't control their urge to go for the kill. To fight."

Ryland twisted the cap off the silver flask and his eyes flashed orange. I saw the glint of fangs in the moonlight before I had to look away—the presence of his wolf, riling mine to a point of no return. When finally I was able to look again, I found his wrist poised over the flask, a dribble of blood running into its opening and down the silver front, slicking it with glimmering crimson.

"With whiskey and blood, the link is formed. Pack magic will bind you to my will for as long as I live. You will drink and speak the binding words. Do you submit?"

"Yes," I growled, my voice taking on the animal quality I knew meant my wolf was close to the surface. It echoed, garbled and inhuman.

The wind changed and a light jasmine smell permeated the air. I stiffened, my heart stopping dead in my chest.

There was only one person I knew who wore that scent.

Jared and Clay caught the scent at the same time, and I whirled at the same time they did, peering into the tree line.

A hushed curse rose from the shadows. I knew that voice, too.

Oh god. Why?

For fuck's sake why?

Across the clearing, another scent emerged. No, not one. Many.

Too many.

Ryland shoved the flask back at Destiny and growled long and low. The others were on edge now too.

From each of the opposite three corners came wolves. A group of three from the north. Two from the east. And...six from the west.

A little squeal came from behind us and Ryland spun, scanning the forest where somewhere, my best friends were hiding in the brush.

The headlights in my eyes. The car that didn't deviate from our winding path even once until we stopped.

The message I'd sent Viv earlier that day flashed in my memory.

Allie: Sorry, can't. There's something I have to do.

See you guys tomorrow, k?

Viv had already been suspicious there was something I wasn't telling her. That I was in some sort of trouble. And by not being honest with my best friends, I may have just inadvertently signed both of their death certificates.

But the car hadn't been Viv's bug. And it hadn't been Layla's parents' station wagon. There was a third person with them. I realized with a shudder that it must be Quinn. It was *his* car, that must've been why I didn't recognize it.

"What is that?" Ryland hissed at Jared and Clay, who both shrugged as though they had no idea, but the tension in their shoulders was a dead giveaway. But Ryland cut his glare back in the other direction, which was where mine now strayed, too as I sent up a silent prayer that Layla and Viv and Quinn would stay still and not make a sound. They were far enough away that I only just caught Layla's scent. Only *just* heard her tiny gasp.

If they didn't move. Didn't speak. They might get out of here alive.

If they did survive, though, I was going to throttle all three of the fuckers...after I was finished apologizing for almost turning them into kibble.

The three sets of wolves approached with measured steps. They snarled at one another. At Ryland. Without knowing for certain, I assumed all the other groups were from different packs.

The reason they called it the four corners became clear a moment later. It was neutral territory. The four corners represented the edge of each pack's land. Ryland and his gang had come from the trees nearby where we emerged from the footpath. To the south. The others from each of the other four corners.

This was the borderlands.

Forrest was the first to burst from his human flesh into wolf form, scattering his clothes to the wind. The girl with the purple hair was next, morphing into a lithe white wolf with a streak of gray on the side of her head, in the exact place where she had part of her hair shaved in human form. I wondered offhandedly if it was done in tribute to her wolf.

Jared and Clay left their positions at my flank and came to stand at my shoulders.

"What's happening?" I breathed. "Layla and Viv—"

"We know," Jared said, hushing me with the words.

Clay shucked off his shirt, baring his steaming chest to the frigid air. His breaths whistled in and out through his teeth, nostrils flaring. "This is bad," he said, his voice brutish and deep, vibrating in behind my breastbone. "We need to get Allie the fuck out of here."

Ryland turned his head, eyes bright as ember. "No one leaves," he ordered, spittle flying from his lips. "Not until I say."

Clay buckled under the order and then stilled, his jaw twitching.

The large wolf leading the pack of six stopped about twenty yards away. A sharp cracking sound sent sleeping birds scurrying from their nests, taking flight into the black sky as he shifted into his human form.

The slate gray wolf became a man at least six feet tall. Naked, his body was coiled with lean muscle. His... package hung like another appendage between his legs. But it was his eyes that I couldn't stop focusing on.

It was as if they were bleached of color and glowed white against his overly tan skin.

"Samson," Jared hissed, shuffling his feet until he had himself positioned more in front of me than beside.

"What are you doing here?" Ryland bellowed across the space between them, his words snatched up by a rogue wind.

"Same thing as you," the naked man shouted back. "Offering this girl a place among my people. With my pack."

Ryland scoffed. "She's already chosen," Ryland growled, but something in his tone told me he wasn't certain of that himself, and the other wolf picked up on his hesitance, too, grinning wickedly.

"Is it true, girl?" The shifter called to me, his white eyes piercing my resolve.

My wolf shook. I braced myself against Clay.

"Have you chosen your pack? Speak now and we'll leave in peace."

And this was it.

My chance to leave. I'd abandoned the idea this morning after talking to Jared. I had myself convinced that running would be the coward's way out. I didn't run. I never did. No matter how much I wanted to sometimes.

I didn't give up just because things got hard. That wasn't me.

That wasn't who I raised to be. But now...

Maybe—

"Is it true?" Another voice joined those of Ryland and Samson, and my gaze drifted to another naked man. This one flanked by two equally massive wolves— both big enough to almost rival Clay in size. "Is her will stronger than yours?"

Ryland balked, skidding a step back as though the other shifter had struck him.

So, they did know.

Clay put his arm around my waist, holding me up as my knees quaked. Jared reached a hand back to brush his fingers against my wrist, reminding me he was there.

"Does she have two tails?" another called. The fourth alpha shifted to ask, revealing a short, thick man in his early forties with silver threaded hair and a thick beard. "Has she mated to *two* shifters?"

My head grew light as my breathing picked up. The short breaths not working to pump oxygen to my brain.

"She cannot be allowed to live among us," The bearded one called into the clearing. "We must cast her out!"

"Pipe down you old crackpot," Samson lobbied back, stretching to limber up his spine. His gaze fixed on me and I found his intent in his stare.

Where the others were wary of me—a shifter who was so far from what was safe and *known*—Samson was the one who saw me as a trophy wolf. Much like Ryland did.

They wanted to collect me. The idea of forcing a being stronger than themselves to kneel before them excited them. I could see it in the wild hunger in Samson's gaze as his eyes roved over my body—over my mates at my sides. As he pulled his bottom lip in between his shining white teeth.

He wanted to own something unownable. I felt sick.

I heard whispers from behind us and coughed to try to cover the sound. The hairs on the back of my neck stood on end as I watched the bearded one and other curiously picking apart the shadows at our back.

Oh shit.

Fuck.

"I've chosen my pack," I shouted with all the force I could muster, shaking as my lower rib popped out of place and the one above it snapped. Clay gripped me tighter around the waist, as if he was trying to hold me together, too.

Knowing the consequences of what could happen if I shifted.

Ryland turned to me with a smile, closing the distance between us to pull my free hand between his own. His acrid peppery scent was magnified from how much he was perspiring, and I choked on it, gagging.

"Repeat after me," he said, his long hand falling forward to curtain off his fiery stare.

I shut my eyes, bristling as his callouses rubbed along the ridges of my knuckles, making me shudder. Making my wolf want to rip his fucking throat out.

Jared and Clay held me between them, acting as my reluctant anchors. Neither could look at me, nor at Ryland as he spoke the words I was to repeat. I could feel their revulsion. They didn't want me to do this any more than *I* wanted to. But to save me—to ensure my safety— they would endure it.

As I would.

"Of my own will—"

The bearded one charged. I gasped, catching the movement just before he launched himself into the air, turning from man to beast faster than I could blink. But before his front paws could connect back with the earth, another wolf tackled him down, his shining jaw clamping around the throat of the other wolf. There was a cry of anguish and a sickening *snap*.

Then the attacking wolf was raising his massive head, jowls dripping with steaming blood and mats of shorn fur. White eyes setting their murderous sights on Ryland.

Samson had killed him. Just like that. Someone had just *died*.

A life had been taken.

Gone.

Did the bearded shifter have children? A mate?

I bent and wretched into the grass. I'd have fallen if it weren't for Clay still holding me up.

The wolf that'd been with the bearded one tucked tail and loped into the brush, retreating from the corpse of its dead alpha with a pain-filled whine.

"I...*can't*," I managed as my human canines began to elongate and sharpen, pressing into my lower lip. Another of my ribs cracked and I screamed from the wrongness of the sensation, the scream itself bringing more pain than the bone breaking. Even breathing was painful now.

I couldn't hold it back anymore. I was losing control.

Ryland shifted and Samson snarled at him, slate gray hackles raised.

"Allie!" Vivian's voice rose above every other sound, shattering any bit of composure I might have retained.

No.

All eyes, canine and human, turned to find the source of the call. A blond-haired head and wide- fearful eyes stared back from the brush. Vivian's hands were fisted at her sides. Her chest heaved. Quinn and Layla quivered beside her.

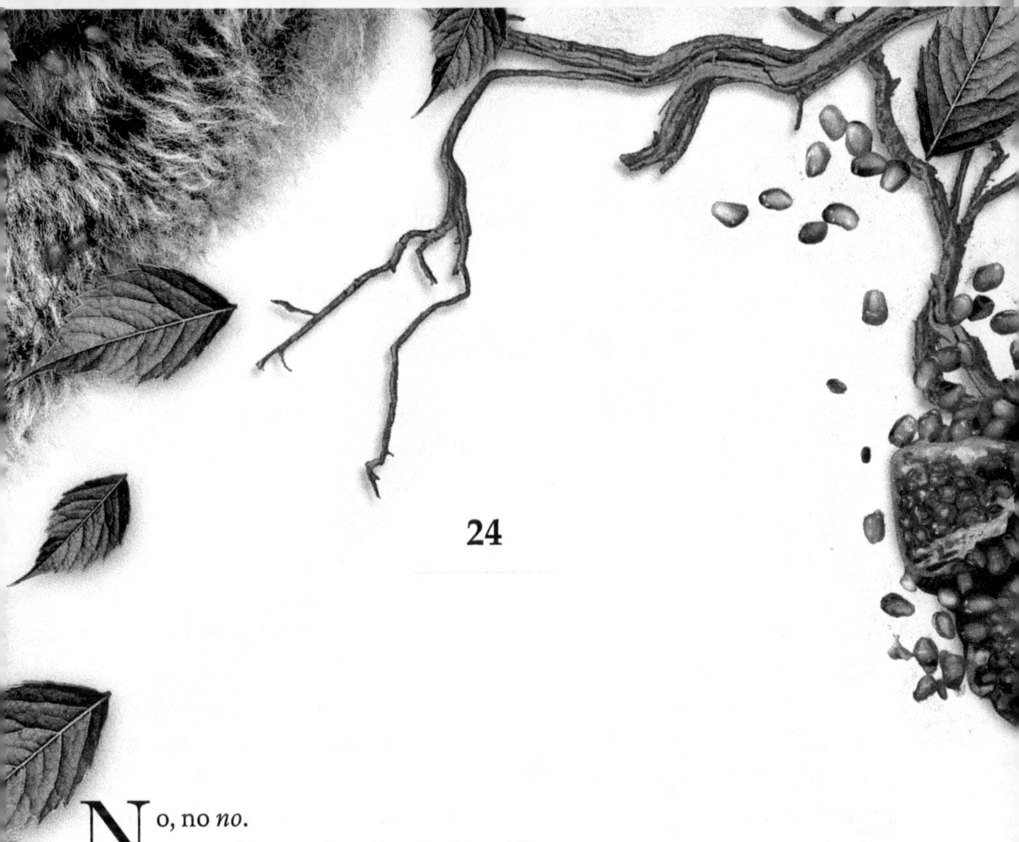

24

N o, no *no*.

Goddamned mother-fucking idiots.

"Run!" I shouted, my face breaking and reforming around the word as I shattered, all my pieces coming back together in a new form. A stronger form.

A false sense of calm flooded my animal body.

I could've kept fighting my wolf's desire for dominance over the other alphas in the clearing. That would have been a thing I could have done, or at least *tried* to do.

But this was something else. I would kill every last person here who would dare harm them, or I would die trying if that's what it took. I never could have taken a life to save myself—hell, I couldn't even bring myself to try to kill Devin when he held me captive. For them, though?

Fighting to save someone you love is different.

Required little to no thought at all.

It's a reaction.

Like how the pulling of the trigger fires the bullet. Action. Reaction.

And I doubted it would be any different whether I was animal or human. My wolf loved my friends as I did. She would die for them too. We were ready for this.

407

We snarled at anyone who dared look our way, lifting our head to assert our power.

We *dared* them to come even a step closer to our friends.

Our mates were at our sides. Their wolves ready to fight too if we needed their help.

Get them out of here, Jared spoke in my mind and we growled at him.

We were *not* going to leave them, either.

Not with one shifter already dead in the grass, his lifeblood flowing back into the earth.

Before Jared or Clay could try to convince us to leave, Samson howled and the pack mates he'd brought with him—the other five who'd been standing patiently by, waiting for a command from their alpha—were taken off leash.

Charity glanced back at me from where she stood, her eyes wide and fearful. *Go,* she mouthed to me before she shifted, running with Harrison, Forrest, Dylan, and Destiny to head off the five attackers while Ryland and Samson circled one another, trying to find weak spots to exploit in each other's languid movements.

This wasn't supposed to happen. It was supposed to be easy.

No one was supposed to get hurt.

An animal squeal of pain assaulted my ears and I bent my head, fighting my wolf's urge to join the all- out brawl under the moon. I could tell Clay was having even more trouble than I was—he was vibrating with the force of his growls, hot saliva foaming at his mouth.

Think Allie. Think! What do we do?

I turned to make sure Vivian, Layla, and Quinn were running. Once they were safely gone, I'd be able to focus. I'd be able to—

A wolf was almost on them.

Layla's black hair whipped around her face as she spotted the wolf, a silent gasp parting her lips. Quinn jumped in front of her just as the wolf descended upon them.

I was running, I was already running, but it was too late. *Too late.* The wolf had wrapped its jaws around Quinn's neck.

Layla—

Where did she go? I couldn't see her in the grass anymore. But I could hear her.

Layla was screaming.

And Vivian. Vivian was on the wolf's back, trying to use her bare hands—her useless *human* hands to pry the beast from Quinn. The rage and fear in her expression tore my heart to ribbons.

She roared as the wolf turned on her and I caught a second wolf racing to aid its friend from the corner of my eye.

Stop it, I shouted in my mind, hoping the thought would reach Jared or Clay. I could sense them a fraction of a second behind me. *At ten o'clock coming fast.*

In a blind rage, I zeroed all my focus in on the wolf lunging at one of my best friends. I pushed myself harder. Faster. So close now. So close.

So far away.

The wolf knocked Vivian to the ground, and I could taste bile in my throat.

It hurt.

It hurt so fucking bad.

Vivian.

In a fury so hot that it burned into my soul I bellowed; *this one is mine.*

The fucker didn't have time to get ready for me. He was too busy with his blood-soaked muzzle in my friend. Without any clue how to work my canine body, I let my animal instinct completely take over, and in case it wasn't obvious to my wolf what I wanted her to do—what I was giving her *permission* to do, I hissed in the darkest part of my mind; *kill.*

Our teeth locked on a chunk of fur and thick flesh behind the wolf's neck. It cried out and bucked us off, shaking itself before it retaliated with teeth bared in a feral snarl and got us with its teeth wrapped around our ankle.

The pain was an explosion of stars in our eyes and we reflexively pulled at the appendage, contorting our body to catch the other wolf under its chin. We felt cartilage and bone in our mouth. It whined, trying to get free. Sharp paws scraping, cutting, slicing.

We didn't let go.

We wrestled it to the ground. We pressed our paw into the hollow beneath its throat. And then we chewed through all that flesh and bone and sinew until it stopped fighting us. Until it did nothing at all.

Until we were reborn of rage and pain and all that kept us tethered to the earth was the foul taste of the creature's blood on our tongue to remind us that we were still alive. Our heart still beat. That a part of us was still human.

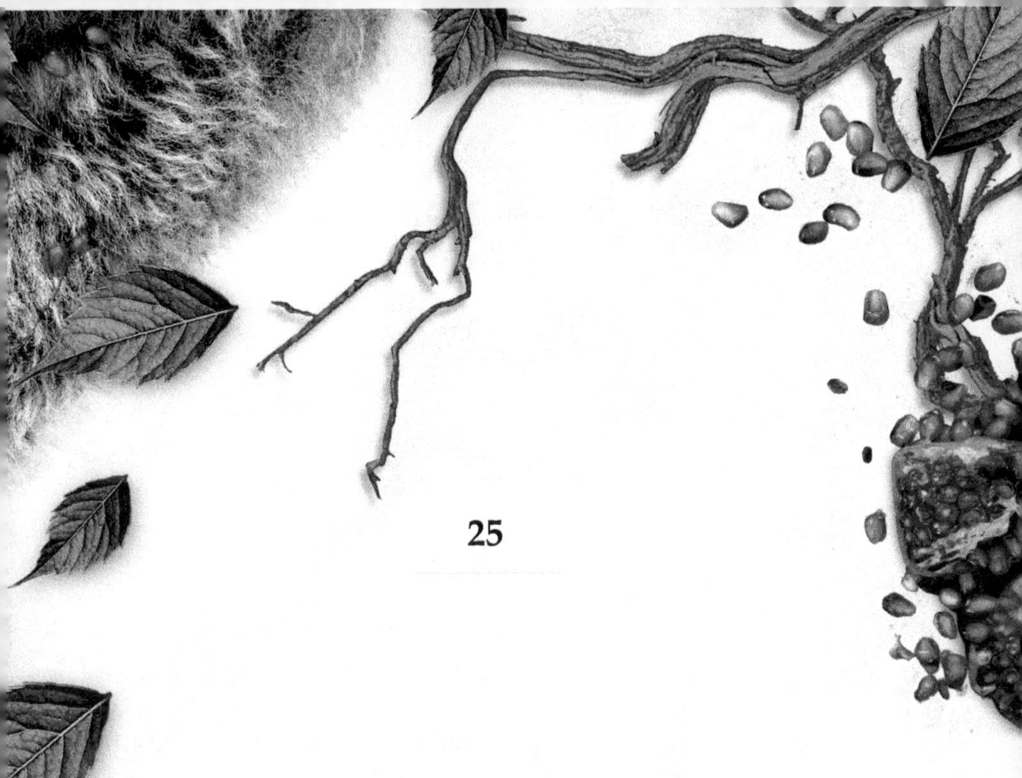

25

There were no more attackers. Not at this end of the clearing.

Jared and Clay were finishing subduing the wolf who'd been racing to aid its friend. I searched to be sure no one else was coming, finding the clearing eerily silent and still.

There came one last terrified yelp out of the wolf Clay and Jared held pinned against the ground.

Clay's brusque voice penetrated my mind in a loud shout, *Allie, you good?*

I struggled to make sense of what I was seeing in the distance. A black wolf rose, its bright orange eyes narrowing on the group of wolves, his and Samson's, who had stopped fighting near the heart of the clearing.

I didn't need to be a rocket scientist to figure it out.

Ryland killed their alpha.

And by rights—in accepting Samson's open challenge and defeating him—Ryland was now *their* alpha too.

The other pack, I realized, was the one who'd taken it upon themselves to attack my friends. Jared and Clay held one against the dirt, and another lay dead at my feet. But their alpha...he seemed to have vanished.

Smart pooch.

Allie, Clay shouted in my mind again, snapping me out of the strange fog trying to claim my mind.

Oh god.

My wolf, understanding my need to go to my friends, relinquished her hold, allowing me to shift back. I retched as soon as I did, hastily wiping my shaking human hand across the back of my mouth before crawling through the grass, searching for my friends.

"Vivian!" I cried, tears blurring my eyes and a burning in my chest. "Viv!"

"Here," A small voice croaked, and I rushed toward it, knees scraping over sharp sticks and tiny rocks.

She lay partially on her side, clutching her arm against her chest—where blood seeped between her fingers, gushing from a wound I *prayed* was not what I thought it was.

She stared at me in horror, and I realized how this all must look. Her best friend had turned into a wolf right in front of her. And another impossibly large wolf had attacked her and her friends. And I was ass fucking naked.

"I'm so sorry," I sobbed, my throat thick with tears and voice watery. "I'm so so sorry, Viv."

"Where's Layla? Quinn?"

I turned to search for them. Viv was the closest to me and I needed to make sure she was alright. "Don't move, okay," I whispered to her harshly before picking up my battered body, finding my mangled ankle was still healing and I had to limp.

"Jared!" I called to the white wolf, his amber eyes finding mine across the short distance between us, completely ignoring whatever was happening on the other side of the clearing. I had bigger problems to deal with right now. "Stay with Viv!"

"Layla!" I called, voice hoarse and broken. "Quinn?"

When no reply came, I stopped to listen, shutting my eyes to focus only on sound. The raucous beating of my heart was almost too loud to hear anything else, but there, not far, was the distant sound of Layla crying.

She's alive.

I rushed toward the sound, dragging my useless leg behind me, until I tripped over something in the grass and fell onto my elbows, wincing as twin trails of electrifying pain raced all the way up my forearms to the tips of my fingers.

I groaned, twisting onto my back to find what I'd tripped over. It had been Quinn's leg. Layla was sobbing into his chest, both of them had been mostly hidden in the grass and the shade of a wide pine next to where they lay.

"Layla," I hedged, reaching out a hand to her, trying to see if she was injured.

"Help him," she moaned, and I gently curled my fingers around her frail shoulders, lifting her from his chest. "He won't wake up."

"I need to see," I said, the threat of bile acrid on my tongue as I took in Quinn's injury.

He was unmoving.

"He won't wake up," Layla repeated, curling her knees into her chest and beginning to rock. "He won't wake up. He won't wake up."

I felt for a pulse, pressing my fingers to the tacky blood marring his neck. It was weak, but it was there. I could feel it. I held my hand in front of his mouth, feeling the barest whisper of breath against my fingers. "He's not dead," I said, more in shock than to reassure Layla.

He was so pale. His lips had lost almost all color. His black hair, flopped over his forehead, only served to make the illusion of his death more pronounced.

"He isn't dead," I said, louder this time. I jumped to my feet.

"Help!" I shouted. "We need help. Please!"

Jared was standing guard near Viv and Clay was still holding the foreign wolf down, so it was Charity who answered my call. I knew it was her, even though she was in her wolf form. She left the group gathering around a blood covered Ryland and came to us, shifting back to human form mid-run.

"What is it?" she asked, and I saw a jagged cut sliced in a wide arc through her breasts. But it was already healing. She would be alright.

"He's hurt," I said. "He needs a hospital." Charity's eyes darkened.

"Charity!" I shouted when she didn't move or answer me.

Her jaw tightened and as though she'd just come to a difficult decision, she growled angrily and kneeled. "Move out of the way."

I did.

She lifted Quinn carefully from the ground as though he weighed nothing at all. And even though he dwarfed her in size, she was able to cradle him to her bare chest.

She didn't ask Ryland for permission, I realized. She didn't even turn around. Ryland was busy with the other wolves—the involuntary new members of the Forest Grove pack.

"I'll do what I can," Charity said solemnly. "But I can't promise anything."

I nodded. "Thank you."

"No, Quinn!" Layla cried, trying to stand, but falling back onto her tailbone.

"Layla?" I kneeled back down as Charity vanished from sight, gone with Quinn to god knew where. "Are you hurt?"

She sobbed quietly. "What's happening?" she asked, her hand reaching down to her left leg and coming away streaked with blood.

I batted her hand away and lifted the hem of her jeans, my blood going cold at what I found.

"La La," I breathed, a fresh wave of tears stinging my eyes. "Layla, did it bite you?"

"Hmm?" she asked, looking at me, but not looking at me at the same time. She was in shock, I realized.

I shook her. "Layla, did it bite you?"

She looked at the wound on her calf with unfocused eyes. "I don't know," she replied numbly, then, "You..." she trailed off. "You were a dog."

Her breaths were heavy and just before she fainted, I realized the signs and lunged to catch her, laying her against my lap.

I hugged her to me tightly, crying over her hair. "I'm so sorry La La. I never meant—" my words were broken by hiccupping sobs.

"Allie," the voice was Jared's and when I looked up, I found him there in all his naked glory, with a hand cupping his junk. Vivian standing next to him, her hand still covering the wound on her arm. I could smell it. It smelled like Layla's wound. The blood laced with something I couldn't name. Not even really a particular smell—it was a mark. Like a small piece of the wolf I'd killed was now imprinted into their blood.

Vivian didn't have to lift her hand for me to know what lay beneath it.

"What have I done?" I choked, not bothering to keep the darkness at bay anymore. I let it consume me. Let all the hateful, ugly thoughts take root.

My fault.

All my fault. It was always my fault. My sister. My mom. My dad.

Quinn.

Layla and Viv.

The dead wolf in the grass fifteen feet away. Everyone around me gets hurt.

It's the rule. It is law.

Every good thing in my life had to be paid for with at least two bad things.

Someone was shaking me, or maybe I was just shaking, I didn't know anymore. It didn't matter. Nothing could undo what had been done here. My friends had been hurt because of *me*. Their lives could change forever because of me. What would happen to them if they didn't shift? Would Ryland kill them?

No. I wouldn't let him. I'd end him if he tried.

The uncertainty of it all swirled like storm clouds, blocking out any rays of hope.

"Allie. Allie!"

A break in the darkness and through a haze of tears I saw Viv, her face hard and worry wrinkling the corners of her eyes. "Allie, snap out of it!"

I tried.

I really tried, but the panic was going to undo me. Already the blackness was seeping in around the edges. I was going to puke or pass out or explode—I wasn't sure which.

My head snapped to one side, my cheek stinging and stars flashing in my eyes. I tasted blood on my tongue. The sobs stopped and I was able to take a breath after the initial shock of Vivian's slap wore off and my brain registered that she was kneeling in front of me, searching my eyes. "Allie, you with me?"

I swallowed hard, swiping a hand over my face to wipe away the snot and tears. I didn't trust myself to speak right away, so I nodded.

She shook her head. "I don't know what the fuck is going on here," she said, looking from me to Jared and back again. "But if anyone gets to lose their shit, it's definitely not going to be *you*."

Her words stung and I recoiled.

"What the hell, Allie?" Vivian added, lifting Layla from my lap to pull our friend onto her own. Vivian held Layla close, brushing her long black hair away from her face as she checked Layla over quickly for injury.

I didn't like the way she was holding her, like *I* was the dangerous one. Like Layla needed protection *from me*. A hard ball formed in my throat and I jumped as something fell across my shoulders. Clay's sweater. I peered up to see him standing behind me, clutching a tattered piece of clothing to him.

I immediately searched for the wolf he'd been pinning down, and Clay met my gaze when I couldn't find it. "Dead," he explained, jaw taut and blue eyes drawn.

When I noticed Ryland and the others were coming this way, I scrambled to put myself in front of my friends like a shield. "What is he going to do?" I hissed the question, imploring either Jared or Clay for a reply.

Jared pulled himself in tighter to me, placing himself on my left side while Clay fell into place on my right, the three of us creating a wall of flesh in front of Layla and Vivian. "He won't hurt them," Jared said, but the uncertainty in his voice would have been evident even if I didn't know him as well as I did.

My mouth went dry. Unable to help myself, I shouted at Ryland before he could get any nearer to us—to them. They were only a stone's throw away now.

It was already too close. "Stay where you are," I barked, shocked by the steadiness of my voice.

This was no time to break down and go spiraling into a panic-fueled oblivion. I needed to keep myself level until both of my friends were safe.

Ryland shifted, revealing a patchwork of slow- healing injuries over his massive muscled frame. A bite mark puckered his cheek on the opposite side to the long scar cleaving the right side. Like the scars of the pups on his chest, I hoped the ugly gashes torn by Samson's fangs would stay there in his cheek, making him as ugly on the outside as I thought him to be on the inside.

"You don't give the orders here," Ryland rebutted, his teeth bared. He turned to shout at the wolves following behind him, "Stay," he growled, and bent to scoop up something from the ground. It glinted in the moonlight and my stomach tightened when I realized what it was. The flask.

"Ry—" Clay warned as his alpha approached alone. "Armstrong, you say another fucking word and I'll have your head on a *pike*. Got it?"

Clay snarled, pressing himself in tighter to my side.

My wolf flared to life and a low growl churned behind my ribcage. I was ready to let her out again if I had to. He just had to give me a reason. One wrong move and I'd let my wolf out—let her do what she'd wanted to do since she first laid eyes on him.

I had no idea if I could beat him. But I would give it my best shot if he lifted a finger to either of my mates or either of my friends.

Ryland stopped in front of us and I had to push myself to standing so my eyeline wouldn't be level with his cock. *Ugh*. I stood in defense, my left foot back and my shoulders squared.

"Allie…?" Vivian called tentatively.

Ryland peered through us at my friends swaddled in the long grass. "They've seen," he said simply.

"It's against the law to kill them," I blurted, trying to remember what exactly it was Jared had told me about the law of the witch's council. The wolf who'd tried to kill them—who'd bitten them— was dead. So, he wouldn't be at their mercy for his crimes. But if Ryland hurt them, I'd find this witch's council and I wouldn't hesitate to tell them what he'd done.

Ryland eyed me with barely concealed disgust. "This is on you," he said, and it was like someone had twisted a knife in my gut.

I grit my teeth together.

I know it is, I thought, but I couldn't say it. I wouldn't admit it to *him*.

Ryland stuck his neck out, sniffing the air as the glow of his wolf returned to his eyes. He snorted and spat into the grass. "They've been bitten."

It wasn't exactly a question, but the alpha was looking at me, waiting for a response.

Ryland's eyes flicker low, to the exposed skin between my breasts and I pulled Clay's sweater tighter around myself, my body clenching as I once again realized I was completely naked beneath the sweater. "*Yes,*" I ground out.

The alpha's lips pursed, and he nodded. "Nothing will be done until the next moon," he announced, raising his voice so it carried not only to us, but to the whole pack at his back.

"You have my word they will not be harmed so long as they can keep the events of tonight and the existence of our kind to *themselves*. If they speak out about what they've seen here tonight, they will have to be... *dealt with*."

"They won't say anything," Jared told his uncle. "See to it that they don't."

"And if they don't shift?" Clay asked, glaring at Ryland. He took the words right out of my mouth.

Ryland paused.

"*If they don't shift?*" I repeated, enunciating every word.

Ryland licked his lips.

"Swear to me they will not be harmed."

A coy smirk and a raised brow twisted Ryland's face into something that made my skin crawl. He stepped forward and pressed the flask into my hand, dipping his head low to whisper in my ear. "Complete the ceremony. Join the pack and I swear to you they will not be harmed."

I shuddered as his putrid breath disturbed the small hairs behind my ear, making a shiver run all the way down to my toes. His peppery smell was laced with something metallic that made my nose wrinkle and my eyes burn.

I blinked and saw over his shoulder, at the edge of the woods, there was a woman in a white nightgown standing amid the grass. Her silvery hair danced in the wind. Her pale blind eyes watched me, unseeing, glowing.

Hazel nodded. Just once.

And when I blinked for a second time and Ryland pulled away, she was gone. As if she was never there at all.

"Do we have a deal?"

My heart beat like a war drum in my chest. My wolf didn't like this. She was battering at my defenses, but she was weak. Subdued. She had given me back the reins willingly and wasn't yet strong enough to take them back.

"Allie?" Layla asked groggily and I turned to find her coming to in Vivian's lap. Viv hushed her and the fear returned to Layla's eyes as what happened came back to her.

I swished the liquid in the bottom of the flask. Most had leaked out into the grass, but it wasn't empty.

"Well?" Ryland snapped, growing impatient.

Jared and Clay both stiffened at my sides. Their outrage and uncertainty—their pain—poured into me.

"We shouldn't do this now—"

Jared tried, but his uncle turned a malicious stare on him. "Dylan is *dead*," he hissed at his nephew. Jared went a shade of green in response and dropped his eyes. "How many more should I sacrifice for your mate's *comfort? Hmm?* Tell me nephew, how many would *you* put at risk?"

The answer was so simple now. My wolf gave one last forceful push before I locked her away completely, gaining back full control.

How had I let this happen?

Maybe Ryland was right. Maybe I was wrong.

"I'll do it."

The fire in Ryland's eyes grew hotter. The excitement in them unmistakable.

"Of my own will, I enter into this pack."

I repeated the words, careful to say them without wavering.

"With the moon and all in attendance here as witnesses, I hereby *submit* myself to the rule of the alpha."

My throat tightened on the last four words, but I managed to grind them out, shaking with the effort.

"*Now drink.*"

I did. The blood and whiskey pooled like acid in my mouth and I coughed, choking on it as it snaked down my throat.

A heaviness settled in my stomach and I blinked past a lancing pain behind my eyes, wincing.

Your will is mine to command, the alpha's voice rang in my skull, clear and all encompassing.

I groaned, forced to my knees beneath him. I knew I shouldn't be able to rise again until he released me, so I didn't even try. This is what Ryland wanted. This is why he killed the other alpha. And if I didn't give him what he wanted, there was no guarantee my friends would get out of this.

Blood of my blood, his voice whispered in my mind while he sniveled down on me.

Then, saying loud enough for all to hear, Ryland released me and lifted his arms as though he were a showman announcing the next act. "Welcome to the pack, Allie Grace."

BONUS SCENE

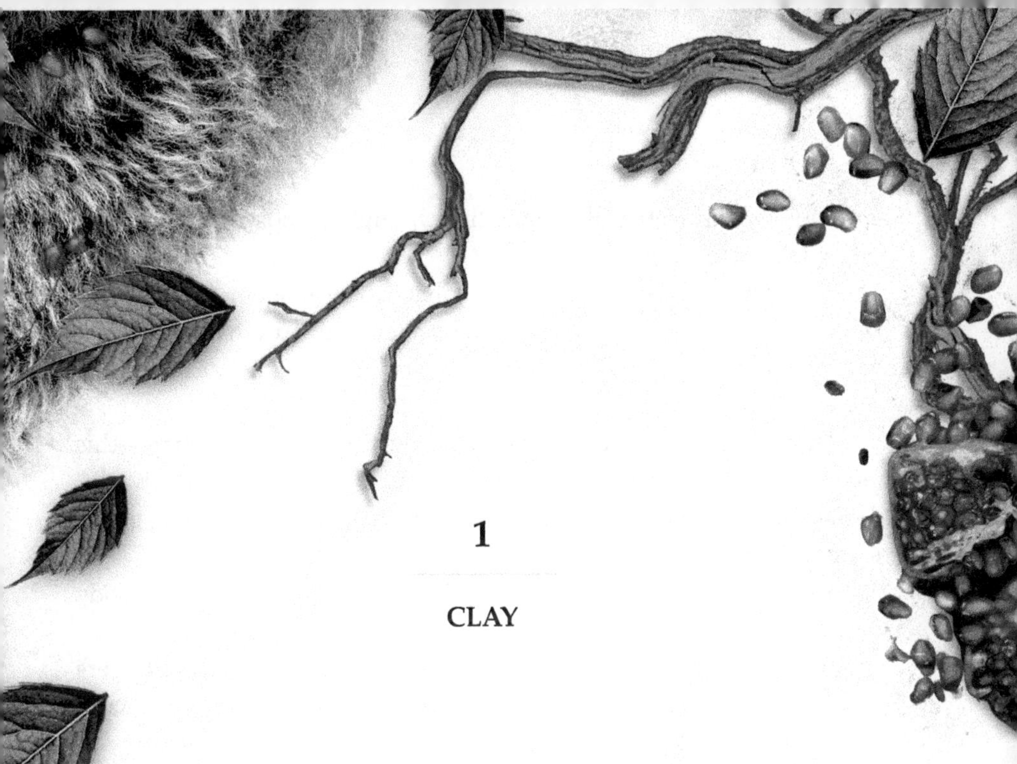

1

CLAY

The groaning creak of old springs sounded behind me and I stilled, my hands still deep in the engine of the bike. The sound came again, this time followed by the crinkle of cheap tarp.

Teeth clenched, I whirled, pulling my hands from the bike's innards and lurching to my feet.

Allie wasn't at the counter anymore, but the area still smelled faintly of the Fast Orange she used to clean the engine grease from her hands. She knelt on the sofa now, her slender fingers peeling back the hanging tarp to reveal what I had concealed beneath.

"Allie, what are you—"

But she'd already jerked the makeshift curtain back. The torque wrench I'd been holding clattered to the ground, the shrill sound of metal ringing against the pavement pushed me forward.

Allie remained speechless and immobile as I stalked toward her, my gaze fixed on the map she was now studying. A series of silver pins and the lines of black string fastened between them covered the map. In the upper right portion was a photo.

A picture taken by the private investigator I hired over a week ago to follow Allie's ex-boyfriend, Devin Wright.

My throat tightened as her panic rushed to fill the room—the emotion raw and restricting. I breathed through my nostrils to quell the roiling in my stomach.

She shouldn't ever have to feel like that. Not ever again.

He was gone, and I was going to make damn sure he stayed that way. It was the best I could do if she wasn't going to let me deal with the son of a bitch.

She peeked up at the only other pin jutting out of the map—this one, unlike the others, was red and stuck in a spot near Fairbanks, Alaska. I swallowed hard, the familiar ache in my chest returning at the red reminder.

"You're tracking him," Allie said in a breathy whisper, her body rigid.

Steeling myself, I knelt beside her, tugging the tarp from her fingers to draw it back closed. She didn't try to fight me, just dropped her hand and her head, her brows drawn.

Silently, she slid from the couch and onto unsteady legs, her arms crossing over her chest, fingers brushing her shoulders as if the room had suddenly chilled.

I stood too, feeling awkward as fuck and wishing I had the right words to say to smooth it all away. Jared would have known what to say. He always knew the right words.

I couldn't imagine what she must have been thinking and I fucking prayed she would just let it be, but then she tilted her head to study me from the corner of her eye and I knew she wasn't going to forget what she saw.

Her gaze, calculated and curious at first, softened, and something in me strained—like an old wooden board about to snap under my weight. Like a storm cloud, black and heavy with rain—the atmosphere thick with the threat of it hanging overhead.

She needed to know, I realized, the nagging ache behind my ribcage spreading.

She deserves to know.

"I may have told Jared I would step back," I told her, fighting the urge to close the short distance between us. Her lily of the valley scent was driving me insane, and somehow the way it combined with the musky smell of engine grease in my shop made it even more brutally intoxicating.

"And I have," I continued, drawing my hands into fists. "But that doesn't mean I won't protect you. I'll *never* allow anyone to hurt you again. Never."

Her bottom lip trembled, and I had to look away.

It didn't dull the crashing waves of her emotions as they tumbled to my shores through the tether of the mate bond. But it helped not to have to look into her light grey eyes.

"Clay—"

She shifted and I backed away as she advanced, her hands outstretched. My name on her lips was a plea I couldn't answer.

"*Don't*," I bit out, unable to keep the word from coming out in a sharp bark. "I can't."

She didn't understand.

She didn't know what she was doing. What it would mean. I *couldn't* have her.

And she shouldn't want me.

"You shouldn't—" I started, but stopped, trying and failing to explain in a way that she would understand. "I'm not—I'm not *good* for you, Allie."

A rough sound escaped her lips. Something halfway between a laugh and a choke.

Her eyes were hard and shining with something I couldn't name when I looked up, bellied by the taut silence between us.

"No," she said firmly, the waver in her voice from a few moments before evaporated. "You're wrong."

My first instinct was to shout. To yell at her and tell her she was crazy if she thought I was anything less than what people thought of me. Hot-headed. An asshole. *A murderer.* I was all of those things and more. I'd *earned* my reputation.

A man like me had no business with someone like her.

None.

And yet, the bond had fused us together like some twisted, gnarled thing. Half beauty and half beast. There was no undoing it.

Did it even matter what I thought? That she deserved someone better? The mate bond took our choice away when it stole a piece of my soul and gave it to her.

...and I was getting tired of pretending it didn't exist.

When Allie closed the space between us the second time, I stilled, forcing myself not to back away again. Not to run.

Her warm palm brushed against the stubble on my cheek, her fingers coaxing me to look at her. I bristled as the connection of flesh on flesh sent a shiver of throbbing pain and ecstasy through me.

This girl was going to be the end of me.

Her lips parted and I couldn't take it for another second. I shook with the effort of keeping myself contained. I wanted to taste those lips. Wanted it more than anything else.

Fuck.

Her eyes flicked to my mouth and it was the only invitation I needed. If she wanted me to kiss her, then I was going to give my girl what she wanted.

Just this once. Just for a second.

I pulled her to me. Shock registered in her eyes for a split second before I found her lips.

Our breaths mingled as I kissed her hungrily, *greedily*, wanting more and less and nothing at all. Just *this.*

Allie moaned against my lips and I almost growled as my wolf burst free from its cage in my chest, reaching across the bridge of our connected bodies, finding its counterpart within her.

She kissed me back.

For half a second, I worried I'd over-stepped. Gone too far. That I read the signals wrong and she didn't want this. Didn't want me after all.

But *she kissed me back.* Her hands squeezed my shoulders, fisted in my shirt, pulling, grasping, begging.

She moaned again and I tipped her head up, gripping the back of her neck to fasten us together. Felt her erratic pulse thud against the pad of my thumb.

Allie felt lighter than air as I lifted her from the ground, wrapping her legs around me as I pressed her into the wall, keeping her elevated so she wouldn't have to crane her neck so much to reach me. And there, with my body pressing hers into the rough pressboard, I thought self-ishly, *savagely*, that I wanted her. Right here. Right now.

And then forever.

There would never be a feeling to rival this one. A man could spend his whole life looking and never find it. Hell, most wolves *did*. But I fucking had it. Right here at my fingertips.

I'd been a damned fool to think I could let it slip through—that it would fade away.

It wouldn't.

Couldn't.

And I didn't want it to anymore.

She let me slide in, her lips parting to allow me entry and I swept in cruelly, stealing all the breath from her lungs. My body was on fire with need as she pressed herself tightly against me and I could feel her warmth on the growing length of my cock.

My fingers dug into her hips, needing something solid to hold onto, to keep my sanity before what little I had left was gone. She moved her hips against me and I shuddered, my body going stiff as a muffled groan passed between us.

I realized what was happening—what was *going* to happen—with a start and jerked myself away enough to get myself under control. This wasn't the time. This wasn't how it should be. Not hard and fast against an auto shop wall. *Christ,* what if she was still a virgin?

I couldn't...

The shock in Allie's eyes cut through me like the sharp edge of a steel blade.

No, not just shock...*horror.*

All the heat from three seconds before was gone, the moment shattered. In its place was a dark, burning sort of cold that stole my breath.

I released her and she fell back against the wall, her chest heaving with labored pants.

With a face twisted in pain, she met my gaze. "We shouldn't have —" she choked out.

I felt her emotions as clearly as if they were my own. Guilt. She was sick with it. My face flushed and I ground my teeth.

Damn.

Jared.

A sob broke free of Allie's chest and I winced, turning back to her just in time to see the first tear fall before she shouldered past me, tripping in her haste to get out of the shop.

To get away from *me.*

I awoke gasping, my stomach turning and chest heavy with a phantom weight. I hissed a string of curses, rolling my aching body from the worn sofa. The springs creaked below me in protest, bringing the dream back into startling clarity in my mind.

Elbows on knees, I rubbed my chapped palms over my face, trying to rid myself of the memory of what happened right here in the shop barely a week ago.

Had it really only been a week? It felt like an age had passed between then and now. Allie barely spoke for the first couple of days after what happened at the Four Corners. Hell, she barely fucking spoke now, either, but at least she responded when spoken to. At least she was eating again.

It was a start.

I couldn't imagine how much worse things would have been if the boy had died. Charity was able to get Quinn to an Alchemist in time to save his life. But there was nothing that could be done for her two best friends.

They were alive and their injuries would heal. It was a small consolation given the fact that by the end of the week their lives could change forever.

The full moon would decide which of them it wanted to claim—for their sakes I hoped it claimed neither.

But for Allie, it was a double-edged knife.

If they changed, she would blame herself for the rest of her life, but she would have her best friends beside her.

If they didn't, Ryland would have their memories of that night and any lingering suspicion erased from their minds. And if he did that, I knew it in my bones that Allie would distance herself from her friends. She would leave them in a heartbeat if it meant saving this from ever happening again. It was just who she was.

Damned if they do. Damned if they don't.

I wished I could make it all go away.

I'd give just about anything to see her smile again.

I rose and stretched, eyeing the flashing red numbers on the clock across the room. It was three in the afternoon, but with the bleak sky and chill air outside, it could have been closer to dusk. Shrugging, I strode to the minifridge and yanked out a beer, popping the cap off with my thumb before taking a long pull.

The bike sat in the middle of the shop. A yellow Yamaha 250 that'd seen better days. I'd gotten it for cheap since it needed some major work done. The guy practically gave it to me.

It was the perfect size for her.

The repairs had taken me the better part of the week, but today was the day I was going to finish it. Just a few more small fixes and a tune up and she'd be good to ride.

If Allie wanted it.

I hoped she'd want it.

That she'd ride with me and find the freedom she craved in rush of wind sailing over her body—in the metal beast propelling her forward. Onward.

Sighing, I set my beer down and got back to work, resigning myself to the possibility that she might not want it.

She might be pissed at me, though.

She'd almost chewed my head off when I paid for her driver's test. And she'd flat out told me she didn't ride anymore.

But I got the feeling it wasn't because she didn't *want* to. It was because she couldn't. I wanted to show her that she *could*.

She was the strongest person I'd ever met, and her wolf had the will to match that strength. It'd damn near gotten her killed, that strength.

It still might.

Good thing Ry's been busy dealing with shit at camp. Now that he'd taken out the eastern alpha and claimed the eastern pack for himself, there was a lot to be dealt with. Our pack was now the largest in the western United States, and expanding pack camp to accommodate the new members was going to be a big job. Not to mention tracking down and wrangling the ones who didn't want to bow to a new alpha.

Once everything calmed down, which would be sooner than I liked, there was no doubt in my mind Ryland would want to teach Allie a lesson. Force her to do his bidding.

She's strong—the strongest wolf in his pack. Ryland would want to use her to his advantage.

I should've *never* let this fucking happen.

My gut twisted and I grunted, cutting my thumb on a sharp edge of rusting metal.

"*Shit,*" I cursed, blood smearing onto the rear shock. I grabbed the oil stained rag from the floor to wipe it off.

"Want a hand?"

I whipped my head around, earning a crick in my neck and damn good case of whiplash. "Allie?" I grunted, rubbing out the sting. "What are you doing here? Don't you have work?"

She shrugged. "Not today. It's Sunday."

Was it really?

"So," she continued, drawing out the word as she brushed her long turquoise hair back from her face, huffing. "You want help or not?"

I smirked, glancing between her and the bike, mouth going dry. "Sure."

"A Yamaha 250," she mused, coming to lower herself into a squat next to the bike, inspecting the work I'd already done, checking its stability. "It's a solid bike."

A rut formed between her brows and her lips pursed, then as quickly as the pinched expression came, it vanished, replaced with a wan look and a long sigh.

"I had one like this once." She curled her hand around the left handlebar as if remembering how her hand had curled around hers. "I know my way around this model really well."

A grin pulled at the edges of my mouth. "Good," I said and passed her the wrench. "Let's get to work then. She just needs a tune up and a new mount kit and she'll be done."

"The shocks need adjusting," she said with a squint at the rear as she pressed forcefully on the seat, testing their give.

A dark shadow crossed her face and I couldn't help asking. "You want to talk about it?"

Her jaw tightened and her gray eyes dampened as tears tried to gather. She rolled her shoulders back. "No. Not really. No point, anyway. I just...want to keep moving. I feel like I'm going to explode if I don't."

Something twisted in my gut. I lifted the half drank beer from the floor by my knee and passed it to her. "Okay," I relented. "No talking."

The tiniest smile pulled at her lips and she took the beer from me, our fingers brushing.

I shivered, doing my best not to let my emotions seep out. She didn't need to know that the way her jeans hugged her thighs and her hair brushed over her long neck, the tips of the strands kissing her collarbone, made me wild with need.

We hadn't talked about the kiss since it happened, but every time we were in the same room, the energy was charged with all the things we didn't say. *Didn't do...but wanted to.*

Or at least, *I* wanted to.

I craved her like the worst sort of addiction. Like she was air and I was suffocating six feet under.

I'd been happy there, once, half-dead and content to suffocate for an eternity.

Now I found myself clawing toward the surface. Hungry for the taste of air again. For freedom.

Because of her.

"What are you staring at?" Allie asked, a strange smirk on her lips, one eyebrow raised.

"Nothing," I coughed and went back to work. "You, uh, had a wasp on you. Fucker flew away, though. You're good."

Allie wasn't buying it. An amused glint in her gaze told me she knew exactly what I was doing but let the lie slide. "Got any more of these?" she asked, shaking the empty bottle above her head.

"Plenty."

SHIFTED RULE

BOOK THREE

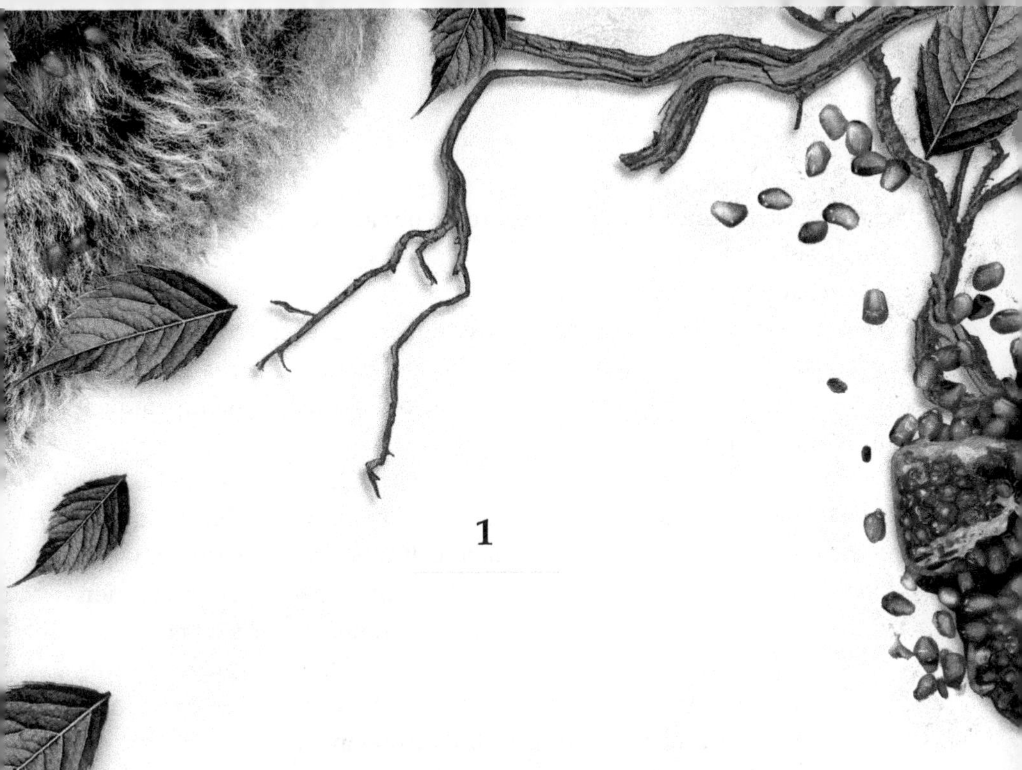

1

Put your body into it," Clay said, studying my form as I squared off to take another swing at his heavy bag.

"I *am* putting my body into it," I hissed in reply, throwing my shoulder into my next hit. The heavy bag swung and the chains holding it in place rattled.

Clay stepped up behind me. "That isn't bad," he said. "But you're still not putting your whole body into it. There's more force you can tap into if you move your whole torso."

His hands settled onto my hips, squaring me off again at the bag. Sweat beaded along my brow and the tops of my breasts. With his hands on me, my body grew hotter. When his fingers brushed over the bare skin where my tank top rode up, I wanted to scream. Not even the cool autumn breeze blowing into the shop was enough to douse the flames.

He moved one hand to tap the side of my right thigh. "Dig your heel in and push off with your legs. Then turn your whole body into it."

Clay guided me into the next swing, showing me how my body should move in slow motion.

"See?"

"Yeah," I gritted out, swallowing and shaking off the tremors caused by his touch. My inner wolf whined audibly in my mind, trying to clamber to the surface so she could reach out and touch him. Since I was too afraid to.

I wasn't sure I could stop if I did.

I continued throwing hits, switching sides every so often. Clay watched with his arms crossed over his thick chest. His sea-glass eyes never leaving me. Every so often, he adjusted my stance, gently nudged my legs back into place.

This was a *tame* selfdefense session with Clay. Usually, he had me run for an hour before we even started. Then he would have me spar with him until my muscles were shaking. It was why I preferred it when Jared taught me, but I knew—despite how much I ached after a session with Clay—that he would push me to learn more. To learn faster.

Where Jared was patient and took more time to explain the *why* behind everything, Clay just shoved me to the edge of my limits. And every day, those limits grew further and further away.

If I were being honest, I preferred to be pushed.

When the initial shock wore off after the Four Corners, I couldn't stop moving. Silence and stillness turned to buzzing, unstoppable energy. If I stopped, I would have to think. To remember.

Charity managed to get Quinn to an Alchemist in time to save his life. She was paying for that kindness now. Ryland was none too pleased that she'd left without asking his permission. That she *saved a human boy* without so much as a word from her alpha.

Lucky for Quinn, he couldn't remember a thing about that night.

I wished Layla and Vivian had been as lucky. They were cursed to remember every awful, blood-soaked moment. After we brought them back to the cabin that night, got them bandaged up, the guys and I did our best to explain things. I'm not sure what they actually digested. They'd been in shock. Angry. Hurt. Terrified.

I explained as best as I could what might happen to them on the next full moon, even though they were the hardest words I'd ever had to speak. I explained how they couldn't tell a soul and that if they did, I may not be able to protect them.

They nodded and sniffled and waited until I was finished. That was when Vivian asked if they could leave. She tucked Layla under her arm and accepted a ride home from Jared. The sound of the screen door banging shut behind them felt like a slap in the face. One I deserved.

They hardly talked to me now. Or each other, really.

We sat together at lunch like we always did, but now the easy laughter is gone. Quinn tried his best to lighten the mood. He always had his arm around Layla. The poor guy didn't understand that there was nothing he could do. I think Layla resented a little that he was the only one blessed with the ability to forget it all.

I'd have left them alone, but Jared insisted we keep an eye on them.

The best part was that after Layla and Viv left around eleven, the night wasn't even over for me. I began to feel the effects of the moon-triggered shift coming on just ten minutes after they left.

I got to learn where the other locked door in the cabin's basement went. A cell. Or I guess they called it a *moon room*. Clay had to be the one to chain me up. Jared couldn't stomach it.

Clay was the one who stayed with me through every aching moment. He listened to me scream in agony as the moon-triggered shift stole all my self-control. Snapped each of my bones. It was *nothing* like a voluntary shift. It was torture.

And when the shift was finished and I was left on all fours, sweating and whining through canine lips, there was only the barest trace of my consciousness remaining. I knew what was happening, but I couldn't control myself. Couldn't control my urges. I nearly tore my arm from its socket that night trying to get free.

The moon released me after a mere twenty minutes, but it felt like hours.

And apparently, I should have been grateful for that. Jared told me most wolves couldn't change back so fast after a moon-triggered shift. Most remained feral in their wolf forms until dawn. At least, that was how it was in the beginning for changed wolves. Or how it should have been, but I guess I had to be an anomaly in all things. In this, at least, I *was* grateful. Twenty minutes was plenty.

"Okay," Clay said, putting his arm between me and the heavy bag. I glared at him.

"You're not here right now, Allie. Your form is all over the place. What's up?"

I gave his arm a little shove and went back to work on the bag. "I'm fine."

I got in three good hits before Clay moved his whole enormous self in front of the bag. I ground my teeth. "No. You're not."

He jutted his chin in the direction of the worn sofa across the shop. "Take a breather."

"I don't want to take a breather." I wanted to keep hitting shit.

Between my early morning bow practice, my early afternoon run, late-afternoon self-defense, and late nights spent helping Clay in the shop with his bike repairs, I'd been doing pretty good keeping busy.

It was only when Jared or Clay forced me to stop that things got shitty again. The emotions kept at bay by busy hands and a focused mind came slowly creeping back in. They whispered things.

Like how I am death incarnate. How everyone I love gets hurt.

Like how every good thing in my life must be paid for by at least two bad things.

And then the most agonizing thought: It's all my fault.

My fault.

My fault.

I shook my head and sighed heavily. "I just need a drink, then we can go again."

"No, Allie. That's enough for the day."

"The hell it is," I retorted, feeling my inner wolf rear her head and my upper lip curl.

Clay just raised a brow and recrossed his arms.

Amused.

The bastard.

He looked me up and down, a frown drawing down the corners of his lips. "You need food," he decided.

It was no secret that I was getting a little on the thin side. With no appetite to speak of and the inability to stop moving, it was bound to happen.

"Come on, we'll make some dinner before Jared gets back from the Quarry."

I groaned, letting my head fall back in frustration as I shoved my wolf back down with a promise to let her out for a good long shift later tonight. I'd been shifting daily now for almost five days. Turned out Clay and Jared were right, the more I shifted, the more cooperative she was willing to be.

And I needed her to cooperate. Now that Ryland wasn't as busy with getting the new pack members into line, he wanted to see me. Tomorrow. Well, not just to see me, really.

How had Clay put it? Oh, right. *He will want to assert his dominance.* I.e. he was going to want to use the pack bond and his rule to control me.

If Clay were right, he'd want to make an example out of me. Bend me to his will. Though Clay had assured me that his interest will fade in time. He made Clay run that gauntlet once, too. Now, Ry pretty much leaves him alone.

I could only pray that his power trip would be over quickly.

"Come on," Clay urged. "I'll get you some ice for those."

He pointed at my hands. Even through the wrappings it was clear how swollen my knuckles were. I had no doubt that if I removed them, they would be an angry red. There really wasn't much point in using ice, though. My body would heal by the time dinner was ready. If not quicker.

It healed the mangled bite in my ankle from the wolf I'd killed at the Four Corners in less than twenty- four hours. A few bruises were nothing.

"Fine," I said, setting to unwrapping my hands, discarding the tensor strips onto the chair pressed against the wall. "But I'm cooking."

Clay rubbed a wide hand over his face but said nothing. He knew better than to argue with me these days. He wouldn't win. I wasn't afraid of his grumpy ass anymore.

I followed Clay from the shop, falling into stride next to him. I didn't miss how he was working his jaw. Or how hidden within the pockets of his jeans, his hands were balled into fists.

"Are you, *uh…*" Clay said, and I could tell he was working through how to say something, as he'd taken to doing more and more lately instead of spewing the first words to come to his mind. "Ready for tonight?"

I dug my fingernails into my palms and licked my cracked lips. A sarcastic laugh bloomed on my lips.

"Are you?" I scoffed.

He inhaled deeply and then shrugged.

That's what I thought.

I still didn't know whose idea it was, but I could guess.

The guys wanted to *have a chat* tonight. About *us.*

As if there weren't a million other more pressing things to fucking worry about.

"We don't have to—"

"No," I interrupted him. "We should."

As much as I didn't want to have this conversation, it needed to be had. Might as well get it over with. I had a pretty good idea where this chat would lead us, and I didn't like it. Not one bit. Though it was probably for the best.

Clay and Jared had been tense with each other since Clay kissed me and then went and confessed to Jared before I could be the one to do it.

Their friendship was more important than whatever this thing was between us. Sacred or not, the mate bond only complicated things. When they told me they'd decided to both keep their distance, to remain only as friends, I'd agree that that was for the best. And I assumed to be able to do that, they would need to ask me to move out. It was too hard to ignore those urges living under the same roof. I'd tell them that was for the best, too.

No matter that it was the last thing in the world that I wanted.

Certainly not what my wolf wanted, either, but I could go back to ignoring it, right? I could pretend like every time Clay touched me, I didn't quake inside. I could act like it wasn't the hardest thing in the world not to allow my gaze to fall to Jared's lips when he spoke to me. That it wasn't impossible not to imagine what it would be like to kiss him, too.

Those were things I could totally do.

"Coffee?" Clay asked, holding open the door for me to walk inside the cabin.

At that, I smirked. "Do you even have to ask?"

A grin that didn't reach his eyes pulled at one side of his mouth as he flicked on the Bluetooth speaker and set to pulling out coffee and what looked like the ingredients to make pasta to go with our nightly steaks.

It had become something of a habit since I came out of my shock coma and Ryland sent Jared away to work at the Quarry—Clay and I cooking together while we listened to music instead of talking. Sometimes, when he forgot I was listening, he would even sing a few lines. His voice deep and yet soft as butter.

"I'm going to wash up really quick and then I'll chop, 'kay?"

Clay nodded, scooping several heaping tablespoons of ground coffee into the filter.

Past him, out the window by the little table pressed against the wall, my wolf sensed Jared approaching. Sure enough, within a few seconds, I caught glimpses of his lithe white wolf snaking through the trees.

"Jared's home," I told Clay, and then rushed the rest of the way upstairs, eager to put off *the talk* for as long as I could.

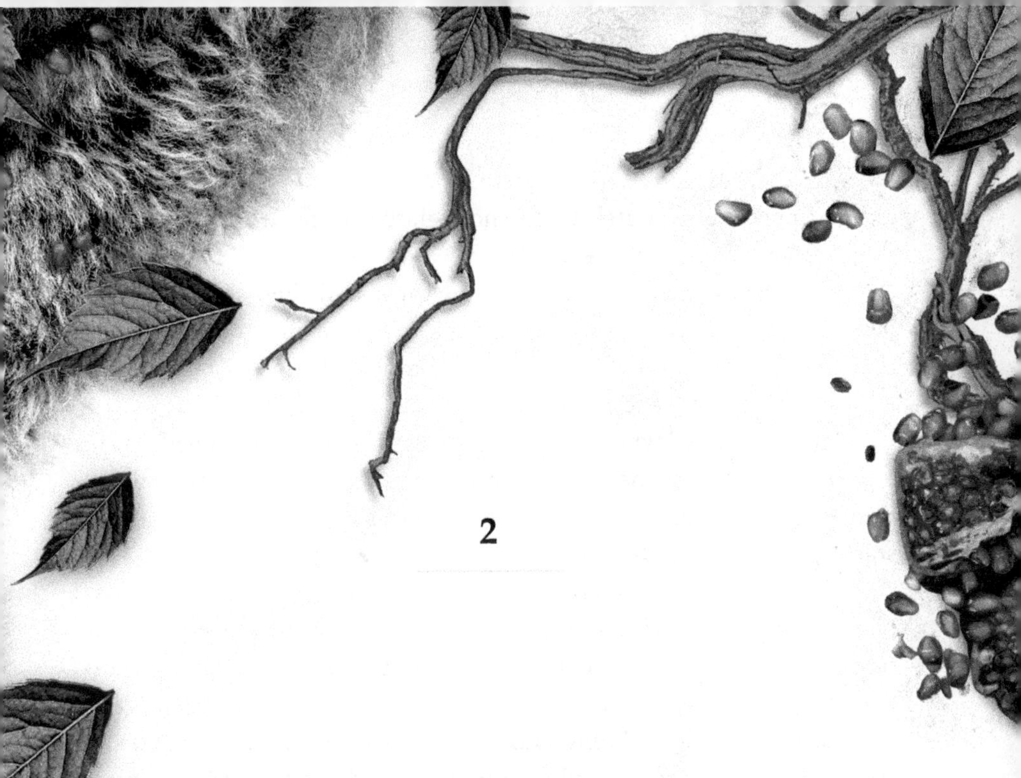

2

Jared didn't seem any more ready for it than I was.

After Clay and I finished with dinner and Jared with showering and getting changed out of his rock-dust coated coveralls, we ate in absolute silence.

The kind of silence that's heavy and suffocating, like there were storm clouds gathering in the air between the three of us. I cleared my throat as I rose to rinse my plate. "So," I said, trying not to let the cocooned butterflies in my belly burst free. "How're things at the quarry?"

"Good," he replied tersely. "Fine."

Oh god, this is painful.

I glanced at him as he finished his last morsel of rare meat, taking in the long line of his neck and those absurdly sexy cheekbones. How his gold-threaded dirty-blonde hair was getting so long that it brushed against them now.

How those green-flecked amber eyes had a tendency to cut through me even when I had my guard up.

"Fuck this," Clay barked, and his chair scraped back against the tile as he rose and stomped out of the kitchen.

Jared and I shared a look before Clay returned with his whiskey decanter and slammed it down in the center of the small table. He

443

nudged past me to snatch three short glasses from the cupboard and then banged those down next to it.

He poured generously into each of them and then shoved one to Jared and moved to pull my chair back out from the table. He stood there, holding the back of it with a white-knuckled grip.

Our eyes locked, and his nostrils flared.

"Sit," he ordered when I didn't move on my own. Jared sighed.

Swallowing past the hard lump in my throat, I set my plate down next to the sink and did as I was told, glad someone had the balls to start ripping this Band-Aid off.

"Thank fuck," I whispered under my breath as I sat down and saw Jared's face twitch with a smirk. Clay shoved my chair back into the table with me in it, and I had to catch myself so I wouldn't be clothes-lined by the wooden edge.

"Here," Clay said, sliding another of the whiskey- filled glasses to me. I caught it before it could tip from the ledge and quirked a brow at him.

If it were possible, he seemed more on edge than I was.

Clay downed his in one long swallow and then knocked his glass back down onto the table and filled it a second time.

Jared and I followed suit.

"So, here's the thing," Clay said after finishing half of his second pour. He paused, a furrow in his brow. "The thing is..." he tried again then sputtered to a stop. He looked to Jared for help, and for a second, it looked like Jared was going to give it to him, parting his lips to explain. But then he shut them again, going pale.

I groaned and leaned back in my chair. Was I really going to have to be the one to do this?

More silence.

...here goes...

"You want me to move out," I stated. "And you want to go back to how it was before I turned. Go back to just being friends. That's it, right? You don't have to make it so ominous—"

"What?" Jared demanded, sitting up straighter in his chair, his eyes narrowed in confusion. "Allie, no. No, that's not—"

"You idiot," Clay muttered to himself, cutting off Jared, and I wasn't sure if he was calling me an idiot or himself. "Did you really think this was about *kicking you out?*"

I choked on a response, suddenly uncertain what to do with my hands. Where to look. "Well, I mean...yeah. What else could it have been about?"

They'd said they wanted to talk about us, hadn't they? Clay and Jared shared a look. Jared's Adam's apple bobbed in his throat and the color returned to his cheeks rapidly, staining them, and the tops of his ears, a shade of pink.

"Clay and I have been talking," he began, squirming slightly in his seat as though it were suddenly the most uncomfortable thing in the world.

Meanwhile, Clay just sat in his chair, stoic still and brooding, his lips slightly pursed.

"About?" I prodded.

Jared took a quick swallow of his whiskey, and his eyes flitted in my direction before landing back onto the table. "About who you should date."

I felt my brows lower, and my wolf began a low growl deep in my belly.

"I suppose you thought it was up to the two of you?" I demanded, my skin bristling. "That I didn't have a say in it at all?"

This was the hard part of being half wolf. Before, I could bottle up my feelings and lock them away. Pretend they didn't exist. Now...not so much.

If someone made me angry, I was *angry*.

"Well?" I prodded when neither replied, both of them sitting there with their eyes trained on knots in the wood grain.

"No." Clay finally joined the discussion, his voice rumbling so deep that I could feel the reverberation of it in my chair. "We want to give you an option that wasn't on the table before. If you'd chill out for a second and hear it."

He cut his brilliant blue eyes to me, and something in them gave me pause. The coolness of them doused the growing flames, and I crossed my arms over my chest with a sudden chill.

I didn't like the vibes they were giving off. The whole emotion-sharing thing was hard enough on a day to day, but this was something else. The nervous energy was making my wolf want to run for the hills. Hell, I may just let her if they didn't hurry up and get this over with.

"Okay, I'm listening."

Jared leaned forward and crooked his head at me. I hated how even as annoyed with them both as I was right now, I couldn't help the near-irresistible desire to reach out and touch him. "Do you remember what Hazel said that night she came for dinner?"

"About how you wouldn't ever mate to anyone else for as long as I'm living?" I asked through gritted teeth. How could I forget?

Clay shook his head. "No, not that part…"

"The part about getting used to the idea of sharing," Jared finished for him.

"I'm not following."

Jared sighed, and I could tell he was getting ready to blurt out the rest. "After what happened between you and Clay," he said with great effort, and I flinched at the reminder. "He and I had a talk. We'd planned to loop you in on it right after you joined the pack but then…" he trailed off.

Then all hell broke loose, and my friends were casualties in the fight.

"Anyway," Jared picked back up where he left off, "we knew it wasn't a good time."

"And you think *now* is a better time?" I prodded, thinking of all the other things we should be talking about but weren't.

Jared didn't seem sure what to say to that, a pained expression crossing his face.

Clay poured more whiskey into my cup and leveled his stare on me. "Look, Allie, if it's even half as hard for you as it is for us to keep your distance, then this conversation needs to happen."

I groaned.

"So, what? Are we really talking about what I think we're talking about here?"

Had they somehow actually agreed to *sharing*?

…to have been a fly on the wall for that painful conversation…

"Yes," Jared said. "We decided that if you're willing to give…three-way dating…a try, then so are we."

"I don't think that means what you think it means," Clay said gruffly, his voice dripping sarcasm.

Jared waved him off. "Whatever, she knows what I mean." Then he turned back to me. "We'll have to be super open about it. Super honest. There will probably have to be rules. It's probably going to be weird for a while—"

I couldn't help a snort at that. "Ya think?"

Jared retreated back into himself a little at that, and the weight of guilt settled in my belly. I was not taking this how they'd hoped, I realized, and tried to school my face. "I'm sorry," I whispered. "This is all just a little out of left field, you know? I thought you were kicking me out. This is...this is not what I was expecting."

"Our options are kind of limited," Clay interjected, swirling his glass.

Jared nodded, but I couldn't help but notice that even now, he was having trouble looking at his friend. "We both have feelings for you Allie. We both did even before you were bitten and turned," he said with a swallow.

My mind raced at that. I looked between Jared and Clay. There was truth in Jared's bright eyes, and even though Clay wasn't looking at me, I could see how his jaw was tightening. He wasn't denying it.

I couldn't believe it. All this time...

"And we think that maybe you have feelings for both of us... right?" Jared continued, his face pinched while he awaited my response.

My throat was suddenly desert dry, and I had to gulp down some more whiskey to wet it, feeling a hot flush crawl up my neck that I knew had nothing to do with the drink.

"I do," I finally managed, heart fluttering in my ribcage like a trapped bird trying to get free.

They both seemed to relax visibly at that. Shoulders lowering and lined foreheads smoothing. I was glad they both seemed so at ease with it. I was still feeling dirty and like I was somehow doing something wrong even though I constantly tried to tell myself that it wasn't my fault. It wasn't like I asked to be mated to two shifters.

And if Jared and Clay wanted to do this, how could I say no? How could I snub their only chance to both be with their intended mate when I knew they would never have another as long as I was living.

Even I had to admit: the idea of dating literally anyone else was absolutely repulsive. I couldn't even imagine it. I had to assume they felt the same.

"So, will you try it or not? Clay demanded. "Will you date both of us?"

"I..." I stammered, taking in both of my mates. My wolf swelled beneath my breast, dying to launch herself up my throat and do zoomies at the mere thought. I could almost hear her in the back of my mind.

Please, she begged.

But she didn't need to.

"If you're sure you want to do this," I told them, gathering up the courage I needed to say the words. "Then...I guess I'm in."

"We should probably decide what the rules will—"

"I think that's enough for one night." Clay interrupted Jared and stood to go trade his whiskey glass for a mug of coffee. He poured a second one and brought it to me. "I have something for you," he said. "But I need you to sober up real quick."

I glared at him. "What is it?"

Sobering up wouldn't be an issue. Ever since I'd turned, my body burned off alcohol at break-neck speeds. Which was really too bad because some nights I'd have liked nothing more than to get stone-cold drunk and sleep through the night.

I took the proffered coffee mug, and Clay grinned at me. One of his rare smiles that stretched wide enough to show teeth.

It was infectious. I found myself blushing again and hating that they could both make me so comfortable and *uncomfortable* at the same time.

"Clay," I growled.

Jared was smiling and I knew whatever it was, he was in on it, too. "Jared?" I tried, knowing that of the two he would be the more pliable.

But the traitor shook his head. "This one was all Clay, Allie girl. I'm not saying a word."

Clay stomped to the door, sipping his coffee. "Hurry up and drink that then meet me around back," he said and then let the screen door bang shut behind him.

Jared stood once Clay was gone and cleared both his plate and Clay's from the table. "I actually have to get back to the Quarry," he said solemnly. "But I promise I'll be back in time to take you to your meeting with Ryland tomorrow."

"You have to go?" I couldn't help sounding disappointed, but that only seemed to make him pleased that I didn't want him to leave. I stood to stop him from trying to wash the dishes. I would do them later, he had enough to worry about lately. "You just got back."

"I know," he said and came to wrap me in a quick embrace, filling all my senses with the heady scents of birch and sandalwood and that trademark *Jared* smell that was his and his alone. He brushed his lips lightly over my cheek, eliciting a shiver from my spine. He seemed to like that, too.

"Back before you know it," he said with a cheeky grin and then slid from the cabin, gone as quickly as he'd arrived. Leaving me with a flutter in my belly and a tickling heat licking up the back of my neck.

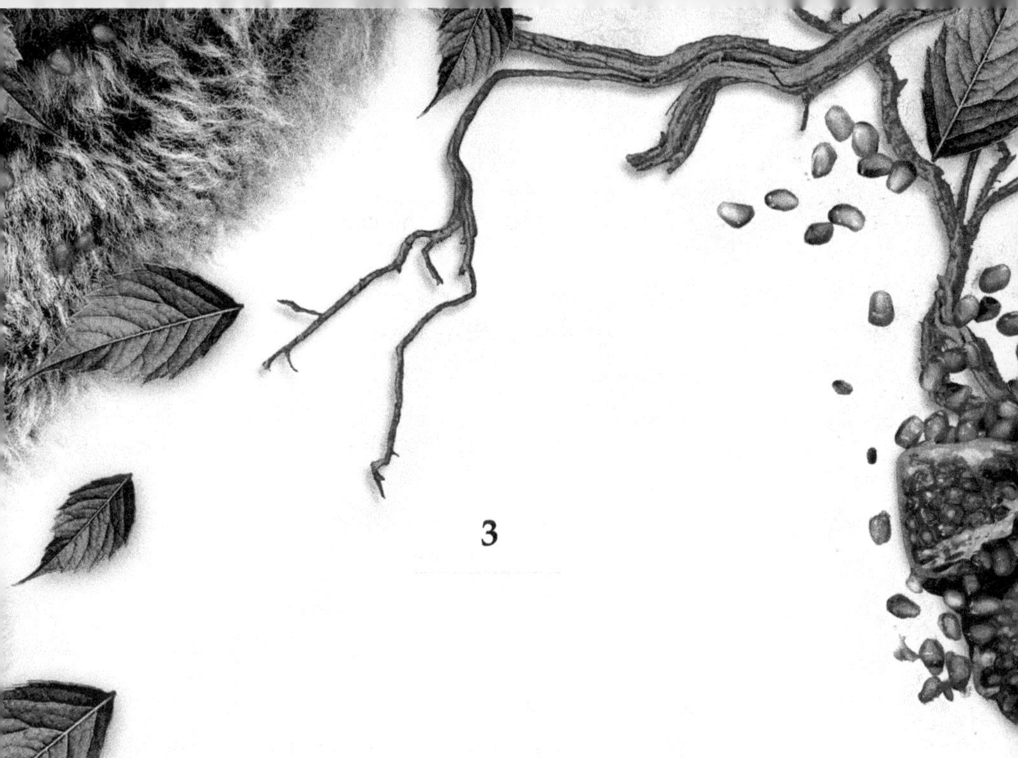

3

Grumbling to myself, I took my time draining my coffee in the kitchen alone, needing a moment to process everything that'd just happened.

I was going to be dating two guys.

Two extremely hot, infuriating, and completely different guys who also happened to be best friends.

I shook my head as I set my empty mug into the sink. This was going to be a complete and utter disaster...and yet, beneath all the layers of unease, there was something else: hope. I wasn't naïve enough to think that it was all going to work out, but there was a calmness in my bones now. A sort of peace that had my wolf rumbling contentedly within.

Hope was a dangerous thing, though. I had hope when my father was sick.

I had hope when Clay and Jared took me under their wing.

It was hope I felt when I escaped from Devin at that awful cave in the mountainside.

And there was hope the day I walked into the bloodbath at the Four Corners—hoping that I could bow and that would be the end of it.

Having hope had never helped me. Better not to hope for anything at all.

Smoothing my rumpled t-shirt and pulling my unruly turquoise hair up into a messy bun, I strode from the cabin and around back to Clay's shop.

When I entered, a leaden weight in my gut, he was standing there in the middle of the shop. In the spot where we'd both had our hands deep in the cavity of an old Harley the night before.

The Harley wasn't there anymore, though. A yellow Yamaha 250 stood next to Clay instead, gleaming as though she'd just been polished to within an inch of her life.

It took me a second, but I recognized it. Clay and I had worked on that bike for a client barely a week before. "We finished with that one days ago," I said, confused. "Did something break again already?"

An uncertain smile twisted at the edges of his lips. "No," he replied. "She's ready to be returned to her owner."

I scrunched my nose. "You...want me to help deliver her?"

He shook his head, a rare laugh blooming on his lips as he kicked the stand away and rolled the Yamaha forward. Understanding widened my eyes as he handed her to me. "No need," he said in a low rumble. "Her owner is already here."

I floundered for words, wanting to cry and punch him and hug him all at the same time.

I can't ride it. I don't ride anymore. Vivid images of riding with my dad bombarded my thoughts and my eyes stung with hot, angry tears.

Picking up on my emotions, Clay settled his wide,

warm hands over my shaking ones on the handlebars. "Hey," he said, waiting until I met his gaze. "It's yours, but only if you want it. If you don't, we can sell her. I got her cheap, *real cheap*—practically free. And you did most of the work fixing her up. We can sell her and split the—"

"Shut up," I said, my voice watery.

Clay's lips pressed into a hard line as I warred with myself over what to do.

My grip tightened on the handlebars and Clay removed his hands from mine, taking a step back while lines formed in his forehead once more.

"Look, if I overste—"

"Shut. Up."

One deep breath. Two. Three.

Craning my neck to one side so he couldn't see, I brushed the back of one hand over my damp eyes and gritted my teeth before speaking. "Thank you," I finally managed around the ball in my throat.

"You want to hit me, don't you?" he asked in a joking tone. "Because if you do, we can spar, and you can take your best shot. I won't even stop you."

"No," I said with a laugh, a sudden surge of adrenaline spiking my blood. No, not just adrenaline... excitement. I smoothed my palm over her nimble body and the supple leather of her freshly polished seat. "Let's ride."

Fire sparked in Clay's eyes.

"For real?" he asked, barely able to conceal his own surprise.

I grinned at him. "Yeah," I said through the bubble of a laugh. "Yeah, for real. I want to ride."

I was even more surprised to find that it was the truth. I *did* want to ride. I hadn't wanted to ride since... No, I wasn't going to think about that right now. I was going to give this beast a proper breaking-in. "I can't believe you had her all this time and didn't say anything."

Clay went and brought his own bike out from the back of the shop, rolling toward me. I knew he owned a big Sportster Forty-Eight. An absolute beast of a Harley. Midnight black with shocks of vivid, shimmering blue and shining silver chrome. But this wasn't that.

This was a flat black ATK Intimidator. One of the fastest and biggest bikes in the world.

Of course, he would have a dirt bike *and* a Harley. I shook my head.

"One day," I said, matching his pace as we rolled both bikes out into the cool autumn night. "You're going to let me ride that thing."

He scoffed. "As if. You'd eat dirt for sure. Not a chance I'd let you ride The Direwolf."

"The *what?*"

"You heard me," he said.

"You named your bike *The Direwolf?*"

"Yeah," he said with a taunt in his tone as we neared the entrance to a narrow trail I'd never noticed at the edge of their property. "And yours is called The Runt."

"Fuck that," I growled, hopping onto the bike's back and starting her engine. She flared to life with a rumbling purr that I felt all the way down to my bones. That adrenaline I was feeling earlier was nothing in the face of this. As I revved her engine, I felt my body tremble with the insatiable need to feel her move beneath me. I was ravenous for it. Didn't realize how much I missed it.

"I'll show you how fast this runt can move."

I took off at breakneck speed, lifting my body as she bumped onto the trail and her back end fishtailed as I got the feel for her size and power. A smile snaked across my lips, and despite all the awful, terrible things that kept me up at night, when I put her into second and then third gear, laughter bubbled up from deep within me.

The whine and rumble of Clay's bike on my tail spurred me faster. My canine vision making the trail clear as if it were early afternoon instead of evening. The cold snap of wind over my body coaxed all my hairs to standing and lit all my nerve endings ablaze. I whooped as I went around a corner and found a small inclined patch of dirt.

I jumped it, reveling in the split second when me and the bike left the ground. The impact of landing coiled up through my arms, my back tire skidding as I bumped around a corner, staying firmly ahead of Clay.

"Allie!" I heard him call over the roar of the wind rushing in my ears, over the sound of my own heartbeat like a drum in my ears.

"Allie, slow down!"

A spark of defiance zipped down my spine.

What? He didn't think I knew what I was doing?

Besides, my new wolf-toughened body could handle a wipeout. I smiled at that, empowered by it. A reckless desire to see how far I could push myself stole through my mind, and heedless of Clay's warning, I kept on, going faster, taking turns sharper. Tuning him out.

There was nothing except me and the bike and chewed earth beneath its tires. There was no Clay. No Jared. No pack alpha.

No best friends who barely spoke to me anymore. No pain.

No fear.

Just wind blowing my hair back and making my eyes water.

Just this bike. This trail. My pulse.

"Allie!" Clay's bellow cut through my walls only an instant before I saw the turn in the trail. This one was sharper. Too sharp. And I was already on top of it.

I kicked her down a gear and twisted the handlebars, trying to drift her rear end enough to make it around the bend. Heart in my throat, I threw my whole body into the maneuver, the sharp edge of panic twisting her blade in my gut.

Almost.

Almost...

The bike kicked out just a little too much to the right, and I fell to the left, taking her with me. We skidded through sharp rocks and gritty earth, her hot as hell exhaust pipe searing into my inner thigh.

"Fuck!" I cursed through clenched teeth, shoving the bike off me once we stopped sliding over the ground.

Clay's bike ground to halt and he let it fall to the ground. I only heard his heavy footfalls before my bike was torn out of my grasp and discarded three feet away as though it were a toy.

His hand came around my thigh where a singed hole was burned into the denim of my jeans, revealing bright red flesh beneath. My left arm was chewed from elbow to shoulder, too. I could feel it, but I didn't move, not wanting him to see.

"Are you hurt anywhere else?" Clay asked in a voice so cold and so threatening that I flinched.

"No," I said breathlessly as I batted his hand away. My thigh was already beginning to heal. The itch of the skin renewing itself made me grit my teeth.

He took me by my right arm, wrapping his hand around my upper forearm to lift me to standing. "What the fuck were you thinking?" he demanded, his blue eyes glowing with the presence of his wolf.

I felt my own wolf rush to the surface in response.

Where I was pissed the hell off, she was preoccupied with the fact that we could smell his leather and engine grease scent, and that his warm callused fingers still brushed over the sensitive skin at our elbow's crease.

I pulled my arm away and took a step back, willing my wolf to be on my side with this.

"Riding," I snapped. "I was riding."

He shook his head and a muscle in his temple twitched. "That wasn't riding, Allie. That was fucking reckless and stupid. You don't know these trails."

I poked him in his big fat chest. "You don't know how I ride," I countered. "I know what I'm doing."

"Do you?" he challenged, stepping in closer. "Because it sure as hell didn't look like it. It looked like you were trying to get yourself hurt."

The truth in his words stung, and I recoiled from them as though they were a physical blow, teeth grinding.

"Don't—"

"No, *you* don't," he interrupted in a growl. "You could have been seriously hurt."

"So what! I would heal."

He stepped in, sealing the gap between us until I could feel the brush of his chest against mine. He leaned his head down to meet my fire-filled gaze with a burning one of his own. I didn't back down.

Didn't back away.

His breath tickled my lips and it took everything inside of me not to give my wolf what she wanted. She pawed and scratched, whined and mewled. She wanted to devour him. I wanted to let her.

Something flipped hard in my belly, and I gasped, hating how I could both *hate* him and *want* him at the same time.

His eyes flicked to my lips and a bolt of white-hot energy shot through me like lightning. I leaned in, ready to surrender.

That's when he pulled back, leaving me unsteady on my feet as his face turned to stone. "I won't watch you do this to yourself," he said in a hard whisper.

Something like acid pooled in my gut and suddenly it was impossible to look him in the eye. My fists squeezed and I bit back a scathing remark.

Clay lifted my bike easily, wrapping his hand around the middle of the handlebars before he went and lifted his own bike back to standing, holding that one up in much the same way. "You can walk back," he said over his shoulder without any remorse. "Then you and I are going to have a little chat."

There were so many things I wanted to say. To shout. To scream as he faded around the bend and all I was left with was an ebbing rage and shaking fists while I listened to the sound of the tires slowly rolling over earth as he walked both bikes back toward the cabin and left me in the dark.

If he thought I was going to fucking follow him like some sad puppy, tail tucked between my legs, the bastard had another think coming.

Right there amid the trees, with pine scented wind stinging my fury-warmed skin, I stripped down until I was naked. Bared to the leaf-dappled moonlight beneath the tree canopy.

Shifting was still painful, but over the last week, it'd become more bearable each time. I was already getting faster at it. Relinquishing the reins to my wolf and letting her overtake me made the transition so smooth I only had to endure a few seconds of agony before I felt my paws pushing into the dirt and the air taking on a crystalline quality.

The sound of the forest magnified in my canine ears. The skitter of a squirrel fleeing up a tree. The buzz and chirp of insects. The sound the wind made when it whistled through needles and branches. And very distantly, Clay, at the trailhead now. I could hear him sigh as the bike's tires rolled to a stop.

He was waiting for me.

He may have been pissed off, but he wouldn't leave me out here all alone.

He could keep waiting.

My wolf strained to go to him, but I asserted my own dominance over her, something else I'd been practicing.

Jared, I spoke in our shared mind.

I had no interest in going back to the cabin with Clay right now. I didn't want to hear what he had to say.

Let's go to the quarry.

Sufficiently satisfied with the alternative, we began to move. Slowly at first, gaining speed until Clay had no hope of catching us. We doubled back twice and ran splashing through creek water part of the way, careful not to mark any trees with our scent.

It was another trick Jared had taught me—how to cover my tracks if I was ever out alone. How to give myself a head start. I was glad my wolf seemed happy to cooperate so long as I allowed her to run in the direction of at least *one* of my mates.

I'd been to the local quarry only once when I was a little girl. Dad had taken me on an errand to buy some flagstone for the curving stone pathway out behind our back deck. But I remembered where it was well enough by the road. Getting there via the forest proved a more challenging route, but my wolf seemed like she already knew exactly where she was going, and I had to wonder if she could somehow sense Jared's location.

It was about twenty minutes later when the last dregs of my anger wore off and I began to regret taking off on Clay. I couldn't say I was ready to admit he had a point, but there was a small bud of guilt poking its head up through my belly and into my ribcage. Soon, it would bloom and grow heavy with seed.

Ugh.

Didn't he understand?

Didn't he get how fucking hard I was trying to hold it all together?

My wolf let out a little yip, and I refocused to find bright lights filtering through the tree branches ahead. The beep and groan of machinery hauling stone and the shouting of men.

We found it.

No point in turning back now. I could ask Jared to send Clay a text telling him where I was. It was the best form of apology I could give. I was still too frustrated to give him any more than that.

Tomorrow at school I was going to have to face Layla and Viv again.

Tomorrow night after work I was going to have to face Ryland. Submit myself to his command.

And by the end of the week, when the full moon reared its ugly head, my friends' fates would be decided and there was nothing at all I could do but wait for the ax to fall.

My painful reminder of what awaited us forced a long howl from my wolf's lips. Our chest ached with it, and when we were finished, a bone-weary exhaustion set in and we lay against the cool earth, resting our chin against our paws.

We didn't have to wait long. Jared found us not more than a couple minutes later. The moment we caught his scent on the wind and began to feel his nearness through the mate bond, a rush of exhilaration brought us back to life.

His silhouette appeared amid the trees, tall and lean. The bright lights of the quarry set his dirty blond hair ablaze, so it looked like a halo rested atop his head.

I gave a little yip of excitement and then my wolf, sated from her long run and the presence of her mate, yielded the reins, putting them back in my hands.

"Allie?" Jared called as he neared, squinting to see me in the dimness. "What are you doing out here?"

I realized, a little belatedly, that I didn't exactly think this through. I bowed my lupine head, examining my fur coated limbs and swishing tails. I hadn't brought any clothes.

Jared kneeled in the leaf-strewn dirt; he reached a hand to me, pushing it into my fur. His eyes blazed vibrant deep amber—that small green fleck like the spark of fire in a rushing verdant river. Unable to help myself, I pushed my head against his touch, letting the pull and give of the mate bond bring a calm clarity to my mind.

He smirked and a dimple formed in his left cheek. I licked it.

He barked a laugh and reeled back.

Mortified, I lowered my head. I hadn't meant to... God, did I really just lick Jared?

"Here," he said and stood, rubbing the back of his hand over the wolf slobber on his cheek before he tugged off his long sleeve gray t-shirt. It was a study in self-control not to drool at the sight of his naked torso. That body belonged to a man. Defined abs and thick biceps. A whisper of light-colored hair disappearing below the belt of his jeans.

Mine, my wolf growled in the furthest reaches of my mind.

I agreed.

"It should be long enough to cover...everything," he prompted, holding it out to me with one arm and turning his head the opposite way to allow me to shift back without him watching. Always the gentleman.

Shifting back had gotten easier since I started letting my wolf out daily, too. Before it was like coming up for breath after suffocating under water. With my insides aching like they were deprived of oxygen and every muscle was on lock.

Now it was just like opening a door and stepping through it. The pain was always less than making the transition *to* wolf.

Still though, I shuddered as I took the t-shirt from Jared's fingers and pulled it over my head. He was right, the hem of the thing came nearly to my mid-thigh. But without panties or a bra, I still felt way too exposed.

"Good?" Jared asked.

I nodded, then realized with a flush that he wasn't looking at me. That he wanted *verbal* confirmation I wasn't naked anymore. "Yeah," I stammered. "Thanks."

He spun with eyes half-closed and his bottom lip caught between his teeth. When his gaze met mine, the tiniest of smiles pulled at my lips.

Jared reached up a hand to scratch the back of his neck and looked me up and down.

"Did you come alone?" he asked, peering into the darkened forest at my back as though expecting company.

I nodded. "Yeah," I told him, pursing my lips. "I know you guys still don't like me going out on my own, but—"

He held a hand up, a knot forming in his brow. "You don't have to explain yourself to me, Allie. I want you safe, but what you do is your business. I'm not here to control you."

I sighed. How could he and Clay be so similar in so many ways, but so very different in others. "Thanks," I muttered. "I just...needed to get away."

He raised a brow at that. "Should I be worried?"

I grimaced. "No, but maybe you should text Clay and let him know I'm here with you. Safe. I kind of took off on him."

Jared stifled a laugh and gave a little nod, as though he wasn't the least bit surprised.

"I take it riding didn't go so well?"

"Understatement of the century," I joked.

"Well, come on," he said and extended his hand to me. "My cell's in the office, and I just made hot chocolate. Stay for a while?"

My belly did a little flip and I took his hand, super conscious that if I bent over even in the slightest, the whole quarry was going to see my lady bits.

"Don't worry," Jared said, squeezing my hand as he led me toward the lights in the distance. "The office is at the edge of the quarry. And it's got a back door."

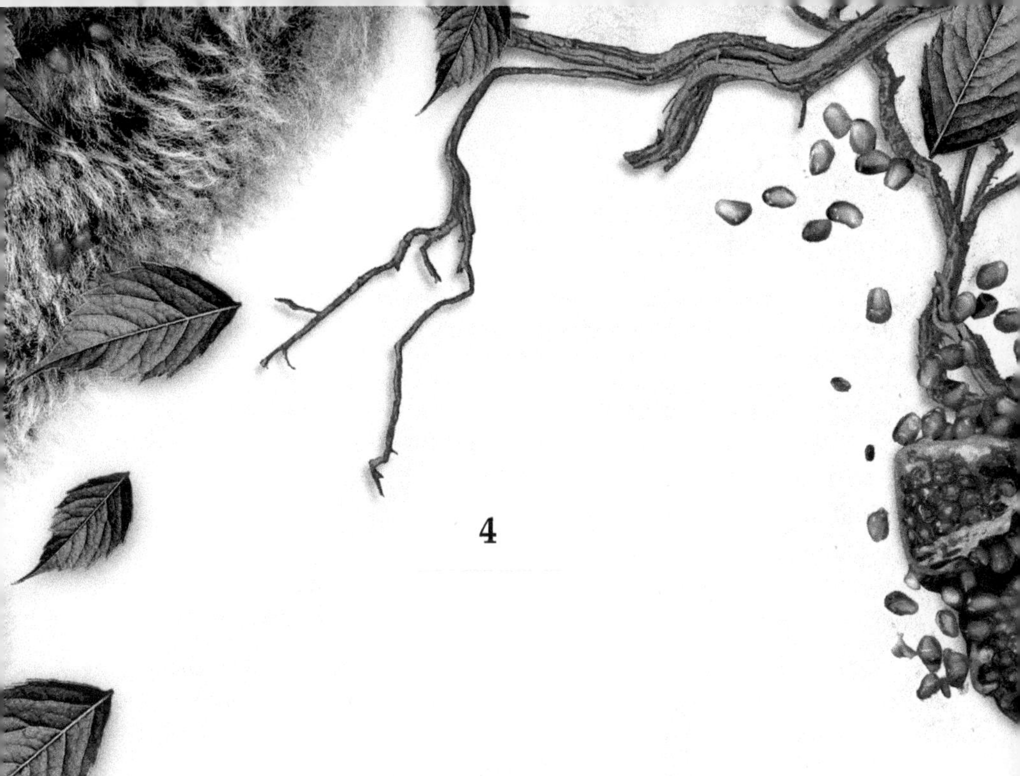

4

Jared busied himself cleaning out an extra mug once he drew the blinds closed at the front of the portable office.

The space was larger than I pictured it to be. With a long desk spaced a few feet ahead of the back wall and a plush leather chair sandwiched between it and the wall. In front of that there were two chairs, for visitors or clients, I assumed. And on the other side of the long space was a makeshift kitchenette, complete with microwave, plug in kettle, and enough ramen noodle cups and hot cocoa packets to last someone at least a year.

Next to the kitchenette was a deep-burgundy sofa. A pillow wadded up on one end and a threadbare taupe blanket folded over the top.

Jared gestured to the sofa once he was finished adding a small handful of marshmallows to the top of two steaming mugs. I couldn't remember the last time I had cocoa, and I salivated at the smell when he pressed the mug into my hand.

With the conversation from dinner still fresh in my mind and Jared right here in front of me, I couldn't seem to think of anything else and easy conversation eluded me.

So, we were dating now. Me and Jared.

Me and Clay.

Weird didn't even begin to cover it.

461

Jared sat and thumbed out a quick text to Clay like I'd asked him.

I opened my mouth to attempt to string together some form of a sentence that didn't giveaway how the twelve inches of space between us was driving me mad, but Jared beat me to it. "How are Layla and Viv?"

Talk about a fucking buzzkill.

Sensing my change in demeanor, his brows lowered. "Sorry."

I shook my head. "No, it's okay. You haven't been at school for a while, so I guess you wouldn't know."

I took a deep breath. "I think they're taking it okay.

I'm not really sure to be honest." His eyes narrowed.

"They aren't exactly talking to me."

He licked his lips, seeming to consider something, as though if he could just think hard enough, he could find a solution to all my problems.

"It'll be over soon," he said. "They might not even shift, and then when they don't, Ry will have them compelled to forget any of this ever happened."

I sighed.

Ah. The mysterious Mr. Grey. The vampire I met briefly in Ryland's house the night of the bonfire. Apparently, they had the ability to *compel,* which from what I understood was just a lax way of saying that they had the ability to fuck with your mind.

The guy already gave me the creeps the first time we met, now he's firmly in *hell-no* territory for ever wanting him near me or any of my friends.

It was what Ryland had planned for me the night I took off only to be captured and turned by Devin. He wasn't going to kill me at all.

Fancy that.

If I'd stayed, I wouldn't have remembered Jared or Clay becoming wolves. Maybe, if Ryland wanted to be extra cautious, I wouldn't even remember that Jared was the one who saved me in the woods. I wouldn't know them. I may not be a shifter right now.

The former are the reasons why I could never wish I'd stayed.

Looking into Jared's kind stare now only reinforces it: I was *meant* to meet them. I knew it as surely as I knew the sun would rise tomorrow morning.

I was *meant* to love them.

I dropped my head. "I know."

"Have you told them?"

"That if they don't shift, they'll be forced to forget it all ever happened? No. Not yet. I think if I tell them vampires are also real right now, they might implode."

Jared nodded his agreement. "What about Quinn?

Has he remembered anything?"

I sipped my hot cocoa, letting my body meld to the worn sofa cushions. This was still painful territory he was poking at, but it was less difficult to talk about. Quinn was the lucky one of the three. He already didn't remember anything from that night. "Nothing at all. He still thinks we're all going to a bush party on the full moon. He has no idea it's a shifter camp."

We'd figure out how to handle that when the time came. Layla was adamant that he not be told anything about what happened. Not until he had to know.

I assumed the waiting to learn their fate was eating at them both. I didn't have that.

I turned mere minutes after I was bitten.

I couldn't even imagine what they must have been going through...

My chest ached, and I set my cocoa down on the rickety side table, stomach suddenly a bit sour.

"That's probably for the best."

"We can trust him, right?" I blurted, needing it to be confirmed at least one more time. "Ryland. We can trust that if they don't turn, he'll let them walk out of there."

Jared's lips pressed into a thin line, and he reached across me to set his mug down, too.

For a second, he seemed to be chewing on a response, then he looked up at me from beneath his caramel colored lashes, gaze flitting to me briefly before falling back down to rest on the sofa cushion between us.

He shifted in his seat and threw a hand through his tousled hair to get it out of his eyes. "When you were little," he started, and I'm confused at where he's going with this. "Do you..."

He paused. Swallowed.

"Do you remember hunting with your dad? You would have been maybe seven or eight."

He waited, and my heart began to pound in my chest. My skin tingled all the way down to my toes.

It couldn't have been...

"You came upon two skinned wolves in the woods."

My eyes welled and a hard ball formed in my throat.

No.

"Huddled against their corpses, there was a young wolf pup."

Beneath the streaks of dried crimson and clotted dirt in its fur, it was the purest white. It'd growled at us. Snarled and swiped. But it was starving. Malnourished. It looked like it had been there for days if not longer. It was all alone. To my eight-year-old self, it was just a little white puppy with sad amber eyes and no one to care for it. How Dad had tried to pull me away, warning me with threats that he'd need to take me to get a rabies shot if it bit me. But I'd fought him.

Dad wouldn't let me take him home. But I wouldn't leave it with nothing.

Jared's jaw twitched as he continued, his hands in fists. "You...you came to me even though your Dad was trying to pull you away," he said with a little laugh of incredulity. "Just this tiny thing...but you had a fire in you even then."

Dangerously close to tears, I dug my fingernails into the palms of my hands, trying to regain control. It wasn't just my own emotions I had to contend with, Jared's sorrow pierced me straight through. Like an arrow of misery burrowing its high carbon steel into my still-beating heart.

"You gave me this little dish from your hiking pack and filled it to overflowing with all the water in your canteen," he said, and some of that sorrow eased. "Then, with your dad groaning at your back, you dumped an entire Ziplock bag of deer jerky onto the ground beside it."

The memory came back so clear it was startling. I remembered how the little wolf had looked at me curiously, edging closer to the jerky and water with an upper lip curled back, ready to attack if he needed to.

"Do you remember what you said to me?" Jared asked, finally lifting his head, amber eyes bright like warm, spiced cider.

I tried to chase the memory, but it was a faraway thing, flying just out of my grasp.

"You told me I was going to be okay," he said with a sad smile. "With this serious little face and tears in your eyes, like you were so sure it was true."

I missed that sense of optimism. It sure would have come in handy now.

At his reminder, the fleeting memory returned, and I remembered how Dad had shaken his head at me. He'd always thought it was strange that I talked to all the animals we came upon in the woods. Little did he or I know that there was one who could truly hear me.

"If it weren't for you..." Jared trailed off and then seemed to come back to himself, as though he'd shucked off the weight of the memory. Put it back behind him where it belonged.

"Anyway," he said. "My point is Uncle Ry picked up the pieces. After you...I gathered the strength to find my way back to the pack. He was there for me when I had no one else. He's an ass sometimes, I'll give you that."

He tipped his head to the side with a short laugh. "But Ry is the only family I've got."

"No, he isn't," I said, moving myself closer to Jared on the sofa. I waited for him to fix those amber eyes back on me before continuing.

The bond between us pulsed. That tether between our two souls grew taut.

I knew, now more than I ever did before, how much this made sense.

My heart broke for that little white wolf in the woods that day. Dad had to deal with my wailing for the rest of the hunting trip. Something in those sad eyes had sliced into me, burrowed deep.

Even then, I think somehow, I knew...

That maybe there was a connection even then, as children, that could not be denied.

"Ry isn't your only family, Jare. You have Clay," I told him, searching his gaze.

He lifted a hand and brushed a length of hair back from my cheek. His fingertips brushed over my cheekbone and I shivered involuntarily, something tightening in my chest.

Jared looked like he was about to disagree, but I wasn't finished.

"And now you have me."

His hand stilled, and I glanced at his full lips, my wolf hedging back to the surface.

I don't know why I ever tried to fight it. It was pointless. This was always going to happen. We were on a collision course, destined for impact. Not a thing in the world could stop it.

"Allie..." My name was a sigh on his lips, and his warm palm pressed against my cheek. I closed my eyes and let out a small sigh of my own, skin bristling.

When I opened them again, Jared's wolf stared back at me. The glow around his irises and the strain in his expression told me all I needed to know.

He was still holding back. Not allowing himself to take what he thought he couldn't have.

But hadn't I always belonged to him? "Allie, I—" he began, but I cut him off. "Just kiss me, you idiot."

Jared's hungry eyes widened for an instant before he let himself loose. The hand on my cheek snaked behind my neck, knotting in the small hairs there. I gasped, but the sound was swallowed by his lips.

Jared kissed me like a man starved. His hands gripped me hungrily, drawing me to him. His lips moved expertly against mine, provoking a shattered moan from my throat. I pressed my hands to his chest, looking for something to hold on to, afraid if I didn't find my grip, I'd fall.

My body came alive with sensation. Heat and tension and electricity swirled and crashed as Jared pulled me onto his lap and my legs fell to either side of his hips.

His hands gripped hard at my waist, holding me there as he swept in with his tongue, the kiss tasting of mint and chocolate. He sat up, wrapping his arms around my middle as he pressed into my chest, making my breasts harden beneath the thin t-shirt.

I was losing it. Losing my grip on reality. On control.

Each of his fevered kisses sent me speeding ever closer to oblivion. My body, naked beneath Jared's shirt, hummed with latent desire, and I realized I didn't want him to stop.

Not ever. This felt *right*.

My hands on his arms trailed lower, reaching between us. I felt his body still as my hands brushed over the top button of his jeans.

"Jared!" A gruff voice called from outside the office and two sobering *thuds* pounded against the front door. The kiss broken, I scrambled from Jared's lap, skin flushed and knees trembling as I tried to get my footing.

"Shit," Jared cursed, rising and readjusting his jeans. "Uh..." he said in a whisper, looking around as though for some means of escape.

The silver knob began to turn, and I spurred into action, rushing around the desk at the back of the office. I'd planned to tuck myself in the nook beneath, but it was already filled with stacks of old files. The door swung open, and I did the only thing I could think of and sat in the chair, pulling it as close to the desk as I was able. Close enough that I hoped the man wouldn't be able to see that I wasn't wearing any pants. I brushed my hair away from my face and straightened my spine, willing my breathing to level out just as he entered.

Jared rushed to grab his mostly empty cocoa and leaned casually against the wall where the kitchenette stood opposite me.

"Oh," the man said, taking in first Jared and then me behind the desk. "Didn't know you had company."

"Nah," he said, clearing his throat. "Allie just popped by to borrow my Jeep," he said and lifted the keys from his pocket to toss them to me.

I scrambled to catch them. "Right," I agreed.

Greg didn't look convinced, but he also looked a hell of a lot like he didn't give a shit one way or the other what we were doing. His chapped hands and coveralls were coated in a thick layer of rock dust, and his eyes told of his exhaustion. He jutted his chin back in the direction of the loud quarry outside the still- open door. "Got a bit of a situation with the skid-steer. She's stuck real good."

Jared's demeanor changed, and he bent to gather a vest and hardhat from a box in the corner, tugging them on.

The look...definitely suited him.

I bit my lower lip, pressing my thighs together beneath the table to keep from making any sound.

"I'll come have a look," Jared told Greg, who turned and left without another word. Jared followed him to the door, pausing in the frame to toss me a wink over his shoulder. "Don't go anywhere," he said with a sly grin. "Back in no time."

I nodded, fully intent on waiting however long it took.

The door swept closed behind Jared, making the blinds rattle against the glass windowpane. Jarring the portable building enough that the mouse atop the desk moved, making the desktop screen come to life.

A web page covered the screen. I was about to look away when the headline of the page caught my eye.

How to use a bow.

A smile tugged at my lips, and I laughed quietly to myself. I wondered offhandedly if he was actually interested, or if he was taking an interest only because he knew how much I liked going out to shoot my bow every morning.

Hesitantly, I scrolled down the page, curious about what it said.

When I got to the end, I noticed the little mail icon flashing on the taskbar and hovered over it, shaking my head at myself when I realized I was about to open it.

What am I doing?

I moved my hand from the mouse but managed to accidentally click the button before I did. An email screen materialized, and I jolted, knowing I should've looked away, but unable to.

Ryland's email address. There was a posed photo of him in the upper right corner. If that weren't enough of a giveaway, there were several already opened emails that showed samples of their hidden content, most of which contained some form of Ry, Ryland, or Mr. Stone as an opening line.

A new email rested at the top, its bold font begging to be clicked on.

A weight settled in my belly and the tips of my fingers tingled as I hovered over it. My palms grew sweaty.

The top three emails were all from the same address. No name in the sender field. Just an *X*. The subject line on the second one down, one of the ones that was already opened read: *The list you asked for...*

The other two didn't have any subject at all.

Before I could think too much about it, I clicked the one about the list and scrolled down through the completely blank email to where there was a file available for download. It said simply: *List.*

Gritting my teeth, I clicked on it. The computer chirped loudly, and I sucked in a breath, staring at a little popup that told me this file was password protected. The empty text box taunted with the flashing black line, as though asking me what the hell I was doing.

Groaning, I exited the popup and clicked over to the next already opened email. That one was blank too, but also contained a file. This one was labeled simply: *Jared.*

An icy chill snaked down my spine at the sight of his name. I tried to tell myself that this was nothing. It could be this person was Ryland's accountant or something. Maybe they were sending out copies of paystubs or lists of expenses.

But then why did I feel like that couldn't have been farther from the truth?

Emboldened, I click on the last email—the one not yet open. This one, blank like the others has two files down near the bottom waiting to be opened. They are image files, but only black squares show where samples would normally be. They must have been password protected, too. Both are labeled with names. One is labeled *Dean,* and the other is labeled *Andreas.*

Footsteps coming back up to the portable door send my pulse skittering into overdrive. With sloppy fingers, I exit out of the email and right click it, marking it as unread and then quitting out of the window.

By the time Jared re-enters the cabin, hands covered in gray dust, I'm leaning back in the plush office chair, doing my absolute best to calm the fuck down before he notices anything is amiss.

"Hey," he said with a grin. "Sorry about that."

I shook my head, standing on leaden legs. "That's okay."

My blood felt near boiling, and I knew that if he looked at me too closely, he would see the evidence of what I'd just done all over my face. *God,* what was I doing?

Snooping on his uncle's—*my alpha's*—computer?

That was a surefire way to earn myself some scorn right off the hop.

I held out his keys to him. "Here."

He pushed them back. "I'd rather you take it," he said. "It'll be safer than running back to the cabin. If you don't mind?"

How could I say no when he was making that face?

The one with the dimple and the sweet smile.

"I really shouldn't," I told him. "I'm supposed to only drive with a licensed driver in the passenger seat."

Jared pursed his lips, considering. "It's all backroads to the trailhead. And you're a fast learner. Already a better driver than I was a few weeks in."

Not wanting to draw this out, I pasted on a wilted grin of my own and curled the keys into my fist.

"It's parked at the edge of the quarry, in the employee lot. I'll walk you through the trees."

"No," I rushed to say. "I mean, that's okay. I'm sure I can find it. How many lifted white Jeeps can there be out there?"

The joke didn't take, and I was left feeling guilty and awkward and wondering if I remembered to exit out of Ryland's email or not. The screen was still lit up and it took all the self-control I had not to lean back and peek just to make sure.

Jared, thankfully, didn't seem to notice my discomfort.

He stuffed his hands deep into the pockets of his jeans and nodded.

"'Kay," I said in a breath. "See you tomorrow night?" I went to turn, ready to make a break for it when he caught me around the waist and spun me back to him. His hand found the back of my head and his other arm kept me from falling as he pressed his lips to mine.

For a brief second, the guilt weighing on my chest turned light as air and I forgot why I wanted to leave so badly.

Then the kiss ended, and it all came rushing back with the air that returned to my lungs.

"Sorry," Jared said, a whisper against my lips. "I couldn't let you leave without doing that one more time."

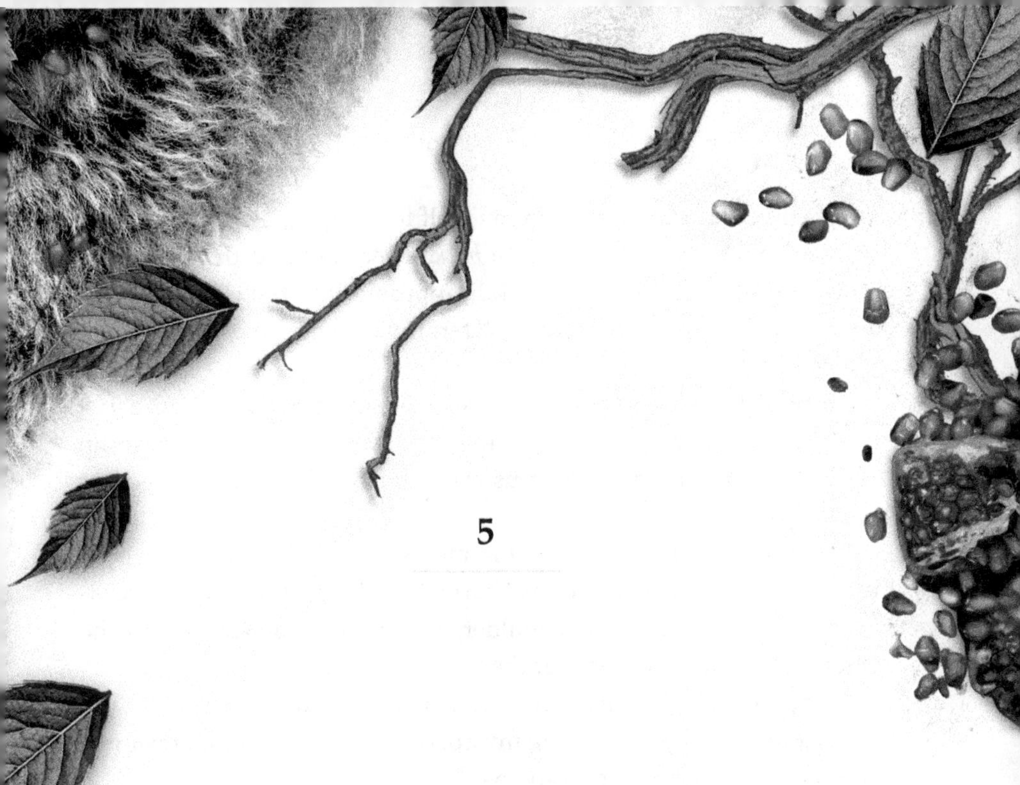

5

I t was time to go.

The day went by in a blur of classes I couldn't focus on and a shift at the bookshop that felt like it was over in minutes instead of hours.

At least Layla and Viv actually spoke to me today. I mean, it wasn't much, a quick conversation about the plan for the full moon, and them asking if we should make plans for my birthday. I shut down the latter, telling them I'd rather not make a big thing out of it. And I did my best to explain everything they needed to know about the former, glazing over the ugly bits.

I knew I should tell them *all* of it, but I just... couldn't. Every time I tried it was like a knife drove deeper and deeper into my chest.

But we talked, and in my book, that was progress. Painful, slow progress, but still progress. The fact that they asked about my birthday —of all stupid things—gave me hope that it was more the situation they were angry at than me.

It didn't erase any of my guilt, but it made it a bit easier to swallow.

I flicked off the lights and dug out the keys to lock up. Clay's burly shadow appeared outside the front window a second later, and I sighed inwardly. Last night when I got home, he was there, sitting on the porch with a beer. Looked like he was ready to wait all night if he had to.

471

When he saw me coming, in my wolf form again, he gave one tight nod, as though to say *good, you're back.* Then he lifted the two other empty bottles from the steps and disappeared into the cabin. When I entered, ass naked, a few minutes later, it was quiet, and his bedroom door was sealed shut.

I'd been thinking about how to explain what happened all day. I knew he was going to be here, that we were going to pack camp together and Jared would meet us there, but I still hadn't figured out what to say.

I tugged the door closed behind me as I stepped outside, the bells rattling at the top of the door as I turned the key in the lock and readjusted my backpack on my shoulder, stuffing the shop keys into the little gap in the double zipper at the top.

"Hey," he said, kicking off from a leaning stance on the wall.

"Before we go," I said, biting my lip, trying to sort through my mess of thoughts. "I just wanted to apolo—"

"Don't," he interrupted, face reddening. "I shouldn't have just left. I should have...I don't know. Tried to make you feel better or some shit."

He took a shaky breath.

"I'm, *uh,* not very good at...at..."

I cocked my head at him, holding in a laugh at his obvious discomfort. "At...being a boyfriend?"

He cringed. "Yeah. I guess."

"Have you never had a girlfriend before?"

I had to ask. He had a reputation at Forest Grove High when he was a senior there. And with that *face* and those *muscles,* I couldn't imagine him not dating.

He shrugged, leveling his bright blue eyes on me with a coy stare. "Depends what you think counts as dating."

A furious blush found its way onto my cheeks, and I dropped my gaze before he could see. He may be inexperienced with the kind of dating I was used to. But I could say with confidence that I was *definitely* inexperienced in the sort of dating he was used to.

"Okay," I said, suddenly eager to end this conversation. "So, I'm not going to say sorry and you're not pissed at me anymore. I guess that means we're good."

Clay smirked. "Yeah, Allie. We're good."

Thank fuck for that. Or this would have been a really awkward drive. Or not...

"Where's the Jeep?"

Clay tipped his head to the sidewalk and began to walk, giving me a little tug on my jacket sleeve as he passed so I would follow him.

"Thought we'd run," he said. "You haven't shifted yet today."

My stomach soured.

Right.

Under normal circumstances I'd be all right to miss a day, but we were going to pack camp. I was going to get my first orders from my alpha. It was easy to read between the lines of Clay's words.

I needed to shift before I faced him so I could keep myself under control.

Ryland wasn't feeling particularly patient lately from what I'd heard when Charity came to visit a few days ago. She got chewed out for helping Quinn and was stuck on security detail, policing the new pack members all week and reporting back to Ry.

"That's probably a good idea."

Clay and I veered off the main road and onto a side street. Another few blocks and it would dead-end in the trees and we could shift.

"Have you spoken to Jared today?" I hedged, wondering if he'd said anything to Clay about what happened between us last night. This whole *sharing* thing was going to take some getting used to. The only way it would work was for us to be honest with each other and to set those ground rules Jared mentioned.

We'd have to have another toe-curling chat to do that soon.

Clay bowed his head. "Yeah. I should've figured you'd go there."

He didn't say it with any ire, just a sort of resigned, careful tone, and I knew right away they'd talked about it. My belly flipped. That was a conversation I was super glad I wasn't there for.

"We kind of established a ground rule," he continued when I didn't comment.

My brows lowered. "What's that?"

"No fucking."

"What?" I choked, a bit shell-shocked at how casually he was just throwing that word out there in that context.

He cut his gaze to me, eyeing me sidelong as we walked. "No. Fucking."

I ground my teeth together, remembering how difficult it had been to stop. Both with Clay and with Jared. I wondered if it was because they were both over eighteen and I was still seventeen?

I mean, I'd be eighteen in just days from now, but neither of them knew that.

Or it could be that neither could stand the thought of the other being that intimate with me.

Then, there was also the possibility that neither of them *wanted* to.

That one hurt the most.

"Fine," I said, unable to keep the biting tone from my words. "It's not like either of you asked me, but..." I trailed off, shrugging.

"Allie—"

"No, it's cool. I get it."

"I don't think you do."

"Can we just not talk about this right now?"

I walked off the streetlamp lit street and stepped into the brush, moving inward to where the shadows hung more heavily to provide us the cover we would need to shift unseen.

Clay grunted and followed me, kicking off his shoes when we stopped. I opened my backpack and put my own shoes inside. Followed by my jeans, sweater, and tank top.

Clay had his shirt and socks off and was just unbuttoning his jeans when he paused, his mouth slightly agape as I unclasped my bra.

Still heated with fury at him and Jared for making a decision like that without my even so much as being present for it, I was feeling a little brazen. Maybe a little vindictive.

The clasp came free, and the chill of the evening brushed over my breasts as I dropped the bra into my bag with the rest of my clothes. A muscle in his neck twitched.

"*Allie,*" he growled, a warning.

"What?" I asked, the word dripping sarcasm as I hooked my fingers into the top of my panties, suddenly grateful I didn't wear my hello kitty ones, but the simple black ones with the sporty waistband. "Your rules. Not mine."

His nostrils flared and a fraction of a second before I worked up the courage to drop my panties, he turned his head to the side, averting his glowing blue stare. His hands clenched so tightly I could see every curve of his knuckles beneath the strained white flesh.

Perhaps a little too pleased with myself, I bent and zipped my backpack and then shifted, only a small cry leaving my lips before my wolf took over and I was staring up at Clay from all fours.

Clay trained his haughty stare on me, his face red. Glad my wolf seemed to be on the same page as me,

we sat still, staring at him with a little crook to our neck. Ready for the show.

Realizing what I was doing, Clay grimaced. "Want to turn around?"

We stared.

His brows lowered, and he turned around, dropping his jeans and shifting in one fluid motion that only afforded the briefest glance at his muscled ass and thick thighs. It was enough.

I lifted the pack from the forest floor with my teeth and took off at a sprint, leaving Clay to fumble to pick up his shoes and follow.

Not cool, Allie, his words floated through my mind as I ran.

Which part? I asked, finding it difficult to be sorry in the slightest.

You know *which part.*

I smiled, buoyant as we ran side by side, taking the long way around the creek and against the mountainside. Both of us needing the extra miles to cool off before we got there.

PACK CAMP BUZZED WITH NOISE AND ENERGY AS WE APPROACHED. MY WOLF could sense all the new pack members. She caught every individual scent on the wind. Clay and I came to a halt close enough to see down into the camp if we really strained our eyes, but far enough away that we could get dressed again without anyone seeing.

Clay might've been used to getting naked in front of the other shifters—it seemed second nature to them—but I had a feeling it would be a while before I got used to it. I may have teased Clay in the woods, but there was no way I wanted to show my goods to an entire pack if I could help it.

I shifted back, falling to my knees as a wave of dizziness washed over me, the world tipping up for a second before it leveled out. I held on to the earth for dear life until the vertigo passed.

"Hey," Clay said brusquely, and I felt his human hands curl over my shoulders and shuddered at the contact. "What just happened? You good?"

I struggled to swallow past a dry lump in my throat and caught my breath. Stars crowded at the edges of my vision.

"Yeah," I managed. "Bullshit."

He turned me to him, careful to keep his gaze level with mine. I can't say I did the same. Even with the stars in my eyes, his...package...was hard to miss.

Clay's index finger lifted my chin, and his blue eyes bored into mine.

"When was the last time you ate?" I blinked.

And as though it was crying out for aid, my stomach growled loudly. I cringed.

"Um. Breakfast."

If a piece of burnt toast on the way out the door counted.

Clay rolled his eyes and handed me my pack, dropping it into my lap. "Get some clothes on. I'll go find you something to eat."

He rose and pulled on his jeans, now with darkened spots of drool on one hip from where he carried them in his mouth and then got his shoes on. "I'll come back and get you."

Before I could get enough breath and clarity of mind to argue with him, he was gone.

I let my head fall back and cursed my own stupidity. I'd been so preoccupied worrying and stressing about Layla and Viv and about tonight's meeting that eating just completely slipped my mind.

Vaguely, I remember pushing around my macaroni salad at lunch while I explained what was going to happen to my friends in mere days. I'm not even sure I had a single bite.

And water? Fuck, had I even drunk any water at all today?

I groaned and pushed myself unsteadily to my feet. I might've been fine if I hadn't shifted and run thirty miles from town. My hands shook with twitching tremors as I pulled on my panties and jeans, followed by my bra and top. Even with my sweater on, I felt cold as I put one foot in front of the other toward the smell of campfire and the low hum of classic rock filtering through the trees.

Seth was the first familiar face I spotted as I stumbled down the decline and onto hard packed dirt. He squinted to make me out at the edge of the trees and a wide grin broke out over his face. "Hey!" he called, running over.

His grin faded when he got a better look at my face. "Shit, Allie, you're looking a bit shit. Nerves?"

I shook my head and immediately regretted it when a spike of pain drilled into my brain. *Ugh.* "Nah," I lied. "Forgot to eat."

"Forgot...to *eat?*" Seth asked as though I were speaking a foreign language.

I nudged his shoulder as we walked together toward where the highest concentration of pack members awaited, nearest to the main fire ring.

"I know," I said. "I'm an idiot."

"I mean, I wasn't going to say it but..."

I made a face of mock insult at him when we came upon the furthest ring of shifters and Seth dragged me over to a smaller group hanging out near the open tailgate of a sleek black truck. Away from the sniveling glares of Harrison, Forrest and the other members of Ryland's merry band of butt sniffers.

"Allie!" Charity called, waving me over to sit on the tailgate's ledge with her. I happily obliged, not sure my legs could hold out much longer. I tossed my pack into the back of the truck and hopped up, accepting a tight hug from Charity. "How are you? You look—"

"Like shit? I know. Seth already told me." She laughed.

"What the hell, Allie?" Clay's growl silenced what remained of the conversations from the small group as he barged in, a steaming plate of barbeque ribs and corn on the cob in his hand.

Oops. Had he asked me to wait?

Clay cleared the gap between us and laid the plate down on my lap, grabbing a bottle of water from his back pocket to set down next to me. "Eat," he ordered. "Ry's just finishing up dealing with some pack bullshit and then he's going to want to talk to you."

"You mean make an example out of me?"

"This one's got claws," Seth commented with a little swipe of an imaginary paw in my direction.

I rolled my eyes at them. "What? It's true, isn't it?

That's totally what's going on here."

Charity bumped my shoulder as I ravenously tore a massive bite out of the piping hot meat, wholly unable to stop myself as the scent of it wafted up into my nose. "He isn't so bad."

I raised a brow at her.

"What?" she said with wide, innocent eyes, and I was reminded of the first time I was ever here at camp. When I went to use the bathroom in Ry's house and ran into the vampire Grey. Ryland had been busy talking to Charity while Creepy McBloodsucker and I had a stare down in the hall.

She'd been blushing while he looked down at her, his forearm pressed into the wall over her head as he looked down into her eyes.

Oh my god. Ew.

"He needs to show the pack who their alpha is to keep everyone in line. If he's lenient with some and not with others, no one would ever listen to him. There would be anarchy." Charity said as she stole a rib from my plate, and I resisted the urge to growl at her, both for sticking up for the fucker and for stealing my food. "And he's just a fucking dickhead," Clay muttered.

At least my mate agreed with me.

"Who's a dickhead?" Jared asked, seemingly appearing from thin air around the back of Clay.

Clay jumped, cursing beneath his breath. "The fuck, man?"

Jared held his hands up in a placating gesture and gave a little shrug. "Sucks getting snuck up on, doesn't it?"

He tossed me a wink while Clay finished fuming and grumbling to himself, and Jared pressed through to lean next to where my legs dangled over the edge of the truck bed. "So, is my Jeep still in one piece?"

I smirked and worked to chew the massive chunk of meat in my mouth before I answered, praying my face wasn't completely covered in barbecue sauce.

"Are you doubting my skills?" He smirked. "Never."

Jared reached in, brushing a thumb over the corner of my mouth and bringing it away covered in a smear of sticky sweet sauce. He popped it in his mouth and his brows went up. "Are there any more ribs?"

The small group quieted. Clay looked like he might throw up.

"If you guys are going to be all cutesy and gross, go find your own flatbed," Seth joked.

Clay grunted.

"I think it's adorable," Charity said wistfully. "I hope I don't have to wait too much longer to find my mate. I thought for sure when the packs merged I would but..."

Seth laughed. "Better hope you don't end up like Ryland. Dude's almost fifty and he still hasn't found his."

"Who would want to mate with that?" I grumbled through another mouthful and Charity elbowed me.

"And how in the hell is that guy over fifty?" I continued once I was finished chewing. "He looks more like, I don't know, maybe thirty?"

The group shared a look, and I got the immediate sense that there was something I was missing. When their stares all turned to me, a heat blossomed in my belly and I cringed back. "What?" I demanded. "Do I have some shit on my face or something?"

Jared bit his lip and muttered to the others, "We, *uh*, we haven't exactly told her yet."

"Oh," both Charity and Seth said in unison.

"Tell me what?" I asked, dragging the back of my hand over my mouth and taking a long pull of lukewarm water from the bottle Clay gave me.

I looked to Jared for an explanation, but it was Clay who spoke, surprising me. "Look, Allie," he said and then seemed to consider how best to phrase what he planned to say next.

Jared's pallor had changed from its usual burnished tan to a sallow shade of green.

A pit yawned open in the bottom of my stomach. I turned my attention to Clay.

"Spit it out already," I urged, setting the plate down next to me. At least I got a few bites in before my appetite vanished again.

Clay wiped a wide hand over the shadow of scruff on his jaw.

"Ryland looks like he's still thirty because... shifters don't age the same way as humans."

"What do you mean we don't age the same?"

A ringing began in my ears. I'd wondered before... I'd wondered why no one at pack camp looked much older than their late twenties. Why hadn't I asked this before?

"Holy shit," I choked out. "Are we...*are we immortal?*" No. There was *no* way that was possible. I mean, I would know, wouldn't I? I would've been able to sense it or something? How could someone not *know* they are immortal?

Clay shook his head, and I took a breath. "Not exactly."

"It's the pack magic," Jared explained, and I turned back to him, liking how his soothing, matter-of-fact voice sounded to my ears right now over the sound of Clay's gruff, unapologetic one.

"Pack magic protects the pack camp from being found by other supernaturals. Sort of like the spell on the cabin that keeps people away and shields it from view, except with pack magic, it's naturally occurring."

He took a shaky breath.

"Pack magic *also* slows the aging process."

"*Slows?*"

Clay pursed his lips. "It stops it."

If my brows rose any higher, they'd get lost in my hairline. "So, you're telling me that as long as I belong to a pack, I won't ever get old? I won't ever die?"

"Well, you can still die," Clay corrected me, though he didn't look pleased allowing those words to leave his lips. "Just not from old age."

"Is that why Grams is the only one who looks old?

Because she doesn't have a pack?" Clay nodded.

"A lot of shifters leave the pack after a hundred years or so, so that they can age out and pass naturally."

"But there are some who are hundreds of years old," Seth added with a swig of his beer. "The oldest on record was over *four hundred* when he died. I plan to break that record." He winked, polishing off his drink.

"Anyone want a beer?"

Numbly, I nodded. "Got anything stronger?"

Seth chuckled. "I'll see what I can find," he said and then took off in the direction of the fire.

Across the blinding orange glow and the curl of dark smoke rising in the air, I could see Ryland exiting his house, the door banging closed behind him as he stared out over his pack. Silver scars in his right cheek glistened in the firelight. The mark from where Samson bit him had left his face puckered and ugly.

I couldn't help but feel a little triumphant seeing it. "We're sorry we didn't tell you before," Jared said,

stuffing his hands in his pockets. Neither of my mates had seemed to notice Ryland scanning the shifters crowded around the fire. "There just never seemed to be a good time, I guess."

"That's bullshit," Clay said, beating me to the exact words I was going to say. "We should have told her, man."

"Yeah," I said grouchily and hopped down from the truck. "You should have."

But right now, I didn't have room in my brain to think about my possible immortality, because Ryland had his burning orange gaze on me, and he was coming this way.

I wasn't about to wait here, cowering as he approached. My wolf sparked to life in my chest and I soothed her softly spoken internal thought.

He's our alpha, I reminded her. *We are just going to get our orders and then we're going to leave. Easy.*

Clay and Jared, realizing where I was staring—*who* I was staring at—fell into step on either side of me as I strode with as much forced confidence as I could to meet him only a few feet away from the fire.

"You made it," Ryland said, the words betraying a note of surprise.

Had he really thought I wouldn't come?

I didn't trust myself to answer without the words coming out dripping acid, so I simply nodded. My wolf was on high alert now, and I was sure Ryland could see her in my eyes. If he couldn't, my clenched fists were probably a dead giveaway as to how hard I needed to fight her.

Clay had been right; the shift and the run had been necessary. I couldn't imagine how much more difficult it would be to stand here and take orders if my wolf had been properly fed, and I hadn't allowed her some time in the light.

"I trust you're...more *adjusted* now?" Fucking prick.

"She's doing great, Uncle Ry," Jared spoke for me.

Ryland grinned, and I couldn't help but notice how the music seemed louder now, clearer.

Because everyone had stopped talking. Everyone was listening.

My spine tingled at the pressure of a hundred phantom eyes watching my every move. My skin bristled.

"Good," Ryland said, never taking his eyes from mine.

A bruising force pressed down on my shoulders, and I had to grit my teeth just to remain standing. A small gasp left my lips.

Jared and Clay turned to check that I was all right and all at once, the pressure lifted, and I glared at Ryland. He was pushing me.

Testing me.

Exerting his dominance in a way no one would notice if he were careful.

He's trying to make sure he still had control of me.

If I ground my teeth any harder, I'm pretty sure one would've snapped.

"There seem to be a few wolves who've...gone astray," Ryland said, steepling his fingers and pursing his lips as though considering something carefully. "I need some help reining them in. Your particular strengths could come in handy for that."

"You mean the shifters from Dave's pack?" Clay asked.

"Charity's group has already searched everywhere for them," Jared said, confused. "They could be halfway to the east coast by now."

"Should I let what's rightfully mine go so easily, nephew?"

Jared, cowed, shut his mouth. My upper lip curled.

"You'll join the search," Ryland told me, and something in his gaze dared me to fight him on this.

He wanted me to, I realized.

A sick feeling spread like sludge in my gut. "When do I need—"

"Tomorrow. You'll meet Charity here at five." Charity appeared a moment later, and I wondered if Ryland used his alpha pull to lure her in. "We usually get back around midnight,"

I shook my head. "I can't," I said. "I have work at the shop six days a week. I could maybe go down to five if I really have to—"

"Are you disobeying a direct order?"

The fire in Ryland's tone could not be mistaken. "*Ry*," Clay hissed.

"Something to say, Armstrong?" Ryland pressed, and I heard someone to our right whistle low and someone else chortle. "I'm in need of my pack. I'm in need of Allie's strong will to wrangle these deserters back to camp so I can deal with them."

A pause and Ryland turned his heated gaze back to me.

"Is this going to be a problem?"

"I can go," Jared offered. "If Charity needs—"

"I need you at the quarry," Ryland barked, and I saw Jared flinch as his uncle used his alpha status to bend him to his will.

"It's fine," I all but growled, realizing all at once that what happened here, right now, hinged on whether or not I would be obedient.

Clay and Jared would stand up for me, and they would get themselves in some deep shit doing it. I couldn't let them. I had enough on my shoulders as it was.

"I'll be here at five."

"What about the shop?" Jared asked, and I could see an uncharacteristic amount of anger in his gaze when I turned to look at him. He was furious.

It took some doing, but I managed to smooth the angered creases in my own forehead and force my shoulders to relax. "It's okay," I told him. "Her niece watches the shop sometimes when I'm sick. I'll call her. It'll be fine."

The last part was a lie.

My boss, Jacqueline, was a kind woman. She was caring and understanding, but she needed someone reliable. It was one of the reasons I even got the job to begin with. I'd volunteered there for three weeks for a school co-op project and had shown her just how reliable I could be. How hard-working.

I was never late.

I didn't leave until everything was finished.

She'd been thinking of extending her hours for a while, and she'd hired me.

Her exact words were, *I've never met a more mature student, and I've hosted a lot of co-ops from the high school. I need someone reliable to close up the shop in the evenings. The job is yours if you want it.*

Someone reliable.

Depending on how long Ryland decided to punish me. I wouldn't be that person she was looking for anymore.

My dreams of renting the apartment above the bookshop—of being self-sufficient when I turned eighteen—would be dashed.

All because of this motherfucker.

"It's settled then," Ryland said with a self-righteous grin. "I'll leave you to work out the details with Charity."

He turned away.

"Ry," Clay called, stopping him.

I cast a warning stare in Clay's direction, urging him to let it go, but he wasn't looking at me. He was glaring at Ryland's back.

Every muscle in his bare arms taut as a bowstring, he waited with a vein sticking a good half an inch out of his temple until Ryland turned.

Ryland spun and raised a brow. "*Clay,*" I whispered harshly.

He seemed to consider something for a moment and then shook his head, sighing. "My sister has requested permission to visit this month. Will you allow it?"

Ryland's eyes flashed for the briefest moment. "Your sister?" he asked, brows narrowing.

"You've never met her," Clay grumbled. "She moved away with my mom before you came back and took over as alpha. She's with a small pack in Alaska now."

Ryland considered the request, a keen interest in his gaze. "I'll allow it," he said after a lengthy silence.

"I appreciate it," Clay managed through clenched teeth.

"But, Clayton," he added before Clay could leave. "You'll be responsible for her while she's here."

Clay nodded.

"Remember this kindness," Ryland called after a retreating Clay as though he'd just given him a wonderful gift. The kind that he expected to be thanked for. The kind that he expected to be repaid.

"Stay," Ryland said, turning to Jared. "The quarry will survive without you for one night, nephew. Have a drink. Enjoy the bonfire."

Jared managed a nod, but the rage in his eyes was still unmistakable. I looped my arm through his and nudged Charity, pulling us away from our alpha. "Come on," I said, a sour taste coating my tongue. "Where's Seth? I don't know about you guys, but I'm going to need that drink."

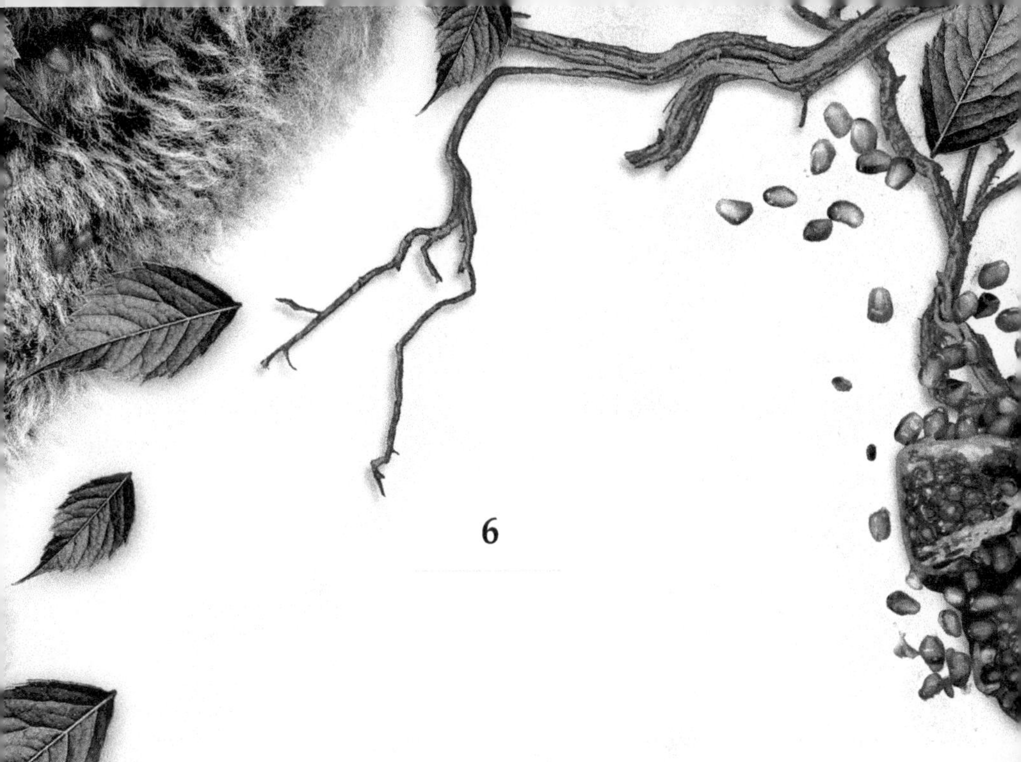

6

How much longer do you think he expects us to keep looking?" I asked Charity as she, Destiny, and I dressed away from the male members of the group so we could head back into camp for a quick bite before we all went home to bed.

Exhaustion clung to every inch of muscle and bone in my body. Over the last three days of nightly searches, we'd covered nearly a thousand miles of land. Not only did we not find the missing wolves, but there wasn't even a *trace* of them anywhere outside the borders of Ryland's territory.

Turned out those names on the password protected files on Ryland's computer were the names of the missing wolves. I had to admit, I was a little disappointed, but also a little relieved to know that. Ryland was obviously asking this '*X*' person for help finding them. The images were likely last known locations or houses they were known to frequent or something like that.

"As long as it takes," Destiny replied as though it were obvious.

Charity rolled her eyes at the purple-haired girl with the perfect tits and sighed. "I don't think he'll make us look much longer. If we'd picked up a trail anywhere at all, then *maybe,* but they're just...gone. It's a waste of pack time and resources to keep looking. Especially when Ry would probably just wind up banishing them anyway."

487

"Pfft," Destiny chided. "Banish them?" she asked. "You really think he'd make us go to all this trouble if he just wanted to send them away himself?"

She asked this like it was the most obvious thing in the whole world.

"He's not going to banish if we find them, Charity. Don't act so naïve. He's going to want to make an example out of them. He'll execute them to send a message to the other new recruits that *no one* leaves the Forest Grove pack without his say so."

She's right, I realized. And I wasn't sure how I didn't realize it sooner.

If we found them, Ryland would want to make an example out of them like he was making an example out of me. Except he couldn't just kill me. Not now that I'd bent the knee.

Though I got the very distinct feeling that that is exactly how he would prefer to handle me, even if Jared disagreed.

"I think you're wrong," Charity replied to Destiny, lifting her chin as she finished pulling on her shirt.

Destiny smirked. "You think you know him just because he let you into his bed, what? Once? He's still the alpha, Charity."

"Oh, fuck off, Destiny," Charity muttered.

Destiny shrugged and moved past Charity to head the rest of the way into camp.

I bumped Charity's shoulder as I passed, trying to get rid of the frown on her lips. I couldn't agree with her, in fact, I was with Destiny on this one, even if I found her to be an abrasive, doesn't-ever-sugar-coat- anything sort of person. "I'm starving," I told her. "Let's eat something before I pass out."

Between school and the nightly searches, I barely know how I managed to stay on my own two feet these days. Even Layla and Viv commented on my new zombie- chic look at school this morning, and that was saying something since we all seemed to share that look lately.

Purple half-moons beneath our eyes. Sallow cheeks and bent spines.

It got worse each day that brought us closer to the full moon. In less than forty-eight hours, it would be here. It felt like time had sped up and we were all being dragged along with it, hurtling toward it.

Clay was at the point where he was threatening to do something about Ryland working me to the bone. I didn't know what that something was, but to avoid it, I'd been staying here with Charity for the last two nights.

Sleeping so close to where Ryland rested his head in the evenings brought me no comfort, but at least Clay and Jared didn't have to see me stumble into bed each night, half dead, and dirty from not having the energy to shower.

There were whispers at pack camp that Clay had been wanting to challenge Ryland for a while now. The only reason he wouldn't is because of Jared. How could he kill his best friend's uncle? And how would Jared feel if his uncle killed his best friend? It was a Catch-

22. Ry took over uncontested from Clay's father after he passed because Clay had been unable to stomach doing anything but to sleep and drink for months. Now that Clay was a bit more stable, it was too late.

But for me...

I didn't want to find out what he would be willing to do.

He or Jared.

I'd seen the rage in Jared's eyes the night at the bonfire. If things kept going the way they were, I wondered if Jared would even try to stop Clay if he challenged Ryland openly.

I shook away the thought. It was barbaric. Savage to even think it.

But my wolf had no problem reminding me every time we saw his scarred face and those creepy orange- tinted eyes: she wanted him dead. Even now, with this will exerted over us, she craved the feel of his wind-pipe in her jowls. The taste of his blood on her tongue. She still wanted to see him under her paws, obedient, submitted. Lifeless.

I shuddered.

"Hey," Charity said as we approached the fire ring, mostly embers now, a few stragglers huddled around it against the chill of the autumn night. "You okay?"

"Hmm?" I said, coming back up for air. "Oh. Yeah.

Fine. Just tired."

"I feel that," Charity agreed and gave me a pat on the back. "I'll run and get us some food and then we can hit it. Want a drink?"

"Just water."

She nodded and then left. The guys, Seth and the mated couple, Trey and Todd came out from the tree line laughing, making their way through tents and cabins of sleeping wolves, probably waking them all up with their raucous laughter. As they passed by the cabin Forrest and Harrison shared, I grudgingly hoped they were loud enough to wake them.

They got back hours ago, having been given the better of the two available search shifts. *Fuckers.* I guess it paid to be a bootlicker in werewolf land.

Sure enough, a muffled shout of *shut the fuck up* filtered through a window as they passed, and they stifled the sound. I giggled.

The tents were a new addition. It was where the new pack members would sleep until more cabins could be built. There were already a few timber frames started around the perimeter. They should be finished before the first snow.

I dragged a few chairs toward the low embers in the pit, eager for some extra warmth. A lone chair was already there, filled with a guy I didn't yet know. He had reddish brown hair that glinted in the glow of the embers and brown eyes that looked near black.

"Hey," I said, trying to make awkward small talk while Seth and the others made their way over to us. "I don't think we've met. I'm—"

"I know who you are," he grumbled, and I noticed the half empty bottle of gin clutched loosely in his hand and the three empty beer bottles at his feet.

Okay then.

"And you are?" I asked, raising a brow. "Sully."

"Which pack were you from?"

He took another swig of his gin and grimaced. "Samson's," he said and then fell back into silence.

This was the other problem with staying at pack camp. I had my small cluster of friends and the rest saw me as something quite the opposite. Being here all the time, it was hard not to notice the way some of them stared. How they whispered. I could hardly blame them.

I was the reason their alphas were dead.

I was the reason their lives were uprooted and they were forced to move to Forest Grove.

But I didn't ask for any of this.

"Nice to meet you, too," I muttered to myself as the guys made it to the fire ring and took the seats I set out for them.

"Oh, don't be like that," Sully said, slurring the words a little. "I know it ain't your fault. Not really, anyway."

"Gee. Thanks."

"This guy bothering you?" Seth asked, flipping his mop of dark hair out of his face to stare unblinking at the drunk guy next to me.

I shook my head. "No, it's fine."

"Is it?" Sully asked. "Because I never asked to be part of that asshole's pack."

He jabbed a thumb toward Ryland's house only fifteen meters or so from where we were sitting. The windows were all dark, but that didn't mean Ryland was asleep. This guy should be careful what he said.

"Ry's not so bad once you get used to him," Seth said, and I could tell he was trying to put an end to this conversation.

"Tell that to Dean and Andreas."

"You don't know what you're talking about, friend."

"What?" I prodded, my interest piqued.

Sully pulled himself upright and pointed two fingers at Ryland's house with a sneer. "Bastard killed them."

"Okay," Seth said, rising. "Where's your tent, dude? I think it's time for you to hit the sack."

Sully laughed. A throaty, hollow sound that gave me chills.

He wiped at his watery eyes. "You really believe the bullshit yarn he's spinning?" Sully asked Seth. "That Dante's pack is to blame for them vanishing? That that *coward* has somehow grown the balls to stand up to anyone?"

Seth opened his mouth to rebut, but I interrupted him. "What is he talking about Seth?"

Seth pinched the bridge of his nose and sighed. "There are whispers that the other pack alpha that was at the Four Corner's that night is trying to pick off our numbers bit by bit."

I remembered the one alpha who ran away when the fighting broke out. The one who looked like he was in his forties. Short and stout. Both the wolves he'd come with had been collateral damage in the fight, and he'd left them to die. Some alpha he was.

"Is that what Ryland said?" I asked.

Seth gave a one-shoulder shrug. "I mean, it makes sense, doesn't it?"

No. I didn't say it, but I glanced at Sully, a question in my stare and the answer in his. I agreed with him. That coward wouldn't be picking off our numbers, but apparently Ryland had the whole pack believing it.

"Then why don't we take the fight to them if Ryland is so sure?" I asked Seth in a whisper, eyeing the alpha's darkened cabin at his back. Being careful of my words.

Seth shrugged again. "No proof. Ry knows it's possible they've just run away, which is why we're looking for them."

"Right," Sully said with a sniffle, dragging the back of his hand over his running nose. "It has nothing to do with the fact that my boys had some dirt on your dirty alpha."

They were his friends then. A vice clamped around my heart. I wanted to ask him what sort of dirt that was, but I got the feeling he wasn't about to tell me even if I asked. Not in front of the others. Especially not now that Charity was approaching with a tray full of steaming dinner. It was common knowledge now that she had the hots for the alpha.

Sully may have thought he could get away with saying some shady shit in front of Seth and the boys, but if he had half a brain cell left in that skull, he would know saying that shit in front of her would not bode well for him.

I'd have to get him alone when he was *less* intoxicated if I planned to find out what it was he thought got his friends killed.

"I'm sorry," I told him instead of pressing further, eager to change the subject before Charity got back. "About your friends. Maybe we'll find them."

Sully shook his head and got unsteadily to his feet. He leaned to one side and nearly fell. Without thinking, I jumped into action and caught him before he could trip backward into the firepit. His head kicked against mine, and he whispered breathily in my ear, his eyes aglow with reddish light. "We both know they ain't coming back."

Then he left, stumbling and nearly falling every few steps as he did, until he vanished from view.

"Allie?" Charity called, eyeing where the drunken shifter had vanished around a cabin at the edge of the camp. "You good?"

"Yeah," I said, gulping down the feeling of dread as the lie slid from my tongue. "I'm good."

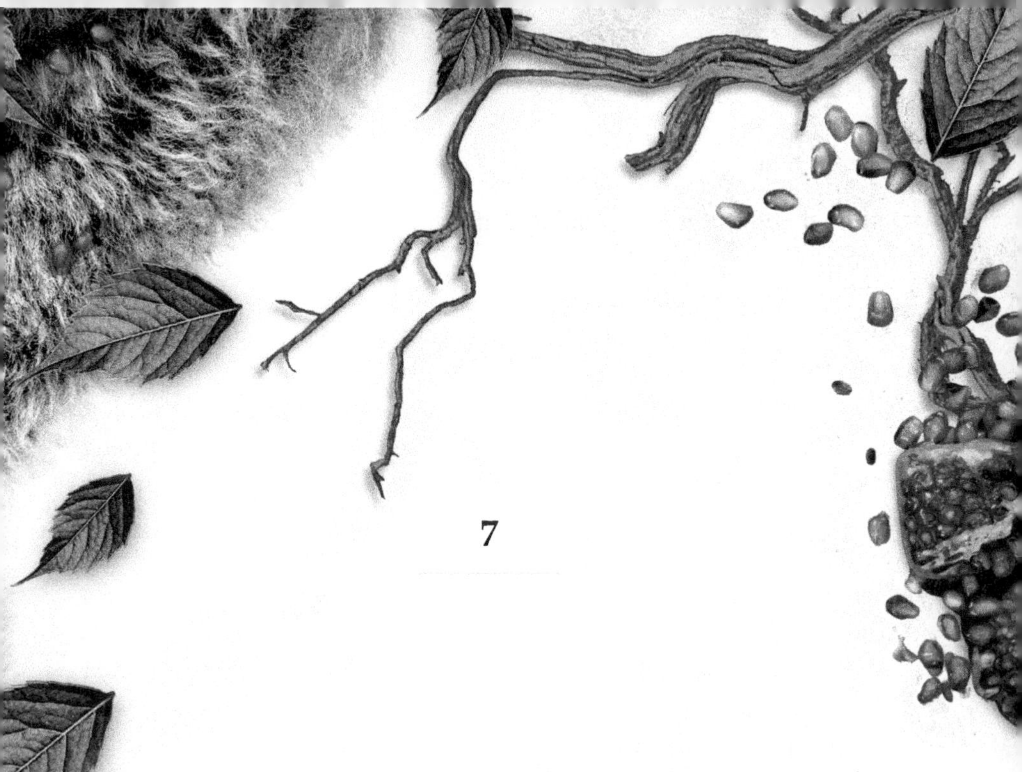

7

Where's Quinn?" I asked Layla when she and Viv came to meet me out front of Viv's place. Jared hovered at my back, and Clay was already waiting for us all at pack camp.

Layla tucked a lock of black hair back behind her ear and shivered as she slung a messenger bag over her shoulder. "He should be here soon."

We were all going to camp together. The full moon would be high enough in the sky to trigger the shift within several hours. It was meant to be a clear, cold night, which apparently would make the shift cleaner. *Nothing worse than having your first shift on a cloudy night,* Jared had told me. It was easier to make the transition in full moonlight. A sky heavy with the burden of clouds slowed it to a crawl.

"Did you bring it?" Layla asked, unable to look me in the eye.

I dug the small bag from my pocket and handed it to her. "Are you sure you want to do it this way? We could explain—"

"No," she cut in. "This way will be easier. If he doesn't shift, then...he'll never have to know."

I nodded gravely and released the pill to her. Charity had gotten it for us from her alchemist friend who healed Quinn. It was an elixir of some kind. None of us had any idea what was inside, but if it did its job, it would knock Quinn out until morning. At least, it would keep him

493

knocked out as long as he didn't shift. Nothing could be strong enough to make someone sleep through *that.*

I still hadn't brought myself to tell them about Grey, and what he planned to do to them if they didn't shift. I supposed, like Layla was trying to protect Quinn, I was also still trying to shield them from as much of it as I could. I had no idea if it was the right thing to do or not.

"What did you tell your parents?" I asked them. "That we're going camping," Viv answered for them both. "They won't expect us back until Monday."

Which gave us four days. If they shifted, would it be enough time for them to get the control they would need to be around their families? I cringed. I didn't think so.

Especially not Layla with her seven younger brothers and sisters at home. There was no way she could be around them all with a testy wolf trying to jump out her throat, was there?

Fuck.

At least I would be there the entire time to help them if it came to that. I'd already left a voicemail for Jacqueline at the shop, explaining that I wouldn't be available until early next week at the soonest. Just another nail in the coffin for my job...

Jared, sensing my emotions, stepped into my side and wrapped an arm around me, rubbing my back. I melded into his touch, letting him push some of his strength and calm into me. I was going to need all I could get.

"There he is," Viv said after a few seconds of strained silence, and we watched Quinn pull his punch buggy up to the sidewalk and step out, bag slung casually over one shoulder while he yanked a big tent bag from his backseat.

"Hey!" he called, rushing over, bright with enthusiasm.

I saw what Layla meant now. How could she do anything to ruin that smile? She did her best when he was around during lunch hours at school to paste on a smile for his benefit, but the one she painted on now looked painfully forced.

She accepted his warm bear hug, digging her fingers into his shoulders. "Hey," she replied and dropped her head as he pulled away.

"So," Quinn said. "We're headed to some place off the map, that right?"

Jared nodded. "It's my uncle's camp," he explained and then seemed to think of something, adding, "He keeps wolves as pets. So, if you see any, don't freak out. They're mostly friendly, just keep your distance."

"No shit!" Quinn said, eyes bugging out of his face. "That is *dope*."

"If only," I muttered.

"What?" Quinn asked, turning a curious look in my direction. Then, as if seeing me for the first time, his eyes widen again. "Shit, Allie. You look terrible. Are you sick?"

I couldn't help rolling my eyes. "*I'm fine,*" I said through gritted teeth. Why was everyone so damned preoccupied with how I looked.

I look like shit. I get it.

"Whoa," Quinn said with a mock defensive stance, his hands raised. "I mean no offense. I just...I have some antacids in my bag if you need them. Just ask."

Rage dissipating, I sighed. "Let's go. Ryland's waiting."

"Who's Ryland?" Quinn asked, falling into step behind Jared and me to walk down the street to where we found an empty spot to park Jared's Jeep.

"He's pack—"

"My uncle," Jared cut in, giving me a pointed look.

Right. No shifter talk.

I supposed we just had to pray no one decided to up and shift in the middle of the camp until Quinn was knocked out. Then we'd have no choice but to explain.

"Hop in," Jared said, taking both Layla and Viv's bags while I went to open the door for them. He and Quinn packed up the back while Layla and Vivian buckled themselves in with shaking fingers. I jumped in the front passenger seat, knowing I was too on edge to drive.

"Does it hurt?" Layla asked, keeping her voice hushed so Quinn couldn't overhear.

I winced.

"If we shift, does it hurt?"

I couldn't lie about that. I was sure she would already be able to see the answer written all over my face. Eyes burning, I nodded mutely, not trusting myself to say too much. "But not for very long."

It was true enough for me. My shift had only lasted seconds, but then, I'd only just been bitten and the moon was already shining. I had no idea what they were in for. I could have asked Charity, she was changed only a couple of years ago, but I didn't have the stomach to find out.

Now, I was regretting that decision. If I found her before we were all taken to the moon room, I would ask. Better to be prepared.

Vivian stared resolutely out the window, her gaze trained on the clear sky. On the iron bars partially blocking her view of the moon already visible perched high in the heavens.

I could already feel its pull. Not very strongly. Not yet. But from the moment I awoke this morning, there had been a noticeable shift in my wolf. She was restless. I wondered if they could feel anything *other* inside of them. Would they even know what it was? Would they notice?

From the way Vivian's jaw was set, her gaze unwavering and spine rigid as she stared at the moon, I thought maybe she could feel its pull, but I was terrified to ask her.

"All right," Jared said with forced cheer as he hopped into the driver's side of the Jeep and started the ignition.

I jammed the button for the sound system and Clay's playlist was picked up from my phone. "Start a Riot" by Banners began to play, and Jared slid his hand over the center console to twine his fingers with mine, squeezing. "You ready?" he asked me, and a sliver of ice lodged itself into my heart.

Clay asked me that just weeks ago in the cabin. Right before we left for the Four Corners. Before my whole world came crashing down around me for the second time.

My response was the same now as it was then, and I tasted the words like an omen of death on my tongue. "Ready as I'll ever be."

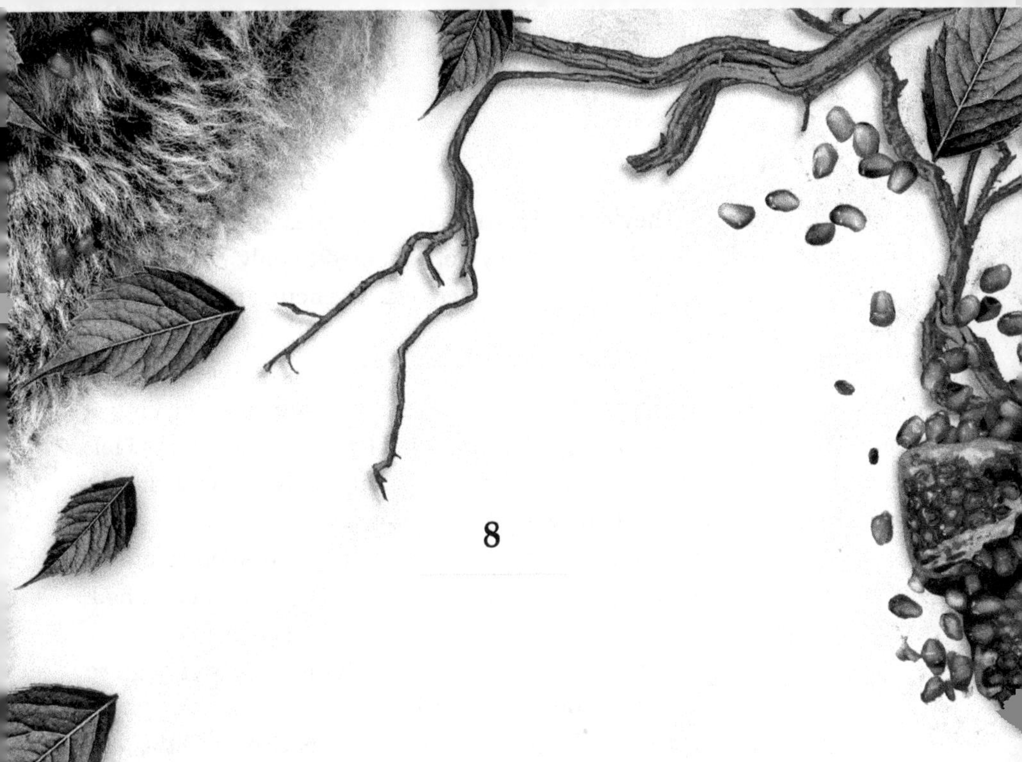

8

How far in is it?" Quinn asked, brushing his dark hair away from his face as he stared dubiously at the tiny deer path snaking out from the inlet where we parked the Jeep on the side of a gravel road. It was as close as you could get to pack camp by car.

It would only take Jared and me about five minutes at a hard sprint in our wolf forms to get there from here, but at a human pace…

"It's about an hour hike," Jared said with an apologetic frown. "I'll carry the tent. Mine and Allie's things are already there."

"I call dibs on your bags," I said, trying to inject some cheer into my voice as I rushed around back to pull both Viv and Layla's bags out of the back of the Jeep.

"Allie, you don't have to—" Viv began, but I cut her off with a shake of my head. Quinn was busy adjusting the steps on the tent bag to better suit Jared's tall, lanky frame, but I kept my voice down anyway.

I pulled on Layla's messenger bag first, and then shouldered Viv's backpack on after that. "I know I don't have to," I replied. "I want to. And honestly? I could probably carry both of you all the way to camp and barely break a sweat, so don't worry about it."

Viv raised a brow. "So, it's not all bad then, I guess.
Super strength would be kind of cool."

It felt oddly like Viv was extending the proverbial olive branch, and I wanted to take it. They'd barely asked me any questions about what would happen if they *did* shift. They both seemed to only want to hold on to hope that they wouldn't. Now there wasn't enough time for me to explain all the...perks.

Thinking on it now, I realized there were a fair few. Speed. Agility. Heightened senses. Strength. Incredible night vision. Fast healing. I could never get sick. I no longer felt like I had to power walk when I left the bookshop after dark in case there were any early evening drunks hanging around the local pub a few blocks down.

"No," I told Viv, feeling like my chest was being cleaved open and all the oxygen I'd been dying for, for *weeks* was rushing in. "It isn't all bad. Not even close."

A smile ghosted across Viv's lips for a second and it was enough to make this all just the tiniest bit less painful.

"What isn't all that bad?" Quinn asked, coming back over to the Jeep to haul his pack out from the back.

I cleared my throat. "The hike," I said. "It'll be over before you know it."

Quinn sidled up next to Layla, sliding his hand into hers as Jared shut the back of the Jeep and locked it up.

"Okay," Jared said, stuffing his keys into his pocket. "Allie and I will lead the way. Stay close. It's easy to get lost out here."

"Aye, aye," Quinn said with a little salute and fell into hushed conversation with Layla as they walked several meters behind us.

Viv rushed to catch up with me and Jared and leaned into my side to speak low so Quinn and Layla wouldn't overhear. "Can you guys tell me a bit more? You know, just in case."

Jared smirked.

I gave her a nod, peeking back to make sure Quinn and Layla were far enough away, but close enough that they wouldn't lose us. "I thought you'd never ask."

"I want it all," Vivian said, and I saw a flash of her usual fiery, take-no-shit-self coming through the dark shell she'd been keeping herself in for weeks. "The good and the bad."

I clenched my teeth. "Okay. All of it."

It took us a little under an hour to get to camp. We kept up a brisk pace as the sun began its rapid descent down the clear blue canvas of the sky. Vivian, still chewing on everything I'd told her, hardly noticed when the camp came into view. It wasn't until Charity, seeing us coming, shouted a greeting. Shouted it *extra* loud so that everyone would know there were mortals entering camp.

"Dude," Quinn said as he and Layla rushed to catch up, and I handed Layla and Viv back their bags. "This is fucking *epic*. Is it like a commune or something?"

Jared snorted. "Something like that."

Unconsciously, I took Jared's hand after he handed the tent back to Quinn and pointed out a spot at the southern edge of pack camp, away from where the new pack members had their tents. Closer to where Charity's cabin was. And the one Seth shared with a few other shifter bachelors. They more than likely wouldn't even get the chance to use the tent, but sending them to set it up would give us a few minutes to run and check on things and warn those who weren't already warned, not to go shifting in front of our mixed company.

"Charity!" Jared called. and she rushed over.

Quinn gave Charity a strange look, and I wondered if she seemed familiar to him. Layla and Viv seemed to recognize her straight away. Layla gave her a grateful, if a little droopy, smile. Viv stared warily.

"Would you mind helping them get set up over there while we go and check on a few things?"

She grinned. "Of course."

"Thanks," I said.

She winked.

"We'll meet you over there in a few and then give you the tour," I explained before we let Charity walk my best friends to the outer rim of the camp. I watched them go, nervously eyeing the area around the spot where they stopped to make sure no one was lurking.

Jared gave my hand a little tug in the opposite direction. "They'll be fine," he said, leaning in to whisper against my cheek. He planted a soft kiss at my temple. "When we find Clay, we'll send him over there to keep an eye on them, too."

"Okay."

I let Jared tow me toward the fire ring and the company gathered there. Ryland was among them for once, lounging on one of the larger

Adirondack chairs like a king on his throne. His eyes sparked with interest when he caught sight of us.

"Well," he said with enough enthusiasm to make my gut twist. What the fuck did he have to be excited about? "Where are they?"

Jared jutted his chin back the way we'd come. "They're setting up their tent on the Southern edge."

Ryland's brows furrowed, the one with the scar through it only lowering halfway. "Bring them over," he said with a wide grin and I caught the scent of whiskey on his breath. "We should give them a proper welcome."

I stiffened, my wolf pawing at the confines of my rib cage, eager to add another scar to the fractured mess of my alpha's face.

"We just wanted to check that everything was ready before we brought them over," Jared told his uncle, a muscle in his jaw jumping as he clenched it.

Ryland cocked his head at his nephew. "Well, of course it is. Nothing but the finest accommodations for our potential new recruits."

I followed Ryland's gaze to the stone structure set next to and behind his house, several meters back, abutting the tree line. It was an ancient looking thing that blended in with the forest behind it. The gray stone was covered in moss. Trees and long grasses sprouted around it on all sides. I made Charity show it to me last night, needing to know what my friends were in for.

Unlike the cave where Devin kept me, or the small cellar moon room in Clay and Jared's basement, this was built specifically for its purpose. It housed enough space for up to eight wolves that needed chaining. A bare space with an icy floor and shackles spaced evenly as they ran along either side of the wall. With enough slack to be able to move a couple of feet once shifted, but not enough to reach any of the other wolves even if the space was filled.

Gratefully, there weren't any that needed the use of the room tonight save for us. The Forest Grove pack hadn't had a newly shifted wolf in nearly a year, and neither had the newly joined packs. As far as I knew, it would only be us, Jared and Clay—because they insisted—and Ryland inside the stone building. When the moon was high enough to trigger a shift, just before midnight in most cases, Ryland would turn a crank on the wall that would open three round holes in the ceiling, letting the moonlight inside to help quicken the transition.

The chains Clay had to clamp around my wrists and ankles at the cabin had been bad enough, pushing memories of Devin and the cave into the forefront of my mind. I had a feeling these chains would be far worse. And even more difficult to endure the sight of my best friends being chained along with me.

"Well, bring them over," Ryland pressed after a moment of tense silence between us. "I'd like to meet them—officially."

"There's one thing," I said, finding my voice. "I'm not sure if you know, but Quinn, the guy with them, he doesn't remember anything—"

Ryland waved off my concern before I could finish. "I've been made aware," he said with an annoyed roll of his ruddy orange eyes. "Don't worry. They're on orders not to shift until you're all safely tucked away in the moon chamber."

I nodded, unable to verbally thank him.

Jared tugged us away from Ryland as another shifter came up next to him, whispering something in his ear.

"Come on," Jared whispered to me. "Let's get a drink and then we'll go back and get them, okay?"

"Yeah. Sure," I replied numbly, letting him pull me over to where Seth was sitting with Trey and Todd next to him on one side and Destiny on the other.

"...what an idiot." Destiny's haughty tone reached through my haze of chaotic thoughts and I perked up, curious who she was talking about. "I can't believe he just left. Like, did he really think Ryland wasn't going to go after him after we've been searching all this time for his buddies. Just watch. He'll probably lead us right to them in the search tonight."

Destiny paused as we came up, eyes widening as though she were surprised to see us. "Oh, hey," she said, the greeting mostly meant for Jared.

"Who are you talking about?" I asked, a sneaking feeling of dread clawing up my back. "Did someone else desert the pack."

"Tried to," Seth corrected me. "I'm sure we'll find him tonight. Too bad you won't be able to run with us. You probably got a good nose full of the fucker's scent at the fire the other night."

"Sully?" I asked, feeling the breath whoosh out of my lungs. "The guy with the red hair that was wasted?"

"Yeah, that one," Trey said with a pointed look. "The douche that almost fell in the fire. Would have too if you hadn't caught his ass."

I shook my head, incredulous. "When did he leave?" Destiny shrugged. "We don't know. He was missing from his tent this morning. We thought maybe he might've just gone for a run, you know, blow off all that extra steam he's carrying around. But he still hasn't come back. Either that's a really long run, or he's gone."

"And no one has gone to look for him yet?" Jared asked, eyeing me curiously. I hadn't told him about Sully at the bonfire. We actually hadn't spoken much other than via text since the hot cocoa night at the quarry.

Destiny made a noncommittal sound and flipped her hair out of her face. "Ry's giving him until dark."

I couldn't believe it. Didn't.

Sully was angry and upset, but he wouldn't have left, would he? I mean, he did have some interesting theories about where his friends vanished to...maybe he thought it was best to get himself the hell out of Dodge before whatever he thought had happened to them happened to him, too.

For some reason though, I wasn't buying it.

"Does Ryland think Adam's pack is behind this one, too?" I asked, trying not to let it show in my tone how unlikely I thought that was.

"Could be," Todd said. "We won't know until we head out after him."

If there's a trail to find...

"Where are your friends?" Destiny asked, changing the subject. She glanced around Jared and me, as though she expected to see them appear out of thin air. "I haven't seen them yet."

"On the south side," Jared told her. "Pitching a tent."

"We should actually get back over there. I was going to send Clay over, but I haven't seen him yet."

Seth jabbed a thumb over his back. "Went that way a few minutes ago. Probably just taking a piss."

"Hey, mind if I come with you?" Destiny asked, directing the question at me. There was none of her usual bite to the question. No hot sarcasm or disdain.

"I guess," I said, studying her suddenly unsure expression. "Just...be nice."

She scoffed, her light grey eyes glinting with the last dregs of sunset. "I can be nice," she said as though offended, but we both knew it was a valid request. Destiny was one of those people who knew exactly what sort of person she was and wasn't afraid to own it.

I admired her that.

She reminded me a lot of Vivian in that way. And just like Vivian, I was sure Destiny would grow on me eventually. Once she got over whatever the hell it was about me she'd decided she didn't quite like.

"I'll believe that when I see it," I joked in return, breaking away from Jared to head back to where my friends were waiting.

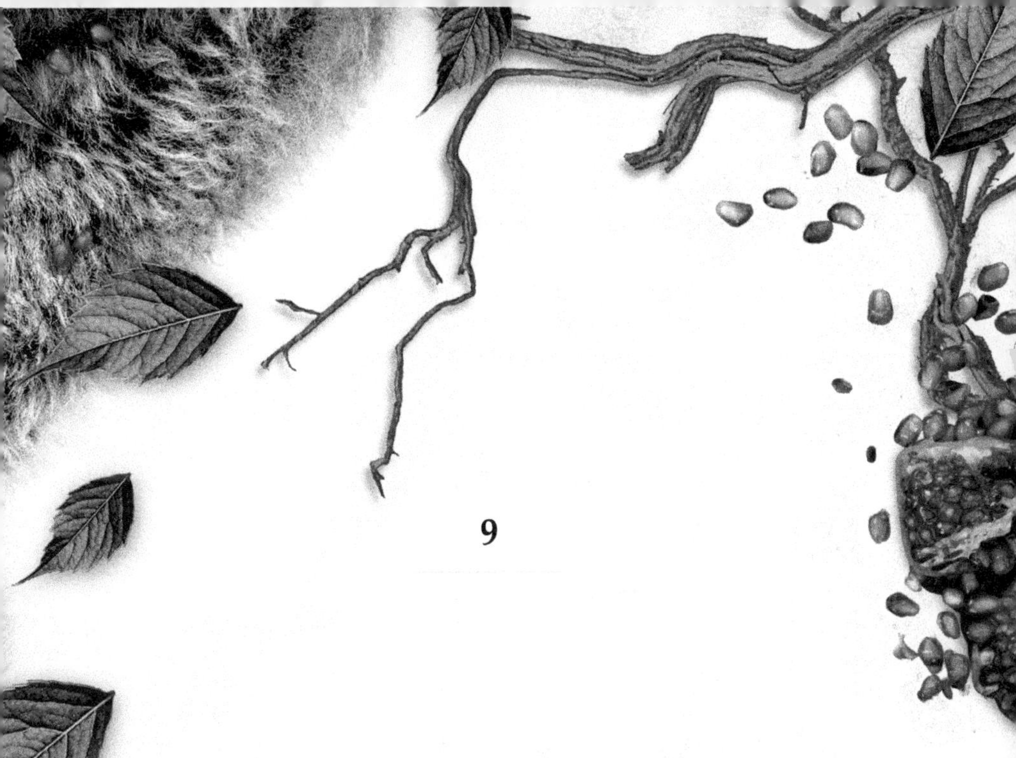

9

Considering how fast the day seemed to pass from waking up to the end of the school day, to mowing down a quick dinner I didn't taste, and picking up Layla and Viv and bringing them here, it was strange how now it felt like time was moving through a thick pile of sludge.

My wolf had become antsy to a point where I knew if someone looked at me the wrong way, I may have growled at them. And I was just done with the waiting.

I needed to get this over with. My anxiety, which had been at a tolerable minimum for a while, was ramping back up to high gear. That awful fluttering behind my ribcage. Spots in my vision. An erratic pulse that skittered and spurted and felt like it may very well stop dead at any second. Oh yeah. It was coming if I didn't calm the fuck down. Soon I'd be shaking all over. Barfing my guts out. That would be a shitty way to have my third shift—in the middle of a full-blown panic attack.

"Allie," Clay growled against my ear. "Come here."

I shook my head, gripping my plastic cup of spirits tighter in my hands. If I weren't careful, I was going to wind up a full-blown alcoholic before I even turned eighteen.

Jared was chatting animatedly with Quinn while Layla looked into

505

the bottom of her own cup, as though hoping it might hold a premonition of her future if she only looked hard enough into the amber liquid.

Vivian, on the other end of the spectrum, was smiling brightly as she and Destiny chatted on the other side of the fire. They both laughed, and Vivian blushed, casting her eyes away from Destiny. They landed briefly on me, and her smile grew tight until it vanished entirely. I frowned.

"Allie," Clay growled again, and I whirled on him, a snarl forming in the back of my throat.

"What?"

"Would you just come here. You're freaking out."

Breathing heavily, I heaved a sigh, forcing the edgy claws of my wolf to retract.

Clay patted his lap, and I cast him one last glare, but sat down, letting his radiating warmth soak into my thighs. I nearly moaned when he wrapped his arm around my waist, pulling me to him. Spice and engine grease filled my nose and his sense of numb calm washed over me like warm summer rain. It took barely a minute before the trembling in my fingertips stopped completely.

"There," he said, his fingers brushing the bare slit of skin at my waist, making me tremble for an entirely different reason. "Better?"

I grumbled to myself but gave him a nod. "Yeah."

"It'll be over soon," he said softly, and I let my gaze fall to his face. To those blue eyes. I let their steadiness calm me.

"Hey," Layla said, and I broke the stare, clearing my throat and pushing Clay's hand away from my waist to turn to her.

She wrung her hands in her long black sweater, sticking her fingers into the wide center pocket to draw something out. She held out the pill meant for Quinn to me and I snatched it quickly before anyone could see.

"What are you doing?"

She paled, her big doe eyes darting from me, to the ground, and back again. "I wanted to be the one to do it, but..." She paused, her throat thickening with tears. "I can't."

I lifted myself from Clay and pulled her hard against me, feeling her frailness beneath my arms as she shook. "I'll do it," I told her in a hush against her cheek. "It's okay. You don't have to."

"Thank you," she muttered into my shoulder and pulled away, sniffling as she tried to erase any evidence of her tears before Quinn could see. "Is there, like, a bathroom or something I can use. I should clean up before..."

She couldn't finish.

"Yeah," I told her, smacking Clay in the knee. "Clay will take you and I'll...I'll take care of Quinn, okay?"

Clay grumbled as he got to his feet, but didn't argue, dutifully taking Layla to Charity's cabin to use her composting toilet. Not even the lure of a real *flushing* toilet could convince me to use Ryland's bathroom ever again—much less allow my friends to go in there. I shivered, thumbing the smooth curve of the capsule beneath the plastic in my palm.

Fuck. I really didn't want to do this.

With my stomach roiling, I picked my way over to the keg and filled two red Solo cups with foamy beer. Then, checking to make sure Quin was good and distracted as he chatted with Seth and Kyle, I cracked open the capsule and let the fine powder fall atop the white foam. It took a minute to sink, and when it did, I swirled the plastic cup, making sure it was good and mixed.

We had to hope this would work fast. I'd been hoping Layla already had given it to him. It would be time soon. *Really* soon. I eyed the cup already in Quinn's hand and rolled my shoulders back, swallowing past the hard lump in my throat.

You can do this.

I went over to the small group of guys and stumbled purposefully when I reached them, knocking my elbow into Quinn's wrist to send his drink sprawling to the dirt.

"Shit, Allie," he said with a laugh. "How wasted are you?"

Not even a little bit. "What? Me? Pfffft." He laughed.

"Here," I said, passing him the cup from my left hand. "Have this one. I was grabbing it for you anyway."

Quinn narrowed his eyes at me for a second, and I just about shit myself, but then a creeping smile moved over his lips, and he took the cup. "Not trying to poison me, are you?"

I laughed, hoping he couldn't tell how I was on the verge of being ill.

"Don't worry," I said, trying to hide my discomfort. "It's the good kind."

I winked and held out my cup for a salute.

He rose to the bait, knocking his cup into mine and lifting it to his lips.

I took a long swallow of my beer, and Quinn followed suit, a furrow forming in his brow as he brought the cup away from his mouth. His eyes went wide. "What did you…" he began, but trailed off, a muscle in his cheek twitching.

"Shit!" Seth cursed as Quinn's eyes rolled back in his head and his body sagged to the ground. I tossed my beer in time to catch him before he could fall too hard, gritting my teeth.

"Fuck. You weren't kidding," Kyle said, his eyes wide with horror. "Why did you—"

"It's how Layla wanted it. He'll wake up if he shifts.

If he doesn't…"

"…then he won't have to ever know that he was chained up in a moon room with a bunch of wolves," Seth finished for me.

I nodded.

"I mean. I get it, but that shit's savage," Kyle said, finishing off his drink and walking away.

I felt Seth watching me as I carried Quinn easily over to a camp chair and set him in it, making sure his head was tipped back so he could breathe unrestricted. "That worked fast," Jared said, appearing behind me and just about earning himself a black eye.

"Whoa," he said as I whirled, my wolf about to crest the surface. "Didn't mean to freak you out."

I settled myself with a staggered breath and slumped into the camp chair next to my unconscious friend. A quick glance around the fire told me that in the last few seconds everyone had somehow found out exactly what I'd done. Suddenly, I was really glad Layla had asked me to do it for her.

I wouldn't have appreciated them looking at her how they were looking at me.

"I thought Layla was going to—"

"She couldn't do it," I snapped before I could get myself back under control. Jared's jaw clenched, and he glanced up at the sky, taking in the ugly white face of the moon. Then he reached into his pocket and drew out his phone, the flare of the screen flashing over his face.

"I think it's time," he said, giving me one last look, studying the glow of my irises. "We should get you guys in there in case the shift is triggered early. It's been known to happen."

Judging by the tremble in my hands and the sudden ache in my muscles, I knew he was probably right.

"Clay went to take Layla to the bathroom," I told Jared. "Can you go bring them back? I'll grab Viv."

He nodded and leaned it to brush a kiss over my temple before he left. His eyes told me what he couldn't say, *everything will be all right.*

The lie made it easier to stand back up and do what I needed to.

"Viv," I said, butting into a conversation between her and Destiny. "It's time."

She visibly paled, her hand clenching around her plastic cup. "Already?'

I nodded.

Destiny reached over and curled a hand around Vivian's shoulder. "I'll go with you," she said.

"You don't have to."

"I want to."

Viv finished her beer and tossed the plastic cup into a nearby metal bin, almost hitting Ryland as he reappeared from behind a cabin, buckling his belt. The alpha raised his eyes to the heavens and grinned, lowering them to meet both Viv's and mine with a challenging stare.

He swept an arm toward the stone moon chamber in the distance, peeking out behind the side of his house. "Shall we, ladies?"

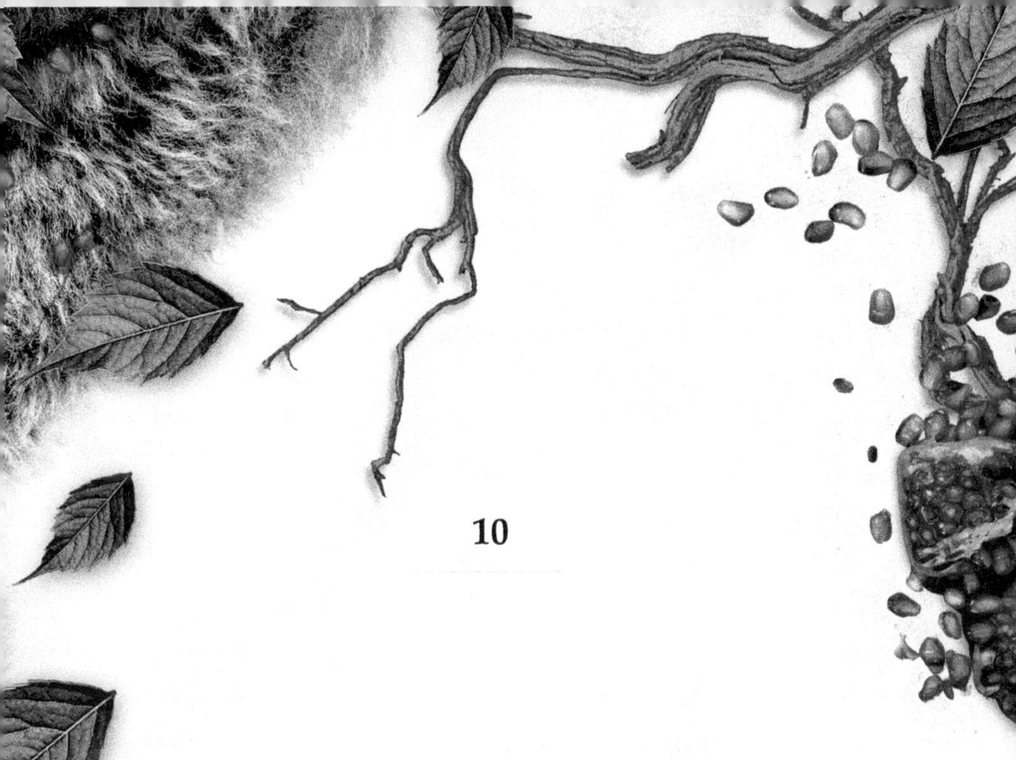

10

The key turned in the lock on the old iron manacle, and I pulled against it, testing its strength. I looked up into Clay's blue eyes, and he set his warm hands atop my shoulders. "Just like last time," he said, never breaking eye contact. "You're safe here. No one is going to hurt you."

Mental images of the chains in the cave with Devin tried to crowd my thoughts, drag me down into the cloying pit of panic, but as long as I looked into Clay's eyes, I knew he was right. I was safe.

"It'll be over before you know it," Jared added from beside Clay, looking like he might be sick.

"I'm not worried about my shift," I said, my voice thick.

I cast a glance to where Destiny was finishing locking up Vivian across from me. Vivian kept her chin up. Her eyes hard and sharp as cut glass.

And to Layla, who was looking at her manacles in terror as silent tears streamed down her face.

My fault.

All of it was *my fault.*

Please don't shift.

Please don't let them shift.

And Quinn, lying still against the stone to my right. He snored

511

quietly, his face a blank sheet of blissful ignorance. If he shifted, would he think it was some kind of nightmare?

He wouldn't be wrong. Except this nightmare wouldn't end by waking. It would go on and on for as long as he would live.

Please don't let them fucking shift.

I'd never been a religious person, but if there was ever a time for prayer, this was it. And I would pray to whatever god or gods would hear me.

Please.

"Hey," Clay barked, and I pulled my focus back to his face. "This is not your fault, okay. No matter what happens."

My throat burned. "You hear me?"

"I hear you."

"We'll be right over there with Ry and Destiny," Jared added, pointing to the open archway of the entrance where Ryland waited with his hand poised on the old wooden crank handle that opened the panels in the ceiling.

The first gut twisting stab of the moon-triggered shift tore through my abdomen, and I struggled to stay on my feet, gaze darting between Layla, Viv, and Quinn to see if anything was happening to them.

They all seemed fine.

"Go," I ground out, the word exiting my lips with a feral, garbled hiss as my vocal cords began to shift.

"*Open it,*" Clay barked at Ryland and began removing his shirt. Jared did the same. Ryland was already stripped bare. Layla and Viv had asked if they should remove their clothes, too, when Ryland had entered buck-ass naked fifteen minutes ago.

He's shrugged and told them not if they didn't care to ruin everything they were wearing. Vivian had removed her jeans and converse shoes. Layla pulled her bra out through the sleeve of her sweater.

Priorities.

I was barefoot in my panties, with just a tank top clinging to my clammy skin. I wore the one with the mustard stain near the hem just for the occasion since I knew I was going to ruin it.

Clay and Jared finished stripping down to their boxers. Except I knew Clay didn't wear briefs normally. He must have dusted some off for the occasion. Pity. It might've been nice to have something to distract me as my insides began to boil and burn.

I clenched my teeth and let the weight of the moon shove me to my knees as the circular panels in the ceiling slid open.

"Allie?" Layla called tentatively, her bottom lip trembling. She was completely fine. Both she and Viv were still standing, watching me with mixed expressions of shock and dread.

"I'm okay," I managed through gritted teeth as I pressed both my fists to the cool stone beside my knees, feeling my spine warp. I bit back a scream, not wanting to frighten them even more. I would endure this shift without so much as a fucking grunt.

I couldn't help my body shaking. I couldn't help the sound of snapping and grinding bones, but I could stopper my voice at the very least.

Jared was the first to shift fully, with barely a hiss of pain as the moonlight cast its eerie white glow over all of us. Clay was next, with a low growl in his throat.

Then came Ryland. His body bending and breaking and sprouting fur so quickly that it seemed as though he went from man to wolf in the span of a single blink.

Destiny had shifted outside and loped in to take up a place next to Ryland, her thick tail wrapping coolly around her to brush her paws.

The four of them waited in their wolf forms, a wildness in their eyes that wasn't normally there. Even with their whole lives as practice, the moon- triggered shift still affected them with a spike of primal, animal instinct. They could just fight it better now. Control it.

One day, I would be able to, as well.

Clay and Jared waited for me to complete my shift.

Ryland's fiery orange stare affixed to my friends, as if willing them to follow.

Baring my teeth, I let go, allowing my wolf to finish what she started. I sent one last glance to Clay and Jared, gaze flicking briefly to Ryland, hoping they understood.

Because there was one other thing I was worried about tonight. Another horrible possibility to add to the list of others: that my wolf would challenge him. It was the first time we'd both been in close proximity in our wolf forms at the same time since the Four Corners. And the moon-triggered shift would give my wolf near full control.

Ryland's orange gaze moved to me as my shift completed, a small sound escaping my half-canine lips at the final stab of anguish.

My canine body shuddered, immediately moving to pull against the chains, to thrash in the manacles. My wolf snapped at Ryland, growling.

Enough.

The alpha's command punched into my chest and I whimpered, still thrashing, but unable to look him in the eye anymore as the weight of his will crushed down on my spine. Pressed hard on my windpipe.

Allie, it's all right, Jared's voice echoed in my skull, sounding foreign and distant. I could understand him, but I wasn't the one in control. Though the sound of his voice seemed to soothe my wolf enough to stop pulling too ferociously on the manacles. If she pulled and twisted much more, she was going to break our ankles.

Look, Clay's brusque voice brushed over my skull and my wolf followed his wolf's gaze to where Layla and Viv and Quinn were all still completely, *perfectly* human.

Even feral as she was with the urge to be free, my wolf settled, seeming to recognize them. To recognize that this was *good*. She whined happily, pulling on her chains with the urge to go to them.

They're okay. They're not shifting.

The part that was still me wanted to shout in triumph. Though there was a small part, a part I promptly told to shut the fuck up, that ached with sadness. Because that part knew that this meant goodbye.

I would never put them in harm's way again. I would never risk this or something worse happening to them.

I just lost my best friends.

But at least they would get to live long, *normal* lives and—

Layla's shriek snapped like a bolt of lightning through the tepid air, piercing me straight through.

"La La!" Vivian screamed, trying to reach Layla as she crumpled to the stone floor, curling in on herself. Vivian's chains snapped tight, and she pulled on them. "Layla!"

But Layla was beyond hearing her. My wolf and I watched, mute, stupefied, and powerless as Layla's wrists snapped backward and she screamed. As her body contorted and she flipped onto her back, her eyes wide and glowing as she stared up at the spiteful moon.

Each of her screams sliced us so deeply, injured us so irrevocably, that I wondered if we'd ever recover.

That was when Vivian began panting and her back hunched, arms wrapped like bars around her stomach. She vomited onto the floor and staggered into the wall. Moonlight glinted on her elongated canines as she turned her bright eyes to the moon.

They're shifting, Ryland spoke in my mind, and I knew he was right. I knew it as my friends broke and reformed, their screams echoing all around me. I wanted to close my eyes. Plug my ears.

I didn't want to watch, but I did. I watched every pain-filled second. I took in every crunch of bone. Every tear. Every bloodcurdling pop of their joints. I didn't look away.

Wouldn't.

I did this.

Layla completed the shift first, scrambling to figure out how to stand on four legs instead of two. Her wolf lifted its black head to reveal a white starburst of fur over her forehead, spreading up behind her right ear. The white socks to match. When she felt my eyes on her, she snapped in my direction, then yelped when her manacles bit in, keeping her from lunging.

Vivian's agonized moan turned abruptly to a growl, and I turned my watery gaze to her, finding her wolf where she'd stood a moment before. She, too, snapped at me, her jowls frothing.

Her wolf was the color of wet sand, with rungs in the shape of a fish's gills around her shoulder blades that shone a pale gold in the moonlight. She snarled and yanked at her chains. Unlike Layla, she found her footing straight away and kicked out her legs and clamped her foamy mouth around the iron manacles, trying to get herself free.

Layla whined low in her throat, and I found her staring at Quinn where he lay, still virtually motionless against the wall. He'd have woken by now if he were going to shift, wouldn't he?

My chest ached as I watched Layla try to get nearer to him. Even in her wolf form, she seemed to know what it meant that she shifted and he didn't.

She'd just lost him forever.

With a quick jerk, Layla's wolf turned its burning eyes on me, her teeth bared and muscles shaking beneath her coat. She snapped in my direction, giving a forceful yank on her chains. The hatred in her gaze cut me deeply, scouring out my insides and burning down my throat.

Vivian, picking up on Layla's distress, abandoned chewing on her iron manacle. When her gaze fell upon me, she lifted her head and howled long and loud into the night before she began to pull on her own binds. Trying to lunge at me.

Their wolves wanted to hurt me, I realized. They were trying to attack.

Layla's sharp claws scratched at the stone floor, leaving jagged white streaks where they managed to form divots in the rock. Vivian battered at her bonds, thrashing and pulling, yelping when the force of her lunges nearly snapped her bones around the manacles.

A cracking sound stole my attention from them for a second and I found a jagged line in the stone around where the chain of Vivian's manacles was bolted deep in the rock wall. Rock dust floated down from it. If she kept pulling, she would get free.

I viewed it all numbly. My friends, their clothes scattered like discarded rags on the ground. Snarling and growling and snapping...*at me*. Their binds beginning to loosen.

Quinn, unconscious and alone on the cold floor.

Jared and Clay, watching with bowed heads and sorrowful eyes.

Ryland sitting regally with a twinkle in his eye.

And Destiny...staring unblinking at Vivian, a whine in her throat.

I could feel my best friends' rage like a fire in my blood and I cowered away from it. It was too much. It hurt *too much*. My sides squeezed painfully, and I realized that awful keening sound was coming from my own lips. My canine eyes were watering, burning.

It's okay Allie, I heard Jared whisper soothingly in my mind.

They don't know what they're doing, Clay's voice joined his brother wolf's.

I shook my head over and over, wishing I could seal my eyes against what I was being forced to witness. To endure.

Their pain was my pain.

And I had a feeling they knew *exactly* what they were doing. This was all my fault. They should be angry. They should hate me.

They should have the right to tear me apart.

With each thought, I retreated further into myself. Deeper into that dark part of my mind where my wolf tucked me away when I gave her the reins. She already had control, but what little I may have been keeping for myself, I gave over. I couldn't do this.

I couldn't be here.

My wolf, fueled by pure animal instinct, gratefully filled all the gaps, helping to shove me back to my dark place. To the safe place where I could survive this storm.

The horrid sounds I'd been making faltered and then stopped. My body rose and instead of a cry of anguish, my chest vibrated with a furious growl.

Allie? Jared questioned, but we were beyond listening, even to our mate.

Letting my wolf take over and shoving myself in the backseat had been unconscious, but even now, from the darkest corner of my mind, I knew what she was doing.

I could feel it ballooning inside of us. That strength.

That need to exert our dominance.

Wait, I whispered within, trying to stop my wolf. But she wouldn't hear me.

Her intent, our instinctual intent, wouldn't allow our friends to harm us. We had things to do yet.

With our front paws pressed hard against unyielding stone, we lifted ourselves up, our shoulders back.

Bow, we snarled, fixing both newborn wolves with withering stares. In the recesses of my mind, I was shouting. Screaming. I didn't want to do this. Not to them. But I knew there was no other choice, so I screamed and shouted to no end. I'd tucked myself too far in and there was no stopping this from happening.

Layla was the first to buckle under the pressure of my stare, her eyes widening as her snarls gave way to tiny yelps.

Vivian was next, fighting it the whole way, steaming saliva dripping from her jowls as her head lowered. As her shoulders shook under the crushing weight of my will.

A primal, snapping growl left my lips, rebounding back to me in the echo of the chamber.

Bow!

Still shaking with the effort of fighting it, Vivian's body finally joined Layla's pressed flat against the stone. Their sounds of rage and pain muted, as though they too were muffled under the weight of my dominance.

But a new contender raced to fill the silence, and I turned my gaze in the direction of the frenzied snarl to find bright orange eyes locked on the bowing wolves.

He snapped at them, moving into a crouch with his hackles raised.

My insides twisted sharply as he lunged, putting himself in front of Vivian. He snapped at her face, and I went full dark.

Lights out. Red.

Everything is red.

Something snapped.

A cry of hurt and there was something in my mouth like old earth and new pennies.

Pain blasted into my side and a sharp knock to my skull replaced the hazy red with shooting stars. Pops of color. My vision returned in spurts and flashes.

Ryland, Clay bellowed.

Don't fucking move.

The command was for more than just me, I realized, and even though I was lying on my side, still trying to clear the stars from my eyes, I found I still could. My paws twitched and I pulled myself back to all fours, keeping my right leg lifted. Something in it didn't feel right. Displaced.

That's when I noticed the manacles around my ankles and wrists. The chains that'd been anchored in the wall lay broken at my feet. Still circling my limbs but attached to nothing. I peered up to inspect the spot where I'd been chained, finding four gouges in the rock where the chains had been rooted.

Destiny stood there now, her wolf breathing heavily as it locked eyes with Vivian. Vivian whined low in her throat, and I felt something shift in the air.

Destiny cleared the gap between them, nipping at Vivian's paws. Her tail began to swish over the stone, and she twisted playfully in her chains, nipping back at Destiny.

They...bonded a faraway voice whispered through my skull.

Then another stole the attention, and I was jarred back to the present.

You dare defy me?

The words were a twisted sneer in my thoughts, and I found Ryland standing over me, looking down into my eyes with such wild anger that it was a wonder he hadn't killed me already.

I'm sure that the wound I saw glistening with crimson in his shoulder is from my teeth. I can still taste him on my tongue.

You dare attack me?

His growl sent tremors racing over my skin, and I could feel his will —the will of my alpha—pressing down on me. I knew it was meant to make me bow. I *should* bow. But I couldn't.

He was going to hurt them.

My alpha didn't like to see them bow to anyone but him.

If I hadn't stopped him, would he have killed them? Jared caught my eye with a little angered groan, and I twisted to see both him and Clay forced into low crouches and remembered they were compelled by their alpha not to move.

Their steady gazes begged me to follow suit.

Please, Clay's voice floated through my thoughts and something in that single word—in his broken plea—got through to me. I came roaring back to the surface, taking some control back from my wolf.

She wouldn't bow. But I could make her.

What other choice was there? Fight him here and now? Injured with stars still dancing through my eyes? Fight him and lose. Fight him and die.

Then what would happen to Layla and Vivian? Who would protect them?

A low hiss skirted past our lips as I sunk into a crouch and lowered my head.

I should end *you,* Ryland's words rattled in my skull.

It was the moon-triggered shift, Jared's frenzied voice joined the conversation.

She wasn't in control, Clay offered. *She wasn't in control, and you know it.*

Except, that wasn't the problem, was it?

I defied my alpha. I *attacked* him. Was that not an outright challenge?

Should I even have been able to do that? I didn't fucking think so.

But I was incredibly glad that I could. What would have become of Layla and Vivian if I hadn't done what I did?

I didn't regret it. I wasn't sorry. But he needed to think I was.

They're right, I managed, pushing the thought toward Ryland, imploring him to hear me. *I should never have...I lost control.*

Ryland snapped at me and it took every last ounce of my self-control to keep my wolf from snapping right back at him. To keep her from tearing his ugly face clean off his skull.

Somewhere at my back, Layla whined softly. The happy sounds Vivian and Destiny were making a moment before vanished.

It wasn't hard to see why. Ryland had begun to pace. His muscled, lithe body flexed. His hackles up. His teeth bared.

Uncle Ry, please— Shut up.

He growled at Jared, who to his credit, didn't so much as flinch.

Clay growled softly, his blue gaze never leaving me. His hard stare warned me not to react without the need for words. This would end badly if I did and we both knew it.

Jared may have been hopeful that his uncle would be merciful. Would forgive. But Clay knew better.

So did I.

In a camp full of wolves who were all sworn to their alpha, if I made one more move against him, I'd never make it out of here alive. Hell, I may not already.

Ryland whirled on me in the blink of an eye. I barely had time to see him, much less react before his jaw clamped around my front leg. The bone snapped and pain unlike anything I'd ever felt screamed in every nerve ending in my body. Horrid, pitiful sounds scratched up my throat. The cadence of my voice changing as the shock of the pain jarred my wolf back enough that I was able to reemerge. The animal sounds turned to human gasps and sobs as I clutched my splintered limb to my chest.

Blood dribbled down my forearm where a knifepoint of white bone protruded from my skin just below my elbow.

I gagged at the sight of it, my stomach turning and vision awash with watery stars again.

The cloying smells of pepper, firesmoke, and whiskey assaulted my senses as Ryland leaned in, naked and steaming in the cold. His human hand curled around my chin, gripping hard enough that I knew there would already be bruises beneath his fingertips.

"That was a *warning*," he spat. "You won't get another."

He shoved my head to the side, and I cried out as my body fell over, crushing my broken limb.

"*Get her out of my sight*," Ryland hissed.

Human hands lifted me. A string of curses tumbled from familiar lips. Clay's voice whistled past my ears. "I'll fucking kill him."

"What was that?" Ryland demanded.

"I'm not leaving them," I managed through gritted teeth, blurting the words quickly before Clay could have a chance to repeat himself and get us all killed. "I won't leave my friends."

Ryland's eyes sparked back to an orange glow and his upper lip curled back. "What did you just say—"

"I'll stay," Destiny's voice rose above all other sounds and I craned my neck to see her standing next to a still canine Vivian, her right hand plunged into the thick fur on Viv's neck as my friend leaned into her human mate.

"What's going on?"

Charity, in a long t-shirt, appeared in the doorway, taking in the blood-soaked stones and my broken limb. The chains and manacles still attached to my wrists and ankles but no longer anchored to the wall.

The jagged bite mark still seeping blood in Ryland's shoulder.

"Charity can stay in your stead," Destiny offered, lifting her chin. She didn't trust Ryland right now, either, I realized. The way she was clutching my best friend to her told me she would die before she saw anything happen to her, too.

Ryland looked like he was about to disagree, staring at Destiny and her new mate in disgust, but Charity spoke first.

"I will not move until you return," she told him, stepping the rest of the way inside and bowing her head to her alpha.

Mollified by her obedience, Ryland snapped, "See to it that you don't," and shifted back into his wolf form, casting one last scathing glare in my direction before loping out of the moon chamber and away into the night.

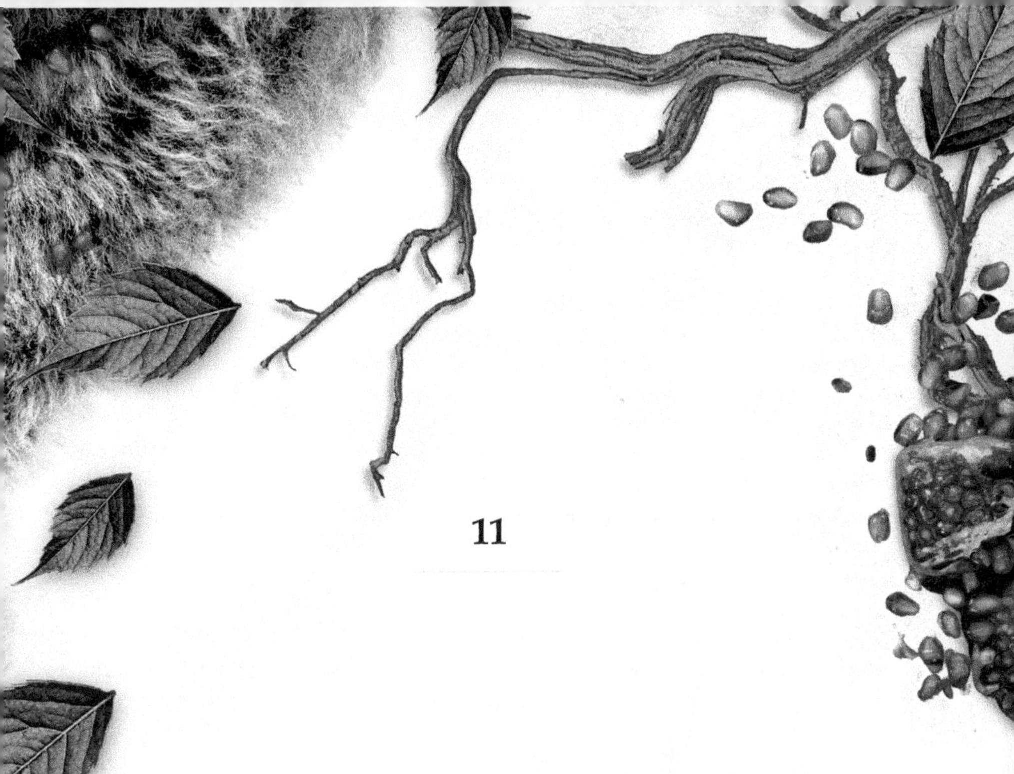

11

W e have to set it," Clay said in a hard monotone, his expression uncommonly drawn. Stiff as stone. "If we don't do it quickly, we'll have to rebreak it and set it again."

I grit my teeth, still clutching my bloodied and broken arm to my bare chest. I shook my head. "I-It's not a clean break," I managed, trying to sound strong and not like the pain was completely unbearable, because it was.

There really was no point in trying though. They were my mates and they were sharing the same airspace. I was willing to bet they could feel my pain as though it were their own.

I took stock again just in case I was wrong. I wasn't. After nine broken bones through my adolescent years, I could tell the difference. This pain was *definitely* not from a clean break.

"Are you sure?" Clay asked. I nodded.

Jared was pacing back and forth, his chest rising and falling rapidly as he worked his jaw, a vein twitching in his forehead. "We'll take her to Stella. She'll be able to heal her faster and set the bone properly."

Jared spoke in a hiss, his eyes never landing on any one thing as he continued to move. I could feel his rage like a fire in my blood, trying to spark the gasoline still in my veins.

"By the time we get there, it'll already be half healed," Clay growled back at him.

"Stella will be able to numb the pain, too. Better than re-breaking it here."

"I won't leave them," I stated plainly. "I won't leave my friends."

Still in their wolf forms, both of them emitted pitchy whining sounds that were like nails on the chalkboard of my heart. I needed to be here when they shifted back. I couldn't leave.

"Besides, I seriously doubt Ry's going to let me go on a fucking field trip right n—"

"I should fucking challenge the bastard. I should do it right now while he's injured," Clay said and the lack of emotion in his tone scared me. This was beyond red-faced, spitting rage. He was pale with it. Sick. His blue eyes glowing and sharp like cut glass.

Murder.

There was murder in his eyes.

Scarier still was how Jared didn't say a word against Clay's intentions. He only continued to pace, his eyes darkening. Would he stop Clay if Clay made good on what he was saying right now?

"Calm down," Charity hissed at Clay, and I had to assume she either didn't see the murder in Clay's stare, or that she truly wasn't afraid of it.

I wasn't sure which.

"I know you're upset but—"

"*Charity*," Clay warned, and she shut up, grumbling something to herself under her breath.

"It isn't up to my uncle," Jared said, finally stopping the conversation. He crouched down to my eye level, and I struggled to keep my gaze on his face and not the coiled masterpiece of his body. His gaze darted to Clay. "Go. Take her to the healer. I'll stay with Layla and Viv. Nothing will happen to them while I'm here."

His eyes found mine again and he brushed a tear away from my cheek. "I promise."

I opened my mouth to protest, but Destiny spoke first. "I'll stay, too. Ry's pissed, but I don't think he'll do anything to hurt your friends."

"If he does?" I challenged her. She was one of Ryland's most loyal followers. Would she really stand up to him?

"*He won't,*" Charity interjected, clearly not happy with where this conversation was going.

Destiny's gaze hardened, and she let it fall back to Vivian, who lay panting in her arms. Completely ignoring Charity, she said fiercely, "I won't let him."

"Look," Charity piped up. "I told Ry I wouldn't leave until he returned. I said nothing about keeping any of you here for him. Jared's right, Allie. You should go to the healer. Your friends are going to be *fine.*"

"I—"

A yelp came from my lips as Clay's thick arms curled around the back of my knees and barred across my back, lifting me to his warm, bare chest. He moved so smoothly that it barely jostled my broken arm, but even the slight movement sent stars blazing over my vision and set my stomach to roiling.

"Sorry, baby," he told me with a frown. "I'm taking you whether you like it or not."

I bit back a biting reply and instead, focused my gaze on Jared, needing him to understand what would happen if I came back to find *anything* had happened to them.

He met my gaze with a furious one of his own and gave one sharp nod of understanding without the need for words from either of us.

If Ryland hurt them, I was going to kill him.

He leaned in and pressed a hard kiss to my forehead. "I'm sorry," he whispered in a breath against my hair, his voice cracking.

"I won't be able to cover our tracks," Clay grumbled, his chest vibrating against my ribcage. "Everyone's probably finished their shift and back at the fire by now, but if they come looking—"

"I'll get Seth and the guys over here," Charity offered. "Tell them what's going on. They'll stall. We'll give you guys as much of a head start as we can. Just get back here quickly. It'll be better for everyone if you come back on your own versus if Ry sends someone to bring you in."

"Thank you," I told Charity, really meaning it. I knew how hard it was for her to go against what she knew Ryland would want. "For everything."

She was always sticking her neck out for anyone who needed it. One of these times, I was afraid she wouldn't be able to avoid the ax.

CLAY STEPPED BACK INTO HIS PANTS WITH CHARITY'S HELP AND DIDN'T WASTE any time leaving. He grunted as Charity removed her t-shirt and draped it over me just before we left, rushing away a second later, taking us deep into the dark forest. I was grateful for the thin bit of fabric. It blocked enough of the frigid midnight air to keep my teeth from chattering.

Like me, Charity still wasn't completely used to the whole being naked all the time thing, but she was definitely more used to it than I was. Besides, she planned to stay in wolf form while they awaited Ryland's return. Better hearing, and the ability to communicate with Seth and the guys made that choice an easy one.

I just hoped we could get to wherever we were going and back again before Ryland returned.

"I can walk," I offered once we got clear of hearing distance from camp. It was my arm that was broken, not my leg, after all.

Clay's jaw twitched.

"Really, it's okay. You don't—"

"I do," he all but barked, a little bit of that fiery anger I knew him for showing through his stony mask. His arms tightened around me, holding me harder against him. "Just...just let me take care of you," he added, pressing his lips into a hard line.

I didn't bother arguing a second time. His nearness and warmth were nearly enough to put me to sleep, even with the scattered battleground of my thoughts and the agony stabbing up my arm with each of his steps. The adrenaline was wearing thin, and a heaviness was replacing it. A sort of numbness that made it hard to hold on to any one thought.

That made my body sag and my eyelids droop.

Clay began to hum softly sometime later when I was nearing the edge of sleep. The rumble in his chest and the deep, rich, baritone of his voice sent me over the edge.

"Clayton?" The voice roused me from a fitful sleep, and I peeled back heavy eyelids only to have my eyeballs seared by a blight blue light flitting back and forth. I groaned, shifting.

A stifled hiss passed through my lips when I jostled my arm.

It didn't feel right.

Not in horrid pain any longer, it just ached dully. At a glance, I found that the bone was still protruding from my flesh, but that it'd stopped bleeding. And inside, I knew that it had somehow fused improperly, or had at least begun to. It felt pulled the wrong way and tight, stretching the muscle and sinew in a way that it shouldn't be.

"Who is that?"

"Allie," Clay replied, and I twisted my neck to find the woman who spoke.

She was maybe in her early thirties, with a shock of silvery white hair that fell in a messy bob to her shoulders. Her petite face was pinched as she took us in, a frown tugging down on the corners of her thin lips.

The blue light that'd burned my eyes, stilled above us. It was...a glowing orb. Like a little blue sun hovering in midair.

"Help her," Clay demanded.

The woman rolled her eyes and gestured to the house at her back. It was a modern looking thing. Not at all what I would've expected from a witch—*er*— alchemist. All black with a boxy shape, it hid like a shadow amid the trees on what looked to be a large property, concealed with high hedges all around it to hide it from view of people passing by on the street.

Though I doubted they were a necessity. I assumed, like Clay's cabin, this home would be warded against curious onlookers, too.

"A simple *please* goes a long way, you know," she said over her shoulder as she made her way to the door. Clay followed, muttering something I couldn't make out to himself.

We passed through the doorway and into a foyer that smelled of patchouli and something vaguely reminiscent of jasmine, but with an undertone of some scent I couldn't place.

"It's a bad break," Clay explained to the woman as he kicked the door shut behind him. "Can you do something for the pain? It'll need to be reset."

"This way," was the woman's only reply as she waved us through the foyer and down a narrow hallway. The warmth inside made me shudder after however long we'd been out in the cold. My skin burned from it, telling me it must've been a lot longer than I thought.

How long had I been asleep?

We followed her through a doorway and down a flight of stairs where the temperature dropped again, and through a dark crowded storage space into a room.

It was unlike anything I'd ever seen before. "*Lucidus*," the woman said and that blue light that'd been hovering over us outside reappeared, lighting the space just long enough for her to set about lighting some candles and flicking on a lamp.

One wall was entirely made up of tiny drawers. Each labeled by means of words scratched directly into the old dark wood. Ingredients, I realized, recognizing a few of the names.

A raised bed sat at the middle of the space and looked to be a recycled hospital gurney. The faux leather covered cushion torn in several places, foam spilling out.

"Sit her down," the woman said, bustling over to a tiny pedestal sink against the far wall to wash her hands.

Clay gingerly slid me onto the lumpy hospital bed and rolled his shoulders back, cracking his neck.

"What are you doing?" he demanded.

"Stella?" he urged when she didn't reply right away. "You want my help or not, boy?"

Clay clamped his jaw shut.

It's okay, I mouthed to him when his gaze fell back on me. *Relax*.

"Are you going to give her some—"

"*Yes*," she said, snatching a bowl from the sideboard next to the sink and taking it over to the wall of drawers to begin filling it with various herbs and little sprinkles of what looked like confetti. "I'll give her something for the pain. It'll cost you, though. Charity already owes me for my help with the boy. She's lucky I have a soft spot for mortals. That boy was as good as dead by the time she got him here."

"Thank you," I blurted, finally finding my voice. "Thank you for helping him. He...he was my friend."

"Hmm," she replied. "Did he shift then? The boy?" My chest squeezed.

"No," Clay answered for me. "But the other two who were bitten did."

"Good," she said, pouring a red liquid into the pewter bowl and beginning to grind everything together with a mortar. "I mean, about the boy. I was hoping my saving him wasn't for nothing."

Okay then.

I was getting the sense this lady didn't particularly like our kind.

As if reading my mind, Clay crossed his arms over his chest and pursed his lips. "Don't take offense," he told me, his tone dripping with disdain. "Stella doesn't like anybody. It's not just us."

Stella smirked. "True enough," she said with a sigh. "I keep to myself, if you know what I mean."

I did.

Probably better than most people.

That's exactly what I was trying to do before Jared and Clay took me in and my life turned into a proverbial shitstorm. Keep to myself. Mind my own business.

That didn't exactly work out for me though, did it?

Looked like it wasn't working out for her either. Judging by the fact that she had two shifters in her witchy cellar asking for help at god only knew what time.

Stella spoke some words I couldn't understand over the mixture in the bowl and strained it into a chipped teacup. She passed it to me, her dark eyes leveling on mine. "Tastes like sour pond water, but it works. Bottoms up."

My nose wrinkled as the tangy earthen smell of it reached me. I could already feel my gag reflex saying a huge *hell no* to drinking it, but I had a feeling I'd regret that choice. Re-breaking a partially healed bone didn't sound pleasant.

Clay gave me a tight, encouraging nod, and I downed the elixir, eager to get this whole ordeal over with and get back to camp. Get back to Layla and Viv and Jared.

Two big swallows got most of it down before I choked, only barely managing to keep it down. It made my tongue feel numb almost instantly, and a warm flush crept over the back of my neck. My chest slicked with cool, clammy sweat.

The floor tipped up as a wave of vertigo took me, and I gripped the edge of the gurney with my one usable hand to keep from falling. Clay was there in an instant, a hand holding onto my shoulder. His steadiness made the strange sensation subside, and I was able to blink back to myself, finding the room had righted itself.

Stella regarded me with a perplexed expression for a moment before stepping in to examine my arm. "That's an ugly one," she said with a little grimace, then sighed, gesturing to Clay. "Hold her steady. The potion should be good and soaked in by now."

She settled her gaze back on me as she gingerly began to draw out from arm from where I had it clutched to my chest. The shirt that'd been laid over me like a shawl fell away and I pulled it back onto my lap, needing at least to have part of myself covered in front of this stranger.

"It'll hurt a bit to be sure, but nothing you can't handle—"

A cry tore from my lungs as she tried to straighten my arm. This was no tiny amount of tolerable pain. Stars danced through my vision, and I had to go back to gripping the table.

"Give her more," Clay hissed at Stella. "You obviously didn't give her enough."

Stella paused, relaxing her hold on my arm. She'd managed to move it a whole six inches from my breast, but no further. She stared curiously into my watering eyes. "I already gave you double the regular dose."

My stomach twisted, and I bent over, grimacing as a tight cramp formed deep in my belly.

"What did you give her?" Clay roared, coming around the gurney to take me by the shoulders. He shook me, trying to get me to sit up. To look at him.

But the pain in my abdomen was only getting worse, and the acid taste of bile in the back of my throat was the only warning I had before I leaned past Clay and vomited onto the floor.

The reddish liquid poured back out of me, the only thing my body expelled.

"Allie? Allie!"

I retched, my sides splitting as my body worked to get the last of it out in dry heaves. Shaking.

Finally, catching my breath, I was able to lean against Clay and slide the back of my hand over my lips. "*Ugh,*" I groaned into his bicep. "I'm okay."

"What the fuck, Stella?"

The woman backed away, staring at me as though I were some sort of foreign creature. Her hands were raised in front of her like a shield against Clay.

"I've never seen someone reject that potion," she said in a whisper, her disbelief clear. It was obvious she hadn't done anything to purposely sicken me, even though I could feel Clay's sense of betrayal pressing into me.

I brushed my fingers over his arm and pushed myself to sitting with more difficulty than I liked. "Chill, crankypants," I told Clay, feeling strangely delirious for a moment while I got my balance back.

Stella hedged nearer, pointing at my arm. "May I?"

"Fuck no."

I glared at Clay then gave Stella a nod.

"I won't touch her," Stella said as she carefully put herself closer to me—and closer to Clay. Stepping around the puddle of regurgitated elixir on the floor.

Sufficiently subdued by her promise, Clay clenched his jaw and let her hover her hands above my busted limb.

Stella shut her eyes and a strange symbol, like a circle with a line through its middle materialized in the air beneath her palms. Crafted of pure light, it shimmered in the air for a moment before drifting down like magical glitter to rain onto my arm.

It felt...warm. But that was it. "Should that have...done something?"

Stella snapped her attention back to me and withdrew her hands as though burned. Her mouth fell open. Her naturally olive-toned skin turned a chalky white. "I can't help you."

"What?" Clay demanded. I deflated. *Well, fuck.*

"*What do you mean you can't help her?*"

In a daze, Stella stepped back and dropped her gaze, staring at her hands as though there may have been something wrong with them.

"Are you all right?" I asked her, much to Clay's annoyance. His upper lips curled.

"Hmm?" she looked back up, blinked. "Oh. I'm fine.

I just—I'm not sure what it means."

"What *what* means?" Clay asked, still seething.

She bit her lower lip, giving me a sorrowful smile. "You seem to be unaffected by alchemist magic."

"Unaffected?"

"Your body rejected the potion. My healing sigil barely breached the outer surface of your skin. I could attempt casting another over you to test the theory, but I don't think…" she trailed off.

"Strange," she added after another moment. "I've never seen anything like this before."

Clay stared at the grotesquerie of my arm and bared his teeth. His eyes sparked with the blue flame of his wolf. "The fuck does it mean?"

"Like I said before," Stella said with the practiced patience a teacher may use to explain something to a kindergartener. "I can't help her. I'm sorry you came all this way."

Clay ran a clawed hand through his hair and groaned. "What the hell am I supposed to do then? Hmm?"

"We'll just have to reset the bone without your witchy magic shit." I held my arm out as best I could. "Let's do it now."

I didn't want to wait to get back to camp and have Layla, Viv, and Jared be party to my pain. I'd do my best to hold it inside for Clay's benefit. But he was the strongest of us. He could take it.

Clay looked like he might be sick, but he didn't argue.

"You're certain?" Stella asked with a raised eyebrow.

I pointed to a wooden spoon beside the sink. "Pass me that."

It was nearer to Clay, but it was Stella who retrieved it for me, pressing it into my palm. Clay just stood there, sweat beading over his brow. "You can wait outside," I offered him, sliding the rounded wooden handle of the long spoon in between my teeth.

Clay shook his head.

"Hold her still then." She ordered Clay, springing into action. She gathered out strips of cloth from a cupboard and dug around in a bin until she came up with a thin plank of wood about two inches wide. "I may not be able to heal you, but I've set a good number of bones in my ninety years. I'll get it set right and splinted. It's the best I can do. It should heal quickly nevertheless."

Did she say *ninety* years?

Clay moved back into position behind me and pulled me back on the gurney until my back was pressed against his chest. The skin to skin contact sent a shiver through me. Then he wrapped his arm around me, placing it like a bar across my chest, using his own body to brace mine from being able to move.

With his other hand he held on to my free arm.

Stella's slender fingers curved around my wrist and just above the break in my forearm.

She looked at me with a question in her eyes. *Are you ready?*

"Just do it," I said around the mouthful of wood, biting down and looking away.

"One," she said, and I bit back a whimper. "Two."

Clay kissed the top of my head and held me tighter. "Three."

Fuck.

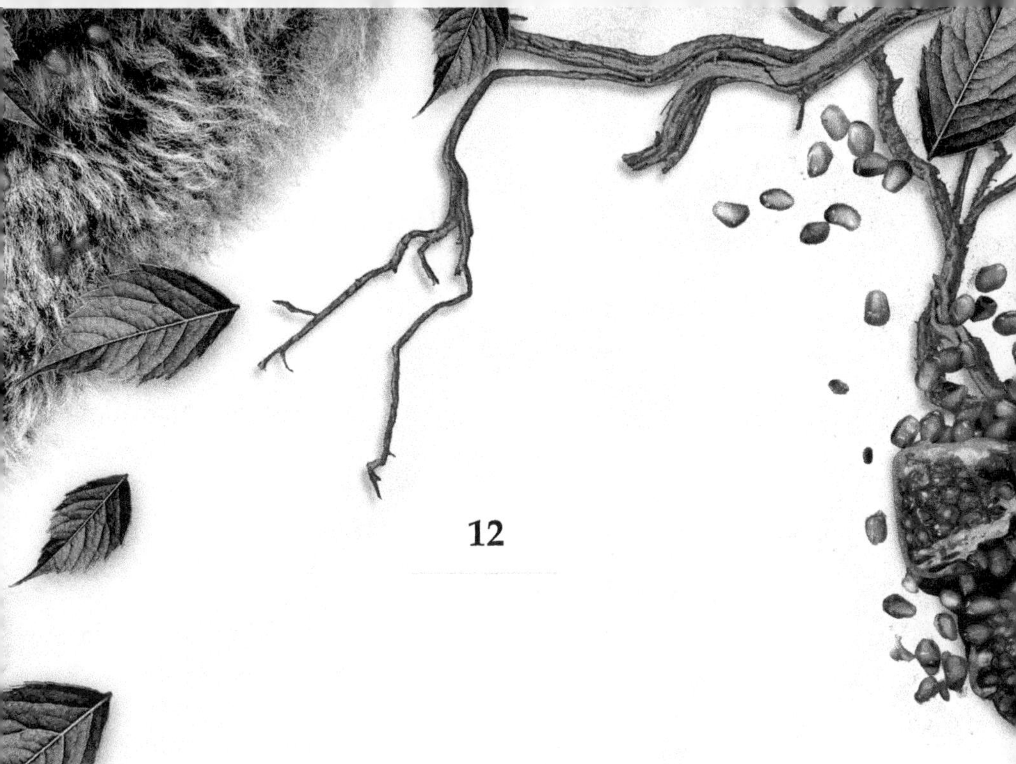

12

W ith the bone set and my arm splinted and in a sling, the pain subsided quickly. Well, quickly enough anyway. The feeling of bone and muscle knitting themselves back together was almost just as bad, though.

Not painful exactly. Just cringeworthy.

Stella lent Clay her niece's bike. Clay wanted to get us back as quickly as possible. Shifting wasn't an option, and running wouldn't allow for my arm to heal properly.

I couldn't remember the last time I sat, perched atop the slim handlebars of a peddle bike. Probably not since I was eleven or twelve. Vivian was the one peddling back then.

Now, it was Clay. His frame dwarfing the bike as he stood up on the pedals to push us up an incline in the road, barely breaking a sweat. The little white basket and frilly ribbons hanging from the front of the handlebars bobbed with each pump of his thighs. The streamers glinted with silver and hot pink, trailing to either side.

His expression was unreadable in the first traces of sunrise.

The chilly air made the tips of my ears burn and clouds of air puffed from my lips. The backroads were entirely clear of traffic at this hour of the morning. Our only company for the ride were the sounds of our own breathing, the beginning of birdsong rising from the trees, and the chirp and croak of insects and other small creatures waking to start a new day.

So peaceful.

I could almost pretend my world wasn't shattered and burning.

I realized where we were a few minutes later, recognizing the slim bus stop sign that Maggie used to drop me off at weeks ago. My lips parted and whirled to face Clay.

"What are you doing?" I demanded. "Why are you taking me to the cabin?"

My pulse spiked as I turned to glare at him, shuffling on the handlebars and jostling my arm. I winced.

"There's not enough room in the Jeep for all of us," he grumbled in reply, not meeting my gaze. "I'll go pick everyone up—"

"Bullshit."

Clay's face darkened, and I lowered my leg enough that if he kept going, he was going to see me knocked to the ground. He grunted and slowed, cursing as he came to a stop.

"Allie," he warned, his eyes glowing a dangerous blue as he tightened his grip on the handles.

I hopped off, grinding my teeth as I held my arm tight to my chest. "*Clay,*" I mocked, using the same dangerous tone.

"I'm going back with you," I told him. "You really think I'm just going to wait at the cabin? Sit there and twiddle my thumbs while you go back there?"

Was he insane?

A muscle in Clay's temple twitched, and in the glow of the early morning, I saw how his tan flesh paled.

Something tugged in my chest, and it took me a minute to realize what it was.

Fear. Clay's fear.

Shared with me through the mate bond. My brows furrowed.

"I don't want you near Ryland right now," Clay began, enunciating each word as though he needed me to understand their full implication.

I tried not to let the bubbling rage in my gut come out my mouth. I wasn't sure I'd ever felt fear from Clay before. Not like this. I couldn't ignore that. But he needed to understand something...

"I don't want you near Ryland right now." His brows lowered.

He knew exactly what I meant.

Groaning, Clay threw a fist through his hair. "Why do you always have to be so goddamned difficult?"

"Why do *you* get to make my decisions for me?

Hmm?"

Exasperated, Clay let his head fall back and sighed. "If you think—"

"I can control myself," Clay said, completely cutting me off. He leveled his blue eyes on me, fixing me with a pointed stare. "I can walk in there, and I can take his bullshit, and I can get your friends back to the cabin."

I opened my mouth to disagree, but he stopped me with a look, continuing. "I can do that as long as you aren't there."

I cocked my head at him, confused.

"If Ry tries to punish you more than he already has...if he," Clay swallowed. "If he hurts you again, I won't be able to stop myself, or my wolf, from trying to rip his throat out. Jared's uncle or not, Allie, if he moved against you again and I haven't been commanded into stillness..." Clay trailed off, shaking his head.

"I need you to stay at the cabin. It's the safest place right now. Everyone's at camp. They'll all be waiting for us to get back."

"And do you think Ryland's going to be happy when you return without me?"

"I don't give a flying fuck," Clay bit out. "And I doubt Jared will, either. If he has a problem with it, he can take it up with us."

I ground my teeth. I didn't like this. Not one bit. Even though I understood why Clay couldn't have me return to camp, I still didn't like the idea of him going back there. Especially due to the fact that he'd be returning without me. Ryland was going to be furious about that. And Clay would be on the receiving end of that wrath.

"Maybe I should just go back and get them alone," I muttered, knowing that the words were going to fall on deaf ears. "Jared and I can—"

"Fuck no."

I sagged and a ball formed in my throat. My chest ached and as much as I tried to hold it back, my eyes burned as they welled with angry, pain-filled tears.

This wasn't supposed to happen.

The crushing weight of everything that'd happened pressed down on me. I'd been numb to it before. It had been easy to focus on the agony of my physical pain, but as that began to wane, the reality of everything was setting in.

Layla and Vivian...

Oh god.

"Allie?"

A sob broke free from my chest, and I clutched at it, gasping at the sensation of a knife twisting somewhere unreachable beneath the bones of my ribcage.

How could this all be happening?

How had I *allowed* this to happen?

The bike fell to the side, crashing into the gravel along the side of the road. Clay's arms circled me gently, being careful of the sling. He tucked my cheek against his chest and wrapped himself protectively around me. His comfort only made me sob harder, my whole body shaking.

I didn't bother trying to keep it in anymore. I didn't bother holding back. I screamed into his chest, clutching at him with hard nails. Needing to feel something solid. Something steady.

I screamed until it hurt to scream anymore. Until my voice was hoarse and my lungs felt like they might give out if I made another sound. All the while, Clay held me there against him, not speaking. Not moving. Just being there.

When my breathing began to even out, he moved just enough to kiss the top of my head. Pressing his warm lips against my temple. "I'm so sorry," he said, his voice a gruff whisper. His body was completely rigid beneath me. I'd been so consumed with my own emotion that I hadn't felt his seeping through until now.

Guilt. Anger. Pain. Fear. Loathing.

I shook my head, smearing tears over his bare chest as I pulled away, wiping my nose. Suddenly eager to be alone with my thoughts, I gulped hard and heaved a sigh.

"I'm sorry," I managed, the words coming out jagged and watery.

Clay's warm hands cupped my cheeks, prodding me to meet his gaze. "Don't you dare apologize," he said, his eyes hard and beginning to glow around the edges. "Not to me. Not ever."

My chest ached again, but this time for an entirely different reason. I pressed my cheek into his palm and gave a little nod.

"I should go," he whispered after a moment more. "Let me get you home and then I promise you, I'll get your friends to you."

I needed him to promise me something else, too. One more thing before I could watch him leave. "I need you to promise me that you'll be with them when they come."

His lips pressed into a firm line, and he dropped his hands.

"I couldn't take it if anything happened to you."

I needed everyone else I loved to be okay. I couldn't take any more of this. The edge of my breaking point was near. That dark place in the back of my mind where the ugly thoughts lived had grown. I'd fought for years to keep that place at bay. To keep it contained.

It was too close to the surface for comfort now. The fluttering in my chest told me that if I wasn't careful, I'd soon be consumed by it. Unable to think. Unable to breathe. The panic would take over until dark spots crowded my vision and I fell into that dark place. Plummeted into the abyss.

And if I fell, this time, I wasn't sure if I would be able to rise again.

"Promise me," I demanded. "Or I'm just going to follow you."

Clay nodded once. A slow, measured movement.

I stood on tip toe and pressed my lips to his. Even a kiss as brief as this sent a wave of ecstasy rolling over my flesh. I broke the kiss and whispered, "Thank you."

Clay shook his head. "Don't thank me yet," he replied. "Thank me when I get all of us back here."

I nodded.

"Come on," he said and lifted the bike from the gravel ditch at the side of the road. "Let me get you home."

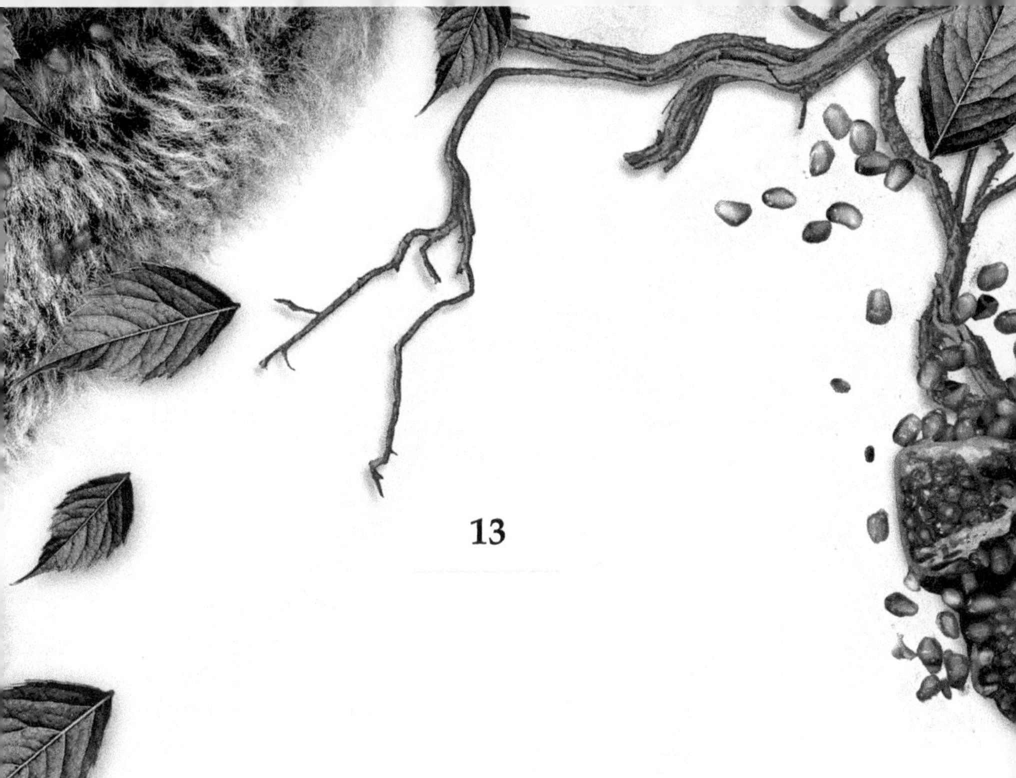

13

The waiting was horrible.

I began to regret giving in and letting Clay go back to camp without me about ten seconds after he left. What if he couldn't help himself? What if Ryland said something to him and he snapped? What if he didn't come home?

And then there were the other worries. Was Jared held responsible for allowing Clay and me to leave without permission? Did his uncle punish him in my stead?

What about Layla and Vivian? Were they all right?

Would they ever speak to me again?

And Charity...

Sticking her neck out for me *again*.

Even though my limbs were heavy with exhaustion, my mind raced to cover every brutal, terrifying possibility. I splashed cool water over my face. Over my arms and down my chest to keep the cloying grasp of panic at bay. I took deep breaths and tried to force myself to stop pacing. But that only made it worse it seemed, so I let myself wear a path into the hardwood between the living room and kitchen while I waited.

It was two hours before I began to hear the sounds of people approaching the cabin. Dawn had emerged in earnest now. No longer just a whisper of pink and purple on the bellies of clouds, the sun was a fat muted orange blob hanging in the sky just above the trees.

My bare feet squished into the dew-covered leaves and glass as I raced across the gravel drive and delved into the trees, following the deer path that led from the cabin to where we parked the Jeep at the tip of the trailhead.

I heard Jared's voice before I saw them. I couldn't make out what he was saying, but it was enough to allow me the first full breath since Clay left me alone to wait.

Clearing the remaining distance with my heart in my throat, I stifled the immediate urge to sob again when I found Jared, Clay, Viv, Layla, and Destiny emerge from the shadows.

Where was Quinn?

Jared's gaze was the first to find me, and he visibly relaxed when our eyes met.

"Viv? Layla."

They looked up, startled until they saw who it was. Vivian's short blonde hair was clotted with dirt.

Layla's already pale complexion was downright scary. But they were all right. They were alive and back in their human forms.

It took every ounce of self-restraint I had not to rush over to them. Layla's gaze passed over me as though barely registering my existence. Vivian glanced at me only briefly before dipping her head to whisper something to Destiny.

Clay brought up the rear, his jaw flexing when no one answered me. There was an apology in his gaze that made my stomach turn.

"Quinn?" I pressed, a sudden, gripping terror seizing me.

Oh fuck.

Had Ryland done something to him?

It was Vivian who answered. "He's okay. We dropped him back at home after..." her brows knitted together. "After the vampire dude did some weird shit to make him forget everything."

A small sound escaped Layla's lips, and she shouldered past me without another word, heading for the cabin.

Her silence cut me worse than she could've done with any words.

Vivian dropped her gaze.

"Can we...can we talk?" I hedged, wringing my hands in the hem of one of Clay's baggy t-shirts I threw on when we got back. "I wanted to—"

"No," Vivian said. "I just want to go to sleep."

"But—"

"I said *no* Allie." She sighed, lifting a hand to pinch the bridge of her nose. "Just...not right now. Okay?"

The finality in her words stung.

"Let's get you to bed," Destiny whispered, rubbing her arm and leading her past me to follow Layla.

"Take my room," I called after them. "It's the last one on the right."

"Mine, too," Jared added, coming to stand next to me. A hand pressed against my back in an attempt to comfort me. "It's across from Allie's. We'll take the couch."

Yeah, right. As if I was going to be able to fucking sleep.

Clay's slow footfalls approached until he was on my other side. He brushed his knuckles against mine. I glanced up at him gratefully. He brought them back just like he promised he would.

But...

Then why didn't I feel any better?

"They just need time," Jared told me in a low voice and there was something in his tone that I'd never heard there before. I craned my neck to look up at him, finding his expression hard and unreadable.

I was almost afraid to ask, but I needed to know. "Is everything okay? Did Ryland..." I trailed off, not really sure what I had planned to ask.

Did he punish you? Get Charity into trouble? Did something else happen while we were gone?

Jared blinked as though coming out of a trance and gave my waist a little squeeze. "No. Nothing like that. He actually passed out about an hour after you left."

I lifted a brow, finding that hard to imagine. After how pissed off Ryland was, how could he just go and pass out? I rationed that he had been drinking pretty heavily earlier in the night and that maybe the drinks had just caught up with him, but it seemed a bit suspicious.

"You look exhausted," Jared said, worry in his eyes. "Let's go try to get some sleep. We'll figure out what comes next in the morning."

I didn't point out that it was already morning, instead letting my body wilt under the force of my exhaustion. I still didn't think I'd be able to sleep any time soon, but resting my eyes didn't sound like a terrible idea. They burned from lack of sleep and the remnants of salt from my tears.

"You coming?" Jared asked Clay when he began to tow me toward the cabin.

I peered back to glance at Clay. He stood unmoving amid the gently swaying naked branches. "No," he said plainly. "Someone should keep watch."

Jared stiffened, but didn't attempt to argue the point.

I was reminded of something Clay had told me once before, when I learned that their cabin was hidden from view by some form of magic. Magic that apparently didn't work on me, just like the alchemist's healing spell hadn't. I asked him why he stayed with me. Wasn't I safe if wolves from other packs couldn't find the cabin?

Some enemies hide in plain sight, disguised as people you trust.

"I can stay up with you," I offered, knowing sleep wasn't an option for me, either.

Clay solemnly shook his head. "No. Jared's right, Allie. You need to rest."

I didn't have the energy to argue with him either, it seemed, because I found myself nodding and submitting to the gentle pull on my waist from Jared.

"Check her arm," Clay called after us before we could completely vanish from view. "Make sure it's healing properly before you pass out."

"I will."

The cabin was already silent when we entered. The only evidence that my friends were inside were their muddy shoes at the door and the faintest scent of Layla's jasmine perfume clinging to the air.

"You can take Clay's bed if you want," Jared offered as he pulled a woolen blanket and a pillow from an ottoman I hadn't known doubled as storage.

Tempting as it was to lie enveloped in Clay's scent and snuggle into his pillow, I didn't think I could take being alone yet. The panic was still there, swimming beneath the surface, ready to boil over if prodded. The only way I was going to be able to lie still and give my body the rest it would need to be able to face tomorrow—or today?—was if I had at least one of my mates close by.

One day, I wouldn't need their strength to support me. But for now, it was the only thing holding me together.

I swallowed hard and shoved strands of dirty hair from my face. "I think the couch is big enough for both of us."

Jared smirked, but it didn't reach his eyes. "I think you're right."

He finished unfolding the blanket and fluffed up the pillow at one end of the sofa and sat down, beckoning me to join him.

"Let me see your arm."

His fingers reached up to untie the knot at the back of my neck, releasing the sling. The pain was no more than a dull, pulsing ache now. That terrible feeling of bone knitting back together had subsided nearly an hour ago, but still, I winced when he folded the cloth back to inspect the damage.

His eyes darkened at the dried blood still marring my arm as he brushed his fingers over where the break had been. "Does this hurt?" he asked, his voice a dangerous whisper.

I stole the cloth back and did my best to knot it again with my one available hand. "It's fine," I replied. "Seriously. I think it's almost healed."

I didn't like the way he was looking at it. At me. His cheekbones flared and his hands curled into fists as he drew them back. "I don't know what to do," he said so quietly I barely heard him.

"What do you mean?"

His Adam's apple bobbed in his throat, and his clenched fists relaxed. "Nothing."

"Jar—"

"Let's get some sleep."

He lay back, scooching as close to the inside of the couch as he could. He opened his arms and the invitation was too welcoming to ignore. I fell into his arms, let him tuck me tightly into his side, and lifted my injured arm so it could lie safely against this chest.

I breathed in his scent, nearly moaning at the comfort it brought. Cedar and birch with an undercurrent of musk. Like my own personal forest. The safe kind. Where there were no monsters lurking in the shadows and no storms could destroy my shelter. I relaxed into him, and even though I hadn't thought it possible, within minutes, his steady breaths lulled me into a deep and dreamless sleep.

546

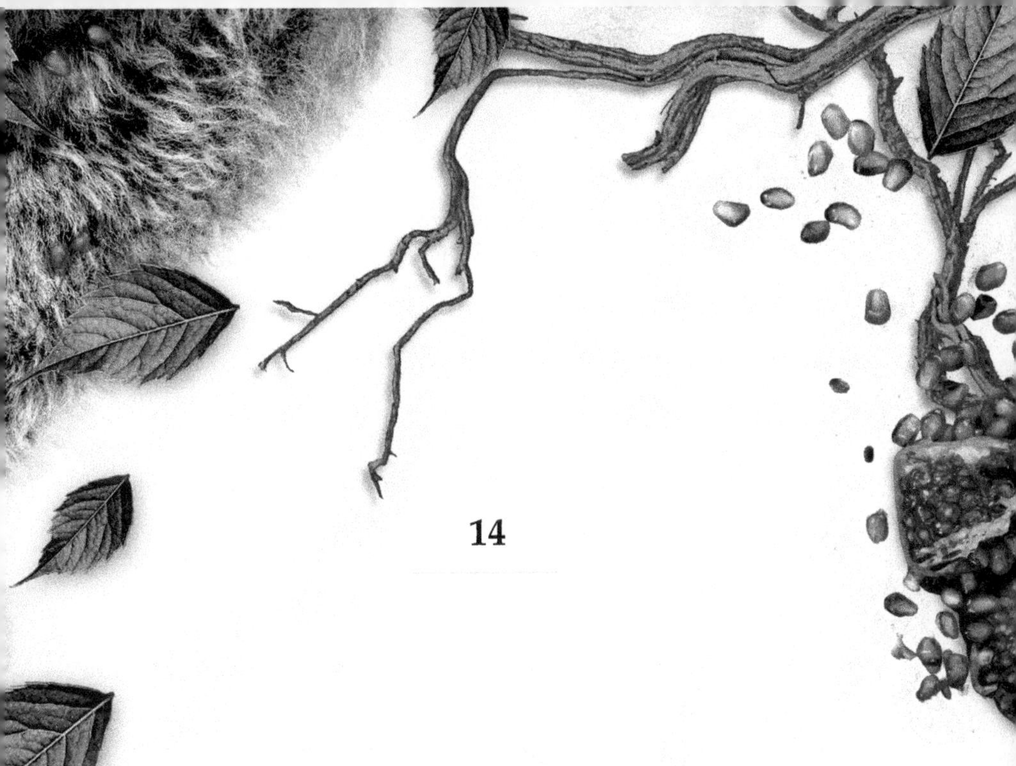

14

The sound of Layla's laughter carried through the cabin like a song. I cringed against the bright light of day, trying to peel my heavy eyelids back from my still-burning eyes. I was on my back on the couch, a low fire in the hearth ten feet away warming my cheek.

Where was Jared?

I must've actually fallen asleep.

The sound came again, Layla's melodic laughter, followed by Vivian's throaty chuckle. Confused and wondering if I was in fact still asleep, I lifted my aching body from the soft cushions and stood on unsteady feet, dark spots dancing in my vision for a second until I got my footing.

My throat was scratchy dry, and my arm and shoulder felt stiff from being held still in the sling for god knows how long. I eyes the kitchen clock, lips parting when I saw that it was somehow already after two in the afternoon.

No fucking way.

I heard Clay's deep timbre outside and followed it along with the mouthwatering smell of seared beef, baked goods, and the invigorating aroma of fresh coffee.

On the kitchen table rested a basket, sun-bleached wicker with a checkered cloth. I didn't have to look inside to find out what it contained. I could smell the burnt butter and brown sugar smell of Hazel's cookies from a mile away. Clearly, I'd somehow also managed to sleep through a visit from Grams.

Damnit.

I really wanted to talk to her. Maybe there was a chance she hadn't left yet.

My feet were still sleep drunk, and I nearly tripped out the screen door, catching myself on the railing of the front porch before I could go sprawling down the stairs and onto the dirt lawn.

"Whoa," Jared's voice rose above the others, and in an instant, he was there, hands steadying me with a firm grip on my elbows. "Looks like someone could use a coffee."

Layla laughed, and I pushed myself back to standing and turned to find her, gaping at what I found.

Clay stood on the furthest edge of the porch deck in front of the barbeque, flipping steaks amid licks of flames. He turned and gave me a tired smirk, waving a pair of tongs.

Vivian sat next to Destiny on the floor of the wood deck, paper plates in both their laps. The only remnants of their steak breakfast a little puddle of red juices on each. Viv's brown eyes were bright as she rested them on me. There was a flush in her cheeks.

Across from them, sitting cross-legged with a mug of coffee pressed between her palms, was Layla. Her black hair shone in the afternoon light with strands of blue and something close to violet. Her complexion was back to a less troubling shade of pale. But what had me entirely baffled was the wide grin on her face.

She set down her coffee and got up, coming over to me.

I couldn't breathe as she wrapped her arms around me, hugging me as tightly as she could without pressing too hard against the sling. Hot tears welled in my eyes.

She pulled away, staring at me curiously.

"What the fuck is going on?" I managed, my voice waterlogged as though there were a physical block in my throat.

I'm dreaming.

I must be dreaming. Why are they smiling?

What the fuck is there to smile about?

"Are you okay?" Layla asked, one perfectly manicured eyebrow raised. "How's your arm?"

"...how's my arm?"

"You're right," Layla said, turning to Jared behind me. "I think she does need a coffee."

"Coming right up."

Layla grabbed my hand and dragged me to where her coffee waited on the deck. Pulled me down to sit next to her.

"Morning," Destiny said, and I glanced down to see her fingers knotted with Vivian's.

Vivian's usually steady gaze flitted to me and back down to her plate as Clay turned from the barbeque to drop another piping hot steak onto her plate. She held her plate out to me instead. "Here," she said with a sheepish grin. "You look like you need it more than I do."

I realized, a little belatedly, how all I had on right now was panties and Clay's massive t-shirt. It was a warm afternoon, so I hadn't really noticed. At least until Vivian's gaze fell on my scrawny legs. The bones of my knees looked strange in my new slimmer body. Clay had been right. I was losing weight. And it definitely didn't suit me.

I took the plate from Vivian, my gaze never leaving her. "Can...someone explain to me what I missed?"

Vivian cocked her head at me.

Were they really going to make me spell it out? "Yesterday, you both wanted to rip my head off." I glanced between Layla and Viv. "Rightly so." Viv pursed her lips.

"And now you're..." How could I put this?

"Happy?" Layla offered and I was sure the shock in my expression was clear.

"Are you?" I asked her, hope and confusion beginning a whirlwind dance behind my breast.

Layla tipped her head this way and that. "Not *un*happy."

"But...*why?*"

I mean, I certainly wasn't complaining. I just didn't understand.

Jared came back out onto the deck and folded himself into a seat next to me, handing me a still- steaming mug of glorious coffee. I took a sip, not caring that it seared my tongue and burned a path all the way down my throat. I needed some fucking clarity, and if they weren't going to give it to me, maybe coffee would.

"We talked," Jared answered for Layla as though it were the simplest thing in the world.

I stared at him, pushing him with my gaze to fucking spit out the rest of the explanation.

His tousled dirty-blond hair fell into his eyes, and he reached up and pushed it back, strands of it catching the sunlight. "We did what we probably should've done for you when you first shifted."

"Which is?"

"Explain shit," Clay butt in.

Layla's cool fingers wrapped around my hand, drawing my attention back to her.

"I'm not sick," she said, her eyes welling and brand- new smile squirming at the corner of her mouth. "I don't have Huntington's. Not anymore."

If my eyes went any wider, they'd bug out of my fucking head.

"It's true," Jared added. "The transition eradicates illness. Most of the time, people who are terminally ill *won't* shift because of those illnesses. The toxin in our bite that triggers the change needs a healthy host. But..." he trailed off, shrugging. "That's not always the case."

"You're really not sick?"

Layla nodded, struggling to keep her tears at bay. Her chin quivered, and she squeezed my hand tighter.

It was my turn to smile. A laugh bubbled up from within me as I shoved my coffee back at Jared, hot black liquid sloshing everywhere so I could hug my friend properly.

"They already had their first voluntary shifts, too," Clay said as I pulled away from Layla after a minute spent shuddering in relief. "They did great."

What? Now they were just making me look bad. I didn't care though, I was grinning ear to ear. "So, does this mean...you don't want to rip my head off anymore?"

Viv barked a laugh and rolled her eyes at me. "We never wanted to rip your head off, Allie. Our wolves did, but Destiny explained that that was probably only because we somehow recognized you as being stronger. A threat."

"It's natural for wolves without an alpha to feel the need to challenge any other wolves they feel threatened by," Destiny confirmed. "Honestly, we should have expected it, but we've rarely had more than one wolf shifting in the chamber at a time before."

No one mentioned the fact that my best friends felt immediately threatened by *my* presence, but seemed to ignore Ryland's entirely. I grimaced, staring down at my hands. It was no wonder he'd snapped at them. He was probably enraged that they felt I was the bigger threat when the alpha who now had the largest pack in the western United States was practically standing right next to me.

It wasn't as if that were my fault though. And honestly, what did he expect? For me to sit idly by while he snapped at them? I thought he was going to *attack* them. I'm still not convinced he wouldn't have if I hadn't been blinded with rage and stopped him.

I shuddered, not wanting to think about that part. Nothing like that had ever happened to me before. I got angry, sure. But never to a point where I entirely lost control. Where one second, I was standing there, chained to a wall and the next I had the taste of blood on my tongue.

It terrified me.

I bowed my head, wondering what would happen now.

They had both completed the transition. They were alive and unharmed and somehow, miraculously, didn't want to see my head on a pike.

All good things. *Very* good things.

But they were still unclaimed wolves in Ryland's territory.

Perhaps sensing where my thoughts had wandered, Clay said, "Ryland already sent Charity over earlier this morning."

I snapped my head up, a vise around my heart.

"He gave us until the end of the weekend to decide if we want to join your pack," Vivian said, a knot between her brows. After a pause, she added, "Could he really make us leave?"

Jared gave her a sympathetic look and answered before I could. "He can and he will. I'm sorry."

"Doesn't matter anyway," Layla said with a shrug. "We already decided we'd join."

"What?"

I was about to lose my shit about the fact that he only gave them two fucking days to decide, but now they were really going to tell me they had *already* decided? In the span of one morning?

Vivian glanced apologetically at Destiny and then lifted her heavy gaze to rest on me. "This is our home," she said. "And I don't want to ruffle any feathers here, but honestly? I think the guy is a power-tripping douche canoe."

Destiny's jaw clenched. Jared paled.

Nobody disagreed.

"Wait. I'm confused. So then why the hell would you want him as your alpha?"

Vivian looked at me like I was daft. "We saw what he did to you, Allie. He fucking *broke* your arm. Without flinching. We aren't going to leave you here with him. Not a fucking chance."

My heart swelled in my chest, and I had to bite down hard on my tongue to keep the sob trying to break free of my chest from getting out. "That's not your problem," I managed in a tight whisper. "Besides, I'm the one who attacked him—"

"Oh shut up," Vivian interrupted. "You want us to stay and you know it."

The playful lilt to her tone told me she was trying to make me feel better, and that only made me want to cry harder.

Layla leaned in to bump her shoulder against mine. "Face it," she said with a chuckle. "You're stuck with us."

I crumpled and Layla pulled me into her side. Vivian left Destiny to come crowd in opposite Layla, wrapping her arm around my shoulders. "This isn't your fault," she told me in a whisper against my filthy hair. "We're stuck in this shit together now."

Clay clapped his hands together a moment later, breaking up the mushy embrace. "Who's game for another shift?"

The weekend went on like that until late Sunday evening. Layla and Viv must have shifted at least a half a dozen times, if not more. They were amazing. Taking it all *mostly* in stride. They knew that to be able to return home to their families they would need to have control, so they worked at it relentlessly.

They already had a plan to meet in the woods before dawn each morning to shift and go for a run before school every day. And each afternoon after school too when they could swing it. Layla was more worried about returning home than Vivian, though. Where Viv only had to endure her parents, Layla had seven brothers and sisters to deal with.

Seven younger brothers and sisters that she was often tasked with babysitting.

The guys and I offered our help whenever she needed it. Even Destiny threw her hat in. Apparently, she'd grown up in a family of six younger siblings before she'd moved away from home and was great with kids. I couldn't see it, but I had to admit I didn't know her all that well. Though I guess I would be getting to know her now whether I liked it or not.

You know, since she bonded to my best friend.

Layla's cell phone vibrated in her hand, and she tilted the screen to see who was calling, thumbing the side button to silence the call before tucking it into her pocket.

"Quinn?" I asked.

She dropped her head. Her non-answer was all the answer I needed.

Layla had been mostly avoiding his calls and texts since they dropped him off at home after the night of the full moon. "I should have had that vampire guy compel him to forget me. Or to break up with me or something."

"Don't say that," I started, but the glare she gave me at the words made me pause.

I sighed. "Sorry, La La. You're right."

She was doing for Quinn what I should have done for them the moment I turned: stayed the fuck away.

Within a few seconds, my own cell phone began vibrating in my pocket, and I grimaced as I drew it out, expecting an incoming call from Quinn looking for Layla. But it wasn't him. It was my uncle. *Again.*

I curled my fingers around the screen, gritting my teeth. We were nearly at pack camp now. It crouched just another half mile through the woods. It wasn't a good time for a lecture from Uncle Tim.

I let the call go to voicemail and watched the missed call notification join the others in a row down the screen.

Over the weekend I'd ignored four calls from Uncle Tim, with only a quick text fired off to explain it was a busy weekend and that I would call him back when I got the chance, so he didn't send out a search party. I'd also missed two calls from my boss. The voicemail icon held the number 3 in a red dot above it since Saturday morning, but I couldn't bring myself to check them.

Uncle Tim would only berate me for not calling him back.

And Jacqueline...I was terrified her voicemail would be the final nail in the coffin for my job. Since Ryland started demanding all my 'free' time I'd missed nearly *all* of my shifts. Jacqueline was a kind woman—understanding—but she would only put up with so much. She needed someone to do the job, and I wasn't doing it. Not anymore.

I'd check the voicemails later, I told myself. When I was alone in my room and could panic in peace. Jared and Clay had done enough comforting this weekend.

"Quinn?" Layla asked as Jared and Clay slowed up ahead for us to catch up and Vivian came bounding through the trees in her wolf form with Destiny snapping playfully at her tail. They nearly knocked into us, and I had to tug Layla out of the way so she wouldn't be bowled over.

Destiny gave a little apologetic *woof* and loped off with Vivian chasing her.

"No," I answered Layla. "Uncle Tim."

Her lips made a little 'o' shape, and she nodded. "Guess you must be getting excited for your birthday. Once you're eighteen you won't have to answer to them anymore, right?"

A hollow laugh passed through my lips. Not too long ago Layla and Viv thought I was still living with my Uncle and his wife out in Seattle. I'd almost forgotten they now knew the truth...about almost everything in fact.

Except how I'd become a shifter. Viv asked me just yesterday, but I'd dodged the question, not ready to tell them yet. No, actually that wasn't it. I didn't have a problem telling them, I just didn't think I could handle talking about it right now.

"Your birthday?" Jared asked, a crook in his brow as he slowed to a stop and cocked his head at me. He glanced between Layla and me. "When's her birthday?"

I opened my mouth to protest but Layla was quicker. "This coming Saturday."

"*Layla*," I hissed.

"What?" she asked innocently. "They didn't know?"

"What the hell, Allie?" Clay demanded. "Why didn't you tell us?"

"Because of exactly *this*," I said, gesturing widely at Jared and Clay. "I don't like to make it a big deal. It's just another day."

Clay's face pinched. "No. It isn't."

"Clay's right, Allie," Jared agreed, turning to Layla. "I'm glad you told us."

"No problem," Layla thrilled sweetly, and I groaned. "You'll thank me later," she stage whispered in my ear, giving Jared a little wink as she walked away, leaving me to the wolves.

"So—"

"Nope. Not important right now," I said, completely cutting off Jared. I could see the gears turning behind his eyes. He was going to ask me what I wanted. Or maybe ask me what I wanted to do. This wasn't the time.

Clay raised a hand to rub the back of his head. "I hate to say it, man, but she's sort of right. Ry's waiting, and we have no fucking idea what we're about to walk into."

Jared lowered his gaze and stuffed his hands into the pockets of his jeans. "I spoke to him earlier," he told us, and I noticed Clay visibly stiffen. "He'll be chill."

"How do you know that?" I asked, cocking my head at Jared.

The fact of it was that Ryland had demanded I come with my friends tonight. I would've gone with them regardless, but the fact that he *ordered* it left a sour taste in my mouth. He wouldn't do that unless he had something planned, right?

We were all hopeful that he might just have some new orders for me or be expecting me to get back to work searching for the deserters with Charity. But something in my gut told me that wasn't it.

"How do you know?" Clay repeated my question to Jared when I didn't answer.

Beneath the thick layer of denim covering his pockets, I noticed how his hands shifted, balling into fists. I could feel his unease, but despite it, his expression remained placid. A bit pale maybe, but calm. Passive. He was playing something down.

"I just...know."

"What aren't you telling us?" I pressed, a sinking feeling in my gut. Or was it a sinking feeling in *his* gut and I was only getting the leftovers through the mate bond?

"Can we just drop this please?" he asked, not sounding the least bit himself. "Like you guys said, we need to focus on what's important. Let's just get Layla and Viv to camp, get them enlisted, and then get home." Clay looked like he was about ready to rip Jared's head off in an attempt to find the answer to what he wasn't telling us. "Jar—"

"You'll tell us later?" I asked, trying to keep my tone level and calm. Neither emotions I was actually feeling. Jared made a noncommittal sound and gave the ghost of a nod before stalking off after Layla who was now a good thirty meters ahead. I could only make out the shadow of her amid the skeletal trees in the distance.

"I don't like this," Clay grunted in a low timbre.

I craned my neck to glance up at him, finding his blue eyes aglow. My mouth was dry when I replied, "Me neither."

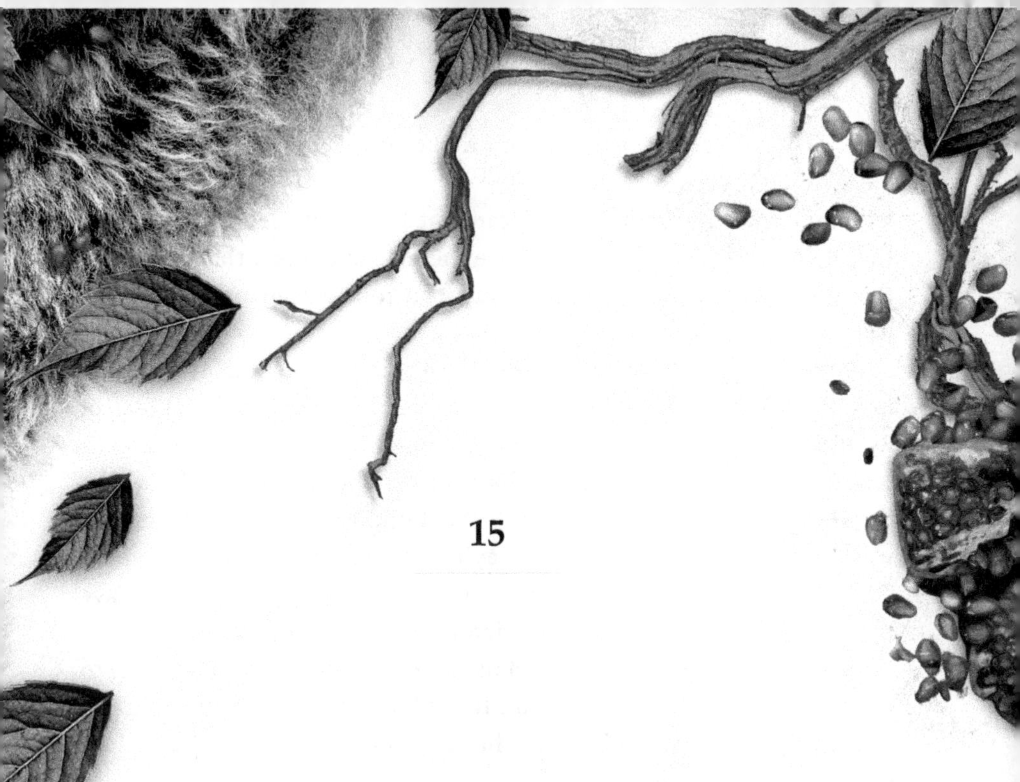

15

I found Charity and Seth among our regular group when we entered the camp. Ryland was nowhere to be seen yet, and I was grateful to have at least a few minutes before I'd need to face him. I got the feeling a simple apology wasn't going to fix anything between us. And truth be told, I wasn't sorry. Not at all, and I was willing to bet he'd be able to sense that if I tried to lie.

Clay stationed himself like a soldier at my side and didn't budge an inch while Jared went to speak with his uncle again before the ceremony could begin. Vivian and Layla, to their credit, didn't seem very nervous. They'd made their choice, and we'd explained to them exactly what would happen tonight, and after, once they became pack.

I envied them their ability to remain chill in the face of it all. Maybe they were just stronger than I was, or maybe it was that they had each other. Whatever the reason, I couldn't be more relieved that they weren't spiraling the way I had at the start. The way I'd been spiraling these past couple of weeks leading up to the full moon...

There was no excuse for that anymore, though. I couldn't fall apart. Not now that they were submitting themselves to Ryland's rule in order to join the Forest Grove Pack. They were joining in part because they wanted to make sure *I* was safe.

They didn't understand that it wasn't me I was worried about. I

557

wouldn't voice it, not in front of Jared at least, but I knew deep down that Ryland wouldn't hesitate to use them against me if that's what he thought it would take to get me under control. To keep me beneath his thumb.

I couldn't give him any reason to use them against me. It was now my job to keep them safe, and if that meant groveling at the feet of Ryland, then that's what I would do. For now.

My wolf would only bend that knee if she knew it wouldn't be forever. I promised her it wouldn't. We'd find a way to leave or maybe we'd just outlive the bastard. Or maybe Clay was right and after Ryland got his fill of rubbing my nose in the dirt, he would get bored and leave me to my own devices. Leave my friends to theirs.

There would be a way for all of us to be free again, and I was going to make it my own personal mission to find it. If that meant playing the docile pup with her tail between her legs for a while, then I could do that.

Or at least, I thought I could do that.

"Where are you right now?" Charity asked, nudging my arm.

"Hmm?" I said, blinking out of the tangled mess of my thoughts and back to the present. "Oh. Just thinking."

"About?"

I shrugged. "Nothing," I said, brushing off her worry and tactfully changing the subject. "How's the search going? I heard Ry had you guys out pretty much all weekend. Is that my fault?"

Charity pursed her lips. "Probably, but the truth is none of us wanted to be here anyway. Ry was in a foul mood all weekend. It was the best punishment he could've given."

I snorted, giving my head a shake. "Fair enough.

Find anything?"

"No. Nothing at all. It's the weirdest thing. It makes no sense that all of them deserted at different times and not a single one of them left even the ghost of a trail. They can't all be that good at covering their tracks.

"Because they aren't the ones doing it," Seth injected, leaning in with a glint in his eyes. "I think Ry is right. It's the eastern pack. It has to be. There's no way they are vanishing into thin air all by themselves."

I was sure the doubt would be clear enough on my face that I didn't need to make a comment, but Seth went on anyway. "I think we need to take the fight to them. Clean house."

"You're drunk," Charity told him with a little sneer, shoving him back. "Hasn't there been enough bloodshed lately?'

Seth gave a one shoulder shrug and resumed sipping whatever awful smelling liquid was in his red Solo cup. "If Ry's right, then they've already declared war."

"I don't think—" I began to disagree when Jared returned, his face ashen and strides purposeful.

"Ryland wants to see you in his office before we start the ceremony."

Layla and Viv had been talking quietly with Destiny, Trey, and Todd across the loose circle of bodies, but fell silent at his words.

"What about?" Vivian demanded before I could speak the words myself.

Jared's gaze flitted to me briefly before training on Vivian. "Don't worry," he told her, and the conviction in his tone settled the flutter beneath my ribcage. "It'll only take a second."

Then finally, he turned to me and something dark in his gaze made my belly flip. "He's going to apologize," Jared told me, as though if he spoke the words forcibly enough, he could make them true. "He realizes that you were not in control, and he shouldn't have punished you the way he did."

Charity's mouth dropped open. Clay was staring at Jared like he may have lost his mind.

"What the fuck did you do?" Clay demanded.

"What I had to," Jared snapped back at Clay and then turned back to me. "Go, Allie. He's waiting. Let's get this over with so we can leave."

I shared a look with Clay, a silent thought passing between us.

We would make Jared tell us what the hell he was up to later. Once we were safely back at the cabin.

"Hang on," Vivian called, breaking away from her mate and Layla to cross the circle. "I'll go in with you."

"He wants to see her alone," Jared said. Viv's nostrils flared.

"My Uncle doesn't do apologies," he explained in a low voice so the others wouldn't be able to hear. His meaning was clear without his needing to explain further. Ryland wouldn't speak to me—definitely wouldn't *apologize* to me—with an audience. He wouldn't want one of his newest recruits thinking him weak.

"Allie will be fine," he added pointedly, his gaze hard. "I made sure of it."

"I'll be back in a minute," I said before Viv could fight Jared on it anymore.

Clay caught my wrist before I could walk away though. "You shout if you need us. I'll hear you a mile away."

I tugged my wrist back and gave him a nod, walking away from the group in a daze. A thousand different thoughts racing to be analyzed in my skull.

Was Ryland actually going to apologize to me?

There was no fucking way that was going to happen, right?

So what was his play?

Apologize now and make me pay for it later?

Or had he just told Jared he would let me off the hook when in fact he planned to punish me in private, and Jared had just given him the perfect opportunity. Was there a gag and new, stronger manacles waiting for me on the other side of that door?

I stepped up onto the porch and through the wide- open screen door into the main lodge. Ryland's peppery scent mingled with the woodsy, mothball odor clinging to the timber walls and dusty cushions in the living room.

The hallway and Ryland's open office door loomed to my right.

Just get it over with, Allie. What's the worst that he could do?

But I knew the real question—the real worry—

wasn't about what he would do, but more about how much I could handle before I snapped.

I soothed the flutter in my chest with a few deep breaths and put one foot in front of the other. The longer I put it off, the harder it would be to go through with.

Just go in there and sit down and shut up and take whatever he gives you.

My wolf elicited a little inward snarl, and I hissed at her to pipe down before entering the room. I thought I heard a sound from some- where else in the cabin, a door opening somewhere maybe? But no one else came down the hall.

Brows furrowed, I turned to face Ryland, a hard ball in my throat.

I swallowed it down and clenched my hands together at my front. "You wanted to see me?" I asked, working hard to keep my voice level.

Ryland sat behind a long rectangular desk. Head bent as he poured over a sheet of paper caught between his hands. His dark hair was half tucked behind an ear on one side and falling forward to cover his face on the other.

He flipped the page over so it was blank side up and raised his head, fiery gaze fixing on me. "Please," he said, as though the word tasted foul on his tongue. "Come in. Sit down."

I glanced around the room, bristling as an odd sensation of being watched washed over me. A strange smell permeated the air and made my nose wrinkle. I knew the scent but couldn't seem to place it.

Fuck, I was being so paranoid.

Shaking my head, I stepped forward and dragged the chair opposite Ryland from the desk, wincing at the scraping sound it made as the metal legs scratched along the old hardwood floor.

I sat like I was told and pleated my fingers in my lap. "About the other night, I—"

Ryland raised his hand to silence me, and I let my lips fall closed.

My alpha pushed his hair back from his face, revealing the newest scar in his cheek, still puckered and ridged in dark pink flesh. The movement made another similar scar catch my eye. One in his shoulder, partially hidden by his undershirt. Though this one healed a little better and was more silver in color than dark pink, it was clear what it was.

A bite mark.

My bite mark.

Ryland, catching me looking, tipped his head to afford me a better view of my handiwork. "My nephew seems to think I owe you an apology," Ryland said, knotting his fingers atop the desk and leaning forward as though he might jump right over the desktop and throttle me at any moment.

I knew the bastard wasn't going to apologize and there was a certain satisfaction in knowing I was right even if that wasn't exactly a good thing.

My wolf moved to high alert, but I willed myself to remain still.

"Nothing to say?" he pressed, his eyes sparking to a dim orange glow. "Do you think I should *apologize* for doling out punishment where punishment was due?"

Asshole.

"No."

"Then we agree."

The silence stretched between us for a few moments until Ryland finally relented, sighing as he leaned back in his chair. "I don't see it," he said, squinting at me as though trying to find something.

I licked my lips, swallowing again to wet my dry throat. "See what?"

"What my nephew sees in you," Ryland said, lifting his hands to pick a small bit of dirt from his nails and flick it onto the floor, as though I was the most inconsequential thing in the room and he found the dirt more interesting.

I wanted to tell him the feeling was mutual. Not only that I didn't understand what Jared and Clay saw in me, either, but also...how I could never fucking comprehend why Jared seemed to believe there was any good left in his uncle. Maybe there was once, but I could feel it like a bad taste in my mouth, like a heaviness in the air around him: cruelness.

The poignant tang of bitterness and the abrasiveness of his tone.

I didn't say any of the things I wanted to, though. I bowed my head like a good little wolfy and remained silent instead, willing this show of dominance to be over.

"You know he threatened me, don't you?" Ryland asked after a few charged seconds and a sizzle of white-hot shock shot up my spine, forcing it ramrod straight.

"He wouldn't—"

"He did. It was quite the surprise, I'll admit. Not once has he ever questioned my methods. *Not once.*"

Ryland let those words hang in the air between us, all the while his gaze darkened. The glow around his irises depleted until they seemed almost black beneath the shadow of his brows.

"I'll speak to him," I offered.

One brow raised, Ryland appraised me, perhaps trying to decipher if I was being truthful.

"I won't have discord in my pack. Loyalty is paramount in our world, Allie Grace. Those who are not loyal do not have a place here. Do you understand?"

Holy fucking shit. Was he threatening me? Or...was he threatening his own nephew?

Scarcely able to breathe, the single word barely skirted past my lips. A whisper. "Yes."

"Good."

Ryland stood and adjusted his belt, righting his undershirt and the shining silver buckle of his belt before he tucked his arms into the sleeves of a crisp navy-blue button up and rolled the sleeves to the creases of his elbows.

Awkwardly, I stood too, unsure if I should ask to leave or just go. Unsure if he was finished with me or not.

"I have new recruits to welcome into the fold," Ryland said as he brushed past me to the door, his entire demeanor changing in the span of a single stride. The mask was back on. He was ready for the curtain call.

I moved to follow him, but his head snapped to the side, a single glowing eye boring into me. "You'll remain here," he ordered, and I felt the weight of the order like a baby grand piano on my chest, his words laced with the command of the alpha. "There are just a few more things Grey will go over with you and then you can join us in the yard."

"What?"

Behind Ryland, a shape disconnected from the rest of the shadows in the hallway, moving stealthily, as though floating on air into the light.

The vampire, Grey came into view. Just as pale as I remembered, with eyes blacker than coal and thick lips mostly bleached of color. Those same warning bells I'd felt earlier came back in a clatter of white noise, ricocheting in my skull.

"Won't you explain to Allie here how things will be from now on?" Ryland asked Grey as he stalked past the vampire and out into the hall. "I don't want to keep her friends waiting. It's late."

Bullshit.

Complete and utter bullshit.

Was anything this fucker said genuine? I was starting to think not.

I would be talking to Jared, but I didn't think Ryland was going to like what I had to say.

"Of course," Grey replied in a hiss, gesturing for me to accompany him back into the office. "It's nice to see you again, Allison."

"It's Allie," I all but snapped. This time when my wolf pressed against my barriers, I let him see her. How close she was to the surface. I wanted him to know that even though I was doing my best to behave for the sake of my friends, that restraint only applied to my alpha. To my mate's uncle. Not to him.

Interest piqued, Grey grinned wickedly, twisting the silver ring on his index finger and as he drew nearer to me. "Allie," he acquiesced. "This will only be a moment."

Grey settled himself on the edge of Ryland's desk and beckoned me forward.

Tightening my jaw and readying myself for any sign of attack, I stayed where I was, unwilling to get any closer to him.

A saccharine smile twisted his lips before he began to speak, holding my gaze. "You will not tell anyone of this meeting," he said, his voice and demeanor changing from dejected politeness to cruel command.

"You will not speak ill of your alpha. You will adhere to his will and command. You will be *obedient*."

I fisted my hands in the hem of my shirt and glared at Grey.

Why couldn't Ryland have given me these orders himself?

Fucking coward.

"That's all for now," he finished, clapping his hands together, forcing me to stumble back a step at the sudden sound and movement, blinking rapidly. "Off you go, little dove. Until we meet again."

Eager to get away from Grey, I spun on my heel and hurried out of the room, rushing down the hall and out of the front door, stumbling outside into the moonlit night. Cold air stung my flushed cheeks, and I gasped for an unrestricted breath, trying to get my bearings.

"Hey," the deep voice boomed from my right, and I stumbled again, this time unable to right myself before my knees struck dirt. I whirled, sagging when I found Clay staring down at me, a worried crease in his brow. "You okay? Was that Grey I heard inside?"

"With the moon and all in attendance here as witnesses." I heard Layla's voice, carried to me on a phantom wind.

I scrambled to my feet and found them. Layla and Vivian standing shoulder to shoulder with the rest of the pack on their flanks and

Ryland standing directly in front of them. An encouraging grin spreading across his lips.

Jared caught my eye as Vivian repeated the oath Layla just finished speaking. His lips parted in silent question at my disheveled appearance, and I struggled to regain composure, the whisper of Ryland's threat still echoing in my ears.

"I hereby submit myself to the rule of the alpha," my best friends spoke in unison, their oaths carrying over the crowd.

Ryland passed the silver flask to Layla first, pressing it into her palm and wrapping his hideous hand around hers. Hesitantly, she brought it to her lips, and I choked on the urge to call out to her, to stop her.

And then it was already too late. The flask was being passed to Vivian, who tipped it back, taking a long pull of the blood-tainted whiskey and grimacing while all I could do was stand and watch in silent horror.

This was a mistake. I could see it now.

Clay wrapped his hands around my shoulders, kneading out the tension there. "They're pack now," he whispered against my cheek. "Family. Forever."

Ryland caught my eye as he turned to cast a shining grin over the pack members in attendance. He paused briefly on me, his grin morphing into something else entirely. Something twisted and conniving. I almost wanted to ask Clay if he'd seen it, to make sure it wasn't my own paranoia making something out of nothing, but the look was gone as swiftly as it appeared, leaving me to guess at whether it had been there at all.

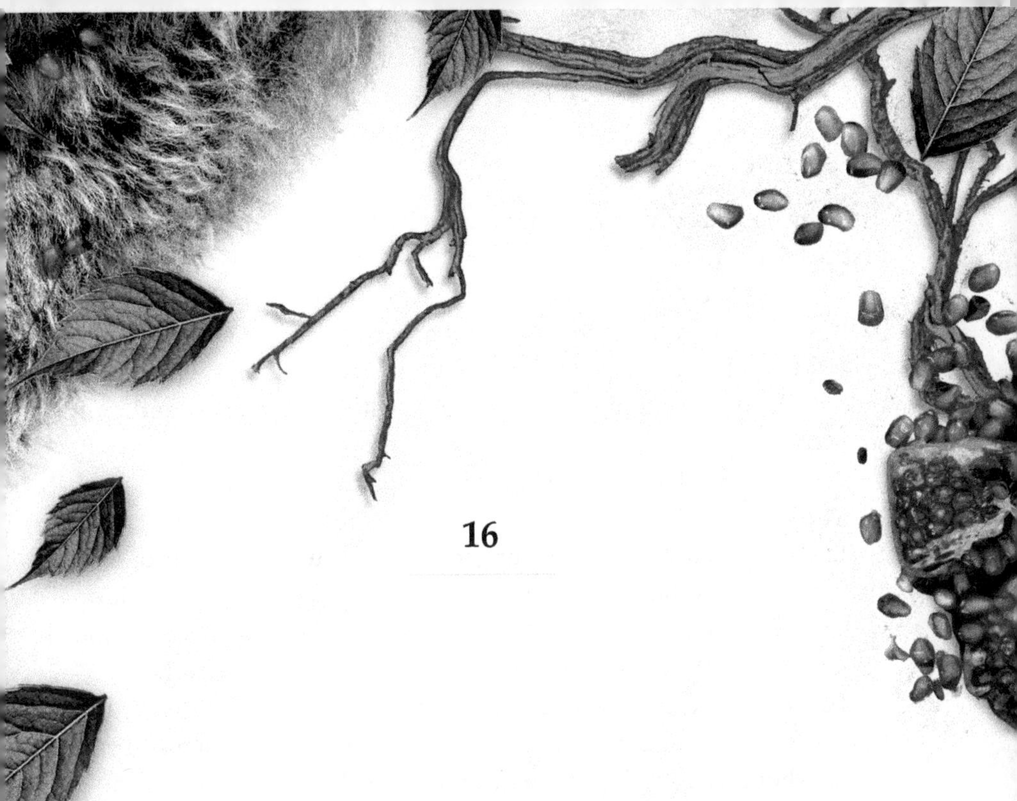

16

I couldn't sleep.

Ever since the ceremony, my thoughts had been erratic. Explosive. Like a minefield I had no way of crossing without getting blown to a thousand tiny pieces.

I checked my phone for the fifteenth time in the last five minutes, gushing a sigh of relief when a text from Vivian flared to life on the screen as though I'd willed it into being.

Vivian: Allie, I'm fine. I'm going to sleep. You should too.

Vivian: See you at school tomorrow, k?

Allie: Have you heard from Layla? She isn't answering my texts.

Vivian: That's probably because it's one in the morning.

She was right. I sat heavily on my bed, the mattress sighing beneath my weight.

Allie: Sorry. See you in the morning.

I chucked my phone onto the bed, losing it in a lumpy pile of blankets and leaned forward to press my palms into my eyes, easing the tension headache knocking at my ocular cavities behind them.

They couldn't fault me for worrying. I remembered what it was like those first few days. I had almost no control.

But then again, I had refused to shift for way too long.

567

They had already shifted more times in three days than I had in my first two weeks.

They'll be fine, I told myself stoically. *Totally fucking fine.*

Them being at home was better than being at pack camp at least. Ryland had offered for them to remain on pack land for a while, until they could both be properly acquainted with their wolves and gain some control.

They'd refused of course. They couldn't just not go home.

They had families.

Layla especially. She had younger siblings counting on her to look after them while her parents worked. Vivian may have been able to swing it. Her mom likely wouldn't notice she was gone for a while, and her dad wouldn't care so long as she gave him a plausible excuse.

I'd worried Ryland wouldn't grant them permission to leave, but he'd simply nodded and gave both my best friends understanding pats on the shoulders. Playing the part of a benevolent and understanding alpha.

He'd warned them of the risks involved with returning home so soon, but they'd both nodded, accepting the risks. And just like that, he'd let them go with only vague orders requesting them to return the following weekend *when they had time.*

Ha!

I'd never received such lenience from Ryland. What was he playing at?

Trying to get them on his good side?

As if that would work after both of them watched him break my fucking arm because he was having a goddamned tantrum.

I barely noticed I'd risen to pace until I was out in the hall, turning back at the stairs to walk back toward my room.

With Jared gone back to the quarry on orders from Ry and Clay busy with something in the shop, I'd been alone with my thoughts since Clay and I dropped off Layla and Viv and returned home.

Now that I had time to think things through, I realized there was a lot not adding up. And I kind of wished I'd pulled Jared away to have that talk with him before he had to leave.

But, like usual, I'd hesitated, developing lockjaw in the span of a single breath.

I needed to think about what I was going to tell him. *How* I was going to say it. I couldn't very well just blurt out that I thought his uncle was a sadistic douchebag who maybe, probably, had something to do with the missing members of the pack.

Loyalty is paramount in our world, Allie Grace. Those who are not loyal do not have a place here.

If the other missing wolves were anything like the one that'd almost fallen drunk into the firepit the week before, then it wasn't a stretch to say that they *weren't* as loyal as Ryland wanted his pack to be.

And to say that the cowardly alpha who ran away that night at the four corners had something to do with it? How was he getting the others to actually buy into that? There was no way it had anything to do with that pack.

Right?

I stopped, chewing my bottom lip as I glanced into the dark, quiet cabin below from the top of the stairs.

There was something going on. Something that wasn't adding up.

The more I thought about it, the more I believed it.

I bowed to my alpha's will to protect my friends and my mates. But would my obedience be enough to save them if he were the monster I was starting to think he was?

I swiped a hand over my face, a jagged sigh tumbling from my lips.

Or was this all just a massive misunderstanding? Was it just that Ryland fucking hated me and was treating me like shit that made me suspicious of him?

Groaning, I raced down the stairs.

There was only one way to find out and put these demons to rest once and for all...

I needed to go to the eastern pack. I needed hard proof. Real, tangible answers.

I needed to know that I didn't just let my friends make the biggest mistake of their lives when they submitted to the rule of Ryland.

The screen door banged shut behind me as I stepped out into the frigid air, my breaths clouding in icy little droplets on my face as I shivered, hugging my arms around myself as I power walked around to the back of the cabin.

The light was still on in the shop. Good.

"Hey," I said, rounding the edge of the garage-style door and entering unannounced. "I need to talk—"

Clay rolled off the couch with a snarl and a thud, flipping onto all fours with his teeth bared and eyes wild and ablaze with blue fire. He spun, searching for an attacker, and I realized all at once that he'd been asleep.

Oops.

His gaze settled on me, great gushes of steamy air puffing past his lips. He blinked, relaxing as he rocked back on his heels and caught his breath.

"The light was on," I said with a wince. "I thought you were still awa—"

"Don't do that," he growled, shakily rising to his feet, his face tinged red. "I almost..." he trailed off, throwing a hand through his sleep-tousled hair.

"I'm sorry. I should've—"

Clay shook his head and his gaze lowered to the floor. "It's fine," he said. "I was just...it was a nightmare. I didn't expect you to—"

"Barge in unannounced at one in the morning?"

"Yeah. That."

"Then clearly you need to change your expectations."

He smirked at that and sat back down on the old sofa, legs spread wide and arms open, one slung over the backrest and the other over the torn armrest. He took up almost half the sofa like that. Sometimes I forgot how massive he was. With arms larger than my thighs and a chest nearly as wide as two of mine.

It didn't help that he was shirtless, exposing every shadowed curve of muscle and a little whisper thing trail of dark hairs disappearing into the rim of his loose fitted jeans from his belly button.

Wasn't he cold?

It had to be less than 60 outside tonight.

"I..." I started but couldn't seem to find the words, or maybe the courage, to start talking. I bit my bottom lip and glanced out at the trees, craving their solace like I haven't craved it in a long time.

"What's wrong?" Clay asked, his casual demeanor shifting as he attempted to study my expression. "Did something happen?"

"Um..."

"Allie?"

"Will you go for a walk with me?" I blurted before I could change my mind. "Not far. Just down the trail and back. Walking sometimes helps me think."

He narrowed his icy blue eyes at me, but stood after a minute. "Sure," he said with a note of suspicion coloring his tone and then snagged a dark sweater from beside the couch to toss in my direction. "Put this on. You're shaking."

I caught it midair and tugged it on gratefully, wilting beneath the instant warmth and the comforting smell that was uniquely Clay enveloping me.

He grabbed a long sleeve t-shirt from the seat of the bike he was working on. One of the ones he used for work that was a deep gray covered in the stain of engine grease.

"Lead the way," he told me as he came to the edge of the shop. "But let's stay tight to the cabin."

I understood what he meant. Let's stay within the perimeter of the spell keeping the cabin and immediate area surrounding it cloaked from view.

I had to wonder if he was worried about the same thing I was, or if he'd bought into the rumors of the eastern pack trying to dwindle our numbers. I shook my head. No. He wasn't that gullible.

Clay didn't press me as we walked slowly over the carpet of fallen leaves coating the forest floor. With the moon still near full and the forest canopy thinned from autumn shed, the path was bright. It had almost a crystalline quality. I could make out every knot of wood. Every flurry of movement. Smell every scent.

I shut my eyes and inhaled deeply, letting the familiar scents of mountain pine and birch soothe the tremor in my bones.

"There's something I need to talk to you about," I started.

"I figured," he said, ever the smart ass.

I gave him a little shove and continued. "This is serious. And I don't want you to freak out, okay? You have to promise you won't."

I chanced a quick peek at him, finding the side profile of his face tight and muscle jumping in his jaw.

"Okay," he said finally.

"Okay, so basically here's the thing...*the thing is...*"

Why was this so hard?

"Spit it out, Allie."

I stopped and turned to face him, my spine going rigid. He stilled, waiting for whatever it was I had to say with a knot in his brow and lips pressed tight. As though bracing for a physical blow.

"So, remember how Jared said that Ryland was going to apologize to me? Well, he didn't. He actually kind of threatened me. Or maybe he threatened Jared. I'm not clear on that. And then he had that Grey asshat try to tell me how things were going to be from now on. And anyway, that's not really important right now, what I really wanted to bring up and maybe get your help with is well...I think Ryland is lying about the missing wolves and the eastern pack being responsible for their disappearances. I think that it's possible that *he* has something to do with them just vanishing into thin air, and he's just trying to shift the blame and—"

"*Whoa*, Allie, slow down. You aren't making any sense."

Clay's hands came around my arms and squeezed. He licked his lips and glanced around us, as though afraid someone might overhear. "Come on, let's go back. We're too close to the edge of the warding spell."

I let Clay take my hand and tug me back the way we'd come. He stopped only when we could see the cabin through the trees and turned to face me.

Sometime in the last few seconds what I'd told him must've sunk in because he didn't look so confused anymore. He looked *pissed*.

Like, not normal pissed. *Clay level pissed.*

With bulging veins and cheeks so red they were verging on purple.

"Calm down," I told him, trying to barricade myself against his raging emotions before they could seep into my own veins, lighting fire to the gasoline already lingering there.

"I'm sorry," Clay spat, his voice dripping sarcasm. "Calm down?"

"Clay—"

"Did you say he *threatened* you?"

Crap. Maybe I should've left that part out.

I grasped for a response that wouldn't set him off even more, choking on several sentence starters that would only lead to more rage.

Exasperated after a minute of trying, I huffed out a curse and gave my head a little shake. "Look, I can't talk to you when you're all murdery. Can you just take a fucking breath, please?"

He reeled back as though stung, but did what I asked, working hard to calm himself enough that he began to look more like a regular human being instead of a mass of veiny stone.

"Better?" he grunted.

It was the best I was going to get. I nodded.

"Good, now can you explain to me exactly what the fuck you're trying to tell me? Maybe at a normal speed this time?"

I ignored the dig and gave him a short glare before launching into a less chaotic explanation. This time, I maybe glazed over the thinly veiled threat Ryland gave, making it sound more like maybe I was just being paranoid and he didn't actually threaten me at all.

It wasn't exactly a lie. I *could* have been blowing it out of proportion. Ryland may not have meant it that way.

But even I had to admit it wasn't as if I was telling the whole truth either.

Anyway, that wasn't the point. The more important bit—the one that I really needed someone to talk to about, was the shifters who'd mysteriously vanished.

I focused on that part when I did my reiteration to Clay. Explaining why I thought it was bullshit and what I wanted to do about it. I got more and more nervous as I spoke, watching Clay's face harden with each word.

I thought he would understand—that if anyone were going to help me do this it would be him. Had I been wrong?

Was this yet another colossal mistake? I wouldn't have been surprised, making mistakes seemed to be all I was good at nowadays. I should just make a sport out of it.

"I want to go to the eastern pack," I told him, praying it wasn't the final nail in my coffin. Clay was either going to be with me on this or he was going to be *firmly* against me. I half wondered if he might lock me up inside just to keep me from trying to go instead of coming with me.

"It doesn't add up Clay," I continued when he didn't immediately reply. "Something is *wrong*. I don't know what it is exactly, but I have this...this *feeling* in my gut that—"

"I think you're right," he interrupted, eyes darting this way and that as he considered.

"You do?"

I wasn't sure if I should have been elated or terrified that someone else agreed with me about this. If I were being honest, it was a bit of both.

"You'll come with me then?" I hedged. "To the eastern territory? To speak to the alpha?"

His face screwed up into a scowl. "You can't go there, Allie," he said incredulously. "They wanted you dead, remember?"

"Which is why I thought it might be wise to bring some *backup*," I replied pointedly, jabbing two fingers at him. "Instead of going alone."

"It isn't safe."

"Safe?" I hissed. "What the fuck is safe anymore, Clay? If you can honestly tell me that I'm safer *here,* then go on, say it, and I'll believe you."

He ground his jaw and cut me a scathing glare, some of the redness blooming back into his cheeks.

"I'm right, and you know it."

"*I'll* go."

"Alone? The hell you will. Either we go together or not at all."

"Why didn't you tell Jared any of this?" Clay asked, seemingly out of the blue until I realized I'd also been thinking the same thing pretty much during this entire conversation.

I should have. I knew I should have.

I should have followed him out to the quarry with Clay after we dropped off the girls, and we should have hashed this out together, but...

"You know why," I told him, and he dropped his head.

Not only was Ryland Jared's uncle, but now we knew the lengths Jared was willing to go to keep me safe. My heart ached just thinking about it.

He'd actually threatened Ryland on my behalf. *Threatened* his own uncle. The last living member of his blood related family.

His alpha.

It was why I couldn't find the words to tell him before he left. I was in shock. I was having a hell of a time rectifying what Ryland told me he did with the visual of him in his uncle's office at the quarry, explaining to me how Ry was the one who helped put him back together after his parents were killed.

They shouldn't be the same person, and yet they were.

He was a fucking idiot for threatening his uncle, but wouldn't I have done the same thing for him?

Wasn't what I was doing right now not in some ways *for him*?

If Ryland was what I thought he might be, then I didn't want Jared or anyone else I loved anywhere near him. I didn't need to hurt Jared more than he was already hurting until I had something more concrete to tell him.

That was why I hadn't been able to speak before he left, him pressing his lips gently to mine in a whisper of a kiss before shifting into his wolf and taking to the trees.

"We can't tell him," I said finally, having worked out the best course of action.

"What?" Clay demanded.

"Not yet. Not until we actually have something to show him. Or something more…I don't know, *real* to tell him. He's already on edge. He fucking threatened Ry." I shook my head in disbelief. "I don't want to lie to him, but if we're wrong, then there's no reason to tell him all my half-baked theories."

Clay thought about it, and his nose wrinkled as though he caught a sour odor on the chill breeze. "I don't like it."

"You think I do? I didn't want any of this shit, but here I am, wading through it all the best I can."

Clay grumbled something unintelligible to himself, and I groaned. "So will you come with me or not?"

"Fine," he hissed. "It's not like you're giving me much of a choice."

I narrowed my gaze at him. "I guess I'm not," I agreed. "But I could have not told you anything and just gone alone."

His eyes darkened and after a moment of teeth- grinding silence, he let his shoulders drop and pulled me into his chest. I was surprised enough to squeak out a little chirp of surprise before we collided.

"Thank you," he whispered against my hair in a rare moment of disarm. "For trusting me with this. I'd have fucking lost my shit if you went alone."

I chuckled against his chest. "I know."

I wrapped my arms around him, pressing my cheek into his chest enough that I could hear the hard, steady beating of his heart. The comfort of his nearness nearly made me forget all the terrible, awful thoughts that'd been dancing and swirling in my mind since the full moon.

Here, amid the trees, with Clay's spicy engine grease scent filling my lungs, I could pretend, just for a minute, that everything would be okay.

"When do you want to go?" Clay asked after a few moments, still holding me tightly against him.

"I was thinking tomorrow after school? Ryland hasn't given me orders to get back on rotation with Charity yet, but I'm assuming he will sooner rather than later."

Clay nodded against the top of my head. "What about work?"

"What work?" I asked, my voice dripping sarcasm. "I'm pretty sure I have a voicemail waiting on my phone from my boss that's going to let me permanently off the hook for that."

"Allie—"

"This is more important, anyway. I'll get another job. It's fine."

"But—"

"I don't want to talk about it."

A tight minute of silence followed my snapped reply before Clay softened beneath me once more and my pulse quieted.

"All right," he said, and I could tell he was working hard to sound understanding but there was a tightness around the words that gave away his anger. "We'll have to be back before eleven. I have to meet my sister at the borderlands and escort her onto our territory."

I'd almost completely forgotten his sister was coming. I didn't want to say it but now wasn't exactly the best time for a visit. Judging by his pained expression when I pulled away to look at him, I could tell he was thinking something similar.

"Do you think she'll like me?"

I wasn't sure why I asked; the words came unbidden to my lips and I didn't realize until after I spoke them how much I dreaded hearing the answer to that question. How much I cared.

Sam was Clay's only remaining relative save for Grams, and I still wasn't even clear on whether or not they were blood related or just really close. I wanted her to like me. To approve of the female her big brother mated with.

Clay quirked a brow at me and a slow smirk tugged at one corner of his lips. I'd surprised him. "That's not something I thought you'd care about."

"You didn't answer the question."

He pondered how to respond for a second before speaking, making me even more on edge. "Sam is..."

Clay trailed off, his face pinching. "How do I say she's a bitch without saying she's a bitch because brothers aren't supposed to say that kind of shit about their sisters?"

I chuckled. "Difficult?"

"Yeah. She's difficult. And opinionated. And after...*what happened...* she finally got the mean streak me and pops thought might've skipped her."

"So, she's going to hate me is what you're saying?" I asked, wincing.

Clay bit his bottom lip, considering. My skin warmed and a flush rose to my cheeks. Fuck, why was that so hot?

"I'm saying," Clay corrected. "That you should take everything she says with a massive amount of salt. Who knows? I haven't seen her in a couple years, maybe she's different now."

He said that last part like he didn't believe it even for a second but had at least a sliver of hope that it might be true.

Clay brushed his palm against my cheek, pushing his fingers deep into my hair until he had me firmly in his grasp with a grip on the back of my neck. He tipped my head back so I would look him in the eyes. "Hey," he said, brows lowering. "I don't care what she thinks. Hell, I don't give a fuck what anybody thinks. You're *mine,* and nobody is ever going to change that."

My thighs squeezed and a violent shudder raced down my spine, making a delicious ache spread through my belly.

My lips parted in a silent plea before I could get control of myself. From somewhere deep within, my wolf came to life, flaring in my eyes and growling in my chest.

Mine, she roared.

Clay's irises flared to twin halos of glowing blue, awakening to my desire. Before I could change my mind, I yanked him to me with clawed fingers knotted into the soft fabric of his shirt and crushed my mouth to his, eager to touch—to taste.

His fingers tightened on my neck while his other hand wrapped securely around my middle, helping to lift me onto my tip toes so I wouldn't have to crane my neck to reach him. Wrapping my arms around his neck, I let him in, the kiss no longer a quick theft beneath the moonlight. Clay swept in with his tongue, drawing a moan from my throat and making my whole body clench, pressing into him as tightly as possible.

I couldn't seem to get close enough. A burning desire to remove every bit of barrier between us had my hands pulling and tugging. Removing his shirt and then mine. Our lips were apart for only a second and it was too long.

I rushed back to him, hungry and grasping. His warm hands gripped my sides, fingers splayed over the back of my bare ribs.

It felt *so* good. I never wanted it to stop.

His lips kissed a hard path down my neck, stopping just above my breasts. A small sound left my lips with my heavy breaths, something like a whine or a pained moan.

I delved my fingers into Clay's dark hair, trying to tell him it was okay—that I didn't want him to hold back. I didn't want him to stop.

His lips brushed over the swell of my left breast and my back arched at the violent sensation that rocked me all the way to my core. The tether linking us together vibrated with tension and heat, getting tighter— *stronger*—the further we went.

I fumbled with the zipper of his jeans, and his grip on my ribs went rigid.

"We can't," he whispered against my neck; the brush of his breath against the tender flesh there driving me insane. "The rules..."

"Fuck the rules."

Clay growled, lifting my feet from the ground. My back knocked into the rough, mossy bark of a tree, and I glared down into the heated gaze of my mate. A war raged beneath his stare. With each puff of hot air clouding the space between our lips, I knew he was considering how much he could bend the rule without breaking it.

I knew because I was thinking it, too.

He leaned in for a rough kiss and pulled back, chest heaving. "I don't think I'll be able to stop," he gritted out through clenched teeth.

The truth was, I wasn't sure if I would be strong enough to stop it, either, but I was beyond caring.

Clay began to robotically pry himself from me and my chest ached with his loss. I knew he was right, but that didn't mean I had to like it.

"Sleep with me," I blurted before he could fully disentangle himself from me. "I mean—not like *that*. Just...sleep."

I hadn't been able to shut my mind off for days. Maybe with him there I could finally get the rest I desperately needed. Tackle tomorrow with a clear head.

Clay's jaw clenched. "I don't cuddle."

I smirked, turning on the pouty eyes. Vivian always said no one could ever say no to me with that look. "For me?"

Clay rolled his eyes, and I grinned, knowing that even the strong and grouchy Clay wasn't impervious to my exaggerated pleading. "Fine."

I began to consider all the different ways I could make this more painful for him. Sleeping nude may have an interesting effect.

Maybe he'd break the rules for me after all.

Clay shook his head. "*Clothed*," he amended, taking the wind from my sails.

I smirked at him. "You're no fun."

"You're going to be the death of me, woman."

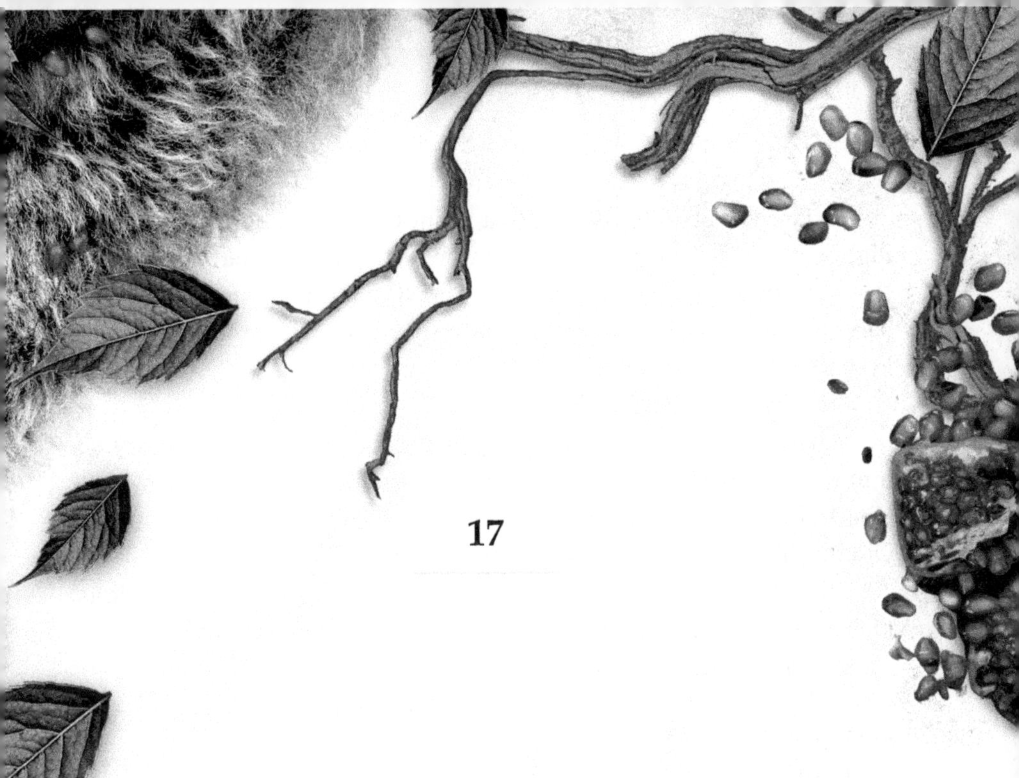

17

It was amazing how much control you could have when you were worried about someone else's more than your own. Monday at school was a shitshow of epic proportions. Even though Layla and Viv had both shifted and run *forty miles* this morning before dawn, they both had a couple near misses throughout the day.

Viv nearly bit off another girl's head in field practice and had to fake a stomachache to get out of participating. And Layla, stuck fending off Quinn's advances all day, nearly snapped her very canine jaws at him in the cafeteria. I expertly shifted the attention to myself with a rather dramatic sweep of my arm across the table, *accidentally* sending all of our lunches falling to the scuffed floor.

We had to get new lunches, which I grudgingly had to pay for, but at least it gave Layla the minute of peace to get control of herself and very politely tell Quinn she *needed some time to herself.*

Miraculously, she didn't seem to have a problem at home with her brothers and sisters.

"It's like my wolf knows them," she explained. "Like it knows it can't hurt them."

She'd shrugged.

"I don't get it, but I don't think being at home is going to be as hard as I thought it would be. School on the other hand…"

Vivian wasn't so lucky. She had to lock herself in her room for the night to keep from barking at her father when he wandered in drunk, but that was par for the course for a Monday night for her. She'd shrugged too, telling me that it was only a little harder than usual to keep from eating him alive.

She'd laughed. I didn't.

When I broke out of my thoughts, telling myself not to worry so much about them, I found Clay watching me curiously. My arms were elbow deep in soapy dishwater, and I gazed without seeing out the window above the sink to the darkening sky outside.

Clay slouched against the counter to my right, a strange, curious look dipping his brows low and pulling at a corner of his mouth.

"What?" I asked, a flush creeping up my neck.

"I don't know what you did to me, but I haven't slept as good as I did last night since I was a kid."

I smiled at that.

I couldn't remember the last time I'd slept as peacefully, either. Except maybe the time I awoke to find Jared curled at the edge of my bed. But this was different. Clay had tucked me in tight against his chest, curling and bending to form his body to mine as though he was the mold and I was the putty.

And I *was* the putty. The way I'd melted into him...

I couldn't be sure, but after the first few moments of trepidation and desire waned, giving way to exhaustion, I was probably asleep within seconds.

His level breaths expanded and contracted against my back. His warm breath caressed my hair. My wolf was in her absolute bliss.

I mean, she might've been happier if he'd given in to us in the woods, but it was the next best thing, so she didn't complain much.

"Good," I told him and bit my lower lip. "I haven't either," I admitted.

His eyes widened. "Maybe..." he trailed off, lifting a hand to rub the back of his neck. "Maybe we could—"

"Just admit it," I teased, flicking bubbles at him. "You *liked* it."

His face twisted into a scowl.

"My big scary mate is actually just a giant teddy bear who likes to cuddle."

His fists clenched. "Take that back." I shook my head. "Nope."

Before I could blink, he was there, one hand on my back and the other plunged into the soapy water. I barely had time to gasp before he splashed water and bubbles all over my face and shirt.

I blinked through the wetness and suds to find him several paces away, grinning like a fool.

"This doesn't change anything," I said, advancing as he retreated up the stairs, away from my dreams of retaliation. "You're still my little cuddle bunches!" I called after him, groaning as I shook my arms, flicking the wetness off the ends of my fingers.

"*Bastard.*"

I heard the shower turn on upstairs and went back to the sink to finish washing up the last few dishes from dinner, secretly hoping that using the water down here would fuck with his temperature up there.

Bugger deserved it.

My phone pinged in my back pocket, and I dried my hands quickly before drawing it out. A message from Clay flashed across the screen.

Clay: I've been called a lot of things. Cuddle bunches is by far the worst.

I began thumbing out a reply, a smirk on my lips,

when my phone pinged again.

Clay: I'll be ready in ten.

Five words and I was right back to where I was earlier today when I got home. On edge and flighty. The caged bird living in my chest trying to break free all over again.

The questions I'd been asking myself all day replayed like an interrogation reel in my head.

What if the wolves from the eastern pack attack us? What if one of us gets hurt?

What if they *are* to blame for the missing wolves? And...

...what if they are not?

If they aren't then that didn't necessarily mean it was Ryland's doing, but it'd be one more tick on the proverbial tally chart on his side.

I huffed out a breath and willed my thrumming pulse to slow.

Allie: I'll wait outside.

Before I could finish the last two dishes, my screen flashed with another message from the countertop. I leaned over to see it was Clay again even though the shower was still running.

Clay: Don't go far.

I rolled my eyes and emptied the sink, guzzling a tall glass of water in preparation for the long run. A run that would normally take us less than an hour would take us nearly two tonight. We'd decided to double back and leave a dummy trail before retracing our steps and cutting through the river.

I shuddered. It was probably colder than ice by now. But it would be worth it if we were right. We couldn't have anyone be able to track where we went. It would raise too many questions that we didn't have the answers to. Not yet anyway.

Deciding to play nice this time, I stripped down to bare skin before the bathroom light in the cabin went out and set my folded clothes on the bottom step of the porch.

"All right girl," I cooed to my wolf. "Your turn."

She surged to the surface, pushing me back so she could take control of the reins. The pain lasted only a brief second before I was staring out through lupine eyes at the sharpness of the evening right after sunset.

We padded around in a circle, wanting to run, but also knowing we needed to wait for Clay. It felt... different this time. I couldn't put my finger on exactly what it was, but my skin felt more sensitive and my movements more jarring.

By the time Clay came outside another minute later, in nothing but a pair of loose khakis, I figured out what it was.

I was still very much *here*. Normally, my wolf tucked me into the back of my own mind like a lone sock tucked into the back of a drawer because it didn't have a match.

Not this time.

My legs felt strong. My chest cavity wide. I felt the outer edges of my being like I'd never felt them before. Foreign but also fitting. Like a coat you forgot you had that fit just like the first day you bought it.

Charity was right.

Hey, Clay's deep timbre rumbled through my thoughts, and I whipped my head up to find him loping down the stairs, doing a lazy circle around me as though appraising me. *You good?*

Great, I replied before taking off at a sprint, eager to feel the push and flex of the earth being chewed beneath my paws.

Clay caught up to me easily and we ran side by side through the night to the east.

Pace yourself, Clay whispered in my thoughts after we got a few miles in. *It's going to be a long night.*

I grinned inwardly.

What? I teased. *Do you need me to slow down? Smartass.*

CLAY HAD BEEN RIGHT AFTER ALL. BY THE TIME WE WERE NEARING THE EASTERN border after doubling back, leaving the dummy trail, and taking the long way around back through the river, I was dead tired.

We paused for a drink in the icy water and most of my drink splashed out of my mouth and dripped down my chin. Wholly unable to close my mouth for the raucous breaths sawing in and out in clouds from my jowls.

Told you, Clay said, and I growled at him.

How much further?

We're nearly there already, Clay told me. *The borders to their territory are just through that copse of trees there.*

He inclined his head toward a thicket, where a natural break was formed to almost look like a doorway. Enchanting and menacing at the same time.

It's not too late to turn back, you know, Clay added.

You're worn out, maybe it isn't such a good idea to—

We're going in, I pressed. I did not almost kill myself running for the past two hours straight just to chicken out now that we were here. If there were answers to be had on the other side of that copse of trees, I would have them one way or the other.

Clay didn't speak, he just looked on toward the entry to foreign territory as though considering his options.

Is there, like, a protocol or something we need to follow?

Or do we just walk through.

He turned his head back to me, his bright blue eyes looking even brighter surrounded by the dark gray— near black—fur of his wolf. I wasn't sure how it was possible, but even in this form, he was drop dead gorgeous. Muscled and wide shouldered with a handsome lupine face. Or maybe it was just my wolf thinking he was attractive?

Who knew.

Normally we'd require permission to enter another pack's territory, but since we can't do that because it requires alpha consent, we're going to have to walk in without it.

Is that dangerous? Can be.

Care to elaborate?

Clay dropped his head and scraped at the dirt with his paw. *Ry keeps wolves at our borders, they run the perimeter. Most packs do that. If one crosses into our boundaries and is caught, they are usually given an opportunity to turn around and leave.*

So you're saying we just go in there, ask permission to enter and if they say no...what? We just have to leave?

Not all packs give foreign wolves the opportunity to leave peacefully.

So...?

If they won't hear us out and they won't give us an opportunity to leave without a fight, then I want you to run. There will only be one—maybe two—running the perimeter. I'll take care of them and then meet you back at the cabin. Run and don't stop until you get there.

I'm not going to leav—

You agree or we walk away right now and forget this whole idiotic idea.

I simpered, holding back a snarl. Why did he always have to be so goddamned infuriating? *Fine.*

Good.

Great.

I followed him as he began to move toward the opening, grumbling internally about how I planned to punish him for this and what an absolute fucking pain in my ass he was.

You know I can still hear you, right? He spoke in my thoughts, and it was like I could see the sarcasm dripping from each consonant and vowel.

I growled. *How the hell do I turn it off?*

No reply.

I did my best to sever the connection myself, thinking about things other than Clay. It seemed to do the trick because by the time we crossed the imaginary line between the two lines of trees, there were only my own thoughts in my head again.

Clay paused about fifteen paces in, rocking back to sit on his haunches.

Now what? Now we wait.

It didn't take long. Within less than five minutes we could hear the telltale sounds of another animal in the forest. Thudding footfalls sending fallen leaves scattering in their wake. The unmistakable heavy breathing of a wolf.

Clay moved, placing himself slightly in front of me while keeping our backs to the border crossing for an easy exit.

Let me do the talking, Clay said just as flashes of movement could be seen hurtling in this direction through the darkened wood.

The wolf slowed, catching sight of us, and lifted his head back in a long howl.

Shit.

Shit. Shit. Shit.

How long would it take for all his eastern pack buddies to come running?

Clay?

I know.

Clay shifted in the blink of an eye, standing in a channel of moonlight. His naked body spotted with dirt and coated in a fine layer of sweat that made him glisten as though his skin was dusted with a metallic powder.

"We aren't here for a fight," Clay called at the wolf, who remained partially hidden in the shadows about thirty paces away. "We have come to request an audience with your alpha. Will you allow us entry?"

A silence so tense and thick hung in the air between them—the question going unanswered for so long that I had to quint my canine eyes to make sure the other wolf was even still there.

A low whine rolled off my tongue. I didn't like this.

We should go.

I nipped at Clay's ankle, trying to get his attention, imploring him to understand my plea. He needed to shift back. He was too vulnerable in his human flesh.

He held a hand out in an attempt to tell me to be still.

Like hell that was going to work.

But just before I could nip him again, harder this time, a flash of dark skin caught my eye, and I peered into the trees where the lone wolf had been hiding to find he'd shifted, too. A tall black man with bright eyes and lips any god or goddess would kill for stepped from the darkness and into the light.

God. When was I going to get used to seeing people naked all the time?

I'd seen more dicks in the past two months than I had in my entire life before now.

"For what purpose?" The man called, his voice colored with a light accent. Southern, maybe? I was shit at figuring out accents. "Permission has not been granted for your entry to these lands."

Clay clenched his fists and I braced myself, coming back to the surface.

My turn.

"Permission couldn't be requested," I said, my voice a tight groan after the shift left me with stars in my eyes and an aching back. I let those words hang in the air, trying to let this guy catch on to their meaning without my having to say it outright that we didn't exactly trust our alpha.

The man's bright eyes narrowed at me and then widened, recognizing who I was. I don't know why the two tails hadn't set him off, but somehow my human form did. Must be the turquoise hair...even though I had a good three inches of new silvery blond growth at my crown now.

Clay's fist clenched at his side. I knew if I could hear his thoughts, I wouldn't like what I heard, but he let me speak.

"You're the twin soul wolf," he said, speaking the name as though it were a moniker of legend or myth.

"The what?"

"The twin soul wolf. The girl who bonded to two of our kind. Who has two tails. *You're*...you're part of Ryland's pack."

"Bravo," Clay said with an annoyed tone. "Your powers of observation are astounding."

"*Clay,*" I scolded.

"Look man," Clay pushed on. "We came for an audience with your alpha. If you don't plan to grant us one *and* promise our protection for the duration of the time we spend here, then I'd rather get the fuck out of dodge before your buddies get here."

The other man considered Clay, eyes flitting over his height and brawn before his gaze slid back to me. "I'll grant it for the girl," he said finally. "You may wait at the border for her return."

"Not a fucking—"

"Done," I chirped.

Clay whirled on me, his face turning from bright red to deathly pale and back again in the span of a single second. A vein in his temple jumped. "*No.*"

"*Yes.*"

"Allie—"

"I came here for answers, and I'm going to get them, Clay. This—hey, what's your name?"

"Toby."

"This *Toby* guy is offering me exactly what we came here for."

It could have been a trick of the light, but I swear I saw his hands begin to shake.

"I can't let you go alone. Don't ask me to."

"I'm not asking."

His expression shifted, his face going momentarily slack as though I'd slapped him.

"If I told you I'd make sure he behaved, would you let him come with me?" I asked, calling the question to Toby without any hope of him giving me that request.

Toby didn't even consider it. "No."

I shrugged, sighing as I let my gaze fall back to Clay. "I tried."

"You swear that she'll be returned to me here, *unharmed* in *any* way."

"By the old laws and the new, you have the word of my pack that she will be returned unharmed," Toby replied, none too politely, crossing his arms over his chest.

"There," I said. "Better?" I brushed my hand against Clay's biceps to get his attention and he reeled back from my touch, casting me a look I couldn't decipher before he stormed away, back toward the border. My chest ached at his rejection.

Didn't he understand that we had to do this?

The alpha of this pack may have wanted me dead a few weeks ago when I was still unclaimed, but he would be an idiot to try to cut me down now. He'd have a war on his hands. A war that he would have no hope whatsoever of winning.

"You have one hour," he warned without turning. "One hour, and I'll end anyone who stands in my way of getting to her."

When Toby didn't voice a reply, Clay paused and turned slightly, just enough to see Toby from the corner of his eye, but not far enough for me to catch his expression. "*Is that clear?*"

"There will be no need," Toby said diplomatically, now clearing the distance between us.

Clay shifted back into his wolf and launched himself through the opening, vanishing on the other side, back into our territory. I knew he wouldn't go far, but without him there to bolster my courage, my pulse began to pound in my ears as Toby shifted back into his wolf form and nudged his head forward. Onward.

Time to go.

With one last glance back to see if I could catch a glimpse of Clay standing sentinel outside, I shifted back and followed Toby, guilt, disappointment, and my own dark thoughts my only companions on the short run.

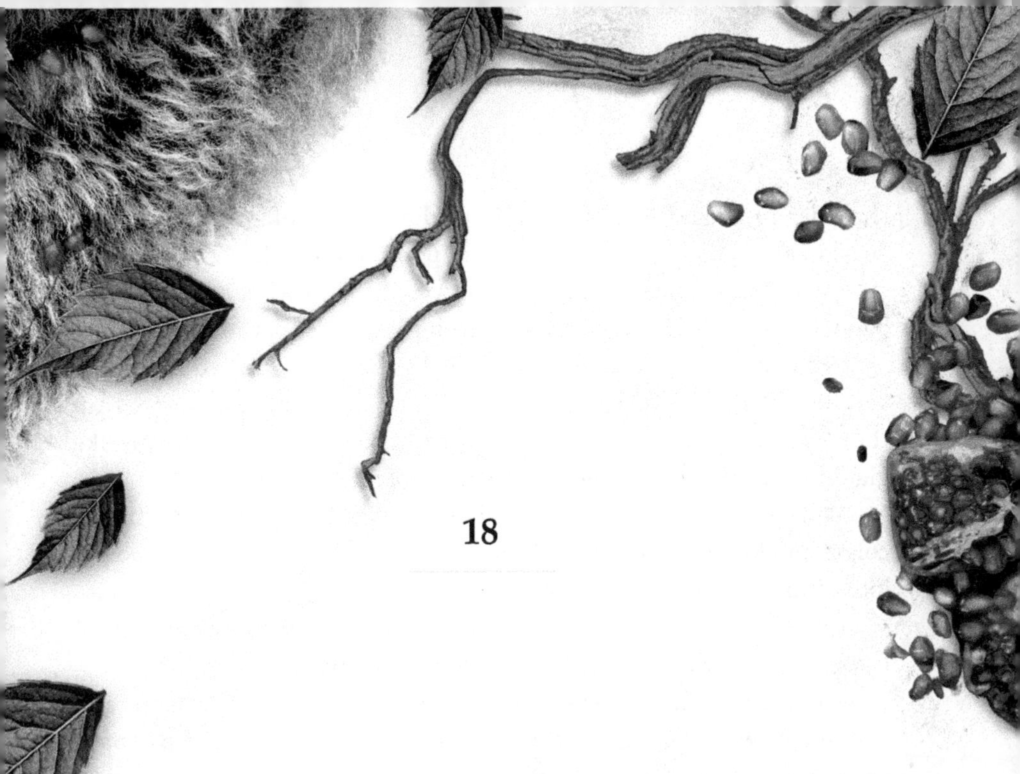

18

Toby's packmates caught up to us on our way. There was a fleeting moment of blood curdling fear as they descended upon us, but then Toby must have communicated with them the deal he'd cut to allow me entry.

I couldn't be sure because I couldn't hear their thoughts. I tried to speak to one of them and tried to listen in, but heard nothing. I figured it must be a pack thing. Like, one pack couldn't get into the heads of another pack. Maybe Jared had told me this already and I'd just forgotten.

But...distantly, I remembered hearing several thoughts the night I was turned and at that time I was not pack. And I could hear my mates' thoughts too, but I assumed that was different.

Maybe they were just blocking me like I'd managed to block Clay earlier at the river.

Toby's matte light-gray wolf slowed, along with the two russet ones on either side of his flank. I slowed with them as we approached what I had to assume was their pack camp.

Fire smoke drifted on the breeze, mingling with a distinct and over-powering foreign animal scent that made my wolf wrinkle her nose. I kept close to Toby as a tall wooden wall came into view.

It had to be at least thirteen feet high, built of wide logs all standing shoulder to shoulder. It went in both directions as far as I could see, curving gently to make a large circle, or perhaps an oval.

I caught my breath, chest heaving as Toby howled and a hidden gateway in the wall swung open, revealing a glimpse of the interior.

What at first glance I thought were weird tents turned out to be various sizes of yurts. Fat bottomed and tapering up to a pointed tip they sat clumped together in places and spaced apart in others, like giant forest fungus or some strange genus of mushroom.

Wolves and humans milled about inside, many wearing bright colors and loose fitted clothes. Thin raw-leather vests and headbands. It looked like the seventies never left this place, if you know what I mean.

And that strange scent on the air I thought was just the smell of foreign wolves revealed itself to be that and something more. Pot.

The skunky odor was easily distinguishable now, and if that weren't enough it was clear from the cluster of three of the eastern pack slouching against the inside of the wall passing a joint around as we entered.

I willed my pulse to stop racing and tried to quiet my mind.

Get in. Get answers. Get out.

The door was pressed shut behind us, and I whirled, holding back a growl as I took in the woman hefting a large wooden plank into place to bar it shut. My tail pressed between my legs and my lip pulled back over my teeth.

"Annie," a familiar voice called, and I spun, antsy and skidding to one side as I took in Toby back in his human form. "Get Adam. The twin soul wolf is here for an audience, and she doesn't have much time."

I relaxed, if only a little, but I wasn't ready to shift yet. I was weak in my human form. Like this, with my wolf holding the reins, I was stronger. Safer. I knew I wouldn't exactly be able to have a conversation like this, but I wouldn't leave myself vulnerable for a single minute longer than I needed to.

It was what Clay would have wanted me to do, I was sure of it.

At the thought of him waiting alone out in the woods, my heart clenched.

Clay? I tried, projecting the thought as forcibly as I could. I needed to know if he could still hear me.

Can you hear me?

Only the echo of my own voice rebounded in my skull. I swallowed hard and my skin bristled. I was alone.

"You idiot," the woman called Annie chastised Toby. "Why the hell would you agree to that?"

"Just get him," Toby snapped back at her. "I think he may want to hear what she has to say."

Toby cut his bright eyes back to me, as though imploring me to have something worthwhile to tell his alpha. I got the feeling he'd be punished if Adam didn't like what I had to say.

Would he be disappointed that I merely came to ask a question that I was fairly certain I already knew the answer to?

I hoped not.

And looking around it was more and more clear to me that I was right without even needing to ask Adam.

There were maybe a total of twenty shifters in the camp that I could see and that was being *very* generous. But that wasn't the dead give-away. They were all so...

So... Peaceful.

A small group played the banjo and sang to a trio of children near a low burning fire in the distance. A pair of younger girls sat together, scribbling in notebooks or maybe sketching.

A few cooked in an open-air kitchen near the fire, and the rest sat or laid in various states of blissful high around the remaining grounds.

These were not people looking for a fight with their neighbors. Nor were they people who would attempt to pick off our numbers one by one without hope of repercussion.

If Adam told me otherwise, I'd call him a liar.

That was when a few flaws in my plan began to emerge from my muddied thoughts.

They could lie to me.

Who was to say that just because I asked if it were them who'd been picking off our numbers that they would tell me the truth?

And who was to say that they wouldn't turn around and tell Ryland themselves that I came here without permission, asking treasonous questions.

Fuck.

Why didn't Clay think of any of this? Jared would've.

Damnit.

Clay was right. We should have told Jared. He should have been a part of this.

I fucked up.

I totally and royally fucked up.

Maybe I should just leave now, say it was all a mistake.

"The twin soul wolf," someone called, and I stilled, recognizing the voice. It was the same voice that'd called for my execution that night at the Four Corners. The same alpha who fled instead of standing and fighting.

He stared at me beneath heavy lidded eyes. His long beard hid most of his face from me. He could have been smiling, or he could be snarling, and I wouldn't be able to tell for the thick bush of salt and pepper hair. He wore a white tunic and loose tan pants. His feet were bare.

He looked for all the world like he was about to welcome me into his commune for an hour of beer yoga. Only his eyes spoke of his status here. Heated. Wide pupils ringed with burning hazel irises.

"Welcome to my territory," he spat like a curse, training a furious stare on Toby who said nothing but dropped his head in shame.

"Well," Adam hissed. "Do you want this audience or not, girl? I heard you have a lad waiting who's primed to explode if you don't return in the next forty minutes."

I wasn't sure if I *did* want to have this meeting anymore, but I was here now. Too late to back out.

I held in a pained cry as I shifted back, the transformation slower going for the fourth time in a day. I cringed to think how the fifth time would treat me when we got home. At least there was a hot bath waiting there.

I clenched my fists against the urge to cover my nakedness from view and forced my spine erect. "Thank you," I managed. "For giving me an—"

"This way," Adam said without letting me finish, waving an arm at me to follow him. "You too, Toby," he added. "I'd like a word with you when our *visitor* departs."

I offered Toby an impish grin, and his face pinched, falling into step behind me as I followed Adam to one of the larger yurts not in a cluster but set apart, with its own little herb garden outside.

Scratch that. Pot garden. With its own little *pot garden* outside.

Adam went inside, holding back a thin white flap for us to follow him. On entry, my senses were assaulted with a myriad of colors and smells. Jasmine and sandalwood. Sage and juniper.

There were patterned carpets and fuzzy blankets of every color. Orange leather and wicker and thick, chunky lace drapes. If I didn't know any better, I'd have guessed the entrance to the yurt was actually a portal through time.

And Adam just sort of blended in with it all. He folded himself down into a wicker seat with bits of the straw-like material fraying and broken in places. It was a wonder the thing didn't collapse under his weight.

"Sit," he ordered Toby, jutting his chin to a chair set next to his, with a small tree stump table placed between them.

He offered me no seat, though if I were being honest, I preferred to remain standing anyway.

Adam gave me one long up and down look, making me shudder and want to cover all the bits and pieces I'd been taught to keep hidden my entire life until now.

He jabbed two fingers at a patterned blue and black blanket cast haphazardly on a lumpy bed jammed against the other side of the yurt. "You can put that on if you want, then I suggest you get talking so we can get you back to your friend before he has a fit."

Grateful, I rushed over and draped the thick blanket over my shoulders, tugging it closed at my front. I tried to ignore the faint scent of body odor clinging to it. It was better than being ass naked in front of two strange men.

Though Toby didn't seem to mind one bit.

"Get on with it, girl," Adam urged, slouching back in his chair with a huff.

An annoyed flush crawled into my cheeks. Now that I was here, exactly where I wanted to be, the question seemed foolish. I knew it wasn't their doing, but maybe they could still give me information I could use. Among the other wolves who had joined our pack after Ryland killed their alphas, there had been a few who seemed to *know* things about Ryland. And it was *those* wolves—supposedly—who'd gone missing.

Maybe there were shifters here who knew some of those things, too.

"Several wolves have vanished from our pack," I began, trying to keep the acid from leaking into my tone. I didn't like how either of them were looking at me. How they were speaking to me. I lifted my chin and waited to see if they would take the bait, tell me something.

Adam's brows lowered at the open-ended statement. "Are you accusing us of something?"

I wasn't exactly sure how to answer that, so I continued, choosing to ignore his question. "They've vanished without a trace. We've searched for weeks, to the outer edges of our borders and far beyond them where we could. They left no trail. Nothing."

His eyes narrowed further, and he made a considering sound in his throat, thinking through something. "And you've come all this way to tell me this...why?"

I swallowed. "Originally, I came to ask if you had something to do with it," I admitted, watching his lips part in surprise, but I wasn't finished. "Since that is what my alpha would have the rest of our pack believe."

The tiniest smirk shifted Adam's beard. His eyes crinkled. "Is that so?'

I nodded.

"It seems he failed to convince at least one of his pack. Maybe two."

I nodded again.

"Let me guess..." Adam trailed off, plunging his thumb and index finger into his beard to rub his chin in an exaggerated pose of thoughtfulness. "These shifters who went missing, they opposed him in some way? Perhaps they knew things about him that they shouldn't have?"

My throat went instantly bone dry, and my stomach dropped.

I prayed that this shifter wouldn't turn around on me and tell Ryland that I came here and everything I said, because the way this conversation was headed, if he did, I was certain I would be the next wolf to vanish into thin air.

"They did," I agreed, wetting my lips. "Or at least, I think they might've."

A long silence stretched between us where I think both were waiting for the other to add something to the conversation. Maybe he didn't want to incriminate himself in case *I* intended to run back to Ryland and tell him all Adam's theories and accusations.

I needed to give him something. Something that would make him trust me.

But that something could also get me killed if he decided to share it.

I inhaled deeply, trying to draw strength in with the oxygen. "I think he killed them."

Adam's eyes widened in surprise, though I didn't think it was because of what I said. More that I'd actually said it.

I couldn't hardly believe I'd allowed the words through my thoughts, never mind freed them from my mouth. I didn't realize *how much* I actually believed it until I voiced my worry aloud.

Adam dropped his gaze, thinking for a moment before he replied.

"You're smart, I'll give you that," Adam said on the back of a sigh. "But also foolish if you think he won't find out you've come here. He has spies everywhere.

And that *damned* vamp friend of his can draw secrets out of anyone with his compulsion."

"I know the risks."

"Bravery is all well and good girl, until it gets you killed."

This coming from the alpha who fled, allowing two of his own shifters to be killed. Hell, the one I killed could have been one of his. I wasn't sure. Though he seemed utterly unconcerned about that.

My so-called bravery may get me killed, but at least I would go down fighting for something. For people I loved. To make sure they are safe.

He was more likely to be stabbed in the back rather than stand his ground against an enemy.

"If I remember correctly, you were the one who wanted me dead at the Four Corners."

Another twitch of his beard, though this time I couldn't tell if he was smirking or scowling. "Aye."

"Then don't fucking preach to me about bravery and risk," I snapped, feeling my wolf surface briefly before settling back down. "I came here for some answers and you can take comfort in knowing that those answers—*should you choose to share them with me*— will more than likely see me to an early grave."

He nodded appreciatively. "True," he agreed, leaning forward to steeple his fingers, pressing his elbows into his knees. "Though I'm starting to think perhaps I was wrong about you."

"Thanks?" I said sarcastically. "That's comforting."

Adam dropped his steepled fingers and sat back once more. "Very well. I'll tell you what I know if you're that determined to hear it, but I do not guarantee the veracity of any of it. Rumors travel through shifters just as swiftly—*and unreliably*—as they do through mortals."

"I understand. Tell me everything you know."

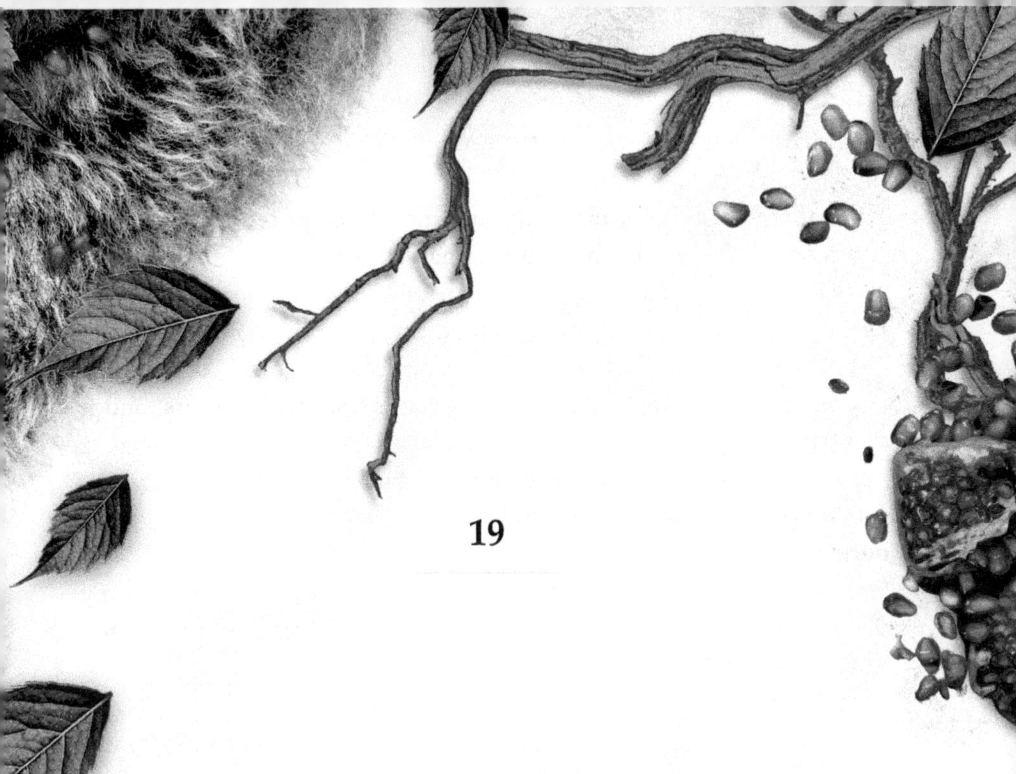

19

We made it back to the border with barely a minute to spare. Clay's wolf was there, steaming in the chill of the evening as he paced, only stilling when he was able to see me in full view.

Adam accompanied Toby and I back to the border. He shifted back to his human form just before I crossed back over to my own territory.

"Don't come back here," he warned. "And if Ryland should ever find out you came here, I will deny everything I told you tonight."

Coward, I thought, and my wolf snarled a little before I could get her in check.

"In fact, I will tell your alpha that you came here for some other nefarious purpose and leave you to clean up whatever mess that makes."

Total fucking coward.

I bobbed my canine head and loped back through the break in the trees, but I didn't feel any less shaky with unease once my paws touched the earth on my own turf. Much the opposite.

My stomach was roiling and my head spinning since leaving the eastern pack camp. Adam hadn't had a massive amount to tell me, but what he had told me... well, let's just say that I was praying it wasn't true.

That the rumor mill birthed it and mouth to ear transit twisted it, turning it even more vile than the original whisper.

Because if it were true... If it were true, I'd kill him.

I may not have been able to defend myself to the point of murder with Devin, but I sure as hell wouldn't hesitate this time. All I needed was one shred of proof of any *one* of Adam's apparent 'rumors' and it would be enough for me.

I peered back and watched Adam shift back, his wolf giving me one last long look before he and Toby turned tail and began the short journey back to camp.

I hope it was worth it, Clay's voice slithered dangerously into my mind and my muscles clenched. There was so much more in that sentence than what it was at face value.

In his voice, I could hear betrayal. Pain. Anger.

He was clearly still pissed at me for leaving him, and I couldn't fault him for it. I didn't have the energy to. Not right now. I needed to process. To decide what the fuck to do with the information I was given.

Well, Clay pressed after a moment. *Are you going to tell me what he said?*

I lifted my face to the wrathful, watchful glare of Clay's burning blue eyes.

I...I don't know where to start.

Some of the fire ebbed away, and he stalked closer, peering through the gap to where Toby and Adam had only just retreated.

Did they hurt you? If they hurt you— No. They didn't hurt me.

At least not in any physical way. Though I was sure my heart and mind would bear the scars of what they told me for as long as it took me to either prove them wrong, or prove them right.

Then what is it?

We should go, I told Clay. *Your sister will be waiting for you. I'll...I'll do my best to explain on the way. I need to move.*

My wolf itched to sprint. She was angry and confused just as I was. We needed to run from those demons, just for a little while. We needed to feel light, or else the heaviness would anchor us in place, and we might never move again.

I didn't wait for Clay to reply. I took off like a round loosed from the barrel of a gun. Clay barely needed more than a few seconds to catch up with me.

He waited, matching my pace, for me to be ready to talk.

I could still sense his rage, but beneath that was something else. Worry.

Good, I thought. *He should be worried.*

For a full five minutes of hard and fast sprinting, I focused only on shielding my thoughts from Clay. I had to think of the best way to tell him all that I needed to, and there was one thing in particular that I couldn't breathe aloud to him. If I did...I didn't think Clay would wait to gather the proof we needed before acting.

Hell, even what I did plan to tell him was enough to send him over the edge. It damn near did for me. The entire run from the eastern camp to the border was spent picturing all the ways I would tear Ryland apart.

It was those *very comforting* images—those promises to myself— that calmed me enough to even consider not going straight to my alpha and demanding the truth in front of the whole pack.

Except...that would end badly for me. I knew it would.

Just like it would end badly for Clay if he were the one to do it.

We have no proof of any of this, I prefaced the first shared thought between our minds. *Adam said himself that all he knows are rumors—that it's possible none of it is even true.*

No reply.

First, they have nothing to do with the missing shifters. How do you know?

Trust me. If there's anything I'm sure of, it's that.

A pause.

Okay. Fine. So what did he tell you then?

I grimaced and relayed all that I could, feeling my gut twist as I spoke. It was so terrible I hardly wanted to say it aloud, let alone tell Clay. It seemed preposterous. A cruel fabrication.

He'd told me that Ryland had his sights set on being alpha of the Forest Grove pack since long before Adam had become alpha of the eastern pack about twenty years ago.

Rumor had it that Ryland had a...*disagreement* with his brother— Jared's father about who was going to succeed him should he fall.

Furious that his brother, Noah, wouldn't leave the pack in his hands, he requested permission to leave the Forest Grove pack and was granted it.

Ryland supposedly ran with a northern pack for a good number of years before returning to Forest Grove, requesting to come home to his pack.

By then his brother had had a son. Jared.

Noah brought Ryland back into the fold and they became brothers once more. Ryland became an uncle to his nephew and indispensable to the pack. But not quite as indispensable as Thomas Armstrong.

That's all true, Clay spoke in my mind. *At least, as far as I know.*

This is where it gets really bad.

The rumors from way back then, all but snuffed out by now, said that Ryland had his own brother murdered along with his wife. The whispers said that he made it look like an accident with the help of a certain vampire friend. They said that he had them shot and skinned to make it look like mortal hunters did it.

Clay's tension rolled off him in waves. I could sense his confusion. His disbelief. And the beginning of a raging fire sparking to life within him. It was a match for my own.

Clay didn't speak. He only waited for me to go on.

From what Adam explained to me, it sounds like Ryland thought that he would be handed the mantle of alpha once his brother was removed from the picture.

But he wasn't, Clay growled in my thoughts. *My father was.*

Were you there then? You would have been so young. I was.

But your sister—

Wasn't, Clay finished for me. I remembered he said Ryland never met her.

There's a lot you don't know about me, Allie, Clay grunted, pushing himself harder and faster as he ran, forcing me to push myself harder too just to keep pace.

What does that mean?

I guess you might as well know, he said, *since you're going to meet her. My sister wasn't a born wolf. She was mortal, like my mom.*

My eyes widened. He'd never really talked about his sister. Hell, I didn't even know he had one until last week. Now, I could see why he never told me about her. His entire body was wired for sound just trying to get out whatever he was trying to say.

She was attacked. Raped. And bitten. Oh my god.

Yeah.

After I killed the bastard who did it, she turned. She and Ma were living up North and after I...did what I did...she didn't want to come to Forest Grove. She found a pack up north and took care of Ma until she passed.

I wondered how he lost his mother but didn't think now was the time to ask.

She knew about our kind, of course. She never *wanted to be like us. She hated shifters. Was terrified of us. It was part of the reason Ma left in the first place, to take her away. To make her feel safe.*

I could feel his pain like a gut punch to my own stomach.

I'm so sorry...

Clay made a strangled half laugh sound in my thoughts and his deep voice rumbled again through my head. *I just told you I murdered someone and that's all you have to say?*

I frowned. Fuck. I honestly hadn't even questioned it. What was I becoming that the casual mention of murder barely phased me? I swallowed back the ugly thought and lifted my head. Shook it.

No. It wasn't wrong. Not for the reasons he did it.

The truth rose up my throat like a brand, but I managed to get the words out anyway. *I'm glad you did it,* I hissed. *He didn't deserve to live.*

Clay ground his claws into the earth, coming to a jarring standstill as dirt was thrown in a wave over the brush. I skidded to a stop, too, breathing heavily.

His burning ice gaze found mine, and he stared openly at me, his head lowered and nostrils flaring with great clouds of steam.

The guy was only sixteen, he snarled. *He already had a pup. A mate.*

I knew what he was doing, but I wasn't going to let him. He wouldn't make himself out to be the monster. Not to me.

And your sister had a life that was taken from her.

I mean *fuck,* it was no wonder she had a temper. I would, too.

Clay tossed his head to the side, making a disgusted sound in his throat.

You can beat yourself up about it all you want, I all but shouted into his head, *but I'm not buying it. You can pretend to yourself that you're some monster, Clay, but I know better.*

I'd killed too. I put down that shifter at the Four Corners without blinking. He was a threat to my friends. He might've killed them.

I didn't know if he had a family, or a mate. But I knew one thing...

I'd do it again.

It may not be the same thing as what Clay did. I'd killed that shifter in the heat of the moment. In defense.

He'd clearly gone looking for the shifter who'd attacked his sister. It wasn't defense. It was vengeance.

That didn't mean it wasn't deserved.

Finish what you were telling me, Clay said, moving back into a walk. We were nearly back at the cabin now. A few more miles and we'd be back on our doorstep.

I bristled, wishing he would talk to me more about what had happened. He didn't need to carry the weight of it alone. But I wouldn't push him. I'd wait until he was ready, and one day, I would make him see that what he did wasn't wrong.

It was justice in a world where most don't get theirs.

If he hadn't done what he'd done, then who was to say that bastard wouldn't have done it again. That he wouldn't have done it over and over *and over.*

That's pretty much it, I explained. *There was already a protocol in place for who was to take over should anything happen to him. Your father, Thomas, was to take over as alpha until his own son, Jared, came of age.*

So what? Clay demanded. *Supposedly, Ry killed Jared's parents to become alpha of the Forest Grove pack and then he just let my dad take over?*

I didn't reply. I couldn't.

Sounds a little too fucked up, don't you think? Doesn't even really make sense.

If he knew the whole story it might.

It could just be a rumor. Is that all then?

I sighed. *There were a couple other rumors that he got a shifter pregnant in one of the northern packs and killed her when he found out. That that was the reason why he came back to Forest Grove. And another rumor that he—*

Stop, Clay seethed.

I let my thoughts go blank, realizing Clay was on the cusp of how much rage he could control.

The other stuff—it's bad—but it doesn't really have much to do with us or with the pack, I explained. In other words, there was no need for both of us to have to be burdened by knowing it. I sure as hell wished I didn't.

We walked onto the cabin's property, and I heaved a relieved sigh when it came into view through the trees. I could hardly believe we'd actually made it, and without anyone catching us.

A small victory, but still a victory.

Clay shifted back once we were on the dirt lawn, showing me his tight backside as he drew up his shorts that were discarded near the bottom step. He tossed me my clothes that were folded nearby and turned around, waiting for me to shift.

I did, whimpering as all my bones cried out in protest. I managed to keep the bulk of my pain under wraps, but I knew Clay would be able to feel it whether I made a sound or not.

It hurt even to pull my t-shirt over my head. The brush of the fabric against my skin felt like sandpaper.

"Done," I ground out when I was no longer naked, my voice gravelly.

Clay turned and met my eyes. In his, I could see his wolf was still on the prowl. And his face, tight and twisted, spoke of the thoughts I could no longer hear.

He pressed his lips into a firm line. "It can't be true," he said.

Though we both knew it very well could be. "For Jared's sake," I said, cutting my fingernails into my palms to keep steady. "I hope it's not."

Clay threw a clawed hand through his hair and rolled his shoulders back, tipping his head to one side to crack his neck.

"You're coming with me," he decided. "I know you're tired, but I'm not leaving you here. I've got to pick up my sister. We'll take the Jeep to meet her. Jared left it for us."

I ached for my bed, but let's be real. Sleep wasn't going to happen whether I laid in it or not.

"There's just one thing," Clay added, his face cut from stone. "I have to bring her to Ry. It's protocol. He needs to officially give her permission to be here. And the pack needs to get a whiff of her scent, so no one ends up on a wild goose chase. We'll drive to the borderlands to meet her so you can have a rest but then we'll have to go on foot into pack camp. Are you good for one more shift?"

My heart thudded hard against my ribcage. Both at the prospect of having to see Ryland face to face *tonight* after having heard what I did, and now I may have to shift *again*. Maybe even twice more before the night was through.

I was going to *live* in the bath for the next two days after this.

I nodded. "I can." A tense pause.

"Can you keep your chill when we get to camp?" I asked Clay.

He raised a brow at me. "Can *you*?" he countered.

I thought about it. "Until we know for sure—yes." He nodded, cracking his knuckles. "Then so can I."

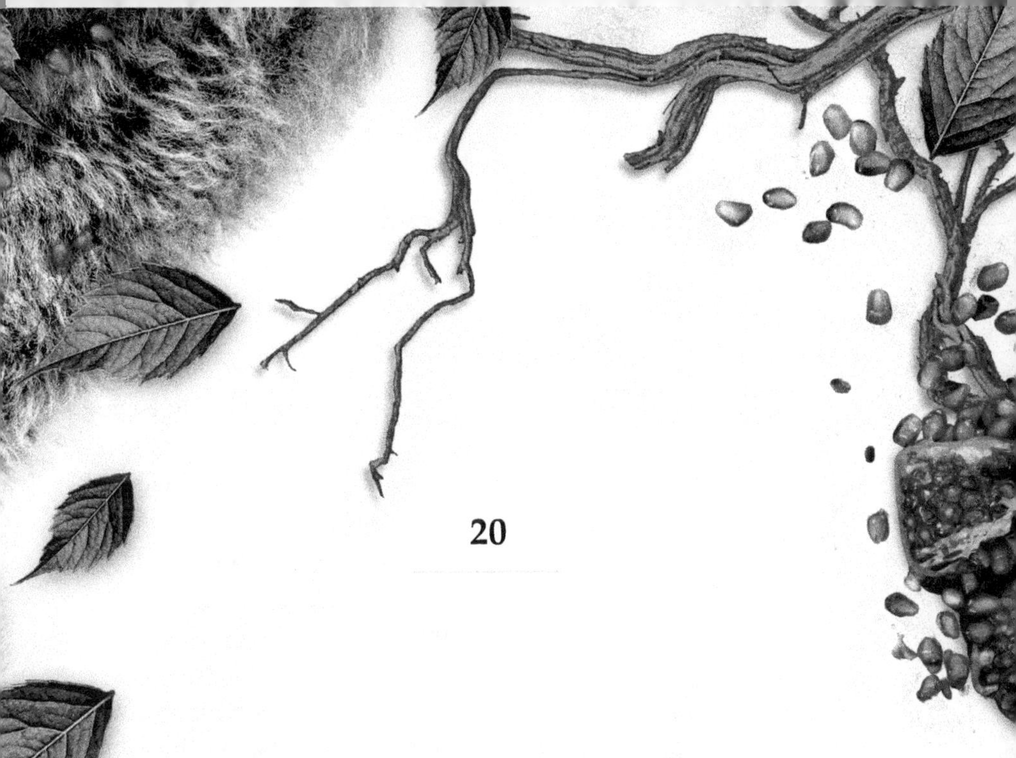

20

The drive to the borderlands took about an hour since Ryland's territory had expanded significantly since the night at the Four Corners. If we'd run, we'd have made it there in a little under thirty minutes. We were late. Not the best first impression I wanted to give Sam. Clay was silent most of the drive, leaving to respond to some texts from Jared and Viv.

Jared would be home tomorrow for good apparently.

And Vivian...Vivian had a lacrosse game coming up. She was asking me if I'd come.

Allie: Lacrosse, Viv?

It pained me to point this out to her, but it had to be done.

Allie: Do you really think that's a good idea?

I didn't expect her to reply, it was well after midnight, but after only a few minutes a response came through.

Vivian: I'm not giving up lacrosse.

Well, that was decided then. I didn't have a choice.

I'd have to go if only to make sure nothing happened.

Allie: When is it? I'll be there.

We parked down a side road. and I left my phone in the car, knowing I wouldn't be able to carry it in my wolf form. We walked the rest of the way into the forest. Me with an armful of clothes for Sam, and Clay with a sour attitude that told me he didn't want to talk. I could sense the foreign wolf was there within minutes. The border was just ahead, I realized, sensing the same shift in the air that I'd briefly experienced when I passed through onto the eastern pack's territory earlier. Like my wolf just *knew* that was where the borders were without having any visual cues.

I supposed that was how everybody knew where they could and couldn't go. I'd usually relied on Charity to lead the way on our searches, and Jared and Clay on our runs, to make sure we didn't encroach on any other pack land.

"Sam," Clay called into the night. "You can cross.
We're here."

A shadowy shape appeared a moment later, growing in size until she was upon us. I squealed as she barreled into Clay, knocking him clean off his feet. She pressed her paws into his chest and bit at his face.

My wolf reacted, raging to the surface in defense of my mate. I dropped the clothes in the dirt and growled at her, ready to shift and go straight for the throat.

Sam whirled on me, as though only just realizing I was there. She snarled at me as Clay cursed to himself, trying to shove her off him. He finally succeeded. "Take it easy," he snapped at me, and my wolf retreated enough for me to shove her the rest of the way back down.

Clay got to his feet, staring down a still-snarling Sam.

She wasn't very big. Not quite Charity's size. Maybe not even quite my size, but I could tell right away she was a spitfire. Lean and angry. Practically foaming at the mouth. And like her brother, she was *fast*. I barely had time to register that she was charging us before she was on top of Clay.

"She *attacked* you," I spat back at Clay, trying to dull the sting of his words.

Ignoring me, Clay glared down at his sister. "*Sam*," he said, his words a warning as his sister continued to growl at me. "This is Allie. *My mate*. Now would you fucking shift already?"

Her snarls quieted, and one second, I was staring at a dark gray wolf with a streak of white like a lightning bolt on her forehead and the next there was a very naked woman standing ten feet away from me. A woman with long, wild black hair and piercing blue eyes. Her pallor was lighter than her brother's, the ivory tone of her skin and darkness of her hair made her look severe.

Her curvy body was a seductress' dream. Large, heaving breasts with dark cherry nipples pebbled in the cool breeze. A thick, muscled frame and wide hips. Legs for days.

I cast my gaze away, blushing.

"*Christ, Sam,*" Clay cursed, lifting a hand to shield himself from seeing his sister in the nude. He snatched up the discarded clothes from the ground and shoved it at her, shielding his eyes all the while.

"Oh stop," she chastised. "It's not like it's anything you haven't seen before."

Her tone was soft as suede, but she wielded it like a whip, leaving a sting.

"You can quit covering your eyes now," she grumbled a moment later. "Hey big bro."

I turned in time to see her tug Clay into a hard embrace. He hugged her back, the scowl on his face quickly changing to something I wasn't sure I'd ever seen there before.

A sort of peace that made my own lips quirk up into a half grin.

"All right," Sam said as she pulled away from her brother. "Introduce me."

She said it like he was about to introduce her to the most unimportant person imaginable. I did my best not to take offense. If this bitch made Clay happy, then I'd swallow what I wanted to say in favor of something a bit less cutting.

"Sam, this is Allie. Allie, meet my kid sister." Sam surveyed me top to bottom.

I did the same.

She should've looked ridiculous in a combination of Clay's baggy sweats and my Naruto t-shirt, but somehow, she managed to rock it.

"Nice to meet you," I said, not bothering with a handshake. A hug was out of the question.

"Right," she said. "I'd say the feeling was mutual, but you kind of fucked up my brother's chance to mate *properly* so...yeah. Hard pass."

"Fair enough."

"Sam," Clay warned. "Be *nice*."

She turned on her brother with a haughty stare. "That *was* nice," she told him. "Do you want to see cruel?"

Clay rolled his eyes but said nothing. "We'll talk about it later," he promised her.

Her nose wrinkled.

I was tempted to ask Clay if she really had to stay with us at the cabin, but thought maybe now wasn't the best time for that. Maybe I could crash at Viv's for a while. Or with Charity.

A sigh left my lips. No. I needed to wear this bitch down. If she was a part of Clay's life, then she was a part of mine.

"Missed you," Sam said, bumping Clay's shoulder with hers.

Clay grunted, neither confirming nor denying that he missed her, too, though I suspected it was the former.

"Still not much for chit chat, huh?" Sam asked, putting a hand to one hip.

"It's late, Sam."

"Well," she replied with a sigh. "Can't argue with you there. I'm pooched. Let's go get this shit over with and head back to the cabin. I can't wait to see my old room."

Clay stiffened and cut me an apologetic look. I held my breath. No, it couldn't be...

My room? I mouthed to him as Sam began to walk away.

Clay grimaced, and it was enough of an answer to make me grit my own teeth. I got the feeling Sam wasn't going to like that one bit.

"Are we walking or running?" Sam asked, calling back over her shoulder. I knew what she really meant was *are we really going to make the trek on human legs? Or can we do this properly?*

Clay looked to me for permission.

Sam made a grossed-out sound in her throat and rolled her eyes at him.

"I'm good," I said in a low voice, not wanting Sam to hear or to think that I was in any way *controlling* her brother. My skin bristled. "Let's run."

I'D BEEN RIGHT ABOUT HOW MUCH TIME WE MIGHT'VE SAVED IF I'D HAD IT in me to use my wolf to run to meet Sam. It took us barely thirty minutes to within ten miles of pack camp. It was late enough that we didn't run into anyone along the way, which I appreciated.

I didn't appreciate that we'd also have to run all the way back to pick up the Jeep at the northern border before making the painfully slow drive home. *Damn.* I really wished I'd just bucked up and run with Clay instead of letting him drive us there. It really backfired. At this rate we wouldn't be home until close to dawn. School tomorrow was going to really suck. And I was meant to work at the shop afterward too, you know, if I still had a job. That voicemail from Jacqueline was primed to expire tomorrow night if I didn't listen to it. I knew I would have to before I went in for my shift, just in case it was her telling me not to bother.

Which I assumed was *exactly* what it would say. At least I'd be able to nap after school...

The painful reality of it made me laugh darkly within the confines of my wolf. For all this new life had given me, it sure didn't seem to want to stop *taking* things, too.

Clay slowed and I saw his ears prick, hearing something I was oblivious to.

What is it? I asked Clay.

Don't know.

Before I could pause to have a better listen myself, curious what it was that had him on edge, another voice entered my thoughts. Sliding in like the sharp edge of a blade.

Stay where you are, Ryland bellowed the command. Clay and I stopped, and Clay let out a little bark for Sam to follow suit. She cocked her head peculiarly at him but didn't make a fuss. In fact, she seemed glad of the break. Her chest heaved hard, and her legs trembled like reeds in the wind.

I remembered she'd run all the way from her pack territory in Alaska and understood why. It made me look like a wimp in comparison.

He must have sensed us, Clay whispered in my thoughts. *He'll want to escort us in, so we don't startle the others.*

I nodded my head to show I understood, though I didn't share any thoughts with him. I was trying to clear them as best I could, not wanting Ry to be able to glean anything off me that I didn't wish to share.

It took a continuous effort to make sure my thoughts were mine and mine alone.

We heard him before we saw him. Ry's footfalls were heavy and coming from the left. Not in the direction of camp. He must've already been out for a run when he realized we were coming.

Sam parked herself beside her brother, sitting with a docile dip to her head and her fluffy tail curled around her paws. Clay had no such chill. He stood next to his sister with a powerful defiance to his stance and a hard stare in his gaze. I wanted to bite his ass to remind him to play it cool, but it was too late, I could already see Ry weaving in and out around tree trunks and brush.

The great black wolf slowed from a sprint to a canine jog as he cleared the last bit of space. His bright orange gaze went first to Clay, and then, without bothering to hide his disappointment, to me.

When his gaze slid from me to Sam, Ryland jerked so violently that his claws dug deep channels in the earth and his hackles went up from the top of his head all the way to the end of his tail.

His eyes were wide. Wild.

Shock was evidenced in the rigidity of his stance. In the quick, short bursts of air filtering in and out through his nostrils.

Sam cried out and all at once I realized what was happening.

Clay saw it, too.

He watched as his sister cringed and buckled, whining as she fought against the invisible force making her head bow just as Ryland's did. And when finally she broke free of it, how she pressed up from the earth, her neck long and chest jutting out as a long howl tore from her mouth. It rose like a scream in the night, tangling the deeper sound of Ryland's own howl.

Clay's blue eyes met mine, panicked and confused. He growled low in his throat, and I lurched over to him, tucking myself in close to his side, trying to soothe him.

Don't, was all I said in his mind, terrified to voice anything else.

Ryland was the first to let the howl fade, dropping his hungry eyes to his new mate. He sauntered toward her like a predator stalking beautiful prey. Like he was strangely disarmed by her beauty but intended to make a meal of her all the same.

It was difficult to look at. Difficult to stomach.

I couldn't even imagine what was going through Clay's mind right now, but I did know he was working *very* hard to hide whatever it was because not a single wisp of a thought broke through his defenses.

I stepped on Clay's paw as Ryland approached, and he grudgingly took a step back, allowing Ryland to stalk a slow circle around a shivering Sam.

Mate, Ryland's throaty roar echoed in my skull, and I knew without needing anyone to tell me that it was a declaration. That it was a single word projected to the entire pack. I buckled under the force of it and Clay flinched.

It was difficult to tell, but I got the sense that Ryland and his mate were having a conversation we couldn't hear. Like when I first mated to Jared and Clay. Even though they weren't my pack yet, the mate bond allowed us to communicate.

Judging by the little sounds they were making, it seemed like it wasn't a horribly unpleasant conversation at least. Sam's shaking began to subside, and her bowed head rose, and she rolled her shoulders back, taking in her new mate like someone would take in a brand-new car.

The fear I'd seen in her for an instant had abated.

She looked...happy.

And like she wanted to take that new car for a test drive.

Ugh.

Clay growled low in his throat, and Ry turned on him with a snarl, but Sam, surprising me, snapped in Ry's direction, earning herself a surprised stare from Ry.

No, surprised wasn't the right word. Shocked, maybe?

Outraged, definitely.

Though Sam didn't back down from his withering stare.

I heard someone else coming and peered into the tree line toward camp, finding several other shifters emerging, awoken from Ryland's declaration. Their approach was enough to tranquilize Ry, who resumed his leering of Sam. *Appreciative* leering, as though she hadn't just done something to offend him a few seconds before.

Charity was the first to reach us. She looked between Ryland and Sam, her eyes watery and her movements stilted. Once she got a good enough eye full, she fled, leaving the other approaching pack members to ogle their alpha's new mate. My heart ached for her even though I would never understand her attraction to him.

Ryland shifted, going from wolf to human in one fluid movement, one step a wolf, and the next on mortal feet. He grinned down at Sam, his look encouraging her to do the same.

When she did, Clay and I followed suit along with many of the other shifters who'd come to investigate.

I barely felt the shift this time, too preoccupied with needing to make sure Clay didn't intend to strangle Ryland. I shivered in the cold and tucked myself into Clay's side, wrapping my hand around his clenched one. For a second, I thought he might shuck me off. I expected it.

He didn't like to be comforted. I knew that.

Which was why I was surprised when he relaxed his fisted hand enough to slide his fingers through mine, gripping tight. For once, I was able to offer him what he always offered me. Courage. And maybe a bit of calmness.

Ryland appraised Sam. His tongue slipped out, licking his lips as though he'd just finished a particularly intoxicating meal. Sam appraised him in turn, and though I could tell she was not wholly satisfied, she seemed at least accepting of what she saw.

I wouldn't say it, but I had to assume it was to do with his age.

From what I knew *generally* the mate bond formed between two shifters nearer together in age naturally, but I also knew that that wasn't *always* the case. It seemed Sam and Ryland were the exception to the rule. From what I knew Sam was only a year older than I was. And Ryland was...what? Close to fifty? Ick.

I felt sick for Clay, and more than ever before, I prayed that what I learned tonight was not true.

Shouted admonishments of congratulations rose from the gathering of my pack mates. Forrest and Harrison whooped, bumping fists with each other before they clapped Ryland on the back and welcomed Sam with open arms and naked embraces. With kisses on her cheeks and shakes of her hand. She grinned broadly through it all, laughing as she kept a seductive eye on her new mate and he on her.

She beamed as he announced a celebration to take place on the weekend. To properly welcome his new mate to the Forest Grove pack.

Not a clue that she may have just mated to the most dangerous shifter here.

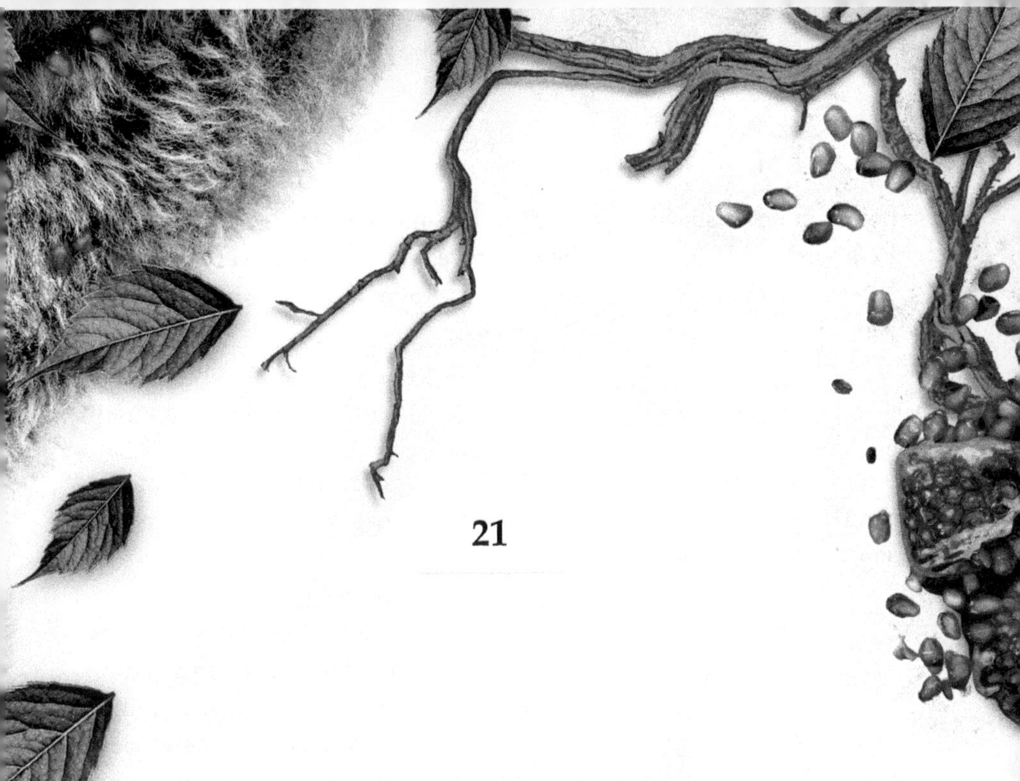

21

I padded down the stairs on leaden legs, my mind in a thick fog. I might have slept even longer had the wafting scent of bacon and pancakes not woken me. I rubbed my burning eyes and did my best to stretch out the awful kink in my neck.

My legs protested every step, threatening to give out under my weight. Seeing Jared flip a pancake into the air and catch it in a sizzling pan in the kitchen brought it all back in a wave.

The reason why I was so sore. The hundreds of miles Clay and I had run. Where we'd gone in secret. What we learned.

My stomach waged a war on itself as I shuffled into the kitchen. Hunger and disgust dueling at the fresh memory of my alpha mating to Clay's little sister. Had that actually happened?

I wished I could believe it was all just a really bad, *really vivid* dream, but I knew better. Clay had been shaking when we finally left. Ryland had insisted Sam stay at pack camp with him. Sam didn't seem opposed to the idea, so what were we to do?

I could tell Clay had *wanted* to do something. *Wanted* more than anything to say something. To warn his sister. But how could he? With his sister smiling and laughing. With the gleam in her eyes.

He wouldn't speak to me on the way back from camp as much as I tried to reach him. Not during the run, or the long drive home. We sat in horror-steeped silence, listening to late-night radio turned down low. He let me hold his hand while we drove, however, and every so often, I felt his fingers twitch, as though he was remembering where his sister was—who she was with—all over again.

I gulped past a hard lump in my throat and glanced around to the living room and out the window to the yard. I couldn't see him anywhere.

I wondered if he slept at all. It took me hours to finally drift off. The thud and rattle of Clay hitting the heavy bag in his shop becoming something of a violent lullaby.

"Morning," I croaked, trying to clear my throat.

Jared spun, just barely catching a pancake he'd been tossing for a second time to flip. He set the pan down on a dormant burner and his lips twitched into a halfway grin. "Hey," he said, taking in my likely monstrous appearance. I'd had a long bath before attempting to sleep last night but tossing and turning with wet hair had left me with a mane that was about the size of a lion's.

A worried crease formed in his brow as he wrapped his arms around me, pressing me into him for a soft hug. I melted into him, shuddering at the intensity of the sensation of his nearness. He was away so much that the feeling was always so strong when he returned. "I missed you," he whispered against my cheek, and I nearly smiled before remembering what Adam had told me. I stiffened and drew back, guilt pooling like acid in my belly. I couldn't tell him now, not with everything else going on.

"Hey," he said, crooking a brow at me as he brushed some warmth back into my arms. "You okay?"

I shook my head, blinking to clear my thoughts. "Yeah. Yeah, I'm fine. Just really tired, and I missed you, too. Where's Clay?"

"He left early this morning right after I got home.

Said he wanted to go and check on Sam." I sighed. Of course, he did. "Did he seem...okay?"

Jared's sandstone eyes fell to the floor. "I think so. It's a little messed up. I mean, she's so young. It's the first time he's seen her in almost four years, you know. He usually goes up to Alaska to visit because she doesn't like coming here. I don't think he expected to be welcoming her back for good, or for her to mate with one of his least favorite people."

I winced. That was putting it lightly.

"Doesn't she need, like, permission from her own alpha to leave?"

Jared nodded. "Yeah, but when it's to do with mating, it's almost never denied. Apparently, she's flying back round trip tomorrow to get her things and then she'll be here to stay."

"So fast?"

Jared gave an uncomfortable shrug. "I guess Ry doesn't want to waste any time. Some of us were starting to wonder if he was ever going to find his mate."

The way Jared said it, like even though the whole thing grossed him out, he was happy for his uncle, made me want to be sick all over again.

Soon, I promised myself. I would tell him as soon as I had something concrete. *Soon.*

If Sam was in any sort of danger with Ry...if that story about him murdering the shifter woman he got pregnant was true...then there wasn't any time left to waste.

"Are you sure you're okay?" Jared asked again, brushing some of my hair away from my cheek.

I brushed my palm over his hand, holding it there, reveling in how blissfully perfect the feel of him was. It was that small thing that gave me enough comfort— enough courage—to nod. I was okay.

We were all going to be okay.

I was going to make sure of that.

"Are you hungry? I made pancakes and about two pounds of bacon."

My stomach burbled between us and he chuckled. "I guess I could eat," I joked, tugging him in for one more hug, admiring how my body just *fit* there with his.

When I opened my eyes again, I gasped, jumping back. "You have got to be kidding me," I groaned, pushing my palms into my eye sockets to rub my eyes. I looked again.

Nope.

Not a cruel joke at all.

The clock above the stove glared at me with angry red numbers.

"It can't actually be one in the afternoon? Please tell me that's wrong," I begged, jabbing a finger in the general direction of the imposing clock.

A strained smile that was more a baring of teeth split Jared's face.

"Sorry?" he offered. "I thought about waking you, but you looked so tired and—"

I moaned, wiping my hands over my face as I slumped into the chair at the little table by the window, hanging my head in my hands. *"Just great,"* I grumbled to myself. "I'm going to lose my job *and* fail all my classes."

And then there was the fact that I'd already been avoiding calls from Uncle Tim. The school would be calling him for sure. *Fuck.* What if he came up?

Four more days until you turn eighteen, I reminded myself.

Just four more days and then you never have to answer a call or text from him again.

Ninety-six hours and he can stop worrying about me and tend to his snooty wife. He can serve her drinks on their beach patio and never think about me again.

Four. More. Days.

"You're not going to fail," Jared said, gently tugging my hands away from my face as he kneeled in front of me. His caramel-blond hair glowed in the muted light from the window.

"I'm *already* failing," I argued.

Jared bit his bottom lip, thinking before he replied, "How about this: I'm really behind on a bunch of stuff right now, too. Let's eat, and then we'll spend the day getting caught up. I'll help you with math and geography and you can help me with English."

My eyes burned at the offer.

There was just one problem, but I doubted it would even *be* a problem anymore once I checked my voicemails. "Okay," I whispered. "Just let me get fired first."

Jared cocked his head at me.

"I'm supposed to have a shift at the shop tonight after school," I explained. "But I'm pretty sure there's a voicemail on my phone that's going to tell me not to bother coming."

Jared's eyes darkened. "I'm so sorry, Allie. Maybe I could talk to her for you? I could explain—"

"How?" I asked, laughing darkly.

He opened his mouth to argue and I pressed two fingers to his lips, effectively cutting him off. "It's fine."

"I hate that word." I lifted a brow.

"*Fine*," he said, heaving a sad sigh. "I never want you to be *fine* Allie. Fine is nowhere near good enough. Not for you."

IT TOOK a solid hour before I could really focus on anything after a few nibbles of breakfast. But when focus finally did find me, Jared and I blew through classwork and overdue projects like a breeze. With his help, algebraic equations looked less like foreign hieroglyphs and more like structures of numeric pyramids. Still confusing, but a lot less like a foreign language.

He made quick work of my geography project, helping me craft an essay from start to finish. With my competence in English and proper essay formatting and his geo knowledge, we finished the whole thing in under an hour.

His own past due English paper got a thorough upgrade and full reference section complete with proper notations and formatting. He was worried his teacher might worry he'd stolen it, but I told him it wasn't against school policy to get help, and I'd take full credit for his improvement, just as I'd give him full credit for mine if asked.

Overall, within about four hours, we were essentially caught up on everything, with only a few smaller assignments and some daily home-work left to complete. I'd have kept going, but I think both of us were starting to run out of gas. Every time I tried to work through a new problem in my textbook it was like my brain choked and sputtered to a stall.

Trying to jam the key in the ignition and pump the gas pedal wasn't working anymore, either. I'd chewed the end of my pen to a disgusting mess, and Jared's hair was sticking out at every angle imaginable.

It looked cute like that.

No, cute wasn't the right word. Rugged, maybe. Sexy for sure.

He glanced up from the philosophy text he was reading and caught me staring. The glaze over his eyes abated and the knot between his brows softened. "What?" he asked, a playful smirk twisting up his lips.

I reached over across the coffee table and ruffled his hair. "Your hair," I joked. "It's getting so long."

The tops of his ears turned pink as he dragged both of his hands through it, trying to finger comb it into place. But it just sprang back into the mess it'd been a second before.

I giggled.

"I guess I could use a trim," he grumbled. I shook my head. "No. I like it like this."

I reached back up to push my fingers into the smooth strands, a bit jealous. Any girl would *kill* to have hair like his. Thick and rich.

"Yours is starting to look different, too," he mused, glancing up at the crown of my head. I'd done my best to tame it with a comb, but had wound up knotting it into a low bun at the nape of my neck. "It's growing out."

I knew he was right. I hadn't dyed it in weeks. No, maybe months? The last time was the night of the party at Thompson's. What was left there for dye had faded to a pale turquoise, more of a pastel color than the vibrant hue I usually wore. And at my roots I had a solid two or three inches of new silvery blonde growth. Truth be told, I couldn't be bothered to keep up with it anymore. Besides that, I couldn't *afford* to buy more dye. As it was, my bank account was dwindling by the week.

Bye-bye dreams renting the apartment above the shop.

Even if I could afford it, I doubted Jacqueline would rent it to me anymore, anyway. Who wanted a flakey tenant who rarely showed up for work.

I'd been right about her voicemail. Though it was much kinder than I thought it ought to be, Jacqueline had let me know, at least temporarily. I believe the exact words were:

I won't pretend to know what's going on, but I have to assume whatever it is, that it's important. I know you wouldn't skip out on work for just any reason. I've brought on a new trainee for the time being and think you should take some time off. We can reassess your position in the summer.

So, not exactly the worst thing ever, but any way you sliced it, my source of income was no more.

I called and left a message at the shop around three o'clock, knowing she would be swamped and wouldn't answer the phone. It was the least I could do to tell her I got her message and apologize. I thanked her for understanding and told her I took full responsibility even though some things were out of my control.

"Allie?" Jared prompted, and I realized I'd missed something he said.

"Sorry. Zoned out. What did you say?"

"Your hair," he repeated. "I like it—the natural color, I mean. Not that the green isn't awesome, too, though."

"*Turquoise*," I corrected, giving him a little swat.

He caught my hand before I could get him, holding me by the wrist. His thumb brushed against the soft skin of my wrist and my body flushed with a warmth not from the low-burning fire in the hearth at my back. "Sorry," he said with a wicked gleam in his eyes. "*Turquoise.* You're right, I don't know what I was thinking. It's clearly not even close to being green."

"Are you trying to charm me, Jared Stone?"

"Is it working?"

His other hand crept onto my thigh beneath the coffee table, and I shuddered, biting the inside of my cheek to hold in a whimper.

When I opened my eyes again, I knew they would be glowing lightly around the edges, my wolf awakening to the touch of her mate.

No...not *hers*.

Ours.

Mine.

I really had missed him all this time. I felt like we'd been robbed of so much of it ever since Ryland started sending Jared away to work at the quarry.

"Are you really back for good?" I asked in a rush, afraid of the answer but needing it all the same. I had to know if he was going to vanish on me again. I needed him just as much as I needed Clay.

Jared was like my sun. Warm and bright even when things were stormy.

Clay like my moon. Shrouded in dark clouds, but still managing to shine despite them.

I couldn't have one without the other.

Jared's cheekbones twitched as he clenched his jaw, but after a second, he gave a single nod. "At least for a while."

It was the best he could do, I realized. None of us could say when Ryland would stick his big ugly head in our lives and rip them from under us. None of us had a say. Not a real one, anyway.

Without another word, I swiped one arm across the coffee table, knocking textbooks and binders and loose note papers to the floor. Jared's eyes widened before narrowing hungrily on me.

"I always wanted to do that," I said in a breath, climbing over the bare table to reach him.

He pulled me into his lap, settling me with my legs around his waist and his hands gripping tightly around mine.

Jared didn't hesitate this time. He pressed himself against me, tipping his chin up to reach my lips before sliding his hands across my back, wrapping both arms securely around me, binding me to him.

With my hands tightly wound in his hair, I kissed him without restraint. Each kiss muting the guilt enough to spur me on. My heartbeat was a wave of dominos falling against bone. My breaths were a broken song, hanging on notes without finding any proper rhythm.

When his tongue slid between my lips, I came undone, my back arching and toes curling.

With me clamped around him, Jared moved, lifting me with him as he stood. His hands moved low, wrapping around my upper thighs to hold me up. Something throbbed low in my belly, twisting and aching. Burning.

I moaned against his mouth as we crested the top of the stairs and gasped when he kicked in the door to his bedroom. The jarring movement broke us apart for an instant, and in it, I saw the burning fire of his wolf in his eyes. The drunken desire making his eyelids heavy.

Jared carried me to his bed, and I let him lay me over the soft gray blanket there. He paused then, drawing back as his eyes traced a lazy trail down the line of my body. His jaw clenched.

"What?" I asked, still breathless and aching to taste him.

I needed him to touch me. I needed to feel him. To erase all the doubt and the pain and the worry with his lips.

"I think I need to reevaluate something," he said, confusing me for a brief second before I caught on to where his mind had gone.

I groaned. "If you mean the *no fucking* rule you have with Clay, then yeah. I think you do."

Jared's lips parted in surprise. "Did he tell you?"

Oh fuck.

I did my best to keep my face blank as I responded. "Yeah."

I could see what he wanted to ask next clear as if it was written on his face in permanent ink. *How did that come up?*

Before he could voice the question and completely ruin the moment,

I sighed and sat back up. "You know, I would've liked to have been involved in that decision."

Jared's expression shifted; some of the fire in his eyes waned, dying out.

Way to kill the mood, Allie.

Jared didn't say anything for almost a full minute, then he sat down, lifting me easily onto his lap again. "You're right," he said. "We should have all talked about it together. It's just..."

"A super fucking weird situation?"

Jared winced.

"At least you're good friends," I hedged. "Imagine if I'd mated to one of you and some other random shifter who you didn't know. Maybe a fifty-year-old alpha with a nasty temper?"

Jared grimaced.

"Too far?" I asked, mirroring his disgust.

"A bit," he replied but wrapped his arms tighter around me. "Why are you so smart, Allie Grace?" he asked. I was going to ask him what exactly he meant, but then he continued. "I didn't imagine this situation to be possible, but again—you're right. I guess it's sort of lucky that it was Clay. He *is* my best friend. I trust him more than I trust anyone else. If I have to share you, then he is the only other man I'd be able to share you with."

"So does that mean we can nix your rule?" I asked with a devilish smirk, purposefully rolling my hips a little on his lap to emphasize my point and then blushed crimson, hardly able to believe what I'd just said and done.

What were these guys doing to me?

He grunted, sucking a breath in through his teeth. When he replied, his voice was husky and low, making my thighs clench. "Maybe," he teased. "Let's have a proper conversation about it. The three of us. Deal?"

"Deal," I said, stealing a kiss from his lips.

He lengthened the kiss, languidly stroking a warm path down the side of my body, caressing my collarbone and the curve of my breast until his fingers found a gap in between the fabric of my shirt and the waist of my jeans. He slid his hand upward, tentatively, as though asking permission.

I pressed my body into his fingertips, my body screaming. How could this feeling be real? I could barely breathe, afraid if I did, it would break the spell keeping us here in this moment. Away from the worry. Away from the pain.

Just...*away*.

Then I remembered.

"I forgot to ask you," I said, digging around in my front left pocket for my cell and thumbing to the conversation with Vivian. With everything else going on, I'd pretty much completely forgotten about it. "Want to come to Viv's lacrosse game with me? I meant to ask Clay too, but..."

I let the sentence trail off, not needing to elaborate on why I hadn't asked him yet. He had enough on his mind right now. Hell, he'd been all day. If he didn't get back soon, or at least answer one of my three text messages, I was going to have to find his ass and drag it home.

"Lacrosse?" Jared asked, not hiding his mild shock or the worried furrow in his brow.

My lips pressed into a thin line. "I know. I tried to tell her it wasn't a good idea. I mean, competitive sports? I still don't even think *I'd* be ready for that and I'm nowhere near as competitive as Viv is."

Jared's lack of immediate reply set my nerves on edge.

"Do you not think she can handle it?"

Jared shook his head. "Honestly? I don't know. Both your friends have adapted better that almost any other shifters I've seen make the transformation."

His gaze slid to me and then away, checking to see if he'd offended me.

I certainly hadn't adapted as well as they had. It was no secret.

"But lacrosse?" he repeated. "Why couldn't she be into horseback riding or chess or something?"

I barked a laugh. I couldn't picture it: Viv staring over a chess board with her fingers steepled, analyzing moves and countermoves. Layla maybe. But not Viv. She needed lacrosse like she needed to breathe. It was her one outlet when life at home wore on her. She was a fucking force of nature on the field.

...which was precisely why this was clearly a terrible idea.

"So, you'll come then?"

Jared inhaled deeply. "Yeah. Of course, I will. And we'll bring Clay, too. Might need him. He's really good at making distractions in a pinch."

I wondered exactly what kind of distractions Clay was so good at making, but Jared yanked me down with him as he lay back, tucking me into his side. His woodsy cedar and birch scent wrapped around me like a cloak of ease, and I sighed.

It barely took more than a few minutes before my mind wandered to darker territory, no longer occupied by math equations and Jared's lips. I shuddered involuntarily as I wondered how Ry and Sam's first night together went, simultaneously grossed out and stressed out. Wondering if she was all right. If that was the reason Clay still hadn't come home... maybe because she wasn't.

But he would've called me if that were the case, right?

"Hey, Allie," Jared said after a few moments spent stroking my arm, lost in his own thoughts.

"Hmm?"

His pulse picked up. I could hear it quicken from a steady drum beat to a discordant patter.

He swallowed. "You know how the mate bond allows us to share our emotions with each other?"

My mouth went dry. "Yeah. Why?"

"I know there's something you aren't telling me. Or maybe there's something going on you don't want me to know about?" He edged the last bit in a question, but he didn't wait for me to answer it.

"I'm not going to push you, but I just wanted you to know—you can talk to me. About anything."

Biting my lip, I kept quiet, trying to work through what to say. I couldn't deny it, but I also wasn't ready to spill all the beans just yet. He would think I was nuts if I told him what Adam had told me. At least until I had something to back it up.

"I just wanted to make sure it isn't something to do with me...or maybe...something I've done wrong or that's offended you—"

I shook my head, my cheek brushing back and forth over his chest before I propped myself up on an elbow to look him in the eye.

"No. You're perfect."

"So, there is something then?" I dropped my gaze.

"You don't have to tell me now. I'll wait. Just promise me you'll tell me when you're ready?"

I groaned, dropping my head heavily to land on his chest with a thud. Why did he have to be so *good?* It made my heart hurt. It made even the prospect of telling him what we found out about his uncle unbearable. How could someone like Jared share the same blood as someone like Ryland?

Please don't be true. Please don't be true.

"Or not?" Jared asked, taking my reaction as a refusal.

I breathed into his shirt in a long exhale and propped myself back up. "There is something I haven't told you," I admitted. Unburdening myself even of that small admission felt like a massive weight lifting from my chest, allowing me a proper breath. "But I *will* tell you, when the time is right."

He pursed his lips but looked otherwise content with my response. Trusting.

"All right. I can live with that."

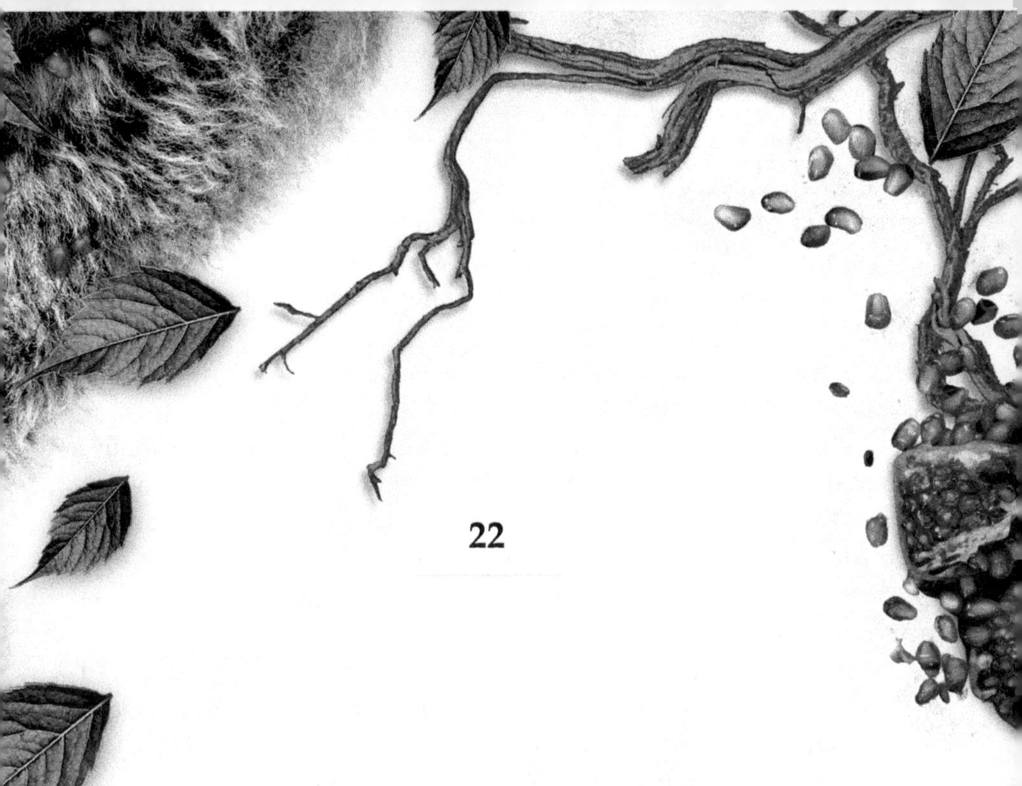

22

"I haven't been to a match in ages," Jared said, sliding onto the bench next to me and passing me a can of soda. I looked past him, searching the crowd of familiar faces all getting ready to take their seats before the match could start. There was no sign of Clay.

I'd met up with Layla and Viv after school, hanging with them until we needed to make our way to the field for warm up. I wanted to see how Viv was beforehand, and she seemed fine. She told me she'd run an extra fifteen miles in the morning, and we all took off for a short sprint between the end of the day bells and the start of warm up.

I was starting to think maybe I'd overreacted, but when I mentioned to her that if she felt at all out of control that she should fake an injury or just run off-field as fast as she could, she'd gotten her hackles up. Her eyes had sparked to light and her jaw had twitched, making me doubt my false confidence.

She was pissed at me now, of course, but it had to be said. There needed to be a backup plan, right? Just in case. Making it through practice was one thing, making it through a competitive match would be a completely other thing.

"Where's Clay?" I asked, still trying to spot him but having no luck.

Jared shook his head, taking a small sip of his soda. "Sam took the

629

red-eye flight last night to get permission to leave her pack. He wanted to be there at the airport to pick her up when she got back."

I furrowed a brow, wondering why Ryland hadn't insisted on picking her up himself.

Jared dug his phone out of his pocket and hit the side button to illuminate the screen. "He should be here, soon."

I sighed. Good, at least he was still coming. I'd only seen him for five minutes since we got home the night after Ry and Sam mated two days ago. Just in passing when I got up for a glass of water in the middle of the night, unable to sleep. He'd been passed out on the couch, his eyes ringed in dark circles and his skin bleached of color. Dressed in loose shorts, his bare feet muddy.

I didn't have the heart to wake him to try to get him to bed, but I'd covered him in a blanket and set a tall glass of water and a wrapped ham sandwich on the coffee table for him, hoping he would eat it before he took off again in the morning like I knew he would.

Sure enough, when I awoke this morning, he was already gone. But his water glass was empty in the sink, and I only found half of the sandwich in the trash, so at least he'd had something to eat and drink before running off again.

"When have you been to a match?" I asked, cracking open the soda and taking a long swallow, letting the carbonated sweetness take some of the edge off my panic.

"Hmmm?"

"You said it's been a while since you've been to one, but I've never seen you at Viv's matches before?"

"Right. It was actually Sam's match I went to last. I went up with Clay and his Dad to Alaska about..." he trailed off, scratching a spot on the back of his head as he considered. "Maybe six years ago? Before Sam was turned and before Clay's dad passed. Sam wasn't very good, but she was one of those kids who had to try everything. Don't tell her I said so."

Jared smirked, and I tried to return it with a grin that I'm sure didn't reach my eyes.

There was something I wanted—no, *needed* to ask Jared, seeing as I couldn't ask Clay. And he'd just given me the perfect entry to that conversation. I needed to know if what Adam told me lined up with what actually happened. If I asked Clay now, he would know why. It wouldn't be hard to put two and two together.

"How did Thomas Armstrong die?" I asked, sipping my soda but not tasting it as I surveyed the field, unable to look Jared in the eye.

I could feel his curiosity at the question. He was wondering why I was asking that now. And why I was asking him and not Clay. I could feel Jared's stare as he replied, speaking the words hesitantly, as though unsure he should be the one to speak them.

"He was shot, actually. It wasn't pack related as far as anyone knows. Just bad luck. A wrong place, wrong time sort of thing. Maybe a case of mistaken identity."

I wondered if he actually believed that. "Did they ever catch the guy who did it?"

Jared shook his head solemnly. "Nah. I think that's what had Clay so messed up for so long. There was no evidence. Not even a shell casing to try to trace the gun. Clay must have scoured that back-parking lot a hundred times looking for it, or any trace of who might've done it. We tried to track by scent, too, but there wasn't anything foreign on Tom's clothes. Whoever did it, did it close range, without contact, and then somehow remembered to pick up their shell casing and any evidence before they left."

"Convenient," I muttered. Jared gave me a strange look.

"Was anyone with him that night?"

Jared's face paled, and he cocked his head at me. "What's going on, Allie?

I shook my head. "Never mind. I was just curious about what happened. That's all."

Jared went back to looking out over the field as Layla made her way up onto the bleachers, a takeaway coffee gripped in one hand her phone to her ear with the other. She held up her hands in a *two minute* gesture and continued speaking to her mother in Spanish as she sat on the bench in front of me.

I pressed a hand to my stomach, trying to quell the urge to be sick and rip out of my skin at the same time. I hoped they were too distracted to notice as the players made their way out onto the field below.

I hoped they couldn't see how my other hand curled into the metal bench beneath me, leaving fingerprints in the ribbed metal. I spotted Clay just as he rounded the edge of the stands and glanced up at me, the mate bond having alerted me to his presence with a sharp tug at my core.

Quickly, I glanced away, afraid my eyes would be a dead giveaway.

The stories matched up. Exactly what Adam told me was what happened to Clay's father. Except Jared and Clay and most everyone else in the Forest Grove pack were missing one vital piece of information —*who* was to blame for his death.

Had Clay just handed his baby sister off to the man who'd killed his father?

"He manufactured his rise to power," Adam said as I stared open mouthed and numb, pulse and mind racing with everything he'd told me. *"And don't think he won't do whatever it takes to keep that position."*

"Hey," Clay grunted, sitting heavily next to me on the opposite side to Jared.

I swallowed back bile and lifted my soda to my lips, sipping a bit to wet my parched throat. "Hey," I croaked, choking on the carbonation.

"Everything good?"

"Yeah," I said, clearing my throat and attempting to lengthen my spine. "How are things with Sam?"

Clay bristled, turning to train his focus on the field as the whistle blew for the first face off. I searched for Viv and found her in her usual attack position. Winced. I'd warned her to take it easy, but this game was going to be the real test.

She was stronger now. Faster. If we were being honest, she had a super unfair advantage, and it was going to be incredibly hard for her not to use it—to tamper herself down to the level of the other mortal players.

"Good I guess," Clay grunted with a curl in his upper lip.

"She's moved in with Ry already," he added, his face contorting as he spoke.

I tried not to gag.

At least everything was all right, and Sam was okay...for now.

I reached over and gave the rigid hand on his thigh a squeeze, reminding him to relax. He did, his body unfurling under my touch. I could tell he didn't exactly want to talk anymore about it—at least not right now, so I dropped it until a time when we could have a more open conversation. As it was, I could tell Jared was more focused on what we were saying than the players below.

"Are you staying home tonight?"

Clay nodded gravely. "Yeah. She told me to quit babying her."

Layla hung up her call just then and turned to face us. "I got out of babysitting later," she announced. "Want to do shakes and fries from Gerry's after the game?"

This time, my grin was genuine. We hadn't been to Gerry's Shake Shack since ninth grade. My mouth watered instantly at the mention, the phantom taste of creamy strawberry and salty grease coating my tongue. "Sounds fucking amazing."

Layla laughed. "Thought you'd be down for that. What about you two? You both look like you could use a pick me up. No offense."

"None taken," Jared said with a grin. Clay growled.

"They'll both come," I decided for them. "No one turns down Gerry's."

A whistle blew below, and the four of us turned our attention back to the game in time to see Viv skid to a stop downfield. She'd been going *fast.* Maybe a bit *too* fast.

I caught her eye from the bleachers and made a *turn it down* motion with my hand. Her lips tightened, but she nodded before moving into position for the next face-off.

"Okay so far?" I asked Jared, since he was the one who'd seemed to be paying the most attention since the game began.

He licked his lips and readjusted himself in the seat. "For the most part," he said in a low voice. "Though I caught a little bit of glow when that chick—number 18— checked her from behind, but she snuffed it out quick."

"That's good, right?"

The question was meant for Jared, but it was Clay who answered, giving me whiplash when I whirled my head back in his direction. "This is fucking stupid," he said, his voice a low, dangerous rumble. "Why did no one tell her this was a dumb fucking idea?"

"I tried," I argued.

"Well, it won't end well," Clay predicted. "She may get through this game, but eventually, something will happen."

"You don't know what for sure," Jared came to Viv's defense, and I loved him for it, even though a part of me worried Clay was right.

"Don't I?" Clay snapped. "Don't you remember senior year?"

"You shouldn't have even joined the team."

"What team?" I asked.

"Yeah. That's what I'm saying," Clay replied to Jared, his tone dripping acid, completely ignoring me. "I learned my fucking lesson. Vivian should've quit when she was turned."

"That's not fair," Layla butt in, twisting to face Clay with a withering look.

Clay fixed her with an uncommonly gentle and understanding stare. "It isn't," he agreed. "But it's what needs to be done."

Layla crossed her arms and turned back to the game, removing herself from the conversation.

"Did you play lacrosse?" I asked Clay, super confused.

He lifted a brow at me. "Football. Coach hounded me for two years about joining the team. I finally gave in. It was a bad call. Someone got hurt. I nearly got found out."

I tried to wrack my brain to remember. I would've been in ninth grade then. A total loner save for my two best friends. But it came to me, nonetheless.

"That kid who almost *died?*" I asked, incredulous and trying to search my mind for the name. "Billy...Billy..."

"Billy Chapman," Clay finished for me. "Yeah. That was my fault. I checked him too hard. He was in a coma for three days."

Clay said this matter-of-factly, but I could feel the stress of the memory radiating off him. I was willing to bet those were some of the hardest three days he'd ever had.

"He was fine, though," Jared interjected. "He woke up and was back at school within two weeks."

Clay turned on Jared in a fury. "That was luck," he snapped. "I could have killed him. Just like *Viv,*" Clay said pointedly, jabbing two fingers at her as she stealthily maneuvered herself downfield, "could accidently hurt anyone on that field."

Damnit.

"We'll talk to her," I said, interrupting Jared before he continued the argument with Clay over me in the middle of them. All their testosterone was going to make me rage if they didn't shut up. "When the game is over, we'll talk to her, *okay?*"

Clay snatched my soda and took a long drink, polishing it off and crushing the can in his hand. Jared brooded in silence.

They made me want to rip my hair out.

Couldn't we just have *one* freaking night of peace?

Just one?

That's all I wanted: a normal night out with my friends. Watch my friend kick ass at her lacrosse game. Get some fries and shakes. Maybe cap the night off with a movie.

But those kinds of nights weren't mine to wish for anymore, I realized. They were a pipe dream in a world of nightmares.

With the mood dampened, we settled in to focus on the game. I noticed Layla taking little snippets of video and pictures throughout and sending them to Destiny. I wondered why she wasn't here watching Viv's game, too, since they were now mated, but couldn't bring myself to ask.

With how things were going, I had a feeling it would be some reason that would only stress me out more. Maybe Ry had her running an errand. Or maybe she was out searching for the so-called 'missing' shifters with Charity again.

I didn't care right now. I didn't want to know. "Sorry," Clay grumbled so quietly beside me that I had to question whether I heard him speak at all.

I peered up at him and found his face hard, his gaze unwavering as he followed Vivian's path down the field. I waited a minute to see if he was going to elaborate on what exactly he was apologizing for, but he didn't say anything else.

I gave his thigh a pat and smirked. "I'll forgive you for ruining the mood if you get me another soda?"

His lips twitched.

"Suppose I could do that," he grunted standing.

A familiar shout rose up from the field, and I jumped, trying to see past a very large and imposing Clay blocking my view. Layla stiffened, rising robotically to her feet at the same time Jared did.

I shoved Clay to the side just as another cry rang out, this one pitched high and broken. *Fuck.*

My eyes locked on Vivian, her hands clawed at her sides as she stared down at a screeching girl clutching the top part of her shoulder. Even from this far away, my canine eyes could see that something wasn't right. Her collarbone jutted out near the top, not through the skin, but it definitely shouldn't look like that.

Vivian shook, staring down at the girl. I could see her fingernails sharpen. Lengthen.

Oh no.

Oh shit.

A whistle blew and players and refs rushed them.

I whirled to Clay, my heart pounding with terror. *What do we do?* I wanted to ask, but I couldn't speak. Could barely move.

Layla dropped her phone and began shoving past the other students in her aisle, trying to get to the stairs.

"Sorry, bro," Clay muttered just before he tossed a fist over my head. I ducked in time to hear the bone- crunching thud of his knuckles knocking into flesh and bone.

I shrieked just as someone shouted, *"Fight!"* and was knocked out of the way, sent tumbling into the spot where Layla had been just a second before.

Clay hit Jared again, this time in the stomach, making him bend forward, a great gust of air leaving his lips and his eyes going wide.

"Clay," I screeched, torn between wanting to stop him and needing to get to my best friend. "Fucking stop it!"

I moved to reach for Clay's arm, to *make him* stop when Jared winked at me and dodged Clay's next swing, shoving Clay hard enough to knock him to the side and get in a good right hook of his own.

...a distraction, I realized. They were making a distraction.

As much as I hated it, with a quick glance around, I could see that all the attention from the stands had been re-directed at them, *not* at Viv.

The same couldn't be said of many of the other players and the refs and coaches. They were all crowding the girl writhing in the grass. Layla was nearly there, hopping from the bottom step.

Vivian's coach whirled on her after checking the other girl, a cell phone raised to her ear. I had to assume an operator was on the other end of the call. The girl was going to need a doctor. A much better one than the nurse practitioner we had on staff at Forest Grove High.

Vivian cast her gaze away from the coach, dropping her head. In the movement, I saw the inhuman glow of her eyes. In her clenched fists, I could see the strain of her wolf like a spirit in her veins. Pulsating. Aching to be free.

With my heart breaking, I shouted down to her,

"Run!"

Her gaze snapped up to meet mine, crazed and ringed in halos of deep ochre. I watched as a single tear fell before she tore away from her shouting coach and fled in a sprint that was definitely too fast, away from the field, toward the woods, with Layla hot on her trail. A crash behind me sent me skittering into action. I raced for the stairs, calling back over my shoulder to Clay and Jared as they fought to the jeers and cries of surprise of the others in attendance. *"Cabin!"*

I couldn't bear to look at them, even knowing their bloody lips and bruises would heal wasn't enough for me to be able to watch them pummel each other. I was going to *kill* Clay when they got back. Couldn't he have done something else?

Literally *anything* else?

Past the point of being able to think about it, I jumped from the bleachers when I was close enough to the bottom not to draw notice and sprinted after Layla and Viv just as the sounds of sirens flared to life in the distance.

It wasn't hard to track them. Layla's jasmine scent made an easy trail to follow all the way through the school lot and onto the hiking trail, then a half a mile in to the east.

"Vivian!" I called, trying to decide if I should shift. My wolf could cover more ground faster. She could sniff them out better.

I groaned, whirling in a circle, trying to tune in to my heightened senses. Listening for the sound of them. Peering into the brush. But twilight made it hard to see. "Layla!"

"Here!" I heard faintly, Layla's voice carrying on the cool breeze.

It took me only a few more minutes to find them. Vivian sitting with her back against a tall, moss- covered stone, her head locked between her knees as she trembled. Layla crouched at her side, rubbing her back while she whispered reassuring words.

A twig snapped under my foot, and Vivian looked up at me, a snarl twisting her face. Even though her eyes still glowed vividly, and her claws and canines were still elongated, she hadn't shifted. She had managed to keep her contained.

Shock wasn't a strong enough word for what I was.

"You were right," Vivian sneered at me. "Go ahead. Say it! You were right, and I was wrong and now Bev has a broken fucking collarbone, and it's all my fault."

She broke into a sob on the last word, her body tightening, her shoulders rolling inward. I could count on one hand the number of times I'd seen Viv cry. Hell, I could count on two fingers. And those two times were both before she turned twelve.

"I wasn't going to say that," I told her, edging closer. I didn't want to spook her, that would only make it harder for her to control her wolf.

"Well you *should*. She'll be out for the rest of the season. Maybe even next year, too."

I wanted to ask her what had happened, but it didn't matter. She'd probably just checked Bev too hard. That's all it would take. "I'm the one who's sorry," I muttered, dropping to my knees beside her and Layla, not caring as a cold wetness seeped into my jeans. "This wouldn't even be happening if...*if*..."

"Oh, fuck off," Viv said. "You don't get to have the blame for this. This was *me*. My stubbornness. I *knew* this would happen, you know that? I fucking knew it, but I convinced myself it wouldn't just so I could keep one normal thing—just *one* and..." she trailed off, her sobs getting too heavy to continue.

Unable to help myself, I leaned in and wrapped my arms around her. Layla did the same, the two of us sandwiching her from either side as tight as we could. I don't know how long we stayed that way, but by the time Layla began to let up, Viv had stopped crying, and her fingernails were no longer jabbing sharply into my forearm. They were back to a more normal, human length and bluntness.

Vivian lifted the hem of her jersey to her face to swipe away her tears. "Maybe Ryland was right," she said. "Maybe I should stay at pack camp for a while. I can probably come up with some sort of excuse for my paren—"

"*No*," I all but growled. Even thinking about Vivian staying at camp, so close to Ryland, gave me goosebumps and made my stomach clench.

"If you want to stay at the cabin, you can, but there's no way in hell you're going back to camp."

Layla cocked her head at me, her brows lifted as though seeing something that'd been there all along, but that she'd somehow managed to miss. On the contrary, Vivian just looked confused. For the moment, it seemed, they'd switched places.

"Allie?" Layla prompted. I sighed.

"Am I missing something?" Vivian asked, digging her palms into the dirt to push herself into an upright seat. "I know the guy is a dick, but—"

"It's not that."

"Then what?" Layla asked, her manicured brows knitting together.

I'd promised them... No more lies.

And if I were going to be able to keep them away from Ryland, they'd have to know why, right?

A million questions stomped and scurried across my thoughts. A million reasons why I *should* tell them everything. And a million reasons why I shouldn't.

I bit the inside of my cheek and sat back into the wet leaves and damp soil. "I'm going to tell you everything," I started, trying to find the right way to begin. "But you can't talk about it. Not with anyone."

Layla sagged, her expression telling me she wasn't the least bit surprised there was more awfulness incoming. Vivian, on the other hand, had grown stiff, the sorrow and guilt that'd been weighing her down lifted in favor of her patented *nobody-fucks-with-my- friends* look. From defense to offense in the blink of an eye. Happy to let the weight of my problems erase her guilt. Distract her from what she'd just done.

"Not even Destiny," I added, before I started, shooting a pointed look Viv's way.

She chewed on that for a second before finally nodding. "All right. I won't say anything."

I told them all of it. My suspicions. Clay and my excursion to the eastern pack to investigate. What we found out. How we didn't have any proof but that I figured it must be true.

Layla was turning a shade of green visible even though the sky was casting shades of orange over the forest. Vivian's reddened cheeks only looked more inflamed beneath the warm hue.

"Please tell me that's all of it," Vivian spoke through clenched teeth.

I wished I could.

I frowned, a mental image of a man shot at point blank range in cold blood flashing in my imagination. "There's one more thing. Not even Clay knows about it—"

"I don't know about what?" Layla screeched like a cat.

"*What the hell?*" Viv demanded, brushing off her knees as she shoved to her feet.

I froze, turning my gaze in horror to find a battered but quickly healing Clay standing barely a stone's throw away. How long had he been there?

A hot flush crept up my neck. It was borne of guilt but quickly morphed to white hot fury when I got a good look at him. His knuckles bloody. His lip swollen and split on the left side.

"Where's Jared?"

"Is he always so quiet?" Layla asked. "I didn't even hear him coming, like, at all. Did you?"

Vivian snorted, and from the corner of my eye, I could see her appraising his wide shoulders and tall, bulky frame. His size thirteen shoes. Viv shook her head.

Clay, completely ignoring my question, let his hard stare pass from me to Vivian, and then to Layla. He came to stand in front of me, fixing me with an accusatory stare that made my blood boil.

"You fucking told them, didn't you?" I cringed.

"*Christ,* Allie, what were you thinking?"

Was it wrong that I was relieved he seemed to have forgotten the part of the conversation he'd interrupted, because *damn,* I nearly pissed myself when I heard him. Clay gnawed his lower lip, throwing his hands through his hair as he stepped to the left, and then back to the right, as though unsure where to go, or what to say, but needing to move anyway.

"Okay," he said, and then more firmly as he paused in his short pacing steps. "*Okay.* I don't like it. Not one fucking bit."

Coming out of his rage, his face turned back from a scary shade of crimson to his normal slightly inflamed pink. He shot a look to Vivian. "You can't say anything about this, not even to—"

"I know," she interrupted, crossing her arms over her chest. "I won't tell Destiny. I already promised."

Clay nodded, satisfied for the moment. He licked his lips, thinking.

I had been about to demand where Jared was again when I heard a howl far in the distance. It was him—I was sure of it. He must've gone to the cabin while Clay followed our trail just in case we were already back there waiting for them. Or, more likely, maybe he went to make sure Bev was going to be all right.

That made sense.

"You shouldn't have told them," Clay growled at me and Viv tipped onto the balls of her feet, looking like she was ready to put the big bastard in his place if I didn't.

Luckily for her, or maybe for Clay, I'd learned to deal with the brute myself.

"They're my *best friends*. I can't lie to them. Not anymore."

Clay made an exasperated sound and clenched his jaw.

"We can trust them."

Clay's cut-glass stare softened as he took me in. He nodded once, turning to face my friends once more. "All right. Then maybe you can help."

"Whatever we can do," Layla said at about the same time Viv said, "Count me in."

"Wait," I said, confused. "Help? Do we have a lead?"

"No," he replied, lowering his voice to a deep rumble. "But I think I know where we can find one."

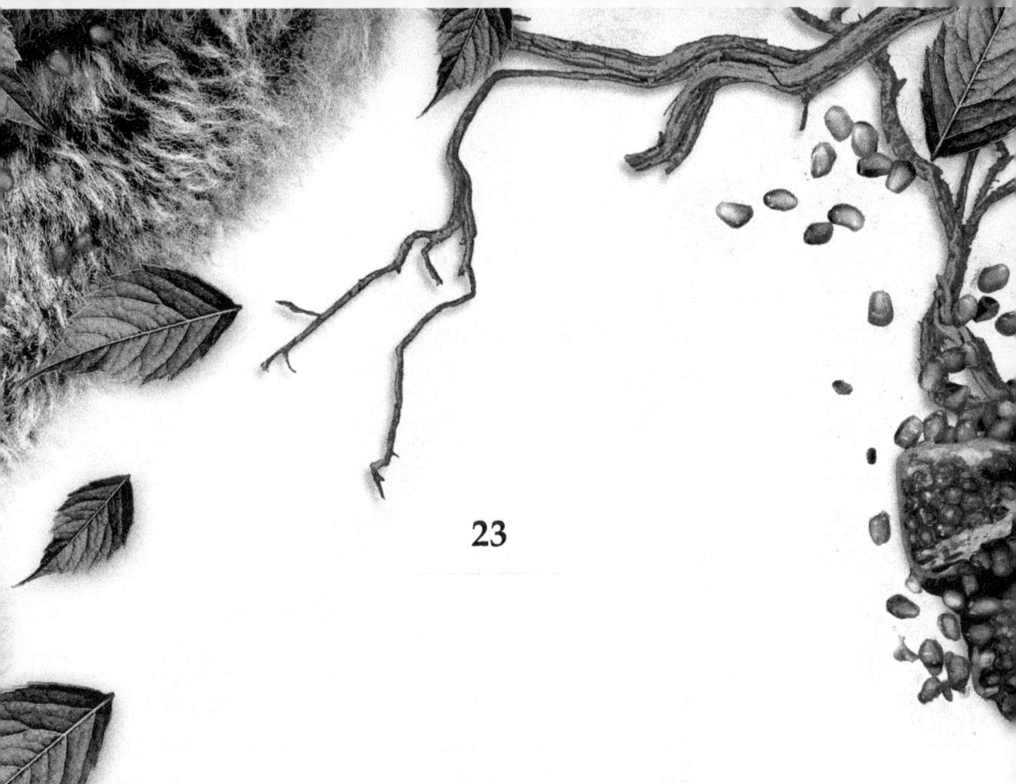

23

My arrow left my bow, sailing through the mist of early morning and into the target, burrowing into its heart.

Damn.

The third bullseye of the morning. That had to be a good sign, right? Maybe it meant today wasn't going to be the epic failure I was dreading it would be.

Stop thinking like that.

Failure wasn't an option. If we failed tonight, it would mean more than losing an opportunity to expose Ryland for what we all thought he was—it could mean we didn't get to see the sunrise tomorrow. That this cool mist caressing my cheeks would be the last kiss I ever received.

I shuddered, shaking off the chill clinging to my bones, and notched another arrow. My shoulder twinged with a sharp pain, and I relaxed it, dropping my arm to roll my shoulder once, twice, three times the charm.

We may have healed quick as a whip, but when you'd been putting your body through what I'd been forcing mine to endure these past three days, it was bound to leave some lasting aches and pains.

The defensive training Clay and I had started weeks ago had started up again.

After coming up with a promising, if a more than a little risky plan

643

to find some evidence of what we feared, Clay had insisted we start again. I agreed, but I'm not sure I would've if I'd known how hard he'd intended to push me. We didn't just train in the mornings anymore. We trained after school, too, since my job was no more. Sometimes he ever insisted on my sparring with Jared in the evenings, to get some actual practice.

Clay was too big for us to be evenly matched. I was getting quicker. Stronger. And he'd taught me some dirty tricks. But there were certain positions he would get me in where I simply had no hope of getting out. His weight was too much for me, especially after he'd already worn me out with a good long run and an icy dip in the stream.

I could best him in strength if I were fresh and ready for it, though, a fact I did *not* let him forget. Whatever strange power allowed me to have two mates and made me strong of will, seemed to also make me stronger than a shifter my size and age should have been. At least, that's what Clay and Jared said, and until I was in a real fight, I'd never know if it was true or if they were just saying it as an excuse because they didn't like being knocked on their asses by a girl. I didn't relish the thought, but I'd admit, I was a bit curious to put their theory to the test.

It made sense, I supposed. As much as anything made sense to me these days.

Finished with a long, rolling stretch of my shoulder, I notched the bow again and sent another arrow soaring. It sank in barely an inch above the bullseye. Not amazing, but still better than last week. I'd take it.

I reached for another and frowned when my fingers grasped empty air. Had I really already used them all? I sighed, snatching up the quiver from where it leaned against my ankle to go and retrieve my arrows, slinging the bow across my back.

This was the first morning I'd woken before Clay in time to come out here before he could drag me away for another lesson, and I breathed deeply. The scents of cold pine and molting leaves were a comforting undercurrent to the stronger scent of the mist itself. Like dew. Or the smell of the earth after it rained.

It reminded me of simpler times.

Of mornings spent ten feet off the ground in Dad's hunting blind, peering out the tent flaps to take in the dawn with a cup of hot oats and huckleberries.

I missed that girl.

Wondered if I'd ever know what it was like to be her again.

I was glad Jared suggested I go shoot some arrows before he had to leave early this morning. It was the best idea anyone had given me in a long time. I'd wanted him to come with me, but he insisted he had a quick errand to run for Ry about the quarry, and I couldn't argue with him.

Especially not when it was to do with his uncle. I was terrified he would see everything that was going on written on my face. I still hadn't told him.

I'd planned to. Especially after telling Layla and Viv. But even they agreed he shouldn't know. Not until there was hard evidence to back it up.

So every day I was just more and more uncomfortable, waiting for the chance to put our half-baked plan into motion so I could finally say *something* to Jared. Even if that something was that I was a complete idiot and that there was nothing to tell.

A blaring chirp from my cell phone killed the calm of the moment, sending a cascade of blackbirds flocking to the sky, crowing their displeasure in their wake.

I fished it out, dropping the quiver near the target.

Clay: Where are you? Training in ten.

I groaned to myself, stuffing my phone back in my pocket without replying.

It chirped again, and I muttered to myself as I pulled it back out. *Seriously?*

Clay: Answer me or I'm going to assume you're dead and need avenging.

Clay: Going once. Clay: Twice.

Allie: I'm coming. Allie: Chill.

I grumpily shoved my phone back into my pocket, flicking the switch on the side to toggle it to silent mode. He could fucking wait. I wasn't going to rush. Not today. He could kick my ass when I was good and ready to receive said ass kicking and not a minute sooner.

I snatched up my arrows and shoved them into the quiver, my chest tight.

"Happy birthday, Allie," I told myself with a sarcastic snort, shouldering the quiver along with the bow for the long walk home.

WHEN I FINALLY MADE MY WAY THROUGH THE LAST OF THE TREES AND ONTO THE dirt lawn, peering up grouchily at the front door, it was eerily quiet.

"Clay?" I called, searching the windows for any sign of him. I'd bumped into Jared on his way out to run an errand at the ass crack of dawn for Ry, and it looked like he still wasn't back yet, either. "I'm back!"

When he didn't materialize, I dutifully checked my phone, assuming because I'd muted him that he'd likely gone on that murderous rampage he'd threatened before I left the clearing. *Shit.*

It buzzed in my hand before I could turn it on.

Clay: Behind you.

I spun, jumping when I spotted him leaning casually against a tree at the far side of the property. The bastard had clearly watched me stomp back onto the property and hadn't said a word.

"What are you doing?" I asked, setting my things down on the porch.

Here I was in sweats, a tank, and loose-fitting sweater, ready for an ass whooping, and he was...

What the hell was he doing?

Clay wore his signature dark wash denim jeans, but these weren't the grease stained ones I'd grown accustomed to seeing on him. These were...well, they looked brand new.

He even had a fitted black button-up on, the sleeves rolled to the crease of his elbows, making his forearms look drool-worthy and biceps like cannons.

And was that *product* in his hair?

"What did you do?" I asked, suddenly *very* aware of the scent of jasmine on the breeze. And the rustle of something coming from behind the cabin. "I *told* you I didn't want—"

"Too bad."

"Ugh."

"Ugh, yourself," Clay countered with a wicked smirk, coming to stand before me.

My shoulders slumped, giving in to whatever horribly embarrassing thing I was clearly going to have to endure whether I liked it or not. At least it looked like I was getting out of training today.

Look at the bright side.

Clay drew me in for a hug, and I let him, giving in as soon as his spicy metallic scent reached my nose. He brushed his lips against the top of my head, and I shuddered in his arms. "Happy birthday, baby."

Despite myself, my lips curled into a grin hidden against him. I fought back a sudden urge to cry and broke the hug, knowing if I stayed there, eventually, it was going to happen.

"Thanks," I muttered, my voice watery. I inhaled sharply and pushed air out through my lips. "Let's get this over with."

"That's my girl," Clay said, scooping me up from the ground and flinging me into his arms as he charged into a sprint, carrying me at a breakneck speed, squealing all the way until we were around the cabin, head on in front of the shop.

My feet touched back down on solid ground at the same time a cheer of "Happy Birthday!" rang out from inside the shop.

I nearly tripped on the gravel but managed to right myself in time to catch a hug from Jared. He lifted me from the ground, spinning me in a circle before putting me back down.

Somewhere in the shop, music began to play. Clay's playlist—now my favorite—starting up at the first song of the list.

Once the shock abated, I wrapped my arms around Jared, hugging him back tightly and whispering in his ear, "You dirty little liar."

He hadn't been going to run an errand at all. The bugger had been here the whole time. He hadn't gone on an errand for Ryland. He'd suggested I go shoot some arrows to get me to leave.

"Worth it," he whispered, his breath tickling my neck. "How was the morning?"

"Peaceful," I replied, my insides quaking as he brushed his lips quickly against the base of my neck before pulling away, purposefully *trying* to drive me mad if his smirk was any evidence.

"That's what I was hoping."

"Hey," Layla called, butting past Jared for a firm hug. "My turn."

She kissed both my cheeks when she pulled away. "So," she asked, gripping me by the arms with a conspiratorial look. "How does it feel? The big one- eight?"

I nodded, grinning. "It's...*liberating*," I said after a moment of thought. I'd texted Uncle Tim this morning and told him I wouldn't be needing his *check in* calls anymore—that he could get back to his glitz and glam life in Florida tending to the every whim of his selfish wife. But, you know, in a much nicer, more mature way than that.

First thing Monday I'd have the school remove him as my parental contact.

How did that saying go?

Oh yes. *I am the master of my own destiny.*

I still hadn't gotten a reply from Uncle Tim, but I assumed he was stewing about what to say. Probably gearing up from a novel-length response with lots of big words and *listen here, Allie Graces.*

The joke was on him, though. I didn't plan to read them.

Layla whooped and Viv stepped up from behind her, ready and waiting with a hug, too. She'd been a wreck at school the last few days, but I was glad to see only a trace of the heavy clouds she'd been carrying around with her since the lacrosse game still lingered.

Her coach and the team all brushed off the incident with Bev as a horrible accident. They didn't even plan to suspend Viv from the team, especially since she seemed too distraught over it herself, running away and all. They had no idea she *had* to run, and for a very different reason.

They took her decision to quit the team hard, but not as hard as she did.

It took two tubs of chocolate panda ice cream from Gerry's on Thursday night before she'd even agree to go back to school at all.

"Love you," she said as she squeezed me tightly. "You're the good shit, Allie cat. Happy eighteen."

"Love you too, Viv."

"Oh, and your gift was a team effort, so you can't be mad at anyone."

My stomach clenched.

I had told them I didn't want anything.

Suppressing a groan, I warily scanned the shop, looking for something wrapped to absolute perfection. Layla wouldn't have let anyone but her wrap whatever it was.

What I found, though, wasn't a boxy shape covered in sparkling ribbons and cleanly folded paper. It was easy to skim over in the shop, just sort of blending in.

Covered in a taupe colored tarp, the telltale shape of a car took up about half of the available space. Clay worked on old cars sometimes, as well as bikes. If it weren't for the very *Layla* black ruffled bow on the hood, I'd have assumed that it belonged to a client.

"Don't get too excited," Jared said with a half laugh, nervously shoving his hands deep into the pockets of his jeans. "She needs work."

"She's practically falling apart," Clay agreed, though I could tell they were only trying to downplay whatever was beneath the tarp and bow to make me feel better.

Layla sauntered over to the side of the car and curled her fingernails into the tarp, readying to unveil what hid beneath.

"Ready?" she asked me with a wide grin, but didn't wait for me to reply. I was too dumbstruck to speak.

My tongue felt swollen, like it didn't quite fit within the confines of my mouth anymore.

Layla tore the tarp off, sending the bow flying across the shop to land with a crinkling thud against the other tarp Clay still kept covering the opposite wall. Covering the map pinned to the wall beneath.

A choked gasp nearly cut off my air supply, and I coughed as I took her in.

"We weren't really sure what you would like," Jared began, his tone tentative, as though he were speaking to a cornered animal instead of his mate. I wondered what my face must have looked like.

"Which is why we asked your friends," Clay finished.

"And *we* told them exactly what you wanted," Viv announced with a warm smile.

Layla patted the roof of the car and leaned against her side. "You've talked about fixing one up since you were, like, twelve," she said. "If you start now, you can probably have her running by the time you get your full license."

"I...I can't..." I croaked, my eyes welling.

Jared wrapped a warm arm around my shoulders, steadying them.

"*You can*," he disagreed. "We all chipped in. Clay and I got her off a guy up in Seattle."

"And we got you a few parts that Clay said you would need—they're in the trunk," Viv continued, gesturing to the black beauty.

"Th-that's where you were?" I asked, my brows lowering as I considered Clay. I thought he'd been with Sam this whole time. Though I'm sure he was for most of it, it seemed like he was also on a road trip to go and pick up a *freaking car*.

Clay lifted his shoulder in a shrug, smirking.

"So," he said, a brow arched. "What do you think?"

I turned back to the car, a sob expanding beneath my breastbone until it was almost painful. A 1970 Chevelle.

Dad had a calendar of old cars in the kitchen growing up. I'd always remember when he flipped the month from October to November and *there*, gleaming on the top of the page was this exact car, albeit shinier, her chrome practically blinding. I knew then that *that* was the car I wanted some day, and it just stuck.

When November rolled to December, I tore that image out of the calendar and taped it to my bedroom wall. It stayed there until Dad passed—the house needed to be sold to cover his hospital bills.

Even in the condition it was, with the start of rust on her fenders, a few dings in her right side, and a missing headlight, I knew she would have cost a small fortune. Certainly, more than I had in my savings account to repay them.

"I know what you're thinking," Clay said, his voice taking on that foreboding tone I knew meant he would accept no argument. "And you are *not* paying us back for it. We'll fix 'er up together, and then I intend to take her for a spin myself. I consider that payment enough."

"I...I don't know what to say," I said, my voice a distant whisper. "I didn't want to accept it. Knew I shouldn't. But fuck if I didn't want that car more than just about anything else in the whole world right now.

"Say thank you," Vivian said with a nonchalant shrug. "Obviously."

"Thank you," I managed as a tear finally escaped, and I swiped it away before anyone could see. "I freaking hate all of you though. I can't believe you hid this from me. And you *know* I *hate* gifts."

I took a long breath and managed to soothe the tremor in my shoulders just as Jared loosened his grip on me, letting me go. "We know," he said. "But we just don't care."

I shoved him and laughed, taking a tentative step toward my new wifey.

"There's one other little thing inside," he said, moving toward the back of the shop where I could see a big white box and plates atop the counter. "Go check her out and then we'll have cake."

Shaking my head, I clenched my hands and tip toed nearer, almost afraid that if I took my eyes off of her that she would vanish before I could ever feel the curve of her steering wheel beneath my fingertips.

Layla opened the door for me, a shrill screech sounding as she did.

She winced. I laughed.

She wouldn't understand that I was *glad* she needed work. I wouldn't have it any other way.

"Maybe I'll just leave it open," she muttered when I inched past her and lowered myself into the driver's seat. "I don't want to snap the door off or something."

Her leather seats were torn on the edges and worn from overuse and sitting too long without proper care, but they formed to my body nonetheless, the smell of dusty carburetor and sun-heated leather filled my nose. I gripped the steering wheel, wringing my hands over it before shifting one to brush a palm over the wide dash.

"Look up," I heard Jared holler and glanced up to see him in the rearview, sticking candles into a chocolate cake. Then something else caught my eye. A photograph, the edges slightly curled.

In it, a woman with long white-blonde hair smiled at the camera, her belly swollen and gray eyes bright as she stared up at the man who held her. His thick arms wrapped tenderly around her from behind, his fingers splayed over her pregnant belly beneath a pretty yellow dress and jean jacket. Dad.

It was dad.

It was a picture of us. All of us.

Before this cruel world stole away the sister I should've had, then my mother, and finally, my father.

I didn't know a picture like this even existed. My throat burned as I tugged it free from the clip holding it in place on the sun visor and shakily brought it closer. They looked so happy together. They had no idea that in a matter of weeks from when this was taken, Diana Grace would be gone forever, and my father wouldn't ever smile quite as widely ever again.

My chest ached as I traced the line of dad's scruffy jaw and found parts of me in mom. I'd only ever seen a handful of pictures of her. Dad had put most of them away after the first couple of years, keeping only the super worn one he always had in his wallet, tucked behind a credit card.

That photo was taken long before this one, when they were still young, before they were ever married or pregnant. She seemed different in this one. Vibrant with life. Beaming as though lit from within.

A tear fell onto the photograph, and I smeared it away, trying to get control of myself. I hugged the photo to my chest, pretending that it was them and not just their likeness captured in mercury infused paper.

I never knew what it was like to be held by my mother, but my Dad had given me all the love he'd had left to give before he passed. Enough for both of them.

Even though I was the one who took her away from him.

If my sister had lived instead of me, would she still be alive? Would they both still be here? Would they be singing happy birthday with smiles on their aged faces, welcoming their daughter to adulthood?

I dropped my head, blinking away blinding tears to stare at the photograph once more, willing myself to see it from another perspective.

It's not my fault, I mouthed the words, tasting them to see if they could be swallowed.

It was what Dad always told me. It was what everyone told me.

Of course, it wasn't your fault, Allie Grace, Dad would say, giving my boney eight-year-old shoulders a squeeze. *Your mom wanted you more than she wanted anything else in the whole world. She's probably up there right now, wishin' you wouldn't be so hard on yourself. I know she wouldn't want you sad. Not even for a second.*

But if she didn't have me, she'd still be here.

There's no way anyone can know that, Allie. Now, come on, buck up. All you can do now is make her proud, 'kay kiddo?

I'd put my tough girl face on and nodded, ignoring how my eyes still watered and spilled over despite my tiny clenched fists and squished together brows.

Dad always knew what to say, with just the right mix of patience and understanding, but also enough tough love to set me straight. I realize with a dawning certainty that there was something I needed to do before tonight. Before Ryland celebrated his new mate under the watchful eye of the moon and we put Clay's plan into motion.

There was someone I needed to talk to. Someone I should have gone to for advice a long time ago. He'd been there all along, waiting for me to come, but I couldn't do it. It hurt too much.

But I could see now that was selfish. Cowardly.

And my dad hadn't raised a fucking coward.

Nodding to myself, I sniffed hard and gently tucked the photo back into place on the visor above my head. I pressed two fingers to my lips and then to the worn photograph.

"Miss you," I whispered before tearing my eyes away from the faces of my smiling parents and swiping my palms over my eyes. I didn't know how I was ever going to thank Jared, and I was afraid to ask where he even managed to find the photo, having a sneaking suspicion he must have broken into the storage unit and gone through about a million boxes to find it.

It took another minute before I was ready, but then I stepped back out of the car, breathing through a bubble of emotion in my throat.

They were all there waiting for me. My family. Standing shoulder to shoulder. Jared held a chocolate cake between his hands, eighteen candles burning down to the base in a wide circle along the outer edge.

"Happy birthday to you," Clay began, and I laughed, shaking two more tears free of my eyes as the others began to sing with him. A tightness made me press my fisted hands to my chest, afraid something within might shatter if I didn't hold it together.

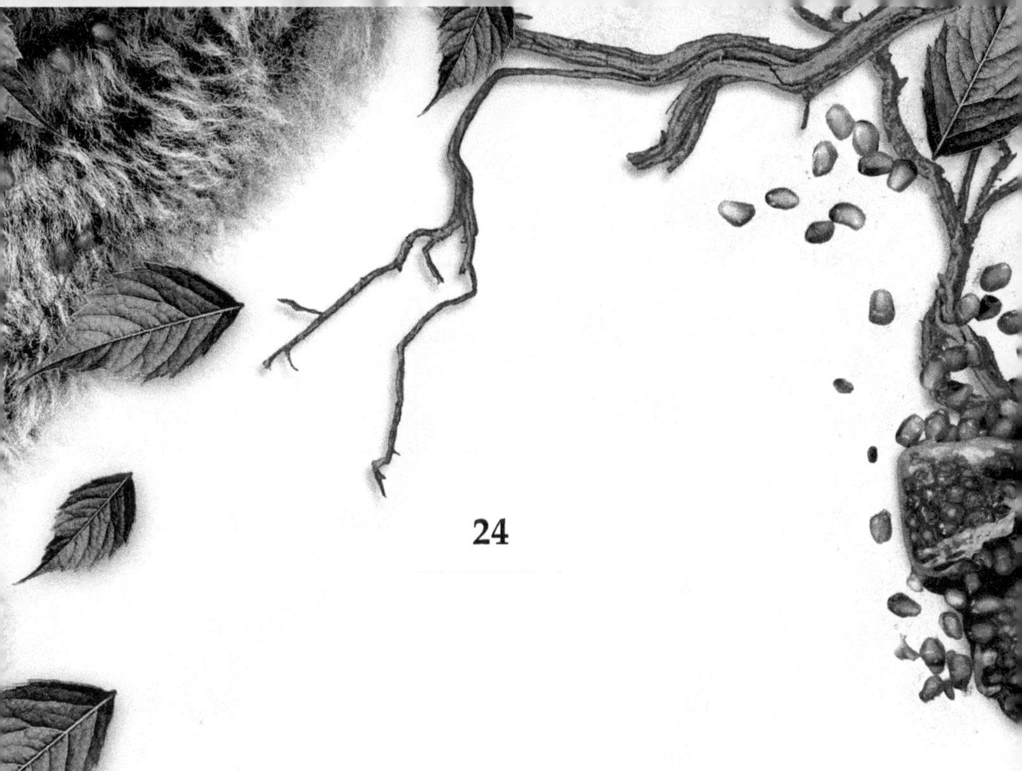

24

W e'll be right here if you need us," Jared said as he put his Jeep into park on the side of Loft Pines Road near the entrance to Pine Grove cemetery.

My skin bristled as I took in the stone grave markers jutting out from the earth in straight lines and winding pathways. The great iron gates standing wide for visitors to come and leave flowers or picture frames next to headstones.

I hadn't been here since the day we buried him. A heavy guilt settled in my stomach like lead.

Shifting uncomfortably, Clay added, "You sure you want to go alone?"

I almost laughed. I *had* wanted to go alone. I'd told them as much once the cake was completely demolished and all the tears had dried up. Later tonight we would all be at pack camp—Ryland had summoned us all to join him in welcoming Sam to the pack. But I needed to do this first, and I needed to do it now.

I should have done it a long time ago.

These two idiots insisted on coming along, promising they would just wait by the car, out of hearing distance. For Jared, I knew the reason was because he wanted to be there for me. To hold me close if I returned to the Jeep broken.

655

Clay may have had similar intentions, but we both knew the main reason he wouldn't allow me to run all the way to the cemetery alone in the hours before sunset: it wasn't safe.

Any minute of any day Ryland could find out what we'd done—where we'd gone. And like Clay, I didn't think he'd hesitate to punish us for it.

"I'm sure," I told Clay, the door creaking as I opened it slowly and stepped out.

We'd dropped Layla and Viv off at their houses to get ready for tonight. They'd both meet us back at the cabin after dark to head to pack camp together. I sort of wished I'd let them come, too, but knew it had to be this way or no way at all.

"I'll be back in a few."

"Take your time," Jared urged, his gaze steady and sincere. "We'll wait for as long as you need us to."

My heart clenched because I knew they would. They'd wait all damn night if I took that long. They'd miss Sam's welcome ceremony and remain there, unchanged until dawn.

I fucking loved the shit out of them for it.

Even though I'd only been there once before, I had no trouble at all finding Dad. The path we'd walked from Uncle Tim's used Lexus into the cemetery would be forever engraved in my memory. Layla and Vivian had come with me that day even though Uncle Tim had tried to insist there be family only at the internment.

I'd flat out told him they were coming and that maybe *he* should be the one who didn't come. He'd barely spoken to dad for the last three years, even while he was sick.

Every step brought with it the urge to panic as I neared his headstone. Quick breaths sawed out through my clenched teeth and that damned fluttering behind my ribcage grew to an intensity that made it a wonder I could even stay on my own two feet.

A chill wind swept through the cemetery, lifting my hair and leaving a lick of cold on the back of my neck. My teeth chattered, catching the first trace scent of winter on the air.

I almost didn't recognize the stone, grown over with moss and vines as it was. Dirty and chipped in one corner. Uncle Tim had chosen the stone, and I'd hated it as much then as I did now. The color of poached salmon with Gregorian script. Dad would have hated it.

But at least the inscription rang with truth.

Loving Father.

"Hey Dad," I said, throat constricting as I bent to my knees in the overgrown grass and began picking vines and scraping moss from the face of the gravestone.

"I'm sorry I—" the words were choked off by a sob, and I had to force it down to continue. "I'm so sorry I didn't come sooner. I just...I just *couldn't.*"

I wiped my face and sat back, straightening. "I know that's no excuse, but...but I'm here now and I need your advice." I barked out a broken laugh. "*God,* you always gave the best advice. It didn't always make sense at the time, and I may not have always listened to you, but I'd give just about anything to hear one shred of advice from you right now."

I grimaced, setting my palms down against the cold earth, slithering my fingers through the grass at the base of the stone. He was right there. Buried somewhere beneath my hands. I'd never been religious. Wasn't sure I believed in heaven or an afterlife, but if people could turn into wolves, then couldn't angels be a thing, too?

Couldn't heaven?

Could he be here right now, listening?

"I fucked up, Dad," I muttered. "A lot of bad shit has happened because of me."

I paused to catch my breath.

"But a lot of good stuff has happened, too."

I thought of Jared and Clay, and the connection that brought the three of us together. No matter that it wasn't normal, I could never see it as being *wrong.* That was the one thing I knew wasn't a mistake.

I told him everything. About what happened with Devin. About Jared and Clay. About Layla and Vivian. About Ryland and what we planned to do. Once I started, it was like I couldn't stop, the whole uncensored story rushing out of me like a flood.

"And I still haven't told Jared," I finished. "But I'm going to. I know that's what you'd tell me to do. Whether or not we find anything. Right? You'd say he had a right to know. I know you would."

In my mind's eye I could almost see him nodding.

Damn straight, he would say.

"I just wish you could give me some sort of sign... or, I don't know... just *something* to tell me what I need to do."

Silence was my reply, and I dropped my head, ready to leave. The sun was nearing the horizon, the autumn evening sky bright with the reddish glow of sunset. Jared and Clay would be getting worried if I didn't go back soon.

I sighed and peered over at the gravestone next to Dad's. In a shade similar to his, my mother's headstone sat in a similar state of neglect. With twitching fingers, I cleared it, too, picking off leaves and vines, brushing over the dirty face of it with the forearms from my sleeve.

"At least you're together again," I whispered, the words snatched up by a rogue wind as it funneled between their tombstones. Only one tombstone was missing, but the ghost of it squatted between theirs. The other daughter they planned for, but never had.

I wondered offhandedly what sort of flowers my mother would have liked, resolving to bring some for her once the things that needed dealing with were through. *Marigolds,* I thought, the flower coming to mind as though it were the easiest choice in the world.

Yes.

I knew she'd like them. "Your parents, I presume?"

The willowy voice broke my focus, and I jarred forward, tripping over myself in my haste to whirl around.

"Now, now, child. I didn't mean to startle you."

"Grams?"

Her blind eyes stared past me as she neared, folding herself into a seat on the grass at my side, tucking the long hem of her deep jade jacket beneath her.

"What are you doing here?"

Hazel tipped her head in the direction of a winding path that led over a grassy knoll in the cemetery. "Visiting my husband," she said. "I sit with him for a few hours every now and again."

Her husband?

"Oh," I said, unsure what else to say, still trying to get my pulse under control.

"Thought your voice sounded familiar," she said, her gaze sailing past me to rest near where my parents' tombstones were. "But I've never heard you here before."

"That's because I've never been here before," I admitted, shame coloring my cheeks in a way that I was glad she couldn't see. "Not since he was buried."

Hazel tipped her head to one side, and her long silvery braid slipped from her shoulder. "I see," she said, falling silent.

We sat there together, both grieving different people, but as one in our sorrow.

"Can I ask you something?" I said after a minute. Hazel dipped her head in a graceful nod.

I'd been waiting for her to come to the cabin. I'd wanted to talk to her after that night at the Four Corners. But I'd been more than a little preoccupied with Viv and Layla, and then afterward, with everything to do with Ryland. Now that she was here, right in front of me, I wasn't sure how to ask what I wanted to.

I had been so sure she'd been there that night. I'd seen her, her silvery hair and white gown billowing in the autumn breeze as she'd inclined her head. Silently helping me make the decision that led me where I was now.

"Why were you there that night?" I asked, shoulders tensing. "Why did you tell me to join the pack?"

For a full minute, a slight downward pull at the corner of her wrinkled lips was the only indication that she'd heard me at all. Finally, she breathed a sigh and reached her hands out to me.

I recoiled, but she managed to snatch up the wrist of my right hand. I let her, breaths coming more feverishly. Her milky gaze lifted, boring into me as though she could see as she flipped my hand over and traced the lines of my palm.

Instead of answering me, her thin brows pulled together, and her lips pursed. My spine tingled.

"I'm sorry that the stars have chosen you to walk this path," she said, her eyes downturned and cheeks growing sallow. "But walk it you must. You're the only one who can."

I swallowed, breath hitching. "What does that mean?"

I *hated* riddles.

Her brow furrowed as she pressed her clammy palm to mine, and I wondered what she was seeing that I couldn't. She'd told me once how she could see the inner workings of people. Their gears and cogs. The way they ticked. Their histories.

A deep and burrowing cold crept like frost over my bones. She knew, I realized. I let her touch me, and now she could see, in her way, what Clay and I were doing. I tugged my hand out of her grasp, my mouth going dry.

I rubbed the chill out of the hand she'd held with my other, hairs on the back of my neck standing on end. "You saw."

Her lips pressed into a taut line.

"Do you know what's going to happen?" I pleaded. "Do you know if we're right?"

She bowed her head, her gaze going back to the unfocused stare of a blind woman. "I can see history," she said, her voice a croak now, and I wondered if her ability exhausted her when she used it. She seemed almost to have aged another ten years in the last five minutes. "Pasts. Presents. Feelings. But...not the future, I'm afraid."

I slumped back, suddenly bone weary and wanting more than anything to be finished with this conversation. What exactly did I hope she could tell me, anyway? If Hazel knew anything, then surely she would have told her grandson. Or Jared directly. I pushed to my feet, casting a silent farewell to my parents.

"There's a reason Ryland forced me out of his pack," she whispered, so quietly I wasn't sure if I heard her. "And a reason he won't allow me near him. Has never allowed me to read him. I have my suspicions, just as you have yours."

She stood, hobbling as she did, and I noticed for the first time how she was barefoot, even in this cold. Maybe we should give her a ride home.

"Hazel, do you—"

"You're different, Allie," she said, interrupting as she brushed past me, headed back in the direction of the grassy knoll. "It's what sets you apart that will see your triumph. Embrace it... and don't forget it."

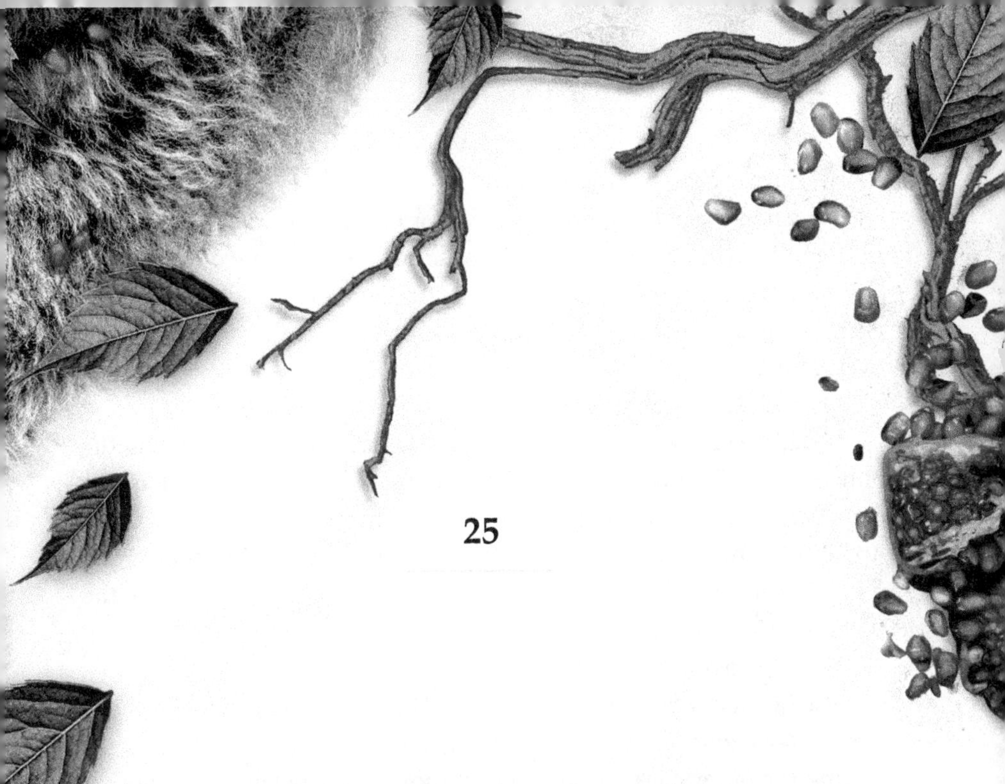

25

"What's this?" I asked, raising a brow at Clay as he handed me a black sweater.

His eyes flitted to Jared, Layla, and Viv where they were walking ahead of us. His hand clamped around my elbow, bringing me to a stall. "It's Sam's."

I lifted a brow. "What do you want me to do with her sweater?"

"Wear it," he replied, giving me a strange look. He rolled his eyes.

"For her scent," he whispered pointedly, gaze darting to Jared and back to me. "To put on when you go in. Make sure you put the hood up and rub your hands in the fabric a bit."

"Oh."

Right. I guess I didn't want to leave my scent all over Ryland's things. Why hadn't I thought of that? I took the sweater, tying it around my waist until I would need to put it on. Clay was still grouchy that we'd decided I should be the one to sneak into Ry's cabin and not him. I could use the excuse of having needed to use the bathroom if I were caught. He couldn't. None of the guys in the pack ever went into his cabin unless invited directly by him.

It was a territorial thing. It would be suspicious if Clay were found inside alone.

And there was no way I was going to allow Viv or Layla to do it.

661

Which left me. With them to cover for me and create a distraction if needed. If anyone were headed toward the cabin, Layla would scream. She had a *great* scream, and a fear of spiders she could blame it on without anyone suspecting anything other than that she was being a bit overdramatic.

"In and out," Clay reminded me. "In and out," I repeated.

It had been Clay's idea to search Ry's office. He and Grey being the only ones ever inside it, it would be the most logical place to look for any clues about the missing wolves or evidence of Adam's rumors. Apparently, most of the pack hadn't ever even *seen* inside that room, with Charity, Jared, and I being the only three ever to step over the threshold of the door.

Which begged the question...why?

Maybe, *hopefully*, because he was hiding something inside. Even I knew it was doubtful, but shy of taking a road trip up north in hopes of finding the other pack Ry ran with all those years ago and hoping that someone remembered—and had evidence of—what he'd done to that shifter woman who supposedly was pregnant with his child...well, this was the only other option.

We'd all agreed that whether or not we found anything tonight, we'd tell Jared all that we'd learned. We'd need him for the next part— to go into Ryland's e- mails at the quarry and open all the ones from the mysterious sender 'X.'

Whoever it was, they'd sent Ryland password protected files and images labeled with the names of the missing wolves. And that one labeled *List,* and the other labeled simply: *Jared.* If anyone were going to be able to figure out the password to open those, it would be his nephew, right?

That was...if Jared actually agreed to help us and didn't think we'd all lost our minds.

My stomach twisted and I winced, falling into step behind Clay as Jared called back to us, "Hurry up! We're already late."

Vivian winked at me as she waved for me to catch up to them. It was her job to see to it that Jared was also distracted. Ry and others may not notice my absence if I weren't gone too long, but Jared would.

I didn't fucking like this, not one bit—leaving Jared in the dark.

After the cemetery, I'd resolved to tell him, knowing that was what

Dad would've told me to do. But I'd been met with resistance from Layla, Viv, and Clay. There wasn't time. And our entire plan could be ruined if we tried to bring him into it at the last second.

I knew they were right, but I still hated it. The guilt gnawed at me, making my mood sour.

"I'm sorry this had to be tonight," Jared said, linking his fingers through mine when Clay and I caught back up to them. Clay eyed our clasped hands but said nothing. I had to hand it to them, they were really handling this whole *sharing* thing pretty well.

Then again, I guess there wasn't much choice. I cringed to think how the next conversation between the three of us would go, though. I didn't know how Clay would feel about taking the relationships to the next level. I mean, I was in no rush, but I didn't want *that* off the table. I was ready. Hell, I was more than ready. But if they needed more time to get used to the idea, I wasn't going to push them.

"Yeah," Viv added. "Having to celebrate someone else on your birthday is lame as fuck."

I shrugged, trying to hide the flush in my cheeks from view.

Get your head in the game, Allie, I scolded myself. I could worry about my relationships with Clay and Jared later. *Not the time. Not the place.*

"Doesn't matter," I said with as much cheer as I could muster. "I had a wicked birthday thanks to you guys. Honestly, I'm kind of relieved to pass off the spotlight. You guys didn't tell anyone else, right?"

I'd sworn them to secrecy, not wanting Seth or Charity or anyone else to make a big deal out of it tonight when the focus was meant to be on Sam, which was exactly where we *needed* the focus to be.

Jared squeezed my hand. "No, but I wish you would've let us. I bet Charity would want to know, and the others, too. Trey and Todd make *amazing* cupcakes. Honestly, you're missing out."

I chuckled. "Next year, okay?"

"I'll hold you to that," Jared said with a wink, giving me a sly look that made my toes curl.

We entered camp together, and I was surprised to see it wasn't the usual bonfire affair. Twinkle lights were coiled around tree trunks and draped like hanging moss from their branches. The pathways and channels between the cabins looked like they'd been swept and picked clean of weeds. Where we could see the fire smoke curling above the rooftops from the main gathering ring, there was also music, louder than we were ever allowed to have it.

Though natural pack magic acted as a sort of repellent for other supernaturals and mortals, keeping them away, I didn't think it could entirely conceal loud thumping music and bright flashing lights that could be spied from passing planes or choppers above or heard at a long distance. Ry was really pulling out all the stops for Sam. It made what we had to do that much harder.

Clay and I shared a look. I could see my own tension mirrored in the tight line of his jaw and the set of his mouth. Even though I didn't know Sam, and she made no secret of her distaste for me, I could tell Clay wanted her to be happy. And now she was.

If we discovered anything to implicate Ryland, we could be jeopardizing that happiness.

But...we could also be saving her. If Ryland had already killed one woman—a *pregnant* woman if you believed the rumors—who was to say he wouldn't kill his own mate? Just because I couldn't imagine ever laying so much as a finger on either of my mates didn't mean he wasn't deranged enough to do it.

Ryland's raucous laughter could be heard around the fire as we approached. He was easy to spot once we drew near enough, too. Sitting in a large wooden chair with Sam on his lap, his face reddened. His slippery grin stretching the puckered skin on his scars.

Sam looked equally joyful, her bitter attitude from when she and I had first met the other night gone. Replaced with an easy smile and a sense of ease about her that wasn't there before. She bantered loudly with Harrison and Forrest, who sat to Ryland's left on low tree stump stools. All of them holding glass steins of frothy beer instead of the usual red Solo cups we always used for weekend drinks around the fire.

I peered around, trying to spot familiar faces, but I didn't see Charity anywhere, or Seth for that matter. But after a minute, I found Trey and Todd standing by the beer keg, Kyle and Destiny with them.

"There's Destiny," I told Viv, pointing her out. Not that I needed to, Viv had already zeroed in on her mate, their eyes locking, matching grins splitting their faces. Viv glanced at me, asking for permission to leave her post distracting Jared for a minute. I nodded, and she and

Layla rushed over with warm hellos. I needed Ry to see that we were all here, including me, before we put the plan in motion.

"Want a drink?" Jared asked Clay and me, releasing my hand to follow Viv to the others and the keg.

"No," Clay and I said at the exact same time. I stiffened.

Jared cocked his head at us, giving Clay a particularly inquisitive stare. "*Okay,*" he said, enunciating the word. "You sure?"

Clay grunted, and I nodded, noticing how Sam's laughter had faded. I quickly glanced over to find Ryland's haughty stare locked on me. Good, he'd seen that I was here. And if he was looking, then I was sure he was listening, too.

"I'll have one in a bit," I told Jared, making sure to speak a bit louder than I needed to so it wouldn't be a struggle for Ryland to hear me. Thinking on my toes, I added, "I'm actually just super thirsty." I cleared my throat, the sound rough and forced. "I think I'm going to go get some water and see if I can find Charity."

Jared's gaze narrowed, and I flinched, quickly checking to see if Ry was still in tune to our conversation. He didn't seem to be. He was whispering something in Sam's ear. I watched as his teeth skimmed over her earlobe, making her shiver and me want to barf.

Jared closed the gap between us and lowered his voice. "Why are you so nervous?"

"What?"

He pulled back enough to search my eyes. I dropped them as quickly as I could, my throat thickening with words I wished I could say.

"Come on, Jare," Clay said, stepping past me to clap him on the shoulder. "I think I will take that beer. Let's let Allie go get Charity."

Jared looked like he wanted to say something else, but Clay's grip on his tightened, and I gave him an imploring look.

Talk later, I mouthed to him. *I promise.*

He paled, but let Clay drag him away, glancing back my way curiously before I tore myself away, forcing my feet into a slow, steady, *I'm-not-creeping-around* walk in the general direction of Charity's cabin.

We'd originally planned to wait until a bit later in the night, but maybe it was better to get it over with now. By the look of Ryland and Sam, they could end the festivities any minute to retreat back to Ry's cabin for an early evening delight.

And if I got it over with now, then I could make more of an appearance later when they did the formal ceremony—where my lack of attendance would be noted. That would be in about thirty minutes. Plenty of time to search an office, cover my tracks, find Charity, and convince her to come back to the fire with me, right?

Right?

Oh god.

Wringing my hands in Sam's sweater, I muttered hellos to a few shifters as they drunkenly stumbled past on their way to the fire and skirted around a cabin near Charity's. I didn't want to get too close to her cabin just yet.

The light was on, which meant she was definitely in there and I didn't want her hearing me or scenting me until I was finished with what I needed to do. I paused behind a quiet cabin and sent a group text to Clay, Viv, and Layla.

Allie: Go time.

A text from Viv came in a fraction of a second later.

Vivian: Already? We just got here.

Clay: Better to get it over with before the ceremony. Go, Allie, we got you.

I made sure my phone was toggled to completely silent and slipped into Sam's sweater, drawing up the hood with trembling fingers.

In and out, I reminded myself.

Easy.

Skirting around the backs of the cabins, I darted into the tree line, following it around camp at a distance far enough that no one would see me unless they looked closely, but close enough that I could see if anyone were to approach. I jogged on quiet feet, aiming for patches of earth and avoiding piles of leaves and twigs as best I could.

I wasn't concerned with leaving a trail, exactly— there were too many shifters here for anyone to decipher mine. I was more worried about making loud noises and alerting anyone to my presence as I came up behind Ryland's cabin, creeping around the moon chamber and into his backyard.

The cabin was lit softly within, Ryland had obviously left a lamp on in the main living area. But the upstairs and eastern side of the house, where his office was, were left in total darkness.

Just like Clay had said there would be, a sliding patio door to the right side revealed a small kitchen I'd never been in. And just like he'd said it would be, it was unlocked. I sighed gratefully as the door rolled away silently, allowing me to step inside with barely a sound and seal the door shut behind myself.

With my heart a thunderous roar in my ears, it was almost impossible to hear anything else inside the cabin. I stayed like that for a minute in the darkened corner of the kitchen, waiting for my pulse to slow so I could make sure there was no one else inside.

Satisfied, I crept to the arched doorway of the kitchen and peered into the living space. Next to me was a staircase leading up into the second level, and across the living room was the hallway that would lead me to Ryland's office.

The front door, mercifully, was closed. Whoever had used the restroom last must have shut it, and I sent whoever that person was my gratitude. Not wanting to waste time, I crept across the living room, nearly jumping out of my skin when I heard someone pass by near the front door.

I did exactly what I shouldn't and froze like a goddamned deer in the headlights. The creak and groan of the wood on the floorboards on Ryland's front stoop faded a second later. Distantly, I could hear Clay's laugh, clearly forced, but whoever he'd used it on to get them away from the cabin, it'd worked.

Thank you, Clay.

Unstuck, I swallowed hard and continued across the living room, practically at a sprint now as I rushed down the hall, opened the office door, and tucked myself inside, shutting it behind myself with fumbling fingers. I'd tried to slip the catch in quietly, turning the knob slowly, but it clicked like a gunshot in the dim office, and I stilled, grimacing as a layer of icy sweat slicked my chest.

Fuck. Maybe I should have let Clay do this.

Who was I kidding? I was not a damned ninja.

My anxiety couldn't handle this shit. I pressed a palm to my chest, willing the fluttering sensation there to take a hike and blew out a breath, steeling myself with eyes squeezed tightly shut before I shoved off from the wall and rushed to the desk. Eager to get this whole debacle over with so I could go back outside and take Jared up on that beer. Or five.

I rubbed my sweaty palms on Sam's sweater, hoping to get as much of my scent off of my hands and as much of *hers* on me as I could. Chances were Sam had been in here already, right? I really hoped so, because if not, Ry may have some questions if he happened to scent her in his office.

Let's just hope he didn't have any reason to come in here before morning, when the scent would most likely have faded beyond recognition.

I touched things as little as I could, easing drawers open to rifle through papers and pens. There was almost an entire drawer of errant receipts and safety pins, none of which looked important, but several that I took note of just in case.

One in particular, a bill from the hardware store that listed tarps and lighter fluid as the only purchases seemed suspect, but he could have used those items for any number of run of the mill things here at camp. I pocketed that one, anyway, thinking he wouldn't miss it in the mess of a hundred others strewn in the deep drawer.

I checked the other three drawers, finding two to be filled with general office fare. Staplers and a hole punch. A few rulers. Pencils. An eraser. A pair of reading glasses I could never have pictured Ryland wearing. A bottle of Advil. Two small bottles of whiskey. One full, the other nearly empty. In the last, largest drawer on the bottom left were files.

Jackpot.

There had to be something in there he was hiding. There were so *many* of them. I fingered through them, jumping at every creak and groan of the cabin to the point I was starting to worry if there actually *was* someone I was just going to wind up attributing the sound of them to Ryland's rickety plumping clattering behind the drywall.

I went through each label *twice* but found nothing that seemed even remotely out of the ordinary. I even took three files out just to see if their titles fit their contents. They did. Purchase orders for lumber for the camp. A generator manual and notes. A bunch of instructions on how to restart the solar system after a bad storm. I didn't even know there *was* a solar system. The panels must've been on the back of Ry's cabin for me to have missed them.

Groaning quietly, I tucked everything back where I'd found it, rolling the drawer shut with a solemn *click*. I checked the papers atop Ryland's desk next, followed by the bookcase on the wall to the right, feeling behind the books that were pushed forward.

If I were a crazy person who killed a bunch of people I was supposed to care about, where would I hide evidence of that?

Apparently, not in my office it would seem.

I knew I was taking too long even before I got the text from Clay. My phone illuminated in my pocket, and I drew it out, my fingertips numb from nerves.

Clay: You're taking too long.

I gripped the phone, pushing my screen to a point where it was near cracking, but I didn't care. There *had* to be something here, right?

A person couldn't just get away with everything Ryland had been accused of getting away with without leaving a shred of evidence behind.

Of course, there was a chance the rumors were just that—*rumors*—but my gut told me otherwise.

Allie: I need a few more minutes. Stall. Clay: Be quick.

There was no computer here, so that option was out, and I could see a cell phone charger plugged into the wall by the bookcase, but there was no phone attached, which meant Ryland must have had it with him.

Unless I was going to start ripping up floorboards, I'd already searched everywhere in the office. I bit my lower lip, letting my gaze sweep over the room one last time. I fixated on the ceiling, looking as though I could see through the wooden beams and plaster to the rooms above.

If I were a crazy person who had something to hide, would I hide it in my office? Or would I hide it somewhere more...private?

Say...my bedroom? Maybe?

A part of me knew I was grasping at straws at this point, but I was nothing if not thorough. *Just a quick look,* I promised myself.

Legs like putty, I crept from the office, pausing to listen for anyone outside. The music drowned out most every other sound, but even from here, I could hear Ryland's laughter and someone shouting for more shots.

Perfect. Hopefully by the time the ceremony started everyone would be too drunk to even realize I was gone at all. Armed with false reassurances, I took the stairs two at a time up to the second floor, grimacing as Ryland's peppery scent grew. It clogged the air, making me want to gag and sneeze in alternating intensities.

A familiar scent also permeated the air near the landing. It was clearly Sam's. It was the scent of the sweater I wore magnified. Juniper and something tangy, like orange juice left out in the sun.

There was only a single room sized door, another, smaller door led to a linen closet after a cursory peek within. I followed the intermingled smells of Ryland and his new mate to the bedroom, nudging the already slightly ajar door open enough for me to slide inside.

A tall king sized bed dominated the heart of the space. It squatted, pushed up against the far wall, two tall open windows on either side served to illuminate the space, casting the moon's glow over matching night tables near each of the extra-long pillows.

The blankets were rumpled and smelled of the deeds that'd been done beneath them. But that wasn't the worst part. The worst part was that Sam's wasn't the only scent clogging my nostrils. Faintly, as though someone had gone to painstaking lengths to remove it, I could also smell Charity.

If I weren't a hundred percent sure they'd been screwing, I was now.

I alternated between feeling sorry for Charity and relieved that she wouldn't ever share this bed with Ryland again.

A mirrored closet coaxed a short chirp from my lips, my own reflection startling me enough that a wave of icy cold stole over every inch of my flesh. In dark jeans and a black hooded sweatshirt, I didn't look myself. But the glow of my light gray eyes within the shadow of the hood were unmistakable. Wide and startled.

Get it together.

I went to the closet first, if only to roll my reflection away behind a non-reflective panel. A suitcase of women's clothes lay half spilled over the floor, clearly rummaged through in a rush. Sam's. Above, in neat rows, Ryland's clothing hung from all black hangers. His jeans were tucked into a shelving unit along one side. Several large-buckled belts hung on hooks next to them.

I felt around on the shelf above where the clothing hung, but my hand came away only coated in a layer of dust and sticky cobwebs. The other side was much the same. More clothes. An overflowing laundry hamper.

Damn. Damn. Damn.

Kneeling, I crawled over to the bed and lifted the corner of the blanket, careful not to touch too much of it. I huffed, finding a wooden board was beneath, sealing off the under part of the bed.

Inching the blanket away from one corner, I lifted the edge of the mattress, squinting to see into the cavity beneath.

Vacant, save for some lost coins and an old sock.

The nightstand was next, and I really wished I hadn't seen what was inside of it. There was no way I was touching any of that to search more in depth.

I padded to the other side, easing out the drawer of the matching nightstand. Within, there was an extra phone charger, some deodorant, cologne, and a tattered copy of a Jack Reacher novel.

I reached my hand into the back of the drawer to feel for anything else when a bloodcurdling scream sliced through the tepid silence, cutting me right down to the bone.

Fuck.

Below, the screen door clattered shut, and Ryland's voice called, "All right over there?"

An indiscernible shout echoed back, Layla telling him it was all right.

Another familiar voice bubbled with a dark laugh. "Hope I didn't scare her," Grey said. "I'm just passing through with my congratulations."

Double fuck.

"Stay for a drink, I have a favor to ask."

"Another one?"

"Possibly. Might be two."

With shaking fingers, I lifted the drawer from the squeaky casters, pushing it back shut, *praying* that they would go to the office for their drink and leave quickly. There was virtually no way I could creep back down the stairs and outside without one of them hearing me. The crinkle of plastic sounded before I could get the drawer shut, and I paused, listening as I lifted the drawer back out and pushed it back in, making it rub against whatever was making the noise a second time. I winced, hoping the sound was faint enough that they wouldn't be able to hear.

The solemn click of the office door closing downstairs gave me the courage I needed to reach my hand back inside the drawer. There hadn't been anything inside that would have crinkled like that. I was sure of it. So then what was making the sound?

I felt around again, biting my lower lip to a point near breaking the skin.

Come on.

Realizing the drawer only made the sound when I lifted it off the casters, I turned my palm upward, feeling the underside of the smooth top of the walnut nightstand. My fingers brushed over thick plastic, and I froze, feeling the rough fabric of Velcro straps holding whatever it was in place.

Lumpy shapes filled the bag. Two large ball-like forms and something small, like a thimble.

Breathless, I tugged gently on the Velcro strap, ignoring the light from my cell phone flashing like a strobe light in my pocket. The crinkle of it coming undone was so loud I gritted my teeth, not daring to so much as breathe.

But when the distant hum of Ryland and Grey's conversation downstairs never faltered, I let the bag drop into my palm and slowly drew it out, careful not to disturb it and end up making even more noise.

The blue-hued moonlight shining in a column through the window above the nightstand caught silvery white fur, and I stilled, my stomach turning. I flipped the bag in my fingers. It was no more than the size of a sandwich bag, but a heavy duty one—the kind we learned drug smugglers used to cover the scent of marijuana during transport.

Another bit of fur pressed against the thick plastic, this one the color of amber, threaded through with gold. I realized what they were with a stomach- churning squeal and dropped the bag as though burned by its contents.

A smear of old blood was matted on the amber fur, right where it was severed from the tail of a wolf.

Tails.

They were the tips of wolf *tails*.

And fuck if that white one didn't look a *lot* like Jared's.

...his parents.

I swallowed back bile, pressing the back of my hand to my mouth to keep it in, sidesheaving. My wolf raged within, awakening with a defensive snarl that came out through my human lips.

Downstairs, the office door creaked open. "What is it Grey?" Ryland asked.

The vampire didn't answer right away, but I heard his long intake of breath. Was he...was he trying to scent me? "Is someone else in here?"

Not wasting another second, I scooped up the bag and gagged as I shoved it down the front of Sam's sweater, beneath the neckline of my shirt, and jammed it between my breasts, shoving the drawer closed.

"Bring them here," Ryland growled, and I did the only thing I could think to do, backing up three steps before sprinting toward the tall, narrow window above the nightstand. I jumped onto the top of the stand and launched myself, knees lifted and elbows out through the screen, popping it out of place as I sailed through.

A breath hitched in my throat as my limbs flailed in midair, trying to position myself for the impact. I hit on the balls of my feet and rolled into standing, grateful my wolf seemed to know how to make that landing because I sure as hell didn't.

I sprinted past the moon chamber and ducked into the trees, not stopping once I had the advantage of tree cover. I kept going, heart thumping, legs pumping.

Panicked, I tried to find a place I could tuck away what I'd found in Ryland's bedside drawer so I could shift. Run faster. *Get away.*

I spied a crook in the base of a tree and skidded, trying to stop too quickly. I fell, sliding over loose dirt and leaves before clamoring back to my feet. I went absolutely still before I could reach for the evidence hidden in my cleavage. There, not more than ten paces from me, stood Grey.

The blue stone of his ring caught the moonlight, glinting almost as menacingly as his black eyes. He tilted his head to one side, a sneaking smirk pulling up one corner of his mouth. "Allie," he said, as though we'd met out here by a happy surprise.

I glanced past him, trying to judge the distance back to camp.

Was it too far for anyone to hear me scream?

Oh god.

I should have run straight for the bonfire.

Stupid.

"Why aren't you at the celebration?" Grey asked, his tone taunting.

"I—I was just—" I stammered, reaching for an excuse that would sound at least plausible, not sure there was a point in even giving one. He knew I was inside. The busted window screen was evidence enough that I'd jumped out, but did he know what I had?

Did I close that drawer or had I left it open?

Would Ryland check to see if his gruesome trophies were missing?

Grey's dark eyes narrowed, and I glanced past him again, searching for Ryland. Surely, he would have followed? Surely, he would want to know what I was doing in his house, alone. In his room.

"Ryland won't be joining us," Grey said, bringing his hands forward to steeple his fingers, tapping them to his lips as he stepped forward. I stepped back in response, my wolf at the ready.

"But don't fret, young one. Better it be me than him."

What the hell did that mean?

A thought crossed my mind, and I gasped, blurting the words before I could stop myself. "You're *X*. Aren't you?"

Surprise widened his eyes for a millisecond before he grinned. "I knew you were trouble from the first time I saw you. I told Ryland as much, but he never listens to me."

He stepped forward again, and a warning growl rose in my throat.

If I could help it, I wouldn't shift. If I did, it would send all my clothes, *and the evidence I found*, scattering to the ground where he could snatch it up.

"You can't best me, Allie. I'm over two hundred years old. If I wanted, I could have you willingly kneel before me. I could sweep that strange hair of yours away from your neck and drink my fill and you wouldn't make so much as a sound."

The reminder that he could compel me to do just that—to do *anything* he wanted—sent a fresh shock of fear pulsing through my veins. I shifted my gaze to his mouth, doing my best not to look him in the eye. That was how it worked, right?

"What do you want?" I demanded, curling my hands into fists.

"What do *I* want?" he asked, seemingly perplexed. "It isn't about what I want, dear one. It's about what must be done."

So, this is it then?

"He wants you to kill me, doesn't he?" I snarled, feeling my canines elongate enough to pierce my bottom lip. A hot dribble of blood rolled down to my chin.

A soft hiss escaped Grey's lips, and I saw his fangs sharpen, growing longer, too. He licked his lips. "He would like that, I'm sure, but no...at least, not yet."

If that wasn't an admission of guilt, I didn't know what was.

"Ryland killed them, didn't he?" I asked, emboldened now that I knew he didn't intend to kill *me*. "The shifters who keep vanishing. They haven't run away at all, have they?"

Grey clucked his tongue.

"*Didn't he?*" I pressed, my voice rising. "Just admit it."

Grey's lips pressed together as he regarded me with a cool sort of interest. Like he was impressed. "I don't think I can rightly give Ryland credit for my work," he said, his voice a sly whisper, smoother than silk.

"For your..." I trailed off, understanding at once what he meant.

"Ryland had *you* get rid of them," I said, more to myself than to Grey. A soft crinkle sounded from my chest as I pointed an accusing finger at him.

But what about...

"And Jared's parents? Did you kill them, too?"

All I needed was his admission of guilt. A nod.

Anything.

Something that would incriminate him and not Ryland. If he gave me that, I'd unleash my wolf.

Grey underestimated us. We were strong. Fast. We could take him.

We would revel in the taste of his blood coating our tongue.

Grey's smile grew. "Some things can be done as favors," he said, the 's' lengthening into a hiss. "But there are some things a man must do himself."

I gasped at the admission, my shock quickly morphing to anger and a dangerous understanding of what was going to happen next.

A bolt of white-hot apprehension seared through my chest as Grey darted forward, too fast for me to react while still dazed by his words.

My eyes met his and his lips parted. "Now..." he cooed, standing over me, his hand reaching up as though he intended to stroke my cheek. I did my best to stand my ground. "You will forget everything we just spoke about."

What?

"You will set aside your suspicions about Ryland, and you will convince anyone else who shares those suspicions that they are unfounded. *Ridiculous.* From this moment on, you will be *loyal* to him in every way."

A strange thought crossed my mind. A whisper of doubt planting seeds in the garden of my mind.

Maybe Ryland was *innocent. Maybe it was all a misunderstanding...*

I realized what Grey was doing with a start I hope he didn't see in my eyes. My clenched fists at my sides steadied me, fingernails digging deeply into flesh.

Stay still, I told myself, pulse thrumming like a hummingbird's wings.

Grey was trying to compel me. How hadn't I seen it before.

Holy fuck, this wasn't the first time, either, was it?

YOU WILL NOT TELL anyone of this meeting, he'd said to me in Ryland's office just over a week before. *You will not speak ill of your alpha. You will adhere to his will and command. You will be obedient.*

Except...I had told Clay of the meeting. And I *definitely had* spoken ill of Ryland. And I certainly was *not* obedient.

Like the spell shielding Clay's family's cabin from view, and the magic the witch had tried to use to heal my arm, apparently, a vampire's compulsion also held no sway over me?

"Do you understand?" Grey asked, a knot forming in his brow, and I realized I may not have been acting like someone compelled would act. I had no idea what that would look like, but I wanted—*no, I needed*—him to think this was working. It was the only way I was going to get out of here without a fight.

I forced my face to slacken, staring unblinking into his dark eyes, fighting my emotions.

"I understand," I replied, trying a slow succinct tone.

Grey bent closer, putting his face a mere three inches from my own. Near enough that I could smell the metallic tang on his breath and the musky scent of his aftershave. He searched my gaze, and I did my utmost best not to move, attempting to slow my erratic pulse.

He tipped his head to one side, brushing the tip of his index finger down from my temple to my jaw. I stiffened at the contact, my jaw twitching with the urge to bite his head off.

"Such a pity the Endurans claimed you first," he purred. "You would have made an *exceptional* vampire."

Don't shift. Don't shift.

"Since we're here," he continued, his gaze following the trail his finger had just made on the side of my face and down lower to my neck. "I don't see why we shouldn't make the most of it. I doubt Ryland would mind."

His fingers came to rest on the side of my neck, pressing against the pulsating artery there as his other hand came around my back, drawing me in closer to him.

No, I roared within. There was no way in *hell* I was going to let this happen. I began unfurling within, letting my wolf know that she was about to take the reins she wanted so desperately, giving her permission to *end* this fucker before he could sink his teeth into us.

On my mark, I whispered within, ready to let go, but not until the right moment.

Let him get a little closer.

Closer.

I held my breath. "Allie?"

Clay's growl rebounded through the woods.

In a matter of less than a second, Grey's hold on me loosened and then vanished entirely.

"Until next time."

His whisper lingered even after he was gone. "Allie! Where the fuck are you?"

"*H-here.*" I whispered, unable to project my voice as the weight of everything came crashing down around me.

We'd been right.

My stomach heaved and just as Clay reached me, I crumpled to my knees, retching into the dirt, my arms quivering beneath my weight.

"Hey," he said, rushing to sweep my hair away from my face.

"*Allie*," he growled. "Allie, what happened?"

Booted feet running through dry leaves sounded somewhere behind Clay, and I flinched, my watery gaze lifting to find the pursuer.

"It's okay," Clay said, rubbing a wide hand over my back. "It's okay, it's just the others."

"What the hell happened?" Jared's voice demanded, and I felt a tug as he gently folded me into his arms, enveloping me in warmth and his woodsy scent.

"Allie?" Layla.

"Did he touch you? I'll fucking kill—"

"Quiet," Clay barked, silencing everyone. "Jared, get her up. It's time for us to leave."

"But their ceremony—" Vivian began just as the hooting of cheers and the clatter of an applause rose from camp in the distance.

"Is already over," Jared snapped, his tone defiant and dangerous and not at all the one that I liked. I wanted my calm Jared. I needed him. As the dark spots crowded in at the edges of my vision, my panic taking root, I clutched him.

"Let's get you home," Jared said, and I felt my body lift from the ground just as my vision began to darken.

I fought against the dark and the fear that if my heart beat any more quickly—more erratically—that it would stop entirely. My wolf prowled, dogged by my panic, but enraged beyond measure.

"No," I muttered, trying to get a grip on myself. "*NO.*"

"Wait, stop," Clay bellowed, and felt Jared jerk beneath me. "What is it Allie?"

My head spun and the cold sweat that had bloomed over my chest earlier was beginning to creep like frost down my arms, leaving a numb tingle in its wake.

We were right.

I tried to say the words. I needed to make him understand that we couldn't leave. Sam was in danger. We were *all* in danger.

But my heart gave one more fitful stammer, and I jerked with the force of it before darkness consumed me.

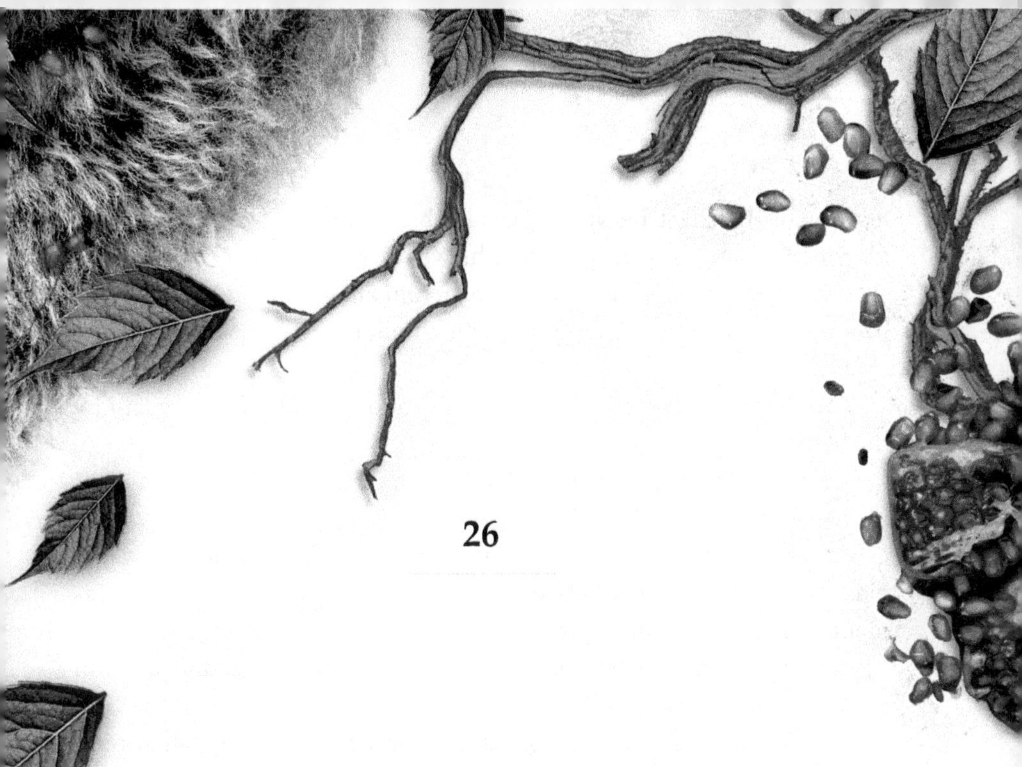

26

My eyes felt like they were filled with sandpaper as I awoke to a barrage of shouting, the flames of hell licking at my face.

No...not hell. They'd set me down on the couch in the living room and there was a wild fire roaring in the hearth, burning my cheeks with the intensity of its heat.

"Guys," Vivian hissed. "*Guys,* she's waking up."

Cool hands fluttered over my arms, and Viv sucked in a breath. "Holy crap, she's on fire."

I felt the couch beneath me move jerkily backward and groaned as a wave of vertigo almost had me leaning over the edge to vomit again.

My head pounded as I tried to push myself to sitting. "Water," I croaked, my throat drier than the Sahara.

An icy glass pressed into my palm, and I gulped it down greedily, breathless when I finally drained it and shivering as the cold water snaked a path down into my belly.

It brought with it a sense of clarity and the hydration my body needed to heal whatever ailed it. I peeled my eyelids back and stared into the worried, angry faces of my friends. Jared's hand closed over mine, and the couch dipped as he sat down next to me.

Clay stood behind Layla and Vivian, his arms crossed over his shirtless torso. His chest heaved with hard breaths as he stared at me, his glowing blue eyes showing the fear he was trying to hide.

I squeezed Jared's hand, trying to let him know that I was all right as I found my voice, swallowing past the diminishing razor blades in my throat.

"You should have told me," Jared said, and I peered up at him, cut by the betrayal in his eyes.

I glanced at Clay, who nodded, telling me that they'd finally let Jared in on everything we'd been looking into.

...they didn't even know the half of it. I dropped my head and the plastic bag still wedged between my breasts crinkled with the movement, reminding me of its presence.

"Are you going to tell us what happened?" Clay demanded. "You scared the *shit* out of us, Allie."

"Would you chill out for, like, two seconds?" Layla snapped at him. "Give her a minute."

"It was a panic attack," Vivian added. "We *told* you that, already. She used to have them all the time."

Clay huffed.

"I'm sorry," I whispered to Jared, ignoring their banter. I waited until his eyes met mine to continue. "It was too awful...all the things Adam told us. I didn't want to tell you until we had proof."

The need to explain overtook me, and burning tears stung in my eyes.

"But you're right. We shouldn't have kept it from you. I wish...I wish..."

Wishing wasn't going to get me anywhere. And nothing was going to soften the blow of this next part. My wolf blazed back to the surface and I grunted, holding her back as my rage erased what remained of the grogginess still clinging to my bones.

Jared tugged my hand. "Is it true?" he asked me, voice hard, and even though his jaw was clenched tighter than a vise, I didn't miss the slight quiver in his chin.

With shaking fingers, I let go of Jared's hand and unzipped Sam's sweater, digging in between my breasts. The bag was coated in slippery sweat, but it was still there, giving life to all the horrible things we'd wished weren't true.

I set it down on Jared's lap as though if I jostled it too much it may explode. He glanced down, brows drawn together as he studied the tufts of fur contained within. For the first time, in the light, I noticed how the tips of the tails weren't the only contents. There was also something shiny, like copper, and small tucked into one corner. And a swath of baby-fine blond hair knotted with a bit of string.

"Is that…" Layla trailed off and her words seemed to break whatever spell had been holding Jared still.

A strangled cry fell past his lips as he lurched to his feet, sending the bag and its contents to the floor. The tails, hair, a bit of shining copper spilled out onto the rug at Clay's feet.

His head shook, as though not believing what he was seeing.

Jared's blatant horror confirmed my suspicions. I'd still been holding onto a shred of hope that the chunks of fur and decayed flesh didn't belong to his parents. I could see now that it was foolish to hope.

I could see now what needed to be done.

Clay stooped, a vein in his neck jutting out, throbbing. With his thumb and index finger he picked the bit of copper from the carpet, rising back to standing. He held it up to the light, turning it between his fingers.

It caught the light, glinting faintly. It wasn't a thimble.

It was a shell casing from a bullet.

"Clay," I said on a breath, seeing the exact moment he realized what it was and why it was in that bag. His face twisted, and in one quick motion, he whipped the casing across the room. The knock of it shattering a perfect circle through the glass window near the door made me jump.

He turned on me with wicked fury, eyes aglow. "*You knew*," he shouted. "You *knew*, didn't you?"

Hurt and scathing fury rippled across his eyes and stained his cheek red.

"Not for certain," I told him, standing my ground. "And you know as well as I do that if I'd told you, you wouldn't have been able to—"

"*Don't*," he snarled, and something inside me crumpled.

Jared knelt on the floor, hesitantly reaching his fingers toward the tufts of crimson-stained fur on the rug. He paused just shy of touching them, unable to. His outstretched hand balled into a fist and he pulled it back.

"Maybe..." he began, his voice oddly detached. "Maybe he just..."

I shook my head, reaching down to put a hand on his shoulder. He flinched at the contact, and I snatched my hand away. "No," I told him. "Grey admitted everything. The missing shifters. Your parents. He told me right before he compelled me to forget it all and be *loyal* to my alpha."

Distantly, I was aware that Clay had begun to pace. I could hear Viv and Layla whispering to him reassuringly, trying to get him to breathe.

"But," Jared said, his eyes widening as realization set in, "you...can't be compelled?"

"Apparently not."

My upper lip curled back as my wolf hedged nearer to the surface. The presence of her mates' wolves— their rage and anguish—stoking her fire. *Our* fire.

"Jare," Clay roared, and Jared tore his gaze away from the last remains of his parents to meet Clay's stare.

Something passed between them. A question unspoken.

Jared's face visibly paled as he dipped his head in a single, solemn nod.

Clay kicked off his shoes and stormed to the front door, Layla and Viv calling after him.

"Jared? What did you just do?" I demanded, getting to my own feet to follow after them.

He didn't look at me when he replied simply, "Gave him permission."

Oh no you didn't.

A terrifying image of Ryland standing with his canine teeth dripping blood over a prone Clay flashed across my mind.

Spurred to action, I hooked a hand beneath Jared's arm and hauled him to his feet, a new kind of panic lodging itself like a blade in my gut. "Well, *ungive* it," I hissed, dragging him to the door with me and out into the cold dawn light.

Jared pulled out of my grasp once we got outside. Layla shrieked as Clay burst from his shorts, coming down on all fours, a vicious growl echoing in the miasmal quiet.

He was past the point of no return. There would be no talking him down. I could see it in his eyes. Wild and hungry. He wouldn't be sated until blood was spilled.

I was knocked onto my stomach as Jared shifted behind me, the hard skull of his canine head slamming against my back. I struggled to get my breath back, rolling out of the way as he launched himself down the steps and onto the dirt lawn with Clay.

Finally, blissfully, I released myself to the power of my wolf, feeling my body bend and break in a matter of a second. I scraped down the steps and placed myself in their path, Layla and Viv taking up posts on either side of me as what remained of our clothes drifted down to land in heaps on the dirt.

Stop, I bellowed in our shared mind. Clay snapped at me. *Move, Allie.*

I won't.

Do as he says, Jared chimed in, vibrating with a level of rage I didn't know he was capable of.

No. I won't let you get yourselves killed. Allie, Jared warned. *Move.*

He needs to be dealt with. Now.

I faltered.

Clay was right.

What am I doing?

It was so obvious. The road laid out as clearly as if it were made out of yellow bricks.

You're right.

Hazel's sad look as she told me *it's what sets you apart that will see your triumph,* came to mind.

Even with a lack of experience, I was the strongest of us. The fastest. But above all, even though I'd accepted Ryland as my alpha, I was the only one of us with a will strong enough to compete with his.

Someone had to put an end to him, but it couldn't be them.

It had to be me.

I think somewhere deep down I'd known that all along. I'd *known* it would come to this; I just didn't want to believe it. And as much as the rational part of me pleaded that we needed to be patient. That we should come up with a plan. The *irrational* part—the part that lusted for Ryland's blood just as much as my mates, demanded to be sated.

Then there was the uncontested fact that if I didn't do it, *they* would. Even if it meant one or both of them died trying.

Vengeance would be had today, but it wouldn't be them who wreaked it upon our common enemy.

I'm going to challenge Ryland, I told them, the panic of a moment before falling away like a discarded skin. The declaration brought with it a sense of calm that stilled the tremor in my paws and evened out my breaths.

It was the simplest thing in the world, that decision.

The hell you are, Clay said, coiling his body to launch past me.

No, I commanded him, letting the full force of my will expand in my core. Letting it infuse my words with power.

Clay buckled, his coiled shoulders lowering.

Jared eyed me warily, glancing between Clay's bared teeth and my unnerving stillness. *Allie, you can't,* he said, the detached tone gone for the moment. *He'll kill you.*

He might, I admitted. *But I'll make sure to leave him weak enough that you can finish what I started.*

Allie! Vivian shouted in my thoughts. *We aren't going to let you do this.*

I whirled on her.

Oh? I hissed, lips pulling back over teeth. *And I should let* them *go instead?*

A startled yelp left her lips, and she bucked backward, cowed.

We need to be rational, Layla said.

Allie, Clay said, strangled. *Let. Me. Up.*

You can't do this, Jared added, taking another tentative step toward me. *Vivian's right. We aren't going to let you.*

That was where he was wrong.

I didn't need them to *let* me do anything.

I dug my claws into the dirt and lifted myself high and proud, letting that bubble of will within grow *and grow* until I knew there was nothing that would stop it.

Layla and Vivian were the first to bow, emitting tiny yelps as their chins bent to rest on the dirt.

No! Clay shouted. *Don't do this. Please.*

I'm sorry, I told them, watching resolutely as Jared and Clay fought against the force of my will. *But no one else is going to get hurt. Not when I can stop it.*

Allie, don't... Jared begged.

Clay shuddered as he fell, his panicked stare piecing me straight through.

Your will won't keep us here, he hissed in my thoughts.

You aren't our alpha!

I don't need it to keep you here, I replied, my heart breaking as I turned away from them to face the trees. *I just need a head start.*

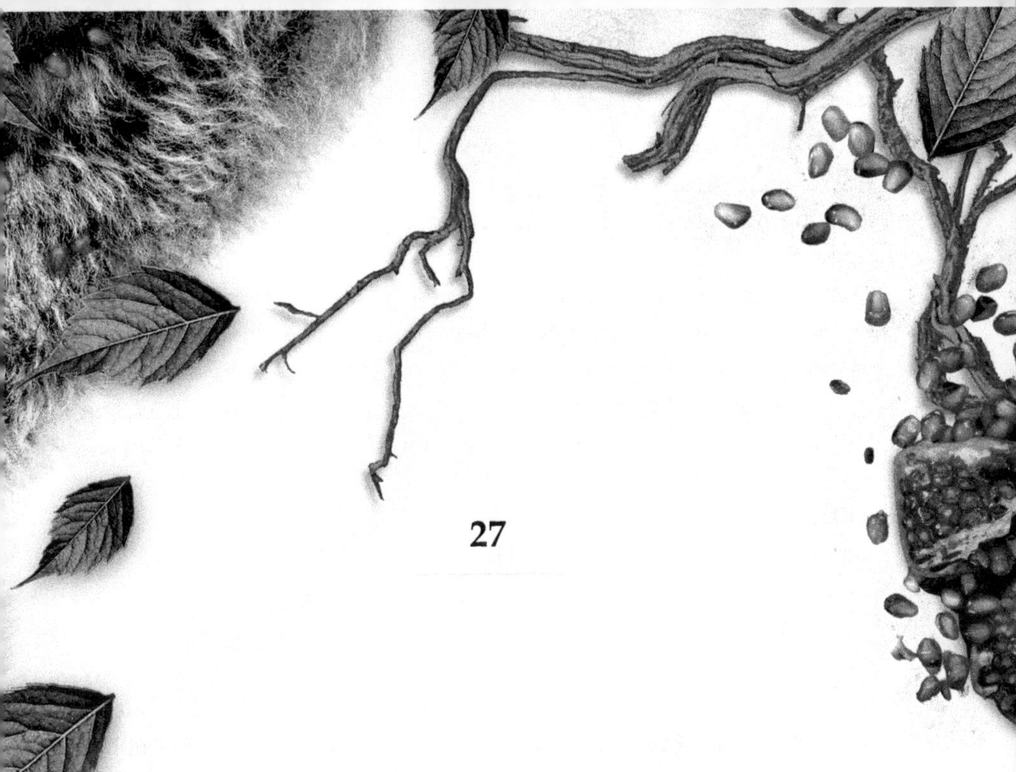

27

It was eerie how quiet it was as I cleared through the tree line and into pack camp, slowing to a quick walk. The camp slept, their untroubled heads resting on pillows. The remnants of last night's drinks keeping them in the comforting bosom of sleep.

Discarded cups and bottles littered the spaces between the cabin, left to be cleaned up another day. The fairy lights that'd been strung through the trees now hung limp and lifeless, their lights gone out.

A stillness in the cool, damp air made my skin bristle. I couldn't do what I needed to do without every single pack member present. I couldn't give Ryland the opportunity to weasel his way out of this. If I challenged him alone in his cabin, there was no telling what he might do.

But challenging him in front of everyone...

He would have no choice but to accept. To play *fair* for once in his miserable existence.

Steeling myself, I crept up to the dead firepit, sending a last prayer up to whatever god would hear me with the last tendril of white smoke twisting upward to the heavens.

Gaze fixed on Ryland's cabin, I shifted, shaking off the wolf as easily as I would a jacket.

"Ryland!" I screamed, hauling in a long, shuddering breath before bellowing his name a second time, making sure my voice would be heard across camp. "Ryland!"

My fists began to shake as the first signs of life awoke in the clearing. The bang of a door shutting somewhere behind me. A shout. The naked shape of a man rushing from the woods to see what was going on. Charity rushing up from my left, in nothing but a long t-shirt, eyes ringed in red and her dreads sticking out at odd angles from how she slept. "Allie?" she asked,

a worried crease in her forehead. "What's happening?" Destiny was the next to approach, with Seth, Kyle,

Trey, and Todd lagging behind her in various states of undress.

Destiny peered around me, searching for signs of Vivian.

"She isn't here," I told her.

Destiny looked between me and the direction I'd come from. In my heightened state, I found I could faintly hear her pulse as it built in tempo. And as she broke into a sprint for the trees, gone in search of her mate, I heard the distinct sound of Ryland cursing and the squeal of Sam as something slammed loudly within the cabin.

I clenched my jaw, willing myself to remain where I was.

"What's going on?" Seth asked, flipping his dark hair away from his eyes.

"Has something happened?" Trey added. "Are Clay and Jared okay?"

My stomach pooled with acid. "No," I growled. "But they will be."

"Go find them," Seth barked at Kyle, and he nodded once to Seth and took off running after Destiny. Then he turned back to me. "Are you going to tell us what happened?"

Just then, Ryland stepped outside, still fastening the large silver buckle of his belt. Barefoot, barechested, and every inch the monster I always knew he was.

"I think I'll let *him* tell you," I replied to Seth, raising my voice to let it carry over the still-gathering pack.

Ryland made no secret of his rage; his eyes flared with ruddy orange light and his muscles rippled. "What is the meaning of this?"

How could he do it?

How could he sit there, smug and haughty with disdain after all that he'd done? As if my appearance here *inconvenienced* him. Fucking *seriously?*

"Where are the missing wolves?" I shouted across the space between us. "Tell them!"

I had the satisfaction of watching his face bleach of color before he recovered, lifting a brow as though I'd just said something that made absolutely no sense to him.

I had to hand it to him. He was *good.*

"I don't know what you're talking about, Allie, but if you'll come inside, we can discuss—"

Ignoring him, I continued, my voice broken and raw but loud enough for all to hear me. "Tell them!" I demanded. "Tell them how you *killed* Jared's parents— skinned them—and kept their tails as souvenirs."

Charity gasped, and from the corner of my eyes, I could see her looking at me like I'd gone and lost my damned mind. I didn't care. I wasn't finished.

"Tell them how you shot Thomas Armstrong in the back of the head and walked away like it never happened!"

Sam, tugging a robe closed over her naked body, froze mid-step as she appeared behind Ryland on the porch. Her face screwed up into a disgusted scowl.

"Ryland," she said. "What the fuck is going on?"

He held up a hand to silence her, never taking his eyes off me. "Those are some pretty serious accusations," he said, his gaze tentatively sliding to the gathered pack, judging their reactions.

I knew I hadn't won them over.

"Allie's lost it," I heard someone mutter just before Charity whispered. "I think you should calm down."

I balked at the suggestion, resisting my wolf's urge to snap at her.

The tether at my core gave a sharp tug and a lick of apprehension skated up my spine. I was running out of time. I could feel Jared and Clay—they were close now. They'd be here soon.

Charity hesitantly curled a hand around my arm, but I shrugged her off. "You can pretend all you want," I hissed at Ryland. "But I know what you've done."

The bastard smirked.

For the first time since he came outside, I tore my gaze away from my alpha and turned to the crowd, making sure they were all paying *very* close attention.

"Ryland," Sam repeated, and I heard him growl at her.

"That's enough," Ryland roared, feeding enough of his alpha will into the words to bend the heads of weaker members of the pack.

"I agree," I said, my chin high.

Something in my eyes must have alarmed him because his lips parted, and I saw understanding flash across his features before I gathered the courage. I needed to say what I came here to say.

"*I challenge you*, Ryland Stone, for the right to rule this pack."

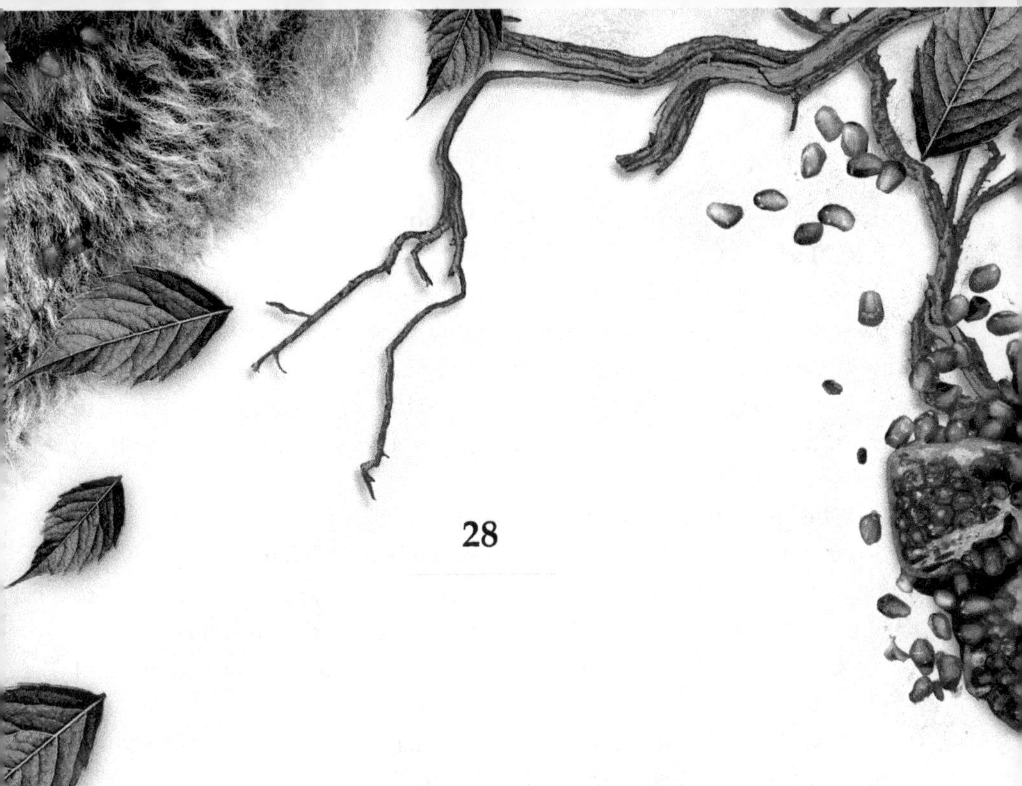

28

A sly smile crept over his lips.

It was there only for the briefest moment, just before he erased all traces of it, but it was long enough to set my nerves on edge. To tell me that he had anticipated this. Was already ready for it.

"Allie!" Charity exclaimed, her voice rising above a barrage of heated whispers at my back. When I finally turned to face her, I found her stricken with fear, her face pale and bright turquoise eyes wide and rimmed with fresh tears. She brought a trembling hand to her mouth, suddenly speechless.

"I'm sorry, Char," I told her. "It has to be done." Charity blinked, and a tear fell. I looked away, unable to watch.

She wasn't crying because I was going to kill the man she mistakenly fell in love with. She was crying because she thought she was going to lose *me*.

I hoped I was going to prove her wrong.

"There's a reason a female shifter has never led a pack on mortal soil," Ryland said, traces of that infuriating smirk still twitching through his mask of phony concern. "You aren't strong enough. You will lose."

Just like he so clearly wanted me to, I rose to the bait. "*Try me.*"

He sighed.

"Allie Grace," Ryland said, his face placid, like a war general coming

693

to terms with a decision he himself did not wish to make but was forced into. "I accept your challenge."

A hush of silence went over the camp, broken only when Sam grabbed Ryland by the arm, wrenching it backward so he would face her. "You can't," she told him. "That's my brother's *mate*."

He shrugged her off. "And like you said," he replied, eyes sliding to me for the briefest second, making sure I was listening. "He will be better off without her."

The blow stung, but I didn't let it shake me.

Hell, if we were being honest here. I agreed with her.

"The others were right," he said, this time lifting his voice for all to hear. "Allie isn't like us. She's...*unnatural*...and clearly unhinged."

Oh, he had no idea...I was about to show him just how *unhinged* I could be.

"*Well*," I hollered, vibrating with anticipation, paying the whispers no heed. "Are you just going to stand there?"

Ryland lifted his chin and stepped down onto the dirt, gaze fixed on me, flitting briefly to something behind me. I spun to look, catching what looked like the hem of a dark jacket as someone skated behind a cabin at the edge of camp.

The echoing snap of a branch in the forest yanked my attention back; my body jerked, anticipating an attack.

Until a dark shape burst from the trees and into camp. Clay. Followed closely by Jared, Viv, Layla, Kyle, and Destiny.

Clay skidded to a stop several paces in front of me, growling ferociously at Ryland. Jared came to stand next to Clay, taking up a similar protective stance at my front. Layla, Viv, and Destiny joined them.

Kyle floundered off to the side, unsure what to do.

Clay and Jared shifted at the same time, the snap and shudder of their bodies over in an instant, leaving me staring at two nude backs. The others remained in their wolf forms. Layla turned, pushing her cold, wet snout against my hand with a low whine.

"You fucking bastard," Clay barked, every muscle in his body tense and rippling beneath a layer of sweat. "I'm going to rip your—"

"*Quiet,*" Ryland commanded, sending Clay skidding back half a step with the force of his alpha's will.

"This is between *us*," Jared spoke, eliciting a new wave of whispers from the pack, this time, their accusing stares turned from me to Ryland, where they belonged. "You will leave Allie out of it."

Ryland frowned, steepling his fingers at his front as he regarded his nephew with a sorrowful stare. "Don't tell me she has you believing all this *nonsense*, nephew?"

Jared stiffened. "I—" he stammered, his whole body shaking.

"I'm afraid you're too late in any case. She's already made an open challenge."

Jared stilled, and Clay, still fighting against Ryland's command with coiled muscle and low grunts, took two running steps at Ry, launching himself over the firepit.

My wolf reacted, rising to the surface like air trapped beneath water.

I growled, going to the balls of my feet for the sprint when Clay was knocked from the air mid shift. Harrison sent him tumbling to one side, and his skull knocked against a wooden bench before he could regain his footing, his body growing still.

"Clay!" I shouted, rushing toward him with Jared close at my heels. I grabbed him, using all my strength to turn him over. "You idiot. You complete fucking idiot. What were you thinking!?"

Clay's eyes slitted open, showing whites as he groaned, his body working to quickly heal what was almost definitely a concussion. Harrison circled at a distance; his teeth bared.

The whispers from the pack had turned to shouts, all of them coalescing into one indecipherable hum of noise that made it hard to think.

Jared's hand clamped around mine on Clay's chest as he slowly blinked awake. "*Allie*," he said in a harsh whisper. "Withdraw."

"What?"

"You have to withdraw. *Please.*"

I shook my head, tugging my hand out from beneath his. "He's been waiting for this, Jared" I whispered back, not caring if Ryland or anyone else heard me. "Even if I did withdraw, he wouldn't honor it."

A muscle in Jared's jaw twitched, and he stood, turning to face his uncle and the pack. "Let me take her place," he demanded, unflinching.

Ryland cocked his head at Jared, a knot between his brows.

"*You* would challenge *me?*" he asked, incredulous. "What has this...

this *filth* put in your head? Would you really attempt to kill your own flesh and blood?"

"I could ask you the same question," Jared spat. "But I already know the answer."

Gasps sounded from the gathered pack members.

Someone shouted, "Is it true, Jared? Is what Allie said the truth?"

"Every. *Disgusting*. Word."

Charity choked off a sob, sinking to her knees. "She's lying!" Sam called, stepping forward to slip her hand into Ryland's, showing their solidarity in a way that made me want to barf.

"She's not," Clay said, his voice garbled and distant as he pushed himself up into a half seat with my help. "He killed dad, Sam..."

Her complexion turned almost green before flaring back to a flushed pink. "That's not true!"

"That's about *enough* of this bullshit," Ryland hissed, nodding to Harrison and Forrest who rushed to flank him left and right as he stalked toward us.

Clay's upper lip curled back, and he winced as he rose, trying to put himself in front of me even though we both knew he wouldn't be protecting anyone as unsteady as he was.

I braced myself, readying for the fight of my life, but Ryland stopped several paces away and his fiery orange eyes weren't trained on me but on Jared and Clay.

Vivian came to my flank and growled, her hackles rising as she watched Ryland warily. I put my hand out, palm down, hoping she got the message to stay put. Stay calm.

If she attacked—if anyone attacked—this was going to get really ugly, really fast.

Clay clenched his right fist and slid his left leg forward, readying himself to swing. I gripped his arm, stopping him before he could.

"You will *not* interfere," Ryland shouted at Clay and Jared, and even my skin bristled from the force of the words, laced with my alpha's will.

"You will *not* speak. You will do *nothing* while I do what I should have done from the start."

Jared looked like he wanted to scream, but with the command of his alpha holding him back, all he could do was breathe hard through his clenched teeth.

I put a hand on each of my mate's backs, trying to soothe them.

"*No*," Clay managed, his eyes bulging with the effort, shocking even Ryland with his ability to directly disobey an order by speaking.

"Ryland, please," Charity said, coming to hover at my left. "There's obviously been a mistake. Allie's confused and—"

"Take her," he ordered Charity before setting his sights back on me.

"You have ten minutes. Use Charity's cabin. Say your goodbyes. When those ten minutes expire, I expect you to be right here," Ryland pointed at the dirt at his feet.

He cut a hateful stare at his nephew. "This is a courtesy I extend for you, nephew," he said. "Don't forget it."

"I don't intend to say any goodby—"

"Come on, Allie," Charity cut me off, tugging at my arm. "Jared. Clay. Let's go."

Ryland turned on his heel and stormed back toward his front porch, where he shouldered past a pale- looking Sam and went inside, slamming the door behind him.

"Come," Charity repeated, her eyes wild. Something in my chest twanged with a sharp stabbing ache.

Layla, Viv, and Destiny padded along beside us as we weaved quickly through the cabins. If I grit my teeth any harder, I was sure they would crack.

I let Charity usher us inside, away from the curious eyes of the others, all of whom remained near the fire ring, waiting for the show to begin.

Jared and Clay made choked off and grunted sounds of exertion, the muscles in their faces trembling. I realized with a sinking in my gut and also a sliver of relief, that they still couldn't speak.

Ryland had ordered them to be silent. He'd told me *I* could say *my* goodbyes. He said nothing about them saying theirs.

Couldn't have them saying anything else that might incriminate him, right? Smart fucker.

If I died today, there was no doubt in my mind that he would have Grey compel them to forget everything I'd told them. Which meant that I *had* to defeat him. I couldn't allow that to happen. They deserved the truth. No matter how ugly.

No matter how painful.

Layla, Vivian, and Charity shifted, rushing inside the cabin as Charity sealed the door shut behind them and turned, frantic, her hands shaking. "You need to leave," she said in a low voice. "You can run. I'll cover for you."

"We can slow him down," Vivian added, clearly liking this plan.

Layla, eyes welling with tears, made wild gestures with her hands. "You can get a head start and—"

"I'm afraid no one will be running away this morning," the rich tone of his voice slithered into the room like a serpent.

Charity started, gasping loudly before Grey caught her by the mouth, stifling her cry. "Silence," he commanded, and the room went quiet.

Jared and Clay rushed forward, poised for the kill, their wolves at the surface but not set free. In this tiny space they risked injuring more than Grey if they shifted.

"Sleep," Grey said, and my mates stilled, unsteady on their feet for a moment before they began to list to one side. I darted forward, trying to break two falls at once. I managed to get an arm around Clay and just caught the back of Jared's skull with the other before it would have hit the floor.

Layla, Vivian, and Destiny fell in a heap at the door and I winced, seeing Destiny's wrist bent at an odd angle beneath Layla's hip.

"*Curious*," Grey hissed, releasing Charity and shoving her to a corner of the cabin, where she fell, stiff as a plank, to the floor. Grey's stare strained as he took me in, still very much *not* asleep as the others were.

I set Jared and Clay down, rising to my feet, feeling the full weight of my wolf like a spirit possessing my limbs.

"*You,*" I said, my voice garbled from a partially shifted throat. My hands claws at my sides.

Grey looked down on me, his head cocked, pupils dilating as he said, "*You will not fight Ryland.*"

Grey's expression tightened. His voice deepening, growing raspy with the force of his words. With how much compulsion he was *trying* to pump into them.

The hairs on my neck raised and my pulse picked up, a rogue thought crossing my mind for a brief second.

I tried to tear my gaze away from him, away from those entrancing dark eyes of his, but I couldn't.

Maybe...

Maybe I shouldn't fight.

My core loosened. My shoulders fell.

"That's it," Grey said, slithering across the bare swath of floor between us, bringing himself within my reach. "There's a good doggy."

Close enough for my nostrils to wrinkle from the cloying scent of his aftershave, he put a single finger beneath my chin, propping my face to his. *"You will beg your alpha's forgiveness for your* unfounded *accusations and then you will kneel before him and accept your fate."*

A slow smile turned up the edges of my mouth. "Like hell I will."

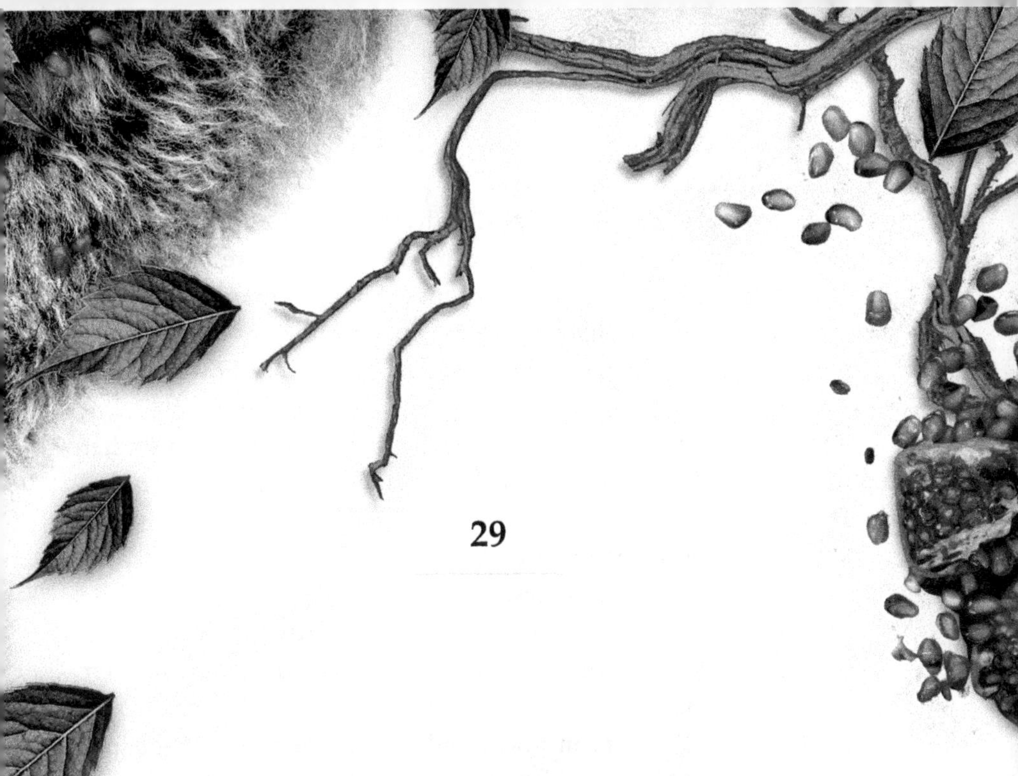

29

I t was heavier than I thought it would be, and more difficult not to
let slide from my fingers because of all the blood. I knotted my fist
more tightly into the hair, the jostling motion sending a scattering of
crimson over the dirt path as I stepped down from the cabin door.

"Back in a jiffy," I called to my still-slumbering mates and friends on
the cabin floor, a strange chuckle bubbling up from my chest. I choked it
back, knowing distantly that this...this was *not* funny.

This was fucked up.

I was fucked up.

A small bark of a laugh escaped, and I bit my lower lip, wondering
offhandedly if this was what it was like to go insane. But no, insane
people didn't know they were going insane, right?

Which meant I was the opposite of *in*sane. I was the most sane I'd
ever been.

Yeah. Let's roll with that.

I shifted my trophy to my other hand, trying to find a better grip
there before I dropped it, doing my best not to limp as I walked. The
bastard had gotten me pretty good in the kneecap before I could finish
shifting, but it was already starting to heal.

The cold air kissed the sweat and blood covering my body and my
hard breaths bloomed in misty clouds around my lips.

701

Heads turned as I approached. Already, the air was tense with anticipation. Some of them might have heard the scuffle before I reemerged from Charity's cabin. They'd likely dismissed it as nothing more than a disagreement, more than likely something to do with Clay.

Any other time, I'd have thought the same. This time, however, they were wrong.

A girl I forgot the name of screamed, her hands moving to cover her mouth as she saw what I carried at my side, bouncing against my naked thigh.

Seth, who'd been rushing forward, slowed to a hesitant walk, his eyes wide and lips parted in shock.

The door to Ryland's cabin opened with a clatter a second later, once I was very nearly at the exact spot he'd indicated I should be after *exactly* ten minutes.

He flew down the steps in a rage, and I tossed the severed head into his path, forcing him to move out of the way or be hit by it. A splatter of vampire blood splashed in an arc over his face, slicing it in two.

"He said I shouldn't fight you," I called, breathless in my rage, wanting him to understand that he had failed. "Said I should take a knee and *accept my fate.*"

I caught my breath, rolling my shoulders back, reveling in how the color bleached from his cheeks, leaving them looking hollow and dark. "As you can imagine, we had a bit of a disagreement on the subject."

His spite-filled eyes locked onto mine, hot with the presence of his wolf.

"Do you have any idea what you've done?" he bellowed.

I tipped my head to the left, cracking my neck, shuddering at the sweet relief.

"No more talking," I snapped, my voice cracking through the morning like a whip as I lowered my body into a fighter's stance like Clay had taught me, pressing into the earth with my heels, ready to let my wolf spring free. I spat what remained of the vile tasting blood from my mouth and dragged the back of one hand over my lips.

"Come on, you coward!" I called, surprising myself with the steadiness of my voice.

The other shifters moved away, giving us space. From the corners of my eye, I saw Seth rush away, back in the direction of Charity's cabin.

Good. I didn't think I'd hurt anyone when I shifted, but it was better to be sure.

"Wait!" Sam called, drawing my attention to where she was, emerging from the front door of the cabin, a fast healing yellowish-purple bruise on her cheek.

Ryland chose that moment to attack, using my distraction to get a cheap hit. His shoulder knocked into my stomach, and I careened through the air.

By the time my feet were back on the ground, they were canine. No longer human. My side ached, the ribs there almost definitely broken, if not at least fractured. But there wasn't time to dwell on that.

He came at me again, this time with fangs and claws. Faster than I ever could have anticipated.

His large black body blotted out the light as he knocked me down, and a deep, penetrating pain ripped through the back of my neck, making me buck and a cry out as a hot wetness slid down my back and shoulders, matting into my fur. I inhaled dirt and gave myself over to instinct, snapping my jaws as I rolled out and away.

Ryland advanced again. His commanding alpha's voice ricocheted through my skull.

Stay.

For a fleeting instant, I couldn't move. My paws were glued to the earth, my heart all but stopped dead in my chest.

For that single second, I didn't think I was going to be able to stop him as he lunged for my throat, his teeth dripping blood as he opened his jaw wide. *Feral.*

I could see the victory in Ryland's predatory stare, as if it were all over and he'd already won.

But something *snapped* inside of me. Something that had been pulled taut for far too long. The bond stretching, cracking, *breaking*.

A veil of red-hot *murder* stole over my eyes, tinging everything in its vermillion hue. I feinted to the right and lurched forward, lifting myself high above him.

Like I knew he would, he turned, realigning himself for the kill, giving me the perfect opening to his jugular. Without hesitation, I sank my teeth through flesh and fur. Deeper, to muscle, sinew, and bone.

An explosion of hot, coppery liquid filled my mouth and I was rewarded with a strangled cry. I pressed him into the dirt, biting down *harder*, an ache throbbing in my jaw.

Delirious with blood lust, I barely registered the loud *crack!* filling my ears and flicking against my teeth in his throat. I barely noticed how he stopped moving. Or how the blood in my mouth had gone cold.

I held on, even as a convergence of thoughts raced through my mind. Mine, and not mine.

He's dead.

She killed him. Ryland!

Allie, let go.

Allie, you need to let go.

I growled, sensing someone coming up on my flank. As though from beneath water, I heard someone else screaming. Not a scream of fear. The bloodcurdling cries of someone in agonizing, torturous pain. It was enough to bring me out of whatever primal thought process had taken over my body and mind.

My growls subsided and my jaws loosened, teeth extracting from deadened meat. Gaining the distance, I needed to see what everyone else saw. The glazed ruddy-brown eyes of a dead black wolf, his throat mangled and gaping, oozing blood over the dirt at my paws.

I yelped and leapt back, eager to put distance between myself and the irrefutable proof of my savagery. Because if I were being honest with myself, it wasn't my wolf that'd done this. I couldn't blame some primal instinct or an uncontrollable second self. Not fully.

Not anymore.

I could see it now. Feel it.

As a single living, breathing being—as I've always been—*I* did this.

Not my wolf. *There is no wolf. There is only...*me.

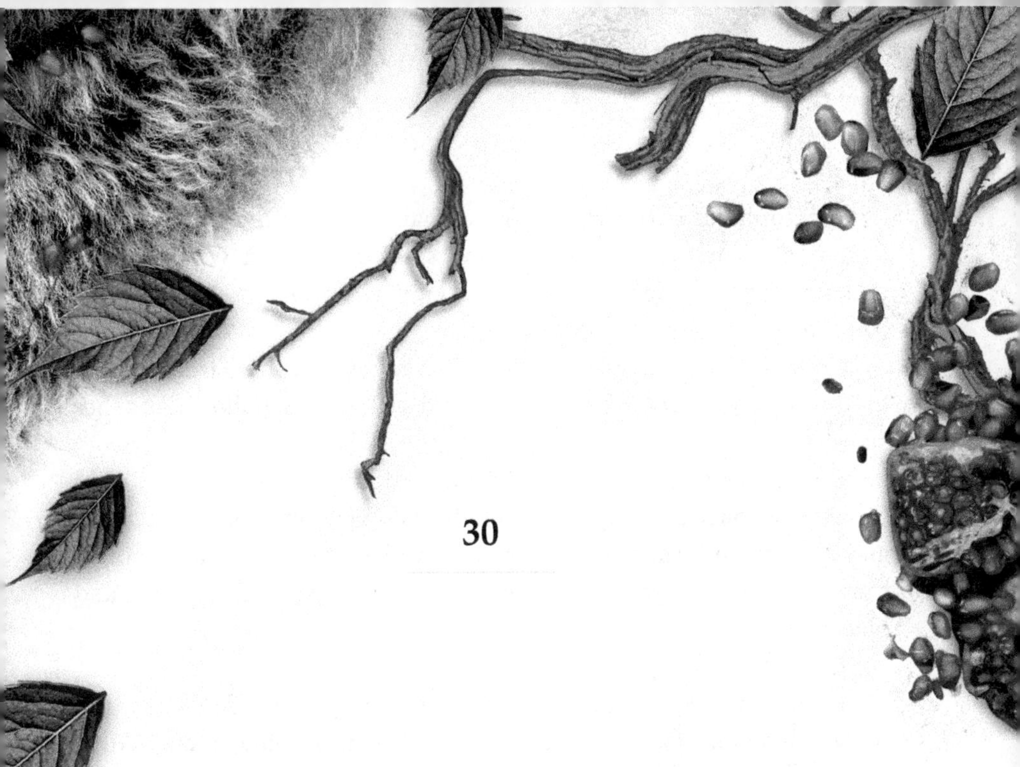

30

A second scream rose to meet the first, this one familiar. I whipped my head in her direction, feeling my insides recoil from her despair. Charity, still in her long shirt, spattered with blood now from what I'd done in her cabin, she rushed forward. Her face a haunting parody of its usual demure expression.

Behind her, down the narrow path from where she'd come, I sensed my mates. Their panic swelling as they woke to find the decapitated vampire lying on the floor. Layla's shriek confirmed it. They were all waking now, coming this way.

"*Watch out!*" Someone—*Seth*—called, and I turned just in time to stare into the acid-filled, too-blue eyes of Sam. Her dark, muscled frame already coiled, sprung. The silvery white streak, like a lightning bolt on her forehead not nearly as shining as her bared teeth.

A shape passed in front of me and a long, ear shattering peal left Charity's wolfen lips as Sam went to the ground with her, teeth gnashing, claws scrambling for purchase on shifting, fur-covered flesh.

Instinctively, I rushed Sam, knocking her off Charity. Using the blunt battering ram of my forehead to stun her well enough that it took her several seconds to get back to her feet. Long enough for a white wolf and a dark gray one to get to their places at my sides. My best friends coming up swiftly behind my mates.

A cacophony of thoughts pushed against the confines of my mind and a cold nose pressed against my side, prodding a wound there, making me flinch. I ignored the voices. I ignored it all.

Charity.

I nudged her, a whine contracting in my lungs. She hardly moved, but I could still hear her breathing. Could still see the shallow rise of her sides.

Not caring whether or not Sam attacked me anymore, I let my need to be heard outweigh my need to fight, allowing my wolf to fall away and my human form to take shape in her place. I cried out as I shifted, the wounds in my upper back and chest protested the shift, tearing and bleeding anew.

I didn't give a shit.

In the myriad of faces I found Seth, hovering undecidedly near the body of Ryland, his face a mask of shock. "Seth," I called, and blinking, he turned. Once he took in the mess of Charity in my arms, he was there, skidding in the dirt to a backdrop of growls and snarls and shouts and whispers.

Trey and Todd followed, helping Seth lift her without injuring her more. "We need to get her to the healer," I told them, ready to rush out of camp as quickly as I'd arrived.

A human hand curled around my wrist, pulling me to a stop.

Jared.

"Take her," he told the others. "Make sure she's going to be okay. *Hurry.*"

I gave them a swift nod. Permission to go without me even though that was the last thing I wanted. Anger flared in a gush of heat up my neck as they raced away, and I turned to face Sam.

I took one step. Two.

A second hand joined the first, gripping me from the other side. Each of my mates holding me back from tearing her apart.

"You fucking bitch!" I snapped. "If she dies..." I couldn't even finish that sentence.

Sam snapped and snarled, hot saliva dripping from her chin. Egging me on.

Do it. I could almost hear her without the need to be in my wolf form. She *wanted* me to attack her. She *wanted,* I realized with a stab, to kill me or die trying.

Inside my chest, my heart gave a violent shudder. Regardless of what he'd done—that he deserved what he got and more—Ryland was Sam's mate. And I couldn't imagine that pain.

Didn't want to even try.

"*Sam,*" Clay barked, his disdainful tone echoing through the camp like a sonic blast.

She shifted in the blink of an eye, pitched forward on the balls of her feet, her stare shining and cruel. Her long black hair wild and painted red on one side with Charity's blood.

"*You could have killed her,*" Clay roared, and suddenly I was no longer the detainee, but the detainer, shifting my wrist out of Clay's grasp to curl it around his wrist instead. Tugging my other one away from Jared in case I needed it to hold him back, too.

Clay shook beneath my hands, and within him I could feel all the things he was too angry to say.

He might have been worried about Charity. In fact, I knew he was. But I also knew he wasn't talking about her. He was talking about *me.*

Sam hadn't meant to hurt Char. Only had because she'd gotten in the way of her intended target.

"Clayton," Sam hissed, still visibly trembling. "*She killed hi—*"

"*Go,*" Clay shouted. "Go before I fucking lose it, Sam."

Stricken by his words as though by a punch to the chest, Sam stumbled back a step.

"Clay," I started, unsure exactly what it was I meant to say. I certainly wasn't going to defend her. Right?

Clay saved me from having to make that choice, turning his burning gaze on me, not with hate. Not with anger. Not with anything I would have expected to find written in the lines of his face.

He looked at me with the face of a man who'd seen the swing of the executioner's blade and somehow, mercifully, managed to get out from under it before it could destroy him. Pure, *raw* relief. His eyes were glassy with it.

It was only a second before he turned back to his sister, but the look was enough to burrow beneath my skin. Tunnel straight through bone. It said more than he ever could with words.

"I won't be back," Sam spat in reply, literally spitting onto the dirt, the wad of her saliva missing my bare foot by an inch. "If you think I'm going to bow to your *bitch,* then you're just as crazy as she is!"

A strange awareness settled over me at her declaration, and I turned my head, taking in my best friends standing right behind me, so quietly, so resolutely, that I didn't even know they were there.

Tears stained their cheeks. A sad grin spread across both of their faces when our eyes met. Vivian reached out and took my hand, knotting her fingers through mine, lending me some of her incredible strength before she let me go.

Past them, I found the alarmed faces of the rest of the pack. *My* pack. Some I knew the names of and others I didn't.

Some, I may never need to learn.

"I won't make you stay," I said, turning back to Sam. "Leave."

Her brows drew together. She looked between Clay and me, still bouncing on her feet, panicking now.

"Go," I reiterated. "You're released from this pack."

She left without another word, only one last glance in the direction of her brother before she shifted back into her wolf and fled from camp. Clay bowed his head, and I slid my hand from his wrist down into his hand, squeezing tight before I let go and turned to address the others.

I found Jared staring down at the corpse of his uncle and pulled him to me, crushing him against my body in a hard embrace. He tentatively wrapped his arms around my middle, softly at first, and then so tightly it was a struggle to breathe. I buried my face into his neck, whispering against his warm skin. "I'm so sorry," before pulling away.

There would be time for him to grieve. And time for me to help him do that, but there was something else that needed to be taken care of right now.

"If there's anyone else who wishes to leave," I called out, my voice hoarse but loud enough for all to hear. "Go now. I won't stop you."

"Allie," Clay said at my side, drawing my attention. "That's not how it works. You challenged Ry and you won."

"It's how it's always worked," Jared agreed, helping Clay to explain. "It's your right to rule them."

"Fuck that," I said, a dark laugh coming unbidden to my lips, and then louder, so everyone could hear me again. "I won't make anyone stay. Honestly? If you don't want to be here, then I don't want you here."

Whispers broke out among the pack, a few near the outer edges tucked tail and left, taking advantage of the moment. Acting fast before I could change my mind.

I wouldn't.

"I will tell you that we do have evidence of the things I *accused* Ryland of doing...I may be *unhinged*," I told them, repeating what Ryland said. "But I am *not* insane. And I may be different, but I am not *dangerous*. Not unless you post a direct threat to the people I care about. Then, *yes*, it seems I can be *very fucking dangerous*."

"It's true," Jared attested, jerking his chin toward a still-stunned Kyle. "Go back to the cabin and bring back the proof. You'll know it when you see it,"

Kyle nodded and shifted quickly before taking off in the opposite direction Sam had.

Forrest and Harrison stood next to each other by Ryland's flank. They were the first to speak, Forrest speaking for them both. "We're leaving."

"And we're taking his body," Harrison added.

Jared opened his mouth as though he were going to protest but then closed it again, his expression darkening. "He wanted to be cremated," Jared muttered. "Just so you know."

Harrison gave a curt nod in Jared's direction before both he and Forrest lifted Ryland's body, taking it with them as they left camp. Without collecting their things. Without so much as a backward glance. Leaving only a puddle of blood where Ryland had been in their wake.

"Anyone else?" I shouted over the gathering.

When no others moved, or even responded, I *finally* let my body relax. Dark spots scattered over the edges of my vision, and I swallowed hard, wobbling a little on my feet.

Jared caught me with an arm around my waist, bracing me against him.

"Go back to your cabins," Jared shouted, his tone shocking me with its authority as he helped me move in the direction of the main house. Ryland's house.

I gave a little whine of protest as Jared tried to weave through the throng of shifters, all of them still standing there, shocked and confused.

"He said *move*," Vivian growled, sending the nearest pack members to us skittering in all directions as she wrapped her arm around me, shifting my weight so it was evenly distributed between her and Jared, as Clay, Layla, and Destiny fell into step behind us.

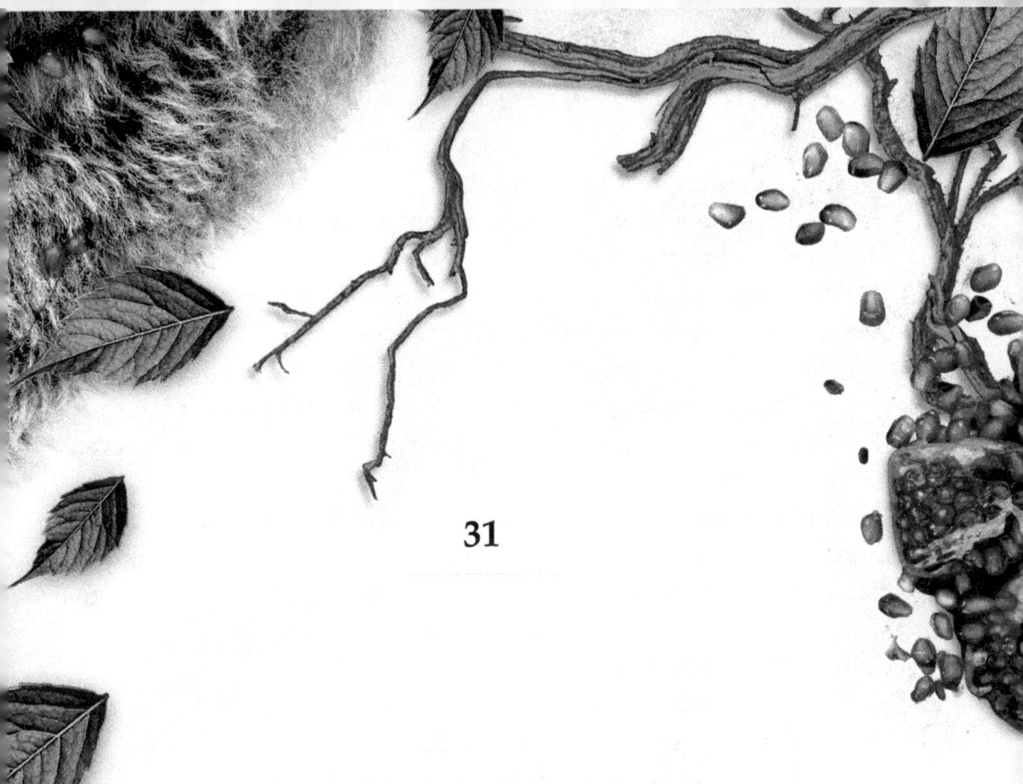

31

O*ne Week Later*

I yanked the pin back out of my hair, pulling a few strands out with it. Groaning, I tried twisting the sides up like Layla sometimes did with her hair, trying to go for the same effortless look. Failed miserably.

Tossing the pin back down onto the vanity, I sighed. There was no way I was going to be able to make my halfway grown out hair look good no matter what I did to it. At least it would be back to its natural shade soon, with my shifter blood helping it to grow nearly twice as fast as it did before.

For the first time ever, I welcomed the return of the silvery blonde. Didn't feel the immediate need to dye it when the roots became too visible. A flash of the smiling woman in the photo with Dad that I still had slipped into the sun visor of my Chevelle came to mind and a weak smile came to my lips. I did look a lot like her. More than I ever looked like dad. For the first time, I didn't think that was such a bad thing.

Giving up, I stepped backward and spread my arms, letting my body fall onto the double bed, the thick duvet puffing around me.

It really didn't matter how I looked. And since when had I cared anyway?

The pack knew who they were accepting as their alpha tonight. I didn't need to pretend to be someone I wasn't.

Movement by the door caught my eye, and I squinted at the tall, lithe form leaning arms crossed against the doorframe.

"Hey," I said, sitting up with a grin and patting the spot next to me.

Jared pushed off from the wall and came over, his lips pulled up into that lopsided smile that drove me mad the very first time he ever flashed it my way.

"You look beautiful," he said in a whisper soft voice, leaning down to brush a kiss softly against my lips. I bit my lower lip, letting the compliment go without trying to oppose it. One day I'd learn how not to squirm whenever someone told me I'd done a good job or looked especially nice. But today was not that day.

"Layla and Viv just got here," he said as he sat down next to me. "They're helping get things ready outside."

Of course, they were. They were here more often than they were at home these days. Helping where and when they could even though I tried to insist otherwise. Layla's second eldest sibling, Katelyn, was turning fourteen this year, and with Layla spending so much time away from home, it had fallen to Katelyn to watch the younger of the bunch. Layla hated that she wasn't there to help anymore but admitted that she would hate it more if she weren't here—with her other family when they needed her.

Jared glanced around the room, showing off the dark circles beneath his eyes and the sallow hue of his skin in the light of the bedside lamp. He was still healing—I knew that—but it didn't make watching the process of his grief any easier.

"I like what you did with it," he mused, gesturing vaguely at the room.

"I still say I would have rather just stayed in one of the cabins."

"It would've been a waste," Jared replied. "Besides, it wasn't always his. And it doesn't even look like the same place anymore."

In that he was right at least. A fresh coat of paint and all new furniture, courtesy of the massive wads of cash Jared found tucked away in Ryland's office at the quarry, really made Ryland's—*no*—*our* cabin a whole new place.

Until they moved out all of Ryland's things, I refused to sleep inside, preferring to crash next to Charity in her cabin. At least for the first few nights after she got home, to make sure she was all right.

She was. Though, since it was a shifter's fangs that had done the damage to her throat and chest, the scars would remain. A gruesome reminder of everything that happened that day.

Every time I saw them, coupled with the smile that never quite reached her eyes anymore, I was reminded of how much I *owed* her. And I wouldn't ever forget it.

"Everyone's almost ready," Clay said, appearing like a ghost in the doorway, but like anything, I was getting used to his random appearances and they barely fazed me anymore.

"Everything all set?" I asked, feeling a wide, dark pit yawn open in the bottom of my stomach. *They* might have been ready down there, but I wasn't, not yet.

Clay nodded, coming to sit on my other side at the edge of the bed, letting out a long breath. "The patrols will shift halfway through the ceremony so we can get through them all tonight."

I pursed my lips, giving a nod. Not that he needed my approval.

Clay had thrown himself into being the unofficial and yet undisputed head of security for the pack. And thank fuck because I had no idea what I was doing in that regard. I'd told him he didn't have to, but he'd insisted. I think he needed something to keep himself busy. For a while he was distant, much like Jared, after everything that happened.

But unlike Jared, it wasn't because of grief. Not really. I couldn't be certain, because much as I tried, he didn't want to talk about it, but I thought it was more that he just didn't know what to do with himself anymore. He was still his same raging, foul-tempered self ninety-nine percent of the time, but he was also...different.

He'd been trying for *years* to figure out what happened to his father. Who killed him. Harboring the sole responsibility for the task since the local police had given up after a measly three months of investigation. Now that he knew the person responsible was gone, there was nothing left to search for.

But he still had something to keep him up at night. Whether he admitted it or not, I knew why he spent the bulk of his evenings out on patrol or sitting on the front porch, staring out at the trees bending in the autumn wind.

Sam had kept her promise.

She hadn't returned. We'd sent word to her old pack up in Alaska, but they told us they hadn't seen her either. It left me to wonder whether he watched and waited because he *wanted* her to come back, or because he didn't.

I would wait until he was ready to talk about it. "You guys sure I can't convince either of you to—"

"*No*," they said at the same time, dashing my last- ditch effort to attempt to pass the torch. I'd offered them the right to rule the Forest Grove pack about fifty times apiece since last week. And all fifty times, they'd both refused. They never wanted it. Still didn't. But for whatever idiotic reason, they thought *I* was somehow going to make a good alpha. I hoped I would be able to prove them right.

I groaned, falling back to lie against the duvet once more, staring at the wood beamed ceiling, and the string lights I'd spent hours twisting around them. They suffused the room in a soft golden glow, deepening the tan skin of my two shirtless mates as they both leaned into my line of sight, making the new soft mattress dip beneath their weight.

"You're going to do great," Jared promised.

"You're going to help me, right?" I asked, not for the first time, shifting my gaze between them. "Both of you?"

"Always," Jared replied. Clay grunted his assent.

I let my body relax a little, unburdened enough to inhale deeply, filling my lungs with engine grease, spice, and warm birch.

My inner wolf purred at their nearness, something tightening deep in our shared belly, making our thighs squeeze.

Above me, propped up on elbows, Clay and Jared shared a look.

"What?" I asked coyly, wondering if they could feel the magnetic draw of our mate bond as strongly as I could right now. Wondering if it affected them in the same way.

"I know I said we'd have the conversation together," Jared said, looking mildly uncomfortable as he shifted position, leaning forward on both elbows instead of just one.

My brow furrowed. "What conversation?"

He stared at me pointedly until my face flushed with heat and I had to avert my stare. "Oh," I said, unable to hide the note of panic from my voice. "*That* conversation."

Clay surprised me by reaching out, stroking his long fingers through my hair, along the side of my cheek, and down my neck, making my body shiver with anticipation. "We almost lost you," he said in a breath, face pinched, his hand stilling when it reached my collarbone.

"Kind of put things into perspective," Jared added, brushing a thumb over my jaw.

The dual sensation of them both touching at the same time threatened to undo me, and I had to clamp my teeth down to keep from setting free the moan trying to claw its way up my throat.

"So," I said, my voice barely above a whisper. "What did you decide?"

Jared glanced up briefly at Clay, checking for something I couldn't see because I was too focused on his lips as he lowered them to mine. The moan I'd been trying to hold back broke free against his mouth, more a whimper.

Clay's fingers curled upward, snaking around the back of my neck. Jared's lips left mine, leaving me bereft only for a second before Clay's grip on me tightened, lifting and turning me until I was on my side. My lips against his.

My head spun as he slid in with his tongue, taking me to new, dangerous heights as Jared's hands found my waist from behind, and I felt the heat of his breath only a second before his lips pressed warm and soft against the back of my neck.

I thought I knew what their answer was, and if I wasn't sure, Jared whispered from behind me, "We decided to leave it up to you."

Barely able to breathe, I gasped between them, my hands trembling as I reached out for them both. One hand knotted in Clay's hair. The other catching the mouth of Jared's pocket, using it as leverage to pull him closer. Close enough that I could feel his pulse racing against my spine. An echo of my own.

Dizzy with desire and drunk on their touch, I wondered if there could ever be anything else that could feel more *right* than this did.

Dismissed the impossibility of the idea.

No matter how...how *unconventional* it was...for us, it couldn't be considered wrong.

I broke away from Clay, breathing heavily. My chest rising and falling against his. His bright blue eyes met mine with *awe* and something else that was more than that. I could feel it from them both so intensely that it threatened to shatter what was left of my damaged heart.

Love.

This was what love felt like.

"I'm sorry this isn't exactly...*normal,*" I told them, worrying that maybe this was still much harder for them than it was for me. I didn't have to *share.* I could have them both.

Jared laughed, his breath tickling my neck as he whispered sweetly against my ear, "We're *not* normal," he said. "We're better than normal."

I chuckled as his hands around my waist turned to tickling fingers, making me shriek and roll into Clay, who wrapped his arms protectively around me, nuzzling his face into the crook below my throat and inhaling deeply.

Downstairs, the screen door creaked open and banged shut. A familiar scent wafted up from below.

Chocolate chip cookies.

"I brought cookies!" Hazel's willowy voice called. "Hope it's not a bad time."

I was wondering when she was going to show up.

Clay snorted, disentangling himself from me to roll off the bed.

I groaned, suddenly eager to get this whole ordeal over with. How many shifters could I swear in per minute? How quickly could we come back up here?

I bit the inside of my cheek, damning myself for where my head was.

Jared caught me around the waist when I tried to get off the bed, pulling me back down to land on his lap, wrapping his arms around me in a long bear hug.

"We'll be right down, Grams," I called, laughter threading through the words.

"Well, hurry up, will you! I'm not getting any younger down here, and I heard there's a pack that could use a stubborn old mutt like me."

I grinned, dragging Jared with me when I moved to stand this time, locking my fingers through his.

Clay offered me a warm smile, jerking his chin in the direction of the door, and what waited on the other side. "You ready?"

"Yeah. I think I am."

SHIFTED SCARS

BOOK FOUR

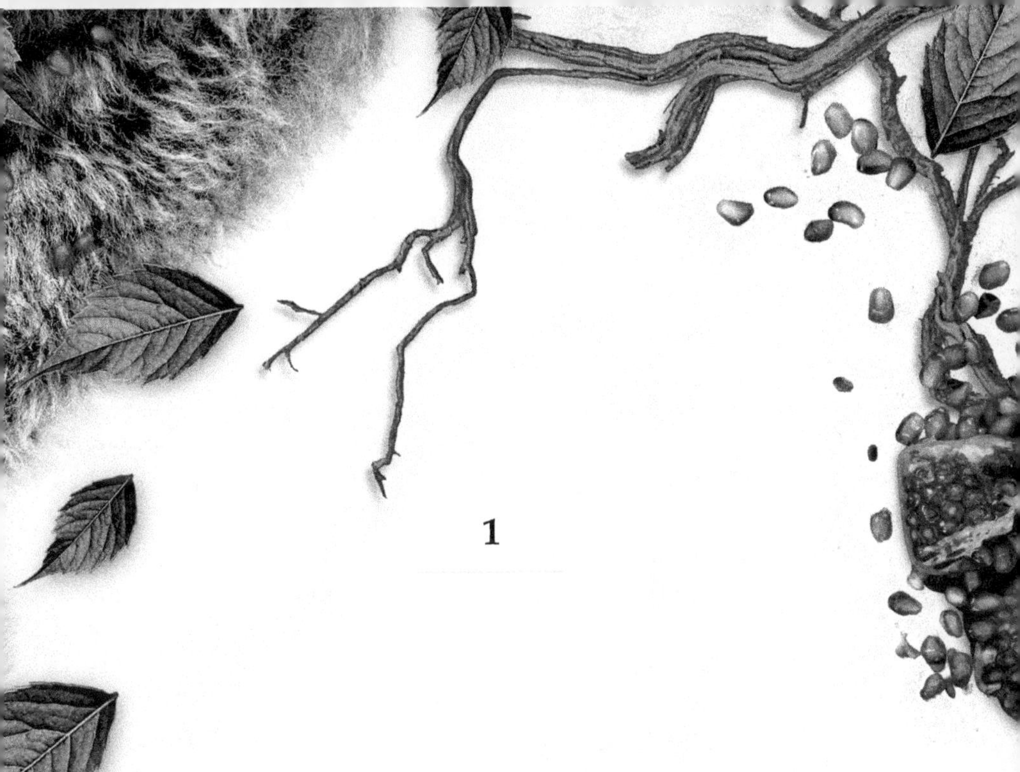

1

Forest Grove had hardly changed in the four years since I'd moved to pack camp.

There were still groups of teenagers hanging out around the entrance to the corner shop, sipping slurpees and sneaking cigarettes.

The restaurant down the block was still somehow open even though I'd never seen a soul go inside, and the old couple who walked arm in arm every afternoon through the town were just taking their break on a park bench near the intersection.

They weren't the reason I came to this part of town, though. The windows of Jacqueline's bookshop reflected the afternoon sunlight in an almost blinding square of gold as I walked up, pausing when a strange scent drifted by on the summer breeze.

Through the small oval window in the door, I could see Jacqueline waving at me to come in and shucked off the distraction. The sweet, musky smell of old books welcomed me as I entered the shop, and I sighed. Wednesday's had to be one of my favorite days.

"Right on schedule," Jacqueline called with a grin from the register. "Your special order came in about an hour ago, and the newest Tate James arrived with yesterday's shipment."

"You're a saint."

I'd been waiting for that book for *months,* and I couldn't wait to devour it, but... "I'm just going to have a quick peek at the shelves before I check out."

"Don't you always?"

I let the serenity of the shop wash over me as I took my time browsing the stacks, finding two more books to add to my pile. I passed over what used to be my favorite section when I worked here four years ago, gaze slipping past bright blues and purples with shining silver fonts.

Paranormal romance was my go-to through all the years of middle and high school. Until Devin took away my mortality, and with it, my ignorance. For a solid year, I hardly read anything at all. Half because I'd lost interest in my favorite genre, and half because I'd been too afraid to come back to Jackie's shop.

The way I had to leave wasn't the greatest. I'd basically forced her into letting me go and replacing me with her niece. Not even able to come in in person and talk to her about why I had to do it. But time mended a lot of things, and when I came in a few years back to get a copy of a new release, she was genuinely glad to see me.

I'd come in every Wednesday since. Books from Jackie's shop were pretty much the only thing I spent my share of the pack's earnings on.

I lifted a new urban fantasy she had prominently displayed and flipped to the back cover. Yellow eyes stared back at me, and the first line promised the reader magic and mayhem. With a shudder, I placed it back on the shelf, turning to the contemporary area.

Once, I'd have snapped up a book like that in a heartbeat. Eager to escape my mundane life into worlds of the supernatural. Now, I needed to escape my supernatural life by reading about normal people and normal problems.

How ironic.

"You know this one is a reverse harem, right?" Jackie asked as I made my way to the front counter as an older couple entered the shop to browse.

Flushing, I nodded, watching her scan my special ordered reverse harem book along with the others and pop them into a bag. She clearly hadn't realized that three out of the four books I was buying today had similar romantic partnerings. At first, I started reading them to feel more normal. Mating to *two* shifters made me an anomaly among my race, but in these books, it was commonplace. Plus, if I were being honest, they were super addictive.

I cleared my throat. "They're really good," I said, trying for nonchalance. She was the one who'd taught me never to judge a reader's tastes. "You should try one."

She lifted a thin brow and smirked. "Maybe I should," she agreed with a wink. "For...*research*."

I laughed as I took the bag from her, shuffling away from the counter to let the older couple pay for their purchases. "See you next week!"

There wasn't a whole lot of time for reading, being the alpha of one of the largest packs in the eastern United States, but I made time. Usually up all hours of the night, binging until one of my mates wrestled the pages from my fingers to force me to get some sleep.

I pulled out the newest book in the darker series I'd been waiting for and anxiously flipped to the first page like an addict looking for a fix. There was no way I could wait until tonight to figure out if the hero were still alive.

The strange smell from before distracted me, and it was too late for me to stop when I looked up from my book before running headlong into the man standing in the middle of the sidewalk.

My book flew from my hands, and like an idiot, I used my supernatural speed and ability to launch five feet to the right and catch it before it could fall into the oily puddle at the side of the road.

Dammit.

I flashed a quick smile at the man I ran into, trying to blind him with it. "Sorry," I said. "Didn't see you there."

"No harm done," he replied brusquely, brushing his palms over his pressed jacket as though my touch had somehow tainted it. *Jackass.*

I snorted, putting my book back in my bag. "You're right on schedule."

I glanced up, wondering who the man was talking to now as I stepped away but there was no one else, and he was staring straight at me. That's when I noticed it.

The odd smell—it was coming from him.

There was an otherworldliness to him I hadn't noticed at first, but it was there. An air of power and knowledge that shouldn't have belonged to a man who looked barely older than thirty.

He isn't human. "What did you say?"

"You must be Alison. I was told I might find you here."

"Allie," I corrected him sharply, hands clenching into fists.

The smell, a smoky odor with an undercurrent of something tangy tugged at a distant memory. But what? My brows rose as I realized where I knew it from. Stella's house. She was a witch who lived just outside Forest Grove and had helped us a time or two.

"You're a witch."

"We prefer *alchemist*, but yes." The man dipped his head in a formal sort of greeting, and I took in his stature, measuring him up. He wasn't very large. A few inches below six feet tall with a clean shaven face and dark brown eyes. "Gregory."

Something he'd said before returned, and I narrowed my eyes at him, feeling my inner wolf surface. I tampered her with a steadying breath and straightened my spine. "You said I was right on schedule. Were you waiting for me?"

His lips twitched into a sly grin as he swept an arm toward the coffee shop next door. "Join me for a coffee?"

"You didn't answer my question."

Heat skittered up my spine and this time when my wolf strained against the confines of my human body, I let him see it. I let him see her in the glow of my eyes.

His smile vanished. "If you'll join me, I'll be happy to explain."

"Hard pass."

Jared and Clay would *kill* me if they found out I went off with some witch to have a private chat, even if it were in public.

"If you have something to say to me, you can do it right here."

I lowered my voice as a few teenagers strolled past, reeking of tobacco and minty chewing gum.

The man, Gregory, dragged his tongue across his teeth, a look of disgust on his face as he considered something. "You've...*how should I put this*...you've piqued the interest of the Arcane Council. My superior would like a meeting with you to discuss your *deformity*."

My upper lip curled back, and I could barely contain it as a low growl reverberated in my chest. "You can tell your *superior* that I have no interest in meeting with him. And you—"

"That's too bad," he interrupted. "He doesn't like to be refused."

A thinly veiled threat in his reply put my teeth on edge. Sweat beaded at my brow, and it had nothing to do with the heat.

"And I don't like being stalked by witches in *my* town," I retorted, meeting him blow for blow with a threat of my own. "If I see you on my streets again, I'll remove you myself."

Surprise flashed quickly in his eyes before his expression settled back to the haughty disdain of a moment before, and he tucked his hands into his pockets.

"Well then," he said with a smirk squirming at the edge of his mouth. "Goodbye for now, little wolf. I'll be seeing you."

"You better hope you don't."

I walked seven blocks, taking the longest possible route back to where I'd parked the Chevelle, needing the time to calm my rattled nerves.

Why were the witches interested in me *now?*

Nothing had changed. I'd been the same Allie Grace— the twin soul wolf—for the last four years. Either they hadn't known about me until now, or they didn't care until now. I assumed the former, but if the latter, what changed to make them curious all of a sudden?

I viscously shoved the thoughts away, locked them up for later inspection. I'd told Clay I'd stop by Grove's End while I was in town, and if I didn't calm my racing heart and break up the mosh pit of worried thoughts in my mind, he would sense there was something up.

No need to worry him. I'd already sent the alchemist prick away, and if he knew what was good for him, he wouldn't come back.

I sighed as I unlocked the door and slid into the seat of my baby, accepting her hug as her leather seats formed to my curves. She'd been a gift from my mates and my two best friends when I turned eighteen. She'd been a wreck then. All rusted out and falling apart. Not anymore. It'd taken almost three years, but she was a sexy thing now. All polished chrome and conditioned leathers and pristine glossy black paint.

It was too bad I only got to drive her on Wednesdays. There wasn't much use for a car on pack land, there being no roads leading in or out.

Being able to run faster than a car also sort of made the use of one a moot point.

"Let's go see Clay," I muttered to her, easing out onto the road, my hands tense on the wheel.

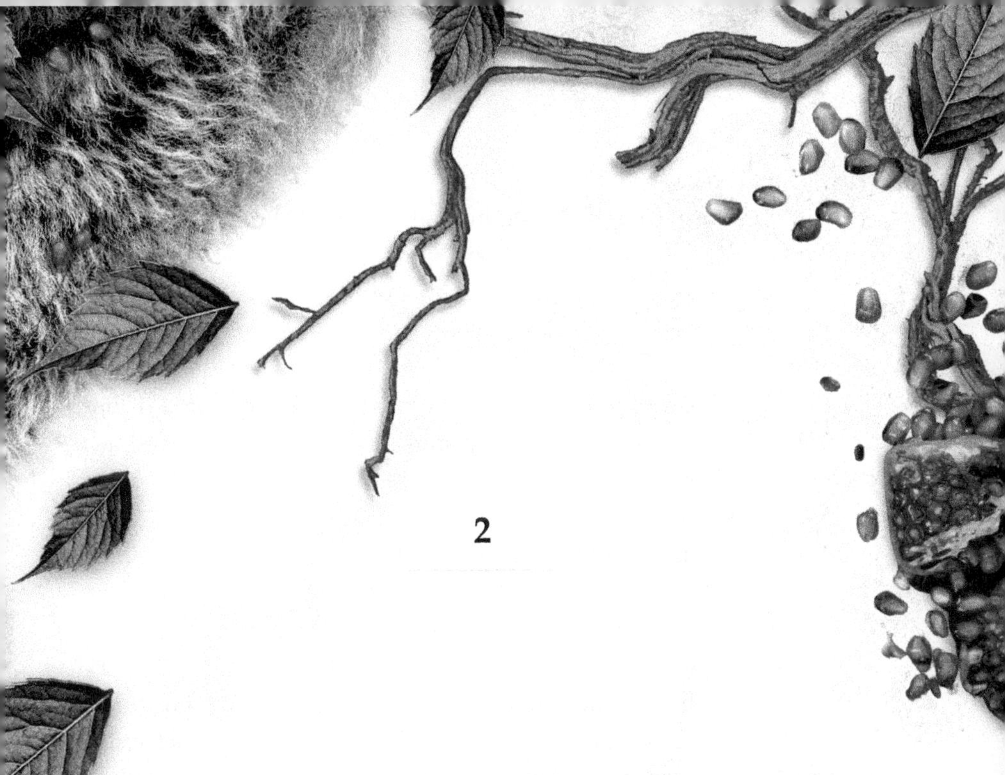

2

It was a short drive to the pub. Well, everything was a short drive in the small town of Forest Grove, but in reality, Grove's End was the furthest you could get without leaving town limits. It sat just on the outer rim, a little down the way from Gerry's Shake Shack.

It didn't look like much on the outside: a tall, slender building with the lower level—the pub— painted all in black with silver lettering for the sign hanging above the door. A tall window gave passersby a glance inside, but keeping it fairly dim made it difficult for mortal eyes to see in without actually entering. The scent of beer and tang of liquor mixed with the mouth-watering salted grease perfume of fresh cut fries as I parked and made my way inside.

It being a Wednesday and smack dab in between lunch and dinner, there were only the usuals seated at the bar. An older gentleman called Tuck, a younger guy named Darren in his construction boots and safety vest from an early morning shift, and Clay.

I grinned at my mate as I made my way to him. He sensed me before he saw me, and I caught the slight upturning of his lips on his side profile before he turned.

"Well if it isn't the queen, herself," he teased, and I leaned down to kiss him, but he yanked me onto his lap instead, making me yelp.

"Hey!" Destiny chastised from behind the bar. "Those stools aren't built for two."

I tried to squirm out of his hold but that only made him hold tighter, his big hands gripping my hips like vises, keeping me pinned against his lap.

"Horseshit," Clay grumbled in reply. "Have you seen some of our customers? If they can hold them, they can sure as hell hold me and this toothpick."

"Have you *seen* you?"

She had a point. Clay was huge. The biggest shifter in the Forest Grove pack by far. Even if he weren't big boned and over six feet tall, the countless pounds of muscle added to his already large frame made him downright monstrous.

Despite myself, I laughed, giving up and letting Clay hold me there. I didn't actually want to move anyway. I hadn't seen him since yesterday and already the nearness of him was settling my nerves and reinvigorating me through the mate bond.

His grip loosened, and he slung an arm around my middle, leaning in to breathe in my scent. His stubble pricked the back of my neck, and I shuddered as his warm breath fanned over my collarbone. Bastard knew exactly what he was doing to me.

"What's wrong?" he asked a moment later as Destiny left to pour another beer for Darren. I didn't dare turn to face him, lifting a shoulder in a little shrug.

"Nothing," I replied, covering the waver in my voice by clearing my throat. "Hey, Des, want to grab me a whiskey?"

She raised a brow at my request. I rarely ever drank at the pub. I definitely didn't during the day. But a whiskey might be just the thing. The Chevelle would be safe parked at Grove's End overnight since we had someone here twenty-four hours for security, and I could use the run back to pack camp.

"Make it two, then," Clay added, giving my side a little squeeze that told me without words that he knew something was up but wouldn't push me.

Not right now anyway. Not with mortal ears four seats down the bar and Destiny hovering.

"So, how's things here?" I asked both Destiny and Clay, sipping my whiskey and letting the burn of it slinking down my throat sear away the last dregs of my unease.

"Good," Clay and Des answered at the same time. "Better than we expected so far," Des added.

"Season doesn't really start for another couple weeks but we're full most nights."

I smiled genuinely at that, throwing Des a wink. "Told you it would be."

Grove's End was Jared and Clay's baby. After I took over for the corrupt former alpha of the Forest Grove pack, Jared took over running his family's quarry. He'd always been good with numbers and over the years, we slowly replaced all the employees as they moved on or retired with shifters from the pack. Business was booming, and when Clay saw that this old building had been listed for sale, the two of them agreed this would be a smart move.

I couldn't even put into words how glad I was to see it thriving. The first year had been rough, like any new business just starting out they ran into pitfall after pitfall. Barriers to getting a food and liquor license. Mold in the ceiling. A burst water pipe a month into the grand opening. Not to mention that the normal people in town tended to shy away from the place based purely on their natural instincts.

They may not be able to physically see the wolves within the owners and employees of the pub, but they could sense it. We were predators. They were prey.

A few months of one-dollar happy hour and two- dollar beers made them set aside their misgivings though. Now we charged full price and they still came. Truth be told, there weren't many half decent places in this town to get a good pint or a half decent burger, and if there were two things shifters did best, it was burgers and beer.

"You're coming to the bonfire later, right?" I asked Clay, tipping back the rest of my whiskey with a shudder.

"For a while. It's my patrol tonight."

A sinking feeling in my gut had me clenching my teeth, and Clay tugged me closer. "Hey," he said, grabbing me by the chin to make me look at him. "I can pass it off to someone else if you'd rather I—"

"No," I stopped him. "No, it's fine. I'm just—I don't know what's wrong with me. Tired, I guess."

He wasn't buying it, I could tell by the way his brows pulled together and his keen blue eyes narrowed. If the witch came back again, I'd tell him. For now, there was no reason to bring it up. There was no reason for me to be worried that he'd be running the perimeter of our lands tonight.

There'd be at least one other shifter with him.

They'd be fine.

I leaned in and kissed him before he could say anything else, lingering there long enough for his lips to soften and for him to reach up and tangle his fingers in my hair. My skin flashed hot from his touch, thighs clenching, before I forced myself to pull away. It was too easy to get carried away with Clay.

"See you soon?"

"See you soon," he confirmed, his face returning to the stoic mask he wore for everyone else but me. I fluffed his hair, trying to bring the smile back, but he only batted my hand away. He'd kept his inky black hair cropped short for so long that the new look, with it longer on top and shaved down to almost nothing on the sides still made me pause every time I saw him. It was severe in a very *Clay* way. It suited him.

I snorted, hopping down from the stool.

"Hey," Clay barked, snagging me by the arm. "Give me your keys."

I frowned at him. "I wasn't going to drive, anyway."

"Then you won't mind handing them over."

Grumbling to myself, I drew them out of my pocket and tossed them to him. He and I both knew that two fingers of Jack weren't enough to really impair my driving. Shifters burned that shit off at least five times faster than mortals. It'd be out of my system in less than twenty minutes. But it was one of his many *rules*, and breaking them had never worked out in my favor.

"Tell Vivian not to wait up if she's tired," Destiny called after me, taking my emptied glass from the bar. "Kyle's on security tonight so I shouldn't be too late, but you know how she gets when she's over-tired."

"Don't we all?"

I'd known Vivian for most of my life. She was one of my best friends, and at first, it'd been hard to share her with Destiny, but there truly wasn't anything that could keep a mated pair apart. Besides, they were so happy that I wouldn't have dared try. Even if Destiny could be one of the most filterless, abrasive people I'd ever met when the mood struck her.

"I'll tell her."

The half-drunk customers lifted their beers to me as I left, and I offered them both a nod. I didn't play a massive role in any of our pack-run businesses, but I was sure that by the way my pack regarded me in public, the general population of Forest Grove probably thought I was some kind of Queenpin.

I chuckled darkly to myself as I made my way down the street toward where the sidewalk ended. If only they knew that I spent the first two—no, really the first three—years in my role as alpha, stumbling through day to day.

I'd had no idea what I was doing, and if I hadn't had Jared and Clay and the others to guide me, I was one hundred percent sure I would have royally fucked something up by now. As it was, we were all still here. Still alive. Wealthier than we'd ever been. More at peace than we'd ever been. And somewhere along the way, it stopped feeling like I was trying to shove my foot into a shoe that didn't fit.

I made my way wistfully past my Chevelle, cursing myself that I forgot to get my books out of the passenger seat before giving the keys to Clay. I supposed I could wait another day to read them. It was better than going back in there now and would only serve to give Clay *two* opportunities to take the keys from me in front of staff and customers. The bastard.

Taking a quick look around the immediate area, I made sure there wasn't anyone watching as I slid from the edge of the concrete and into the tree line. My wolf awoke at the scent of damp earth and warm pine, making my skin bristle and a little rumble quake in my chest.

I cracked my neck, moving to our spot further in to be sure I was away from any prying eyes before stripping down to my birthday suit. I crudely folded the clothes and set my boots atop them, shoving the leaves and bramble away from the nook between the tree and midsize boulder to tuck them inside.

My clothes from the last time were still in there, and I'd have to remember to come and fetch them before my whole damned wardrobe ended up here.

I carried them home sometimes in my mouth, but they usually ended up with holes that way. I'd need to remember to bring my pack if I wanted to get them back to camp.

Replacing the branches over our makeshift locker, I cracked my neck again and took off at a run, pounding my bare feet against the earth as my wolf took hold. When I was first changed, the transformation was painful. Excruciating. The first couple of times it had taken hours. Now, I could shift between one footfall and the next with only a split second of agony that was easy enough to endure.

I launched forward, giving over that part of myself that would allow my wolf to be free. She took the reins, bursting out from within me with a snarl. Our twin tails bobbed behind us as she carried us swiftly toward home. Once, she'd felt like a separate entity from me. Like a force I could neither control nor understand.

Even though her instincts didn't always align with mine, I knew now that we were one. She was merely an extension of me. A shadow self that ran on primal instinct and raw emotion instead of logic and limits.

I luxuriated in the feel of the cool, shaded breeze running through channels of our black and silver fur, giving us a reprieve from the scorch of the sun.

The borders of our land now extended far beyond the boundaries of Forest Grove, encompassing two other pack territories that had been absorbed into ours during the battle of the Four Corners before I ever became alpha. But the border I crossed now was the border of our pack camp.

The inner ring. One of three that always had a constant patrol.

We didn't anticipate any attacks. Only a fool would try something against what was now one of the largest packs in the US. Though if I'd learned anything from the time I was bitten by my psychotic ex-boyfriend until now, it was that you could trust no one. That when you feel you're the most safe, is often when you're the most in danger.

My ears pricked as another wolf approached from the west, and my wolf recognized them as pack. I slowed as they approached, my sides heaving from the long sprint. Layla came into view a moment later, her all-black wolf offset with a starburst of silvery fur on her forehead and socks to match. Her trademark jasmine scent clung to her even in wolf form.

Seth was only a few seconds behind, loping up to greet me with his long tongue lolling out to one side.

They were dating now. Had been for a few months, and even though Layla was one of my best friends along with Vivian, I couldn't say I saw it coming.

Where Layla was quiet, reserved, and preferred to dress in all black to match her long dark hair and near- black eyes, Seth was the complete opposite. With hazel eyes often set in a mischievous stare, and a loud ass personality.

A case of opposites attract, I supposed.

Did you leave the Chevelle in town? We didn't see it on the way past the garage, her voice slipped into my mind as her wolf cocked its head.

I did. Had a drink at Grove's End, so...

Clay take your keys? Seth butted in, bumping my shoulder with his as he stalked around me playfully, making me skid to one side to avoid his snapping jowls.

You good, Allie? Layla asked before I could answer, and I was reminded just how well my besties knew me even if we didn't have a mate bond allowing us to sense one another's emotions. Truly, I'd all but put the encounter with the witch out of my mind, but the lingering aftereffects of it kept my muscles taut and strained.

I'd expect the inquisition from Vivian, but Layla would let it go.

Yeah, you guys should get back to your patrol. Is Jared back yet?

No, Seth replied. *But I talked to him earlier. He said he'd be back in time for the festivities.*

I gave Seth a nod and looked north toward camp.

How are they settling in, do you know?

They've already started work on their cabin, Layla told me. *A bunch of the pack are helping, including Viv and the guys, so they should have it built within the week.*

Some of the weight lifted from my shoulders at that, and I let out a relieved chuff. *If Viv is on it, I doubt it'll take more than a few days,* I joked. With her barking orders, no one would be getting any breaks.

Come on, babe, move that cute tush, we have work to do.

Seth snapped at Layla's behind, making her yip before they took off to continue their rounds. No doubt Seth had orchestrated it so that they could take the earlier shift and not miss the party. He never missed an opportunity to feast and drink. *Ever.*

The new shifters we were welcoming tonight were from a pack further to the south. They'd been forced out by their alpha when they mated. It was the same old story. Once word spread that we were accepting of same sex mated pairs in our pack, they started seeking us out.

Four mated pairs had joined us already over the last four years and that was a lot, considering how few shifters remained. The fact that they couldn't procreate was the reason given when their alphas forced them to blood out, but I knew better. They were backward thinking asshats with antiquated principles who wouldn't understand the concept of love even if it got them by the jugular.

This new couple had it rough, though. One of them, Callum, was a freshly turned wolf, and their alpha mangled him when he blooded them out, going for the face instead of the usual shoulder, arm, or leg that inflicted less damage and left a less noticeable scar.

I'd have been pissed too if I knew I was going to lose a shifter as strong and able as Archer when he mated to Callum, but that was his choice to cast them out...and there was no excuse for that sort of behavior. If they hadn't come over two-hundred miles to be here, I'd go show him exactly what I thought of his barbaric methods.

Shifters healed quickly, and often without scarring. The only thing that *did* scar us was a bite from another wolf. Something in the venom prevented proper healing, hiding away beneath the tissue and lingering there, keeping the scars from ever truly healing.

I had several of my own I would bear for the rest of my life, and I knew that if I held the position of alpha, there would be a great many more to come.

Just like Seth and Layla said, there was a small crew hard at work on the new cabin at the edge of the massive clearing. Soon, we'd have to clear more forest if the pack kept growing.

Viv waved as she saw me pass, her short blonde hair catching the last rays of the sun before it would slip down below the trees. She stopped for only a second before spinning to bark more orders at her small group of conscripted helpers. The newbies waved too, nervously, and with smiles that were too broad and didn't reach their eyes.

They were nervous. Didn't know what to think of me. Of how I ran my pack. They would see soon enough that they were more than welcome and the only things I expected from those under my command, other than their loyalty, was for them to pull their own weight and not start shit with other pack members. That was it.

I shifted back at the sliding door to the rear of the cabin I shared with Clay and Jared. Even after four years, I preferred being naked without an audience, though it didn't bother me much when the need arose anymore. Not like it used to.

"Do you think they'll like chocolate chip or peanut butter better?" Grams asked as I slid the door closed, unsurprised to find her baking in my kitchen. It was the only one with a working oven. We'd have sprung for her to have one in her own cabin, but I think she liked the excuse to come by just as much as she liked to bake. "Or should I just do a cake?"

"If they're anything like the rest of us, they'll eat whatever you want to make."

When it came to Hazel's baking, we didn't discriminate. For an old blind woman, she really knew what she was doing.

"*Hmph*," she grunted, pulling out the ingredients for both kinds of cookies like I'd suspected she would. No matter how many she made, they'd all be gone by morning.

"You see my grandson today?"

"Yep. He'll be by for the welcoming ceremony before he goes on patrol."

"Good," she huffed. "Between that damned *bar* and him patrolling every night and sleeping all day, I never see him."

"You and me both, Grams." I slid past her to grab a drink from the fridge, going for the cold brew. She brushed my shoulder and stilled, turning on hobbling legs to yank my hand away from the handle on the fridge door and pull it into hers.

She squished my hand between her palms and then turned it face up as though she could see the lines in the surface of my skin with her milky white eyes. I knew what she would see, or sense more like.

Grams had been blind since birth and that affected the senses of her wolf when she made the transition. Heightening them in a way that allowed her to glimpse emotions and snippets of the past and present events that spurred them.

"Who was it?" she asked, tilting her head. Her long gray braid shifted behind her shoulder as she stared at me, unseeing. There was no sense in lying to her. Never was.

"A witch," I told her, gently pulling my hand away from her grasp. "I sent him away. He won't be back."

She pursed her lips.

"Don't mention it to the guys?"

Her hands went to her hips, and I could already anticipate the talking to I was about to get and rolled my eyes. "Look," I added before she could get a word in. "If he comes back, I'll tell them. There's no reason to worry them over nothing. Deal?"

"What did he want?"

"A meeting. With someone from the Arcane Council."

Her expression soured. It was a truth universally known and acknowledged that the witches didn't exactly get along with the other three races. They hadn't ever since the original voyagers left their veiled homeland of Emeris and sailed to the mortal lands.

Ancient history if you asked me, but old grudges died hard it seemed.

"I don't like it," she replied, clucking her tongue before turning back to her task at the counter with a flustered blush in her pale cheeks.

I patted her on the shoulder as I passed. "Save me a few chocolate chips before they're all spoken for?"

A grunt was her only reply as I went to get ready for the night ahead, a new kind of anxiety taking root next to the other one still blooming. A sense that something was coming. Something out of my control. Maybe it was just the visit from the witch putting me off, but my gut hadn't ever been wrong before.

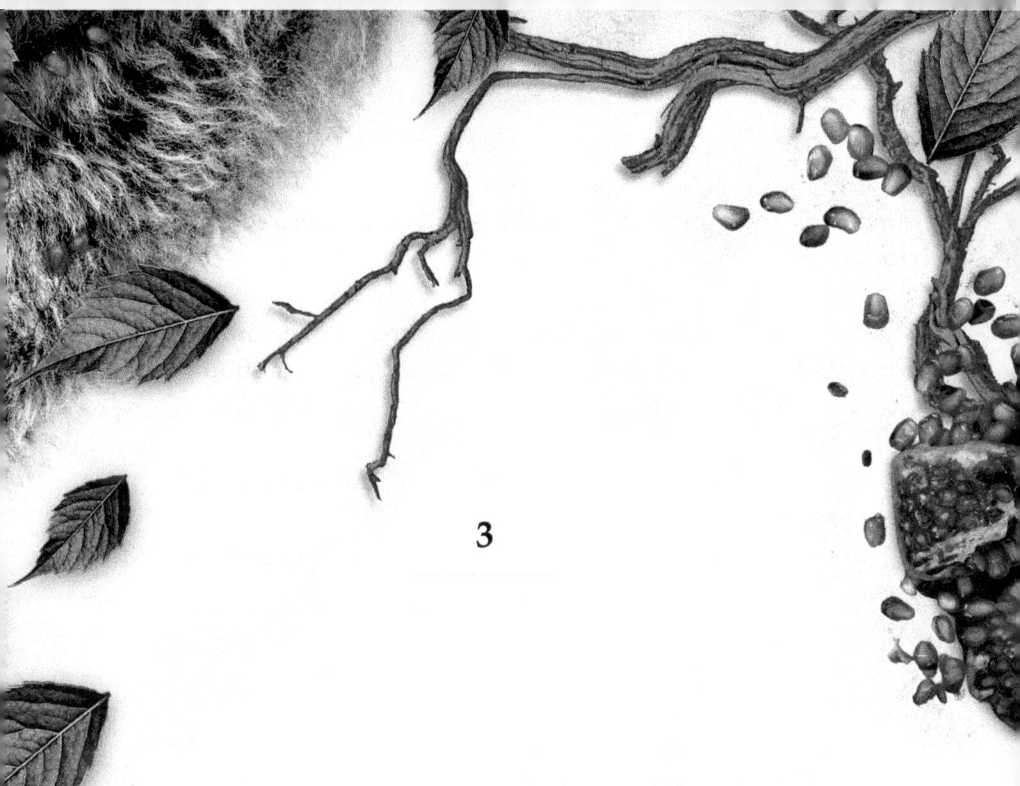

3

Clay still wasn't back from Grove's End.

It was full dark now, and Jared had returned an hour ago, though he was still in the cabin getting ready. I liked a good hot shower as much as the next person, but he liked to drain every drop out of the hot water tank. Good thing I'd already showered before he got home from the quarry.

"Have you seen Clay yet?" I asked Viv as she came over to sit next to me, passing me a beer I wasn't sure I could stomach, but I took anyway.

Though the bonfire warmed my skin and baked the fronts of my jeans, there was a coldness within that had me hunching, arms tucked in against it. I hadn't been able to shake it for hours.

She frowned and shook her head. "Why? His patrol isn't for another couple hours."

"No reason. Just thought he'd be back by now."

Viv narrowed her eyes at me but didn't pry for once. I drew my phone out of my pocket and fired off a text to set my mind at ease.

Allie: Have you left yet?

When my phone didn't ping with a reply straight away, I clutched it tighter as though willing a reply message to appear.

I'd checked to make sure the witch hadn't followed me to Grove's End. My eyes had been glued to the rear- view in the Chevelle just as much as they were on the road. And I hadn't picked up his scent anywhere around the pub when I left.

He left town, I reassured myself.

I turned him down so he had no reason to hang around. With a resigned sigh, I put the red cup to my lips and sipped the frothy beer, my head a million miles away.

"You want to talk about it?"

I blinked, almost having forgotten Viv was there. "You guys fighting or something?"

I chuckled a little at that. It wouldn't have been unheard of if we were. Clay and I had some of the most epic arguments. He once slept outside in his wolf form for an entire month when he was pissed at me. But he never left pack camp, and he slept only a stone's throw from the cabin, unable to stay too far away.

"Nah," I told her. "Just on edge today."

"What is it? The new recruits?"

My phone pinged a moment later, and I fumbled to lift it, thumbing the screen to life to view the message.

Clay: I already grabbed your books from the car, woman. Chill. Leaving now.

I sat up and tucked my phone away, taking a longer swallow of my beer this time. "Nah. Everything's good."

"Want me to get everything set up? We should start soon."

"Thanks Viv."

"No problem, Allie cat," she said with a wink, rising to clear a space and fill the ceremonial bowl Layla had bought for the pack a couple years back with whiskey.

The brass combined with the amber liquid that reflected the flames from the roaring bonfire made the drink look like liquid fire. It was such an archaic tradition, but at least blooding in a new pack member was less barbaric than blooding them out. I'd only had to release two shifters since I became alpha four years ago. And they only left because they mated to shifters from other packs whose alphas wouldn't release them to join us.

Someone had to be the bigger person, but the fact that it seemed it always had to be me got old.

The screen door of our cabin clattered shut, and I turned to find

Jared bounding down the steps, his dirty blonde hair still damp from the shower. His toned chest and abs glistened from the flicker of the firelight as he strode toward me in only a pair of low hanging gym shorts that left nothing to the imagination.

His smile radiated the warmth I felt as my inner wolf felt him draw near, banishing the rest of the coldness from my bones.

I shuddered as he settled himself onto the arm of my chair, snaking a hand through my hair to brush over the back of my neck. Like he always did, Jared swept the immediate area before leaning down to press his lips to mine. Where Clay was all hard edges—the darkness that harbored my moon—Jared was the complete opposite. He was my sun.

He was warmth and comfort. A steadying presence that I could always count on no matter what.

His hand tugged lightly at my hair, tipping my head back more so that he could sweep in with his tongue and steal my breath away from my lungs.

"Get a room," Viv teased, and Jared broke the kiss, leaving me to glare at my best friend.

She smirked before passing me the matching blade to go with the ceremonial bowl.

"Are we waiting for Clay?" Jared asked, running a finger down the side of my neck in the way that he *knew* drove me insane until I shied away, giving him an accusing look to which he just chuckled.

"No need," Clay grunted, appearing as though from nowhere like he always did. For a guy his size, he was insanely light on his feet. If it weren't for our mate bond tugging at my core whenever he was near, he'd scare the ever-loving shit out of me on a daily basis.

As it was, he still did sometimes, but only when I was distracted. Like when I was just kissing my other mate.

"Great, we're all here then. I'll grab the guys."

Viv fled to go and wrangle the newbies while Clay, barefoot and bare chested, in only a pair of dark jean shorts, dropped my book bag onto my lap.

He ran a hand through his tousled black hair, clearing his throat as he fell into the chair next to mine. "How's it going at the pub?" Jared asked, starting a conversation with his best friend and removing his hands from my body, making a muscle twitch in my jaw and a hollow feeling settle in my gut.

As they bantered back and forth with me between them, we reverted to what I dubbed *stasis mode*. At first, when we decided it was time to stop trying to fight our instincts and take the relationships to the next level, it seemed like I was going to be able to have it all. Both of my mates. The three of us together in the way that I desperately craved.

That was not how it happened though. They tried at first, but in the end, their territorial instinct made it almost impossible. Especially when sex was put on the table.

Their inner wolves couldn't be subdued, plus, I suspected, on some level, it was also to do with the very *human* notion that you're not supposed to share a lover. But who the fuck came up with that rule, anyway?

If what I felt for *both* of my mates was unnatural, then I didn't want to be natural.

I'd have fought their decision to keep things separate. I wanted to, but I wouldn't risk putting any more strain on their friendship than there already was.

I could wait.

As long as it wasn't forever.

Layla rushed in with Seth from their patrol, both of them ass naked, as several others were, preferring to remain in the nude to allow for easier shifting back and forth. Seth made a beeline for the beer keg and Layla came to greet the three of us.

"All clear," she reported, her long dark hair covering her nipples as she settled herself onto a stool by the fire.

It always was these days. I was so glad to be done with the constant trespasses on our land. They'd happened frequently when I first took over as alpha. Mostly spurred by curiosity. There hadn't ever been a female alpha. And there definitely hadn't ever been one who had mated to two other shifters and sported two tails.

Vivian walked Archer and Callum into the ring, putting her fingers to her lips to give one of her signature ear-splitting whistles to get everyone's attention.

I rose and tucked my books away behind the chair, as far from the fire as I could get them and lifted the bowl and dagger from the stump where Viv had left them.

Shaking off my unease, I walked them to the cleared area where Viv waited with them. Clay, Jared, and Layla on my heels. Charity fell in line behind them, standing in as the fourth official witness.

Callum grinned widely, stretching the skin of the gnarly scar in his cheek. Somehow, it didn't diminish his good looks, but rather seemed to almost enhance them—give them an edge to make him look just as intimidating as his massive mate.

"You know the words?" I asked them, accepting Viv's help as she stepped forward and took the bowl from my hand, holding it out to me as I put my hand over it, readying the blade.

They both nodded and the gathering quieted. The air still, save for the rush of heat from the fire and crackle of the wood burning.

"Of my own will I enter into this pack," they said as one, their eyes betraying no hint of uncertainty.

One after another, they spoke the final binding words.

"With the moon and all in attendance here as witnesses, I hereby submit myself to the rule of the alpha."

I sliced the blade into the flesh of my palm, grimacing as my blood dripped down to mix with the whiskey in the bowl. The stream slowed and stopped a moment later, the wound already healed, leaving only an annoying itch behind.

I took the bowl from Viv, trading it for the blade, and gave it first to Archer for a drink, and then Callum. Closing my eyes, I felt the connection form like a growing thing inside of me. Like another branch of a tree, or perhaps a new root sinking deeper into the earth. I sighed as the sensation passed, my wolf hedging to the surface to greet her new kin, her twin souls flushed with raw energy vying for release.

"Welcome to the pack," I told them, and they shared a look, embracing as cheers and whoops rose all around. Foamy beer sprayed in our direction, and I lifted an arm to shield my face from the brunt of it as Viv clapped the new recruits on the backs and called for a round of shots.

I'd have to tell them the rest tomorrow unless someone else spilled the beans first. I wished I could explain it all up front, *before* they joined the pack, but no one outside of this territory knew and we liked to keep it that way.

Much like how Grams' blindness gave her the ability of a different form of sight, my twin soul afforded me some...*perks.* Depending on how you looked at it.

The magic of the other races could hold no sway over me. I couldn't be compelled by a vampire. Or bespelled by a witch. When I became alpha of the pack, those abilities became shared by all who blooded in.

We didn't even realize it'd happened until someone got *really* hurt. She was a relatively new wolf. Just changed a few months before, a victim of one of the shifters I cut loose when I took over. She wasn't healing quickly enough on her own, and like the pack had done on many occasions before, we took her to Stella, the witch who lived alone at the edge of town, and offered her money or favors in exchange for her help.

Only, Stella couldn't heal her. Just like she couldn't heal me. The girl's body rejected the potions. Repelled her cast spells.

The girl died on her table.

It was a good thing we'd realized the change soon after I became alpha or we would've had a boon of shifter babies running rampant on our territory. We were back to good old human methods of birth control now, the pill in particular being the only usable kind since we could no longer take the once monthly witchy alternative the pack had used for generations prior.

So as a whole, we all agreed the perks outweighed the pitfalls. There was a reason we were more careful now. Careful who we allowed to join. Careful who we allowed to be cut loose.

Stella would keep quiet; I didn't think she even spoke to other people, mortal or immortal, but if the vampires or witches found out...

Well, our pack agreed that in this case, different was good, but the others wouldn't see it that way. Shifters who were immune to their magic? Immune to compulsion? There was a good chance they'd want us gone.

Which was precisely why I didn't want a fucking high and mighty alchemist prick running around my town asking questions.

"Hey," Jared said, dragging me back to the present. I flinched as his hand pressed to my lower back and a worried crease formed between his brows. "What's up?"

Before I could come up with a reply, Clay stood with a grunt, downing the rest of his beer in one long swallow before tossing the cup into a bin. "I'm heading out for patrol," he announced, his cold blue eyes alighting on Jared's hand on my waist as he passed.

"Be careful," I blurted before I could stop the words from coming out, earning myself a raised brow and a smirk from the big oaf before he gave his head a shake.

He curled two fingers at Charity behind me. "Let's move."

Charity groaned as she passed. "Rest in peace legs," she muttered to herself, making Layla laugh and Jared and me grin.

We had to switch out who had to run patrol with Clay every night because he set a punishing pace and refused to slow down, expecting everyone to keep up no matter how much their bodies protested.

I was the only one he didn't enjoy running with, because I was the only one who could beat his ass in speed and strength.

Thank you twin soul.

Once Clay and Charity vanished into the tree line, I sagged against Jared, giving in to the comfort of his touch. He brushed a hand down my back, and I nuzzled into his neck, breathing in his scent of smooth cedar and musk.

"Take me to bed," I whispered into the hollow beneath his chin. As alpha, there was always something I was worried about. New builds at pack camp, keeping everyone fed and happy, maintaining all three rings of our territory at all times.

And now a stupid motherfucking witch.

I sighed, needing the one thing that always worked to ease the tension and send me sailing off into a solid sleep.

Jared shuddered at my light touch on his chest, catching my hand before I could trail it too low and pressing it against his lips.

"Your wish is my command," he replied in a husky whisper against my fingertips, making my belly squeeze.

I let out a little yelp as he swung me up into his arms, his eyes brightening with the presence of his wolf. I could feel it rumbling against the cage of his chest, a low growl that was echoed within me as he carried me away from the bonfire to a chorus of hoots and hollers.

Nothing was private here. Did you know arousal has a very distinct scent? Different for both males and females, but once I learned to identify it, I could see what they were talking about. And right now? I was sure I reeked of it.

Jared spirited me through the cabin and upstairs with ease, kicking the bedroom door shut behind him.

I reached for him, but he was already there, dipping his head low to steal a kiss from my lips as he lowered me to the rumpled blankets. His hands moved to my hips, and I lifted for him, letting him hook his fingers into the loops of my jeans to drag them off.

The kiss broke as he tugged my shirt over my head, and he laid a trail of hot kisses down my neck, brushing the inside curves of my breasts as he moved lower.

His touch sent shivers skating over my skin, leaving goosebumps in their wake as I moaned, digging my hands into his soft hair, needing something to hold on to.

My wolf prowled within, her eagerness to be joined with her mate so strong it made my head spin as Jared gripped me by my thighs. He pulled them apart, lowering himself to his knees on the floor at the edge of the bed.

"Jared." I gasped as he pressed his lips to my inner thigh, driving me wild with anticipation as he teased my panties away from the heat of my sex.

I released his hair, reaching for something else to hold on to as he settled his mouth over my sex, making my hips buck as his tongue slid over my clit. My hands fisted in the sheets, my nails elongating in a way that I knew would leave holes in them, but I didn't care.

Jared's tongue drove all impeaching thoughts from my mind, and when his fingers dug into the muscle of my thighs, holding me open even as I tried to squirm, I knew I was nearing the edge.

So close.

So close.

Jared's tongue slowed, bringing me back from the edge and making me cry out. In one swift movement, he lifted my hips, rising from his knees and thrusting until the length of him was buried deep in my throbbing sex.

"Fuck!" I shouted, stars bursting against the dark curtain of my eyelids as I reveled in the glorious fullness of having him seated inside me.

I wrapped my legs around his hips, locking him to me as he began to thrust against me. He groaned at his own ecstasy as my sex clenched around him, and the small sound only drove me wilder. Frantically, I moved my hips, meeting him stroke for stroke as he pumped into me.

When he added his fingers to the mix, rubbing my clit as he gripped me hard with his other hand to hold me in place, I knew I was a goner.

"That's it," he panted in the dark, his eyes glowing a steady, scorching amber in the dark. "Come for me, Allie."

Knowing he was close to his own release shoved me over the edge, and I went with him, plummeting into oblivion as he fell over me. We howled our release in a tangle of shuddering limbs. In that moment, there was nothing but me and Jared. No problems to solve. No witches to burn. Just us. Just this moment.

He cuddled me to his heaving chest, kissing me on the forehead as he drew the sheet up around my back. "I love you," he breathed into my hair, making a new warmth grow in my chest. I squeezed him tight.

"I think you're pretty cool, too," I muttered, eyes growing heavy already. His chest shook with quiet laughter, and I smiled, feeling more at peace than I had in days.

I pressed a sleepy kiss to his chest. "Love you more."

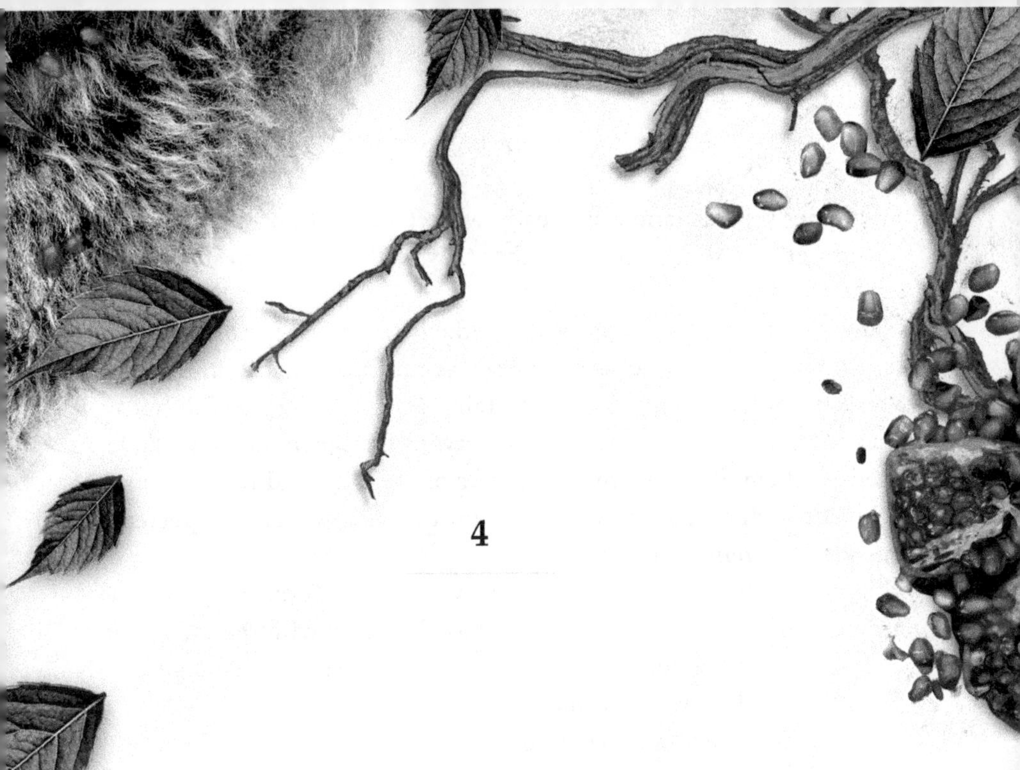

4

The first rays of morning sunlight woke me, streaming in through the window to pool over Jared's toned chest and caress the side of his face.

Making him look every bit the angel he was. My guardian angel. He always had been. Even after the betrayal of his uncle, when he went dark for a while, he never missed an opportunity to make me feel safe. Loved.

I carefully slid out of his grasp, distributing my weight so I wouldn't jostle the mattress too much. He still had a few hours until he needed to leave for the quarry to check on things. Even though I knew the light wouldn't wake him—hardly anything could rouse him when he was this deeply asleep—I slid the curtains closed, peering outside to check for Clay first.

Sometimes after a patrol he would go sleep in the studio above Grove's End. Most nights, though, especially in summer, he preferred to nestle in the shrubbery below the window and sleep in his wolf form.

I didn't blame him. I'd joined him a few times, in fact, and had to admit it was just as comfortable as the bed. Maybe even more so with the soft breeze and forest sounds lulling you to sleep.

But he wasn't there.

I rustled around in my closet for something to throw on, settling on a Banner's t-shirt and my already worn twice but not dirty enough to wash yet jean shorts. The ones that Clay could never stop staring at my ass when I wore.

It went without saying that it made them my favorite ones.

Something pricked at my senses as I slipped my cell into my back pocket and made my way downstairs. My hackles rose, and my wolf surged to the surface. There wasn't anyone foreign in the cabin, I'd have sensed them. Only the regular scents of the pack and the container of chocolate chip cookies Grams left on the counter for me greeted my nose in the main living area.

"Allie!" Vivian called from somewhere far off outside, and I was immediately put on high alert, my blood singing with the urge to shift as I raced out the door, clearing the porch and steps in two bounds. My hands turned to clawed daggers at my sides.

Protect, my wolf snarled within.

Kill.

Frantically, I scanned the dead campfire ring, finding it and the cabins beyond it quiet.

I sensed her approach from my right and took off into the trees like a bolt loosed from my bow. "Viv!" I hollered, adrenaline pulsing through my veins. If she were hurt...

A mental image of Gregory the witch choking on his own blood as my teeth sank into his jugular flashed through my thoughts before her scent hit me.

Not Vivian's.

I slowed, seeing them walking toward me. Vivian and Archer with a girl between them.

Vivian's eyes met mine with an apology. "I was just showing Arch the ropes and..." She trailed off, gesturing at the girl with the familiar dark hair.

Her scent reached me at about the same time my wolf recognized her as unclaimed, and she lifted her head to meet my gaze head on.

"*Sam?*" I asked, incredulous. It'd been four years, but I would know that bone structure—those eyes— anywhere. They were traits she shared with her brother. My mate. Clay.

Her lips pressed into a thin line as her gaze roamed over my body, no doubt taking note of the scars and the way the new muscle bulked up my frame. The last time she'd seen me I'd just *killed* Ryland. The former pack alpha. *Her mate.*

I'd been only eighteen then. A scrawny, anxiety ridden teenager with turquoise hair and not a clue what I was doing other than trying to protect the people I cared about.

Though where I'd filled out, grown the turquoise out of my hair in favor of embracing the silvery color inherited from my mom, she didn't seem to have fared so well since she'd walked out on this pack.

I didn't begrudge her leaving. I couldn't, not knowing how it would tear me apart to lose either of my mates. But I *did* blame her for trying to kill me before she went.

"It's been a while," she said as though we were old friends instead of...whatever the hell we were.

Her cheeks looked sallow, and her eyes dark rimmed. If I didn't know any better, I'd say they almost seemed bruised. Once, I'd been envious of her curves, but now, standing before me in her birthday suit, I could see that the world hadn't been kind to her.

Her muscle and flesh clung to her bones so tightly that I was afraid if she didn't get a drink of water soon she would begin to prune.

"What are you doing here, Samantha?"

Her upper lip curled at my use of her full name but her wolf remained confined within. Not so much as a spark rising to her bright blue eyes.

Her head dropped, making her messy dark hair fall forward to shield her face. Her shoulders shook. "I...I didn't know where else to go."

My lips parted, but I didn't know what to say. My fingernails were digging half-moons into my palms and my wolf still called for blood, making my ability to stay level headed shaky at best.

"Look," Sam snapped, seeming to get a hold on her emotions. Flipping the switch from *poor me* to *fuck you* in an instant.

"I just want to see my brother, okay? I'm...I'm *sorry* for what I did," she gritted out through bared teeth. "Just let me see him, and then you can chase me out of your territory if that's what you want."

My jaw clenched at her request, and it took everything I had not to lay into her.

Did she have any idea what her betrayal did to him? Had Charity not gotten in the way of her attack, and nearly died in the process,

Sam might've succeeded in taking me out. The pain in Clay's eyes when he roared at his sister to leave, his hands shaking with the need to protect his mate, even against his own blood, still haunted my nightmares.

He'd patrolled every night since. For four fucking years.

He didn't say so, but I knew, at least in the beginning, that he was waiting for her to come back.

Not knowing whether she'd come back tail between her legs or claws and fangs poised to finish what she started ate at him. It ate at him almost as much as the prospect that she might keep her promise and never come back at all.

"Save your apology," I hissed, taking a shaky breath to steady my nerves. "I'm not the one you owe it to."

I gestured to Archer and Vivian to bring her. "Bring her inside. Don't take your eyes off her."

They nodded and left, leaving me to whisper a string of curses under my breath alone.

With trembling fingers, I drew out my phone as they walked away, finding Clay's name in my call history and hesitating for an instant before jamming the screen.

I paced as it rang.

"Allie?" Clay's voice came over the receiver. "What's wrong?"

Leave it to him to know something was up before I could even get a word in.

"Are you at Grove's End?"

"What happened?" he growled, and I could already hear him moving, muttering to himself how he *knew* he should have stayed at camp. "Allie, start talking."

"No one's in danger," I told him, mentally adding, *at least I don't think anyone's in danger.* "Just get here, 'kay?"

"Already on my way."

The line went dead, and I sighed. I guessed we had about ten minutes before he got here. He was just that fast.

The telltale clatter of a screen door back at camp was followed by several others, and I knew that there wouldn't be a soul at camp who didn't know she was here within the hour.

A flash of light hair caught the sun through the trees, and I sensed him coming. It took a lot to wake up Jared, but camp just got a whole lot louder than it normally was on a Thursday morning.

Jared's hands were in fists at his sides, and his eyes glowed with the light of his wolf begging to be freed as he came into view. His fury only served to reignite my own, and I had to work twice as hard to keep myself in control.

"Want to tell me why Samantha fucking Armstrong is in our kitchen right now?"

"She just showed up wanting to see Clay," I explained, throwing a hand in the air. "What was I supposed to do, Jare?"

"*She tried to kill you.*"

He grabbed me by the arm, forcing me to face him. The contact sent a rush of angry heat pulsing into me, and I had to disentangle myself from his grasp.

"*I know,*" I lobbed back. "But that was four years ago and Clay—"

"Do you honestly think Clay is going to be glad to see her? He's just going to send her away all over again."

What he wasn't saying hurt more than anything he could've said. Clay was going to have to grieve her all over again.

"Maybe not," I argued. "It's been four years. Maybe she—"

"Please tell me you're not that stupid."

I narrowed my eyes at him, trying and failing to find the Jared from last night in his stare. My steady wolf. My rock. The thing I held on to when things got messy.

This was a hard limit for him, though. He trusted our inner circle and had a wary trust of the rest of the pack, but he harbored no faith in anyone else. Not ever. Not since his uncle's betrayal.

Not only had Ryland been to blame for the death of Clay's father, the pack alpha before him, but he'd also been responsible for the death of Jared's parents. The former gave him control of the pack. The latter gave him the deed to the quarry and control of all of its income.

I wouldn't trust anyone anymore, either, but he needed to calm the fuck down.

"Maybe you should go," I suggested, doing my best not to take his comment to heart. If he stayed, he might just end up saying more things he might later regret.

My words seemed to get through his erected barriers, and I saw a crack form in his facade. His lips parted and the strain around his eyes eased. *There* he was.

"*Shit*," he cursed, throwing a fist through his bed- rumpled hair. "I'm sorry, Allie, I just..."

I nodded. "I know. It's okay."

"I'm not leaving," he announced a second later. "I'll have Todd go take care of things for me. I'm not leaving until she's gone."

I could see that there was no room for argument, so I didn't bother trying. "Clay should be here any minute," I told him, earning myself a scowl.

"You should have let me question her first."

"And put you at the mercy of Clay when he found out you didn't call him the instant she arrived?" I scoffed. "I'd be cleaning your guts up off the kitchen floor by noon."

The joke fell on deaf ears as a knot formed between Jared's brows, and we both made our way back to the cabin. Side by side, but miles apart.

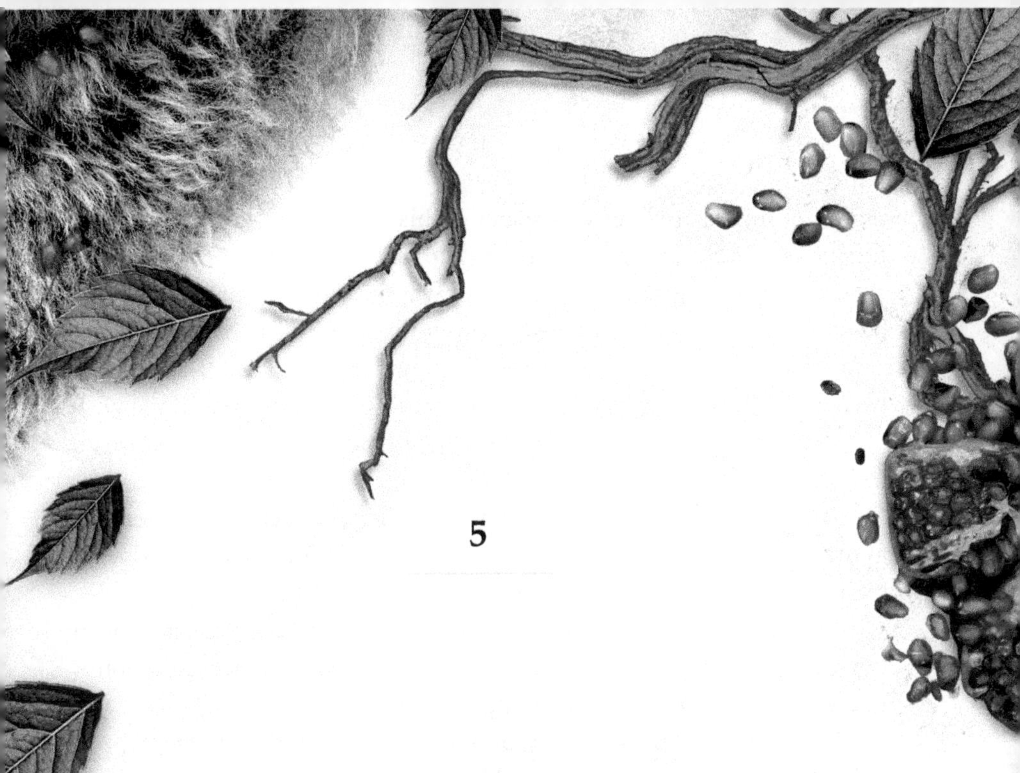

5

J ared and I dispersed the growing crowd of curious shifters and went inside to wait for Clay to show up. I half wondered if I should put away the breakables but decided it really didn't matter right now if some shit wound up broken. We had bigger things to worry about.

But the thought that he would either be utterly relieved to see his sister or murderous left me antsy as fuck.

"You guys can go back on patrol." I dismissed Viv and Archer, holding the door open for them as Jared and I took over babysitting.

Sam made herself comfortable on one of the barstools next to the kitchen island. She had one of my chocolate chip cookies in her hand and a half drunk glass of milk at her elbow.

"You got something I can wear?" she asked with a mouth full of cookie.

"You sure you're good?" Viv asked, her gaze hard as she paused in the doorway to read my stare.

I gave a terse nod. "Peachy."

My stomach soured as I closed the door behind Viv and Archer. "Stay with her while I find something for her to throw on."

"Jared crossed his arms over his tan chest and leaned against the refrigerator, not making any secret of his distrust as he watched her unblinking while she annihilated my cookies. The bitch.

I found my ugliest dress tucked away in the back of the closet. I never wore dresses, but I owned a sum total of two of them, and I didn't care about getting this one back. She could keep it, and if she didn't want it, it'd make half decent bonfire kindling when she was done with it. There was no way I'd be wearing it again once her scent was clogged into every inch of the fabric.

My wolf shifted within, sensing her mate approach. I could feel his apprehension like a spike through my own chest. I rushed back downstairs, thrusting the dress at Sam.

"He's here," I muttered, and she dropped the cookie she'd been munching on and tugged the dress over her head, grimacing no doubt at the lingering scent of me clinging to the fabric.

Clay burst into the cabin a moment later and got about two steps in before he froze in place. He would've known it was her. Clay had an *insane* sense of smell. He would've scented her within a mile of camp.

His burning blue eyes flicked to me for an instant, his jaw clenched so hard I thought he might shatter his teeth.

"Hey, big bro," Sam said in a voice that was trying to sound nonchalant, but I could sense her fear. The sweet, sour smell of it wrinkled my nose.

Clay's dark hair was still rumpled from sleep, and his dark shorts hung low on his hips. Every bulky muscle in his body coiled as though expecting an attack. Clay was already one of the largest shifters in the pack four years ago. Now, no one could compare to his monstrous size.

Sam looked up at him, and I could tell she wasn't breathing. Her face a pale mask of calm.

"Did you miss me?" she added in a joking tone, making his eyes narrow.

For a split second, I thought he was going to kill her.

I felt his anger flare like a lit match meeting a pool of gasoline, and my wolf rose to meet his, a snarl curling my upper lip. But as quickly as it came, it began to wane.

"Where the fuck were you?"

Sam's face pinched. "Does it matter?"

Clay glared at his sister, and I could see his muscles shudder with rage. "*Sam,*" he warned.

She rolled her eyes and gestured vaguely with her hand. "Here and there," she replied. "I was running with a pack out east for a while, but..." She trailed off, and Clay seemed to notice the state of her for the first time. Some of his fury fizzled out, taking in her thin, dirty hair. The way my dress hung from her bony frame. Her gaunt face and hollow eyes. "...let's just say it didn't work out."

Clay sniffed the air, scenting his sister and likely picking out any other lingering scents of her pack. He grimaced. "You're unclaimed."

It wasn't a question, but she answered it anyway. "I left them two weeks ago."

Clay's expression shifted and he took in the room, probably sensing my unease. "She try to hurt you?"

I shook my head, admitting the truth through gritted teeth. "She actually...apologized."

"You want to stay then? Is that it?" Clay demanded of his sister. "You come crawling back after four fucking years—after you tried to kill my mate—looking for what? Pity?"

Sam reeled back as though the blow of his words were a physical one and something in my chest ached at the sight of her pain.

"Clay," I said, giving my head a small shake when our eyes met.

Sam deserved everything she got wherever she'd been for the past four years, but if someone killed either of my mates, I could say with confidence that nothing on this earth could stop me from ripping the culprit's head off.

Ryland may have been a psychopath, but I could see her forgiving a lot for her mate. Besides, she never really got a chance to see the worst of him before it was too late.

The door opened again, and Grams hobbled through, muttering something about the *damned* stairs before she nearly ran into Clay's back.

"Sam?" she asked, her unseeing eyes widening as she sensed the presence of her granddaughter. She shoved past Clay and carefully stepped toward her, hand outstretched.

Sam bristled, jumping from the chair before Grams reached her. For a heartbeat, I thought she was going to bolt, but her chin quivered, and when Grams wrapped her arms around Sam, they both began to cry softly.

Sam broke the embrace first, stepping away from Grams who was now leaning against the countertop, her hand to her chest.

"Is that what you're after?" I pressed, leveling my stare on Sam. "You want to stay? Rejoin the pack?"

I didn't want to break up the reunion, but the fact remained: she was an unclaimed wolf on our lands. She couldn't stay here, not unless she was pack, and I was the only one with the power to make that happen.

Her teeth ground together, and she looked to her brother instead of me as she replied, "Yes. If you'll have me."

I nodded to myself, wondering how the hell I should handle this.

"Allie," Jared interjected, piping up for the first time. "I don't agree with this. We should talk about—"

I lifted a hand to hush him, realizing that this shouldn't be up to me after all. There was only one person who should be the one to make this call, and he was staring at his sister like he still couldn't decide if he wanted to chase her out of our territory himself or wrap her up in his arms. I ached for him.

"This shouldn't be up to us," I told Jared, turning my attention to Clay and his sister. "Your brother will decide your fate."

Clay's head snapped up, his cut-glass eyes sharp and accusing.

"It should be your choice," I told him. "Not mine. If you decide you want her here, then I'll honor that. If you would rather she leave, then I'll escort her off our territory myself. It's your call."

Jared cursed under his breath and shoved off from the fridge, storming out the door.

"I'll give you some privacy," I offered, lifting myself up on tiptoe to kiss Clay's cheek and squeeze his shoulder as I passed. "Take your time. I'll get someone to cover your patrol tonight."

He grunted his assent.

"Text me if you need me."

I hardly got more than ten feet from the front porch when Layla and Vivian came out of the woodwork. No doubt they'd been waiting since word spread of Sam's arrival.

"Is it true?" Viv demanded. "Is she actually trying to rejoin the pack?"

Layla's eyes flared to a fiery glow.

I supposed Jared had already told them what was up before he took off wherever.

"It is," I told them. "I'm leaving it up to Clay to decide."

Vivian looked like she was going to argue. Hell, Layla seemed like she might get in on that action, but seeming to sense my tension, they both thought better of it. Sharing a look and then falling silent.

"Did you see where Jare went?"

"To get someone to take his shift at the quarry so he can stay at camp with you. He said he'd be right back," Layla supplied, wringing her slender hands. "Are you sure this is a good idea?"

"What else am I supposed to do? If I force her out..."

Maybe it was foolish, but I didn't want Clay to hold it against me for the rest of our immortal lives.

"I get it," Viv said, gripping me around my shoulders for a sideways hug before sighing. "But that doesn't mean *we* forgive the bitch. I wouldn't trust her as far as I can throw her."

"Bet you could toss her pretty far, though." I smirked, and Viv released me to punch me in the arm.

Layla shook her head at us, lifting her gaze to the heavens.

I shoved at Viv, feeling the weight on my shoulders shift free, if only for a second. "Thought I sent you back on patrol, huh? What are you still doing here?"

"Leave and miss the most dramatic thing to happen in years? I don't think so. I sent the next patrol out early. Said you needed me for something."

"And the second and third ring patrols?"

"All still doing their rounds. Third ring patrol were the ones who brought her in to us."

Good to know our patrols were doing what they were meant for. I'd been wondering if Sam had somehow snuck through the first two rings to get Viv's first ring patrol route. It would have been a massive failure if she had.

"Who was running it?"

I meant to give them a few words of commendation for their good work when they got back, but before Viv could reply, my cell buzzed in my pocket.

My face screwed up at the name on the screen. I assumed it'd be Jared letting me know he had to go to the quarry after all.

"It's Jacob."

"They were on patrol," Viv blurted. "Answer it, what if—"

I had the phone to my ear before she could finish.

"Jake, what is it? Did someone else break the lines?"

Immediately, my wolf was on the defensive. If Sam's coming were some sort of distraction so that others could slip through our ranks, she would be fucking sorry. My cell phone crunched in my fingers, and I cursed inwardly at having broken yet another damned screen.

"No, it's not that. The ring is solid, no one else has been around. It's…"

I could barely hear him, a strange sound in the background drowned him out.

"Spit it out."

"It's Sal's. We smelled smoke and deviated a little from the route to check it out. Sal's was burning."

That's what it was, in the background of the call.

Fire.

Sirens sounded in the distance, and I felt both relieved and devastated all at once.

Sal's Butcher Shop was where we'd been going for our meat for years after the last butcher in town closed up shop and retired. We went weekly for meat runs. We were due to go tomorrow.

Layla and Viv were already whispering, having heard Jacob from where they stood.

"You're there now?"

"Yeah."

"Then who the hell is on third ring patrol?"

"Danny is on it alone," he rushed to say. "I'm heading back in a minute. I just wanted to let you know about Sal's."

Bits of glass cut into my fingers as I released my grip on the phone, finding that I could smell the ghost of smoke on the breeze even from here. "Was Sal hurt?"

"I don't think so."

"Okay. Get back to your route. I'll see if we can send a few of ours to help."

I tapped my shattered screen to end the call.

"Kind of fucking suspicious isn't it?" Viv hedged, her hands in claws at her sides. "Not an hour after she shows her face and Sal's is up in smoke?"

Bad timing?

My gut said no, but what else could it be? The witch from town? Gregory? My pulse skittered at the thought. *No.* He left. What reason could he have for attacking a local?

None.

Get your head on straight, Allie.

"You busy?" I asked them.

Viv glanced longingly back toward her cabin—the one she shared with Destiny. No doubt Des was still asleep inside after her long shift at Grove's End. Like Jared, she tended to sleep like the dead. And the fact that their cabin was near the fringes of camp would make it easier for her not to hear the commotion of the morning.

"Stay if you want," I offered. "I can grab Seth."

Layla winced, and I knew at once that her beau was very likely a little worse for wear this a.m. He tended to overdo it and not even shifters were impervious to hangovers, though they tended not to last as long at least.

"No. I'll come. Just let me leave a note for her." I nodded. "Hurry."

Viv ran off just as Jared reappeared, jogging over with concern in the line of his brows. "What is it?"

"Sal's," I told him, bracing for the same suspicion Viv had. "It's burning."

His nose wrinkled, perhaps able to smell it just as I could. His amber eyes slid to the cabin where Clay was inside with his sister and grand-mother. The fleck of jade green in his left eye catching the light.

He didn't say it, but through the mate bond I could feel his dread.

"Is Sal—"

"He's fine. But we're going to see if there's anything we can do to help."

Sal had taken care of us for years. If not for him, we'd have had to travel all the way to Portland for our meat every week. I supposed now that was exactly what we'd have to do. *Fuck.*

We could lend him some lumber and equipment though. We could spare a few bodies to help him rebuild. It was the least we could do after the countless rush orders of entire sides of beef.

"Wait, you're leaving?" Jared demanded, his eyes narrowing to slits. He jabbed two fingers at our cabin. "With *her* here?"

"You should stay, keep an eye on things for me." I gave him the option, knowing before the words even left my lips that he would refuse. "But if you'd rather come, then I think Clay has it handled, don't you?"

His lips pressed into a hard line. "I'm with you."

Thought so.

I thumbed a quick text to Clay before discarding my phone on a vacant wooden stool.

Allie: Something came up. Back in a few hours.
I'm with Jared. Don't worry.

I knew he would worry, but chances were he wouldn't even read the text for a while. He was clearly distracted enough to not sense my distress when Jacob told me about Sal's. He would be distracted enough not to notice anything was amiss until I got back.

Or at least I hoped so. He had enough to worry about.

"We'll pick up Viv on the way out," I said, shucking off my clothes and letting my soul awaken to my wolf. "Let's move."

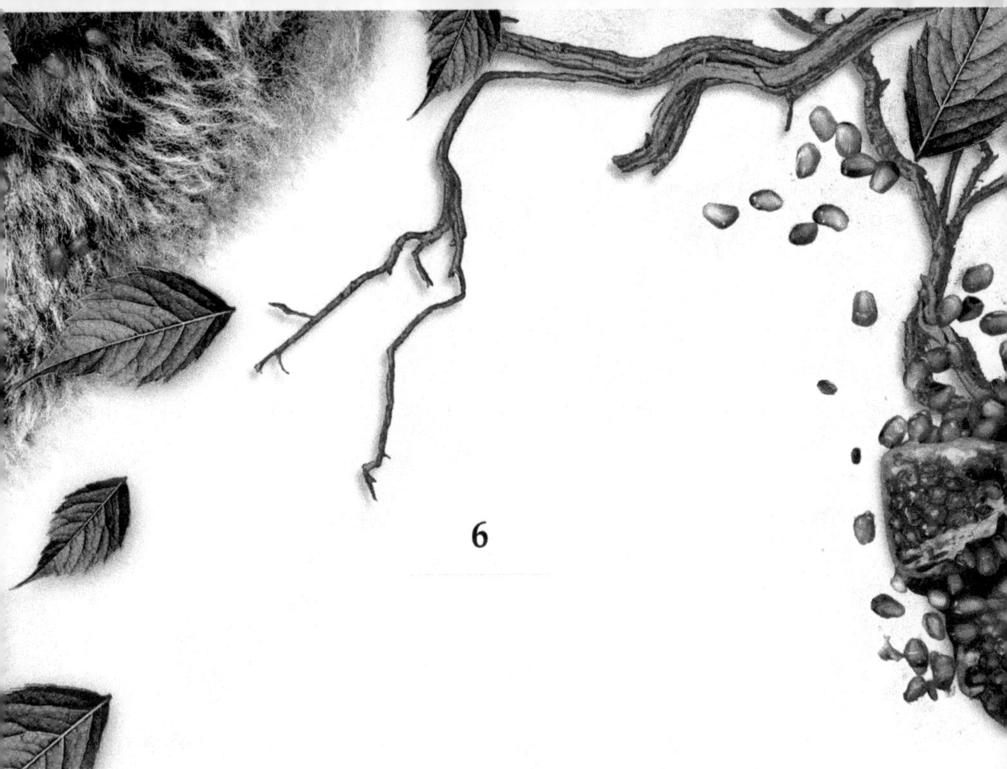

6

There was nothing to save by the time we got there. We'd been quick, passing through the first two rings within ten minutes. Sal's sat just between the second and third rings, on the outskirts of the next town.

Firefighters still worked to smother what remained of the embers with their hoses, but it was too late. I'd hoped...hell, I don't know what I'd hoped. That we could save some of it for him, maybe.

We weren't fireproof, but we healed quickly and could take a lot more than mortal fire rescue in terms of handling the heat.

The structure that was once a squat log house with a bright red roof was now a mess of ash and half burnt wood. Bits of the red roof could be mistaken for more embers where they hid among the black soot choking the earth.

I coughed, inhaling a little too much smoke and batted some rogue ash away before it could get in my eyes.

"It's gone," Jared breathed, staring agape at the wreckage. He was the one who usually picked up the orders from Sal, using his silver Jeep to haul the meats as close to camp as he could before the pack would help unload, taking everything the rest of the way in coolers since no roads led inside the heart of our territory.

We could see Sal standing with two officers across the road. It was odd to see him in something other than a bloodstained apron. His burly frame strained at the plaid button-up he wore as he paced back and forth, pinching the bridge of his nose before running a thick hand down the beard on his chin.

"We'll help him rebuild," I promised. "We can afford it, and I'm assuming his insurance will cover most of the cost of the repairs, anyway. We'll have it back up in no time."

Jared nodded solemnly.

"Come on, we should go talk to him. See what happened."

"We'll go see if there's anything we can do," Viv offered, dragging Layla with her as they went to inspect the damage a little closer.

With a single look, we communicated what else she should be looking for before she rushed away. Any evidence that this may not have been an accident.

Coincidences happened, but having Sam show up and then this happen an hour later seemed...odd.

Paranoid didn't even begin to cover what I was when it came to the safety of my pack. I didn't like loose variables. Already I could feel the beginning of my anxiety flaring up. I'd tampered it over the years and hadn't had an attack in ages, but now it tended to manifest itself in other ways.

Fists squeezed so tight that I bruised them without knowing. Insomnia. Knees bouncing beneath tables.

It was better, but not gone. I didn't think it ever would be.

"Sal," Jared called, and the big guy spun, his unfocused eyes catching sight of us. I was sure we looked strange in our hastily thrown on clothes. Jared bare- chested and both of us barefoot, but shoes just weren't practical for shifters.

"Jared. Allie. What are you doing here?"

"We heard," I said with an apology in my voice. "I'm so sorry, Sal."

"What happened?" Jared pried, stepping past the curious police officers chatting to themselves while they jotted something down in their notepads.

Like most mortals did, they stepped casually away as we approached Sal, their senses telling them they had been demoted on the predator scale.

Sal dropped his head, throwing a hand up in frustration at the carcass of his baby. "Fucking gas leak," he growled. "Of all the bullshit luck."

"Will insurance cover the damages?"

"They damn well better. Just had an inspection not two months ago and everything got the green light."

He groaned, lifting his head to stare up at the sky.

Poor guy.

"Your order was inside. I'm sorry, but—"

"Don't worry about that," Jared interrupted. "We can get what we need elsewhere for now. We came to help."

Sal glanced up, looking between us, a bit confused.

I jabbed a thumb back in the direction we came from. "We have some handy friends and some equipment from the quarry that we can spare. You just tell us what you need. We'll make sure you get it."

His eyes went glassy, and it took him a full fifteen seconds to get control of his emotions, clearing his throat twice before he spoke again. "Right. I'd, *uh...* I'd appreciate that, but I don't expect any handouts. I'll pay for the labor. Most of what I got is your money anyhow."

I chuckled a bit at that. We were *definitely* his best customers.

"We take care of our own," I told him with a wink, trying to bring a smile to his grim features. "The sooner you're back up and running the sooner we're back to eating the best steaks in the west."

It seemed it really was an accident after all. Even though Layla and Viv had already scoped out the smoldering wreckage of Sal's shop, Jared and I did a sweep as well before we left. There was nothing to indicate foul play. Nothing to indicate it could have been a witch *or* a shifter.

Of course, there was a good chance that whatever evidence might have been there burned away. And if it were somehow Sam's doing—for whatever mad reason—that her scent would be erased by the thick black smoke clogging the air.

She hadn't come from this direction though, and if Sal and the officers were right about the timing of when the fire started, then Sam was already at pack camp with us. She couldn't have had anything to do with it.

And if that witch fucker knew what was good for him, he was already long gone.

Guilt ate at me all the way back to camp. For immediately thinking the worst of Sam, and for being so paranoid that I failed to see what was right in front of me. Sam was a lone wolf. A lone malnourished wolf in need of help who lost her mate. Who made a mistake four years ago that maybe I didn't need to make her pay for now.

When we arrived back at camp, Sam was seated on the front steps of the cabin with Clay. He lurched to his feet as we neared, and I knew before he even opened his mouth what his decision was.

I could feel it. His resignation. His nervous energy. His desire to protect his blood even after what she did. He wouldn't forgive her so easily. And it would take a long time for him to trust her, but I could see it in his eyes; he was willing to try.

"I just heard about Sal's," he said. "What happened?"

"Gas leak," Jared explained, his jaw twitching as his amber gaze slid to Sam. Clearly, some of us didn't feel as guilty as others for thinking she was to blame.

Clay scrubbed a hand over his jaw. "Shit. How bad?"

"Bad. It's pretty much gone. I offered to lend a hand to help rebuild if Sal wants it. Maybe you could get a crew together this weekend. There has to be at least four or five bodies we can spare."

His lips tightened, but he nodded.

I gestured to Sam still sitting mutely on the stairs behind him. "I take it she's staying?"

I hadn't meant for it to come out the way it did, like an accusation, making Clay's expression sour.

"Clay, I didn't mean—"

"It's fine, Allie," he said in a low rumble. "I don't like it either."

Sam's shoulders slumped as she looked up at her brother like he was breaking her heart. It kind of hurt to see.

"But she has nowhere else to go. She's been through some shit, and she's sworn to me that she doesn't hold Ryland against you anymore."

At that, Sam tensed, and I wondered if just the sound of his name triggered her still. She tucked her bony fingers under her thighs, sitting on them as though she didn't trust what they might do.

There I went again, being all fucking paranoid. It didn't help that Jared's distrust was rolling off of him in waves from right next to me.

I sighed.

"Then we'll do it tonight. With the shit going on with Sal and the welcoming ceremony for Archer and Callum just last night—"

"I don't want a ceremony," Sam finally piped up. "I just want a shower and a bed."

"We can do that. You can use our shower now if you want. We'll see where there's a free bunk to put you. We're a little tight for space, so unmated pairs share cabins."

She stiffened at the reminder, and feeling momentarily empathetic, I added a hasty apology. "Sorry."

I turned to Clay. "That work?"

He grunted his assent, and it was settled. Samantha Armstrong was back for good. I hoped he made the right choice.

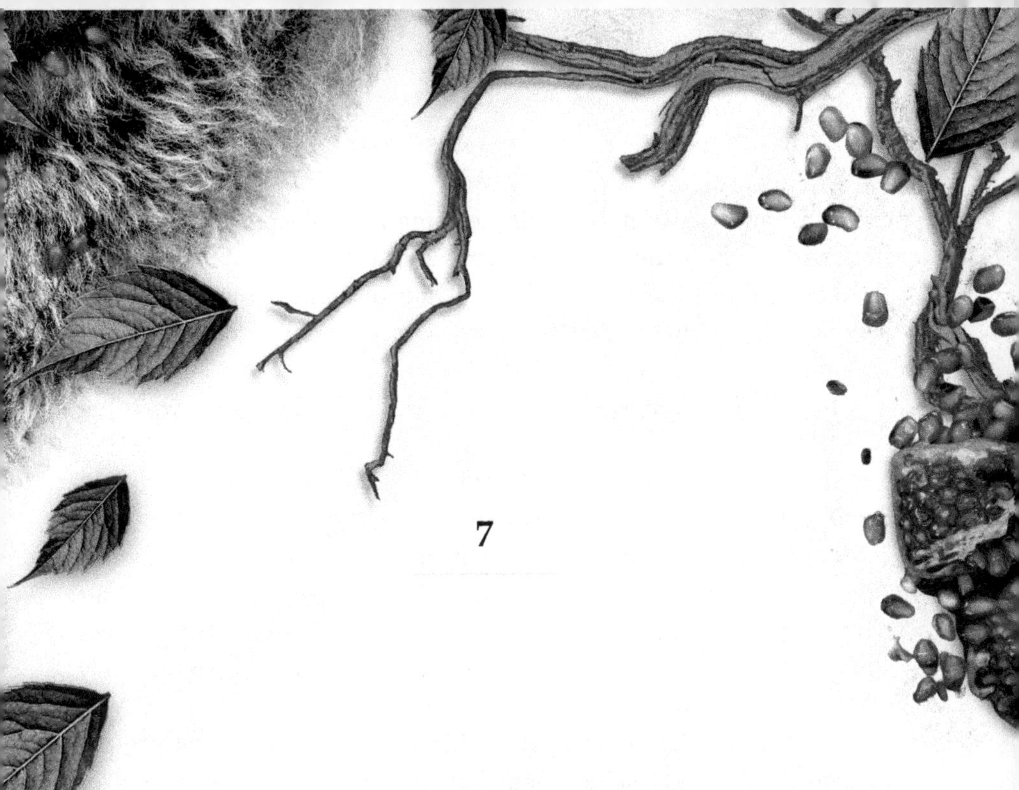

7

I t took a week to secure a new supplier for our meat. We had some frozen in the deep freeze in the main cabin, thankfully, but even that had dwindled to almost nothing the past six days. Seth was on his way to Portland to pick up our order from a butcher there and soon we'd have more meat than we knew what to do with.

Aside from some grouchy shifters forced to eat smaller portions though, things had been almost—*dare I say it*—back to normal. Camp had returned to the quiet bustle of tasks to complete and day to day life.

There had been no more visits from the mysterious Gregory. Nothing else burned to the ground. And Sam kept mostly to herself, preferring to stay in her shared cabin most of the day, only leaving for runs or to visit Clay at Grove's End some afternoons.

She'd asked him to give her a task or some sort of assignment like the others, but as much as I tried, I still didn't trust her enough for that. Much like we decided it wasn't safe to trust her with the secrets of our pack just yet either. No one really spoke to her, so I doubted she'd find out unless we told her directly.

And she definitely wasn't going to be on any of the patrols, but maybe there was something I could have her do around camp to keep her busy.

I'd even managed to finally finish the books I bought last week. They came in handy since my anxiety kept me from sleeping most nights since the visit from the witch and Sam's arrival.

Having things back to some semblance of normalcy was great and all, but I still couldn't shake the feeling eating at me that something was wrong. No matter how hard I tried.

"Allie Grace," Grams said, lifting her gaze from the warm dirt at her knees. "Come to help?"

I smirked to myself but tied my hair in a loose bun and crouched down, gaze sweeping over the garden.

Hazel had started it when she joined the pack after I took over as alpha. A vegetable garden that she coaxed to life each spring and fed our ranks well into fall. It'd come in handy over the last week, and she was already replanting new seeds to make up for what was prematurely taken.

"Actually, I came to ask if you could use another hand to help in the garden. Sam's been asking about having a job. Guess she's tired of sitting around already."

I took the trowel Hazel offered and copied her movements, digging up shallow trenches for her to drop two seeds in each before gently recovering them. Peas, I thought. This early in the season there were only so many things that would grow and ripen quickly. Most of the vegetables had barely just begun sprouting. We had a store of potatoes and onions from last season in the cellar beneath the Moon Room though. Between that, the early greens, and a couple trips to the supermarket, we've made due.

"*Hmph*," Grams snorted, packing some dirt over a hole. "You could ask her, I suppose, but I doubt she'll want to be spending her time with me."

If she said something rude to Grams... My wolf growled within.

"Why? What do you mean?"

Grams sighed, dragging her long silvery hair away from her face with muddy fingers. "She's been through something, that's for sure. I think she's afraid I'll see the awful truth of whatever it is if she gets too close to me."

"She's afraid you'll read her, you mean?"

Grams nodded. "That girl and I have never seen eye to eye really. I was here while she was away up north with her mother most of her life.

We aren't close like I am with Clay. Maybe it's that she's embarrassed about it, or maybe it's that she thinks it's none of my business. I sensed a bit of both from her that first day."

Well that was settled then. If Sam wanted a job, then she would be working with Grams in the garden. Grams clearly wanted to be closer with her granddaughter, and maybe sharing some of her pain would help Sam break out of the shell she'd been living in since she got here.

The pack was already whispering about her, but her shutting herself off to everyone wasn't helping them find anything even remotely close to trust toward her. Especially not now that they all knew she once tried to off me.

"She probably just needs more time."

"Time, I've got now, thanks to you." Grams patted my hand in the dirt with a crooked grin, warming me.

Living without a pack for so long had aged her. She'd been at peace with her choice to live out the rest of her days as a lone wolf until the years caught up with her and death finally found her. But when I took over the Forest Grove pack, she'd asked to join.

"Speaking of time. About how long until you'll give me grandbabies? This pack hasn't seen young wolves in far too long, and I'm not getting any younger."

A furious flush crawled up into my cheeks. She never missed an opportunity to remind me that she fully expected about a thousand grandkids, and I'd better get cooking them.

"Well, you've stopped aging now, so I suppose you can wait as long as it takes."

So long as she remained in the pack, the natural pack magic would keep her at the ripe old age of...however old she was. I knew it was much older than she looked. In truth, she wasn't Clay's grandmother, but his great *great* grandmother. Pack magic had seen her through at least a century by now.

She grumbled something unintelligible to herself, and I leaned back on my elbow for a moment, basking in the warmth of the sun as it found its highest peak in the sky. I closed my eyes, inhaling the scents of the forest and damp earth soaking into the ass of my shorts.

My phone pinged in my pocket, ruining the peace of the moment. Should've left the damned thing inside.

A text from Seth flared to the screen, and I cut myself on the busted glass while opening it to read what it said. I *really* needed to get Charity to fix it for me, but as she was heading up the crew helping Sal clear out the wreckage of his shop, it'd have to wait.

"That my grandson? Tell him to bring me a bottle of that whiskey I like, would you?"

"No, it's..."

I trailed off, reading the text and groaning.

Seth: The order's not ready. Going to be another week. Their supplier had some kind of hold up. What should I do?

"Fuck."

"*Language.*"

"Sorry, Grams. Looks like we're going to need to raid your garden some more. The order's been held up."

Allie: Take whatever they have available in the storefront for now. I'll head into town and raid the grocery again. That should be good for another week.

Seth: Yeah. Until the townies go hungry because all their meat's been stolen by wolves.

I snorted.

Allie: Just hurry back. Seth: Will do.

"How long?" Hazel demanded. "I haven't got much that's ready. Some more lettuce and radishes. Potatoes from the cellar."

"Then we'll have salad and stew for dinner. Seth's grabbing whatever the butcher has on hand, and I'll go into town to pick up some things."

"Send a hunting party out," Grams all but ordered. "Hungry wolves are dangerous wolves."

I knew she was right, but I'd hoped not to resort to that. The wildlife in our territory was already sparse, driven away from the scent of predators in their midst. I'd have to send them further afield to be able to find any game large enough to do more than feed a single shifter.

"I will."

I rose, dusting off my hands on my jeans.

"Don't forget my whiskey," she reminded me just as I sensed Clay returning to camp from an early morning check on Grove's End.

"I just brought you a bottle last week, Grams," Clay chastised her. "Don't tell me you've finished it already?"

"Would you deprive an old lady of her vices, grandson? Have I not earned the right to—?"

"Yeah, yeah," Clay interrupted, giving his head a shake. "Fine, I'll bring your whiskey. Stubborn old bat."

"I don't have to wonder where you get it from," I joked, earning myself glares from the both of them.

That was my cue.

I tucked my cell into my pocket and jerked my head toward town. "I have to pick up some things. Our meat order's been delayed. Need anything?"

His brows lowered. "Why's it delayed?" I shrugged. "Not sure. Seth didn't say."

Clay licked his lips in a way that made something low in my belly tighten as he considered something. He'd been either sleeping with me —on the nights Jared stayed at the quarry—or outside the cabin barely a stone's throw from the window. He'd even given up some of his night patrol shifts this week, further cementing my suspicion that all this time he'd been wary of Sam returning.

It was odd to see him up so early in the day when he usually slept well past noon. I wasn't sure how much sleep he was actually getting at night though; his eyes had dark circles to rival my own.

"I'll come with you," he decided. "I've been meaning to check on the old cabin and my shop. We can make a pit stop on the way back. Maybe take the bikes for a rip if there's time."

I grinned at that. We hadn't taken out the dirt bikes in a while. Not since last fall, actually. Though Clay regularly checked on things at the old cabin where I'd lived with him and Clay before shit hit the fan here — tuning up the bikes and making sure the pipes didn't freeze in the winter.

Jared slept out there sometimes, still, needing the solitude every now and then.

It was where I lost my virginity after I'd finally had enough of their testosterone and forced them to rock paper scissors for it. Looking back now, it was ridiculous how we handled it, but we were just a bunch of horny teenagers, and I was tired of waiting.

Jared won, and Clay didn't speak to either of us for weeks after. Until one *very* heated argument led to us tearing each other's clothes off and...

I swallowed hard. Not the time. Definitely not the place. I eyed Hazel warily from the corner of my eye and found her smirking at me. Likely scenting my pheromones and daydreaming about all the grandbabies. "Such a good idea," she said, jostling to her feet to pat Clay on his thick shoulder, leaving a smear of dirt over the tanned muscle. "You two go on then. Take your time."

Clay raised a brow at me, and I tucked some loose strands of hair back from my face, hustling past him. "I'll grab a couple duffels to carry the groceries back. We'll buy some bags of ice to keep it cool if you want to take the bikes out, but—"

"We won't be long, Allie," he interrupted, fixing me with a knowing stare. I never left pack camp for more than a few hours at a time. Being away for too long made me restless. Made my wolf itch to check on the others. To make sure they were safe.

"Such a worrier, that one," I heard Hazel murmur to Clay as I swerved through the cabins and back into the heart of camp. "She'll worry herself to death one day. Mark my words."

I lifted another stack of overpriced beef into the cart, grimacing as some of the juices leaked onto my palm. The quality was shit and it was twice the price of buying in bulk from Sal's, but it would have to do for now.

"Want to go grab the whiskey for Hazel?" I asked Clay, starting to pick through the whole chickens for the largest of them. We had a lot of mouths to feed, but I couldn't take all of them. There were only two small grocery stores in this town, and if we depleted them of all their meat, people would ask questions.

As it was, the cart just looked like we were going to have a real big barbeque. Which was exactly what I would say if asked. I even added a couple bags of corn on the cob for good measure.

Clay stalked off down the aisle in search of the whiskey Grams liked, and I smirked at his backside, feeling a lick of heat roll across the back of my neck.

I so rarely saw him fully clothed anymore. In shoes and a shirt. The way the black tee clung to his muscled frame made me bite my lip. He looked so out of place among the packaged meats and pyramids of packaged foods. Like a giant in a dollhouse.

Or a bull in a china shop.

It was at that instant he accidentally knocked the edge of a display, unable to squeeze between it and the endcap on the next aisle. Several boxes scattered to the floor and an employee rushed to scoop them up, apologizing to Clay as if *they* were the one who'd done something wrong.

He had that effect on people.

"One of your two mates, I presume?"

His strange scent tickled my nose before I locked eyes on him, my hackles raising and an anvil dropping in my gut.

"Thought I told you to stay out of my territory, witch?"

Gregory cocked his head at me from where he leaned near the door leading to the stock area of the grocery. "You did. But my superior doesn't like taking no for an answer, so here I am, back in the wolves' den for round two."

Clay came crashing back through the store with a bottle of whiskey in his fist, eyes burning a fiery blue as they locked on to Gregory. Customers scattered like roaches from his warpath, and I had to hand it to Gregory, he hardly flinched as Clay reached my side, his upper lip curling in distaste at the sight of the witch.

"Clayton, I presume?" Gregory inquired with a raised brow as he sized up my mate.

"Who the fuck is this clown?" Clay demanded, glancing between us. My unease likely wreaking havoc on his own nerves as well.

"An emissary of sorts," Gregory responded before I could. "Alison here was just about to turn me down for the second time."

"What is he talking about?"

"I—"

"She didn't tell you?" Gregory asked, seeming to be thrilled at this new discovery. His eyes gleamed as he launched into an explanation even though my wolf was looking at him like she might rip his throat out right here in the meat section of the Forest Grove grocery.

"I work for a delegate of the Arcane Council, and they would like an audience with your darling mate. Just a few questions, you know. Perhaps they'll want to take some blood to run tests. Perform an origin spell on her. That sort of thing. Standard stuff, really. But your mate here didn't even allow me to explain the last time. Told me to leave and not to return."

Clay slammed the bottle of whiskey into the cart and stepped toward Gregory, his massive frame hulking over the shorter witch. "And you should've listened," he growled, his eyes flaring to a vivid blue glow.

A little girl down the way gasped, tugging on her mother's sundress to get her attention. Her little finger pointing at Clay. *Shit.*

"Clay," I hissed between gritted teeth. "Not here."

He trembled with the urges of his wolf, and my own wolf responded, battering against the cage of my human form.

"Get out of here," I spat at Gregory. "Tell your superior that I have no interest in meeting with them and if you come back here again, you won't ever leave. Got it?"

Clay's gaze never left the witch as he tipped his head in a sarcastic farewell, a smirk playing over his lips before he turned and lazily wandered back toward the exit of the store. Like he didn't have a worry in the world. Like the largest shifter in my pack wasn't staring after him like he might be lunch.

Clay's balled fists ached for a release as he whirled on me, his face a red mask of fury. A vein jumped in his temple, and I took a cursory glance around, checking to make sure no one could hear.

"I was going to tell you—"

"*When?* When were you going to tell me, Allie?

When did this happen?"

I swallowed hard, cold dread frosting over my chest. "About a week ago. He confronted me at Jackie's shop."

Clay's eyes widened. "He knew you'd be there, then?" He edged the words in a question, but I could tell he was already formulating the answer himself. His rigid hand dove through his dark hair as he fumed, his eyes still flickering with the light of his wolf.

"*Fuck, Allie,*" he roared, and from the corner of my eye, I could see a tall, slender man with a manager badge on his button-down approaching cautiously, trying to look more in control than I could sense he felt.

"Everything all right here, miss?" he asked me, his kind eyes slipping to Clay before returning back to me. "Is this man bothering you?"

"Mind your fucking business," Clay growled, and when the store manager's eyes locked on his again, getting a glimpse of what lay dormant within, the man buckled in the knees, stumbling back three steps with horror in his eyes.

Fuck this.

Abandoning the cart, I took off, rushing out of the store with my heart in my throat and my wolf snapping at my heels.

"Miss!" the manager called.

"*Allie,*" Clay hissed, chasing me out like I knew he would.

I didn't stop when I hit the pavement outside, though. I broke into a run, making for the trees at the edge of the lot, flip flops flying off before I could even make it past the tree line.

"Allie, *stop.*"

My wolf took hold, crashing into my mind and taking over my body in the span of a single breath. Flaying my clothes to ribbons.

*Allie, stop or so help me…*Clay's seething voice slunk into my thoughts as he shifted, too.

Or what? I taunted, unable to help myself before taking off at a sprint that I knew he wouldn't be able to outrun. I hardly knew where I was headed until the old cabin came into view through the trees and my wolf began to slow.

A whine sounded in my throat, making my heaving chest tighten as I bounded up the steps and onto the front porch. Clay burst through the brush not more than a few heartbeats later, his dark wolf lumbering over to me with quick, sure steps.

Allie, what—

I let my wolf fall away and shifted back before he could finish the thought in my mind, furless skin bristling in the chill breeze sweeping over the clearing.

Clay shifted back, too, and I pushed my way into the cabin, going straight for the kitchen to get a glass of water.

"How could you not tell me there was a *witch* tailing you?" he demanded in his I'm-trying-to-be- calm voice. It only ever managed to make him sound menacing instead of angry, but I appreciated the effort.

I guzzled the water, taking a long breath before replying, setting my glass into the sink. "Because it wasn't a big deal," I replied. "I told him to get fucked. Not to come back."

"Oh yeah?" he asked, his shoulders going rigid. "How'd that work out for you?"

"Don't be a dick. I didn't want to worry anyone, and I thought I'd dealt with it myself."

"Clearly, you didn't. And if you think that fuckwad won't be back, you're an idiot."

I cleared the gap between us in two strides, our combined frustration and fury getting the better of me. Where Jared was a balm to my nerves, Clay was the match that often set me ablaze. Jared and I flowed. Clay and I burned.

He staggered back as I shoved at his sweat-slicked chest. "You're the idiot who almost got us caught in the fucking grocery store!"

His cheekbones and nostrils flared as he clenched his jaw.

"You might as well have held up a big ass sign that said *hey, look at me, look how not human I am.*"

"Don't try to spin this on me. If you'd just told us about the witch then—"

I threw my hands up, growling. "Fine. I'm sorry, okay? I should've told you. Happy now?"

Clay jerked forward, wrapping a hand firmly around my biceps to pull me close. "*No,*" he hissed, breath fanning over my cheek. "My *mate* kept something from me. Something that could put her and all of us in danger. No, Allie, I'm not fucking *happy.*"

His eyes darkened, and my breath caught at the pain showing through those cut-glass eyes. It made a ball form in my throat. I didn't want to feel guilty, though. I shouldn't have to. I was just doing what I thought was right.

But was it...?

I shook my head and pulled my arm from his, stomping out of the kitchen to go upstairs. I still kept some of my old clothes here, and I was going to need to get changed and go back to the grocery store and get all the meat we left behind. And apologize to the goddamned store manager for my brute of a mate.

"Where the hell are you going?" Clay bellowed, his rough voice practically reverberating the floorboards as I made my way to my old bedroom.

Normally silent as a cat, he didn't bother trying to conceal his steps as he stormed after me, the stairs creaking and groaning beneath his weight.

I entered my room and whirled to slam the door, but he was there, catching it before it could click into the doorframe. Venom in his stare.

"I wasn't finished," he said through gritted teeth. "Well, I was."

I turned on my heel and went to tug open the drawers of my old dresser, searching for something that would still fit my new filled out frame.

Clay batted the drawer closed, nearly catching my fingers.

"What the fuck, Clay?"

"Look at me, Allie."

Heat washed up my back, pooling in my cheeks as I spun to face him again, resisting the very persistent urge to shift again.

I softened when I saw the haunted look on his face. How his breaths evened out. For a second, I saw the fear hidden beneath all the anger he wore like armor.

"I..." he started and trailed off, a vein throbbing in his temple. "I *need* you to be safe, Allie."

My throat burned at his whispered admission.

"I can't protect you if I don't know what you need protecting from."

He scrubbed a hand over the dark stubble on his jaw. "All this shit with Sam and now...I can't fucking handle both, babe."

A crack in his facade revealed what I'd suspected since Sam arrived back at camp. He still didn't trust her. Might not ever. It was why he was staying at camp through the nights even when Jared was the one sharing our bed. Why he never moved from the spot just below the bedroom window.

Why he couldn't handle another separate threat from the one he was already trying so hard to make sure I was safe from.

The fact that it was his own flesh and blood he was worried about just added another hundred pounds of pressure and stress to his already weighted down shoulders.

"I..."

I felt like an asshole.

"Don't say sorry," he offered. "Just tell me you won't lie to me again."

I nodded, eyes watering as the guilt found a toehold in my core and began to scrape my throat raw.

My arms were iron rods at my sides when Clay bridged the gap between us and yanked me to his chest, pressing our naked bodies against one another. My head bent into the crook beneath his chin. My curves fitting perfectly into the mold of his body.

I felt the exact moment his emotions began to twist. Felt it in the way his middle finger drew a soft line down the length of my spine to my tailbone, making me shiver against him.

We hadn't been intimate since Sam came to camp. Even a little while before that, actually. I felt his need pulse through me. An all-consuming thing, like he was starving. Like he might die if he didn't take a bite.

His fingers trailed back up my spine and curled into my hair at the back of my skull. He fisted them there, tugging my head back, tipping my chin up. I arched, pressing my breasts against him as my nipples pebbled. "No more lies," he demanded, staring hard into my soul.

A fractured breath stuttered from my lips.

"No more lies," I agreed, and his lips stole the words from my mouth, consuming them and every last bit of sanity I possessed.

I moaned against his mouth, and he used the opportunity to slip inside, tasting me, robbing me of breath. Claiming me.

His hands dropped to my hips, fingertips digging into flesh and bone as he lifted me with ease, prodding me to wrap my legs around his waist.

Clay's hardened length brushed against my folds, and I reared back from his kiss, a small cry falling from my lips that turned into a gasp as his mouth closed over my nipple.

Heat rushed through me as he circled his tongue, biting down enough to make me shudder.

His soft growl vibrated through my ribcage as he moved to my other breast, hands gripping my ass to hold me tight against him.

With one arm, Clay swept the objects from the top of the dresser, sending clothing and a lamp clattering to the floor before he sat me atop it. His rock-hard cock nudged at my belly, and when his mouth moved to my neck, biting down on the sensitive skin there, I saw stars.

"I want you," I breathed, feeling like if I didn't have him right here and now I would lose my goddamned mind.

Clay angled himself, bending at his knees so the tip of his large cock flicked against my clit, making me jump. Making my legs cling around his hips tighter, pulling him to me.

He lifted his head to stare into my eyes. His lips parted as he curled his hands around my thighs and spread me open for him. His gaze never faltered as he pushed into me, giving me a moment to adjust to his size as he thrust the full way in, expelling the air from my lungs.

I clenched around his length inside me, fingernails biting down into his thick biceps, searching for something—anything—to hold on to.

Clay eased out, and I felt him tremble under my touch, his ecstasy further fueling my own. When he didn't immediately push back inside, I whimpered, trying to push him deeper. Needing him to fuck me as badly as I sensed his urge was to do just that.

"Clay," I gasped. "*Please.*" He came unhinged.

Whatever thing had been holding him back broke like a dam, and he surged back to himself. To me.

His upper lip curled as he tipped his back and drove his cock into me, shaking the dresser beneath us with the force of his thrust.

I moved against him, urging him faster. Harder.

I moaned loudly against his mouth as he kissed me again. His breaths came heavier as he wrapped his mammoth hand around the back of my neck, securing me in place.

He knew just the right way to hold me. Like I was caught in a vise from which there would be no hope of escaping even if I wanted to. As he leaned his body back to get a better angle, he released his hold on my thigh to circle against my clit as he pounded into me.

The dual sensation had me coming apart at the seams almost instantly, and I bucked and writhed, but Clay's grip on the back of my neck, with his arm braced against my back, kept me in place. Making me bend to the will of my body as he brought me ever closer to an orgasm that might just rip me apart.

"Come on, baby," he said in a husky whisper, bending to join his forehead with mine as he worked relentlessly on my pussy, his own orgasm reaching a peak.

Unable to contain myself as my wolf's natural urge to fight back against the coming storm took over, I unwrapped my legs from his waist and pushed off from the dresser, ejecting him from me for only an instant before he had me again.

He spun me, bending me over the dresser and sheathing himself inside of me once more. His hand splayed over my back, pressing me against the warm wood as he fucked me from behind. He used his weight to hold me in place as he reached around and continued his merciless rubbing of my slit.

I cried out as my climax surged to its peak, gripping the edge of the dresser for dear life as Clay annihilated me in every sense of the word. I came hard, wood splintering where my fingers tore giant chunks from the dresser.

My body coiled, tightening like the flex of a bowstring right before being shot. Sending me sailing in oblivion as I shuddered against him, crying out as my release ripped through me like a fucking hurricane. Clay didn't stop, his hands going to my hips to bear down hard as he continued to fuck me, making my one orgasm fall into another as he howled his release and we both sagged against the mangled dresser.

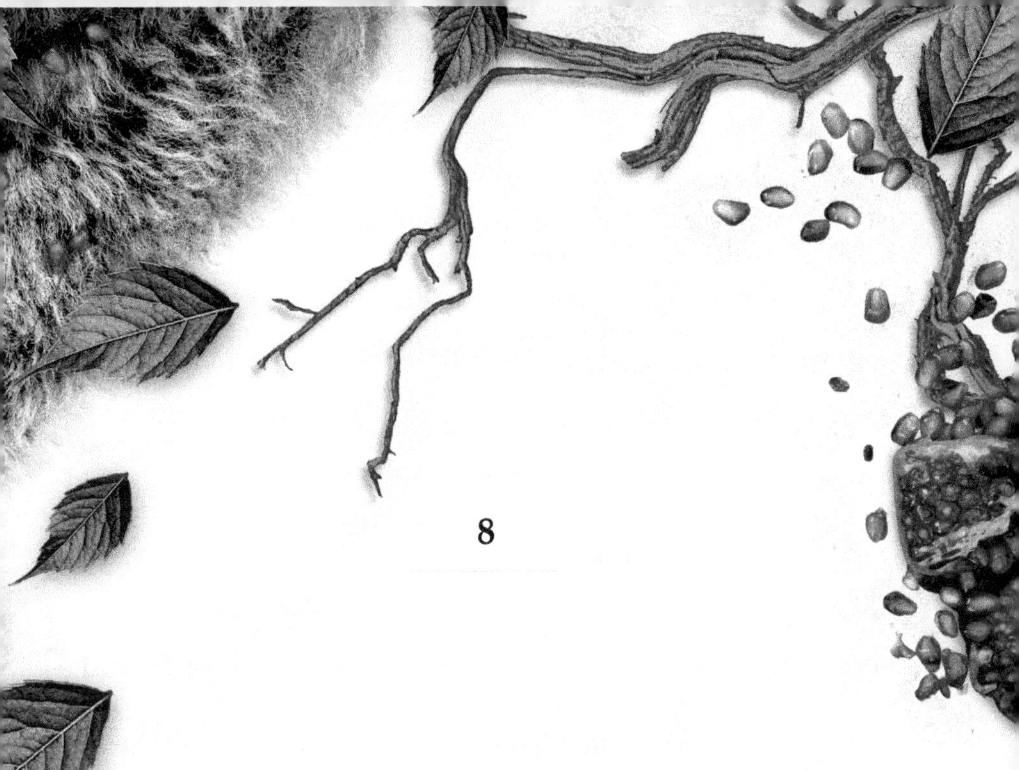

8

I pushed the stew around in my bowl. It was mostly potatoes and carrots, but if I lookedhard enough I might find at least one more piece of beef.

Clay smirked, watching me slyly from the corner of his eye as he drained the remnants of his own bowl. It'd been a few days since the most recent incident with the witch and our stores of meat were getting low again. The hunting party managed to bag a deer and a few hares, but when you were talking about feeding a pack of nearly fifty wolves. That didn't last very long.

I sighed, resigning myself to finishing the potatoes and carrots.

"When are Seth and Layla getting back?" Clay asked, sliding the back of his hand over his hips as he set his bowl down on the picnic table.

The chatter of conversation from the other tables around us hushed a little. No doubt everyone was just as eager for them to get back as I was. We'd sent them into Portland to do one last grocery run before our butcher order came in on Monday. We couldn't keep clearing out the Forest Grove grocery, and we'd need a fair amount more to last us the next few days.

Hazel had been right. Hungry wolves made for grouchy wolves. And

781

grouchy wolves tended to cause some problems. We'd already had to break up two fights in the last day alone.

"They'll be back later tonight. Probably in the next few hours. I told them to go to a few stores so they'd be able to get enough for everyone to eat a real dinner tomorrow. The steaks won't be as good as Sal's, but..."

"Hell, I'd take one *well-done* right now," Destiny said on a sigh and Viv nodded, agreeing with her mate.

"I'd even take one with that awful blue cheese sauce on it."

I barked a laugh at that, but their admission cut me deep. I was the alpha. It was my job to make sure my pack was cared for. Safe. *Fed.*

"Another bowl?" Clay asked, lifting my now empty bowl from in front of me. I shook my head. There wouldn't be much left, and I needed to make sure everyone got some.

Grimacing, Clay brought both of our bowls to the outdoor sink under the new canopy we built earlier this spring to rinse off. I hated that he would also go without seconds just because I did, but I couldn't fault him for it.

Jared and Clay had been my right and left hands since the start. Together, we formed a united front and truly, it was more like we were all the alpha, even if I was the one who formally made all the calls.

Sara emerged from the tree line a bit breathless, with her patrol mate close in tow. She was a newer recruit, having just joined the pack last year. But...they weren't on patrol until dark. Sara and Tyler had been taking over most of the overnights now that Clay was hanging around camp more often.

They came straight for the tables and made a beeline for me.

"What is it?" I demanded before they could get a word in, my hand fisting in my lap beneath the table.

"It's Luke," Sara told me, glancing around before taking the seat opposite me. I didn't like the way she was keeping her voice hushed and sensing my unease. Clay rushed back to slide into the seat next to me.

"What's going on?"

"Luke didn't come back last night," Tyler replied. Luke...

Being pack alpha and absolute shit with names was not a good combo. I knew all of their faces. My wolf recognized theirs as pack, but with names I was pretty much useless.

"Tall. Skinny. Light hair. Scrappy. Joined the pack when Ry killed Samson," Clay filled in the blanks for me in a whisper.

I gave a tight nod and turned my attention back to Sara and Tyler. "When was the last time you saw him?"

"At dinner yesterday. He left for a run before dark. I don't think he's been back since then."

I mulled over the info, Clay and I sharing a look, and the stew in my stomach soured.

"Luke's left before, hasn't he?" Clay asked, fixing Luke's friends with a hard stare that told them they'd better be honest.

Ty winced but nodded. "Yeah. He's got a temper. He usually just goes into the city and gets smashed, but he wasn't upset about anything."

"Not that you know of," Clay snapped back, and I had to put my hand on his thigh beneath the table to steady him.

"Charity," I called and saw her head pop up at the next table, her dreads bobbing as she got up and made her way over, mouth full of stew.

She leaned over the table, glancing between Sara and Ty and me and Clay. Her face fell. "What's up, Allie?"

"Luke didn't come back to camp last night."

"He's probably sleeping off a massive hangover somewhere," Charity told me with a shrug, obviously she had no trouble remembering who he was.

I nodded, wanting to agree with her, but something in my gut told me this wasn't that. It was worse. "You're probably right," I agreed, "But if he's not back by morning, could you get a small party together and track him. Bring him back?"

"We already tried to track him," Ty argued. "His trail went cold a few miles past the third ring."

I swallowed past the lump in my throat. Fuck, I really hated being put on the spot.

"Well..." I trailed off, thinking of how best to handle this.

"I'll go with Charity," Clay offered without a second's hesitation. "You might have lost his trail, but I should be able to pick it up."

I gave him a grateful smile, and he covered my hand with his, squeezing. Jared and Clay were the best trackers we had. Better even than I was even with the advantage of my twin soul wolf's extra strong sense.

Tyler and Sara seemed satisfied with that and gave me a pair of tight, thankful nods before leaving.

"He'll be back by morning," Charity assured us. She gripped my shoulder, giving me a meaningful look. "Don't sweat it. I don't know the guy very well, but he's a loose cannon on the best of days. Probably just got riled up about something and went to blow off steam."

If that were all it was, I'd be relieved as hell, but Luke would be getting an earful. Pack members weren't allowed to leave territory without notifying me or Jared or Clay first. It wasn't a control thing, it was a safety thing, and I rarely ever denied any requests to leave pack land. We just needed to know when they left and where they went so that if they didn't come back we'd know where to look.

"Thanks, Cherry."

She grinned at the nickname and spun on her heel. "Let me get you guys a couple of beers, yeah? You both look like you could use one."

"You don't think it's…" I muttered under my breath, not daring to meet Clay's stare or speak the word *witch* aloud for fear of anyone overhearing and word spreading. I told Jared about Gregory, and Hazel already knew. That was enough for now.

"Nah. His kind aren't that stupid." He squeezed my hand again. "*Relax* before you give yourself an aneurysm."

Scanning the tables, I mentally went through the faces of the pack, counting to make sure everyone who should be here was. Save for those asleep now from night patrol and those on active patrol. Or working at the quarry with Jared or at Grove's End.

Several other faces were missing. Likely they were just gone for runs before dinner or out on errands, but it set me even more on edge. I couldn't help but notice the lack of one face in particular and my brows lowered. Sam wasn't at dinner. In fact, I didn't think I'd seen her all day.

That wasn't unheard of for her, though. She seemed to think that she could outrun the ghosts haunting her and was gone sprinting through our territory more often than she was here.

"You seen Sam today?"

Clay grunted his thanks as Charity plopped two frothy mugs down in front of us and took a long swallow of her own, leaving a foamy white mustache on her upper lip.

"Out for a run. As usual. She's supposed to check in before dark."

She'd fucking better.

I WRITHED IN BED LIKE I NEEDED AN EXORCISM MOST OF THE NIGHT. IT WAS A good thing it was Jared next to me instead of Clay or he'd have tied me down by now. As it was, I knew there would be no chance of sleep.

Running my hands through my sweat dampened hair, I sat up, dropping my tired head into my palms. There was no point in lying there. When my insomnia hit me this hard, I could be up for days without sleep. Maybe if I just went and checked to see that Luke was back, I would be able to grab a few hours of shut-eye before dawn.

I slipped from the bed, pausing to admire the work of art next to me for a moment before tugging on a pair of jeans to go with Jared's over-sized shirt and padded barefoot out of the room.

The heat of the early summer day still lingered, making the night air damp with humidity as I crept through the cabin and out the front door. I'd forgotten to check if Clay was sleeping in his wolf form around back of the cabin, and made an extra effort to silence my steps, leaving the front door open behind me to avoid the noise of shutting it.

Much as he tried to hide it, or brush it off, I saw his dark circles too. He needed his sleep and I didn't want to be the one to wake him.

Pack camp was always quiet this close to dawn. The only wolves awake the ones out on patrol. The first ring wasn't far from the borders of camp, but it was far enough that I couldn't see or hear whoever was running it.

I shivered as I picked over the dew-dampened dirt near the fire pit and around the foot-trails through the cabins to where I thought Luke's cabin was. Hushed conversation met my ears as I approached the edge of camp and I saw the girl from dinner, Sara, sitting with Archer on the small front stoop jutting out from the cabin on my right a little further down.

"Sara?" I called quietly, hurrying my steps. "What are you doing out here? It isn't dawn yet."

"Is he back?"

Sara's face fell and something twisted in my gut.

Damn.

She jabbed a thumb behind her at the darkened windows of the cabin to her back. "I just came to check," she explained. "I thought maybe he'd have slipped back in sometime in the night, but..."

"The other guys said they hadn't seen him."

I remembered now. Luke shared a cabin with two other unmated males, though for the life of me, I couldn't remember their names.

I pinched the bridge of my nose and sighed. "We'll give it another hour," I told her. "And if he isn't back then I'll wake Charity and go with her."

"We'll come too," Sara offered, and even though it was clear she hadn't slept either, I was in no position to deny her. If it were my friend missing, I'd want to go, too.

Archer nodded his agreement and rubbed his wide hand over Sara's back. I got the feeling she liked Luke. Maybe as something more than just a friend and fellow packmate. Though I couldn't remember ever seeing them together.

That was generally how it went though. Other than casual sex, most shifters preferred not to date. Getting serious with someone who wasn't your mate could spell disaster and heartbreak for all those involved if one wound up mating to someone else.

Better to just wait and hope that you won't be one of the unlucky few who have to wait decades if not longer to find their mate.

I scanned the trees as though if I looked hard enough I'd be able to see Luke rushing over the moonlight-dappled forest floor. Coming home. But other than the sounds of nighttime insects and an owl far off in the distance, there was nothing to be seen or heard.

Except...I realized there was a light on in one of the cabins in the next row. Or at least, I assumed there was.

I could see the glow of it tinting the dirt a muted gold from here. Was that Layla's cabin?

"Have you been awake long?" I asked Sara, already moving away from them and toward the light with slow steps.

"Did you see Layla and Seth get back from Portland?" I added before either of them could answer, wondering if they'd only just returned. I could think of no other reason why Layla's light would be on this late. Squinting, I tried to see if the cabin Seth shared with Kyle and Jake also had a light on, but couldn't tell from this far away.

"I don't think they came back yet," Sara told me, making my throat tighten and my steps falter.

"What do you mean? They should have been back just after dark at the latest."

I'd spent the evening reading before bothering to try to sleep. Why hadn't I come out to check that they'd returned? Why hadn't I realized they may not have when they didn't come into the main cabin to tuck the meat away in the deep freezer in the basement?

Fuck.

Footsteps followed me as I rushed toward Layla's cabin, heart in my throat. *Please be there.*

Please be there.

I didn't pause to knock, flying through the cracked open door of the cabin to sweep the interior. Charity and Danny blinked at me, startled, their inner wolves immediately on the defensive as I invaded their territory. At least until they saw who I was.

"Allie?" Charity asked. "What's going on?"

"Where's Layla?"

My hands twitched at my sides, and my sleep- deprived brain was already swiftly moving into kill- mode. If someone didn't speak the fuck up *right now...*

"We tried calling," Charity supplied. "She texted earlier and said they might be a bit late so we went to sleep, but they still aren't back."

Don't panic.

Don't fucking panic.

I am the alpha. I need to be calm.

"I left my phone at the cabin," I said in the most level voice I could muster, lying to myself with an inner monologue of reassurances. Layla was fine. Seth was fine. *Everything was fine.*

Charity rushed to grab hers from the nightstand and hand it to me, coming to stand in the middle of the space. Layla's trademark jasmine scent clung to everything in here and it was easy to tell which bunk was hers. Deep navy sheets rumpled on her top bunk had little silver stars on them. Long, silver-chained necklaces were strung over the edge of the ladder, pointed gemstones dangling from their tips.

My fingers fumbled over the screen of Charity's phone, and I had to move out to the porch where Sara and Archer hovered to be able to make the call. We had reception out here, but in certain areas of camp it was spotty at best.

"We already called twice," Charity said, wrapping a shawl around her bare breasts to come outside and join me.

I thumbed to her recent calls and jammed Layla's name in the list of calls, resisting the urge to pace along the foot trail as the call connected.

"Hey."

"Layla, thank—"

"It's Layla. Leave a message if you must or just text me like a normal person, and I'll get back to you."

Damn.

A lump formed in my throat, and it was impossible to get any air past it. My head spun as I jammed her name again and put the phone back to my ear.

"Pick up," I muttered. "Pick up, dammit."

When it went to voicemail again, I went to Charity's contacts and searched for Seth.

"Allie, what's going on?" Sara asked, and I could hear the accusation in her tone without having to look up and see it on her face. I'd somehow begun to pace, and I hadn't even noticed it, and I had to force myself to stop.

Charity came down the step to join me standing barefoot in the dirt and lifted her hand to my arms. "Hey. I'm sure they just got held up or whatever."

My throat burned as I met her steady gaze. "I can't find Seth," I said, still scrolling through contacts.

"He's under Dirty McFlyboy."

I raised a brow and she smirked. "Long story."

"Allie?"

Whirling, I found Clay approaching and something inside of me snapped a little.

His brows drew together as he took in the small group of us, the moonlight casting deep shadows over his every muscle as he stalked forward.

"It's Layla and Seth," I managed around the still- growing lump of dread blocking my airway. "They haven't come back yet."

His lips parted in surprise, and just as I had, he scanned the trees and squinted toward Seth's cabin, searching for signs of life.

"And Layla isn't answering her phone," Charity added, tossing her dreadlocks over her shoulder with a frown.

"I'm trying Seth now."

Clay's warm hands folded around my arms, lending me some strength. He leaned in to my side and whispered breathily against my cheek. "Breathe, Allie."

I pressed the screen to call him and waited, vibrating more and more with unease as each ring went unanswered.

"He isn't answering," I hissed, my voice trembling. "Here," Clay said and held out his hand for the phone. I passed it to him and he listened for a second before hanging up and placing another call. "If she doesn't answer then—"

"Charity?" I could hear Layla's voice connect on the other end of the call and snatched the phone back from Clay.

He flinched as I put it to my ear. "Where are you?"

"Allie?"

"Are you guys all right?"

"Yeah," Layla replied, some trepidation in her voice. "We just stopped at the barrens to stargaze. Don't worry, we packed the meat with tons of ice so it'll be fine—"

"I don't care about the fucking meat," I snapped, unable to help myself as my entire body sagged with relief and a muscle below my eye began to twitch. "Why weren't you answering your phones?"

"It was on silent."

"And Seth's?"

"Can't find the damn thing anywhere," I heard him call in reply.

"Just...get back here, okay? Now, please."

"On our way," she said, and the line went dead.

"I'm losing my fucking mind," I muttered to myself, forgetting there was an audience surrounding Clay and me. Ugh.

Charity stepped in and rubbed my back. "Girl, I think you need some sleep."

She wasn't wrong. I nodded numbly, and let Clay guide me into his side, relishing in the comfort of his body pressed along the side of mine.

"Wait," I said on a breath. "Luke still isn't back."

Clay stiffened against me but grunted that he understood. "Charity and I will take care of it," he said and then turned back to face her and the others. "Just let me get her back to bed and then we'll track him."

"We're coming, too," Sara and Archer piped up. "Meet you at the fire ring?"

Clay grunted his agreement again and even though I knew what the answer would be, I tipped my head up to him as he guided me away and asked anyway. "I won't be able to sleep, maybe I should just go with—"

"Not a chance. You're having a stiff whiskey and then going to bed. You're fucking shaking, baby." He pulled me in tighter, and I let him, needing him to hold me together for just another second before I put myself back together.

The door opened before we could even make it to the front porch, and Jared stepped out, all sleep rumpled hair and downturned eyes. "Allie? Clay? It's like four in the morning, what are you guys—"

"Luke still isn't back," Clay interrupted him, helping me up the steps to place me into Jared's arms. I shuddered against his heat.

"She hasn't slept. Give her a whiskey and put her to bed, yeah?"

"*Allie*," Jared chastised, "You should have woken me up if you couldn't sleep."

I sent a glare to Clay who only shrugged innocently, as though he didn't just ensure that I would be babied until I finally forced myself to sleep. No, not babied, that wasn't the right word. Taken care of, I supposed, but he knew I *hated* anyone doting on me. He knew because he was the exact same damn way.

I'd take the whiskey, though, if only to calm my nerves.

"Careful out there," I warned Clay, giving him a meaningful look as I saw the others gathering around the fire ring to head out for the search. "And I want you back before breakfast."

He raised a brow. "That an order?"

"You're damn right it is," I barked back, though I didn't bother lacing the command with the power of my alpha status to strong-arm him into complying. I rarely did. He just better fucking listen or he wouldn't get any nookie for a goddamned month.

He smirked, but leaned in and brushed his lips over my forehead, eyeing Jared, who surprisingly didn't show any discomfort at the gesture. "Don't worry, babe. Everything'll shake out all right. You'll see."

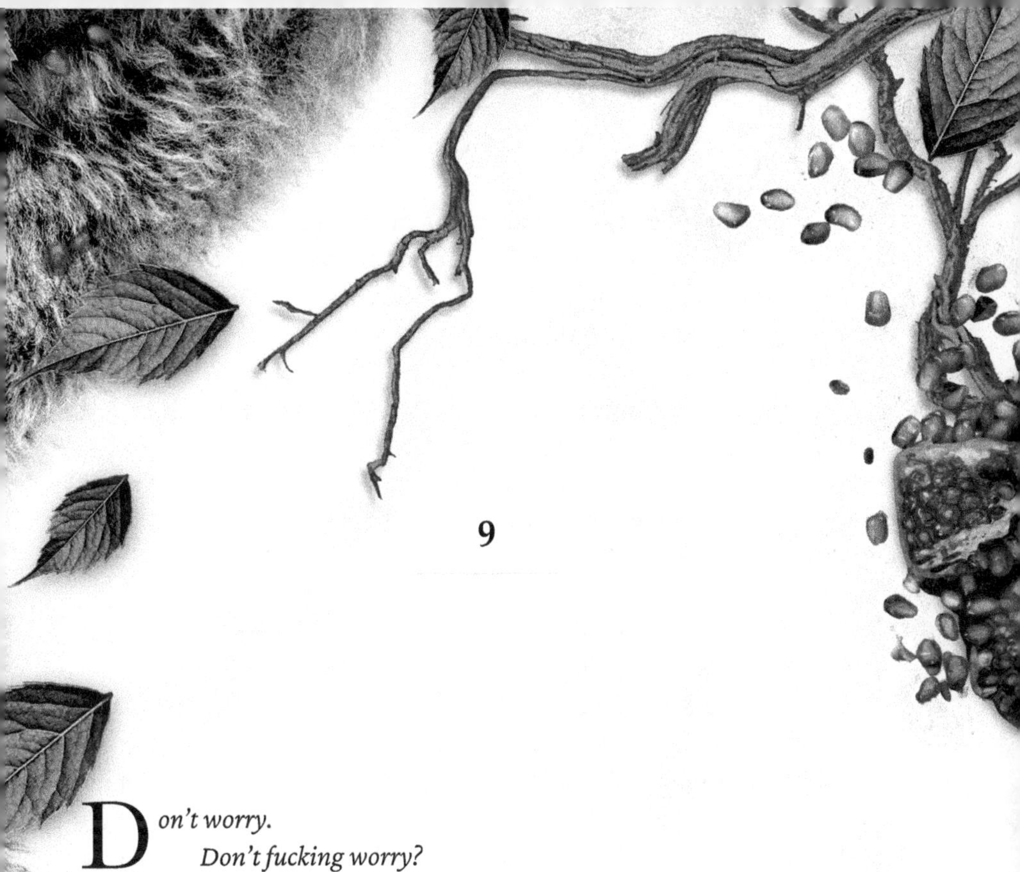

9

D on't worry.

Don't fucking worry?

Well, how about now?

"We need to find them," I snarled, my breaths coming in pants as I struggled to maintain a solid hold on my inner wolf. She'd been restless ever since Charity had barged into the cabin to tell me Trey and Todd still hadn't been found.

They'd been here since the start and were a mated pair. They welcomed me into the Forest Grove pack with open arms when the vast majority had shunned me because of Ryland's distaste for me. And now they were gone, without a trace.

We'd tried calling. Texting. Tracing their phones. The patrol teams on each ring had been notified and were keeping an eye out, but their scent seemed to just vanish somewhere to the east.

Charity followed me outside into the rain, and I breathed in the heady scent of petrichor, letting it soothe me. Letting the cool water running down my face and body shock me into mental clarity.

"They can't have gotten too far," I said over the roar of the downpour. We'd just seen them at dinner last night.

We all pretended not to know how they liked to go out past the third ring some nights to rut in their wolf forms and that was exactly what they'd done. They'd snuck past third ring patrol and Charity pretended not to notice just like she always did. Except they hadn't come back.

Worse, Luke still hadn't returned either, and it'd been two days since we sent out the first search party for him. We'd sent four more since then but came up empty handed each time.

Not even Clay's tracking skills were good enough to find him. His trail went stone cold not far outside the third ring.

And of course now it was fucking raining. Any trace of Luke's scent that may have remained was now gone, and if we didn't move quickly, any trace of Trey's and Todd's would be gone, too. There wasn't any time to waste.

My phone buzzed in my pocket, and I swiped water off the cracked screen to read a text from Clay.

Clay: Trey and Todd back yet?

He'd had to go to Grove's End to deal with a few things this morning and still hadn't returned. I didn't realize I'd been worried about him, too, until I saw his message.

When Luke went missing, it wasn't shocking. In fact, there were a few who even believed he may have deserted us, fed up with pack life. More built for life as a lone wolf. But now...

Trey and Todd would never leave us. Especially not without saying something.

Allie: No. I need you. We're going out to search before the rain washes away their scent.

Clay: Coming now. Don't go anywhere without me, got it?

I didn't bother answering. If he wasn't back in the next fifteen fucking minutes, I was leaving.

"What do you want to do, Allie?" Charity asked, antsy on her feet as she awaited my orders. Charity had known Trey and Todd much longer than I had, and I could see the worry etched into her stare and the knot between her brows.

I blinked away the rainwater leaking into my eyes, trying to focus through the noise of panic in my skull. Over the rumbling in my stomach that was becoming more and more difficult to ignore. Thank the stars Seth was going to pick up the massive meat order from the butcher in Portland the day after tomorrow. We could stretch what we had until then, but it would make searching that much harder.

How far could we run, for how long, without proper fuel?

"Clay is on his way back. You, me, him and Viv will take point. We'll search to the east, where patrol said they lost their scent. Between the four of us, we should be able to pick something up and track where they went."

"The guys from the crew helping Sal took a rain day. Want me to beef up patrol in case we can pick up anything?"

I should've thought of that. "Good idea. Double each ring and give them something of Trey's or Todd's to scent."

She nodded. "'Kay."

"And Seth," I added. "Wake him up. I need him to keep an eye on things for me here while we're gone."

Charity vanished a moment later, rushing through the mud to do as I asked as I stood there, useless in the rain. I pressed a hand to my rumbling stomach, but even if we had anything that would sate my hunger, there was no way I could eat right now.

Not even Hazel's cookies, which she'd been baking nonstop to try to make up for the fact that we had barely enough meat to get through another day.

I squinted, senses piquing as I heard running footsteps approach. It wasn't Charity, she'd gone the other way. And it wasn't Clay, I'd have been able to feel him.

Unable to contain my wolf any longer with all riot of emotions rattling the cage of my bones, I tossed my cell back onto the porch and removed my clothes in one fluid motion, letting the shift take me.

I shuddered as the rain wet my fur a moment later, bristling against the momentary shock of pain as my body broke and reformed. I scented the air, catching her scent before I saw her coming.

It was Sam.

What is it? I demanded, shoving the question into her skull. I could sense her panic. The smell of it tainted her natural juniper smell.

The quarry, her panicked voice came into my mind.

Jared sent me for—Jared.

I launched past her, gone before she could finish.

Allie, wait! Her voice echoed inside my skull, but I couldn't hear it over the agonizing whine of my wolf as our lungs collapsed even as they were filling with air, pushing us forward.

Sam fell behind, and through the pandemonium in my head I managed to bark out an order for her to stay at camp. Being sure to lace it with the power of my status so she wouldn't follow me. We didn't need something happening to her right now. Clay was already on the verge of snapping.

I was already on the verge of snapping.

I plowed through the foliage, sliding in the muck but not caring even as I came up coated in dirt and debris with each skid of my paws over the earth.

A vivid image of my mate in my mind kept me going. If anything happened to him...

If he were hurt... If he were *gone...*

I'd tear this world apart to find him, and I didn't care who had to get hurt in the process. The logical part of my mind warred against that thought, but my wolf wanted blood.

I veered around a tall oak and skidded through second ring patrol, turning heads as I flew down the sloping terrain toward the quarry.

Relief flooded me like a sedative injected into my veins as my wolf recognized the feel of Jared's soul nearing ours. Not gone, then. And I'd feel it now if he were hurt. I picked up on a feeling of unease from him, but nothing more.

I shifted as I made it to the portable where his office was, rushing through the rain and up the steps to the front door on human feet. Steam lifted from my heated flesh as I brushed hair out of my face and stepped inside.

Jared's amber eyes snapped to me in the dark, his wolf glimmering just beneath the surface. "Allie, what are you doing here?"

I blinked, confused as to why he was sitting in the dark until I flipped the light switch and found that the overhead light didn't illumi-nate. "Sam said..." I trailed off, panting a little from the long run.

Jared rounded his desk and came to me, tugging off his t-shirt with one arm and pulling it down over my head.

What had Sam said? I supposed I left before she could really say anything at all.

"She seemed panicked. I just...I just ran."

Jared pushed my wet silver hair back from my face and sighed just as I sensed Clay approaching. I twisted just in time to see him barge in the door, ass naked with his eyes full of malice. "What the fuck happened?"

His glare cut to me. "Patrol said you flew by like a bat out of hell."

"The power lines were cut," Jared said, drawing my attention back from Clay. "We thought it might've just been a fluke, but I went and checked it out myself. The cuts were clean."

"Show me," Clay barked, already turning to go back out into the rain with Jared and me on his heels.

"You don't have any clients here today, right?" Clay checked before shifting. Something I should have done before waltzing into the portable office in my birthday suit, but I wasn't thinking straight.

We ran on foot through the quarry, only shifting once we were clear of the main operations area, where members of our pack—the employees of the quarry— huddled beneath the covered lunch area, waiting out the rain.

We followed the power lines almost all the way out to the main road before Jared slowed, veering into the trees and shifting back to his human form. Clay and I followed suit, and Clay went to inspect a mess of wires Jared was pointing out to him while I kept an eye on the surrounding woods.

Cars passed in the distance on the main road and the pelting of rain on leaves drowned out most everything else. I shifted back, letting my wolf takeover again as a familiar scent filled my nose. There was no denying, it was Sam's scent. I circled the entire area, searching for any other scents in the shrubbery or clinging to the waterlogged earth, but finding none.

"Why was Sam here?" I asked Jared as I shifted back, shivering.

Clay's eyes narrowed at Jared. "Sam was here?"

"Yeah, she was passing by on her run when she noticed the power was out. She came with me to check the lines."

That explained why her scent was all over the place, but it didn't explain why she was out running this way *in the rain* while there were a million other places for her to run.

Jared's eyes flickered to mine for an instant before falling away, and I could tell he was thinking the same guilty thought I was. It was clear from the clean cuts that this wasn't an accident, but who would want to do this to us? And why?

I could think of only two potential culprits. Sam or the witch, Gregory.

"You think it's that witch fucking with us because you didn't do what he wanted?" Clay asked, water dripping in a steady stream from his chin.

"You don't think he would mess with our pack, too, do you?"

He picked up on what I was referring to. There had to be a reason Trey and Todd were missing. What if Gregory snatched them up to use as leverage to get me to do what he wanted? To meet with the asshole he works for. One of the twelve Arcane Council delegates. "There's only one way to find out," Clay said in a low, dangerous voice that made my skin crawl and my toes curl all at once. "How much you want to bet he's still stalking Forest Grove waiting to corner you again?"

Jared frowned, seeing where this was going and clearly disagreeing with this angle. But I saw the sense in it.

"This could've been a local," Jared tried to argue, but Clay and I were beyond listening, and Jared would see that this was the easiest, and fastest way to rule out the witch.

We needed to get searching for Trey and Todd before their scent began to disintegrate, but after that, we needed to come up with a plan to catch us a witch.

"Do you know how to neutralize a witch, by chance?"

Clay grinned. "Hell yeah, babe."

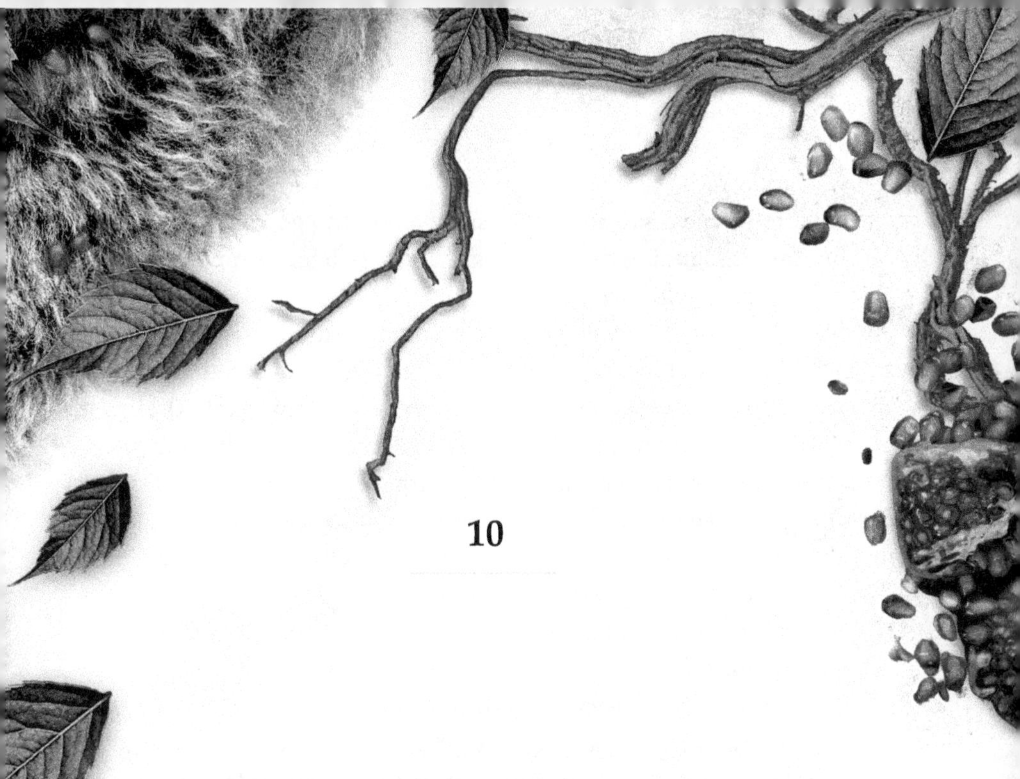

10

"He's coming to," Jared informed me, his face placid as an early morning lake, even though I could sense how he truly felt.

It was how we were all feeling. It'd now been almost forty-eight hours since Trey and Todd vanished without a trace. Luke was still missing. It was going to take *days* if not longer for the power company to come out and restore the lines, effectively pausing all operations at the quarry and putting our finances in a chokehold. Not to mention we were all fucking starving.

Seth would be leaving in about an hour to go pick up our order from the butcher in the city, though, so there was that at least.

"Clay used the bindstone on him like we were taught, but I've never actually seen it work before so just...be careful, all right?"

I inhaled deeply, unclenching my fists as I rose from the kitchen island where I'd been sitting with Layla and Vivian.

"Want me to go with you?" Layla offered as I got up, but I shook my head. "You need to go with Seth. I don't want anyone going anywhere alone right now. He'll be leaving soon."

Layla hopped down from her stool and came around to pull me into a jasmine scented hug. She didn't say anything. She didn't need to.

"I'm staying actually," she said as she pulled away. "We wanted to be here for you."

Viv offered me a sad smile. "Destiny offered to go with him for the pickup. Sara is manning the bar tonight at the pub for her and you know how my girl is a night owl."

I smirked. That she was. Their pick up time was later in the evening so they likely wouldn't be back until after dark. I debated sending a third body with them just in case, but then it was possible the meat order wouldn't fit in the Jeep. They'd need all the space they could get.

They didn't push me on coming with, and I was grateful. They didn't need to see this. Hell, *I* didn't even want to see this, but this was my job now. I was the alpha, and I needed to keep my pack—my family —safe. "Thanks, you guys," I muttered, leaving them behind in the kitchen as I let Jared lead me out to the moon chamber where we were keeping Gregory.

It'd been relatively easy to grab him. Just like Clay thought, he'd been loitering outside Jacqueline's shop earlier today. Waiting to ambush me again when I left with this week's book order. But it was him who was ambushed. One good clock to the back of his skull by Clay and we had him in the back of the Jeep.

The pack kept a small store of bindstone in the safe in Ry's old office. It didn't look like much except a hunk of rock, but apparently if worn around a witch's neck, it prevented them from accessing their powers. Blocked their ability to draw energy from the earth. I wouldn't pretend to understand how it worked, but I was grateful it did.

The only other way, by my understanding, was to blind them and sever their hands, and I wasn't quite prepared to go that far, even if my wolf heartily disagreed with me.

"I still don't think we should've brought him here," I groused to Jared, the tension returning to my muscles as we rounded the edge of the cabin and the moon chamber came into view, the stone painted in gold from the setting sun.

"There was nowhere else to take him," Jared replied. "We'll make sure he's either blindfolded or unconscious when we bring him back to town and cut him loose. He won't be able to get back here on his own, and if he tries, then it'll be his funeral."

I hadn't needed to use the moon chamber for a long time. Another perk of being the twin soul wolf. But Layla and Viv had to use it for their first year of moon-triggered shifts, give or take. In the beginning, it was almost impossible to control the inner wolf during a moon-forced shift. Which was why they needed to be chained, to keep them from lashing out or hurting anyone, or god forbid, wind up biting another human.

Now, the only being chained in the moon chamber was a witch. He slouched against the wall about halfway down the length of the chamber. His hands chained at his back, anchored into the wall. A rock on a leather cord strapped around his neck, resting against his clavicle.

Clay's upper lip curled as he watched the witch slowly come to. Moaning and squirming like a babe.

I shucked off the weaker Allie and left her at the threshold, barring her from following me inside. This wasn't the time to let my anxieties get the better of me. I needed answers, and I needed them now.

For Trey and Todd. For Luke.

"Gregory," I said by way of greeting, barely recognizing my own voice as I went to stand next to Clay in front of our captor. "Thought I told you to stay out of my town?"

He spat on the dirt floor and squirmed against his binds, glancing down at the stone resting below his throat. He grimaced, looking pale as he realized what it was.

"Bindstone? Where did you get it? I thought we'd destroyed all that was left."

Clearly they hadn't, but I wasn't here to talk about a stupid rock.

"I'm going to cut to the chase," I said, lowering into a crouch to put myself at eye level with him. "We seem to be short a few members of our pack."

I studied his expression, searching for any evidence of falsehood while I asked the direct question. "Are you responsible for their disappearances?"

His brows scrunched together, brown eyes flaring with something I couldn't name beneath the surface. My wolf growled and the sound came from my still- human lips.

"Answer me," I gritted out between my teeth, a tremor rattling down my spine and raising the hairs on my arms.

"What is this?" he asked, and I scented the first whiff of fear evaporating from his flesh. "You have no right to hold me here. If you release me now, I will not report this to the council."

Rage tightened my core, heating me from the inside out as I resisted my wolf's urge to bite his head off and be done with it.

"Allie," Jared warned in a low voice from somewhere behind me, probably sensing my murderous intent. I didn't care.

"If you don't tell me what I want to know, you won't be going anywhere."

My voice came out stone cold and so devoid of emotion I had to wonder if it was even my own. I would not stand for anyone hurting the people I cared about. I would not allow my family to be messed with. It was my job to protect them, and it was the one thing I would not fail at. Not while I was still breathing.

Gregory seemed to be judging my sincerity, his gaze narrowing while his breathing picked up a tick.

"Fine," I muttered when he didn't speak. "Have it your way."

Clay darted forward like he would stop me, but I already had my hand wrapped firmly around the witch's ankle, and a beat before Clay could reach me, it snapped beneath my palm and Gregory's scream echoed into the night.

His eyes welled, and he cursed repeatedly, staring wide-eyed at his broken ankle like he could heal it by sheer force of will. For all I knew, maybe he could. But he wouldn't be doing that with a hunk of bind-stone around his neck.

"Allie, we should—"

"Don't," I snapped at Jared, raising a hand to silence him. My rage was enough to chase away the guilt of not allowing him to rein me in. I didn't need to be reined in right now. I needed to be let loose.

My wolf ached for freedom. She wanted to see how his slender neck would feel with our jaws around it. I licked my lips.

"Talk," I barked at him. "Talk or I break the other one."

"You crazy bitch!"

Wrong answer.

This time, Clay and Jared didn't bother stopping me as the bones in his other ankle crunched and then snapped. They did nothing even when a bit of jagged white tore through his flesh and bright crimson glinted in the moonlight as it ran down into the earth.

Bile rose in my throat, and I gagged on it, but managed to keep it down. Managed to keep a straight face. The weaker Allie I left at the door was begging me to stop, but I couldn't.

This bastard was a threat to us. My bones sang with the truth of it. My heart recognized a snake in the grass when it saw one.

Trust your gut.

It was what my dad always used to tell me. What Hazel told me. And it hadn't steered me wrong yet.

"Still think I'm bluffing, asshole?"

I reached for his kneecap, and he dragged himself back from me, wincing and shaking, until he was pressed up against the stone wall.

"Stop," he cried. "You fucking heathen, just stop and I'll tell you whatever you want to know."

"Everything," I hissed.

His lips parted and a worried crease formed in his brow, but then he sighed and dropped his head. Resigning himself to betraying whatever confidence the Arcane Council member had in him.

He sucked a breath in through his teeth as a cool breeze funneled through the moon chamber, whistling over his broken skin.

"Start with where the fuck my friends are."

His jaw twitched and I couldn't see his expression because of the shadows from his hair falling over his forehead, but he shook his head. "I don't know where your missing shifters are."

"Liar!"

He snapped his gaze back up and glared at me. "It's the truth!"

I didn't believe him, not for one second, but I'd play along for a minute.

"What are you doing here?"

"It's like I said; I'm here to bring you to speak to a representative of the Arcane Council."

"Get Hazel," I shot to Jared. This clown may be able to lie to me, but he wouldn't be able to hide his nature from her.

He left a second later, and I stood, taking a steadying breath. It was a damn good thing Hazel was blind. I didn't want her seeing what I'd done to the witch, though I was sure she'd be able to smell the sweet tang of his blood soaking into the earthen flood.

I pinched the bridge of my nose. "Why? Why does he want to speak to me?"

The witch slouched against the wall, his breathing evening back out. If he thought I was out of danger just because I'd stood up and moved two steps away, he was mistaken.

"Please," he moaned. "Let me heal myself."

He pulled against the chains holding his arms behind his back and choked out a wet cough, turning to spit on the ground.

"Not until we're finished." A lie.

I was starting to realize our mistake and what I'd need to do to fix it...

Gregory couldn't leave Forest Grove. He could never be allowed to walk out of here. Even the smallest possibility of his retribution—of the retribution of the Arcane Council against my pack...

I shuddered.

It wasn't a risk I was willing to take.

Jared walked just behind Hazel as she made her way inside, walking straight to where I stood, her milky gaze sweeping the ground.

"I need you to read him," I explained. "Can you do that?"

Hazel ran her tongue over her teeth, considering, before she finally nodded.

I looked to Jared and then to Clay. "Unbind him. Hold him steady."

Jared's face was a mask of horror as he knelt to do as I asked. I had to block out his emotions as he passed. They threatened to crush my resolve. I gravitated to Clay as he also moved to Gregory, on his opposite side. He was brooding and furious, shocked, worried, but not disgusted.

Jared unlocked the manacles and my mates each took one of Gregory's arms while he pulled against their hold, protesting in indeterminate mutterings.

"What..." he breathed, his hands balling to fists. "What is she going to do to me?"

"Open his hand," I ordered Clay, and he forcibly unfurled the witch's fingers. Not wanting to wind up with more broken bones, the bastard didn't fight him much.

I led Hazel to Gregory's left side and guided her hands to his open palm.

"What is she doing?" Gregory demanded, baring his teeth.

I crossed my arms and waited as Grams ran her fingertips over the uncallused skin of his palm. As her body hunched in on itself and her features twisted. Her milky eyes lit with the glow of her wolf, and Clay ripped her away, clutching her by her wrist while he held Gregory steady with his other hand.

"What is it?" he asked in a snarl, and Hazel's murderous stare found Gregory through her blindness.

"He has wolf blood on his hands," she said in a low whisper. "Vampire, too."

His eyes went wide.

"He likes the thrill of it," Hazel continued, not knowing that each of her words was hammering a new nail in this fucker's coffin. I was feeling less ill at the thought of ending this monster's life by the second.

"Even though he's acting on orders and not of his own mind."

"Can you tell if he's hurt Trey and Todd? Luke?"

She solemnly shook her head. "No. I can only sense his darkness. Feel the texture of it. His emotions. No specifics."

I ground my teeth.

"Thanks, Hazel. You can go."

"Think I'll stay," she said, her face pinched as she backed out of my way to stand sentinel behind me, crossing her wrinkled arms over her long nightdress.

I didn't have it in me to argue. She could think of me what she wanted. This needed to be done.

"I'd start explaining if I were you," I growled. "Where are my friends?"

"I d-didn't touch them," he argued, and I saw Clay's grip on his arm tighten, making him grit out a little squeal. "It's the truth! I *have* done what she said, but it was orders, nothing more. I was sent here to bring you in—*for testing*. Because you're different than the others. Rumor has it that a vampire's compulsion has no sway over you. That you can see through a witch's ward. It's unnatural." His upper lip curled back. "I'm not here to kill you or anyone else. Just to bring you in."

"So that your superior can do what?" Clay demanded, twisting his arm. "Torture her with some fucked up testing *and then* kill her."

Gregory's lips sealed closed, and it was as much an admission of guilt as if he'd spoken.

"There can be no evidence," he muttered so low I wasn't certain I heard him correctly. It didn't matter though, I'd heard enough.

"If you don't know the whereabouts of my missing pack mates, then you are of no more use to me."

I waited, allowing those words to soak in. Allowing the weight of my stare to convey my intention until the reek of his fear permeated the air. He opened his mouth to speak a few times before closing it again for good.

Either he truly didn't know or he was willing to die to protect the secret. I was starting to assume the former, but there was one way I could be sure to prevent further harm to my pack: eliminate him from the equation. He said he was working for *one* of the Arcane Council members.

I had to assume it was a corrupt one. That no one else except that singular alchemist knew Gregory was here. And he wouldn't go reporting his missing assassin to anyone if Gregory never returned because that would be tantamount to admitting what he was doing.

Round and round the thoughts parried and lunged in my mind. Trying to find the best—the safest— option. I had to trust that this option was the one that would lead to the least amount of harm. Other-wise...I didn't want to think about *otherwise*.

Trust your gut.

"There isn't any way I can trust your word," I spoke in a low rumble, lengthening up through my spine as I sized up the blade clipped to the waistband of Clay's dark denim jeans. "But there is one way I can make sure that if you are responsible, you can hurt no one else."

"Y-you said you'd let me go," he croaked, his face twisting just as much as he tried to twist in Clay and Jared's grip.

I shook my head solemnly. Giving him a moment to make peace with my choice. To say a prayer if he wished. He did neither of those things though as I numbly knelt in front of him, drenching my knees in the cool damp of his blood in the dirt.

"Allie, we can't..." Jared pleaded, his Adam's apple bobbing as he looked between the witch and me. His heart beat hard against his ribcage; I could hear it from here. Like a caged beast smashing against iron bars.

"Let me do it," Clay offered, cutting me a hard stare from the corner of his eye while Gregory devolved into racking sobs and the smell of urine prickled my nose.

"*Clay,*" Jared snapped. I looked at the blade on Clay's waistband, a question in my stare. His jaw tightened, but he nodded, giving me permission.

Jared's wolf crashed to the surface, urged almost to bursting free from his heightened emotion." We aren't seriously going to—"

In one swift movement, I leaned forward, freed the knife from Clay's waist. The solemn *click* of the blade flicking open came only an instant before I dragged the honed edge against the witch's throat.

Hot blood spurted and spilled down his neck, and his eyes went wide with shock as he fought for air, burbling and croaking his last as his body convulsed and then began to sag.

Jared dropped his arm as though stung and skidded backward, looking green.

Clay gently leaned the dead witch against the ground and closed his still-staring eyes, pressing down with his thumb and index finger on the witch's eyelids.

I stared mutely at the evidence of the lengths I would go to in order to protect my pack and felt...

Nothing.

For once, the awful flutter of anxiety in my chest had eased. The shaking was gone, and I felt an unfamiliar stillness in my bones that I hadn't for some time now. The gore made me a bit queasy, but that was the only bit of discomfort I felt.

My brows drew together as a darkness crept into my thoughts, whispering how I must be a monster to feel this calm, this at peace, with the body of a man I'd just killed not even cold yet at my feet.

I eliminated the threat. I'm not sorry.

I hadn't even realized I'd spoken aloud until Jared lurched to his feet and left the moon chamber, chucking the manacle keys to the dirt before he vanished.

Light hands landed on my shoulders, and I breathed in Hazel's baked goods scent, letting it chase away the shadows with dreams of gooey chocolate and warm brown sugar. "You did what you needed to," she told me, and for some strange reason, it was those words that undid me. A stinging pain raked up my throat and burned in my eyes. My stomach twisted.

Hazel patted my shoulders, and her long silver hair tickled my cheeks when she leaned in. "Go rest now. Let me and my grandson clean up here."

Clay grunted as he rose to his feet and pulled me up with him, tugging me into his chest and out of Hazel's grasp. My tears wet his shirt as I inhaled his familiar scent, letting it wash over me and take away the sting.

"It was the right choice," he reassured me, whispering against my hair. "The only choice."

He pushed me back to hold me at arm's length, jutting his chin out to gesture to where Jared had just left through the door. "He knows that, too. Just give him some time to realize it."

I nodded even though I didn't fully believe that. "I should help. We'll bury him on pack land. Somewhere no one else will come snooping. The second ring maybe? Out by the caves?"

Clay squeezed my arms before letting go. "Go be with your girls. They're waiting for you inside. We'll clean this up and then I'll stay with you tonight."

It went without saying that Jared would spend the night elsewhere. Whether at the quarry or the old cabin in the woods was anyone's guess. I really hoped he was smart enough to go to the cabin and not the quarry though. He'd be alone there and the nearest patrol route was a mile and a half out. At least the cabin was warded. Only members of our pack could find it, and only because my ability to see through witch's wards now extended to them.

I sighed and gave in, the prospect of a nice cold whiskey enough to get my legs moving even though an emptiness was forming in my chest, hollowing out my bones. With each mile I felt Jared move away from camp, from me, a hole formed in my soul, and I had to wonder if I was any better than the previous pack alpha.

A knot formed between Clay's brows, and he shook me, getting my attention again. "Hey. What's going on in there?" he demanded, bright blue eyes flicking between my gray ones.

"It's nothing," I replied, swallowing past the lump in my throat as I slipped out of his grasp. "Get back soon?"

"I will."

"And take at least two others with you. If he was telling the truth, then the threat is still out there. We may not be safe. Not yet."

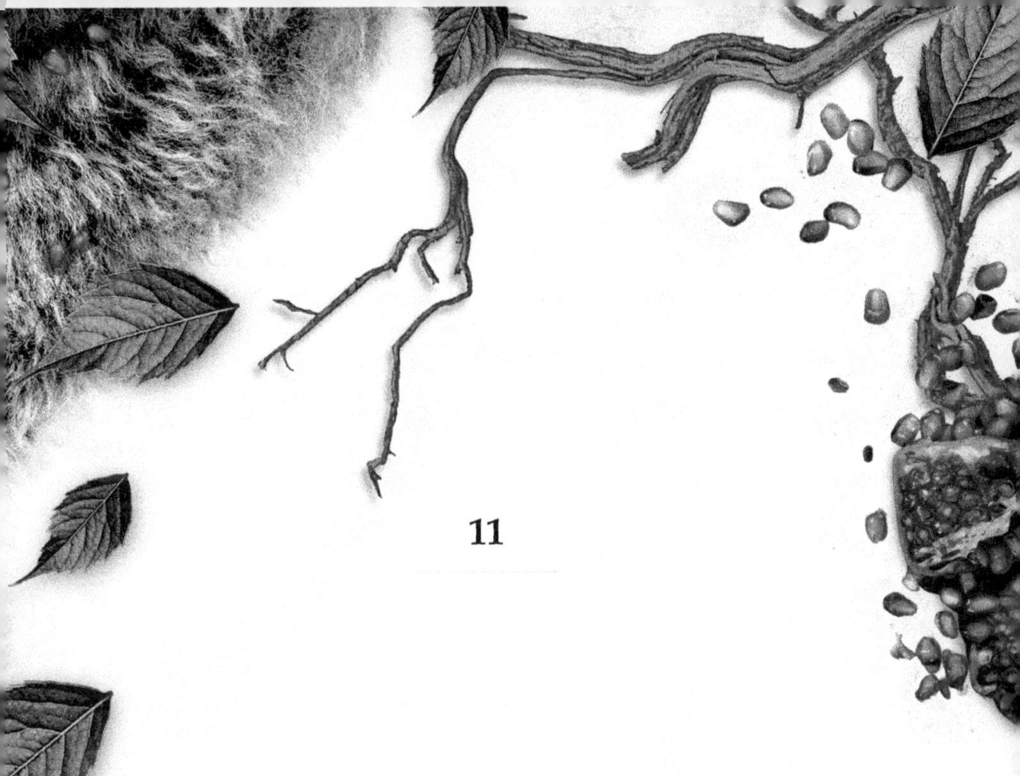

11

Layla and Viv were there for me when I dragged my suddenly very heavy feet through the front door. They'd curled themselves up on the couch in the living room and had a movie playing on the tv that really didn't ever get much use.

They didn't ask me any questions as I strode past them and up the stairs to shower the blood off my hands and discard my crimson splattered shirt. They still didn't ask me a damned thing when I came out of the bathroom and found them both on my bed waiting for me with an icy cold whiskey and understanding expressions.

Maybe it was the fact that they didn't ask, or maybe that I saw no judgement in their eyes, that made me want to tell them, but after a time—and two whiskeys—I did just that.

They didn't try to hide their surprise, but I got no sense from them that they thought what I did was wrong. I didn't stop at admitting I'd just killed a witch, though. I'd already told them how he'd been following me, trying to get me to go with him to speak to an Arcane Council member. The whole pack knew that now, otherwise bringing him to the moon chamber for questioning would have led to too many questions of their own. But I also shared with Viv and Layla my suspicion that Gregory was to blame for the missing wolves and my fear that they wouldn't be coming back.

That I'd failed them.

We had planned to wait up until Seth and Destiny returned from Portland and Clay from burying the witch's corpse, but by the time Clay returned, the three of us girls had fallen asleep in my bed. The whiskey sending us off with a wave and a warmth deep in our bellies.

I awoke to the soft press of lips against my forehead and the shifting of blankets as Clay drew them up to cover me and the girls. He whispered to me to go back to sleep, brushing a knuckle down the length of my jaw in a way that made me shiver before he left. I wasn't able to fall back asleep until the shower had stopped running and I sensed Clay shifting and curling up to sleep below the window outside in his wolf form.

Knowing he was close, not only so that he could protect us, but also so I could protect him if needed, allowed me to drift back into a black and dreamless sleep.

I SENSED HIM COMING AS THE GRIP OF A RESTLESS SLEEP EASED AND I BLINKED into the barely-there light of early morning. Jared. A sigh of relief blew out through my lips as I carefully maneuvered myself from the bed, careful not to wake Layla and Viv just yet.

I tiptoed to the door and down the stairs, skipping all the boards that I knew creaked underfoot so I wouldn't wake Clay outside, either. I inched the door open and shut behind me and took off toward the trees at the edge of camp, where I could sense him approaching on quiet bare feet over the hard packed dirt.

The sun hadn't begun to rise in earnest yet, and a chill still clung to the air that told me it was likely not even five am yet. I shivered, wrapping my arms around myself as I slipped past a few of the smaller cabins and into the trees. The scents overwhelmed my still- waking senses, and I breathed in the grounding bouquet of wet earth and cold pine as I waited for Jared to find me.

It didn't take long. About a minute later I spotted him walking through the foliage in his human form. A pair of khakis riding low on his hips.

"Hey," I said lamely when he was close enough to hear, fighting a blush.

He smirked, sighing as he came to a full stop a couple of feet away. "Hey."

"We should talk—"

"I couldn't sleep—"

We spoke at the same time, and Jared bit his lower lip, tucking his hands deeply into his pockets. "You first."

"No, you go."

He pursed his lips. "Okay. I..."

He scratched the back of his head, making some of the dirty blond strands stick straight up. "I'm sorry I freaked out. I shouldn't have left."

My jaw set of its own accord, and my wolf woke within, prowling. Usually, my guys could do no wrong in her eyes, but on this one, she agreed with me. Neither of us were fucking happy.

"I'm not what you seem to think I am," I replied, my hands clenching, drawing his attention. "You...you put me on this pedestal like I'm perfect—like I can do no wrong, you always have. But that's not true. That's *not* who I am, Jare."

His brows drew down, shadowing his amber eyes as a muscle in his jaw ticked. "That's not fair, Allie."

"Not fair?" I demanded, hating how my voice was growing in volume but completely unable to help it. He'd hurt me last night. Just leaving like that. Making me feel his disgust. His shock. His fucking *dismay* at what *I had to do.*

"What's not fair is having to feel your judgement after I did something you knew damned well needed to be done. I am willing to do whatever it takes to protect my family."

My voice broke on the last word, remembering what it was like before. Living with the ghost of my dad after my mom died giving birth to me until he died too, succumbing to his illness without putting up a fight. Hell, even my aunt and uncle ditched me within a few months of taking me in after he was gone.

For years Layla and Viv had been my only family while I lived alone out in the woods, barely surviving on berries and oatmeal because I didn't want to burden anyone.

Things were different now, though. I had a family. A real one. This pack meant more to me than I could ever express in words and it wasn't just my alpha wolf that felt fiercely protective over them, it was my human side, too.

I'd die for any one of them. And I wouldn't stop at killing Gregory if the threat against them persisted. I'd end the life of *anyone* involved in hurting my pack. Not just because it was my job, but because I wanted to. Needed to. I wanted to earn their respect, their friendship. Their loyalty.

"Whatever. It. Takes," I reinforced when Jared made no reply, instead, staring at me like there were a thousand things he wanted to say but had no idea where to begin.

Fine, if he didn't want to talk this through then I wasn't going to make him. A short snarl fell from my lips as I spun on my heel, ready to go back to the cabin and dump half a bottle of Bailey's into a coffee so I could get through whatever the fuck today decided to throw at me. His hand closed around my wrist, stopping me dead, and I tore my arm from his grip, baring my teeth.

"What?"

His lips parted but no sound came out. Pain ripped through me, sent like a vibration down the mate bond straight from his heart to mine. I winced, guilt hedging in to blot out the anger trying to take hold.

"What, Jared?" I asked again, more softly this time, my chest heaving. Then even more softly, "I needed you. I needed you to support me, to be there for me, and you weren't."

"There's nothing I can say to make up for that," he gritted out, lifting his hard gaze to mine. "But you're wrong about something."

I waited for him to continue, trying to keep a level head and not make this worse than it already was.

"You are exactly who I thought you were," he said finally. "Stronger than I could ever be."

His Adam's apple bobbed in his throat.

"You're right that it was hard to watch you do what you needed to—"

"Eliminate the threat," I amended, speaking the words he was clearly too afraid to voice aloud.

He nodded. "It was hard to watch, not because I was disgusted at you or horrified or any shit like that. It was hard because I'm not sure I'd have had the strength to do it myself."

My nose wrinkled, confusion muddying my thoughts.

"The mantle of alpha was always meant to eventually pass to me from Ry. And…I can't help thinking that I would've been absolute shit at it. I'm weak, Allie. A coward. You barely flinched while you took out the most likely threat against our pack. I felt your resolve like a cement wall. No cracks. No second guessing. You knew in your bones it was the right thing. The only thing."

He shook his head, letting his gaze finally drop.

"I don't think any less of you, Allie. I envy you. I envy your strength. And it fucking eats at me that you have to be the one to deal with all this shit when it should've been me."

"No," I choked out, stepping in closer and forcing him to look at me. "You don't get to do that. If it weren't for you, I'd be dead or worse by now. My psycho ex would've killed me when I didn't mate him after he bit me. If not for you, I'd have remained homeless. Alone. You've given me more than I've ever had."

"And taken away more than I could ever replace."

"Shut the fuck up."

His eyes narrowed.

"You *are* strong, Jared. I know it even if you don't because I can feel it here." I pounded a fist over my heart. "And because I've seen it with my own eyes. If I wasn't here I know you'd be able to step up and do whatever you needed to for this pack, but I am here, and I'm glad it's me."

I realized how much it might hurt me if I had to watch him do something that might taint his self- image or moral views. If I had to watch a darkness creep over his soul like the one that had already begun to creep over mine long before I had to kill Gregory.

It was a callusing of the spirit. A building of resilience. Born of understanding that in the many *many* years to come there would be trials you needed to face and you needed to face them head on without apologizing.

Jared looked doubtful at my admission, but he didn't argue.

"Does that mean you'll forgive me for being an ass and taking off on you?" he asked with a hopeful gleam in his eye. I knew he was just trying to get out of the conversation, and I was hesitant to let him, but when he threaded his fingers through mine, I gave in.

I licked my dry lips and tugged on his hand. "I forgave you about three seconds after you left, but I fully expect at least a week's worth of groveling."

His full lips tipped up at one corner and a short laugh escaped. "Done. How about I start with making coffee and breakfast. I have a couple of hours before I need to be getting to the quarry."

My stomach rumbled loudly at his suggestion. "Only if you make those banana pancakes."

"The ones with the chocolate sauce?"

I nodded, salivating already, and Jared chuckled. I could already feel his inner turmoil easing as we made our way back to camp.

The fire pit was just coming into view when my wolf sensed danger approaching. I tugged Jared to a stop and listened to the sounds of the forest. "Do you feel that?"

"I don't—"

"*Shh.*"

I closed my eyes, wondering if I should shift, my heart lurching into my throat. There was something...

My eyes snapped open.

"Seth," I growled before drawing on my wolf. I ran toward the east, following the faint sound of his approach. It was him. My wolf recognized the feel of his pack bond. But what was he doing out here? He should have been sleeping still.

My stomach twisted as I shifted and a yelp left my canine mouth as I barreled onward, heading straight for him.

Allie, came Jared's voice in my mind, his wolf right at my heels. *Where are you going?*

He must've heard or sensed Seth a moment later because his voice in my mind ceased. I howled, calling to my other mate in case we needed help, my chest tightening.

I couldn't explain it, but I just knew something was wrong. Seth was never up this early. Seth wouldn't be running toward pack camp from the east before five a.m. He just wouldn't. Not unless...

My eyes bugged wide as I caught sight of him in his wolf form, limping as he ran through the foliage. Archer at his side. He must have left his patrol station on the first ring to escort Seth in case he didn't make it. I skidded to a stop as our paths met, my wolf wrinkling its nose at a foreign smell clinging to his broken body.

What happened? I demanded, circling him as Clay found his way to us, churning up dirt as his claws scraped over the earth.

What's going on?

We were attacked, came Seth's reply as he bowed his head, his sides heaving and bloody saliva leaking from his jowls. *Just outside the third ring. We didn't even see them coming.*

My heart in a vise, I scanned the forest behind him, reeling, a million questions vying for dominance in my mind, but there was one I needed the answer to first. Before anything else.

Where's Destiny?

Seth's wolf whined, its sides squeezing in as his tail tucked low between his legs.

No.

Is she...

They took her.

Who took her? Jared growled, stamping a thick paw to the earth as his hackles rose and his upper lips curled back to reveal his canines. His white fur vibrating with malice to rival Clay's.

I don't know, Seth admitted with another whine, his face pained. I realized his rear right ankle was broken and had set improperly. He was mostly healed now though streaks of dried crimson still matted his fur, but that ankle would need to be rebroken before he could walk on it properly.

As much as I wanted to get him back to camp—get him properly cared for, that would just have to fucking wait.

Seth, I urged, not realizing that I'd laced the word with the authority of my alpha status. He buckled under the pressure of it, lowering into a bow.

I tried to ease up, hot breaths pushing out through my nostrils. *Was it witches?*

He lifted his head to meet my eyes, and I found a sadness there laced with so much guilt it made my stomach turn. *It was shifters. A foreign pack.*

Not Dante's? Clay demanded, but we already knew the answer to that. Dante was too much of a coward to try anything against us. He and his pack lived peacefully beyond the third ring of our territory to the northwest. Seth had come from the east.

No. I didn't recognize any of them.

I circled Seth again, picking up the foreign scent still clinging to his jet black fur. Clay and Jared joined me, committing the unique scent to memory.

I'm so sorry, Allie... Seth trailed off, practically shaking, and I couldn't tell if it was the pain or the guilt that brought it on. But if he thought he was in pain now, wait until Vivian...

Vivian.

A whine pushed up my throat and my eyes burned, making my wolf shake her head to try to rid herself of the sensation. Her mate had been fucking *taken*. Taken by a foreign pack. But why?

Why take her. Attacking another pack to try to gain new territory wasn't uncommon among shifters from what I'd learned, but this happened outside of our territory, and we had to assume they hadn't killed Destiny. Vivian would have felt it if her mate's life had been snuffed out. No matter the distance. But her fitful sleep last night now made a hell of a lot more sense.

Why take her? Did they plan on using her as ransom to gain some territory? Who the fuck were they?

My wolf snarled viciously as I made up my mind. There wasn't only one thing to be done. Get Destiny back. Retaliate. Retaliate strong and fast. Strike hard. Show whoever these fuckers were that we were the strongest pack in the eastern USA and we were *not* to be messed with.

How many were there?

I-I'm not sure. Maybe seven?

Think harder, I growled and Seth lowered his head, flinching away at my tone, but I was beyond keeping myself in control.

He paused, sealing his eyes shut to recall the information.

Eight, he finally said. *There were eight. I'm almost certain.*

Where.

He explained the location and Clay stepped forward, his gaze already set on the trees due east. *I know it. I can lead.*

He already knew what I intended and he was on board. Good. One less person to convince.

Get a team together, I shot at Jared. *Ten of our strongest and fastest. Fighters. Tell Charity I need her to bring in third ring patrol and triple patrols on the first two rings. I want everyone awake and ready in case anyone tries anything while we're gone.*

He hesitated, but only for a moment. I thought he might fight me on it, but his eyes narrowed to slits and he nodded. *Don't leave without me.*

Hurry.

He took off in a flash of white and vanished through the trees.

Archer, get him to the cabin and see to it that he gets some help setting that ankle.

The new pack member brushed against Seth's side,

getting him moving and giving him the ability to lean on him if needed. I watched them as they passed and cocked my head, considering Archer for the first time since he and his mate joined the pack no more than a couple of weeks ago now.

Since the pair of them arrived, our butcher had gone up in flames. Three shifters had gone missing, and the power lines to the quarry were cut. Now, one more had been taken. This one forcibly under attack.

Our food source. Our numbers.

Our income.

I met Clay's icy stare and let him in on my thoughts. His gaze darkened as my realization settled in his mind and his lips pulled back to reveal bared teeth.

You think this has something to do with them? No, I don't.

It was the truth. Archer and Callum came here seeking asylum and to live without being judged for their same sex bond. Why would they do anything to interfere with that? I'd never felt even the slightest animosity from them. I had to believe they were innocent, though you could bet your ass I'd still be looking into the possibility.

This next part was going to hurt to admit, but I'd only just promised Clay I wouldn't lie to him and there was one other shifter who'd recently rejoined the Forest Grove pack.

They aren't the only ones who joined recently...

I let the weight of that sink in for a moment before continuing, feeling the sinking in his gut as though it were in my own.

I'm not saying it's to do with her for certain, I hedged.

But—

But it fucking looks that way, he finished for me. *Dammit,* he growled, paws scraping against the ground in fury. *If it's her...fuck! If it's her, I'm going to—*

We don't know for sure yet, Clay.

A human howl of pain stole our attention and both of us turned our heads on a swivel toward camp a fraction of a second before we began running.

My chest ached as she howled again, this time it was her wolf crying out. Vivian had just found out her mate was taken. This was not fucking good.

We broke through the tree line and entered the main ring in front of the cabin just as Vivian lunged for Seth's throat, her sandy brown wolf sailing through the air from the front porch with jaws wide.

Stop! I commanded, but it was too late.

Seth didn't even try to move or to fight back as Vivian's jaws clamped on to the back of his neck and she tossed him like a doll toward the dead fire ring.

I raced forward, but Layla got there first, her dark eyes wide and wild as she put herself between her injured boyfriend and her best friend. Viv growled at her, snapping in her direction, but didn't move to attack Seth again. Her initial rage was already wearing off, being replaced by a bone deep fear that I could scent even from twenty yards away.

Others were gathering now, shifting to communicate with Seth and find out what was happening.

Viv, I called to her, pulling her attention from Seth and Layla and the growing crowd at their backs.

Vivian! I called again when she fought my demand.

She turned, her muscled legs trembling beneath her fur.

We're going after her, I promised. *Right now. I need to know if you can get your head straight. I can't have you with us if you're a loose cannon.*

Who took her? she demanded, her tongue slipping out between her bared teeth. Ridges forming on her snout at the force of her snarl. *Where is she?*

I shook my head, acid pooling in my gut. *We don't know. But we know where she was last. Jared is getting a group together. We're going after her. We will get her back.*

You can't stop me from coming, she snapped at me.

I can, I corrected her, hating myself for it but knowing that if she didn't at least try to calm down she'd be more of a liability than a help. She was always a firecracker, but right now she was a fucking nuclear bomb ready to explode. *Don't make me.*

Her snarls quieted and within another moment, she cracked, dissolving into agonizing whines that struck my own heart like blades. My throat burned as I closed the distance between us and put my snout to her neck, just being there for her for a second.

She's okay, right? Her voice slipped weakly into my mind. *She'll be okay?*

If she weren't, you would sense it. The severing of the bond wouldn't go unnoticed, Viv. She's alive. And as long as she's alive, we can bring her home.

I'm going to kill them, she admitted to me. *Anyone who touched her. Anyone who hurt her. I will* end *them.*

I know, I told her, imagining if it was one of my mates who were taken. The things I would do to the people responsible. I couldn't begrudge her that. *And we're going to help you.*

I sensed Clay approaching us as Layla shifted to help Seth inside, sending a glance our way as tears streamed freely down her cheeks. *I'm sorry,* she mouthed to me, and I gave a tiny nod of acknowledgement. She was staying behind, I gathered, and I would've made her even if she hadn't made the call herself.

Layla was smart. Lithe. Sly. But she wasn't even close to being the strongest of us. She was better off here.

Clay fixed Vivian with a hard cold stare as she drew away from our canine embrace. *Whoever is responsible for this will pay for their sins in blood,* he promised, aching internally as the cabin door closed behind Layla and one of his best friends. He lifted his head in a long howl, calling to Jared to let him know we were leaving and he'd better move his ass if they didn't want to wind up miles behind us.

Jared's returning howl told us he was already on his way back over from the other side of camp, and Clay turned tail and made for the tree line to the east, Viv and me on his heels.

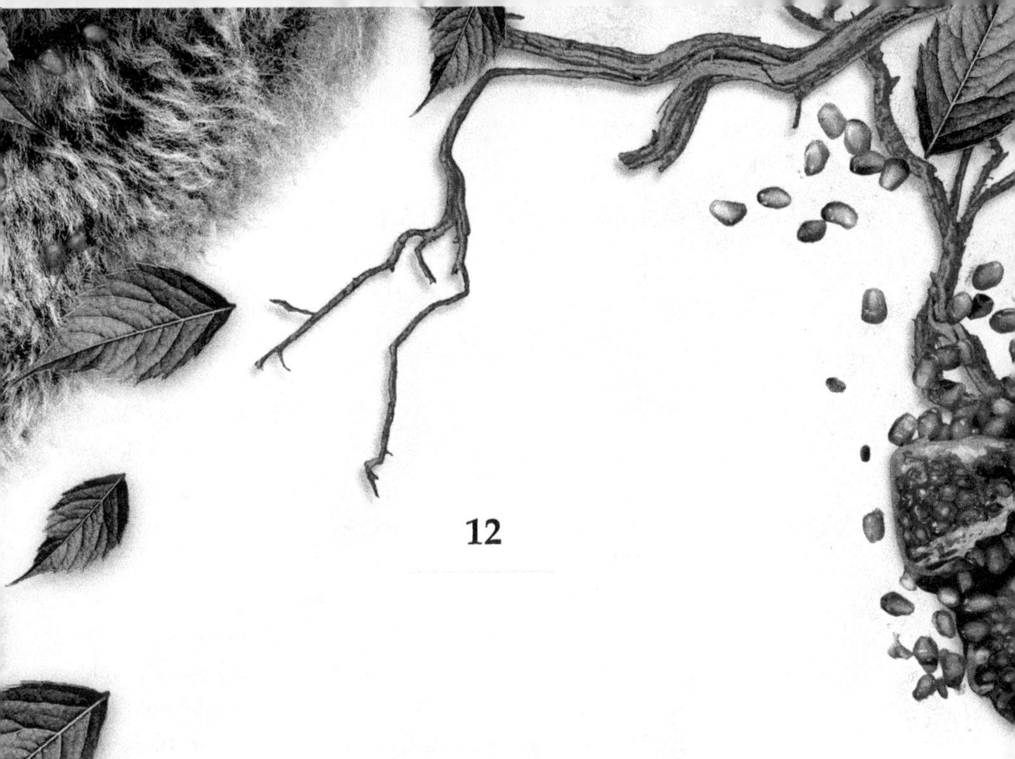

12

lay, Jared, Vivian, and I led the charge toward where the attack took place. It took a lot of willpower to keep my strides on par with those of the rest of the shifters accompanying us. Much like I felt Clay's urge to sprint ahead and scout for danger, the same desire twisted in my gut, tried to push my legs faster. But we needed to stay together. We were a group of twelve, which should be more than enough if we came upon the group of eight attackers along the way, but if we split up our odds would drastically decrease.

Almost there, Clay spoke in my thoughts. *Be ready.*

I sent the information out to the others through the alpha bond, and their returning growls of *ready, let's fucking do this shit,* and *bring it on,* sent shivers racing down my canine spine.

Vivian was the only one who remained silent, her brown eyes fixed ahead. I picked up Destiny's scent on the early morning breeze only a second before she did. I always thought Clay was the fastest of the pack besides me, but Vivian sprang forward like she'd been catapulted, churning up dirt and pollen in her wake as she sped on.

Clay and I shared a look before speeding to catch up with her. There was no use telling her to wait, she wouldn't listen, and I wasn't prepared to hold my will over her. Not now.

The rest of the pack hustled to gain on us as the tree line broke ahead, showing the cleared space of the backroad we usually took from Portland. It was paved about three quarters of the way, but then turned to a dirt road too bumpy for most to want to drive on. It made transporting goods to the edge of our territory easier, and also provided us a safe place to park the Jeep.

My nose wrinkled as I picked up the scent my guys and I had caught on Seth. It had been faint on him, but here, it was ripe, permeating the air and clinging to the earth. The very distinct smell of foreign wolves on our turf. Nearly as strong as the odor of spoiled meat.

A growl reverberated behind my breastbone as we launched onto the road a second behind Viv.

Her nose pressed to the earth as soon as we were clear of the trees, searching for her mate. The area was void of life, and I couldn't help feeling deflated even though I knew this would likely be the case. I'd half hoped they'd leave an emissary behind to negotiate terms, but even that hope had now been dashed.

The Jeep lay on its side in the middle of the road. The rear window smashed and its contents spread over the dirt. An entire fucking cow and enough bacon for at least a month sat spoiling under the still-rising sun. The red butcher paper torn and shredded. Chunks of ground beef and hunks of steak sprinkled all around like morbid confetti.

They hadn't taken it. By the look of it, they hadn't even eaten any of it, either. But their intent to destroy it was unquestionable, leading credence to my growing worry that the fire at Sal's butcher shop was no accident after all.

A couple of the pack shifted to help Jared right the Jeep as I ordered the others to spread out and find their exit trail. We needed to keep tracking them. They had a solid hour head start at this point and we were going to need to cover a lot of ground really fucking fast if we had any hope of catching up to them.

A pang shot through my gut at all the risk that could lead to, but I did my best to silence that part of me. If their trail led to another pack's territory, we would decide what to do when the time came. We couldn't cross into it without risking being slaughtered for trespassing. And I wouldn't send an emissary in, and there was no way Jared and Clay would let me enter alone. Though I could make them if I had to...

Just like I would have to force Vivian to back down if we did follow the trail to another pack's borders.

Fuck.

Let's just hope they haven't gotten that far yet and we can still head them off.

I followed my nose to the east, sticking close to Vivian as the pack spread out, but remained close enough to one another that no one would be blindsided by an attack.

This way, Viv hissed in my mind and I left the trail that had been going cold beneath my nose to follow hers, sending out a message to the others to come with us and leave the Jeep for now. Though I could feel that it pained Jared to leave her half busted in the middle of a road. Pained him and made him even more furious than he already was. That thing was his baby.

Hell, it was mine, too. Clay and Jared taught me how to drive in that car.

Jared? I called back, making sure he was following as Clay caught up, but I didn't sense him near.

Coming.

Hurry the fuck up, Clay shot back at him as we raced to the east, pausing every few miles to make sure we still had the trail right. Doubling back twice when we almost lost it.

Where the fuck are they taking her? Viv cried in my mind as the miles vanished beneath our feet and I was beginning to think we wouldn't be able to catch up before we lost the trail. The other issue being that we were getting *way* too far away from our own territory.

I don't know, Viv.

It wasn't safe to be in no-man's-land this long, and I was feeling the distance between myself and the others back at camp like a black void growing in my chest.

I needed to be there. To make sure no one else was hurt. No one else taken.

We couldn't keep going east forever.

Viv, seeming to sense my trail of thought growled through the pack bond, *I am* not *turning back, Allie. Don't you dare make me.*

I said nothing as we neared civilization, the sounds of tires on a freeway rushing in my ears. The trail led straight to it, and we slowed as we approached the edge of the forest, crouching low so as not to be seen.

You think they crossed it? Jared asked, and I'd just been considering the same, but it didn't make sense. Even in the dark hours of the morning there would still be traffic on this road. Not a lot maybe, but some. They wouldn't risk being seen. Unless...

A snarl ripped from Vivian's lips as she darted out from the cover of the forest and right into oncoming traffic. My heart squeezed in my chest, and the blood in my veins ran cold as she weaved through both directions of traffic, using her strong hind legs to sail over a car at the last second. A flurry of honking bombarded my senses, and I bared my teeth, calling back an order to stay there as I chased after her.

The southbound traffic was at a complete standstill because of the three car pileup Vivian had caused, and it was easy enough to launch myself over the two lanes of slow-moving traffic going northbound to get to the other side.

Someone screamed at the sight of me, and I cursed, hoping I was too fast for them to get much of an eyeful. Rule number fucking one—do *not* be seen by humans. And I just broke it.

I flew headlong into the trees at the other side of the road, snarling Vivian's name in my mind as I picked up her trail and followed her back into the shadows.

Her frantic thoughts reached me a second later, and I tried to rein in my fury at her carelessness as I slowed to a walk and strode to her.

It's gone, her panicked voice skated through my thoughts. *It's gone. The trail is gone. What the... No! NO!*

She pressed her nose to the earth, to the surrounding trees, searching for any trace of her mate's scent. I guessed she was also using the bond to try to sense the distance, or at the very least the direction they went, but her frantic thoughts told me what she couldn't. She couldn't feel Destiny anywhere.

Allie! Allie, help me! Help me find it. I have to find it! Viv...

Don't just stand there, it has to be here. We just lost it.

She rushed to the right and then the left, scraping her paws furiously over bushes and digging beneath a log to try to find any traces. She wouldn't find any though. It was exactly as I'd feared and in another minute, once she'd calmed down, she'd understand it, too.

Vivian, their trail went cold at the roadside. No. No it didn't! It's here, we just have to...

She lifted her head, her wide eyes meeting mine as heavy breaths ballooned and compressed through her strong ribcage.

It has to be...

I shook my head.

No, Viv. Their trail died at the roadside because they— Don't say it!

I didn't want it to be true any more than she did,

but there wasn't even a lick of their scent anywhere on this side of the road and that could only mean one thing.

They knew we'd track them, Viv. They ran to the highway and they got into a car, or several cars and they—

Shut up!

We won't stop looking, I promised her, my heart splintering apart at the look in her eyes. At the tremble in her legs. *We'll have search parties out day and night. We still might pick up her scent, or the scent of the foreign pack someone outside our territory. We can still find her.*

Like we've found Luke? She barked, her hackles rising and tail going erect. *Like we found Trey and fucking Todd?*

Her words stung like a slap to my soul, but I took it standing. I deserved it.

We can—

Save it, Allie. I'm going to go back to where the trail started and see if there were any other routes.

I nodded, jerking my chin back toward the highway still buzzing with honking and now, the sound of sirens approaching in the distance. *But we go around.*

She at least had the decency to look guilty at that, and took off to the north, where I remembered there being a wildlife crossing tunnel beneath the highway that we may be able to sneak through if we were stealthy.

No trail here. They took a car. We're going the long way round, I shot back across the road to my guys. *Meet us at the exit.*

Careful, came Jared's reply.

Heading there now, came Clay's, and I raced to follow Vivian back up the highway to go back and do this all over again. I had a horrible sinking feeling that it would only lead to the exact same result.

It was another four hours before Vivian relented, realizing that the only trail was the one leading to the highway, and that it did, in fact, die there. With no trace left to follow.

The pack members who joined us were winded, hell, we all were, and we took it slow on the way back to camp. We wandered in a long arc around the third ring, triple checking to make sure there was no trace of the foreign scent anywhere.

We'd already come to the conclusion that the group responsible for the disappearances of Luke, Trey, and Todd was the same as the one who took Destiny and likely also burned down Sal's and cut the power to the quarry. There *should* have been some trace of them, but it'd rained twice since then. Whatever might've been there had likely washed away by now.

I had to wonder if they were using the rain to their advantage. Striking when they knew it would erase their trail.

So many random pieces of fractured thoughts and ideas churned in my mind that I almost missed it. A scent I recognized. Faint. But I was almost certain of it. I slowed and Clay slowed with me as I went to investigate the scent, giving the green light for the others to continue. We had been breaking off from the main formation often to investigate potential scents, so it wasn't a big draw of attention, and I was grateful because if I were right...

Clay had to have scented it, too, because he trailed me silently as we traced it up toward Glenwood, a town just inside of our third ring.

Find something? Jared's voice slipped down the line of our bond, and I could already sense him breaking off from the others to join us.

Stay with the pack, I told him, not wanting to leave them too thin. *It's not their trail. It's something else. Just checking it out real quick.*

Clay grunted unhappily beside me as we sped up, both of us on edge as we followed the thread of his sister's scent up a hill and peered over it, breathless as we took in what lay beneath.

About 100 yards away, through the sparse trees, lay a quiet depot with a bus idling near the exit. A few passengers disembarked, while a few others stepped on, headed to new destinations. We waited until the bus left and saw the shopkeep flip a sign in a small window near the entrance. I couldn't make out what it said, but judging by the time, it was likely some form of 'back after lunch.'

The straggly young man got into a beat up Camry and sped away, blasting rap music a moment later, leaving the place utterly desolate save for some warring chipmunks near the trash bin and a swarm of bees congregating around a mess of yellow flowers poking through the cement at the base of a phone booth.

It's her, right? I asked even though I was almost certain already. I just needed him to confirm it.

Yes.

I had about a thousand things I wanted to say. Questions I wanted to ask. But I didn't. There could be a perfectly good reason why Sam's scent could be lingering out here. She went for regular runs. Even I came out this far some days when I really wanted to stretch my legs. But why risk getting this close to a bus depot. Sniffing the air, I could tell her scent was stronger here than it should've been.

Not enough that most of the pack would have even picked up on it. But between Clay's nose and mine, there was no doubt. Even from a distance, I knew she'd been here.

Her scent had been on the wind, but not on the ground, which meant that she didn't come to the bus depot the way we did. She likely came from the other direction, which would make sense since that was closer to camp. But for her scent to be lingering this strongly just on the air, it meant that she'd either spent a great deal of time here recently, or she came here a lot.

We should get back, Clay grumbled, and I risked a look in his direction, taking in the set of his jaw. The worry in his cold stare.

Yeah, I replied, able to stave off my curiosity with a promise to bring this up again as soon as we were alone. As soon as our thoughts weren't at risk of being heard by other shifters. It was generally easy to keep what we liked to ourselves, but sending thoughts as telepathic speech to only a single shifter instead of all those nearby was an art form I hadn't quite perfected yet.

Clay nipped at my heels when I didn't move, stuck in my own thoughts like a stick in the mud.

Move, Allie, he nudged, and I yipped, taking off at breakneck speed back to our search party while a new worry took root in my bones.

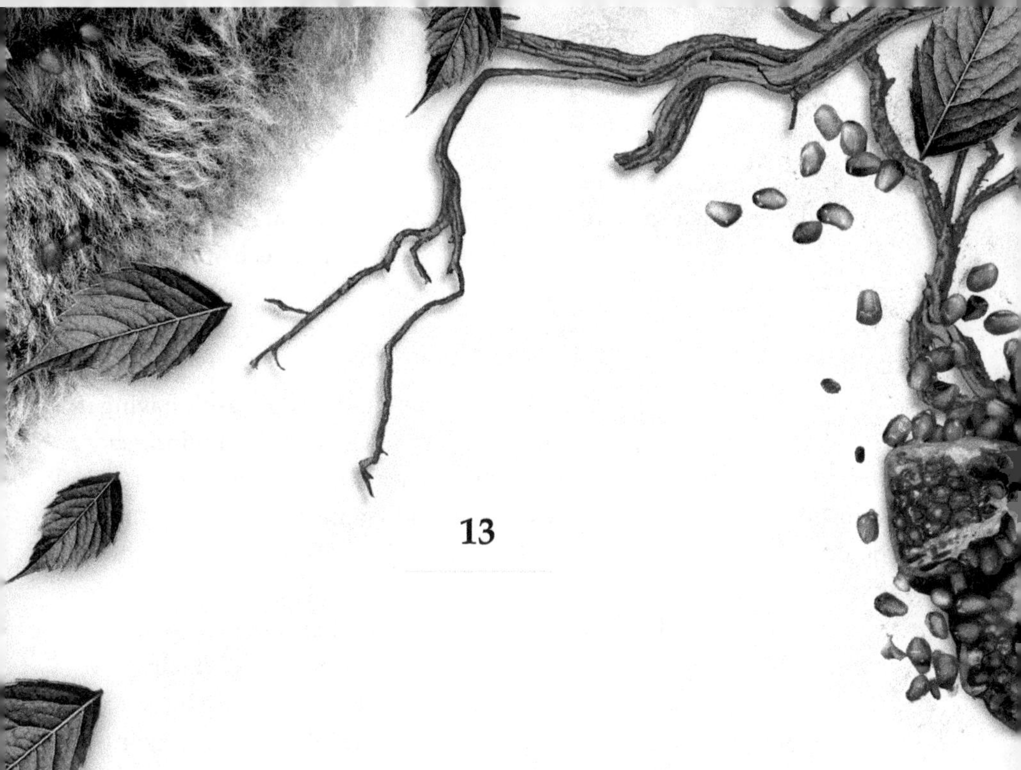

13

"What's taking so long?" Vivian demanded, pacing the length of the living room in the main cabin. "If they aren't ready to go soon, then I'll just go myself."

She seemed like she might shift back at any second, but after the long search and taking her anger out on a few trees at the edge of camp, I had to trust that she wouldn't. At least she would be able to hold off to get herself back outside if she did. Not that I was all that worried about broken lamps or furniture right now, but I didn't need any more shit on my plate than was already piled there.

"They need to get a full group, Viv," I rationed. "We can't leave camp unprotected, and the shifters who were out with us all morning need to rest. We're pulling our guys back from helping Sal. Half will stay here to bolster patrol and half will go with you on another search."

She groaned, pushing her fingers into her short blonde hair and yanking on it from the roots so hard I thought she may actually rip it all out, but I stopped her. Stepping it to place my hands on her arms and gently tug her arms back down. "They'll be back any minute," I promised. "Just be patient. I can't have you going out after her alone."

"I'll go with her," Seth offered from where he was lying on the couch with Layla kneeling on the floor near his head. "My ankle is almost fully healed already. I can run on it."

Vivian's upper lip curled and her hands clenched at her side. Just the sound of his voice was setting her off. "If you had been watching her back like you were supposed to, this wouldn't be fucking happening!"

"Viv!" Layla snapped harshly, her bright eyes darkening at her best friend. "That's not fair, and you know it."

"It's okay, La La," Seth tried to interrupt, but Layla wasn't having it. She stood in a huff, her face pinching. I didn't have to be a mind reader to see that she was having a difficult time walking the thin line between wanting to be there for her best friend and wanting to stand up for her boyfriend. In the end, though, Layla would always side with whatever she deemed to be the 'right' thing. She was good like that.

"No, it's not," she told Seth before turning her attention back to a still-fuming Vivian. "There were eight of them, Viv. Eight against *two*. Are you telling me you would've held up any better than Seth?"

Her jaw ground in response, and I winced, thinking she was going to crack a tooth.

"I hate that this happened. I hate that she's gone, too, but don't put this all on him, Viv. It isn't fucking fair, and you know it."

She inhaled sharply and seemed to make a decision. "I'll go with you for the next search." She spun to glare at Seth. "And *you* will go back to your cabin and take a goddamned nap so you can heal properly."

Seth opened his mouth like he meant to argue the point, but Layla's brows rose in challenge, and he shut his mouth before uttering a word.

Layla could be scary like that. I didn't blame him for not wanting to cross her. She gave a cold shoulder like no other.

Vivian's lower lip trembled and Layla's rigid facade crumbled as she sighed and closed the gap between them, pulling Vivian into a violent hug that she didn't return at first. But as her tears began to fall, her arms lifted to wrap around Layla and her fists clenched into the dark fabric of her long black dress. "It's okay," Layla cooed, rubbing her palm up and down Viv's back. I went to join them and Layla pulled me in so I had an arm around her and one around Viv.

We held Vivian until her sobs quieted, and I had to choke back tears of my own at my friend's anguish.

Layla sniffled as she pulled away just as the guys entered the cabin. They froze in the entryway, clearly wondering if they should turn around and go back the way they came to give us some more privacy. I shook my head to tell them it was okay to come in, and Jared cleared his throat.

Their bare chests glistened with sweat from the run to get the guys back from Sal's, and Clay wrapped a hand around the back of his neck, tipping it into a loud crack. With all the running they'd done already today, I wouldn't doubt they would both be sore as shit by morning.

"They're packing up," Jared told us. "Should be back in the next twenty or so."

Vivian stiffened. "Twenty minutes?"

She didn't seem fucking happy, scrubbing a hand over her face.

Sam entered behind the guys a second later, her dark hair slicked back from her face in a severe ponytail that made her face look even more gaunt than it had when she'd arrived.

"Where have you been?" I blurted, unable to help myself. The suspicion clear in the inflection of my voice. I couldn't remember seeing her this morning when all that shit went down. Or last night for that matter.

Her face screwed up into a scowl at my tone, and she glanced at Clay as though he might stick up for her, but he only stepped away from his sister. Not even bothering to look her way.

"I was in my cabin," she said with a shrug. "I was out late for a run last night and slept through the commotion this morning. I came to see if I could help."

I pinched the bridge of my nose and tried to shuck off my animalistic urge to jump down her throat. I needed to be smart. If she actually had anything at all to do with this and we let on that we suspected something, we could spook her. She would take off before we could get the intel we needed to get our missing pack mates back.

Be smart, Allie.

"No," I ground out. "We're good here. Maybe see if Hazel needs a hand in the garden, though. Our meat order was destroyed in the attack. It'll be fucking potato pie again tonight."

"Right," she said with a gulp. "Sure."

She left a moment later and Vivian fell hard into the armchair opposite Seth, who was sitting up, testing his weight on his injured ankle.

"I can't just sit here," Vivian lamented, dropping her head into her hands. "I have to keep looking. Every minute we waste, she could be getting further away. She could be getting hurt." Her voice broke on the last word, and I realized something I should've from the start.

Vivian wasn't going to quit. She never had at anything in her entire life, and she wasn't about to with this, either. Especially not this.

She was going to go off alone if no one would go with her or if there was a lull between search parties. She was going to get herself taken or killed. She was going to run herself into an early grave.

I could hardly blame her, but I couldn't let that happen, not when I had the power to ensure it didn't.

"Viv," I said, stepping over to the armchair and bending into a crouch. I set my hands on her knees, and she dropped hers from her face to look at me.

Her dead stare pierced my soul, and I hardened myself against the ugly emotions wreaking havoc in my core. "I need you to promise me you won't go looking for Destiny alone."

I held her stare, even as it soured against me. "I can't promise you that, Allie."

I sighed, closing my eyes against what needed to be done as I drew on that well of authority deep in the chasm of my soul. The power of the alpha flashed through my eyes as I opened them again, fused to the sound of my voice. "If they took her for ransom, they'll be sending someone with the terms of her release. We need to be smart about this, Viv. We'll keep searching, but it might take some time—"

"I won't stop looking for her. You can't ask me to do that."

"I'm not," I argued. "I'm asking you to be fucking smart about it."

Her gaze hardened, and I knew that it didn't matter what I said. If she felt like she needed to, she wouldn't hesitate before going out after Des alone. She was leaving me no choice...

"You will not go after her alone," I commanded, releasing my physical hold on her in favor of one much deeper. Using all the alpha energy I'd drawn on, I let it flow through the pack bond and bind her to my will.

"*Allie.*" Vivian growled, and I could feel her fighting it, like a mental game of tug-o-war she was destined to lose.

"I'm sorry, Viv. I won't lose you, too."

She got up and stormed past me, pushing into my shoulder as she went with a bruising force. She cursed under her breath as she shoved through Jared and Clay at the door and shifted less than a second after she was through it, sending up a howl at the afternoon sun.

"Was that necessary?" Layla asked gently and guilt piled onto my shoulders, weighing down my already heavy as fuck soul.

"You know it was," I replied and Layla gave a sad nod, brushing her long black hair back to tuck it behind one ear.

"I'll go see if I can try to get her to eat something before the next search party goes out."

I stalked to the kitchen and pulled out the last bag from my jerky stash in the back of the top cupboard. I'd gone through the whole damned pile over the last few weeks, passing it out to members of the pack on patrol who needed it most. "Here," I said, tossing it to Layla, who caught it with ease before giving me a tight- lipped smile and leaving.

I sank onto a barstool at the counter and resisted the sudden desire to smash my forehead into the marble surface at the impossibility of it all. I groaned loudly and Seth, perhaps sensing that it was time for him to scram, stood on his good leg and hopped to the door.

"You need help getting back to your cabin, man?" Jared asked, opening the door for him.

"Nah. I'm good," he said as he went outside and was immediately bombarded with one of Layla's trademark screeches for walking on his own.

Clay shut the heavier wooden door behind him before both my mates came to join me in the kitchen.

Jared rubbed my back while Clay leaned over the counter opposite me, his face a stormy mask that made me wonder what was going on behind those sharp as glass eyes.

"I should probably go check on things at the Quarry," Jared said, breaking the silence. "Call all the guys back to camp for now. There's no sense in them being there while there's no power to work."

"What, so that whoever took out the power can do worse while it's unguarded?" Clay asked, incredulous, and I had to admit, he was right.

Jared chewed his lower lip, realizing his mistake. He was usually the thinker of the three of us, but I couldn't blame him for not thinking straight right now. None of us were. It was a good thing we had each other to fill in the gaps where needed.

"Clay's right. You should go check on things there but leave the crew and tell them to be on high alert and to stick together. We can't risk the Quarry, the pub isn't enough on its own to keep us all afloat."

"Speaking of," Clay grunted. "With Destiny…gone…I'll need to train up another bartender. And we should probably double security there, too."

I nodded, agreeing, and then shivering as my blood chilled at the realization that Clay was talking as though Destiny wouldn't be back anytime soon. I couldn't believe that, even if all the signs pointed that way. I wouldn't.

"Before either of you leave, there's something we need to talk about."

They waited for me to go on, and I saw the flicker in Clay's gaze that told me he knew what I would say and he was bracing himself against it.

"Clay and I caught Sam's scent out near Glenwood," I said before I could change my mind. "It was on the air. We tracked it to the old bus depot there."

"What was she doing out there?"

"Maybe nothing," I admitted, keeping a wary eye on Clay as I explained things to Jared. "Maybe something. I'm not sure, but I'd be lying if I said I didn't think it was a bit suspicious."

"You think she's been taking a bus out of town?"

I shook my head. "I honestly don't know. But it would allow her to leave our territory unnoticed. Her scent would die near the bus depot inside of our third ring, and if she traveled back and forth through the same spot then…"

"Then it would seem like she never left."

"But if she was going to meet with a foreign pack, we'd know," Clay said, not so much argument as a statement of fact. "We'd scent them on her."

"Not if she were careful. If she's half as good of a tracker as you, she would know how to cover their scent."

"Not well enough that I wouldn't catch the stink," he bit back.

Jared stood quietly for a moment, and I could sense his unease ramping up within him, quickly morphing into hot, savage sort of hatred, fueled by a feeling of betrayal he knew far too well.

"What do we do?" Jared asked in a dangerous timbre, licking his lips like he wished he could taste Sam's blood on them.

Clay pushed off from the counter and stood, towering over us as he rolled his shoulders back and set his jaw. "I'll camp out near the depot in case she goes back there. She's here most of the day so she has to be going there at night. I'll cover my tracks and stay far enough away and downwind so she won't scent me."

That could work.

"I'll go with you," I decided. "I'm not going to fucking sleep anytime soon, anyway."

"I could—"

"No." I stopped Jared before he could finish. "I need you here. I need her and everyone else to think I'm asleep upstairs with you. I can mask my scent with Clay's to go into town, and we can take the Chevelle to Glenwood and go on foot from there." The pan began to take shape in my mind, accounting for any possibility of error. "She won't scent us as easily in our human forms."

"You should stay," Clay argued. "I can do this myself.

It might not be safe."

"Which is exactly why I won't let you go alone. And also why it needs to be me. I'm the strongest. Besides, we don't even know what we'll find, if anything. If I send someone else with you then the whole camp will be talking. They already don't trust her, imagine if they knew we suspected she had something to do with this, too?"

He paled.

They'd fucking eat her alive.

"Why not just confront her?" Jared asked, a crease forming between his brows.

I explained to him how she could get spooked and take off and how we couldn't risk that—not with Destiny and the others on the line.

"If she has anything to do with this, then we need whatever information she has. It might be the only way we can get them all back."

"I can think of other ways to get information..." Jared argued and I saw malice flash in his amber eyes like flames and an image of Gregory, bloody and cold at my feet sprang into my head, making me cringe.

Surprisingly, Clay didn't say a word against the idea, though I could feel his stress like an elastic band pulled taut to the point of snapping.

"No," I shook my head. "That's off the table."

This was Clay's sister we were talking about. His flesh and blood. We had to give her the benefit of the doubt, at least for now. Until we had some form of proof of her intentions. If we got it, though, all bets were off. That bitch was going *down*.

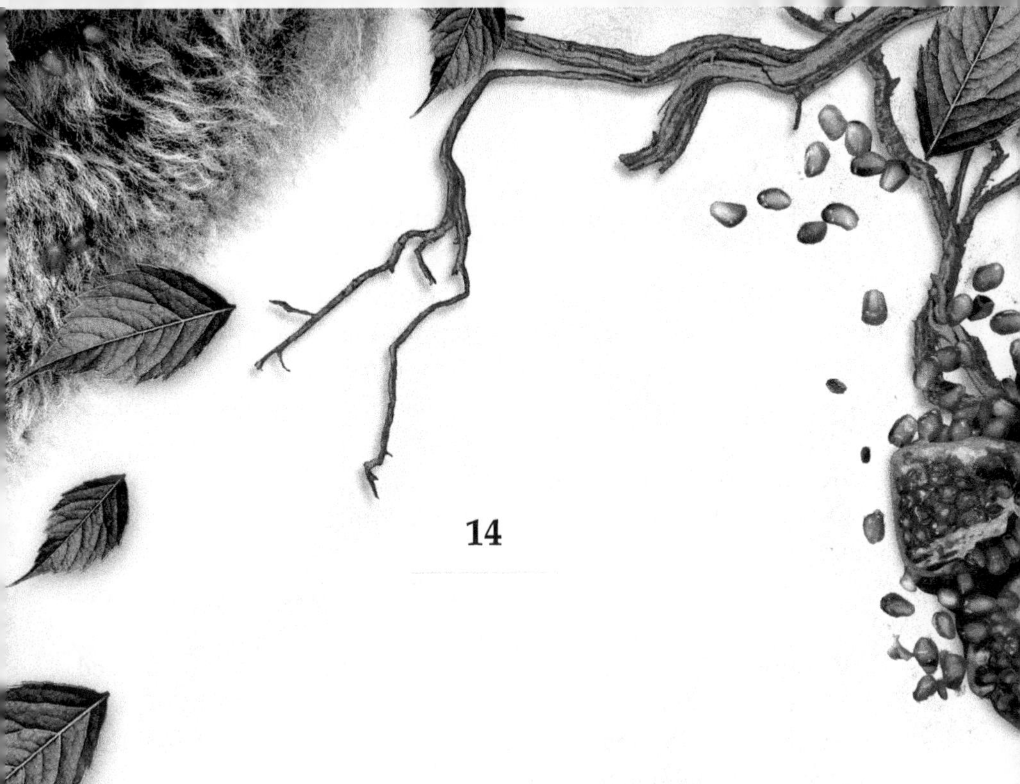

<h1 style="text-align:center">14</h1>

By the time we made it to the top of the hill looking down over the quiet bus depot in the distance, it was full dark. Just like we'd planned it. We settled into the shadows beneath the bottom branches of a tall pine tree, nestling in against the trunk to wait.

I pulled my small pack from my back and set it on my lap, drawing out a bottle of water for a drink after the hike out here. We'd been very careful to carve a path keeping downwind of the bus depot, and we'd driven in as closely as we could to reduce our trail just in case.

There was still the possibility that Sam would scent us, even with all the precautions, but we had to stay optimistic. This was the only possible lead we had so far, and I didn't want it to pan out almost as much as I *did* want it to.

I had Jared keeping a wary eye on Archer and Callum, and the entire pack now knew to be on the lookout for witches, and we'd found nothing suspicious with either. That left Sam. And if she weren't to blame for any of this, then we had to start from ground zero and pray one of the search parties picked up the scent of the foreign pack again.

Vivian was pushing them to go further each time, and I let her, for the most part, knowing we would need to widen our net if we were going to find anything. But it didn't make me any less uneasy to think that the search parties were too far away for us to be able to get to them if something were to happen. At least not before it would inevitably be too late.

Clay sniffed in my direction, distracted momentarily by the scent leaking out through my pack. "What'd you bring? Is that...donuts?"

I grinned, peeling back the zipper to reveal a pack of the powdery white donut holes he loved, a thermos of coffee, and binoculars. "What's a stakeout without donuts, right?"

He smirked despite the pent up tension that'd been building inside of him since this morning. Since long before that if we were being honest.

"You think we're downwind enough?" I asked as I popped open the plastic packaging and passed him a donut.

He turned it in his fingers, as though he wasn't really sure he wanted it. But in the end, hunger won out. The potato pies that we'd had for dinner might have temporarily filled the void in our stomachs, but they did little to sate our hunger.

These would help get us through the night.

I took a big bite of one myself, and Clay followed, shoving the entire thing in his mouth in one bite, leaving a smear of white powder just below his lower lip.

Without thinking, I leaned over and brushed it away, kissing the spot where it'd been and tasting the sugary sweetness on my lips.

He dropped his head, his brows pinching.

"She might just like running out this way," I attempted to reassure him, but the sentiment fell flat. He knew how I felt just like I knew how he felt. Clay knew I didn't trust his sister. Hadn't since the moment she'd arrived. But he also knew I was trying my best to. "We might feel like total idiots when this night is over."

He swallowed hard, swiping the back of his hand over his mouth and reaching for the thermos. "Yeah," he said solemnly. "Maybe."

We settled into a tense silence as we watched the sleepy little bus depot down below, listening for sounds of approach. Waiting to see a flash of dark fur passing beneath a streetlamp.

"When did you say the last bus is?" Clay asked after two buses came and went without picking up a single passenger, though each dropped one off.

"Midnight. There's a red-eye that goes from here to Portland."

Clay tugged his phone from his pocket and checked the screen. There was still another hour or so until then.

The minutes seemed to pass as though each their own hour, the time ticking down to midnight. And with each one, Clay grew even more tense. His muscles straining. Veins popping on his wrists and in his temple. I had to erect a wall to block the flow of his discomfort from reaching me through the mate bond.

I had no idea how he was managing to hold himself in human form with all that pent up anger and stress filling him to the brim. Sighing, I scooched closer to the big fucker, pressing myself against his side and shivering a little at his warmth. The night wasn't all that cold. In fact, it was the perfect temperature for my wolf. But for my human flesh...well let's just say a sweater might've been a good idea.

Clay grunted at the chill of my bare arms and tugged me closer, wrapping his big arms around me with a sigh of his own. "How you're always this cold, I'll never understand," he grumbled to himself. "Wolves are supposed to run hot. In wolf form and out of it. It's unnatural."

A quiet laugh pressed against my sealed lips as I tried to remain quiet, and I gave my head a little shake before resting it on his shoulder. "What about me has ever been normal?"

"Fair enough."

I inhaled his spicy scent, finding it lacked the signature undercurrent of engine grease and orange hand scrub that it once had. He was so busy between the pub and the pack that he hardly spent any time working on bikes anymore. I wondered if he missed it. I knew I did.

Hell, we hadn't ridden in ages, either.

"Hey, you remember that time a couple of winters ago when we decided to ditch camp for the night?"

His chest rumbled with an almost laugh in reply. "You mean when we had to spend the night in that cave up north because of the storm and you almost died of hypothermia?" he replied, mostly teasing, but even to this day there was a tension in his voice when he recalled it. He'd been so worried, even if he had put a brave face on for me. "How could I forget? I'd had to hunt down wood for a fire to keep you warm in a fucking blizzard."

"And you kept the fire going for hours with damp wood somehow. We reeked of smoke for weeks after that."

I didn't mention the other part. How after I'd stop shaking so much and Clay's fire and body heat had started to warm my bones, we'd turned to *other* methods of keeping warm until the storm passed and we could start the journey home.

We were stuck there for two days, and Jared had been frantic trying to find us, but between the storm and how far we'd accidentally wandered, there'd been no hope of that.

Jared had been so pissed at Clay. He hadn't realized it had been my idea to go off for the night with my other mate. It wasn't my fault a storm came unannounced to ruin my plans.

"We sure did," Clay said, squeezing me tight. "It was stupid. I never should've agreed to take off like that. I don't know what got into me."

"I do," I teased. "You just can't say no to me."

He barked a disapproving sound, but didn't deny it. Once, he had no problem denying me anything. And he definitely never hesitated to tell me just what he thought when I had a particularly stupid idea, but when push came to shove, I knew I could convince him to go along with just about anything. He knew it, too, though he would never admit it.

Clay stiffened as the sound of a bus engine rumbled down the road, and we separated as we watched it enter the depot, eyes peeled for any sign of a dark wolf or a black-haired girl.

"You see anything?" Clay asked in a hushed tone, leaning forward to army crawl closer to the edge of the dugout-like space beneath the tree.

"No. Not yet."

If I shifted, I might've been able to sense her, but then there would be too great of a chance of her sensing me, too. Not worth the risk. I pulled the binoculars out of the bag and put them to my eyes, lowering myself next to Clay until the smell of cold dirt filled my nose. While in human form, our eyesight was heightened, just like the rest of our senses, but the distance we needed to keep from the depot was a stretch even for my twin soul eyes.

I scanned the area, starting from the tree line cozying up to the western side of the depot and all the way through the platform and in every nook and cranny. I saw nothing amiss.

Once again, no passengers got on the bus when it finally pulled to a stop against the platform, but two did get off. I scrutinized them with the binoculars, but they were clearly human. A younger couple with tattoos who grabbed guitars from the compartment beneath the bus as they departed, walking away up the road as they chatted.

We waited with bated breath as the bus's air brakes hissed and the doors closed. "She didn't come." I whispered, more to myself than for Clay, but he answered anyway.

"Doesn't mean she still won't."

"That was the last bus," I muttered as it pulled away and disappeared around the back of the building in the direction of the main road.

Clay ground his teeth, and I could tell by the faraway look in his eyes that he was thinking hard about something. His blue eyes flared with the glow of his wolf, and I reached out to rub a hand up his back.

"Hey, we can stay. Might as well wait out the night to see—"

"Shh!" he hissed a second later, tensing under my hand, and my heart lurched into my throat as I followed his line of sight. A flash of movement caught my eye in the shadowy channel between bus terminals, and I pressed myself into the dirt, putting the binocular back to my face, barely daring to breathe for fear that I'd be heard.

A sick feeling made my throat slick with the acrid taste of bile as I spotted her. It was hard to be sure at first that it was her, but as the lonely streetlamp caught her in its glow, I became violently certain of it.

My wolf growled within, immediately battering at my defenses, wanting to assert her alpha dominance over Sam without the need for any further proof.

She peered around the depot as she made her way on bare feet down the platform in nothing but a long t- shirt. One that I recognized as Clay's. That only served to stoke the flames of my rage, and my upper lip curled back. Clay curled a clammy fist around my arm, silently urging me back into silence.

I clenched my teeth hard enough to crack one as I watched, white knuckle grip unfaltering on the binoculars as I recited what I was certain were lies to calm me down.

This doesn't mean she's guilty. This doesn't mean anything. She didn't get on the bus.

She might just like hanging out at vacant bus depots in the middle of the night.

Bull-fucking-shit.

The glow of Sam's eyes flashed our way as she scanned the area one last time before closing herself inside of the phone booth. She dropped a few coins into the slot and dialed. The glass panes of the booth were so clouded from age that I couldn't see her very well.

Clay cursed as she began to speak. I listened as hard as I could, but wasn't able to pick out anything discernible. I pulled back from the binoculars for a second to look at Clay, wondering if he could hear.

He shook his head sharply, and I went back to watching, grinding my teeth to dust.

She shouted something angrily that sounded like *'fine?'* Or maybe *'mine?'* It was too smothered by the glass encasement of the phone booth to tell. Right after she shouted, she slammed the receiver down and shoved out the doors of the booth, stamping back toward the shadows where she came from.

I opened my mouth to ask Clay something, but he clamped a hand tightly over my lips to stop me and put a finger to his own to silence me. I realized only a few seconds after he did how the wind had shifted directions. He gently nudged my head toward the earth and began quietly rubbing dirt into my silvery hair, pressing both of us to the ground as we carefully slid backward to get beneath the cover of the wide branches of the pine. Between it and the dirt, she shouldn't be able to scent us.

My scalp itched as we waited for what felt like ages before finally daring to move or speak. She had to be far enough away by now that it was safe.

"You think she scented us?" I mouthed more than said, just in case, and Clay ran a hand through his own dirt-clogged black hair and blew out a breath.

"Don't know. Doubt it, though. She looked distracted."

His eyes darkened.

"Do you think we can star-69 the call she made?"

"I doubt that works on a payphone, and if we go anywhere near it and she comes back—"

"She'll scent us." He nodded.

I mulled over the possibilities for a few minutes before asking the question I knew both of us wanted the answer to. "Who do you think she was calling?"

Clay began gathering our things back into my small pack with a grim expression. "I don't know, but we need to find out."

"This may not even mean anything."

He looked at me like I might be daft, and I had to admit, it sounded stupid even to my own ears. There was something shady going on— there was no denying it. But was it regular shady or the really bad kind?

Clay was right, we needed to find out.

"We know she's been here more than once. For all we know she comes every damned night. She'll be back. We just have to be ready."

I lifted a brow as Clay reached out a hand to help me stand and brushed his fingers roughly over the top of my head, scattering bits of dirt back to the earth before moving to take my jaw into his grip, tipping my head up.

"How?" I asked, genuinely wondering what the actual fuck we could do here without blowing our cover or resorting to the interrogation Jared craved.

"We bug the phone booth," Clay said like it was the simplest thing in the world.

"Are you serious?"

He dropped his hand and turned to head back the way we'd come from the Chevelle, making me scurry to follow him.

"I know a guy," he muttered, careful of where he was stepping to avoid making any unnecessary sounds. I tried to follow his footsteps, but still managed to sound like a drunk elephant by comparison. For a guy so damned massive, I'd never understand how he could be so deadly silent.

"How very mysterious." I rolled my eyes. "Care to elaborate?"

"His name's Joe. He's the private investigator I hired to follow Devin when we ran him out of town."

I shuddered at the reminder of that psycho, remembering the map and images I'd discovered hidden in Clay's workshop. How he told me that he had needed to make sure that Devin had truly left. That he wasn't ever coming back. To make certain I was safe. It was the only compromise he could make with himself to keep his wolf from going full protector and hunting the bastard down.

Devin had wound up several states over. He was probably beating up on another girl these days and it made me sick to think that, but it was the truth. The madness I'd seen in his eyes the night he turned me, and many nights before that one couldn't be cured.

The best anyone could hope was for that fucker to get hit by a bus.

"You're still in contact with him? I thought you cut him loose a few years ago?"

"I did, but I still have his info. He said he could get me anything I needed. I'll have him bug it so Sam won't recognize his scent."

"How soon do you think he could do that?"

"For the right price?" Clay asked with a raised brow, considering. "I think I could have him do it by tomorrow."

I chewed my lower lip, imagining another night without finding Destiny. Without Luke, or Trey, or Todd. I sealed my eyes against a lancing pain in my chest and nodded.

"Okay. Call him. Do it now. We don't have any time to waste."

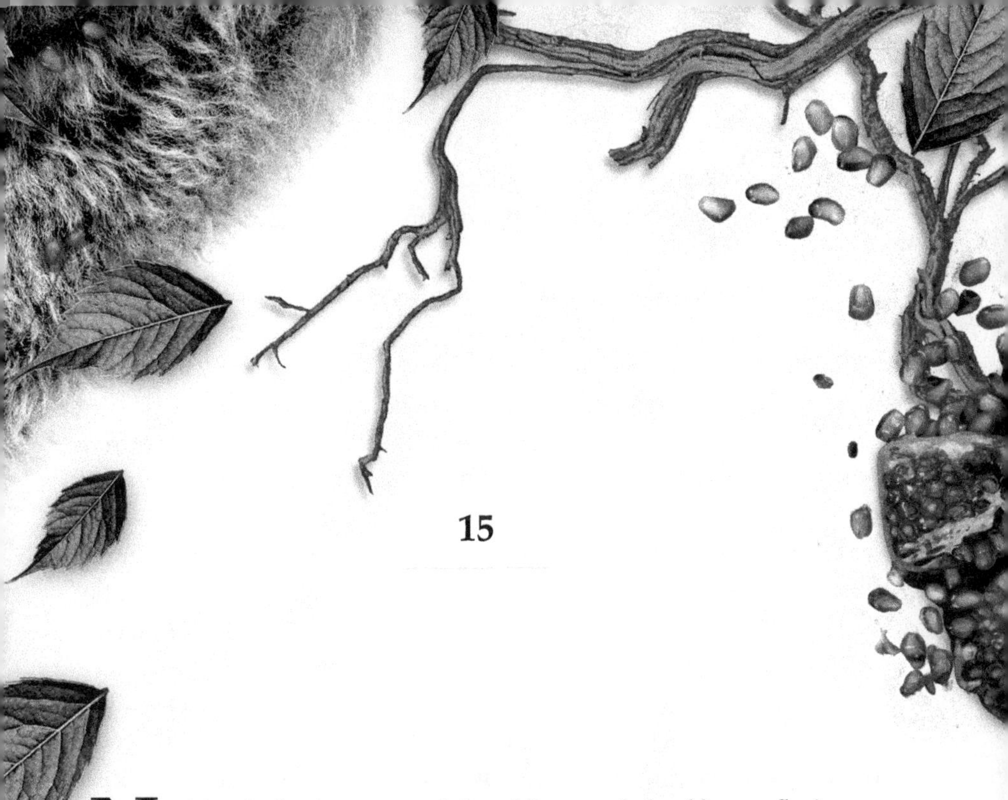

15

"Nothing," Charity reported, head bent and cheekbones flaring as she clenched her jaw. "Not a fucking thing."

Vivian stalked away from the search party, going to return to her cabin with a black cloud hanging over her head. She hardly left her cabin anymore, unless it was to join a search. She ate in there. Slept in there. I didn't think she'd showered at all since Destiny vanished.

I sighed and gripped Charity's shoulder, trying to lend her strength that I didn't even have to give. "Thanks. Go get some rest and some food."

"Want me to get a new party out while we're taking a break?"

I ground my teeth, staring in the direction Vivian went. We'd had at least one search party going every minute of every day since Destiny vanished, but we were all at the end of our rope. The pack was exhausted. Underfed. Worn out.

We all needed a reprieve.

"No," I said finally, though it hurt me to force the word out. "Take a rest. It's almost noon now. We'll send out another search party after dinner."

Charity grimaced and pushed her heavy dreadlocks back from her face with a nod before departing. The others dispersed, too. Gone to fall into their bunks for a long nap. No one looked particularly excited for food, and I couldn't blame them. One could only eat so many goddamned potatoes.

The hunting party managed to snag a deer in the early hours of the morning, though, so tonight at least, the pack would be well fed. Tomorrow, too, if we stretched it out. But I had a mind to let everyone eat their fill. They'd earned it. They needed it.

And in a few more days, we'd have our replacement meat order from Portland. Hopefully, we'd only need to order from them a few more times before Sal had his cooler installed. We'd had to pull back our pack from helping him for the time being, but he assured us that all he really needed was a workable space and his cooler and he could at least supply us with what we needed, even if he couldn't operate for the general public yet.

I hesitated before heading after Vivian, wanting to check on her even though I knew I was probably the last person she wanted to see right now. A ball formed in my throat and sweat beaded at my brow that had nothing to do with the sweltering heat beating down on me from the afternoon sky.

I knocked twice on the door before entering, finding her sitting on the edge of the double bed she and her mate shared, her back bent. Head resting in her palms. She'd put on a t-shirt that I recognized as Destiny's, and my heart ached at the sight of her in it.

"Viv," I hedged. "Can I get you anything?"

She dropped her hands and twisted her head to flick her cutting gaze to me. "What do you want, Allie?"

"I just..."

What did I want?

To help her. But I knew damn well that there was nothing I could do except get Destiny back. Nothing else would ease the pain.

Vivian's brown eyes narrowed on me, and her upper lip curled. "Just go, okay. Tell someone to come get me when the next search goes out."

I stepped into the shadows inside and closed the door behind me, swallowing hard to try to rid myself of the still-growing lump trapping all the words I wanted to say from coming out. "The next search isn't going out until after dinner. You should rest and eat, while you can."

It seemed to take a moment for her to register what I was saying, moving slowly until her spine was erect, showing me just how much she *needed* to eat. She looked rail thin. The hollows beneath her eyes were turning a bruised purple, and her hands were shaking even though she was clearly trying to force them still, clutching at her thighs.

"What the fuck are you talking about?"

My lips parted, but I wasn't sure what she meant. "What do you—?"

"You're not sending another party out?" Her tone was accusing, haughty with disdain that made my skin crawl. I'd heard Vivian use that tone on others. Her father. Assholes at school. But never me.

I steeled myself against the rise of panic in my chest and leveled what I hoped was a calm stare on my friend. "They need rest. Between the doubled patrols, the hunting party, the search parties, and extra security at camp, the quarry, and the pub, we are at the end of our—"

"No," she seethed, getting unsteadily to her feet. Her face paling. "You aren't giving up on her, Allie. You can't."

I held my hand up. "I'm not, Viv. I just need to keep us whole. We can't find her or protect ourselves if we're spread too thin."

The pale tone of her skin quickly turned green, and I only just made it to her side before she fell to her knees and hugged a small trash bin to her chest, heaving bile into it. I rubbed a hand up her back, bracing her as her body wracked and squeezed, twisting every last drop of whatever she'd managed to consume today out.

When she was finished, she wiped the back of her hand over her mouth and sat back heavily, uncaring as she knocked hard into the wood of her bed. "Please, Allie," she begged, a deadness in her eyes. "I need to find her. I can't...I can't..."

Her shoulders shook, and I pulled her in tight, hugging her to me as she began to cry. My own eyes burned too, sharing the pain of my friend, but they burned with fury, as well. My wolf and I not at war for once, but at peace with the promise to *destroy* whoever did this to us.

"She's gone..." Vivian sobbed. "She's really gone..."

She sniffled, clutching on to me so tight I thought she might leave bruises, but I didn't care. "What if she never comes ba—?"

"Don't say that," I interrupted, squeezing her tighter and then unable to help it, I did the thing I promised I wouldn't. Vivian deserved to know. She had to know or else she was going to go insane. I couldn't give her details or a name, but I could give her this little piece of hope.

"We have a lead," I whispered so low that I wasn't sure if she heard me until she stiffened, my words registering.

She pulled back, still shaking, but the tears at least had stopped. "What do you mean? Who? Who is it? Do you know?"

I shook my head. "I can't tell you more than that yet."

I implored her to understand with a look I hope conveyed everything I couldn't say. Viv was always the best at understanding what I meant with a single look, but she was also the first one to beat the details out of me when she knew I was hiding something from her.

"I can promise you that as soon as I know something concrete, you will be the first to know."

She opened her mouth, and I could see the fire of a coming argument in her eye and stood, shaking my head once, sharp. "Don't say anything to anyone. Not yet. This stays between us. I should know more in a day or two and then, if I'm right, we might know exactly where Destiny is."

Her eyes went wide at that and some color returned to her cheeks. "Okay," she said simply, the complete opposite of what I was sure she wanted to say, and it just made me love her even more. When push came to shove, Vivian knew that I would do everything within my power to get her mate back. That there was very little I wouldn't sacrifice to do it.

"Okay," I repeated then gestured to her bed. "Get some rest. I'll have someone bring you in some venison when it's ready."

"And wake me up when it's time to leave?" she added, and I could tell by the hard set of her stare that she wouldn't even dare try to sleep unless I promised her.

"Yes. I will."

She nodded solemnly to herself, and I watched as she pulled herself back up onto her bed and took a long drink out of a bottle of water before lying down. I shut the curtains and grabbed the stinking trash bin from the floor before closing the door behind me and sighing. I set the bin down outside and took a moment to compose myself before heading back across camp.

I sensed their eyes on me as I passed. From the windows of the cabins. From the footpaths, their footfalls pausing, not daring to come near as I wandered on numb legs through the zigzagging pathways.

The guilt gnawed at me. I didn't have to be in my wolf form to know what they were thinking. They blamed me for what was happening. They wondered why I hadn't found our missing kin yet. Why I wasn't doing more.

My fault.

All of it was my fault.

How could I have let this happen?

I startled as someone appeared at my side and broke free of the dark thoughts swirling within at the sight of silvery hair pulled into a loose braid. The lightest of the strands reflecting the sunlight. Hazel hobbled along next to me, a sour look on her face as she bared her teeth at a trio of shifters near the fire ring who all ceased their conversation to stare openly as we passed.

"Little heathens," she muttered. "Don't pay them any mind."

She patted my elbow and glanced up at me with her blind eyes. "You're doing great, child," she said. "You'll find them all. I know you will."

I smirked coldly at her, wishing I could be as confident in myself as she seemed to be. "Thanks, Grams."

"You go rest now. Seth and I are whipping up a nice venison bourguignon. I'll be sure to put extra wine in it. Everything tastes better with booze in it."

A small laugh escaped my lips at that, and she clapped me on the ass, sending me off toward the cabin. "There you go. You'll be right as rain after some rest and food. Get some nookie, too, while you're in there. I'm still waiting on those grandbabies."

I flushed scarlet, wishing she could see the glare I shot her way before traipsing up the stairs and inside. Jared and Clay were sitting at the kitchen island, the pair of them sending me knowing looks that told me they'd heard everything Grams had just said.

"Grandbabies, eh?" Jared asked, a brow raised as he peeled a label off of his beer bottle. "How long has she been pushing you for pups?"

I rolled my eyes. "Awhile."

"Fucking terrifying," Clay grumbled, shuddering as he took a swig of his beer, earning himself a hard elbow from Jared.

"She's right, you know," Jared said, ditching his empty bottle in the sink to come around the counter.

My brows knotted.

"About having kids?" I asked, incredulous and a little terrified myself now. I was *not* ready for that.

He snorted. "No. About you needing rest. You've hardly slept at all in over a week, Allie. And I'm assuming you and Clay are going out to Glenwood again tonight?"

Clay and I shared a look that told Jared all he needed to know. We'd been out there the last three nights in a row, and we were definitely going to be there again tonight. Sam had only come back to the phone booth again once since three days ago, but right about now Clay's guy was at the Glenwood bus depot, bugging the place. There was no way we weren't going to be there.

The guy set it up so that we could listen in to the bug through an app on Clay's phone, but it only worked if we were within range of the signal. We wouldn't have to go quite so close this time. We could stay a few miles away in the Chevelle, lessening the chance of her catching our scent even more.

At least it would be more comfortable.

"The booth is being bugged right now," Clay confirmed in a low voice, ears pricked to make sure no one else was around to hear. "We'll be parking a few miles out from the depot to listen in."

Jared nodded. "Then now is your only chance to get some rest."

I tried to picture myself actually closing my eyes.

Lying still.

Couldn't.

"I really don't think I can."

"Try," Clay urged, and Jared nodded his agreement. I squinted at Clay, a muscle ticking in my jaw.

"You've barely slept, either," I accused him.

"And *you,*" I jabbed a finger in Jared's direction, "are taking the night shift on security at the quarry tonight."

I crossed my arms over my chest. "You want me to rest? Then you can both take a fucking nap, too."

They shared a look, expressions hardening. Clay's nostrils flared. "Fine," he gritted out. "You're right," Jared added.

Wait...that wasn't supposed to happen. They were supposed to let me get out of taking a stupid ass nap because they were both too stubborn to take one themselves.

Jared grinned like a cat, realizing my intention and how they'd just thwarted it. The fucker.

"I'll go to Seth's cabin," Clay muttered, tipping his head to one side to crack his neck before making for the door.

"No," I said on a whim, stepping in his path. "I need you."

He cocked his head at me.

"I need both of you if I'm going to be able to sleep.

Stay. Please?"

His bright blue eyes flicked over my head to Jared before settling back on me. "Okay, baby. If that's what you need."

"It is."

The tension in the room grew, but nothing could subdue the high tingling in my blood at the idea of sharing our bed together. The three of us.

Just knowing they were both there with me. Both safe. All of us, together. It was what I'd been lacking for a long time.

I poured a glass of water before following Jared upstairs, dragging Clay with me by his arm.

Jared had just finished hanging the blackout curtains on the windows and turned on the lamp to the low setting while I undressed to get into bed.

"Aren't you going to, like...?" Clay rubbed his knuckles over the back of his head, eyeing my naked body like a hungry predator. "Put on some pajamas or something?"

I cocked my head at him, confused. I never wore clothes to sleep. Why bother when we were all naked most of the time around here, anyway? "Um. No. But you can if you want to."

He cleared his throat as I climbed into the middle of the bed and lifted the sheet to cover most of my body, leaving my breasts exposed, maybe kind of sort of on purpose.

Jared was the first to slide into bed with me, fully clothed to my utter dismay.

Clay, seeming to agree to some unspoken bullshittery between them, *also* lay down without bothering to remove his dark wash denim jeans. Without even bothering to get beneath the sheet.

Really?

Judging by the lustful emotions in the undertow beneath his waves of discomfort and macho need to claim me as his and *only* his, I'd say that he didn't get beneath the sheet because he didn't trust himself.

Jared pressed his leg against mine, and his hand came to rest on my stomach as he turned onto his side, making me shudder. I bit down on my lip to control the sudden overwhelming need to be closer to them.

Maybe Grams was right. I could use some...*nookie.*

I ran a hand down Clay's arm, making the latent muscle tense and bulge as goosebumps rose over the trail where I'd touched him. I tugged gently on his arm, guiding him closer. He obliged, shuffling nearer on the bed so that both of my mates pressed in close to either side of me.

Nothing beat this.

Having them both this close settled my soul in a way that nothing else could. I sighed breathily, nuzzling against Clay's shoulder and twining my fingers with Jared's beneath the sheet. Their combined scents of cedar, birch, whiskey, and spice washed over me like a drug, dulling the sharpness of the stress I'd been shouldering for weeks. Making everything seem softer. Easier. Until, for just a moment, I was able to forget it all and just be here.

I pushed Jared's hand lower on my belly, until his knuckles brushed the sensitive inner corner of my thigh. As I did that, I snaked my hand around Clay's neck, pulling him around. He turned with only a little hesitation, meeting my drugged gaze with pure blue flame.

My lips parted, and with one more tug, he bent to my will, bending as he turned to press his lips to mine. A soft moan was smothered between our lips as Jared's hand brushed my hot core, sending flashes of intense pleasure coursing through my blood.

A growl reverberated in Clay's chest, and his and Jared's testosterone levels spiked, breaking down the wall I'd tried to erect against their feelings.

Clay pulled back and Jared's hand slipped from mine, making my thighs press together with the loss of his touch. A pained sound came from the back of my throat as I squeezed my eyes tightly shut and pressed my forehead to Clay's.

"Please," I murmured, searching beneath the sheet for Jared's hand again. When I found it, I re-twined my finger with his and squeezed.

"*Please*," I repeated more clearly this time in case they didn't hear. "I need you. I need both of you."

"Allie..." Jared trailed off in a hollow whisper that threatened to break me from the inside out. "You know we can't do that. We tried before and—"

"It's been *years*," I all but snapped, trying to rein in my inner wolf's urge to jump down both their throats at the gall of denying her. "Try *again*."

I peered up at Clay, finding him staring off into the dimness of the room, a furrow in his brow. "Clay?" I asked, living on a hopeless prayer that he would take my side on this and together we might sway Jared.

His gaze hardened, and I knew before he opened his lips to speak what his reply would be. I suppressed the ridiculous urge to cry, and he surprised me by wrapping an arm around the back of my neck and pulling me into his side. He nodded to Jared, who came closer until he was pressed along the line of my back, his arm around me, tucked up between my breasts to hold me tight.

I shuddered, glancing up at Clay curiously.

"Can this be enough for now?" he asked with a pain in his eyes that broke my heart. I stopped trying to block out their feelings and gasped at the rawness of it all as it came crashing in.

Even this—just being this close with me—*together* was incredibly difficult for them. Guilt twisted my lungs up in a vise, and I bowed my head, unable to look him in the eyes anymore.

"Don't feel guilty," Jared whispered against my bare back, his warm breath skating down my spine in a way that made me shiver. "This is on us. I...I wish we could give you what you want, Allie. I really do."

"But we'll try," Clay gritted out, making both Jared and me stiffen. "It'll just take some time."

Jared didn't make any comment to the contrary, and it was as much of an agreement as I would get out of him. Between the two, strangely enough, Jared was the more possessive. The one who was more territorial.

In the beginning, I would've thought it to have been Clay, but that was until I got to know him better. He didn't think he deserved me. Didn't think he was good enough. He wanted me to be with someone kinder, more patient, less hot-headed. So, when I told him I *did* want him and that I wouldn't take no for an answer, he was just glad to have any part of me he could.

I could tell, even after almost four years, he still felt the same way. Stupid fucker.

"I love you," I whispered.

"Us too," Jared replied while Clay shoved my head down into the crook of his arm and brushed my hair back from my face, sighing.

"Close your eyes," Clay demanded. "You're supposed to be resting, not making us horny as fuck. Don't make me smother you with a pillow."

I let out a short laugh, convincing myself that Clay was right. This was enough. At least for now. But I wouldn't forget his promise to try for more. It was more than I'd dared hope for in longer than I could remember.

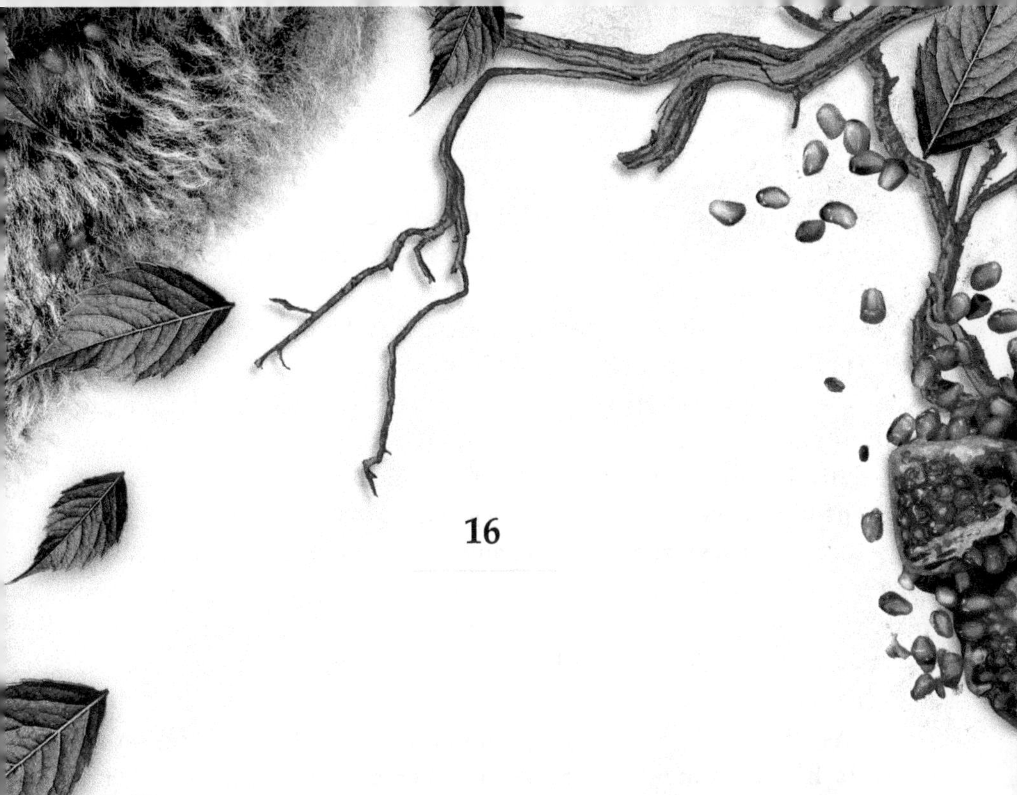

16

"Y ou sure you know how to work that?" I asked for the third time since we parked.

Clay fiddled with the app on his phone that should allow us to hear inside of the phone booth. We were hoping it would allow us to hear both ends of the conversation, given our very heightened sense of hearing, but the guy who installed it said it was unlikely.

He jammed a few more buttons and got another error screen. I rolled my eyes and took the phone from him. "Let me see."

He relinquished it with a frustrated sigh and leaned back in the passenger seat, glaring at me.

"If I can't figure it out, then you—"

"Done," I announced, passing the phone back to him with the correct screen within the app open. It showed that the device was recording, and we could even hear the wind and the slight rattle of the phone booth doors.

"How did you...never mind."

"You're welcome."

I cozied up in my seat with the blanket I brought, peering out the windshield at what I could see of the starry night sky through the fingers of the tall pines reaching high above.

We found a side road to park on, tucking the Chevelle in a small

857

drive that looked like it'd been months if not years since anyone had used it. It kept us hidden from any road traffic and boxed in with closely clustered pines and shrubbery.

I rolled the window down a little, letting a bit of cool night air in to try to clear the quickly fogging windows.

"Think she'll go tonight?" I asked after a few minutes listening to the drone of the wind through the app on Clay's phone.

His lips pressed together into a tight line to match the ones carved deep into his forehead. "Guess we'll just have to wait to find out."

If the last several nights were any indication, there was likely about a fifty-fifty chance she would show. She didn't come every night from what we saw, but she also didn't seem to miss more than a night or two at a time. She missed yesterday, so we hoped that meant she would be here tonight.

As much as I loved snuggling up in my Chevelle, with her leather seats hugged around my curves and her old car smell settling my nerves, this wasn't exactly my idea of a chill time with my mate.

Getting a wicked idea, I licked my lips and slid my hand over the center console, walking my fingers over his muscled thigh toward the fly of his jeans.

He caught my hand before I could undo the button, cocking his head at me, a question in his stare.

"She usually doesn't come until after midnight," I whispered into the shadows between us, wanting to ease some of the tension from his soul, and maybe some of my own as well. It was only eleven. We had time.

For a moment, I thought he might reject me again, like he had with Jared earlier before we'd all fallen asleep in the afternoon, but...he released my hand, groaning appreciatively as I let it glide over his growing length through his jeans.

"We need to stay focused," he breathed as his button popped and his fly slid down. He wasn't fighting me though, so I knew I'd already won.

"Fine," I said with a sly grin. "Then you keep an eye on that," I nodded to the phone clenched tightly in his mammoth hand. "And *I'll* keep my attention...elsewhere."

"*Baby,*" he groaned, but his words cut short on a growl as I freed his cock from his jeans and stroked its length.

I hushed him as I leaned over, positioning myself to take him into my mouth. His hand on the phone loosened, falling, and I *tsked* him, nudging it back up into his view. "Focus," I teased.

His head fell back as I closed my lips over his tip, suckling lightly in that spot I knew drove him wild before taking him all the way in.

"*Fuck,*" he hissed, and his free hand came to rest on the back of my head, fingers twisting into my hair. He pushed up into my mouth, hips bucking as he found the back of my throat and shuddered.

He was too big to take all the way in so I slid my hand around his base, stroking up and down slowly at first, but picking up speed as I bobbed my head in time with the thrusts of his hips as he fucked my mouth.

His pleasure was my own as his ecstasy passed through the mate bond, making my core tighten as his did. I moaned against his cock, jerking when his hand slid out from my hair to reach beneath my crouched form, finding the waistband of my joggers and slipping beneath.

His fingers flicked aside my panties, finding me already slick as he rubbed the rough pads of his fingers over my clit, making my body come alive with sensation.

"That's it, baby," he whispered, circling the sensitive bundle of nerves quicker. His expert touch driving to the edge of my own release just as surely as our shared pleasure through the bond.

He thrust into my mouth harder, and I worked to pump the base of his cock with wild abandon until I felt him harden to bursting under my tongue.

"*Allie,*" he moaned as he found his release, and I came with him, crying out against the girth of his cock as I came hard on his fingers. His warmth slid down my throat, and he jerked beneath me.

I licked his crown wickedly, drawing another shuddering groan from his lips as I came up for air. Before I could pull away, his fist found the front of my t-shirt and he yanked me up to his mouth, crushing his lips against mine.

I breathed in sharply in surprise, letting the brutal press of his lips unwind me.

"Damn," he muttered as our lips came apart and he pressed his forehead to mine. "That was..."

"Hot as fuck?" I supplied, and he smirked as I settled back in my seat and patted the Chevelle's dash. "I figured it was about time we popped her cherry," I joked.

Clay's eyes narrowed on me. The glow of his inner wolf receding as his heartbeat returned to a more normal rhythm. "You mean you never...not even with Jared?"

I shook my head. "Nope."

He chuckled softly, giving a one shoulder shrug that told me he was more than a little pleased with himself and trying to play it cool. "At least I got a first *something*," he joked, but I sensed something more serious lingering beneath the surface level sentiment.

Jared had been the first one I slept with.

But, thinking back, I realized there was another first Clay and I had shared. "You were the first one to..." I let him put the pieces together, glancing down at my still throbbing core and biting my lower lip.

The first time Clay and I had done it, he'd been so insistent on making me come first. He didn't say as much, but I got the feeling it was because he was worried he wouldn't last more than a hot minute once he got inside me. Turned out he did just fine. First with his tongue and then with his cock. He'd gotten me twice that night.

I flushed at the memory. At how awkward we both were at first until we just gave in to our baser instincts and let our bodies do the talking. Then it was as easy as breathing. Just like it had been with Jared.

A clattering noise in the car made me jerk my attention back to the phone.

"Is it...?" I said in a breath, afraid to speak too loudly for fear Sam could somehow hear me from her end of the bug, which I gathered was absolutely ridiculous, but I couldn't help it. Fuck, I'd make a terrible spy.

Clay hushed me and lifted the phone between us like it might spontaneously combust in his hands.

Please be her, I thought. But also...

I hope it isn't her.

We listened as metal gears groaned with the closing of the payphone door and a receiver was lifted. A rustling sound and the clatter of coins shoved into the metal slot blocked out all other sound except for the chirp of numbers being pressed on the dial pad.

"Breathe," I reminded Clay in a quiet whisper, noticing how his face was going a very vivid shade of crimson. He took a breath and some of his regular tan pallor returned.

I gestured to the phone, offering to take it, but even though his hands were shaking, he shook his head.

"It's me." A voice that was unmistakably Sam's filled the cab of the Chevelle, shoving out any last hope that it might've been someone else and ushering in the reality that she was *definitely* doing something she wasn't supposed to. Now we just needed to figure out what the fuck that was.

Clay and I shared a look as someone on the other end of the call spoke. It was way too quiet for us to hear much more than the garbled drone of a male voice on the other end.

"I know, I'm sorry," Sam said, her voice low and shaky, making me all the more confused.

"I wasn't able to get away or else I would—" A pause.

"I know. There's no excuse. I'm sorry." Another pause, this one longer.

I nudged Clay. "Can you hear anything from the other end?"

He shook his head once, sharply.

Fuck.

"Well, they have a new meat order coming in. They're picking it up on Friday, and I think I heard Seth say Jared was going to be the one to collect it."

Fucking little bitch.

"I don't know. I doubt they'll take the backroads again after what happened. They'll probably take the main highway and go around through Forest Grove and hike in."

"*I'm going to kill her...*" Clay said in a violent whisper so low that it shook deep in my belly and sent shivers racing up my spine. A vein throbbed in his temple and he was beginning to bend the metal case around his phone.

I peeled his fingers back and took it from him, feeling sick as we continued to listen to the conversation. Praying that she would say something that could be of use to us. A name. A location. Fucking *anything*.

"I don't really know about that," Sam said after a moment. "They're still sending out search parties, but they usually decide the routes right before, not in advance. I could try to—"

The male voice rang through the receiver in a clipped tone. It was distant, far away, but he must've been shouting real loud for us to be able to make out the words *find out*.

Something about the tone was familiar, and I immediately racked my brain, trying to place it. Could it be Forrest or Harrison? Still pissed about Ryland and looking for revenge after four fucking years? Seemed unlikely, but I would consider every option.

"I'll try," Sam replied, and then after a second. "I will. I promise."

"Something isn't right," I muttered at the next pause, gaze flitting to Clay's stony expression. "She sounds...*scared*."

"You think someone's forcing her to do this?"

I shrugged. "I don't know, but she doesn't sound like the Sam I know."

He nodded like he agreed, but his cheekbones flared as he clenched his teeth. "Doesn't matter," he decided. "I don't give a fuck if someone's forcing her. If she were in some sort of trouble, she should have told us. She should have told *me*."

He was right, so I didn't say anything else, falling back into silence as Sam cleared her throat on the other end of the receiver.

"Okay," she said in a sad whisper. "I'll try to come back tomorrow after I find out more."

Clay's hand lifted to the door handle of the Chevelle, and I snatched his arm, holding him in place. This was *not* the time to fly off the goddamned handle. If he killed her, he would be sacrificing a beautiful opportunity to play this to our advantage. He was just too pissed off to see that.

"I love y—" her words were cut short and through the phone we could hear the blaring sound of a dead line wailing on the other end of her call before the solemn click of the receiver silenced it.

The door of the payphone booth clattered open and shut again, and I hit the side button on Clay's phone to turn it off, mind racing with possibilities.

Clay tugged on his arm, trying to wrench it free of my grip. "If we leave now, we can catch up to her," he seethed. "Looks like Jared's going to get his wish after all."

I shuddered at the reminder of what Jared had wanted to do to get information from Sam but composed myself again. "I have a better idea," I told him, meeting his gaze with a rock solid resolve.

He cocked his head at me, and I licked my lips, trying to put together how best to say this so that he would go for it.

"Allie, spit it out or I'm going after her."

"Okay," I hissed, releasing his arm to sit back in my seat and reorganize the chaos in my skull. "We can use this. She's definitely guilty, but we still have no idea who it is she's working with. We don't know where the shifters who were taken are. And we don't know when they will strike next other than the fact that they may try to intervene with another meat order."

I could see the gears turning behind his eyes now, too, shifting his focus away from blind rage and toward more useful thinking.

"What are you suggesting then? We just let her get away with this? Let her keep feeding whoever the fuck was on the other end of that call information that could hurt us in the hope that the next time they talk we'll be able to figure out more?"

No. He wasn't seeing the opportunity here.

"No. I'm suggesting we *feed her* information that would be useful to us. Like, say, a false lead about when and where the meat order is being picked up."

His brow rose. "So that we can actually get it to camp," he supplied, catching on.

"Yes, but also so that *we* can be the ones lying in wait when they walk right into the trap we set for them."

"A Trojan horse?"

"A motherfucking Trojan horse," I agreed with a wide grin and his brows drew together, eyes lit from within with the spark of his wolf and something like wicked delight.

"We take them out," he supplied, chewing his bottom lip as he considered my plan and removing his hand from the door handle of the car, making me sag a little in relief that he wasn't beyond reasoning. "Make them pay for what they've done."

"All but one," I amended. "To find out who is behind these attacks and why."

"Sam will—"

"No." I interrupted. "We need Sam to think we don't know she's against us for as long as possible. So long as she thinks she hasn't been found out, we can use her."

I leveled my gaze on him, thinking that he might challenge me on this, but after a beat of tense silence, his head bobbed in a grudging nod.

"Fine."

"You think you can face her? Pretend shit's all good?"

His jaw clenched. "Not like I have a choice."

I brushed a hand down the length of his arm reassuringly until he looked at me. His dark hair swept low over his glowing eyes, making them appear even brighter amid the shadows.

"We'll have blood for this," I promised him. "When this is all over, whatever you want to do about Sam, I'll support you."

I didn't add the other bit I was thinking, not wanting to voice it aloud. If he wanted her dead after we set things straight and brought home the missing pieces of our makeshift family, then *I* would deliver the killing blow.

I wouldn't let him be the one to do it. If there was anything I'd learned from killing Ryland, it was that that shit never left you. I still had trouble dealing with the fact that I was the cause of the death of my sibling…and I'd unconsciously killed her in the fucking womb. Absorbed her into me.

This would be worse. Sam was his little sister. He'd grown with her as a child. Cared for her. Protected her. Killed for her.

He couldn't be the one to do it.

His lips pressed into a hard line at the unspoken promise in my gaze before he stuffed his phone back into his pocket and faced forward. "Let's get out of here."

He didn't have to tell me twice.

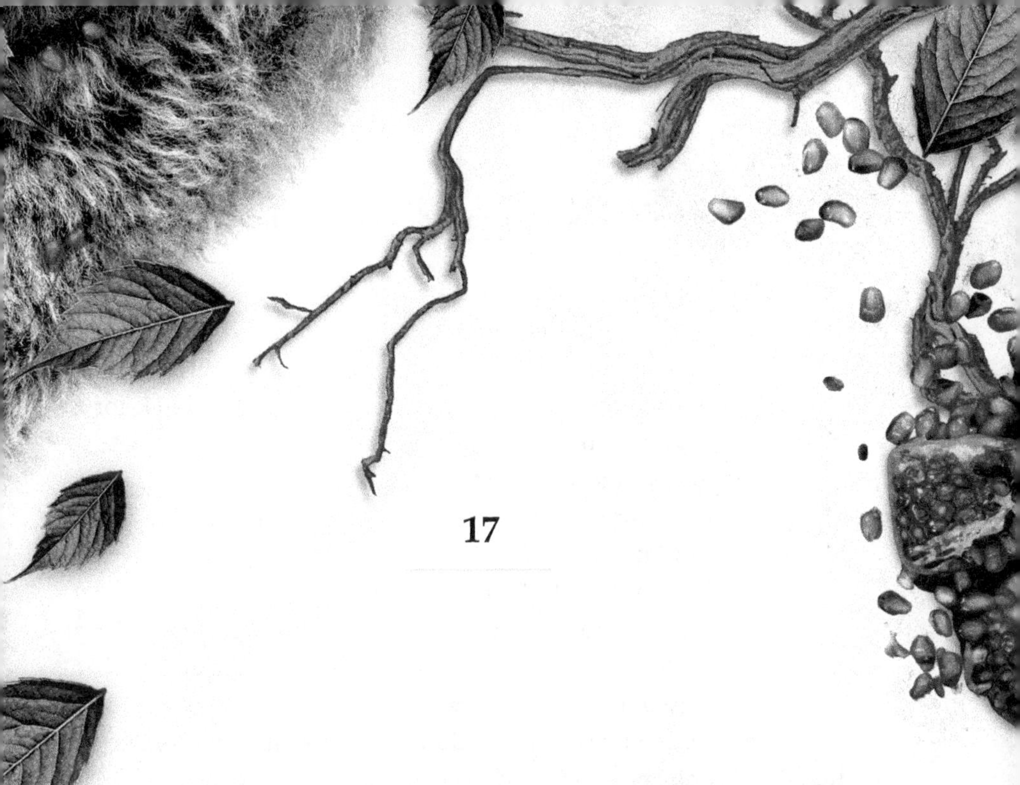

17

I could hardly believe the plan we put into motion was working. Sam didn't suspect anything, though she seemed a little put off that Clay was avoiding her. I couldn't blame him, though. Even I couldn't stand to be falsely civilized in her presence for more than a minute or two at a time.

It was a good thing she kept mostly to herself.

"Are they there yet?" Clay asked, his nostrils flaring as he paused in his pacing of the living room floor. "They should have been there by now."

"Give them a few more minutes," I said, holding my hands up in a placating gesture I knew would do absolutely nothing to soothe him.

Jared's phone pinged, and Clay and I both whipped out heads to where he leaned against the counter in the kitchen, staring down at the illuminated screen of his phone.

"They made it," he said in an exhale, throwing a shaky hand through his tousled hair.

I almost shouted out in relief, but settled for a grin that both my guys shared. "We did it."

We'd casually spoken about the new order pick-up date and time in front of Sam yesterday, and like a good little snitch, she fed the information to the person on the other end of the phone just after midnight last night. We were even so kind as to include our plans for a route for the return trip.

Our order was in fact *not* delayed by a day as we'd allowed her to think. In fact, it'd just been delivered without a hitch to Grove's End's hastily cleared out walk-in freezer in town. And that was where it would stay for now. We would make a trip later tonight to grab enough for a few days and smuggle it into our deep freeze in the cabin.

As far as anyone would know until we could tell them otherwise, the meat came from a last-minute trip to the K-Mart in Hillsborough.

Jared clapped Clay on the shoulder, and the big oaf nodded to his best friend with a pained smile. "Damn. I thought for a second..."

He let the sentence trail off, but we both knew what he was thinking because we were thinking it, too. He thought they were caught. That they were taken and our meat order was destroyed *again*.

"I told you this would work." I couldn't help but rub it in just a little. If I thought Clay had been hesitant to go along with my crazy idea, Jared had been even more combatant about it. He wanted to drag Sam in here by her hair and force her to talk. He didn't think trying to outwit whoever was behind this was smart. Or safe.

Which told me that neither of them were going to like what I had to bring up next.

"Okay," I said, getting myself back in planning mode. "We finally got some food, so that's good, but that's only part one of the plan."

I slid my gaze to each of them in turn, and their grins dropped, replaced with a stoic determination to see the rest of the plan through to completion.

Clay sat heavily in the armchair, and Jared leaned against the wall just behind him, folding his arms over his chest and putting his tan biceps on display.

I closed the distance between us, easily lifting the couch from its bottom ledge and dragging it closer to where they waited. We needed to speak quietly. It wasn't just Sam we had to worry about overhearing; until we figured this out, no one else could know what was happening.

"Part two," I started, pressing my callused fingers together in front of my face. "We know they're going to try to head off the jeep on the way back from Portland."

"We'll do it like we talked about," Jared continued.

"Turn the Jeep into a Trojan horse."

"Jared drives. You and I coat ourselves in meat scent and hide in the back. When they attack, we'll be ready."

I bit my lower lip.

"I think we should bring a few others into this," I blurted before I could change my mind. "The last time they attacked with eight. If they have the same number, maybe more, it'll be a hard-won fight."

"But we'll have the element of surprise," Clay reminded me, but I could already feel the change in the air between us. They both knew I was right. Likely had been thinking the same thing as me. I'd risk myself, but I wouldn't risk them.

And they'd risk themselves, but they wouldn't risk me.

Which meant that if we were serious about doing this, we'd need help, and they would have to know what they were signing up for.

"If we tell others, we risk Sam finding out she's been made," Jared put in, not an argument, just stating a fact. "And if she's going to find out anyway, then we may as well just get what we need from her."

"No," Clay and I growled at the same time, making Jared narrow his eyes on Clay.

"I know she's your sister, man, but if it's between Allie and her—"

"You don't think I get that," Clay snapped, looking at Jared like he didn't even recognize him. "That's not it."

"Then what is it?"

"First off," I butt in, giving them both a cutting look that said to keep their goddamned voices down. "It's not worth the risk of losing our ability to be one step ahead. There *is* a chance that she could find out, but she may not, and if she doesn't, then we can still use her."

Jared's face pinched, and I could tell he was holding back from saying whatever it was that fought to be set free from his lips. "And second?" he gritted out. "I'm assuming there's something else I don't know."

He shot me a glare, and I tried not to take it personally. He'd been stuck covering my and Clay's asses every night here at camp when we left. I knew he was feeling left out of the loop, but his role was equally as important as the role Clay and I played when we went to listen to the bug in the Chevelle.

I made a mental note to send him with Clay next time. As much as I hated the idea of either or both of them being out there without me, it was only fair.

"Second," I said, trying to rein in my wolf as she growled quietly within, put off from the vibe in the room. "She lied to him."

"What?" Jared asked, frustrated and confused. "Don't snap at her, man," Clay shot at Jared, and seeing them in weirdly opposite roles from normal really made my head spin.

Jared ground his teeth together before repeating himself, more calmly this time. "What do you mean?"

"Sam lied to whoever was on the other end of the call last night." Clay was the one who answered, leaning over the front of the armchair with his finger knotted between his knees. "She was asked about the search party routes and said she didn't know where they would be."

I remembered that moment clearly. The both of us so confused in the car when she said that she couldn't find out without seeming too suspicious. But we both knew that she'd been there at dinner, sitting just two seats down from Charity as she briefed Clay and a few others on this morning's search party route.

We'd of course quietly suggested to Charity after dinner that she go the complete opposite way from which she was planning, but Sam had definitely heard.

I'd even seen her peek up at Charity halfway through, her gaze flitting back and forth over her barely touched macaroni salad as Char gave away her entire search plans.

"I think it's because Clay was going to be with her," I admitted, sending an apologetic glance his way.

He snorted as though that was highly unlikely, but said nothing to the contrary.

"You think she doesn't want Clay getting hurt or taken?"

I nodded solemnly. "Either that, or she's having second thoughts about helping whoever's orchestrating all of this."

Jared shoved off from the wall. "Don't tell me you're starting to feel bad for that lying piece of trash."

Clay bristled but didn't contradict Jared, and the tension in the room grew.

I held my hands up. "I don't know what to think right now, Jare. I'm just saying I think we need to keep Sam in our back pocket. Go ahead as planned and keep her thinking she's safe."

"Fuck," Jared muttered, shaking his head at nothing in particular as he toed the carpet. "So, who do we bring in, then? Another two or three would even our odds."

"Seth," Clay said straight off. "Maybe Charity. I trust them both more than anyone else here."

I agreed with him. Vivian would've been another obvious choice had it not been her mate that was taken. She couldn't know about Sam or she'd kill her. But I was tempted to let her unleash her fury on those responsible for what happened to her mate. It's what I would want if it were either of mine. Maybe...

"Maybe no one really has to know anything just yet," I mused aloud. "Maybe we get a small team together. Seth, Viv, and Charity—"

"Allie," Clay interrupted, giving me a look.

"Hear me out," I urged him. "We tell them we have a lead on where and when the people responsible for this shit will strike, but we don't tell them how we know. We don't tell them about Sam. We swear them to secrecy."

Jared sighed heavily, and it looked like he'd aged five years in the last few days. I was sure Clay and I didn't look much better. "I don't know about this, Allie."

"It's too risky otherwise," I pressed.

"There's risk involved either way," Clay grumbled to himself, lifting his head with a decision set in his eyes. "But Allie's right. I'd rather the kind of risk that might see Sam killed than the kind that might hurt any of us."

Jared had nothing to say to that, working his jaw as he mulled over the less than perfect options on either side.

"Okay, but just Viv, Seth, and Charity. And we bring them to Grove's End with us and tell them there. Then there's no way of anyone over-hearing."

"And Layla," I amended with a wince. "Someone here needs to know where we're going and what we're doing just in case...just in case we don't come back."

Jared's face darkened at that, but grudgingly, he nodded.

"And I want to tell Layla about Sam."

Clay's eyes bugged out at me. "You're kidding, right?"

I shook my head. "No. Layla is one of the most level-headed people I know. She will know better than to tell Vivian, and once I tell her why it needs to remain a secret, she'll understand why she can't tell anyone, and she won't. I trust her. And we need someone here who knows the whole truth just in case we—"

"Stop saying that," Clay demanded, his voice growing in volume and agitation. "We're coming back, Allie. With all the information we need to take whoever is doing this to us out. End of story."

I wouldn't upset him more by pushing the point, but I needed them to agree to this. I promised no more secrets, and so my intent to tell Layla everything had to be shared even if my first instinct had been to do it without saying a word to them about it so they couldn't stop me.

"We need to do this. We need someone here who knows the truth while we're gone. What if Sam tries something, hmm? What if she cries wolf and the pack goes running into a trap because I'm not there to give them orders otherwise?"

Jared pursed his lips. "That's a good point," he acquiesced. "Maybe...maybe *you* should stay behind. Then we don't have to tell Layla anything and camp will have more protection."

"Ha!" I scoffed. "You won't be rid of me that easily. There's no way in hell I'm letting the two of you go running into an ambush without me at your sides. *Period.*"

"I don't know, Allie," Clay started, his shoulders tensing. "Maybe Jared's right—"

"*Period*," I repeated, enunciating every syllable of the word.

They both quieted at that, and I realized my wolf was dangerously close to the surface, battering at my defenses for a good long run. I hadn't joined the search parties for a day or two and with everything going on, going for my daily run didn't really seem like a priority. And now, my wolf was the one paying the price.

She was chomping at the bit for some freedom.

"I'm going to go for a run," I said, changing the subject. "Can you guys handle wrangling Seth, Char, and Viv? I'll meet you all at Grove's End later"

"You aren't going anywhere alone," Clay all but hissed, eyes slanting in a way that dared me to disagree with him.

"I'll go with her," Jared offered. "Think you can handle getting everyone together, brother?"

Clay nodded. "Yeah. I got it."

"What about Layla?" Jared asked. "When are you going to tell her?"

I tried not to think too hard about it before replying in a heavy breath, "Now, I guess. Before my run. No point in waiting."

I'd like to say that Layla was shocked at my admission about Sam, but the truth was that she didn't seem surprised at all. She even told me in confidence that she'd heard several others whispering that they thought she might be the one to blame for everything that was happening.

I guessed Sam might've already hung herself before we even had the chance to untie her noose. Oh well, she'd dug her own grave. I just hoped we could get what we needed from her before the rest of the pack swapped out false niceties for their claws and fangs.

Just like I'd thought, though, Layla completely understood the reason for the secrecy and easily promised not to tell anyone anything. Especially Vivian. At least for now. I'd promised her the truth would be coming out soon whether we wanted it to or not, and I'd take the full force of Vivian's rage and all of the blame for keeping it from her when the time came.

Our friendship had weathered many storms since third grade. We could get through this, too. Or, at least, I hoped we would because I couldn't imagine my life without my two best friends.

"So you're going to the pub now?" Layla asked as she walked alongside me down the stairs and to the door. Jared nodded to us from where he stood near the front window, making sure no one drew too near to the cabin while we had our little talk upstairs.

"Going for a run first, then we'll head over."

She gave my arm a squeeze and tugged me in for a hug that enveloped me in her jasmine scent. I didn't know what it was about hugging your bestie when your life was falling apart all around you, but the instant her arms closed around me, a ball formed in my throat. My eyes burned, and I had to work extra hard not to let myself cry.

I was afraid if I did, I wouldn't be able to stop.

"Be careful," she said as she pulled away. "I'll take care of things here."

"I know you will."

"Ready?" Jared asked from the doorway and the way half his face was cast in moonlight and the other in the dim shadows of the room made him appear to be two people instead of one. The Jared I fell in love with four years ago, and the one I loved now.

I wished he'd never had to go through what he did to create that second shadow self, but without it, he wouldn't be who he was now, and I wouldn't change a thing about him. Darkness and all.

My lips tipped up into a grin, and the knot between my mate's brows softened. "Yeah," I said. "I am."

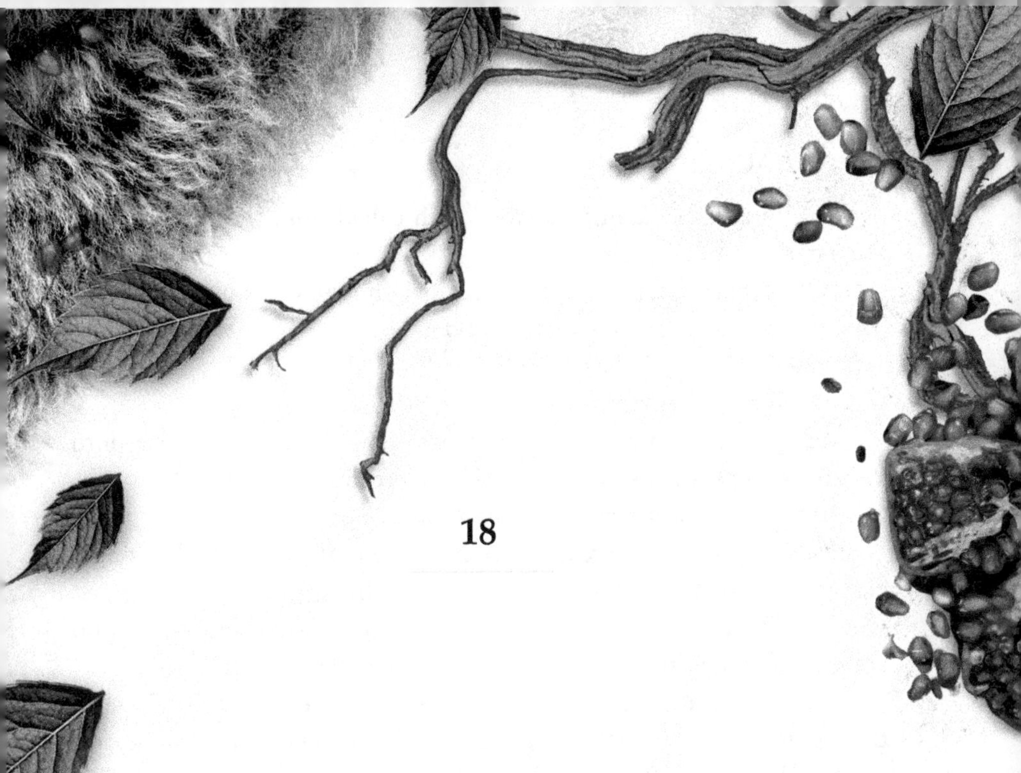

18

J ared and I crashed through the door to Grove's End sopping wet, our bare feet sliding on the polished hardwood in the entryway. He caught my elbow to steady me as the door closed behind us, muting the rushing sound of the downpour outside.

"You made it," Charity called from the bar, a frosty pint in her hand and a grin on her lips that didn't reach her eyes. "Clay was about to go looking for you."

Clay shoved through the swinging doors to the kitchen at the back of the narrow pub with a scowl on his lips. He stalked toward us, scrutinizing gaze passing over first me and then Jared, checking for injury. "Where the fuck have you been?"

A flush warmed my rain-chilled cheeks, and I cleared my throat as I looked away, afraid what Jared and I had been up to in the rain beneath the moon would be written all over my face.

"Sorry, man," Jared said, not bothering with any real explanation. "Just lost track of time."

Clay's scowl only intensified, but he seemed to be willing to let it go for now, we had bigger problems on our plates. I peered around Clay's hulking form to find Viv sitting two stools down from Charity at the bar, looking into the bottom of an empty shot glass like it might hold all the answers.

"So, what's this about exactly?" Seth called from the other side of the bar, and I rolled my eyes.

"Who let him back there?" I demanded, though without any mirth.

He shot me a look in reply that told me he knew he was the absolute last person who should be bartending. We'd all be on our asses within the hour if his heavy hands were mixing drinks.

Seth poured another measure of whiskey, the top shelf shit, into Vivian's shot glass. She nodded mutely before draining it dry.

Better get to it before everyone's too drunk to hear me.

Even though I was already acutely aware that there wasn't a single customer in the pub, I did my due diligence checking anyway. I stepped around Clay to peer into the five booths lining the right side of the pub and stood on my tiptoes to see into the kitchen.

There was still another twenty minutes until we'd officially close for the night, but it seemed the rain had kept all the townsfolk away. Good.

"I already sent the others home," Clay told me, and I spun to find him crossing his arms over his chest. "It's just us here."

"'Kay," I said, nodding to Jared who was still hovering in the doorway, shaking the rain from his hair and trying to wring the water from the hem of his gray t-shirt. Our clothes had been dry for all of five seconds after we put them on. I was grateful I'd had a dress in the clothing stash near town. Nothing more uncomfortable than heavy ass wet jeans.

"Lock it," I told him. "And flip the sign."

Jared did as I asked him, and I heard Seth whisper something behind me that sounded like, *this should be interesting.*

I pushed my wet hair back from my face and made my way to the bar, lifting the section of counter to get behind it and kick Seth out.

"Awe, come on," he complained. "Let me get you a drink, boss."

"I'll get it myself," I muttered, shoving him out to the other side to take the seat between Charity and Vivian. Clay and Jared found seats at the bar, too, filling what remained of the vacant ones.

"Beer?" I asked, and both of them shook their heads no.

"Well, I'm having one." I sighed and poured myself a pint of the good shit from the local brewery and took a long swig.

"You found something out, didn't you?" Charity asked, her turquoise eyes boring into me.

Vivian perked up at her words, hazed eyes clearing with the promise of hope.

"Yes and no," I admitted, earning myself a glare from Clay and Jared. "We have intel about where and when the next attack will be."

Vivian's eyes widened, and her mouth opened to speak, but I silenced her with a raised hand.

"I can't give much information right now. I'm sorry. But this is a chance to find out who is behind our missing brothers and sister. This is a chance for retribution, but I need to know that you'll help us, and that everything we're planning stays between us."

The three of them shared a look before each nodded in turn.

Vivian was the first to speak. "Okay," she said tensely, shoving away her shot glass. "I don't care about the details anyway, I just want her back." Her eyes went glassy with angry tears as her face hardened, upper lip curling back to reveal low-growing fangs. "I want fucking blood."

"And you'll have it," I promised her. "But our first priority is to find out who is orchestrating these attacks and *where* they are."

"You know I'm in," Charity said, licking her lips as though she could already taste the blood of her enemies there.

Seth nodded quietly to himself, all traces of his jokester persona sloughed off for a moment of brutal reality. "It's my fault she was taken," he said. "I'll do whatever it takes to set that right."

"It's not—"

"Thank you," he interrupted. "For letting me try to make it right."

I sealed my lips shut and nodded back instead of berating him. If it were me, I know I'd feel just as guilty, no matter if the reasoning behind that emotion was sound or not.

"All right," I decided, glancing at Clay and Jared for confirmation. They each gave the all clear to continue, and I settled myself with a breath before leaning over the bar. "It'll happen tomorrow night, just before the sun sets."

"Not going to lie," Seth whispered. "I feel like a total badass. This is some fall of Troy shit."

"Yeah and I feel like a damned pin-cushion," I lobbied back, squirming to get his elbow out of my ribs.

"Quiet back there," Jared hissed from the front seat. "We're almost to the location."

The Jeep veered off the main highway, and the tires slowed as we came onto the road that would eventually lead into Forest Grove. In about three minutes, we'd take a turn onto a side road. The side road Sam thought we were taking to drive a 'meat order' as close to pack camp as we could.

If our assumption was correct, they'd want to attack us outside of our territory, which left only a small stretch of side road where that could be possible.

My heartbeat pounded in my chest, sending the sound of blood rushing in my ears.

Someone's stomach growled noisily, and I heard Charity groan to herself. "Did we really have to cover ourselves in the smell of raw meat? I'm fucking starving. It's making me want to gnaw off my own arm."

I suppressed a laugh and gave her a soft kick in the thigh. We'd all had prime rib for dinner from our hidden stash at Grove's End, but much like my stomach, Charity's was bottomless and never really got 'full.' "Shut up, Char," Clay growled, and I could feel his tension and frustration like a fucking spike in my chest. He had it the worst of any of us. Folded into the narrow space on the floor between the front seats and backseats. Meanwhile, Charity, Vivian, Seth and I shared the roomy trunk area.

Well, it had seemed roomy anyway, until we had to fit four shifters into it.

Our bodies were little more than a mass of tangled limbs. I was actually starting to worry we wouldn't be able to spring out of this bitch as easily as I'd originally planned. At least Clay had managed to repair the latch at the back so we could actually open it after it was damaged in the last attack.

Once they'd managed to flip it back upright, that seemed to be the only thing that was truly busted aside from the windshield. The white Jeep was almost good as new now, though she'd need a paint job to buff out all the scratches and scuff.

"This is it," Jared said in a low whisper. "Get ready."

A fire burned in my blood, the lit match striking the gasoline in my veins. *Fuck.*

Viv let out a short whine as a popping sound filled the trunk area. She was working hard to keep herself from shifting, but her wolf was winning out.

"Not yet," I hissed, searching for her hand around Charity's back. I found it and squeezed her clammy palm tight. "Wait for it."

She squeezed back, nearly breaking bone, but I didn't care. We needed to keep hidden until they attacked. If we were found out, they could flee. I'd still fucking catch at least one of them, but call me greedy, I wanted them *all*.

Please work, I sent a silent plea to the heavens. To the stars who might hear me as they became visible in the rapidly darkening pink and orange sky. *Please. Don't let anyone be hurt.*

I closed my eyes, listening carefully over the sound of the tires slowly chewing pavement, surprised when I heard a car approaching from the opposite direction and passing us by. It was rare to see another vehicle on this road, there being no housing in the area for miles. It was why I'd chosen it for a decoy. Less chance of human collateral in the fight.

Once I couldn't hear the other car anymore, my hackles rose and my wolf awakened with a growl that shook behind my ribcage. She could sense them.

"They're here," I mouthed to Charity, and she nodded that she understood, setting her jaw.

Seth went still where he was crouched next to me, and I knew that he sensed them too, now.

Why weren't they attacking?

Vivian's bruising grip on my hand turned crushing, and I bit down on my tongue to stifle a cry of pain, needing her to keep herself under control more than I needed her to let go.

Come on you fuckers, I thought. *Take the bait. Take it!*

Scraping paws over dirt. A growl.

Yes.

A force as strong as a fucking wrecking ball barreled into the side of the Jeep, denting in the metal. Drilling into Seth's side as the Jeep spun out of control. I said nothing as I released the latch, stomach in my throat as we swerved off the road and came to a shattering stop against a tree. The windows rained broken glass over us a second before the latch clicked free and we sprang out.

I smashed into Seth as I shifted, letting my inner wolf free in the cramped tree-clogged space at the rear of the Jeep. He skidded to the side, dazed as a startled foreign wolf bared his teeth, coming for him with bloodlust in his eyes.

Shit. I moved to intervene, but Clay was faster, his massive dark wolf checking the attacker and sending him sailing into the white skin of a birch tree, staining it red.

You good? I sent to Seth through the pack bond, not pausing to check for myself as I got into position in front of him, covering his flank from any other attack.

Good, he replied, and I charged left of him, moving around the other side of the Jeep where the feral snarls and cries of shifters in battle bombarded my ears. The scent of fresh blood wetting my jowls.

Jared streaked past only a second before Clay and Seth joined ranks with me, rounding the sacrificial Jeep to the bloodbath on the other side.

Two shifters lay motionless around Vivian and Charity's feet while five more attacked viciously. One got a hold on the back of Vivian's neck and an ear splitting cry of pain assaulted my ears before my wolf all but blacked out with rage.

I tore the beast from her back with a lock on *its* neck in retaliation. It was easy to overpower him, and I didn't stop as blood gushed into my mouth or as his cries rang loud in my ears. I cut off the sound with a sharp jerk of my head, snapping his spine and leaving him to grow lifeless on the forest floor.

Something slammed into my side, and I grunted in pain before rearing up on my hind legs to attack.

The wolf's ears lowered in submission only a moment before my strike fell, but I couldn't stop myself. There would be no mercy. Not from me and definitely not from my wolf.

My jaws clamped around his shoulder, taking him down with ease until I had him pinned beneath me. Still, he didn't move to fight. He lay there prone beneath my paws and teeth, snout pressed to the dirt, a sickly whine humming between his lips.

I growled at him, putting my face in his, my need for blood temporarily nullified by the sight of the pathetic creature beneath me.

They're getting away! Jared called, and I snapped my head up, seeing what they saw. Three more corpses lay on the ground now, making a total of five. The remaining two were fleeing and Vivian was hot on their heels, her sandy fur matted with the blood of her enemies. An all-consuming rage gleaming in her eyes.

Stop! I demanded. *We stick together, Viv. I've already got one here. Let them go.*

I can't. Vivian!

Clay bolted after her, *I'll bring her back,* he promised,

and I had to believe they'd be fine. That Clay would catch the fleeing wolves and help Vivian end them before they got too far away.

My other mate approached, a slight limp in his right leg. *I'll take him,* he offered, and I grudgingly relented my hold on the shifter still blowing dirt with his incessant whining.

Everyone whole? Charity asked, and I lifted my head to her, checking her over. She seemed all right save for a gash in her collar that was already quickly healing.

I tested my legs, afraid that the hit to my flank might've broken some shit, but it seemed I was only badly bruised.

Yeah. All good.

I allowed a momentary flash of pride at what we'd managed to accomplish here today. We'd been outnumbered and had come out whole anyway. I credited the element of surprise, but not above the skill of my packmates.

For what I'd asked them to sacrifice here today, there were no words. In the battles we've had to face in the years past, there had been death, but never before now had I asked them to fight for me, for our pack. To shed blood in the name of our family.

And not one of them looked as though they regretted it, though I sensed it may haunt them for a time, regardless.

We waited for Clay and Vivian to return before doing anything. The rest of us waiting in patient silence as we collected ourselves. Let our bodies settle and heal.

It didn't take long. Within a few minutes, they returned. Both of them looking a little worse for wear, but mostly unharmed. Vivian loped over to me with her ears pressed down against her head while Clay followed only a few steps behind. A darkness rolling off him in waves.

Sorry, Viv sent through the pack bond. *I couldn't...I couldn't seem to stop myself.*

I shook my canine head. *It's all right.*

It wasn't, really, but what was done was done and they were both all right. Next time, and I fucking *prayed* there wouldn't be a next time, I'd need to command her to stay with the group.

Have you questioned him yet? Clay asked, leaning down over the still-keening wolf pressed to the dirt beneath Jared's white paws.

I was waiting until you got back.

Let him up, I instructed Jared, and everyone formed a ring around the shifter as Jared lifted his paw.

The shifter didn't even try to get up. He kept his head pressed flushed to the earth, sides heaving with even more alarm now that he was released.

I shifted back, grunting as the transformation made something in my hip pop where a bone must have been slightly knocked out of the joint.

"*Fuck,*" I groaned, earning myself a worried look from Clay which I waved off. "I'm good," I assured him before turning my attention back to the shifter on the ground.

"Shift," I ordered him. "We need to have a little chat."

The wolf let out one last sniveling whine before shifting, turning into a tan boy with short black hair who couldn't have been older than fifteen or sixteen. His dark brown eyes peered up at me from where he lay, slightly covering his face as though anticipating an attack.

"I'm not going to hurt you," I decided, pity spurring the words from my lips. "Not if you tell me what I want to know."

He nodded, lowering his hands from his face with twitching slowness.

"I-I can't," he stammered. "He'll kill me."

Clay growled, and I bared my teeth at the boy. Pitiful fucker or not, I would have the answers I needed to protect my pack. No matter the cost. A hollowness formed in my gut, and I winced at the thought of hurting the boy, but steeled myself against the feeling.

This is what it means to be alpha.

"If you don't tell me what I want to know, *I'll* kill you," I promised him, shocked at the sincerity in my voice.

His red-rimmed eyes welled up and honestly I had to wonder who the hell sent this *child* on an attack errand. There was no fucking way I'd have sent someone like him. He clearly wasn't ready.

"P-Please, I just—"

"Start talking. I want to know who sent you. I want to know where they are. What they're planning. How large their pack is. And where the hell he's keeping the shifters he captured."

His brown eyes widened. "*Now.*"

Vivian punctuated my demand with a fierce snarl that sent the boy to shaking again.

"Okay!" he shrieked. "Okay, I'll tell you."

I crouched down closer to his level, putting the full weight of my stare on him.

"H-his name is Devin."

It took me a moment to register what the kid said, my mind refusing to translate the syllables of his name into anything meaningful.

What. The. Fuck.

Clay charged the kid, knocking him from his side to his back and pressing his paws down into his shoulders. His claws drawing blood as he snarled in the boy's face, hot saliva dripping from his jowls. His bright blue eyes crazed with fury.

"Clay!" I barked, drawing his attention just long enough for him to get ahold of himself and step off the sobbing teenager and stalk away into the trees. Not far enough that he couldn't hear, but far enough that he could hopefully stop himself from killing the kid. He began to pace between the trees.

"I want to make sure I'm understanding you," I said, swallowing down my knee-jerk reaction to scream. "Your pack alpha is Devin *Wright?*"

He lowered his gaze from mine, wiping at the snot beneath his nose. "Yes."

Yes.

Fucking *yes.*

Devin Wright.

My high school boyfriend. The one who slapped me around and

called me a whore. The very same sadistic psychopath who kidnapped me and shackled me in a fucking *cave* because he was convinced I was his one true mate. The same Devin Wright that sunk his canines into my shoulder and sealed my fate.

Absently, my finger trailed over the scars on my shoulder. The jagged edges of them from where his fangs tore open my flesh beneath the full moon.

I swallowed back bile, my stomach simultaneously filling with dread and burning with a rage so hot I feared it would consume me. My wolf battered at my defenses, feral with rage of her own. Her focus narrowing until inside, all we could see was his face...and how we would absolutely mutilate it.

"Keep talking," I said, my voice a distant monotone. "O-our pack is the largest in the whole state. He took over five other packs in the last year alone by challenging their alphas."

How had we not fucking heard of this? And how had he even managed that? He must've had something up his sleeve. Some secret weapon. Otherwise succeeding in the takeover of five different packs in *one* year would be downright impossible.

I shared a look with Jared in his wolf form, whose amber eyes looked more like fire in this moment than they ever had.

"How many?" I demanded.

"I...I don't know exactly. Maybe seventy."

I couldn't conceal my gasp of alarm at the insanity of that number. I'd never even heard of a pack so large. We had close to fifty and were considered the largest pack in the western United States.

"What does he want?"

Vivian snarled impatiently, and I knew she was getting antsy not knowing where Destiny was. I shot her a look that I hoped conveyed that was what I was going to ask next and she needed to chill for a sec.

"How should I know?" the boy asked in a shrill voice. "I just j-joined when he took over my p-pack a few weeks ago."

I glared at him.

"*I don't know,*" he insisted, and the scent of his fear wrinkled my nose even in my human form. All sour and sweet. "But I know that y-you...that your pack is his endgame. He's been g-getting us all ready for this s- since my pack joined."

I nodded, surmising that he was telling the truth. If he knew more, I had no doubt he'd say it. "Okay," I gritted out, my teeth near cracking at the tension in my jaw. "Fine. Where is he keeping the shifters he captured?"

He curled in on himself, lowering his head as though waiting for the blade to drop.

"Hey!" I shouted. "You tell me where they are or I'll—"

"I don't know!" he cried, panting, his entire body trembling. "I *s-s-swear* I don't. Th-This was my first run with the attack crew. We were supposed to t-take that one," he glanced briefly at Jared, his Adam's apple bobbing, "straight to the alpha. He said he wanted to handle him himself."

My wolf almost leapt out from my throat and swallowed the kid whole, but I managed to rein her in at the last second, my own body trembling with the effort of keeping her caged.

Just wait, I urged myself. Urged my wolf. *We'll have our revenge. We just need to wait.*

"The others he c-captured aren't at pack camp. He keeps them s-somewhere else. Nobody knows where except his inner circle."

Sam. Would Sam know?

Vivian shifted in a lupine cry of anguish that morphed into a very human shriek in the span of one shared breath.

"He's lying!" she hissed, stepping forward with her hands extended, her fingers tipped with deadly sharp claws that didn't look at all like they were receding.

"Viv!" I warned, and she hesitated, her chest rising and falling rapidly. Guilt lashed through me like the biting edge of a whip at the sight of her ribcage, clearly visible through her pale skin.

I turned my attention back to the boy. "If you're lying—"

"I'm not," he choked out through sobs. "I p-promise.

I would tell you if I knew. *I would.*"

Vivian's glowing eyes met mine, frantically searching my gaze as though I might have a better answer for her than this boy did.

"Where is his camp?"

"We move every c-couple of days. We're on the eastern s-side of Mt. Hood right now."

Far, but not that far. Jared told me that Mt. Hood was home to more than three small packs a long time ago, but after a battle between them leaving only one the victor, none wanted to remain there anymore. They abandoned their camp and moved south. Mt. Hood was no-man's-land now.

"Devin wants something," I muttered, trying to think through the red haze of my rage tainting my every thought. *Think, Allie.*

"And he's not going to stop until he gets whatever it is."

I bit my lower lip so hard I tasted blood, and the tang of it combined with the sharp bite of pain brought me the clarity I needed to make the call.

"Tell your alpha I want to meet."

"Allie, what the fuck are you doing?" Clay's growl came from the trees as he charged back to where the rest of us stood, his face a shade of red that might've scared me once upon a time.

I clenched my fists and stood my ground. "I'll meet him at the eastern border of my territory. There's a lacrosse field there at the college in Beaverton. Saturday at noon. I'll be waiting at the northern entrance under the bleachers. He knows the spot."

Bile rose in my throat at the memory of his hands on my body. How I'd craved his touch. How I'd let him in. How I let him drag me beneath the bleachers when I should have been watching my best friend's lacrosse championship game.

The boy looked like he was either going to shit himself or pass out in relief. "Y-you're letting me go?"

"Run. Before I change my mind."

He pressed himself up from the ground on shaky legs, cautiously glancing at the giant wolves and furious humans who all looked like they'd rather take a bite out of him than let him leave.

"This is a mistake," Clay hissed under his breath as Jared shifted back to his human form, a vacant look in his eyes.

"Go!" I all but screamed at the boy and he tripped in his haste to flee, scrambling to get back to his feet and shift back into his wolf form.

"We should have killed him," Jared said plainly. His face pale. "Clay wanted to and I stopped him. If we'd killed him—"

Clay hauled off and slammed his fist into the nearest tree, sending wood splinters scattering into the air with the force of the blow. A bloody smear was left in the mangled trunk, but he didn't even seem to feel the injury as he tore the lowest branches clean off the thing and threw them to shatter against other trees.

His emotions wreaked havoc on my already chaotic thoughts and my tenuous hold on my control. I clenched my body tighter, willing my wolf to give me the inner peace I needed right now. The level headedness of an alpha. A leader.

"Clay," I called in a low voice, waiting as he unleashed his rage on the forest around us while Charity and Seth dutifully remained in their wolf forms, keeping their ears pricked to any sign of approach and Viv and Jared stood mutely by. Angry and numb.

"Clay," I tried again, and he whirled on me, face a mask of pain.

"What?" he demanded in a voice not quite fully human.

"You were ordered to let him leave pack territory by Ryland. *That* was his punishment. If you had disobeyed—"

"And what about after?" he demanded, stepping up to me until he was so close I could smell his sweat. Hear the hammering pulse of his heartbeat. He put his face in mine. "After you became our alpha and I stopped keeping tabs on him, hmmm? I should have gone after him. I should have *ended* him."

"I wouldn't have let you."

His upper lip twitched as he rolled his shoulders back, challenging me. Clay would never hurt me, I knew that, and yet for a fleeting second I wondered if he might really lose his control this time.

Guilt crushed me as his hands gripped my arms and yanked me to his chest, pressing me against the dirt and sweat, tucking my head beneath his chin. "This is my fault," he said in an exhale, his body twitching as the muscles attempted to relax with the adrenaline still flowing through them.

I pushed him away. "No, it's not."

I sent a pointed look at Jared, urging him to meet my gaze. "It isn't either of your faults. It's mine."

Jared opened his mouth like he might disagree, but I shook my head. "It doesn't fucking matter now, does it? I'm assuming he wants some kind of revenge against us for forcing him out of Forest Grove. For me denying him."

"Then you can't go there," Vivian said. "You can't meet him. It might be exactly what he wants."

I knew it must have pained her greatly to admit that, especially since meeting with him might've been the only way for us to find Destiny and the others. But there was one other possibility…

"I'm not," I told her, making all the others turn spurious looks my way. "Haven't you ever seen a movie? Read a book?"

"What are you saying?" Jared asked, his brows lowering.

"We're going to plant a phone there. And at noon on Saturday, we're going to call it."

Surprise flashed across Clay's eyes, and he cocked his head at me like he never knew I could be so crafty. *Dick.*

"Guess there is a use for all those books you read besides getting you all hot and—"

"Ew," Vivian interrupted, looking like she might vomit.

"Everyone cool with this plan?"

They all nodded, Seth and Charity included with slight inclines of their lupine heads.

"Good. There's just one more thing."

I sent an apologetic look Clay's way, but this was it. It couldn't be avoided any longer. They needed to know. And as soon as we got back, we needed to find out what Sam knew.

If she knew where Destiny and the others were being kept this whole fucking time, I would feed her to Vivian.

"What?" Vivian asked, and I could tell she was internally bracing for what I'd say next.

"It's Sam. She's been lying to all of us."

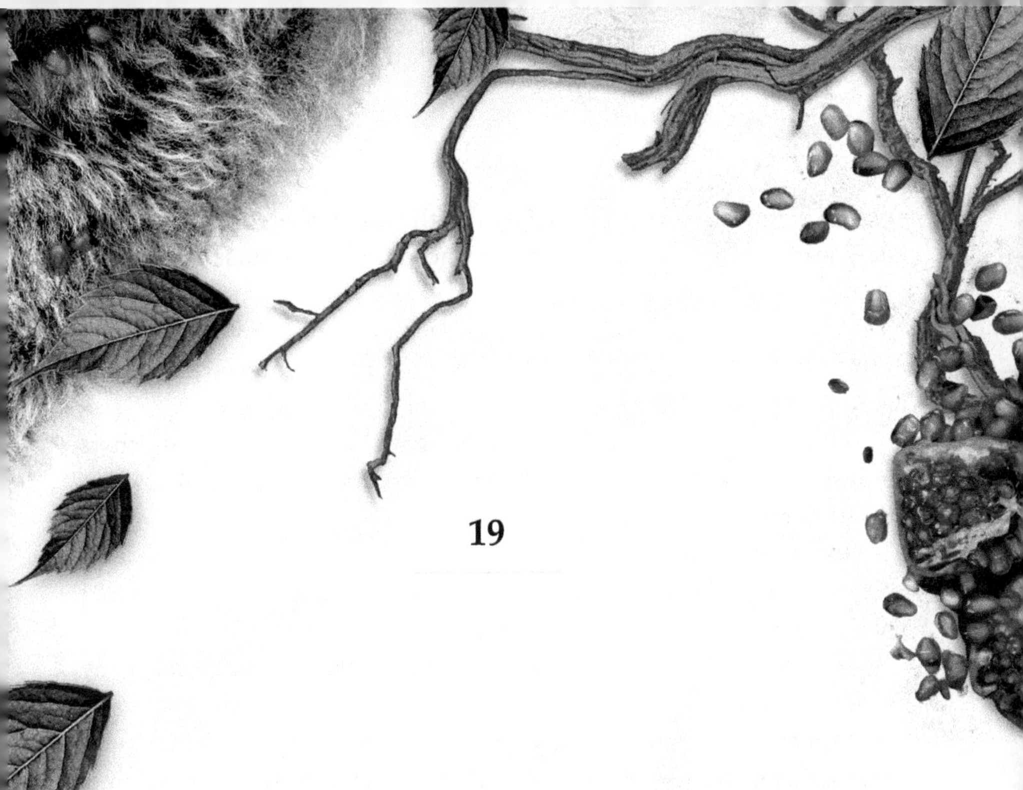

19

I sensed something was wrong before we could even cross back over into our territory, and by the time we got to second ring patrol, I was certain of it.

The patrol wasn't out. The scents of Archer, Jacob, and Danny were there, but they were faint. They hadn't run this section of the ring in a while. Maybe an hour. Could be more.

Something's wrong, Clay said through the pack bond, causing the others to slow, catching on to what my and Clay's noses already had.

Where's the patrol? Jared asked, as though one of us might have an answer. We didn't.

Hurry, I growled through the bond. *We have to get back* now.

Clay and I led our small group back to camp. Me just ahead of Clay, and Clay just ahead of Vivian and Jared with the others behind them. It was a study in fucking patience to keep myself from taking off ahead of them all. I could. My legs were ready, willing to push me faster, and I had to tamper them down. Unable to leave anyone behind or without sufficient backup.

I hear them, Clay spoke in my mind and I realized I could hear them, too. As we blew past the first ring and onto the edges of camp, I could hear the sounds of people talking. There was no screaming. No growls or burning buildings. But in my gut, I could feel that something wasn't right. There was a heaviness in the atmosphere, and it pressed down on me, filling me with dread and making my pulse flutter and spurt.

As we cleared the trees and burst back into camp, my hackles high and body on full alert, we found Layla standing amid a half-naked group of shifters near a slow burning fire in the pit.

As soon as her eyes locked on to me, she shoved through the others in her path to get to us. I shifted back, shivering despite the warmth in the early evening air at the loss of my fur.

Her eyes roved over my dirt and blood streaked skin for an instant before lifting back to my face as the others entered camp and shifted back, too, all of them coming to flank me.

"I'm so sorry," Layla said, her chin quivering in a way that made my heart leap into my throat.

"What happened?" Jared demanded while Clay's piercing gaze roamed over the rest of camp, searching for attackers. For something, *anything* amiss.

"They just didn't come back," she said in a watery voice, holding back tears with a faraway look in her eyes.

Vivian shouldered past me and grabbed onto Layla's shoulders, giving her a little shake to get her to snap out of it. "Who?" she demanded. "Who didn't come back?"

"The search party," she said, finding her strength and shucking off Vivian's hands as she lifted her chin and pushed her long dark hair back from her face. "They were supposed to be back an hour ago, but they haven't returned. I sent a small scout party as far as the third ring, but they just got back."

One of what I presumed was the small scout party of four stepped up behind Allie. A guy named Dillon. "There was no sign of them," he confirmed. But near the outer edge of the third ring near Glenwood we, *uh*, we think we picked up the scent of some foreign shifters."

"Fuck," Clay groaned, scrubbing a hand over his face. "Who was it?"

Dillon filled us in on the names. There had been six of them.

We were down another *six* shifters.

My stomach turned sour, and I hunched as it twisted, seeing stars.

"Someone bring me Sam," I hissed before spinning on my heel and taking off toward our cabin.

Distantly, I registered them calling after me, but I needed to get away. I needed...

Oh shit.

I forced myself not to hunch any more as I took the stairs two at a time and blew through the front door, making for the main floor bathroom at a near-sprint. The instant I crossed the threshold, I kicked the door closed and fell to my knees, spewing bile into the toilet until there was nothing left.

Until the hot tears staining my eyes from retching turned to fat droplets of pure fury, fear, and frustration.

Devin motherfucking Wright. This *was* my fault after all. All of it was.

I should've known. I'd had too many years of peace. Too many years of *good things.* Now it wouldn't be only me who paid for my happiness, it would be my pack, too. Just like Mom. Just like Dad. Just like Vivian and Layla. Clay and Jared. No one close to me was safe from the havoc my life wreaked on others.

The door creaked as it opened, and I glanced up from the porcelain goddess to see Jared quietly pushing himself inside.

"You don't want to see this," I groaned, heat crawling up my neck as I closed the toilet lid and flushed, sagging against the vanity. "I just need a minute."

He sat next to me, closing the door behind him and pulling me into his arms. My chest tightened at the immediate sense of comfort and fresh tears spilled onto my cheeks. "I've got you," he said in a low whisper, tugging a towel down from the rod to wrap around my naked, shuddering body.

I clutched on to him, allowing myself just a moment to feel all the pent up emotions roiling within. I'd hardly slept in weeks. And even though I was forcing down food on the regular and I knew my wolf was strong and swift, I felt empty inside. Hollow and frail. Like a strong breeze might blow me away.

"What do we do?" I croaked, trying unsuccessfully to stop the deluge of tears as I allowed the warmth of his body to seep into my icy bones.

"We do what we always do," Jared said in a soft, reassuring voice, squeezing me tighter. "We figure it out. One step at a time. Clay's already gone to town—"

I stiffened.

"*With* a *large* amount of backup," he added and some of the new tension eased. "To pick up a burner phone. It's supposed to rain overnight tonight and that'll make it hard for anyone to find or track them in case Devin gets cocky enough to attack us on our own turf. He'll go with a crew to plant the phone beneath the bleachers like you said and come straight back."

There were still two days until Saturday. Forty-eight hours. Why did it feel more like a decade to have to wait.

As the fluttering behind my ribcage quieted, I was finally able to take a full breath and rid the dark edges from my vision and the dizziness from my head.

"You're doing so amazing, you know that?" Jared said, surprising me.

No I fucking wasn't.

I'd gotten, what? Ten wolf shifters captured. I'd killed an innocent witch. I'd gotten Sal's butcher shop burned to the ground and Jared's Jeep smashed almost beyond repair now.

Which reminded me, we still needed to get that towed back to the garage. Ugh.

"I don't mean what you're doing or what's happened," he said, pressing a soft kiss to the knot between my brows. "I mean in here."

He tapped my forehead.

"You haven't had any real panic attacks. I can feel your anxiety every day, but you keep pushing through. You keep putting on a brave face. You've come so far. I'm proud of you."

Well, that's just fucking rude. Now I want to cry again. "Why'd you have to go and say that?" I croaked. "Love you, too."

I nuzzled back into him for a moment before remembering my last order to them before I gave in to my anxiety. Shit. We really didn't have time for this. I straightened, coming out of Jared's arms and letting the towel fall to pool around my waist.

"Where's Sam? We need to find out what she knows. She might be able to tell us where Devin is keeping the others. We could get them back. We could—"

Jared's amber eyes darkened, and he bowed his head, his hair shadowing his expression from view.

"Jare?"

"She's gone, Allie. She must've figured it out. I don't know how, but..."

"No." I stood up, my knees weak but waking with a new flood of adrenaline. "No, she can't be gone. She was our best chance of finding them. Where did she go? When? What direction?"

I wrenched open the door and stalked down the hall. "We can still catch her. We *have* to catch her."

"She's *gone*," Jared called behind me, rushing to catch up, his footfalls echoing in the empty cabin. "Allie, wait."

His hand closed around my elbow, jerking me to a stop. "Layla was keeping an eye on her shared cabin all day, but she managed to slip out the window during the commotion when they realized the search party hadn't come back."

A chill rattled down my spine. If that was true, then she'd been gone for hours already. We'd never catch up to her.

"She's gone back to him, isn't she?" I asked, though it was obvious that was exactly what she'd done.

And I was the idiot who let it happen.

I tipped my head back in a quiet roar of frustration, kicking the nearest object to me to get out the pent up rage that felt near bursting inside of me. "*Dammit!*" I shouted as the hall table smashed against the opposite wall, sending wooden legs and a glass bowl shattering in every direction.

"I should have listened to you. We should have chained her up and questioned her as soon as we found out what she was doing."

Jared's lips pressed into a thin line. He wasn't disagreeing with me. Why should he? It was the truth. *I let this happen.*

"I'm going to kill her," I growled. "I'm going to find her, and I'm going to fucking destroy her. Right after I tear Devin's goddamned head off."

"I know," Jared said calmly. "I know you will. And we'll help you do it."

Less than fifteen minutes stood between now and noon. The last two days had been the hardest so far. Vivian was beside herself with worry and stress. The other pack members were on high alert. We only patrolled the first ring now, keeping the remaining wolves we had as close as we could.

We moved the meat from the pub and closed it temporarily.

The quarry had also been shut down and a human security service that cost us so much money I didn't even want to look at our account balance was watching over both venues.

Not even Devin was stupid enough to risk exposure to mortals and bring the wrath of the Arcane Council down on him.

It was the only option that kept everyone as safe as possible, even if it would take months for us to recover financially. That was a worry for another time, though. "I've been thinking," Layla said, lifting her head with a furrowed brow. "He had to have been planning this for a long time, right?"

I nodded. "Yeah. Attacking our food supply, our income, and reducing our numbers…" Even I had to admit it. "It was well thought out."

"Don't forget using my kid sister as a fucking spy to get all the info he needed to do it," Clay grunted, crossing his bulging arms over his bare chest where he leaned against the fridge.

"That too."

"What are you getting at?" Vivian asked, her jaw working as she ground her teeth in a way that made my skin crawl.

Layla pursed her lips. "I don't know. This can't just be about payback, right? It has to be something more."

I nodded to the slim black flip phone at the heart of the kitchen island. "That's what we're going to find out. He has to want something otherwise he would be killing the shifters he took, and Viv would know if Destiny was…"

I couldn't bring myself to say it, but Viv nodded anyway. "She's not dead," she confirmed. "I would know. I would feel it."

That didn't mean she was all right. Not in the least, but I wasn't about to say that.

"I think I might have an idea what he's after," Jared said, staring at the phone like he might rather smash the thing to dust than let me make the call.

"What?" Layla asked and Jared's eyes darted first to her and then to Clay, whose upper lip twitched into a snarl. Eventually, his glowing amber eyes slid to me, and I saw and felt so much hatred within him that my pulse quickened.

"You," he said simply, as though it were the obvious answer, but also the most disgusting one he could imagine. "Do you remember what he said to me at Jacqueline's bookshop the day I asked you to come home with me?"

I thought back to that day. When Devin had come to confront me at work and Jared had made him leave and convinced me to stay with him.

"You're mine," I repeated the words Devin said to me that day, shivering and sick at the memory.

"And he believed that," Jared continued. "It's why he kidnapped you. Why he turned you. He thought that when you shifted, you would mate with him and be bound to him forever."

"But I didn't. I mated with you, and with Clay."

And the rage and utter betrayal I'd seen in Devin's eyes that night told me that nothing had ever hurt him more than bearing witness to that.

"So you think this is all some ploy to get to Allie?" Vivian asked, her face turning a sickly shade of green.

Jared shrugged. "I don't know. It's the only thing that makes sense. At least, a fucked up kind of sense. The guy's a psychopath."

"And not the fun kind," Layla muttered, drawing curious looks from the others. She and I shared a look and I remembered that she had been borrowing books from my library.

"No," I agreed with her. "Definitely *not* the fun kind."

Devin was no Viper or Saint. He was an *actual monster*. The kind that didn't deserve to be understood or forgiven. The kind that needed to be killed. End of story.

Clay snorted his agreement and tapped the clock on the stove. "It's time. Let's see what this fucker has to say."

I snatched up the phone and went to the only contact in the list—the other burner cell—and hit call, afraid I'd lose my nerve if I hesitated even for a second. Devin needed to know that I meant fucking business, and I wouldn't bend to whatever it was he wanted. If it was a war he wanted, then I might just give it to him.

I put it on speakerphone as it began to ring and let it clatter back onto the counter, leaning over and winding my hands together to keep from shattering the marble countertop with my grip.

The call connected and there was a brief pause when I thought he might've hung up, but then a familiar voice filtered through the speaker, lifting the hairs on my arms and filling my stomach with acid.

"Smart girl," Devin said. "Though I expected no less."

He sounded almost the same as I remembered. That same smooth voice that haunted my nightmares for almost a year after what he put me through, now colored by age. It had a deepness to it that hadn't been there before. A gruffness that suited him far better than his smooth tongue ever had.

"You're a dead man," I spat, unable to form anything more articulate just yet. I needed him to know what I intended to do to him.

"Now that just hurts my feelings, and we both know you wouldn't dare launch an attack against me. Not while I have so many of your pack under my thumb."

"Get to the point, asshole. What the fuck do you want?" Vivian shouted, and I sent her a look. They all promised to be quiet.

"Vivian, is that you? Destiny's been asking for you, you know—"

Vivian's eyes went saucer wide, and she launched for the phone, her wolf bursting out from within. "You fucking bastard!"

I managed to snatch it before she could, and she sailed over the smooth counter and landed in a heap on the floor, scrambling to her feet with claws instead of fingernails.

"Get her outside," I ordered, and Layla dutifully herded Viv out, muscling her in a way I didn't know Layla was even capable of.

Laughter echoed from the line and the amount of venom in my blood was making my vision darken. He was *laughing* at her. At us.

The only thing that allowed me to remain even remotely calm was thinking *in detail* about everything I was going to do to him once I got my hands on him.

After a moment, his laughter quieted. "No? Not funny? Well shit, hope I didn't offend..."

"Where are they?" I asked. "What have you done with them?"

"They're alive," he replied. "For now. So long as you do as I ask, they will remain that way."

Clay bristled, his body tensing in a way that told me his wolf was also on the verge of breaking free.

"And what is it that you want?" A pause.

"You."

"*Motherfucker*," Jared cursed under his breath, shoving away from the countertop to walk into the living room, arms braced behind his head. Every muscle taut as a bowstring.

"You belong to me, Allie. You always have. You always will. One day, you'll see it, too. I promise you that."

My own stomach turned at his admission, but I supposed I shouldn't have been surprised. And honestly? This might work to our advantage. He wanted me? The twin soul wolf.

As far as any of us knew, I was the strongest shifter to have ever lived thanks to having ingested my would- be twin sister in my mother's womb.

If he wanted me, he would get me. I'd *end* him.

"When and where?" I asked, drawing furious and shocked looks from my mates.

"Now, now, my pet. Don't be hasty. I know you miss me but there's no rush."

"I want this over with," I told him, trying to ignore the way Clay and Jared were staring daggers at me. But beneath their trepidation I felt their curiosity. They were wondering what my ulterior motives were with this.

I loved them for realizing I wasn't stupid enough to just walk into a trap.

"Me for the shifters you took and full immunity from future attacks against my pack. Do we have a deal?"

The crackle of a fire somewhere near him on the other end of the line popped and hissed before he replied, his voice taking on the dangerous tone I remembered from the times he hurt me.

"You think I'd play right into your hand?"

"What do you mean?"

"Don't play dumb with me, Allie. I know you too well."

My tongue slid across my teeth, passing over where my canines were slipping out from my gums, elongating.

"If you challenge me openly, I will kill them all," he promised me, and I dropped my head, clenching my teeth together in frustration. That had been *exactly* what I planned to do.

It was an easy fix. I knew I was stronger than him. I would win, and he would die. And this fucking madness would end.

"How do you propose this works then?" I ground out, imagining plucking his stupid green eyes out of his skull with nothing but my bare hands.

"You'll see, my love. I have plans. Big plans. You'll have to be...*neutralized*. Can't have my wife trying to kill me at every turn, now can I? First, though, there's something I need you to do for me. A gesture of good faith so that I know you're serious about your offer to leave your pack and take your place with me, where you belong."

"Oh yeah?" I asked, fully unable to keep the sarcasm out of my voice any longer. "What's that?"

"It's a small thing, really. You see, I can't very well have you while you're still... mated to those *mutts*. Reject them."

My heart gave a panicked start at the very idea of that without meaning to, I let out a hiss that turned into a very growly *"Fuck you."*

That wasn't even a consideration. If I rejected the bond, it would destroy me. And it would relegate them to spending their entire lives alone. A wolf only mated once. The only thing that could permanently and fully sever a mate bond was death. Only then could a shifter find another mate.

As long as I lived, if I rejected Clay and Jared, they would never find other mates. And nor would I.

"Tsk tsk," Devin said with a gleeful ring to his voice. "I thought you were serious about saving the lives of the shifters I've borrowed from your pack, Allie? Shall I send you a token of the seriousness of my intentions? A hand perhaps? Or a head? Perhaps Destiny's?"

"You *monster*."

"You have one week. In the meantime, I give you my word that they will not be harmed. But if you haven't done what I've asked you to by then..."

"I'll call you at this number with further instructions in a few days."

Dark clouds swirled through my thoughts, ridding myself of the ability to respond. My wolf growled within, backed into a corner from which she couldn't see a way out.

One week, I whispered within. *A lot can happen in one week. We can find him. We can kill him. It won't come to that.*

"Oh, and Allie? I'll expect you to answer the phone when I call. If you don't, I'll have to punish one of your pack, and I'm sure you wouldn't want that."

"Is that all?" I gritted out. "For now."

I clicked the phone shut and pulled back my shaking hands before I could knock it from the counter and risk breaking it.

"He's a dead man walking," Clay swore, his face red.

A vein in his temple jumping with his quick pulse.

Jared's eyes locked on mine. "We have to find them," he said. "We have to find them and bring them home before he..." He didn't finish, his throat bobbing while his brows lowered, shadowing his eyes from view.

I shook my head. "I would *never* do what he just asked me to do," I told them both, a pit yawning open in my stomach. But even as I said it, I realized it might not be the truth.

If it was a choice between rejecting my mates and saving people from being killed? From saving my entire pack from Devin's wrath? It would be the most selfish thing I'd ever done to refuse the request.

Jared came to wrap his arms around my shoulders and press a hard kiss to my temple. "We know."

Over his shoulder, I could see Clay watching me. In his icy eyes I could see that he wasn't fooled. More than that, I felt the challenge in his stare. *Just fucking try it,* he seemed to be saying. *I'll never let you go.*

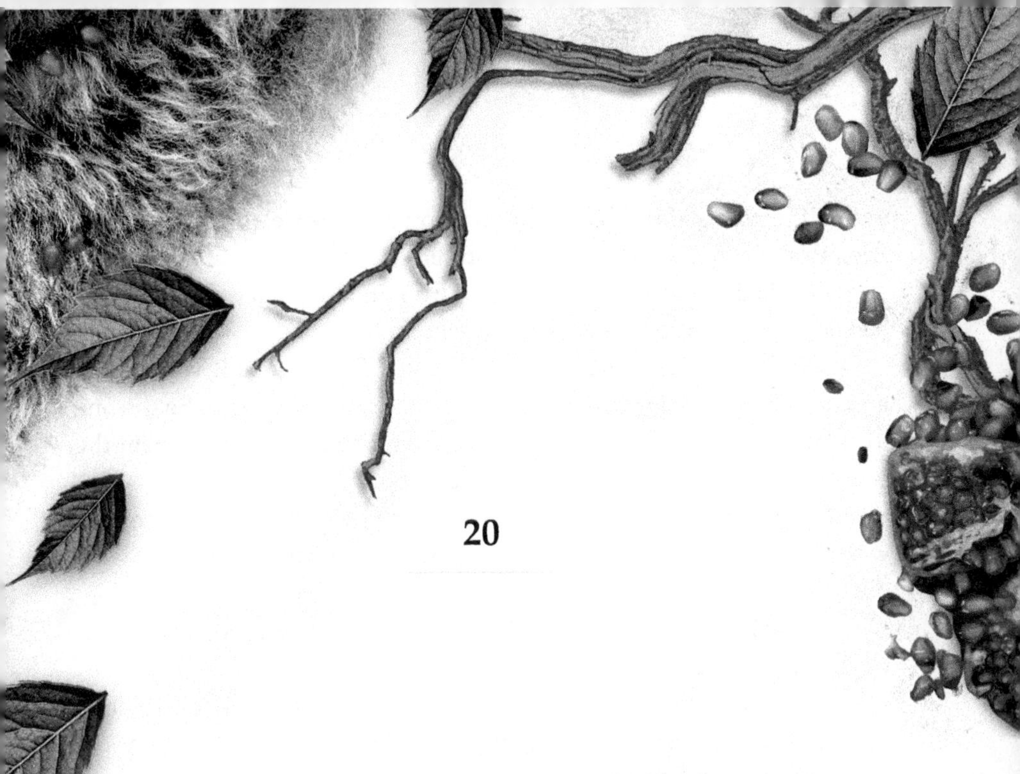

20

Finding our missing kin proved to be easier said than done. Not that I expected any less. We couldn't spread ourselves too thin in case Devin launched another assault or tried to capture any more of our pack. Which meant that we only patrolled the first ring now. The quarry and pub remained shuttered and guarded by hired mortal help. And when we did send out scouting parties, it was in varying directions, at varying times, and *only* in large numbers.

Not so large that we would be leaving pack camp inadequately protected. But not so small that they would be easily overcome if set upon by Devin's pack.

In the two days since Devin had declared his terms to me, we'd scouted as far as we dared to go and had turned up empty handed every time.

We'd even approached Dante's pack requesting aid. As I expected there too, we were denied. Dante and his pack bordered our lands to the west and preferred to remain comfortable and safe behind the thick walls surrounding their camp. It was a lost cause, but it was worth trying. Anything was worth trying at this point.

We had five more days until Devin would expect me to do something so horrible I couldn't even imagine it. Though my mind came up with all sorts of painful scenarios on its own, while sleeping and awake. Even though I did very little of the former.

"We need to tell them," Jared said, rubbing long circles in my back. "If you don't want to, then Clay and I can do it for you."

I shook my head, causing my hair to fall from where it was tucked behind my ear and form a curtain between us. "No. I have to be the one to do it. I should've been honest with them about everything from the start. Maybe if we had been, this wouldn't be—"

"Don't think like that. This is where we're at now. We have to deal with it. It doesn't matter what might've happened if things were different."

But it did matter to me. And I got the gut twisting feeling that it might matter to the pack, too.

They'd all followed orders just fine this whole time. They'd joined the scouting parties led by Charity, Jared, Clay, or myself. They'd asked little questions. But they deserved answers.

Jared pushed my hair back, draping over my shoulder so he could see my face again. I did my best to school it into something less worried. Failed.

"Are they all gathered?"

"They are," Jared confirmed. "But we don't have to go out yet."

Glasses clinked behind me and I jumped out of my skin, whirling on the couch to find Clay in the kitchen setting three glasses down on the counter. How in the hell he managed to not only get inside, but get into the kitchen and open a cupboard right behind us was beyond me. But I'd long since stopped questioning how he was so unnaturally light on his size thirteen feet.

"How about a whiskey first?" he offered.

I blew out a breath, and he smirked at me, knowing he got my heart hammering double time and had spooked me out of my dark thoughts.

"A double I think," I agreed. "Please."

He poured three and carried the small glasses in his mammoth hands to the living room, passing them out one to each of us.

"To..." he trailed off, lifting his glass.

Knowing there was absofuckinglutely *nothing* to be celebrating right now, I muttered a quick "To surviving through the night," and tossed my whiskey back, grimacing as it carved a searing path down my esophagus and pooled warmly in my belly.

Jared and Clay shared a look before following suit, all of us discarding our glasses on the low coffee table behind Clay.

"No one is going to blame you," Jared assured me as I stood up, giving me one last pat on the back.

"And if they do, I'll set 'em straight," Clay added, tipping his head to one side to crack his neck.

I rolled my eyes at him and stepped past the pair of them to the firing squad waiting outside.

Viv and Layla hushed the congregation of shifters surrounding the fire ring as I stepped out into the brisk night air. All I could see as I approached them was the ones *not* here.

Vivian, without Destiny.

Seth, without his usual partners in crime—Trey and Todd.

Sara without Luke.

And so many others looking bereft and forlorn at the party of shifters that was lost only two days ago. Some of which I didn't even recall their full names. If— no, *when*—I got them all back, I was going to make an effort to get to know each and every one of them.

"*Um,*" I started, the fire and crickets the only sounds besides the bleating of my heart pounding in my head.

Viv gave me an encouraging look and she and Layla along with my mates came to stand at my sides, lending me their strength.

"You all know how absolutely terrible I am at this sort of shit, but you deserve to know everything that we do, and I'm...I'm sorry I didn't explain it all sooner."

My instinct to find a spot on the ground and stare at it was overruled by my need to make them understand. I needed to look them in the eyes when I told them everything. They deserved that much.

My gaze roamed over the crowd, finding mated pairs and other couples. Brothers and sisters. Parents. Grandparents. And for a second, I was so utterly grateful that our pack hadn't seen any young in more than fifteen years. I'd *hate* to put a child through what I feared we as a pack were about to endure.

"Our missing brothers and sisters have been taken from us by someone some of you may remember. He was once a member of this pack, but he was cast out and banished for breaking one of our most sacred laws."

A few whispers broke out, and I wondered if they already knew. Many likely did. Vivian mostly kept to herself and Layla was good at keeping secrets, but a few others *in the know* weren't the best at keeping things to themselves.

Looking at you, Seth.

He pursed his lips as my gaze swept over him.

"His name is Devin Wright. He is the one who triggered my transformation. Ryland ordered that he be banished from Forest Grove for that crime."

"He's come back?" a male voice called, and I nodded.

"Yes. And he is the alpha of his own pack now. If what we've been told is true, it's...it's the largest pack in the country."

"Bigger than ours?" a girl maybe about seventeen asked, her nose wrinkling and face screwing up as though I might have bad intel.

"Yes."

Especially now that we've lost ten shifters, I thought but didn't say aloud.

"By about thirty shifters," I added, wanting to be as transparent as I could. They needed to know what we were up against here.

A few gasps sounded from the group and whatever I'd been about to say next vanished with the need to reassure them that I would do whatever I needed to protect them.

"We can't go up against that," someone cried.

"I heard two packs to the south got taken over. I wonder if it was him." Another mused to his friend.

"So then he wants revenge because Ryland banished him?"

"We could never win. Not without all the shifters he took."

"Are they even alive? How do we know he hasn't killed them already?"

"How are we going to get them back?'

The fluttering began behind my breastbone at the panic coming from all those looking to me for the answers.

"Hey!" Clay barked, surprising me and shocking all the others back to silence. "Let her fucking finish."

"*Clay*," I hissed, but he just crossed his arms over his chest and stared down each and every one of them.

"We know they're still alive," I assured them. "There's something he wants, and until he gets it, he won't risk the only bargaining chips he has."

"What does he want?" Tyler asked, his thick brows knotting together. "Can't we just give it to him?"

"It's not that simple," I said, my mouth suddenly dry as hell. "But I can promise you I'm going to do everything within my power to get our missing kin back and to keep everyone safe. This won't come to a battle. I won't ask anyone to fight."

"*Allie*," Clay growled, and I shot him a look.

"You said you wanted to be honest with them," Jared added. "Go on, tell them what he wants."

My stomach turned, and I swallowed back nervous bile, unable to speak.

"Devin wants your alpha," Clay said, and I bit down hard on the inside of my cheek, drawing blood. Angry that they were undermining me. Angry at myself for not being able to be 100% honest with my pack.

"He wants Allie," Jared continued. "Some of you don't know the whole story, but let me fill you in real quick. This guy is a monster. He kidnapped her."

He jabbed two fingers in my direction, and I winced, my inner wolf waking as though personally attacked.

"He chained her up in a cave and poisoned her. Abused her. And then to top it all off, he attacked her. *Bit her*."

"And then *Ryland* let the fucker go," Clay finished for him. "Devin thinks Allie belongs to him."

"Stop," I muttered.

"He's told her to reject us," Jared admitted to our pack and a barrage of whispers followed. "And if she doesn't do what he's asked, he's told her he'll hurt the shifters he's keeping hostage."

"Stop," I repeated, heat rushing through my veins. "And once she's rejected us, he wants her to submit to him. Leave this pack. For good. Have her all to himself. To torture. To rape. To make her bow."

"I said *stop*," I all but screamed, panting, my bones near snapping from the pressure of my wolf.

Jared reached out for me, but I flinched away, too angry to be calmed. "I won't let him hurt us," I promised them in a voice so fierce I had to question whether it came from my own lips. "I'll do whatever I have to. It's my *job* as your alpha."

Silence followed. Faces fell. Tensions rose.

"I'm so sorry," I murmured. "I brought this on us, and I *swear* to you that I will fix it."

Shuffling steps drew my attention, and I glanced up to find Hazel gently shouldering through the throng. She walked straight for me, hands outstretched until she found me and tugged my shaking fists into her wrinkled palms.

"*We'll* fix it," she said, her milky gaze sad and searching as she read me through the soft touch of her fingers. "You are our alpha, girl. If you think we'll allow you to sacrifice yourself to save any one of us, you are sorely mistaken."

She lifted my hands to her lips and kissed the back of my palm. "I'd sooner die than see you harmed, granddaughter. And I don't think I'm the only one."

My throat burned, and Hazel held my hands tighter in hers when they began to shake.

"She's right," a familiar voice called, and I peered up to find Archer standing next to Callum. "You took us in when no other pack wanted us. You gave us a home. A purpose."

"It doesn't matter if we're outnumbered," Callum agreed and a female mated pair who joined our pack last year moved to stand next to the two mated males, nodding their agreement.

"We'll fight with you if it comes to that. The last year we've been here has been the best of our lives," the one named Lily said, squeezing the hand of her mate.

"We won't let that bastard hurt you," Seth agreed. "And if you think we would, then you're an even bigger idiot than I thought."

"*Nice*, asshole," Layla said, giving him a playful shove.

Whispers of agreement spread through the pack like wildfire, until the whispers turned to louder shouts of affirmation. Until my heart was so full I feared it might burst in my chest. Until it hurt unlike anything I'd ever felt before.

It was a bittersweet sort of anguish.

I loved each and every one of them for being willing to fight and maybe die trying to defend me and this pack, but…

It only cemented my decision to do everything in my power to save them. These were good people. The best of shifter-kind. My family. And I would not allow them to be hurt.

Not while there was something I could do about it.

Grams released my hands just as the tears spilled over, carving hot trails down my cool cheeks. "Don't do anything foolish," she whispered, the roar of the others behind her all but drowning her out.

"I won't."

She tutted. "Don't lie to me, girl."

"Hazel…"

"If you go getting yourself hurt I promise to haunt you for the rest of your miserable life. And not the fun kind of haunting. I'll go full poltergeist on your ass. Got it?"

An unwilling smile stole its way onto my lips as I shook my head at her. "Got it."

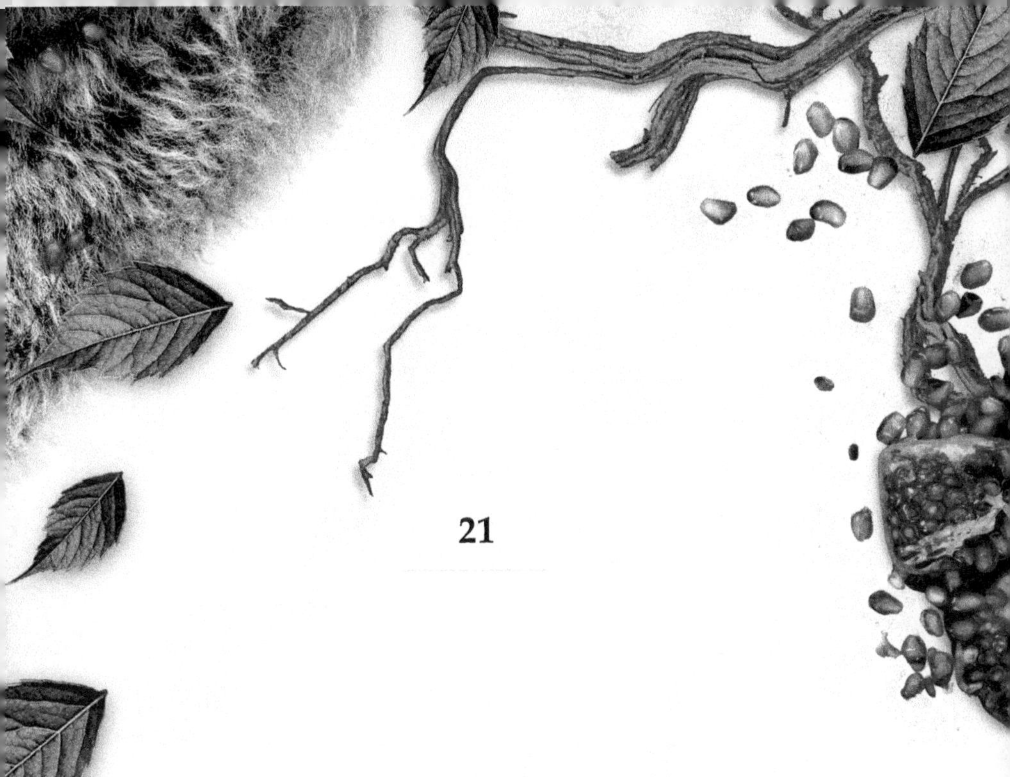

21

W e watched the fire burn down from the steps on the front porch of the cabin. I was still reeling from the meeting several hours before, and a few too many whiskeys had eradicated any desire to get up, move, or do much of anything but sit here and watch the flames try and fail to lick the clouds.

"Cookie?"

My brows crinkled, and I lifted my heavy head from the fist propped up on my knee to find Hazel exiting the cabin behind me, a plate of cookies in between her hands.

That explained why my stomach had been rumbling for the last hour.

"Why are you making cookies at midnight?" I asked but didn't hesitate for even a second to snatch a few still-warm chocolate chip ones from the plate before the guys descended on them.

Clay stole what looked like five with one scoop of his hand, leaving Jared only one remaining on the plate.

I thought they'd both been asleep, honestly. They'd been quiet for so long. Clay sprawled over the rough wood of the porch with his head in my lap. And Jared was sitting on the dirt, two steps below mine, his head resting heavily against my thigh.

It was official, I was certain Hazel's cookies could even wake the dead.

I stuffed one in my mouth, moaning at the melty chocolate goodness.

"There, see? Nothing a good cookie can't fix."

Something cold nudged my shoulder and I spun to see Hazel pressing a cold glass of water to my skin. "Drink this. You'll thank me tomorrow."

I huffed, but gratefully accepted the glass, draining in in two long swallows. Wincing as the chill of it stung my teeth.

"Thanks, Grams."

She ruffled my hair and turned to go back inside. "Don't clean up," I insisted. "Let us do it in the morning."

"Oh, it's already clean dear. I'm just going to get another plate of cookies. Seems I underestimated how hungry you beasties would be this late."

Despite myself, I grinned as I watched her feel her way back to the door and vanish back into the cookie scented cabin.

"Come on, Clay," Jared said, leaning over my lap to where Clay had himself propped on an elbow, demolishing his cookies. "I only got one."

"Your own damned fault you weren't fast enough."

"*Dude.*"

"Here," I offered, sadly looking at my only remaining cookie before passing it to Jared. He didn't take it, though.

Clay snatched it away from him and not so gently stuffed it into my mouth.

"Hey," I muttered around the mouthful, glaring at him.

"That's *your* cookie," he growled, casting a venomous glare in Jared's direction. "Here, you fucking tortoise."

He tossed Jared one of his cookies. "Don't say I never gave you anything."

"You spit on it, didn't you?" Jared asked, his face pinching as he turned the cookie over in his hands.

Sometimes I forgot that they were just a bunch of overgrown twenty-somethings that had been best friends their whole lives. A lightness stole some of the weight from my shoulders, and a small giggle escaped my lips that had absolutely nothing whatsoever to do with the empty bottle of whiskey at our feet.

Nope. Nothing at all.

Not two seconds after Clay set his head back down in my lap and I let my fingers delve into his soft dark hair, something shifted.

The screen door creaked open, and I felt the *pause* not just in her step, but also in Clay's stiffening shoulders against my thighs.

A cool night breeze brought with it a familiar scent that I hadn't been quick enough to catch first. Probably because I didn't know it as well as they did.

"Sam," Hazel said on a breath, and the plate of cookies shattering behind us spurred us all into action.

Clay leapt up from the porch, his inner wolf immediately taking over.

He shifted before I could blink and was chewing dirt as he sped off into the trees in the direction of her scent.

"Clay!" Hazel called. "Don't kill her!"

I snapped out of my daze and grabbed Jared's elbow as I stood. "It could be a trap," I blurted, my pulse thundering in my ears as my wolf awoke with a vicious need for bloodshed fueled by the lick of whiskey in my veins.

We raced after him, and I mourned the loss of yet another favorite pair of jean shorts as they flayed to ribbons in my haste to shift.

My wolf nearly ran headlong into a tree, disoriented from the taint of alcohol still lingering in our bloodstream.

Fuck.

I'll never drink again, I promised myself.

"Allie!" Vivian shouted, panicked from somewhere behind me. I knew she'd follow. So would anyone else still awake, or anyone woken by the commotion.

Shit. Shit. Shit.

I needed to get to her before Clay did. If it was a trap, he'd need backup.

If it wasn't, someone would need to stop him from tearing his sister's throat out. Not that she didn't deserve it, but if she were really back, then we might need her. Any information she dumped from her poisonous mouth when I let Vivian beat it out of her was better than the big fat fucking nothing that we had now.

Clay, I shouted down the length of the bond, spurring my sloppy run into a full on sprint. *It could be a trap. Wait!*

No reply.

I said wait, I growled within, injecting the words with an alpha's venom to which I heard Clay howl ahead, forced to slow by my will alone. It wouldn't stop him entirely, I needed to be closer for that. Needed eye contact. But it would make it a hell of a lot harder for him to run.

Stall him, Jared spoke in my mind. *The others and I are just behind you.*

Got it.

Mentally thanking Hazel for the cookies and water to sop up some of the booze in my gut, my vision began to clear. My wolf burning off the last dregs of it with her heat and power. Once our head was clearer, we could run full tilt.

A dash of shadow ahead told me we were right on top of him now. And ahead, I could hear the plaintive cry of an injured wolf. Sam's scent permeated the air now. Tainted every heavy breath I drew.

A savage snarl proceeded the pitched cry of an animal as Clay attacked his sister.

I got there just in time before he got his jaws around her slender neck and knocked him off, finding Charity and Syd flanking Sam's wolf.

Calm the fuck down, I hissed. *We need her.*

Vivian was the next to arrive, all fangs and claws and fury.

You fucking cunt! She screamed through the pack bond, launching at Sam.

I stepped into her path, blocking her and earning myself a stare of cutting betrayal.

She may know something, I reminded Vivian, my own desire to tear Sam's throat out almost winning out over rational thought.

A few years ago, my wolf would've had her way no matter what I wanted, but not now. I respected and validated her need for pain and punishment. For retribution. And she respected my need to retain my authority and to do whatever I needed to serve my pack in the best, *smartest* way. Even if she didn't always agree.

I faced Sam as Jared and the others crowded in around, ears pricked for signs of attack. We were still within the first ring, so if I had to wager, I'd say we were safe here.

Clay growled ferociously at his sister, his emotions a chaotic mess of anguish and fury that was starting to taint my own thoughts enough that needed to actively block him out.

Please, Sam pleaded and I was disgusted at the reminder that I never officially cut her out of this pack.

It was then that I noticed all the blood. The scent of it alerting me before the sight of it in the dark.

Blood coated every inch of her dark fur, making it glimmer in a red hue under the light of the moon. Her rear quarter looked awkward, too. And her left leg was twisted at an odd angle, showing bone through the skin.

Her face, too.

A long gash ran six inches from her temple down to split her lips wide open on the right side.

She was utterly grotesque with injury, and despite all my loathing, something in my stomach grew cold with pity at the sight.

Clay was noticing it now, too, bending low to sniff at her back.

With a long, broken howl that tore open the wound on her lips afresh, she shifted back into her human form, bones rebreaking and wounds bleeding anew.

It was easier to see the injuries against her pale flesh and my canine stomach heaved at the severity of it all.

Broken ribs for sure.

One eye running completely red from burst blood vessels.

A foot facing the wrong way.

What are you doing? I demanded through the bond, not even realizing at first that she couldn't hear me anymore as she screamed her pain.

She'd have healed better and faster in her wolf form. The bones would've had to be rebroken but...shifting was the stupidest idea in her state. She could die from the blood loss alone.

Her scream choked off into a sob, and she bent forward, wincing at the broken ribs and letting her long black hair fall to cover her face. "All my fault," she said in a distant, watery voice. "All my fault. All my fault."

I shifted, careful to keep my distance as I knelt naked onto the earth. "What happened?"

"So sorry," she muttered, beginning to rock back and forth despite the discomfort that must have brought her. "All my fault. All my...all my fault. Shouldn't have done it. Lies! He lied to me."

She snapped her head up and I saw madness in her eyes as she fixed them on me. "He lied! *He lied, he lied, he lied!*"

My upper lip curled and Jared appeared at my right shoulder, shifted back to his human form.

"She's fucking delirious," I spat, hating that I felt sorry for her after what she'd done. "Let's get her back to the cabin. If she bleeds out, she's no good to us."

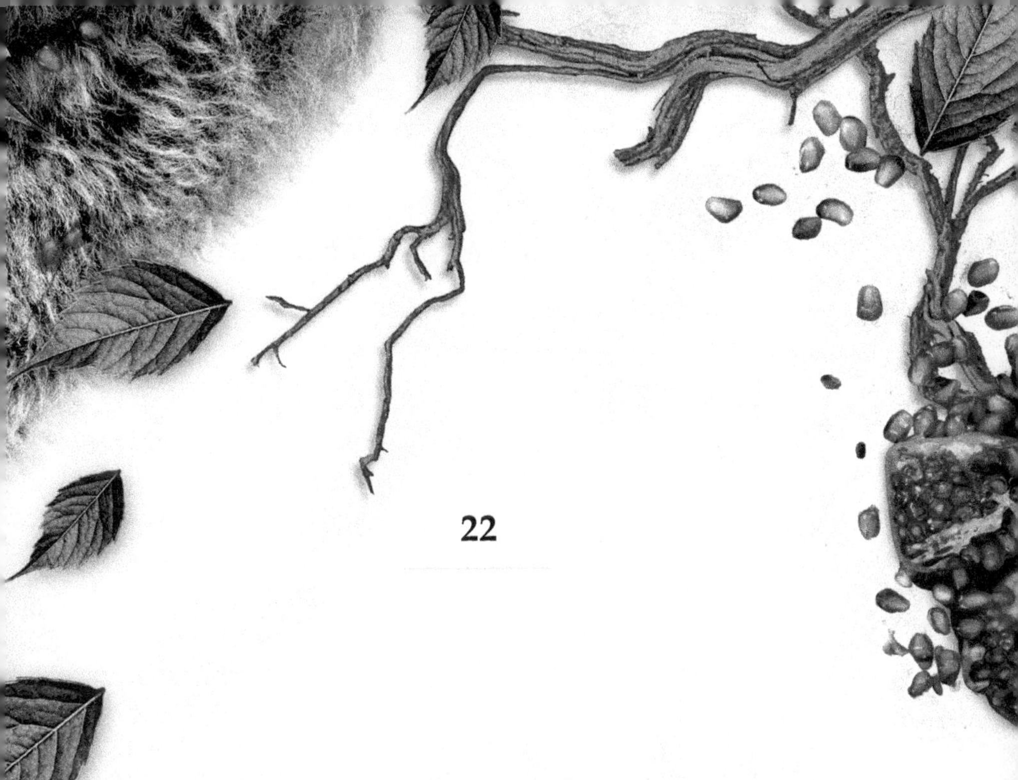

22

Despite how weak she appeared, it took four of us holding her down to re-break and set each of her bones. She could do nor say anything useful in her state and as soon as we had her bones set, wrapped, and splinted, she passed out.

Much as I would have liked to slap her awake, I knew she needed to mend not just her bones, but her mind before she could help us.

"I really don't know why we bothered setting her bones," Jared grumbled, leaning cross-armed against the wall by the sofa where Sam slept fitfully, covered in a layer of her own sweat and blood. Ruining my goddamned couch.

"*Jared*," Hazel tutted, swatting his arm and missing save for the tips of her fingers.

He lifted a brow at Hazel. She'd been the one to order us about when we carried a delirious Sam back to the cabin. Before we knew it, she had us mending Sam's bones, and I didn't fight her on it.

We needed to get her talking, and in the amount of pain she was in, that was unlikely.

Fixing her up a bit was a means to an end and did *not* for one second mean I wouldn't rebreak each and every bone I mended to get the information I needed if she didn't give it to us.

"She's fucked up," Vivian said, watching Sam like she might like to snap her bones all over again, too. "You suppose Devin did that to her?"

My nose wrinkled as memories of that vile bastard crowded my thoughts. The *slap* of his knuckles against the bones of my cheek. The feel of his hands around my throat.

I had little doubt it was him. The question was...*why?*

Was she not his spy. Had she not said over the phone that she loved him? Clearly he didn't share that sentiment with her.

But then again...he always did have a warped idea of what *love* was.

Sam stirred and Clay lifted his head to watch her from where he was hunched over, head bent and fingers splayed on the kitchen island.

"She's waking up," Layla said in a breath.

Sam muttered something, and I strained to hear it, carefully stepping closer to better hear.

"Water," she croaked, her eyes slitting open.

Layla and I shared a look, but I nodded, giving her permission to go fill a glass from the sink for her.

Layla handed her the glass a moment later and Sam spilled most of it over her chest and the couch trying to drink it with shaking hands and weak limbs.

Clay was the only one who stayed fixed where he stood in the kitchen vehicle the rest of us crowded closer as she peeled her eyelids back, seeming to see all of us around her for the first time. Her pulse began to pound, and my inner wolf began to pace within.

I was about to speak when Hazel came around the head of the couch and Sam locked her blue eyes on her grandmother's milky ones. Growing pale at Grams' hard expression.

"I'm disappointed in you, Samantha."

I don't think any of us could say a single thing that would hurt her more than Hazel saying those five words. She looked like she'd been bitch slapped and had her heart carved out all at the same time. Shock and anguish showing in her eyes.

"Our sins have a way of catching up to us...but I'll not see you die today."

Hazel reached down to pat Sam's sweaty shoulder, but she flinched away from her grandmother's touch. "Not if I can help it."

She lifted her head, and her loose silver-streaked hair fell back away from her face. "Do with her what you must, but I ask that you spare her life as a favor to me."

Sam began to sob. "Thank yo—"

"*Hush up*," Hazel snapped.

My fists clenched, and even though I knew she couldn't see me, I had a hard ass time looking Hazel in the eyes. Instead, I fixed my wrathful stare on a trembling Sam. "I can't promise you that," I admitted. "But if she gives us what we need..."

Sam bowed her head until her chin was pressed against her chest. I'd never seen her so broken. She was a firecracker, just like her brother. This was...embarrassing.

"The pack will want retribution," I told Sam as Hazel stepped away from her granddaughter to brush past me.

"If you decide her fate will be to meet the stars, then I would say goodbye first," Hazel said, showing no emotion at all on her aged face.

"You have my word."

Hazel lifted a hand to give my shoulder a squeeze, and my stomach dropped to my toes at the realization that one granddaughter was at the mercy of another. I vowed to *try* not to kill her, if only for Hazel as she found her way outside into the pre-dawn air.

"Start fucking talking," Vivian snarled, and Layla snatched her wrist before she could dart forward.

"No one touches her unless I say so," I gritted out, meeting the stares of each of my mates and each of my best friends before letting the full weight of it fall on my would-be sister-in-law.

She squirmed on the stained cushions until her head was propped against the armrest, her face betraying how much pain she was still in.

"I don't want to hurt you," I lied. "But I will if—"

"I was supposed to say I was attacked," she blurted before I could finish, her bloodshot eyes going wide as though she herself was shocked at her own admission.

Her eyes welled anew, and her face pinched. "He told me that I should say I was attacked by his pack and return to you. To be his little pawn. His *spy*."

I settled into the armchair usually reserved for Clay, dragging it round so it faced her head on. Leaning over my knees, I knotted my fingers together and waited for her to go on. I didn't necessarily believe a single word she said, but if I had to bring Hazel back here to read her, then I would.

"I can't..." she trailed off on a choking sob. "I can't do this anymore."

"Do what?" Vivian demanded. "Betray your pack?

Betray your own fucking family?"

"He never loved me," Sam said in a distant voice. "I know that now. You don't...you don't hurt people you love. Not like this..."

Her weary eyes swept over her battered body, and I knew for sure. It was Devin who'd done it. If she were telling the truth, he'd done it just to make us think that her story of having been attacked was believable. And he was so confident in Sam's feelings for him that he thought she would still love him—still do his bidding— even after he'd beaten her.

Honestly, I wouldn't have been surprised if she had.

It surprised me more that she saw his true colors. "I-I overheard him before...before he..."

She swallowed hard, glancing at her brother, whose jaw flexed and eyes burned with hot blue flame.

"Overheard what?" I demanded, urging her to get to the fucking point. We needed to know everything she knew. But most of all, I wanted to know if she had any idea where our missing wolves were.

Her lip pulled at the new scar running down her face. It didn't look like it was going to heal properly at all. It must have been inflicted by Devin's fangs, otherwise it would heal. She was going to be marred like that for the rest of her life.

As though she could sense where my thoughts had gone, she lifted a hand to touch the pink skin above her mouth and frowned. "He said he'd spare my brother," she replied in barely a whisper. "He promised me. But I heard him. He means to kill him and Jared. He thinks once he does..."

Her upper lip curled, and venom seeped back into her eyes as she lifted them back to mine.

"He thinks once they're out of the way that he'll be able to form the mate bond with me," I finished for her, and she nodded.

"You dumb bitch," Jared growled, and Clay slammed a fist down on the counter. I'd be surprised if he didn't at least crack it.

"Enough of this," he barked. "Tell us where he's keeping them Sam, or so help me..."

She flinched away from her brother's words.

"All right," she murmured, that one word rendering us all deadly silent. Each of us afraid to break the spell of this moment.

It was almost too good to be true. My throat grew thick with emotion.

"Where?" I managed after a second, and Vivian closed the distance to Sam in the blink of an eye, throwing herself onto her knees at the side of the couch and snatching Sam by her shoulders. She shook her violently, her eyes wild.

"Where?" she shouted. "Where are they?"

Sam, startled, tried to wriggle out of Vivian's hold.

I pulled Viv back, making her fall heavily onto her backside against the rug.

Sam swallowed. "Follow White River south," she told us, and if it were possible, she went even paler than she already was. "Follow it down to where it meets with Iron Creek. That's where you'll find them. There's an abandoned mill there. That's where he has them."

Of course. He used the rivers to hide their trail.

Stupid.

Why hadn't we thought of that?

Jared shoved off from the wall, drawing Sam's attention to him. "How do we know she isn't lying?"

"I'm not," she promised, and though I felt she was being sincere, it was impossible to be certain.

"Layla," I called, and she nodded, knowing already what I wanted and heading for the door.

Hazel couldn't give us a definitive yes or no as to whether or not she was lying. But she could help us to be more certain of her intentions here.

As though she were just as guilty as we all assumed she was, Sam closed her eyes and shuddered as Layla left.

"If you're lying to us," I warned her. "I won't be able to save you from this pack."

We waited out the five minutes until Hazel returned listening only to the sound of Vivian pacing the floor. None of us daring to hope we might *finally* have gotten a win.

Hazel hobbled through the door with Layla on her heels, and Vivian immediately took Grams by the hand and led her Sam's side. I didn't miss how Grams flinched at the contact with Vivian. I wouldn't want to feel that hurricane of emotion, either.

She tugged out of Vivian's grasp as her shins knocked against the couch, and she reached down, waiting for Sam to give her her hand as opposed to taking it.

Like she was giving her granddaughter a choice to do the right thing.

It took a second, but Sam did lift her hand, tentatively slipping it into Hazel's with a grimace.

The old woman closed her other hand over Sam's for barely an instant before dropping it as though scalded.

She cocked her head at her granddaughter, shock registering on her face.

"What is it?" I demanded impatiently. Glaring between grandmother and granddaughter.

"I can't be certain," Hazel told me, wringing her hands as though she could wash them of whatever she felt at Sam's touch. "But I believe she's telling the truth. She fears Devin. And with good reason. But there's resolve there, too. Her desire to protect her kin is stronger than her fear of denying him."

A derisive snort came from the kitchen, and I turned to find Clay shaking his head, running his tongue over elongated teeth. He wasn't fucking buying it. But even if he wouldn't show it to the others, I could feel his deep seated hope that his sister wasn't entirely lost to that monster. That he wished he could believe her.

Hazel made as though to console Sam before snatching her hand back to her chest with a sad look in her eyes that made me wonder what it was she saw. I could guess, though. Having been under Devin's thumb once myself.

"What are we waiting for then?" Vivian declared, her voice growing in pitch. "We have to go and free them. We have to bring them home."

I cast my best friend what I hoped was a reassuring stare. "Yes," I agreed. "But we have to be smart about it." I turned my attention back to Sam. "If you want to prove your loyalty remains here with this pack— with your family—then there's something I need you to do." Her brows wrinkled.

"I need you to go back to him."

She gasped. "I can't," she pleaded, a note of panic returning to her voice. "He'll kill me."

"He might," I agreed.

"Why send her back?" Hazel asked in a flat monotone, not betraying how she felt on the matter. "If I'm wrong about her intentions, then..."

Then she could destroy us. It was a risk.

But I trusted Hazel's judgement. Could sense Sam's remorse.

"It's a bad idea," Jared argued. I held up a hand.

"You will tell Devin that I've done as he asked. That I've severed the bond with Clay and Jared and you personally witnessed my rejection of them. And that I plan to give myself up as he requested."

"I don't get it," Vivian snapped. "What's the play here?"

"We'll discuss it once she's gone."

"Please don't ask me to do this," Sam pleaded. "I'll do anything else you want."

"*This* is what this pack needs from you." Her lower lip trembled.

"You'll leave as soon as you're able to walk on your own."

"What are you doing, Allie?" Clay demanded, his jaw working again.

Trust me, I tried to tell him without saying the words aloud and his lips parted, but no other argument fell out.

"If you betray us again," I warned Sam. "*Devin* won't be the one you need to fear...and that beating he gave you will look like a fucking mercy. Do you understand?"

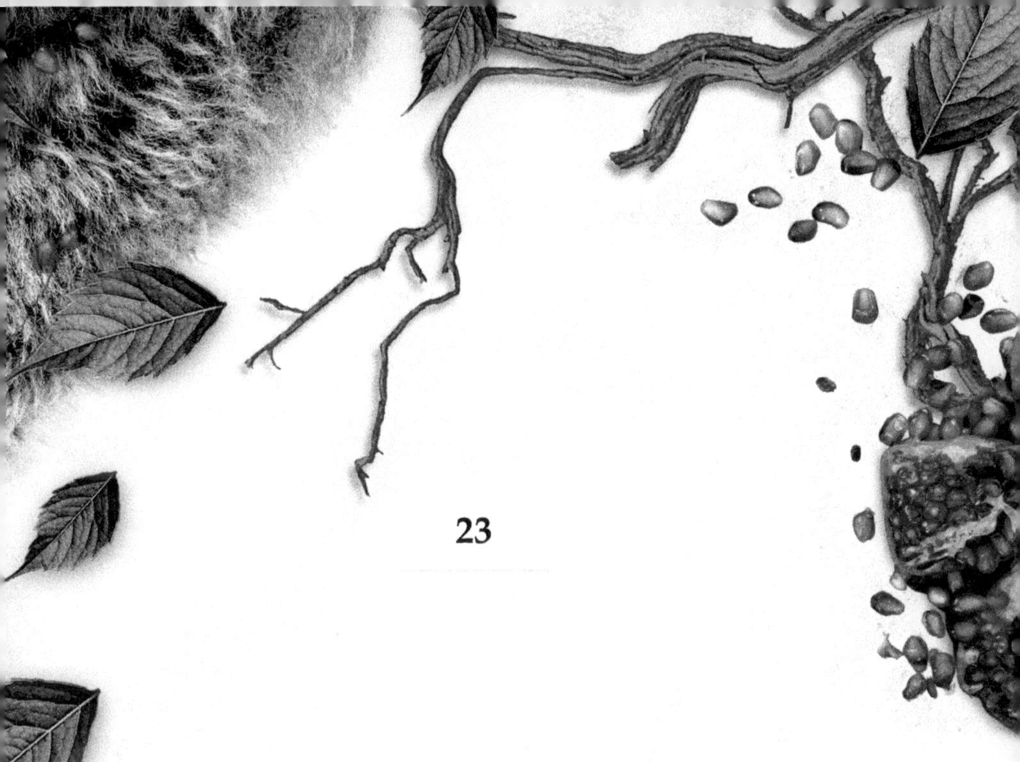

23

"S he's right, you know," Hazel said during the meeting barely six hours after I made my choice to send Sam back to Devin. "He might kill her the moment she returns."

"He might," I agreed. "But if she survives, you'll get what you asked for. I'll pardon her from her crimes. She'll be excommunicated from this pack, but not killed."

Hazel fell silent, gazing blindly toward the north east, where Sam limped into the trees only thirty minutes before. My mind still reeled from everything she told us, and everything she didn't. I got the sense there was more. That there was something she was desperate for us to know but couldn't say.

Maybe Devin had commanded she keep something else a secret when she was still part of his pack? Would the effects of his alpha dominance persist even after she joined our pack?

Fuck. Why did I still feel like there was something more to this than I was seeing? *Damn* my fucking over- paranoid brain.

"Let's get to the point," Jared cut in. "What's the plan, Allie? I know you wouldn't have let her go back to him unless you had one."

Nodding, I cringed inwardly, hoping they didn't think this was the stupidest idea in shifter history. Normally, I'd have brought them in on a decision of this magnitude, but there was no way to have that discussion with Sam present, and honestly? I was afraid they'd try and stop me.

"Whatever it is," Clay said in a low, dangerous voice, his eyes flicking to me and away. "I already don't fucking like it."

"How about a little faith?" I said, trying not to be stung by his words.

Layla jabbed Clay with an elbow. "Don't be an asshole."

Clay grumbled something unintelligible, laced with curses, but I paid him no mind.

"Okay," I said on a breath. "Once Sam has returned and told Devin that I've done as he's asked, I'm going to call him to set up a meet."

"The fuck you are," Jared hissed.

I sent him a glare, urging him to wait for the rest. "He'll be so preoccupied with readying for the meeting that he might not notice the shifters he has stationed at the mill with the captured wolves haven't been checking in."

We'd wrung every morsel of information out of Sam last night before allowing her a couple hours of fitful sleep to heal enough to be able to leave. She wasn't a fountain of information, but she was able to tell us that he kept somewhere between six and ten shifters on guard at the mill depending on whether he needed them elsewhere.

To her knowledge, they were all still alive, but weak. He fed them enough to keep them alive, but that was it.

It was a good thing we had a shit ton of beef just waiting to be eaten. We already had about fifteen pounds of it thawing.

"We need this distraction for this to work. If he figures out we're going to free them, he could intercept the rescue attempt and we'll lose even more shifters."

"Right," Jared said, and I could tell he was holding back from saying something much less calm. "But this whole *plan* hinges on Sam *not* betraying us again. If she does—"

"I don't think she will," I interrupted. "And my gut has never been wrong before."

They all knew it was more or less true.

"And this meeting?" Clay cut in. "Who's to say he won't bring his entire pack and slaughter us all?"

"I'm counting on it," I bit back, making everyone shut up. "We'll send a team to free the shifters from the mill. Five or six."

"I'm going," Vivian said. "I want to lead it."

"Fine," I replied. "But you'll go with Seth and Charity as well."

She nodded.

"You'll travel with supplies to get them fed and mend any who are injured after you take out the guards."

"Okay," Viv said, catching on.

"As soon as you have them strengthened and ready to go, you'll join us."

"Our numbers still won't be enough to defeat him," Clay roared, not seeing what was right in front of him.

"We don't have to defeat them all," I corrected him. "With our pack freed, he won't have his bargaining chip anymore."

Layla gasped. "You're going to challenge him."

"You're damn right I am," I replied with a grin. "And I'm going to end that motherfucker once and for all."

Everything was set into motion quickly after that. Viv, Seth, and Charity gathered three others to join them on the raid to free our kin.

I briefed the rest of the pack on the plan, promising that if this went down how I hoped it would, not a single soul would be harmed. I needed them all with me as a show of strength, to keep Devin's attention on *us* and not behind him where we planned to drive in the knife.

Let him think I planned to attack him with my inferior numbers. Let him relish in the thought of having his chance to rid me of my mates.

And then pull the carpet out from under him with a challenge he couldn't refuse.

It *had* to work.

There was no other plan. This was it.

For now at least, it seemed Sam had kept her word. I made the call to Devin early this morning, and when I told him I wanted to meet, he was overeager to agree.

He even promised me that if I had truly rejected them as I said, that he would consider releasing his captors. We just needed to work out the 'terms' first.

Ha! The only term I would accept would be his psychotic head on a fucking pike.

The bastard had no idea what he was in for. My wolf was ready. *I* was ready.

As a little extra added bonus we thought we'd like to see him kneel before we killed him. Just to rub a little salt in the wound, you know?

If we made Ryland kneel to us, we were certain we could utterly *break* the pathetic shifter that was Devin Wright.

"Everything is set," Clay said. "But I don't like leaving camp abandoned."

I didn't, either, but we couldn't afford to split up with our numbers already so small. "And Hazel?"

"Stubborn old bat is insisting she come with us."

"She'll be safer at the old cabin. It's warded."

"Try telling her that."

A slap on my arm had me tripping forward on the dirt lawn in front of our cabin. "I'll tell you the same thing I told my grandson," Hazel chided. "I'm coming with you whether you like it or not."

"Grams…"

"You say it won't come to a fight," she argued. "So then what's the problem, hmm?"

"Why do you have to be so damned difficult?" Clay groaned, scrubbing a palm over his face.

I lifted a brow at him. "Now I know where you get it from," I said, tossing a wink. "Not that I ever had any doubt."

Hazel smirked and left. "Send someone to fetch me when it's time to leave," she called back. "I'll just go check on my garden first."

I shook my head, chuckling quietly to myself.

"You seem…" Clay trailed off, cocking his head at me. "…different today. Happier."

I bit my lower lip. "Hopeful is more like it," I corrected him. "I think this is going to work. By the end of today, this all might finally be over."

Clay's lips pressed into a hard line that told me he didn't think it would be so easy, but he nodded. "And what will you do if you succeed?" he asked. "If you take him out, you become rightful alpha of his pack."

My mood soured.

"I'll do what I did when I took over this pack," I decided. "I won't force anyone to stay."

Clay didn't seem particularly supportive of the idea, but he didn't argue the point. We needed to get through steps one through five before we started worrying about step ten.

Jared came out from the cabin a moment later in a pair of low hanging cargo shorts, his chest and hair glistening with water from the shower. He looked up as he approached. "Hey. Everything good?"

"You've been gone for fifteen minutes," I reminded him. "Not much has changed."

He lifted a brow at me. "Around here? A lot can happen in fifteen minutes."

"Well, Hazel's coming now," I relented. "So there's that."

"Stubborn old bat," Jared grumbled, and Clay and I nodded our agreement.

Just then, I sensed Viv approaching and found her, Seth, Charity, Archer and two other shifters weaving through the trails of pack camp toward us. Viv looked better than I'd seen her in weeks. She'd force fed herself all three meals the day before and accepted some extra strength sleeping pills from Charity to help her get the rest she desperately needed.

It would've been a lot easier if we'd been able to use the store of magical potions from Stella, the witch who'd been a friend to the pack for generations. But you know, immunity from witch and vampire magics had its drawbacks just as well as it had its advantages.

"You look good," I commented and Vivian gave me a partial smile and a nod.

I could tell she was feeling it, too. The hope that today, this would all be over. That she'd finally get her mate back. And I got the feeling Viv was never going to let Destiny out of her sight again.

"We're ready to go," she announced, her resolve clear on her face.

A pang in my chest told me that despite my trust in this plan, I was still terrified of something going wrong. I didn't want her to leave. Not without me for backup.

I grimaced. "All right. Go now then. We'll be leaving in about an hour which should give you enough time to get to them, see them fed, and make your way to where we're to meet."

"Just make sure you come up on the barrens from the—"

"Yes, from the west. We know," Viv answered Jared. "We'll follow the creek as far as we can to hide our trail. We know the plan."

He gave her a terse nod and tugged her into a hug that had her light brown eyes widening. "Be careful, Viv."

"Well, fuck, if we're going to be dramatic about it."

Clay rolled his eyes before taking his turn wrapping Viv in a big bear hug while Jare moved on to embrace Charity and give Seth a clap on the back.

"You be careful, too," Viv whispered against my cheek as she hugged me, her long arms crushing my ribcage.

"We will be," I promised her.

She fixed me with a pointed stare as she pulled away, as though she didn't believe I would be careful at all and *fuck,* did no one have any faith in me?

I gave her a pronounced eyeroll and a little shove. "Get out of here."

Seth saluted me and Viv flashed me a grin I had been starting to think I would never get to see again.

"Come back whole," I demanded, calling out to them as they vanished into the tree line and my gut twisted.

Jared pulled me into his side, lending me some of his strength. "They're going to be all right. They can do this."

I nodded.

"I know they can."

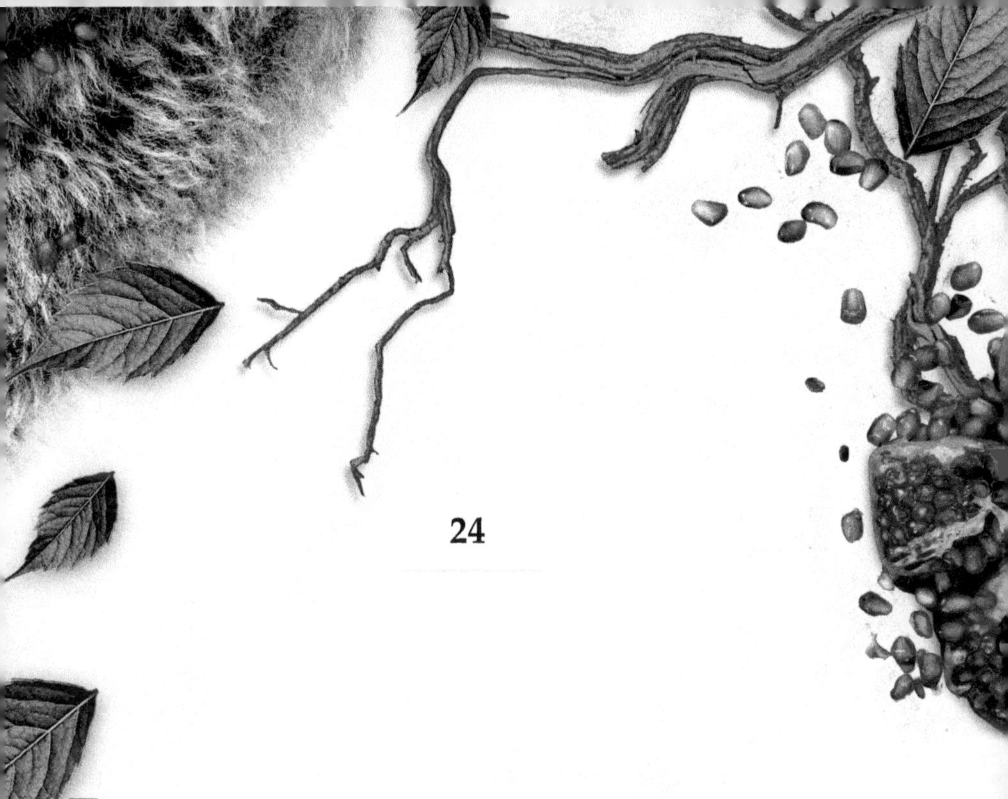

24

It was hard to imagine that only a few weeks ago Seth and Layla came to this very spot for something as innocent as stargazing.

Now, returning to the barrens, Layla looked anything but innocent. In her wolf form, she was lithe and alert. Vividly aware that her boyfriend would have arrived at the mill where the white river met the iron creek over an hour ago.

If everything went to plan, they would already be on their way here. Layla had wanted to go with them, but saw the sense in coming with us instead. I could account for Vivian's absence if we met with Devin before they arrived. I could say that she couldn't be trusted not to attack first and ask questions later, given he had her mate. But Layla not being present would raise suspicion. Especially when I had the entire pack at my back.

Though there was still the chance he might wonder at the absence of Seth and Charity, having known them too when he was still with the Forest Grove pack.

Please, I sent the silent prayer to the heavens as we cleared the trees and stepped out onto the wide expanse of patchy dirt and grass known as the barrens. *Please let this work.*

My pulse picked up at the prospect of seeing Devin again and *not* being able to immediately go for his throat. I was really hoping Viv would show up with all of the others in tow before Devin got here so I wouldn't have to hold back.

I came to a stop just outside the tree line and the rest of the pack stopped with me, their nervous energy ramping up.

Where is he? Clay asked, and I peered with my canine eyes across the expanse to the trees on the other side. Seeing nothing.

Late?

My hackles rose at what that could mean, and I soothed myself in the thought that perhaps we were just early. Judging by the positioning of the sun, sunk beneath the tree line but not fully drowned just yet, we were right on schedule.

Pretty, isn't it? Layla said, distracting me from my thoughts.

I turned to find her just behind me, staring up at the sky with hopeful eyes.

She was right, though I hadn't noticed it. The sky awash with the colors of a summer sunset in the mountains. Clouds with pink stained bellies in a hazy purple sky. A wash of amber light over the floor of the barrens. Tipping the tops of the trees in a gold so bright they appeared to be on fire.

My gaze snapped forward as the stench of foreign wolves was carried our way on a westward breeze.

They're here.

Blood rushed in my ears, and I dug my paws into the earth, rooting myself still until the moment when I could spring ahead. My wolf bristled at the feel of the earth beneath us. The slight tremble of it as the enemy approached.

Easy, Jared warned and I reined in my wolf with a long exhale.

I still don't sense him, Callum sent from somewhere behind us and my blood chilled.

It may not mean anything, I told myself. They may just be slightly out of range. It was handy having one half of a mated pair of shifters with us. Callum could tell us when Archer was near. He was also the reason we knew they were all still alive. Or, at least, Archer was.

We'll stall, I decided. *I'm sure the asshole will want to preen first anyway.*

Just then, a wolf broke through into the barrens. A wolf with dark fur the colors of stone and wet earth, with eyes brightest emerald. A silent gasp parted my lips at the sight of him.

There was no mistaking who he was. I'd know those eyes anywhere. They were the same ones that stared into mine as he hurt me. Bit me. Changed my life forever.

But this wolf was twice the size of the one who was run out of Forest Grove over four years ago. And as his pack emerged from the shadows of the forest, I saw that his numbers were not exaggerated as I'd hoped.

Perhaps not seventy, but there was no denying the number was painfully close to that. On closer inspection though, I found young shifters much like the one who gave us the information we needed. There seemed to be many more teenagers and even younger juveniles than I'd anticipated. Though none seemed older than their mid-forties.

Though, if they'd been running with a pack for any length of time, they could all be much older than they appeared.

My initial relief at seeing so many younger, more inexperienced wolves was quickly replaced by a horrid hollowness in my stomach.

There are so many young… Jared trailed off in my thoughts, mimicking my worry.

They were just kids. We couldn't kill them…could we?

I shook my head.

It won't come to that.

Anything? I sent to Callum, setting my jaw as Devin and his pack came to a standstill fifty years away.

No, he replied, and I could hear the worry in the inflection of his voice even though he was trying to hide it. *Nothing.*

Goddamn it.

Devin shifted along with the two wolves to either side of him and I gasped, recognizing one of them.

Is that…? Clay asked, and I felt the tension radiating off him in waves.

It's Forrest, Jared confirmed.

He was at Ryland's right hand four years ago, before I became the twin soul wolf and everything changed. I'd let him go along with a small group of others who couldn't bear to stay under my command.

So it seemed Sam wasn't the only one who came back to bite me.

Forrest wanted his revenge, too.

"Come," Devin called across the clearing. "Let's talk."

I stifled a growl and my wolf retreated, letting me take the reins for a minute. I shifted, and though I'd gotten used to being naked in shitty situations, I couldn't remember the last time I'd felt so *exposed*.

Once, Devin had proclaimed my body *his*.

Once, I'd had to wonder if he'd touched me while I was drugged in that cave.

I clenched my fists and stood taller.

"You really filled out," he called appreciatively, and I ground my teeth, trying *not* to pay any more attention than I needed to his naked body.

Jared and Clay bent low at my sides, their tails going rigid as they growled at him.

Devin fixed his cutting stare on my mates next.

"It seems my intel was mistaken," he said, his brows lowering, and I wondered at how he could possibly tell whether I'd rejected them or not. Being an outsider of this pack, there was no way he could know for certain.

He lifted a hand, beckoning to someone further back in his three line formation.

I turned briefly to find Callum several yards behind me. He shook his head, and I stiffened.

Where the fuck were they?

Barely a second later, I sensed Clay's alarm and heard Hazel's low whine before I spotted her. Two shifters in their human form held a struggling, naked Sam between them as they pressed through the rest of their pack, dragging her to Devin's side.

She bucked against their hold, and despite the piece of silvery tape covering her mouth, I still heard her muffled pleas.

A pitched keen came from down the line, and I found Hazel stepping out ahead of the others. Her silvery gray wolf tilting its head to better hear what she could not see.

"Hazel," I called, drawing her attention.

Don't, I implored her, and she fell silent as she slipped back into line.

My first thought was that she'd betrayed us and my wolf nearly stole back the reins. But then if she'd told Devin everything, why did she look so much like a prisoner between the bodies of the two shifters holding her. Why did she look so afraid?

"I thought it a bit suspicious," Devin said as the two men came to a stop next to their alpha, and Sam's panicked gaze found me across the barren field.

"Aren't you going to ask me *what* I found suspicious?" Devin called, tipping his head to one side as he steepled his fingers.

How had I ever thought he was anything less than a total psychopath?

"I'm sure you're going to tell me whether I give a shit or not."

He grinned, flashing two rows of shining white teeth in an angular jaw. "I found it suspicious that Samantha returned to me even after I told her to remain with your pack."

I realized that his offhanded admission should have shocked me. I wasn't supposed to know that Sam was working with Devin to destroy us, but it was too late now, and he only grinned wider.

"Where's he going with this shit?" Clay whispered harshly, having shifted in the span of a single breath.

"I don't know," I admitted, keeping my voice low. "But I don't like it."

"So, like any rational person would, I questioned it. I thought her loyalty knew no bounds, but it seems I was mistaken there, too."

Devin's appraising green eyes passed over Sam, and she looked away, her shoulders curling in defensively.

He reached out to trail a hand down her cheek, and she bucked, trying to escape his touch. Despite my fury at Clay's sister, I seriously considered how I might bite off that hand for daring to lay a finger on her. On any woman who didn't want it.

"Without my little Piper, I might never have known the truth."

As though on command, a girl of no more than eighteen stepped forward, her mousy brown hair a mess of mats and tangles down her chest to her belly button.

She stepped around Sam and lightly touched her cheeks.

"Does Samantha have anything she'd like to say?" Devin asked, and I glanced to Clay for clarity. What exactly was happening right now?

The girl called Piper dropped her fingers a moment later and turned to face her alpha with a bowed head and a pronounced tightness in her jaw.

Her hands moved in a sequence of patterns, and I realized after a second that she was signing something. "She's deaf," Clay said, confirming my suspicion,

and my mind began to race.

Hazel was blind and could see a person's past experiences and feelings through touch.

I had a twin soul and mated to two shifters instead of one.

This girl, it seemed, was deaf to the world around her, but could hear the inner thoughts of those she touched.

Devin had used her to read Sam's thoughts. *Fuck.*

This was it. *She* was it. The secret weapon he'd used to get the upper hand and takeover five other fucking packs. The thing Sam couldn't tell us about.

Sam *knew* this could happen. She tried to warn us, but we didn't listen.

Jared shifted at my side.

"What did she say?" Clay asked.

Jared visibly paled. "Sam's asking for you to forgive her."

Devin nodded to the girl, and she moved back to her place in the line behind him.

"Such a shame," Devin said, and my mouth opened in shocked horror as he stabbed into Sam's stomach with partially shifted claws. Her body sagged as he lifted her heart to shine in what remained of the dying light as though it were a trophy to be placed on a mantle and admired.

Clay's anguish hit me only a moment after the sinking realization that Sam was dead. He fell to his knees, catching himself with two fists pressed flat against the earth as he roared his pain. The heart-wrenching sound of it echoed back to us as the two men holding Sam discarded her onto the ground. Her limp body bent at an odd angle, but her face...her face was clear as day. Two familiar blue eyes wide with fear. A mouth sealed forever.

Clay bellowed again, and Hazel's canine cries almost undid me.

"Clay," I whispered, holding back bile as I bent to touch him.

Jared snatched me back before I could, and I gasped as Clay ripped free of his human form. He let loose a haunting howl filled with everything he never said. Every hope he'd had for his sister to be redeemed. To return home. For real.

Hazel's cracked howl rose to join Clay's, and their raw melody seeped into my bones. Would stay there forever.

Clay looked ready to charge, and I felt an unimaginable amount of pride in him for holding his ground even though I could feel every fiber of his being screaming *kill*.

Once I was certain he wasn't going to budge, I flicked my hate-filled gaze back to Devin. "You're going to die," I promised him, glancing back at Callum for confirmation that our missing shifters were almost here.

But he shook his head again, a low whine on his lips.

"Not waiting for your packmates, I hope?"

I spun back around, a pounding so loud in my ears I wasn't sure I heard him correctly. I better have *not* fucking heard him correctly.

"You know, poor Samantha might not have known your plan, but once Piper was able to figure out that she told you where I was keeping your pals...well, it was easy to figure out. It's what I would have done: distract your enemy while you steal from right under their nose. You and I are so similar."

"I am nothing like you."

The unease from my mates and my pack ramped up to the point it felt like every inch of my skin was crawling.

Layla shifted. "What have you done with them?" she demanded, shaking, her small fists clenched so tight I knew her painted black nails would be carving half- moons into her palms. "Where's Vivian? Where's Seth?"

Devin's eyes narrowed on Layla, alight with malice. "My men got there just in time to stop them."

"Where are they?" Jared echoed. "Allie didn't honor our agreement..." My stomach turned.

"So, they're dead, of course. All but a few. I'll let you guess which lives I spared."

My vision narrowed until all I could see was a pinprick of light in a dark tunnel of naked horror. Layla screamed somewhere in the distance, but all I could see was the tunnel. And at the end of it: his face. Laughing. Cold. Victorious.

"*Allie,*" Jared was saying, and my body shook. I wasn't sure if he was the one shaking it or if it was doing it all on its own. I had no awareness of my limbs. No sense of the moments passing.

Callum's mate wasn't dead. He would have felt it.

Callum's mate was the one of the ones he *spared.* His last bargaining chips.

Which meant...

Which meant...

My mind rejected the thought. Refused it.

No.

If Vivian was... And Seth... Destiny... Charity...

No. *No.*

"You're lying," I hissed, finding my voice again as my vision returned and Jared helped me up from the ground.

Devin tossed Sam's heart onto her corpse with a shrug of indifference. "Afraid not."

"*Shit,*" Jared said, and he left my side to tend to Layla, who was sitting mutely on the ground, her face a mask of shocked terror. "Layla, come on, snap out of it."

But even Jared's voice was watery with emotion. He was just better at keeping his pain inside.

I stepped forward with purpose, my wolf on the brink of absolute feral combustion. If only I could catch my breath. If only I could *breathe.* But each short sharp inhale scarred my lungs, making me dizzy with dread so potent that it blotted out fury. Replaced it with a hollowness that ate at me from the inside out.

My fault.

This is all my fault.

No.

His fault.

I took another purposeful stride forward, my skin hot and bristling with the urge to shift.

"*Uh uh,*" Devin called in a sing-song voice, wagging his finger back and forth as though scolding a child. "I wouldn't do that if I were you."

He gestured to the pack behind him. The pack that was now easily double our current size. There was no need for him to say it. If I attacked, we'd all be slaughtered.

The guy to his right held up a cell phone and Devin pointed to the illuminated screen. "And if you get any *funny* ideas, then the shifters I have guarding the remaining hostages will know. They have orders to finish them off if anything should happen to me or anyone else here today."

If I challenged him, the rest of them would die.

In a twisted, rage-fueled place in my mind, doing it anyway almost made sense. A sacrifice in exchange for tearing his head from his shoulders...but the idea of even *one* more innocent life being taken cut me to my core. I couldn't do it.

What if one of the still-surviving ones was Vivian?

Could I sacrifice her to ensure the safety of the rest of my pack?

Maybe a better alpha would have said yes, but I could *never* do something like that. Not while I still had one card left to play.

Clay pressed into my side, his lupine body vibrating with a visceral need to protect his pack. To protect me. Perhaps sensing my intent.

"This ends now," Jared said, leaving Layla to return to my side. "This madness needs to stop. We attack. Now."

Callum broke out into a panicked whine, and I looked to find a few others attempting to console him.

"No," I replied, lifting a hand absently to stroke the line of his jaw. He really was the most beautiful man I'd ever seen. Would ever see again. "No one else is going to die today."

He caught my hand as I pulled away, his brows lowering. "Allie?"

Clay growled next to me, and I hushed him, delving my fingers into his fur until I felt his warm body against my palm. "It's all right."

Jared jerked me back to face him, his amber eyes wild in a face set of stone.

"We aren't going to let you do this."

"Yes," I told him, gently prying his fingers from my wrist. "You are."

"What guarantee do I have that you won't harm any of my pack if I agree to go with you?" I called, squinting into the twilight as Clay thrashed against my side, turning to snarl at me.

Devin licked his lips. "My word."

"Because that's always been so trustworthy in the past..."

"Allie, you really don't have any other choice."

My stomach iced over at the reality of the situation. We'd walked right into this trap. I thought we'd been the ones holding all the cards. That we'd play him to our advantage and take him for all he was worth.

That's not what happened here. We were the ones who got played.

And now it was time to pay the price for that mistake.

Already my mind raced with possibility. Maybe I didn't have to be his captive for long. I *was* stronger than him. I could kill him. I just needed an opening. A split second where he let his guard down and I could take him out.

But I remembered his vague threat on the phone before. *You'll have to be neutralized.* What had he meant? Did he mean to...what? Lobotomize me? Drug me?

Fucking hypnotize me or some shit? Would that work?

"My mates," I called, shuddering as I felt their accusing eyes turn on me. "If you harm either of them, I will never stop fighting you. I will live and breathe for the sole purpose of making you suffer."

"No, Allie..."

"*But,* if you let them live...and if you release your hostages...and let my pack go free to live in peace—"

"That's an awful lot of conditions for a woman without anything to bargain with."

It was my turn to smirk now, because there *was* one thing I still had, and my mates were the only two souls on this earth I would trade it for.

"If you do as I've asked, I *won't* fight you. I'll go willingly. I'll be yours."

"But never truly mine until they are dead," Devin argued, a muscle ticking in his cheek.

"And if I don't mate to you once they're dead? Which I *won't*. Then you will have me at my worst forever. Your choice."

Devin fell silent as though considering this new variable very carefully while I fended off every sort of awful emotion from my mates.

"Very well," he said, finally. "We'll *try* it your way."

"If you do this..." Jared said, his amber eyes aglow with his wolf as he searched mine. "We'll never stop coming for you."

I didn't say what I was thinking, because if I did, he'd stop me. They both would, because I didn't intend to give them a choice.

"I won't let you do this," Clay growled, his voice still half wolf as his fur vanished from beneath my fingertips, replaced with hard, sweat-slicked naked flesh. "We can take them. We can—"

"And let his pack kill whoever he still has at the mill? Or wherever the fuck they are now?"

"What if he's lying? What if he's already killed them all?"

"Allie," Vivian's choked voice came over the cell phone across the barrens, the guy holding it having put it on speaker.

My heart leapt into my throat and I had to throw out an arm to stop Layla from rushing forward.

"Vivian!" she cried.

"Kill him!" Vivian's rough voice called down the line. "Kill the fuckin—"

Her voice was cut off by a thud and a shuffling sound before the buff guy holding the phone jammed the screen to deactivate the speaker.

"She's still alive..." I didn't realize I'd spoken aloud until Layla's fingernails dug sharply into my forearm, making me release her.

My best friend stared at me in horror, looking between me and the phone across the field with clear desperation in her eyes.

"It's okay," I assured her, gripping her by the shoulders to stop her shaking. "It's okay. She's going to be fine."

I hugged her to me. "I promise."

And then lower, for only her to hear. "I'm going to kill him. I don't know how. But I *promise* you I will do it. Take care of them. Don't let them do anything stupid."

"Just come back," she sobbed against my shoulder. "You have to come back."

I nodded as I pulled away.

"You can't ask me to sacrifice Vivian," I told Clay, sniffling as I swiped angry tears from my eyes, and he looked at me like a man staring down the barrel of a gun.

"I'll kill him," he promised, and I gave him a sad smile.

"You won't come after me," I said, lacing the words with the absolute authority of an alpha wolf.

"No, Allie, don't you fucking dare—"

"You will take care of our pack."

"You can't do this to us," Jared grunted, already bending to the weight of my will until he was forced to take a knee, his head bowing.

It was only seconds before Clay followed, pure hate burrowing from his eyes directly into my soul as he fought my command. Every muscle flexing and bulging.

"Lead them together."

Hazel whined, coming forward to press her cold nose into my stomach. At least she wasn't fighting me.

"Take care of them for me?"

She rubbed her forehead against my belly before bending to nuzzle against her grandson's side, making him flinch.

The rest of the pack watched me with canine eyes, sad, but unwavering. It was a salute, I realized, a show of unity. Of thanks. My throat burned at the sight of them, and I had to turn around before I showed them my weakness. In the face of their strength, I felt like the biggest impostor of us all.

"If you're nearly finished with this very entertaining spectacle, I think we should be going," Devin said, stretching out a hand to me. A test. To see if I would comply.

"*Go*," I commanded my pack, and I swear the earth beneath my feet trembled at the power behind the command.

"*Fuck...*" Clay gritted out between his clenched teeth, his veins popping as he fought me tooth and nail. Jared didn't budge, either, but I could see how his body trembled.

The others moved back, bowing at my authority as they sunk further back into the trees as the last dregs of sunlight left the sky and they were all cloaked in shadow.

"I said *go*," I repeated, raising my voice until it was a shrill awful thing that hurt my own ears to hear.

"*I won't...*" Clay managed as he dragged his half-wolf claws in the ground to try and stop himself from leaving. "*...forgive you for this.*"

"Good," I blurted before I could stop myself. "Be angry. Blame me. *Hate me.*"

Anything would be easier for them than admitting this was the only way. Anything would be easier than living with the pain of my loss. Hate was easier. Hate would keep them going.

I shoved Jared back first before moving to Clay until they were both forced to standing—to moving two steps back.

But instead of snarling at me like I wanted them too. Instead of looking spiteful and angry, they just looked like a beautiful tragedy. My heart clenched painfully in my chest until I couldn't look at them anymore for fear of looking permanently undone.

"Never," Clay promised.

Jared winced as my command finally won out, and he began to be absorbed into the shadows of the trees. "We couldn't hate you. Not for this. Not for anything."

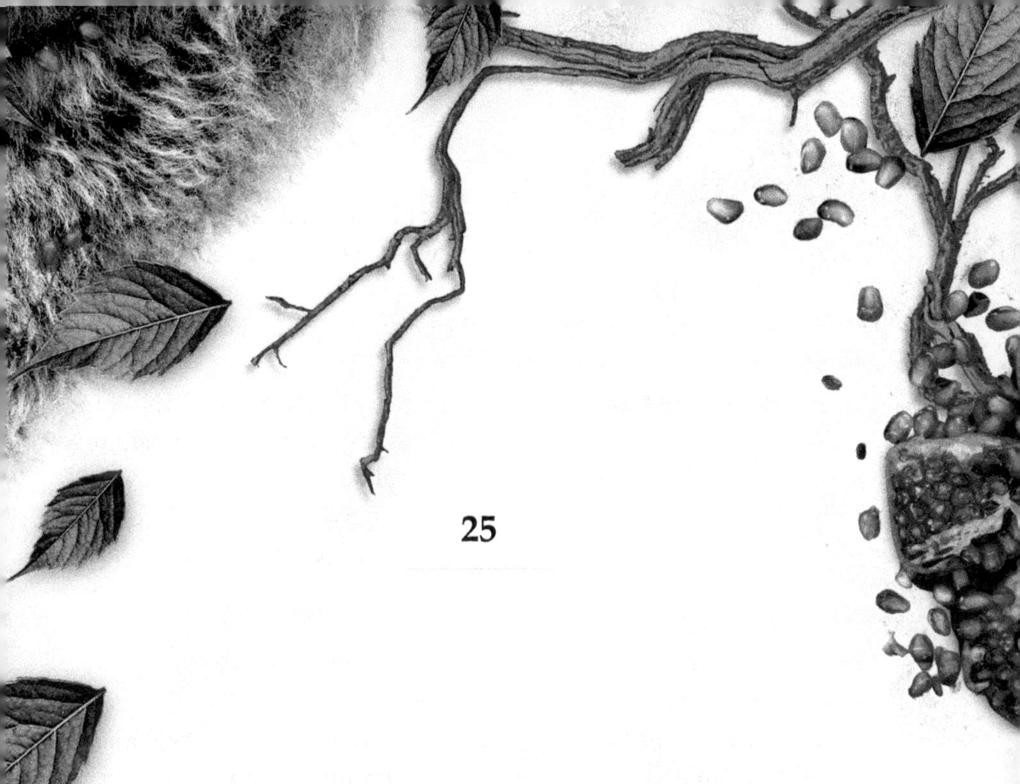

25

I couldn't be sure how long I stood there as my pack, family, retreated from the barrens. It might've been hours, but more likely it was only minutes.

I didn't move so much as an inch until their howls of anguish echoed over the valley and I knew that they were outside of his reach. At least for now. At least for as long as I kept up my end of our deal.

That was my hope, but Devin could just as easily decide he'd rather I kept on trying to fight him. Hell, maybe it turned the psycho on.

Once even the echoes of my pack's call faded, I crossed the barrens. Each step felt like another nail in my coffin, but I reminded myself that this wouldn't be forever. He wouldn't always have the upper hand, and as soon as that power shifted, I would be ready.

My wolf went dormant as I approached Devin, his hand still outstretched, waiting for me to take it. I silently thanked my inner beast for allowing me to do this, whether she would bear witness to it or not.

Even that primal, reactive part of myself knew this was the right thing, for now. To save the ones we loved. Devin had always been taller than me, but the bulk he'd added to his once slender frame made him absolutely dwarf me in all ways now. Though we both knew who was the stronger wolf here, I sensed that in human form, I may have more difficulty fighting him off than I originally thought.

I grimaced, slipping my fingers over his callused palm. He gripped me tightly, hauling me in until his face was level with mine. "There," he said. "Was that so hard?"

My gut instinct was to strike, my fist clenched and ready at my side, but I held myself back.

Devin lifted two fingers to caress the tender flesh beneath my chin. "So much fire," he said, gazing into my eyes in a way that made my stomach turn. "We'll have to do something about that."

He snapped his fingers, and Forrest tugged a small sack from a leather cord around his neck and dumped its contents into Devin's waiting palm.

Four white pills.

"Open," Devin said with a grin, his gaze slipping to my lips.

"What are they?"

He pursed his lips for a moment, considering me before he replied. "A paralytic. Can't have you running off or trying anything before I can even get you home."

Fear spiked my blood with a fresh wave of adrenaline, and my heart began to pound anew.

As though he knew exactly where my thoughts had wandered, he let his predatory gaze slip down the length of my body and licked his lips. "Don't worry, my pet. I won't touch you. Not until you want me to."

My brow furrowed, confused at the easy way he spoke. Like he really expected me to crave the touch of a narcissistic psychopath like him.

I glanced at Forrest and the coward let down his gaze and stepped away. It was one thing to stand by an asshole like Ryland, a man Forrest had known and befriended for upward of twenty years, even after his truth came out. It was why I'd let him and a few others go free instead of forcing them to bow.

I understood misplaced loyalty.

Once, I'd placed that same faith in the man standing before me now.

But *this*. Standing with Devin. Helping him crush a pack that he once defended. I shook my head, and even though he wasn't looking at me, I knew he could feel my disgust radiating from me in waves. He would die for this, too.

I would make sure of it.

I flinched away as Devin leaned in, his warm breath fanning over my ear. "I might let you kill him if you want," he whispered conspiratorially. "Call it a wedding gift."

"You're insane."

My head jerked back as the sharp rap of the back of his hand found my cheek. The tang of blood bloomed over my tongue, and I blinked the dark spots from my eyes.

"*You will not speak to me that way,*" he hissed, looking every bit the crazed lunatic I knew he was, but only for a beat before he slicked his dark hair back from his face and sighed.

"Now. *Open wide.*"

I groaned as I resurfaced from the drug, my head heavy and ears filled with cotton. My fingers twitched over something smooth, like velvet or suede, and I worked hard to peel back my eyelids, but they wouldn't cooperate.

It was dark wherever we were. A suffused orange glow was the only light that flickered behind my shuttered eyelids.

Taking stock, I realized there was something brushing against my chest and shoulders. I could feel it against my flesh, and yet I couldn't move to touch it.

It took more effort than I ever would have thought possible to get my eyelids even a fraction open, but I did. Grunting like a rabid animal.

Where was I?

A smooth carpet coated the earthen floor beneath me. Propped behind my back was a small mountain of suede pillows. An old kerosene lantern hung in one corner of what looked like a really big tent. The dark tactical style canvas of it at odds with the plush interior.

I rocked my head to one side, gaining back another modicum of movement and found a bed. What looked like a real mattress on top of some kind of cot-like structure to keep it up off the floor. A rumpled green blanket hung half on and half off, and my nose wrinkled as the smell hit me.

Devin's scent. That strange combination of smooth musk and sharp pine that I'd once loved, but now thought smelled like a bog in the forest. The kind that housed algae and toads and smelled absolutely rank when it got too hot out.

Yeah. I didn't know how I'd ever actually *enjoyed* that smell.

As though on cue, Devin swept into the tent, pushing through a flap opposite me. He was still full naked, his body glistening with sweat in the lamplight.

Judging by how dark it was outside, I had to guess it'd been at least a few hours since the barrens, which meant I could be literally anywhere within a two- hundred mile radius. Not a comforting thought.

"You're awake."

No shit, I wanted to reply, but my tongue wasn't ready to work yet and sat uselessly on the floor of my mouth.

He turned back and lifted the flap, calling out into the night, to where I could hear the distant sounds of people and animals milling about, setting up camp.

"Bring him," he demanded, and the shadow of a tall man moved from beside the entrance, his footsteps fading as he moved away.

Devin moved to the corner of the tent where a basin was placed high on a collapsible camp table. He splashed the water on his face, scrubbing away the last splatters of what I had to assume was Sam's blood from his cheeks.

He took a cloth from the top of a stack next to the basin and soaked it in the water, wringing out the excess before coming to me.

I cringed inwardly as he knelt at my side, cocking his head, considering my face, my neck, and then lower, to where someone had mercifully dressed me in what looked like a white nightgown.

"You're even more beautiful than I remembered," he told me, lifting a finger to twirl it in my long silvery hair, making my blood pump faster. The spark of fear doing enough to burn off some more of the paralytic from my blood, enabling me to twitch my hand into a loose fist and close my gaping mouth.

Devin lifted the cloth to my cheek, scrubbing away what felt like a mat of blood even though I couldn't remember being hurt. When the cloth came away brown instead of red, I sighed inwardly, glad to see it was only dirt.

"I didn't touch you," he said, and I wanted desperately to believe him.

"W-what..." I tried, the word coming out as if I had a ball in my mouth.

"Hush," Devin chided me, dragging the cool cloth down to my collarbone. "It'll be a while yet before your strength returns. Be patient."

I narrowed my eyes on him, wondering what the fuck he was playing at with this bullshit *nice guy* act.

"The alchemist," someone announced from outside as the feeling returned to my toes.

"Let him in."

A man entered a moment later. Tall, with broad shoulders and silver strands in his dark hair that caught the light as he moved through the tent.

"This is the bitch?"

"Don't call her that," Devin snapped at the man, whirling on him with a warning in his stare and muscle coiled to strike.

The man, to his credit, didn't so much as flinch at Devin's threat, instead surveying him as one might survey a specimen beneath a microscope. Finding it particularly lacking.

When he looked at me, though, the same disinterest was not present in his cutting stare.

"Shall I proceed then?" the alchemist asked Devin, not bothering to pay him any mind as he brushed past to stand before me.

"This...this *spell* you're casting, how long will it last?"

"It is permanent." A spell?

Devin was having this fucking alchemist prick cast a spell on me?

I had to clench my jaw as tightly as I could to stop myself from smiling. Being the twin soul wolf allowed me to mate to two shifters, but it had also allowed me to be somehow impervious to the magic of other immortal races. And that ability hadn't only extended to me, but to my entire pack when I became alpha.

It was a secret I knew wasn't safe if shared. People like this alchemist, with his clear status in the witching community, apparent in his dress and confidence, wouldn't allow shifters like me to live if they knew the truth.

And this one, *clearly,* didn't.

The alchemist inhaled sharply through his nose and tipped his head to one side, cracking his neck and flexing his fingers until each one popped.

"I'll need a moment in private," he said, closing his eyes and spreading his hands at his sides, palms down to draw magic up from the earth.

"No."

The alchemist's eyes flew back open to glare at Devin.

"Either you leave, or you will not get what you've asked for. This magic is ancient. Forbidden. Known only to a handful of my kind. Its knowledge cannot be—"

"I don't give a fuck about your magic. Besides, I'm not in the business of leaking information that could harm my kind."

The alchemist seemed to consider this and then nodded. "Very well, but if you tell a soul, I'll have to kill you."

The corner of Devin's mouth lifted into a grin as though he welcomed the challenge, and he was even more the fool than I thought he was. Too cocky. That cockiness would be the very thing that killed him.

Without warning, the alchemist raised his hands and sparks of blue-hued light flew from his fingertips, forming a blazing symbol in the air. Intricate with lines and curves and runic symbols twisting and locking into place as though he was playing a puzzle game with electricity and the universe was the game board.

I'd seen magic before. But not like this. Never like this.

Someone gasped, and it took me a moment to realize it was me as I shied away from the blazing glow of the alchemist's spell.

It won't work on me, I told myself. The words a mantra on repeat in my skull. *It won't work. It won't work.*

"*Liraveris Bestiam,*" he said, and the blue hued light splintered into a thousand tiny pieces, shooting straight for me. They stabbed into my flesh, sinking down through muscle, sinew, and eventually, bone.

My stomach roiled at the attack. His magic filled me until I was near bursting. My insides feeling too big to be contained by my outsides until my eyes were bulging. Until I was choking on it.

"What's happening?" Devin demanded, and as I vomited, he caught me, turning me onto my side to prevent me from choking as putrid bile flowed from my lips and bright spots of light crowded my vision.

"Her twin soul, I imagine," the alchemist said without feeling. "It'll be harder to contain than a normal shifter. The magic will do its work, though, you can be certain of that."

Hot tears pricked my eyes as my sides stopped squeezing and the horrible sensation of the magic invading my body seemed to leech away back to the earth.

"There, see? She's just fine."

Devin's hands left me, and I let my tensed muscles sag against the carpet, focusing on breathing. On getting air into my lungs and the light bursts out of my eyes so I could see.

"What..." I hissed, finding that the alchemist's magic had burned off even more of the drug still lingering in my bloodstream. "What did you...do...to me?"

The alchemist knelt, careful to avoid the pool of bile, until I could see his face. "I've bound your wolf," he told me with a grin, lifting his gaze back to Devin.

"She won't be able to access the strength of her inner beast. Nor will she be able to shift...though I'm afraid nothing will stop her from shifting during a full moon. However, she will be feral during a moon-triggered shift. Acting on instinct alone. Like a wild animal. Best to have her chained."

Devin nodded, his face falling as though he didn't relish the thought of taking a part of me away. Like he didn't just try to hack off part of my soul.

But I could already sense it, the last of the witch's magic leaving my body and returning to the earth. And though she was muted, hampered by all the drugs still lingering in my system, I found I could still feel her. I couldn't be certain, but it was enough to hope that whatever magic this bastard had tried to use on me hadn't worked.

Even if I needed them both to think it had.

"How much?" Devin asked, going to retrieve a stack of bills from a low table next to his bed.

The alchemist shook his head, standing. "She killed my nephew," he said. "We'll call it even."

A river of ice flooded my veins as I considered the alchemist for a second time. Recognizing the sloping nose and wide jaw. They were features he shared with his kin: the witch we captured, tortured, and killed.

The one we'd found to be innocent of the crimes we accused him of, but guilty of so many others committed at the behest of his master. His *uncle*.

I committed his face to memory, vowing to kill him too if I ever saw his ugly face again.

"Fucking bastard," I spat, my voice still softer than I would've liked but growing in strength all the same.

"It goes without saying," the alchemist said as he made to depart, holding open the tent flap to cast one more disdainful glance in my direction. "I was never here."

Devin didn't bother replying as the man left, bending to lift me from the ground instead, setting me back against the pillows while he tugged the dirtied carpet out from under me and tossed it outside.

"Get rid of that," he barked. "And bring me the girl."

"Yes, sir."

"Now what?" I asked, wiggling my toes and flexing my shoulders. Hoping he didn't notice just how much feeling was returning to my limbs while his back was turned to me. I rolled my ankles, stopping as he came back to me.

"We live happily ever after?" I asked, my voice dripping with sarcasm. "You the mad king and me, the chained bitch at your side?"

His brows lowered, confused.

"No, Allie. I won't have to keep you chained. That's the beauty of it, don't you see? The council member was only the first visitor. There will be another. One who will make you irrevocably mine. Forever. Unless you hold up your end of the bargain."

"Let me guess? A vampire?"

So predictable. Also, so *so* fucking perfect.

Devin took hold of my jaw, forcing my still-rolling eyes to focus on him instead. His rough touch sent shivers of disgust rolling through me, and I had to stop myself from spitting in his face.

"You made me a promise," he said, neglecting to respond. "You swore to be mine if I allowed your *mates* to live."

He cast my face to the side with a sharp jerk of my chin, leaning in to inhale deeply beneath my jaw. "*That smell...*"

"*Fuck off*," I growled.

His fist came around my throat, squeezing just enough to prove what he could do if he wished. "We can do it my way if you prefer? I have a crew ready to go after them. And I wouldn't stop at your mates, Allie. I'll kill them all."

My breath wheezed through the pinhole of my throat, and he relaxed his hold just enough for me to respond. "No," I croaked, testing my arms while he was distracted. I could lift them, but I was afraid they'd still be of little use.

"Then show me you mean it," he demanded, his eyes falling to my lips while he licked his own. "Don't fight me. Just give in to it. I know you can feel it, too. We're the same, Allie."

I closed my eyes as he leaned in, thinking of Clay. Of Jared. Of my pack. I would kill Devin, but right now, he still had the upper hand. He could send that crew of shifters after them. For all I knew, he might have already.

Right now, I needed to play this part. Be what I promised him I would. Keep my guys safe. Keep us whole even though it felt like something inside of me was breaking as Devin's lips brushed mine.

He pulled away a second later, and I sagged, thinking it was over, but when I saw the look in his eyes, the way they slanted with lust, I knew it was far from being over. "You can do better."

This time he wasn't gentle.

This time, his lips were hard and demanding, almost bruising as he deepened the kiss, slipping his tongue into my mouth until I gagged on it.

He snarled as he pulled away, rising to rake clawed fingers through his hair as though he might rip it from his scalp. "Why do you fight me?" he shouted. "Why must you *always* fight me?"

In the blink of an eye he had me up on my feet, supporting my weight between himself and a tent post with an arm barred against my chest. "You. Are. Mine."

I bit back a scathing retort, trying to suss out whether or not I could stand on my own if he released me.

"I will have you, Allie, whether you want it or not, but for your own sake, *don't* fight me. I don't want to have you compelled. Don't make me."

If I could be compelled, it was about the only way he'd *ever* have me, because promise or no, I would *not* let this motherfucker rape me.

Devin pressed in against me, making his naked body flush with mine until I could feel the press of his hardening cock through the thin white fabric of the gown I wore and shuddered.

He ran his free hand up my thigh, finding the hem of the nightgown and pressing beneath it. "That's it," he cooed. "Just give in."

His fingers gripped my hip, knocking my tailbone hard into the post at my back, and it was the perfect opportunity. In a knee jerk reaction, *literally,* just as his hand moved down to lift the hem of the gown, I drove my knee into his erection.

Perhaps not with as much strength as I could've done had I not been drugged, but it had the intended effect. His hold against my chest weakened as he buckled, holding his junk.

I slipped free of his grasp, but misjudged how much of my strength had returned. I managed two rocky steps to the left before my knees gave out under the weight of my body and I crashed to the floor. He was on me barely a second later, flipping me onto my back until his knees were pressed tightly to either side of my hips, his cock hovering over my belly button. Somehow still partially hard.

"Bitch!" he snarled, his eyes showing the wolf that lingered within. Devin's fingers splayed over my chest, trying to hold me down while he stroked his cock back to a full head. And all the while I squirmed, thrusting weak jabs at his chest with my heavy fists.

"*Get...off...me,*" I managed through fits of panicked breath, gasping when I finally wiggled high enough to dislodge a leg. With everything I had, I planted my heel to his chest and kicked, sending him rocking backward far enough for me to get my other leg free and repeat the motion while he was still surprised.

Using the hard packed earth as leverage I slammed both feet into his chest and this time he flew back...right into a girl who'd just stepped through the door, a guard holding her tightly by the arm.

She shrieked as he knocked into her, and they both fell to the ground.

"Sir!" the male shifter called, grabbing Devin by the arm to try to help him up, but Devin knocked away the shifter's hand and turned his fury on the girl.

Piper cried out as he slapped her hard across the face. "*Never* enter my tent unannounced," he hissed at her as she whimpered. "And *never* put your filthy hands on me again."

The girl choked on a sob and tried to sign something, but Devin wasn't paying attention.

"I'm sorry, sir, we heard the shouts and she just darted in. Slipped right out of my fingers for a second—"

"Get out," Devin said to the guard, settling a glare on him so malicious that I wondered if Devin might strike him down right there and then for not having stopped the girl from entering.

The shifter vanished back the way he'd come, and by the time Devin faced me again, I'd managed to army crawl nearly all the way to the back of the tent. A useless endeavor, but still, I had to try.

"You," he hissed at Piper. "Get over there and read her."

The girl's dark watery gaze flicked to me in muted horror.

When she didn't move, he kicked her, and she winced at the pain while scrambling to her feet only to fall to her knees again in front of me.

"Does she have *any* intention whatsoever of making good on her promise to me?" The question was for Piper, but his luminous eyes remained locked on me. And then after another moment, his upper lip curling back, he said, "Does she intend to kill me?"

My jaw clenched as I found some last morsel of strength, and I hauled myself up to a seated position so I could scooch away from the girl. I shook my head at her, feeling my wolf waking from a too-long slumber within. She was weak though, muted, and I couldn't seem to draw on her strength.

The realization that the alchemist's spell may have somehow worked made me sick to my stomach, and I shoved away the idea. Pulling harder on that little flicker of her I could still feel deep within.

I couldn't let this girl read my thoughts. I didn't think I would be able to hide them from her, and if she told Devin my intentions—that I would *never* let him have me, and that I fully fucking intended to not only kill him but make him suffer—then the deal was off, and my mates, my entire pack, were as good as dead.

Why hadn't I seen this bullshittery coming? Damn.

Damn. Damn. *Damn.*

"Do it!" Devin growled and the girl darted forward, making a grab for my hands. I shoved her back, and she looked to Devin for guidance.

He rolled his eyes before coming over and settling himself behind me. I wasn't able to fight him as he locked my arms with his and hauled my body against his so that my back was pressed to his chest and his hot breath skated down the back of my neck.

"What are you waiting for?"

I wriggled as Piper leaned in and placed her clammy hands on either side of my face, a hopeless sob expanding in my chest.

No. Please. Please.

Don't think. Don't think.

I implored her for mercy, begged her for it with my eyes, and watched as her chin quivered.

Clear your mind, Allie.

But even in trying to clear it, the edges of my subconscious thoughts were still there. Dancing around my conscious desire for them to shut the fuck up.

"Well?" Devin demanded.

Piper dropped her hands to wring them together in her lap. Her long hair fell back as she lifted her gaze to her alpha's and began to sign.

I studied each vague movement, studying the symbols and *praying* to be able to understand something of what she was telling him, but it was no use. I'd read a book on sign language once as a teen with good intentions of learning, but I'd never stuck with it. I barely remembered how to sign the letters of my goddamned name.

"*Hmmm.*" Devin's chest rumbled with the curious sound as his hold relaxed and Piper rose on shaking legs to take a step back from me. "Interesting."

Interesting? What was fucking interesting?

"That'll be all, Piper. Go back to your tent and stay there. I'll see to it that you're brought a proper meal for your *assistance* today."

Piper nodded her head and cast me an apologetic look before she scampered back outside.

I jerked out of Devin's grasp and nearly fell on my face, only catching myself at the last second as he rushed to follow Piper to the door. "Is it ready?" he asked someone outside.

"Yes. Shall I take her?"

"No. I'll do it myself."

Before I knew what was happening, Devin lifted me with a firm grip on my arm.

"Let go," I snapped, still wobbling on my feet.

He jerked me steady and put his face in mine. "Keep fighting me and I'll not just kill them, Allie, I'll make you watch."

So he knew...

He knew.

I felt nothing as Devin dragged my only half-functioning body from the tent out into the night. I barely registered the stares or the whispers as we passed rows of small tents and groups of naked bodies surrounding metal barrel campfires.

As pine branches slapped across my cheeks and thorny shrubs carved small wounds into my knees, I pieced together that we were entering a thicker part of the forest.

And then we were inside. It smelled of wood. Of old cedar and mothballs and metal.

Chains rattled, and I wasn't able to claw back to myself from the pits of my despair in time to stop it.

I stared down into a dark hole in the wooden floor of what I assumed was some sort of old hunting cabin. The cloying smell of damp earth filled my nose as Devin released me with a shove and I fell.

The ground rushed up to meet me, expelling all the air from my lungs. I wheezed as I tried to get air, fingers clawing into the damp wood beneath me, trying to flip around.

Devin pulled the ladder up and discarded it somewhere up there as I fell onto my back, staring up, still unable to get a full breath.

There was a creak as the door above, *so far above*, began to close, and I blinked, trying to judge the distance. It had to be at least twelve feet.

"There's something I have to take care of," Devin told me, and the implication in his words made every inch of my flesh prickle and the back of my throat burn.

"You...you motherfucker," I stammered, my chest still aching from the blow of the fall. "Don't...don't you dare—"

But Devin only smiled as he sealed me into the cellar with the smells of earth and wood rot as my only company.

Chains drew across the wooden exterior of the hatch and the *chink* of a lock clicking into place burrowed into my heart just as surely as a bullet might. "I'll be back before you know it," Devin called, his footsteps retreating until another door closed and I heard the muffled drone of low conversation outside. "I'm going…" I coughed, my voice still so low that I doubted he could hear me. "…to kill you. I swear."

26

It took far longer than I would've imagined, but eventually I was able to stand. To walk.

Not that it helped much. In the pitch dark of the cellar the only things I could find were cobwebs and mouse droppings. They'd been careful, it seemed, to remove everything from the space.

There wasn't any way I could reach the hatch above, either. I'd tried. If I could shift, then maybe...but my wolf lay dormant inside, leaving me all alone.

For so long, I'd wished to never have been changed. In the beginning I'd fought that new foreign part of myself. Hated it, even. But without her I felt lost now. Bereft.

Abandoned.

Though that wasn't the reason I'd begun to pace. Nor was it the reason my skin was crawling, my heart fluttering against the bones of my ribs like a bird beating against a sealed window. No escape.

No escape.

Panic twisted my guts and made breathing so much of a chore that every few moments I had to gasp for it, to force it down into my lungs just to keep from passing out again.

He's going after them.

Piper had told Devin what I was thinking, what I planned, and now he was going to kill them. He would kill them all.

I choked as bile tried to force its way up my throat, my stomach heaving, but there was nothing in there to be expelled. It didn't stop my body from trying though, making fresh tears sting my already burning eyes.

I need to get out. Get up, Allie.

Get. Up.

My head spun as I found my footing again, going back to the wall to search for any sort of handhold nearest to where I could see the tiniest bit of light filtering through a fissure in the wooden hatch above. Judging by the light, it was day. Had been for some time, though I could only recall a few hours. I'd passed out not long after Devin locked me inside.

My body folding to the first wave of anxiety like a cheap tent.

I wouldn't let that happen again.

I knew they were still alive. I could feel it in my bones. And as long as my mates drew breath on this earth, there was no way in hell I was going to stop fighting to save them.

My shaking hands brushed over the rough wooden surface of the wall, catching a couple of splinters I ignored. There were no shelves. No tables. Nothing.

If I didn't know any better, I'd have to assume I was in an oversized wooden coffin. Sure as fuck felt like one.

Getting an idea, I steeled myself, spreading my legs wide and swinging my clenched fist into the wood paneling. The wood splintered and snapped and my fist went through. My triumph was quickly muted as my knuckles smashed into hard brick.

"*Fuck!*" I cradled my fist to my chest, testing the knuckles for breaks. It seemed fine, but the pinky was questionable. I'd have to worry about setting it later.

I gripped the edge of the wood, and a small grin pulled up at the corner of my lips. I'd made a handhold. If I could just do that about eight more times, I could reach the hatch.

My smile faltered.

Then what, genius?

The hatch was chained shut. And every twenty minutes or so someone entered the cabin above, did a sweep, and then exited the front door again. I had to assume there were at least two out there at all times.

If I made a ruckus trying to break through the goddamned hatch, they'd just come and stop me. And the commotion from that would draw even more of them.

Doesn't matter, I told myself. *You still need to try.*

I shook out the sting still lingering in my split knuckles, giving it another couple of seconds to heal before throwing it through the wood again.

I whimpered as my knuckles struck the brick, the pain radiating up through my forearm.

I could use a little help, I whispered inwardly, still drawing on my inner wolf. I'd all but forgotten how bullshit human strength was. At least I was healing quickly though, at least there was some sign that the alchemist hadn't succeeded in binding my wolf. At least not fully.

Footsteps charged inside from above, and I crouched, eyeing the hatch, holding my breath.

"You hear that?" one asked another. A pause.

"Nah, what was it?"

"Not sure."

Silence.

"It's gone now. Probably just the bitch throwing herself against a wall."

"A lot of good that'll do."

They shared a laugh, and rage burned through my veins as they retreated back to their posts outside the old hunter's cabin.

There was no way I was going to be able to punch seven more holes in this damned wall to reach the top without them coming to investigate. But...maybe that was a good thing.

If they opened the hatch...

Ugh.

Without my wolf, I was useless, who the hell was I kidding.

I leaned back against the wall and sank, pulling my knees into my chest and closing my eyes to focus.

"I can feel you," I whispered. "I know you're still in there."

She was in pain. *We* were in pain.

But we would *keep* being in pain for the rest of our miserable lives if we did nothing to save them.

Please.

A scratching sound, like tiny claws on wood, brought me back out of my head.

I squinted into the dark, trying to figure out where it was coming from and wondering absently if I was hungry enough to eat a raw rat. Shudder. I may not be, but if my wolf would cooperate, she wouldn't hesitate to gobble it up.

Feeling my way, I crawled across the dirty floor, listening intently as the sound came again. Louder this time and followed by the familiar sound of dirt and small stones trickling down to the ground. Along with the *knock* of one brick being set atop another.

A dim light shone through one of the hollow knots in a panel of wood, and I gasped, hearing someone grunt on the other side.

Hurriedly, I pressed my eye to the notch, peering through to see the silhouette of someone moving. Behind them I could make out what appeared to be a stretch of space and stairs leading up.

It was another entrance to the cellar. One the hunter would've used to haul in big game so he wouldn't have to track it through the house. I wanted to smack myself for not thinking to check for it, but clearly this entrance had been sealed up a long time ago.

I tried to get a better look at who was attempting to burrow into my makeshift cell, but when they moved, dirt sprayed into my eye and I fell back, trying to blink it clear.

The wood panel groaned as though they were pushing on it, and I scrambled to my feet, readying myself for a fight.

It looked like there was only one. Even without my wolf, I could take them. I *had* to.

The panel snapped free, and I clamped my jaw shut to silence the sounds of my haggard breathing, praying the shifters guarding the cabin upstairs didn't hear.

A slender shape slipped through the opening, and I blinked into the second-hand light, bending low in preparation to tackle them.

Piper held up her hands, her eyes going wide at the sight of me. She put her finger to her lips.

I looked past her to the short tunnel and stairway, unable to stop myself from moving toward it.

The girl launched herself at me, gripping my arms frantically to stop me from leaving. I shook her off, resisting the urge to shout. Couldn't draw any more attention than Piper likely already had.

She moved her hands, trying desperately to tell me something that I wasn't understanding. I shook my head, confused. "I don't understand."

Not just what she was trying to tell me, but what the hell she was doing here. I had to assume she was helping me, but...why?

"I need to go. He's going to kill them if I don't."

She shook her head, and I cocked mine at her in response. She clenched her jaw and tugged a tiny chunk of pencil shaved almost all the way down to the eraser end out of her pocket. She searched for something to write on, and I hurriedly pulled off my nightgown, thrusting it at her.

Her eyes lit up, and she pushed the gown against the wall, beginning to write something.

Not safe yet. Need to wait. Trust me.

My brows drew together as I glanced between her and my freedom. The leafy pattern lying in shadows against the stairs told me she was at least smart enough to have camouflaged the opening. But the covering was sparse. If someone looked too closely...

"Is there someone on patrol nearby?" I asked in a whisper.

Piper squinted at me and I realized she was looking at my mouth, trying to understand what I was saying. I repeated the question more slowly, giving her ample opportunity to read my lips.

She nodded and held up four fingers. Four of them.

In my wolf form, *maybe* I could take them. But definitely not like this.

She then held up two fingers with one hand and made a zero with the other before pointing to her wrist as though she were wearing a watch.

"Twenty minutes?"

She nodded again and went back to writing on the white shift for a painfully long minute before turning it to face me again.

He was never going to let any of them live no matter what. I'm sorry. I thought he was different. I didn't know how far he would go.

I remembered how Devin knocked into her in the tent and how he warned her off ever touching him again. She definitely got a good earful of his thoughts during that quick exchange, and it was obvious he'd never allowed her to read him before. Otherwise, I was willing to bet she wouldn't have been so eager to help a psychopath.

I held up a hand. "It doesn't matter. I just have to get back to my pack. If I'm fast enough, then maybe I can still save my mates and the rest of them."

Her lips parted, and she hurriedly scribbled out two more words.
Still alive.

"I know," I replied, confused. "I would feel it if my mates were dead."

She shook her head, flustered.

The other ones, she wrote. *He said he killed them, but they are not dead yet. They are still alive. He sold them to the witch.*

My wolf stirred within.

Still alive?

"Are you sure?"

She nodded and I tried to count the hours between when the witch cast his spell on me and now. Would that be enough time for him to arrange pick up and transport of that many shifters?

"Do you know where they are?"

She nodded again, and I snatched her up, pulling her hard to my chest for an awkward, trembling embrace. My heart squeezed in my chest. *Alive.* They were all still alive.

"Why are you helping me?" I asked in a watery voice. "Why betray your pack?"

She chewed her bottom lip and wrote something out near the hem of the gown and passed it to me.

You're good. He's not.

She had that all wrong. The part about me being good anyway, but I didn't argue. "How much longer?"

Piper considered, listening closely to the sounds of the forest outside. She held up a one and five apologetically, and I ground my teeth. How the fuck was I supposed to sit here uselessly for fifteen more minutes.

"Do you know where he went? Where Devin went?" She shook her head, and a chill snaked through me.

I had to believe he wasn't going after Clay and Jared, at least not yet.

Piper settled into silence, sinking down to sit cross legged with a fresh swath of gown in her lap. She set to drawing something, and I peered over her shoulder in the dim light to find the beginnings of a map.

"Hey," I interrupted, crouching down to her level. "You can't stay here. He'll know you helped me. Your scent is bound to be all over this room by now."

She frowned, though it certainly didn't seem like news to her.

I wrinkled my nose. She knew he'd kill her and still helped me anyway. I couldn't say I condoned what she'd likely done in helping him build this army, or in getting my mate's sister killed for switching sides, but...

I understood what it was like to feel like you didn't have a choice. I knew the urge for self-preservation above all else was the hardest thing to give up.

"Come with me."

She cocked her head at me.

"Come with me, and if we survive...if I can kill him...you'll have a place with my pack."

Her eyes filled with unshed tears and instead of trying to write anything, she snatched my hand, squeezing it in what I could only assume was a form of thanks.

"Don't thank me, yet," I muttered. "There's a pretty good chance neither of us will survive until tomorrow." A lump formed in my throat as I tried to come up with some semblance of a plan. I needed to rescue my packmates before anything else, even though my heart yearned to make a beeline straight for my mates. I owed it to them to save them and once that witch had his hands on them, there was no telling where they'd wind up.

I may not be able to find them then. I couldn't risk that.

Okay, find the shifters Devin has captive, free them, then what?

The taste of blood filled my mouth as I bit down too hard on my cheek trying to think of a way out of this, but I was coming up empty.

Fuck.

Okay, first things first. Get the hostages freed and then work out the rest.

Like Jared would've said: one step at a time.

A gentle tap on my arm drew my attention back to Piper and the new message she had written over the top of the map.

I was coming to find your pack when he found me first, it said. *He promised me safety if I helped him. If it weren't for me, he wouldn't have so many shifters in his pack. He used my ability against them.*

She signed that she was sorry and it was one gesture I did remember from that old textbook.

"You were coming to find *my* pack?" I asked, not needing the explanation of the rest. Devin could be very convincing and quite charming when he needed to be. Besides, I had no doubt this poor girl was hated everywhere she went. No one wanted someone being privy to their private thoughts. I could imagine the trials she would've had to face in trying to find a pack, and everyone knew that being a lone wolf wasn't the safest way to live as our kind.

I heard you took in same sex mated pairs and that you had a seer and had mated to two shifters. I thought if anyone could understand, it would be you. I had no idea Devin was after you. None of us knew until it was too late to do anything to stop him.

She didn't have to tell me the rest. The way he treated Piper now told me all I needed to know. She'd helped him of her own free will at first, not knowing the truth that hid behind carefully crafted smiles and an easy laugh. And when she decided she didn't want to help him anymore, he made her anyway.

I patted her leg, practically bouncing on the balls of my feet in anticipation of getting the fuck out of here. "You don't need to explain to me. I know him. I understand. I may not be able to promise you safety, but I can promise you freedom."

She nodded resolutely, discarding the remaining nub of pencil with the shirt on the floor. She held up five fingers.

Five more minutes.

Thunder rumbled in the distance and both of us jumped at the sound, sharing a look. I was almost afraid to breathe and break the spell.

If it rained, our scent would be harder to track. Hell, if it rained hard enough, it would be near impossible.

We listened intently as the first droplets began to fall, a dark cloud passing over the sun above, erasing the shadows on the stairs.

A wide grin split my face and deep within, awoken by a new hope, my wolf lifted her weary head.

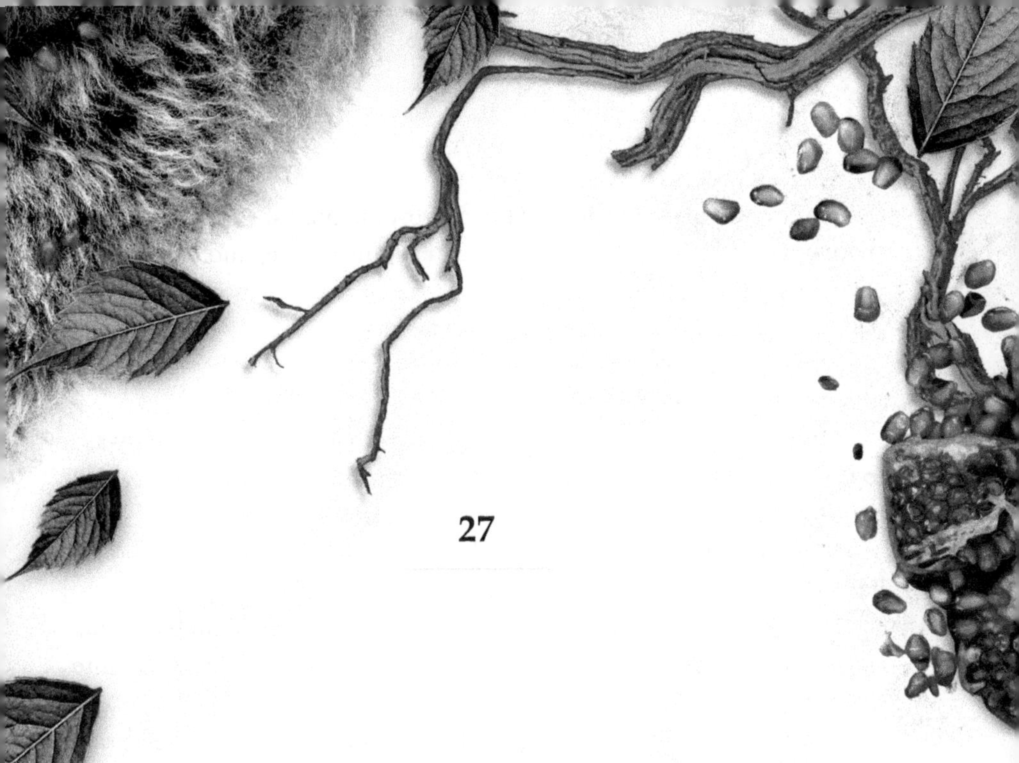

27

Piper gave me a loaded look when it was time, her jaw clenching tightly. I could hear her heartbeat from a foot away, and erratic as it was, it was a comforting notion. My wolf was breaking through whatever kept her walled away at my center.

But I didn't think it had anything to do with the witch and everything to do with having lost hope. Of not wanting to bear witness to what she thought we'd have to endure at the hands of Devin for the sake of our mates.

I truly had meant to give in to him if it meant saving them, but even without my wolf to influence me, I just couldn't do it.

"Ready?" I asked, listening to the sounds of the rapidly darkening forest outside. I heard nothing save for the pelting of rain on leaves and earth. The patrol had moved on, or perhaps they were switching out.

I just had to hope there weren't several rings of patrol we'd need to get through, or if there were, that Piper knew a way through undetected.

It wasn't lost on me that I was putting a lot of faith in a person that I'd only truly met today. Someone without whom none of this might even be happening.

My wolf bristled within, making my upper lip twitch into a snarl, but this teenage girl was not the enemy. At least, she wasn't anymore.

I followed Piper out through the narrow opening she created toward the wet cement steps. A curved shape caught my eye, and I paused to pry a rusted meat hook from the wall near the exit, clutching the bar end in my palm to wield as a weapon if needed.

I wasn't sure yet if my wolf was strong enough to take over and I'd need to be prepared if she weren't.

Piper raised a brow at me but quickly recovered, gesturing upward to the covered opening and then to the northeast with two quick jerks of her fingers. We needed to exit quickly and run in that direction.

I nodded that I understood and my body flooded with adrenaline, hairs standing on end as the chill air met my flushed skin.

Piper inhaled sharply and cleared the steps in a single bound, shoving the branches and bramble from her path as she vanished into the rain.

I cleared the exit only a second after her, shivering as cold rain coated my naked body, pressing my hair flat to my scalp.

For a little thing, she was *fast*.

Piper kept in a low crouch as she weaved through the trees, her footfalls so light they were almost inaudible above the rush of the rain.

I kept my eyes fixed to her simple gray paper-bag dress, but it blended in so well with the shadows that I nearly lost sight of her a couple times and had to keep right on her heels to keep from losing her completely.

My tan flesh was definitely better than the white gown I'd been wearing as far as camouflage went, but I'd still be spotted easily in comparison to her. The white blonde hair wasn't helping, either.

I rushed to tap Piper on the arm and held up a hand, mouthing *one sec* as I set down the meat hook and dug my fingers into the earth at my feet, scooping up two fistfuls of muck. I smashed it into my hair and rubbed the excess down my arms and chest, remembering another time I'd done the same. While trying to escape the very same monster who would hunt me the moment he noticed I was gone.

Except last time I wasn't ready. I didn't know what I was up against. And he'd won.

This time would be different.

"Okay," I whispered, grabbing my meat hook and gesturing forward. "Lead on."

She nodded grimly, and I wondered why she hadn't shifted yet. Surely we were far enough from camp now that no one would sense her or catch her wolf's scent? If she weren't shifting, I had to assume there was still at least one more patrol ring we'd need to pass through.

We'd be faster on four legs, though, if my wolf would allow the shift. I had no idea how long Devin would be gone, nor how long it would be until someone noticed I was gone or stumbled upon the exit Piper had found hidden in the trees.

Not long, I guessed. Not long at all.

A head start was the best we could hope for, and I prayed it would be enough.

I almost ran into Piper when she stopped dead in her tracks, lowering herself down until her fingertips kissed the mud.

My body went rigid as I heard what had given her pause. A sort of snuffling sound. Like a wolf trying to track a scent.

They were close, and getting closer every second. They'd caught our scent even through the rain. We must have walked right into them.

I closed my eyes and listened, separating the sounds of two distinct canters. Two. There were only two of them.

I held up two fingers for Piper to see, and she nodded then shrugged as though to say *what now?* It was clear she wasn't a fighter. Her frame too wiry and thin beneath the baggy dress.

I swiped the rain from my eyes and mouthed *stay here,* before creeping past her, careful not to disturb the brush at the base of a wide oak—the rusted meat hook clenched tightly in my palm.

She caught me by the wrist, signing something I couldn't understand. I shook my head to tell her as much but that only made her hold tighter, making me have to jerk myself free.

I held up a hand. "This isn't your fight," I mouthed as clearly as I could, watching her read my lips.

Her face fell, but she didn't move to stop me again, instead hunching down lower in the brush to wait for my return.

I slipped through the foliage, squinting through the rain and shadow for them. My vision narrowed, helped along by my inner wolf, until I caught sight of one snuffling the base of a tree no more than twenty yards away.

So busy watching the shifter's every movement, I wasn't prepared for the other one to attack from behind. Good thing he wasn't as light on his feet as another shifter I knew or else I'd be dead. The squish of his paws in the mud were enough to alert me to his presence a split second before he attacked.

Without thinking, I whirled, arm outstretched, until the rusty hook clenched in my palm sunk deep into the throat of the wolf tumbling atop me.

Hot blood sprayed across my chest as we fell. Stars burst in my eyes as my head connected with something hard, and I was crushed under the weight of the shifter.

A horrible gurgling sound dug into my ears as the wolf thrashed and then began to still.

I called on my wolf, drawing her out as I worked to get the dying wolf off of me, knowing the other would be coming. But I'd only just managed to roll the beast from my chest when the other descended on me. I cried out as its teeth sliced into my forearm, dragging me back.

My body bumped over a tree root as I swung at him, unable to land a single blow. I switched tactics, fighting for something to grab hold of to stop him dragging me back. Each vicious tug of his jaws tearing deeper into my flesh.

Why hadn't I pulled the hook back after that first goddamned swing?

I cried out as the shifter bit harder and a gush of heat slid down my arm faster than the rain could wash it away.

My shoulder was near coming out of its socket as I fought his hold, and he was so focused on not letting go that he didn't see her coming.

Piper slammed into his side with a wet smack, managing to get her slender jaw around his throat before he could buck her off. But he was quickly gaining the upper hand, their enormous bodies twisting and tumbling together until I could hardly tell where one of them ended and the other began.

Piper let out a sharp whine, and I felt around in the mud for something to use, the only thing I could come up with a small boulder that I could barely lift. One of my arms useless with blood loss and severed nerve endings.

I hefted it above my head with a shaking grip, willing my body to heal faster. As soon as I saw an opening, I smashed it down. It *cracked* against the shifter's skull, dazing him long enough for me to hit him again.

And again.

Until I was left staring down at a grotesquerie of bone and I didn't want to consider what else.

I dropped the stone with a thud at my feet and hurried to kneel next to Piper, feeling her out for injury. Her collarbone was broken, and I gave her an apologetic look before using my full body weight to hold her down and guide it back into place for her to heal.

A broken cry came from her canine lips, but after a minute, her breathing evened out and I was able to release her. It definitely wouldn't be the best setting I'd ever done, but it would have to do for now. If we lived long enough to get back to camp, I'd have it set properly.

"You good?" I asked as she got to her feet, needing to repeat myself a second time for her to interpret the movements of my mouth.

She nodded shakily and nudged her nose to my chest before tipping her head to gesture behind her. No, not behind her, to her back.

"No," I replied. "You can't carry me while that's still healing."

Piper's lupine face screwed up in a scowl as she tipped her head to one side. Not understanding. Clearly she thought the witch's magic had worked on me. Forrest had always been a loudmouth. I was willing to bet everyone in his hellhole of a camp thought they'd seen the last of my wolf.

They were wrong.

Now or never.

I crouched to one knee, planting my fists against the earth.

Wake-up, I commanded, tipping my head back to regard the moon, studying its near-full curve during a break in the cloud cover.

"*Come on,*" I commanded through gritted teeth, offering myself to the power of my beast. Offering her the full control she always craved but I never gave.

I need you. Wake!

She shattered through whatever barrier had been erected around her, surging to the surface like a bolt of white-hot fire.

A guttural growl forced hot steam to cloud around my mouth as my body broke and bent, being reclaimed. Reforged.

Reborn as the wolf I was always meant to be.

I snapped at Piper, and she took off running, leading the way as fast as her legs could carry her.

Failure was not an option anymore. Not even a thought in our shared mind. Our purpose narrowed to a single focus, punctuated only by the steady beating of our heart in our chest and of our paws against the earth: revenge.

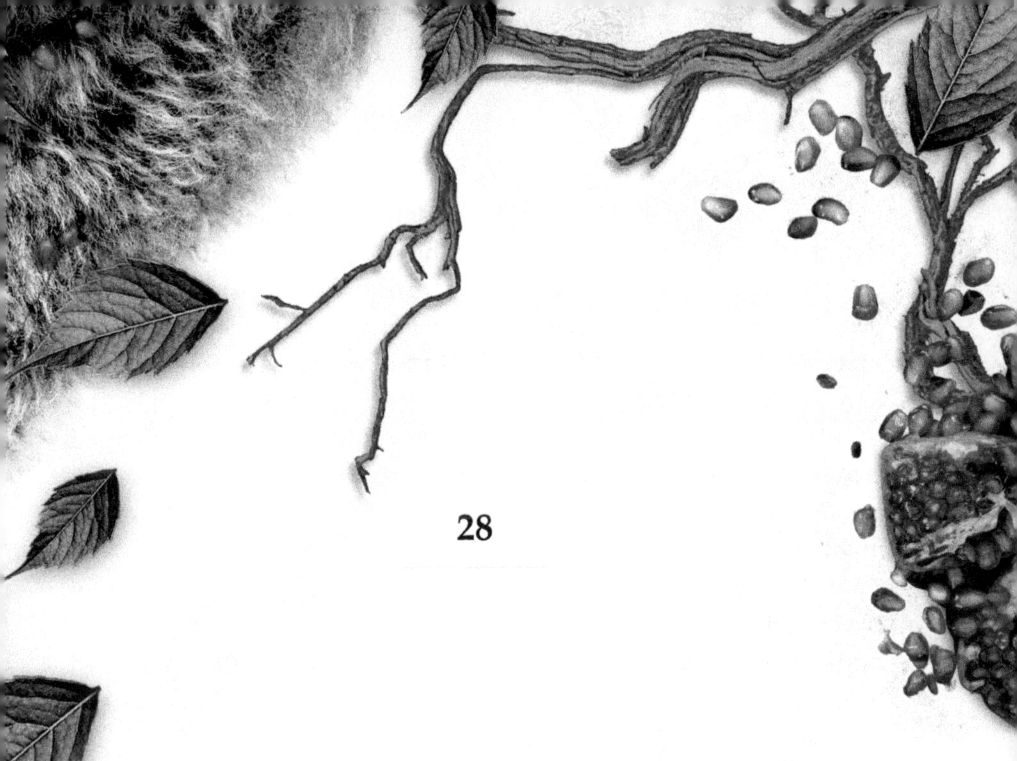

28

I recognized the route we were taking after we diverted from our northern heading to turn sharply south. Piper was smarter than I gave her credit for. She'd only headed north to leave the camp, but as our path converged with White River, she'd skated down to the edge of the bank and continued south.

The bastard hadn't even moved his captives yet. He was just that cocky that I wouldn't be able to escape and that Clay and Jared wouldn't dare make a play for them after everything else that'd happened.

It was his cockiness that was going to be the end of him.

When Piper began to slow after nearly an hour of running, I knew we were getting close. It was still raining pretty hard and that would be to our advantage, but in the distance, I could see the clouds breaking up.

If we wanted to get them out and make any sort of clean getaway, we'd need to do it right now.

There was just the tiny problem of us being *heavily* outnumbered, but I was filing that under *minor detail* in my already overflowing worry bank.

Piper stopped, jerking her head to the southwest. I nodded.

I wouldn't have blamed her for staying behind, but as I jumped up from the riverbank, she followed, keeping right on my heels.

971

We crept through the brush in the dark, and distantly I could hear the sloshing of a watermill turning double-time in the rain and wind.

We found a good place to stop and observe from a distance, tucking ourselves in next to the wide trunk of a fallen tree. It reeked of rot and fungi, which was perfect to help conceal our scent even more than the rain already would.

The mill was situated off to the right of the intersecting river and creek. A quiet stone building almost entirely covered in moss and young ivy, the stones chipped and yellowed with age. The windows broken or missing entirely.

At first we saw no one, and I had to wonder if they'd moved on. If Devin had already returned and discovered I was gone and sent word for them to move. Or perhaps the bodies of the two shifters I'd killed barely an hour ago had been discovered already and it was someone else who set word.

But then...

Two shifters exited the building, standing under a stone awning to keep their cigarettes from getting spoiled by the downpour.

I listened carefully, trying to pick out their voices, or any other noises from the building.

Snippets of their conversation floated my way and to my surprise it seemed they were still thinking they were on schedule for a pick up by the witch's lackeys sometime before dawn.

It was barely midnight now. We had lots of time on our side at least.

Piper cocked her head at me in question, a small whine of protest on her lips that made my wolf want to bite her head off. *Quiet,* I commanded, and even though she couldn't hear it, she felt the weight of my alpha dominance and fell silent.

Six.

The more I listened, the more I was certain of it. There were six of them. Two outside sharing a cigarette. One in wolf form down the creek. And three more inside.

Unless the ones I heard talking and shuffling about inside were actually my packmates, then I supposed there were only the three. I doubted I was that lucky, though.

There was just one more thing I needed before I could even *think* about finding a way inside. There was no way in hell I was walking blindly into another trap.

It came several minutes later, the scrape of chains over stone. A low moan so familiar it made my blood sing with relief.

"She's waking up again," someone said, their words all but drowned out by the pelting rain.

"Bitch doesn't know when to quit."

"I'm going to stuff your useless balls down your goddamned throats," came Viv's biting retort, clear as a bell, sharp as the business end of a blade.

They were keeping them unconscious, then, which wasn't exactly fucking ideal but...

Work with what you've got.

A thump preceded a gasping emittance of pain and my hackles raised.

Wait, I beseeched my wolf, but I'd given her the reins, and she'd just decided the element of surprise was all we needed.

One of the shifters huddling under the awning stubbed the cigarette butt out on a wall, sending bright red cinders scattering into the wind and rain. He didn't even see me coming.

He didn't make so much as a squeal before I had him pressed flat to his back and cut off his air supply with a feral thrust of my paws. The other one I caught mid-shift, his bright green eyes reminding me so much of Devin's that there could be no holding back.

His neck snapped under my jaws and the coppery tang of blood filled my mouth as he went down, twitching as he grew limp.

The door burst open, and I charged before I could think, my jaws clamping down on a corded shoulder as I tumbled into the mill. The man still locked between my teeth.

"Get her!" someone shouted, and I snarled viciously, sinking my teeth further into the man to make him scream.

Come near me, I dared them without the need for words. *I fucking dare you.*

The two remaining men shifted, narrowly avoiding injuring my pack, who lay in a tangle of pale limbs and chains against the far wall. They were so still that for a heart wrenching moment I thought they might be dead. But their heartbeats filled my ears, the sound like a balm to my soul.

My gaze locked on Vivian's for an instant, her gaping mouth closing as she immediately went into action, trying to wake the others as she pulled mercilessly on her shackles.

No mercy, my wolf decided. *I decided.*

The one in my grip was dead in the next instant, spurring the remaining two to charge. I growled, letting the power of my alpha spirit fill me to near bursting. They barely cleared half the space to me before they buckled under the pressure, bending, breaking, bowing.

In my periphery, I could see Piper in the doorway, staring aghast at the scene before her, paralyzed with fear.

There was no stopping now, though. I charged them, checking the one on the right so hard that he sailed into the stone wall with a deafening *clap!* And fell to the ground, unmoving.

My twin tails whipped around me as the other of the two cowered, head bent low and ears pressed flat.

No. Piper!

The shifter who'd been down the creek fell on her a second before I might've warned her, knocking her out of the doorway and back into the brush.

Fuck.

I howled as a lancing pain shot through my ankle, my distraction allowing the other one to launch an attack.

"Allie!" Vivian cried, and the wolf yipped in surprise as a long bolt of chain whipped into its rear end, giving me the opportunity to break free. My counterattack was swift and merciless, going straight for the quick kill.

I ran for the door.

Stumbling over myself in my haste to get to Piper, I nearly bowled her over as she reappeared in the doorway, panting heavily. Bloody but uninjured. The victor.

Impressive.

I jerked my head to the door, requesting that she remain there to alert us of any others, and she spun around dutifully, scanning the shadows.

"Allie?" the groggy voice of Seth found my ears and I yipped excitedly, rushing back to the group as the scent of stale urine clogged my nostrils, replacing the tang of blood that'd been clogging them before. Trey and Todd were still unconscious near his feet, but I could tell they were alive. They were okay.

We were all going to be okay.

"Allie, quit it, you're disgusting," Seth griped as I licked him up the side of his face.

"Are you hurt?" Viv asked, still tugging on her chains as the others all began to come to.

I barreled into her chest, stepping on someone else's leg in the process and knocking the wind out of her.

"Whoa," she said. "Easy or you'll break a damn rib."

My wolf, soothed by the knowledge that her charges were all here, all still alive, gave over the reins.

I shifted back, jerking Vivian's chin up to the see in the moonlight jutting into the room from one of the broken windows above. She batted my hand away. "I'm fine."

She wasn't, but I knew she would be. There was dried blood on her cheeks and below her nose, and I had no doubt there had been many bruises that'd since healed as well. She put up a damn good fight.

"I'm so glad you're okay," I choked out, hugging her. "Where's—"

I scanned the waking shifters and found a bright streak of purple as Destiny lifted her head from across the pile. She blinked into consciousness, her shock at seeing me clear on her face. "Allie? But they said..."

"They said you gave yourself up," Seth finished for Destiny when she trailed off. "That Devin had you."

"He did," I admitted. "I escaped."

"How long until he comes after us?" Seth asked, jerking at the chain around his wrist.

"I don't know. But he'll know I'm gone, or at least that something is up, soon. I had to put down two of his patrol on my way out."

"So when the patrol switches..."

"Yeah. And I have no idea when that is. At best, a few more hours. At worst, the bodies have already been discovered."

A groan drew my attention to a mop of dirty blond dreadlocks as Charity awoke, radiating feral rage. "The fuck is going on," she hissed, violently wriggling out from beneath a few others who were still knocked out."

"It's okay," I said, catching her eye as I gazed at all my packmates who had already awoken. "It's all going to be okay, but we need to move."

Charity snapped herself to full attention, finding the corpses of the dead shifters strewn around the other end of the mill. "*Shit, Allie. You went to work.*"

"Where are the guys?" Seth asked. "The rest of the pack?"

I left Viv to find the keys to their shackles, knowing that time may not be on our side.

"I'll explain everything," I promised. "But first, let's get you all free."

"Then what?' Viv asked, trying to reach for her mate, but Destiny was still too far away.

It made sense why they kept them all in a big pile like that, jammed them all so close together that if any dared to shift, they would be injuring others in the process.

Motherfuckers.

"We'll gather some food," Charity supplied. "And water. They have a bit here, but Seth, Viv, and me, we're stronger than the others. We haven't been here as long. Fifteen minutes to gather some supplies and get everyone fed and then we move? Yeah?"

"Yeah," I replied, finding the keys in the pocket of the one lying limp by the wall and tossing them to Charity. "Go. Hurry."

"Then where will we go?" Archer asked, coughing and wincing in a way that had me worried he might have a few displaced ribs. I hoped not. I didn't have the skill to set them without help. At least not here without the proper supplies.

I knew he was likely eager to get back to his mate. To know where he was. "Callum is fine," I assured him, praying that I was right. "And we're going back to camp...or...to wherever the rest of the pack went."

I had to admit I had no idea if they would have returned back to camp. Not knowing that Devin knew exactly where it was and could strike at any time.

"Did any of them have a cellphone?" I asked, already rifling through the dead shifter's other pocket.

"The tall one," Luke said, barely able to stand on his own as Charity cut him loose from his chains. "He's usually outside."

One of the smokers then. I raced for the door and found the phone buried deep in a side pocket of the guy's cargo shorts. It was wet from the rain, but still worked as I tapped the screen.

Shit. Facial recognition.

I knelt down and pried back the guy's head with a fist in his hair and opened the screen a second time, hoping the moonlight would be enough for the phone to pick up his face.

It took two more tries, but it unlocked, and I heaved a sigh, thumbing Jared's cell number into the illuminated keypad as I stepped back inside.

I began to pace when he didn't answer on the second ring or the third. I ended the call as it went to voicemail and tried Clay's phone instead, convincing myself that his not answering didn't mean anything.

But Clay didn't answer, either. Or Layla.

"*Fuck*," I cursed, my fingers hovering over the keypad, trying to think of another phone number I could try, but theirs were the only three I knew by heart aside from Vivian's, and she was already here.

Deep breaths, Allie.

I scrolled through the call log on the phone, checking the numbers there. Then the text messages. Other than a raunchy sexting convo with a girl named Candy, there was nothing of note.

And if this was the only phone and no one had called yet to sound the alarm, then that had to mean we were still in the clear. It wasn't a lot to go on, but it was something.

I pocketed the cell for now, resolving to keep it just until we left, at which point I'd smash it to pieces and leave it behind. If someone called or sent a message, then we'd at least have a heads up.

Vivian held Destiny close as Charity and Seth limbered up to go collect some water and whatever they could find for food. "You coming?" Charity asked her, and she turned to whisper something to Destiny.

"Leave her," Archer said, rising with a slight limp. "I'll go with you."

Vivian sent him a grateful half smile and went back to picking debris out of her mate's hair.

Piper shifted out of the way as they passed, each of the three giving both her and me curious looks. "She helped me," I explained. "She's with us now."

That was all that needed to be said. They gave Piper thankful nods and tight smiles before departing.

"Want to fill us in?" Viv asked, settling a weak- looking Destiny into her lap. Her head rolled back onto Viv's shoulder, and her chapped lips parted as though she hadn't the strength to keep them shut. My stomach twisted at the sight, and I searched the space for anything that might help, gaze settling on a half-full water bottle discarded in a corner of the room. I brought it to her, using my palm to tip up her chin as I poured small mouthfuls of water in, slowly so she could swallow and catch her breath.

"Thank you," Vivian mouthed, and I sighed, falling onto my backside on the cement floor. I did my best to fill her and the rest of them in, feeling guilt like a ten- ton weight on my chest with each word.

It was odd, though, how not a single one of them looked angry or seemed to hold any hostility toward me. They all looked...grateful. Relieved. Like I was their savior and not the one who got them all into this damned mess in the first place.

"So we find the others then?" Destiny croaked, the water doing its work to moisten her throat and allow her body to begin to heal from everything it'd endured here.

"That's the plan. We'll head west toward our territory. If they're there, I'll sense them. If not, then if we can just get close enough to wherever they are, then the mate bond should guide me."

"Or we'll be able to pick up their scents and track them," Vivian supplied, and I agreed.

Her eyes hardened, sparking with the fire she always harbored deep within. I knew what she was thinking. "And then?"

"Then the bastard pays for his sins."

There would be no white flag. No deals struck or trades made. Not this time.

It was him or me. Live or die.

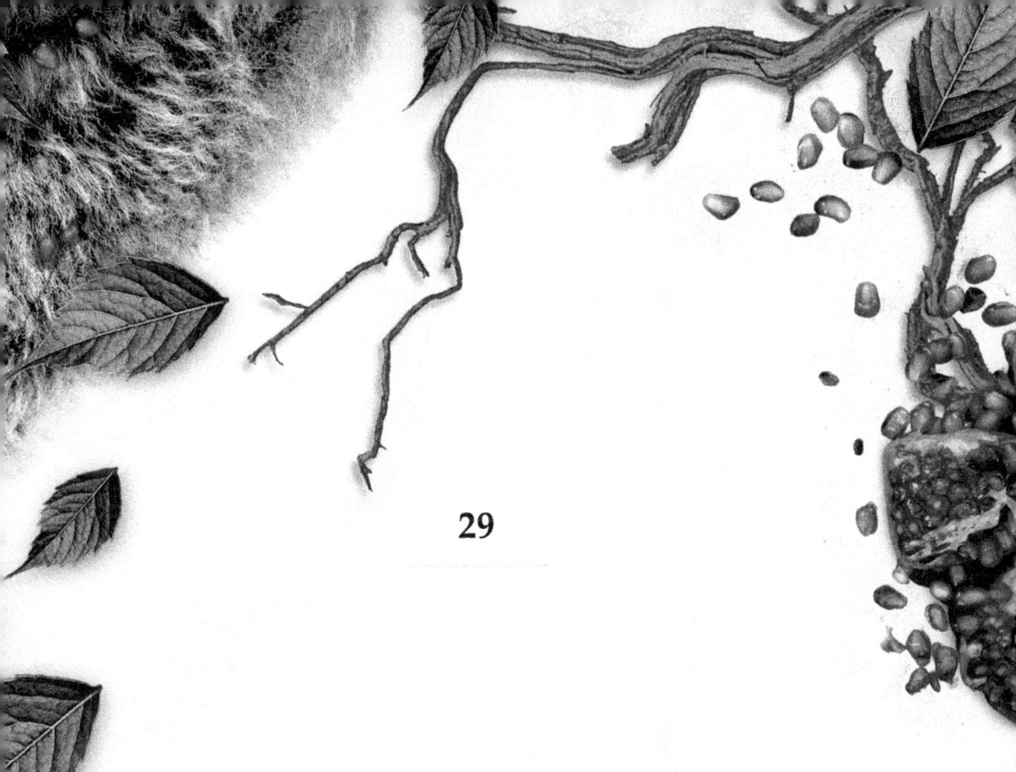

29

Just a little farther, I sent through the pack bond, trying to reassure the ones still weak with hunger and exhaustion. Still stiff with soreness from not moving for so long.

If we didn't pick up any trace of them soon, we'd find a safe place to make camp and rest for a few hours, but I couldn't give up yet. Our pack camp was only twenty more miles northwest. We were getting close to the edge of the third patrol ring now, though I didn't expect it to be manned, whether they were at camp or not.

Not with so few of them remaining.

The rain had let up almost thirty minutes ago, but my pelt was still weighed down with moisture just as much as the branches of the trees and water-soaked plant life.

Do you sense them yet? Vivian asked, flanking me with a weary Destiny at her side.

No.

She didn't say it, but I knew what she was thinking because the same thought had occurred to me already. If my mates were at camp, I'd have sensed them by now.

Which meant they weren't. Which meant there was virtually no reason to go there, to the one place our enemy would undoubtedly look.

It's almost dawn, she said. *We should turn to the south, follow the*

Willamette River to cover our tracks. Make camp until we figure out what our next move will—

I stopped, lifting my head as the first rays of pink dawn light brightened the navy sky.

What is it? Charity asked, loping ahead, her body rigid with alertness, her cutting eyes searching out the misty, dawn-stained foliage for attackers.

I lowered my head, listening, trying to figure out what had made me pause.

There it was again. A pull in my center.

A tether between souls.

It's them, I blurted, moving in a wide circle on clumsy paws, trying to figure out which direction. I assumed it was camp, but when I moved in that direction, the tether slackened. The sensation weakening.

South!

They were approaching from the south, I was certain of it.

A whine forced its way out of my mouth and my wolf rocked back on her heels, moving forward only to stop again. Needing to go to them but also needing to remain with the weakest of her pack. To protect them.

Go on, Todd said, bumping my side with his shoulder.

We'll be right behind you, Trey finished for his mate.

I charged ahead, hearing the others pick up their pace behind me.

My wolf did her best to temper her speed, but as that tether grew shorter and shorter, drawing us closer to them, we couldn't help but sprint.

The miles flew away beneath my paws, the scent of petrichor filtering through my lungs in great gusts of breath. Until I could make out other scents floating to me on the northbound breeze.

Cedar and Birch. Spice, and the unmistakable perfume of motor oil that somehow always clung to Clay no matter how long it'd been since he tuned up a bike.

They appeared like ghosts from the mist, exploding through the brush with a scattering of dew. One wolf white, and one so dark a gray that he could almost be mistaken for black.

Distantly, I could hear the others trailing behind them, unable to keep pace, but trying their best.

Allie! Jared's exclamation in my mind made another whimper tumble from my lips, and as they reached me, churning up loose earth on a hard stop, we collided.

What happened? Are you hurt?

Were you followed?

Their voices in my mind spoke over one another, a barrage of worried, frantic, and heated questions, all of them demanding answers, though I could give none.

I leaned into my mates, needing the quiet solace of their touch, just for a minute. Needing *them* before I could form another rational thought.

Allie, talk to us. What's going— Holy shit.

I heard the others approaching behind me and watched as my mates gaped at their arrival, shock and relief etched into their expressions.

My wolf released after she had her minute, letting me come forward, emerging from our shared flesh. I shifted with a sob in my throat and choked it back as my body reformed.

"I found you," I whispered, my voice shaking almost as much as my body as I wrapped my arms around Clay's neck, burying my face in his damp dark fur. "I found you."

"Hey." Jared's soft touch on my back was the only thing that could've been tempting enough for me to let go of Clay, turning to let my other mate wrap me up in his human arms.

"Hey, it's okay," he crooned as my relief became too much for me to contain and I let the tears fall. "It's okay, you're safe. We've got you."

A jerk on my arm and Clay had me out of Jared's embrace and into one of his own, crushing me against the hard expanse of his chest. "Don't you *ever* do anything like that again. You almost..." He choked off. "You could've..."

"I'm sorry."

"Did he touch you? Is the bastard still alive?"

I guessed I had a lot of explaining to do, but as the others emerged from the south, another reunion drew my attention as a still-limping Archer knocked his mate to the ground, the two of them yipping and licking one another as they collided.

Bodies shifted and both human and wolf embraces were had all around as our pack became whole again, though I hated to think what might've become of them if I was even just a few hours later in rescuing them.

Destiny had been near complete dehydration. So had some of the others.

Piper was the only one who seemed out of place, lagging behind the others as they all joined together.

I saw Layla practically jumping on Vivian with joy and smiled as her gaze found mine, latching on with an unspoken rush of relief. I nodded to her, telling her with a look that I was okay and she should stay where she was, at least for the moment.

"I'll explain everything," I told my mates, the lump leaving my throat as I swiped the tears from my eyes.

"But first, we need to get someplace safe. They need rest. And food and—"

My spine tingled as I recognized a group of shifters standing apart from the rest. Removed. They weren't from this pack.

My upper lip curled, and I darted away from Clay, putting myself between us, when I realized that I recognized one of them.

"Is that...?"

"Dante," Clay confirmed. "And about half of his pack."

I whirled on my mates, eyes narrowed. "What are they doing here? I already sent word asking him for help. He denied me."

Jared nervously scratched at a phantom itch on the back of his neck, unable to meet my gaze. "We might have...threatened him a little..."

My lips parted in surprise as a rush of fury zipped down my spine like liquid fire. I looked between them, waiting for the *real* truth to come out.

Clay bristled under the weight of my stare. "Fine," he seethed. "We threatened him *a lot.*"

"What did you expect us to do?" Jared asked, getting defensive. "We weren't going to leave you with that fucking psychopath."

"But I *commanded* it."

Jared glanced guiltily at Clay, and the pair of them shrugged.

"Guess you're losing your touch, babe."

I pressed my lips together against a retort that I really didn't have the right to sling at them right now. Not after what I'd done. What I'd made *them* do. "I'll deal with the two of you later," I told them, going to the pack alpha waiting away from the raucous celebration taking shape in the middle of the forest.

I bowed my head to him, waiting for him to shift so that we could speak plainly. Dante nodded his lupine head to the shifter at his right hand and together, both of them shifted.

"The twin soul wolf," Dante said by way of greeting. "We were told we were to go to war in an effort to rescue you."

I shot a nasty glare back at my mates before responding, keeping my tone as diplomatic as I could. We'd always had an understanding with Dante's pack, since they bordered our lands to the west and generally kept to themselves.

"It was wrong of my mates to try to pressure you into this fight."

"Pressure us?" Dante scoffed. "They said they'd..." He groaned, shaking his head. "You know what, it doesn't matter."

"I apologize for their rash thinking, but I hope you understand what prompted them to do it."

Dante frowned, nodding to himself. I didn't know much about him personally, but one thing I did know was that his mate died a number of years ago. He still hadn't re-mated, and I could see the loss of her in his haunted stare. Knew it was a large part of the reason for the tall walls surrounding his camp. And why he never got involved with the affairs of other packs unless he thought them a direct threat to his own.

"Aye, I do."

"I won't ask you to fight with us, but I will tell you that if this threat is not dealt with now, it will affect you and your pack. If we do not succeed, I have no doubt in my mind that the man responsible for all of this will take over Forest Grove and snuff out any pack who refuses to join him."

Dante rolled his shoulders back, his round face growing red at the insinuation, but it was the truth. And I think he knew that.

"Perhaps there's something else we could offer..." I added, sensing his hesitation. "With you and the shifters you've brought, our numbers will be even with his. It may not even come to a fight, not if Devin can see that he is matched in strength and numbers. I'll challenge him, and *I'll win.*"

"And what are you offering for us to partake in this *show of strength?*"

"The quarry," Jared said, appearing at my side. "We'll give you a stake in the earnings. Jobs for any of your pack who wish them. But…if it *does* come to a fight. We'll expect you to stand with us then, too."

We knew Dante and his pack led a simple life. A life of farming and meditation, promoting a oneness with the earth, but they still had needs, right?

Dante whispered something to his right hand, and the man nodded, agreeing with him.

"Are you sure?" I asked Jared in a whisper, searching his eyes for the truth.

He nodded easily. "I am."

"Twenty-five percent," Dante demanded.

"Twenty," Clay growled, appearing at my other side with a scowl on his handsome face. "And not a nickel more."

He eyed Clay for a moment and then inclined his head. "Twenty then, and you'll have our help in this fight. This fight alone and no others."

I walked forward, some ancient part of my still human mind recoiling at shaking hands with a naked man while being entirely nude myself.

The ridiculousness of the thought almost made me smirk. Almost.

"We have a deal then," I said, my calluses rubbing against his, feeling more confident now than I had been in a very long time.

"I assume you have a plan?"

I swallowed hard. "We need to strike now, before he has any opportunity to undermine us or get one step ahead."

Dante jutted his chin in the direction of the rest of my pack. "They don't look battle ready."

"They will be," Clay argued. "I'll see to it. We have supplies. Enough for everyone to have a full meal. We can hunt, too, if we have to."

"Okay. We strike tomorrow," I decided. "Take tonight to make preparations and ensure everyone's ready. Sound good?"

Dante nodded, and turned to walk away without another word. He would wait for my orders with the members of his pack, but he wasn't about to get cozy with a bunch of foreign wolves. I couldn't blame him.

My brow furrowed as I searched through the shifters all coming off the temporary high of being reunited again, waiting for orders. "Where's Hazel?"

Clay dropped his gaze, visibly paling. "She's preparing Sam for burial. She was a bottle of whiskey deep at the old cabin when we were ready to leave pack camp with our supplies."

"Even if she was coherent," Jared put in. "I don't think it would've been hard to convince her to stay behind. She'll be safe there."

My chest ached anew as I ran a hand down the corded muscle of Clay's arm, drawing his attention. "I am *so* sorry, Clay. I—"

"We knew it was a risk," he interrupted, clearing his throat. "When we sent her back. We knew something like this could've happened."

Not *we*, I wanted to correct him. It was *me* who ordered her to return. I hadn't given her a choice. It was *me* who sent his sister to her death.

"She made her bed," Jared said in a low grumble, his jaw ticking as he looked between me and Clay.

"Jare—" I hissed.

"No, he's right." Clay ran a hand through his tousled black hair, sighing. "But if it's all right with you, I'd like to have her buried on pack land. I want her close."

"Of course," I replied, tugging him down to press a soft kiss to his lips. "And when we get home, we'll give her a proper send off."

Clay grimaced. "I'm not sure if the pack—"

"She made mistakes, Clay, but in the end, she realized what she'd done. She tried to make it right. She's *pack*. She'll be sent off as one of us."

He dropped his head onto my shoulder, hunching as he drew me close. "I'll never deserve you, woman."

I smiled, nuzzling into his neck to whisper into his ear. "Fate seems to think you do. And I agree with her."

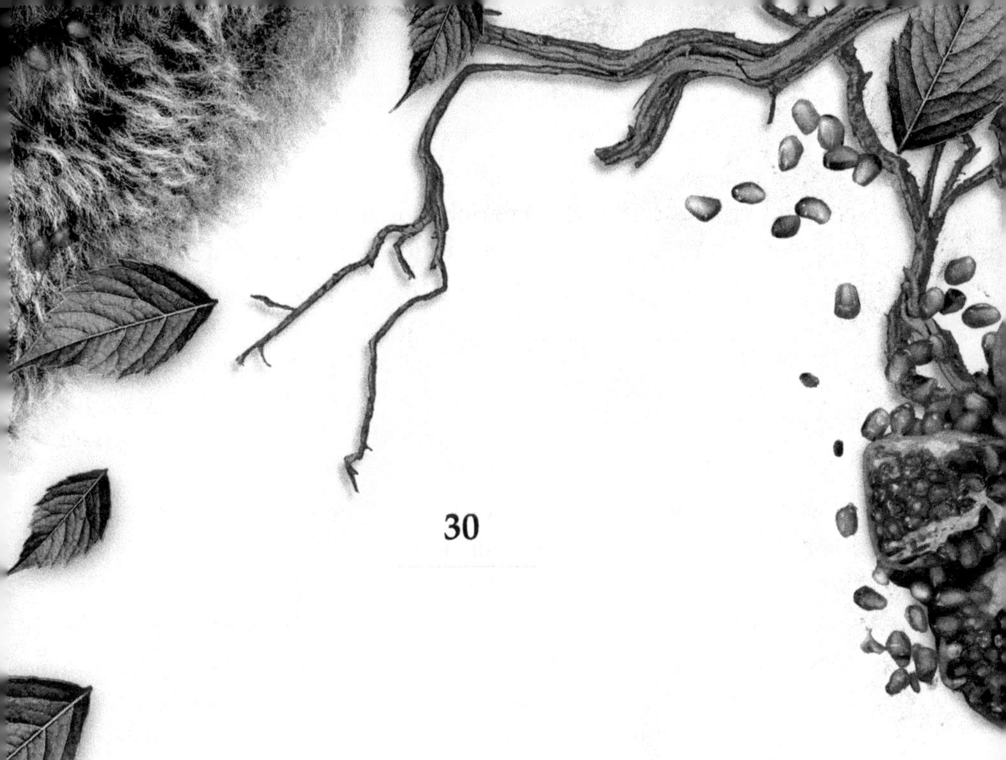

30

"So does this mean all is forgiven then?" I asked them as Jared passed me another cut of meat from the makeshift spit over the fire. I'd just finished explaining everything to them and answering their million questions and was ready to finally eat.

We'd have to put the fire out when the sun went down, and it was already on its descent down the sky. We had maybe twenty minutes of burn time left and still a good bit of meat left to cook. Though many didn't mind eating it raw in their wolf forms, and that was exactly what most of the weakest of them did.

They'd heal faster that way, without expending the energy needed to shift back.

"Not even close," Clay growled, tossing me a tall bottle of water from the pack at his feet. "Drink," he ordered. "You can put on a strong face for them, but we know you need it."

Jared tapped the meat on the bit of cloth in my hand, and I obediently took a bite, moaning as the flavor coated my tongue.

"Don't look so smug," I said between bites and sips of water. "I was *fine*. Now I'm just...better."

"Mhmm," Jared hummed. "If you say so."

The truth was I'd been trying to make sure everyone else had their fill first, but Jared and Clay were right. I had no idea how long I'd been passed out in that cellar and the journey to the mill had been long. I hadn't touched a single morsel of the supplies Charity and Seth managed to wrangle for the others, knowing we wouldn't get more than a few miles if they didn't regain a good amount of strength first.

Not for the first time, I thanked whatever fuckery allowed for shifters to heal quickly. Without it, I didn't know where we'd be. Where *I'd* be right now.

As it was, by my third bite of the juicy meat and about halfway through the liter of water, I was already feeling back to my regular self. Minus a few pounds maybe, but that didn't matter.

"Hey, Allie, mind if—" Charity started, coming over from one of the other cook fires when Clay interrupted her.

"Not now, Char," he growled. "Let her eat."

She held up her hands in a placating gesture and stepped away.

"Char, wait," I called after her, but she was already gone.

"What did you do that for?" I demanded, elbowing Clay in the ribs.

He grunted but didn't reply.

"I'll deal with it," Jared offered, rising and passing his retractable metal skewer to Layla. "Probably just wants clarification on something. You just eat. I'll be back in a sec."

I shook my head absently as he left, catching Layla's raised brow. "See what I mean?" she whispered to Seth, who was seated behind her, his arms loosely wrapped around her middle. He chuckled, making me think I was more than likely the butt of some private joke between them.

I didn't care though. I'd be the butt of all the damned jokes in the world so long as everyone was okay.

Once I'd polished off the entire bottle of water and every last morsel of meat on my makeshift plate, I sighed, leaning back against a tree. I put a hand to my contented stomach and jumped when something poked me in the ribs.

Clay held out a toothbrush and small tube of paste for me, and I grinned, taking them with a curious tilt of my head. "A toothbrush?" I asked, unable to conceal my smirk.

When they were busy gathering supplies to run far and fast away from camp, he'd dubbed a toothbrush necessary?

He shared my smirk. "Yeah. I was...we were *all* a mess, Allie. I somehow remembered my toothbrush but not a single scrap of clothing, or even the water. It was Layla who thought to fill a bunch of bottles and wrap some of the meat to take with us."

He heaved in a breath, looking haunted by the memory still, even with me back here, right in front of him.

I rested a hand on his thigh, shivering at the contact as his passion speared through me from the mate bond, awakening a primal urge deep within that pooled heat between my thighs.

"She's really great you know. Both of them are. I'm glad they're with us."

"Aww, love you, too, Clay," Layla said with a cheeky wink, having overheard.

He rolled his eyes at her and crossed his arms over his naked chest.

"Don't let it go to your head."

"Wouldn't dream of it."

"Let's go share this around," Seth said, maybe taking Clay's subtle hint at wanting a modicum of privacy to talk to me. He took the rest of the meat that'd finished cooking and together he and Layla kicked dirt over the fire until it snuffed out before moving on to share the meager supplies.

"Hey, make sure Piper gets some, will you?"

She had found a place sitting with Archer, Callum, and a few others, but by the way she was sitting, with her knees hugged into her chest, I could tell she wouldn't be asking for any handouts.

"Will do," Seth said with a little salute.

"Have fun," Layla called back, giving me a knowing look that made a hot flush creep up my neck to roost in my cheeks.

Clay cleared his throat. He'd settled one of the large packs they'd brought to transport supplies into his lap to conceal his junk and was now adjusting it. Shoving it down with the palm of his hand.

"Problem?" I asked him knowingly. "You're wicked, woman."

I wrinkled my nose, playing it off. "I have no idea what you're talking about."

Jared returned a second later, making me dangerously aware of just how flushed my skin was. How my thighs squeezed together, and I fought to maintain composure.

Now that we were here, together, and everyone was all right. Resting and fed. And we had a plan. I could think of nothing else on this earth that I wanted more than I wanted them right now.

Nothing.

"Sorry, I was just..." He trailed off, sensing the vibe through the mate bond. His Adam's apple bobbed as he slowed to a stop right in front of me. "I, uh, was just going over everything with them one more time. A bunch of them are going to try to sleep now while the rest take the first watch."

I glanced between him and Clay, biting the inside of my cheek to keep myself in check. "Oh. Okay. Yeah, that's good. Thanks."

"I can go and, *uh*...I mean, if you guys want some privacy."

He stuffed his hands into his pockets, looking virtually *anywhere* but at me. It seemed Jared *had* remembered to pack a pair of jeans, and suddenly I was wishing he hadn't, noticing the bulge begin to form beneath the strong denim.

I licked my lips.

"No," I said on a breath. "I don't want you to leave."

His amber gaze flicked up to meet mine first, and then Clay's, his lips parting in silent question.

Please.

Clay let out a low rumble beside me, and I turned to see his blue eyes lit from within, his face stormy.

He nodded to Jared, just one tight bob of his head, before moving to stand, taking the pack with him. "I'm up for a walk..." he said, a muscle in his neck straining. "...if you are."

My gaze snapped back to Jared and something in my expression must have undone him because his rigid stance loosened and the look in his eyes softened. He held out a hand for me, offering to help me stand. "Yeah," he said. "I could go for a walk."

 didn't say as much, but the knowing smirks wriggling at the corners of their mouths told me they knew *exactly* what we were up to. And being some of my best friends, they *also* knew I'd been wanting this for as long as I could remember.

The night crept over the forest swiftly, the last dregs of sunset sucked away by the shadows. We didn't speak as we wandered through the foliage, not heading in any direction really except *away*. Far enough away that we wouldn't be heard, but close enough that we could be back in a flash if we needed to.

Jared slid his hand into mine as we neared a gnarled old beech tree, its branches low lying, reaching out near its base like waiting arms.

The sounds of the nighttime forest droned in my ears, humming almost as loud as my own heartbeat. I shivered, even though I was anything but cold. The late summer night just the right temperature to be comfortable. At least, for a shifter.

Jared tugged sharply on my hand, making me spin as we walked up to the tree until my backside met the low branch and he helped me sit atop it, the cool bark surprisingly soft against my skin.

Some unspoken thing passed between my mates as they regarded each other, each seeming to have made a decision I wasn't privy to.

"We're…" Jared began, trailing off to tug his lower lip in between his teeth, considering the right thing to say. Reminding me of the Jared I'd first fallen in love with.

"We're going to try," Clay finished for him. "But if this doesn't work—"

"It's okay," I blurted, my pulse spiking with an injection of adrenaline and something far more potent. "Just try. That's all I want."

All I needed.

Had *been needing* for so damn long it felt like forever.

Jared stilled as Clay brushed his strong fingers down the line of my neck, making me tremble with need. A moan was already building in my chest, but I worked to contain it, not wanting to spook either of them away.

"Don't hide from us," Clay demanded, sensing me holding back. "We can feel you."

I bit down on my tongue as his hand swept lower, passing over my breast to pebble my nipple.

When Jared leaned in to press a hot kiss to my throat, I swear I saw stars, light, and color bursting around the edges of my vision as I gasped at the dual sensation. Of three souls joining into one.

He kissed a path down my throat, pausing briefly at my collar before delving lower, his fingers tripping up my spine until he pressed his palm flat to the middle of my back. Holding me in place while he took my aching breast into his mouth, making a stuttering moan tumble from my lips.

All the while, Clay's fingers continued their downward descent, teasing lightly around my hips, my thighs, until they inched toward their mark. He groaned at the first touch of his knuckles against my core, already so wet for them both.

"*Fuck*," he groaned, reaching out his free hand to clutch on the low hanging branch, the pads of his fingers indenting the wood. Eyes like blue fire watched me as I tipped my head back in a cry of ecstasy. His fingers expertly circled my entrance, making my body writhe against the tree, against his hand, against Jared's mouth.

When his fingers pushed in, I cried out, every inch of my body electrified with desire. Jared's lips came off my breast with a pop, gone for only an instant before they claimed my mouth instead.

He kissed me with a brutality I didn't know he possessed as Clay worked me to the edge of a climax I couldn't have stopped even if I'd wanted to. His tongue slipped in, deepening the kiss until I was dizzy with need and a lack of air. Completely unable to remember the last time I took a breath. If I was breathing at all.

"That's it," Jared whispered against my mouth, and I gasped for air. His amber eyes glowed with the power of his wolf as he palmed my breast, tugging lightly on my nipple. Rolling it between his thumb and index finger.

"Come on, baby," Clay grunted, dangerously close to shredding through the tree branch with how hard he was gripping it to maintain control. His eyes sparked to life with the presence of his wolf, and my own wolf responded, awakening with a primal need to claim her mates the way she'd been waiting to for four long years.

"Come for us," Jared commanded in a breathy whisper, his lips finding mine again as my body surged to the apex. Tightening and splintering apart all at once as I came, moaning into Jared's mouth as

Clay held me down, mercilessly drawing the climax out until I squirmed beneath them, the sensation almost too much to bear.

I gripped tightly to Clay, snatching up his arm as he tried to pull back. Jared, too, moved to back away, but I pinned him with a lusty stare.

"*No,*" I muttered, still panting. "I want you. I want both of you."

I knew this was pushing it to the limits of what they could take, but I had to try. Greedy bitch or not, I'd waited for this for far too long for them to stop now.

Jared's cheekbones flared, his fiery gaze passing over the shadowed ground while Clay stared openly at me, a question poised on his parted lips.

"Are you sure that's what you want?" he asked.

I swallowed, finally able to catch my breath, my pulse still pounding, but less erratic than the moment before. "*So* fucking sure."

Clay's bright gaze passed over to Jared, but my other mate didn't acknowledge him. Though after a second, he uttered a shaky, "All right. I just need a second to get control."

He backed away a step, turning away from us to take a few shallow breaths. I'd give him all the fucking seconds he needed if he would just *try* for me.

And I could tell he was already. I could feel the effort he was exerting to maintain control. From both of them.

Was I awful for forcing this? Was I being selfish?

I cringed inwardly, dropping my head as a darkness crept into my thoughts, hollowing out my insides.

"Hey," Jared said, spinning back to face us. "Don't do that. We want to give you this."

Clay nodded his agreement, and I took solace in the fact that I felt very little discomfort from them. Only a visceral need to claim their mate that overshadowed everything else. A need to be the *only* one, even though there were two souls bonded to my own instead of one.

I understood it, even if I wished it weren't like that. "Brother," he said, facing Clay, his sharp stare skating between us. "I'm sorry in advance if I rip your head off."

"Apology accepted. So long as you know it'll be you who ends up on his ass."

Jared smirked and some of the tension lifted as he nodded to Clay, giving the go ahead.

The instant Clay turned his attention back to me, my core began to throb with need again, a beautiful ache spreading like wildfire through my belly.

He snatched up my chin, jerking my mouth up to meet his with the rough brush of his thumb. I moaned against his lips, my arms rising on their own to find something to hold onto, tangling in his hair and gripping at the solid muscle of his back.

He jerked against my touch, shuddering as I slipped a hand between us, circling his proud length. He was already rock hard as I slid my hand up his shaft, teasing his sensitive head until he bit down hard on my lower lip, making me gasp.

"Not so fast," he growled, fingers clenching my hips as he lifted me from the branch, twisting me around so I had to grip the underside so as not to fall face first over the other side.

His hand explored the curve of my ass, coming down with a little slap that sent shivers of pleasure coasting over the planes of my body. Bent over the thick branch, I could turn around enough to see Jared, but it was enough knowing he was there, watching as Clay pressed two fingers to my opening, readying me for him.

"*Jare*," I gasped as Clay slipped them inside and my thighs clenched tight, trying to hold him in.

"*Fuck!*" I shouted as Clay removed his fingers and thrust into me in a movement so quick I didn't see it coming. He filled me to bursting, making my back arch, trying to adjust to the size of him.

A low growl that I knew to be Jared's broke the sound of our panting breaths as Clay carefully eased out a bit, settling himself inside me as his fingertips bruised my waist with their hard grip.

I reached out blindly, beckoning to my other mate. "Come," I called. "Please."

As he came into view, ducking beneath the branch so that he was on one side while Clay was on the other, I licked my lips. I ached to smooth the knot between his brows. To relieve the tension lifting his muscled shoulders high.

I looped a finger into his jeans, drawing him closer, asking silently if this was all right.

He helped me when I fumbled with the button, my hands sloppy as Clay began thrusting into me, alternating between painfully slow and quick jabs that hit me in just the right spot.

Jared's cock sprang free as his jeans fell to pool around his ankles, and it was a lesson in restraint that I didn't immediately jerk him closer.

I wanted *him* to do it. I needed him to be comfortable or else I didn't want it.

I jerked as Clay quickened his pace, groaning his own pleasure as he fucked me from behind.

And maybe it was Clay's display of pleasure that made Jared give in to it as he slipped his long fingers into my hair, curling them into a loose fist at the base of my skull as he stepped forward, easing his cock to my lips.

I took him in slowly at first and then with a hunger unlike any I'd felt before. He glided over my tongue, finding the back of my throat and shuddering.

"*Shit, Allie,*" he sighed, his grip on me tightening as he rocked into my mouth and I slid my tongue over his head again and again as I felt the tension leak out of him with each passing second.

Clay shifted his grip, splaying one hand over my back while the other slipped between our joined bodies and the branch to rub my clit.

I convulsed as the already building pressure in my core spiraled to new heights, almost choking on Jared's cock.

My nails dug into Jared's hips, spurring him on faster, needing him to fuck my mouth just as rapidly as Clay was fucking me. I ground against Clay's hand, knowing I was near the edge and wanting—no, *needing*—them to come with me for the fall.

I cried out against Jared's cock, my toes curling into the earth as my world shattered into a million tiny pieces. Propelled by my mates reaching climaxes of their own.

Clay growled, hunching over me as he thrust his last, his breath fanning over the back of my neck. Jared came only an instant later, his warmth filling my mouth as every muscle in his lower back tightened beneath my clenched fingers.

I sagged, utterly spent but still jerking with the aftershocks of the best orgasm of my life as Jared slid from my mouth, crouching down to lovingly caress my face between his palms.

His wolf had receded, the glow no longer a fiery halo in his eyes. I smiled sleepily, unable to remember a time where I'd ever felt as content as I did in that moment.

"I love you," I murmured, and he dipped his head down, pressing his forehead to mine.

"Always."

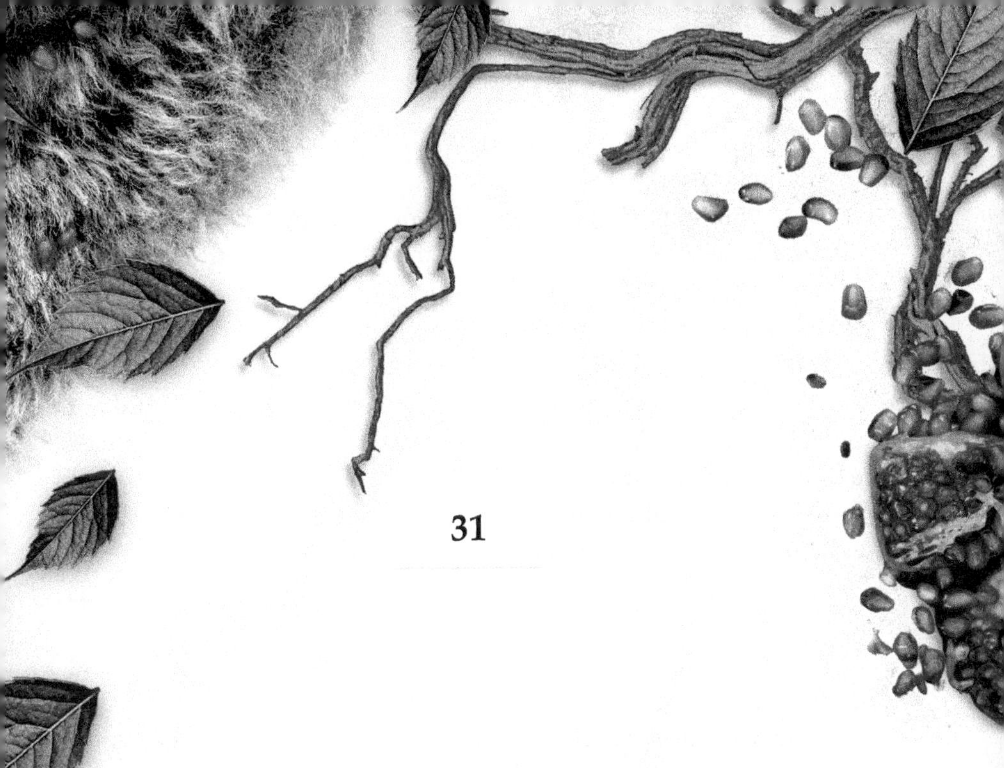

31

The barrens seemed as good a place as any to make our stand.

Once I'd gotten my bearings after escaping Devin's temporary camp, I'd realized that he hadn't been all that far from the barrens after all. Barely forty miles. Likely closer to thirty.

Making him come to us here had other benefits, too. The benefit of having our own pack land and Dante's to our back, discouraging an attack from behind. With the bonus benefit of being the first ones here, giving us time to prepare and preventing him from having the ability to set any sort of trap for us.

He'd have to approach head on, from the east, and we would be ready for him.

I'd spill his blood on the same ground where he'd spilled Sam's.

An eye for an eye.

Or in this case a heart for a heart.

"We're ready," Layla said, handing me a slender flip phone and giving my arm a squeeze before stepping away. Distantly I could hear Viv and Destiny arguing about her staying out of the fight. She was one of the weaker few, but would still be an asset if this came to a fight. Destiny had almost no match for her fiery will, except maybe her mate.

Hopefully, there wouldn't be a need for any of them to fight and their argument would prove utterly useless. That was my one hope for this bleak morning. That only one life would end by the time the dawn mist lifted and the sun rose to drink up the moisture from the earth.

My gaze flicked to my mates, their steadying presences bolstering my strength.

"Make the call," Clay urged. "Let's end this."

I flicked the burner phone open, tension making my fingers stiff as I flicked through the missed call log, seeing that Devin had already tried to call twenty-six times.

A few more and he might've drained the battery to nothing. As it was, there should be just enough juice for this one last call.

I jabbed the button to call, a flash of heat rushing down my back as my untethered fury warred with my need for sound logic.

It didn't even complete the first ring before the line connected and my jaw clamped tight.

"Where the fuck is she?" Devin hissed down the line, his tone manic. Completely unhinged.

"Right where she should be," I replied, shocked at the even cadence of my tone.

He paused. "You've been a naughty girl, Allie. Eight of my men are dead—"

"And a great many more will die along with them if you don't listen to me *very* carefully."

I had no illusions that Devin cared at all for the members of his pack, but I had something he wanted. I *was* something he wanted, and I had no doubt that he would put each and every single life under his command in danger to get me.

"*You ungrateful cunt—*"

"Shut up," I roared, my voice coming out double with the presence of my wolf. "Now, let's try this again, shall we? I'm at the barrens with...a few friends."

The phone chirped, telling me the battery was critically low.

"If you want me," I spat. "Come and fucking get me." The line went dead a beat later, cutting off whatever Devin had been about to say as I clapped the phone closed, letting Jared take it from my grasp.

He removed the sim card and battery and tossed the pieces to someone in the line behind us to get rid of.

My body hummed with anticipation, rocked with little tremors as my wolf knocked at the door to my soul. Letting me know that she was there. She was ready.

"You think he'll come?" Jared asked, hard gaze already set on the other end of the barren field.

"I know he will."

They emerged just as we thought they would. Not even two hours after I made the call, Devin and his pack slipped through the trees and into the barrens like water from a sieve. But this time, his numbers weren't overwhelming. They didn't make my insides quake with unease.

They didn't matter anymore.

This was a battle between him and me and no others.

His eyes glinted in the light of the rising sun like sharp cut gemstones. Hard and unyielding at first, but then, as he noticed the breadth of my pack with the addition of Dante's shifters, I had the satisfaction of watching his smug smirk falter.

He recovered quickly, though, lifting his chin as he stepped ahead of his pack, all of them already in their wolf forms, as most of my own were.

"What now, love?" he called across the expanse, and the taunting tone of his voice gave me a moment's pause. He seemed way too pleased with himself for someone going to their death.

Unable to hold it in for even another second, I curled my hands into fists at my sides and shouted loud enough for all to hear. "Devin Wright, I hereby challenge you for the right to rule your pack."

Truth be told, I didn't give a flying fuck about his pack, but I did give all the fucks about tearing him into a thousand pieces. And this was how it needed to be done.

Unnervingly, he smiled at my challenge, lifting a hand to tap a finger against his chin.

"*Hmm*," he purred, brows crinkling as my pulse picked up speed. "I think not."

My lips parted as I looked to my mates for clarification. Their grim faces told me everything I needed to know. Though as a general rule it was never done, an alpha had every right to refuse a challenge from another. But such a refusal meant only one thing.

"I prefer the *other* option," he stated, his slippery gaze tracking to my mates with a fiendish gleam.

Did he really still think that if he killed them, I would mate to him? Did he really think that even if I *did* mate to him that I wouldn't kill him for the things he'd done?

His ego really knew no fucking bounds.

"I refuse your challenge, Allie Grace," he declared, lifting his arms high as though he were a priest or a saint. "But I have a counteroffer: return with me now and there will be no fight. Your pack will live. None will be injured, and none will die except for *those two*."

A savage growl ricocheted through my chest as he pointed two fingers at my mates, my wolf vibrating with unspent rage as she backed herself into a corner.

My pack had already pledged to stand with me if this came to a fight. They'd reaffirmed that pledge just last night. They were ready and willing, but that didn't mean I wanted any of them in harm's way.

"Allie..." Clay's low growl brought me back to the surface, up out of the darkness and into the light.

I just had to *kill him*. And quickly. Then the rest of his pack would cease fighting.

I wondered if he still believed that my wolf was bound. Wouldn't it be a wonderful surprise to show him just how little he knew me.

Instead of answering Devin, I glanced over the pack forming two neat lines behind him.

"We will give no quarter," I called to them. "If you stand with him, I will not hesitate to cut you down if you get in my way...but if you step away now, you will not be harmed. You have my word."

The wolves shifted uneasily at their alpha's back, several tucking tail and several more looking like they may truly back out of the fight.

Devin whirled on them, one scathing look from him rooting those most uncertain back into place. I couldn't imagine what it was like for them living under his thumb, at least, those of them who weren't just as fucking psycho as he was.

Forrest snarled at Devin's right hand, and I locked his wolf's markings into my memory. The strong bands of rusty brown curving up around his ears, the only lick of color in his black pelt.

When none retreated, I bowed my head to the suffocating ache taking root at my core. I needed to protect my family. No matter the cost.

"Is this your answer?" Devin asked, a muscle in his cheek twitching over a flash of bared teeth. "Are you refusing me?"

He clearly hadn't anticipated this, I could see his resolve shaking. His hold on that damnable smugness wavering.

I glanced back at my pack, finding nothing but absolute certainty in the set of each face. Vivian let out a guttural snarl, lowering her head for the charge with her mate at her side.

My lungs filled as I released myself to my wolf. When my eyes opened again, I knew they would be aflame with her unbroken spirit.

"So be it."

I raced ahead of the pack, getting in only two leaping bounds before my wolf exploded out from within, shattering me apart to stitch me back together as something stronger. Our twin tails whipped around our side as we hit the earth, our eyes locked on target.

I had the satisfaction of seeing Devin's eyes widen in mortified shock before he shifted, bursting into his wolf form. His deep gray coat rippled with the flex of hard muscle beneath as he shook his canine head with a primal snarl, his hot tongue sliding over his bared teeth.

Five others stepped forward, pushing ahead of their alpha, leading the charge and those psychotic green eyes vanished from view, swallowed up by the crush of canine bodies rushing across the barrens.

"No mercy!" I heard Devin call over the din of hundreds of paws pounding against the earth.

I sensed my own pack at my heels and sent up one last silent prayer to keep them all safe as I let my wolf do her worst. But the eyes of the five Devin sent ahead weren't fixed on me. They split off. Two to one side and three to the other, distracting me just enough so that another coming with the wave of shifters behind was nearly able to catch me around the throat. I put her down before she even knew what hit her. A strangled cry the last sound that would ever leave her mouth.

More of them swarmed, and I knocked them back, the sound of hounds at war filling my ears until there was nothing else.

Jared! I called through the bond, trying to find the telltale streak of white fur in all the chaos while fending off two more attacks. Raking claws found purchase in my thigh, and I roared, launching up on my hind legs despite the pain to come down on my attacker with no mercy.

A flash of white and I spun, racing out of the melee and back the way I'd come, realizing a moment too late where Devin had sent his best. His strongest. He'd sent them straight for my mates, his prime targets.

Fuck.

No reply came from my mate, and I surged forward, reaching center-field just in time to buck a shifter off the back of Destiny, letting her up from under its jaws. I met her frantic gaze for an instant, acknowledging her thanks before pressing on.

Help Clay! Came Jared's frantic call, echoing in my skull, and I shifted paths, letting my mate bond tether guide me to him.

On it.

Clay's roar of pain stabbed into me like a bullet, piercing straight through the ragged fabric of my soul. *Hold on!*

A hit from the right sent me sailing off course and I smashed against the ground, a rib cracking from the blow.

Motherfucker.

I shook the daze from the edges of my vision, catching sight of him just in time to roll onto my back and kick the shifter sky high as he raced to mount me for an attack.

He was the one sent sailing then, landing in a cloud of dirt against the hard packed earth with a cry. As he tried to get up, I let the full force of my alpha wolf flood my veins, lifting my head with a pride I hadn't felt in a long time.

Stay down, I warned, whether he could hear me or not and he buckled under the pressure of my stare, whining as his body bent to my will.

He wouldn't be getting up any time soon.

Behind me was absolute chaos. A pandemonium of snapping jaws and snarls and howls of misery. Too many lay dead on the field, and I didn't dare look too closely, terrified of what I might find in the faces of the dead.

This ends now.

I spotted Clay and sprinted back into the fray, my jaws tearing into the scruffy neck of a sandy brown shifter, tearing the fucker off my mate's back.

I put my back to Clay's, blocking his blind spot as he blocked mine.

You good? Fucking peachy. Do you see him?

Clay's body tensed for the strike as the shifter came again, injured but not giving up.

No, he hissed in my thoughts, pushing his claws into the throat of the shifter after getting him easily on his back. With his windpipe crushed, the wolf choked, its eyes widening fearfully as it tried for air.

I left Clay's back to snap the shifter's neck, unable to watch him die slowly when I could make it quick.

Clay nodded to me, his dark head marred with the reddish tint of still-wet blood.

Haven't seen him since the charge, Clay said. *Fucking coward.*

Watch out! I launched forward, colliding with Forrest before he could attack Clay. A hard punch to my throat made me gasp for breath as warm fluid coated my chest.

I lost my sense of gravity, of balance, as I tumbled to the earth, bouncing and skating over dirt and stone, spinning until my vision doubled.

Two Clays fought off four attackers twenty paces away, and I blinked, trying to get my vision to clear as a cry pierced the atmosphere. The sound unmistakable. *Layla.*

Jaws clamped around my throat, holding me down, or trying to, and away to the east, I saw a dark shadow emerge from the trees. A monster coming to claim his prize.

Fat fucking chance.

I braced myself for the pain as I ripped out of Forrest's grasp, allowing his canines to tear a deep channel into muscle and sinew. But he wouldn't kill me. Not with his alpha watching.

It was a gamble. But it seemed it was one I would win as Forrest's jaws came free, letting me up. Before he could mount another attack, a lightning quick spear of deep gray shot into his side, knocking him away.

Piper.

They kicked up dirt in a flurry of scraping claws and feral snarls, but my attention was fixed elsewhere. On the wolf waiting by the trees. The one letting his pack fight and die so that he could claim a prize he had no right to.

Layla's cry came again, drawing me back. My wolf ached for vengeance, vibrated with it. She wanted the taste of his blood on her lips. She wanted to look into his eyes while his life left him.

She would have to wait.

We raced back, narrowly tripping over a familiar corpse as we dodged and dipped around wolves locked in battle. Until we found her.

Charity got there first, her attack drawing the heat from Layla.

I went straight for my best friend, nudging her with my snout to force her to get up. *Go!* I commanded, seeing her injuries. Too many. Far too many. She limped to standing, a pitched keening tumbling from her lips. *Go! Get the fuck out of here.*

I lifted my head. *Seth! Here.*

Take her. Get out!

He barreled ahead, tracking at Layla's side as they retreated from the fight, taking a direct route to the western tree line. I was too distracted watching their backs that by the time I turned around, it was too late to save her.

Charity had taken care of Layla's attacker, who lay lifeless beneath her, but another was already on top of her. One with bands of brown curving up around his ears. Charity's eyes widened as her neck snapped beneath his jaws.

My heart spluttered in my chest, my wolf's immediate need for revenge at war with the splitting ache in my chest at her loss.

My vision tunneled, fixating on Forrest as he lifted his blood-stained maw from the limp neck of my friend. One second I was standing there, shocked still by the sudden loss of Charity's life, the next I was on top of him. Blacked out with the burning need for retribution. My muscles burned and my chest heaved.

I felt pain. I delivered it.

Until he stopped moving and I blinked, coming back to myself with disgust roiling in my stomach at the sickening lump of flesh and bone that was once Forrest.

The others came back into view incrementally, like a curtain drawing slowly open over a stage to reveal a tragedy unfolding within. But this was no act played by men and women of the theater. This was real. The bodies leaking life's blood into the earth, the fighting, the pain.

All of it was real.

I caught my breath, my gaze finding Charity's blank stare and crumpling from within.

My wolf tipped back her head in a howl, pouring her pain and frustration into the world for all to hear.

I caught sight of my mates, back-to-back in a brawl against four others. And Vivian, tearing through the throng like a fucking hurricane.

With a whimper, I shifted back, the cuts that had begun to heal reopening with the reformation of my body. I gasped at the pain, bright spots arcing through my vision like shooting stars.

"Come out, you fucking coward!" I called, scanning the tree line in search of him. "*Come on!*"

One of the attackers got a hold of Jared's leg, taking him to the ground, and I charged ahead on human legs, slipping beneath Viv as she vaulted overhead to stop a shifter from reaching me.

Clay went down next, his vivid blue eyes hard as steel as he tried to get back to his feet against the brutal attacks of two shifters.

"*Get back!*" I hollered, lacing my alpha power into the words. I may not have been their alpha, but my authority knew no equal. It was just enough for them to let up. Enough time for me to shift back and reach them.

Devin, seeing his chance, entered the fold and I sensed his own authority overtaking mine, forcing his packmates to fight until they had no fight left to give.

Make sure he doesn't get away! I called through the pack bond to anyone that could hear me and help. I needed to take care of the ones attacking my mates, but I'd be damned if I would let him get away again.

With the playing field leveled by my insertion, my guys and I made quick work of the last of Devin's strongest shifters.

My ears pricked, hearing the sound of retreat.

No.

Not this time, you bastard.

I'd rather *die* than let him get away.

He could have *killed* one of my mates. He *had killed* I didn't even want to consider how many of my own. Too many. Whether he delivered the killing blows or not.

I've got him, Clay bellowed, tearing off at a pace that made him appear almost as a blur in the scorching light of the sunrise.

Devin hightailed it back the way he'd come, but my pack was already there, skidding to a halt to block his path into the trees. He made a swipe at Destiny but missed. She was too fast for him.

I sped toward them, a prickle of unbridled fucking *glee* skating down my spine as Clay tackled him from behind. Glee and jealousy that the hit wasn't mine.

The two dark wolves clashed and wrestled, flipping over one another as they fought.

Clay, I heard Jared calling to his brother wolf. *This one belongs to Allie.*

I grinned, letting Jared lope ahead of me.

Go and help the others, I called to Destiny and Archer where they still blocked any chance of Devin's escape. *We got this.*

I darted in, narrowly missing Clay's ass as I clamped my jaws around the bony length of Devin's hind leg, dragging him out.

A keening sound filtered into my ears like music as he fought against my hold.

Hold him, Jared said, the order meant for a panting Clay as his prey was tugged out from beneath him.

He did as Jared asked, scuffling with Devin until he was pressing both his face and neck into the dirt while Jared nudged me off Devin's leg to hold him at the other end.

Devin snarled into the earth, blowing bits of dirt with each hard pant through his nostrils. Fear flashed through his eyes as he struggled and thrashed, trying to break free of my mates' hold on him.

What are you waiting for? Wait Allie, don't—

But I already was. My wolf bowed to my request for dominance, seeing victory and retribution within our grasp. I shifted, grimacing as something internal twanged with injury.

It would heal though. We would all heal. After this was finished.

I eyed my mates, making sure they had a strong enough hold on him before I stepped forward, kneeling at Devin's side.

"Look at me," I said, drawing his attention.

His upper lip curled, froth gathering at the corner of his canine lips as he fought.

"I said look at me, you son of a bitch."

He did, and I didn't waste any more time. I inhaled and twisted my entire body into the thrust of my fist, punching through the hollow beneath his ribcage.

He cried out, a wet sound that turned my stomach.

I fought the urge to recoil in disgust, a singular focus driving me forward. Toward the jackhammer of his heart racing deeper within.

As my fingers found its edge, and curled around the delicate membrane, I had the absolute satisfaction of seeing him realize what was about to happen. A plea of mercy humming through his lips.

"No mercy," I mocked and ripped my fist from his chest, letting the useless organ tumble from my fingertips right before his deadening eyes.

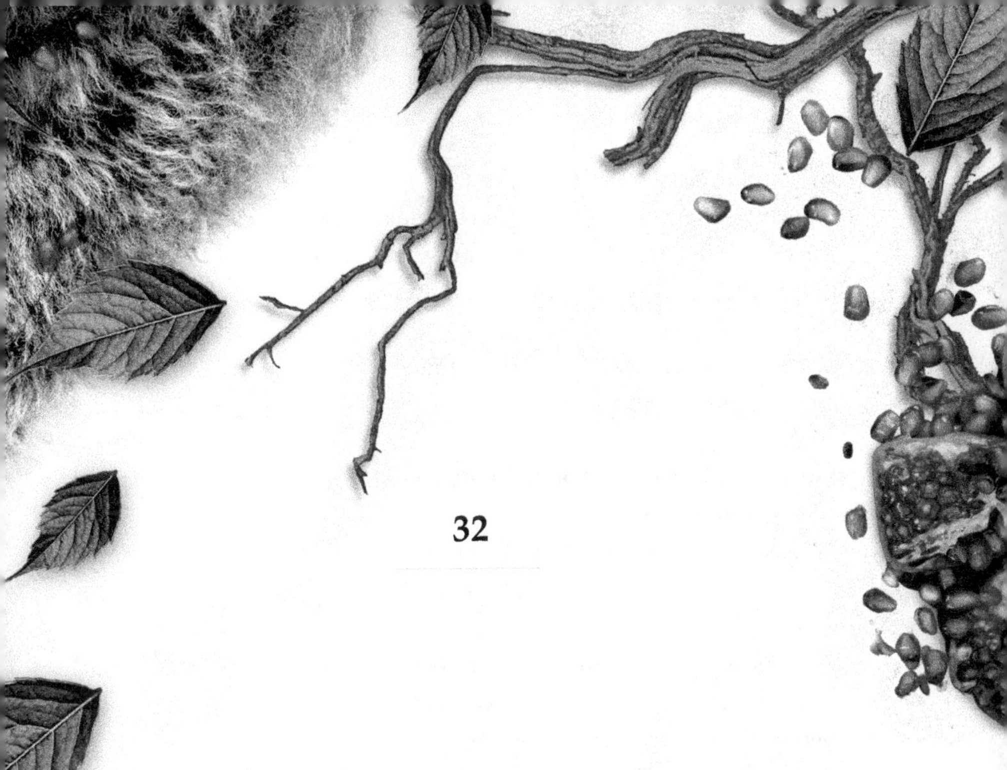

32

My skin itched as Devin's blood began to dry, crusting on my forearm rapidly in the growing heat of the morning.

"*Enough*," I demanded, rising to face the shifters still locked in battle behind us. "*I said that's enough!*"

Yips of surprise and frightened yelps rang out all around as claws retracted and bodies moved, separating one pack from another under the threat of my command.

My chest heaved, feeling oddly hollow. Limitless. Like no amount of air could ever properly sustain my need to breathe. But still I tried, panting as I slowly regained control.

Countless sets of wolfish eyes turned to me, waiting. Some afraid, others still amped up and looking to spill more blood. They might just get their wish.

Through familiar and unfamiliar faces, I searched the features of both the living and the dead. Bile burned in my throat, finding Charity across the barrens. And next to her, Luke. And closer, Sara, and Tyler.

All of them dead. And there were more, though I couldn't see their faces.

I found Layla and Seth re-emerging from the trees and sighed, nearly moved to tears when I found Vivian lying next to an injured, but alive, Destiny.

My jaw clenched as I considered the next move.

Pack law dictated that *I* was now the alpha of the wolves who fought under Devin's command, but right now...

Right now I was just as likely to rip every single one of them to pieces than force them to bow to command. "Allie?" Jared hedged, rising on human legs to stand at my back. "We don't have to do this now."

"Yes we do."

Uneasy wolves shifted on their feet, wistful gazes looking for escape. I fucking dared them to try it.

"Please," came a soft voice, and I searched the crowd to find her. A girl about my age. With reddish hair and freckles over her nose. Not my pack. *His.* "Have mercy on us. He commanded we fight. He forced us."

I shook my head, curling my hands back to fists. "Not all of you," I corrected her, thinking of Forrest. Of the others who seemed all too keen to shed the blood of my family.

A middle-aged man shifted, casting his dark eyes down to the earth as he took a knee and bowed his head. "It would be an honor to be accepted into your pack."

My teeth ground with the urge to tell him to go fuck himself. To *look* at what they'd done! Forced or not.

I didn't even realize I was shaking until a steadying hand curled around my shoulder, lending me his support. "Breathe, baby. It's over."

I latched on to Clay, squeezing his hand as I fought for a full breath through the damnable flutter in my chest. "Not yet. I won't put my family in danger again. I won't let *anyone* hurt them. We've already lost too man..."

I choked on a sob, clearing my throat and forcing my spine erect to stop myself from being overcome.

Be strong, Allie.

The girl who first spoke knelt with the older man, and as we watched, the rest of them followed. Some shifted to kneel on human knees over the blood- soaked soil. Others remained in their wolf forms, putting their bellies to the earth in a show of submission.

My own pack followed, awaiting orders.

One thing was absolutely certain, I would *not* be letting anyone walk away from this field today. Last time I allowed shifters to leave instead of bow as they were meant to, two of them returned to betray me. If I'd never let Sam or Forrest go, Devin may not have had the intel or the resources to do what he did.

This may never have happened.

I searched the gathering, thinking there may be one possible way that didn't end in the complete decimation of Devin's pack.

"Piper!" I called out, worry creasing my brow when I didn't find her.

"Has anyone seen Piper?"

"Here," Trey called, and I rushed back across the field, my mates at my sides.

Trey and Todd muscled a large gray wolf off of a smaller, dark coated one.

Piper lay unmoving save for the slight rise and fall of her chest.

"Hey." I pried back her eyelid, checking for dilation. "Piper?"

"I don't think she's fatally injured," Todd said, the voice of reason in the maelstrom in my head.

Jared snatched me back as Piper came to, nearly taking my damn ear off as her eyes widened in panic and she scrambled to her feet, body trembling.

I held my hands up to her. "Hey, it's okay."

"It's okay..." I repeated a second time, making sure she understood from the movement of my lips.

Piper's gaze jerked over the scene, searching until they landed on Devin.

She shifted, falling to her knees, her big eyes watering as she blinked rapidly to clear them. She signed something, and Jared translated for me, kneeling to speak into my ear.

"She's asking if it's really over now."

"Almost," I told her, and her brows crinkled.

"There's something I need you to do for me, and then it will be."

Jared stumbled through signing my words, and I stopped him, placing a hand over his. "She can read lips. Really well, actually."

Piper smirked and signed something else. "She says okay. She'll do whatever you need."

My chest squeezed, and something in my face must have given away my pain because she signed again, concern lining her forehead.

I didn't wait for Jared to translate this time, launching into an explanation of my own. "I need you to read them," I told her. "I need you to read each and every one of them and tell me if they did this willingly or if they were forced."

Her lips parted and her face, already pale, became impossibly paler.

"This is bullshit!" Someone shouted behind me, moving to leave.

"*No one leaves,*" I hissed, jerking my chin to the retreating man, giving the order to stop him. "Restrain him."

"You are not the executioner," I assured Piper, swallowing past the hard lump in my throat. "I am."

I felt the certainty in my decision, backed up by the solidarity of my mates through the bond. They agreed with me. This was the only way.

"It's how it has to be. It's the only way for me to keep everyone safe."

Piper's jaw flexed, considering her role in what would effectively be the murder of several of her previous packmates.

She nodded once, a sharp bob of her head and the full weight of what I had to do next crashed down on my shoulders. But at least I wouldn't have to do it alone.

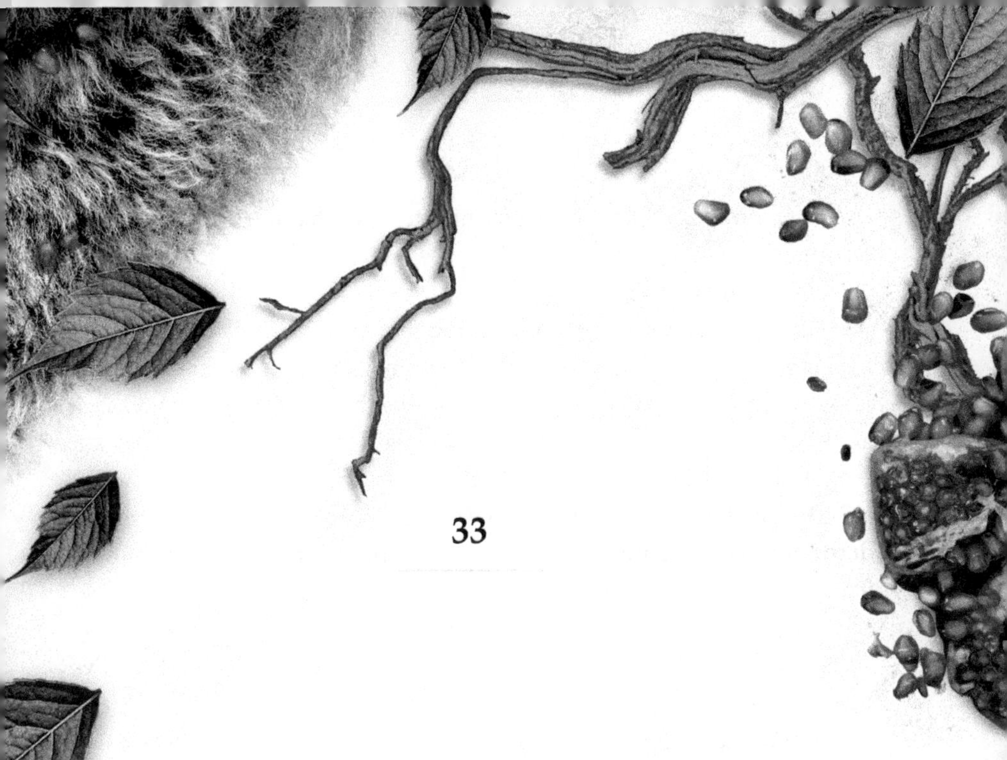

33

My dead were carried home on the backs of the living.

The traitors and murderers were left behind in shallow graves on the barren field. Only one was left to rot—to be picked at by the sharp shiny beaks of crows and other scavengers until he was only bone.

A risk, to leave him out in the open, even if it was a place that didn't recognize the touch of mortal souls. But I couldn't stomach the alternative. He didn't deserve it.

A total of eight shifters from my pack would never see another day, but Devin's losses were far greater. Nearly twenty graves had needed to be dug for them, and the work took us until dusk to complete.

Then came the long journey home after splinting broken bones with the little supplies we had on hand and seeing everyone properly hydrated.

It still hadn't hit me: the loss of them. The hours passed in a flurry of halfhearted orders and miles passed through the tree covered landscape. All the while the reek of blood clung to the inside of my nose, reminding me of the additional lives I'd had to take even after the battle was fought. Six.

But I tried to remind myself that their deaths would pave the way for peace. The others had, in fact, been commanded to fight until they could no longer. They were repentant. They hadn't wanted to kill anyone.

They were welcome.

The smell of campfire broke through the hard shell of numbness keeping me shriveled inside, and I lifted my gaze from the carpet of the forest for the first time in hours. The weight of Charity on my back ached as I came back to myself, and I winced.

Jared and Clay carried two others over their canine backs at my sides while the rest walked behind. Most as wolves, though a few shouldered the packs containing our supplies and walked along on human feet, heads bent as we approached camp.

Wait here, Clay spoke in my thoughts.

There shouldn't have been a fire in the pits at camp. It should've been vacant.

No, I replied. *We go together.*

"This is where we part ways," Dante said, tipping his head west to give his packmates the order to head in the direction of home. He looked wistfully after a dark wolf who carried a lighter gray one slung over his back.

His only loss in the fight. But even one was too many, I understood.

I nodded, trying to convey the depth of my gratitude without the need to shift.

"We'll be in touch," he added before veering off to join his pack, shifting on the fly until their shadows vanished.

It's Hazel, Clay said from several paces ahead, peering through the trees. *I can smell her scent.*

Sure enough, her floral aroma found me on the breeze, and despite everything, a comforted half smile stole onto my lips.

Stubborn woman, Jared put in. *She was supposed to stay at the warded cabin until we returned.*

When have you ever known her to listen, I asked them both, giving a pointed look.

Clay grunted and began walking again, pausing near the edge of camp, where the moon chamber crouched low in the grass. He gently knelt, bowing his head to allow Luke to slide gracefully from his shoulders and onto the ground next to the moss coated stones.

I nodded, looking at the small patch of land next to the chamber. It was perfect.

The rest of us followed suit, and I paused to push my snout against Charity's forehead after setting her down, feeling the gravity of her loss like a thousand pounds on my shoulders.

Goodbye, my friend.

A ball grew in my chest as I pushed through my wolf to the surface, feeling her aches in my smaller human muscles as I opened my eyes again.

A muscle in my jaw twitched as I took in the cabin, and the quiet camp beyond. Barely forty-eight hours ago I'd been forced to wonder if there was a chance I'd never make it back here. Seeing it now, I thought I'd never seen anything more beautiful in my whole damn life.

This was home.

My home.

"We'll take care of the graves," came Archer's voice from behind me, and I turned to see several of them already marking out an area to inter our friends. "When they're ready to be...*uh*...buried, I'll send someone to get you."

"I should help," I muttered, my voice sounding far away even to my own ears.

A strong arm slipped around my back, and I inhaled warm spice, sighing as the exhaustion finally began to set in. "You've done enough, baby. Come on, you need to rest."

I hadn't the strength to fight Clay as he guided me around the cabin and the smell of cooking meat and sharp vinegar assaulted my senses.

My brows drew together as my mates and I rounded the cabin to find Hazel, sweat beading over her forehead as she worked two barbeques near the crush of picnic benches where stacks of paper plates were weighted down with heavy stones and bowls sat piled high with cabbage slaw and macaroni salad.

Trays of steaming steaks and chicken piled higher as she pulled them from the grill, dual wielding tongs like a ninja.

She barely turned around as we approached, casting a narrow-eyed stare over her right shoulder. "Took you long enough," she tutted, and I stared openly at her.

The woman who didn't doubt for even a second that I would return with both my mates in tow and mostly unharmed. So sure of it that she'd cooked a damned feast to welcome us back.

"I assume we have guests? How many? I need to know how many steaks need cooking. And we'll have to put in another order, this is pretty much the last of—"

I looped my arms around her back, squeezing tight as my throat tightened and my eyes burned, overflowing with stinging tears that dampened the back of her long dress.

She tensed at first, but then relaxed, patting my trembling arms.

"Now, now, it's all going to be—" Her hand stilled on my wrist.

Tongs discarded, Hazel twisted in my embrace, holding me at arm's length and drawing my hands into hers.

"Oh!" she exclaimed, trading in my hands to press two palms to my stomach.

"Um...Hazel?"

I shared a look with my mates as a wide grin broke over Hazel's face, her blind eyes searching as though she could see something we couldn't.

"*Hazel*," I exclaimed when her lips quivered and a tear fell from her chin. "What's wrong?"

She sniffed and stepped back, her shoulders shaking with something halfway between laughter and sobbing. "You're with child, my daughter."

"No," I uttered uneasily. "I can't be, I take pills for..." Oh fuck. When was the last time I'd taken them?

With everything going on, swallowing a tiny pill every morning wasn't exactly high up on my priority list.

"Are you sure?" Clay asked, his jaw clenching and unclenching just as rapidly as his fists.

"As sure as I'm standing here," she replied as whispers bloomed behind us, and I sensed the rest of the pack join.

"You're going to be a mom?" Layla asked hopefully, a crooked grin showing the dimples you could almost forget she had. She wrapped me up in a big hug, her jasmine scent erasing whatever remained of the stench of blood from my nose.

"We're going to be aunties?" came Viv's exclamation. Her eyes turned red-rimmed as she clenched her hands together and fought back against the urge to cry.

My heart pounded in my chest, a whole new kind of fear taking root in my belly.

Hesitantly, I placed a hand to my belly, trying to feel what Hazel felt.

"Where there is death, there is also life," Hazel whispered, almost inaudibly.

Jared's hand slid over mine, and I looked up to see him smiling, his amber eyes alight with an astonished kind of joy that made the dark emotions flee from my mind.

I looked to Clay, my throat desert dry.

"Clay?" I hedged, concerned at the red tint to his face. At the distant look in his eyes.

He cleared his throat and lifted his chin, swallowing a breath. "So," he said, his voice thick with emotion as he glanced at his best friend. "What are we going to name our son?"

My chest ached as a hard laugh left my lips that quickly turned into an aching sob of relief.

Jared laughed, too, pressing a hard kiss to my temple.

"*Hey*," I sniffed. "Who said it's a boy? What if she's a girl?"

"*Pfft*, that's easy," said Jared, wrapping an arm loosely around my waist.

"We'd name her after the strongest woman we know."

I glanced at Hazel as though she could feel my eyes on her; she shook her head.

"They mean you, stupid," she said, swiping at the papery skin beneath her eyes.

Another laugh-sob twisted in my chest and I snatched Clay, drawing him close until the bond connected all three of us. He brushed my dirty hair back and pressed a soft kiss to my mouth that made my belly flutter and my toes curl.

A speck of light formed in all the darkness and I smiled against his lips. Terrified, but knowing that no matter what happened, I'd always have them. Together, we could do this.

It was time for a new kind of adventure.

BONUS SCENES

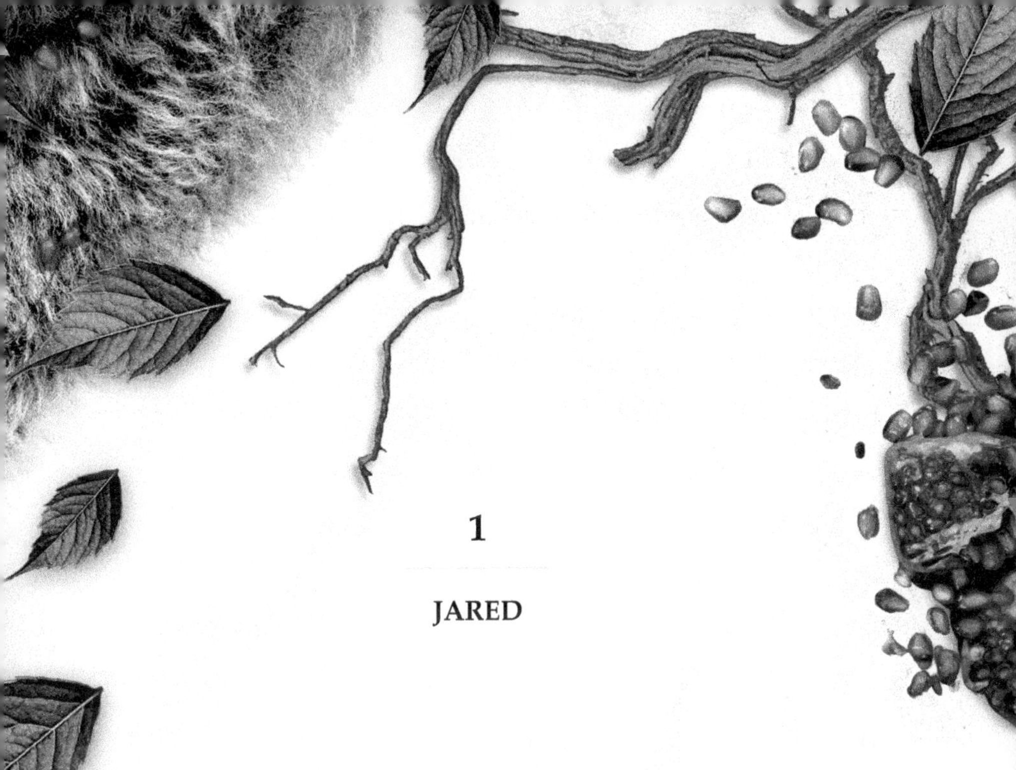

1

JARED

The pain radiated down my spine and ricocheted through my entire body. It rose and crested, forcing me to hunch down and grip the edge of the counter to catch my breath. Like a wave, it broke, white spray blotting out my vision before the clenching ache subsided, leveling out into an even roar of discomfort.

"*What the fuck...*" I muttered breathily, clenching my stomach.

My phone pinged loudly, yanking me out of my daze. Shakily, I reached for it in my pocket, thumbing the screen to see a single text message glowing in the shadowy kitchen.

Layla: It's time.

No.

It couldn't be time yet.

Allie wasn't due for another two weeks.

I nearly tripped over my own feet running up the stairs to check our bedroom, bursting through the door to find it entirely vacant. The bedsheets rumpled. A wet stain on the carpet next to Allie's side of the bed.

I'd just gotten home from wrapping up a big order at the quarry. Clay must have still been at the pub. Allie had to be at Hazel's cabin. That was where we'd planned to do the delivery.

My pulse spiked, pushing adrenaline through my veins and awakening my wolf.

Were they ready? Did we have everything?

Layla had thrown herself into learning everything there was to learn about midwifery and how to care for a shifter in childbirth. Hazel was a seasoned vet, too, having delivered several babes in her time. Everything was going to be fine.

Totally fucking fine.

Right?

I gripped twin fistfuls of my hair, trying to think clearly. Was there anything I was supposed to grab before I headed over there? I was sure there was something but...

Shit.

I sloppily swiped at my phone, punching *Clay* in the contact list. It rang twice before he answered.

"I'm already on my way," he growled down the line, his voice garbled with the presence of his wolf. "Give me five minutes."

The line went dead before I could even get a word in.

Another message flashed across the screen, this time from Vivian.

Vivian: Where the fuck are you? Patrol says you passed through fifteen minutes ago. Get your ass over here. Now.

My throat felt near closing, but I didn't hesitate another second, rushing down the stairs and out into the chill of the early spring night. Sweat dripped from my hairline, and I winced, doubling over halfway to Hazel's cabin as another wave of pain gripped me, making every muscle in my back rock solid as I gasped to breathe through it.

Contractions, I realized. Allie was having contractions, and I was sharing in her pain.

Cool fingers curled around my arm, and I flinched, ripping away from the helping hand.

"Jare?" came a familiar voice, and I blinked through the wetness stinging my eyes to find a lick of dark hair and Seth's concerned face. "Layla just sent me to look for you, man. You okay? You look like fucking shit."

I coughed, tasting the tang of bile at the back of my throat as I let him help me straighten. "I can feel it," I gritted out. "Hazel was right."

Seth's eyes went wide. "I didn't think you'd feel it *that* much."

I groaned, rushing forward once I had my footing. The sound of Clay's wolf howling in the distance chased Seth and me across the camp.

The lights were bright in all the windows, and I sensed her inside. Her fear. Her anguish.

Stupid. I shouldn't have taken the shift at the quarry. Not this close to the day. I should've been here.

I shouldered through the door, my eyes locking on her across the room. Allie schooled her face the moment I entered, slapping her lips shut to breathe heavily through her nose. Locking down her fear.

Didn't she know that she didn't have to hide from us anymore?

"Allie," I breathed, crossing the floor to where she was lying at the center of Hazel's bed over several layers of thick blankets and sterilized surgical pads.

"You," Layla barked, glaring at Seth while she dipped a cloth in a large basin of cool water. "*Out.* There's already too many people in here."

He took one look at Allie, gave an apologetic, if a little pained, smile and saw himself out.

"Hey," I said, unable to dislodge the lump from my throat as I took her hand in mine and pressed it to my lips.

"Hey," she replied, trying on a smile.

Layla shoved the basin at me, sloshing icy water over my feet and the floor. "Here. Try to keep her comfortable, would you? I have to get some more things ready."

I nodded, setting to the task of wiping down Allie's brow with the damp cloth. She shivered gratefully as I glided the cloth down to her neck, leaning into my touch.

"Where's Clay?"

"*Here.*"

He stood in the doorway, steaming lightly from the exertion of his run, his muscles bunched with tension and eyes dark with the same emotion I was feeling.

My jaw clenched as a silent moment passed between me and my best friend. We hadn't spoken about it, but I knew he was thinking the same thing I was ever since we found out Allie was having twins.

Hazel was clever to keep it from us. She didn't say a word until both the babies' heartbeats were strong enough for us to be able to discern that there were two beating within her womb. And by that stage, the chances of vanishing twin syndrome occurring were so low that Allie only *kind of* flipped out.

But the chance of Allie not surviving the birth, however low, was an ever present fear since the beginning. Her mother hadn't survived Allie's birth. What if…

"It's too soon," Clay grunted, his nostrils flaring as he keenly took in every inch of the room, as though in search of an enemy or at the very least, something he could punch.

"He's right," I agreed, gulping as I dipped the cloth back into the water and let Allie snatch it from my hand to wring over her bare chest with a sigh. "Isn't that too early, what if—"

"There's nothing to be done about it now," Hazel interrupted, readying the table with supplies and clean cloths. "Besides, two weeks early isn't so bad. Not for twins."

Allie grunted, her hand gripping my forearm as another wave of muscle spasming pain rocked us both.

Clay doubled over across the room, growling.

When Allie finally let go, yellow bruises colored my flesh, and she winced apologetically. "Sorry."

"Break it if you want," I offered. "I don't care."

She barked a laugh, growing more serious as Layla draped a thin sheet over her swollen belly and helped her get her knees upright. "How long?" she asked, breathless.

Layla peered beneath the sheet, swiping her arm over her brow. "*Um*…I'm not sure. Looks like five centimeters. It's happening too fast."

Clay swayed unsteadily on his feet, blinking rapidly as he braced his hands on his knees. "What does that mean?" he demanded.

"It means we need to be ready for anything."

"I'm back, got the ice," Viv called, barging in and nearly tripping over Clay's hunched form in the entry.

Ice cubes scattered to the hardwood, and she cursed, thrusting the bucket of ice at me so she could help Clay.

"What are these for?"

Allie stuffed her hand into the bucket and popped two into her mouth, moaning as they began to melt.

Guess that's what.

"Hey," Viv said, snapping her fingers in front of Clay's reddened face. "Hey, snap out of it."

He knocked her hands away as she tried to help him unfurl back to his full height.

"Clay?" Allie said around a mouthful of ice. "Is he okay?"

"Am *I* okay?" he hissed. "*Christ, babe.*"

"Okay, come here you big idiot," Viv ordered, finally getting a hold on him. "Come get some air."

"Wait," Allie blurted, looking after Clay with a pained expression on her face as Layla took another measurement beneath the sheet.

Vivian shoved Clay through the door and spun around with a wink. "Don't worry," she assured my mate. "I'll bring him right back. Promise."

My stomach twisted uneasily as Layla gave me a meaningful look from between Allie's legs. It was happening too fast. Layla's already pale complexion turned an almost sickly white as she swallowed hard, rising to whisper something to Hazel that I didn't catch.

What the fuck was happening?

I set to stroking Allie's hair back from her flushed cheeks, the repetitive motion calming us both. I could still hear her heart beating strong in her chest. Feel the life flowing through her. Through the mate bond. She was strong. The strongest woman I'd ever known. She would get through this.

She was going to be an incredible mother.

She *had* to make it through this.

I didn't know if I could do it without her.

"Your nerves are giving my nerves hives," she muttered, stuffing more ice cubes into her mouth as she gave me an angry side-eye.

My throat went dry, and I tried to get a handle on myself, trying to be the calm eye of her storm. Trying to be the solidity she needed when all around us was chaos.

Hazel nodded to Layla and lifted a tray from beneath the table. A metal tray with a whole bunch of scissor looking things and scalpels and...

"What the hell is that for?"

Hazel shot daggers at me from across the room, and you'd almost think she could see again from the accuracy of her stare. It was clear she wasn't going to answer me, but I felt Allie stiffen beside me when she noticed the tray.

Outside, I could hear the roar of Vivian shouting at Clay. Telling him that Allie needed him to keep his cool. That he wasn't allowed to fall apart. That Allie was going to be *fine,* but that if he missed the birth of his own children, Allie would kill him, and then *he* would be the one that wasn't fine.

"*Fuck!*" Allie shouted as another contraction hardened her belly and raced across my lower back like the swipe of a red hot blade.

I gritted my teeth, trying not to bend to it. Trying to be strong for her.

If what Hazel said was true, what we could feel was only a *taste* of the pain Allie was feeling. The echo of it. I had no right to be a wreck when she was handling this like a champ.

Baring her teeth through the pain and then sagging to catch her breath when it was over. Even managing a tiny smile in my direction.

"Eight centimeters," Layla announced a minute later, her pulse almost on par with Allie's pounding drumbeat. "We should see a head, right? Where's the head?"

"Move!" Hazel shoved Layla out of the way, her long braid falling forward as she reached beneath the sheet to feel what she could not see.

I took Allie's hand, and she squeezed tightly, her gray eyes flitting between Layla's haunted expression, the hunch of Hazel between her legs, and me.

"What is it?" she asked. "What's wrong? Are they okay? Are my babies okay?"

As though she could feel for herself, she flattened a palm against her impossibly large stomach, and I watched as a limb moved beneath the surface of her skin. Like a tiny hand trying to reach out for the touch of his mother.

Hazel rocked back on her heels and rose, putting a bloodied hand to her temple. "He flipped," she said. "He isn't in the right position."

"Can we turn him?" Layla asked hopefully, rushing to flip through several pages of the birthing bible she'd been carrying around for months. "There's a section in here that explains—"

"It's *twins*," Hazel cut her off. "Packed in there like a couple of sardines. We can't turn him."

"We should've had the birth at a hospital," I all but growled, my wolf flooding me from the inside, making my heated flesh prickle with agitation. It had been a sticking point from the start. Births had always been done on pack land. Try explaining rapid healing and glowing eyes to a mortal doctor... but I'd have handled it. Hired a vampire to compel the doc to forget. Whatever we had to do to make sure something like *this* didn't happen.

"If they'd come on time, then Katie would have been here," Layla argued. Katie was a surgeon from a southern pack who'd be here on standby in case of an emergency. She was meant to arrive in just two days.

Two days too late now.

I pinched the bridge of my nose and inhaled deeply, hating how the scent of her blood was all I could smell. It permeated my nostrils, filled my lungs like poison.

"What do we do?" Allie asked, her words trailing off into a cry as another contraction nearly put me on my knees. Allie almost snapped my index finger from her grip.

Clay raced back inside, his eyes lit with his wolf as he glared at Hazel and Layla as though they were somehow to blame for her pain. "What's happening?"

"Clay," Allie choked out, sagging back against her mountain of sweat-stained pillows.

He came to her, shaking the cabin with each stomp of his feet until he was hunched over the side of the bed opposite to me. He bent and took her other hand, putting his forehead to hers. "I'm sorry," he muttered. "I'm here now. I'm here."

She nodded against him and then pulled away, gasping, her hands going to her stomach. "Something's wrong," she said, all the color draining from her face.

"Something's wrong," she repeated, frantic, her hands moving over the surface of her belly. "I can't hear her. I can't hear her heartbeat."

Hazel rushed to the bedside, almost barreling into me as she listened at Allie's belly, her hunched back showing a knobby protrusion of spine under her surgical gown.

"It's there," Hazel said after the longest moment of my entire fucking life. "But faint."

"Get them out," Allie said, her whole body shaking. "Get them out *now*."

Her fear crept over my heart like frost, and it was like all my worst fears were coming true before my eyes and there was nothing I could do to stop it.

Hazel went for the surgical tray, cutting herself as she rifled through polished utensils until her wrinkled fingers found the blunt end of the scalpel.

"Fuck that," Clay growled, standing between Hazel and Allie. "*No*, Grams. You aren't cutting them out of her."

Vivian sagged against the wall in the doorway, blinking like she might pass out.

Layla just stood there, frozen still by the realization of what was happening.

The one thing we weren't prepared for.

"Move, Clay," Allie all but hissed, trying to sit up so she could move him herself.

"No, Allie."

"Clay!"

She looked to me, her eyes pleading. Lower lip quivering. "They'll die…"

She couldn't ask me to do this.

I *wouldn't* do this.

"Please."

Fuck.

I left her side and tackled Clay to the ground, getting a good elbow hit into his ribs before he went down, the air rushing out of his lungs. He fought back, trying to get the upper hand.

"Viv!"

She was there in a split second, helping me get a hold of Clay. "Hey!" I shouted, trying to get his attention as Layla and Hazel crowded in behind us.

"Okay, hun, you're going to have to do this," Hazel was saying, the scalpel glinting in the lamplight as she passed it to a stunned Layla. "I'll talk you through it."

"Get the fuck off me," Clay bellowed, knocking over a nightstand.

"Stop it!" Allie screamed, making Clay pause just for a second. The second we needed to get through to him.

"Man, listen," I ground out, my muscles burning with the effort of keeping him on the ground. *"Listen!"*

The fight went out of him, a little at first, but more as the seconds passed. "She can't leave us, man. She *can't.*"

"She won't, you big idiot," Vivian snapped in his face. "She heals faster than all of us. She's got this. She can do this. You need to *let her* do this."

I lowered my mouth to his ear, speaking low so only he could hear. "If something happens to them because you wouldn't let Hazel and Layla do this, she'll never forgive you."

He knew it was true, but the last of his fight left him and my chest ached at the hatred in his stare. He bared his teeth. "But at least she'd be alive."

Allie cried out and a sharp pain skated over my nerves, making the three of us come apart in a tangle of limbs on the floor. I scrambled to my feet, rushing back to her side.

"Don't look," she insisted, gripping my hand. "Look at me."

Clay held her other hand, and I saw his face harden in a mask of stone as his gaze swept low over Allie's belly where Hazel was coaching Layla where to cut.

"At me!" Allie demanded, tugging Clay's hand to get his attention.

He watched her in muted horror as they sliced through her stomach and she barely made a sound. Silent tears and a wire-tight jaw the only outward proof of her torment.

This pain wasn't shared, but we could still sense her resolve. Stronger than her fear.

"I love you so much," I told her, lifting her hand to my lips. "So much."

She grunted and sagged, her body jerking before her grip on my hand softened and her head rolled back.

"Viv!" Layla cried. "Take him."

Allie looked down, and I followed her gaze to the mess of her stomach and the tiny thing Layla passed into the hands of Vivian.

"Is he...okay?" Allie asked groggily, and I turned to find her pale, her eyelids heavy.

"Allie?" I prodded, brushing my knuckles over her cheek to try to rouse her.

"Is he okay?" Clay echoed, her voice gruff. "Vivian! Is he okay?"

"I...I don't know."

"Help him," Allie muttered, and Clay looked between her and Vivian frantically, trying to find a place to lay the infant down.

"Clear his airway," Layla ordered, her tone steadier than it had any right to be.

Clay was across the room in half a second, his hands shaking as he took the baby from Vivian. A few seconds later a strangled cry rose, filling the cabin with its perfect sound, drawing on something deep inside my core.

"He's okay..." Allie breathed, her body jerking again as Layla tugged another baby from her. Her brows pinched, and she sighed, her eyes fluttering.

Droplets fell over Allie's cheek, and it took me a minute to realize they were tears. My tears.

"He's okay," I repeated, pushing her hair back. My fingers stilled as they brushed her forehead. Flushed only a second before it felt cool. Too cold.

A second cry rose to meet the first, this one higher in pitch, drawing my attention away from my mate to find her. Little Charity Grace, impossibly small. A tuft of white blonde hair on her squirming head in the arms of Layla.

"Allie, they're okay. Look, they're—"

Her eyes fluttered to a half close, showing whites.

"Layla!" I called, releasing her limp hand to grip both sides of her clammy face instead. "Wake up, Allie. You need to stay awake."

"Here," I heard Clay say, and then he was there, elbowing me out of the way and tapping Allie on the cheek harder than I'd like.

"Babe?" he said, voice a distant monotone. "Babe, wake up."

I stepped back, an odd sensation making everything hazy. Like I was watching from a shelf high up in the corner. Like I wasn't really here.

Like this was just a dream

A nightmare.

Chapter 1

Soon, I'd wake up.

Wake up.

Wake. Up.

Clay was shouting something I couldn't understand.

Layla worked on Allie's stomach. The *chink chink* of the staple gun like gunshots to my lungs. Was I breathing?

Did it matter?

"Look!" Vivian shouted, cradling the still crying baby to her chest. "She's healing. She's already healing."

I blinked, coming back to myself like a soul sucked back into a body and caught myself on the headboard before my knees could buckle.

"She's healing," Layla confirmed, and I found the edges of her wound, a strange laugh blooming on my lips as I watched her skin slowly knit itself back together, helped on by the staples keeping her skin and muscle and sinew together.

I could kiss the fucking stars.

She groaned, and Clay and I leaned over her, both of us breathless as her eyes fluttered back open, trying to focus.

"Where…" she muttered, her voice small and faraway. "Where…"

Vivian tapped me on the shoulder, and I spun, my lips parting at the baby in her arms. "Here," she said while Hazel brought the other one to Clay.

I took her into my arms, terrified that I wasn't doing it right. You're supposed to support the neck, right? What if I drop her? What if…

My chest ached at the sight of her, twinging even more as she nuzzled into my collarbone, settling as though she already knew who I was.

"Hi, Charity," I managed in a watery voice, running a finger down her tiny nose.

"Jared?" Allie pleaded, and I swallowed hard, trying to get my arms to stop shaking so I could set her down with my mate.

I settled Charity into the crook of Allie's arm while Clay nestled a fussing Liam against her chest. Christ, it must've taken us four months to decide on his name. Liam was the only name none of us hated and looking at him now, it fit. We made a good choice.

Allie began to sob, her weak arms trying to draw them in closer.

"They're perfect," she said after a minute, lifting her gaze to me, and then to Clay. "We did it."

"You did it," Clay corrected her, pressing a kiss first to Liam and then to her forehead.

Outside Hazel's cabin, cheers erupted from the pack. A cacophony of whoops and hollering. Of laughter and of clapping hands.

Welcome to the pack little ones.

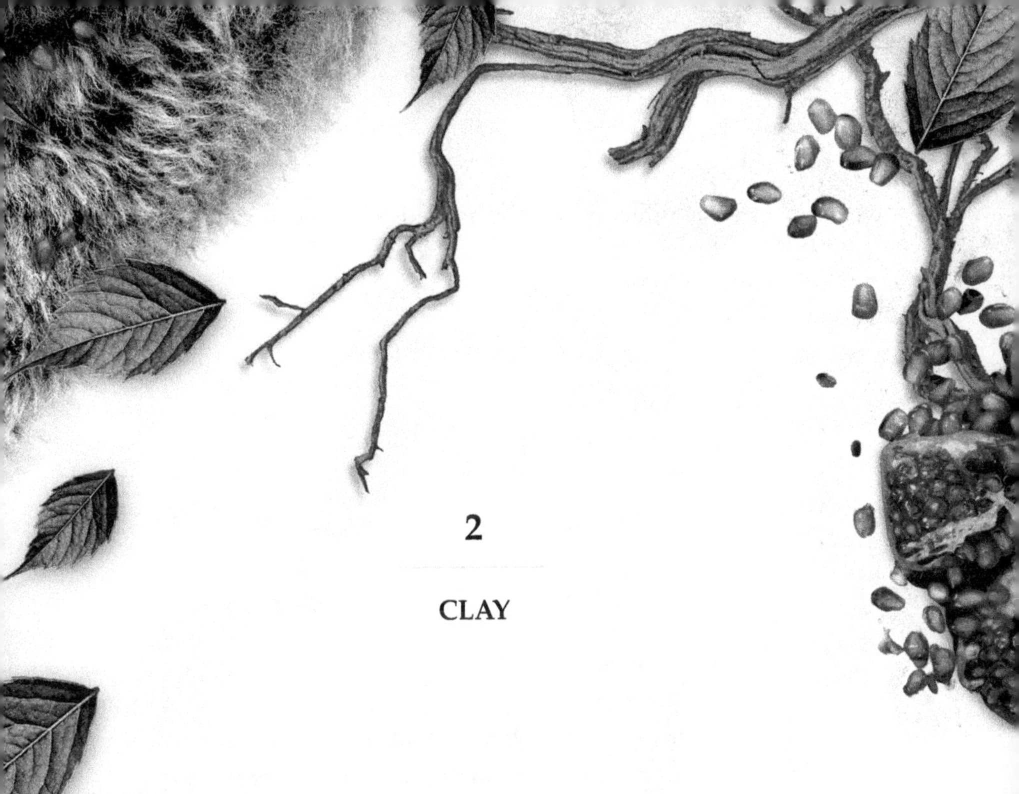

2

CLAY

"Hey, have you seen my--"

The sentence cut short as I nudged the bedroom door open to find her asleep. I smirked, stepping into the room quietly and easing the door closed behind me.

Layla and Viv must have the kids. They often took them out for hikes on the weekends so Allie could rest and this Sunday was no different. I licked my lips, wondering how long it would be until they returned.

I'd just come back from patrol, and Jared was filling a large order at the quarry. It was so rare to have a minute with her alone. I'd learned the hard way that three-year-olds had absolutely no respect for privacy or personal space. I wouldn't change it, but fuck if I didn't *miss* her.

I dragged a hand over the stubble on my jaw, inching closer to the woman strewn across the king size bed. Her tan legs tangled in the white sheets. Her hair a wild mane of silvery blonde. The curve of her naked hip and swell of her breasts.

I'd caught her evaluating her new body in the mirror more times than I'd like since she had the twins. More often than not with a frown. But I saw something different. A woman who nearly died to protect the new life inside of her. Who would've without question if fate had deemed it a necessary payment for their birth. I saw beauty. The kind that can't be manufactured or enhanced with fucking injections and shit. Hers was the raw kind. The perfect kind.

She muttered something unintelligible in her sleep and I lowered myself to lay next to her, breathing in her scent. The same scent I'd fallen in love with almost eight years ago. So many things had changed, but I hoped that never did.

"Clay…" Allie murmured, tucking herself into me with a sigh.

I brushed my fingers through her hair, biting down hard on my lip when her ass brushed against my cock. "*Shhh*," I demanded. "Go back to sleep."

"Not…tired…" she lied, the words broken up by a yawn.

"Bullshit."

The twins had kept her up most nights this week and because she was more stubborn than an ox she rarely let us get up with them. Especially since Jared started running night patrols and I took over security for the evening shifts at Grove's End after the twins started sleeping through the night.

They only recently started to think that 3:00am was a perfectly reasonable time to wake up for the day.

Allie tugged on the sheets, removing the only thing separating us and groaned as her tailbone pressed against my cock.

I grunted, gripping her hip to hold her steady.

"How long do we have?" she murmured, twisting to face me while she continued teasing my erection with her bare ass. Her fingers skated down the length of my jaw, coaxing my face closer to hers.

My lips pulled up at the softness of her stare, still glazed with sleep and downturned at the edges.

"Not long enough," I told her, stealing the breath from her lips with a hard kiss that made her back arch and a gasp hitch in her throat.

It was never long enough.

Would never be long enough.

Her lips parted for me to sweep in and I lifted her by the hips, seating her on my cock and making her shudder as the length slid over her slick core.

"Hurry," she pleaded, eyeing the clock on the nightstand. "They'll be back soon."

She didn't have to fucking tell me twice.

I pushed inside, groaning as she clenched around me, a short cry of release on her lips that made her turn away to twist her fingers into the sheets.

I eased out, thrusting back in gently even though every fibre of my being wanted me to take her hard and fast. To leave her blissfully undone in a puddle of sated desire. To fuck her until she couldn't feel her legs.

Christ, it had been too long since I'd had her alone.

Sharing her with Jared had gotten easier, but I'd be lying if I didn't say I missed this. *Craved* this.

"Harder," she urged, and I obliged, gritting my teeth as I increased the pace, thrusting into her as deep as I could go, whispered curses falling from my lips as I felt the beginning of my release.

Not yet.

Allie's hand snaked low and I felt her fingers brush the base of my cock with each thrust as she touched herself, breathing heavily. Making me even more fucking turned on.

I moaned into her hair, fingers digging into her hips to keep myself from falling from the edge. "Come on, baby," I whispered harshly, the words fanning over her neck. "I need you to cum."

She clenched, her pussy tightening and body writhing as she found her release in a long, broken exhale. I tugged her waist, flipping her from her side onto her belly to get deeper, lengthening her climax and spurring my own to a head.

Her shout of ecstasy was muffled by the pillows as I thrust my last, pouring into her with a held breath, teeth grinding.

I pressed a kiss to her back and she shivered, flipping around to wrap her arms tightly around my neck and lock me against her.

"Good morning," she said in a cheeky voice, biting at my ear.

I snorted. "You mean afternoon?"

She shrugged, sagging, her arms relaxing around me.

"Do we have to get up?" she asked hopefully, nuzzling against my chest. "Can't we just stay like this?"

"*We* can't," I said. "But you can."

I slid off and drew the sheet up to cover her. "I'll go make lunch for when they get back."

"*No,*" she argued, reaching for me as I deftly slid out of her reach and off the bed. "Stay."

I dug around in my dresser for a pair of jeans and cursed, snatching some up off the floor instead when I found none. "I'll take care of the laundry, too."

I grabbed the long black t-shirt I'd been wearing yesterday from the chair by the bed but Allie snatched it from my hand before I could put it on, drawing it over her head pulling the collar to her nose to breathe deeply of my scent.

I didn't like the look of those dark circles under her eyes, but I was glad they weren't there for worse a reason. It'd been years since we had an incident worth losing sleep over, but even now I could see Allie was just waiting for the hammer to drop.

Some nonsense about having to pay for everything good in her life...

"You should--"

"Nope," I interrupted. "Go back to sleep."

Fire raced up my neck as I swiveled to face the window, wincing at a hard tug in my chest.

Allie sat bolt upright, and my nostrils flared, glancing between her and the window.

"Did you feel--"

Charity's shrill cry sounded like a siren in the distance, the aching soundwaves burrowing deep into my bones.

I'd never moved so fast in my whole damned life.

Liam's voice rose to meet his sister's in a howl of pain and as the front door burst from its hinges I realized I could hear Layla and Viv shouting, too.

Allie transformed, launching over my head as though I was the most pitiful hurdle she'd ever had to jump. A spear of black and silver fur locked on target.

I was right behind her, my wolf taking over before I fully gave over to him.

We nearly barreled into several pack members as we wove through camp towards the treeline, skidding to a stop as a small head of silvery blonde hair flashed in the afternoon sun.

Charity thrashed in Vivian's arms, blood dripping from her chin. Her cutting grey stare fixed on her brother.

"Liam!" Layla snapped, snatching him by the arm to stop him trying to charge at his sister.

His right eye was swollen and he swung his little fists in the air as though he could somehow hit her even though they were several paces apart.

I shifted, kicking off the remains of my favorite jeans. "What's going on?" I growled and Charity broke out of Layla's grip, running straight for me.

"*Daddy,*" she whined, her little arms lifted.

I scooped her up into my arms, wiping at the blood beneath her nose. She immediately stuck her damp face into my shoulder and hid as I rubbed circles into her back.

"Hey, *shhh*, it's okay. Want to tell Daddy what happened?"

She shook her head against my shoulder and Allie sent me a deadpan look that conveyed everything she didn't say. She thought I coddled her too much. When Charity wanted something, she didn't go to Allie, not even to Jared, she came to me first.

How the hell was I supposed to say no?

She had me wrapped tightly around her little finger--we all knew it.

I was working on it.

My jaw ticked as I turned my attention to Liam, who dropped his eyes with shame the moment mine connected with his.

Allie shifted, going to Liam.

"I don't know what happened," Layla said, looking to Vivian for support. "One second they were hunting for huckleberries, the next they were--"

"Like this," Vivian interrupted, gesturing vaguely at the pair of them.

Liam no longer tried to pull away from Layla, but just stood there with his arms crossed, a pout on his lips and a knot between his brows.

Allie knelt down next to him, placing a comforting hand on his arm. "What's this all about?"

"Dominance," came a willowy voice and I spun, readjusting Charity in my arms.

Hazel came around a cabin with Piper on her heels. "It's time, I think."

"Time?" Allie asked, looking to me for clarification.

Hazel swatted my arm as she passed, crossing her arms over her chest. "Do you not remember? You and Jared were the same. Always scrapping when the time came. I mended many a broken nose and bruised knuckles when you two came of age."

"You mean...?" Allie trailed off, paling as she drew little Liam into her arms. "But I thought that wouldn't be for another year or two."

"They're like their mom, I suspect," Hazel said, bending down to her knees in the grass. "Come here little ones."

My jaw tightened, but I let little Charity down, giving her a little push to her great grandmother.

Allie didn't let go of Liam at first, holding him tighter instead.

I gave her an encouraging look even though my heart was pounding, making my face heat and a muscle twitch in my temple.

"It's okay," I told her. "They should do it now if they're ready. The longer they hold it back the worse it will be. Hazel can help them."

She shook her head and I felt her need to protect them wash over me, dousing my fire with a biting cold that made me grit my teeth.

Her head snapped up at the sound of footsteps approaching and I found Jared rushing over, his amber eyes wide and hair disheveled from a run. He must have sensed it, too.

His face hardened at the sight of us. Of Allie holding tight to a fussing Liam. Of Charity sitting on Hazel's knee while Piper wordlessly pulled her wild silvery hair back into a braid.

"It's time, isn't it?" he asked, his adams apple bobbing in his throat as he ran a shaky hand through his hair, pushing it out of his face.

I nodded.

"They're too small," Allie argued. "They should wait."

Jared's cheekbones flared and he cleared the space between him and Allie, stooping to drop a kiss to the top of her head and whisper something into her ear that I couldn't hear.

He squeezed her shoulder, lending her the strength I couldn't, and within a moment, she released her tight hold on Liam, letting Jared lead him by the hand to Hazel.

I went to Allie, lifting her up from the ground to pull her into my side. "They'll be okay."

A choked sob to our left was followed by a hard sniff.

"Viv?" Allie asked, peering around me to see her best friend.

Vivian swiped at the snot beneath her nose and tried to conceal the way her chin wobbled. "They're just growing up so fast," she croaked.

Layla wrapped her arms around Viv. "Come here you big cry baby," she teased, even though her eyes were already welling, too.

I cleared my throat, trying to get rid of the burn there and held Allie tighter.

Jared came to stand with us, giving Hazel some space as she talked in hushed tones with our babies. Charity nodded at something she said and Liam shrugged, sending angry stares at his twin sister.

Hazel took them both by the hand and stood. "Now do what Grandma Hazel said."

"Won't it hurt?" Charity complained, skipping her r sounds like always.

"I want to keep him in," Liam said. "He don't want to come out."

"He is *you,* my boy," Hazel contradicted. "And if you don't let him out now, he might come out when you really don't want him to. Or the moon might force him out. He might even hurt Charity. You don't want that, do you?"

Liam glared at his sister for a moment before his expression softened and his shoulders slumped. "No."

"Good boy."

Hazel squeezed Charity's hand. "It'll hurt for a minute. But only a minute. I promise."

She nodded resolutely, her light gray eyes hardening in a way that reminded me so much of Allie it took my breath away. She would be a force to be reckoned with as she got older. I almost felt sorry for my future self.

Hazel let them go and gave them each a little nudge, stepping back. "Remember what I said. Deep breath, and then step back. Don't fight it."

Allie latched onto my hand, nearly popping joints with the force of her hold even though Jared was doing his best to soothe her.

Little Charity and Liam looked to their mom for the final word and she gave them a strong nod, forcing an encouraging smile.

They moved apart and I clenched my jaw, seeing the exact moment our Liam let go. His eyes widened as though he wished he could take it back the moment his wolf surged to the surface, but couldn't.

My stomach turned as he cried out and I had to tighten my grip on Allie to keep her on her feet. Charity's high pitched keen quickly followed, her dirt-streaked face contorted as her inner wolf took root, breaking free.

I looked away when the first bone snapped, and if it weren't for the fact that I needed to hold Allie up, I might have fallen myself. But Allie...I watched her watch them. Stoically.

Without blinking.

She would bear witness to their first shift, to their pain, no matter how much it hurt her to do it.

It was over in barely a moment. The first shift for a born wolf was painful, it would be for a while, but it was nothing compared to the agony of the first shift of a changed wolf. The breaking and realigning of fully formed adult bones made the process *much* worse.

A tear rolled down Allie's cheek as a little hissing snarl sounded before us. Her frown cracked into a relieved grin and she released her death grip on my hand.

A little ball of silver and black fur barreled into my legs, nearly taking me out, sharp claws scraping over my ankles.

"*Shit,*" I cursed, staring down at her viscous face. She growled at me, her hackles raised and gray eyes narrowed in challenge.

Her wolf wanted to play.

Liam howled. A tiny little sound that brought a smile to my face.

He padded toward Jared, his coat the exact replica of his sisters.

I shared a look with Allie.

You'd never know they were twins to look at them in their human forms. With Liam's dark hair and taller frame, and Charity's white blond mane lighter eyes.

But as wolves...

Charity set her sights on her brother, beginning to chase him in circles around us.

"Come on," Allie said, her eyes alight with mischief as she shrugged out of my embrace and looked to Jared and the others.

"They need to run."

She whistled sharply and took off for the trees, shifting mid-stride to lope into the brush, her twin ails bobbing.

Charity yipped, abandoning her efforts to cage in her brother to chase her mom, Liam right behind her.

Layla and Viv shared a look before taking off after them, laughing as they shifted.

Hazel came to stand between Jared and I, patting us both on the arm. "You did good," she said absently. "They're strong. Like their fathers."

Jared scoffed and I shook my head.

"Not like us," Jared corrected her. "Like their mom."

She pursed her lips, nodding. She knew he wasn't wrong.

"Well?" she snapped after a second, rolling her shoulders back. "What are we waiting for? Let's show those pups how it's done."

THE END

www.ingramcontent.com/pod-product-compliance
Lightning Source LLC
Chambersburg PA
CBHW070828020826
48982CB00015B/815

* 9 7 8 1 9 8 9 7 2 3 5 6 2 *